ALSO BY GARDNER DOZOIS

ANTHOLOGIES

A DAY IN THE LIFE
ANOTHER WORLD
BEST SCIENCE FICTION STORIES OF THE
    YEAR #6–10
THE BEST OF ISAAC ASIMOV'S SCIENCE
    FICTION MAGAZINE
TIME-TRAVELERS FROM ISAAC ASIMOV'S
    SCIENCE FICTION MAGAZINE
TRANSCENDENTAL TALES FROM ISAAC
    ASIMOV'S SCIENCE FICTION MAGAZINE
ISAAC ASIMOV'S ALIENS
ISAAC ASIMOV'S MARS
ISAAC ASIMOV'S SF LITE
ISAAC ASIMOV'S WAR
ROADS NOT TAKEN (with Stanley Schmidt)
THE YEAR'S BEST SCIENCE FICTION, #1–29

FUTURE EARTHS: UNDER AFRICAN SKIES
    (with Mike Resnick)
FUTURE EARTHS: UNDER SOUTH AMERICAN
    SKIES (with Mike Resnick)
RIPPER! (with Susan Casper)
MODERN CLASSIC SHORT NOVELS OF
    SCIENCE FICTION
MODERN CLASSICS OF FANTASY
KILLING ME SOFTLY
DYING FOR IT
THE GOOD OLD STUFF
THE GOOD NEW STUFF
EXPLORERS
THE FURTHEST HORIZON
WORLDMAKERS
SUPERMEN

COEDITED WITH SHEILA WILLIAMS

ISAAC ASIMOV'S PLANET EARTH
ISAAC ASIMOV'S ROBOTS
ISAAC ASIMOV'S VALENTINES
ISAAC ASIMOV'S SKIN DEEP
ISAAC ASIMOV'S GHOSTS
ISAAC ASIMOV'S VAMPIRES
ISAAC ASIMOV'S MOONS

ISAAC ASIMOV'S CHRISTMAS
ISAAC ASIMOV'S CAMELOT
ISAAC ASIMOV'S WEREWOLVES
ISAAC ASIMOV'S SOLAR SYSTEM
ISAAC ASIMOV'S DETECTIVES
ISAAC ASIMOV'S CYBERDREAMS

COEDITED WITH JACK DANN

ALIENS!	SORCERERS!	DRAGONS!	HACKERS
UNICORNS!	DEMONS!	HORSES!	TIMEGATES
MAGICATS!	DOGTALES!	UNICORNS 2	CLONES
MAGICATS 2!	SEASERPENTS!	INVADERS!	NANOTECH
BESTIARY!	DINOSAURS!	ANGELS!	IMMORTALS
MERMAIDS!	LITTLE PEOPLE!	DINOSAURS II	

FICTION

STRANGERS
THE VISIBLE MAN (Collection)
NIGHTMARE BLUE
    (with George Alec Effinger)

SLOW DANCING THROUGH TIME
    (with Jack Dann, Michael Swanwick, Susan
    Casper, and Jack C. Haldeman II)
THE PEACEMAKER
GEODESIC DREAMS (collection)

NONFICTION

THE FICTION OF JAMES TIPTREE, JR.

THE YEAR'S BEST

SCIENCE FICTION

thirtieth annual collection

edited by Gardner Dozois

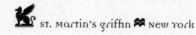 st. martin's griffin ❧ new york

These short stories are works of fiction. All of the characters, organizations, and events portrayed in these stories are either products of the authors' imaginations or are used fictitiously.

THE YEAR'S BEST SCIENCE FICTION: THIRTIETH ANNUAL COLLECTION.
Copyright © 2013 by Gardner Dozois. All rights reserved.
Printed in the United States of America.
For information, address St. Martin's Press, 175 Fifth Avenue, New York, N.Y. 10010.

www.stmartins.com

Library of Congress Cataloging-in-Publication Data

The year's best science fiction : thirtieth annual collection/edited by Gardner Dozois.—First edition.
    pages cm
  ISBN 978-1-250-02805-1 (hardcover)
  ISBN 978-1-250-02913-3 (trade pbk.)
  ISBN 978-1-250-02804-4 (e-book)
1. Science fiction, American.   I. Dozois, Gardner R., editor of compilation.
  PS648.S3Y44 2013
  813'.0876208—dc23

                                                    2013009319

St. Martin's Griffin books may be purchased for educational, business, or promotional use. For information on bulk purchases, please contact Macmillan Corporate and Premium Sales Department at 1-800-221-7945 extension 5442 or write specialmarkets@macmillan.com.

First Edition: July 2013

10 9 8 7 6 5 4 3 2 1

contents

PERMISSIONS ... *ix*

ACKNOWLEDGMENTS ... *xiii*

SUMMATION: *2012* ... *xv*

WEEP FOR DAY • *Indrapramit Das* ... *1*

THE MAN • *Paul McAuley* ... *15*

THE STARS DO NOT LIE • *Jay Lake* ... *27*

THE MEMCORDIST • *Lavie Tidhar* ... *71*

THE GIRL-THING WHO WENT OUT FOR SUSHI • *Pat Cadigan* ... *80*

HOLMES SHERLOCK • *Eleanor Arnason* ... *96*

NIGHTFALL ON THE PEAK OF ETERNAL LIGHT • *Richard A. Lovett*
and *William Gleason* ... *111*

CLOSE ENCOUNTERS • *Andy Duncan* ... *160*

THE FINITE CANVAS • *Brit Mandelo* ... *182*

STEAMGOTHIC • *Sean McMullen* ... *202*

IN THE HOUSE OF ARYAMAN, A LONELY SIGNAL BURNS • *Elizabeth Bear* ... *223*

MACY MINNOT'S LAST CHRISTMAS ON DIONE, RING RACING,
FIDDLER'S GREEN, THE POTTER'S GARDEN • *Paul McAuley* ... *259*

TWENTY LIGHTS TO "THE LAND OF SNOW" • *Michael Bishop* ... *273*

ASTROPHILIA • *Carrie Vaughn* ... *316*

WHAT DID TESSIMOND TELL YOU? • *Adam Roberts* ... *331*

OLD PAINT • *Megan Lindholm* ... *349*

CHITAI HEIKI KORONBIN • *David Moles* ... *366*

KATABASIS • *Robert Reed* ... *376*

THE WATER THIEF • *Alastair Reynolds* ... *415*

NIGHTSIDE ON CALLISTO • *Linda Nagata* ... *426*

UNDER THE EAVES • *Lavie Tidhar* ... *438*

SUDDEN, BROKEN, AND UNEXPECTED • *Steven Popkes*   448

FIREBORN • *Robert Charles Wilson*   486

RUMINATIONS IN AN ALIEN TONGUE • *Vandana Singh*   501

TYCHE AND THE ANTS • *Hannu Rajaniemi*   514

THE WRECK OF THE "CHARLES DEXTER WARD" • *Sarah Monette*

    and Elizabeth Bear   526

INVISIBLE MEN • *Christopher Barzak*   555

SHIP'S BROTHER • *Aliette de Bodard*   570

EATER-OF-BONE • *Robert Reed*   580

HONORABLE MENTIONS: 2012   647

THE YEAR'S BEST

SCIENCE FICTION

permissions

Well, the physical print book didn't die in 2012, although some commentators have been predicting that it would be totally extinct by 2015. Nor have e-books proved to be a transitory "fad," as the more wishful thinking of the print purists once asserted that they would turn out to be.

Instead, something interesting seems to be happening. More people are reading than ever before, and it may be that rather than driving print books into extinction, the two forms are complementing each other in a synergistic way, one helping to boost the other. It may be that the more you read, in either print or electronic form, the more you *want* to read.

The average American adult read seventeen books in 2012, the highest figure since Gallup began tracking the figure in 1990.

A Pew Research Center survey said the percentage of adults who have read an e-book rose over the past year, from 16 percent to 23 percent. But 89 percent of regular book readers said that they had also read at least one printed book during the preceding twelve months.

Although comprehensive overall figures for 2012 won't be available for some time yet as I type these words, according to Stephen Marche, writing in *Esquire*, revenue for adult hardcover books is up 8.3 percent in the January-June 2012 period from the same period in 2011, from 2.038 billion dollars to 2.207 billion. Paperback sales were up 5.2 percent (other figures suggest that this growth was mostly in trade paperbacks, while mass-market paperbacks declined, suggesting that a significant proportion of those who used to buy mass-market paperbacks are now buying e-books instead; see the novel section below for further breakdowns), while book sales for young adults and children grew by 12 percent.

According to Nicholas Carr, writing in *The Wall Street Journal*, "Hardcover books are displaying surprising resiliency. The growth in e-book sales is slowing markedly. And purchases of e-readers are actually shrinking, as consumers opt instead for multipurpose tablets. It may be that e-books, rather than replacing printed books, will ultimately serve a role more like audio books—a complement to traditional reading, not a substitute." The Association of American Publishers reported that the annual growth rate for e-book sales fell during 2012, to 34 percent, still impressive, but a decline from the triple-digit growth rates of the preceding four years. Sales of dedicated e-readers were down by 36 percent in 2012, while sales of tablet computers such as the iPad and the Kindle Fire exploded.

Not that e-books are going to go away, either. A survey by children's publisher Scholastic Inc. indicated that 46 percent of responding kids aged nine to seventeen had read an e-book, and that around half of those who have not yet read an e-book say that they want to do so, going on to state that the rise of iPads and other tablets has helped to vastly expand the availability of picture books and other children's books in electronic format. But 80 percent of those kids who read an e-book in 2012 *also* read a print book.

My guess is that in the future, rather than one mode driving the other out of existence, most readers will buy books both in electronic and print forms, choosing one format or the other depending on the circumstances, convenience, their needs of the moment, even their whim. There are strong indications that in some cases people will buy both e-book *and* print versions *of the same book*. It may be true that a rising tide floats all boats.

The biggest story in the publishing world in 2012 was probably the merger of publishing giants Random House and Penguin to form Penguin Random House (and prompting wiseasses everywhere to say it should have been called "Random Penguin" instead). The merger still needs government approval to go through, but if it does, the so-called "Big Six" publishing houses will be reduced at a stroke to the "Big Five." Since there were rumors at the end of 2012 that HarperCollins' parent company, News Corp, is interested in acquiring Simon & Schuster's book business, that number may be reduced even further in the near future. All this merging has, of course, prompted the usual fears that formerly independent and competing imprints will be consolidated, spelling the loss of editorial jobs and perhaps a reduction in the number of overall titles released. Elsewhere: Angry Robot launched a YA imprint, Strange Chemistry, and will launch a crime-fiction imprint, Exhibit A, later this year. PS Publishing is launching a mass-market paperback imprint, Drugstore Indian. Penguin/Berkley/NAL added a graphic novel imprint, Inklit. Orbit will launch a new "commercial fiction" imprint, Redhook. Random House announced four new digital imprints: Alibi, to publish mysteries/thrillers/suspense; Hydra, to publish SF/fantasy; Loveswept, to publish romance; and Flirt, to publish "New Adult" fiction targeting women in their twenties and thirties. HarperCollins announced a new digital YA imprint, HarperTeen Impulse. Pearson, the parent company of Penguin, acquired self-publishing company Author Solutions, Inc. Barnes & Noble has put its Sterling Publishing arm up for sale. Amazon made a deal to acquire over four hundred titles from Marshall Cavendish Children's Books. Betsy Mitchell has been hired by e-book publisher Open Road Media as a "strategic advisor" for their SF and fantasy titles. Patrick Nolan became editor in chief and associate publisher of Penguin Books. Madeline McIntosh became Chief Operating Officer for Random House. Devi Pillai was promoted to executive editor at Orbit, and Susa Barnes to associate editor. Therese Goulding was hired as managing editor for Ann and Jeff VanderMeer's Cheeky Frawg Books imprint. Editor David Pomerico left Del Rey to become an editor at Amazon.com's SF imprint, 47North. Steven H. Silver resigned as editor and publisher of ISFiC Press.

It was a mostly stable year in the professional print magazine market. After years of sometimes precipitous decline, circulation figures are actually beginning to creep back up, mostly because of sales of electronic subscriptions to the magazines, as well as sales of individual electronic copies of each issue.

Asimov's Science Fiction had another strong year, publishing excellent fiction by Elizabeth Bear, Jay Lake, Indrapramit Das, Megan Lindholm, Steven Popkes, Robert Reed, Gord Sellar, Tom Purdom, and others; their SF was considerably stronger than their fantasy this year, with the exception of a novella by Alan Smale. For the third year in a row, circulation was up. *Asimov's Science Fiction* registered a 10.8 percent gain in overall circulation, up from 22,593 in 2011, to 25,025. There were 21,380 subscriptions; Newsstand sales were 3,207 copies, plus 438 digital copies sold on average each month in 2012. Sell-through jumped sharply from 28 percent to 42 percent. Sheila Williams completed her eighth year as editor of *Asimov's Science Fiction*, and won her second Best Editor Hugo in a row.

Analog Science Fiction and Fact published good work by Richard A. Lovett and William Gleason, Michael Alexander and K.C. Ball, Linda Nagata, Michael Flynn, Sean McMullen, Alec Nevala-Lee, and others. *Analog* registered a 4.9 percent rise in overall circulation, from 26,440 to 27,803. There were 24,503 subscriptions; newsstand sales were 2,854; down slightly from 2,942, but digital sales were up sharply, from 150 digital copies sold on average each month in 2011, to 446 in 2013. Sell-through rose from 30 percent to 31 percent. Stanley Schmidt, who had been editor there for thirty-three years, retired in 2012, and has been replaced by Trevor Quachri. The year 2012 marked the magazine's eighty-second anniversary.

The Magazine of Fantasy and Science Fiction was almost exactly the reverse of *Asimov's Science Fiction*; lots of good fantasy work appeared there in 2012, including stories by Ted Kostmatka, Rachel Pollack, Peter S. Beagle, Felicity Shoulders, John McDaid, Alter S. Reiss, and others, but little really memorable SF, with the exception of stories by Robert Reed and Andy Duncan. The magazine also registered a 20.4 percent drop in overall circulation, from 14,462 to 11,510. Print subscriptions dropped from 10,539 to 8,300. Newsstand sales dropped from 6,584 to 5,050. Sell-through rose from 38 percent to 39 percent. Figures are not available for digital subscriptions and digital copies sold, but editor Gordon Van Gelder said that they were "healthy," and that "our bottom line in 2012 was good." Gordon Van Gelder is in his sixteenth year as editor, and his twelfth year as owner and publisher.

Interzone is technically not a "professional magazine," by the definition of *The Science Fiction Writers of America* (SFWA), because of its low rates and circulation, but the literary quality of the work published there is so high that it would be ludicrous to omit it. *Interzone* had good work by Aliette de Bodard, Sean McMullen, Lavie Tidhar, Elizabeth Bourne, and others this year. Exact circulation figures are not available, but is guessed to be in the 2,000-copy range. TTA Press, *Interzone's* publisher, also publishes straight horror or dark suspense magazine *Black Static*, which is beyond our purview here, but of a similar level of professional quality. *Interzone* and *Black Static* changed to a smaller trim size this year, but maintained their slick look, switching from the old 7¾" by 10¾" saddle-stitched semigloss color cover and 64-page format to a 6½" by 9¼" perfect-bound glossy color cover and 96-page format. The editors include publisher Andy Cox and Andy Hedgecock.

If you'd like to see lots of good SF and fantasy published every year, the survival of these magazines is essential, and one important way that you can help them survive is by subscribing to them. It's never been easier to do so, something that these days can be done with just the click of a few buttons, nor has it ever before been possible to subscribe to the magazines in as many different formats, from the traditional print copy arriving by mail to downloads for your desktop or laptop available from places like Amazon.com (www.amazon.com), to versions you can read on your

Kindle, Nook, or i-Pad. You can also now subscribe from overseas just as easily as you can from the United States, something formerly difficult to impossible to do.

So in hopes of making it easier for you to subscribe, I'm going to list both the Internet sites where you can subscribe online and the street addresses where you can subscribe by mail for each magazine: *Asimov's* web address is www.asimovs.com, and subscribing online might be the easiest thing to do. There's also a discounted rate for online subscriptions; its subscription address is *Asimov's Science Fiction*, Dell Magazines, 267 Broadway, Fourth Floor, New York, NY 10007-2352. The annual subscription rate in the U.S. is $34.97, $44.97 overseas. *Analog's* site is at *www .analogsf.com*; its subscription address is *Analog Science Fiction and Fact*, Dell Magazines, 267 Broadway, Fourth Floor, New York, NY 10007-2352. The annual subscription rate in the U.S. is $34.97, $44.97 overseas. *The Magazine of Fantasy & Science Fiction's* site is at www.sfsite.com/fsf; its subscription address is *The Magazine of Fantasy & Science Fiction*, Spilogale, Inc., P.O. Box 3447, Hoboken, NJ 07030. The annual subscription rate in the U.S. is $34.97, $44.97 overseas. *Interzone* and *Black Static* can be subscribed to online at www.ttapress.com/onlinestore1 .html; the subscription address for both is TTA Press, 5 Martins Lane, Witcham, Ely, Cambs CB6 2LB, England, UK. The price for a twelve-issue subscription is 42.00 Pounds Sterling each, or there is a reduced rate dual subscription offer of 78.00 Pounds Sterling for both magazines for twelve issues; make checks payable to "TTA Press."

Most of these magazines are also available in various electronic formats for the Kindle, the Nook, and other handheld readers.

In truth, there's not that much left of the print semiprozine market; in 2011, several magazines transitioned from print to electronic format, including *Zahir* (which subsequently died altogether), *Electric Velocipede*, and *Black Gate*, and in 2012 they were joined by criticalzine *The New York Review of Science Fiction*. I suspect that sooner or later most of the surviving print semiprozines will transition to electronic-only online formats, saving themselves lots of money in printing, mailing, and production costs.

The semiprozines that remained in print format mostly struggled to bring out their scheduled issues. Of the SF/fantasy print semiprozines, one of the few that managed all of its scheduled issues was the longest-running and most reliably published of all the fiction semiprozines, the Canadian *On Spec*, which is edited by a collective under general editor Diane L. Walton. Another collective-run SF magazine with a rotating editorial staff, Australia's *Andromeda Spaceways In-flight Magazine*, managed four issues this year, as it had in 2011. *Lady Churchill's Rosebud Wristlet*, the long-running slipstream magazine edited by Kelly Link and Gavin Grant, managed only one issue in 2012, as did fantasy magazines *Shimmer*, *Bull Spec*, and Ireland's long-running *Albedo One*. *Neo-opsis* managed two issues, as did *Space and Time Magazine*, before being sold. The small British SF magazine *Jupiter*, edited by Ian Redman, produced all four of its scheduled issues in 2012, as did the fantasy magazine *Tales of the Talisman*. *Weird Tales* also managed two issues, one compiled by the old editor, Ann VanderMeer, and one compiled by the new editor, Marvin Kaye.

The fact is that little really memorable fiction appeared in any of the surviving print semiprozines this year, which were far outstripped by the online magazines (see below).

With the departure of *The New York Review of Science Fiction* to the electronic world in mid-2012, the venerable newszine *Locus: The Magazine of the Science Fiction and Fantasy Field* is about all that's left of the popular print critical magazine market. A multiple Hugo winner, it has long been your best bet for value in this category anyway, and for more than thirty years has been an indispensible source of news, information, and reviews. Happily, the magazine has survived the death of founder, publisher, and longtime editor Charles N. Brown and has continued strongly and successfully under the guidance of a staff of editors headed by Liza Groen Trombi, and including Kirsten Gong-Wong, Carolyn Cushman, Tim Pratt, Jonathan Strahan, Francesca Myman, Heather Shaw, and many others.

Most of the other surviving print critical magazines are professional journals more aimed at academics than at the average reader. The most accessible of these is probably the long-running British critical zine *Foundation*.

Subscription addresses are: **Locus, The Magazine of the Science Fiction & Fantasy Field**, Locus Publications, Inc., P.O. Box 13305, Oakland, CA, 94661, $76.00 for a one-year first-class subscription, 12 issues; **Foundation**, Science Fiction Foundation, Roger Robinson (SFF), 75 Rosslyn Avenue, Harold Wood, Essex RM3 ORG, UK, $37.00 for a three-issue subscription in the U.S.; **On Spec, The Canadian Magazine of the Fantastic**, P.O. Box 4727, Edmonton, AB, Canada T6E 5G6, for subscription information, go to Web site www.onspec.ca; **Neo-opsis Science Fiction Magazine**, 4129 Carey Rd., Victoria, BC, CanadaV8Z 4G5, $25.00 for a three-issue subscription; **Albedo One**, Albedo One Productions, 2, Post Road, Lusk, County Dublin, Ireland; $32.00 for a four-issue airmail subscription, make checks payable to "Albedo One" or pay by PayPal at www.albedo1.com; **Lady Churchill's Rosebud Wristlet**, Small Beer Press, 150 Pleasant Street, #306, Easthampton, MA 01027, $20.00 for four issues; **Andromeda Spaceways Inflight Magazine**, Web site www.andromedaspaceways.com for subscription information; **Tales of the Talisman**, Hadrosaur Productions, P.O. Box 2194, Mesilla Park, NM 88047-2194, $24.00 for a four-issue subscription; **Jupiter**, 19 Bedford Road, Yeovil, Somerset, BA21 5UG, UK, 10 Pounds Sterling for four issues; **Shimmer**, P.O. Box 58591, Salt Lake City, UT 84158-0591, $22.00 for a four-issue subscription; **Weird Tales**, Web site www.weirdtalesmagazine.com for subscription and ordering information.

The world of online-only electronic magazines has become increasingly important in the last few years, and in 2012 electronic magazines continued to pop up all over like popping-up things that suddenly pop up. How long some of them will last is yet to be seen.

Late in the year, in one of the more interesting developments of 2012, Jonathan Strahan announced that his critically acclaimed anthology series *Eclipse* was transforming itself from a print anthology to an online magazine, *Eclipse Online* (www.nightshadebooks.com/category/eclipse), which would release two stories every month throughout the year; three issues appeared in 2012, and the literary quality was very high, with excellent stories by Lavie Tidhar, Eleanor Arnason, Christopher Barzak, K.J. Parker, and others published.

Fireside (www.firesidemag.com), edited by Brian White, debuted in 2012, as did

Michael Moorcock's New Worlds (www.newworlds.co.uk), edited by Roger Gray, and *International Speculative Fiction* (http://internationalsf.wordpress.com), edited by Correio do Fantastico.

Promised for next year are *Galaxy's Edge,* a bimonthly e-zine edited by Mike Resnick, *Waylines,* edited by David Rees-Thomas and Darryl Knickrehm, and a re-launch of *Amazing Stories,* edited by Steve Davidson.

Lightspeed (www.lightspeedmagazine.com), edited by John Joseph Adams, had a good year, featuring strong work by Vandana Singh, Linda Nagata, Keith Brooke, Marissa Lingen, Ken Liu, Sarah Monette, Sandra McDonald, and others. Late in the year a new electronic companion horror magazine, *Nightmare,* was added to the *Lightspeed* stable.

Clarkesworld Magazine (www.clarkesworldmagazine.com), edited by Sean Wallace and Neil Clarke, also had a strong year, featuring good stuff by Carrie Vaughn, Aliette de Bodard, Indrapramit Das, Theodora Goss, Yoon Ha Lee, Xia Jia, and others.

Subterranean (http://subterraneanpress.com), edited by William K. Schafer, was a bit weak overall this year, but did publish some first-class work, mostly at novella length, by Jay Lake, K. J. Parker, Maria Dahvana Headley, Nnedi Okorafor, Ian R. MacLeod, and others.

Tor.com (www.tor.com) had good work by Elizabeth Bear, Andy Duncan, Michael Swanwick, Brit Mandelo, Paul Cornell, Pat Murphy, and others. Ellen Datlow and Ann VanderMeer joined Patrick Nielsen Hayden and Liz Gorinsky on the editorial staff.

At this point, *Strange Horizons* (www.strangehorizons.com) is probably the oldest continually running online magazine on the Internet, started in 2000; they publish SF, fantasy, slipstream, horror, the occasional near-mainstream story, and the literary quality is usually high, although I'd like to see them publish more science fiction. This year, they had strong work by Molly Gloss, Louise Hughes, Ellen Klages, Benjamin Rosenbaum, Kate Bachus, Samantha Henderson, and others. Longtime editors Jed Hartman and Susan Marie Groppi have stepped down, to be replaced by Brit Mandelo, An Owomoyela, and Julia Rios.

Following in the footsteps of last year's *TRSF,* an all-fiction magazine produced by the publishers of *MIT Technology Review,* in 2012 the publishers of *New Scientist* magazine created *Arc,* edited by Simon Ings and Sumit Paul-Choudhury, and described as "a new digital magazine about the future," featuring both fiction and a range of eclectic nonfiction, and which exists mainly as various downloadable formats for the Kindle, the iPad, iPhones, Windows PC and Mac computers. Three issues of *Arc* appeared in 2012, featuring good work by Paul McAuley, Alastair Reynolds, Nancy Kress, Robert Reed, and others. A new issue of *TRSF* is promised for 2013 as well.

Former print semiprozine *Electric Velocipede* is now an electronic magazine (www.electricvelocipede.com), still edited by John Kilma. They published an excellent story by Aliette de Bodard this year, as well as good stuff by Ann Leckie, Ken Liu, Derek Zumsteg, and others.

Apex Magazine (www.apexbookcompany.com/apex-online) had good work by Kij Johnson, Mary Robinette Kowal, Ken Liu, Jay Lake, and others. The new editor is Lynne M. Thomas.

Abyss & Apex (www.abyssapexzine.com) ran interesting work by Colin P. Davies, Genevieve Valentine, Jay Caselberg, Arkady Martine, and others. The longtime editor there is Wendy S. Delmater, although Carmelo Rafala is "transitioning" in to take over that position.

An e-zine devoted to "literary adventure fantasy," *Beneath Ceaseless Skies* (http://beneath-ceaseless-skies.com), edited by Scott H. Andrews, had a strong year, running nice stuff by Richard Parks, Chris Willrich, Cory Skerry, Karalynn Lee, Margaret Ronald, and others.

Long-running sword and sorcery print magazine *Black Gate* transitioned into an electronic magazine in September of 2012 and can be found at (www.blackgate .com), where they publish one new story per year, to date featuring stories by Judith Berman, Sean McLachlan, Aaron Bradford Starr, and others.

The Australian popular-science magazine *Cosmos* (www.cosmosmagazine.com) is not an SF magazine per se, but for the last few years it has been running a story per issue (and also putting new fiction not published in the print magazine up on their Web site), and interesting stuff by Michael Greehut, Richard A. Lovett, Margo Lanagan, Barbara Krasnoff, and others appeared there this year. The new fiction editor is SF writer Cat Sparks.

Ideomancer Speculative Fiction (www.ideomancer.com), edited by Leah Bobet, published interesting work, usually more slipstream than SF, by Rachel Derksen, Sara K. Ellis, Wendy N. Wagner, and others.

Orson Scott Card's InterGalactic Medicine Show (www.intergalacticmedicine show.com), edited by Edmund R. Schubert under the direction of Card himself, had another fairly weak year, although they still ran interesting stuff from the ubiquitous Ken Liu, Tony Pi, Eric James Stone, Nancy Fulda, and others.

New SF/fantasy e-zine *Daily Science Fiction* (http://dailysciencefiction.com) publishes one new SF or fantasy story *every single day* for the entire year. Many of these were not really up to professional standards, unsurprisingly, but there were some good stories here and there by Ken Liu, Lavie Tidhar, Ruth Nestvold, Sandra McDonald, Robert Reed, Eric Brown, and others.

Redstone Science Fiction (http://redstonesciencefiction.com), edited by a collective, hasn't updated their site since June, and may well have gone out of business.

GigaNotoSaurus (http://giganotosaurus.org), edited by Ann Leckie, published one story a month by writers such as Ken Liu, Ian McHugh, Patricia Russo, Ben Bovis, and others.

The World SF Blog (http://worldsf.wordpress.com), edited by Lavie Tidhar, is a good place to find science fiction by international authors, and also publishes news, links, roundtable discussions, essays, and interviews related to "science fiction, fantasy, horror and comics from around the world."

A similar site is *International Speculative Fiction* (http://internationalSF.word press.com), edited by Roberto Mendes.

Weird Fiction Review (http://weirdfictionreview.com), edited by Ann Vander-Meer and Jeff VanderMeer, which occasionally publishes fiction, bills itself as "an ongoing exploration into all facets of the weird," including reviews, interviews, short essays, and comics.

Below this point, it becomes harder to find center-core SF, or even genre fantasy/ horror, and most of the stories are slipstream or literary surrealism. Sites that feature those, as well as the occasional fantasy (and, even more occasionally, some SF) include Rudy Rucker's *Flurb* (www.flurb.net), *Revolution SF* (www.revolutionsf.com), *Heliotrope* (www.heliotropemag.com); and the somewhat less slipstreamish *Bewildering Stories* (www.bewilderingstories.com).

In addition to original work, there's also a lot of good *reprint* SF and fantasy stories out there on the Internet. *Fictionwise* and *Electric Story*, the two major sites that made downloadable fiction available for a fee, seem to have died, perhaps from competition from the e-book market, but there are sites where you can access formerly published stories for free, including *Strange Horizons*, *Tor.com*, *Lightspeed*, *Subterranean*, *Abyss & Apex*, and most of the sites that are associated with existent print magazines, such as *Asimov's*, *Analog*, and *The Magazine of Fantasy & Science Fiction*, make previously published fiction and nonfiction available for access on their sites as well, and also regularly run teaser excerpts from stories coming up in forthcoming issues. Hundreds of out-of-print titles, both genre and mainstream, are also available for free download from Project Gutenberg (http://promo.net/pc/), and a large selection of novels and a few collections can also be accessed for free, to be either downloaded or read on-screen, at the *Baen Free Library* (www.baen.com/library). Sites such as *Infinity Plus* (http://www.infinityplus.co.uk), and *The Infinite Matrix* (www.infinitematrix.net) may have died as active sites, but their extensive archives of previously published material are still accessible.

There are still plenty of other reasons for SF fans to go on the Internet, though, even if you're not looking for fiction to read. There are many general genre-related sites of interest to be found, most of which publish reviews of books as well as of movies and TV shows, sometimes comics or computer games or anime, many of which also feature interviews, critical articles, and genre-oriented news of various kinds. The best such site is easily *Locus Online* (http://www.locusmag.com), the online version of the newsmagazine *Locus*, where you can access an incredible amount of information—including book reviews, critical lists, obituary lists, links to reviews and essays appearing outside the genre, and links to extensive database archives such as the Locus Index to Science Fiction and the Locus Index to Science Fiction Awards—it's rare when I don't find myself accessing *Locus Online* several times a day. The previously mentioned *Tor.com*, though, rivals *Locus Online* as one of the most eclectic genre-oriented sites on the Internet, a Web site that, in addition to its fiction, regularly publishes articles, comics, graphics, blog entries, print and media reviews, book "rereads" and episode-by-episode "rewatches" of television shows, as well as commentary on all the above. The long-running and eclectic *The New York Review of Science Fiction* has ceased print publication, but can be purchased in PDF, epub, and MOBI formats, and POD editions through *Weightless Books* (http://weightlessbooks.com; see also www.nyrsf.com for information). Other major general-interest sites include *SF Site* (www.sfsite.com), *SFRevu* (http://www.sfsite.com/sfrevu), *SFCrowsnest* (www.sfcrowsnest.com), *SFScope* (www.sfscope.com), *io9* (http:io9.com), *Green Man Review* (http://greenmanreview.com), *The Agony Column* (http://trashotron.com/agony), *SFFWorld* (www.sffworld.com), *SFReader* (http://forums.sfreader.com), and *Pat's Fantasy Hotlist* (www.fantasyhotlist.blogspot.com). A great research site, invaluable if you want bibliographic information about SF and fantasy writers, is *Fantastic Fiction* (www.fantasticfiction.co.uk). Another fantastic research site is the searchable online update of the Hugo-winning *The*

Encyclopedia of Science Fiction (www.sf-encyclopedia.com), where you can access almost four million words of information about SF writers, books, magazines, and genre themes. Reviews of short fiction as opposed to novels are very hard to find anywhere, with the exception of *Locus* and *Locus Online*, but you can find reviews of both current and past short fiction at *Best SF* (www.bestsf.net), as well as at pioneering short-fiction review site *Tangent Online* (www.tangentonline.com). Other sites of interest include: *SFF NET* (www.sff.net), which features dozens of home pages and "newsgroups" for SF writers; the Science Fiction Writers of America page (www.sfwa.org); where genre news, obituaries, award information, and recommended reading lists can be accessed; *Ansible* (http://news.ansible.co.uk/Ansible), the online version of multiple Hugo-winner David Langford's long-running fanzine *Ansible*; *Book View Café* (www.bookviewcafe.com) is a "consortium of over twenty professional authors," including Vonda N. McIntyre, Laura Ann Gilman, Sarah Zittel, Brenda Clough, and others, who have created a Web site where some of their work—mostly reprints, and some novel excerpts—is made available for free.

An ever-expanding area, growing in popularity, are a number of sites where podcasts and SF-oriented radio plays can be accessed: at *Audible* (www.audible.com), *Escape Pod* (http://escapepod.org, podcasting mostly SF), *The Drabblecast* (www.drabblecast.org), *Star Ship Sofa* (www.starshipsofa.com), *Pseudopod* (http://pseudopod.org, podcasting mostly fantasy), and *PodCastle* (http://podcastle.org, podcasting mostly fantasy). There's also a site that podcasts nonfiction interviews and reviews, *Dragon Page—C Cover to Cover* (www.dragonpage.com).

It was a somewhat weak year for original anthologies, although there were still a few that were worth your money.

Without a doubt, the best SF original anthology of the year was *Edge of Infinity* (Solaris), edited by Jonathan Strahan. True, original SF anthologies were light on the ground this year, but *Edge of Infinity* would be a standout in any year. Unusually, in these days when it seems almost de rigueur for editors to sneak some slipstream or fantasy stories into even ostensibly "All SF" anthologies, everything here actually *is* pure-quill core SF, some of it hard SF at that, and the literary quality is uniformly excellent across the board. There's nothing that's bad here, again unlike most anthologies, which makes it difficult to pick favorites, but among the strongest stories are those by Pat Cadigan, Paul McAuley, Gwyneth Jones, Hannu Rajaniemi, and Bruce Sterling, although there's also excellent work here by Elizabeth Bear, James S.A. Corey, Sandra McDonald and Stephen D. Covey, John Barnes, Kristine Kathryn Rusch, Stephen Baxter, Alastair Reynolds, and An Owomoyela, any of which would have been among the standout stories in any other SF anthology of the year.

None of the other original SF anthologies of the year were in this league, but there was some interesting stuff.

An odd item was *Solaris Rising 1.5: An Exclusive ebook of New Science Fiction*, edited by Ian Whates, and available only in e-book form. An original SF anthology designed to act as a "bridge" between 2010's *Solaris Rising* print anthology and 2013's upcoming *Solaris Rising 2* anthology, it features good fiction by Adam Roberts, Aliette de Bodard, Paul Cornell, Paul Di Filippo, and others. *Armored* (Baen), edited by John Joseph Adams, is an all-original anthology of military SF, stories about armored fighting suits, and wearable tanks, more or less, probably first popularized by Robert A. Heinlein in his novel *Starship Troopers*, seen subsequently in lots of SF, including movies such as *Avatar*, and currently hovering right on the edge of becoming an actuality; certainly it won't be more than ten or fifteen years at most before we have them prowling the battlefields in the real world. The best stories here are by David Klecha and Tobias S. Buckell, Alastair Reynolds, Ian Douglas, Simon R. Green, Karin Lowachee, and Sean Williams, although there's also solid work here by Carrie Vaughn, David D. Levine, Jack McDevitt, Genevieve Valentine, Michael A. Stackpole, Tanya Huff, David Sherman, and others.

Other good original SF anthologies included *Going Interstellar* (Baen), edited by Les Johnson and Jack McDevitt, which contained an excellent novella by Michael Bishop, as well as solid work by Jack McDevitt, Ben Bova, and others, in addition to nonfiction essays about possible designs for interstellar spaceships by Dr. Gregory Matloff, Dr. Richard Obousy, and Les Johnson himself. (Simon & Schuster), edited by John Joseph Adams, a tribute anthology in which modern writers get to play with Edgar Rice Burroughs's Mars and its characters and generate Barsoom stories of their own. There is a noticeable split in approach to the material here. Some authors write straightforward John Carter adventures with lots of swordplay and mayhem, chases, captures, hairsbreadth cliff-hangers, and daring escapes, much as Burroughs himself might have (although all of the authors in the book are much better writers line by line than Burroughs ever was). The best stories in this mode are probably those by S. M. Stirling and Joe R. Lansdale. The best stories here are those that take the other approach, and add a dab of playful postmodernism to the mix, including stories by Peter S. Beagle, Garth Nix, Theodora Goss, Catharynne M. Valente, Tobias S. Buckell, and Genevieve Valentine.

There were two post-Apocalyptic anthologies, *After: Nineteen Stories of Apocalypse and Dystopia* (Hyperion Books), edited by Ellen Datlow and Terry Windling; and *Epilogue* (Fablecroft Publishing), edited by Tehani Wessely, and an anthology of dystopian YA stories, *Diverse Energies* (Tu Books), edited by Tobias S. Buckell and Joe Monti. There were two steampunk anthologies, *The Mammoth Book of Steampunk* (Running Press), edited by Sean Wallace, and *Steampunk III: Steampunk Revolution* (Tachyon), edited by Ann VanderMeer. There were two shared-world anthologies, *Man-Kzin Wars XIII* (Baen), edited by Larry Niven, and *Grantville Gazette VI* (Baen), edited by Eric Flint. *Postscripts Anthology No. 26–27: Unfit for Eden* (PS Publishing), edited by Nick Gevers and Peter Crowther, was one of two *Postscripts* editions this year, the other, *Postscripts 28–29*, being a special "Gothic Fiction" edition guest edited by Danel Olson. *Postscripts 26–27* was a bit weak compared to some of the earlier volumes in this series, but still contained good work by Michael Swanwick, Jessica Reisman, Steven Utley, Michael Bishop, Eric Brown, Michael Bishop, and others.

This was a very good year for anthologies that afford a view of what's happening in fantastic literature in other countries, outside the usual genre boundaries. Anthologies of this sort included *The Future is Japanese* (Haikasoru), edited by Nick Mamatas and Maumi Washington; *Breaking the Bow: Speculative Fiction Inspired by the Ramayana*, edited by Anil Menon and Vandana Singh; *Afro SF: Science Fiction by African Writers* (StoryTime Press), edited by Ivor W. Hartmann; *Three Mes-*

sages and a Warning: Contemporary Mexican Short Stories of the Fantastic (Small Beer Press), edited by Eduardo Jiménez Mayo and Chris N. Brown; Lauriat: A Filipino-Chinese Speculative Fiction Anthology (Lethe Press), edited by Charles Tan; Walking the Clouds: An Anthology of Indigenous Science Fiction (University of Arizona), edited by Grace L. Dillon; and The Apex Book of World SF 2 (Apex Publications), edited by Lavie Tidhar.

L. Ron Hubbard Presents Writers of the Future Volume XXVIII (Galaxy Press), edited by the late K. D. Wentworth, is the most recent in a long-running series featuring novice work by beginning writers, some of whom may later turn out to be important talents. Wentworth died in 2012, and her replacement has yet to be named.

Noted without comment is Rip-Off! (Audible), an audio anthology of SF and fantasy stories edited by Gardner Dozois.

Jonathan Strahan, who had an excellent year in 2012, also edited the year's best fantasy anthology, a YA anthology about witches, Under My Hat: Tales from the Cauldron (Random House Books for Young Readers), which means that Strahan has pulled off, in my own estimation, anyway, the difficult task of editing both the best fantasy anthology and the best science fiction anthology of 2012. Not surprisingly, since it's aimed at a YA audience, Under My Hat is not as substantial and chewy as Strahan's Edge of Infinity, but it has a very pleasing wit and lightness of tone about it (for the most part, there are a few darker stories) that ought to appeal to the adult fantasy-reading audience as well. The best stories here include work by Peter S. Beagle, Margo Lanagan, Ellen Klages, Garth Nix, Jane Yolen, and Holly Black, although there are also good stories here by Ellen Kushner, Delia Sherman, Jim Butcher, M. Rickert, Patricia A. McKillip, Isobelle Carmody, Tim Pratt, Tanith Lee, Charles De Lint, Frances Hardinge, and Diana Peterfreund, as well as a poem by Neil Gaiman. A (mostly) reprint anthology on the same subject was this year's Witches: Wicked, Wild & Wonderful (Prime Books), edited by Paula Guran.

Other original fantasy anthologies were Magic, An Anthology of the Esoteric and Arcane, edited by Jonathan Oliver (Solaris); Elemental Magic: All-New Tales of the Elementary Masters (DAW), edited by Mercedes Lackey; and Hex Appeal (St. Martin's Griffin), edited by P. N. Elrod. There was a tribute anthology to Ray Bradbury, Shadow Show: All-New Stories in Celebration of·Ray Bradbury (William Morrow Paperbacks), edited by Sam Weller and Mort Castle; mostly fantasy with an admixture of horror, and a tribute anthology to Charles Dickens, Pandemonium: Stories of the Smoke (Jurrasic London), edited by Anne C. Perry and Jared Shurin; which had a similar fantasy/horror mix. Other books on the borderland between fantasy and horror included An Apple for the Creature (Ace), edited by Charlaine Harris and Toni L. P. Kelner; The Alchemy Press Book of Ancient Wonders (Alchemy Press), edited by Jan Edwards and Jenny Barber; The Alchemy Press Book of Pulp Heroes (Alchemy Press), edited by Mike Chinn; and Westward Weird (DAW), edited by Martin H. Greenberg and Kerrie Hughes; which also mixed in elements of the Western.

The most prominent original horror anthology this year seemed to be A Book of Horrors (St. Martin's Griffin), edited by Stephen Jones, but there was also a big zombie anthology, 21st Century Dead: A Zombie Anthology (St. Martin's Griffin), edited by Christopher Golden; Danse Macabre: Close Encounters with the Reaper (EDGE), edited by Nancy Kilpatrick; and *Dark Currents* (NewCon Press), edited by Ian Whates; and *The Weird: A Compendium of Strange and Dark Stories*, edited by Ann VanderMeer and Jeff VanderMeer.

Lavie Tidhar, Aliette de Bodard, Ken Liu, Elizabeth Bear, and (as usual) Robert Reed were all highly prolific this year, publishing good stories all over, in many different markets.

SF continued to appear in places well outside accepted genre boundaries, from the science magazines *Cosmos* and *Nature* to *The New Yorker*, which surprised everybody by releasing a "Special SF Issue" this year.

(Finding individual pricings for all of the items from small presses mentioned in the Summation has become too time intensive, and since several of the same small presses publish anthologies, novels, *and* short-story collections, it seems silly to repeat addresses for them in section after section. Therefore, I'm going to attempt to list here, in one place, all the addresses for small presses that have books mentioned here or there in the Summation, whether from the anthologies section, the novel section, or the short-story collection section, and, where known, their Web site addresses. That should make it easy enough for the reader to look up the individual price of any book mentioned that isn't from a regular trade publisher; such books are less likely to be found in your average bookstore, or even in a chain superstore, and so will probably have to be mail-ordered. Many publishers seem to sell only online, through their Web sites, and some will only accept payment through PayPal. Many books, even from some of the smaller presses, are also available through Amazon.com. If you can't find an address for a publisher, and it's quite likely that I've missed some here, or failed to update them successfully, Google it. It shouldn't be that difficult these days to find up-to-date contact information for almost any publisher, however small.)

Addresses are: **PS Publishing**, Grosvener House, 1 New Road, Hornsea, West Yorkshire, HU18 1PG, England, UK www.pspublishing.co.uk; **Golden Gryphon Press**, 3002 Perkins Road, Urbana, IL 61802, www.goldengryphon.com; **NESFA Press**, P.O. Box 809, Framingham, MA 01701-0809, www.nesfa.org; **Subterranean Press**, P.O. Box 190106, Burton, MI 48519, www.subterraneanpress.com; **Old Earth Books**, P.O. Box 19951, Baltimore, MD 21211-0951, www.oldearthbooks .com; **Tachyon Press**, 1459 18th St. #139, San Francisco, CA 94107, www.tachyon publications.com; **Night Shade Books**, 1470 NW Saltzman Road, Portland, OR 97229, www.nightshadebooks.com; **Five Star Books**, 295 Kennedy Memorial Drive, Waterville, ME 04901, www.galegroup.com/fivestar; **NewCon Press**, via www.newconpress.com; **Small Beer Press**, 176 Prospect Ave., Northampton, MA 01060, www.smallbeerpress.com; **Locus Press**, P.O. Box 13305, Oakland, CA 94661; **Crescent Books**, Mercat Press Ltd., 10 Coates Crescent, Edinburgh, Scotland EH3 7AL, UK, www.crescentfiction.com; **Wildside Press/Borgo Press**, P.O. Box 301, Holicong, PA 18928-0301, or go to www.wildsidepress.com for pricing and ordering; **Edge Science Fiction and Fantasy Publishing, Inc. and Tesseract Books, Ltd.**, P.O. Box 1714, Calgary, Alberta, T2P 2L7, Canada, www.edgewebsite.com; **Aqueduct Press**, P.O. Box 95787, Seattle, WA 98145-2787, www.aqueductpress.com; **Phobos Books**, 200 Park Avenue South, New York, NY 10003, www.phobosweb.com; **Fairwood Press**, 5203 Quincy Ave. SE, Auburn, WA 98092, www.fairwoodpress .com; **BenBella Books**, 6440 N. Central Expressway, Suite 508, Dallas, TX 75206, www.benbellabooks.com; **Darkside Press**, 13320 27thAve. NE, Seattle, WA 98125, www.darksidepress.com; **Haffner Press**, 5005 Crooks Rd., Suite 35, Royal Oak, MI 48073-1239, www.haffnerpress.com; **North Atlantic Press**, P.O. Box 12327, Berkeley, CA, 94701; **Prime Books**, P.O. Box 36503, Canton, OH, 44735, www.prime books.net; **Fairwood Press**, 5203 Quincy Ave. SE, Auburn, WA 98092, www.fair woodpress.com; **MonkeyBrain Books**, 11204 Crossland Drive, Austin, TX 78726, www.monkeybrainbooks.com; **Wesleyan University Press**, University Press of New England, Order Dept., 37 Lafayette St., Lebanon NH 03766-1405, www.wesleyan .edu/wespress; **Agog! Press**, P.O. Box U302, University of Wollongong, NSW 2522, Australia, www.uow.ed.au/~rhood/agogpress; **Wheatland Press**, via www.wheat landpress.com; **MirrorDanse Books**, P.O. Box 3542, Parramatta NSW 2124, Austra-lia, www.tabula-rasa.info/MirrorDanse; **Arsenal Pulp Press**, 103-1014 Homer Street, Vancouver, BC, Canada V6B 2W9, www.arsenalpress.com; **DreamHaven Books**, 912 W. Lake Street, Minneapolis, MN 55408; **Elder Signs Press/Dimen-sions Books**, order through www.dimensionsbooks.com; **Chaosium**, via www.chao-sium.com; **Spyre Books**, P.O. Box 3005, Radford, VA 24143; **SCIFI, Inc.**, P.O. Box 8442, Van Nuys, CA 91409-8442; **Omnidawn Publishing**, order through www. omnidawn.com; **CSFG**, Canberra Speculative Fiction Guild, www.csfg.org.au/ publishing/anthologies/the_outcast; **Hadley Rille Books**, via www.hadleyrillebooks .com; **Suddenly Press**, via suddenlypress@yahoo.com; **Sandstone Press**, P.O. Box 5725, One High St., Dingwall, Ross-shire, IV15 9WJ; **Tropism Press**, via www.tro pismpress.com; **SF Poetry Association/Dark Regions Press**, www.sfpoetry.com, send checks to Deborah Flores, SFPA Treasurer, P.O. Box 4846, Covina, CA 91723; **DH Press**, via diamondbookdistributors.com; **Kurodahan Press**, via www .kurodahan.com; **Ramble House**, 443 Gladstone Blvd., Shreveport LA 71104; **In-terstitial Arts Foundation**, via www.interstitialarts.org; **Raw Dog Screaming**, via www.rawdogscreaming.com; **Three Legged Fox Books**, 98 Hythe Road, Brigh-ton, BN1 6JS, UK; **Norilana Books**, via www.norilana.com; **coeur de lion**, via http://coeurdelion.com.au; **PARSECink**, via www.parsecink.org; **Robert J. Sawyer Books**, via www.sfwriter.com/rjsbooks.htm; **Rackstraw Press**, via http://rackstraw press; **Candlewick**, via www.candlewick.com; **Zubaan**, via www.zubaanbooks.com; **Utter Tower**, via www.threeleggedfox.co.uk; **Spilt Milk Press**, via www.electric velocipede.com; **Paper Golem**, via www.papergolem.com; **Galaxy Press**, via www.galaxypress.com.; **Twelfth Planet Press**, via www.twelfhplanetpress.com; **Five Senses Press**, via www.sensefive.com; **Elastic Press**, via www.elasticpress.com; **Lethe Press**, via www.lethepressbooks.com; **Two Cranes Press**, via www.twocranes press.com; **Wordcraft of Oregon**, via www.wordcraftoforegon.com; **Down East**, via www.downeast.com; **ISFiC Press**, 456 Douglas Ave., Elgin, IL 60120 or www.isfic press.com.

According to the newsmagazine *Locus*, there were 2,951 books "of interest to the SF field" published in 2012, down 4 percent from 3,071 titles in 2011, the first year of decline after five years of record numbers. Overall, new titles were down 5 per-cent to 2,030 from 2011's 2,140, while reprints dropped 3 percent to 921 from 2011's 931, cumulatively down 4 percent to 2,951 from 2011's 3071. Hardcover sales were actually up, from 867 to 875, while the number of trade paperbacks sold saw only a slight decline, from 1,355 to 1,343; the big drop was in mass-market paperbacks, which dipped 14 percent from 849 to 733, probably because of competition with e-books, which seem to be cutting into mass-market sales more than any other category. The number of new SF novels was up 4 percent to 318 titles as opposed to 2011's 305. The number of new fantasy novels was up by 2 percent, to 670 titles as opposed to 2011's total of 660. Horror novels were down 10 percent, after a 9 percent drop in 2010, to 207 titles as opposed to 2011's 229 titles. Paranormal romances were down to 314 titles as opposed to 2011's 416 titles (although sometimes it's almost a subjective call whether a particular novel should be pigeonholed as paranormal romance, fantasy, or horror).

Young adult novels continued to boom in SF, while declining in fantasy. YA fantasy novels made up 33 percent of the overall fantasy novel total, down from 35 percent in 2011, while YA SF novels rose from 24 percent of the overall SF novel total in 2011 to 28 percent in 2012. Most of this increase was in dystopian and post-apocalyptic YA SF novels, perhaps driven by the success of *The Hunger Games* novels and films.

(It's worth noting that these totals don't count e-books, media tie-in novels, gaming novels, novelizations of genre movies, or print-on-demand books—all of which would swell the overall total by hundreds if counted.)

As usual, busy with all the reading I have to do at shorter lengths, I didn't have time to read many novels myself this year, so I'll limit myself to mentioning that novels that received a lot of attention and acclaim in 2012 include:

Blue Remembered Earth (Ace Hardcover), by Alastair Reynolds; *2312* (Orbit), by Kim Stanley Robinson; *Intruder* (DAW), by C. J. Cherryh: *The Fractal Prince* (Tor), by Hannu Rajaniemi; *The Hydrogen Sonata* (Orbit), by Iain M. Banks; Red Country (Orbit), by Joe Abercrombie; *Range of Ghosts* (Tor), by Elizabeth Bear; *In the Mouth of the Whale* (Gollancz), by Paul McAuley; *Redshirts* (Tor), by John Scalzi; *The Drowned Cities* (Little, Brown), by Paolo Bacigalupi; *Be My Enemy* (Pyr), by Ian McDonald; *Dodger* (Harper), by Terry Pratchett; *Existence* (Tor), by David Brin; *The Long Earth* (Harper), by Terry Pratchett and Stephen Baxter; *The Great Game* (Angry Robot), by Lavie Tidhar; *Apollo's Outcasts* (Pyr), by Allen Steele; *The Apocalypse Codex* (Ace), by Charles Stross; *Some Kind of Fairy Tale* (Doubleday), by Graham Joyce; *Harmony* (Solaris), by Keith Brooke; *The Inexplicables* (Tor), by Cherie Priest; *Kitty Steals the Show* (Tor), by Carrie Vaughn; *The Rapture of the Nerds* (Tor), Cory Doctorow and Charles Stross; *Empty Space* (Gollancz), by M. John Harrison; *Bowl of Heaven* (Tor), by Larry Niven and Gregory Benford; *Captain Vorpatril's Alliance* (Baen), Lois McMaster Bujold; *Shadows in Flight* (Tor), by Orson Scott Card; *Slow Apocalypse* (Ace), by John Varley; *Caliban's War* (Orbit), by James S.A. Corey; *Sharps* (Orbit), by K. J. Parker; *City of Dragons* (Harper Voyager), by Robin Hobb; *Great North Road* (Del Rey), by Peter F. Hamilton; *The Fourth Wall* (Orbit), by Walter Jon Williams; *Ashes of Candesce* (Tor), by Karl Schroeder; *Whispers Under Ground* (Del Rey), by Ben Aaronovitch; *Queen's Hunt* (Tor), by Beth Bernobich; *The King's Blood* (Orbit), by Daniel Abraham; *Triggers* (Ace), by Robert J. Sawyer; *Forge of Darkness* (Tor), by Steven Erikson; *Sea Hearts* (Allen & Unwin), by Margo Lanagan; *Railsea* (Del Rey), by China Mieville; *Crucible of Gold* (Del Rey), by Naomi Novik; *Hide Me Among the Graves* (William Morrow), by Tim Powers; *The Coldest War* (Tor), by Ian Tregillis; and *Boneland* (Fourth Estate), by Alan Garner.

For at least fifteen years now, I've been hearing the complaint that all the SF books have been driven off the bookstore shelves by fantasy books, but there's still plenty of it around. On the list above, although there's a number of fantasy titles, there are quite a few undeniably core SF titles there as well: the Robinson, the Reynolds, the McAuley, the Steele, the McDonald, the Bacigalupi, the Schroeder, the Corey, the Cherryh, the Banks, the Hamilton, and many others. Many more could be cited from the lists of small-press novels and first novels. Yes, fantasy is popular, but science fiction has not vanished yet—there's still more good core SF out there than any one person could possibly have time to read in the course of a year.

Small presses are active in the novel market these days, where once they published mostly collections and anthologies. Novels issued by small presses this year included: *The Eternal Flame: Orthogonal Book Two* (Night Shade Books Books), by Greg Egan; *Time and Robbery* (Aqueduct Press), by Rebecca Ore; *Zeuglodon* (Subterranean Press), by James P. Blaylock; *Black Opera* (Night Shade Books), by Mary Gentle; *Ison of the Isles* (ChiZine), Carolyn Ives Gilman; *Worldsoul* (Prime Books), by Liz Williams; *Everything Is Broken* (Prime Books), by John Shirley; *Swallowing a Donkey's Eye* (ChiZine), by Paul Tremblay; *The Architect* (PS Publishing), by Brendan Connell; *Against the Light* (47North), Dave Duncan; *Hitchers* (Night Shade Books), Will McIntosh; *Bullettime* (ChiZine), Nick Mamatas; *The Croning* (Night Shade Books), Laird Barron; and *Crandolin* (Chomu Press), by Anna Tambour.

The year's first novels included: *The Games* (Del Rey), Ted Kosmatka; *Throne of the Crescent Moon* (DAW), by Saladin Ahmed; *Grim* (Scholastic), by Anna Waggener; *Above* (Arthur A. Levine Books), by Leah Bobet; *Enchanted* (Harcourt), by Alethea Kontis; *Alif the Unseen* (Grove Press), by G. Willow Wilson; *Hidden Things* (Harper Voyager), by Doyce Testerman; *A Once Crowded Sky* (Touchstone), by Tom King; *The Minority Council* (Orbit), by Kate Griffin; *So Close to You* (Harper Teen), by Rachel Carter; *Blackwood* (Strange Chemistry), by Gwenda Bond; *Glitch* (St. Martin's Griffin), by Heather Anastasiu; *Albert of Adelaide* (Twelve), by Howard L. Anderson; *Something Strange and Deadly* (HarperTeen), by Susan Dennard; *Three Parts Dead* (Tor), by Max Gladstone; *Through to You* (Balzer + Bray), by Emily Hainsowrth; *Seraphina* (Random House), by Rachel Hartman; *Shadows Cast by Stars* (Atheneum), by Catherine Knutsson; *Blood and Feathers* (Solaris), by Lou Morgan; *Fair Coin* (Pyr), by E. C. Myers; *Year Zero* (Del Rey), by Rob Reid; *The Man from Primrose Lane* (Sarah Crichton), by James Renner; *Something Red* (Atria), by Douglas Nicholas; *Strange Flesh* (Simon & Schuster), by Michael Olson; *Starters* (Delacorte), by Lissa Price; and *Living Proof* (Tor), by Kira Peikoff. None of these novels generated an unusual amount of buzz; the most frequently reviewed were probably *The Games* and *Throne of the Crescent Moon*.

The strongest novella chapbooks of the year included *On a Red Station, Drifting* (Immersion Press), by Aliette de Bodard; *Gods of Risk* (Orbit), by James S. A. Corey; *The Boolean Gate* (Subterranean Press), by Walter Jon Williams; *The Yellow Cabochon* (PS Publishing), by Matthew Hughes; *After the Fall, Before the Fall, During the Fall* (Tachyon), by Nancy Kress; *Mare Ultima* (PS Publishing), by Alex Irvine; *Starship Winter* (PS Publishing), by Eric Brown; *An Account of a Voyage from World to World* (Jurassic), by Adam Roberts; *Indomitable* (Subterranean Press), by Terry Brooks; *Face in the Crowd* (Simon & Schuster), by Stephen King and Steward O'Nan; *When the Blue Shift Comes* (Phoenix Pick), by Robert Silverberg and Alvaro Zinos-Amaro; *The Thorn and the Blossom* (Quirk Books), by Theodora Goss; *From*

Whence You Came (d.y.m.k. Productions), by Laura Ann Gilman; *The Pit of Despair* (PS Publishing), by Simon R. Green, and *ad eternum* (Subterranean Press) and *Book of Iron* (Subterranean Press), both by Elizabeth Bear.

As you can see, this category is largely dominated by Subterranean Press and PS Publishing.

Novel omnibuses this year included: *American Science Fiction: Nine Classic Novels of the 1950s* (Library of America), edited by Gary K. Wolfe; *Ride the Star Winds* (Baen), by A. Bertram Chandler; *Thunder in the Void* (Haffner), by Henry Kuttner, edited by Stephen Haffner; *The Chalice of Death* (Paizo/Planet Stories), by Robert Silverberg; *The Planet Killers* (Paizo/Planet Stories), by Robert Silverberg; *A Song Called Youth* (Prime Books), by John Shirley; *The Ghost Pirates and Others: The Best of William Hope Hodgson* (Night Shade Books), by William Hope Hodgson, edited by Jeremy Lasson (contains short stories as well); *Earthblood and Other Stories* (Baen), by Keith Laumer and Rosel George Brown (contains short stories as well); and *Ice and Shadow* (Baen), by Andre Norton. Novel omnibuses are also frequently made available through the Science Fiction Book Club.

Not even counting print-on-demand books and the availability of out-of-print books as e-books or as electronic downloads from Internet sources, a lot of long out-of-print stuff has come back into print in the last couple of years in commercial trade editions. Here are some out-of-print titles that came back into print this year, although producing a definitive list of reissued novels is probably impossible. Tor reissued: *Mother of Storms*, by John Barnes; *Earthseed*, by Pamela Sargent; *After the King: Stories in Honor of J.R.R. Tolkien*, edited by Martin H. Greenberg; *Foundation's Friends*, edited by Martin H. Greenberg; *The Eye of the World*, *The Fires of Heaven*, *The Great Hunt*, and *Lord of Chaos*, all by Robert Jordan. Orb reissued *Peace*, by Gene Wolfe; *Downward to the Earth*, by Robert Silverberg; and *The Long Price: The Price of War*, by Daniel Abraham. Baen reissued *When the People Fell*, by Cordwainer Smith; *Voyage Across the Stars*, by David Drake; *Strangers*, by Gardner Dozois; *Nightmare Blue*, by Gardner Dozois and George Alec Effinger; *The Forerunner Factor*, by Andre Norton; and *An Assignment in Eternity*, *Sixth Column*, and *The Star Beast*, all by Robert A. Heinlein. Subterranean Press reissued *Dying of the Light*, by George R. R. Martin; *Phases of Gravity*, by Dan Simmons; and *Stranger Things Happen*, by Kelly Link. Ace reissued *Illegal Alien*, by Robert J. Sawyer. Bantam reissued *Windhaven*, by George R.R. Martin and Lisa Tuttle. William Morrow reissued *Stardust: The Gift Edition—Deluxe Signed Limited*, by Neil Gaiman. Ballantine/Del Rey reissued: *The Annotated Sword of Shannara: 35th Anniversary Edition*. Houghton Mifflin reissued *The Hobbit*, by J.R.R. Tolkien; *A Wizard of Earthsea*, by Ursula K. Le Guin; and *Counter-Clock World*; *Flow My Tears, the Policeman Said*; *Gather Yourself Together*; and *Solar Lottery*, all by Philip K. Dick. Harcourt/Mariner reissued *The Man in the High Castle* and *Time Out of Joint*, by Philip K. Dick. The Library of America reissued *A Princess of Mars* and *Tarzan of the Apes*, by Edgar Rice Burroughs. Fairwood Press reissued *Brittle Innings*, by Michael Bishop. Roc reissued *Majipoor Chronicles*, by Robert Silverberg. Arc Manor reissued *The Masks of Time* and *Thebes of the Hundred Gates*, by Robert Silverberg. Chicago Review Press reissued *Roadside Picnic*, by Arkady and Boris Strugatsky.

PM Press reissued *Byzantium Endures* and *The Laughter of Cathage*, by Michael Moorcock. Farrar, Straus and Giroux reissued *A Wrinkle in Time*, by Madeleine L'Engle. Grand Central reissued *The New Moon's Arms*, by Nalo Hopkinson. Scribner reissued *Black House*, by Stephen King and Peter Straub. Wesleyan University Press reissued *Starboard Wine: More Notes on the Language of Science Fiction*, by Samuel R. Delany. Open Road reissued *Alien Sex*, edited by Ellen Datlow. Underland Press reissued *Glimmering*, by Elizabeth Hand. HiLoBooks reissued *When the World Shook*, by H. Rider Haggard.

Many authors are now reissuing their old back titles as e-books, either through a publisher or all by themselves, so many that it's impossible to keep track of them all here. Before you conclude that something from an author's backlist is unavailable, though, check with the Kindle and Nook stores, and with other online vendors.

2012 was a strong year for short-story collections. The year's best collections included: *The Best of Kage Baker* (Subterranean Press), by Kage Baker; *Other Seasons: The Best of Neal Barrett, Jr.* (Subterranean Press), by Neal Barrett, Jr.; *Shoggoths in Bloom* (Prime Books), by Elizabeth Bear; *The Pottawatomie Giant and Other Stories* (PS Publishing), by Andy Duncan; *At the Mouth of the River of Bees* (Small Beer Press), by Kij Johnson; *Eater-of-Bone and Other Novellas* (PS Publishing), by Robert Reed; *The 400-Million-Year Itch* (Ticonderoga), by Steven Utley; *Win Some, Lose Some: The Hugo Award Winning (And Nominated) Short Fiction of Mike Resnick* (ISFIC Press) by Mike Resnick; *Fountain of Age: Stories* (Small Beer Press), by Nancy Kress; *A Stark and Wormy Knight* (Subterranean Press), by Tad Williams; and *The Dragon Griaule* (Subterranean Press), by Lucius Shepard. Also good were: *Captive Dreams* (Arc Manor), by Michael F. Flynn; *Neil Gwyne's On Land and At Sea* (Subterranean Press), by Kage Baker and Kathleen Bartholomew; *First and Last Contacts* (NewCon), by Stephen Baxter; *Flying in the Heart of the Lafayette Escadrille and Other Stories* (Fairwood Press), by James Van Pelt; *Angels and You Dogs* (PS Publishing), by Kathleen Ann Goonan; *Errantry* (Small Beer Press) by Elizabeth Hand; *Crackpot Palace* (Morrow), by Jeffery Ford; *Birds and Birthdays* (Aqueduct Press), by Christopher Barzak; *Jagannath* (Cheeky Frawg Books), by Karin Tidbeck; *Near + Far* (Hydra House Books), by Cat Rambo; *Master of the Galaxy* (PS Publishing), by Mike Resnick; *Resnick's Menagerie* (Silverberry), by Mike Resnick; *Moscow But Dreaming* (Prime Books), by Ekaterina Sedia; *Cracklespace* (Twelfth Planet), by Margo Lanagan; *Confessions of a Five-Chambered Heart* (Subterranean Press), by Catlin R. Kiernan; *You Will Meet a Stranger Far from Home* (Lethe Press), by Alex Jeffers; *Trapped in the Saturday Matinee* (PS Publishing), by Joe R. Lansdale; *Report from Planet Midnight* (PM Press), by Nalo Hopkinson; *The Janus Tree and Other Stories* (Subterranean Press), by Glen Hirshberg; and *Earth and Air: Tales of Elemental Creatures* (Big Mouth House), by Peter Dickinson.

Career-spanning retrospective collections this year included: *The Unreal and the Real: Selected Stories Volume One: Where on Earth* (Small Beer Press), by Ursula K. Le Guin; *The Unreal and the Real: Selected Stories Volume Two: Outer Space, Inner Lands* (Small Beer Press), by Ursula K. Le Guin; *Dream Castles: The Early Jack Vance, Volume Two* (Subterranean Press), by Jack Vance, edited by Terry Dowling and Jonathan Strahan; *The Collected Kessel* (Baen), by John Kessel; *The Collected*

Stories of Robert Silverberg, Volume 7: We Are For the Dark (Subterranean Press), by Robert Silverberg; *The Best of Robert Silverberg: Stories of Six Decades* (Subterranean Press), by Robert Silverberg; *The Door Gunner and Other Perilous Flights of Fancy: A Michael Bishop Retrospective* (Subterranean Press), by Michael Bishop, edited by Michael H. Hutchins; *A Blink of the Screen: Collected Short Fiction* (Doubleday UK), by Terry Pratchett; *The Collected Stories of Philip K. Dick Volume Three Upon the Dull Earth (1953–1954)* (Subterranean Press), by Philip K. Dick; *Kurt Vonnegut: Novels and Stories 1950–1962* (Library of America), by Kurt Vonnegut, edited by Sidney Offit; *Sex and Violence in Zero-G: The Complete "Near Space" Stories: Expanded Edition* (Fantastic Books), by Allen Steele; *Store of the Worlds: The Stories of Robert Sheckley* (New York Review Books Classics), by Robert Sheckley; *A Song Called Youth* (Prime Books), by John Shirley; *Wonders of the Invisible World* (Tachyon), by Patricia A. McKillip; *Where the Summer Ends: The Best Horror Stories of Karl Edward Wagner, Volume 1* (Centipede), by Karl Edward Wagner, edited by Stephen Jones; *The Ghost Pirates and Others: The Best of William Hope Hodgson* (Night Shade Books—also contains a novel), by William Hope Hodgson, edited by Jeremy Lasson; and *A Niche in Time and Other Stories: The Best of William F. Temple, Volume 1* (Ramble House), by William F. Temple.

As has been true for at least a decade now, small presses again dominated the list of short-story collections, with only a few trade collections being published. Subterranean Press was particularly active in this area this year.

A wide variety of "electronic collections," often called "fiction bundles," too many to individually list here, are also available for downloading online, at many sites. The Science Fiction Book Club continues to issue new collections as well.

The most reliable buys in the reprint anthology market, as usual, are the various Best of the Year anthologies. At the moment, science fiction is being covered by three anthologies (actually, technically, by two anthologies and by two separate half anthologies): the one you are reading at the moment, *The Year's Best Science Fiction* series from St. Martin's, edited by Gardner Dozois, now up to its thirtieth annual Collection; the *Year's Best SF* series (Harper Voyager), edited by David G. Hartwell and Kathryn Cramer, now up to its seventeenth annual volume; by the science fiction half of *The Best Science Fiction and Fantasy of the Year: Volume Six* (Night Shade Books), edited by Jonathan Strahan; and by the science fiction half of *The Year's Best Science Fiction and Fantasy: 2012 Edition* (Prime Books), edited by Rich Horton (in practice, of course, these books probably won't divide neatly in half with their coverage, and there's likely to be more of one thing than another). The annual Nebula Awards anthology, which covers science fiction as well as fantasy of various sorts, functions as a de facto Best of the Year anthology, although it's not usually counted among them; this year's edition was *Nebula Awards Showcase 2012* (Pyr), edited by James Patrick Kelly and John Kessel. (A similar series covering the Hugo winners began in 2010, but swiftly died.) There were three Best of the Year anthologies covering horror: *The Best Horror of the Year: Volume Four* (Night Shade Books), edited by Ellen Datlow, and *The Mammoth Book of Best New Horror: 23* (Running Press), edited by Stephen Jones; and *The Year's Best Dark Fantasy and Horror: 2012 Edition* (Prime Books), edited by Paula Guran. Fantasy, which used to have several series devoted to it, is now, with the apparent death of David G. Hartwell and Kathryn Cramer's *Year's Best Fantasy* series, covered by the fantasy halves of the Strahan and Horton anthologies, plus whatever stories fall under the Dark Fantasy part of Guran's anthology. There was also *The 2012 Rhysling Anthology* (Hadrosaur Productions), edited by Lyn C. A. Gardner, which compiles the Rhysling Award-winning SF poetry of the year.

It was a somewhat weak year for large stand-alone reprint anthologies this year, especially in SF, although there were a fair number of good reprint theme anthologies.

Robots: The Recent A.I. (Prime Books), edited by Rich Horton and Sean Wallace, is a strong mixed reprint (mostly) and original anthology of, just as it says, recent stories about robots and A.I. (Artificial Intelligence, for those of you who haven't read any science fiction since the '50s). The one original story is a fine one, Lavie Tidhar's "Under the Eaves," included in this anthology, but the reprint stories are also strong, including stories by Catherynne M. Valente, Elizabeth Bear, Cory Doctorow, Ian McDonald, Rachel Swirsky, Benjamin Rosenbaum, Aliette de Bodard, Mary Robinette Kowal, James L. Cambias, Robert Reed, Tobias S. Buckell, Ken Liu, and others, all of which makes this one of the strongest reprint SF anthologies of the year.

Another good mixed reprint (mostly) and original SF anthology, by the same editorial team, is *War and Space: Recent Combat* (Prime Books), edited by Rich Horton and Sean Wallace, an anthology of recent Military SF, although their definition of Military SF seems a bit broader than it sometimes is. As with *Robots: The Recent A.I.*, there is one good original story here, Sandra McDonald's "Mehra and Jiun," as well as strong reprints by Ken MacLeod, David Moles, Charles Coleman Finlay, Yoon Ha Lee, Paul McAuley, Tom Purdom, Nancy Kress, Alastair Reynolds, Robert Reed, Kristine Kathryn Rusch, Geoffrey A. Landis, Cat Rambo, and others. Another good value for the money.

Rock On: The Greatest Hits of Science Fiction & Fantasy (Prime Books), edited by Paula Guran, is another mixed reprint (mostly) and original anthology featuring both SF and fantasy. Some of the best stories here are by Howard Waldrop, Michael Swanwick, Pat Cadigan, Norman Spinrad, Edward Bryant, Lewis Shiner, Lucius Shepard, Bruce Sterling, Alastair Reynolds, Elizabeth Bear, Bradley Denton, Elizabeth Hand, Marc Laidlaw, Caitlin R. Kiernan, John Shirley, and others, including original stories by Del James and Lawrence C. Connolly.

A good reprint anthology of parallel or alternate world stories is *Other Worlds Than These* (Night Shade Books), edited by John Joseph Adams, which featured good work by Ian McDonald, Alastair Reynolds, Kelly Link, Michael Swanwick, Yoon Ha Lee, Pat Cadigan, George R. R. Martin, Vandana Singh, Paul McAuley, Stephen Baxter, and others.

The Posthuman/Singularity story was never quite cohesive enough to function as a subgenre all its own, but there were *lots* of them throughout the '90s and the oughts, including some of the best work of those periods, and the form is still very much an important part of the current SF scene today. *Digital Rapture: The Singularity Anthology* (Tachyon), edited by James Patrick Kelly and John Kessel, a reprint anthology, does a good job of providing a historical overview of the Posthuman/Singularity form, taking us from an excerpt from Olaf Stapledon's *Odd John* in 1935, through perhaps the first modern posthuman story, Frederik Pohl's "Day Million," in 1966, through the cyberpunk days of the '80s, represented here by Bruce

Sterling, and on through the rich harvest of such stories from the '90s and oughts to the present. The best stories here, other than those already mentioned, are probably the ones by Charles Stross, Greg Egan, Cory Doctorow and Benjamin Rosenblum, Robert Reed, Justina Robson, and Hannu Rajaniemi. The anthology also contains a reprint of Vernor Vinge's seminal essay, "The Coming Technological Singularity: How to Survive in the Post-Human Era," an immensely influential bit of speculation that set many of the concerns and shaped much of the content of this kind of story, and which popularized the term "Singularity" itself; there are also speculative essays by Ray Kurzweil and J. D. Bernal, and other stories by Isaac Asimov, Rudy Rucker and Eileen Gunn, Elizabeth Bear, David D. Levine, and Vinge himself.

Retro SF is represented by *Tales from Super-Science Fiction* (Haffner), edited by Robert Silverberg, which features pulp stories from Jack Vance, Daniel F. Galouye, James Gunn, and Silverberg himself.

Substantial reprint fantasy anthologies included *The Sword & Sorcery Anthology* (Tachyon), edited by David Hartwell and Jacob Wiseman, and *Epic* (Tachyon), edited by John Joseph Adams. For those not familiar with Sword & Sorcery, *The Sword & Sorcery Anthology* is a good place to start, providing a historical overview of the Sword & Sorcery subgenre, from its beginnings in the *Weird Tales* of the 1930s up to the present day, with original stories by Michael Swanwick and Michael Shea. Unsurprisingly, the best stories here are classics by Robert E. Howard, C. L. Moore, Fritz Leiber, Poul Anderson, Michael Moorcock, and Joanna Russ, but there's also good stuff by Glen Cook, Rachel Pollack, George R. R. Martin, and others. *Epic: Legends of Fantasy*, is another meaty, solid anthology, this one all reprint, that will be valuable to beginning fantasy readers as a sampler of various fantasy styles; the best story here, and in fact one of the best fantasy novellas of the decade, is probably George R. R. Martin's "The Mystery Knight," an enormous novella set in the same general milieu as his bestselling A Song of Ice and Fire novels, but there are also strong stories by Robin Hobb, Patrick Rothfuss, Ursula K. Le Guin, Tad Williams, Orson Scott Card, Paolo Bacigalupi, Carrie Vaughn, Brandon Sanderson, Trudi Canavan, Aliette de Bodard, Kate Elliott, N. K. Jemisin, Juliet Marillier, and others.

Other reprint (mostly) fantasy anthologies included two books of Christmas stories, *Season of Wonder* (Prime Books), edited by Paula Guran, and *A Cosmic Christmas* (Baen), edited by Hank Davis; *Witches: Wicked, Wild & Wonderful* (Prime Books), edited by Paula Guran; and *Circus: Fantasy Under the Big Top* (Prime Books), edited by Ekaterina Sedia.

There were a lot of reprint horror anthologies, some of which included a few original stories, and occasionally an admixture of fantasy in varying strengths: *The Book of Cthulhu II* (Night Shade Books), edited by Ross E. Lockhart; *Ghosts: Recent Hauntings* (Prime Books), edited by Paula Guran; *The Mammoth Book of Ghost Stories by Women* (Running Press), edited by Marie O'Regan; *Extreme Zombies* (Prime Books), edited by Paula Guran; *Obsession: Tales of Irresistible Desire* (Prime Books), edited by Paula Guran; and *Bloody Fabulous* (Prime Books), edited by Ekaterina Sedia.

Anthologies of gay SF and fantasy and/or erotica included *Heiresses of Russ 2012: The Year's Best Lesbian Speculative Fiction* (Lethe Press), edited by Connie Wilkins and Steve Berman; *Fantastic Erotica: The Best of Circlet Press 2008–2012* (Circlet), edited by Cecilia Tan and Bethay Zaiatz; *Beyond Binary: Genderqueer and Sexually*

Fluid Fiction (Lethe Press), edited by Brit Mandelo; and *Wilde Stories 2012: The Year's Best Gay Speculative Fiction* (Lethe Press), edited by Steve Berman.

It was a somewhat weak year in the genre-oriented nonfiction category, mostly notable for books of essays by genre authors, including *An Exile on Planet Earth: Articles and Reflections* (Bodleian Library, University of Oxford), by Brian W. Aldiss; *Distrust That Particular Flavor* (Berkley), by William Gibson; *London Peculiar and Other Nonfiction* (PM Press), by Michael Moorcock, edited by Michael Moorcock and Allan Kausch; *Some Remarks* (William Morrow), by Neal Stephenson; *Reflections: On the Magic of Writing* (Greenwillow Books), by Diana Wynne Jones; and two books of essays and film reviews by Gary Westfahl, *The Spacesuit Film: A History* (McFarland) and *A Sense-of-Wonderful Century* (Borgo Press).

There were several critical studies of various genres, including *Science Fiction: The 101 Best Novels* (NonStop Press), by Damien Broderick and Paul Di Filippo; *Strange Divisions and Alien Territories: The Sub-Genres of Science Fiction* (Palgrave Macmillan), edited by Keith Brooke; *Unutterable Horror: A History of Supernatural Fiction [Volume II] (Twentieth and Twenty-first Centuries)* (PS Publishing), by S. T. Joshi; *The Cambridge Companion to Fantasy Literature* (Cambridge University Press), edited by Edward James and Farah Mendlesohn; *As If: Modern Enchantment and the Literary Prehistory of Virtual Reality* (Oxford University Press), by Michael Saler; and *Utopian Moments: Reading Utopian Texts* (Bloomsbury), by Miguel A. Ramiro Avilés and J. C. Davis. There were several studies of the work of individual authors, including a study of the work of Gene Wolfe, *Gate of Horn, Book of Silk: A Guide to Gene Wolfe's The Book of the Long Sun and The Book of the Short Sun* (Sirus Fiction), by Michael Andre-Driussi; *Judith Merril: A Critical Study* (McFarland), by Diane Newell and Victoria Lamont; *Turtle Recall: The Discworld Companion . . . So Far*, by Terry Pratchett and Stephen Briggs; *Scanned Clean: An Analysis of the Work of Michael Marshall Smith* (PS Publishing), by David Sweeney; and *The Manual of Aeronautics: An Illustrated Guide to the Leviathan Series* (Simon Pulse), by Scott Westerfield.

All Yesterdays: Unique and Speculative Views of Dinosaurs and Other Prehistoric Animals (lulu.com), by John Conway, is not technically genre oriented, but since I've never meet an SF fan who wasn't interested in dinosaurs, I'm including it anyway. If you haven't read anything about dinosaurs for the last decade or so, this book will be an eye-opener—these definitely aren't your father's dinosaurs, or even the dinosaurs you used to know as a kid when you marched a plastic T. rex across the living room rug while making growling sounds; for one thing, most of them have feathers! Another book that will interest most genre readers (and which makes for a nice segue into our next section) is *Dinosaur Art: The World's Greatest Paleoart* (Titan Books), edited by Steve White.

Speaking of art (see what I did there?), 2012 was a pretty weak year in the art-book market. As usual, your best bet was probably the latest in a long-running Best of the Year series for fantastic art, *Spectrum 19: The Best in Contemporary Fantastic Art* (Underwood Books), edited by Cathy Fenner and Arnie Fenner. Also good were *Expose 10: The Finest Digital Art in the Universe* (Ballistic Publishing), edited by Ronnie Gramazio; *The Art of the Hobbit by J. R. R. Tolkien* (Houghton Mifflin Harcourt), art by J. R. R. Tolkien, edited by Wayne G. Hammond and Christina Scull; *Art of the Dragon PB: The Definitive Collection of Contemporary Dragon Paintings*

(Vanguard Productions), edited by Patrick Wilshire and J. David Spurlock; *Trolls* (Abrams), by Brian Froud and Wendy Froud; *M. W. Kaluta: Sketchbook Series 1: Sketchbook* (IDW Publishing), by Michael William Kaluta; and, a bit on the edge of genre, but still vaguely justifiable because of its fantastic imagery, *In Wonderland: The Surrealist Adventures of Women Artists in Mexico and the United States* (Prestel USA), edited by Ilene Susan Fort and Tere Arcq, with Terri Geis.

According to the Box Office Mojo site (www.boxofficemojo.com), nine out of ten of the year's top-earning movies were genre films of one sort or another (if you're willing to count animated films and superhero movies as being "genre films"), as were sixteen out of the top twenty, and forty-five out of the top one hundred.

Like last year; four out of five of the year's top five box-office champs were genre movies—and if you're willing to accept the James Bond movie *Skyfall* as a genre film, as some would be, then all five were (I'm not willing to go that far myself, thinking that it stretches the already somewhat stretched definition of a "genre film" past the useful point, although it certainly could be argued that some of the impossible physical action would qualify as fantasy). Two of the top five were superhero movies, *Marvel's The Avengers* and *The Dark Knight Rises*, and one was a dystopian science fiction movie based on a bestselling YA series, *The Hunger Games*. *Skyfall* finished in fourth place, and a supernatural vampire romance, *The Twilight Saga: Breaking Dawn Part II*, came in fifth. The following five of the top ten were made up of the cinematic version of a classic fantasy novel, *The Hobbit: An Unexpected Journey*, a relaunch of a superhero franchise, *The Amazing Spider-Man*, an animated fantasy movie, *Brave*, a slob comedy about a living, talking teddy bear, *Ted*, and a new addition to a successful animated franchise (also about talking animals), *Madagascar 3: Europe's Most Wanted*. Further down the list were animated film *Dr. Seuss's The Lorax* at eleventh place, SF comedy *Men in Black 3* at twelfth place, animated films *Wreck-It Ralph* and *Ice Age: Continental Drift* at thirteenth and fourteenth places, fantasy film *Snow White and the Huntsman* in fifteenth place, animated horror comedy *Hotel Transylvania* in sixteenth place, and, finishing disappointingly in twentieth place, *Prometheus*, the prequel to *Alien*. The only nongenre movies in the top twenty were *Skyfall*, in fourth place, and *Lincoln*, *Taken 2*, and *21 Jump Street*, at seventeenth, eighteenth, and nineteenth places, respectively.

None of this should be surprising, and is the reason why a shitload (this is a precise critical term) of genre films are coming up in 2013. Genre films of one sort or another have dominated the box office top ten for more than a decade now. You have to go all the way back to 1998 to find a year when the year's top earner was a nongenre film, *Saving Private Ryan*.

The year's number-one box office champ was *Marvel's The Avengers*, which so far has earned an amazing $1,511,757,910 worldwide. Directed by cult-favorite Joss Whedon, creator of the TV classic *Buffy the Vampire Slayer*, it was also a pretty entertaining movie, as even those who are lukewarm about superhero movies, like me, had to admit. Next was the finale of the Christopher Nolan–directed *Batman* trilogy, *The Dark Knight Rises*, which raked in $1,081,041,287 worldwide, and which I was less enthusiastic about, not that anyone cares. There's a long fall thereafter to the movie in third place, *The Hunger Games*, which earned a "mere" $686,533,290 worldwide.

The Hobbit: An Unexpected Journey, a prequel of sorts to the Lord of the Rings movies, was released in mid-December to scathing reviews and a moderately sluggish domestic box-office start, reaching only sixth place in the 2012 ranking; by the second week in January 2013, though, it had recovered—in my opinion, because positive word-of-mouth reviews had had a chance to kick in, balancing the critical drubbing—and has already earned $824,820,000 worldwide overall, with probably a lot more to come in the rest of the year. I liked it quite a bit myself, although it's hard to argue against the opinion that it's too long, and would be a better movie with at least a half hour trimmed out of it (this seems to be a weakness of Peter Jackson movies; Jackson's *King Kong* had a good movie buried in it, but would have greatly benefited from having an hour cut from it). Martin Freeman was marvelous as Bilbo, as were (as usual) Andy Serkis as Gollum and Ian McKellan as Gandalf. In a controversial move, director Peter Jackson decided to stretch *The Hobbit* into three movies rather than one, or even two, and the second movie, *The Hobbit: The Desolation of Smaug*, will be out late in 2013.

I also enjoyed another of the year's most critically savaged movies, *John Carter*, a film version of Edgar Rice Burroughs's famous adventure novel, *A Princess of Mars*, which sends a heroic swashbuckler from Virginia to Mars to cross swords with the ferocious alien warriors who live there. Effectively sabotaged by its own studio (which dubbed it "the biggest bomb of all time" while it was *still in theaters*), critically drubbed, and given little real promotional or advertising support, it failed at the box office, unsurprisingly, although even so it came close to earning back its enormous production budget, earning $282,778,100 worldwide, and might have been a blockbuster with some studio support. In contrast to most reviews, word-of-mouth about it among many fans has been good to excellent, and although it's hardly without flaws, it's a solidly entertaining movie that deserved better.

The much-hyped *Dark Shadows* remake ended up in only thirty-sixth place on the box-office list, and the similarly hyped *Frankenweenie* made it only to ninetieth place. Josh Whedon's other 2012 movie, the clever postmodern horror film *The Cabin in the Woods*, made it only to seventy-eighth place, but got a lot of critical respect and some great reviews.

As usual, there were few movies that could be considered *science fiction* movies, as opposed to fantasy movies and superhero movies. Two of them have already been mentioned, *The Hunger Games*, the most successful SF movie of the year at the box office, and *John Carter*. Perhaps the most eagerly awaited SF movie of 2012 was *Prometheus*, a prequel of sorts to *Alien*; unfortunately, it underperformed at the box office, and was widely savaged in both professional and word-of-mouth reviews, proving a disappointment to many, although it did have a few avid supporters. The only other SF movies were a continuation of the *Men in Black* SF comedy franchise, *Men in Black 3*, which finished in twelfth place on the box office list, a convoluted time-travel thriller, *Looper*, which placed fortieth, an alien invasion movie loosely based on—or at least inspired by—a children's board game, *Battleship*, in forty-second place, and a perhaps ill-advised remake of *Total Recall*, which managed to make it only to fifty-first place. The reincarnation saga *Cloud Atlas*, which had a section set in the future, and so could be considered an SF movie of sorts, got some good reviews, but finished dead last in the list of a hundred bestselling movies. *Argo*, one of the most critically acclaimed movies of the year, has a tenuous connection to SF: the book the real-life conspirators claimed to be making as a cover story was Roger Zelazny's *Lord of Light*. However, it would be too much of a stretch to claim it as an SF movie, or even as a genre film.

As some of these immense sums should indicate, it wasn't a bad year at the box office for the movie industry. Overall profits were up 6.5 percent, to 10.83 billion from 2011's 10.17 billion, and ticket sales were up to 1.36 billion, from 2011's 1.28 billion—still a fair distance from 2002's record 1.58 billion. In spite of the recession and the price of tickets, which keeps inching up, and the availability of movies on TV and via the Internet, many people are still willing to buy tickets—although I suspect that they're more willing to shell out for widescreen big-budget spectaculars with lots of splashy special effects than they are for quieter movies, for which they might be willing to wait until they come out on DVD.

Most of the buzz about upcoming films seems to center around the new *Star Trek* film, *Star Trek Into Darkness*, and the second *Hobbit* movie, *The Hobbit: The Desolation of Smaug*, but I suspect that the giant robots-fight-Godzilla-like-monsters film, *Pacific Rim*, is also going to make a bazillion bucks, and there's also a fair amount of anticipation about the movie version of Orson Scott Card's novel *Ender's Game* and the new *Hunger Games* movie, *The Hunger Games: Catching Fire*. There'll also be a big-budget reimagining of *The Wizard of Oz*, called *Oz the Great and Powerful*.

There are so many fantasy/SF shows on television now that, like cowboy shows in the '50s, it's sometimes hard to keep track of them all. As was true of 2011, the big success story of 2012 was probably HBO's *A Game of Thrones*, based on the bestselling Song of Ice and Fire series of fantasy novels by George R. R. Martin, which managed to become even more popular than it had been the year before, and is now a full-fledged Cultural Phenomenon—*Game of Thrones* references are now understood by just about everybody, even those who don't usually self-identify as fantasy fans, and pop up everywhere, from *The Big Bang Theory* to *Saturday Night Live*, which ran a satire of the show, complete with a satirical take on Martin himself. Needless to say, it's coming back in 2013. HBO's other genre show, the campy vampire show *True Blood*, is also coming back in 2013, for what may or may not be its last season, depending, I would imagine, on whether or not it pulls itself out of the ratings slump that has eaten (sucked?) away its audience during the previous two seasons. The show could still be turned around, but the quality of the writing needs to improve from an awful fifth season and an only so-so sixth season to the level of the first couple of seasons.

That other Cultural Phenomenon, *Dr. Who* (which has won so many Hugo Awards by now that fans joke that the Best Dramatic Presentation, Short Form category should be renamed the *Dr. Who* category), is, of course, also returning in 2013.

The two big debut SF shows of the last couple of seasons were *Terra Nova* and *Falling Skies*, both boasting unusually high budgets for television, and both produced by movie director Steve Spielberg. *Falling Skies*, in which embattled gue-rilla militiamen battle alien invaders, has survived and become moderately successful, but *Terra Nova*, in which refuges flee through time to the dinosaur era, never really did catch on, and has died. Another Spielberg-produced show, the hor-ror series *The River*, also died. One big-budget TV show upon which a lot of hopes were pinned, *Alcatraz*, by *Lost* creator J. J. Abrahms, died as well, after a disap-pointingly short run, as did *Last Resort*, supernatural show *666 Park Avenue*, *A Gifted Man*, *The Secret Circle*, *The Event*, and *Ringer*, which had excited some fans by bringing *Buffy the Vampire Slayer*'s Sarah Michelle Gellar back to the small screen. Long-running supernatural shows *Medium* and *Ghost Whisperer* died, as did *Legend of the Seeker*, *Merlin*, and *Camelot*, as well as the SF comedy *Eureka*. Cult favorite SF show *Fringe* will run its last few episodes in 2013, and then die, too, after five seasons.

Supernatural, *The Vampire Diaries*, *The Walking Dead*, *Teen Wolf*, *Being Hu-man*, the animated *Star Wars: The Clone Wars*, and *American Horror Story* are all coming back, as are the dueling fairy-tale series, *Grimm* and *Once Upon a Time*. SF comedies *Warehouse 13* and *Futurama* are returning, as is semi-SF (a straight thriller, really, other than the heroes having a super-advanced computer that helps them spot crimes before they happen) show, *Person of Interest*. *Touch* is returning, but is said to be "on the bubble," and may not last much longer. Coming up some-time in 2013 is a TV movie prequel to *Battlestar Galactica*, called *Battlestar Galac-tica: Blood and Chrome*.

Of the new shows already on the air, the most buzz so far seems to be generated by *Arrow*, a gritty reboot of D.C. Comics long-running superhero character, Green Arrow. *Revolution*, set in a world in which electricity no longer works and people are reduced to using horses, swords, and bows (think *Hunger Games*, set in a post-apocalyptic, no-technology future), has also generated some buzz, but seems a bit shaky in the ratings, as is the new version of *Beauty and the Beast*.

New shows coming up include *Defiance*, an SF/western described as "*Deadwood* with aliens," *Orphan Black*, a clone drama, *Zero Hour*, an *X-Files*-like show that tackles conspiracy theories, *Under the Dome*, which follows people imprisoned un-der a dome by mysterious forces, *Continuum*, about a time-traveling cop, *Lost Girl*, which explores the problems of fairies exiled in the modern world, supernatural show *Da Vinci's Demons*, and a new version of Dr. Jekyll and Mr. Hyde, *Do No Harm*. The most fan anticipation seems to be building for a rumored *Avengers* spin-off series to be directed by Joss Whedon, *S.H.I.E.L.D.*

Miniseries versions of Kim Stanley Robinson's *Red Mars*, Joe Haldeman's *The Forever War*, and Philip Jose Farmer's *Riverworld* have been promised for so long now that I begin to wonder if we'll ever see them at all.

Chicon 7: The 70th World Science Fiction Convention, was held in Chicago, Illi-nois, from August 30 to September 3, 2012. The 2012 Hugo Awards, presented at Chicon 7, were: Best Novel, *Among Others*, by Jo Walton; Best Novella, "The Man Who Bridged the Mist," by Kij Johnson; Best Novelette, "Six Months, Three Days," by Charlie Jane Anders; Best Short Story, "The Paper Menagerie," by Ken Liu; Best Related Work, *The Encyclopedia of Science Fiction, Third Edition*, by John Clute,

David Langford, Peter Nicholls, and Graham Sleight; Best Editor, Long Form, Betsy Wollheim; Best Editor, Short Form, Sheila Williams; Best Professional Artist, John Picacio; Best Dramatic Presentation (short form), *Doctor Who*: "The Doctor's Wife"; Best Dramatic Presentation (long form), *Game of Thrones—Season 1*; Best Graphic Story, *Digger*, by Ursula Vernon; Best Semiprozine, *Locus*; Best Fanzine, *SF Signal*; Best Fan Writer, Jim C. Hines; Best Fan Artist, Maurine Starkey; plus the John W. Campbell Award for Best New Writer to E. Lily Yu.

The 2011 Nebula Awards, presented at a banquet at the Hyatt Regency Crystal City hotel in Arlington, Virginia, on May 19, 2012, were: Best Novel, *Among Others*, by Jo Walton; Best Novella, "The Man Who Bridged the Mist," by Kij Johnson; Best Novelette, "What We Found," by Geoff Ryman; Best Short Story, "The Paper Menagerie," by Ken Liu; Ray Bradbury Award, *Doctor Who*: "The Doctor's Wife"; the Andre Norton Award, *The Freedom Maze*, by Delia Sherman; Solstice Awards to Octavia E. Butler and John Clute; the Service to SFWA Award to Clarence Howard "Bud" Webster; and the Damon Knight Memorial Grand Master Award to Connie Willis.

The 2012 World Fantasy Awards, presented at a banquet on November 4, 2012 in Toronto, Canada, during the Twenty-First Annual World Fantasy Convention, were: Best Novel, *Osama*, by Lavie Tidhar; Best Novella, "A Small Price to Pay for Birdsong," by K. J. Parker; Best Short Fiction, "The Paper Menagerie," by Ken Liu; Best Collection, *The Bible Repairman and Other Stories*, by Tim Powers; Best Anthology, *The Weird*, edited by Ann and Jeff VanderMeer; Best Artist, John Coulthart; Special Award (Professional), to Eric Lane; Special Award (Non-Professional), to Raymond Russell and Rosalie Parker; plus the Life Achievement Award to George R. R. Martin and Alan Garner.

The 2011 Bram Stoker Awards, presented by the Horror Writers of America on April 1, 2012 in Salt Lake City, Utah, were: Best Novel, *Flesh Eaters*, by Joe McKinney; Best First Novel, *Isis Unbound*, by Allyson Bird; Best Young Adult Novel, *The Screaming Season*, by Nancy Holder and *Dust & Decay*, by Jonathan Mayberry (tie); Best Long Fiction, *The Ballad of Ballard and Sandrine*, by Peter Straub; Best Short Fiction, "Herman Wouk Is Still Alive," by Stephen King; Best Collection, *The Corn Maiden and Other Nightmares*, by Joyce Carol Oates; Best Anthology, *Demons: Encounters with the Devil and his Minions, Fallen Angels and the Possessed*, edited by John Skipp; Best Nonfiction, *Stephen King: A Literary Companion*, by Rocky Wood; Best Poetry Collection, *How to Recognize a Demon Has Become Your Friend*, by Linda Addison; plus Lifetime Achievement Awards to Rick Hautala and Joe R. Lansdale.

The 2012 John W. Campbell Memorial Award was won by *The Islanders*, by Christopher Priest and *The Highest Frontier*, by Joan Slonczewsk (tie).

The 2012 Theodore Sturgeon Memorial Award for Best Short Story was won by "The Choice," by Paul McAuley.

The 2012 Philip K. Dick Memorial Award went to *Equations of Life/Samuel Petrovitch*, by Simon Morden.

The 2012 Arthur C. Clarke award was won by *The Testament of Jessie Lamb*, by Jane Rogers.

The 2012 James Tiptree, Jr. Memorial Award was won by *The Drowning Girl*, by Caitlin R. Kiernan, and *Ancient, Ancient*, by Kiini Ibura Salaam.

The 2011 Sidewise Award went to *Wake Up and Dream*, by Ian R. MacLeod (Long Form) and "Paradise Is a Walled Garden," by Lisa Goldstein (Short Form).

The Cordwainer Smith Rediscovery Award went to Katherine MacLean.

Dead in 2012 or early 2013 were:

RAY BRADBURY, 91, one of the best-known and most iconic of all SF/fantasy writers, winner of the World Fantasy Award for Lifetime Achievement, the SFWA Grand Master Award, the Stoker Life Achievement Award, and many other honors, author of such famous books as *The Martian Chronicles*, *Fahrenheit 451*, *Dandelion Wine*, and *Something Wicked This Way Comes*, as well as hundreds of short stories and essays; **HARRY HARRISON**, 87, another giant of the SF field, author of *Make Room, Make Room* (filmed as *Soylent Green*), *Deathworld*, *Bill, the Galactic Hero*, the many *Stainless Steel Rat* books, and dozens of others; **GORE VIDAL**, 86, prolific author, essayist, political commentator, and media celebrity, whose twenty-five books include SF novels such as *A Visit to a Small Planet*, *Kalki*, and *Messiah*; **BORIS STUGATSKY**, 79, who, writing with his late brother **ARKADY**, became perhaps Russia's best-known SF writer, internationally renowned for the novel *Roadside Picnic*; **CHRISTOPHER SAMUEL YOUD**, 89, British SF author who wrote as **JOHN CHRISTOPHER**, best known for the novel *No Blade of Grass*, as well as the YA *The Tripod Trilogy: The White Mountains, The City of Gold and Lead*, and *The Pool of Fire*; **CARLOS FUENTES**, 82, famous Mexican magical realist; **JIM YOUNG**, 61, SF writer, actor, longtime fan, diplomat, a personal friend; **MARK BOURNE**, 50, SF writer, creator of planetarium shows and museum exhibitions, longtime fan, a personal friend; **STEVEN UTLEY**, 65, one of the most acclaimed and prolific authors at short-story length of his generation, someone who sold dozens of brilliant stories to practically every market in existence, best known for his long-running series of Silurian tales, a friend; **K. D. WENTWORTH**, 61, SF writer and editor, longtime fan, a friend; **KEVIN O' DONNELL, JR.**, 61, SF writer with ten novels and more than fifty short stories to his credit, former SFWA officer; **JOSEPHA SHERMAN**, 65, SF writer, editor, folklorist, longtime fan, a friend; **SIR PATRICK MOORE**, 89, astronomer, TV presenter, science popularizer, and author; **JANET BERLINER**, 73, SF writer, editor, anthologist; **ARDATH MAYHAR**, 81, SF writer; **MICHEAL ALEXANDER**, SF writer and Clarion West graduate; **SUZANNE ALLÉS BLOM**, 64, SF writer; **PETER PHILLIPS**, 92, SF writer; **STUART J. BYRNE**, 97, SF writer; **GENE DeWEESE**, 78, writer of SF and media novels; **ROLAND C. WAGNER**, 51, French writer, translator, editor; **PAUL HAINES**, 41, Australian SF writer; **CHRISTINE BROOKE-ROSE**, 89, novelist and scholar; **MARGARET MAHY**, 76, children's book author; **NICK WEBB**, 63, British publisher and author; **JEFF MILLAR**, 70, writer of the long-running syndicated comic strip *Tank McNamara*, as well as the occasional SF story; **ADAM NISWANDER**, 66, author and bookseller; **GRETTA M. ANDERSON**, 55, editor and publisher; **HILARY RUBINSTEIN**, 86, literary agent and editor; **JACK SCOVIL**, 74, literary agent; **WENDY WEIL**, 72, literary agent; **JACQUES GOIMARD**, 78, French critic and editor; **LISTER MATHESON**, 63, academic who was the former director of the Clarion Workshop; **STUART TEITLER**, 71, bookseller and collector; **JEAN GIRAUD**, a.k.a. **MOEBIUS**, 73, internationally renowned French artist and illustrator, widely influential with his work in comics, books, and films, inducted into The Science Fiction Hall of Fame; **RALPH Mc-QUARRIE**, 82, artist, conceptual designer and illustrator largely responsible for the look of the *Star Wars* films; **LEO DILLION**, 79, artist and illustrator, with his wife and collaborator Diane Dillion part of a Hugo-winning artistic team who illustrated a huge number of children's books, fantasy novels, and SF novels; **MAURICE SENDAK**, 83, children's author and artist, best known for *Where the Wild Things Are* and *In the Night Kitchen*; **MICHAEL EMBDEN**, 63, British cover artist and illustrator; **DAVID GROVE**, 72, SF cover artist and illustrator; **ALAN HUNTER**, 89, British fan artist; **CYNTHIA GOLDSTONE**, 90, artist, writer, and longtime fan; **NEIL ARMSTRONG**, 82, astronaut, the first human being to walk on the moon; **SALLY RIDE**, 61, astronaut, the first American woman to travel into space; **JONATHAN FRID**, 87, television actor, best known for playing vampire Barnabas Collins on the original TV supernatural soap opera version of *Dark Shadows*; **ERNEST BORGNINE**, 95, television and movie actor, best known to genre audiences for roles in *Ice Station Zebra*, *Small Soldiers*, and *SpongeBob SquarePants*; **LARRY HAGMAN**, 81, television actor, best known for his role as J.R. on *Dallas*, but also known to genre audiences for his role on *I Dream of Jeannie*; **JACK KLUGMAN**, 90, television actor best known for roles in *The Odd Couple* and *Quincy*, who also appeared in *The Twilight Zone* and *The Outer Limits*; **HERBERT LOM**, 95, movie actor, best-known these days for his role in the Inspector Clouseau movies, but who also played The Phantom of the Opera, Professor Van Helsing, and Captain Nemo; **CHARLES DURNING**, 89, movie actor, known for his roles in *Twilight's Last Gleaming*, *The Muppet Movie*, and *The Last Countdown*; **MICHAEL CLARKE DUNCAN**, 54, movie actor, star of *The Green Mile*; **MICHAEL O'HARE**, 60, television actor, best known for his role on *Babylon 5*; **RICHARD DAWSON**, 79, longtime game show host of *Family Feud* who also costarred in *The Running Man*; **HARRY CAREY, JR.**, 91, veteran movie actor mostly known for his roles in many Western movies, who also costarred in *Back to the Future Part III*; **RICHARD ZANUCK**, 77, movie producer, producer or coproducer of such genre films as *Jaws*, *Cocoon*, and *Planet of the Apes*; **GERRY ANDERSON**, 83, creator of British television shows for children such as *Supercar*, *Fireball XLS*, *Thunderbirds*, and *Captain Scarlet*; **JAY KAY KLEIN**, 80, photographer, artist, longtime fan; **JANE FRANCES GUNN**, 87, wife of SF writer and critic James Gunn; **RICHARD S. SIMAK**, 64, son of SF writer Clifford D. Simak and occasional SF writer himself; **HELEN SAPANARA KEARNEY**, 92, mother of SF writer Pat Cadigan.

THE YEAR'S BEST

SCIENCE FICTION

weep for Day

INDRAPRAMIT DAS

Indrapramit Das is a writer and artist from Kolkata, India. His short fiction has appeared in Clarkesworld, Asimov's Science Fiction, Apex Magazine, Redstone Science Fiction, The World SF Blog, Flash Fiction Online, *and the anthology* Breaking the Bow: Speculative Fiction Inspired by the Ramayana. *He is a grateful graduate of the 2012 Clarion West Writers Workshop, and a recipient of the Octavia E. Butler Memorial Scholarship Award. He completed his MFA at the University of British Columbia, and currently lives in Vancouver, working as a freelance writer, artist, editor, game tester, tutor, would-be novelist, and aspirant to adulthood. Follow him on Twitter at @IndrapramitDas.*

Set on a tidally locked planet where the frozen and eternally dark Nightside is slowly being explored—and conquered—by explorers from the Dayside, this is an evocative, sensitively characterized, and lyrically written story that reminds me of something by Gene Wolfe—no faint praise in my book.

I was eight years old the first time I saw a real, living Nightmare. My parents took my brother and I on a trip from the City-of-Long-Shadows to the hills at Evening's edge, where one of my father's clients had a manse. Father was a railway contractor. He hired out labor and resources to the privateers extending the frontiers of civilization towards the frozen wilderness of the dark Behind-the-Sun. Aptly, we took a train up to the foothills of the great Penumbral Mountains.

It was the first time my brother and I had been on a train, though we'd seen them tumble through the city with their cacophonic engines, cumulous tails of smoke and steam billowing like blood over the rooftops when the red light of our sun caught them. It was also the first time we had been anywhere close to Night—Behind-the-Sun—where the Nightmares lived. Just a decade before we took that trip, it would have been impossible to go as far into Evening as we were doing with such casual comfort and ease.

Father had prodded the new glass of the train windows, pointing to the powerlines crisscrossing the sky in tandem with the gleaming lines of metal railroads silvering the hazy landscape of progress. He sat between my brother Velag and I, our heads propped against the bulk of his belly, which bulged against his rough crimson waistcoat. I clutched that coat and breathed in the sweet smell of chemlis gall that hung over him. Mother watched with a smile as she peeled indigos for us with her fingers, laying them in the lap of her skirt.

"Look at that. We've got no more reason to be afraid of the dark, do we, my tykes?" said Father, his belly humming with the sound of his booming voice.

Dutifully, Velag and I agreed there wasn't.

"Why not?" he asked us, expectant.

"Because of the Industrialization, which brings the light of Day to the darkness of Night," we chimed, a line learned both in school and home (inaccurate, as we'd never set foot in Night itself). Father laughed. I always slowed down on the word "industrialization," which caused Velag and I to say it at different times. He was just over a year older than me, though.

"And what is your father, children?" Mother asked.

"A knight of Industry and Technology, bringer of light under Church and Monarchy."

I didn't like reciting that part, because it had more than one long "y" word, and felt like a struggle to say. Father *was* actually a knight, though not a knight-errant for a while. He had been too big by then to fit into a suit of plate-armor or heft a heavy sword around, and knights had stopped doing that for many years anyway. The Industrialization had swiftly made the pageantry of adventure obsolete.

Father wheezed as we reminded him of his knighthood, as if ashamed. He put his hammy hands in our hair and rubbed. I winced through it, as usual, because he always forgot about the pins in my long hair, something my brother didn't have to worry about. Mother gave us the peeled indigos, her hands perfumed with the citrus. She was the one who taught me how to place the pins in my hair, both of us in front of the mirror looking like different sized versions of each other.

I looked out the windows of our cabin, fascinated by how everything outside slowly became bluer and darker as we moved away from the City-of-Long-Shadows, which lies between the two hemispheres of Day and Night. Condensation crawled across the corners of the double-glazed panes as the train took us farther east. Being a studious girl even at that age, I deduced from school lessons that the air outside was becoming rapidly colder as we neared Night's hemisphere, which has never seen a single ray of our sun and is theorized to be entirely frozen. The train, of course, was kept warm by the same steam and machinery that powered its tireless wheels and kept its lamps and twinkling chandeliers aglow.

"Are you excited to see the Nightmare? It was one of the first to be captured and tamed. The gentleman we're visiting is very proud to be its captor," said Father.

"Yes!" screamed Velag. "Does it still have teeth? And claws?" he asked, his eyes wide.

"I would think so." Father nodded.

"Is it going to be in chains?"

"I hope so, Velag. Otherwise it might get loose and . . ." he paused for dramatic effect. I froze in fear. Velag looked eagerly at him. "Eat you both up!" he bellowed, tickling us with his huge hands. It took all my willpower not to scream. I looked at Velag's delighted expression to keep me calm, reminding myself that these were just Father's hands jabbing my sides.

"Careful!" Mother said sharply, to my relief. "They'll get the fruit all over." The indigo segments were still in our laps, on the napkins Mother had handed to us. Father stopped tickling us, still grinning.

"Do you remember what they look like?" Velag asked, as if trying to see how many questions he could ask in as little time as possible. He had asked this one before, of course. Father had fought Nightmares, and even killed some, when he was a knight-errant.

"We never really saw them, son," said Father. He touched the window. "Out there, it's so cold you can barely feel your own fingers, even in armor."

We could see the impenetrable walls of the forests pass us by—shaggy, snarled mare-pines, their leaves black as coals and branches supposedly twisted into knots by the Nightmares to tangle the path of intruders. The high, hoary tops of the trees shimmered ever so slightly in the scarce light sneaking over the horizon, which they sucked in so hungrily. The moon was brighter here than in the City, but at its jagged crescent, a broken gemstone behind the scudding clouds. We were still in Evening, but had encroached onto the Nightmares' outer territories, marked by the forests that extended to the foothills. After the foothills, there was no more forest, because there was no more light. Inside our cabin, under bright electric lamps, sitting on velvet-lined bunks, it was hard to believe that we were actually in the land of Nightmares. I wondered if they were in the trees right now, watching our windows as we looked out.

"It's hard to see them, or anything, when you're that cold, and," Father breathed deeply, gazing at the windows. "They're very hard to see." It made me uneasy, hearing him say the same thing over and over. We were passing the very forests he travelled through as a knight-errant, escorting pioneers.

"Father's told you about this many times, dear," Mother interjected, peering at Father with worried eyes. I watched. Father smiled at her and shook his head.

"That's alright, I like telling my little tykes about my adventures. I guess you'll see what a Nightmare looks like tomorrow, eh? Out in the open. Are you excited?" he asked, perhaps forgetting that he'd already asked. Velag shouted in the affirmative again.

Father looked down at me, raising his bushy eyebrows. "What about you, Valyzia?"

I nodded and smiled.

I wasn't excited. Truth be told, I didn't want to see it at all. The idea of capturing and keeping a Nightmare seemed somehow disrespectful in my heart, though I didn't know the word then. It made me feel weak and confused, because I was and always had been so afraid of them, and had been taught to be.

I wondered if Velag had noticed that Father had once again refused to actually describe a Nightmare. Even in his most excitable retellings of his brushes with them, he never described them as more than walking shadows. There was a grainy sepia-toned photograph of him during his younger vigils as a knight-errant above the mantle of our living-room fireplace. It showed him mounted on a horse, dressed in his plate-armor and fur-lined surcoat, raising his longsword to the skies (the blade was cropped from the picture by its white border). Clutched in his other plated hand was something that looked like a blot of black, as if the chemicals of the photograph had congealed into a spot, attracted by some mystery or heat. The shape appeared to bleed back into the black background.

It was, I had been told, the head of a Nightmare Father had slain. It was too dark a thing to be properly caught by whatever early photographic engine had captured his victory. The blot had no distinguishing features apart from two vague points emerging from the rest of it, like horns or ears. That head earned him a large part of the fortune he later used to start up his contracting business. We never saw it, because Nightmares' heads and bodies were burned or gibbeted by knights-errant, who didn't want to bring them into the City for fear of attracting their horde. The photograph had been a source of dizzying pride for my young self, because it meant that my father was one of the bravest people I knew. At other times, it just made me wonder why he couldn't describe something he had once beheaded, and held in his hand as a trophy.

My indigo finished, Mother took the napkin and wiped my hands with it. My brother still picked at his. A waiter brought us a silver platter filled with sugar-dusted pastries, their centers soft with warm fudge and grünberry jam. We'd already finished off supper, brought under silver domes that gushed steam when the waiters raised them with their white-gloved hands, revealing chopped fungus, meat dumplings, sour cream, and fermented salad. Mother told Velag to finish the indigo before he touched the pastries. Father ate them with as much gusto as I did. I watched him lick his powdered fingers, that had once held the severed head of a Nightmare.

When it was time for respite, the cabin lights were shut off and the ones in the corridor were dimmed. I was relieved my parents left the curtains of the windows open as we retired, because I didn't want it to be completely dark. It was dim enough outside that we could fall asleep. It felt unusual to go to bed with windows uncovered for once.

I couldn't help imagine, as I was wont to do, that as our train moved through Evening's forested fringes, the Nightmares would find a way to get on board. I wondered if they were already on the train. But the presence of my family, all softly snoring in their bunks (Velag above me, my parents opposite us); the periodic, soothing flash of way-station lights passing by outside; the sigh of the sliding doors at the end of the carriage opening and closing as porters, waiters, and passengers moved through the corridors; the sweet smell of the fresh sheets and pillow on my bunk—these things lulled me into a sleep free of bad dreams, despite my fear of seeing the creature we'd named bad dreams after, face-to-face, the next vigil.

When I was six I stopped sleeping in my parents' room, and started sleeping in the same room as my brother. At the time of this change, I was abnormally scared of the dark (and consider, reader, that this was a time when fear of the dark was as normal and acceptable as the fear of falling from a great height). So scared that I couldn't fall sleep after the maids came around and closed our sleep-shutters and drew the curtains, to block out the western light for respite.

The heavy clatter of the wooden slats being closed every respite's eve was like a note of foreboding for me. I hunkered under the blankets, rigid with anxiety as the maids filed out of the room with their lanterns drawing wild shadows on the walls. Then the last maid would close the door, and our room would be swallowed up by those shadows.

In the chill darkness that followed, I would listen to the clicking of Nightmares' claws as they walked up and down the corridors of our shuttered house. Our parents had often told me that it was just rats in the walls and ceiling, but I refused to believe it. Every respite I would imagine one of the Nightmare intruders slinking into our room, listening to its breathing as it came closer to my bed and pounced on me, not being able to scream as it sat on my chest and ran its reeking claws through my hair, winding it into knots around its long fingers and laughing softly.

Enduring the silence for what seemed like hours, I would begin to wail and cry until Velag threw pillows at me and Mother came to my side to shush me with her kisses. To solve the problem, my parents tried keeping the sleep-shutters open through the hours of respite, and moved my brother to a room on the windowless east-facing side of the house when he complained. Unfortunately, we require the very dark we fear to fall asleep. The persistent burning line of the horizon beyond the windows, while a comforting sight, left me wide awake for most of respite.

In the end Velag and I were reunited and the shutters closed once more, because Father demanded that I not be coddled when my brother had learned to sleep alone so bravely. I often heard my parents arguing about this, since Mother thought it was madness to try and force me not to be afraid. Most of my friends from school hadn't and wouldn't sleep without their parents until they were at least eleven or twelve. Father was adamant, demanding that we learn to be strong and brave in case the Nightmares ever found a way to overrun the city.

It's a strange thing, to be made to feel guilty for learning too well something that was ingrained in us from the moment we were born. Now nightmare is just a word, and it's unusual to even think that the race that we gave that name might still be alive somewhere in the world. When Velag and I were growing up, Nightmares were the enemy.

Our grandparents told us about them, as did our parents, as did our teachers, as did every book and textbook we had ever come across. Stories of a time when guns hadn't been invented, when knights-errant roved the frigid forest paths beyond the City-of-Long-Shadows to prove their manhood and loyalty to the Monarchy and its Solar Church, and to extend the borders of the city and find new resources. A time coming to a close when I was born, even as the expansion continued onward faster than ever.

I remember my school class-teacher drawing the curtains and holding a candle to a wooden globe of our planet to show us how the sun made Night and Day. She took a piece of chalk and tapped where the candlelight turned to shadow on the globe. "That's us," she said, and moved the chalk over to the shadowed side. "That's them," she said.

Nightmares have defined who we are since we crawled out of the hot lakes at the edge of fiery Day, and wrapped the steaming bloody skins of slaughtered animals around us to walk upright, east into the cooler marches of our world's Evening. We stopped at the alien darkness we had never seen before, not just because of the terrible cold that clung to the air the farther we walked, but because of what we met at Evening's end.

A race of walking shadows, circling our firelight with glittering eyes, felling our explorers with barbed spears and arrows, snatching our dead as we fled from their ambushes. Silently, these unseen, lethal guardians of Night's bitter frontier told us we could go no farther. But we couldn't go back towards Day, where the very air seems to burn under the sun's perpetual gaze.

So we built our villages where sun's light still lingers and the shadows are longest before they dissolve into Evening. Our villages grew into towns, and our towns grew into the City-of-Long-Shadows, and our City grew along the Penumbra until it reached the Seas-of-Storms to the north and the impassable crags of World's-Rim (named long before we knew this to be false) to the south. For all of history, we looked behind our shoulders at the gloaming of the eastern horizon, where the Nightmares watched our progress.

So the story went, told over and over.

We named bad dreams after them because we thought Nightmares were their source, that they sent spies into the city to infect our minds and keep us afraid of the dark, their domain. According to folklore, these spies could be glimpsed upon waking abruptly. Indeed, I'd seen them crouching malevolently in the corner of the bedroom, wreathed in the shadows that were their home, slinking away with impossible speed once I looked at them.

There are no Nightmares left alive anywhere near the City-of-Long-Shadows, but we still have bad dreams and we still see their spies sometimes when we wake. Some say they are spirits of their race, or survivors. I'm not convinced. Even though we have killed all the Nightmares, our own half-dreaming minds continue to populate our bedrooms with their ghosts, so we may remember their legacy.

To date, none of our City's buildings have windows or doors on their east-facing walls.

And so the train took us to the end of our civilization. There are many things I remember about Weep-for-Day, though in some respects those memories feel predictably like the shreds of a disturbing dream. Back then it was just an outpost, not a hill-station town like it is now. The most obvious thing to remember is how it sleeted or snowed all the time. I know now that it's caused by moist convective winds in the atmosphere carrying the warmth of the sun from Day to Night, their loads of fat clouds scraping up against the mountains of the Penumbra for all eternity and washing the foothills in their frozen burden. But to my young self, the constant crying of that bruised sky was just another mystery in the world, a sorcery perpetrated by the Nightmares.

I remember, of course, how dark it was. How the people of the outpost carried bobbing lanterns and acrid magenta flares that flamed even against the perpetual wind and precipitation. How everyone outside (including us) had to wear goggles and thick protective suits lined with the fur of animals to keep the numbing cold of outer Evening out. I had never seen such darkness outdoors, and it felt like being asleep while walking. To think that beyond the mountains lay an absence of light even deeper was unbelievable.

I remember the tall poles that marked turns in the curving main road, linked by the ever-present electric and telegraph wires that made such an outpost possible. The bright gold-and-red pennants of the Monarchy fluttered from those poles, dulled by lack of light. They all showed a sun that was no longer visible from there.

I remember the solar shrines—little huts by the road, with small windows that lit up every few hours as chimes rang out over the windy outpost. Through the doors you could see the altars inside; each with an electric globe, its filament flooded with enough voltage to make it look like a hot ball of fire. For a minute these shrines would burn with their tiny artificial suns, and the goggled and suited inhabitants of Weep-for-Day would huddle around them like giant flies, their shadows wavering lines on the streaks of light cast out on the muddy snow or ice. They would pray on their knees, some reaching out to rub the faded ivory crescents of sunwyrm fangs on the altars.

Beyond the road and the slanted wet roofs of Weep-for-Day, there was so little light that the slope of the hill was barely visible. The forested plain beyond was nothing but a black void that ended in the faint glow of the horizon—the last weak embers in a soot-black fireplace just doused with water.

I couldn't see our City-of-Long-Shadows, which filled me with an irrational anxiety that it was gone forever, that if we took the train back we would find the whole world filled with darkness and only Night waiting on the other side.

But these details are less than relevant. That trip changed me and changed the course of my life not because I saw what places beyond the City-of-Long-Shadows looked like, though seeing such no doubt planted the seeds of some future grit in me. It changed me because I, with my family by my side, witnessed a living Nightmare, as we were promised.

The creature was a prisoner of Vorin Tylvur, who was at the time the Consul of Weep-for-Day, a knight like Father, and an appointed privateer and mining coordinator of the Penumbral territories. Of course, he is now well remembered for his study of Nightmares in captivity, and his campaigns to expand the Monarchy's territories into Evening. The manse we stayed in was where he and his wife lived, governing the affairs of the outpost and coordinating expansion and exploration.

I do not remember much of our hosts, except that they were adults in the way all adults who aren't parents are, to little children. They were kind enough to me. I couldn't comprehend the nature of condescension at that age, but I did find the cooing manner of most adults who talked to me boring, and they were no different. Though I'm grateful for their hospitality to my family, I cannot, in retrospect, look upon them with much returned kindness.

They showed us the imprisoned Nightmare on the second vigil of our stay. It was in the deepest recesses of the manse, which was more an oversized, glorified bunker on the hill of Weep-for-Day than anything else. We went down into a dank, dim corridor in the chilly heart of that mound of crustal rock to see the prisoner.

"I call it Shadow. A little nickname," Sir Tylvur said with a toothy smile, his huge moustache hanging from his nostrils like the dead wings of some poor misbegotten bird trapped in his head. He proved himself right then to have not only a startling lack of imagination for a man of his intelligence and inquisitiveness, but also a grotesquely inappropriate sense of levity.

It would be dramatic and untruthful to say that my fear of darkness receded the moment I set eyes on the creature. But something changed in me. There, looking at this hunched and shivering thing under the smoky blaze of the flares its armored gaolers held to reveal it to its captor's guests, I saw that a phantom flayed was just another animal.

Sir Tylvur had made sure that its light-absorbent skin would not hinder our viewing of the captured enemy. There is no doubt that I feared it, even though its skin was stripped from its back to reveal its glistening red muscles, even though it was clearly broken and defeated. But my mutable young mind understood then, looking into its shining black eyes—the only visible feature in the empty dark of its face—that it knew terror just as I or any human did. The Nightmare was scared. It was a heavy epiphany for a child to bear, and I vomited on the glass observation wall of its cramped holding cell.

Velag didn't make fun of me. He shrank into Mother's arms, trying to back away from the humanoid silhouette scrabbling against the glass to escape the light it so feared; a void-like cut-out in reality but for that livid wet wound on its back revealing it to be as real as us. It couldn't, or would not, scream or vocalize in any way. Instead, we just heard the squeal of its spider-like hands splayed on the glass, claws raking the surface.

I looked at Father, standing rigid and pale, hands clutched into tight fists by his sides. The same fists that held up the severed head of one of this creature's race in triumph so many years ago. Just as in the photograph, there were the horn-like protrusions from its head, though I still couldn't tell what they were. I looked at Mother who, despite the horrific vision in front of us, despite her son clinging to her waist, reached down in concern to wipe the vomit from my mouth and chin with bare fingers, her gloves crumpled in her other hand.

As Sir Tylvur wondered what to do about his spattered glass wall, he decided to blame the Nightmare for my reaction and rapped hard on the cell with the hilt of his sheathed ceremonial sword. He barked at the prisoner, wanting to frighten it away from the glass, I suppose. The only recognizable word in between his grunts was "Shadow." But as he called it by that undignified, silly nickname, the thing stopped its frantic scrabbling. Startled, Sir Tylvur stepped back. The two armored gaolers stepped back as well, flares wavering in the gloom of the cell. I still don't know why the Nightmare stopped thrashing, and I never will know for sure. But at that moment I thought it recognized the nickname its captor had given it, and recognized that it was being displayed like a trophy. Perhaps it wanted to retain some measure of its pride.

The flarelight flickered on its eyes, which grew brighter as moisture gathered on them. It was clearly in pain from the light. I saw that it was as tall as a human, though it looked smaller because of how crouched into itself it was. It cast a shadow like any other animal, and that shadow looked like its paler twin, dancing behind its back. Chains rasped on the wet cell floor, shackled to its limbs. The illuminated wound on its back wept pus, but the rest of it remained that sucking, indescribable black that hurt the human eye.

Except something in its face. It looked at us, and out of that darkness came a glittering of wet obsidian teeth as unseen lips peeled back. I will never forget that invisible smile, whether it was a grimace of pain or a taunting leer.

"Kill it," Velag whispered. And that was when Mother took both our hands tight in hers, and pulled us away from the cell. She marched us down that dank corridor, leaving the two former knights-errant, Father and Sir Tylvur, staring into that glimmering cell at the specter of their past.

That night, in the tiny room we'd been given as our quarters, I asked Velag if the Nightmare had scared him.

"Why should it scare me," he said, face pale in the dim glow of the small heating furnace in the corner of the chamber. "It's in chains."

"You just looked scared. It's okay to be scared. I was too. But I think it was as well."

"Shut up. You don't know what you're saying. I'm going to sleep," he said, and turned away from me, his cot groaning. The furnace hissed and ticked.

"I think papa was scared also. He didn't want to see a Nightmare again," I said to Velag's back.

That was when my brother pounced off his cot and on top of me. I was too shocked to scream. My ingrained submission to his power as an elder male authority figure took over. I gave no resistance. Sitting on my small body, Velag took my blanket and shoved it into my mouth. Then, he snatched my pillow and held it over my face. Choking on the taste of musty cloth, I realized I couldn't breathe. I believed that my brother was about to kill me then. I truly believed it. I could feel the pressure of his hands through the pillow, and they were at that moment the hands of something inhuman. I was more terrified then than I'd ever been in my entire short life, plagued though I'd always been by fear.

He held the pillow over my head for no more than four seconds, probably less. When he raised it off my face and pulled the blanket out of my mouth he looked as shaken as I was. His eyes were wet with tears, but in a second his face was twisted in a grimace.

"Never call papa a coward. Never call papa a coward. Papa was never afraid. Do you hear me? You never had to sleep alone in the dark, you don't know. I'm going to grow up and be like papa and kill them. I'll kill them," he hissed the words into my face like a litany. I started crying, unable and probably too scared to tell him I hadn't called Father a coward. I could still barely breathe, so flooded was I with my own tears, so drunk on the air he had denied me. Velag went back to his cot and wrapped himself in his blanket, breathing heavily.

As I shuddered with stifled sobs, I decided that I would never tell my parents about this, that I would never have Velag punished for this violence. I didn't forgive him, not even close, but that is what I decided.

I was seventeen the last time I saw Velag. I went to visit him at the Royal Military Academy's boarding school. He had been there for four years already. We saw him every few moons when he came back to the City proper to visit. But I wanted to see the campus for myself. It was a lovely train ride, just a few hours from the central districts of the City-of-Long-Shadows to the scattered hamlets beyond it.

It was warmer and brighter out where the Academy was. The campus was beautiful, sown with pruned but still wild looking trees and plants that only grew farther out towards Day, their leaves a lighter shade of blue and their flowers huge, craning to the west on thick stems. The sun still peered safely behind the edge of the world, but its gaze was bright enough to wash the stately buildings of the boarding school with a fiery golden-red light, sparkling in the waxy leaves of vines winding their way around the arched windows. On every ornate, varnished door was a garish propaganda poster of the Dark Lord of Nightmares, with his cowled cloak of shadows and black sword, being struck down by our soldiers' bayoneted guns.

I sat with Velag in a cupola in the visitors' garden, which was on a gentle bluff. In the fields adjacent, his fellow student-soldiers played tackleball, their rowdy calls and whistles ringing through the air. We could see heavy banks of glowing, sunlit storm-clouds to the west where the atmosphere boiled and churned in the heat of Day, beyond miles of shimmering swamp-forests and lakes. To the east, a faint moon hung over the campus, but no stars were visible so close to Day.

Velag looked so different from the last time I saw him. His pimples were vanishing, the sallow softness of adolescence melting away to reveal the man he was to become. The military uniform, so forbidding in red and black, suited his tall form. He looked smart and handsome in it. It hurt me to see him shackled in it, but I could see that he wore it with great pride.

He held my hand and asked about my life back home, about my plans to apply to the College of Archaeology at the University of St. Kataretz. He asked about our parents. He told me how gorgeous and grown-up I looked in my dress, and said he was proud of me for becoming a "prodigy." I talked to him with a heavy ache in my chest, because I knew with such certainty that we hardly knew each other, and would get no chance to any time soon, as he would be dispatched to the frontlines of Penumbral Conquest.

As if reading my thoughts, his cheek twitched with what I thought was guilt, and he looked at the stormy horizon. Perhaps he was remembering the night on which he told me he would grow up and kill Nightmares like Father—a promise he was keeping. He squeezed my hand.

"I'll be alright, Val. Don't you worry."

I gave him a rueful smile. "It's not too late. You can opt to become a civilian after graduation and come study with me at St. Kataretz. Ma and papa would think no less of you. You could do physics again, you loved it before. We can get an apartment in Pemluth Halls, share the cost. The University's right in the middle of the City, we'd have so much fun together."

"I can't. You know that. I want this for myself. I want to be a soldier, and a knight."

"Being a knight isn't the same thing as it was in papa's time. He was independent, a privateer. Things have changed. You'll be a part of the military. Knighthoods belong to them now and they're stingy with them. They mostly give them to soldiers who are wounded or dead, Velag."

"I'm in military school, by the saints, I know what a knighthood is or isn't. Please don't be melodramatic. You're an intelligent girl."

"What's that got to do with anything?"

"I'm going. I have more faith in my abilities than you do."

"I have plenty of faith in you. But the Nightmares are angry now, Velag. We're wiping them out. They're scared and angry. They're coming out in waves up in the hills. More of our soldiers are dying than ever before. How can I not worry?"

His jaw knotted, he glared down at our intertwined hands. His grip was limp now. "Don't start with your theories about the benevolence of Nightmares. I don't want to hear it. They're not scared, they *are* fear, and we'll wipe them off the planet if need be so that you and everybody else can live without that fear."

"I'm quite happy with my life, thank you. I'd rather you be alive for ma and papa and me than have the terrible horde of the Nightmares gone forever."

He bit his lip and tightened his hand around mine again. "I know, little sister. You're sweet to worry so. But the Monarchy needs me. I'll be fine. I promise."

And that was the end of the discussion as far as he was concerned. I knew it was no point pushing him further, because it would upset him. This was his life, after all. The one he had chosen. I had no right to belittle it. I didn't want to return to the City on bad terms with him. We made what little small talk was left to make, and then we stood and kissed each other on the cheek, and I hugged him tight and watched him walk away.

What good are such promises as the one he made on our final farewell, even if one means them with all of one's heart? He was dispatched right after his graduation a few moons later, without even a ceremony because it was wartime. After six moons of excited letters from the frontlines at the Penumbral Mountains, he died with a Nightmare's spear in his chest, during a battle that earned the Monarchy yet another victory against the horde of darkness. Compared to the thousands of Nightmares slaughtered during the battle with our guns and cannons, the Monarchy's casualties were small. And yet, my parents lost their son, and I my brother.

In death, they did give Velag the knighthood he fought so hard for. Never have I hated myself so much for being right.

When Velag was being helped out of Mother by doctors in the city, my father had been escorting pioneers in the foothills. I see him in his armor, the smell of heated steel and cold sweat cloying under his helm, almost blind because of the visor, sword in one hand, knotted reins and a flaming torch in the other, his mount about to bolt. A new metal coal-chamber filled with glowing embers strapped to his back to keep the suit warm, making his armor creak and pop as it heated up, keeping him off-balance with its weight and hissing vents but holding the freezing cold back a little. Specks of frozen water flying through the torch-lit air like dust, biting his eyes through the visor. His fingers numb in his gloves, despite the suit. The familiar glitter of inhuman eyes beyond the torchlight, nothing to go by but reflections of fire on his foes, who are invisible in the shadows, slinking alongside the caravan like bulges in the darkness. The only thing between the Nightmares and the pioneers with their mounts and carriages weighed down by machinery and thick coils of wire and cable that will bring the light of civilization to these wilds, is him and his contingent.

How long must that journey have been to him? How long till he returned alive to see his wife and new son Velag in a warm hospital room, under the glow of a brand-new electric light?

By the time I was born, armorers had invented portable guns and integrated hollow cables in the suit lining to carry ember-heated water around armor, keeping it warmer and enabling mercenaries and knights-errant to go deeper into Evening. The pioneers followed, bringing their technology to the very tops of the foothills, infested with Nightmares. That was when Father stopped going, lest he never return. They had new tools, but the war had intensified. He had a son and daughter to think of, and a wife who wanted him home.

When I watched Velag's funeral pyre blaze against the light of the west on Barrow-of-Bones cremation hill, I wondered if the sparks sent up into the sky by his burning body would turn to stardust in the ether and migrate to the sun to extend its life, or whether this was his final and utter dissolution. The chanting priest from the Solar Church seemed to have no doubts on the matter. Standing there, surrounded by the fossilized stone ribs of Zhurgeith, last of the sunwyrms and heraldic angel of the Monarchy and Church (who also call it Dragon), I found myself truly unsure about what death brings for maybe the first time in my life, though I'd long practiced the cynicism that was becoming customary of my generation.

I thought with some trepidation about the possibility that if the Church was right, the dust of Velag's life might be consigned to the eternal dark of cosmic limbo instead of finding a place in the sun, because of what he'd done to me as a child. Because I'd never forgiven him, even though I told myself I had.

How our world changes.

The sun is a great sphere of burning gas, ash eventually falls down, and my dead brother remains in the universe because my family and I remember him, just as I remember my childhood, my life, the Nightmares we lived in fear of, the angel Dragon whose host was wiped out by a solar flare before we could ever witness it.

Outside, the wind howls so loud that I can easily imagine it is the sound of trumpets from a frozen city, peopled by the horde of darkness. Even behind the insulated metal doors and heated tunnels of the cave bunkers that make up After-Day border camp, I can see my breath and need two thick coats to keep warm. My fingers are like icicles as I write. I would die very quickly if exposed to the atmosphere outside. And yet, here I am, in the land of Nightmares.

Somewhere beyond these Penumbral Mountains, which we crossed in an airtight train, is the City-of-Long-Shadows. I have never been so far from it. Few people have. We are most indebted to those who mapped the shortest route through the mountains, built the rails through the lowest valleys, blasted new tunnels, laid the foundations for After-Day. But no one has gone beyond this point. We—I and the rest of the expeditionary team from St. Kataretz—will be the first to venture into Night. It will be a dangerous endeavour, but I have faith in us, in the brave men and women who have accompanied me here.

My dear Velag, how would you have reacted to see these beautiful caves I sit in now, to see the secret culture of your enemy? I am surrounded by what can only be called their art, the lantern-light making pale tapestries of the rock walls on which Nightmares through the millennia scratched to life the dawn of their time, the history that followed, and its end, heralded by our arrival into their world.

In this history we are the enemy, bringing the terror of blinding fire into Evening, bringing the advanced weapons that caused their genocide. On these walls we are drawn in pale white dyes, bioluminescent in the dark, a swarm of smeared light advancing on the Nightmares' striking, jagged-angled representations of themselves, drawn in black dyes mixed from blood and minerals.

In this history Nightmares were alive when the last of the sunwyrms flew into Evening to scourge the land for prey. Whether this is truth or myth we don't know, but it might mean that Nightmares were around long before us. It might explain their adaptation to the darkness of outer Evening—their light-absorbent skin ancient camouflage to hide from sunwyrms under cover of the forests of Evening. We came into Evening with our fire (which they show sunwyrms breathing) and pale skins, our banners showing Dragon and the sun, and we were like a vengeful race of ghosts come to kill on behalf of those disappeared angels of Day, whom they worshipped to the end—perhaps praying for our retreat.

In halls arched by the ribcages and spines of ancient sunwyrm skeletons I have seen burial chambers; the bones of Nightmares and their children (whom we called imps because we didn't like to think of our enemy having young) piled high. Our bones lie here too, not so different from theirs. Tooth-marks show that they ate their dead, probably because of the scarcity of food in the fragile ecosystem of Evening. It is no wonder then that they ate our dead too—as we feared. It was not out of evil, but need.

We have so much yet to learn.

Perhaps it would have given you some measure of peace, Velag, to know that the Nightmares didn't want to destroy us, only to drive us back from their home. Perhaps not.

Ilydrin tells me it is time for us to head out. She is a member of our expedition—a biologist—and my partner. To hide the simple truth of our affection seems here, amidst the empty city of a race we destroyed, an obscenity. Confronted by the vast, killing beauty of our planet's second half, the stagnant moralities of our city-state appear a trifle. I adore Ilydrin, and I am glad she is here with me.

One team will stay here while ours heads out into Night. Ilydrin and I took a walk outside to test our Night-shells—armored environmental suits to protect us from the lethal cold. We trod down from the caves of After-Day and into the unknown beyond, breath blurring our glass faceplates, our head-lamps cutting broad swathes through the snow-swarmed dark. We saw nothing ahead but an endless plain of ice—perhaps a frozen sea.

No spectral spires, no black banners of Night, no horde of Nightmares waiting to attack, no Dark Lord in his distant obsidian palace (an image Ilydrin and I righteously tore down many times in the form of those Army posters, during our early College vigils). We held each others' gloved hands and returned to Camp, sweating in our cramped shells, heavy boots crunching on the snow. I thought of you, Father, bravely venturing into bitter Evening to support your family. I thought of you, Brother, nobly marching against the horde for your Monarchy. I thought of you, Mother, courageously carrying your first child alone in that empty house before it became *our* home. I thought of you, Shadow—broken, tortured prisoner, baring your teeth to your captors in silence.

Out there, I was shaking—nervous, excited, queasy. I wasn't afraid.

I have Father's old photograph with the Nightmare's head (he took it down from above the mantelpiece after Velag died). I have a photograph of Mother, Father,

Velag, and I all dressed up before our trip to Weep-for-Day. And finally, a smiling portrait of Velag in uniform before he left for the Academy, his many pimples invisible because of the monochrome softness of the image. I keep these photographs with me, in the pockets of my overcoat, and take them out sometimes when I write.

So it begins. I write from the claustrophobic confines of the Night-Crawler, a steam-powered vehicle our friends at the College of Engineering designed (our accompanying professors named it with them, no doubt while drunk in a bar on University-Street). It is our moving camp. We'll sleep and eat and take shelter in it, and explore farther and longer—at least a few vigils, we hope. If its engines fail, we'll have to hike back in our shells and hope for the best. The portholes are frosted over, but the team is keeping warm by stoking the furnace and singing. Ilydrin comes and tells me, her lips against my hair: "Val. Stop writing and join us." I tell her I will, in a minute. She smiles and walks back to the rest, her face flushed and soot-damp from the open furnace. I live for these moments.

I will lay down this pen now. A minute.

I don't know what we'll find out here. Maybe we *will* find the Dark Lord and his gathered horde of Nightmares. But at this point, even the military doesn't believe that, or they would have opposed the funding for this expedition or tried to hijack it.

Ilydrin says there's unlikely to be life so deep into Night—even Nightmares didn't venture beyond the mountains, despite our preconceptions. But she admits we've been wrong before. Many times. What matters is that we are somewhere new. Somewhere other than the City-of-Long-Shadows and the Penumbral territories, so marked by our history of fear. We need to see the rest of this world, to meet its other inhabitants—if there are others—with curiosity, not apprehension. And I know we will, eventually. This is our first, small step. I wish you were here with me to see it, Velag. You were but a child on this planet.

We might die here. It won't be because we ventured into evil. It will be because we sought new knowledge. And in that, I have no regrets, even if I'm dead when this is read. A new age is coming. Let this humble account be a preface to it.

The Man

PAUL McAULEY

Born in Oxford, England, in 1955, Paul McAuley now makes his home in London. A professional biologist for many years, he sold his first story in 1984, and has gone on to be a frequent contributor to Interzone, *as well as to publications such as* Asimov's Science Fiction, SCI FICTION, Amazing, The Magazine of Fantasy & Science Fiction, Skylife, The Third Alternative, When the Music's Over, *and elsewhere.*

McAuley is at the forefront of several of the most important sub-genres in SF today, producing both "radical hard science fiction" and the revamped and retooled widescreen Space Opera that has sometimes been called The New Space Opera, as well as Dystopian sociological speculations about the very near future. He also writes fantasy and horror. His first novel, Four Hundred Billion Stars, *won the Philip K. Dick Award, and his novel* Fairyland *won both the Arthur C. Clarke Award and the John W. Campbell Award in 1996. His other books include the novels* Of the Fall, Eternal Light, *and* Pasquale's Angel, Confluence—*a major trilogy of ambitious scope and scale set ten million years in the future, comprised of the novels* Child of the River, Ancients of Days, *and* Shrine of Stars—Life on Mars, The Secret of Life, Whole Wide World, White Devils, Mind's Eye, Players, Cowboy Angels, The Quiet Wars, *and* Gardens of the Sun. *His short fiction has been collected in* The King of the Hill and Other Stories, The Invisible Country, *and* Little Machines, *and he is the coeditor, with Kim Newman, of an original anthology,* In Dreams. *His most recent book is a novel,* In the Mouth of the Whale. *Coming up is a new novel,* Evening's Empire, *and a big retrospective collection,* A Very British History: The Best of Paul McAuley.

Here—in a story set off at a bit of a tangent to McAuley's "Jackeroo" series, where humanity has been gifted with a number of sub-standard worlds to colonize by an enigmatic alien species who probably have agendas of their own—he takes us to a newly settled colony world, a bleak and somewhat insalubrious place, and introduces us to a tough-minded old woman who lives by herself in the depths of a hostile alien forest, making a precarious living scavenging artifacts left over from a previous failed colony attempt by an unknown race millennia before and who, on one stormy night, finds a mysterious stranger seeking refuge at her door—one who looks human, but, as soon becomes obvious, is clearly not . . .

He came to Cho Ziyi at night, in the middle of a flux storm.

It was as dark as it ever got, in the sunset zone. Low, fast-moving clouds closed off the sky. Howling winds drove waves onshore and blew horizontal streamers of snow into the forest, where the vanes of spin trees madly clattered and coronal discharges jumped and crackled. Ziyi was hunkered down in her cabin, watching an ancient movie about a gangster romance in Hong Kong's fabled Chungking Mansions. A fire breathed in the stone hearth and her huskies, Jung and Cheung, sprawled in a careless tangle on the borometz-hide rug. The dogs suddenly lifting their heads, the youngest, Cheung, scrambling to his feet and barking, something striking the door. Once, twice.

Ziyi froze the movie and sat still, listening. A slight, severe woman in her late sixties, dressed in jeans and a flannel shirt, white hair scraped back in a long ponytail, jumping just a little when there was another thump. It wouldn't be the first time that an indricothere or some other big dumb beast had trampled down a section of fence and blundered into the compound. She crossed to the window and unbolted the shutter. Pressed her cheek against the cold glass, squinted sideways, saw a dim pale figure on the raised porch. A naked man, arm raised, striking the door with the flat of his hand.

The two dogs stood behind her, alert and as anxious. Cheung whined when she looked at him.

"It's only a man," Ziyi said. "Be quiet and let me think."

He was in some kind of trouble, no question. A lost traveller, an accident on the road. But who would travel through a storm like this, and where were his clothes? She remembered the bandits who'd hit a road train a couple of years ago. Perhaps they'd come back. He had managed to escape, but he couldn't have gone far, not like that, not in weather like this. They might be here any minute. Or perhaps they were already out there, waiting for her to open the door. But she knew she couldn't leave him to die.

She fetched a blanket and lifted her short-barrelled shotgun from its wall pegs, unbolted the door, cracked it open. Snow skirled in. The naked man stared at her, dull-eyed. He was tall, pale-skinned. Snow was crusted in his shock of black hair. He didn't seem to notice the cold. Staring blankly at her, as if being confronted by an old woman armed with a shotgun was no surprise at all.

Ziyi told him to move off the porch, repeating the request in each of her half dozen languages. He seemed to understand English, and took a step backwards. Snow whirled around him and snow blew across the compound, out of darkness and back into darkness. Fat sparks snapped high in a stand of spike trees, like the apparatus in that old Frankenstein movie. Ziyi saw the gate in the fence was open, saw footprints crossing the deep snow, a single set.

"Are you hurt? What happened to you?"

His face was as blank as a mask.

She lofted the blanket towards him. It struck his chest and fell to his feet. He looked at it, looked at her. She was reminded of the cow her grandmother had kept, in the smallholding that had been swallowed by one of Shanghai's new satellite towns in the last gasp of frantic expansion before the Spasm.

"Go around the side of the cabin," she told him. "To your left. There's a shed. The door is unlocked. You can stay there. We'll talk in the morning."

The man picked up the blanket and plodded off around the corner of cabin. Ziyi bolted the door and opened the shutters at each of the cabin's four small windows and looked out and saw only blowing snow.

She sat by the fire for a long time, wondering who he was, what had happened to him. Wondering—because no ordinary man could have survived the storm for very long—if he was a thing of the Jackaroo. A kind of avatar that no one had seen before. Or perhaps he was some species of alien creature as yet undiscovered, that by an accident of evolution resembled a man. One of the Old Ones, one of the various species which had occupied Yanos before it had been gifted to the human race, woken from a sleep of a thousand centuries. Only the Jackaroo knew what the Old Ones had looked like. They had all died out or disappeared long ago. They could have looked like anything, so why not like a man? A man who spoke, or at least understood, English . . .

At last she pulled on her parka and took her shotgun and, accompanied by Jung and Cheung, went outside. The storm was beginning to blow itself out. The snow came in gusts now, and the dark was no longer uniform. To the southeast, Sauron's dull coal glimmered at the horizon.

Snow was banked up on one side of the little plastic utility shed, almost to the roof. Inside, the man lay asleep between stacks of logs and drums of diesel oil, wrapped in the blanket so that only his head showed. He did not stir when Cheung barked and nipped at the hem of Ziyi's parka, trying to drag her away.

She closed the door of the shed and went back to her cabin, and slept.

When she woke, the sky was clear of cloud and Sauron's orange light tangled long shadows across the snow. A spin tree had fallen down just outside the fence; the vanes of all the others, thousands upon thousands, spun in wind that was now no more than the usual wind, blowing from sunside to darkside. Soon, the snow would melt and she would go down to the beach and see what had been cast up. But first she had to see to her strange guest.

She took him a cannister of pork hash. He was awake, sitting with the blanket fallen to his waist. After Ziyi mimed what he should do, he ate a couple of mouthfuls, although he used his fingers rather than the spoon. His feet were badly cut and there was a deep gash in his shin. Smaller cuts on his face and hands, like old knife wounds. All of them clean and pale, like little mouths. No sign of blood. She thought of him stumbling through the storm, through the lashing forest . . .

He looked up at her. Sharp blue eyes, with something odd about the pupils— they weren't round, she realized with a clear cold shock, but were edged with small triangular indentations, like cogs.

He couldn't or wouldn't answer her questions.

"Did the Jackaroo do this to you? Are you one of them? Did they make you?"

It was no good.

She brought him clothes. A sweater, jeans, an old pair of wellington boots with the toes and heels slit so they would fit his feet. He followed her about the compound as she cleared up trash that had blown in, and the two Huskies followed both of them at a wary distance. When she went down to the beach, he came too.

Snow lay in long rakes on the black sand and meltwater ran in a thousand braided channels to the edge of the sea. Seafoam floated on the wind-blown waves, trembled amongst rocks. Flecks of colour flashed here and there: flotsam from the factory.

The man walked down to the water's edge. He seemed fascinated by the half-drowned ruins that stretched towards the horizon, hectares of spires and broken walls washed by waves, silhouetted against Sauron's fat disc, which sat where it always sat, just above the sea's level horizon.

Like all the worlds gifted by the Jackaroo, Yanos orbited close to the hearthfire of its M-class red dwarf sun; unlike the others, it had never been spun up. Like Earth's Moon, it was tidally locked. One face warm and lighted, with a vast and permanent rainstorm at the equator, where Sauron hung directly overhead; the other a starlit icecap, and perpetual winds blowing from warm and light to cold and dark. Human settlements were scattered through the forests of the twilight belt where the weather was less extreme.

As the man stared out at the ruins, hair tangling in warm wind blowing off the sea, maybe listening, maybe not, Ziyi explained that people called it the factory, although they didn't really know what it was, or who had built it.

"Stuff comes from it, washes up here. Especially after a storm. I collect it, take it into town, sell it. Mostly base plastics, but sometimes you find nice things that are worth more. You help me, okay? You earn your keep."

But he stayed where he was, staring out at the factory ruins, while she walked along the driftline, picking up shards and fragments. While she worked, she wondered what he might be worth, and who she could sell him to. Not to Sergey Polzin, that was for damn sure. She'd have to contact one of the brokers in the capital . . . This man, he was a once-in-a-lifetime find. But how could she make any kind of deal without being cheated?

Ziyi kept checking on him, showed him the various finds. After a little while, straightening with one hand in the small of her aching back, she saw that he had taken off his clothes and stood with his arms stretched out, his skin warmly tinted in the level sunlight.

She filled her fat-tyred cart and told him it was time to put on his clothes and go. She mimed what she wanted him to do until he got the idea and dressed and helped her pull the cart back to the cabin. He watched her unload her harvest into one of the storage bins she'd built from the trimmed trunks of spike trees. She'd almost finished when he scooped up a handful of bright fragments and threw them in and looked at her as if for approval.

Ziyi remembered her little girl, in a sunlit kitchen on a faraway world. Even after all these years, the memory still pricked her heart.

"You're a quick learner," she said.

He smiled. Apart from those strange, starry pupils and his pale poreless skin, he looked entirely human.

"Come into the cabin," she said, weightless with daring. "We'll eat."

He didn't touch the food she offered; but sipped a little water, holding the tumbler in both hands. As far as she knew, he hadn't used the composting toilet. When she'd shown it to him and explained how it worked, he'd shrugged the way a small child would dismiss as unimportant something she couldn't understand.

They watched a movie together, and the two dogs watched them from a corner of the room. When it had finished, Ziyi gave the man an extra blanket and a rug, and locked him in the shed for the night.

So it went the next day, and the days after that.

The man didn't eat. Sometimes he drank a little water. Once, on the beach, she found him nibbling at a shard of plastic. Shocked, she'd dashed it from his hand and he'd flinched away, clearly frightened.

Ziyi took a breath. Told herself that he was not really a man, took out a strip of dried borometz meat and took a bite and chewed and smiled and rubbed her stomach. Picked up the shard of plastic and held it out to him. "This is your food? This is what you are made of?"

He shrugged.

She talked to him, as they worked. Pointed to a flock of windskimmers skating along far out to sea, told him they were made by the factory. "Maybe like you, yes?" Named the various small shelly ticktock things that scuttled along the margins of the waves, likewise made by the factory. She told him the names of the trees that stood up beyond the tumble of boulders along the top of the beach. Told him how spin trees generated sugars from air and water and electricity. Warned him to avoid the bubbleweed that sent long scarlet runners across the black sand, told him that it was factory stuff and its tendrils moved towards him because they were heat-seeking. "Let them touch, they stick little fibres like glass into your skin. Very bad."

He had a child's innocent curiosity, scrutinising ticktocks and scraps of plastic with the same frank intensity, watching with rapt attention a group of borometz grazing on rafts of waterweed cast up by the storm.

"The world is dangerous," Ziyi said. "Those borometz look very cute, harmless balls of fur, but they carry ticks that have poisonous bites. And there are worse things in the forest. Wargs, sasquatch. Worst of all, are people. You stay away from them."

She told herself that she was keeping her find safe from people like Sergey Polzin, who would most likely try to vivisect him to find out how he worked, or keep him alive while selling him off finger by finger, limb by limb. She no longer planned to sell him to a broker, had vague plans about contacting the university in the capital. They wouldn't pay much, but they probably wouldn't cut him up, either . . .

She told him about her life. Growing up in Hong Kong. Her father the surgeon, her mother the biochemist. The big apartment, the servants, the trips abroad. Her studies in Vancouver University, her work in a biomedical company in Shanghai. Skipping over her marriage and her daughter, that terrible day when the global crisis had finally peaked in the Spasm. Seoul had been vapourised by a North Korean atomic missile; Shanghai had been hit by an Indian missile; two dozen cities around the world had been likewise devastated. Ziyi had been on a flight to Seoul; the plane had made an emergency landing at a military airbase and she'd made her way back to Shanghai by train, by truck, on foot. And discovered that her home was gone, the entire neighbourhood had been levelled. She'd spent a year working in a hospital in a refugee camp, trying and failing to find her husband and her daughter and her parents . . . It was too painful to talk about that; instead, she told the man about the day the Jackaroo made themselves known, the big ship suddenly appearing over the ruins of Shanghai, big ships appearing above all the major cities.

"The Jackaroo gave us the possibility of a new start. New worlds. Many argued against this, to begin with. Saying that we needed to fix everything on Earth. Not just the Spasm, but global warming, famines, all the rest. But many others disagreed. They won the lottery or bought tickets off winners and went up and out. Me, I went to work for the UN, the United Nations, as a translator," Ziyi said.

Thirty years, in Cape Town, in Berlin, in Brasilia. Translating for delegates at meetings and committees on the treaties and deals with the Jackaroo. She'd married again, lost her husband to cancer.

"I earned a lottery ticket because of my work, and I left the Earth and came here. I thought I could make a new start. And I ended up here, an old woman picking up alien scrap on an alien beach thousands of light years from home. Sometimes I think that I am dead. That my family survived the Spasm but I died, and all this is a dream of my last second of life. What does that make you, if it's true?"

The man listened to her, but gave no sign that he understood.

One day, she found a precious scrap of superconducting plastic. It wasn't much bigger than her thumbnail, transparent, shot through with silvery threads.

"This is worth more than ten cartloads of base plastic," she told the man. "Electronics companies use it in their smart phones and slates. No one knows how to make it, so they pay big money. We live off this for two, three weeks."

She didn't think he'd understand, but he walked up and down the tideline all that day and found two more slivers of superconductor, and the next day found five. Amazing. Like the other prospectors who mined the beach and the ruins in the forests, she'd tried and failed to train her dogs to sniff out the good stuff, but the man was like a trufflehound. Single-minded, sharp-eyed, eager to please.

"You did good," she told him. "I think I might keep you."

She tried to teach him t'ai chi exercises, moving him into different poses. His smooth cool skin. No heartbeat that she could find. She liked to watch him trawl along the beach, the dogs trotting alongside him. She'd sit on the spur of a tree trunk and watch until the man and the dogs disappeared from sight, watch as they came back. He'd come to her with his hands cupped in front, shyly showing her the treasures he'd found.

After ten days, the snow had melted and the muddy roads were more or less passable again, and Ziyi drove into town in her battered Suzuki jeep. She'd locked the man in the shed and left Jung and Cheung roaming the compound, to guard him.

In town, she sold her load of plastic at the recycling plant, saving the trove of superconducting plastic until last. Unfolding a square of black cloth to show the little heap of silvery stuff to the plant's manager, a gruff Ukranian with radiation scars welting the left side of his face.

"You got lucky," he said.

"I work hard," she said. "How much?"

They settled on a price that was more than the rest of her earnings, that year. The manager had to phone Sergey Polzin to authorise it.

Ziyi asked the manager if he'd heard of any trouble, after the storm. A missing prospector, a bandit attack, anything like that.

"Road got washed out twenty klicks to the east is all I know."

"No one is missing?"

"Sergey might know, I guess. What are you going to do with all that cash, Ziyi?"

"Maybe I buy this place one day. I'm getting old. Can't spend all my life trawling for junk on the beach."

Ziyi visited the hardware store, exchanged scraps of gossip with the store owner and a couple of women who were mining the ruins out in the forest. None of them had heard anything about a bandit attack, or an accident on the coast road. In the internet café, she bought a mug of green tea and an hour on one of the computers. Searched the local news for a bandit attack, some prospector caught in the storm, a plane crash, found nothing. No recent reports of anyone missing or vehicles found abandoned.

She sat back, thinking. So much for her theory that the man was some kind of Jackaroo spy who'd been travelling incognito and had got into trouble when the storm hit. She widened her search. Here was a child who had wandered into the forest. Here was a family, their farm discovered deserted, doors smashed down, probably by sasquatch. Here was the road train that had been attacked by bandits, two years ago. Here was a photograph of the man.

Ziyi felt cold, then hot. Looked around at the café's crowded tables. Clicked on the photo to enlarge it.

It was him. It was the man.

His name was Tony Michaels. Twenty-eight years old, a petrochemist. One of three people missing, presumed taken by the bandits after they killed everyone else. Leaving behind a wife and two children, in the capital.

A family. He'd been human, once upon a time.

Someone in the café laughed; Ziyi heard voices, the chink of cutlery, the hiss of the coffee urn, felt suddenly that everyone was watching her. She sent Tony Michaels' photo to the printer, shut down the browser, snatched up the printout and left.

She was unlocking her jeep when Sergey Polzin called her. The man stepping towards her across the slick mud, dressed in his usual combat gear, his pistol at his hip. He owned the recycling plant, the internet café, and the town's only satellite dish, and acted as if he was the town's unelected mayor. Greeting visitors and showing off the place as if it was something more than a squalid street of shacks squatting amongst factory ruins. Pointing out where the water treatment plant would be, talking about plans for concreting the air strip, building a hospital, a school, that would never come to anything.

Saying to Ziyi, "Heard you hit a big find."

"The storm washed up a few things," Ziyi said, trying to show nothing while Sergey studied her. Trying not to think about the printout folded into the inside pocket of her parka, over her heart.

He said, "I also heard you wanted to report trouble."

"I was wondering how everyone was, after the storm."

He gazed at her for a few moments, then said, "Any trouble, anything unusual, you come straight to me. Understand?"

"Completely."

When Ziyi got back to the cabin she sat the man down and showed him the print-out, then fetched her mirror from the wall and held it in front of him, angling it this way and that, pointing to it pointing to the paper.

"You," she said. "Tony Daniels. You."

He looked at the paper and the mirror, looked at the paper again and ran his fingertips over his smooth face. He didn't need to shave, and his hair was exactly as long as it was in the photo.

"You," she said.

That was who he had been. But what was he now?

The next day she coaxed him into the jeep with the two dogs, and drove west along the coast road, forest on one side and the sea stretching out to the horizon on the other, until she spotted the burnt-out shells of the road train, overgrown with great red drapes of bubbleweed. The dogs jumped off and nosed around; the man slowly climbed out, looked about him, taking no especial notice of the old wreckage.

She had pictured it in her head. His slow recognition. Leading her to the place where he'd hidden or crawled away to die from grievous wounds. The place that had turned him or copied him or whatever it was the factory had done.

Instead, he wandered off to a patch of sunlight in the middle of the road and stood there until she told him they were going for a walk.

They walked a long way, slowly spiralling away from the road. There were factory ruins here, as in most parts of the forest. Stretches of broken wall. Chains of cubes heaved up and broken, half-buried, overgrown by the arched roots of spine trees, and thatches of copperberry and bubbleweed, but the man seemed no more interested in them than in the wreckage of the road train.

"You were gone two years. What happened to you?"

He shrugged.

At last, they walked back to the road. The sun stood at the horizon, as always, throwing shadows over the road. The man walked towards the patch of sunlight where he'd stood before, and kept walking.

Ziyi and the two dogs followed. Through a thin screen of trees to the edge of a sheer drop. Water far below, lapping at rocks. No, not rocks. Factory ruins.

The man stared down at patches of waterweed rising and falling on waves that broke around broken walls.

Ziyi picked up a stone and threw it out beyond the cliff edge. "Was that what happened? You were running from the bandits, it was dark, you ran straight out over the edge . . ."

The man made a humming sound. He was looking at Sauron's fat orange disc now, and after a moment he closed his eyes and stretched out his arms.

Ziyi walked along the cliff edge, looking for and failing to find a path. The black rock plunged straight down, a sheer drop cut by vertical crevices that only an experienced climber might use to pick a route down. She tried to picture it. The road-train stopping because fallen trees had blocked the road. Bandits appearing when the crew stepped down, shooting them, ordering the passengers out, stripping them of their clothes and belongings, shooting them one by one. Bandits didn't like to leave witnesses. One man breaking free, running into the darkness. Running through the trees, running blindly, wounded perhaps, definitely scared, panicked. Running straight out over the cliff edge. If the fall hadn't killed him, he would have drowned. And his body had washed into some active part of the factory, and it had fixed him. No, she thought. It had duplicated him. Had it taken two years? Or had he been living in some part of the factory, out at sea, until the storm had washed him away and he'd been cast up on the beach . . .

The man had taken off his clothes and stood with his arms out and his eyes closed, bathing in level orange light. She shook him until he opened his eyes and smiled at her, and she told him it was time to go.

Ziyi tried and failed to teach the man to talk. "You understand me. So why can't you tell me what happened to you?"

The man humming, smiling, shrugging.

Trying to get him to write or draw was equally pointless.

Days on the beach, picking up flotsam; nights watching movies. She had to suppose he was happy. Her constant companion. Her mystery. She had long ago given up the idea of selling him.

Once, Ziyi's neighbour, Besnik Shkelyim, came out of the forest while the man was searching the strandline. Ziyi told Besnik he was the son of an old friend in the capital, come to visit for a few weeks. Besnik seemed to accept the lie. They chatted about the weather and sasquatch sightings and the latest finds. Besnik did most of the talking. Ziyi was anxious and distracted, trying not to look towards the man, praying that he wouldn't wander over. At last, Besnik said that he could see that she was busy, he really should get back to his own work.

"Bring your friend to visit, some time. I show him where real treasure is found."

Ziyi said that she would, of course she would, watched Besnik walk away into the darkness under the trees, then ran to the man, giddy and foolish with relief, and told him how well he'd done, keeping away from the stranger.

He hummed. He shrugged.

"People are bad," Ziyi said. "Always remember that."

A few days later she went into town. She needed more food and fuel, and took with her a few of the treasures the man had found. Sergey Polzin was at the recycling plant, and fingered through the stuff she'd brought. Superconductor slivers. A variety of tinkertoys, hard little nuggets that changed shape when manipulated. A hand-sized sheet of the variety of plastic in which faint images came and went . . . It was not one tenth of what the man had found for her—she'd buried the rest out in the forest—but she knew that she had made a mistake, knew she'd been greedy and foolish.

She tried her best to seem unconcerned as Sergey counted the silvers of super-conducting plastic three times. "You've been having much luck, recently," he said, at last.

"The storm must have broken open a cache, somewhere out to sea," she said.

"Odd that no one else has been finding so much stuff."

"If we knew everything about the factory, Sergey Polzin, we would all be rich."

Sergey's smile was full of gold. "I hear you have some help. A guest worker."

Besnik had talked about her visitor. Of course he had.

Ziyi trotted out her lie.

"Bring him into town next time," Sergey said. "I'll show him around."

A few days later, Ziyi saw someone watching the compound from the edge of the forest. A flash of sunlight on a lens, a shadowy figure that faded into the shadows under the trees when she walked towards him. Ziyi ran, heard an engine start, saw a red pickup bucket out of the trees and speed off down the track.

She'd only had a glimpse of the intruder, but she was certain that it was the manager of the recycling plant.

She walked back to the compound. The man was facing the sun, naked, arms outstretched. Ziyi managed to get him to put on his clothes, but it was impossible to make him understand that he had to leave. Drive him into the forest, let him go? Yes, and sasquatch or wargs would eat him, or he'd find his way to some prospector's cabin and knock on the door . . .

She walked him down to the beach, but he followed her back to the cabin. In the end, she locked him in the shed.

Early in the afternoon, Sergey Polzin's yellow Humvee came bumping down the track, followed by a UN Range Rover. Ziyi tried to be polite and cheerful, but Sergey walked straight past her, walked into the cabin, walked back out.

"Where is he?"

"My friend's son? He went back to the capital. What's wrong?" Ziyi said to the UN policewoman.

"It's a routine check," the policewoman, Aavert Enger, said.

"Do you have a warrant?"

"You're hiding dangerous technology," Sergey said. "We don't need a warrant."

"I am hiding nothing."

"There has been a report," Aavert Enger said.

Ziyi told her it was a misunderstanding, said that she'd had a visitor, yes, but he had left.

"I would know if someone came visiting from the capital," Sergey said. He was puffed up with self-righteousness. "I also know he was here today. I have a photograph that proves it. And I looked him up on the net, just like you did. You should have erased your cache, by the way. Tony Daniels, missing for two years. Believed killed by bandits. And now he's living here."

"If I could talk to him I am sure we can clear this up," Aavert Enger said.

"He isn't here."

But it was no good. Soon enough, Sergey found the shed was locked and ordered Ziyi to hand over the keys. She refused. Sergey said he'd shoot off the padlock; the policewoman told him that there was no need for melodrama, and used a master key.

Jung and Cheung started to bark as Sergey led the man out. "Tony Daniels," he said to the policewoman. "The dead man Tony Daniels."

Ziyi said, "Look, Sergey Polzin, I'll be straight with you. I don't know who he really is or where he came from. He helps me on the beach. He helps me find things. All the good stuff I brought in, that was because of him. Don't spoil a good thing. Let me use him to find more stuff. You can take a share. For the good of the town. The school you want to build, the water treatment plant in a year, two years, we'll have enough to pay for them . . ."

But Sergey wasn't listening. He'd seen the man's eyes. "You see?" he said to Aavert Enger. "You see?"

"He is a person," Ziyi said. "Like you and me. He has a wife. He has children."

"And did you tell them you had found him?" Sergey said "No, of course not. Because he is a dead man. No, not even that. He is a replica of a dead man, spun out in the factory somewhere."

"It is best we take him to town. Make him safe," the policewoman said.

The man was looking at Ziyi.

"How much?" Ziyi said to the policewoman. "How much did he offer you?"

"This isn't about money," Sergey said. "It's about the safety of the town."

"Yes. And the profit you'll make, selling him."

Ziyi was shaking. When Sergey started to pull the man towards the vehicles, she tried to get in his way. Sergey shoved at her, she fell down, and suddenly everything happened at once. The dogs, Jung and Cheung, ran at Sergey. He pushed the man away and fumbled for his pistol and Jung clamped his jaws around Sergey's wrist and started to shake him. Sergey sat down hard and Jung held on and Cheung darted in and seized his ankle. Sergey screaming while the dogs pulled in different directions, and Ziyi rolled to her feet and reached into the tangle of man and dogs and plucked up Sergey's pistol and snapped off the safety and turned to the policewoman and told her to put up her hands.

"I am not armed," Aavert Enger said. "Do not be foolish, Ziyi."

Sergey was screaming at her, telling her to call off her dogs.

"It's good advice," Ziyi told the policewoman, "but it is too late."

The pistol was heavy, slightly greasy. The safety was off. The hammer cocked when she pressed lightly on the trigger.

The man was looking at her.

"I'm sorry," she said, and shot him.

The man's head snapped back and he lost his footing and fell in the mud, kicking and spasming. Ziyi stepped up to him and shot him twice more, and he stopped moving.

Ziyi called off the dogs, told Aavert Enger to sit down and put her hands on her head. Sergey was holding his arm. Blood seeped around his fingers. He was cursing her, but she paid him no attention.

The man was as light as a child, but she was out of breath by the time she had dragged him to her jeep. Sergey had left the keys in the ignition of his Humvee. Ziyi threw them towards the forest as hard as she could, shot out one of the tyres of Aavert Enger's Range Rover, loaded the man into the back of the jeep. Jung and Cheung jumped in, and she drove off.

Ziyi had to stop once, and throw up, and drove the rest of the way with half her attention on the rear-view mirror. When she reached the spot where the roadtrain had been ambushed, she cradled the man in her arms and carried him through the trees. The two dogs followed. When she reached the edge of the cliff her pulse was hammering in her head and she had to sit down. The man lay beside her. His head was blown open, showing layers of filmy plastics. Although his face was untouched you would not mistake him for a sleeper.

After a little while, when she was pretty certain she wasn't going to have a heart attack, she knelt beside him, and closed his eyes, and with a convulsive movement pitched him over the edge. She didn't look to see where he fell. She threw Sergey's pistol after him, and sat down to wait.

She didn't look around when the dogs began to bark. Aavert Enger said, "Where is he?"

"In the same place as Sergey's pistol."

Aavert Enger sat beside her. "You know I must arrest you, Ziyi."

"Of course."

"Actually, I am not sure what you'll be charged with. I'm not sure if we will charge you with anything. Sergey will want his day in court, but perhaps I can talk him out of it."

"How is he?"

"The bites are superficial. I think losing his prize hurt him more."

"I don't blame you," Ziyi said. "Sergey knew he was valuable, knew I would not give him up, knew that he would be in trouble if he tried to take it. So he told you. For the reward."

"Well, it's gone now. Whatever it was."

"It was a man," Ziyi said.

She had her cache of treasures, buried in the forest. She could buy lawyers. She could probably buy Sergey, if it came to it. She could leave, move back to the capital and live out her life in comfort, or buy passage to another of the worlds gifted by the Jackaroo, or even return to Earth.

But she knew that she would not leave. She would stay here and wait through the days and years until the factory returned her friend to her.

The stars do not lie

jay Lake

Highly prolific writer Jay Lake seems to have appeared nearly everywhere with short work in the last few years, including Asimov's Science Fiction, Interzone, Jim Baen's Universe, Tor.com, Clarkesworld, Strange Horizons, Aeon, Postscripts, Electric Velocipede, *and many other markets, producing enough short fiction that he has already released four collections, even though his career is only a few years old:* Greetings from Lake Wu, Green Grow the Rushes-Oh, American Sorrows, Dogs in the Moonlight, *and* The Sky That Wraps. *His novels include* Rocket Science, Trial of Flowers, Mainspring, Escapement, Green, Madness of Flowers, *and* Pinion, *as well as three chapbook novellas,* Death of a Starship, The Baby Killers, *and* The Specific Gravity of Grief. *He's the coeditor, with Deborah Layne, of the prestigious* Polyphony *anthology series, now in six volumes, and has also edited the anthologies* All-Star Zeppelin Adventure Stories, *with David Moles,* Other Earths, *with Nick Gevers, and* Spicy Slipstream Stories, *with Nick Mamatas. His most recent books include* Endurance, *a sequel to* Green, *and a chapbook novella,* Love in the Time of Metal and Flesh. *Coming up are new novels* Kalimpura *and* Sunspin. *He won the John W. Campbell Award for Best New Writer in 2004. Lake lives in Portland, Oregon.*

Here he takes us to a world whose inhabitants have forgotten (and, in fact, vehemently deny) their origins, for an elegant and somewhat steampunkish tale, evocatively written and peopled with characters of real psychological complexity, all embroiled on one side or another in a political and religious war between those who want to reveal the truth and those who want to surpress it.

In the beginnings, the Increate did reach down into the world and where They laid Their hand was all life touched and blossomed and brought forth from water, fire, earth and air. In eight gardens were the Increate's children raised, each to have dominion over one of the eight points of the Earth. The Increate gave to men Their will, Their word and Their love. These we Their children have carried forward into the opening of the world down all the years of men since those first days.

—Librum Vita, *Beginnings 1:1—4; being the Book of Life and word entire of the Increate*

Morgan Abutti; B.Sc. Bio.; M.Sc. Arch.; Ph.D. Astr. & Nat, Sci.; 4th degree Thalassocrete; Member, Planetary Society; and Associate Fellow of the New Garaden
Institute, stared at the map which covered the interior wall of his tiny office in the
Institute's substantial brownstone in downtown Highpassage. The new electricks
were still being installed by brawny, nimble-fingered men of crafty purpose who
often smelled a bit of smoke and burnt cloth. Thus his view was dominated by a
flickering quality of light that would have done justice to a smoldering hearth, or a
wandering planet low in the pre-dawn sky. The gaslamp men were complaining of
the innovations, demonstrating under Lateran banners each morning down by the
Thalassojustity Palace in their unruly droves.

He despised the rudeness of the laboring classes. Almost to a man, they were
pale-faced fools who expected something for nothing, as if simply picking up a
wrench could grant a man worth.

Turning his attentions away from the larger issues of political economy and surplus value, he focused once more on history.

Or religion.

Honestly, Morgan was never quite certain of the difference any more.

Judging from the notes and diagrams limned up and down the side of the wide
rosewood panel in their charmingly archaic style, the map had been painted about
a century earlier for some long-dead theohistoriographer. The Eight Gardens of the
Increate were called out in tiny citrons that somehow had survived the intervening
years without being looted by hungry servants or thirsty undergraduates. Morgan
traced his hand over the map, fingers sliding across the pitted patina of varnish and
oil soap marking the attentions of generations of charwomen.

Eufrat.
Quathlamba.
Ganj.
Manju.
Wy'east.
Tunsa.
Antiskuna.
Cycladia.

The homes of man. Archaeological science was clear enough. Thanks to the
work of natural scientists of the past century, so was the ethnography. The Increate had placed the human race upon this Earth. That was absolutely clear. Just
as the priests of the Lateran had always taught, nothing of humanity was older
than the villages of the Gardens of the Increate.

Nothing.

Sick at heart, Morgan turned back to his photographic plates, their silver oxide
bearing indubitable evidence of ephemeral nature of such faith in the Increate.

The stars do not lie.

"Gentlemen of the Planetary Society . . ." Morgan Abutti let his voice trail off a moment. His next words once uttered could never be taken back. Not before this august assemblage of the greatest scientific minds of the modern era. He drew in a deep breath and plunged recklessly onward. "On examination of considerable evidence from fields as varied as paleontology, archaeology, and astronomy, I have been compelled to confront the distinct likelihood that we, the human race, are not of this world."

He paused to give the audience a moment to consider the proposition. The racket of the city of Highpassage echoed from outside the Society's Plenary Hall— steam whistles, horses, motorcars, the grumble of the new diesel engines powering the latest generations of airships. The seven hundred faces staring at him included a scattering of the paler-skinned northern folk, who were finally entering academe and the sciences thanks to the same progressive policies that had helped pave Morgan's own way to the exclusive University of Highpassage. That women had been allowed to study a generation earlier had cracked open the door that later admitted the traditionally inferior white race.

The world was growing more open-minded by the decade in spite of itself. Were his colleagues in the Planetary Society ready for this, his grand conclusion?

What he'd thought to be shocked silence degraded into murmuring, muttering, even outright laughter in a few corners. Some delegates rose from their seats, ready to move onward to more fruitful pursuits. Others struck up conversations with their seatmates, or commenced making notes, in some cases with deliberate ostentation.

Morgan had lost the audience, waiting for their reaction to his news.

"I have . . . have assembled a précis of the evidence . . ." he began, but his voice trailed off. A moment later Doctor Professor the Revered Lucan Matroit, Secretary-General of the Planetary Society, plucked at Morgan's sleeve.

"My deepest regrets, ah . . . Doctor Abutti," Lucan said quietly, his tone as formal and disinterested as if the two of them had never met before. "The Society thanks you for your contributions." He quite effectively twisted Morgan's arm and propelled him toward the heavy maroon velvet curtains marking stage left.

"Dear ones," Lucan called out to the audience, which immediately stilled its unrest at his piercing voice. "Let us now offer praise to the Increate, as redress to Them for the caprice and responsibilities of free will . . ."

Morgan did not hear the rest of the invocative prayer. Two of the Society's burly porters—like most of their fellows, former Thalassojustity Marines—seized him by the upper arms, shoved his despatch case into his hands, jammed his bowler hat upon his head, and escorted him to a service entrance from which he was summarily ejected into a dung-spattered alley under the doleful gaze of a brace of hinnies hitched to a rag man's cart.

At least they had not thrown him bodily into the muck. No, even that embarrassment had been trumped with a few mere words by Lucan Matroit.

Gathering the shreds of his dignity, Morgan resolved to retreat to the shelter of his office at the New Garaden Institute. The Avenida Tram line ran past the Plenary Hall, and would deposit him within two blocks of his destination.

Waiting for the next street car to arrive, Morgan noticed one of the porters watching him. The man leaned on a pillar of the rococo façade of the Plenary Hall, smoking a fat cigar and making no effort to hide himself, or pretend interest in anything but Morgan. After adjusting his collar tabs and fussing with his shirt front, Morgan held his leather case to his chest as if it could armor him, and waited among the ladies' maids and banker's daughters for the tram.

Riding among a crowd consisting mostly of servants summoned memories that Morgan had expended some effort at setting aside. The human odor of painfully starched cleanliness and faint malnutrition within the tram was far too reminiscent of his own childhood. He stared out at the streets of Highpassage, ignoring the people around him with their muted gossip and wondered what he'd been about.

Seeking truth, *science*, had been his path out of ungenteel poverty. That the good universities admitted scholarship boys at all was still a strange novelty when Morgan had first enrolled. He'd studied beyond reason to qualify, understanding perfectly clearly he would have to do twice as well to be thought half as good as someone of monied birth and good family.

Even now, with his doctorate and his post at the New Garaden Institute, far too few listened with ears of reason. People only saw and heard what they wished. If he'd been a titled scion of some ancient house, Matroit would not have been able to rush him out of the Planetary Society.

The most important discovery of the modern age was being crushed by pettiness. No different from the rough back alley games of his youth. The strongest ones, the ones with the most friends, always prevailed.

Head pressed against the glass, feeling the shudder of the tracks through the tram's iron wheels, Morgan almost wept to realize the world's unfairness had no end. He could never be good enough, never have possession of enough facts, to surpass that barrier.

The New Garaden Institute's offices occupied the majority of an elegant building that had been designed and constructed during the height of the Neoclassical Revival at the beginning of the previous century. It had been one of the first structures in Highpassage built with the intention of being gas lit and centrally heated. Plumbing stacks, gas valve closets, ventilation shafts for the introduction of fresh air to the innermost precincts of the structure—the building had been a truly visionary project from the century's most famous architect, Kingdom Obasa. A brilliant Iberiard educated outside the top-ranked university system, Obasa had very much gone his own way in both engineering and aesthetics. As a result, for all of its brownstone glory the New Garaden Institute nonetheless resembled nothing so much as a cathedral which had been somewhat melted.

The recent addition of an array of rooftop electrickal signaling devices for the propagation and reception of radio waves had done nothing to alleviate the building's strangeness.

Stung, embittered, saddened by his setback, but firmly in command of himself once more, Morgan stumbled through the vestibule into the receiving parlor only to find the Desk Porter in close consultation with a pair of on-duty Thalassojustity

Marines. His view of the wide expanse of maroon carpet, delicate settees and brass rails telescoped into a horrified vision of another ejection from his barely attained positions of privilege. The Marines' formal red tunics contrasted oddly with the firearms borne by both of the large men. While Morgan had little familiarity with weapons, even he could see that these were not the long-barreled, wooden-stocked rifles carried on parade, but rather short, snub-nosed bits of machined steel slung tight on well-worn leather straps. Businesslike tools of violence, in other words.

"Ah, Dr. Abutti," one of the Marines said, even before he'd turned from the Desk Porter's podium. A large man, his purple-blue eyes were like grapes squeezed into the unnaturally pale, ruddy flesh of his face.

Morgan was impressed for about three beats, until he realized the man had seen his reflection in the glassed-over painting of the Battle of Mino Harbor behind the podium.

"Indeed. I do not believe we have been introduced." Morgan glanced pointedly at the Desk Porter. The Desk Porter—was his name Philas? Phelps?—just as pointedly failed to meet Morgan's eye.

"No need, sir. You're to come with us. Thalassojustity business. You're being called before the Lesser Bench, sir." The Marine favored Morgan with a warm smile that did not meet the eyes. His fellow favored Morgan with the blank stare of a gun barrel casually swung to bear.

"Now?" Morgan asked with an involuntary swallow.

"Now." And after a moment too long, "Sir."

"I may be some time," Morgan told the Desk Porter.

"I'll make a note, Doctor." This time he did raise his eyes with a faint flash of malice.

> When first they hanged the pirate Black upon the beach
> Little did the captains trow what they set upon the sea
> Neither haunt nor hollow, down the long years between
> Justice for the open waves, and a fire upon the deep
> —Lords of the Horizon, *Ebenstone (trad. attrib.)*

By sharp contrast with the New Garaden Institute, the Thalassojustity Palace was arguably the oldest building in Highpassage. It was certainly the oldest building still in regular use. The legal and sovereign relationship between the Thalassojustity and its host city were ambiguous, strained by two millennia and more of precedent, treaty, and occasional open warfare.

In other words, arguably not in Highpassage proper. The Increate, as always, manifested Their power on the side of the big battalions.

Morgan Abutti was treated to a close view of the Pirate's Steps, the ancient risers that led to the formal portico. A temple of the sea, the palace had been looking out across the Attik Main for over a third of recorded history. He knew the building well—impossible not to as a fourth-degree Thalassocrete. The initiation ceremonies stressed history above all else.

Normally he used a discrete side door for the alternate Thursday lodge meetings.

Only criminals and heads of state paraded up the Pirate's Steps. He knew which he wasn't.

"What have I done?" he asked of the two Marines for at least the sixth time. For at least the sixth time, they gave him no answer. Even the false smiles had vanished, to be replaced by a firm grip on each arm and the banging of one Marine's firearm against Morgan's hip.

At the top of the steps, he was hoisted around and faced outward, so that he stared at the bottle-green waters of the Attik Main. Shipping crowded the waves, as always at Highpassage, one of the busiest ports in the world. Great iron steamers from the yards at Urartu far to the east passed above dish-prowed fishing boats whose lines had not changed in a thousand years of beachfront ship building. A white-hulled Thalassojustity cutter cruised past barges and scows waiting for their dock pilots. Overhead, a pair of the new Iberiard dirigibles beat hard against the wind, engines straining as they slung urgent deck cargo to landfall from a vessel waiting too long for a slip.

Highpassage, crossroads of the world.

But the message wasn't that, Morgan knew. He'd sat through too many initiations not to see the point the Marines were making. The hanging tree, the ultimate symbol of both justice and power across the world's maritime extents, stood on beach below him, memorialized as a granite monument to the largely legendary death of the largely legendary pirate Black. That angry court of captains and bosuns had met on a firelit beach in the teeth of a rising storm over two thousand years past to take justice in their own hands after the King of Highpassage had declined to act. The sailors had broken Black, so the story ran, and unintentionally founded a line of power that controlled the high seas to this day, serving as a pragmatic secular counterbalance to the widespread spiritual and temporal influence of the Lateran church.

Drawing on that tradition to this day, justice, as untempered by mercy as the sea itself, was the purpose of the Thalassocretes.

"You're a man of keen wit and insight," said the pale Marine in a startlingly soft tone, to Morgan's surprise.

"I am likely blind to much in this life." He felt as if he were uttering his last words. "Science is both my mistress and my muse. But even I can still see history."

Like estranged lovers met on a sidewalk, the moment swiftly passed. A rough adversity resumed. Morgan found himself pushed within, toward the upper halls and the quiet, incense-reeking rooms of the Lesser and Greater Benches of the Thalassojustity.

The Most Revered Bilious F. Quinx; B.Th. Rhet..; M.Th. Hist. & Rit.; Th.D. Hist. & Rit.; 32nd degree Thalassocrete; and master of the Increate's Consistitory Office for Preservation of the Faith Against Error and Heresy, watched carefully as His Holiness Lamboine XXII paged through one of the *prohibitora* from the Consistitory's most confidential library.

The two of them were alone—unusually so, given His Holiness' nigh everpresent retinue—in the aerie of the Matachin Tower of the Lateran Palace. This room was Quinx' private study and retreat, and also where his most confidential meetings were held. The latter was due to the architecture of the tower walls that rendered the usual methods of ecclesiastical eavesdropping futile.

Quinx, in both his official capacity and from his well-developed personal sense of curiosity, worried about the possibility of spying via the new electricks. For that reason, he had thus far forbidden any lights or wires to be installed in the Matachin Tower. He preferred instead to rely on traditional oil lamps tended by traditional acolytes who damned well knew to keep their ears shut. And besides which, wore nubble-soled slippers so they could not sneak.

Privacy was both a commodity and a precious resource within these walls of the Increate's highest house. Quinx made it his business to control the available privacy as much as possible.

Still, having His Holiness leaf so casually through a *prohibitorum* was enough to give a thoughtful man a galloping case of the hives.

Lamboine—who had once been called Ion when they were boys together in a mountain village plentifully far away from the Holy Precincts—raised his eyes from the page. "There is nothing in this world I am not entitled to know, Bili."

"You understand me perfectly as always."

Those words summoned a small, sad smile, one that Quinx also remembered far too well from a youth lost six decades past. "That is why I am the Gatekeeper and you are my hound," Lamboine replied. As ever, his voice was preternaturally patient. "I have always wondered why our friends among the Thalassocretes have never sought to place a man on the Footstool of the Increate."

Ion was one of the few remaining alive who could provoke Quinx to unthinking response. "Do you honestly suppose they never have done so? I am numbered among their rolls, after all."

"They think you their spy in the house of the Increate." Another small smile. "In any event, I should think I would know if one of them had ever held my throne. My opinion is that they have never felt a need to. Truth is a strange commodity."

"Much like privacy," Quinx almost whispered, echoing his own, earlier thoughts.

The Gatekeeper shook his head. "Privacy is just a special case of truth, or its withholding. This . . ." His hand, palsied with the infirmity of age that had yet to overcome Quinx, swept over the open book. "This is truth of a different sort."

"No, Your Holiness. It is not. It is only the Thalassocretes' story. We have the Increate and the evidence on our side."

"What makes you think there are sides, Bili?"

In that moment, Quinx saw Lamboine's death. Flesh stretched tight and luminous across his face, the deep, natural brown of his skin paling to the color of milk in coffee, his eyes brittle as cracked opals. The man's fires were guttering. "There are always sides, Ion. That has been my role these long years here, preserving and defending your side." He paused a moment, then added: "Our side."

The Gatekeeper waited several measures of silence too long for comfort before replying. "I am glad you did not claim a side for the Increate. They are all, and They are everything."

"Of course." Quinx bowed his head.

A trembling hand descended in surprising blessing. Quinx had not even realized that the Gatekeeper had set the book down. "Do not rely too much on evidence, my oldest friend. It has a way of turning against you in time. Proof can change with circumstance. Faith is the rock upon which we must always build."

Quinx remained bowed until the Gatekeeper had departed, shuffling far enough down the spiral stairs to summon his attendants who bore him away on a wave of soft whispers and perfume. After a time, he rose and set some incense alight before kneeling on a bolster with a small, ricepaper copy of *Librum Vita* in his grip. It had been made in distant Sind, something of a curiosity, copied out in a firm hand by a man wielding a brush comprised of only a single hair. Act of faith? Dedication to art?

It did not matter. The Increate's words fit in the palm of Quinx' hands. From there, he drew comfort as surely as he had from his mother's grasp once so long ago. *Or Ion's.*

The relief of prayer drew him in then, toward the dim inner light that always filled Bilious Quinx when he sought the Increate in honest, faithful silence with open heart and empty thoughts.

Much later he trimmed the wicks in his office and lit the night lamp. Darkness had descended outside, the evening breeze bearing the itching scent of pollen and spring chill off the mountains to the east and north. Quinx opened his windows, their red glazing parting to let the tepid lamplight spill out to compete with the distant stars.

The Lateran Palace had its own observatories, of course. Someone must demarcate the lines of the world. Even the almighty Thalassojustity had in the past been willing to leave the skies to the church. The irony of that was not lost on Quinx in these late days. He was certain it was no less lost on the Thalassocretes in Highpassage and elsewhere.

No matter his own initiations into their ranks; the Thalassojustity had always known who and what Quinx was, and whose creature he had been, body and soul. That Ion was dying now changed nothing of Quinx' loyalties.

He considered the *prohibitorum*, lying so carelessly open where the Gatekeeper had left it on one of the round room's several curve-backed writing desks. The book was open to a map of the Garden of Ganj, annotated only as the heretics of the Thalassojustity would bother to do. This particular volume was a first printing of the *Revised Standard Survey, Th. 1907*. Almost a hundred years old, and their color plates a century past were as good as anything the Lateran presses could manage even today.

Ion had left a scrap tucked in the center crease. Quinx plucked it out, his own hand trembling. It was a short note that must have been written before the Gatekeeper had come up to see him, in Ion's lifelong careful copperplate hand, rendered edgy and strange by the exigencies of age.

> Dearest—
> Do not let them elect you to the Gatekeeper's throne after me. And do not
> be afraid of what may be proven. Farewell, I regret that I must go before.
>   Always yours.

So he had seen truly into the Gatekeeper's face. And *Dearest*. They had not used that word between them in over five decades. Quinx carefully burned the note, then stirred the ashes. After that he trimmed his night lamp back to darkness, closed and sealed the *prohibitorum* with a black ribbon, and took a chair by one of the open casements to watch the stars wheel slowly until just after midnight the Lateran tower bells began to ring their death knells.

When the great, iron bell of the Algeficic Tower tolled last and slowest of all, his tears finally flowed.

> Love is the sin that will not be denied.
> —Librum Vita, Wisdoms 7:23; *being the Book*
> *of Life and word entire of the Increate*

The funerary rites for His Holiness Lamboine XXII began at Matins as the first flickering sweep of dawn glowed like coals in the eastern sky. In his role as Preserver of the Faith, and therefore fourth-ranking priest in the Lateran hierarchy, Quinx could have insisted on being the celebrant. The two men above him were already closeted deep in the electoral politics of the Primacy, those same delegates from around the world having received the Gatekeeper's death notice by telelocutor for the first time in Church history.

Quinx had a sick feeling that he would soon grow very weary of that last thought: *the first time in history.*

Instead of celebrating, he chose to attend as a congregant, a man, a priest, a mourner. The Deacon of the Lateran High Chapel led the first round of services. He was a young man with a perpetually surprised expression now properly dressed in a sweeping black cassock embroidered in gold and silver thread, though he'd begun the services in a nightshirt before being rescued by an acolyte with the right set of chamber keys.

Incense, again, and the familiar tones of the chimes indicating the order of service. As the deacon struck them in turn, Quinx tried to put the memory of the tower bells away. Not to forget, for nothing could be forgotten by a man in his office, but to be set aside.

Prayer was a valve opened to the comfort of the Increate, from Whom all things sprang and to Whom all things flowed. There were times when he could understand the attraction of the Aquatist Heresies, for all that their pernicious metaphors had nearly fatally tangled the Lateran Church in its own liturgies. There were times when he wondered what the Increate truly intended, as if They would speak directly to him in response. There were times when quiet refuge was the greatest gift They could give him. Quinx let the deacon's droning voice lead him from grief to some other place where his cares could wait on the attentions of his heart.

Somewhere in memory, two young men on a hillside scattered with sheep, goats, and bright blue flowers laughed under a summer sky and spoke together of all things great and small.

When fingers touched his shoulder, Quinx was briefly startled. He'd gone so far into meditation that he'd lost himself in the well-worn rituals of the service. *Become the liturgy,* as they used to say in seminary.

He looked around. Brother Kurts, his lead investigator, stood as always just a bit too close.

"Sir," the monk growled. A big man, one of those pale northerners who somehow never seemed to advance far in the Church hierarchy, Kurts carried far more than his own weight. The man was a boulder in a snowfield. Here, in the midst of service, his blocky frame and the dark brown rough-spun habit of his Sibellian Order made him a brutal shout against the soaring of the silk-robed choir who must have filed in to the loft while Quinx had been meditating.

"Kurts?"

"You must come, sir. We have an urgent dispatch from Highpassage. By air."

"By air?" Briefly, Quinx felt stupid—an unusual sensation for him. Of late, matters of great urgency were transmitted via telelocutor. His own office had approved such innovation only three years earlier, well after the undersea cable had been laid between Highpassage and the Lateran, crossing beneath the Attik Main. Matters of great secrecy were handled quite differently, and always with utmost discretion.

Sending an airship across the sea the night of His Holiness' death was tantamount to lighting a flare.

"By air, sir," Kurts confirmed. "Matroit dispatched the messenger."

Matroit. The man was the very model of probity, and no more likely to panic than he was to fly to the moon. But the timing of the thing . . . It stank of politics. Quinx felt briefly ill. "Was the vessel a Thalassojustity airship?"

The monk shook his head. "A racing yacht. I understand it was put about to have been sent on a dare by some of the young wastrels of the city."

Not an utterly unreasonable cover story, Quinx had to admit, for all that such defiance of the Thalassojustity was outrageous. *Outrageous* served as the stock in trade of a certain set in Highpassage. He set aside for later consideration the issue of how Lucan Matroit was connected to that set in the first place. For now, a dispatch this urgent would be a distraction to his grieving heart.

How welcome or unwelcome remained to be seen.

He did not bother to ask if Kurts had read it. The man would not have done so. In his entire life, Quinx had only ever trusted two men utterly. The first of those had passed on into the hands of the Increate last night. The other was here before him. Whatever Kurts' many flaws, the monk was loyal to the bone. *Blood and vows, vows and blood,* as they used to say.

Quinx gathered the skirts of his cassock and rose from the prayer bench. He gave an approving nod to the deacon, now well into the third iteration of the funerary mass and looking distinctly tired, before withdrawing from the High Chapel in the wake of his man.

They closeted themselves in a tiny dining room from which Quinx had by virtue of his office ruthlessly evicted four hungry priests. Plates of plain eggs and blackbread toast still steamed. He considered the contents of envelope presented by Kurts. The seal had been genuine enough to the best of Quinx' rather well sharpened ability to determine. For something that had come rushing over hundreds of miles of open water, the letter within was sufficiently sparse as to seem laughable. A single sheet of crème-colored Planetary Society paper, with that slick finish favored by the very wealthy though it would take few inks. A rushed hand, script rather than copper-plate, the pigments a curious green that was one of Matroit's affectations. And only a very few words indeed.

But such dangerous ones.

It was dated the previous day though no time was given. He realized on reflection that this missive must have been written before Ion's death could have been known, just by judging the miles the message had flown even at the speed of the fastest air-racing yacht.

> Revered—
> The Externalist heresy was proclaimed again today in the Plenary Hall. To my surprise, the Thalassocretes have taken custody of the young man in question, but I have secured his work for the nonce. There is a possibility of empirical evidence.
>
> M.

Evidence.

Proof.

Had Ion known last night this letter was coming, known as he was dying? Or was it simply that now happened to be the world's time for such trials? The cloying smell of cooling eggs provided no answer.

Still, Quinx felt a swift trip to Highpassage would be in order. With their profound challenge to the roots of Lateran doctrine, Externalists were a far more troublesome heresy than the dissenters such as the Machinists or the Originalists. Putting paid to this renewed outbreak of Externalism before it had a chance to establish and multiply was an utmost priority. And that errand in turn would keep him safely away from the deliberations of the Assemblage of Primates, who would surely be meeting *in camera* the moment the Gatekeeper's body had been sufficiently blessed. Death was an unfortunate pause in events, but politics continued forever.

There was a young man to see, and a Thalassojustity to face down. *Again.*

Why people insisted on resisting the obvious and holy truths of the Increate was one of those mysteries of free will that a priest could spend his lifetime contemplating without any success. If all the saints of ancient days could not answer such a question, surely Bilious Quinx would be no wiser.

Questions he could not answer, but problems he could solve.

"Brother Kurts . . ."

"Sir?"

"Does the airship pilot perhaps await our pleasure?"

There was the briefest pause, then the slightest tone of satisfaction in the monk's reply. "I have already made certain of it, sir."

> The advantages of the reflecting telescope over the refracting telescope cannot be understated, and should be obvious to any thinking man. While the great refractors of the past century have multiplied our understanding of the Increate's work amidst the

heavens, the practical exigencies of glass-making, gravity and the engineering arts limit the refracting mirrors to less than fifty inches of diameter. Advances in the philosophy of the reflecting telescope have produced designs by such luminaries as Kingdom Obasa's son and successor Brunel for mirrors of a hundred inches or greater! Even now, the Planetary Society raises a subscription for such a heavenly monster to be placed upon Mount Sysiphe north of Highpassage, that we might enumerate the craters of the moon and count the colors of the stars to better understand the glories of Creation. A true union of Science and Faith can only prosper from such noble endeavors.

—*Editorial in the* Highpassage Argus-Intelligencer,
November 2nd, *H.3123, Th.1997, L.6011*

"Lesser Bench" was a misnomer. Morgan knew that. *Everybody* knew that. The Greater Bench met only in solemn conclave on the beach to hear capital cases, and certain classes of piracy accusations. Everything else that transpired in the Thalassojustity took place under the purview of the Lesser Bench.

The question was which of those benches.

The two Marines dragged Morgan into the interior of the Thalassojustity Palace. The main nave soared to the roof, some eighty feet above, and was lined with enormous statues of sea captains and Thalassocretes through the ages. The joke ran that the bodies remained the same and the heads were switched from time to time. Whatever the truth, the sculpture represented one of the greatest troves of Classical art in the world, with continuous provenance stretching back well before the onset of consistent recordkeeping.

Glorious, strange, and too large for the world—that was the majesty of the Thalassojustity, encapsulated in the world of art.

At the moment, Morgan was feeling inglorious, ordinary, and far too small. Even the marble flags were oversized, designed to intimidate.

He was scooted a bit too fast past the massive altarpiece at the far end of the nave, through a bronze door wrought with an overly detailed relief of some long-forgotten naval battle, and into a far more ordinary hallway that could have been found in any reasonably modern commercial building in Highpassage. Electricks flickered overhead, giving a reddish-yellow cast to the light. Entrances lining each side of the hallway were so mundane as to be aggressive in their plainness—dark brown, two-paneled doors, each relieved with frosted glass painted with the name of some bureau or official. Cocked-open transoms above each provided some relief from a warmth that must be stifling in high summer.

Only the carpet, a finely napped deep blue that Morgan could not put a name to, betrayed the true wealth of this place.

Well down the hall he was propelled into an intersecting corridor with doors set much farther apart. Larger rooms for larger purposes? The Courts of the Lesser Bench, he realized, as they passed a door where gold-flecked lettering proclaimed "EXCISE BENCH."

The door he was pushed through was marked "LOYALTY BENCH."

Morgan's heart stuttered cold and hard. *The treason court.* Where offenses against the Thalassojustity itself, or against the common good, were tried.

The door slammed behind him. No Marines. Morgan whirled, taking in the small gallery, the judge's podium, stands for witness and examiner, the interrogation chair, glass cabinets where evidence or exhibits might be stored.

And no one present. No judge, no advocates, no clerks of the court, no bailiffs, no witnesses, no one at all but himself. Defendant?

The walls rose high, two or three storeys, though not as tall as the nave. These were paneled in inlays of half a dozen different colored woods to create a pleasing abstract pattern. Electrick chandeliers dangled overhead. Their fat iron arms signaled their gaslamp history.

Morgan ceased gaping and sat down in the gallery. He had no desire to approach the front of the courtroom. As nothing seemed to be taking place, he simply closed his eyes for a moment. His heartbeat calmed for the first time since stepping to the podium back at the Plenary Hall of the Planetary Society.

Without seeing, other senses sharpened. He smelled the furniture polish and floor wax of the courtroom, along with the faint ozone scent of the electricks. All of it masked the underlying accumulation of human stress and fear. Perspiration had left its indelible mark in the air.

The sounds of the room were similar: a faint buzz from the lights, the creak and sigh of old wood, the footfalls of someone approaching.

Morgan's eyes shot open and he stiffened.

The newcomer—no door had opened, had it?—was gloriously dark-skinned as any king of old, gray eyes almost silver in a cragged and noble face. His hair was worked back in prince-rows, each set with tiny turquoise and silver beads so that he seemed almost to be wearing a net upon his head. A silver hoop hung from his left ear, the conciscrux of the Thalassojustity tiny in his right. Barefoot, he wore a laborer's canvas trousers and shirt, though dyed a deep maroon rather than the usual blue or grubby tan. Despite the attire, this one would not have fooled any thinking observer for more than a moment, not with his bearing.

After a moment, Morgan finally registered how *small* the man was. Barely shoulder high, four foot nine at the most. That was when he knew who he faced—Eraster Goins, presiding judge of the Lesser Benches. *The* Thalassocrete.

"Pardon my state of undress," Goins said politely. "I was attending to some physical matters when I was informed of the requirement for my presence."

"I . . . Sir . . ." Morgan made the hand-sign of his lodge.

A crinkling smile emerged that was entirely at odds with the power at this man's word. Goins could summon fleets, lay waste to cities, claim the life of almost anyone, at his mere whim. "Of course I know that, Dr. Abutti. You do not need to demonstrate your loyalty or training at this time."

At this time.

"Wh-what, then, sir?"

"Well . . ." Goins cracked his knuckles, took a moment to find great interest in the beds of his nails. Morgan did not think this was a man ordinarily at a loss for words. "So far as anyone in the city of Highpassage is concerned, you are in here being thrashed within an inch of your now-worthless life. This matter will be of specific interest to certain Lateran observers."

Morgan was moved to briefly study his own hands. He was under threat, certainly. No one talked to Goins or his ilk without placing themselves at great risk. A single false word could misplace an entire career, or a lifetime's work. *Or freedom.*

"This is about my speech at the Planetary Society, isn't it?"

"Your perspicacity shall soon be legendary." Goins' tone managed to be simultaneously ironically airy and edged with a whiff of fatality. "Perhaps you would care to explain to me what you thought you were about?"

"Am I on trial?" Morgan regretted the words the instant he'd blurted them out.

"No, but you certainly could be." Goins eyes narrowed, his smile now gone to some faraway place. "You would enjoy the process far less than you're enjoying this discussion, I shall be pleased to assure you."

"No, I didn't mean . . ." Morgan stopped stumbling through reflexive excuses and instead summoned both his courage and his words. Proof was proof, by the stars. He couldn't explain *everything*, but he could explain a great deal more than was comfortable. "I have new evidence concerning the Eight Gardens, and the origins of man."

"I do not believe that is considered an open question. Are you a Lateran theologian, to revisit Dispersionism? That is a matter for our contemplative competitor on the southern verge of the Attik Main."

Morgan made the sign of the Increate across his chest. "I do not presume to challenge faith, I just—"

"No?" Goins voice rose. "What precisely did you intend to present to the Planetary Society, then?"

He was sweating now, his gut knotted. This had always been the crux of the matter. The world was so *true*, so *logical*. Until it wasn't. His newly summoned courage deserted Morgan, apparently to be followed by a fading sense of self-preservation. "A mistake, sire. I intended to present a mistake."

"Hmmm." Goins took Morgan's attaché case from his unresisting hands, tugged open the flap. "A mistake. That's better. You still haven't answered my question, however." The presiding judge leaned close. "What was the mistake?"

Morgan opened his mouth, to have his lips stopped by the single tap of his inquisitor's finger.

"Heed me carefully, Dr. Morgan Abutti. We have no copyist present. No autonomic locugraphitor hums nearby. No clerks of the court labor at my elbow to give later inconvenient testimony. I do not ask you this from my seat of responsibility at the head of the Pirate's Steps. I do not wear my robe and chain of office. No oaths have been sworn beyond those we both live under every day of our lives." Goins leaned close. "At this moment, I am merely a man, asking a simple question of another mere man. Both of us stand before the Increate now as always clad only in our honor. After you have answered, we may make other decisions. Other testimonies may be required, each suitable to their intended audiences. For now, I only listen. To the truth entire as you understand it.

"So tell me. What was the mistake?"

"I believed something I saw of significance in the heavens," Morgan said simply. "Though what I found runs against the word and the will of the Increate, and everything that has been taught to us in the six thousand years since They first placed man in the Eight Gardens and awoke us to Their world."

"Mmm." Goins stepped away from Morgan, paced briefly back and forth before turning to face him again. "I trust we are not so lucky that this mistake in the heavens was presented to you by an eight-winged angel with glowing eyes? Or perhaps the voice of the Increate Themself whispering in your sleeping ear? I am going to assume that your . . . mistake . . . arrived borne on the back of evidence derived from the latest and most pleasing artefacts of Dame Progress, objective and empirical in the hand."

Morgan stared at Goins, appalled. "Had an angel told me what I have learned, you could call me both blest and crazed. Almost all would smile behind their hands and carry on."

"Precisely."

"'Twas no angel, sir. No miracle at all, except that of optics, patience, and an emulsion of silver salts painted onto a glass plate to be exposed to the night sky before moonrise could flood the world with pallid light."

"Mmm." This time Goins did not pace, but stared instead at Morgan. "And what do you think this photographic *truth* signifies? Speaking in your professional capacity, of course."

Morgan's heart sank further. He was close to tears, torn. "I c-cannot deny the Increate."

"Why not? You were prepared to do so in front of seven hundred people in the Plenary Hall not two hours past."

"Forgive me. I . . . I did not understand what it was I was about." He wanted to groan, cry, shriek. It was as if he were being torn apart. "Is not truth part of Their creation?"

Goins leaned close. "What you *did* was take some photographs of the night sky, study them, and draw conclusions. You did this being the good scientist that you are, trained at the University of Highpassage and the New Garaden Institute. One of our New Men, concerned with the evidence of the world before them rather than the testimony of tradition. I don't want to know what the innocent boy who prayed to the Increate every night believes. I want to know what the educated man peering into the telescope thinks."

The words poured out of Morgan Abutti with the strength of confession. "There is something artificial at the Earth's trailing solar libration point. A small body, similar to one of the asteroids. I believe it to be a vessel for traveling the aether. I speculate it to be the true home and origin of mankind. Whatever I believe does not matter, for all will be revealed in due time. This artificial world has begun to move, and will soon be visiting us here in our own skies."

Goins' response shocked Morgan. "It has begun to *move*?" he asked in a voice of awed surprise.

Morgan's heart froze. The presiding judge's words implied that he'd known of this. He fell back on the most basic refuge of his profession. "The stars do not lie, sir. We may misunderstand their evidence, but the stars do not lie."

Goins sat heavily, his face working as if he too sought to avoid tears. Or terror. "You have the right of that, my son. But we may yet be forced to lie on their behalf."

The racing aeroyacht *Blind Justess* was so new that Quinx could smell the sealants used to finish the teakwood trim of the forward observation cabin. Her appointments were an odd combination of luxurious and sparse. Like the airship's rakish exterior form, the interior of fine craftwork minimally applied stood in strong contrast with the lumbering, gilded monsters of the Lateran's small aerial fleet. Those wallowing aerial palaces served as ecclesiastical transports and courts-of-the-air for peregrinations to distant sees where the dignified estate of the Gatekeeper might not be so well honored.

Quinx had claimed the forward observation chair by sheer presence. The captain-owner of *Blind Justess*, one young gallant by the name of Irion Valdoux, was a scion of the Massalian aristocracy, and very much a traditionalist when it came to handling his own weapons and equipage.

And doubtless his women, too, Quinx thought with a distinct lack of charity.

Valdoux was as dark-skinned as any comely lass might hope for in a suitor, with a smile unbecoming a man of serious parts. He had bowed Quinx into the button-tucked seat, upholstery so well-stuffed that a horse could likely have taken its ease there. A glass-walled pit opened between Quinx' feet. At the time of boarding this curious portal revealed a view of dawn over the Attik Main, the ocean opaque with night's last shadows as they plucked at the tumbled ruins along the shoreline beneath the Lateran's airfield masts. Though his head for heights was excellent—Quinx had lived in a tower for some decades now—he found the open space beneath him a trifle unnerving.

"When we're racing for pips under Manju rules," Valdoux explained, "I keep a spotter here with the grips for the electrick harpoons." He cleared his throat. "Open class, no restrictions. 'Justity hates it, they does.'"

"I do not suppose the Lateran entirely approves either," Quinx replied.

Valdoux, who knew perfectly well that the word of the Consistitory Office was quite literally ecclesiastical law, and that the word of Quinx was quite literally the word of the Consistitory Office, fell silent.

"Long explanations wear on the soul," Quinx supplied a few moments later. "I shall oversee our progress from here." He favored Valdoux with the sort of smile that reminded some men of small bones breaking. "It would please me to examine your harpoon grips, however."

"N-not running under Manju rules here over the Attik Main, sir," Valdoux managed. "But I'll send the boy for'ard with 'em, sir. Will that be all?"

"No." Quinx withdrew his smile. "I expect you to break airspeed records bringing me to Highpassage. The Lateran will be most . . . grateful. As will my office. Brother Kurts shall assist you as necessary."

Valdoux wisely withdrew to the bridge, which was a deck below the observation cabin.

Quinx had managed a decent view of *Blind Justess* on the way up the airship's mooring tower. Her envelope was of very unusual design, more of a flattened vee shape than the usual billowing sausage of an airship. Though he was no engineer, he could appreciate the effort at linestreaming in a racing vessel. Some of the fastest water yachts shared that look. Likewise the high-speed locomotive that ran the express routes between the Lateran and Pharopolis far to the east, the largest city on the south shore of the Attik Main.

The gondola below the envelope was just as unusual, resembling nothing so much as a sleek wooden knife. She boasted a sharp keel that split the air, a fine array of viewing ports in smoked glass, and very few of the usual utilitarian protrusions so common on airships. Just before boarding, he'd noted a profusion of small hatches and ports along the outside of the gondola's hull—clearly this vessel kept many of her secrets from prying eyes.

Within was that odd combination of wealth and efficiency. The carpets felt thick and cool, of the finest wool and not yet showing any signs of wear. Grab rails and spittoons were brass polished to a painful brightness. Most furniture was gimbaled and latched away against violent manoeuvres, or possibly just to save space. Her most salient characteristic was *narrowness*.

He wondered what to make of that.

Narrow or not, the great diesels encapsulated into nacelles along the lower curve of the gas bag coughed swiftly to life before growling deep in their throats. *Blind Justess* cast off from the tower smoothly enough, but within minutes she was moving faster than Quinx ever had done while airborne, nearly to railroad speeds.

Kurts had reported a promised velocity of over fifty miles per hour through the air. Quinx had considered his man to be mistaken or misinformed, but as the Attik Main slipped by beneath his feet, his mind was changing.

How much progress had taken place in the factories and laboratories of Highpassage, Massalia, and the other great cities of the world while he'd spent his life laboring among books and sweating priests and accusations of error? A ship like this, any airship in truth, had been inconceivable when he and Ion were boys. That he could now fly with the speed of storms was . . .

A miracle?

Perhaps the Increate had always intended this for Their creation. Another generation would have to answer that question, Quinx knew. His was growing old and become too tired to look much further ahead.

Externalism.

His mind had avoided the point of this journey, dwelling on the mysteries of a machine in which Quinx in truth had no interest.

Heresies were for the most part quite boring, even mundane. And the Lateran of these later days was nothing like the Lateran of centuries past. His own predecessors in office had routed out sin and error with a vigor at which Quinx could only marvel. And sometimes shudder at.

Not that he hadn't broken more than a few men, some of them quite literally. But peculation and sins of the flesh seemed to be the flaws in his generation. Not the bonfires of the heart that had sent armies marching across entire continents in ages past, not to mention setting the Lateran time and again in opposition to the Thalassojustity.

No one *cared* so much any more. The role of the Increate in man's tenure on Earth was undeniable—even the poor, deluded atheists were little more than dissenters against a preponderance of evidence from scriptural to archaeological. The rise of science had only reinforced what the Lateran had always taught.

Except for the damned Externalists.

Every time that heresy had arisen, it had been viciously suppressed. Somewhat to Quinx' continued surprise, even the Thalassojustity had cooperated in the panicked months over the winter of L.5964 and L.5965, when he was new in his place as head of the Consistory Office and Brother Lupan had grown regrettably public in his insane claims of having found the Increate's Chariot on an island in the Sea of Sind.

There were a dozen theological problems with Brother Lupan's theory, but the most practical problem was that he'd had such a vivid, imaginative presentation of his claims that the human race, already birthed elsewhere, had descended from the skies in the hand of the Increate. People *listened*, at least at first.

Quinx still believed that the Thalassojustity had intervened in what was logically a Lateran internal dispute simply to protect their Insular Mandate. Trade flowed over the world's oceans under their protection. In return, unless otherwise ceded by treaty, islands belonged to the Thalassojustity. All of them, from the smallest harbor rock to the great, jungled insulae scattered across the eastern verges of the Sea of Sind.

Brother Lupan had been trespassing not only on theology, but also on the private property of the greatest military and economic power on Earth.

Quinx examined the electrick grips the boy had brought forward. Huge things, built into oversized rubber gloves lined with some felted mesh. He wondered where the harpoons were, how one aimed. Was there a reticule to be used here?

It was a silly, juvenile fantasy, and beneath him as a servant of the Increate. No Lateran vessel had sailed armed since the Galiciate Treaty of L.5782, over two centuries ago. In that document the Thalassojustity had guaranteed the safety of all Lateran traffic, as well as the persons of the Increate's servants here on Earth. *Blind Justess*, not being a Lateran vessel, and practically papered over with the money required to build her, doubtless carried a somewhat more robust defensive proposition to accompany her rakish lines and inhuman speed.

Quinx let his thoughts go and stared into the wave-tossed sea swiftly passing far below his feet. Externalism was the worst sort of heresy, because it denied the very basis of the relationship between man and the Increate. That Lucan Matroit had seen it openly declared was frightening. From where did such evil arise, and how so swiftly?

Ever was that the nature of his office. To seek out evil and lay it to rest.

Still, he wondered what Ion had known. Now was not the time for a crisis, not with a new Gatekeeper to be elected and elevated and begin setting his own mark upon the church of their fathers.

It is the considered opinion of this subcommittee that the study of astronomy and the related arts be placed under much closer supervision than has heretofore been believed advisable. The impressionable minds and irresponsible imaginations of some of our younger researchers may be influenced towards paths of thought not consonant with this institution's devotion to the spirit of scientific inquiry. A Review Committee is proposed as an adjunct to the Board of Governors, consisting of senior faculty, a representative of the Planetary Society, and by invitation if they so desire to accept, representatives from both the Thalassojustity and the Lateran. We may thus guide the research and observations of our

more impetuous young faculty and students along lines fit for
men of good social standing, character, and faith.

— *Undated memorandum, University*
of Highpassage faculty senate

"Show me," Goins said quietly.

"Show you what?" A surge of recklessness overtook Morgan. "I thought you were
forcing me to silence."

The judge grimaced. "Show me what you found. Because if you can find it, anyone can find it."

Morgan paused, attempting to sort out if he'd just been insulted. "I hardly think
that just anyone could—"

Goins interrupted. "I cast no aspersions, merely indicate that you are not unique.
Rather, a man of your time. Or possibly your technology."

"May I please have my case back then, sir?"

Morgan took the leather bundle from Goins, opened the clips, and slipped out
the beribboned folder he'd meant to present for review at the end of his failed lecture. Such a mistake it had been to surprise the Planetary Society. His presentation
had been posted as an overview of new observational techniques with attention to
some exciting discoveries. Morgan had slyly left all the critical information out of
both the proposal and the abstract.

He'd wanted his moment.

Well, now he had his moment.

"You are familiar with the idea of astronomical photography? That we can expose a plate coated with silver salts through a telescope to study the night skies?"

Goins favored Morgan with a flat stare. "Yes."

"Good." Morgan tugged the ribbon's knot loose. "Some astronomers study the
planets and their satellites this way. Arguing over the true count of moons about
Deiwos Pater is very nearly a club sport among my colleagues."

"Yes."

Glancing at Goins again, Morgan saw something very flat and dangerous in the
man's eyes. Here was someone who could start a war on the far side of the world
with a mere word. Power was his beyond reckoning. "I am not stalling, sir. Rather,
leading you to the point."

"Yes."

No more stalling, he thought. "I have been studying the Earth's libration
points, both with respect to the moon and the sun. You are, ah, familiar with the
concept?"

"First described by LaFerme in 1873."

Thalassocratic reckoning, of course. "I did not realize you were an astronomer,"
Morgan said, surprised.

"A presiding judge must be many things, Dr. Abutti. Not the least of which is a
step ahead of the ambitious and rebellious men around him."

Which of those categories did Goins consider him to fall into? "Very well." Morgan
held out a series of photographic prints. "The first two are the trailing and leading
libration points in the Earth-Moon system, traditionally accounted the fourth and

fifth positions. Each is sixty degrees in advance or in retard of the Moon. Note the photographs show only clouds of dust."

Goins frowned as he studied the images. "I shall have to trust your word on this. A man can only be so far ahead. With what instrument were these photographs taken?"

"The eighty-eight inch refractor at Mount Sysiphe," Abutti said, pride leaking into his voice.

"Of which you were one of the principal architects, is that not the case?"

A combination of natural modesty and self-preservation governed Morgan's reply even in the face of a flush of pride. The Mount Sysiphe project had been much of his doctoral work. He'd even put time in on the manufacturing of the mirrors themselves, as well as supervising the great instrument's initial installation at the site, beneath the enormous iron dome delivered by the shipwrights. "I would hardly say 'principal,' sir. Far more learnéd and experienced men than I sat as members of the projects Board of Governors."

A wry smile flitted across the judge's face. "I am aware of the distinction, Dr. Abutti. Carry on, please."

"Your question was important to understanding my . . . evidence. No one has ever seen the heavens so well as those of us with access to Mount Sysiphe."

"Which has been restricted these past three years." Goins' tone made it clear he was in full support of such scientific censorship.

"Yes. Even *my* access was challenged, as an associate fellow of the New Garaden Institute rather than a University faculty member." The very mention of the incident recalled all too vividly his stung pride.

"Still, you no doubt persevered in the face of great pressure."

Once more, Morgan found himself wondering if he were being mocked. "As you say, sir. In the end, the Board of Governors found it difficult to deny one of the principal architects access to his own work."

"Ever has common decency paved the way to uncommon folly. You are forestalling your revelation, Doctor Abutti."

"I show the Earth-Moon libration points in order to set the expectation. Of interest to orbital mechanicians, but consisting only of a few clouds of dust, and perhaps small rocks. Now, here are the Earth-Sun libration points the fourth and fifth." He handed another set of photographic prints to Goins, then fell silent.

The presiding judge studied the new images, then compared them to the first set. He was silent a while, but Morgan did not mistake this for confusion or hesitation. Eventually, Goins looked up from the sheaf of prints in his hand.

"The fourth libration point appears to me to be little more than dust."

Morgan nodded.

"A body is present at the fifth libration point." Goins' tone had gone dangerously flat again.

The man truly had known all along. "Yes."

"What can you tell me about that body?"

"Two things," Morgan said slowly. "First, that spectrographic analysis of its reflected light tells us that the body is a composite of metals, carbides, and oxides. A composition that is literally unique among observed bodies in the solar system."

"And second . . . ?"

"Sometime in the past three weeks, the body has begun to move in contravention to its known orbit. Without the influence of any observable outside force."

Goins simply stared.

Eventually Morgan filled the silence. "Under its own power, sir. Toward Earth, as best as I can determine."

"What does that mean to you? As a scientist?"

"That . . . that there is an artificial object at the fifth libration point. It has been there for an unknown amount of time. It is now coming to Earth."

"Is that all?"

"I . . . I have deduced that this artificial object is an aetheric vessel, a ship of space, as it were. Achman's Razor compels me to believe that six thousand years ago it brought us to this Earth. Otherwise I must conclude the Increate placed *two* intelligent species here in our world, ourselves and some other race to build this aetheric vessel. I find that even less likely than the deduction I reached from the evidence before me."

In the silence that followed, Morgan's own heartbeat thundered.

Finally: "And you were going to announce this to the Planetary Society?"

"Yes, sir. I told them we were not of this Earth, originally." He took a deep breath, and added in a rush, "All of the scientific evidence that points to the Increate just as logically points to my hypothesis. It is well established across many disciplines of science that humanity simply *arrived* six thousand years ago. The question is how. Created whole from the dust of the world by the hand of the Increate, or aboard this aetheric vessel?"

Goins studied him carefully. "You expected to leave the building alive?"

Morgan stopped a moment. "We are all scientists there."

"Of course." Goins shook his head. "You are what, a fifth-degree Thalassocrete?"

Taken aback by the swift change of subject, Morgan shook his head. "Fourth-degree, sir. Alternate Thursday meetings of the Panattikan Lodge here in Highpassage."

Goins made a flicking motion with his left forefinger and thumb. "Congratulations, you're now a thirty-second degree Thalassocrete. By the power invested in me as Presiding Judge I so declare. Someone will teach you the secret handshake later."

Morgan was stunned. "Sir?"

"There are some things you need to know, right now. Truths that carry the death penalty for those not of rank." Goins leaned close. "You are now of rank. Second-youngest ever to reach this height, I might add."

Still grasping at the change in the conversation, Morgan stammered the first question that came into his head. "Who . . . who was the youngest?"

"That is left as an exercise for the astute observer." Goins' swift, savage grin left no doubt in Morgan's mind as to the answer.

Though sea piracy has long been largely the stuff of legend, air piracy is a novel menace for which our society has not yet developed an appropriate response. The terrestrial powers are rightly jealous of their prerogatives with respect to the Thalassojustity, so the solutions which have long kept the sea lanes clear and active do not translate well to the requirements of this new century, where an enterprising rogue with some funds and few good mechanics and sharpshooters may set up an illicit aerie in rough country, then cross national borders and Thalassojustity waters to raid shipping and towns with impunity. The White Fleet may not purse our villain overland away from the coastlines, while few nations yet have the resources to mount their own aerial response, or the willingness to allow their neighbors to pursue miscreants under arms across their own skies.

—*Editorial in the* Highpassage Argus-Intelligencer, *January 18th, H.3124, Th.1998, L.6012*

Blind Justess approached Highpassage from west of south. They'd swung their course that way, Valdoux had explained to Quinx and Brother Kurts, to make best use of the shore breeze in their approach to the masts at the airfield.

All three of them were on the bridge now, which was crowded as a result. Admittedly, Brother Kurts was a crowd all to himself, with his looming height, muscled breadth, and glowering pale visage. Still, the man's loyal service to the Lateran and especially to the Consistitory Office made him a credit to his race.

Quinx studied the duty stations of the bridge. As a racing yacht, *Blind Justess* was designed to be operated with a minimal crew—as he understood it, the captain-pilot, an engineer up in the gas bag tending to the temperamental high-performance diesels on their wide-slung cantilevers, and a ship's boy to serve as runner and temporary relief.

Yet here were a navigator's station, a wireless telegrapher's station, two weapons stations, and the pilot's station. Compact, almost ridiculously so, but elegant in their gleaming brass instruments, the lacquered loudspeaker grills, bright bells and tiny colored electricks signifying the state of more parts and processes than he'd imagined one airship to have. Except for the pilot, all the stations had small leather saddles for their now-absent operators, presumably to economize on space. The pilot had a real chair, meant for long, comfortable occupation, though it was currently clipped back as Valdoux stood at the helm. His head nearly brushed the cabin roof as he made a great study of Highpassage from their position about two miles offshore.

"See," the captain said, pointing toward a cluster of multistorey buildings connected by an aerial tramway, "since the Pharic Mutual Assurance put up that blasted office tower near the airfield, the approach has been tricky. It breaks the wind off the hills, and we sometimes get a rotten shear. Old Piney's widows are suing them over the crash of *Unfettered* last year."

Quinx had no idea who Old Piney was, but he vaguely recollected reading of an airship crash in Highpassage. There had been a scandal, that he did remember. He'd spent little time in this city the past few years, which might have been a mistake. If nothing else, it had grown taller.

Something still bothered him. *Why did a racing yacht have two weapons stations, in addition to the gunner in the forward observation cabin?*

The instrument and control labels were unmistakable. Forward battery. Aft battery. Long chasers. Port bomb rack. Starboard bomb rack.

There must be observers as well, to guide these releases.

"Highpassage is your home port?" he asked casually. Where had Lucan Matroit found this pilot? And with what had Valdoux been bribed? The man was clearly not one of the Planetary Society's operatives. His connection to the Lateran was non-existent.

Quinx would have known otherwise.

"No, the Racing Society has got a private field a few miles up the coast. Well away from buildings and such."

He sat down in one of the weapons saddles and began to regret spending most of the trip in the observation cabin. There was more to be learned here. Quinx' blunt, manicured fingers caressed the port bomb rack release.

"Those don't do nothing now," Valdoux said without turning his attention from their approach.

"Then why are they here?" asked Quinx.

"Because when we run with a full load and all her crew, they do just what you think."

Quinx heard a hardness in the young bravo's voice. "Because sometimes you're racing for pips under Manju rules," he said softly. *Whatever that argot was intended to actually signify.*

"Exactly."

An air pirate didn't need a hidden mountain base, Quinx reflected. That made good copy in those scientific romances which sold so well at street corner kiosks, but the logistics of fuel and spare parts were improbable. All a pirate really had to do was keep an honest face. With that he could hide his airship in plain sight. Who knew, later?

Then they were pitching and turning to approach the mast. "Have you down in ten, sir," Valdoux called out.

"I want you to stay aboard," Quinx quietly told Kurts as the ship's boy laid out a narrow board to connect *Blind Justess* to the mooring mast. "At the least, I shall require a swift return to the Lateran, possibly quite soon, depending on what Matroit is able to tell me. I can imagine several other outcomes as well, for which a fast ship might be of service."

"Sir," Kurts said, quiet acknowledgement.

"And one more thing. Tell Valdoux that he can ready his ship under Manju rules. I may be playing for pips myself shortly."

"What precisely is a pip, sir?" Kurts asked.

"I'm sure I don't know," Quinx replied. "But it's something Valdoux and his set are willing to kill for. If Lucan hasn't already suppressed this outbreak of Externalism, we may be pressed for hard solutions ourselves."

"Yes, sir." Kurts stepped back into the cabin as Quinx left the ship for the platform.

He didn't bother to count the steps in the mooring mast. Far too many, to be sure. Quinx lived in a tower for several reasons—privacy had been the original, of course—but he'd long since recognized the value of having to ascend and descend one hundred and twelve steps every time he wished to do more than stare out the window or piss in a chamber pot. He didn't *think* he was old, but his body had other ideas after a sleepless night, a long day aboard a speeding airship, and now this.

Ion is dead, which is as old as one ever gets.

At least he was still walking. By the time he reached the soil, Quinx' heart was pounding like a fist inside his chest. His knees had become rubber. He rather thought he might be joining Ion soon.

Instead he found awaiting him a rat-faced young man with an unfortunately pale cast of skin. wearing an ill-fitting maroon suit. "Dr. Matroit sent me, your worship," the fellow said, bobbing about like a cork slipped down into a wine bottle. The motions made Quinx vaguely ill, which in turn reminded him that he'd not eaten all day.

He did not even have the energy to put this fool in his place. "Please take me to him."

The quadroon led Quinx to a motorcar. The priest groaned inwardly. Those beastly things were never comfortable, and tended to break down as often as they ran. This one was an open-topped steamer, already stoked up from the sound of the boiler. It was pretty enough, he had to admit, with the deep blue lacquer on fenders, hood and body, and a pleasing amount of brightwork for trim.

"Here, sir, in the back. I gave you some cushions. No luggage being sent down?"

"Just myself." Quinx carried a small satchel, but this trip had been so sudden that he'd brought no trunks or wardrobes. "Please, take me to Matroit."

A few minutes later, they rumbled off to the accompaniment of an ear-piercing shriek of a release valve. Quinx looked up and back at *Blind Justess* now shadowed in the encroaching dusk. She was just a shape in the last light of day, a hawk hovering over the city looking for her next prey.

Lucan Matroit had the good sense to arrange a meal for Quinx at the Plenary Hall. The foolish steamer driver had managed not to kill them or anyone else on the way, and kept the thing running smoothly enough to avoid destroying Quinx' appetite, so he tucked into the cold pickle and pudding as soon as possible after the basic pleasantries were dispensed with.

The matter at hand was so critical that they met alone, without the nigh ubiquitous secretaries, clerks, or servants. Quinx briefly regretted leaving Kurts aboard *Blind Justess*, but he'd wanted badly to keep Valdoux under observation. He also truly had foreseen several potentially critical uses for the airship and her equipage.

Lacking servants, the meal was sparse and strange, something that novices in the seminary might have prepared for themselves. Quinx had grown up on fresh cabbage, preserved peppers, and the occasional bit of goat meat, so even this was welcome. The cold pickle was a fairly ambitious tray of vegetables along with a few regrettable cheeses. The pudding was one of those curious northern dishes that had become popular in Highpassage the past few years, all chewy breading around plums and bits of organ meat.

Still, he ate, and listened to Lucan's sadly incomplete story.

". . . so I had Dr. Abutti shown out immediately," the Secretary General was saying. "In the moment, I was somewhat concerned for his safety, but far more concerned with settling the audience."

"Would they have done him a mischief?" Quinx asked around a mouthful of pungent eggplant.

"In the Plenary Hall?" Matroit shrugged. "Unlikely. But anything is possible. There have been three murders in this building since its dedication, and almost a dozen suicides. The Planetary Society itself is not ordinarily a risk to life and limb. Passions here tend to be more, ah, individualized."

"Three murders?"

"Surely you recall the death of Drs. Messier and Ashbless? They fought a duel on the rooftop over a dispute concerning the orbits of the moons of Mars. We had only the twenty-eight inch reflector back then, and observations were inconclusive."

"I take it both men lost."

"Or won, as it may be. Choice of weapons went to Dr. Ashbless, who unaccountably decided on carboys of high molar sulfuric acid fed into spray pumps."

"Never mind," Quinx said. "I believe I'd prefer to finish my dinner. Please continue your tale."

"Well, I quickly realized I should have detained Dr. Abutti rather than sending him out into the city. I sent two of our porters over to the New Garaden Institute, where they determined that Dr. Abutti had been taken away by Thalassojustity Marines."

Oh Increase, grant me strength now. "That would not be the outcome I might have prayed for."

"Nor I, sir."

If the Thalassojustity held Abutti, anything was possible. Their concerns were largely orthogonal to those of the Lateran—the two institutions had coexisted in varying states of competition for the better part of two thousand years, after all—but this was not the Externalist crisis of L.5964, when the Thalassojustity's interests had been directly compromised.

Presiding Judge Eraster Goins was in charge these days. The Consistitory Office had little information on him, none of it sufficiently damning to serve as any leverage. And under his leadership, the Thalassojustity had showed some remarkable innovations.

Quinx' heart grew leaden at the thought of what innovations Goins could derive from Abutti's madness. "I am a Thalassocrete of the highest degree," he said, something very unusual for a Lateran priest, and in his case rarely spoken aloud. "I believe I shall have to pay my respects at the Thalassojustity Palace quite shortly."

His body cried for sleep, but his soul cried panic. Despite what Ion had told him, Quinx was very much afraid of what might be proven.

And by whom.

The quadroon managed to navigate the steam car from the Plenary Hall to the outer entrance of the Thalassojustity Temple, once more without actually inflicting material harm on Quinx or anyone else. The hour was nearly nine o'clock when they chuffed to a shuddering halt outside the tall, studded gates.

Prior centuries had brought more than one angry mob here. Not to mention a few armies. Though most of the old walls were long gone, replaced with timber lots and gardens of roses and blackberries, the fortified gatehouse itself still blocked the only public road connecting Highpassage to the Thalassojustity's territory. This was an international border, and by and large, casual tourists were neither welcomed nor wanted.

The Revered Bilious Quinx was neither casual, nor a tourist. And he was exhausted.

Staggering from the car over the protestations of the driver, he yanked on the bell pull beside the main gate. A pale, idiot face peered from a darkened window in the gatehouse proper.

"Public hours is closed!" the man shouted through the glass.

Quinx leaned close, gathered his fist inside his vestments, and punched out the glass. Cursing rose from within, as the priest leaned close and spoke in the low, calm voice that he'd used for delivering judgments these past forty years. "I am a thirty-second degree Thalassocrete on urgent business to the Presiding Judge. I do not have time for visiting hours, and I will have you swabbing decks in frozen Hyperborea if you do not open the gates now."

Scrambling noises emitted from within, followed by the distinctive whir of a telelocutor. A few hushed words, then more scrambling, then the gates creaked open.

Resuming his seat in the back of the steamer, Quinx told the quadroon, "Drive on, boy."

"Yes, *sir!*" The man's voice quavered somewhere between horror and awe.

Their tyres crunched up the crushed coral drive that led to the Thalassojustity Temple. The New Buildings lurked beyond, thousand-year-old fortifications that served as an office complex. Two more recent, taller structures rose past them. Those contemporary buildings were simply referred to as "the towers."

Know your friends; know your enemies better. The Thalassojustity had been both to the Lateran over the centuries.

Otherwise the grounds were as gardened as any cemetery of the wealthy. Cypress trees spread low in the moonlight, hares and deer cropped, barely attending to the wheezing of the steamer as it passed. The sea lay to Quinx' left, its murmuring unheard over the racket of the steam car as the waters lapped at the bottom of a sharp decline down which a man might easily lose his footing. The crescent of Black's Beach, at the foot of the stairs from the Temple, gleamed pale ahead of him.

No one was around. Not a Marine, not a night watchman. The lights of the Temple portico were doused, and only a few stray glimmers showed from shuttered windows in the New Buildings or the towers.

Which was odd. Lodge meetings tended to run into the evenings. There were always late-working bureaucrats scurrying about, along with the servants who tended them. Quinx had visited the Thalassojustity Temple more than a few times over the decades, on a variety of errands from the deeply secretive to the bloodily public. He'd never seen it look so, well, abandoned.

The quadroon slowed his steamer to a halt where the drive met the Temple steps. Quinx climbed out of the car again, regretting his long walk down the airship mooring mast. He was desperately tired he realized.

Where *was* everyone?

One step at a time. Up. And up. And up.

The great doors at the top, bronze castings forty feet high chased with elaborate friezework, stood open as they always did. Lore held that the doors would only be closed in times of utmost crisis. Quinx had always figured it for a problem with the hinges. A slight man in a crisp, dark suit sat just within the threshold on an office chair that very much did not belong in the nave. "May I help you?"

"I'm looking for Goins," Quinx said, too much of his irritation creeping into his voice.

"The Presiding Judge is not available. Who is asking?"

"Me." Quinx glared at him. "Get a lot of men in red and white robes calling late at night?"

"You are clad in the sartorial estate of a prince of the Lateran, sir, but I have not had the prior pleasure of your acquaintance, so for all of my knowledge you might be a lad about on a lark."

"With *this* hair?" Quinx had to laugh, his foul mood broken for a moment. "It's been fifty years since I could pass for a lad. And believe me, Eraster will talk to me once he knows I'm here. I am the Revered Bilious Quinx, and I am pursuing some very dangerous questions."

"Revered Quinx." The door warden gave the name some thought. "Your fear-some reputation precedes you, sir. If memory serves, you are also an initiate of our own Lodges, and as such should not be required to seek admittance at the public portals."

"I did not arrive by the hidden paths, and time may be of the essence." He moved his hands in the recognition signs of a thirty-second degree Thalassocrete. "And yes, I am the highest level initiate who also serves in the church's senior hierarchy."

"Who is known to serve," the door warden corrected mildly, words that gave Quinx serious pause. "You were answering the Presiding Judge's call, then? I am afraid you are too late by hours. All of the available senior initiates sailed on the afternoon's tide, aboard Th.S. *Clear Mountain*."

"With Dr. Morgan Abutti aboard?"

"Of course." The man seemed surprised. "Who else?"

Quinx leaned close. "And where were they bound?"

"Thera, I believe. But rumors are often put out to obscure the truth of such missions as this."

Quinx' heart sank. The entire leadership of the Thalassojustity had just abandoned their headquarters. *Why?* Such a thing had never happened, even during the worst wars of the last century.

Whatever Abutti had found must have proven extremely convincing. Ion's prophesied proof was happening, almost before his very eyes. *Externalism . . .*

Even his thoughts failed. "I must to Thera, and swiftly," he said.

"*Clear Mountain* is very nearly the fastest of ships."

"Oh, *I* can travel faster."

Stumbling down the steps to the quadroon's steamer once more, Quinx wondered how difficult it would be to convince Valdoux to mount his weapons on *Blind Justess*.

The traditional association between vulcanism and the Eight Gardens is a folk myth not borne out within the received text of the Librum Vita. Neither do any of the Lateran's formal teachings support it. Yet like most folk myths, it likely arises from some transmuted memory of history. Each Garden is seen to be paired with a smoking mountain—Cycladia has its Thera, for example, Wy'East has the volcano of the same name. The Thalassojustity has been notoriously reluctant to permit full surveys of the relevant sites under their control, so most of what can be said about this association arises from ethnography and the study of more primitive folkways than the modern world can boast. Still, it does not require much speculation to see how the Increate's children, early in their tenure upon this Earth, might have associated Their power with the world's own fiery exhalations.

"Contemporary Survey of Myths and Legends Concerning the Eight Gardens"; B. Hyssop, F. Jamailla, A. Serona; Ouragan Journal of Ethnographic Studies, *Vol. XCVII, Issue 7*

Morgan sat in *Clear Mountain*'s forward lounge, a gin fizz in hand, and marveled at the events of the past day. Goins had wasted no time in calling his entire senior hierarchy to witness this . . . unfolding? Apparently the Thalassojustity has been waiting for his revelation for a very, very long time. Ancient secrets indeed, to bring all these old, powerful men so swiftly to arms. Even this vessel was something between a warship and a royal yacht, as the wide, forward facing windows with their armored shutters testified.

The Attik Main by moonlight was dark as an old grave and restless as risen lust. He watched the sea move as if lifted by a thousand submerged hands, and wondered whether land or clouds occluded the horizon. Within, all was as lush as man might ask, better appointed than a fine gentlemen's club, but still with that certain rough readiness of any ocean-going vessel.

The Thalassojustity treated its leaders very well indeed. Even the upper halls of the Planetary Society were not so nice as this, and at the University of Highpassage one would have to ascend to the Chancellor's estate to find similar quiet luxuries.

He could grow accustomed to the privileges of a thirty-second degree Thalassocrete, if only he better understood the associated duties.

After their initial conversation, Goins had pressed Morgan to provide his evidence and theories to several more audiences. Almost all of the men with whom he spoke were as engaged as the judge had been. No one was shocked, or even surprised.

He felt like a prophet speaking in tongues only others could understand.

Still, it was not his place to ask. Not when serious-faced men with sword-sharp eyes kept questioning him about everything from the construction of refracting telescopes to the proper maintenance of spectrographic analyzers. Oddly, none of them questioned his basic observations, or his conclusions.

It was increasingly clear to Morgan that he was telling some of these men a secret to which they were already privy. *That* was frightening. The rest simply took in what he said, then moved on.

Within hours, the ship was readied, and his impromptu seminars on astronomy, photography, and light had moved aboard *Clear Mountain*. Then suddenly, shortly after dusk, they were done with him. Everyone retreated to some meeting room belowdecks. Morgan was left to drink alone, attended only by a handful of solicitous stewards who went conspicuously well-armed as they brought him drinks, canapés, and cigars.

He'd never even learned any name but Goins'. He did not know where they were bound, or why. No one had told him anything. Only asked him endless questions, which had swiftly become repetitive.

The experience so far was in many respects much like being an undergraduate.

Goins finally found him, somewhere near midnight.

"We will make landfall shortly after dawn."

"Where?" Morgan asked, not particularly expecting an answer.

"Thera."

The name sounded familiar. "That's near the Garden of Cycladia, yes?"

The Presiding Judge appeared vaguely pained. "Yes. A volcanic island under Thalassojustity jurisdiction."

"If I may be permitted a further question, why?"

"So we can show you something."

"All of you? There must be three dozen senior Thalassocretes board."

"All of us." Goins sighed. "This matter lies at the heart of our historical purposes. It must be witnessed."

This time, Morgan heard the grim tone in Goins' voice. Had it been there all along? "So close to one of the Gardens," he began, then stopped. His thoughts were tangled by the lateness of the hour and the alcohol, but there was a next link in this chain of logic that was decidedly unpretty.

"You are a very intelligent man, Dr. Abutti. Pray that on the morrow you are wise enough for what will come next."

With that, Goins departed. Lacking a stateroom, or even a bunk, Morgan kicked off his shoes, propped his feet on the ottoman, and proceeded to drink himself into sleep.

Valdoux was at the base of the mooring mast, negotiating with a small whippet of a man who managed to look furtive while standing still and empty-handed. The moon had risen, lambent through a veil of clouds that rendered the night sky into a dark rainbow. The scent of water rode the wind as well, harbinger of a distant storm.

Reluctantly dismounting from the steam car, Quinx dismissed the quadroon and his device. The whippet, who had ignored the vehicle's chuffing approach, turned to take note of the priest. The man was another pale-skinned northerner.

Quinx was too tired to wonder why the airship captain surrounded himself with inferior servants. "Valdoux, dismiss your man and take me aboard," he said firmly. Where was Brother Kurts? "We have urgent business to attend to." *And I need to lie down*, he thought. From lifelong habit, he would never confess a weakness before others.

Such confessions were something Ion had never seemed troubled by. Somehow his oldest friend had still managed to become the Increate's vicar here on Earth. Quinx swallowed a shuddering breath that threatened to become a sob.

Tired, too damned tired.

"I don't think—" Valdoux began, but the whippet raised a hand to silence the captain. "Do you know who I am, Revered?"

"No," Quinx said shortly. "Nor do I particularly care."

"Perhaps you should care," the whippet said in a quiet, almost wondering voice. "For I do know who you are. I am all too sadly familiar with the mission of the Consistitory Office. Once I was a novice, Revered, before being turned out upon the path of what you call the Machinists' Heresy."

"Then I sorrow for you, my son, that you have strayed so from the Increate. But still, I must aboard with Captain Valdoux."

"You will not go without me," the whippet warned. "A man in your hurry is always in want of weapons. I am master gunner of *Blind Justess.*"

Quinx, who had apologized to no one but Ion in at least five decades, held back his next words. What this Machinist deserved and what the priest was in a position to mete out to the man were far different things. He had his priorities. After a moment, he found suitable alternatives. "That is between you and the captain, master gunner. My hurry is my own, and all too real."

"Speak, then," Valdoux said, finally in voice again. "There ain't nothing you can say that I won't tell to Three Eighty Seven here. He's got to know what it is I hire us out to do."

"You are already hired," Quinx pointed out.

"Not to push off into the sky armed and rushing." Valdoux's eyes narrowed. "East, I reckon. I've heard talk of who took ship today and where their course was laid to."

Enough, thought Quinx. There was small purpose in fencing with these two. And he was exhausted besides. If they crossed him over much, he could have them taken on an ecclesiastical warrant later. The Thalassojustity would simply laugh at such paper, but the government of Highpassage recognized Church writ.

"Yes, east. I must to Thera, and quite promptly. And we should fly under arms."

"Afraid of pirates?" The thrice-damned Machinist was positively smirking.

"Afraid we might need to become pirates," Quinx admitted.

"Sailing into the red under the banner of Holy Mother Church?" Three Eighty Seven touched himself forehead, mouth, and navel; the sign of the Increate. "We should ever be so honored." He turned to Valdoux. "Are you planning to take this commission? Ninety Nine will be here shortly, but I must go see to the armaments, unless you think the churchman here cannot afford your hire."

Valdoux laughed aloud. "The Revered here could buy me out ship, sail, and shoes, if he set his sights on that. The question is whether I figure to take his coin." He winked at Quinx. "Best go to your station, master gunner. One way or another, we'll be playing at the hardest game soon enough, I reckon."

The whippet grinned and trotted up stairway that wound foursquare around the interior of the mooring mast.

"There are no pirates, are there?" Quinx said. "Just airships and airships."

"The lines on the map ain't visible from up in the sky." Valdoux cocked his head. "But someone of your experience can't possibly be surprised at what is true being hidden in plain sight."

"No one raids the Gatekeeper's air fleet, so the Gatekeeper's minions do not attend so closely to such matters as others doubtless must," the priest admitted. "Besides which, we have been disarmed these many years, and would be required to apply to the Thalassojustity for relief."

"*Their* borders are perfectly clear from above. More's the pity. Ain't too many would make such a fight as a Thalassojustity crew trained and ready for action." Valdoux squatted. "You look like the death of a priest. Even the Grand Inquisitor must sleep sometimes."

"This is the hour I would pass over into sleep, yes," admitted Quinx. As if it were not too obvious from his face, surely. "But I need you to take me to Thera, swiftly. And I need to be certain you will attend to my orders, should that become necessary."

"You won't have no say over my weapons. No one does. But I'll take you to Thera. We'll fly armed and ready." Valdoux paused, chewing his lip. Something warred within. Then: "I will also listen to your counsel, should we come to be fighting."

"And . . . ? There is always an 'and' at the end of such sentences."

"More of a 'but', I reckon." This time Valdoux smirked, while Quinx pretended to misunderstand the jest. "But I got to know why you want to chase after the Thalassojustity's biggest brass. All hot up and ready to fight, at that. This ain't something a thoughtful priest would be doing. Or even a thoughtless priest."

"I fear a great heresy is about to be unleashed. Tonight. Or perhaps tomorrow. And it may sweep the world. If I can reach one man aboard *Clear Mountain* and stop him, I may be able to halt a rising tide before the damage is done."

"Ain't no one stops the tide," Valdoux observed. "That's why I fly over the waters. Let the Thalassocretes argue with the waves. Storms don't trouble the top of the sky." He stuck his hand out. "I'll take you for a single silver shekel. That seals a contract. Learning what comes next will pay your balance. You're a mighty strange man, Revered, on a mighty strange errand."

"A shekel it is." Despite the process. Quinx was afraid he'd somehow got the wrong end of the bargain nonetheless.

"Look at it from my bridge." Valdoux grinned again. "Either I'll get to see the beginning of tide that floods the world, or I'll get to see a lone man stop the tide. History before my eyes either way, no matter how the play lands. Or maybe you're a madman. Even so, I reckon you're mad with the entire power of the Lateran behind you. Watching that should be good sport, likewise."

Ninety Nine loomed out of the darkness at those words. Quinx was startled again—from the name he'd expected another Machinist, but not a female. She was clad immodestly in a tunic and sailor's dungarees.

Valdoux bowed her wordlessly up the tower. She favored Quinx with one cold, incurious glance, then clattered upward.

He stared after her a long moment, trying to sort his feelings from his fatigue, then surrendered the effort and began the slow, aching climb himself.

As Quinx mounted the stairs, Valdoux called after him. "We sail under Manju rules now, Revered. Be sure you really want what you're asking after."

Quinx slept the remainder of the night away while *Blind Justess* set her course and left Highpassage ahead of the impending storm. He awoke to a pearlescent pink dawn gleaming through the tiny porthole of his tiny cabin. Most of the available space not occupied by his bunk was filled with Brother Kurts, who snored gently while sprawled upon the deck.

He could not remember ever having seen the monk asleep.

There was no getting up without disturbing the other man, so Quinx lay still a while and watched the sky shift tone from pink to blue. They would be heading very nearly into the sun, he realized, and surely not so far from Thera now unless the winds had been notably unfavorable.

Tiny though the cabin was, it had been appointed with the same odd combination of frugality and luxury as the rest of the airship. The paneling was some wood he did not recognize, doubtless a rare tree from the waist of the world. Brightwork and electrics ran across the walls like veins. Even the sheets were silk, which seemed a bit perverse.

Soon he realized he must be awake and about. Valdoux was mercurial, likely to take any number of strange actions in the absence of his direction. "Brother Kurts," Quinx whispered.

The monk's head snapped forward with a gust of garlicky breath. "Revered," he said, his hand falling away again from something beneath his robes.

A weapon, of course, though such was forbidden by the Galiciate Treaty. Kurts worked for Quinx, not the Thalassojustity. The Consistitory Office had its own requirements, for all that he must at times pretend to a long lost innocence as to means and methods.

"Everything is well, Brother Kurts. I must have some coffee, and mount to the bridge to consult with our fair captain."

"Six others aboard, sir," Kurts replied. "Two of them Machinists. The captain, his ship's boy from before. An engineer and his boy as well. The heretics serve as gunners and artificers, best as I can tell."

"I met one of them last night. He styled himself Three Eighty Seven."

"The master gunner." The monk nodded slowly. "Gunner's mate is a female name of Ninety Nine."

"I briefly saw her yesterday evening." Somehow Ninety Nine's dubious femininity seemed doubly blasphemous by the late of day, though in truth, Quinx was rapidly losing his capacity for surprise at what might transpire aboard *Blind Justess*. "I doubt she will challenge anyone's virtue. She is both offensive and unlovely."

"And what do you know of a woman's loveliness, Brother Kurts?" Quinx asked with a small smile.

The monk was not amused. "As little and all as the Increate allows a man of my vows."

"Fair enough. I apologize for troubling you. But I must find my way to coffee before I become more trouble."

They slipped into the short companionway on this upper deck. Brother Kurts led Quinx the half dozen steps to the tiny galley. This was indeed a racing yacht, not intended for full meal service. Or really, any other full service. The coffee machine, however, was an elegant marvel of brass and copper, festooned with a maze of pipes and valves and small, decorative metal eagles screaming for their freedom.

It smelled like a slice of heaven.

"Truly the Increate did bless mankind when They caused the coffee bean to grow," said Quinx.

Kurts grunted, studying the machine for several long moments before launching into a rapid set of seemingly random manipulations that shortly produced a steaming cup of coffee so deep brown Quinx thought he might be able to see the reflection of last year's breakfasts in it.

Five minutes later, fortified by caffeine and a rather stale sticky bun of dubious provenance, Quinx headed for the bridge on the deck below. He was trailed by a bleary-eyed Brother Kurts.

"Good morning to you, Revered." Valdoux seemed as chipper as if he'd just had a week at a Riveran resort. The ship's boy was present, as well as another lad whom Quinx took to be the engineer's boy. To his profound relief, neither Machinist was on the bridge.

"Captain, the pleasure is all mine." Quinx slipped up to the fore, where Valdoux piloted *Blind Justess* with a wheel and a set of levers. Gauges were arrayed to either side of him, but before and sweeping down to his feet was a wall of curved glass. The pale green of the Attic Main loomed vertiginously below, the ripples of waves like crumpled foil.

An oblong island with a sharp-peaked central mountain lay before them. A small settlement nestled on one shore—the south?—dominated by its docks. The rest of the island was heavily forested. Clearly not settled, beyond whomever lived there to service the sea traffic.

"Thalassojustity territory," Quinx observed.

Valdoux made a tsking noise. "Ain't no airship masts. They're behind the times, our naval friends."

Quinx glanced sideways. "You hold no brief for the *Pax Maria*?"

"What do I care for the sea? The air is my place. They can't make neither peace nor war in the skies. And they ain't made no real effort to claim what power might be theirs up here."

"Where one grasp fails, another will reach," muttered Brother Kurts behind them.

"Exactly," said Valdoux. "And here is Thera, Revered. We overflew a fast ship on the water late in the night. I reckon they'll be here by midmorning."

"*Clear Mountain*?"

"I didn't figure on stopping to ask. But that does seem to be a sensible thing to assume."

How to proceed? Quinx badly wanted to confront this fool Morgan Abutti before more damage could be done, but the man had spent almost an entire day closeted with the senior Thalassocretes. A more focused assemblage of the powers in the world he had trouble imagining, short of another Congress of Cities and States being called.

How much harm had already been levied? Was the Externalist heresy loose for good and all? Or had the Thalassojustity seen through the madman and contained him?

Valdoux's voice interrupted Quinx' whirling thoughts. "No."

"No? No what?"

"I can't land you in force aboard *Clear Mountain*."

"That was not my . . ." Quinx let his voice trail off. He didn't know what he should do next. He thought quickly. "I would meet them at the dock. Brother Kurts will guard my back."

"With *Blind Justess* circling overhead? Or standing off?"

That took a long moment of consideration. Aerial force was not a strength of the Thalassojustity, especially not in this place. "Overhead. Awaiting my signal."

Valdoux reached down to the bottom of his wheel column and unclipped a fat-barreled pistol. "Fire this. I'll come down hot and fast, guns at the ready."

Quinx looked in wonder at the weapon in his hand. He'd never held a firearm before, any more than he'd ever held a viper.

Brother Kurts reached around and took it from him. "A flare gun," he explained. "But you can still harm yourself with it."

"Or someone else," Valdoux offered cheerfully. "A shot to the chest from that won't likely kill nobody, but the other fellow might wish it had."

"Give me back that flare, Brother Kurts," Quinx said, suddenly tired all over again. "Only I can decide when to use it."

The monk looked unhappy, but he returned the weapon.

It fit awkwardly within Quinx' robes. "Take me down," he told Valdoux.

"I can't land here. You got to go down by rope. I'll send Ninety Nine along to look after your safety."

Quinx' fatigue shifted to a sense of nausea, or perhaps outright illness. He would be confronting heresy under the protection of a female Machinist. Any priest who came before the Consistitory Office with such a story would spend long months under the Question, or at the very least in quiet confinement to pray over his errors of judgment and resultant sins.

The expression on Valdoux' face made it clear the captain was testing Quinx. And Quinx knew that here and now, he held no leverage.

"Let us do this thing," he gasped, forcing out the words before the last tatters of his certainty vanished.

Holy Mother Church was infinitely patient. There was always a later. Even for a man such as Captain Valdoux.

Especially for a man such as Captain Valdoux.

> The Thalassojustity has served for centuries as a check upon the powers of the Lateran. Church history documents a much earlier era when the Gatekeepers asserted economic, political, and even military dominance over many of the societies of the Earth. The aggressively secular founders of the Thalassojustity held no patience for the divine right that many of the kings and princes of Earth claimed for their power, and less patience for the generations-long schemes of the Lateran to convert or subvert them. Indeed, there is considerable evidence that the establishment of the secret societies of the Thalassocretes was precisely a

countermove against Lateran infiltrations as well as more overt cozenings of their rivals. For make no mistake: this tension between lords spiritual and the lords of the sea is two thousand years in the making, but neither of them has ever misunderstood who their true competition is. Should a significant number of the land-based states around the world ever achieve meaningful confederacy, the power of Thalassojustity and Church alike would be undermined much more deeply than anything either rival could do the other.

> *From the introduction to* Common Interests,
> Uncommon Rivals, *P.R. Frost, University*
> *of Massalia Press, M.2991, Th. 1994, L.6008*

There was a great deal of excitement aboard *Clear Mountain* as they approached Thera. Morgan was not sure what the fuss was, as no one had paid him much attention since he'd finished explaining his thesis the night before, but he eventually padded out to the foredeck to find a number of the Thalassocretes staring at the clouds above the island.

Goins wordlessly handed him a set of field glasses. "See for yourself," the Presiding Judge growled. "Watch the cloud formation that rather resembles a camel."

Morgan scanned the sky, not seeing anything he would consider a camel, but pointing his instrument in the direction everyone else was looking. He caught a glint and sense of motion.

"Bastard's hiding in the cloud bank," someone else said, then cursed in a language Morgan did not speak, though the intent of the words was clear enough from the tone.

"Airship?" he asked.

"Anyone care enough about you to chase you out here?" Goins made the question sound casual, but the rapid silence around them told Morgan quite clearly what was at stake.

"Not even my own mother," he said. "Not this place."

"Hmm." Goins sounded unconvinced. "The area is under absolute prohibition."

"Can you not force them down?"

"We don't even allow our *own* airships here."

"Mistake." That was someone behind Morgan.

"The question will be re-opened, you may be sure," Goins said loudly. "Unless it has been rendered irrelevant in the mean time."

"Why are we here?" asked Morgan. "Why do we care about an airship?"

Goins reached up to grab Morgan's shoulders. His fingers were vises, his eyes drills. "I am about to show you the deepest, darkest secret known to mankind."

"Me?"

"It is a puzzle, to which you may have found the key."

Morgan only knew one secret of his own, and he'd already shared it. "My photographic plates. The aetheric vessel at the libration point."

"Precisely."

"Precisely *what*?"

Another senior Thalassocrete snatched Morgan's arm even as Goins released him. "Precisely shut your yap and see what is to come," growled the other man.

It took Morgan only a moment to realize these very powerful men were all frightened.

Clear Mountain approached the dock at Thera at dead slow. Waves slapped her hull, while mewling gulls circled overhead. Someone waited at the end of the pier, but beyond them was a puzzling scene. Several people sprawled at the head of the pier, while two more stood guard, their backs to the sea. A smaller crowd clustered inland, at the village, in a standoff with the guardians.

A fight had taken place, though Morgan could not imagine who would fight here, or over what. Not in this place. Presumably anyone here was in on Goins' great secret.

A great racket arose around him. Crewmen rushed to the teakwood foredeck with rifles. Two set up a Maxim gun on a pintle at the bow. Several relatively junior Thalassocretes were directing preparations for a possible offense.

Morgan debated going below, or at least retreating to the lounge where he could fortify himself with alcohol and be out of the line of fire. But Goins was at his side again. "This is *your* fault," the Presiding Judge said with a growl.

"Mine?" Morgan was astonished. "What does this have to do with me?"

"Everything." Goins gave him another of those long, hard stares. "What did you think would happen when you presented your evidence?"

"I dreamt that my reputation would have been made," Morgan said sadly. "The spirit of scientific inquiry is one of the most powerful forces known to man. With a bit of luck, I could have launched a generation of research."

"Fear is one of the most powerful forces known to man," retorted Goins. "And nothing inspires fear like attacking people's faith. Doesn't matter what kind of faith—faith in the order of the world, faith in themselves, faith in the Increate. And you, Dr. Morgan Abutti, are attacking all of those faiths."

Amid a swash of saltwater, *Clear Mountain* growled to a slow, rolling halt by the pier without any gunfire being exchanged. Goins didn't look to shore, just kept staring down Morgan.

"I . . ." Morgan's voice faltered. "No. People are better than that." His heart fell. "The Increate did not put us on this Earth so that we could pretend away the natural world."

"You, sir, have averred that the Increate did not put us on this Earth at all," Goins said. "And though everyone will cry you down for saying that, the damnedest thing is that you are *correct*."

He turned and looked over the rail, at the man on the pier. Abutti looked with him to see a priest waiting. Two-dozen rifles and the Maxim gun were trained down on the Revered, who seemed unperturbed. He stared back up at them, clearly identifying Goins as the authority aboard ship.

"If it is not the Presiding Judge," the priest called up.

Goins appeared positively sour. "Revered Quinx."

"*Quinx!?*" hissed Morgan. "The Inquisitor?"

"The Lateran refers to that as the Consistitory Office," Goins told him quietly. "And I know what that oily little bastard is doing here. I just don't know how or why."

Morgan nodded. "The airship your people were looking at."

"Do you have a Dr. Morgan Abutti aboard?" Quinx called up. "I am very much fain to speak with him if so."

"How—" Morgan began, but Goins cut him off. "Don't be an ass, man."

"Ah, I see you have him with you," Quinx said. "I would be much obliged if you'd set the doctor ashore for some private discussions with me."

"On whose authority?" Goins waved the riflemen to port arms.

"I could claim the authority of the Lateran, but our writ does not run here."

"No." This time Goins grinned. "Have a better offer?"

"Remember your history, Judge. Brother Lupan died not so long ago."

Goins shook his head. "This tale does not fly on wings of madness, Revered. It creaks atop the edifice of science."

"Are they truly so different in the face of the Increate?" Quinx stared at Morgan. The man's eyes were like steel, even from this distance. Morgan shuddered at the thought of being alone in a small room, under the Question.

"I . . . I have never denied the Increate," he shouted. "Nor did I intend to."

Goins jabbed Morgan in the ribs. "If you are so eager to treat with the Revered, I can put you ashore. *Alone.*"

Courage seeped back into Morgan's heart like the tide rising beneath a sandbar. "Bring him aboard."

"What?"

"You made me a thirty-second degree Thalassocrete. That means I have voice in this floating conclave. Bring him aboard."

"Well, well," said Goins. "Who realized you would have such backbone, Dr. Abutti? No, despite your entreaties, I believe we shall put you ashore. But in company. We did come here for a reason, in all good haste. I do not propose to abandon our mission for the sake of a chaffer with a single churchman, no matter how highly placed. As he is also a thirty-second degree Thalassocrete, the Revered may accompany us up the mountain and amuse himself in discourse with you along the way."

"Where?"

"To where the stars do not lie."

Abutti followed Goins down the gangplank. A line of armed men observed from *Clear Mountain*'s rail, but no one among the assembled Thalassocretes or ship's crew objected when the Presiding Judge had ordered them to stand down and remain aboard.

Morgan couldn't see how one priest would be so immediately dangerous, even this one. Still, people were sprawled at the head of the pier. Injured? Dead?

"Bilious," Goins said, shaking hands with the priest, then embracing him.

"Eraster." The Revered wore a grudging smile that bespoke the bond that only two ancient enemies could share.

"You know one another?" Morgan asked.

The priest turned to him. "The most powerful man in the Thalassojustity and the most feared man in the Lateran? Of course we know one another, Dr. Abutti." He extended his hand. "The Revered Bilious Quinx."

"Revered," said Morgan, shaking the man's hand. Though rather larger than Goins, Quinx was still a small man, in that compact way that suggested strength, even at an age that must be approaching seventy. His eyes were sea-gray, set deep in a face dark-skinned enough for any debutante's ball in Highpassage. He wore a cassock, faded with wear and laundering, but highly serviceable. A small silver Lateran orbicrux hung around his neck. He was otherwise unadorned with the Earthly riches that Morgan associated with high churchmen. "And now I am acquainted with the both of you."

"To our great mutual pleasure," Quinx said in a tone of voice that promised quite the opposite.

Goins nodded sharply, glancing down the pier. "Enough. We are on an errand of some urgency. Call off your men down there, and you may accompany us. If you simply must interview Dr. Abutti, feel free to do so on the march."

"Amid your mob?" Quinx' voice dropped to a very soft, easy threat. "I am far more accustomed to my own chambers, and *tools*, for such interviews."

"This island is *my* chamber, Bilious," Goins snapped. "I'll thank you not to soil it with my colleague's vital fluids."

"Oh, we gave up soiling with vital fluids generations ago," Quinx replied. "Our tools are more subtle now. The arts of the mind are powerful."

"Call off your men, or the arts of the mind will be powerless this day."

Quinx nodded, then walked up the pier toward his guardians.

"He's mighty energetic for such an old man," Morgan said.

"That old man is the sharp point of a very long blade. We do not fear him, but we have immense respect for his power."

Morgan thought for a moment. Then: "I am too young to remember Brother Lupan. But I have read of him."

"They teach that in history classes now?" Goins sounded surprised.

"Not in public school, or even when I was working to my baccalaureate. But in my graduate days, we covered him in a seminar on science, myth, and the public mind. The book about him was in manuscript. It had not yet passed before the censors."

The Presiding Judge snorted. "I marvel that you learned nothing from that." Ahead of them, the priest had reached his deadly minions. Goins tugged on Morgan's arm again, a habit that was quickly wearing in its novelty and charm. "We go now."

They walked up the pier, followed by a parade of Thalassocretes and servants. Approaching Quinx, who was deep in hurried converse, Morgan was shocked to see that his servants were a pair of white people—a hulking, brutish male and a hard-looking female.

She glanced up at him. Her eyes were reptile cold, and seemed preternaturally alert. *Danger*, they said, though Morgan never thought to encounter such menace in any woman born.

His capacity for astonishment had been played out. "Strange company the Revered Quinx keeps, for a priest."

"Oh, the Lateran is blind to the color of a man's skin." Sarcasm ran thick as mud in Goins' voice. "But I cannot possibly explain the woman given the Church's view on their proper role in society." His hand dropped, flickering through a quick series of motions signaling someone behind them.

"What of your people?" Morgan pointed toward the bodies beyond.

"There will be a reckoning," Goins said. "Quite soon. But not in this moment."

The priest and his servants hurried ahead of them, so that Morgan was the first of the Thalassocratic party to reach the downed men. They were four, two with broken necks and the pallor of death upon them already, the other two groaning and bloody.

He bent to look, but a squad of sailors pushed past him, a pair of them medics with canvas bags bearing the Red Orb.

Morgan straightened again and followed Goins.

Fuming, Quinx fell into step beside the heretic Abutti. They were already well above the tiny dockside village, following a path that was not much more than a goat track up the slopes of the island's central mountain. He could do little about whatever foolishness Goins had in mind. The closer they came to the top of the mountain, the closer they were to rescue—or brute force—courtesy of *Blind Justess*. Brother Kurts and the woman were under close guard behind him, but the Thalassojustity party did not seem to be armed.

When this business was over, all he needed was a shot from the flare gun. And perhaps a convenient fall for Dr. Abutti.

"Revered," said the heretic. Polite but nervous.

Quinx had a lifetime of working with those cues. "Dr. Abutti." And to hell with the listeners crowded not so subtly close around them.

The path ahead narrowed to little more than a foot's width, rising sheer on the left and dropping sheer on the right. A chain was fastened to the rock, to which the party clung as they climbed. Almost thirty of them, strung out like flies on a wall.

"H-how may I be of service to you?"

Quinx took the matter by the knob. "This is a complex affair. Much history and passion is caught up in what I understand you are even now pursuing. I would have liked to invite you to present your findings at the Lateran before making your thesis public."

"I am not yet so public, Revered." Abutti sounded oddly sad. "I was ejected from the Planetary Society. And, well, these Thalassocretes are not so indiscrete with their confidences."

Honeyed words flowed from Quinx' lips. "So you are saying we could put this affair to rest without widespread comment?"

A moment of rough breathing and dizzying fear as they crept around a bulge in the side of the mountain. Then Abutti responded. "Would that be a permanent rest for me, Revered? I saw those men at the dock. I know who you are in the hierarchy."

"No fool you," Quinx replied. "To be blunt, you have poked your telescope into matters much better left undiscussed. Externalism is no trifling affair."

"So I've been told." Abutti's breath huffed a bit. "Should you wish your thugs to shove me off a cliff top, Revered, I surely cannot stop you. But I am not the only astronomer on Earth with a telescope. The facts will out. Even your Increate cannot deny this truth written in the skies."

"*My* Increate?" Quinx was both amused and frustrated by the assumptions embedded in that phrasing. "And yes . . . I can hardly ban telescopes across the world. Regardless of whatever you think your truth is."

Abutti stopped, turned back to Quinx, clinging to a stanchion as pines whispered in the wind hundreds of feet below him. "Do you not know what I have found?"

"Not precisely, no," Quinx admitted. "And in truth, it does not matter. You seek to unseat the holy truth of the Increate and reinstate the Externalist heresy. That is enough for me."

"You accuse me of ecclesiastical crimes when all I pursue is the objective truth!"

"Move it along," shouted one of the Thalassocretes from behind them. Abutti turned and hurried along to where the path widened to a ledge, then waited in ankle-high grass for the priest to catch up.

Quinx did, breathing hard as much from the stress of the heights as anything. "Do you not fear I will toss you off myself?" he asked, glancing past Abutti at the slope beyond.

"No. Men like you do not toss people off cliffs. You have people tossed off cliffs. That's why you have that monster monk and the dreadful woman." Abutti paused, obviously chewing on his next words. "Not so long ago, you would have had a tall stake and a hot fire awaiting someone like me."

"Holy Mother Church never burned anyone," Quinx replied, stung.

"No, you merely passed sentence and had the secular authorities carry it out. I have trained in logic, Revered. I know who holds the responsibility there."

A line of Thalassocretes pushed past them, though both Brother Kurts and the woman were pulled aside by their guards rather than go ahead of Quinx and Abutti.

"When one raises rebellion against the Increate, one bears responsibility for one's penalty."

"Rebellion against the Church is not rebellion against the Increate," Abutti grumbled. "And I raise neither. Only truth."

Quinx had no answer to that, but he knew he had the measure of this man now. Smart but weak. Too willing to be turned aside.

Still, the astronomer had the right of it. There *were* more telescopes in the world.

"What did you find?" he asked as they began following the line of march again, finally drawn back to the question despite himself.

"Evidence of an aetheric vessel." A stubborn pride swelled in Abutti's voice. "The Increate's ship of space, that brought us to this world."

"I do not believe you," Quinx replied. "Simply not possible."

"Then why are we tramping up the side of Thera?"

They both looked ahead, to where Goins was long vanished at the head of a receding column of Thalassocretes variously in their blue-green robes and khaki excursion wear.

> Archaeology represents one of our greatest challenges in unraveling the mysteries of the human experience. Geology tells us much about the age of the world, and through the sciences we understand that the Creation narrative of the *Librum Vita* is a grand

metaphor for the natural processes of the universe. Yet archaeology shows us a literal view of the Increate's placement of human beings upon this Earth. How to integrate the inarguable inerrancy of the Increate's word with the interpolations of the geological sciences remains one of the greatest doctrinal challenges of our century, and perhaps centuries to come.

—*His Holiness Lamboine XXII*, Posthumous Commentaries

Morgan drew away from the priest as the group summited the crest of Thera and began clambering down into the crater within. Quinx' retainers, for all that they were under guard, frightened him. He was certain that at a word from the Revered, the two would tear free of their bonds and throw him from the cliffs.

Goins gathered his group in a sloping meadow a few hundred feet below the rim. Already the Presiding Judge was talking, urgently and low. Not an exhortation. Morgan hurried to catch up and hear. They knew *his* evidence already, everyone who had been in the lounge of *Clear Mountain* the night before.

Whatever Goins had to show them here fit with Morgan's own work like a ratchet into a gear.

". . . passed into our trust with the foundering of the Bear Cult at Truska."

Thalassocretes nodded in return.

"Only certain among you know anything of this secret. None of us, not even me, have ever come to this place. Even those who maintain the upward path along the outer face of the mountain are forced to spend their lives on this island." His voice dropped. "Until Dr. Abutti's telescope opened the heavens to our eyes, this was without doubt the deepest truth upon this Earth. Brother Lupan had the right of it."

"The Increate's Chariot?" Quinx stepped up next to Morgan. "A ridiculous fantasy embedded in a foolish heresy."

"A truth, embedded in the heart of each of the Eight Gardens," Goins replied, his voice booming now. "I give you the Chariot of Cycladia."

He turned, walked across the meadow, and began tearing at the vines that draped a grove there.

Quinx reached into his robes and pulled out a firearm. A fat-barreled gun. Morgan stared a moment, incredulous, then tackled the priest as he raised his weapon and fired it into the sky.

The next few moments were blinding confusion. Something hissed high before popping—fireworks? Shouting echoed around Morgan as the enormous monk and the woman with him broke free of their guards as he'd feared. Morgan stumbled back to his feet, fleeing the priest and the lopsided fight behind him toward the dubious safety of Goins and the Thalassocretes who were tearing down plants to reveal a mottled wall of . . . something?

Engines strained overhead as an airship circled low in the sky. He looked up to see a narrow bag with a knife hull beneath. Copper lances protruding from the hull crackled with visible energy.

Morgan ran toward the Chariot. "Judge Goins, we are betrayed!"

Goins turned, stared into the sky a moment, watching in apparent disbelief as lightning forked across the sky to ground into the trees behind him with a series explosive cracks. He began to laugh as smoke rose. Now his voice boomed like a parade sergeant's. "Quinx, you are a greater fool than even I thought. Do you doubt the Increate's Chariot can defend itself?"

Another bolt lanced from the airship, striking down half a dozen shrieking Thalassocretes in a groaning mass. Quinx scuttled toward Goins, trailed by his dangerous guardians. Above them, the airship strained lower, barking bullets that sprayed across the meadow in a scythe of flying dirt that somehow claimed no lives on the first pass.

The flash of light erupting from the trees blinded Morgan for a moment. A sizzling noise followed, which terminated in a thunderclap. He rolled over, rubbing his eyes, to see the airship aflame and lurching toward the other side of Thera's crater. Quinx was still on his feet but stumbling. The monk was down, while the woman howled at the sky a long moment before rushing toward Morgan and Goins.

"You are all mad," the doctor shouted. "All of you!"

The woman headed straight toward him. Her eyes glowed with a death-madness that Morgan had never before witnessed, having only read of such things in his scientific romances. Goins simply stood, staring down a hundred and fifty pounds of racing anger. Above them, something exploded aboard the airship.

Still running, the woman caught up to Quinx, grabbing the priest by the arms. She continued to sprint toward Morgan and Goins, carrying the shuddering Quinx over one shoulder. Instead of plowing into them, she pulled up short, her breath a bellows.

"Show me the Chariot," she demanded. Her voice was a deep, threatening growl. Behind her, the monk arose and stumbled toward them.

"Who are you to ask?" Goins asked.

"A Machinist." Her voice was a growl. "This is my future. The future of my faith."

"The past," Morgan said, correcting her. "The future is coming in the sky."

Behind them, the mottled wall whirred. He turned to see a section slide upward to create an opening. Faint crimson light glowed beyond. The airship crashed in the distance with another whoosh of flame and heat.

The Machinist continued to stare them both down. "My lover is dead, as is my captain. You allowed them to die. You owe me this."

The monk caught up to her, tackling from behind with his hands spread wide to catch her eyes and the edges of her mouth. The woman dropped Quinx, who bit off a scream as he hit, then she bent to seize the monk and wrestle him to the ground in front of her.

He bounced up, obviously rattled, but ready to engage. Goins tugged Morgan's arm. "Back," he hissed. "This is not our fight."

"None of this is *my* fight," Morgan growled.

Goins tapped the wall of the Increate's Chariot. "This is one of eight aetheric ships here on Earth. You have found their origin, the great ship that is their mother. You were right all along. Do you now doubt that our history is coming home in the sky, from your libration point?"

"No, I do not doubt." Behind them, a screech. The monk and the Machinist were circling dangerously as Quinx staggered to his feet.

Strangely, Goins was ignoring the battle, focusing his entire attention on Morgan. That in turn drew Morgan's gaze back to the judge. For all his curiosity, he was terribly loath to step within. He hadn't wished to be *this* right, to confront the meaning of his discovery so personally. "But I did not summon it."

"Then who did?" the judge asked impatiently.

That, he could answer. "All of us. With our telelocutors and our airships and our engines, sending rays of energy into the aether as surely as if we'd lit a bonfire in the night. If this Chariot knows enough to defend itself, doubtless the mother ship can watch our Earth for us to rise high enough to see it in return. We have had electrickifcation for a generation. It can see that."

With a flicker of his eyes, Goins drew a gun of his own and shot past Morgan in one motion. Startled, Morgan turned to see the monk falling to the ground, his face bloody. The woman was on her hands and knees. Quinx lurched slowly toward the two of them with a slightly unfocused look on his face.

The Presiding Judge handed the pistol to Morgan. "You choose. The past, or the future."

Morgan promptly dropped the weapon into the grass. He'd wanted the truth, by the Increate, not such a mess of power and violence. "I am a *scientist*. I do not have people thrown off cliffs."

Quinx reached for Morgan's hand. "Ninety Nine," he gasped. "Brother Kurts. Please . . . Stop it. You didn't need to do this."

The Machinist shuddered to her feet. One eye was gouged loose, and her mouth bled. Morgan glanced at the dying monk and wondered just how tough a human being could be.

Her eyes were no longer mad. Instead, they were haunted. "Stop," she said, echoing Quinx' words.

"Go," Morgan replied. He had just lately learned the measure of his own courage, and was not sure he could step into the chariot himself. "Go into the future. It cannot be stopped. The stars do not lie, and they are coming toward us."

"They are my stars." She stared at them with her remaining eye. "Ours. Not yours."

The woman stumbled weeping through the opened door. Quinx turned away from Morgan. "It cannot be," the priest gasped. "I must go where Ion has already led." Face twisted in some inner agony of the spirit, he followed after her.

"And you?" asked Goins. "Do you choose the future as well?"

Afraid, he stood unmoving a moment. Then: "I would have thought to . . ." The doctor's words ran out as he marshaled his thoughts. "No. I've come to understand that the future is here with us. Whatever comes, comes."

Morgan Abutti looked up at the smoke trailing into the blue sky from the ruined airship. Goins squatted next to him, pistol still in hand. The door into the Chariot had slid shut.

"What next?" the scientist asked.

"Surely the Increate knows," said Goins.

"Quinx would have said that the Increate knows all." Morgan thought about those words. "It seems to me that They do not think to warn us of the truth."

The remaining Thalassocretes gathered around. Some tended the wounded and the dead, others discussed the advisability of sending a party to look into the crash of the airship.

The Chariot began to whine, a low hum that built slowly in volume. Goins rose, gestured for a general retreat. It seemed wisest.

Morgan was slow to move, staring at the chance of greatness which he'd abandoned. He was the first to see the Chariot break from the trees and rise into the sky. The rest stopped to watch as clouds of dust and steam spiraled beneath it.

"Good luck, Revered Quinx," muttered the doctor.

Goins tugged at his arm. "The choices are made. You were correct. We must go."

"You have it almost right," said Morgan. "*His* choices are ended. *Ours* are just begun." His courage returned to him once more, like a whipped dog coming home. "This is what I get for uncovering the truth. What I had declined to see clearly before. There are great consequences to be accounted for." He glanced away from the departing chariot. "Are you ready to face those, Judge? I am."

"Remember, your aetheric vessel was coming anyway, whether or not you had seen it first. You did not cause this." Goins paused a moment, searching Morgan's face as if for some truth. "Science finds the path where the light of faith has shown the way."

Morgan could not tell if the judge meant to be ironic or not. That did not matter. He patted the other man's shoulder. "Let us go, then. There is work to be done."

Above them, the future rose ever higher, shedding six thousand years of mud and plants and tradition as it climbed to meet the oncoming stars.

the memcordist

Lavie Tidhar

Lavie Tidhar grew up on a kibbutz in Israel, has traveled widely in Africa and Asia, and has lived in London, the South Pacific island of Vanuatu, and Laos. He is the winner of the 2003 Clarke-Bradbury Prize (awarded by the European Space Agency), was the editor of Michael Marshall Smith: The Annotated Bibliography, *and the anthologies* A Dick & Jane Primer for Adults *and* The Apex Book of World SF. *He is the author of the linked story collection* HebrewPunk, *the novella chapbooks* An Occupation of Angels, Gorel and the Pot-Bellied God, *Cloud Permutations, Jesus and the Eigh-fold Path, and, with Nir Yaniv, the novel* The Tel Aviv Dossier. *A prolific short-story writer, his stories have appeared in* Interzone, Clarkesworld, Apex Magazine, *Sci Fiction,* Strange Horizons, *ChiZine,* Postscripts, Fantasy Magazine, *Nemonymous,* Infinity Plus, Aeon, The Book of Dark Wisdom, Fortean Bureau, *and elsewhere, and have been translated into seven languages. His latest novels include* The Bookman *and its sequel* Camera Obscura, Osama: A Novel, *and, most recently,* The Great Game. Osama: A Novel *won the World Fantasy Award as the year's Best Novel in 2012. Coming up is a new novel,* Martian Sands. *After a spell in Tel Aviv, he's currently living back in England again.*

It's been said that everyone is the hero of their own drama. Here's a poignant look at a future where everyone else gets to watch as well. . . .

POLYPHEMUS PORT, TITAN, YEAR FORTY-THREE

Beyond the dome the ice-storms of Titan rage; inside it is warm, damp, with the smell of sewage seeping through and creepers growing through the walls of the above-ground dwellings. He tries to find her scent in the streets of Polyport and fails.

Hers was the scent of basil, and the night. When cooking, he would sometimes crush basil leaves between his fingers. It would bring her back, for just a moment, bring her back just as she was the first time they'd met.

Polyphemus Port is full of old memories. Whenever he wants, he can recall them, but he never does. Instead he tries to find them in old buildings, in half-familiar signs. There, the old Baha'i temple where they'd sheltered one rainy afternoon, and watched a weather hacker dance in the storm, wreathed in raindrops.

There, what had once been a smokes-bar, now a shop selling surface crawlers. There, a doll house, for the sailors off the ships. It had been called Madame Sing's, now it's called Florian's. Dolls peek out of the windows, small naked figures in the semblance of teenage boys and girls, soft and warm and disposable, with their serial numbers etched delicately into the curve of a neck or thigh. His feet know the old way and he walks past the shops, away from the docks and into a row of box-like apartments, the co-op building where they'd first met, creepers overgrowing the walls and peeking into windows—where they'd met, a party in the Year Seventeen of the Narrative of Pym.

He looks up, and as he does he automatically checks the figures that rise up, always, in the air before him. The number of followers hovers around twenty-three million, having risen slightly on this, his second voyage to Titan in so many years. A compilation feed of Year Seventeen is running concurrently, and there are messages from his followers, flashing in the lower right corner, which he ignores.

Looking up at her window, a flower pot outside—there used to be a single red flower growing there, a carnivorous Titan Rose with hungry, teeth-ringed suckers— her vice at the time. She'd buy the plant choice goat meat in the market every day. Now the flower pot is absent and the window is dark and she, too, is long gone.

Is she watching too, somewhere, he wonders—does she see me looking up and searching for her, for traces of her in a place so laid and overlaid with memories until it was impossible to tell which ones were original, and which the memory of a memory?

He thinks it's unlikely. Like the entire sum of his life, this journey is for his benefit, is ultimately about him. We are what we are—and he turns away from her window, and the ice-storm howls above his head, beyond the protective layer of the dome. There had been a storm that night, too, but then, this was Titan, and there was always a storm.

ON BOARD THE *GEL BLONG MOTA*, EARTH-TO-MARS VOYAGE, YEAR FIVE

There are over twenty million followers on this day of the Narrative of Pym, and Mother is happy, and Pym is happy too, because he'd snuck out when Mother was asleep, and now he stands before the vast porthole of the ship—in actuality a wall-sized screen—and watches space, and the slowly moving stars beyond.

The *Gel Blong Mota* is an old ship, generations of *Man Spes* living and dying inside as it cruises the solar system, from Earth, across the inner and outer system, all the way to Jettisoned and Dragon's World before turning back, doing the same route again and again. Pym is half in love with Joy, who is the same age as him and will one day, she confides in him, be captain of this ship. She teaches him asteroid pidgin, the near-universal language of Mars and the belt, and he tells her about Earth, about volcanoes and storms and the continental cities. He was not born on Earth, but he has lived there four of his five years, and he is nervous to be away, but also happy, and excited, and it's all very confusing. Nearly fifty million watched him leave Earth, and they didn't go in the elevator, they went in an old passenger RLV and he floated in the air when the gravity stopped, and he wasn't sick or *anything*. Then they came to an orbital station where they had a very nice room and there was gravity again, and the next day they climbed aboard the *Gel Blong Mota*, which was at the same time very very big but also small, and it smelled funny. He'd seen the aquatic tanks with their eels and prawns and lobster and squid, and he'd been to the hydroponics gardens and spoken to the head gardener there, and Joy even showed him a secret door and took him inside the maintenance corridors beyond the walls of the ship, where it was very dry and smelled of dust and old paint.

Now he watches space, and wonders what Mars is like. At that moment, staring out into space, it is as if he is staring out at his own future spreading out before him, unwritten terabytes and petabytes of the Narrative of Pym, waiting to be written over in any way he wants. It makes him feel strange—he's glad when Joy arrives and they go off together to the aquatic tanks—she said she'd teach him how to fish.

TONG YUN CITY, MARS, YEAR SEVEN

Mother is out again with her latest boyfriend, Jonquil Sing, a memcordist syndication agent. "He is very good for us," she tells Pym one night, giving him a wet kiss on the cheek, and her breath smells of smoke. She hopes Jonquil will increase subscriptions across Mars, Pym knows—the numbers of his followers have been dropping since they came to Tong Yun. "A dull, provincial *town*," Mother says, which is the Earth-born's most stinging insult.

But Pym likes Tong Yun. He loves going down in the giant elevators into the lower levels of the city, and he particularly loves the Arcade, with its battle droid arenas and games-worlds shops and particularly the enormous Multifaith Bazaar. Whenever he can he sneaks out of the house—they are living on the surface, under the dome of Tong Yun, in a house belonging to a friend of a friend of Mother's—and goes down to Arcade, and to the Bazaar.

The Church of Robot is down there, and an enormous Elronite temple, and mosques and synagogues and Buddhist and Baha'i temples and even a Gorean place and he watches the almost-naked slave girls with strange fascination, and they smile at him and reach out and tousle his hair. There are Re-Born Martian warriors with reddish skin and four arms—they believe Mars was once habituated by an ancient empire and that they are its descendants, and they serve the Emperor of Time. He thinks he wants to become a Re-Born warrior when he grows up, and have four arms and tint his skin red, but when he mentions it to Mother once she throws a fit and says Mars never had an atmosphere and there is no emperor and that the Re-Born are—and she uses a very rude word, and there are the usual complaints from some of the followers of the Narrative of Pym.

He's a little scared of the Elronites—they're all very confident and smile a lot and have very white teeth. Pym isn't very confident. He prefers quiet roads and places with few people in them and he doesn't want anyone to know who he is.

Sometimes he wonders who he is, or what he will become. One of Mother's friends asked him, "What do you want to be when you grow up?" and he said, "A spaceship captain—" thinking of Joy—and Mother gave her false laugh and ruffled his hair and said, "Pym already *is* what he is. Isn't that right, sweetheart?" and she gathered him in her arms and said, "He's *Pym*."

But who is Pym? Pym doesn't know. When he's down at the Multifaith Bazaar he thinks that perhaps he wants to be a priest, or a monk—but which religion? They're all neat.

Fifteen million follow him as he passes through temples, churches and shrines, searching for answers to a question he is not yet ready to ask himself, and might never be.

JETTISONED, CHARON, YEAR FIFTY-SIX

So at last he's come to Jettisoned, the farthest one can get without quite leaving completely, and he hires a small dark room in a small dark co-op deep in the bowels of the moon, a place that suits his mood.

Twenty-three million watch, less because of him and more because he'd chosen Jettisoned, the home of black warez and wild technology and outlaws—the city of the Jettisoned, all those ejected at the last moment from the vast majestic starships as they depart the solar system, leaving forever on a one-way journey into galactic space. Would some of them find new planets, new moons, new suns to settle around? Are there aliens out there, or God? No one knows, least of all Pym. He'd once asked his mother why they couldn't go with one of the ships. "Don't be silly," she'd said, "think of all your followers, and how disappointed they'd be."

"Bugger my followers," he says now, aloud, knowing some would complain, and others would drop out and follow other narratives. He'd never been all that popular, but the truth was, he'd never wanted to be. Everything I've ever done in my life, he thinks, is on record. Everything I've seen, everything I've touched, everything I smelled or said. And yet had he said or done anything worth saying, anything worth doing?

I once loved with all my heart, he thinks. Is that enough?

He knows she'd been to Jettisoned in the past year. But she'd left before he arrived. Where is she now? He could check, but doesn't. On her way back through the outer system—perhaps in the Galilean Moons, where he knows she's popular. He decides to get drunk.

Hours later, he is staggering along a dark alley, home to smokes bars, doll houses, battle arcades, body modification clinics, a lone Church of Robot mission, and several old-fashioned drinking establishments. Anything that can be grown on Jettisoned gets fermented into alcohol, sooner or later. Either that or smoked. His head hurts, and his heart is beating too fast. Too old, he thinks. Perhaps he says it out loud. Two insectoid figures materialise in the darkness, descend on him. "What are you—?" he says, slurring the words, as the two machines expertly rifle through his pockets and run an intrusion package over his node—even now, when all he can do is blink blearily, he notices the followers numbers rising, and realises he's being mugged.

"Give them a show," he says, and begins to giggle. He tries to hit one of the insectoid figures and a thin, slender metal arm reaches down and touches him—a needle bite against his throat—

Numb, but still conscious—he can't shout for help but what's the point, anyway? This is Jettisoned, and if you end up there you have only yourself to blame.

What are they doing? Why have they not gone yet? They're trying to take apart his memcorder, but it's impossible—don't they know it's impossible?—he is wired through and through, half human and half machine, recording everything, forgetting nothing. And yet suddenly he is very afraid, and the panic acts like a cold dose of water and he manages to move, slightly, and he shouts for help, though his voice is reedy and weak and anyway there is no one to hear him . . .

They're tearing apart chunks of memory, terabytes of life, days and months and years disappearing in a black cloud—"Stop, please," he mumbles, "please, don't—"

Who is he? What is he doing here?

A name. He has a name . . .

Somewhere far away, a shout. The two insectoid creatures raise elongated faces, feelers shaking—

There is the sound of an explosion, and one of the creatures disappears—hot shards of metal sting Pym, burning, burning—

The second creature rears, four arms rising like guns—

There is the sound of gunshots, to and from, and then there's a massive hole in the creature's chest, and it runs off into the darkness—

A face above his, dark hair, pale skin, two eyes like waning moons—"Pym? Pym? Can you hear me?"

"Pym," he whispers, the name strangely familiar. He closes his eyes and then nothing hurts any more, and he is floating in a cool, calm darkness.

SPIDER'S HOLD, LUNA, YEAR ONE

Not a memory as much as the recollection, like film, of something seen—emerging from darkness into a light, alien faces hovering above him, as large as moons—"Pym! My darling little Pym—"

Hands clapping, and he is clutched close to a warm, soft breast, and he begins to cry, but then the warmth settles him and he snuggles close and he is happy.

"Fifty-three million at peak," someone says.

"Day One," someone says. "Year One. And may all of your days be as happy as this one. You are born, Pym. Your narrative's began."

He finds a nipple, drinks. The milk is warm. "Hush now, my little baby. Hush now."

"See, already he is looking around. He wants to see the world."

But it isn't true. He only wants to sleep, in that warm, safe place.

"Happy birthday, Pym."

He sleeps.

POLYPHEMUS PORT, TITAN, YEAR SEVENTEEN

The party is crammed with people, the house node broadcasts out particularly loud *Nuevo Kwasa-Kwasa* tunes, there is a lot of Zion Special Strength passing around, the strong, sweet smell latching on to hair and clothes, and Pym is slightly drunk.

Polyport, on his own: Mother left behind in the Galilean Republic, Pym escaping—jumping onto an ancient transport ship, the *Ibn-al-Farid*, a Jupiter-to-Saturn one-way trip.

Feeling free, for the first time. His numbers going up, but he isn't paying any attention for once. Pym, not following the narrative but simply living his life.

Port bums hanging out at Polyport, kids looking for ships for the next trip to nowhere, coming from Mars and the Jovean moons and the ring-cities of Saturn, heading everywhere—

The party: a couple of weather hackers complaining about outdated protocols; a ship rat from the *Ibn-al-Farid*—Pym knows him slightly from the journey—doing a Louis Wu in the corner, a blissful smile on his face, wired-in, the low current tickling his pleasure centers; five big, blonde Australian girls from Earth on a round-the-system trip—conversations going over Pym's head—"Where do you come from? Where do you go? Where do you come from?"

Titan surface crawlers with that faraway look in their eyes; a viral artist, two paint-ers, a Martian Re-Born talking quietly to a Jovean robot—Pym knows people are look-ing at him, pretending not to—and his numbers are going up, everybody loves a party.

She is taller than him, with long black hair gathered into moving dreadlocks—some sort of mechanism making them writhe about her head like snakes—long slender fingers, obsidian eyes—

People turning as she comes through, a hush of sort—she walks straight up to him, ignoring the other guests—stands before him, studying him with a bemused expression. He knows she sees what he sees—number of followers, storage space re-ports, feed statistics—he says, "Can I get you a drink?" with a confidence he doesn't quite feel, and she smiles. She has a gold tooth, and when she smiles it makes her appear strangely younger.

"I don't drink," she says, still studying him. The gold tooth is an Other, but in her case it isn't truly Joined—the digital intelligence embedded within is part of her memcorder structure. "Eighty-seven million," she says.

"Thirty-two," he says. She smiles again. "Let's get out of here," she says.

JETTISONED, CHARON, YEAR FIFTY-SIX

Memory returning in chunks—long-unused backup spooling back into his mind. When he opens his eyes he thinks for a moment it is her, that somehow she had rescued him from the creatures, but no—the face that hovers above his is unfamil-iar, and he is suddenly afraid.

"Hush," she says. "You're hurt."

"Who are you?" he croaks. Numbers flashing—viewing figures near a hundred million all across the system, being updated at the speed of light. His birth didn't draw nearly that many . . .

"My name's Zul," she says—which tells him nothing. He sees she has a pendant hanging between her breasts. He squints, and sees his own face.

The woman shrugs, smiles, a little embarrassed. Crows-feet at the corners of her dark eyes. A gun hanging on her belt, black leather trousers the only other thing she wears. "You were attacked by wild foragers," she says, and shrugs again. "We've had an infestation of them in the past couple of years."

Foragers: multi-surface machines designed for existing outside the human bub-bles, converting rock into energy, slow lunar surface transforms—rogue, like every-thing else on Jettisoned. He says, "Thank you," and to his surprise she blushes.

"I've been watching you," she said.

Pym understands—and feels a little sad.

She makes love to him on the narrow bed in the small, hot, dark room. They are somewhere deep underground. From down here it is impossible to imagine Charon, that icy moon, or the tiny cold disc of the sun far away, or the enormous field of ga-lactic stars or the shadows of Exodus ships as they pass forever out of human space—hard to imagine anything but a primal human existence of naked bodies and salty skin and fevered heartbeats and he sighs, still inexplicably sad within his excite-ment, for the smell of basil he seeks is missing.

KUALA LUMPUR, EARTH, YEAR THIRTY-TWO

At thirty-two there's the annoyance of hair growing in the wrong places and not growing in others, a mole or two which shouldn't be there, hangovers get worse, take longer to dissipate, eyes strain, and death is closer—

Pym, the city a spider's web of silver and light all around him, the towers of Kuala Lumpur rise like rockets into the skies—the streets alive with laughter, music, frying mutton—

On the hundred and second floor of the hospital, in a room as white as a painting of absence, as large and as small as a world—

Mother reaches out, holds his hand in hers. Her fingers are thin, bony. "My little Pym. My baby. Pym."

She sees what he sees. She shares access to the viewing stats, knows how many millions are watching this, the death of Mother, supporting character number one in the Narrative of Pym. Pym feels afraid, and guilty, and scared—Mother is dying, no one knows why, exactly, and for Pym it's—what?

Pain, yes, but—

Is that relief? The freedom of Pym, a real one this time, not as illusory as it had been, when he was seventeen?

"Mother," he says, and she squeezes his hand. Below, the world is spider-webs and fairy-lights. "Fifty-six million," she says, and tries to smile. "And the best doctors money could buy—"

But they are not enough. She made him come back to her, by dying, and Pym isn't sure how he feels about it, and so he stands there, and holds her weakened hand, and stares out beyond the windows into the night.

POLYPHEMUS PORT, TITAN, YEAR SEVENTEEN

They need no words between them. They haven't said a word since they left the party. They are walking hand in hand through the narrow streets of Polyport and the storm rages overhead. When she draws him into a darkened corner he is aware of the beating of his heart and then her own, his hand on her warm dark skin cupping a breast as the numbers roll and roll, the millions rising—a second feed showing him her own figures. Her lips on his, full, and she has the taste of basil, and the night, and when they hold each other the numbers fade and there is only her.

JETTISONED, CHARON, YEAR FIFTY-SIX

When they make love a second time he calls out her name and, later, the woman lies beside him and says, her hand stroking his chest slowly, "You really love her," and her voice is a little sad. Her eyes are round, pupils large. She sighs, a soft sound on the edge of the solar system. "I thought, maybe . . ."

The numbers dropping again, the story of his life—the Narrative of Pym charted by the stats of followers at any given moment. The narrative of Pym goes out all over space—and do they follow it, too, in the Exodus ships, or on alien planets with unknown names?

He doesn't know. He doesn't care. He rises in the dark, and dresses, and goes out into the night of Jettisoned as the woman sleeps behind him.

At that moment he decides to find her.

DRAGON'S HOME, HYDRA, YEAR SEVENTY-EIGHT

It feels strange to be back in the Pluto system. And Hydra is the strangest of the worlds . . . Jettisoned lies like a sore on Charon, but Hydra is even farther out, and cold, so cold . . . Dragon's World, and Pym is a guest of the dragon.

When he thinks back to his time on Jettisoned, in the Year Fifty-Six—or was it Fifty-Seven?—of the Narrative of Pym, it is all very confused. It had been a low point in his life. He left Jettisoned shortly after the attack, determined to find her—but then, he had done that several times, and never . . .

Dragon's World is an entire moon populated by millions of bodies and a single mind. Vietnamese dolls, mass-produced in the distant factories of Earth, transported here by the same *Gel Blong Mota* he had once travelled on as a child, thousands and tens of thousands and finally millions of dolls operating with a single mind, the mind of the dragon—worker-ants crawling all over the lunar surface, burrowing into its hide, transforming it into—what?

No one quite knows.

The dragon is an Other, one of the countless intelligences evolved in the digital Breeding Grounds, lines of code multiplying and mutating, merging and splitting in billions upon billions of cycles. It is said the dragon had been on one of the Exodus ships, and been Jettisoned, but why that may be so no one knows. This is its world—a habitat? A work of strange, conceptual art? Nobody knows and the dragon isn't telling.

Yet Pym is a guest, and the dragon is hospitable.

Pym's body is in good shape but the dragon promises to make it better. Pym lies in one of the warrens, in a cocoon-like harness, and tiny insects are crawling all over his body, biting and tearing, sewing and rearranging. Sometimes Pym gets the impression the dragon is lonely. Or perhaps it wants others to see its world, and for that purpose invited Pym, whose numbers rise dramatically when he lands on Hydra.

The *Gel Blong Mota* had carried him here, from the Galilean Republic on a slow, leisurely journey, and its captain was Joy, and she and Pym shared wine and stories and stared out into space, and sometimes made love with the slow, unhurried pace of old friends.

Why did you never go to her?

Her question is in his mind as he lies there, in the warm confines of Dragon's cocoon. It is very quiet on Hydra, the dolls that are the dragon's body making almost no sound as they pass on their errands—whatever those may be. He thinks of Joy's question but realises he has no answer for her, and never had. There had been other women, other places, but never—

POLYPHEMUS PORT, TITAN, YEAR SEVENTEEN

It is the most *intimate* moment of his life: it is as if the two of them are the center of the entire universe, and nothing else matters but the two of them, and as they kiss, as they undress, as they touch each other with clumsy, impatient fingers the whole universe is watching, watching something amazing, this joining of two bodies, two souls. Their combined numbers have reached one billion and are still climbing. It will never be like this again, he thinks he hears her say, her lips against his neck, and he knows she is right, it will never—

KUALA LUMPUR, EARTH, YEAR TWO

Taking baby-steps across the vast expanse of recreated prime park land in the heart of the town, cocooned within the great needle towers of the mining companies, Pym laughs, delighted, as adult hands pick him up and twirl him around. "My baby," Mother says, and holds him close, and kisses him (those strange figures at the corner of his eyes always shifting, changing—he'd got used to them by now, does not pay them any mind)—"You have time for everything twice over. The future waits for you—"

And as he puts his arms around her neck he's happy, and the future is a shining road in Pym's mind, a long endless road of white light with Pym marching at its center, with no end in sight, and he laughs again, and wriggles down, and runs towards the ponds where there are great big lizards sunning themselves in the sun.

DRAGON'S HOME, HYDRA, YEAR ONE HUNDRED FIFTEEN

Back on Dragon's Home, that ant's nest whose opening rises from the surface of Hydra like a volcanic mouth, back in the cocoons of his old friend the dragon—"I don't think you could fix me again, old friend," he says, and closes his eyes—the cocoon against his naked skin like soft Vietnamese silk.

The dragon murmurs all around him, its thousands of bodies marching through their complex woven-together tunnels. Number of followers hovering around fifty million, and Pym thinks, They want to see me die.

He turns in his cocoon and the dragon murmurs soothing words, but they lose their meaning. Pym tries to recall Mother's face, the taste of blackberries on a Martian farm, the feel of machine-generated rain on Ganymede or the embrace of a Jettisoned woman, but nothing holds, nothing is retained in his mind anymore. Somewhere it all exists, even now his failing senses are being broadcast and stored—but this, he knows suddenly, with a frightening clarity, is the approaching termination of the Narrative of Pym, and the thought terrifies him. "Dragon!" he cries, and then there is something cool against his neck and relief floods in.

Pym drifts in a dream half-sleep, lulled by the rhythmic motion of his cocoon. There is a smell, a fragrance he misses, something sweet and fresh like ba—a herb of some sort? He grabs for a memory, his eyes opening with the effort, but it's no use, there is nothing there but a faint, uneasy sense of regret, and at last he lets it go. There had been a girl—

Hadn't there?

He never—

He closes his eyes again at last, and gradually true darkness forms, a strange and unfamiliar vista: even the constant numbers at the corner of his vision, always previously there, are fading—it is so strange he would have laughed if he could.

POLYPHEMUS PORT, TITAN, YEAR FORTY-THREE

He walks down the old familiar streets on this, this forty-third year of the Narrative of Pym, searching for her in the scent of old memories. She is not there, but suddenly, as he walks under the dome and the ever-present storm, he's hopeful: there will be other places, other times and, somewhere in the solar system, sometime in the Narrative of Pym, he will find her again.

the girl-thing who went out for sushi

PAT CADIGAN

Here's a fast-paced story about a spacefaring construction-worker injured in an accident in orbit around Jupiter who must not only deal with recovery but with the problems and benefits of changing your species altogether . . .

Pat Cadigan was born in Schenectady, New York, and now lives in London with her family. She made her first professional sale in 1980, and has subsequently come to be regarded as one of the best new writers of her generation. Her story "Pretty Boy Crossover" has appeared on several critic's lists as among the best science fiction stories of the 1980s, and her story "Angel" was a finalist for the Hugo Award, the Nebula Award, and the World Fantasy Award (one of the few stories ever to earn that rather unusual distinction). Her short fiction—which has appeared in most of the major markets, including Asimov's Science Fiction *and* The Magazine of Fantasy & Science Fiction—*has been gathered in the collections* Patterns *and* Dirty Work. *Her first novel,* Mindplayers, *was released in 1987 to excellent critical response, and her second novel,* Synners, *released in 1991, won the Arthur C. Clarke Award as the year's best science fiction novel, as did her third novel,* Fools, *making her the only writer ever to win the Clarke Award twice. Her other books include the novels* Dervish Is Digital, Tea from an Empty Cup, *and* Reality Used to Be a Friend of Mine, *and, as editor, the anthology* The Ultimate Cyberpunk, *as well as two making-of movie books and four media tie-in novels. Her most recent book was a novel,* Cellular.

Nine decs into her second hitch, Fry hit a berg in the Main ring and broke her leg. And she didn't just splinter the bone—compound fracture! Yow! What a mess! Fortunately, we'd finished servicing most of the eyes, a job that I thought was more busy-work than work-work. But those were the last decs before Okeke-Hightower hit and everybody had comet fever.

There hadn't been an observable impact on the Big J for almost three hundred (Dirt) years—Shoemaker-Somethingorother—and no one was close enough to get a good look back then. Now every news channel, research institute, and moneybags everywhere in the Solar System was paying Jovian Operations for a ringside view. Every JovOp crew was on the case, putting cameras on cameras and back-up cameras on the back-up cameras—visible, infrared, X-ray, and everything else. Fry was pretty excited about it herself, talking about how great it was she would get to see it live. Girl-thing should have been watching where she wasn't supposed to be going.

I was coated and I knew Fry's suit would hold, but featherless bipeds are prone to vertigo when they're injured. So I blew a bubble big enough for both of us, cocooned her leg, pumped her full of drugs, and called an ambulance. The jellie with the rest of the crew was already on the other side of the Big J. I let them know we'd scrubbed and someone would have to finish the last few eyes in the radian for us. Girl-thing was one hell of a stiff two-stepper, staying just as calm as if we were unwinding end-of-shift. The only thing she seemed to have a little trouble with was the O. Fry picked up consensus orientation faster than any other two-stepper I'd ever worked with but she'd never done it on drugs. I tried to keep her distracted by telling her all the gossip I knew and when I ran out, I made shit up.

Then all of a sudden, she said, "Well, Arkae, that's it for me."

Her voice was so damned final, I thought she was quitting. And I deflated because I had taken quite a liking to our girl-thing. I said, "Aw, honey, we'll all miss you out here."

But she laughed. "No, no, no, I'm not leaving. I'm going out for sushi."

I gave her a pat on the shoulder, thinking it was the junk in her system talking. Fry was no ordinary girl-thing—she was great out here but she'd always been special. Back in the Dirt, she'd been a brain-box, top-level scholar *and* a beauty queen. That's right—a featherless biped genius beauty queen. Believe it or leave it, as Sheerluck says.

Fry'd been with us for three and half decs when she let on about being a beauty queen. The whole crew was unwinding end-of-shift—her, me, Dubonnet, Sheerluck, Aunt Chovie, Splat, Bait, Glynis, and Fred—and we all about lost the O.

"Wow," said Dubonnet, "did you ask for whirled peas, too?" I didn't understand the question but it sounded like a snipe. I triple-smacked him and suggested he respect someone else's culture.

But Fry said, "No, I don't blame any a youse asking. That stuff really is so silly. Why people still bother with such things, I sure don't know. We're supposed to be so advanced and enlightened and it still matters how a woman looks in a bathing suit. Excuse me, a biped woman," she added, laughing a little. "And no, the subject of whirled peas never came up."

"If that's how you really felt," Aunt Chovie said, big, serious eyes and all eight arms in curlicues, "why'd you go along with it?"

"It was the only way I could get out here," Fry said.

"Not really?" said Splat, a second before I woulda blurted out the same thing.

"Yes, really. I got heavy metal for personal appearances and product endorsements, plus a full scholarship, my choice of school." Fry smiled and I thought it was the way she musta smiled when she was crowned Queen of the Featherless Biped Lady Geniuses or whatever it was. It wasn't insincere, but a two-stepper's face is just another muscle group; I could tell it was something she'd learned to do. "I saved as much as I could so I'd have enough for extra training after I graduated. Geology degree."

"Dirt geology though," said Sheerluck. It used to be Sherlock but Sheerluck'll be the first to admit she's got more luck than sense.

"That's why I saved for extra training," Fry said. "I had to do the best I could with the tools available. You know how that is. All-a-youse know."

We did.

Fry had worked with some other JovOp crews before us, all of them mixed—two-steppers and sushi. I guess they all liked her and vice versa but she clicked right into place with us, which is pretty unusual for a biped and an all-octo crew. I liked her right away and that's saying something because it usually takes me a while to reso-nate even with sushi. I'm okay with featherless bipeds, I really am. Plenty of sushi—more than will admit to it—have a problem with the species just on general principle, but I've always been able to get along with them. Still, they aren't my fave flave to crew with out here. Training them is harder, and not because they're stupid. Two-steppers just aren't made for this. Not like sushi. But they keep on coming and most of them tough it out for at least one square dec. It's as beautiful out here as it is dangerous. I see a few outdoors almost every day, clumsy starfish in suits.

That's not counting the ones in the clinics and hospitals. Doctors, nurses, nurse-practitioners, technicians, physiotherapists, paramedics—they're all your standard featherless biped. It's the law. Fact: you can*not* legally practice any kind of medicine in any form other than basic human, not even if you're already a doctor, supposedly because all the equipment is made for two-steppers. Surgical instruments, operat-ing rooms, sterile garments, even rubber gloves—the fingers are too short and there aren't enough of them. Ha, ha, a little sushi humor. Maybe it's not that funny to you but fresh catch laugh themselves sick.

I don't know how many two-steppers in total go out for sushi in a year (Dirt or Jovian), let alone how their reasons graph, but we're all over the place out here and Census isn't in my orbit, so for all I know half a dozen two-steppers apply every eight decs. Stranger things have happened.

In the old days, when I turned, nobody did it unless they had to. Most often, it was either terminal illness or permanent physical disability as determined by the biped standard: i.e., conditions at sea level on the third planet out. Sometimes, how-ever, the disability was social, or more precisely, legal. Original Generation out here had convicts among the gimps, some on borrowed time.

Now, if you ask us, we say OG lasted six years but we're all supposed to use the Dirt calendar, even just to each other (everyone out here gets good at converting on the fly), which works out to a little over seventy by Dirt reckoning. The bipeds claim that's three generations not just one. We let them have that their way, too, because, damn can they argue. About *anything*. It's the way they're made. Bipeds are strictly binary, it's all they know: zero or one, yes or no, right or wrong.

But once you turn, that strictly binary thinking's the first thing to go, and fast. I never heard anyone say they miss it; I know I don't.

Anyway, I go see Fry in one of the Gossamer ring clinics. A whole wing is closed off, no one gets in unless they're on The List. If that isn't weird enough for you, there's a two-stepper in a uniform stuck to the floor, whose only job is checking The List. I'm wondering if I'm in the wrong station, but the two-stepper finds me on The List and I may go in and see La Soledad y Godmundsdottir. It takes me a second to get who she means. How'd our girl-thing get Fry out of that? I go through an airlock-style portal and there's another two-stepper waiting to escort me. He uses two poles with sticky tips to move himself along and he does all right but I can see this is a new skill. Every so often, he manoeuvres so one foot touches floor so he can feel more like he's walking.

When you've been sushi as long as I have, two-steppers are pretty transparent. I don't mean that as condescending as it sounds. After all, I was a two-stepper once myself. We all started out as featherless bipeds, none of us was born sushi. But a lot of us feel we were born to *be* sushi, a sentiment that doesn't go down too well with the two-steppers who run everything. Which doesn't make it any less true.

My pal the poler and I go a full radian before we get to another air-lock. "Through there," he says. "I'll take you back whenever you're ready."

I thank him and swim through, wondering what dim bulb thought he was a good idea, because he's what Aunt Chovie calls surplus to requirements. The few conduits off this tube are sealed and there's nothing to hide in or behind. I know Fry is so rich that she has to hire people to spend her money for her, but I'm thinking she should hire people smart enough to know the difference between spending and wasting.

There's our girl, stuck to the middle of a hospital bed almost as big as the ring-berg that put her in it. She's got a whole ward to herself—all the walls are folded back to make one big private room. There are some nurses down at the far end, sitting around sipping coffee bulbs. When they hear me come in, they start unsticking and reaching for things but I give them a full eight-OK—*Social call, I'm nobody, don't look busy on my account*—and they all settle down again.

Sitting up in her nest of pillows, Fry looks good, if a little undercooked. There's about three centimetres of new growth on her head and it must be itchy because she keeps scratching it. In spite of the incubator around her leg, she insists I give her a full hug, four by four, then pats a spot beside her. "Make yourself to home, Arkae."

"Isn't there a rule about visitors sitting on the bed?" I say, curling a couple of arms around a nearby hitching-post. It's got a fold-out seat for biped visitors. This place has everything.

"Yeah. The rule is, it's okay if I say it's okay. Check it—this bed's bigger than a lot of apartments I've had. The whole crew could have a picnic here. In fact, I wish they would." She droops a little. "How is everyone, really busy?"

I settle down. "There's always another lab to build or hardware to service or data to harvest," I say, careful, "if that's what you mean." The way her face flexes, I know it isn't.

"You're the only one who's come to see me," she says.

"Maybe the rest of the crew weren't on The List."

"What list?" she says. So I tell her. Her jaw drops and all at once, two nurses appear on either side of the bed, nervous as hell, asking if she's all right. "I'm fine, I'm fine," she snaps at them. "Go away, gimme some privacy, will you?"

They obey a bit reluctantly, eyeing me like they're not too sure about how safe she is with me squatting on the bedspread.

"Don't yell at *them*," I say after a bit. "Something bad happens to you, it's their fault. They're just taking care of you the best way they know how." I uncurl two arms, one to gesture at the general surroundings and the other to point at the incubator, where a quadjillion nanorectics are mending her leg from the marrow out, which, I can tell you from personal experience, *itches*. A *lot*. No doubt that's contributing to her less-than-sparkly disposition—what the hell can you do about itchy *bone marrow?*—and what I just told her doesn't help.

"I should have known," she fumes, scratching her head. "It's the people I work for."

That doesn't make sense. JovOp couldn't afford anything like this. "I think you're a little confused, honey," I say. "If we even *thought* JovOp had metal that heavy, it'd be Sushi Bastille Day, heads would—"

"No, these people are back in the Dirt. My image is licensed for advertising and entertainment," she says, "I thought there'd be less demand after I came out here—out of sight, out of mind, you know? But apparently the novelty of a beauty queen in space has yet to wear off."

"So you're still rich," I say. "Is that so bad?"

She makes a pain face. "Would you agree to an indefinite contract just to be rich? Even *this* rich?"

"You couldn't get rich on an indefinite contract," I say gently, "and no union's stupid enough to let anybody take one."

She thinks for a few seconds. "All right, how about this: did you ever think you owned something and then you found out it owned you?"

"*Oh . . .*" Now I get it. "Can they make you go back?"

"They're trying," Fry says. "A court order arrived last night, demanding I hit the Dirt as soon as I can travel. The docs amended it so *they* decide when it's safe, but that won't hold them off forever. You know any good lawyers? Out here?" she added.

"Well, yeah. Of course, they're all sushi."

Fry lit up. "Perfect."

Not every chambered Nautilus out here is a lawyer—the form is also a popular choice for librarians, researchers, and anyone else in a data-heavy line of work—but every lawyer in the Jovian system is a chambered Nautilus. It's not a legal restriction the way it is with bipeds and medicine, just something that took root and turned into tradition. According to Dove, who's a partner in the firm our union keeps on retainer, it's the sushi equivalent of powdered wigs and black robes, which we have actually seen out here from time to time when two-steppers from certain parts of the Dirt bring their own lawyers with them.

Dove says no matter how hard biped lawyers try to be professional, they all break out with some kind of weird around their sushi colleagues. The last time the union had to renegotiate terms with JovOp, the home office sent a canful of corporate lawyers out of the Dirt. Well, from Mars, actually, but they weren't Martian citizens and they went straight back to No. 3 afterwards. Dove wasn't involved but she kept us updated as much as she could without violating any regulations.

Dove's area is civil law and sushi rights, protecting our interests as citizens of the Jovian system. This includes not only sushi and sushi-in-transition but pre-ops as well. Any two-stepper who files a binding letter of intent for surgical conversion is legally sushi.

Pre-ops have all kinds of problems—angry relatives, *rich* angry relatives with injunctions from some Dirt supreme court, confused/troubled children, heartbroken parents and ex-spouses, lawsuits and contractual disputes. Dove handles all that and more: identity verification, transfer of money and property, biometric resets, as well as arranging mediation, psychological counselling (for anyone, including angry relatives), even religious guidance. Most bipeds would be surprised to know how many of those who go out for sushi find God, or something. Most of us, myself included, fall into the latter category but there are plenty of the organized religion persuasion. I guess you can't go through a change that drastic without discovering your spiritual side.

Fry wasn't officially a pre-op yet, but I knew Dove would be the best person she could talk to about what she'd be facing if she decided to go through with it. Dove is good at figuring out what two-steppers want to hear and then telling them what they need to hear in a way that makes them listen. I thought it was psychology but Dove says it's closer to linguistics.

As Sheerluck would say, don't ask me, I just lurk here.

The next day, I show up with Dove and List Checker looks like she's never seen anything like us before. She's got our names but she doesn't look too happy about it, which annoys me. List-checking isn't a job that requires any emotion from her.

"*You're* the attorney?" she says to Dove, who is eye-level with her, tentacles sedately furled.

"Scan me again if you need to," Dove says good-naturedly. "I'll wait. Mom always said, 'Measure twice, cut once.'"

List Checker can't decide what to do for a second or two, then scans us both again. "Yes, I have both your names here. It's just that—well, when she said an attorney, I was expecting—I thought you'd be . . . a . . . a . . ."

She hangs long enough to start twisting before Dove relents and says, "Biped." Dove still sounds good-natured but her tentacles are now undulating freely. "You're not from around here, are you?" she asks, syrupy-sweet, and I almost rupture not laughing.

"No," List Checker says in a small voice. "I've never been farther than Mars before."

"If the biped on the other side of that portal is equally provincial, better warn 'em." Then as we go through, Dove adds, "Too late!"

It's the same guy with the poles but when Dove sees him, she gives this crazy whooping yell and pushes right into his face so her tentacles are splayed out on his skin.

"You son of a bitch!" she says, really happy.

And then the Poler says, "Hiya, Mom."

"Oh. Kay," I say, addressing anyone in the universe who might be listening. "I'm thinking about a brain enema. Is now a good time?"

"Relax," Dove says. "'Hiya Mom' is what you say when anyone calls you a son of a bitch."

"Or 'Hiya, Dad,'" says Poler, "depending."

"Aw, you all look alike to me," Dove says. "It's a small universe, Arkae. Florian and I got taken hostage together once, back in my two-stepper days."

"Really?" I'm surprised as hell. Dove never talks about her biped life; hardly any of us do. And I've never heard of anyone running into someone they knew pre-sushi purely by chance.

"I was a little kid," Poler says. "Ten Dirt-years. Dove held my hand. Good thing I met her when she still had one."

"He was a creepy little kid," Dove says as we head for Fry's room. "I only did it so he wouldn't scare our captors into killing all of us."

Poler chuckles. "Then why you let me keep in touch with you after it was all over?"

"I thought if I could help you be less creepy, you wouldn't inspire any more hostage-taking. Safer for everybody."

I can't remember ever hearing about anyone still being friends with a biped from before they were sushi. I'm still trying to get my mind around it as we go through the second portal.

When Fry sees us, there's a fraction of a second when she looks startled before she smiles. Actually, it's more like horrified. Which makes *me* horrified. I told her I was bringing a sushi lawyer. Girl-thing never got hiccups before, not even with the jellies and that's saying something. Even when you know they're all AIs, jellies can take some getting used to no matter what shape you're in, two-stepper or sushi.

"Too wormy?" Dove says and furls her tentacles as she settles down on the bed a respectful distance from Fry.

"I'm sorry," Fry says, making the pain face. "I don't mean to be rude or bigoted—"

"Forget about it," Dove says. "Lizard brain's got no shame."

Dove's wormies bother her more than my suckers? I think, amazed. *Lizard brain's not too logical, either.*

"Arkae tells me you want to go out for sushi," Dove goes on chattily. "How much do you know about it?"

"I know it's a lot of surgery but I think I have enough money to cover most of it."

"Loan terms are extremely favorable. You could live well on that money and still make payments—"

"I'd like to cover as much of the cost as I can while my money's still liquid."

"You're worried about having your assets frozen?" Immediately Dove goes from chatty to brisk. "I can help you with that whether you turn or not. Just say I'm your lawyer, the verbal agreement's enough."

"But the money's back in the Dirt—"

"And *you're* here. It's all about where *you* are. I'll zap you the data on loans and surgical options—if you're like most people, you probably already have a form in mind but it doesn't hurt to know about all the—"

Fry held up a hand. "Um, Arkae? You mind if I talk to my new lawyer alone?"

My feelings are getting ready to be hurt when Dove says, "Of course she doesn't. Because she knows that the presence of a third party screws up that confidentiality thing. Right, Arkae?"

I feel stupid and relieved at the same time. Then I see Fry's face and I know there's more to it.

The following day the crew gets called up to weed and re-seed the Halo. Comet fever strikes again. We send Fry a silly cheer-up video to say we'll see her soon.

I personally think it's a waste of time sowing sensors in dust when we've already got eyes in the Main ring. Most of the sensors don't last as long as they're supposed to and the ones that do never tell us anything we don't already know. Weeding—picking up the dead sensors—is actually more interesting. When the dead sensors break down, they combine with the dust, taking on odd shapes and textures and even odder colorations. If something especially weird catches my eye, I'll ask to keep it. Usually, the answer's no. Recycling is the foundation of life out here—mass in, mass out; create, un-create, re-create, allathat. But once in a while, there's a surplus of something because nothing evens out exactly all the time, and I get to take a little good-luck charm home to my bunk.

We're almost at the Halo when the jellie tells us whichever crew seeded last time didn't weed out the dead ones. So much for mass in, mass out. We're all surprised; none of us ever got away with doing half a job. We have to hang in the jellie's belly high over the North Pole and scan the whole frigging Halo for materials markers. Which would be simple except a lot of what should be there isn't showing up. Fred makes us deep-scan three times but nothing shows on Metis and there's no sign that anything leaked into the Main ring.

"Musta all fell into the Big J," says Bait. He's watching the aurora flashing below us like he's hypnotized, which he probably is. Bait's got this thing about the polar hexagon anyway.

"But so many?" Splat says. "You know they're gonna say that's too many to be an accident."

"Do we know *why* the last crew didn't pick up the dead ones?" Aunt Chovie's already tensing up. If you tapped on her head, you'd hear high C-sharp.

"No," Fred says. "I don't even know which crew it was. Just that it wasn't us."

Dubonnet tells the jellie to ask. The jellie tells us it's put in a query but because it's not crucial, we'll have to wait.

"Frigging tube-worms," Splat growls, tentacles almost knotting up. "They do that to feel important."

"Tube worms are AIs, they don't feel," the jellie says with the AI serenity that can get so maddening so fast. "Like jellies."

Then Glynis speaks up: "Scan Big J."

"Too much interference," I say. "The storms—"

"Just humor me," says Glynis. "Unless you're in a hurry?"

The jellie takes us down to just above the middle of the Main ring and we prograde double-time. And son of a bitch—is this crazy or is this the new order?—we get some hits in the atmosphere.

But we shouldn't. It's not just the interference from the storms—Big J gravitates the hell out of anything it swallows. Long before I went out for sushi (and that was quite a while ago), they'd stopped sending probes into Jupiter's atmosphere. They didn't just hang in the clouds and none of them ever lasted long enough to reach liquid metallic hydrogen. Which means the sensors should just be atoms, markers crushed out of existence. They can't still be in the clouds unless something is keeping them there.

"That's gotta be a technical fault," Splat says. "Or something."

"Yeah, I'm motion sick, I lost the O," says Aunt Chovie, which is the current crew code for *Semaphore only*.

Bipeds have sign language and old-school semaphore with flags but octo-crew semaphore is something else entirely. Octo-sem changes as it goes, which means each crew speaks a different language, not only from each other, but also from one conversation to the next. It's not transcribable, either, not like spoken-word communication because it works by consensus. It's not completely uncrackable but even the best decryption AI can't do it in less than half a dec. Five days to decode a conversation isn't exactly efficient.

To be honest, I'm kinda surprised the two-steppers who run JovOp are still letting us get away with it. They're not what you'd call big champions of privacy, especially on the job. It's not just sushi, either—all their two-stepper employees, in the Dirt or all the way out here, are under total surveillance when they're on the clock. That's total as in a/v everywhere: offices, hallways, closets, and toilets. Bait says that's why JovOp two-steppers always look so grim—they're all holding it in till quitting time.

But I guess as long we get the job done, they don't care how we wiggle our tentacles at each other or what color we are when we do it. Besides, when you're on the job out here, you don't want to worry about who's watching you because they'd *better* be. You don't want to die in a bubble waiting for help that isn't coming because nobody caught the distress signal when your jellie blew out.

So anyway, we consider the missing matter and the markers we shouldn't have been picking up on in Big J's storm systems and we whittle it down to three possibilities: the previous crew returned to finish the job but someone forgot to enter it into the record; a bunch of scavengers blew through with a trawler and neutralized the markers so they can re-sell the raw materials; or some dwarf star at JovOp is seeding the clouds in hope of getting an even closer look at the Okeke-Hightower impact.

Number three is the stupidest idea—even if some of the sensors actually survive till Okeke-Hightower hits, they're in the wrong place, and the storms will scramble whatever data they pick up—so we all agree that's probably it. After a little more discussion, we decide not to let on and when JovOp asks where all the missing sensors are, we'll say we don't know. Because the Jupe's honest truth is, we don't.

We pick up whatever we can find, which takes two J-days, seed the Halo with new ones, and go home. I call over to the clinic to check how Fry's doing and find out if she managed to get the rest of the crew on The List so we can have that picnic on her big fat bed. But I get Dove, who tells me that our girl-thing is in surgery.

Dove says that, at Fry's own request, she's not allowed to tell anyone which sushi Fry's going out for, including us. I feel a little funny about that—until we get the first drone.

It's riding an in-out skeet, which can slip through a jellie double-wall without causing a blow-out. JovOp uses them to deliver messages they consider sensitive—whatever that means—and that's what we thought it was at first.

Then it lights up and we're looking at this image of a two-stepper dressed for broadcast. He's asking one question after another on a canned loop; in a panel on his right, instructions on how to record, pause, and playback are scrolling on repeat.

The jellie asks if we want to get rid of it. We toss the whole thing in the waste chute, skeet and all, and the jellie poops it out as a little ball of scrap, to become some scavenger's lucky find.

Later, Dubonnet files a report with JovOp about the unauthorized intrusion. JovOp gives him a receipt but no other response. We're all expecting a reprimand for failing to detect the skeet's rider before it got through. Doesn't happen.

"Somebody's drunk," Bait says. "Query it."

"No, don't," says Splat. "By the time they're sober, they'll have to cover it up or their job's down the chute. It never happened, everything's eight-by-eight."

"Until someone checks our records," Dubonnet says and tells the jellie to query, who assures him that's a wise thing to do. The jellie has been doing this sort of thing more often lately, making little comments. Personally, I like those little touches.

Splat, however, looks annoyed. "I was joking," he says, enunciating carefully. They can't touch you for joking no matter how tasteless, but it has to be clear. We laugh, just to be on the safe side, except for Aunt Chovie who says she doesn't think it was very funny because she can't laugh unless she really feels it. Some people are like that.

Dubonnet gets an answer within a few minutes. It's a form message in legalese but this gist is, *We heard you the first time, go now and sin no more.*

"They *all* can't be drunk," Fred says. "Can they?"

"Can't they?" says Sheerluck. "You guys have crewed with me long enough to know how fortune smiles on me and mine."

"Spoken like a member of the Church of The Four-Leaf Horseshoe," Glynis says.

Fred perks right up. "Is that that new casino on Europa?" he asks. Fred loves casinos. Not gambling, just casinos. The jellie offers to look it up for him.

"Synchronicity is a real thing, it's got *math*," Sheerluck is saying. Her color's starting to get a little bright; so is Glynis's. I'd rather they don't give each other ruby-red hell while we're all still in the jellie. "And the dictionary definition of serendipity is, 'Chance favors the prepared mind.'"

"*I'm* prepared to go home and log out, who's prepared to join me?" Dubonnet says before Glynis can sneer openly. I like Glynis, vinegar and all, but sometimes I think she should have been a crab instead of an octopus.

Our private quarters are supposed to have no surveillance except for the standard safety monitoring.

Yeah, we don't believe that for a nano-second. But if JovOp ever got caught in the act, the unions would eat them alive and poop out the bones to fertilize Europa's germ farms. So either they're even better at it than any of us can imagine or they're taking a calculated risk. Most sushi claim to believe the former; I'm in the latter camp. I mean, they watch us so much already, they've gotta want to look at something else for a change.

We share the typical octo-crew quarters—eight rooms around a large common area. When Fry was with us, we curtained off part of it for her but somehow she was always spilling out of it. Her stuff, I mean—we'd find underwear bobbing around in the lavabo, shoes orbiting a lamp (good thing she only needed two), live-paper flapping around the room in the air currents. All the time she'd spent out here and she still couldn't get the hang of housekeeping in zero gee. It's the sort of thing that stops being cute pretty quickly when you've got full occupancy, plus one. I could tell she was trying, but eventually we had to face the truth: much as we loved her, our resident girl-thing was a slob.

I thought that was gonna be a problem but she wasn't even gone a day before it felt like there was something missing. I'd look around expecting to see some item of clothing or jewellery cruising past, the latest escapee from one of her not-terribly-secure reticules.

"So who wants to bet that Fry goes octo?" Splat says when we get home.

"Who'd want to bet she doesn't?" replies Sheerluck.

"Not me," says Glynis, so sour I can feel it in my crop. I'm thinking she's going to start again with the crab act, pinch, pinch, pinch but she doesn't. Instead, she air-swims down to the grotto, sticks to the wall with two arms and folds the rest up so she's completely hidden. She misses our girl-thing and doesn't want to talk at the moment, but she also doesn't want to be completely alone, either. It's an octo thing—sometimes we want to be alone but not necessarily by ourselves.

Sheerluck joins me at the fridge and asks, "What do you think? Octo?"

"I dunno," I say, and I honestly don't. It never occurred to me to wonder but I'm not sure if that's because I took it for granted she would. I grab a bag of kribble.

Aunt Chovie notices and gives me those big serious eyes. "You can't just live on crunchy krill, Arkae."

"I've got a craving," I tell her.

"Me, too," says Bait. He tries to reach around from behind me and I knot him.

"Message from Dove," says Dubonnet just before we start wrestling and puts it on the big screen.

There's not actually much about Fry, except that she's coming along nicely with another dec to go before she's done. Although it's not clear to any of us whether that means Fry'll be *all* done and good to go, or if Dove's just referring to the surgery. Then we get distracted with all the rest of the stuff in the message.

It's full of clips from the Dirt, two-steppers talking about Fry like they all knew her and what it was like out here and what going out for sushi meant. Some two-steppers didn't seem to care much but some of them were stark spinning bugfuck.

I mean, it's been a great big while since I was a biped and we live so long out here that we tend to morph along with the times. The two-stepper I was couldn't get a handle on me as I am now. But then neither could the octo I was when I finished rehab and met my first crew.

I didn't choose octo—back then, surgery wasn't as advanced and nanorectics weren't as commonplace or as programmable so you got whatever the doctors thought gave you the best chance of a life worth living. I wasn't too happy at first but it's hard to be unhappy in a place this beautiful, especially when you feel so good physically all the time. It was somewhere between three and four J-years after I turned that people could finally choose what kind of sushi they went out for, but I got no regrets. Any more. I've got it smooth all over.

Only I don't feel too smooth listening to two-steppers chewing the air over things they don't know anything about and puking up words like *abominations*, *atrocities*, and *sub-human monsters*. One news program even runs clips from the most recent re-make of *The* Goddam *Island Of* Fucking *Dr. Moreau*. Like that's holy writ or something.

I can't stand more than a few minutes before I take my kribble into my bolthole, close the hatch, and hit sound-proof.

A little while later, Glynis beeps. "You know how way back in the extreme dead past, people in the Dirt thought everything in the universe revolved around them?" She pauses but I don't answer. "Then the scope of human knowledge expanded and we all know that was wrong."

"So?" I grunt.

"Not everybody got the memo," she says. She waits for me to say something. "Come on, Arkae—are *they* gonna get to see Okeke-Hightower?"

"I'd like to give them a ride on it," I say.

"None of them are gonna come out here with us abominations. They're all gonna cuddle up with each other in the Dirt and drown in each other's shit. Until they all do the one thing they were pooped into this universe to do, which is become extinct."

I open the door. "You're really baiting them, you know that?"

"Baiting who? There's nobody listening. Nobody here except us sushi," she says, managing to sound sour and utterly innocent both at the same time. Only Glynis.

I message Dove to say we'll be Down Under for at least two J-days, on loan to Outer-Comm. Population in the outer part of the system, especially around Saturn, has doubled in the last couple of J-years and will probably double again in less time. The civil communication network runs below the plane of the solar disk and it's completely dedicated—no governments, no military, just small business, entertainment, and social interaction. Well, so far, it's completely dedicated but nobody's in any position for a power grab yet.

OuterComm is an Ice Giants operation and originally it served only the Saturn, Uranus, and Neptune systems. No one seems to know exactly where the home office is—i.e. which moon. I figure even if they started off as far out as Uranus, they've probably been on Titan since they decided to expand to Jupiter.

Anyway, their technology is crazy-great. It still takes something over forty minutes for *Hello* to get from the Big J to Saturn and another forty till you hear, *Who the hell is this?* but you get less noise than a local call on JovOp. JovOp wasn't too happy when the entertainment services started migrating to OuterComm and things got kind of tense. Then they cut a deal: OuterComm got all the entertainment and stayed out of the education business, at least in the Jovian system. So everything's fine and JovOp loans them anything they need like a big old friendly neighbor but there's still plenty of potential for trouble. Of *all* kinds.

The Jovian system is the divide between the inner planets and the outer. We've had governments that tried to align with the innies and others that courted the outies. The current government wants the Big J officially designated as an outer world, not just an ally. Saturn's been fighting it, claiming that Big J wants to take over and build an empire.

Which is pretty much what Mars and Earth said when the last government was trying to get inner status. Earth was a little more colorful about it. There were two-steppers hollering that it was all a plot by monsters and abominations—i.e. us—to get our unholy limbs on fresh meat for our unholy appetites. If Big J got inner planet status, they said, people would be rounded up in the streets and shipped out to be changed into unnatural, subhuman creatures with no will of their own. Except for the most beautiful women, who would be kept as is and chained in brothels where—well, you get the idea.

That alone would be enough to make me vote outie, except the Big J is really neither outie nor innie. The way I see it, there's inner, there's outer, and there's us. Which doesn't fit the way two-steppers do things because it's not binary.

This was all sort of bubbling away at the back of my mind while we worked on the comm station but in an idle sort of way. I was also thinking about Fry, wondering how she was doing, and what shape she'd be in the next time I saw her. I wondered if I'd recognize her.

Now, that sounds kind of silly, I guess because you don't recognize someone that, for all intents and purposes, you've never seen before. But it's that spiritual thing. I had this idea that if I swam into a room full of sushi, all kinds of sushi, and Fry was there, I would know. And if I gave it a little time, I'd find her without anyone having to point her out.

No question, I loved Fry the two-stepper. Now that she was sushi, I wondered if I'd be in love with her. I couldn't decide whether I liked that idea or not. Normally I keep things simple: sex, and only with people I like. It keeps everything pretty smooth. But in love complicates everything. You start thinking about partnership and family. And that's not so smooth because we don't reproduce. We've got new sushi and fresh sushi, but no sushi kids.

We're still working on surviving out here but it won't always be that way. I could live long enough to see that. Hell, there are still a few OG around, although I've never met them. They're all out in the Ice Giants.

We're home half a dec before the first Okeke-Hightower impact, which sounds like plenty of time but it's close enough to make me nervous. Distances out here aren't safe, even in the best top-of-the-line JovOp can. I hate being in a can anyway. If anyone ever develops a jellie for long-distance travel, I'll be their best friend forever. But even in the can, we had to hit three oases going and coming to refuel. Filing a flight plan guaranteed us a berth at each one but only if we were on time. And there's all kinds of shit that could have made us late. If a berth was available we'd still get it. But if there wasn't, we'd have to wait and hope we didn't run out of stuff to breathe.

Bait worked the plan out far enough ahead to give us generous ETA windows. But you know how it is—just when you need everything to work the way it's supposed to, anything that hasn't gone wrong lately suddenly decides to make up for lost time. I was nervous all the way out, all through the job, and all the way back. The last night on the way back I dreamed that just as we were about to re-enter JovOp space, Io exploded and took out everything in half a radian. While we were trying to figure out what to do, something knocked us into a bad spiral that was gonna end dead center in Big Pink. I woke up with Aunt Chovie and Splat peeling me off the wall—*so* embarrassing. After that, all I wanted to do was go home, slip into a jellie, and watch Okeke-Hightower meet Big J.

By this time, the comet's actually in pieces. The local networks are all-comet news, all the time, like there's nothing else in the solar system or even the universe for that matter. The experts are saying it's following the same path as the old Shoemaker-Levy and there's a lot of chatter about what that means. There are those who don't think it's a coincidence and Okeke-Hightower is actually some kind of message from an intelligence out in the Oort cloud or even beyond, and instead of letting it crash into Big J, we ought to try catching it, or at least parts of it.

Yeah, that could happen. JovOp put out a blanket no-fly—jellies only, no cans. Sheerluck suggests JovOp's got a secret mission to grab some fragments but that's ridiculous. I mean, aside from the fact that any can capable of doing that would be plainly visible, the comet's been sailing around in pieces for over half a dozen square decs. There were easier places in the trajectory to get a piece but all the experts agreed the scans showed nothing in it worth the fortune it would cost to mount that kind of mission. Funny how so many people forgot about that; suddenly, they're all shoulda-woulda-coulda, like non-buyer's remorse. But don't get me started on politics.

I leave a message for Dove saying we're back and getting ready to watch the show. What comes back is an auto-reply saying she's out of the office, reply soonest. Maybe she's busy with Fry, who probably has comet fever like everyone else but maybe even more so, since this will be like the big moment that kicks off her new life. If she's not out of the hospital, I hope they've got a screen worthy of the event.

We all want to see it with our naked eyes. Well, our naked eyes and telescopes. Glynis is bringing a screen for anyone who wants a really close-up look. Considering the whole thing's gonna last about an hour start to finish, maybe that's not such a bad idea. It could save us some eyestrain.

When the first fragment hits, I find myself thinking about the sensors that fell into the atmosphere. They've got to be long gone by now and even if they're not, there's no way we could pick up any data. It would all be just noise.

Halfway through the impacts, the government overrides all the communication for a recorded, no-reply announcement: martial law's been declared, everybody go home. Anyone who doesn't is dust.

This means we miss the last few hits, which pisses us off even though we all agree it's not a sight worth dying for. But when we get home and can't even get an instant replay, we start wondering. Then we start ranting. The government's gonna have a lot of explaining to do and the next election ain't gonna be a love-fest and when did JovOp turn into a government lackey. There's nothing on the news—and I mean, *nothing*, it's all re-runs. Like this is actually two J-days ago and what just happened never happened.

"Okay," says Fred, "what's on OuterComm?"

"You want to watch soap operas?" Dubonnet fumes. "Sure, why not?"

We're looking at the menu when something new appears: it's called the Soledad y Gottmundsdottir Farewell Special. The name has me thinking we're about to see Fry in her old two-stepper incarnation but what comes up on the screen is a chambered Nautilus.

"Hi, everybody. How do you like the new me?" Fry says.

"What, is she going to law school?" Aunt Chovie says, shocked.

"I'm sorry to leave you a canned good-bye because you've all been so great," Fry goes on and I have to knot my arms together to keep from turning the thing off. This doesn't sound like it's gonna end well. "I knew even before I came out here that I'd be going out for sushi. I just couldn't decide what kind. You guys had me thinking seriously about octo—it's a pretty great life and everything you do matters. Future generations—well, it's going to be amazing out here. Life that adapted to space. Who knows, maybe someday Jovian citizens will change bodies like two-steppers change their clothes. It could happen.

"But like a lot of two-steppers, I'm impatient. I know, I'm not a two-stepper any-more and I've got a far longer lifespan now so I don't have to be impatient. But I am. I wanted to be part of something that's taking the next step—the next *big* step—right now. I really believe the Jupiter Colony is what I've been looking for."

"The Jupiter Colony? They're cranks! They're suicidal!" Glynis hits the ceiling, banks off a wall, and comes down again.

Fry unfurls her tentacles and lets them wave around freely. "Calm down, whoev-er's yelling," she says, sounding amused. "I made contact with them just before I crewed up with you. I knew what they were planning. They wouldn't tell me when, but it wasn't hard to figure out that the Okeke-Hightower impact was the perfect op-portunity. We've collected some jellies, muted them, and put in yak-yak loops. I don't know how the next part works, how we're going to hitch a ride with the comet—I'm not an astrophysicist. But if it works, we'll seed the clouds with ourselves.

"We're all chambered Nautiluses on this trip. It's the best form for packing a lot of data. But we've made one small change: we're linked together, shell-to-shell, so we all have access to each other's data. Not too private but we aren't going into exile as separate hermits. There should still be some sensors bobbing around in the upper levels—the Colony's had allies tossing various things in on the sly. We can use what-ever's there to build a cloud-borne colony.

"We don't know for sure it'll work. Maybe we'll all get gravitated to smithereens. But if we can fly long enough for the jellies to convert to parasails—the engineers fig-ured that out, don't ask me—we might figure out not only how to survive but thrive.

"Unfortunately, I won't be able to let you know. Not until we get around the in-terference problem. I don't know much about that, either, but if I last long enough, I'll learn.

"Dove says right now, you're all Down Under on loan to OuterComm. I'm going to send this message so it bounces around the Ice Giants for a while before it gets to you and with any luck, you'll find it not too long after we enter the atmosphere. I hope none of you are too mad at me. Or at least that you don't stay mad at me. It's not entirely impossible that we'll meet again some day. If we do, I'd like it to be as friends.

"Especially if the Jovian independence movement gets—" she laughs. "I was about to say, 'gets off the ground.' If the Jovian independence movement ever achieves a stable orbit—or something. I think it's a really good idea. Anyway, good bye for now.

"Oh, and Arkae?" Her tentacles undulate wildly. "I had no idea wormy would feel so good."

We just got that one play before the JCC blacked it out. The feds took us all in for questioning. Not surprising. But it wasn't just Big J feds—Dirt feds suddenly popped up out of nowhere, some of them in-person and some of them long-distance via comm units clamped to mobies. The latter is a big waste unless there's some benefit to having a conversation as slowly as possible. Because even a fed on Mars can't do anything about the speed of light—it's still gonna be at least an hour between the question and the answer, usually more.

The Dirt feds who were actually here were all working undercover, keeping an eye on things, and reporting whatever they heard or saw to HQ back in the Dirt. This didn't go down so well with most of us out here, even two-steppers. It became a real governmental crisis, mainly because no one in charge could get their stories straight. Some were denying any knowledge of Dirt spies, some were trying to spin it so it was all for our benefit, so we wouldn't lose any rights—don't ask me which ones, they didn't say. Conspiracy theories blossomed faster than anyone could keep track.

Finally, the ruling council resigned; the acting council replacing them till the next election are almost all sushi. That's a first.

It's still another dec and a half till the election. JovOp usually backs two-steppers but there are noticeably fewer political ads for bipeds this time around. I think even they can see the points on the trajectory.

A lot of sushi are already celebrating, talking about the changing face of government in the Jovian system. I'm not quite ready to party. I'm actually a little bit worried about us. We were born to be sushi but we weren't born sushi. We all started out as two-steppers and while we may have shed binary thinking, that doesn't mean we're completely enlightened. There's already some talk about how most of the candidates are chambered Nautiluses and there ought to be more octos or puffers or crabs. I don't like the sound of that but it's too late to make a break for the Colony now. Not that I would. Even if Fry and all her fellow colonists are surviving and thriving, I'm not ready to give up the life I have for a whole new world. We'll just have to see what happens.

Hey, I told you not to get me started on politics.

Holmes sherlock

ELEANOR ARNASON

A *HWARHATH* MYSTERY

Eleanor Arnason published her first novel, The Sword Smith, *in 1978, and followed it with novels such as* Daughter of the Bear King *and* To The Resurrection Station. *In 1991, she published her best-known novel, one of the strongest novels of the '90s, the critically acclaimed* A Woman of the Iron People, *a complex and substantial novel that won the prestigious James Tiptree Jr. Memorial Award. Her short fiction has appeared in* Asimov's Science Fiction, The Magazine of Fantasy & Science Fiction, Amazing, Orbit, Xanadu, *and elsewhere. Her most recent books are* Ring of Swords, Tomb of the Fathers, *and* Mammoths of the Great Plains. *Her story "Stellar Harvest" was a Hugo Finalist in 2000. She lives in St. Paul, Minnesota.*

Here, in one of her long-running series of stories about the alien hwarhath *people, part of the same sequence as* A Woman of the Iron People, *she gives us a story about an alien woman who becomes intrigued with a human fictional character—with intriguing results.*

There was a woman who fell in love with the stories about a human male named Holmes Sherlock. Her name was Amadi Kla, and she came from a town on the northeast coast of the Great Northern Continent. It became obvious, when she was a child, that she was gifted at learning. Her family sent her to a boarding school and then to college in the capital city. There she learned several languages, including English, and became a translator, working for a government department in the capital.

She did not translate military information, since that was done by *hwarhath* men in space. Nor did she translate technical information, since she lacked the requisite technical knowledge. Instead, she translated human fiction. "There is much to be learned from the stories people tell," the foremost woman in her department said. "If we are going to understand humans, and we must understand them since they are our enemies, then we need to study their stories."

The fiction came out of computers in captured human warships. At first the Department of Translation picked stories out of the human computers randomly. Most were as bad as the novels read by *hwarhath* young men and women. But it turned out that the humans made lists of important stories, so their young people would know the stories they ought to read. Once these lists were found, the Department began to pick out famous and well-considered works for translating.

The foremost woman said, "It may be possible to learn about a culture by reading trivial fiction. There are people who will argue that. But humans are not a trivial species. They are clearly dangerous, and we should not underestimate them. If we study their least important work, we will decide they are silly. No one who can blow apart a *hwarhath* warship is silly."

After nine years in the capital, Kla began to long for the steep mountains, fjords and fogs of her homeland. She requested permission to work from home.

"This is possible," the foremost woman said. "Though you will have to fly here several times a year for meetings."

Kla agreed, though she did not like to fly, and went home by coastal freighter.

Her hometown was named Amadi-Hewil. It stood at the end of a fjord, with mountains rising above it. Most of the people belonged to one of two lineages, Amadi or Hewil, though there were some members of neighboring lineages; the government kept a weather station on a cliff above the fjord. The two men who cared for the station were soldiers from another continent. Of course they were lovers, since there were no other men of their age in the town. Almost all young males went into space.

Most of the people in the town—women, girls, boys, old men and old women—lived off fishing. The cold ocean outside their fjord was full of great schools of silver and copper-colored fish, insulated with fat. There was a packing plant at the edge of the town, that froze the fish or put it in cans; smaller operations made specialty foods: dried seaweed and smoked or pickled marine animals.

The town had rental apartments and rooms for fishers whose family homes were farther in the mountains. Kla decided to take one of these, rather than move back into one of the Amadi houses. She had gotten used to living on her own.

Her room was furnished with a bed, a table and two chairs. There was a bathroom down the hall. She had a window that looked out on a narrow street that went steeply down toward the harbor. There were plenty of electrical inlets, which was always good. She could dock her computer and her two new lamps on any wall. A shelf along one side of the room gave her a place for books and recordings. She settled in and began to translate.

It was in this period that she discovered Holmes Sherlock. There was little crime in her town, mostly petty theft and drunken arguments. But there was plenty of fog, rain and freezing rain. The street lamps outside her window glowed through grayness; she could hear the clink and rattle of carts pulled by *tsina*, coming in from the country with loads of produce.

The human stories seemed to fit with her new life, which was also her childhood life. Much human fiction was disturbing, since it dealt with heterosexual love, a topic the *hwarhath* knew nothing about. Holmes Sherlock lived decently with a male friend, who might or might not be his lover. While the male friend, a doctor named Watson John, eventually took up with a woman, as humans were expected to, Holmes Sherlock remained indifferent to female humans.

The stories were puzzles, which Holmes Sherlock solved by reason. This appealed to Kla, who was not a romantic and who had to puzzle out the meaning of human stories, often so mysterious!

After a while, she went to a local craftsman and had a pipe made. It had a bent stem and a large bowl, like the pipe that Holmes Sherlock smoked in illustrations. She put a local herb into it, which produced an aromatic smoke that was calming when taken into the mouth.

Holmes Sherlock wore a famous hat. She did not have a copy of this made, since it looked silly, but she did take an illustration that showed his cape to a tailor. The tailor did not have the material called "tweed," but was able to make a fine cape for her out of a local wool that kept out rain and cold. Like Holmes Sherlock, Kla was tall and thin. Wearing her cape, she imagined she looked a bit like the famous human investigator.

For the rest, she continued to wear the local costume: pants, waterproof boots and a tunic with embroidery across the shoulders. This was worn by both women and men, though the embroidery patterns differed.

Twice a year she flew to the capital city and got new assignments. "You are translating too many of these stories about Holmes Sherlock," the foremost woman said. "Do it on your own time, if you must do it. I want stories that explain humanity. Therefore, I am giving you *Madame Bovary* and *The Journey to the West*."

Kla took these home, reading *Madame Bovary* on the long flight over winter plains and mountains. It was an unpleasant story about a woman trapped in a life she did not like. The woman—Bovary Emma—had a long-term mating contract with a male who was a dullard and incompetent doctor. This was something humans did. Rather than produce children decently through artificial insemination or, lacking that, through decent short-term mating contracts, they entered into heterosexual alliances that were supposed to last a lifetime. These were often unhappy, as might be expected. Men and women were not that much alike, and most alliances—even those of women with women and men with men—did not last a lifetime. The *hwarhath* knew this and expected love to last as long as it did.

Bored by her "husband," a word that meant the owner of a house, Bovary Emma tried to make herself happy through sexual liaisons with other human males and by spending money. This did not work. The men were unsatisfactory. The spending led to debt. In the end, Bovary Emma killed herself, using a nasty poison. Her "husband" lived a while longer and—being a fool with no ability to remake his life—was miserable.

A ridiculous novel! Everyone in it seemed to be a liar or a fool or both. How could humans enjoy something like this? Yes, there was suffering in life. Yes, there were people who behaved stupidly. But surely a story this long ought to remind the reader—somewhere, at least a bit—of good behavior, of people who met their obligations, were loyal to their kin and knew how to be happy.

Maybe the book could be seen as an argument against heterosexual love.

When Kla was most of the way home, she changed onto a seaplane, which landed in her native fjord and taxied to dock. The fishing fleet was out. She pulled her bag out of the plane and looked around at the fjord, lined by steep mountains and lit by slanting rays of sunlight. The air was cold and smelled of salt water and the fish plant.

Hah! It was fine to be back!

She translated *Madame Bovary* and sent it to the foremost woman via the planet's information net. Then she went on to *Journey*, an adventure story about a badly behaved stone monkey. But the monkey's crimes were not sexual, and it was obvious that he was a trickster, more good than bad, especially after he finished his journey. Unlike Bovary Emma, he had learned from experience. Kla enjoyed this translation, though the book was very long.

While she was still working on the monkey's story, she met a woman who lived on another floor of her rooming house. The woman was short and stocky with pale gray fur and almost colorless gray eyes. She was a member of the Hewil lineage, employed by the fishing fleet as a doctor. She didn't go out with the boats. Instead, sick and injured fishers came to her, and the fleet paid her fees. Like Kla, she preferred to live alone, rather than in one of her family's houses. She walked with a limp, due to a childhood injury, and she enjoyed reading.

They began to meet to discuss books. The doctor, whose name was Hewil Mel, had read some of Kla's translations.

"Though I don't much enjoy human stories. They are too strange, and I can't tell what the moral is."

"I'm not sure there is one," Kla said and described *Madame Bovary*.

"I will be certain to avoid that one," Doctor Mel said firmly. "Do you think your translation will be published?"

"No. It's too disturbing. Our scientists will read it and make up theories about human behavior. Let me tell you about the story I am translating now."

They were walking along the docks on a fine, clear afternoon. The fleet was in, creaking and jingling as the boats rocked amid small waves. Kla told the story of the monkey.

"What is a monkey?" asked Doctor Mel.

"An animal that is somehow related to humans, though it has fur—as humans do not—and lives in trees."

When she finished with the story, leaving out a lot, because the book really was very long, Doctor Mel said, "I hope that one is published in our language."

"I think it will be, though it will have to be shortened, and there are some parts that will have to be removed. For the most part, it is decent. Still, it seems that humans can never be one hundred percent decent. They are a strange species."

"They are all we have," Doctor Mel said.

This was true. No other intelligent species had been found. Why had the Goddess given the *hwarhath* only one companion species in the vast darkness and cold of interstellar space? Especially since humans was more like the *hwarhath* than anyone had ever expected and also unpleasantly different. Surely if two similar species were possible, then many unlike species ought to be possible, but these had not been found; and why was a species so like the *hwarhath* so disturbing? Kla had no answer. The Goddess was famous for her sense of humor.

In the end, Kla and the doctor became lovers and moved to a larger apartment in a building with a view of the fjord. When she had free time, Kla continued to translate stories about Holmes Sherlock and handed them around to relatives, with the permission of the foremost woman. Some stories were too dangerous to spread around, but these were mostly safe.

"People need to get used to human behavior," the foremost woman said. "But not all at once. Eh Matsehar has done a fine job of turning the plays of Shakespeare William into work that we can understand. Now we will give them a little more truth about humans, though only in your northern town. Be sure you get your copies back, after people have read them, and be sure to ask the people what they think. Are they interested or horrified? Do they want to meet humans or avoid them forever?"

When Kla and the doctor had been together almost a year, something disturbing happened in the town; and it happened to one of Kla's remote cousins. The girl had taken a rowboat out into the fjord late one afternoon. She did not come back. In the morning, people went looking for her. They found the rowboat floating in the fjord water, which was still and green and so clear that it was possible to look down and see schools of fish turning and darting. The rowboat was empty, its oars gone. People kept searching on that day and days following. But the girl's body did not turn up, though the oars did, floating in the water only a short distance away.

The girl was a good swimmer, but the fjord was cold. She could have gotten hypothermia and drowned. But why had she gone out so late in the afternoon? And how had a child from a town full of skilled sailors managed to fall out of a boat and been unable to get back in? Where was her body? It was possible that the ebbing tide had pulled it out into the ocean, but this was not likely. She ought to be in the fjord, and she ought to float to the surface.

All of this together was a mystery.

After twenty days or thereabouts, Kla's grandmother sent for her. Of course she went, climbing the steep street that led to the largest of the Amadi houses, which was on a hill above the town. The house went down in layers from the hilltop, connected by covered stairways. Kla climbed these to the topmost building. Her grandmother was there, on a terrace overlooking the town and fjord. The day was mild. Nonetheless, the old lady was wrapped in a heavy jacket and had a blanket over her knees. A table with a pot of tea stood next to her.

"Sit down," the grandmother said. "Pour tea for both of us."

Kla did.

"You still wear that absurd cape," the grandmother said.

"Yes."

"I have read some of your stories about the human investigator."

"Yes?" Kla said. "Did you like them?"

"They seemed alien." The grandmother sipped her tea, then said, "We have a mystery in our house."

Kla waited.

"The girl who vanished," her grandmother said after a moment. "People are saying she must have weighted herself down and jumped into the water deliberately. Otherwise, her body would have appeared by now. This is possible, I think. But we don't know why. She had no obvious reason. Her mother is grieving, but refuses to believe the girl is gone. I would like you to investigate this mystery."

"I am a translator, not an investigator."

"You have translated many stories about investigation. Surely you have learned something. We have no one else, unless we send to the regional government or the capital. I would like to keep whatever has happened private, in case it turns out to be shameful."

Kla considered, looking down at the green fjord, edged with mountains. Rays of sunlight shone down through broken clouds, making the water shine in spots. "I will have to talk to people in this house and look at the girl's computer."

"The girl erased all her files and overwrote them. We have not been able to recover anything. That is a reason to think she killed herself."

"Then she must have had a secret," Kla said.

"But what?" the grandmother said. "It's hard to keep secrets in a family or a small town."

Kla could not refuse. Her grandmother was asking, and the woman was an important matriarch. In addition, she wanted to see if she could solve a mystery. She tilted her head in agreement and finished her tea. "Tell the people in the house I will be asking questions."

"I will do that," the grandmother said. "The girl was only eighteen, not yet full grown, but she was clever and might have become an imposing woman. I want to know what happened."

Two days later, Kla went back to the house and questioned the women who had known the girl, whose name was—or had been—Nam.

A quiet girl, they told her. She had no close friends in the family or elsewhere. When she wasn't busy at household tasks or studying, she liked to walk in the mountains around the town. She always carried a camera and did fine landscape photography.

One aunt said, "I expected her to go to an art school in the capital. She had enough talent."

"Can I see her work?" Kla asked.

"Most is gone. It was on her computer. You know she erased it?"

"Yes."

"But some of us have photographs she gave us. I'll show you."

Kla followed the woman around the Amadi house. The photographs hung on walls in public and private rooms. They were indeed fine: long vistas of mountain valleys and the town's fjord, close-ups of rocks and low vegetation. The girl had potential. It was a pity she was gone.

Kla went home to her apartment and filled her pipe with herb, then smoked, looking out at the docks and the water beyond. When Doctor Mel came home from looking at a fisher with a bad fracture, Kla described her day.

"What will you do next?" Mel asked.

"Find out where the girl went on her walks. Do you want to come with me?"

"With my leg? I'm not going to limp through the countryside."

"Let's rent *tsina* and ride," Kla said.

They went the next day, which was mild though overcast. Now and then, they felt fine drops of rain. The *tsina* were docile animals, used to poor riders, which was good, since neither Kla nor the doctor was a practiced traveler-by-*tsina*.

They visited the town's outlying houses. Most were too far away to be reached by walking. Nonetheless, they contained relatives, Amadi or Hewil, though most of these were not fishers. Instead, they spent their days herding or tending gardens that lay in sheltered places, protected by stone walls. Some of these people remembered the girl. They had seen her walking along farm roads and climbing the hillsides. A shy lass, who barely spoke. She always carried a camera and took pictures of everything.

Some had photographs she had given them, fastened to the walls of herding huts:

favorite livestock, the mountains, the huts themselves. The girl did have an eye. Everything she photographed looked true and honest, as sharp as a good knife and balanced like a good boat that could ride out any storm.

"This is a loss," Doctor Mel said.

"Yes," Kla replied.

After several days of exploring the nearby country, they returned their *tsina* to the town stable and went home to their apartment. A fog rolled in at evening, hiding the fjord and the neighboring houses. Streetlights shone dimly. Sounds were muffled. Kla smoked her pipe.

"What next?" the doctor asked.

"There are paths going up the mountains above the fjord. No one lives up there, except the two soldiers at the weather station. We'll ask them about the girl."

"It's too steep for me," Doctor Mel said.

Kla tilted her head in agreement. "I'll go by myself."

The next day she did. The fog had lifted, but low clouds hid the mountain peaks. The fjord's water was as gray as steel. Kla took a staff and leaned on it as she climbed the narrow path that led to the station. Hah! It seemed perilous! Drop offs went abruptly down toward the gray water. Cliffs hung overhead, seeming ready to fall. She was a townswoman, a bit afraid of heights, though she came of mountain ancestry. Her gift was language and a curious mind.

The station was a prefab metal building, set against the cliff wall. Beyond it was a promontory overlooking the fjord. Equipment stood there, far more complicated than an ordinary weather station. Well, it was maintained by the military. Who could say what they were watching, even here on the safe home planet? No doubt important women knew what was going on here.

A soldier came out of the prefab building, a slim male with dark grey fur. He wore shorts and sandals and an open jacket.

Casual, thought Kla.

"Can I help you?" he asked.

She explained that she was looking for people who had met Amadi Nam, a shy girl who loved to photograph.

"No such person has been here," the soldier replied.

"Hah!" said Kla and looked at the magnificent view of the fjord beyond the equipment.

Now the second soldier appeared. He was the same height as the first male, but much broader with thick, white fur that was lightly spotted. He also wore shorts, but no jacket. His fur must be enough, even on this cool, damp day.

He agreed with the first man. The girl had never been to the station.

Kla thanked them and went back down the mountain. She arrived home at twilight. Lamps shone in the apartment windows. The electric heater in the main room was on. Doctor Mel had bought dinner, fish stew from a shop in town.

They ate, then Kla smoked, settled in a low chair close to the heater. Doctor Mel turned on her computer and watched a play on the world information net, her injured leg lifted up on a stool. Kla could hear music and cries of anger or joy. But the dialogue was a mumble, too soft to understand.

The play ended, and Doctor Mel turned the computer off. "Well?"

"I have a clue," answered Kla.

"You do?"

Kla knocked the dottle out of her pipe. "It is similar to the dog that made noise in the night time."

"What is a dog?"

"A domestic animal similar to a *sul*, though smaller and less ferocious. The humans use them to herd and guard, as we use *sulin*. In this case, in a story you have apparently not read, the dog did not make any noise."

"Kla, you are being irritating. What are you trying to say?"

"The dog did not do what was expected, and this was the clue that enabled Holmes Sherlock to solve the problem."

"You met a *sul* on the mountain?"

"I met two young men who said they never met my cousin, though she climbed every slope in the area and loved to photograph splendid vistas."

"They are lying?"

"Almost certainly."

"Why?"

"I have no idea."

Doctor Mel looked confused. "They belong to far-off lineages and have no relatives in town. Why would they become involved in something here? If Amadi Nam had been a boy, one might suspect a romance. But she was a girl, and the soldiers are lovers, as everyone knows."

"This is true," Kla replied. "But I am certain the soldiers are lying. I need to confront them."

Doctor Mel rose and went to pour two cups of *halin*. She gave one to Kla and settled back in her chair. "If they are telling the truth, they will think you are crazy and may tell people in town. You will have to endure joking. More important, if they are lying, then they are crazy and may be dangerous. I'd go with you, except for the climb."

"I'll go to my grandmother tomorrow and explain the situation. She will know what to do."

"Good," said Doctor Mel.

The next day was clear and cold. Ice rimmed puddles in the streets and made the street paving stones slippery. Kla could see her breath.

Her grandmother was inside, next to an old-fashioned brazier full of glowing coals.

"Help yourself to tea and pour a cup for me," the old lady said. "Then tell me what you have found."

Kla did as she was told. When she had finished her story, the matriarch said, "The soldiers must be confronted."

"My lover has suggested that they may be dangerous."

"Hardly likely. But this story is disturbing. Something unpleasant has happened." Her grandmother drank more tea. "I want to keep this in the family. I'll pick two of your cousins, large and solid fisher-women. They'll go with you up the mountain. Even if the soldiers are crazy, they will hardly do harm to three women, all larger than they are, though you are thin. The fishers will not be."

A day later, Kla went back up the weather station. It was another clear, cold day. The fjord sparkled like silver.

The two fisher-women were named Serit and Doda. Both were second cousins to Kla, and both were tall and broad, with big knives in their tunic belts. Serit carried a harpoon gun, and Doda had a club.

"Is that necessary?" Kla asked.

"Always be prepared," Serit replied in a deep, calm voice.

"The soldiers have been trained for war," Doda added. "But the war they were trained to fight is fought by ships in space. How can that help them here? We, by contrast, have struggled with many large and dangerous fish, while the fish thrashed on the decks of our boats. If the soldiers threaten us, though that does not seem likely, we will know what to do."

When they reached the station, both men came out.

"How can we help?" the dark soldier asked.

"We are certain Amadi Nam came here," Kla said. "Since you lied about this, we are going to search your building."

What did she hope to find? Some evidence that Nam had been there—a picture that had been printed out or her camera, full of pictures. People did not easily throw away Amadi Nam's work.

The dark soldier frowned. "This is a military installation. You can't examine our equipment or building until you get permission from the officers in front of us."

Serit lifted the harpoon gun. "This is not space, where your senior officers make decisions. This is our town, our country and our planet. Our senior women are in charge, and you are here on this mountain with their—and our—permission. If we want to know what you do in your building, we have the right."

"We will go in," Kla said.

"Women do not fight and kill," the dark soldier said, as if trying to reassure himself.

"What nonsense," Serit replied. "Doda and I fight large and dangerous fish and other sea animals."

"But not people," the dark soldier said.

"Of course not. We are fishers, and we are still young. But who decides which newborn children will live? Who gives death to those who have nothing left but suffering?"

"The old women," said the spotted soldier in a resigned tone.

"So," Serit continued in a tone of satisfaction. "Women can fight, and we are able to kill. We will go into this building."

Kla felt uneasy. As a rule, men and women did not interfere with each other's activities. If it had been up to her, she would have waited for the soldiers to consult their senior officers, though she suspected they were stalling. What did they have hidden which could be better hidden, if they had time?

But her grandmother had picked Serit and Doda. She must have known how aggressive they were.

The spotted soldier exhaled. "I will not fight women, Perin, even for you."

The dark soldier made the gesture that meant be quiet!

So, thought Kla, there was a secret. "I will go in and search. The two of you watch the soldiers."

Doda made the gesture of assent, and Serit tilted her head in agreement.

Kla entered the building. It was messy, as was to be expected, with two young men living alone, no senior officers near them. Unwashed dishes stood on tables. The beds were unmade. Kla saw no sign of the girl, even in the closets and under the beds. But there were pieces of paper tucked between one bed and the wall. She pulled them out, surprised that she had noticed them. Printouts of photographs. They showed the green fjord, the black and white surrounding mountains, and the dark soldier, Perin.

She took the printouts into sunlight. "What are these?"

"I took them," the spotted man said quickly.

This was almost certainly a lie. Kla knew Nam's work when she saw it. She gave the printouts to Doda and went back in the building, going through it a second time. An uncomfortable experience! She was a translator, not someone who poked around in other people's homes.

This time she found the girl, wedged into a low cabinet and folded over like the kind of scissors that bend back on themselves, the blade points touching the handles.

"Come out," said Kla.

"No," said the girl, her voice muffled.

"Don't be ridiculous," Kla replied. "I might not be able to get you out, but I have two large, strong fisher-women with me. They can easily pull you from that hole."

After a moment or two, the girl squeezed herself out, groaning as she did so. Once she was upright, Kla could see her clearly. A plump young woman with badly rumpled clothing and fur. She looked miserable and angry.

Kla gestured, and the girl followed her outside.

"Now," Kla said to the girl and the soldiers. "What is this about?"

The girl looked sullen. The soldiers looked more unhappy than before. No one spoke.

"Very well," Kla said. "We will all go to see my grandmother. If the girl has a jacket, get it."

The spotted soldier did.

"Put it on and pull the hood up," Kla said to the girl. "I don't want people to know you are alive, until Grandmother has made a decision."

The girl obeyed, and they all went down the mountain, Serit last, holding the harpoon gun ready.

Once again her grandmother sat by an old-fashioned brazier, though it was difficult to see the glow of the coals this time. The room was full of sunlight, coming in through east-facing windows. The red floor tiles shone, and it was easy to see the paintings on the walls: flowers and flying bugs.

Doda pushed the girl in front of the old woman, then pulled back her hood.

"Well," the old lady said. "You've had all of us worried, Nam." Then she glanced around at everyone. "Pull up chairs. I will hurt my neck, if I look up at you."

The men brought chairs from the walls and arranged them in front of the old woman.

"Sit!" Kla's grandmother said. "You found Nam at the weather station. That much is evident. But why was she there? Why was the boat left floating empty? And why was her computer erased?"

"I think the soldier with spots might tell us," Kla answered. "He seems to be the most reasonable of the three."

The man clasped his hands tightly together. "I know I am dead. May I tell this the way it happened?"

"Yes," said the grandmother. "But try to be brief. And tell me your name."

"I am Sharim Wirn."

"Go on."

"My lover always took walks. I did more of the work than he did, but willingly, out of love. Recently, he has taken longer walks, and I began to notice food was disappearing. I do the accounting. I knew how much food we bought and how much we usually ate." The man paused, glancing briefly at his comrade. "I thought he might have a new lover. But where had he found the man? And why would he feed him? It made no sense. So I followed Perin. He went to a cave in the mountains. I went inside after him, expecting to find Perin with another man. Instead, I found him with the girl, sitting by a little fire and sharing food. Not eating with her, that would be indecent, but giving her food from our supplies.

"I asked what this was about. At first he refused to speak. At last, he told me the story. He had met the girl during his walks. They both liked the mountains, and they were both solitary. The girl had no one to love, apparently, and Perin had only me. I was not enough." The soldier's voice was bitter. "They began by talking and ended by having sex."

The two fishers drew breath in sharply. Kla's grandmother hissed. Kla was too shocked to make a noise. Men and women had mated in the past, before artificial insemination, but only after their families had agreed to a breeding contract, and only to make children. Of course there had been perverts. But they were not common, and she had never expected to meet any. She certainly had not expected to have one in her family.

"Go on," the grandmother said, sounding angry.

"The girl became pregnant and came to Perin, insisting on his help," the spotted soldier went on. "He knew he would be told to kill himself, if this story became known. So he hid the girl, until I found them. I insisted on bringing her to our building. The cave was cold and damp. She would become sick. I was not willing to be responsible for the death of a woman, even one as foolish and selfish as this girl."

He lifted his head, glancing briefly at the old lady. "I know that I should have told my senior officers, but I loved Perin. I knew he would die for what he did, and it would be my fault for telling. I could not bear the idea of him dying."

"How could you love him after he had sex with a woman?" Serit asked.

The man looked down at his clasped hands. "I don't know. But it became obvious to me, after spending time with her, that the girl has the stronger will. I believe she seduced him; and then she entangled him with her plan."

This did not seem likely. Nam was only eighteen, two years away from adulthood.

Kla looked at the girl and saw her grim, determined, angry face.

"What plan?" asked the grandmother.

"She emptied her computer, so no one would know where she had been and what she photographed; and then she left evidence of her death—the boat, floating in the fjord, empty. Then she went to Perin and insisted on his help. He had no choice. If she told her family—you—what had happened, he would die. Or if not that—his family has influence—he would get a really bad assignment.

"She could not stay here in this town, because her family would discover what she'd done. And she could not travel while pregnant. A woman alone in that condition would arouse too much interest and concern. People would stop her and offer help or ask about her family. Where were they? Why was she alone?"

"You say that you love this man Perin, but now you tell this terrible story," Kla's grandmother said.

"There is no good ending," the spotted soldier replied. "If the girl gave birth, she would do it alone, with no one to help except Perin and me. Hah! That was frightening! If the child lived, what would happen to it? Children don't appear out of nowhere. They are the result of breeding contracts. They have families. No mother with a child is ever alone."

"This is true," Kla's grandmother said.

"It became apparent to me that the child would die, even if it was healthy. How else could Perin and the girl hide what they had done?" He paused and took a deep breath. "The girl said she would travel to the capital after the child was born. There are people there who live in the shadows and make a living in irregular ways. She planned to become one of those. She never spoke of the child.

"All the time, while this was happening, my love for Perin was wearing away. How could he be so stupid? It was obvious to me that the girl had the stronger will. He was acting the way he did out of weakness and fear of discovery. I would have told your family or my senior officers, except by this time I had gotten myself entangled. I was at fault. I would be told to kill myself, once this was known."

"True," said Kla's grandmother. She looked at Nam. "Well, child, why did you do this?"

"I love him," Nam said stubbornly, though Kla was not sure the girl meant it. How could love endure this mess?

"How can you?" the old lady asked. "He is male."

"I cannot change what I feel."

"Certainly you can."

"No," the girl replied.

"Tell them all to kill themselves," Serit put in. "They are disgusting."

The old woman looked at Kla. "You have studied human crimes. What is your advice?"

"Two suicides close together would cause talk," Kla replied. "Though we might say it was some kind of lovers' quarrel. But why would both commit suicide? No one was stopping their love. It would be a mystery. There would be talk and wondering and possibly an investigation by military. We don't want that.

"As for the girl, everyone thinks she is dead. But we would have to hide her body, if she killed herself. Otherwise, people would wonder where she had been before her death. And she is pregnant. That's another problem. If Sharim Wirn is right, the girl planned to kill the child or let it die. We have no reason to believe the child is defective. I am not comfortable doing what the mother planned to do."

"Yes." The grandmother leaned back in her chair and closed her eyes. "Be quiet, all of you. I need to think."

They sat, as sunlight moved across the floor and out of the room. Kla needed to pee and would have liked a cup or tea or *halin*. But she kept still.

At last, the grandmother opened her eyes. "The important thing is to keep this story secret. One solution would be for all three of you to die. But as Kla says, that might cause talk and wondering; and there is the problem of the child. So—" She gestured at the two soldiers. "You will volunteer for service in space, far out in the war zone, where you will not meet women. My family has relatives who are important in the military. They will make sure you get the assignments you desire.

"As for you, Nam, you will stay in this house until your child is born. You have a cousin who is pregnant now. We will say that she had twins. I am not comfortable with this, since I will be deceiving the lineage that provided semen for your cousin. But we do what we have to do; and I hope you are ashamed at the lies you are forcing your relatives to tell."

Kla looked at the girl. She did not show any evidence of shame.

"After the child is born—" the grandmother said. "I will give you two choices. Either you can stay here and study art on the world information net, or you can leave and go into the shadows. If you stay here, we will watch you for further signs of misbehavior. We cannot trust you, Nam. You have initiative, a strong will, no self-control and no sense of family obligation. This is a dangerous combination."

"I will go," Nam said.

The grandmother exhaled. "If you want to live in the shadows in the capital, fine! But don't tell anyone your family name."

"I won't," the girl said. "I despise all of you and this town."

"Why?" asked Kla, surprised.

"Look at you," the girl said. "In your silly cape, pretending to be a human."

"What harm does it do?" Kla asked.

"And you," the girl stared at Kla's grandmother. "Pretending that none of this happened, because you are afraid of gossip."

"Gossip can cause great harm," the old lady said.

"The world is changing," Nam said. "There are aliens in the sky! But your lives remain the same, full of fear and pretense."

"There are no aliens in the sky," Kla's grandmother said firmly. "The humans remain a long distance from our home system." She paused for a moment. "I hope your child has your gift for art, without your difficult personality. This has been an unpleasant conversation. I'm tired now. I want to take a nap. Everyone go."

"You stay in the house," Serit said to Nam. "We don't want anyone outside the family to know you are alive."

The girl made the gesture of assent, though she looked sullen.

Kla left the house with the soldiers. "Thank you," the spotted soldier said before they parted. "You said that our suicides would cause talk. For this reason, Perin and I will remain alive."

"Behave better in the future," Kla said.

The man showed his teeth in a brief smile. "We will have no chance to behave badly in a war zone." He glanced around at the mountains. "I will miss this country. But space may be safer."

The two men took off, walking rapidly. They kept well apart, as people do who have quarreled.

Kla went back to her apartment. It was late afternoon by now, and the sun was behind the mountains, though the light still touched the high peaks, streaked with a little snow. The fjord was still and gray.

Doctor Mel was in the main room, drinking tea. Kla sat down and told the story. Even though Mel belonged to another lineage, she was a doctor and knew how to keep secrets.

At the end, Mel said, "You have solved your mystery."

"It's an ugly story," Kla said. "I wish I still believed the girl had drowned."

"That is wrong," Mel said firmly. "Her life may be hard, but she still has a future. The dead have nothing." She refilled her cup and poured tea for Kla. "Most likely, she will give up her unnatural interest in men. If she does not—well, there are people in the shadows who know about contraceptives."

"There are?" Kla asked.

Mel grinned briefly. "You know more about crime in the ancient human city of London than you know about bad behavior here. Of course there are *hwarhath* who behave in ways we do not find acceptable; and of course these folk learn to deal with the consequences of their behavior. Doctors know this, though we rarely talk about it."

"In the stories I have translated, the solution to the puzzle is satisfying. The ending seems neat and finished, though—of course—I don't understand everything. Humans are alien, after all. I can translate their words, but not their minds. This ending does not satisfy," Kla said.

"How could it? Most likely the young men will be fine, once they are in a military unit with officers to watch them; and most likely the child will be fine, born in your grandmother's house and raised by members of your family. But the girl is an unsolved problem. Maybe she will decide to stay here and study photography. Her work is full of possibility."

"I don't believe she'll stay. She is angry, though I don't know why. Maybe it is shame. She said our lives are full of fear and pretense."

"We live with rules and obligations," Doctor Mel said. "Most of us fear what will happen if we break the rules; and we may—as in this case—pretend that a rule has not been broken, rather than deal with the idea of broken rules. Is this wrong? I don't think so. I would not like to live in chaos, without the net of kinship that holds us all, and without front-and-back relations. The girl may want more honesty. However, most of us want a comfortable life."

Mel paused, obviously thinking. "The girl is right about one thing. Our universe is changing in ways that people could not have imagined a century ago. Look at your job, translating human literature. It did not exist in the past. Now, through your work, we learn about Holmes Sherlock and the shadows of London, also that irritating woman who lived in her own shadow."

"Bovary Emma. That translation will never be released. It is too disturbing."

Mel smiled briefly. "See how we protect ourselves!"

"Rightly!"

Mel gave Kla a look of affectionate amusement, then continued her line of thought, like a *sul* following a scent. "There have always been people who feel constrained by our rules. Most stay in their families and are unhappy. Others leave, going into the shadows. Some are criminals. Others are outcasts or eccentrics. Doctors know about them, because we must watch everyone—even people who are difficult—for signs of illness. Public health requires that we treat everyone, even those we don't approve of.

"Is it possible to be happy in shadows? I think so. Holmes Sherlock was happy, though he lived outside a family and made his own rules, and so was Watson John, who was odd enough to enjoy living with Holmes Sherlock. The irritating woman—remind me of her name."

"Bovary Emma."

Doctor Mel tilted her head in thanks. "Was unhappy, but she does not sound—from your description—like a person able to live a difficult life. Or even an ordinary life."

"These are humans, and they are imaginary!"

"We can still learn from them. We can always learn from other people."

"Are you saying the girl might be happy, even among outcasts?" Kla asked.

"Happier than in her—your—family. I will give you a name. Please give it to Nam before she leaves home. It's a doctor in the capital city, a good woman who treats people in the shadows and collects art. She can help Nam get settled. If she likes Nam's work, she can find a dealer-in-art. A good photographer should not be wasted."

Kla looked at Mel with speculation. This woman she loved, who lived in a small town and treated the injuries of fishers, knew more about people than she did, although she had lived in the capital city and had been translating human novels for years. People were more difficult to understand than she had believed, even the people she loved. But Mel was right. A good photographer should not be wasted. Maybe this situation would work out. Best of all, the disturbing girl would be gone from Kla's life.

Doctor Mel got up and limped to the room's window. After a moment, Kla joined her. The street lamps were on, and lights shone on the fishing boats anchored by the docks. High up on the mountain, a gleam showed that the soldiers were home.

nightfall on the peak of eternal light

RICHARD A. LOVETT
AND WILLIAM GLEASON

Richard A. Lovett is a former law professor, astrophysics major, and Ph.D. economist turned science and science fiction writer. The author of forty-eight short stories, he is the winner of a record eight AnLab (reader's choice) awards from Analog *magazine, for which he also writes a popular series on how to write short fiction. He's written more than three thousand newspaper and magazine articles for such publications as* Science, Nature, NewScientist, Psychology Today, *and others, and is a distance-running coach whose trainees range from local competitors to Olympic Trials contenders. His short-story collection,* Phantom Sense & Other Stories, *was released in 2012 by Strange Wolf Press. Find him on the Web at www .richardalovett.com.*

William Gleason is a freelance editor, writer, and poet based in San Antonio, Texas. A relative newcomer to science fiction, he has sold five pieces to Analog *since 2008. When not writing fiction, he works for a company that develops test materials for grade schools and high schools. If parts of his fiction have a distinctly working-class feel, it's because he himself knows the process. "I'm the guy who starts in the mail room and works his way up," he says. Literally, in the case of his day job, in which he rose from the mail room to senior director of editing before going freelance.*

Here they combine forces to bring us a taut thriller about a man on the run from something so dangerous that he flees all the way to the Moon to escape it—which may turn out to be not anywhere far enough away.

I

Drew Zeigler was finally alone.

People, people, everywhere. That had been his life for so long he'd forgotten what alone was like. First Earth, then the spaceport, then the shuttle. People whose presence made his skin itch, like the emergency suit he'd been forced to wear for the last ten days.

The suit never let him forget what would happen should the shuttle hit a century-old chunk of space debris. The vision of it exploding from beneath his clothes like the swelling chest of Superman was a reminder he always needed to keep track of the nearest air tube, so he could plug in before it ran out. A mental itch to go with the physical.

The people were a different type of itch, one that made him feel not as though he were about to explode, but always on the brink of collapse. So many. Always there, always strangers. Everyone else was gone, always would be if he'd done things right. If nobody found the childhood friends who knew he'd once dreamed of space. If . . . too many ifs. Better just to keep his distance, hyper-vigilant for unknown faces in an unknown crowd.

It was impossible. But it had to be done. And it wasn't impossible. It was like running the 5,000 meters, back in college, before life launched the collapse that had landed him here, alone. Running—at least at the level that paid your tuition—isn't something you just do, like a kid on a playground. *Relax the arms. Lower the shoulders. Don't try too hard or you'll wind up working against yourself.* You get that so drilled into you that you can't run without self-monitoring. It was how you became good. No . . . how you went from good to the best you could be. A small difference but significant.

Now that he'd landed, he could at least get rid of one of the itches. From now on it was his decision when to wear the emergency suit, and in most of Luna C there wasn't much more risk of being caught in a blowout than of dying of botulism from a plasti-sealed meal. On the periphery . . . well that was his choice. Itch and be safe, or don't itch and maybe die. Here, a man could make his own choices.

But the people-itch? Could he let that go too?

I am Drew Zeigler. This is who I am, who I always will be. I am Drew Zeigler, and this is a new life.

After ten days of Velcro gloves and slippers, Drew had been looking forward to the pleasure of weight. But the Luna C grab plates felt peculiar, as though the simulated gravity was pulling him down through the center of his bones rather than weighting his body more evenly. Not to mention that you were under Earth-normal grav only when actually touching a plate. It felt like the Velcro slippers, only more so.

Customs was a formality. Nobody who'd not been pre-cleared made it aboard a shuttle. Still, getting through was a relief. *I am Drew Zeigler*, he told himself again. *I am on the Moon and I am a new man.*

The grab plates were for tourists. The locals avoided them. A macho thing, Drew had figured when he first heard about it. Like not carrying an umbrella in Seattle or never complaining about cold in Minnesota. Or maybe their muscles had simply atrophied to the point where full Earth gee was uncomfortable.

The guidebooks warned that walking the plates was a skill and cautioned against trying to move too quickly. Each had its own term for what could happen if you missed a plate. *Ceiling bait* was the most colorful although *Ping-Pong* also got the idea across. He'd wondered why they didn't just convert the plates to strips, or plate the entire corridor. Then he looked up the power requirements. Yowsa, as his no-longer-gramps would have said. It said something about the Moon's power economy that there were any of the things at all.

In the spaceport, in fact, there were three aisles of them, marching down one side of the corridor. One was too close for his natural gait, another too far apart. The third was just right. He was on the Yellow Brick Road to the city of the Three Bears.

He couldn't remember what happened to Goldilocks, but suddenly he felt an overwhelming need to act like a Loonie. He angled off the plates, stepped into native lunar grav . . . and launched the next step straight upward. Happily, he didn't bounce off the ceiling, though he did float for what seemed like forever, windmilling like an ice skater on a badly launched triple axel.

Everyone noticed, though most were polite enough to pretend they didn't. He might as well have painted *newby* across his forehead. When he finally came down, the next stride was more *bounce* than step and now he was indeed the off-balance skater, moments from crashing. He lunged for the nearest grab plate . . . only to regret it as the force yanked him into itself with a jerk.

Not exactly his most inconspicuous moment.

Collecting himself, he fiddled with the strap of his duffel bag while watching his fellow passengers. Some had been met by guides. Tourists, on short-term visas. Technically that was him too, but it wasn't who he needed to be. Others had been met with hugs, kisses. As they headed into the corridor, their strides were low—a slow-rhythmed, shuffling glide.

One of the early astronauts, he'd read, had been a cross-country skier who claimed skiing taught the best motion for low-gee. Since most tourists didn't come from Norway, it wasn't anything the guidebooks had latched onto. "Use the grab plates," was all they'd said. "You'll find them everywhere you need to go." But Drew didn't want to be a tourist, so he studied what the Loonies did. Cock the knee, dip low, then push backward, making sure the force drove you forward, not up. It worked on the grab plates, too, he discovered, though you needed to take three at a time. In fact, with the extra traction, leaping the plates should be the fastest means of locomotion. But nobody was doing it. "Don't run," was advice all the books agreed on.

Still, for a few glorious paces, he couldn't resist, zipping by everyone in the corridor, Terran or Loonie. Back home, life was a cocoon of don't-dos, but the Loonies really didn't care if you broke an ankle, so long as you could pay the bill. Which, unfortunately, he couldn't. The joy faded, and he slowed to a walk, alternating between practicing his Loonie glide and Terran plate-walk. He wasn't sure which he'd need, but he wanted to have both down pat.

Other than the gravity, the shuttleport might as well have been on Earth. A terminal full of uncomfortable-looking seats and a corridor leading to the real world. Underground, of course. Everything here was underground except the domes and some of the trains.

The nearest dome was a transit hub, a full klick away. From there, you could catch the rail to Luna C's central domes. But for the moment, there was only the corridor. No carts or moving walkways. If you couldn't walk a klick, you weren't fit enough to ride the shuttle anyway.

Everything was purely utilitarian. *Airport ordinaire a' la neglect.* Winnemucca, Nevada, not Heathrow or O'Hare.

The transit hub was more of the same, as was the train. Only the fare was out of the ordinary: thirty-five credits—the first dent in finances never designed for this adventure. Drew would have preferred to walk, but the spaceport was a dozen klicks from the rest of Luna C. Nothing like living in a vacuum to make you leery of things falling out of the sky.

But the dome his thirty-five-credit train ride eventually spilled him into—that was a different matter. It was as though he'd stumbled from Winnemucca into Universal City or the Mall of the Arctic. Or maybe Las Vegas. He was at the edge of a plaza, several hundred meters across, limned by storefronts and cafes with the jingling of slot machines beckoning from the center. Many tourists never made it farther than this dome, though why people would travel so far to lose their money here rather than on Earth, he'd never understood . . . until he looked up.

The guidebooks had given him facts. Now the Skyview pulled at his vision the same way the grab plates pulled at his feet.

Windows were rare on Luna C. The transparent nanoweave that made large ones possible wasn't cheap. But the city planners had decided that if they were going to do it, they were going to do it right. And the Skyview was the rightest of the right.

Beginning just behind the shops, the windows—there were four of them— blossomed like tulip petals, spreading wide, then returning to an apex two hundred meters above. It was like being inside a giant puffball—with windows.

On the shuttle there was always one set of windows pointed toward Earth, another shuttered against the Sun. From here, only klicks from the Moon's south pole, the Sun was never visible. Nor was the Earth. Outside was permanent shadow, colder than the nitrogen snows of Pluto. Inside was light, warmth, food, and frenetic fun. Above was endless night, the stars hard, diamond-bright, and oddly renewing.

Drew wasn't sure he had a soul. But the view, more than anything else, told him the past was a memory. Earth was gone, the life ahead new.

If he would be allowed to live it.

He ducked into a kiosk and bought a download, then treated himself to a sandwich and the cheapest beer available. There were too many people here—not as tightly packed as on the shuttle, but still too many—and as he scanned the want ads he also found himself looking for exits.

Always know your lines of escape; that rule had become so engrained it was like monitoring his running form in college. It was something you automatically did, like old Wild Bill Hickock's rule of never sitting with his back to a door because if you do, they'll wind up naming aces and eights for you as the dead-man's hand. Only in Drew's case, it would be ham-and-provolone on rye. And how the hell do you keep your back to the wall in a damn dome, where corridors, storefronts, and store*backs* spilled in all directions like goddamn tentacles?

He forced himself to take a deep breath and close his eyes, imagining he was back in college, an hour from the start of a big race, high on adrenaline that would do no good until needed. Slow your breathing, hear your pulse, take control and feel your heart rate reduce—that was the trick.

When he did open his eyes again, it was to look upward, at the stars. Earth was gone. The life ahead was new.

If he would allow himself to live it.

In theory he had four weeks to find a job before his visa expired. In practice he was going to need one sooner than that.

He studied the download, trying to ignore the activity swirling around him. He didn't know this place well enough to spot a threat, anyway. The job listings weren't laden with options but there were glimmers. Would retail pay enough for provisional residency? What about a temp agency? Could that lead to something permanent, soon enough? And what the hell was a sun harvester?

Too late to find out today. What he needed now was a safe place to sleep. Preferably cheap.

The Overway to Central was clearly marked, as were the routes to a half-dozen other domes. Anyplace would be cheaper than here and the trains weren't the only way around. Most of the central domes were only a klick or two apart, separated by underground passages, some of which would have grab plates. Even the richest tourists didn't always take the train.

Maybe one of the tentacles that had so frightened him before would offer a hidey-hole for a quick nap. Maybe he could grab a snooze on one of the benches beneath the Skyview.

He chewed the last of his sandwich, looking for a recycler for the wrapper. It was still too early for sleep. Better to do some exploring. He'd once been an athlete. He could walk.

II

Artemis Razo was drinking coffee, watching vids of the afternoon shuttle spitting out its occupants.

Most were tourists: rich, young, and trying to don that been-there/done-that look that said being here was no big deal. Although there were always a few who hadn't believed the warnings about synth-gee or thought they were too tough for spacesick meds. Part of being young and rich, he supposed, especially if you were male. Once he'd been full of young testosterone, but that was a long time ago and it had gone elsewhere, along with a lot of other things.

One idiot was trying to run the plates. Raz had seen that before, too. Maybe this one wouldn't wind up in an emergency room. He should care, but that too had gone with the years. The guy had the right to break his bones if that was what he wanted.

But there were always a few who were different. Rich and young, yes, but trouble in Luna C's more permissive clubs. Low gee and alcohol were a poor combination for the uninitiated. If you threw in a world where most people worked hard and blew steam even harder—well, it sometimes gave Raz more reasons than he wished for wanting to blow steam himself at shift's end.

Then there were the dreamers, hoping to find places on the Moon before their visas expired. Raz had seen these a thousand times, too. Even in the low-quality vid, you could sometimes see it in their eyes. They wanted this place too much— enough that not getting it would crush them. Twenty years before, that had been him, though in his case it had been getting the dream that had crushed him. Still, for years he'd been sympathetic to other wannabes. But that too was long ago.

This one's name was Fidel Franko. Son of a strip-mall mogul from Philadelphia. A lot of F sounds there. Why do parents do that to their kids, he wondered, then flicked off the image.

Unless they had jobs lined up in advance, most wannabes failed. He couldn't let himself care. Better to just wish the guy luck in a vague sort of way—about as personal as how, as a child in South Jersey, he'd wished well to the frogs that every spring insisted on trying to hop across the highway. Some made it. Most didn't. That's the way it was, always would be. Every spring, the frogs would hop. Statistically, not a good bet, but enough would make it to ensure there were always more frogs.

The last Raz had heard, Jenn was still in Perth. That's where she'd gone when her visa ran out, taking his unborn baby with her. They'd not known she was pregnant until they got here, and for her, pregnancy and low-gee were an even worse mix than low-gee and alcohol. Nobody would hire her, throwing up all the time.

He'd thought that once he got established, he could bring her and the child back up. But Loonie immigration was a lot less permissive than its clubs. Had he and Jenn been married when they left Earth, it might have been possible. As it was, she'd had the same one-time shot as anyone else. It was a game of chance with much bigger stakes than any in the casinos, and she'd lost. She could come as a tourist as often as she wanted, but there were no second chances on immigration. Raz could have gone back and joined her once he'd figured that out. But he hadn't. And in a dark recess of his mind, he wondered if he'd have done the same even if he'd known from the start.

His com buzzed.

"I'm on site, boss," came the hoarse voice of Officer McHaddon.

McHaddon's natural tone was a soft tenor—an embarrassment to an increasingly paunchy man who thought it undercut his authority. For the past three loons, McHaddon had been trying to intensify his tone. Overcompensation? Raz wasn't about to ask. All he knew was it didn't have the desired effect. The man now sounded like perpetual laryngitis.

How long had McHaddon been on the force? At least since Jenn's final disappearance, when she told him it was better if his daughter thought her father dead than unreachably distant, and he'd realized no amount of guilt would ever return him to Earth.

McHaddon's voice was unusually raspy. Maybe he'd been up all night. "The plates are still there," he said, "but we've got about ten meters of corridor in Luna gee, right off the Skyview. Looks like somebody crowbarred the plates up, snapped the wires, and put 'em back. Luckily, no one was seriously hurt. Just a few bruises, plus some folks threatening to sue you, me, the city, whatever. You want for me to call City Services?"

"I already did." Raz sighed. "Sounds like kids. Use your discretion."

Sometimes the worst thing you could do to a juvenile was throw the book at him. Raz had always wished he could thank the cop who'd remembered that when he was sixteen and set him on the path that got him away from his mother and her boyfriends and eventually to a fresh start. Except . . . the fresh start had come at such a price. Why hadn't he and Jenn been more careful? What would have happened had he gone back? A lifetime of resentment? Or just a different lifetime? Damn that wannabe. Raz might not want to care anymore, but even the effort of not-caring stirred up memories.

Luckily he'd put McHaddon on voice only. Or maybe it wasn't luck. It wasn't like he hadn't been feeling this way more and more often of late. Not the type of thing you want your subordinates to see.

He reached again for his coffee. There were days when he might as well mainline the stuff the way his mother and her boyfriends did the crackerjack. "But if it's some drunk tourist, I want him out of my domes." The coffee was cold. He drank it anyway. "Even if you have to put him in an emergency suit and roll him out an airlock."

"Got it, boss."

"Emergency suit optional."

McHaddon's laugh forgot to sound tough. "We all know you're the baddest of badasses."

Despite himself, Raz smiled. "Someday, someone's going to push me too far. Just wait."

Another laugh. "Whatever you say."

That was the trouble with the Moon. Everyone knew you too well. Or thought they did. Nobody knew about the crackerjack. Or Jenn.

The security vid was still playing. Raz reached for the off button, just as a cough at his office door announced he wasn't alone.

Caeli Booker was leaning against the doorframe as if she owned it. Which, on occasions, it almost seemed she had. Tall, with frizzy red hair, green eyes, and a pale, oval face flirting on the border between pleasant and pretty, she was an imposing enough figure she usually got what she wanted—and a frequent enough visitor that none of his subordinates was going to challenge her.

With a twitch of Earther-strong shoulders she shoved herself upright, walked in, and settled into the visitor's chair. "You ever miss an offloading?"

He wasn't sure if she'd detected his mood but she always brightened his day. "Not when you're flying. Gotta keep you out of trouble."

"Or in it?"

The green eyes sparkled and Raz had to fight to hold back his own smile. "I've never done that."

"Yeah, right."

"Those seeds were a controlled substance!"

"If you're a flower pot. They weren't opium poppies for God's sake!" When she smiled her face definitely kicked over the border into pretty.

"And probably allergenic as hell." The seeds were how they'd met. "The council would have had my ass if the Vantage Vista had been stupid enough to plant them. You finally going to tell me how you got them through?"

The grin was pure wolf. "Gal's gotta have her secrets."

Then the smile slipped, revealing a trace of something that lasted just long enough for him to realize she might have other secrets. Like him and Jenn. Him and the baby—Lily, who would never know him. In space, everyone had something. Some talked. Most didn't.

Then the deeper glimpse was gone as quickly as it had come. Caeli glanced over her shoulder, leaned in conspiratorially. "Oh, hell. I just walked through with them. Called 'em baking supplies. You know, for muffins."

Raz knew more than he wanted about hiding from deeper truths. Light conversation was safer. Flirting better yet. "That's a damn lot of muffins!"

"And who the hell thinks flowers are toxic waste? Though I guess I wouldn't have planted 'em on my shuttle. Had a damn cigarette smoker a couple of runs ago. And I have no idea how she got *those* through customs."

"So, how long you up for?"

"Twenty-five days, can you believe it? Nearly a whole loon of sleep and R'n'R. But first, I wanted to tell you I think you've got a gwipp."

"A what?"

"Gwipp. G-W-I-P-P. Government Witness in Personal Protection."

"You made that up."

"Yeah. Sounds good, though, doesn't it?" She leaned close, for real this time. "I'm trusting you, okay. If I'm right, I wasn't supposed to figure it out."

"Got it." His tone startled him. It didn't matter that he didn't know her story. "What can you tell me?"

"Not much, specifically. I've got a friend at the other end. Someone in Immigration who has been known to . . . imbibe. She told me that putting together the passenger list was odd. Said they weren't allowed to do more than standard checks." She cocked her head, looking for words. "Usually they pick a few passengers at random and work like hell to dig up skeletons."

Lily. Everyone had them. Immigration might not care, but nobody wanted them found.

"Anyway, she told me the order seemed to come from very high up. Said she'd never seen anything like it. A gwipp's the only thing I can think of."

"Any idea who?"

"Nope. Those folks don't just get a new past, right? They get plastic surgery, bodywork. I bet they can make a twenty-year-old look fifty. I wish they could do it vice versa."

"You're nowhere close to fifty."

She laughed. "How do you know? Maybe I'm not really me and I'm a hundred-year-old crone from . . . where is it they live practically forever? Moldavia?"

"Yeah, with the legs of"—he tried to think of the latest vid phenom, but came up blank. At first, he'd ignored them all because they reminded him of Jenn. Then he was out of the habit.

She leaned back, crossing said legs for his inspection.

They'd played this type of game before but suddenly he was uncomfortable. "Maybe it was the Lebdekov assassination."

"No way!" Caeli uncrossed her legs and leaned forward, the debater returning. "Whoever that was is long gone or dead! More likely some refugee from the mob crackdown in Philadelphia."

That was interesting. Could it be that easy? McHaddon would probably have the grab-plate vandals within the hour. Would the Feds leave such an obvious trail?

Meanwhile, Caeli needed her rest. "Thanks," he said. "You're the best."

She leaned forward again, but instead of a peck on the cheek deposited the barest touch, right on the lips. "Be good to yourself," she said. Then, before he could react, she turned to go, auburn mane blazing in a halo of backlight.

III

He called himself Beau Guest. He liked it when people laughed. As far as he knew, no one knew his real name. Sometimes he'd been the one to make sure they could no longer remember it.

This assignment was lucrative but a bitch. If the intel was right, the hare had gone to the Moon: a move both stupid and smart. The smart part was that Luna-Shuttle security was as tight as it got. So, once the hare made it off Earth, it had reason to feel safe. Not to mention that here, even the cops didn't carry guns. Earth might never figure out gun control but the Loonies knew bullets and vacuum made a bad combo. In the domes, there could be no clean kill from afar.

On the stupid side, there were plenty of other ways to kill. And if you had enough money, you didn't need to deal with shuttle security. All you needed was a spacesuit, a private launch, and a willingness to hike. And then, the target would have nowhere to run.

IV

Finding a place to sleep proved harder than expected. Eventually, Drew wound up back in the Skyview, where dimming lights heralded the official sleep shift. Not that it seemed to matter to the bars and slots.

Above, the view was grander than ever, the stars simultaneously closer and more remote. For the first time he noted that there was more to the view than the sky. By climbing to the Overway platform, he was able to see the lights of Luna C's other domes—bright curves rising above the regolith. And not everything else was dark. High on the crater rim, sunlight etched brilliance—a wire-thin slice of heat and light that would always be up there, never down here. Higher yet, set back far enough from the rim to be barely visible from this angle, dark rectangles rose on enormous stilts: power panels for grab plates, casinos, dome lights, farming, and everything else.

Then fatigue hit and the awe faded. He needed a place to sleep. But he wasn't sure what would happen if he tried to duck into a side passage. Would cameras bring police to roust him out? Would Loonie derelicts roll him for what little cash he had?

Anger at his handlers helped wake him up. All he needed was a bit more money. As a kid, wanting to get as far from the things he'd been born to as possible, he'd dreamed of space. And now, if he was going to do this, then by hell, space was where it was going to be. But he'd been too confused to think of that, back when he'd turned traitor to all he'd been born to protect. And now, while they'd reluctantly agreed to let him try, they'd insisted it be as the person they'd already created.

Drew Zeigler barely had the assets to get to the Moon. He certainly wasn't going to be able to live in luxury.

He studied the hotels, eventually picking the Grand Eclipse. Back home, its twenty stories would have been minimal, but in the Skyview, it rose halfway to the stars.

Getting into the hotel was easy. Drew slipped through as a guest was leaving, found a stairwell, and started climbing. At this hour, most floors were quiet, although one echoed with voices and clattering dishes. Up was high-rent territory. Lower was cheaper. Eventually, he found a dark corner, hugged his duffel to his chest, and dropped asleep.

After what seemed like only an instant, he was awakened by voices.

—"I dunno. A guest . . . ?"

—"Or a drunk Loonie Too. Didn't the BelleView get one last week? Maybe we ought to ask Erin."

A door closed and Drew was up like a shot. Down, he headed. Down and out. But on the second floor he spotted a men's room, and moments later was inside. Time to get back to the plan. Clean up, get out of the hotel, start calling about jobs.

Using hand soap, he washed his hair and face over a miserly spigot of slow-falling water. At long last, he peeled off his emergency suit, sponging off as best he could. He stuffed the suit into his duffel, found a semi-clean shirt, and tried to assume the guise of a tourist. But it was only once he was outside the building that he again breathed normally.

The light was still dim. He glanced at his watch but couldn't remember when he'd bedded down. Four hours ago? It would have to be enough. His stomach growled, so he bought a candy bar along with the latest download from a sleepy-eyed clerk who assured him his shop wasn't hiring.

Job. Any job. He needed a job.

There was a bank of public coms on the far side of the dome. Calling up the news holo before him, he headed that way to wait for the start of the business day.

Seven hours, no food, and twenty-eight calls later, he was talking to a male voice—no holo—at SEA Technologies, which was seeking a "solar-panel maintenance technician, EDA experience preferred." He had no idea what SEA was—much less EDA—but he was running out of prospects.

"Yeah, the job's still open," the man said. "You've got to come in, fill out an app, then interview. You got experience?"

"No. But—"

"Well, come in anyway. Luna II, west side, third tier, room 312. Got that?"

"Yeah, but—"

"Okay, then." And the line was dead.

Luna II snuggled in the bottom of a secondary crater that broke the main rim's symmetry like a giant divot. It wasn't all that far away, but it was a long way up, which meant Drew had no option but to splurge on rail fair on a train whose backward-facing seats tilted at a forty-degree angle that only made sense when it started to climb. It moved at a decent clip, however, and he reached Luna II still in early afternoon, hoping his quick follow-up would show sincerity. Only then did he realize he hadn't had a real bath since leaving Earth orbit. But didn't that also show sincerity?

"Hi," he said to an impressively tattooed and nose-ringed man behind a metal counter. "I called about the job."

Nose Ring motioned to a com station. He appeared to be in his mid-fifties. "Fill out the app and hit 'send.'"

This was probably the best chance Drew would ever get. Everyone else had turned him down cold. *Earther. Nah. Why you when we got plenty of locals? But good luck elsewhere.* As if any of them really meant it. None of the others had even suggested he show up in person.

But the form was full of potential traps.

Name? No problem. Immigration number? Easy.

El Paso would stand scrutiny as place of birth and he could answer questions about it, even though he'd never been there. Desert. Yucky rock mountains. A good place to leave, even if the university did have history as a track powerhouse. Though on his official resume, he'd never been an athlete. Next question?

That was the problem. His official employment history was an eclectic mix, mostly designed to make him marginally employable in anything other than the fields in which he was actually qualified, the theory being that anyone chasing him would think he'd be stupid enough to still bill himself as a CPA/lawyer. Why couldn't he have been *either* a CPA or a lawyer? And what the hell use, here on the Moon, was a stint as a taxi driver? Though he had to admit the Moon hadn't been where they'd wanted to send him.

But that was just the beginning. There were also questions he had no idea what they meant. What the hell was photovoltaic rehab technology? Eventually, he said a prayer to a God who might or might not be in the answering mood and figured he'd done the best he could. If experience in photovoltaic rehab technology was critical, he was screwed. At least he now knew that EDA was exta-domal activity. That wasn't on his resume, either.

"You have to list an address," Nose Ring said a moment later. During the twenty minutes Drew had been struggling with the form, the man had been busy with a computer, but, Drew realized, the com had never buzzed. What kind of job had he just applied for that nobody wanted?

"I, uh, don't have one."

The man studied his screen.

"I'm on a tourist visa." Drew hesitated, then poured out his cover story, which involved the recent deaths of his father, a brother, and what seemed like half his extended family. "So you can see I'm very motivated. Your ad said experience preferred, not required. I'm a fast learner and I need a new life."

The man hesitated. "Okay, kid."

Drew started to object that at thirty-six he was nobody's "kid" but thought better. *Surgery*, he reminded himself.

"Show up at 0730 tomorrow and we'll start your training. Show up at 0731 and you're on the shuttle back to Earth. We'll know soon enough if you can hack it. On the pel, it's my rules, or no rules. Leave now if you can't take it."

"The pel?"

"You really are desperate, aren't you?"

Drew hesitated, then nodded. "I want to stay here."

For the first time, the man seemed to look at him, not his application.

"Good. That's probably better than a decade's experience steaming gas, driving EDA donkeys, or punching tunnels." Another look. "We really don't care about your past. You do the work, you're one of us."

The man looked again at his comp. "The PEL is the Peak of Eternal Light. No surprise you ain't heard of it. It's not in the travel guides. The guy you're replacing snagged his suit on a panel bracket and vacuum-froze his arm and half his shoulder." He paused again and Drew wondered if this was an attempt to scare him. If so, Nose Ring had a surprise coming.

The silence stretched. When it broke, Drew had won something, though he wasn't quite sure what.

"It's supposedly the only place on the Moon that's always in sunlight," Nose Ring said. "The Peak of Eternal Light, get it? Bullshit, of course, but near enough true, not counting eclipses and a couple of damn big mountains."

Drew wanted to ask about salary, but didn't. He had no other options, and they both knew it. "See you at 7:30," he said instead.

V

There is a song they sing in Loony Too, where the workers toil on the Peak of Eternal Light and wish for shade. Razo had heard it many times on visits to the outlying dome.

Back in Central, most people disdained Luna II's working-class culture, but Raz found himself drawn to it ever more strongly as the years mounted and pains refused to fade. Could he have gone back to the life he'd left? It wasn't Jersey he'd fled, per se. It was the family that wasn't a family, the life that was a living death. It had taken years of working two jobs to save enough, but he'd *had* to get a new start or the nameless cop had saved him in vain. Then Jenn couldn't handle it, and he'd had to choose.

At its best, Luna II reminded him of childhood—the good parts, of which there had been a few—though if you looked hard enough you could still find the crackerjack. But not much, even though here the stuff was legal. People who'd worked that hard to escape to a new world didn't hide in a chemical one.

But that didn't mean they didn't like their synthanol. At shift's end, you could find them, the stench of suit still thick upon them, descending from the always-day above to this dome on the edge of the never-light below.

We drink from the Sun but we eat from the Earth,
Ain't many here standing who've been here from birth;
One of these days we'll all say goodnight,
But from now unto then just leave on the light!

They were singing as he walked into Archie's, one of two bars in Luna II's main lobby, the other being the Waddup Widdat.

The dust never falls to the cold lunar ground,
It spins and whirls like a Loonie-go-round;
One of these days we'll be buried all right,
But from now unto then just leave on the light!

It was one of the better verses, referring to the way the photovoltaics drew dust, even though the eggheads claimed it wasn't possible. Nothing like an egghead who got it wrong to make the workingman happy—that was another thing Raz remembered from youth. Even though the egghead was never the one who had to clean up the mess.

Archie Skaggs was behind the bar. He and Raz had known each other for years, the respect more than grudging. Arch ran a business. Raz ran the domes. Neither liked trouble.

Archie smiled, reaching for a shelf under the bar where Raz knew he kept the good stuff, but Raz shook his head. *Sober tonight.* Then, before he could speak, Archie's patrons launched into another verse. There were a lot of verses, not to mention those invented on the spot. Sometimes the new ones even made sense.

The river Sol flows and the panels they burn,
One of these days they'll be done to a turn;
We'll switch off the churners and wrap 'em up tight,
But from now unto then just leave on the light!

Raz stepped for the courtyard, motioning for Arch to follow.

"Hey, Art," Archie said when they'd reached the relative quiet beyond the bar.

Arch had never explained why he refused to call Raz by his nickname. He certainly wasn't formal about anything else. Perhaps he too had a secret. Before Jenn, there'd been a woman who wouldn't call him Art. For her, that name would always be her abusive father. To her, Raz had always been Artemis. Secrets didn't have to be deep. Just painful.

"Long time, no see," Archie continued. "I got up some Johnny Walker, couple a' shuttles ago. Nobody better to drink it. Where ya' been?"

"Busy. Damn council won't hire new cops. We're all working overtime. They figure as long as the tourists keep coming we can get along with the force we had a decade ago."

"So is this business or pleasure?"

"Business, I'm afraid. There's a young man just up from Earth, trying to hook on with SEA. Drew Zeigler. You heard of him?"

"Can't say's I have."

"Well, he's the kid with the duffel bag, over there." Raz hooked a thumb toward a dome-side table.

He had no proof Drew was Caeli's gwipp but Philadelphia Fidel had not only been too obvious, he'd been applying for top-line jobs at places like Lunar Nanosystems and Vacuum Molecular BioSyn. Zero-prospect applications: not the type of thing a well-schooled "gwipp" would do. Zeigler was the next-best guess.

"So do me a favor and let me know if you hear anything."

"Anything like what?"

Raz flapped a hand. "You know, if he's doing okay with Lum. If he gets into trouble. Stuff like that."

"Is he trouble?" Archie feigned a disinterested glance. "Kinda scrawny for an Earther. He do somethin'?"

"No. And this is just between you and me, okay? No reason to make trouble for him."

Archie leaned back, took a sip of whatever drink he'd carried from the bar. Probably nonalcoholic. There's a difference between making your customers feel at home and blending in too well. "Sure."

Behind them, the song showed no sign of winding down. Raz wondered if anthropologists back on Earth, the ones who loved to prattle about what the Moon "meant," had ever tried to count verses to songs like this, and if so, how they distinguished "official" ones from those made up on the fly. If it even mattered.

Some say the Earth is the place to plant roots,
But we plant ourselves on the Moon with our boots;
Maybe we're loony, but we'll see who's right,
But from now unto then just leave on the light!

VI

For the second time in a row, Drew had no idea where he was spending the night. He'd remained in the Luna II dome because he'd not known where else to go, but he still needed a place to stay. Not that there were hotels in Luna II. It was just a dome full of people who worked for a living, sans Skyview, casinos, and fancy restaurants.

He'd never been this broke before. Never been truly broke at all, actually, though going into the program certainly felt like it at first. For good or ill, he'd gotten used to the money he'd once shunned. Odd. Work like hell for that track scholarship so he didn't have to let the family buy him college . . . then let them buy him again afterward, until eventually he was laundering their damn money for them. Though that final step hadn't just been the money. *It's time to step up,* they'd insisted. Because blood was thicker than water. Because it was his duty. Duty to do what, he only asked later. Throw away his life as though "family" was some kind of disease everyone succumbed to eventually? If that was family, who the hell needed it?

The Moon was his chance to prove nobody owned him. If only he'd thought of it before he went in the program. When he'd suggested it afterward, his handlers had been livid. Too risky, they'd said. We can't protect you there. You can't afford it. Even if we gave you the cash, any sudden source of money isn't going to pass unnoticed. Better to disappear into suburban . . . where? St. Paul? Spain? Seattle? Not a place where real, true new starts were the name of the game. Live or die, it was useless without the new start.

"Don't tell me I can't do it," he'd said, shocking himself with his vehemence. Everyone had told him he couldn't do things, all his life. First, running in middle school. Then high school. Then college. It had only been in the Olympic Trials that he'd finally hit his limit. *I will save enough money*, he'd told them. But making it last now that he was here—that was a different problem. Middle class people who visited the Moon saved for years. Immigrants cashed everything and rolled the dice.

Luna II wasn't a good place to hide. Every centimeter seemed to be in use, making him realize just how profligate the tourist area was, with its Skydome, promenades, and hotels. Here, there was open space, but not a lot. When the locals wanted more they went and rubbed elbows with those whose travel dollars paid for it.

If only Loonie immigration hadn't forced him to buy a return ticket. Then he'd have money to stay anywhere. But to claim a refund he'd have to be able to convince them he was securely employed . . . by which time he wouldn't really need it. Nothing like a perfect Catch-22.

How long could he remain awake and still functional? Could he get by with bits of sleep here and there, with a real hotel every second or third day? At least the pseudo-beer was cheap. Cheap-tasting too, but better than nothing.

A voice startled him from his reverie. "Hi, Drew. I'm Detective Razo."

He turned to see a large man behind him. Not fat, just big. Tall and broad, with most of his strength in his shoulders. Where'd he come from? Since the shuttle, Drew had definitely let down his guard. Or maybe it was the fatigue. Still, even half-asleep, he didn't need the introduction to know the guy was a cop. In the last couple of years he'd seen just about every imaginable type. Good, bad. Friendly, gruff. This one seemed to be going for world-weary.

"Mind if I sit down?" the cop said. "Just like I would if I were asking friendly like about what a tourist like you is doing here in Luna II?"

Drew nodded cautiously.

"Good." The detective eased onto the bench beside him. "But I don't need to ask any of that because I already know."

There were a lot of responses to that. Drew went for the simplest. "Oh?"

"Yeah. Sleeping in hotel stairwells, by the way, isn't legal, even on the Moon."

"Oh." Briefly, Drew thought about saying he hadn't done it, but another rule that had been drilled into him was never to deny the undeniable.

The detective said nothing, but Drew had seen that one before, too. He took the tiniest sip of his beer. Eventually the detective gave up. "You're a cool customer."

Drew didn't feel like it but he'd become good at acting. "I figured there'd been a camera."

"No. We don't have a lot of those. We may live crammed together, but Loonies like their freedom."

This time, Drew saw no reason not to bite. "So how'd you know?"

"Locator beacon on your emergency suit."

"And you just happen to track those things?"

The detective chuckled. "So now you're curious. Let's just say I don't care about a little bit of vagrancy, so long as you don't break anything."

"I didn't."

"Didn't think so." The detective leaned back, to all appearances totally relaxed. "And while I have to admit you make me curious, there are a lot of things that make me curious."

"Such as?"

"Oh, I don't know. Whether there's life at other stars. Why frogs cross the road. What makes for quiet, cautious types like you."

"I'll keep out of stairwells."

The detective gave a theatrical sigh. "Well, I don't know everything, but sad to say, I don't rule the universe. If you've got secrets, kid, as long as you keep your nose clean, that's none of my business. Folks here, most of us came to start over." He glanced at Drew's duffle. "And by the way, those transponders are never off. Luna Tourism is dead-set against losing tourists. Though, of course, you're no longer a tourist, right?"

The detective levered his bulk off the bench, grunting even in the plaza's Luna-gee.

"And when Grace asks, be smart and say yes. Lousy sunner but that woman can cook."

What the hell had that been about? Drew picked up his beer, preparatory to nursing it for a long time. Inexpensive, yes. Free, no. It was odd how the liquid sloshed, slow motion, as he raised it. So much about this place was similar to what he'd grown up with, but so much was different. And not just the gravity.

Maybe it was the fatigue, but this cop seemed different. He'd practically told Drew that someone—his handlers perhaps—had tipped him to . . . well, something. Then, the cop had hinted that he really could have a fresh start. And what was the bit with the emergency suit? Why give away his advantage by telling him he could be traced simply by carrying it around?

He took another sip of the beer. It would take a long time to figure this place out. As long, perhaps, as it might to discover who he really was and re-invent himself in its image.

Detective Razo was barely out of sight when Drew became aware of yet another person heading his way. What was this, Grand Central Station? Or was it just that he was new in what amounted to a small town, where anything new drew attention?

This one was a gray-haired woman in coveralls, nearly as large as Detective Razo but moving with a much more purposeful-seeming stride. No cop-act world-weariness here.

"You Zeigler?" Even in the continuing racket from Archie's, her voice had no trouble covering the distance.

Don't lie beyond the cover unless absolutely necessary. But nothing said caution wasn't good. "Last time I checked."

If smiles were in her, she didn't offer one. "You need a place to stay, right?" She turned and started walking away, her gait as quick as Detective Razo's had been slow. "You hungry? I'm starving."

"Who—? Why—?"

She twisted back without bouncing out of contact with the ground, oddly graceful in the low gee. "You always been this stupid or you been practicing? I'm Grace. Grace Dorfman. Lum asked me to keep an eye out for you. Said to give you a hand if you looked all right. My husband Bernie says it's okay and Raz didn't arrest you, which means you must be all right."

Too much information. He grabbed one bit. "Who's Lum?"

"Geez you really were born stupid. Luckily, he's got a soft spot for wannabes 'cause he was one himself. Likes to make sure they got a place to stay, first coupla' a nights till they get on their feet. So c'mon if you're coming." She did the pirouette thing again and started off, again at the surprisingly brisk pace. Maybe on the Moon extra mass was an advantage.

That night Drew ate better than he had in weeks. It left him feeling wonderful, then sick, then hurled him into slumber on the Dorfmans' couch.

The next thing he knew it was 8:00 am.

How could he have been so stupid as to not set the alarm? But no, he remembered setting it.

It must have been the food. Or maybe that for the first time in years he'd felt safe, the first time he'd felt truly content since the day Coach happened to be walking by as he was getting out of the car he should have known better than to accept. The gift car from his uncle. The bright red Python all the girls had loved, with its gyroscopic suspension, full-immersion senses, ultracapacitor electrics that recharged nearly as fast as they went zero to ninety.

He knew what gifts meant in his family. But somehow he'd pretended "no strings attached" was for real. Until, in a series of steps he later could never quite reconstruct, he found himself turning his back on the family-away-from-family he'd worked so hard to build. He could still see the slump of Coach's shoulders when he'd dropped his scholarship and sold his soul back to his birthright—the tightlipped disappointment that was the only rebuke Coach ever needed to give. Coach knew Drew's past, had helped him escape it. And then Drew had gone back because . . . because of the damn car. Or maybe the girls. They really had liked it. Enough that most never wanted to know about the lifestyle that paid for it. Enough that most never really wanted to know Drew.

The good thing about sleeping on a couch is that you're already dressed. Drew yanked on his shoes, the resulting gravity bounce reminding him in the nick of time not to move too abruptly. Then he was in the corridor, hitting the grab plates at full stride.

That at least was the plan. He'd not gone twenty paces before he nearly crashed into a tattooed man with a nose ring, dodged, lost the grab-plate trail, hit a wall, and bounced ignobly to the opposite side of the corridor.

Nose Ring appeared above him, as Drew tried to find a graceful way to lever himself off the floor.

"I'm Lum Arbuckle, and the only reason you still have a job is because you were running. What, Gracie get you drunk?" He laughed and hauled Drew to his feet, like a fisherman landing a big one. "Of course, if I ever catch you running the grab plates again there better be a damn good reason. I don't like paying workers' comp for stupid injuries. You got me?"

There was only one response. "Yes, sir."

A few minutes later Drew found himself in a chamber that looked and smelled like the locker rooms that had once shown the path to something better than the life he'd thought himself strong enough to flee. Though this locker room's ancestors must have mated with a dry-cleaners. Looping behind the benches and stools ran one of those overhead chains used by dry-cleaners the world over to recall sweaters, slacks, and blazers from the establishment's bowels. But rather than pinstripes and tweeds, this one carried spacesuits. None of which, apparently, were his.

"Sarah, your new trainee is here!" Lum called toward the doorway from which the suits emerged.

He cocked his head, nose ring dangling, as if looking at Drew from an angle gave him a better shot at sizing him up. "What are you? A little over one-eighty cm?"

"One-eighty-three."

Lum turned back to the doorway. "Get him a trainer. Medium ought to do."

Wherever Sarah was, her voice echoed. "One medium glowball coming up."

Drew didn't like the sound of that. "I went through the class, back on the shuttle . . . "

"Obviously," Lum said. "But it's different to work in one all day. You get the training suit. The controls are simpler and people know to keep an eye on you. You'll be less likely to get yourself killed before your first paycheck."

Then the overhead chain was whirring.

Drew looked around. "This place is . . . kind of large."

"And you're kind of late."

The suit arrived. A near-fluorescent lime green, larger than the others—not for a bigger man, but in design. Built for safety, not mobility. Behind it came a woman in a skinsuit built more for mobility. Or maybe exhibition. With the helmet off, it didn't leave much to the imagination, even with the billow of blonde hair that tumbled semi-discreetly across its formfitting torso.

Lum had obviously seen this reaction before. *Surprise, the most beautiful woman on the planet is about to be your boss. Even if it is a small planet.* Maybe it was a test. Stare too much and you're too easily distractable for the job.

"Drew, this is Sarah," he said. "Sarah Janes. When you're here, consider her God."

More like a goddess, but that was clearly the wrong thing to say. "Uh, sure."

Once, he'd been good with beautiful women. Now they made him nervous. Past attacking present. Maybe that was how it always went.

And maybe this really was a test. It couldn't be like she didn't know the impact she'd just had. She had to be at least thirty. No woman like her got to that age without knowing the effect she had on men.

If so, he apparently hadn't failed yet. She pulled the suit off the rack, shoved it in his arms. "No way you'll get lost in that."

"I'll never be able to walk far enough to get lost."

"Hah, he's a quick one." Sarah turned to Lum. "You want me to take him all the way up?"

"No, just to the rim. Walk him around, make sure he's not a vomiter. Cut him loose when swing shift shows up. He can go to the PEL tomorrow." He turned to Drew. "See me in the office when you're done. If Sarah doesn't shitcan you, I'll give you an advance. Can't have you mooching off Gracie forever."

VII

Razo was reviewing shift reports when Archie rang his private line.

Nobody used that line for chitchat. "What's up?" he asked.

"Remember that guy Zeigler?"

"He in trouble?"

"No. I mean, I don't think so. But Leo just told me a guy came by asking about him. Definitely not a local; called himself Beau Guest."

"And?"

"Well, that's a novel, not a name. Beau Geste, get it?" Archie pronounced the G the soft, French way. Like *gendarme*. "It's a classic. About mercenaries, among other things."

"Really?"

"Yeah, don't you read?"

Raz snorted. "Wish I didn't have to. Nothing worse than admin stuff. What's the point?"

"It's like he thinks we're stupid. What kind of guy names himself after a novel?"

"What did Leo tell him?"

"Whaddya think? Told him to get vacced."

Raz laughed. He wasn't sure who Leo was, but he knew about the hello outsiders got from Looney Toos protecting their own. It spoke well of Zeigler that the boy had gotten so far in only a few days. "He still up there?"

"This Jester guy? I've not seen him."

"Damn, I was hoping for a—"

"Picture?" Archie was all grin. "All you gotta do is ask. Gimme a moment and I'll zip over what my bar cam got."

Raz chuckled. "Thanks."

"No problem. But be careful. This guy gave Leo the willies and Leo's seen a lot. You and your folks may take a lot of flak out here, but fact is, not much of it amounts to much. Without you, a lot of us would've long ago packed it in and moved central. Leo says this guy's serious as a pressure leak."

VIII

When he'd had the car and all the things that eventually went with it, Drew knew why beautiful women were attracted to him. Scrawny guys who ran cross-country and track didn't get them. Football players did. Or people with hundred-thousand-credit cars.

Drew still wasn't a football player. And he no longer had the car. But Sarah seemed to like him. Off-duty anyway. She was always there, in Archie's or the Wad-dup or just sitting in Dome Gardens. Twice, he'd spent no-longer-so-precious credits to take the Overway back to Central, with all that a night on the town entailed.

For his new identity, it was perfect. They were simply two of 17,000 residents, blending in with the other 16,998. Him because his life depended on it. Her . . . well, he wasn't quite sure. All he knew was that when she fell asleep on the Over-way, which she did both times on the return, her mouth dropped slightly open, re-vealing ever-so-slightly crooked teeth. Teeth that on Earth would have been fixed, but which here didn't matter. More than anything else, her sleeping face revealed total, complete trust. Trust in him as protector? Or simply that the Moon was a safe place—safer, for sure, than anything he'd known on Earth?

Off-shift, that is. On-shift, both Sarah and the Moon were different. In the case of the Moon, the reasons were obvious. The job involved vacuum work, with heavy equipment and sometimes-long hours. Tourism wasn't Luna C's only cash cow. Lunar industries relied on power. But power generation had never been the safest work. And the damn solar panels were dust magnets—even the rim-side reflectors for the volatiles stills down on the crater floor, where the only sunlight in four bil-lion years was that focused in by the panels' adaptive optics.

Nobody knew why every grain of dust seemed to wind up on the panels—which, of course, everyone found immensely amusing, at least when they weren't stirring up more dust, changing out panels for refurbishing or hoisting new ones onto the ever-growing array.

For once, Drew was glad his cover gave him a degree in political psychology. It spared him from being the brunt of egghead jokes. "Four years of campusology," he explained, risking a word he'd picked up from his maternal grandfather, who'd al-ways managed to stay at least a bit aloof from the family business. "With just enough basket-weaving to graduate."

Meanwhile, on-shift-Sarah was his boss.

"Darkness," she was saying. "How long until it starts?"

In his prior life, he'd have had such things memorized. But the new Drew had a degree in political uselessness that probably meant otherwise. And he was stuck in a bright-colored pressure suit that marked him as too . . . green . . . to have yet gotten beyond it.

"Um—"

There was a click and Sarah's voice switched channels. To a more private one, reserved for personal conversations . . . or scoldings.

"Listen," she said. "Last night was last night." Not that anything more than an almost-kiss had happened. Before she fell asleep on the train. "Here, your life de-pends on paying attention. Lum doesn't care what we do off-shift. Hell, he's probably hoping we'll marry and have two thousand kids, so long as they're all sunners. But when you put on the suit, you've got to keep your mind on the job. If you don't, you won't just get shipped back to Earth. You'll get yourself killed. Maybe along with someone else. Got it?"

"Yeah."

"So, Darkout. When is it?"

Drew knew. "Drew" wouldn't. Which pretty much sucked when he wanted to impress both his boss and an increasingly interesting woman.

He gazed around the horizon, his suit automatically blotting out the Sun's unviewable glare. Two big peaks to the . . . what do you call it when all directions are north? A smaller one, thirty degrees to the right. The Sun barely above the horizon, as it had been for billions of years and always, ever, would be.

Three hundred sixty degrees in twenty-eight days was a bit less than fifteen degrees per day: that's how fast the Sun would move. He made a show of holding his hand against the horizon, counting handspans. Ninety degrees was eight, maybe nine. Was he supposed to be able to figure that out? Screw it, he was tired of playing the role he'd been assigned. "Wednesday?"

Sarah's expression was unreadable through her suit visor. "Care to be more specific?"

He went back through the show again. "Maybe 1100? A bit before noon. Though I might be off."

Sarah turned so she was facing him, her visor de-opaquing, though her face was still unreadable. "Not bad. Not bad at all. It's 1122 to be precise. You know, the suit electronics do allow you to look it up."

"Oh." Damn the handlers who'd decided to make him blandly useless. Of course he knew it. It was how he'd made his "guess."

He and Sarah were standing a couple of klicks from the rim, the nearest of the PEL's solar panels rising just behind, like the Solar System's largest billboards. Hectares upon hectares of cells atop spindly stilts like old-fashioned fire towers. Towers that were sturdy enough here because there were no windstorms, tornadoes, or earthquakes to knock them down. Tall because "up" meant more light, shorter Darkout, better power for industries that gobbled it like a kid with Halloween candy.

"Keep on the lights" was a joke. The lights would run a long time off batteries. The real industries, the power-hungry ones, couldn't. Three times a month they took expensive shutdowns. Not that the employees minded. Or the owners of the clubs where they partied. But they weren't the ones who drove Luna C's economy. Every new hectare of cells brought in new, power-hungry industries . . . new voices clamoring for the PEL to live ever closer to its name. And the higher it went, the shorter the shutdown became. The PEL was ever expanding and would ever expand so long as Luna C herself did the same.

"What's Darkout like?" he asked.

"It sneaks up on you. Kind of like a really slow sunset on Earth, from what I've heard. Then poof, all of a sudden the light is gone." She waved a gloved hand at the crater below. "Like suddenly being down there. Kind of disconcerting, even when you're expecting it."

Drew stared across the crater floor. Luna II was invisible, tucked out of sight behind the rim of its own crater. But the other domes were clustered below, their lights like swarms of fireflies. Elsewhere, the crater floor was dark as only vacuum shadows can be, except at the volatiles mines, where the rimtop reflectors focused giant beams of sunlight wherever it was required. No electricity needed for the mines; just pure, concentrated light to bake everything from water to mercury and silver out of soils that hadn't seen heat in four billion years.

"Those shut down too." Sarah had seen the direction of his gaze. "We're pretty much the only ones who don't get to party when the Sun goes away."

There was just a hint of a smile visible in the backlight seeping through her visor, a trace of off-work twinkle in her eyes. Enough to say that next time they went to Central the kiss would be there if he wanted it.

Suddenly, he felt crushingly tired. If he did kiss her, he wanted it to be without pretense.

"Sarah, there are things I need to tell you."

She read his mood right but mis-guessed the cause. The twinkle vanished, replaced by Sarah-boss.

"Damn right. Where's the nearest emergency shelter?"

"Sarah—"

"Uh-uh. Use the suit's weblink if you have to. If your suit suddenly sprung a leak, where would you go? Hell, if my suit sprang a leak, where would you take me? *Now.* Hiss-hiss. Time's wasting. You'd better have grabbed an emergency patch by now, or we're already in trouble. Quick now!"

Screw being "Drew." He probably wouldn't know. Drew did.

"Over there." He pointed to the base of the nearest pylon "Though the one over that way isn't much farther."

IX

The Loonie Toos weren't the only ones whose workload increased during Darkouts. Razo's tended to as well, especially during First Darkout, when the biggest of the three mountains blocked sunlight for a full thirty-seven hours. By Second Darkout, most of those inclined to do so had already blown their paychecks, and by Third, only the diehards were left. But First Darkout? "It's kind of like TGIF on steroids," he told Caeli the first time she'd joined him on one of his pre-Darkout soirees. "And normal off-shifts can be bad enough."

Which meant that just before Darkout was a bad time for Raz to blow steam. That would come later. Pre- was for true relaxation. Although this time he might have relaxed the wrong way.

"I'd never have taken you for the ballet type," Caeli was saying as they found their seats.

"You ever been before?"

"Once. Swan Lake, I think. That's the one they do at Christmas, right?"

"No, that's The Nutcracker. Though not here. The classics just don't work well in low-gee unless you grab-plate the entire floor. Earth ballet is all about defying gravity. Up on the toes, lifts, leaps, and all that. If you try that stuff here it just comes out weird, probably because anyone can do it, so what's the point? This is a bit more . . . gymnastic."

"How so?"

This particular ballet was one he'd seen before. It was a tale of loss and longing and things abandoned forever in a chase for a pot of gold that kept receding—like a lot of Loonie art and music, really. Powerful chords in minor keys, with always a hint of major-key resolution just a few bars in the future, but never quite found. The art-crowd answer to the bar tunes that tried to revel in this frontier that drew so strongly but demanded so much. Had frontiers always been like that? Raz wasn't historian enough to know. There was a day when crossing an ocean was more permanent than going to space. But the Moon wasn't just a new continent. There was nothing here except what you brought . . . or invented.

Like the ballet.

"You see the checkerboard parquet on the floor?"

"Yeah . . . "

"Well, the dark pieces are grab plates. The light ones are Luna gee. You use the dark for traction, the light for bounce." In some productions, the grab plates even led up the walls onto the ceiling.

Earth ballet wasn't merely about defying gravity. It also involved occupying space. Ballerinas with heads held high, shoulders spread, arms swept in grand, passionate gestures. Here, it was *all* about occupying space. Pun fully intended. "The good ones spend a lot of time upside down," Raz said. "Handsprings are a big part of it."

"And heaven help them if they hit a grab plate?"

He chuckled. "They call that the Lunar dip. Not a good move. But you're not really all that interested, are you?"

She shrugged. "If you're interested, I am."

Suddenly, he felt uncomfortable. "That's not necessary."

She stared at him a moment, then changed the subject. "Did you find my gwipp?"

"Maybe. Why?"

"Oh, I'm just worried about him."

"Him?"

"Ha! It's a him, isn't it?"

"Maybe."

"Maybe, hell! But is he safe? Guys like that . . . I'd hate to see him draw the wrong attention."

She hesitated, stared at him again. "Why are we doing this, Artie?"

"Doing what? Going to the ballet?"

"No. Everything else. You, me, this type of conversation. How long have we been doing it? I won't hang on the shelf forever."

"So you don't like ballet?"

"No, you can't hide like that!" There was fire in her eyes. "We click. We have fun. Then you arm's-length me. Just like you did there! Why? What is it you're so afraid of?"

"Well, you do cut an imposing figure."

"*Don't* give me that. What the hell is going on?"

Raz tried to meet her gaze. Flinched away. Just like the guiltiest of guilty perps. Tried again, gave up. He'd known her for two years, but always through a self-created screen of flirty confidence. A pretense, not the real him.

"I had a daughter."

"Had?"

"Yeah."

"She died?"

"No."

And then the story. The two-decade secret he'd never told anyone—never thought he would—tumbling out until the music started, underscoring the loss, the longing, and the unreachable pot of gold that didn't really matter because it's the being here that trumps everything, and which you'd sell your soul to achieve . . . all over again. That was when he leaned close, lowered his voice, and dared the words he feared even to ask himself. "What if I did it all over again? To you?"

Caeli's breath was warm in his ear. "You couldn't. Because I'd never ask you to go back to Earth. This place . . . it's who you are."

Then the dance began and conversation was impossible.

Sarah was glistening in sweat, fresh off the dance floor, her golden hair limned in blue, red, and green from the Waddup's synthband diodes. Drew took her hand to lead her back to their table for drinks and a rest.

Darkout was tomorrow. Thirty-seven hours of dusting, looking to bring as many panels as possible back to optimum efficiency before the Sun returned and made the main arrays too hot even for the best skinsuits to handle. The busiest time of the month, because each panel dusted was 1,700 credits in Luna C's industrial bank, as best Drew could calculate. As if "Drew," without the MBA, had a chance of figuring such things out.

He was tired. Tired of the pretense. If he couldn't trust Sarah, who would he ever be able to trust?

She must have read his mood. A moment before, she'd been the one who was going to kiss him. Now she drew back, let herself be escorted to the table.

"You know, you're a real conundrum," she said.

"How so?"

"Sharp as a tack one moment, dumb as a post the next. I mean, there you were last week, gazing at the Sun and estimating Darkout within minutes, and then, next thing, not knowing you could have simply answered the question by calling up the weblink on your suit. And you're one hell of a good dancer. I mean, I've been around more than I'd like to admit. Comes with spending too much of your life in places like this. I know the difference between the barroom grope and an actual dance. You were trying to hide it, but you've taken some lessons. I know because Lum made me do it."

"Lum?"

"It figures you wouldn't know. He's just like you: wonderful one moment, idiot the next. He's my father. Which I gather he didn't tell you. Janes is my mother's name. Long story. But he's always trying to set me up. Usually with idiots. Well-meaning idiots, but idiots. So . . . what are you? You try to act dumb, but you aren't. In case you're wondering, dumb doesn't impress women. At least not this one."

Drew laughed, though it sounded forced, even to him. "I was beginning to figure that."

His gaze swept the bar. Caught the eye of a pale, hawk-nosed man who suddenly developed an interest in his menu. Probably nothing. Probably just staring at Sarah. But suddenly his Wild Bill reflexes were on full alert.

"Let's get some air."

They moved to the courtyard, the stranger not following. *False alarm*, Drew thought. You're safe here. Relax. They couldn't follow you even if they knew where to go. Immigration would get them before they even tried to board the shuttle.

That was too close, Beau thought as the quarry and woman moved outside. It had taken two weeks to find him, and now he'd almost blown it. But who would have thought the guy would stuff his suit transponder beneath an Overway seat cushion? Beau had followed the damn thing to hell and gone before he realized the hare wasn't on an endless job hunt. Then nobody in Luna II would talk to him, and there wasn't anything he could do to improve their cooperation because there weren't any good places for a nice, private talk.

That was also when he realized that making a hit on the Moon was going to be harder than anticipated. The place was simply too crowded. The kill would be easy enough. But getting away—that was the rub. Until he saw the quarry with the woman. LunaNet security was a joke, but she'd done nothing to hide her profile, anyway. The quick holo he'd snapped before they'd seen him was all he needed. Sarah Janes Arbuckle, shift sub-supervisor for SEA Industries, PEL Division. The rabbit had been idiot enough to accept a job that took him outside.

Beau prided himself on being good at his work, but sometimes, when it all came together, it was almost too easy.

He rose, remembering at the last instant to do so slowly lest his Earther legs reveal him as an outsider. Not that he ever expected to be back here again.

If he left now, he had time to climb the rim and hike to the scooter that would take him back to his hidden crawler. Not that it was hard to hide things in this land of eternal shadows.

The crawler had everything he needed. Beau had never been one to head out on an assignment without being as prepared as possible. If he hurried, there was time to make the trip, do the job, and be back in civilization next week. A million credits richer, to boot.

Beau often smiled. It made people like him. But the social smile rarely touched his eyes. He'd practiced but could never quite get it. Now, though, he knew his smile was genuine.

"So what the hell is going on?" Sarah's eyes were a cool grey, but that didn't mean they couldn't spark with anger. "And why couldn't you tell me about it in there?"

"Too much noise." Drew paused. "No. I just don't like crowds."

All the way out of the Waddup, he'd been looking for words.

"I'm not who you think I am."

Sarah's eyes clouded. "Oh-oh. Who is she?"

"No, that's not it."

"You're married."

"*No*. It's nothing like that. It's me. I'm not *Drew*."

Her expression was unreadable. "Who are you then?"

It was amazing how hard it was to make himself say the words. His indoctrination had been thorough. *Never, never, never.* Never trust. Never bond. Always float on the surface. But they were wrong. Ultimately, there came a time when it was better to risk. What was the point in being not dead if you were never alive?

"I'm Dimitri. Or I was, until last year. Dimitri Katsaros."

Her eyebrows rose. "That's a mouthful. I can see why you might prefer Drew." But there was no humor in it. The Sarah he knew was on hold.

"Son of Leander Katsaros."

Her headshake was quick. "If that's supposed to mean something it doesn't." Her lips thinned. "Or maybe that just makes me a dumb Loonie."

"No. It just means you have better things to do than follow the Greek mob in Baltimore."

It wasn't just her eyes that were unreadable now.

"I betrayed my family."

Darkout was only hours away and Razo should be thinking about sleep. Instead, as he and Caeli left the theater he turned toward Central and the soul-searching infinities of the Skyview.

She was right, this place was part of him. Had been, really, since before he left Earth, since the nameless cop's compassion had shown him a glimmer of hope. Jenn had given him an impossible choice. No—not Jenn. Loonie laws. They were all about fairness and equal chances. But fairness and hope weren't always compatible. Maybe that was why Raz wound up in law enforcement. He'd thought it had just kind of happened, but his first job had been driving EDA donkeys for the solar stills, helping Lunar Air & Water capture precious resources as the rimtop mirrors baked them out of the soil. Police work came later, when he'd found there was no way to bring Jenn back. He'd thought he'd just kind of drifted into it, but he'd never forgotten the compassionate cop who'd saved him.

Caeli squeezed his hand. "You're quiet."

"Sorry. Just thinking." He wasn't sure how long they'd been walking, but her hand had been in his since they'd left the theater.

"You okay?"

"Yeah."

More than okay, in fact. What he felt was a sudden lifting of age. For some time, he'd been feeling increasingly run down. Thinking, even, of taking early retirement and doing . . . well, something else. But that might have to wait.

"Talking about it after all these years . . . I feel . . . It's going to take a while to process I guess."

"That's okay. Trust me, I know all about processing." He gave her a sharp glance, but she shook her head. "Some other time."

Then the Skyview was overhead.

"You know," she said, "I never tire of this place."

"Is this what it's like piloting a shuttle?"

"Yes. And no. This has more grandeur. The shuttle has . . . freedom. You know, you can come with me sometime."

The thought brought back a touch of the old pang. Yesterday he'd have said no way. Now . . . well, who knew? Though there was a practical concern.

"I'd never be able to handle the gravity."

"Oh, pfoo! You'd just need to work out a bit."

"More than a bit." He paused. "You weren't all that fond of the ballet, were you?"

They were leaving the Skyview now, heading down a corridor toward . . . Raz wasn't sure where. Just heading. For the moment that was enough.

"Not really. But that's okay." She laughed. "And it does give some interesting ideas." She stepped on a grab plate, shoved off sideways and bumped hips hard enough to make him stagger. Then she stepped on the next plate and pulled him back. "I never realized the plates could be so much fun!"

"Only if you're an Amazon!"

"A Celtic Amazon. We're not into ballet. We're into feasting, Finagal, Fimbulwinter . . . or was that the Vikings? Damn, I shoulda' paid more attention somewhere along the line."

He laughed, too. It was the old banter, but somehow different. Fun for fun's sake, not for hiding.

"Not to mention blarney," he said.

"Got me there. I was raised in Duluth for God's sake. On the shores of Gitchegume with lutefisk. And Finns. For some reason they all went to Lake Superior."

"I didn't know that."

"What, the Finns? It's true—"

"No. About you." Was confession really this good for the soul? It was like something long-pent, suddenly released.

She braked on a grab plate, so suddenly that again her Earth strength nearly pulled him off his feet.

"That's because you never asked."

"I—"

She leaned in. Gave him a gentle kiss. Friendly, not passionate. Though with a suggestion of more.

"You can't relive old decisions forever." She was gripping both his hands now. "That was twenty years ago. You are who you are now. Not who you were."

He started to kiss her back, but suddenly his mind clicked over. "Oh, hell. The gwipp."

"What about him?"

"He's not who he is now. Not to those he left behind. And those folks never give up."

His mind was spinning. The stranger asking Leo about the kid. Where do strangers come from? Would a hit man really risk Immigration?

Celtic Amazons. Ballet. Earther strength.

He'd spent hours combing immigration records. If there was a hit man, his record was as well forged as the gwipp's. Raz had put traces on every incoming passenger who'd come close to matching the holo (which wasn't as good as Archie had thought; the guy had done a good job of staying in shadows), but none had done anything out of tourist-ordinary. Nor had anyone named Guest, Gueste, Jest, Beau, Beauregard, or pretty-boy-anything thumbed an ident or registered at any of the hotels. Raz had about come to the conclusion the whole thing was a figment of Leo's imagination.

Chasing rainbows.

Chasing, with Earther strength.

Grab plates on the walls.

"Hell," he said again. "Double hell." He tapped his com. "McHaddon? I don't know where you are, but we've got work to do."

He squeezed Caeli's hand, gave her a quick, more-later peck on the cheek that was more than he'd once planned, less than he now wanted. "I think the guy's really in trouble."

She kissed him back—again more than he'd once expected but less than he now dreamed of.

"Go. Save a life."

It was, he realized, the best possible atonement.

"The Greek mob in Baltimore?" Sarah's voice was still cool.

"Yeah."

"Did you kill people?"

Drew shook his head. "No. I just accepted money from those who did."

"Why?"

"They were family. And it was a *lot* of money."

How could he explain?

"When I was young, I wanted free of it. I even found a way out." Track scholarships, universities clamoring after him. "But it didn't quite work." Olympic prospects fading away. Then the car. The girls. No strings, just come back. *That's what family is for.* Except, of course, there were expectations. Because those too are what family was for.

"And then . . . I would have lost me. No, I *was* losing me. When I was a kid, it was mostly gambling and protection. Loans to people dumb enough to take them. Nothing Darwin wouldn't approve of. Would you believe my father actually told me that?"

Sarah shook her head. "That sounds . . . my life always centered around the PEL. Without us there'd be no Luna C. Just a big, dark crater. It always made me feel like a hero."

Drew was still in the past. Trying to expunge it. Trying to atone. No, to justify his atonement.

"Darwin was actually a theologian of sorts. Did you know that? He wouldn't have approved of what my father said. Me learning that was part of what the family got for letting me go to college. Though by then they were into prostitution, drugs, whatever else would make a credit."

He'd been staring across her shoulders at the accelerating pulse of dance lights. Now he forced himself to meet her gaze.

"Eventually, I knew I'd start helping make the money more directly. In my family, it's what you *do*. So when the Feds got a handle on a couple of killings . . . that was my second way out. And this time I made it stick."

"So you didn't kill anyone."

"No." Unless his uncle really did get the death penalty.

"Didn't sell drugs?"

"No."

"So what's the problem?"

"I took the easy way out."

"What, the one that didn't quite work?"

"No, I wasn't strong enough for that." It wasn't like he'd lost his place on the team. He'd been the star. Then quit. "My father is in jail because of me. Plus my uncle and a couple of cousins."

"And that makes you a bad guy?"

"It sure as hell doesn't make me son of the year."

Sarah was looking at him oddly, but Drew no longer cared. If he didn't come clean, he'd be no better than he was before. And he needed to be better. Even if it cost him the only decent woman—the only real friend—to come his way since he'd accepted the car.

"My father and uncle killed six people I know of. If they did one good thing in their lives, I don't know what it was."

He started to turn away, but Sarah's voice called him back. "Your father did at least one that wasn't half-bad."

"What?"

"You."

Beau didn't mind hiking. It cleared the mind, gave him time to think. On Earth, his favorite place was the desert. Nobody there but himself, nothing to disturb him but the occasional snake, scorpion, or tarantula. A simple land. A land where people might never have existed.

Which meant he particularly didn't mind hiking on the Moon. Especially now that he knew what he was doing. The quarry had a job outside the dome. A job that would guarantee he'd be outside in a few hours and would remain there until Beau could get back.

Beau was again smiling. Ultimately, most assignments were like this. Wait, gather information, and the hit itself was trivial.

Outside the dome, he didn't need special skills to make the kill. Even if he didn't score a bull's-eye, the Moon would finish the job for him. It was amazing how stupid the rabbits could be. It was as if they were begging him to do his job. End the chase and put them out of their misery.

In a few hours, the rim and its Peak of Eternal Light were going to be dumped into thirty-seven hours of darkness. If Beau couldn't make the hit then, it was time to retire.

A few minutes after Razo reached his office, Caeli showed up.

"Sorry, I got bored." She was leaning against the doorframe again, her theater wear swapped for blue jeans and a nondescript tee. "Anything I can do to help?"

Raz started to shake his head, then changed his mind. "Yes. Can you get me coffee? There's a pot—"

"I know."

A minute later, she was back, nose wrinkling.

"I think it's been there a while."

"Doesn't matter, so long as it's got caffeine."

"You might also want one of these." She offered him a pink pill. "I don't know about you, but the drink I had at intermission was still with me a bit."

"Thanks."

He swallowed the pill, took a swig of coffee, grimaced. "It's been there more than a while." He took another swig. "But it'll do the trick."

"So, what's up? Or would you rather I made myself scarce? Don't worry about me."

"No." Two heads and all that. "Your gwipp's got a stalker. I'd gotten a hint, but how could a really bad guy get through immigration?" He leaned back in his chair. Talking it out beat searching the net, anytime. "I mean, your gwipp made it in, but he had help."

"So you're saying this other guy's also got a government behind him?"

"No. Just that I've been stupid."

Here he was, a ballet fan, of all things. Ballet required remaining Earth-strong. But it wasn't until Caeli's talk of going back to Earth and the hip-bump that nearly knocked him off his feet that he'd fully realized what Earthers could *do*. Like Drew—the gwipp—running the plates. Everyone knew Earthers did stupid things in low gee. But they were also strong. And fast.

He tried to organize his thoughts. "He's got a lot of money behind him. And he's smart. He didn't come through security. He went around it."

"How's that?"

"He has his own ship. Not that that's uncommon."

"Of course. There are always a few at the port."

"But this guy didn't land at the. He must have come in low behind the rim, probably way out, and landed somewhere out there. Maybe drove some kind of buggy as close as he dared. Then walked. How far could you walk in this gravity?"

Caeli shrugged. "Quite a ways. But he'd have to get down from the rim. Kinda steep."

Raz noted that she'd not said high. What's 4,000 meters to an Earther?

"And dark," he added. "Even here that could make a nasty fall. And if he took much of a light, he'd stand out like a radar beacon. I'd bet you credits to cranberries he had grab boots."

"Grab boots?"

"Like grab plates, but portable."

"What powers them?"

"Battery." A big battery, which was why they weren't common. "They use them sometimes in the ballet, but not much. Any battery that lets you do more than a few moves isn't the most graceful thing to carry."

"So he's not going to get very far with it."

"But he could get far enough. He only has to use the boots when he needs them." And he was an assassin, not interested in grace. An Earther. He could carry one hell of a battery.

Raz's phone chimed.

"I've got him," McHaddon said. "He registered at the Ambassador as Barton Fink."

"You sure he's our man?"

"If not, we've got two of 'em. That's another damn movie."

Despite himself, Razo laughed. "You've been talking to Archie."

McHaddon returned the chuckle. "Who doesn't? Anyway, this guy blew the hell out of a whole floor's power stats two weeks ago."

"Nice job," Raz said. Then to Caeli's unasked question he added, "That's what we were looking for. We knew he'd been nosing around two weeks ago, so we were looking through hotel guests who'd not yet checked out."

"That's still a lot of people," Caeli said.

"Yeah, but I figured he'd recharge as soon as he could, which narrowed it down. And"—nothing like a guess that panned out—"he just seemed the type who'd be at the Ambassador. Or maybe the Grand. If your client has that much money to spend on a grudge, why not live it up?"

He picked up the coffee cup, downed the last dregs. "Only problem is, where's he got to now?"

X

Like all good hits, it was indeed proving easy. Even the long hike had been uneventful, though more time-consuming than Beau had expected. Topping off the boots' battery pack from the crawler's generator had been worthwhile, but frustratingly slow. Then, just about the time he'd closed in on them, the sunners finished cleaning one set of towers and trooped off to another—irritating because shifting positions this close, he couldn't risk more than the dimmest of lights. Just enough for his heads-up to amplify to a grainy image of the rocks he was about to trip over.

At least with his radio locked on receive-only, nobody could hear him curse. The sunners, on the other hand, chattered endlessly on a dozen channels, the hare's voice prominent among them. Even when he switched channels, Beau's state-of-the-art eavesdropping equipment tracked him seamlessly.

One of the rules of his trade was never to ask why. The hare had done something that meant he deserved to die. That was all Beau needed to know. But while some jobs were pure business, this one smacked of revenge. His clients might like to hear the hare's last, unsuspecting, words. There might even be a tidy bonus. He twitched a cursor with a shift of his eye, ordering his suit to record everything that came in over the radio.

Drew was dusting. Not the way his mother once made him do it during a brief between-maids phase, but with an electrostatic wand that made the dust fly off in a fountain of motes that sparkled in his suit lights. He wondered how much would eventually end up on other panels he'd wind up dusting next Darkout. Nobody knew how the dust found the panels, though he'd been told that when power generation was at max, the stuff practically seemed to climb the towers. Luckily his job wasn't to figure out why. It was just good, physical work that left him feeling like he'd actually accomplished something useful.

Dozens of other workers were spread across the array like sailors on an ancient frigate, but somehow Sarah had wound up next to him on the same panel. "Just looking after the newby," she said. But Drew knew better. Not to mention that he was no longer the newby. That honor, along with the ridiculous spacesuit, had been handed over to Damien something-or-other. Drew was now in a professional skin-suit that not only made him feel like a full member of the team, but finally, bless-edly, allowed him to *move*.

"Why don't they just make panels that do this automatically?" he asked.

They were on their first break, sitting on a scaffold fifty meters above the surface. She shrugged. "Why do they do anything?"

In Darkout, her face was unreadable. A black void behind her helmet light, just as everything beyond the range of his lights was now dark as the pit of Hell. But she'd been here her whole life, knew how to communicate when vision failed and voice was all you had.

Maybe her shoulders shrugged. Maybe not. Her voice did. "You'd never have asked that on Earth. There, you'd just know labor is cheap, technology expensive. Here, nothing is cheap, but I guess we're cheaper than redesigning the panels. And hey, it's a job." She touched his arm. "With a view." Again the maybe shrug. "When you can see it. Would you really rather be inside?"

"No way."

Sarah checked her tether. A reflex. She'd not unclipped during break, never would. Most accidents, she'd told him more times than he could count, came simply from falling off. Even in lunar gee, that could be deadly.

"Me neither," she said. Then she shifted to the general com-channel. "Break over."

Beau was finally in position. He unlimbered his rifle, set up the tripod. Watched, looking for surprises. Not that he expected any, but it was the watching and waiting that kept it that way.

He removed his overglove—the inner would be enough for thirty or forty sec-onds, more than enough time. Dialed the range into his autoscope.

Three hundred forty-two meters. He couldn't miss. He'd made hits from three times that range. He put the outer glove back on to warm his hands. The hare was on the scaffold far above, doing nothing. *Break over.* The perfect epitaph.

He removed his glove again. Slipped his finger over the trigger. Lined up on the helmet, just below the visor light. Breath in. Hold it. Pulse low, hands steady. Squeeze the trigger, not pull it. Nothing new. He'd done this countless times.

"Damn it, Damien!" At Sarah's shout, Drew's head swiveled to the new guy, at the far end of the scaffold he'd been sharing with Sarah. "What kind of idiots is Lum hiring these days? Tether up! Never unclip this high off the ground. You got me?"

Drew stood up, glad he himself had graduated from beginner to journeyman, or whatever you became when you no longer had to wear the training suit. Damien clipped in and started to wave a desultory hand. Drew knew what he was thinking. *Yeah, yeah. Sorry boss.* Only, of course, he wouldn't be truly repentant because the scaffold was wide, the railing secure, the tether a nuisance. How could you fall off?

Then, suddenly, the panel shattered. Cracks ran across it in a starburst ripple and sections began falling away in a slow-motion scattering of giant daggers.

Drew's first thought was that he himself had somehow broken it. But he'd barely moved, hadn't even touched the panel. If they were this fragile, why hadn't Sarah told him?

The unthinkable had happened. Beau had missed. At first he was simply stunned. Then he realized: the autoscope was calibrated for Earth. Six times higher gravity. The damn shot had gone high.

For the first time in his career, he'd made a mistake. Two, actually. Trusting the autoscope was the second. The first had been going for the head shot. Yeah, it was the classic kill. But in a vacuum? Any hole should be good enough.

Luckily, the hare was frozen in confusion. Beau lowered his aim. Forget finesse, go for the center. His fingers were cooling, but still comfortable. He tuned out the explosion of chatter pouring in over the radio, squeezed the trigger again. Once. Twice. Three times.

Drew was staring at the panel, trying to fathom what had happened. Then Sarah's voice was in his ear. "Meteorite. If something had to get hit . . ." She switched to the all-suits channel. "Just a bit of rock. Nothing to worry about . . ."

Then Damien jerked and a strangled gasp came over the radio, fading as the training suit went flaccid. He staggered back, then slumped forward, restrained only by his tether.

Later, Drew would wonder if he already knew. If so, it hadn't yet penetrated his thinking brain. But even on mental autopilot, he was remembering Sarah's safety drills. Vacuum wasn't death. Not instantly. And he and Sarah were closest to the victim. Faster than even she could react, he unclipped his tether and sprinted for the newby, being careful not to run so hard he hurled himself over the rail into a long fall.

"Hang in there!" he yelled, as if the guy could hear him with a suit full of vacuum. At the same time, he was ripping a patch from his emergency pouch, letting the vacuum activate its glue for instant application.

The holes in Damien's suit were round, about a centimeter in diameter, a fog of frozen red spicules still jetting out of them. Three holes in a tight triangle, only centimeters apart. What kind of meteorite did that?

Then his thinking brain clicked in.

He'd always wondered how he'd react if the long arm of his family found him. Sometimes he'd deliberately pondered it, uselessly trying to plan. More often he dreamed it in time-frozen nightmares. But now time wasn't frozen, although there was the stark clarity he'd once known just before the starter's gun, when you were simultaneously aware of everything and nothing.

He braked hard just before another bullet shattered more of the panel, right where his head would have been.

He wanted to yell a warning, but there wasn't time. Instead, he yanked the emergency release on Damien's tether, while more shards erupted around him, fragments stinging like angry bees. Then he was pushing off like a sprinter out of the blocks, grabbing a stanchion with one hand, Damien's suit harness with the other, swinging around toward the far end of the panel just as he saw a quick succession of tiny flashes in the darkness below. The stanchion vibrated with impact, but if he'd been hit, he couldn't feel it.

Then he was on the backside, as more sniper rounds pierced the panel above him. No scaffold here, just a maze of braces connecting panels to machinery that kept them always pointed at the sun.

In the bulky training suit, navigating this would have been impossible, but now it was like monkey bars on a Jersey playground, made easy in the low gravity. He wedged Damien in an angle between two braces and slapped on a patch. Then he yanked another from his kit, the biggest available, holding this one for a slow count of three, as Sarah had instructed, so the vacuum could fully activate the glue. He was feeling lightheaded, but ignored it. Damien needed him to focus. Sarah needed him to focus.

He slapped the patch over the two remaining holes, then reached behind Damien to turn his air up full blast. Blood spicules continued to escape, even as the suit inflated, but before Drew could pull a third patch from his kit, Sarah was with him, slapping on one of her own. Then she turned to him. "You're leaking," she said. "Raise your arm."

The lightheadedness was back with a vengeance, fireflies now flickering at the edges of his vision. But Sarah's voice was an anchor. "Shit," she said. "There must be a dozen little holes!"

He looked down, saw fog. Air, not blood. But the fireflies were multiplying.

Sarah's voice pulled him out of a mounting daze. "One-one-thousand. Two-one-thousand. Three-one-thousand. Okay, that got the biggest ones. Stay with me Drew! One-one-thousand, two-one-thousand, three-one-thousand . . ."

His head was clearing, drawn back partly by the urgency in her voice, partly by the rapidly thickening air in his suit.

"—one-one-thousand, two-one-thousand, that's the worst. The rest are just nicks. You still there?"

He nodded. The emergency patches were contracting, as the glue pulled the holes together. Putting pressure, too, on any wounds. Not that they'd be major. He'd been hit by shards, not bullets. He could even feel the patches warming him as they did their job to ward off frostbite.

"I'll be fine."

Sarah's voice carried the smile he couldn't see.

"Good. You scared the hell out of me there for a moment. Damn this place. How can you love it so much, only to . . . Never mind. Still got a leaker. One-one thousand, two—"

Beau's hand was near-frozen, his aim useless. Time to put the outer glove back on while he still could. What the hell had happened? He'd seen the impacts, watched the blood fog, seen the suit deflate. And still the hare's voice kept coming through the radio. First he'd shot high, then he'd shot the wrong man. How could he make so many mistakes?

Briefly he'd thought of just shooting everyone he could see, hoping one might be the hare, just as he'd shot, on general principles, at the two who'd snatched the original target and dragged him out of sight. But whatever his clients wanted, it was either business or vengeance. Neither thrived on that kind of publicity. His job was a hit, not a massacre.

Meanwhile, he listened to the radio chatter, filtering voices.

"Meteorite swarm," the one called Sarah was saying. "Do you have any idea how rare those are? Damn! Second day on the job and he was standing in the wrong place at the wrong time. Damn."

Beau remembered the image of the two of them in the bar, heads together. A couple, incipient. If the woman came into his sights, shooting her might be useful. Apparently she and the hare had been the ones who'd dashed to the rescue of that Damien guy. What would he do for the woman if she was hurt? Shooting her could be a very good idea.

"Is he alive?"

Drew's brush with vacuum had left him oddly energized. Like the time he'd gotten tripped and fallen in the 10,000-meter nationals. Get up, take control, and move, move, move, back into the race. But methodically, not purely on emotion, or you burn out and crash a different way before you reach the end. He'd gotten a school record for that one.

"I don't know." Sarah's voice seemed kilometers away. "Damien, can you hear me?" Her light illuminated his face, but if he was breathing, it was impossible to tell.

Drew didn't need to consult the web to know the nearest shelter was the access passageway beneath the array. "Gotta get him down."

He pulled the emergency release on his own tether, clipping it to Damien's suit. Wrapped the other end around his wrist. Thank God for lunar gravity. How much could the man weigh here, even with the training suit? Thirty pounds? Surely no more than forty. "I'll lower, you steady." Suddenly he remembered who was boss. "If that's okay."

"Sounds like a plan." Sarah switched channels. "Christophe, Andrea, get your butts over here. We're on pylon—"

"No!"

Drew grabbed her gloved hand, switched off his suit mike, leaned over to touched helmets. Waited until a click told him she'd done the same.

"Damien was shot. Whoever did this is still out there. People need to keep out of sight. Damien wasn't his target."

"Who was?" A pause. "Oh."

"I'm sorry. I thought I was starting over. I don't know who got bought out, where . . . I never thought I was putting anyone else in danger. When we get him down, maybe I should just walk out and announce myself. Get it over with."

"No." There was surprising fire in her voice. "And that's an order."

He nearly laughed, but was already bracing to lower Damien to the next level.

"Yes, boss."

Even in one-sixth gee, fifty meters of Jungle Gym wasn't easy. Especially because Sarah had ordered everyone to extinguish their lights, forcing him to work by enhanced starlight. But five minutes later they were down, and moments after that, they were bundling Damien into an airlock, a half-dozen other sunners crowding in with them. Then there was air, someone had a first aid kit, and he and Sarah were stripping off Damien's suit.

He was alive, but not by much, his chest making awful noises as air went in and out through the bullet holes.

"Shit," Sarah said. "We need a medic, now."

Someone reached for a panel marked *emergency com*, but Drew stopped him. "No." He flipped the latches on his helmet and took it off. Sarah understood immediately and did the same, while the others, puzzled, slowly followed suit.

"Is there any way to make that com private?"

Sarah shook her head. "No. It's designed to bring help even if you're too badly hurt to know your location."

"And no way to lock that door?"

"Crap. You think whoever did this is still out there."

"'Who'?" one of the others asked. "I thought it was a—"

Sarah waved him to silence. "Later."

"Right now," Drew said, "he may think we're still out there too." He tried to remember what they'd said over the radio, bringing Damien inside. "Either way, we need to give him as little information as possible."

He tried to think like the type of man his family would entrust with making sure he paid for his betrayal. But Sarah was a step ahead. "Eventually, he's going to figure it out."

"Yeah." His mind was functioning again. All that time he'd spent wondering . . . even the nightmares had prepped him for this.

But again, Sarah was ahead of him. "So we need to get Damien somewhere else." She turned to the rest of her crew. "Take him outward, away from the dome. At least two or three pylons out. Far enough nobody'd expect us there. And if you run into anyone from Snellman's or Wang's crews, for God's sake, no radios."

"Good." Drew said. "I'll go get help."

There were grab plates along one side of the corridor. He had no idea why. Maybe they were for traction, hauling loads. Sarah had been right. Even on the Moon, labor was sometimes cheaper than equipment, but power was one thing sunners had aplenty.

This part of the PEL was ten klicks from Luna II. Drew had once run that far in twenty-eight minutes, fifty-four seconds. And that had been in full Earth gravity— the day he'd fallen.

He stepped to the nearest plate and started to jog. Found his rhythm and stretched it to a long, low lope. Four plates per stride. Five. Six.

Beau wished he knew more about the hare. What had he done? What type of man was he? If he was right that this was about vengeance, then it was about someone who'd done something stupid back on Earth. And there was only one kind of stupid that could produce a hit as expensive as this.

Stupid people stayed stupid. Which meant there was really only one thing the hare would do now. Character and geography constrained him.

Not for the first time, Beau was glad he wasn't similarly constrained. His grab boots still held a fifty-two percent charge. He knew where he needed to be next and had been running for it from the moment the suit radios went quiet. That should give him enough of a head start.

For reasons known only to the tunnel drillers, no corridor in Luna C was perfectly straight. Maybe it was fear of staring endlessly into vanishing-point distances. Maybe it was simply a desire to avoid monotony. Whatever the reason, they progressed in short straights, bounded by easy curves, like a gently meandering road or trail.

Drew was rounding one of these curves when a figure loomed in front of him.

A man in a jet-black skinsuit.

A man with a rifle, emerging, as if by magic, from an airlock a scant thirty meters ahead.

Drew attempted to brake, missed the next plate, and slid across the lunar-gee floor, flailing until his hand caught a plate with a jerk, just as a bullet pinged the floor and zinged down the tunnel behind him.

Then something he belatedly registered as a spacesuit helmet flew over his head in a fast, flat arc, smashing hard into the black-suited man's hand.

"This way!" Sarah yelled, waving him back around the curve he'd just rounded. "What, you think you're the only one who ever tried to run the plates? Move!"

More bullets pinged, but these were wild, barely aimed, as he and Sarah dived around the curve. A moment later she ducked into an airlock, pulling him after her as the door shut. Already the air was cycling for space.

"Wait!" he yelled, scrambling to lock down his helmet. "You don't have any air!"

But she'd already grabbed a helmet from an emergency locker. "One size fits all." She clamped it down. The outside door opened, and they were on the surface. Alone, in the dark.

He stared back into the airlock, wondering how much lead they had. Not much, but maybe he could extend it a bit. He grabbed another helmet out of the emergency locker and used it to wedge the outer door open.

"Good move," Sarah said. Then she was on the broadband. No need for silence now. "Base, we have a casualty in pylon corridor four, near airlock twenty-seven. Please send a medic. And be careful. We have an assassin with a gun. Repeat, assassin with a gun." She paused. "And you, creep, if you're listening, you leave my crew alone. If you want me, come get me. You know where I went."

She cut out. Touched helmets with Drew. "I guess it's just you and me. Any brilliant ideas?"

XI

"Assassin?" Raz was on his fourth cup of coffee but the sleepiness he'd been fighting was suddenly gone. "Where?"

He clicked off the com. "McHaddon. With me. Caeli—" Damn, what could he give her to do? "Duty roster. On my computer. Password Booker2Much@ Earth."

He caught her glance.

"Yeah, I know. Call everyone. Tell them to get their butts on the com to me now. Okay, that might not be the best metaphor. But get them off whatever they're doing and in touch with me, no excuses."

He was already half out the door. "And if you come up with some brilliant way to stop an invisible sniper in the dark, give me a call."

Then he was in the corridor. Not that dashing off to Luna II really did much good. But where else could he go? Luna II was where the action was.

At the last moment, he stopped, hurried back to his desk. Thumbed the lock on the bottom drawer and fumbled inside until he found his sidearm. He couldn't remember the last time he'd touched it. In the domes it just wasn't safe.

He wondered if the damn thing even worked. Not that it mattered. If it came to a shootout, a professional assassin would have him before he even knew he was under attack. But he strapped the holster beneath his jacket, even as he was back on the com, demanding that the Luna II Overway be at the station, *now.*

For one brief moment, he was glad Caeli was here, in the office. She'd have his back, as best a civilian could do. He wasn't sure when it had happened, but sometime in the past few hours he'd realized she would always do that, even if the person she was defending him against was himself. And here in the office she was only a com call distant, while still out of harm's way.

Both mattered. A lot.

Drew stared across the regolith. Lights off, vision enhancement at max. Rocks were grainy blurs, slopes indistinct, tripping easy.

Somewhere beyond was the crater rim. A 4,000-meter drop into the land of eternal dark. Not that at the moment it would be any darker there than here.

His air gauge told him he was good for forty-seven hours at minimal exertion. Maybe he and Sarah could just hide.

Then he looked down. Even enhanced, his footprints were barely visible. But they were there.

"Leave me," he said. "Circle back. It's me he wants."

"No." There were a lot of things in her voice, not all of which he could parse.

Then light burst from an exit 400 meters down-tunnel.

Running for Luna II was no longer an option, and circling back would get them trapped at the PEL. The only choice was into the void ahead.

Drew pulled away, breaking the tenuous helmet-to-helmet contact. His family wanted to kill him. Sarah was willing to risk dying with him. Just as he'd risked dying for Damien, who he'd never even met. He hoped he lived long enough to figure out what it all meant.

Meanwhile, they had to move. A one-time runner and a born-and-bred Loonie in a marathon of unknown length: one that only ended when they escaped and lived . . . or didn't.

Raz was in Archie's, the only place he could come up with for his informal field office. Archie didn't even try to offer him Scotch. Coffee was the order of the night.
Technically it was a breach of regulations not to pay, but paying would be a mortal
insult. Especially since Archie had chased out a sea of Darkout revelers, many of
whom still hovered in the plaza, wondering what was happening.

"So let me get this," Archie was saying as he filled Raz's mug. "Some Earth
goon's chasing him, up on the rim?"

"Something like that."

"So why doesn't he just come back in here?"

"Maybe because he can't. We're pretty sure the bad guy's got grab boots, so he
can move pretty fast. He also shot up the PEL pretty good." The story was still gar-
bled, but it sounded like a miracle Damien was even barely clinging to life. "If you
were him, would you lead someone like that back here?"

"Hell no. These folks are like family to me. You get that bastard, okay?"

"If I can, Arch."

For the nth time, Raz pulled up a holo of the PEL. Smooth ground, sloping toward the rim. A few boulders, but nowhere to hide. Drew and Sarah had shut off
their transponders, presumably fearing their pursuer could home in on them. But
where would they be going?

He flipped on the com. "Harken?" She'd been one of the first to check in, so he'd
made her com coordinator, relieving Caeli. "How many folks you got up on the
PEL, so far?"

"Three. Two more coming."

"ETA?"

"Fifteen minutes."

"Don't wait." Drew, Sarah, and the bad guy could be halfway to anywhere. "Tell
them to track footprints and keep us posted. No lights. And for God's sake, tell them
to be careful. Follow, not engage."

"Got it. No lights. No contact. You know they'll never catch up, anyway."

"I know. I just want to know where everyone's going. I don't want to recycle a
bunch of dead cops."

Drew was counting advantages and disadvantages. His advantage was that he'd
once been a runner. He knew how to marshal his energy efficiently. Sarah's was that
she knew how to move in lunar gee. Their disadvantage was that that they could
barely see where they were going. Much of the time, their image enhancement was
good enough, but then a boulder would loom, and they'd have to veer, leap, or
brake to avoid it. A waste of energy that their pursuer, following their tracks, could
avoid. The bastard could even use lights if he needed. Not to mention that he had
some kind of tech that allowed him to run just like he was on Earth. Drew had seen
him burst into the corridor, stop, raise the rifle, never touching a plate. Without
Sarah's helmet-pitch Drew would be dead.

Every runner had heard how unarmed hunters once ran prey into the ground,
killing them with their bare hands. An antelope might be faster, but the hunter,
whether Native American, Kalahari bushman, or sport-hunting ultramarathoner,
was more efficient.

As far as Drew could tell, the dis- advantages outweighed the ad-s. Sarah had saved him in the tunnel, but had she condemned herself by doing it? Now they were the antelope, running in energy-wasting spurts and lunges.

Think, he commanded himself. *Think.*

Meanwhile, he did the only thing he could, and ran as fast as visibility allowed. Maybe he and Sarah were fitter. Maybe they could outlast their stalker, even if he had more advantages. Maybe that was how the antelope thought, right up to the moment the hunter's hands closed on its neck.

Raz was out of ideas.

Not that he'd had many to begin with. Outside, it was dark as only Darkout could be. Sarah and Drew, or whatever his real name was, would try to hide, but on the Moon, footprints are forever—or as close to it as made no nevermind. If this Jester guy was on their trail—and Raz had no doubt he was—he'd gradually run them down . . . then fade off into the dark. On Earth, they had IR tech to track him, but here, nobody'd ever seen a need for that stuff. As long as he stayed in shadows, the guy might as well be invisible. And odds were that his crawler was even better stealthed.

Drew was also thinking about footprints. The antelope only lost if the hunter knew where it went. He tapped Sarah's shoulder, pulled her to a stop. Behind, a pale wash of light blinked on, then off. A suit light on ultra-dim, just enough for easier pursuit. He'd seen it several times before, a little closer each time.

"We can't beat him this way," he said. "We've got to do something about the footprints."

"What?"

"I don't know. Find firmer terrain. Or a beaten path. Anything that at least makes him work to follow us."

The helmet-to-helmet contact stuttered as Sarah looked around—for what little good that did in the dark.

"—Too bad . . . cut off from the PEL, but . . . harder rock and boulders . . . if we can find a break in the rim."

The light appeared again. He could feel the panic rise. If the antelope bolted and escaped a hundred and one times, but got caught on the hundred and second, it made no difference. The end was the same, either way.

"How far?"

"Two, three klicks." Her shoulders were already turning.

And then the antelope were off again.

Razo stared at Archie's walls. Like any bar's, they were cluttered. Sports vids, not only from Luna C and Earth but also the O'Neils, as if any ground-dweller could figure out the sports played in their zero-gee hubs. A pair of carved-wood carousel horses, all the way from Earth. Dozens of soccer shoes. What in the world would

Arch want with soccer shoes? Holos of the first PEL: a single tower on a rotating platform. Flat pics of the construction of the Luna II dome. More, showing a row of reflectors on the crater rim, paired with shots of miners under banks of construction lights, building the solar stills, far below.

A rustle of motion brought him back to the present. Caeli. She'd turned up several coffees ago, when Harken had relieved her on the com, and had been helping Archie serve drinks to the revelers on the plaza. At first Razo had been worried, but wherever the action was headed, it clearly wasn't going to wind up in Archie's. Still, he should send her away, tell her to get some sleep. Instead he motioned her to sit beside him.

"I'm going to lose them," he said. "Everything we've got is aimed at finding people who *want* to be found. I never dreamed of anything like this. How could I have been so stupid?"

"Because you're human?" Her gaze shifted, then returned. "And just because we do things we regret, way back—it doesn't mean we've got to be perfect ever after. No matter how badly we want to atone."

"Do you have regrets?"

"Who doesn't? But most weren't things I could control." She smiled. "Right now, I only wish we could have had these conversations loons ago. Though then, we wouldn't be doing it now, and I'm not sure I'd wish that away."

There was nothing accusing in her gaze—which made it all the harder to hold. Instead, he looked back at Archie's photo collection. Bright lights and ultimate darkness: the contrast was what produced the drama, especially in the construction photos, with all the workers under the lights. Perhaps it was the contrast that made the Moon itself worthwhile. Forging a home out of the most inhospitable place humanity had yet reached.

Caeli must have read his mind. "The kid's right, you know. This is a place for starting over. However many times it takes. And quit beating yourself up for not anticipating this. Nobody thinks of everything."

Then abruptly she was back to business. "So how much air does our bad guy have?"

"I have no idea, but you can bet it's more than Drew and Sarah."

XII

They'd had to use lights at the rim. A quick flash, as dim as possible, then move before their pursuer could draw a bead. Another flash and another move.

One of the many things Drew knew that "Drew" might not was that much of the escarpment dropped at nearly a forty-degree angle. Not vertical, but steep enough they couldn't just descend anywhere. But within 300 meters, they had what they needed. A boulder-choked crack, perhaps an ancient fault, where exposures of solid rock looked like they might not roll underfoot and at least some of the wedged boulders looked free of footprint-holding dust. Not that this would fool their follower for long. When there is only one way down, that has to be the way they went. But it was the best chance they were going to get.

No need to speak. Drew took Sarah's hand and gave it a quick squeeze. Then they started down. Together.

"They're heading for the crater," Raz said. Caeli was still sitting with him, nursing a cola. "Harken's team says their footprints are making for the rim, looking like they're moving fast. They probably reached it quite a while ago."

"Wow," Caeli said. "It's steep on that side. Landing, I never have much time to gawk at the scenery, but if the Sun's on the rim, it's hard not to notice. I sure wouldn't want to climb down."

"I don't think they have much choice."

Raz closed his eyes and rubbed his fingertips across them, brightness shooting in a starburst as he did. When he opened them again, everything seemed brighter but fuzzier, with nothing to see but the clutter on Archie's wall, slowly coming back into focus.

That's when it hit. Probably impossible, but when all else is impossible, the probably impossible looms as a beacon of hope.

Archie was behind the bar, wanting to help but also wanting to keep out of the way. Raz tapped the rim of his cup, the universal signal for a refill. "Thanks," he said as the bartender drew near.

"For what?"

"Giving me room to think."

Arch shrugged. "Anyone would do that."

For the first time in hours, Raz felt himself smile.

"And for collecting things."

Then he was back on the com, feeling the energy mount within him as he watched his friend's puzzled face. "Get me McHaddon," he said.

He turned to Caeli. "Can you do a calculation for me?" It was five hours, give or take, until the end of Darkout. The Sun wouldn't be fully up until a couple of hours after that, but he didn't need full Sun. Just enough of it—whatever that might be. "Figure out how much air Drew and Sarah have left."

Then his com came alive again.

"McHaddon, I need you to roust some folks out of bed, parties, or wherever they are." He rattled off a list of names and titles. "Don't waste time on the ones you can't find. Get those you can and turn 'em over to Lum.

"Arch—can you find Lum? He's got to be around here somewhere. And Caeli, find out who's into astronomy. I need the biggest-ass portable telescope we can get, ASAP."

Beau flexed his hand. Back at the PEL, he'd left the outer glove off too long, and his hand had been only beginning to warm again when the woman hit it with that damn helmet. For a bit, he'd thought she'd broken it, but it was just the pain of a hard blow on near-frozen digits.

Maybe he'd kill her first. His clients wouldn't mind. Even if he was wrong about this being a revenge job, killing the guy's friend/lover/whatever-she-was would send a warning that his clients weren't to be messed with.

He flexed the hand again. It had taken hours, but he was sure he could make the shot now, even from a thousand meters. On Earth, anyway. Why the hell hadn't he thought to reprogram the autoscope? But there was nothing to do about it now. He'd always prided himself on clean kills, but this might be better. He flexed his hand yet again. That had *hurt*. Damn lucky bitch.

He checked the power on his grab boots. Still thirty percent. He'd been conserving, waiting for his hand to return to normal, using the boots only when he had to, to make up time lost when he had to stop, looking for tracks. Which hadn't been all that often. Yes, there were fewer footprints here, but no matter how careful you were, you couldn't move fast without dislodging rocks . . . and those too left marks.

Keep 'em moving. That was the goal. Moving and dislodging rocks. Moving and burning air. They had to be running low, and there were only two places they could go for more. One was the domes of Luna C Central, and the moment they got within a klick of those, there'd be enough light from the windows for his night vision to have them like bugs on a carpet. He could feel his lips pull in a smile. He'd heard their silly song. *From now unto then, just leave on the lights.* How fitting if their own motto was their undoing.

Drew was running out of gas, both literally and figuratively. Slipping downslope without dislodging any more rock than he could was painstaking, thigh-burning work. It didn't matter that the gravity was one-sixth what he'd once been used to. Thousands of meters of downgrade were still thousands of meters of downgrade. Brake, brake, brake, brake, brake. Slip, and brake again, hard enough he could feel the energy draining from his legs, even as he knew he was yet again leaving telltale marks. He wondered how Sarah did it. Women were just plain tough. There'd been one on the track team named Becky who ate mile repeats for breakfast. He himself always had to fight off butterflies before anything longer than 800s.

Meanwhile the lights of Luna C beckoned like the warm glow of a campfire. But it was a dangerous glow he knew they could never approach, even though his air gauge seemed to drop each time he looked at it. They had to flee, but flee efficiently, until Sarah could lead them to more gas. If they lived long enough to reach it. And then, they had to run, yet again.

Maybe he should just quit. Behind him he could occasionally see light, appearing and disappearing, relentlessly following. The man was a machine, indefatigable. Nothing could stop him, nothing could tire him.

Which was exactly the thinking that had lost him the conference championship his sophomore year in college. The guy chasing him then hadn't been superhuman. Drew had just thought he was. A year later, he'd come back with more confidence and had the pleasure of watching the other guy puke at the finish. Some people only looked indefatigable. When they broke, they broke totally.

Keep going, he told himself.

Meanwhile, his air gauge crept lower.

First Darkout was ending. Beau watched as light blazed a crescent on the rim: a mere hairline, but enough to change everything. Here in the shadows it was still dark, but soon the backwash would be a hundred times brighter than the light of the stars. Dislodged rocks and footprints would no longer need to be sought out.

The crater floor was still a thousand meters below, but already Beau could see better. It was time to use the grab-boot power he'd been sparing—get in close enough that even the damn autoscope would score a hit in this gravity that wasn't real gravity.

The prey was down there somewhere. Running out of air. With him following their tracks, they couldn't simply hole up and hide. And on the move, their standard-white suits would show up a lot better to him than his would to them.

The time had come.

"What do you mean you can't see him?"

Yelling at McHaddon wasn't doing anyone any good, but Raz could apologize later. He desperately wished he could be up on the rim with him, looking through the damn telescope himself. But delegating was the cost of being in charge. Which meant he was still in Archie's, five hours more tired, five coffees more wired. Caeli had never left his side.

The only place Drew and Sarah could be going was the volatiles mines, and they had to get there soon or run out of air. Or get shot. But just because he knew where they were going didn't mean McHaddon could spot them in the damn scope.

"Too many rocks," McHaddon said. "Or maybe the scope's not big enough." The biggest portable Caeli had been able to find had only been forty centimeters. "The image isn't exactly bright."

Raz thought a moment, then shifted from the scrambled channel he and McHaddon had rigged up with the help of one of Raz's hastily roused techs to the all-police band. Com security was another of those things he'd never had to worry about before. In the main domes, the com was private. But emergency coms and suit radios were meant to be found, not hidden.

"Barker, Kowalski, Gardner," he called to Harken's crew. "Turn around, and flash your lights. Just once. Then move, in case this guy wants to take a pot at you."

"Got 'em," McHaddon said, a moment later. "They're definitely heading where we thought they would."

"Good. The folks we're looking for should be in the same direction, farther ahead."

The silence stretched, nearly broke.

"Sorry. Still too dark."

"Damn."

Raz checked his watch. Time was running out. How soon, he didn't know, but his gut told him he couldn't wait much longer. He flicked on the com.

"Lum, tell your folks we need some light." He hated to do this because the Geste guy might have lost Sarah and Drew's trail, and he might just lead him back onto it. But somehow he doubted that. The guy'd had them out-teched all along.

"Still working on it. How much?"

"Not a lot, but over as broad an area as you can handle." He gave the coordinates. "They're down there somewhere but McHaddon can't see them. We need to give him a little help."

Lum's voice was clipped, tense. Not for the first time, Raz wished he'd been able to find someone who didn't have so much at stake. But Lum knew everything above the rim better than anyone else in the domes, even the parts that weren't technically his domain.

Beau heard the radio chatter, saw the headlamps.

Hours before, the cops trailing him had wised up and shut off their radios, but not before it had become clear they did *not* like descending endless talus and had no experience at it. Now, the distant lights confirmed what he'd suspected, that he, the hare, the girl . . . all were moving twice as fast as the best cop.

When it came time to get away, that too would be easy. The bottom of the crater was a maze of crawler paths and bootprints, and not by coincidence, his boots were identical to a thousand others. Once he hit those trails they'd never find him.

Which, of course, was the hare's plan, too. But first he and the girl had to get more air. And there were only two places to go . . . one of which was suicide. That left the one they were indeed heading for. Was it also suicide if you were simply outsmarted?

Five minutes later, Beau had them. By now the backwash from the slowly widening crescent on the rim was ten times brighter than before, and while his targets were still grainy blobs even in his top-of-the-line visor, they were clearly there. Closing in on their destination, but too far from it to have any chance of getting there.

He ran/walked/skidded another couple of minutes, as fast as the terrain permitted. That wasn't all that fast because it was still godawful steep, but it was faster than the prey could go without the boots.

The range was now 600 meters. Close enough. He found a convenient rock, unlimbered his tripod, and set up the rifle.

Briefly, he wished he knew which blob was which. But even through the scope, they were merely blobs. He picked the leader, aimed low in a vague effort to compensate for the 'scope, and squeezed. One. Two. Three. Four. Five.

At least one connected.

Whoever he'd hit went down in remarkably slow motion. As long as he lived, he was never going to get used to this place.

He shifted aim to the other, but this one was making it easy. He—she?—ran to the fallen companion. Again, Beau felt the grin. He really hadn't enjoyed a hunt this much since his early days. Let them stop the leaks. One was now hurt enough to be a burden. The other should run, but wasn't going to. He switched on his vid recorder. His clients would like this.

He picked up the tripod, not bothering to unbolt the gun, and moved forward again, grab boots on full power. If anything weird happened, he wanted to be able to react fast. But there was nowhere for the prey to hide. If it ran, Beau would shoot. There was all kinds of time to make the kill, and nobody here but the three of them. Beau had long ago checked the work schedule—leaving an active worksite between him and his crawler was not part of his escape plan. Apparently, ramping up and shutting down for each Darkout wasn't worth the effort: the folks who worked here were gone for a week. Some triumphs were worth savoring. And the cops on the rim were impossibly far behind.

The survivor didn't run. Rather, it stood up, and, in the increasing light, waved its arms over its head.

"It's me you want." The voice came in over the all-band radio. "She's done nothing to you, never heard of the Katsaros family until I told her. She's just my boss."

Beau restrained his laugh only by habit. Not that the noise would have mattered, with his suit telemetrics fastidiously set to "off."

She was a lot more than boss, from what he could tell. Unconsummated love, left so forever because one of them had foolishly angered the wrong people. His clients really were going to like this.

He kept walking. The lighting was getting better by the second. Now, even from 400 meters, he could tell that the one on the ground was female. He folded the tripod up against the stock of the rifle. Lowered the gun and fired from the hip. A miss. But not by much. He'd seen the dust puff behind the hare. On Earth the man might have flinched, but here, unless he saw the muzzle flash, he might not even have known he'd been shot at.

Beau continued to walk. As long as the guy didn't run, Beau could be as nonchalant as he wished. And the guy clearly wasn't going to leave the woman. Stupid because she was dead, no matter what. Maybe Beau would even get to record his face as he blew her brains out.

Two hundred meters away, and suddenly he realized he had a shadow. That wasn't right. No way was the image enhancement that good. He turned it off and the shadow was still there. How could there be a shadow here in the land of eternal night?

He wheeled back to look at the top of the crater rim behind him. The crescent of sunlight was still there, a bit thicker than before, but not much. But above it was a flare of unbelievable brightness; so bright his suit's sunshield automatically kicked in to dim it.

He wheeled back toward the prey, but could no longer see them. He fired vaguely in the right direction, but he was now in the center of a spotlight, so bright everything outside was impenetrably dark.

The one good thing was that he could now truly see his footing. He tried to run, but the light followed him, the beam contracting by the second.

It was getting warm. Not just warm, but *hot*. He dodged right, then left, but the intolerable brightness remained. There were voices yelling at him to do something, but he tuned them out.

Belatedly he realized that the way to go was toward the prey: force the operators of this blinding, searing light to aim it not only at him, but at them. But he was in a land of brightness surrounded by dark and he no longer knew where his targets were. The brightness contracted, the darkness drew closer, and the heat rose and rose until the ground steamed, as ices, trapped for a billion years, felt the light of a thousand suns they'd never seen before and Beau's suit, black as the night he'd hidden in, absorbed every erg. As did the gun. Stumbling, burning, he dropped it. Zigged. Zagged. Tried to get into the dark.

Then, blessedly the light was fading.

But his suit was still burning, burning, burning, and he needed out, out. Needed a breath of coolness. Just a whiff. Anything but the fabric that still burned his skin, the air that still seared his lungs, even as the light faded to that which he'd remembered from a distant Earth.

He couldn't think. He was confined in something. A suit. That was it. A hot, horrible suit. All he needed was air. Cool air. Just a breath. He'd stripped off his outer gloves some time ago; he couldn't remember when. Now he fumbled at the latches for his helmet. Cool. He had to have cool . . .

Razo hadn't needed McHaddon's telescope to watch the assassin die. Once the light got bright enough, there were plenty of perfectly ordinary cams near the volatile mines to use as Lum's crew put the adaptive optics of the stills' mirrors through tricks they were never intended to do. Pure, raw sunlight, stolen from an area a hundred meters on a side and focused into a beam of blinding heat. So what if, up on the rim, only a sliver of sun was yet above the horizon?

"Poor bastard," he said.

Caeli gripped his hand.

"In twenty years, I've never had to kill anyone. Never thought I'd have to."

Caeli didn't say anything, which was probably best. He squeezed back. Then it was time for business.

"Sarah?" he said on the all-suits channel. "Drew? You still with us?"

"Yeah." Drew's voice seemed surprisingly close. "Though we could use some help. What the hell was that?"

"Home-made heat ray." Suddenly he felt unbearably tired. "Ask Lum."

Ask your future father-in-law, he'd almost said. Some tea leaves were easy to read. Even with Caeli still holding his hand, Raz felt old.

He shut off the com. "He went back for her. He could have run, but he went back."

"Of course."

"I didn't."

It took her a moment to get it. "It's not the same, Artie. Nobody was pointing a gun at her and your situation was absolutely no-win."

"He didn't leave her."

"Yeah, and look how it worked out. He'd have been dead if he had, shot before he took two steps. Would you concede, for just a minute, that had you gone back to Earth you might have died? Not the same way, but in some other?"

"Or how about this. If you had, Drew and Sarah would be dead. Give yourself a break, Artie. Sometimes good things come out of bad. And new starts don't have to be instantaneous."

XIII

"How's Damien?"

By now, Drew knew Sarah well enough not to be surprised that these were her first coherent words once she'd recovered from surgery. The bullet had shattered her femur, narrowly missing the femoral artery, and it had taken eight hours and a hardware store's worth of titanium to put it back together. Still, the docs had assured Drew she'd not only walk again, but someday challenge him at running the plates. Bones knitted well under low gee.

But of course Sarah hadn't asked about that. Oh, she would eventually. Descending into the crater with her, Drew had been amazed by how gracefully she moved, how easily she maintained the effort. On Earth, she'd have had a sport. Gymnastics, perhaps. Or maybe tennis. Something that demanded poise and strength.

Or maybe he was just biased.

Meanwhile, the issue was Damien.

"It looks like he's going to make it. The docs gave him a seventy-five percent chance, last I heard. They're really stunned he even got back to the tunnels alive."

The meds made her voice groggy. "We're a good team."

Drew grinned. "Never doubted it." Though it wasn't just them. When the assassin had blocked his and Sarah's run for help, the rest of the PEL crew had done everything else as close to perfectly as humanly possible. A lot of hands had worked to save Damien, a lot of folks who'd never before met him. Hell, Drew had never met him. He was just a guy who'd accidentally taken a bullet—three bullets, actually—for him, and been saved by a clan of folks he'd never known before.

Drew finally knew why he'd come to the Moon. It wasn't just a new start. It was a new family. The real thing. Bound by . . . well, he wasn't sure what. But something thicker than blood.

Meanwhile he had other news.

"I'm dead."

Sarah was recovering quickly from the meds. "You don't look it."

"Good." He laughed. "I wasn't meaning it literally. But while you were under . . ." Briefly, he choked up. Even though the docs had been optimistic, there'd always been a chance she'd never wake up again . . . "While you were under, Razo—he's a good guy, you know—he told me that as long as the guy trying to kill us was dead, he was putting out the word that there were two casualties, Drew Zeigler being the other. The official story is that I got killed before Razo and Lum got him."

Unexpectedly, he felt smothered in a confusing mix of emotions. Gratitude. Relief. The dregs of leftover fear. Saving him would have been the pinnacle of Razo's career: the stuff of tabloids from here to Ceres. Instead, he'd given it up to truly save him.

Razo, Lum, the folks who'd worked to save Damien. Blood wasn't thicker than water, whatever that meant. Blood was simply genetics. This—this had been choice.

"Anyway," he said, "he's going to need some help keeping the secret."

"No problem. Nobody's going to have any trouble with that."

"And I'm going to need a new name. Something Loonie would be good."

Sarah's smile was tired and he knew that sleep beckoned. But not yet. "Janes?"

XIV

"When you go back to visit, I want to meet her too," Caeli said.

She and Raz had wound up in his quarters, still too wired to make more than the most chaste moves toward that which they'd joke/flirted about so often.

"Who?" Raz was still thinking about fresh starts, good-coming-from-bad.

"You know. Your daughter. She's got to be in college now, right?"

"Yeah. She's a sophomore at Macquarie, majoring in Renaissance literature."

"Really?"

He shrugged. "What makes you think she'll even talk to me?"

Caeli's eyes were far away. "Oh, she will." She hesitated. "You're not the only one to hit space with secrets."

"Don't say anything you don't want to. It's the real you that matters." He tapped his chest. "The one that lives in here."

"Yeah. That's what I've been trying to tell you. But this is part of what made me who I am. And probably brought me to space." She paused. "You would have brought Jenn and Lily back here if you could. My daddy . . . well, let's just say I'd give my right arm to have him show up from wherever he went." Her eyes were moist. "I might beat him black and blue with it, but I'd give it up. But I'd not give up space. Not for all the daddies in the world."

Her mood brightened. "I've got a better idea. Don't go visit her. You didn't want to train for the gravity, anyway. Invite her here. How could she resist?"

"And who, pray tell, would fly her up?"

She raised her eyebrows. "Oh, I bet you could find someone."

He stared at the com. It would take a while to work up the courage. But family—true family anyway—was more than the accident of birth. It was about choices. Maybe sometimes you could choose both.

ANDY DUNCAN

Andy Duncan made his first sale, to Asimov's Science Fiction, *in 1997, and quickly made others, to* Starlight, Sci Fiction, Amazing, Science Fiction Age, Dying For It, Realms of Fantasy, *and* Weird Tales, *as well as several more sales to* Asimov's. *By the beginning of the new century, he was widely recognized as one of the most individual, quirky, and flavorful new voices on the scene today. His story "The Executioner's Guild" was on both the Nebula Awards Final Ballot and the final ballot for the World Fantasy Award in 2000, and in 2001 he won two World Fantasy Awards, for his story "The Pottawatomie Giant," and for his landmark first collection,* Beluthahatchie and Other Stories. *He also won the Theodore Sturgeon Memorial Award in 2002 for his novella* The Chief Designer. *His other books include an anthology coedited with F. Brett Cox,* Crossroads: Tales of the Southern Literary Fantastic, *and a nonfiction guidebook,* Alabama Curiosities. *His most recent books include a chapbook novella,* The Night Cache, *and a new collection,* The Pottawatomie Giant and Other Stories. *A graduate of the Clarion West Writers Workshop in Seattle, he was born in Batesberg, South Carolina, and now lives in Frostburg, Maryland, with his wife, Sydney. Duncan is an assistant professor in the Department of English at Frostburo State University. He has a blog at http://beluthahatchie .blogspot.com.*

The simultaneously sad and funny story he offers us here is a treat for anyone who grew up in the flying saucer–mad days of the '50s and stayed up late, eyes wide, reading battered old paperback copies of Donald E. Keyhoe's The Flying Saucers Are Real. . . .

She knocked on my front door at midday on Holly Eve, so I was in no mood to answer, in that season of tricks. An old man expects more tricks than treats in this world. I let that knocker knock on. *Blim, blam!* Knock, knock! It hurt my concentration, and filling old hulls with powder and shot warn't no easy task to start with, not as palsied as my hands had got in my eightieth-odd year.

"All right, damn your eyes," I hollered as I hitched up from the table. I knocked against it and a shaker tipped over: pepper, so I let it go. My maw wouldn't have approved of such language as that, but we all get old doing things our maws wouldn't approve. We can't help it, not in this disposition, on this sphere down below.

I sidled up on the door, trying to see between the edges of the curtain and the pane, but all I saw there was the screen-filtered light of the sun, which wouldn't set in my hollow till nearbouts three in the day. Through the curtains was a shadow-shape like the top of a person's head, but low, like a child. Probably one of those Holton boys toting an orange coin carton with a photo of some spindleshanked African child eating hominy with its fingers. Some said those Holtons was like the Johnny Cash song, so heavenly minded they're no earthly good.

"What you want?" I called, one hand on the deadbolt and one feeling for starving-baby quarters in my pocket.

"Mr. Nelson, right? Mr. Buck Nelson? I'd like to talk a bit, if you don't mind. Inside or on the porch, your call."

A female, and no child, neither. I twitched back the curtain, saw a fair pretty face under a fool hat like a sideways saucer, lips painted the same black-red as her hair. I shot the bolt and opened the wood door but kept the screen latched. When I saw her full length I felt a rush of fool vanity and was sorry I hadn't traded my overalls for fresh that morning. Her boots reached her knees but nowhere near the hem of her tight green dress. She was a little thing, hardly up to my collarbone, but a blind man would know she was full growed. I wondered what my hair was doing in back, and I felt one hand reach around to slick it down, without my really telling it to. *Steady on, son.*

"I been answering every soul else calling Buck Nelson since 1894, so I reckon I should answer you, too. What you want to talk about, Miss—?"

"Miss Hanes," she said, "and I'm a wire reporter, stringing for Associated Press."

"A reporter," I repeated. My jaw tightened up. My hand reached back for the doorknob as natural as it had fussed my hair. "You must have got the wrong man," I said.

I'd eaten biscuits bigger than her tee-ninchy pocketbook, but she reached out of it a little spiral pad that she flipped open to squint at. Looked to be full of secretary-scratch, not schoolhouse writing at all. "But you, sir, are indeed Buck Nelson, Route Six, Mountain View, Missouri? Writer of a book about your travels to the Moon, and Mars, and Venus?"

By the time she fetched up at Venus her voice was muffled by the wood door I had slammed in her face. I bolted it, cursing my rusty slow reflexes. How long had it been, since fool reporters come nosing around? Not long enough. I limped as quick as I could to the back door, which was right quick, even at my age. It's a small house. I shut that bolt, too, and yanked all the curtains to. I turned on the Zenith and dialed the sound up as far as it would go to drown out her blamed knocking and calling. Ever since the roof aerial blew cockeyed in the last whippoorwill storm, watching my set was like trying to read a road sign in a blizzard, but the sound blared out well enough. One of the stories was on as I settled back at the table with my shotgun hulls. I didn't really follow those women's stories, but I could hear Stu and Jo were having coffee again at the Hartford House and still talking about poor dead Eunice and that crazy gal what shot her because a ghost told her to. That blonde Jennifer was slap crazy, all right, but she was a looker, too, and the story hadn't been half so interesting since she'd been packed off to the sanitarium. I was spilling powder everywhere now, what with all the racket and distraction, and hearing the story was on reminded me it was past my dinnertime anyways, and me hungry. I went into the kitchen, hooked down my grease-pan and set it on the big burner, dug some lard out of the stand I kept in the icebox and threw that in to melt, then fisted some fresh-picked whitefish mushrooms out of their bin, rinsed them off in the sink, and rolled them in a bowl of cornmeal while I half-listened to the TV and half-listened to the city girl banging and hollering, at the back door this time. I could hear her boot heels a-thunking all hollow-like on the back porch, over the old dog bed where Teddy used to lie, where the other dog, Bo, used to try to squeeze, big as he was. She'd probably want to talk about poor old Bo, too, ask to see his grave, as if that would prove something. She had her some stick-to-it-iveness, Miss Associated Press did, I'd give her that much. Now she was sliding something under the door, I could hear it, like a field mouse gnawing its way in: a little card, like the one that Methodist preacher always leaves, only shinier. I didn't bother to pick it up. I didn't need nothing down there on that floor. I slid the whitefish into the hot oil without a splash. My hands had about lost their grip on gun and tool work, but in the kitchen I was as surefingered as an old woman. Well, eating didn't mean shooting anymore, not since the power line come in, and the supermarket down the highway. Once the whitefish got to sizzling good, I didn't hear Miss Press no more.

"This portion of *Search for Tomorrow* has been brought to you by . . . Spic and Span, the all-purpose cleaner. And by . . . Joy dishwashing liquid. From grease to shine in half the time, with Joy. Our story will continue in just a moment."

I was up by times the next morning. Hadn't kept milk cows in years. The last was Molly, she with the wet-weather horn, a funny-looking old gal but as calm and sweet as could be. But if you've milked cows for seventy years, it's hard to give in and let the sun start beating you to the day. By first light I'd had my Cream of Wheat, a child's meal I'd developed a taste for, with a little jerp of honey, and was out in the back field, bee hunting.

I had three sugar-dipped corncobs in a croker sack, and I laid one out on a hickory stump, notched one into the top of a fencepost, and set the third atop the boulder at the start of the path that drops down to the creek, past the old lick-log where the salt still keeps the grass from growing. Then I settled down on an old milkstool to wait. I gave up snuff a while ago because I couldn't taste it no more and the price got so high with taxes that I purely hated putting all that government in my mouth, but I still carry some little brushes to chew on in dipping moments, and I chewed on one while I watched those three corncobs do nothing. I'd set down where I could see all three without moving my head, just by darting my eyes from one to the other. My eyes may not see *Search for Tomorrow* so good anymore, even before the aerial got bent, but they still can sight a honeybee coming in to sip the bait.

The cob on the stump got the first business, but that bee just smelled around and then buzzed off straightaway, so I stayed set where I was. Same thing happened to the post cob and to the rock cob, three bees come and gone. But then a big bastard, one I could hear coming in like an airplane twenty feet away, zoomed down on the fence cob and stayed there a long time, filling his hands. He rose up all lazy-like, just like a man who's lifted the jug too many times in a sitting, and then made one, two, three slow circles in the air, marking the position. When he flew off, I was right behind him, legging it into the woods.

Mister Big Bee led me a ways straight up the slope, toward the well of the old McQuarry place, but then he crossed the bramble patch, and by the time I had worked my way antigoddlin around that, I had lost sight of him. So I listened for a spell, holding my breath, and heard a murmur like a branch in a direction where there warn't no branch. Sure enough, over thataway was a big hollow oak with a bee highway a-coming and a-going through a seam in the lowest fork. Tell the truth, I wasn't rightly on my own land anymore. The McQuarry place belonged to a bank in Cape Girardeau, if it belonged to anybody. But no one had blazed this tree yet, so my claim would be good enough for any bee hunter. I sidled around to just below the fork and notched an X where any fool could see it, even me, because I had been known to miss my own signs some days, or rummage the bureau for a sock that was already on my foot. Something about the way I'd slunk toward the hive the way I'd slunk toward the door the day before made me remember Miss Press, whom I'd plumb forgotten about. And when I turned back toward home, in the act of folding my pocketknife, there she was sitting on the lumpy leavings of the McQuarry chimney, a-kicking her feet and waving at me, just like I had wished her out of the ground. I'd have to go past her to get home, as I didn't relish turning my back on her and heading around the mountain, down the long way to the macadam and back around. Besides, she'd just follow me anyway, the way she followed me out here. I unfolded my knife again and snatched up a walnut stick to whittle on as I stomped along to where she sat.

"Hello, Mr. Nelson," she said. "Can we start over?"

"I ain't a-talking to *you*," I said as I passed, pointing at her with my blade. "I ain't even a-*walking* with you," I added, as she slid off the rockpile and walked along beside. "I'm taking the directedest path home, is all, and where you choose to walk is your own lookout. Fall in a hole and I'll just keep a-going, I swear I will. I've done it before, left reporters in the woods to die."

"Aw, I don't believe you have," she said, in a happy singsongy way. At least she was dressed for a tramp through the woods, in denim jeans and mannish boots with no heels to them, but wearing the same face-paint and fool hat, and in a red sweater that fit as close as her dress had. "But I'm not walking with you, either," she went on. "I'm walking alone, just behind you. You can't even see me, without turning your head. We're both walking alone, together."

I didn't say nothing.

"Are we near where it landed?" she asked.

I didn't say nothing.

"You haven't had one of your picnics lately, have you?"

I didn't say nothing.

"You ought to have another one."

I didn't say nothing.

"I'm writing a story," she said, "about *Close Encounters*. You know, the new movie? With Richard Dreyfuss? He was in *The Goodbye Girl*, and *Jaws*, about the shark? Did you see those? Do you go to any movies?" Some critter we had spooked, maybe a turkey, went thrashing off through the brush, and I heard her catch her breath. "I bet you saw *Deliverance*," she said.

I didn't say nothing.

"My editor thought it'd be interesting to talk to people who really have, you know, claimed their own close encounters, to have met people from outer space. Contactees, that's the word, right? You were one of the first contactees, weren't you, Mr. Nelson? When was it, 1956?"

I didn't say nothing.

"Aw, come on, Mr. Nelson. Don't be so mean. They all talked to me out in California. Mr. Bethurum talked to me."

I bet he did, I thought. *Truman Bethurum always was a plumb fool for a skirt.*

"I talked to Mr. Fry, and to Mr. King, and Mr. Owens. I talked to Mr. Angelucci."

Orfeo Angelucci, I thought, now there was one of the world's original liars, as bad as Adamski. "Those names don't mean nothing to me," I said.

"They told similar stories to yours, in the fifties and sixties. Meeting the Space Brothers, and being taken up, and shown wonders, and coming back to the Earth, with wisdom and all."

"If you talked to all them folks," I said, "you ought to be brim full of wisdom yourself. Full of something. Why you need to hound an old man through the woods?"

"You're different," she said. "You know lots of things the others don't."

"Lots of things, uh-huh. Like what?"

"You know how to hunt bees, don't you?"

I snorted. "Hunt bees. You won't never need to hunt no bees, Miss Press. Priss. You can buy your honey at the A and P. Hell, if you don't feel like going to the store, you could just ask, and some damn fool would bring it to you for free on a silver tray."

"Well, thank you," she said.

"That warn't no compliment," I said. "That was a clear-eyed statement of danger, like a sign saying, 'Bridge out,' or a label saying, 'Poison.' Write what you please, Miss Priss, but don't expect me to give you none of the words. You know all the words you need already."

"But you used to be so open about your experiences, Mr. Nelson. I've read that to anyone who found their way here off the highway, you'd tell about the alien Bob Solomon, and how that beam from the saucer cured your lumbago, and all that good pasture land on Mars. Why, you had all those three-day picnics, right here on your farm, for anyone who wanted to come talk about the Space Brothers. You'd even hand out little Baggies with samples of hair from your four-hundred-pound Venusian dog."

I stopped and whirled on her, and she hopped back a step, nearly fell down. "He warn't never no four hundred pounds," I said. "You reporters sure do believe some stretchers. You must swallow whole eggs for practice like a snake. I'll have you know, Miss Priss, that Bo just barely tipped three hundred and eighty-five pounds at his heaviest, and that was on the truck scales behind the Union 76 in June 1960, the day he ate all the silage, and Clay Rector, who ran all their inspections back then, told me those scales would register the difference if you took the Rand McNally atlas out of the cab, so that figure ain't no guesswork." When I paused for breath, I kinda shook myself, turned away from her gaping face and walked on. "From that day," I said, "I put old Bo on a Science Diet, one I got from the Extension, and I measured his rations, and I hitched him ever day to a sledge of felled trees and boulders and such, because dogs, you know, they're happier with a little exercise, and he settled down to around, oh, three-ten, three-twenty, and got downright frisky again. He'd romp around and change direction and jerk that sledge around, and that's why those three boulders are a-sitting in the middle of yonder pasture today, right where he slung them out of the sledge. Four hundred pounds, my foot. You don't know much, if that's what you know, and that's a fact."

I was warmed up by the walk and the spreading day and my own strong talk, and I set a smart pace, but she loped along beside me, writing in her notebook with a silver pen that flashed as it caught the sun. "I stand corrected," she said. "So what happened? Why'd you stop the picnics, and start running visitors off with a shotgun, and quit answering your mail?"

"You can see your own self what happened," I said. "Woman, I got old. You'll see what it's like, when you get there. All the people who believed in me died, and then the ones who humored me died, and now even the ones who feel obligated to sort of tolerate me are starting to go. Bo died, and Teddy, that was my Earth-born dog, he died, and them government boys went to the Moon and said they didn't see no mining operations or colony domes or big Space Brother dogs, or nothing else old Buck had seen up there. And in place of my story, what story did they come up with? I ask you. Dust and rocks and craters as far as you can see, and when you walk as far as that, there's another sight of dust and rocks and craters, and so on all around till you're back where you started, and that's it, boys, wash your hands, that's the Moon done. Excepting for some spots where the dust is so deep a body trying to land would just be swallowed up, sink to the bottom, and at the bottom find what? Praise Jesus, more dust, just what we needed. They didn't see nothing that anybody would care about going to see. No floating cars, no lakes of diamonds, no topless Moon gals, just dumb dull nothing. Hell, they might as well a been in Arkansas. You at least can cast a line there, catch you a bream. Besides, my lumbago come back," I said, easing myself down into the rocker, because we was back on my front porch by then. "It always comes back, my doctor says. Doctors plural, I should say. I'm on the third one now. The first two died on me. That's something, ain't it? For a man to outlive two of his own doctors?"

Her pen kept a-scratching as she wrote. She said, "Maybe Bob Solomon's light beam is still doing you some good, even after all this time."

"Least it didn't do me no harm. From what all they say now about the space people, I'm lucky old Bob didn't jam a post-hole digger up my ass and send me home with the screaming meemies and three hours of my life missing. That's the only aliens anybody cares about nowadays, big-eyed boogers with long cold fingers in your drawers. Doctors from space. Well, if they want to take three hours of my life, they're welcome to my last trip to the urologist. I reckon it was right at three hours, and I wish them joy of it."

"Not so," she said. "What about *Star Wars*? It's already made more money than any other movie ever made, more than *Gone With the Wind*, more than *The Sound of Music*. That shows people are still interested in space, and in friendly aliens. And this new Richard Dreyfuss movie I was telling you about is based on actual UFO case files. Dr. Hynek helped with it. That'll spark more interest in past visits to Earth."

"I been to ever doctor in the country, seems like," I told her, "but I don't recall ever seeing Dr. Hynek."

"How about Dr. Rutledge?"

"Is he the toenail man?"

She swatted me with her notebook. "Now you're just being a pain," she said. "Dr. Harley Rutledge, the scientist, the physicist. Over at Southeast Missouri State. That's no piece from here. He's been doing serious UFO research for years, right here in the Ozarks. You really ought to know him. He's been documenting the spooklights. Like the one at Hornet, near Neosho?"

"I've heard tell of that light," I told her, "but I didn't know no scientist cared about it."

"See?" she said, almost a squeal, like she'd opened a present, like she'd proved something. "A lot has happened since you went home and locked the door. More people care about UFOs and flying saucers and aliens today than they did in the 1950s, even. You should have you another picnic."

Once I got started talking, I found her right easy to be with, and it was pleasant a-sitting in the sun talking friendly with a pretty gal, or with anyone. It's true, I'd been powerful lonesome, and I had missed those picnics, all those different types of folks on the farm who wouldn't have been brought together no other way, in no other place, by nobody else. I was prideful of them. But I was beginning to notice something funny. To begin with, Miss Priss, whose real name I'd forgot by now, had acted like someone citified and paper-educated and standoffish. Now, the longer she sat on my porch a-jawing with me, the more easeful she got, and the more country she sounded, as if she'd lived in the hollow her whole life. It sorta put me off. Was this how Mike Wallace did it on *60 Minutes*, pretending to be just regular folks, until you forgot yourself, and were found out?

"Where'd you say you were from?" I asked.

"Mars," she told me. Then she laughed. "Don't get excited," she said. "It's a town in Pennsylvania, north of Pittsburgh. I'm based out of Chicago, though." She cocked her head, pulled a frown, stuck out her bottom lip. "You didn't look at my card," she said. "I pushed it under your door yesterday, when you were being so all-fired rude."

"I didn't see it," I said, which warn't quite a lie because I hadn't bothered to pick it up off the floor this morning, either. In fact, I'd plumb forgot to look for it.

"You ought to come out to Clearwater Lake tonight. Dr. Rutledge and his students will be set up all night, ready for whatever. He said I'm welcome. That means you're welcome, too. See? You have friends in high places. They'll be set up at the overlook, off the highway. Do you know it?"

"I know it," I told her.

"Can you drive at night? You need me to come get you?" She blinked and chewed her lip, like a thought had just struck. "That might be difficult," she said.

"Don't exercise yourself," I told her. "I reckon I still can drive as good as I ever did, and my pickup still gets the job done, too. Not that I aim to drive all that ways, just to look at the sky. I can do that right here on my porch."

"Yes," she said, "alone. But there's something to be said for looking up in groups, wouldn't you agree?"

When I didn't say nothing, she stuck her writing-pad back in her pocketbook and stood up, dusting her butt with both hands. You'd think I never swept the porch. "I appreciate the interview, Mr. Nelson."

"Warn't no interview," I told her. "We was just talking, is all."

"I appreciate the talking, then," she said. She set off across the yard, toward the gap in the rhododendron bushes that marked the start of the driveway. "I hope you can make it tonight, Mr. Nelson. I hope you don't miss the show."

I watched her sashay off around the bush, and I heard her boots crunching the gravel for a few steps, and then she was gone, footsteps and all. I went back in the house, latched the screen door and locked the wood, and took one last look through the front curtains, to make sure. Some folks, I had heard, remembered only long afterward they'd been kidnapped by spacemen, a "retrieved memory" they called it, like finding a ball on the roof in the fall that went up there in the spring. Those folks needed a doctor to jog them, but this reporter had jogged me. All that happy talk had loosened something inside me, and things I hadn't thought about in years were welling up like a flash flood, like a sickness. If I was going to be memory-sick, I wanted powerfully to do it alone, as if alone was something new and urgent, and not what I did ever day.

I closed the junk-room door behind me as I yanked the light on. The swaying bulb on its chain rocked the shadows back and forth as I dragged from beneath a shelf a crate of cheap splinter wood, so big it could have held two men if they was dead. Once I drove my pickup to the plant to pick up a bulk of dog food straight off the dock, cheaper that way, and this was one of the crates it come in. It still had that faint high smell. As it slid, one corner snagged and ripped the carpet, laid open the orange shag to show the knotty pine beneath. The shag was threadbare, but why bother now buying a twenty-year rug? Three tackle boxes rattled and jiggled on top of the crate, two yawning open and one rusted shut, and I set all three onto the floor. I lifted the lid of the crate, pushed aside the top layer, a fuzzy blue blanket, and started lifting things out one at a time. I just glanced at some, spent more time with others. I warn't looking for anything in particular, just wanting to touch them and weigh them in my hands, and stack the memories up all around, in a back room under a bare bulb.

A crimpled flier with a dry mud footprint across it and a torn place up top, like someone yanked it off a staple on a bulletin board or a telephone pole:

SPACECRAFT
CONVENTION
Hear speakers who have contacted our Space Brothers
PICNIC
Lots of music—Astronomical telescope, see the craters on the Moon, etc.
Public invited—Spread the word
Admission—50c and $1.00 donation
Children under school age free
FREE CAMPING
Bring your own tent, house car or camping outfit, folding chairs, sleeping bags, etc.
CAFETERIA on the grounds—fried chicken, sandwiches, coffee, cold drinks, etc.
Conventions held every year on the last Saturday, Sunday and Monday of the month of June
at

BUCK'S MOUNTAIN VIEW RANCH
Buck Nelson, Route 1
Mountain View, Missouri

A headline from a local paper:

"SPACECRAFT PICNIC AT BUCK'S RANCH ATTRACTS 2000 PEOPLE."

An old *Life* magazine in a see-through envelope, Marilyn Monroe all puckered up to the plastic. April 7, 1952. The headline: "There Is A Case For Interplanetary Saucers." I slid out the magazine and flipped through the article. I read: "These objects cannot be explained by present science as natural phenomena—but solely as artificial devices created and operated by a high intelligence."

A Baggie of three or four dog hairs, with a sticker showing the outline of a flying saucer and the words HAIR FROM BUCK'S ALIEN DOG, "BO."

Teddy hadn't minded, when I took the scissors to him to get the burrs off, and to snip a little extra for the Bo trade. Bo was months dead by then, but the folks demanded something. Some of my neighbors I do believe would have pulled down my house and barn a-looking for him, if they thought there was a body to be had. Some people won't believe in nothing that ain't a corpse, and I couldn't bear letting the science men get at him with their saws and jars, to jibble him up. Just the thought put me in mind of that old song:

> The old horse died with the whooping cough
> The old cow died in the fork of the branch
> The buzzards had them a public dance.

No, sir. No public dance this time. I hid Bo's body in a shallow cave, and I nearabouts crawled in after him, cause it liked to have killed me, too, even with the tractor's front arms to lift him and push him and drop him. Then I walled him up so good with scree and stones lying around that even I warn't sure anymore where it was, along that long rock face.

I didn't let on that he was gone, neither. Already people were getting shirty about me not showing him off like a circus mule, bringing him out where people could gawk at him and poke him and ride him. I told them he was vicious around strangers, and that was a bald lie. He was a sweet old thing for his size, knocking me down with his licking tongue, and what was I but a stranger, at the beginning? We was all strangers. Those Baggies of Teddy hair was a bald lie, too, and so was some of the other parts I told through the years, when my story sort of got away from itself, or when I couldn't exactly remember what had happened in between this and that, so I had to fill in, the same way I filled the chinks between the rocks I stacked between me and Bo, to keep out the buzzards, hoping it'd be strong enough to last forever.

But a story ain't like a wall. The more stuff you add onto a wall, spackle and timber and flat stones, the harder it is to push down. The more stuff you add to a story through the years, the weaker it gets. Add a piece here and add a piece there, and in time you can't remember your own self how the pieces was supposed to fit together, and every piece is a chance for some fool to ask more questions, and confuse you more, and poke another hole or two, to make you wedge in something else, and there is no end to it. So finally you just don't want to tell no part of the story no more, except to yourself, because yourself is the only one who really believes in it. In some of it, anyway. The other folks, the ones who just want to laugh, to make fun, you run off or cuss out or turn your back on, until no one much asks anymore, or remembers, or cares. You're just that teched old dirt farmer off of Route One, withered and sick and sitting on the floor of his junk room and crying, snot hanging from his nose, sneezing in the dust.

It warn't all a lie, though.

No, sir. Not by a long shot.

And that was the worst thing.

Because the reporters always came, ever year at the end of June, and so did the duck hunters who saw something funny in the sky above the blind one frosty morning and was looking for it ever since, and the retired military fellas who talked about "protocols" and "incident reports" and "security breaches," and the powdery old ladies who said they'd walked around the rosebush one afternoon and found themselves on the rings of Saturn, and the beatniks from the college, and the tourists with their Polaroids and short pants, and the women selling funnel cakes and glow-in-the-dark space Frisbees, and the younguns with the waving antennas on their heads, and the neighbors who just wanted to snoop around and see whether old Buck had finally let the place go to rack and ruin, or whether he was holding it together for one more year, they all showed up on time, just like the mockingbirds. But the one person who never came, not one damn time since the year of our Lord nineteen and fifty-six, was the alien Bob Solomon himself. The whole point of the damn picnics, the Man of the Hour, had never showed his face. And that was the real reason I give up on the picnics, turned sour on the whole flying-saucer industry, and kept close to the willows ever since. It warn't my damn lumbago or the Mothman or Barney and Betty Hill and their Romper Room boogeymen, or those dull dumb rocks hauled back from the Moon and thrown in my face like coal in a Christmas stocking. It was Bob Solomon, who said he'd come back, stay in touch, continue to shine down his blue-white healing light, because he loved the Earth people, because he loved me, and who done none of them things.

What had happened, to keep Bob Solomon away? He hadn't died. Death was a stranger, out where Bob Solomon lived. Bo would be frisky yet, if he'd a stayed home. No, something had come between Mountain View and Bob Solomon, to keep him away. What had I done? What had I not done? Was it something I knew, that I wasn't supposed to know? Or was it something I forgot, or cast aside, something I should have held on to and treasured? And now, if Bob Solomon was to look for Mountain View, could he find it? Would he know me? The Earth goes a far ways in twenty-odd years, and we go with it.

I wiped my nose on my hand and slid Marilyn back in her plastic and reached for the chain and clicked off the light and sat in the chilly dark, making like it was the cold clear peace of space.

I knew well the turnoff to the Clearwater Lake overlook, and I still like to have missed it that night, so black dark was the road through the woods. The sign with the arrow had deep-cut letters filled with white reflecting paint, and only the flash of the letters in the headlights made me stand on the brakes and kept me from missing the left turn. I sat and waited, turn signal on, flashing green against the pine boughs overhead, even though there was no sign of cars a-coming from either direction. *Ka-chunk, ka-chunk,* flashed the pine trees, and then I turned off with a grumble of rubber as the tires left the asphalt and bit into the gravel of the overlook road. The stone-walled overlook had been built by the CCC in the 1930s, and the road the relief campers had built hadn't been improved much since, so I went up the hill slow on that narrow, straight road, away back in the jillikens. Once I saw the eyes of some critter as it dashed across my path, but nary a soul else, and when I reached the pullaround, and that low-slung wall all along the ridgetop, I thought maybe I had the wrong place. But then I saw two cars and a panel truck parked at the far end where younguns park when they go a-sparking, and I could see dark-people shapes a-milling about. I parked a ways away, shut off my engine and cut my lights. This helped me see a little better, and I could make out flashlight beams trained on the ground here and there, as people walked from the cars to where some big black shapes were set up, taller than a man. In the silence after I slammed my door I could hear low voices, too, and as I walked nearer, the murmurs resolved themselves and became words:

"Gravimeter checks out."

"Thank you, Isabel. Wallace, how about that spectrum analyzer?"

"Powering up, Doc. Have to give it a minute."

"We may not have a minute, or we may have ten hours. Who knows?" I steered toward this voice, which was older than the others. "Our visitors are unpredictable," he continued.

"Visitors?" the girl asked.

"No, you're right. I've broken my own rule. We don't know they're sentient, and even if they are, we don't know they're *visitors.* They may be local, native to the place, certainly more so than Wallace here. Georgia-born, aren't you, Wallace?"

"Company, Doc," said the boy.

"Yes, I see him, barely. Hello, sir. May I help you? Wallace, please. Mind your manners." The flashlight beam in my face had blinded me, but the professor grabbed it out of the boy's hand and turned it up to shine beneath his chin, like a youngun making a scary face, so I could see a shadow version of his lumpy jowls, his big nose, his bushy mustache. "I'm Harley Rutledge," he said. "Might you be Mr. Nelson?"

"That's me," I said, and as I stuck out a hand, the flashlight beam moved to locate it. Then a big hand came into view and shook mine. The knuckles were dry and cracked and red-flaked.

"How do you do," Rutledge said, and switched off the flashlight. "Our mutual friend explained what we're doing out here, I presume? Forgive the darkness, but we've learned that too much brightness on our part rather spoils the seeing, skews the experiment."

"Scares 'em off?" I asked.

"Mmm," Rutledge said. "No, not quite that. Besides the lack of evidence for any *them* that *could* be frightened, we have some evidence that these, uh, luminous phenomena are . . . responsive to our lights. If we wave ours around too much, they wave around in response. We shine ours into the water, they descend into the water as well. All fascinating, but it does suggest a possibility of reflection, of visual echo, which we are at some pains to rule out. Besides which, we'd like to observe, insofar as possible, what these lights do when *not* observed. Though they seem difficult to fool. Some, perhaps fancifully, have suggested they can read investigators' minds. Ah, Wallace, are we up and running, then? Very good, very good." Something hard and plastic was nudging my arm, and I thought for a second Rutledge was offering me a drink. "Binoculars, Mr. Nelson? We always carry spares, and you're welcome to help us look."

The girl's voice piped up. "We're told you've seen the spooklights all your life," she said. "Is that true?"

"I reckon you could say that," I said, squinting into the binoculars. Seeing the darkness up close made it even darker.

"That is so cool," Isobel said. "I'm going to write my thesis on low-level nocturnal lights of apparent volition. I call them linnalavs for short. Will-o-the-wisps, spooklights, treasure lights, corpse lights, ball lightning, fireships, jack o'lanterns, the *feu follet*. I'd love to interview you sometime. Just think, if you had been recording your observations all these years."

I did record some, I almost said, but Rutledge interrupted us. "Now, Isobel, don't crowd the man on short acquaintance. Why don't you help Wallace with the tape recorders? Your hands are steadier, and we don't want him cutting himself again." She stomped off, and I found something to focus on with the binoculars: the winking red light atop the Taum Sauk Mountain fire tower. "You'll have to excuse Isobel, Mr. Nelson. She has the enthusiasm of youth, and she's just determined to get ball lightning in there somehow, though I keep explaining that's an entirely separate phenomenon."

"Is that what our friend, that reporter gal, told you?" I asked. "That I seen the spooklights in these parts, since I was a tad?"

"Yes, and that you were curious about our researches, to compare your folk knowledge to our somewhat more scientific investigations. And as I told her, you're welcome to join us tonight, as long as you don't touch any of our equipment, and as long as you stay out of our way should anything, uh, happen. Rather irregular, having an untrained local observer present—but frankly, Mr. Nelson, everything about Project Identification is irregular, at least as far as the U.S. Geological Survey is concerned. So we'll both be irregular together, heh." A round green glow appeared and disappeared at chest level: Rutledge checking his watch. "I frankly thought Miss Rains would be coming with you. She'll be along presently, I take it?"

"Don't ask me," I said, trying to see the tower itself beneath the light. Black metal against black sky. I'd heard her name as *Hanes*, but I let it go. "Maybe she got a better offer."

"Oh, I doubt that, not given her evident interest. Know Miss Rains well, do you, Mr. Nelson?"

"Can't say as I do. Never seen her before this morning. No, wait. Before yesterday."

"Lovely girl," Rutledge said. "And so energized."

"Sort of wears me out," I told him.

"Yes, well, pleased to meet you, again. I'd better see how Isobel and Wallace are getting along. There are drinks and snacks in the truck, and some folding chairs and blankets. We're here all night, so please make yourself at home."

I am home, I thought, fiddling with the focus on the binoculars as Rutledge trotted away, his little steps sounding like a spooked quail. I hadn't let myself look at the night sky for anything but quick glances for so long, just to make sure the Moon and Venus and Orion and the Milky Way was still there, that I was feeling sort of giddy to have nothing else to look at. I was like a man who took the cure years ago but now finds himself locked in a saloon. That brighter patch over yonder, was that the lights of Piedmont? And those two, no, three, airplanes, was they heading for St. Louis? I reckon I couldn't blame Miss Priss for not telling the professor the whole truth about me, else he would have had the law out here, to keep that old crazy man away. I wondered where Miss Priss had got to. Rutledge and I both had the inkle she would be joining us out here, but where had I got that? Had she quite said it, or had I just assumed?

I focused again on the tower light, which warn't flashing no more. Instead it was getting stronger and weaker and stronger again, like a heartbeat, and never turning full off. It seemed to be growing, too, taking up more of the view, as if it was coming closer. I was so interested in what the fire watchers might be up to—testing the equipment? signaling rangers on patrol?—that when the light moved sideways toward the north, I turned, too, and swung the binoculars around to keep it in view, and didn't think nothing odd about a fire tower going for a little walk until the boy Wallace said, "There's one now, making its move."

The college folks all talked at once: "Movie camera on." "Tape recorder on." "Gravimeter negative." I heard the *click-whirr, click-whirr* of someone taking Polaroids just as fast as he could go. For my part, I kept following the spooklight as it bobbled along the far ridge, bouncing like a slow ball or a balloon, and pulsing as it went. After the burst of talking, everyone was silent, watching the light and fooling with the equipment. Then the professor whispered in my ear: "Look familiar to you, Mr. Nelson?"

It sure warn't a patch on Bob Solomon's spaceship, but I knew Rutledge didn't have Bob Solomon in mind. "The spooklights I've seen was down lower," I told him, "below the tops of the trees, most times hugging the ground. This one moves the same, but it must be up fifty feet in the air."

"Maybe," he whispered, "and maybe not. Appearances can be deceiving. Hey!" He cried aloud as the slow bouncy light shot straight up in the air. It hung there, then fell down to the ridgeline again and kept a-going, bobbing down the far slope, between us and the ridge, heading toward the lake and toward us.

The professor asked, "Gravitational field?"

"No change," the girl said.

"Keep monitoring."

The light split in two, then in three. All three lights come toward us.

"Here they come! Here they come!"

I couldn't keep all three in view, so I stuck with the one making the straightest shot downhill. Underneath it, treetops came into view as the light passed over, just as if it was a helicopter with a spotlight. But there warn't no engine sound at all, just the sound of a zephyr a-stirring the leaves, and the clicks of someone snapping pictures. Even Bob Solomon's craft had made a little racket: It whirred as it moved, and turned on and off with a *whunt* like the fans in a chickenhouse. It was hard to tell the light's shape. It just faded out at the edges, as the pulsing came and went. It was blue-white in motion but flickered red when it paused. I watched the light bounce down to the far shore of the lake. Then it flashed real bright, and was gone. I lowered the binoculars in time to see the other two hit the water and flash out, too—but one sent a smaller fireball rolling across the water toward us. When it slowed down, it sank, just like a rock a child sends a-skipping across a pond. The water didn't kick up at all, but the light could be seen below for a few seconds, until it sank out of sight.

"Awesome!" Isobel said.

"Yeah, that was something," Wallace said. "Wish we had a boat. Can we bring a boat next time, Doc? Hey, why is it so light?"

"Moonrise," Isobel said. "See our moonshadows?"

We did all have long shadows, reaching over the wall and toward the lake. I always heard that to stand in your own moonshadow means good luck, but I didn't get the chance to act on it before the professor said: "That's not the moon."

The professor was facing away from the water, toward the source of light. Behind us a big bright light moved through the trees, big as a house. The beams shined out separately between the trunks but then they closed up together again as the light moved out onto the surface of the gravel pullaround. It was like a giant glowing upside-down bowl, twenty-five feet high, a hundred or more across, sliding across the ground. You could see everything lit up inside, clear as a bell, like in a tabletop aquarium in a dark room. But it warn't attached to nothing. Above the light dome was no spotlight, no aircraft, nothing but the night sky and stars.

"Wallace, get that camera turned around, for God's sake!"

"Instruments read nothing, Doc. It's as if it weren't there."

"Maybe it's not. No, Mr. Nelson! Please, stay back!"

But I'd already stepped forward to meet it, binoculars hanging by their strap at my side, bouncing against my leg as I walked into the light. Inside I didn't feel nothing physical—no tingling, and no warmth, no more than turning on a desk lamp warms a room. But in my mind I felt different, powerful different. Standing there in that light, I felt more calm and easeful than I'd felt in years—like I was someplace I belonged, more so than on my own farm. As the edge of the light crept toward me, about at the speed of a slow walk, I slow-walked in the same direction as it was going, just to keep in the light as long as I could.

The others, outside the light, did the opposite. They scattered back toward the wall of the overlook, trying to stay in the dark ahead of it, but they didn't have no place to go, and in a few seconds they was all in the light, too, the three of them and their standing telescopes and all their equipment on folding tables and sawhorses all around. I got my first good look at the three of them in that crawling glow. Wallace had hippie hair down in his eyes and a beaky nose, and was bowlegged. The professor was older than I expected, but not nearly so old as me, and had a great big belly—what mountain folks would call an *investment*, as he'd been putting into it for years. Isobel had long stringy hair that needed a wash, and a wide butt, and black-rimmed glasses so thick a welder could have worn them, but she was right cute for all that. None of us cast a shadow inside the light.

I looked up and could see the night sky and even pick out the stars, but it was like looking through a soap film or a skiff of snow. Something I couldn't feel or rightly see was in the way, between me and the sky. Still I walked until the thigh-high stone wall stopped me. The dome kept moving, of course, and as I went through its back edge—because it was just that clear-cut, either you was in the light or you warn't— why, I almost swung my legs over the wall to follow it. The hill, though, dropped off steep on the other side, and the undergrowth was all tangled and snaky. So I held up for a few seconds, dithering, and then the light had left me behind, and I was in the dark again, pressed up against that wall like something drowned and found in a drain after a flood. I now could feel the breeze off the lake, so air warn't moving easy through the light dome, neither.

The dome kept moving over the folks from the college, slid over the wall and down the slope, staying about twenty-five feet tall the whole way. It moved out onto the water—which stayed as still as could be, not roiled at all—then faded, slow at first and then faster, until I warn't sure I was looking at anything anymore, and then it was gone.

The professor slapped himself on the cheeks and neck, like he was putting on aftershave. "No sunburn, thank God," he said. "How do the rest of you feel?"

The other two slapped themselves just the same.

"I'm fine."

"I'm fine, too," Isobel said. "The Geiger counter never triggered, either."

What did I feel like? Like I wanted to dance, to skip and cut capers, to holler out loud. My eyes were full like I might cry. I stared at that dark lake like I could stare a hole in it, like I could will that dome to rise again. I whispered, "Thank you," and it warn't a prayer, not directed *at* anybody, just an acknowledgment of something that had passed, like tearing off a calendar page, or plowing under a field of cornstalks.

I turned to the others, glad I finally had someone to talk to, someone I could share all these feelings with, but to my surprise they was all running from gadget to gadget, talking at once about phosphorescence and gas eruptions and electromagnetic fields; I couldn't follow half of it. Where had they been? Had they plumb missed it? For the first time in years, I felt I had to tell them what I had seen, what I had felt and known, the whole story. It would help them. It would be a comfort to them.

I walked over to them, my hands held out. I wanted to calm them down, get their attention.

"Oh, thank you, Mr. Nelson," said the professor. He reached out and unhooked from my hand the strap of the binoculars. "I'll take those. Well, I'd say you brought us luck, wouldn't you agree, Isobel, Wallace? Quite a remarkable display, that second one especially. Like the Bahia Kino Light of the Gulf of California, but in motion! Ionization of the air, perhaps, but no Geiger activity, mmm. A lower voltage, perhaps?" He patted his pockets. "Need a shopping list for our next vigil. A portable Curran counter, perhaps—"

I grabbed at his sleeve. "I saw it."

"Yes? Well, we all saw it, Mr. Nelson. Really a tremendous phenomenon—if the distant lights and the close light are related, that is, and their joint appearance cannot be coincidental. I'll have Isobel take your statement before we go, but now, if you'll excuse me."

"I don't mean tonight," I said, "and I don't mean no spooklights. I seen the real thing, an honest-to-God flying saucer, in 1956. At my farm outside Mountain View, west of here. Thataway." I pointed. "It shot out a beam of light, and after I was in that light, I felt better, not so many aches and pains. And listen: I saw it more than once, the saucer. It kept coming back."

He was backing away from me. "Mr. Nelson, really, I must—"

"And I met the crew," I told him. "The pilot stepped out of the saucer to talk with me. That's right, with me. He looked human, just like you and me, only better-looking. He looked like that boy in *Battle Cry*, Tab Hunter. But he said his name was—"

"Mr. Nelson." The early morning light was all around by now, giving everything a gray glow, and I could see Rutledge was frowning. "Please. You've had a very long night, and a stressful one. You're tired, and I'm sorry to say that you're no longer young. What you're saying no longer makes sense."

"Don't make sense!" I cried. "You think what we just saw makes sense?"

"I concede that I have no ready explanations, but what we saw were lights, Mr. Nelson, only lights. No sign of intelligence, nor of aircraft. Certainly not of crew members. No little green men. No grays. No Tab Hunter from the Moon."

"He lived on Mars," I said, "and his name was Bob Solomon."

The professor stared at me. The boy behind him, Wallace, stared at me, too, nearabouts tripping over his own feet as he bustled back and forth toting things to the truck. The girl just shook her head, and turned and walked into the woods.

"I wrote it up in a little book," I told the professor. "Well, I say I wrote it. Really, I talked it out, and I paid a woman at the library to copy it down and type it. I got a copy in the pickup. Let me get it. Won't take a sec."

"Mr. Nelson," he said again. "I'm sorry, I truly am. If you write me at the college, and enclose your address, I'll see you get a copy of our article, should it appear. We welcome interest in our work from the layman. But for now, here, today, I must ask you to leave."

"Leave? But the gal here said I could help."

"That was before you expressed these . . . delusions," Rutledge said. "Please realize what I'm trying to do. Like Hynek, like Vallée and Maccabee, I am trying to establish these researches as a serious scientific discipline. I am trying to create a field where none exists, where Isobel and her peers can work and publish without fear of ridicule. And here you are, spouting nonsense about a hunky spaceman named Bob! You must realize how that sounds. Why, you'd make the poor girl a laughing stock."

"She don't want to interview me?"

"Interview you! My God, man, aren't you listening? It would be career suicide for her to be *seen* with you! Please, before the sun is full up, Mr. Nelson, please, do the decent thing, and get back into your truck, and go."

I felt myself getting madder and madder. My hands had turned into fists. I turned from the professor, pointed at the back-and-forth boy and hollered, "You!"

He froze, like I had pulled a gun on him.

I called: "You take any Polaroids of them things?"

"Some, yes, sir," he said, at the exact same time the professor said, "Don't answer that."

"Where are they?" I asked. "I want to see 'em."

Behind the boy was a card table covered with notebooks and Mountain Dew bottles and the Polaroid camera, too, with a stack of picture squares next to it. I walked toward the table, and the professor stepped into my path, crouched, arms outstretched, like we was gonna wrestle.

"Keep away from the equipment," Rutledge said.

The boy ran back to the table and snatched up the pictures as I feinted sideways, and the professor lunged to block me again.

"I want to see them pictures, boy," I said.

"Mr. Nelson, go home! Wallace, secure those photos."

Wallace looked around like he didn't know what "secure" meant, in the open air overlooking a mountain lake, then he started stuffing the photos into his pockets, until they poked out all around, sort of comical. Two fell out on the ground. Then Wallace picked up a folding chair and held it out in front of him like a lion tamer. Stenciled across the bottom of the chair was PROP. CUMBEE FUNERAL HOME.

I stooped and picked up a rock and cocked my hand back like I was going to fling it. The boy flinched backward, and I felt right bad about scaring him. I turned and made like to throw it at the professor instead, and when he flinched, I felt some better. Then I turned and made like to throw it at the biggest telescope, and that felt best of all, for both boy and professor hollered then, no words but just a wail from the boy and a bark from the man, so loud that I nearly dropped the rock.

"Pictures, pictures," I said. "All folks want is pictures. People didn't believe nothing I told 'em, because during the first visits I didn't have no camera, and then when I rented a Brownie to take to Venus with me, didn't none of the pictures turn out! All of 'em overexposed, the man at the Rexall said. I ain't fooled with no pictures since, but I'm gonna have one of these, or so help me, I'm gonna bust out the eyes of this here spyglass, you see if I won't. Don't you come no closer with that chair, boy! You set that thing down." I picked up a second rock, so I had one heavy weight in each hand, and felt good. I knocked them together with a *clop* like hooves, and I walked around to the business end of the telescope, where the eyepiece and all those tiny adjustable thingies was, because that looked like the thing's underbelly. I held the rocks up to either side, like I was gonna knock them together and smash the instruments in between. I bared my teeth and tried to look scary, which warn't easy because now that it was good daylight, I suddenly had to pee something fierce. It must have worked, though, because Wallace set down the chair, just about the time the girl Isobel stepped out of the woods.

She was tucking in her shirttail, like she'd answered her own call of nature. She saw us all three standing there froze, and she got still, too, one hand down the back of her britches. Her darting eyes all magnified in her glasses looked quick and smart.

"What's going on?" she asked. Her front teeth stuck out like a chipmunk's.

"I want to see them pictures," I said.

"Isobel," the professor said, "drive down to the bait shop and call the police." He picked up an oak branch, hefted it, and started stripping off the little branches, like that would accomplish anything. "Run along, there's a good girl. Wallace and I have things well in hand."

"The heck we do," Wallace said. "I bring back a wrecked telescope, and I kiss my work-study goodbye."

"Jesus wept," Isobel said, and walked down the slope, tucking in the rest of her shirttail. She rummaged on the table, didn't find them, then saw the two stray pictures lying on the ground at Wallace's feet. She picked one up, walked over to me, held it out.

The professor said, "Isobel, don't! That's university property."

"Here, Mr. Nelson," she said. "Just take it and go, okay?"

I was afraid to move, for fear I'd wet my pants. My eyeballs was swimming already. I finally let fall one of my rocks and took the photo in that free hand, stuck it in my overalls pocket without looking at it. "Preciate it," I said. For no reason, I handed her the other rock, and for no reason, she took it. I turned and walked herky-jerky toward my truck, hoping I could hold it till I got into the woods at least, but no, I gave up halfway there, and with my back to the others I unzipped and groaned and let fly a racehorse stream of pee that spattered the tape-recorder case.

I heard the professor moan behind me, "Oh, Mr. Nelson! This is really too bad!"

"I'm sorry!" I cried. "It ain't on purpose, I swear! I was about to bust." But I probably would have tried to aim it, at that, to hit some of that damned equipment square on, but I hadn't had no force nor distance on my pee for years. It just poured out, like pulling a plug. I peed and peed, my eyes rolling back, lost in the good feeling ("You go, Mr. Nelson!" Isobel yelled), and as it puddled and coursed in little rills around the rocks at my feet, I saw a fisherman in a distant rowboat in the middle of the lake, his line in the water just where that corpse light had submerged the night before. I couldn't see him good, but I could tell he was watching us, as his boat drifted along. The sparkling water looked like it was moving fast past him, the way still water in the sun always does, even though the boat hardly moved at all.

"You wouldn't eat no fish from there," I hollered at him, "if you knew what was underneath."

His only answer was a pop and a hiss that carried across the water loud as a firework. He slung away the pull top, lifted the can, raised it high toward us as if to say, Cheers, and took a long drink.

Finally done, I didn't even zip up as I shuffled to the pickup. Without all that pee I felt lightheaded and hollow and plumb worn out. I wondered whether I'd make it home before I fell asleep.

"Isobel," the professor said behind me, "I asked you to go call the police."

"Oh, for God's sake, let it go," she said. "You really *would* look like an asshole then. Wallace, give me a hand."

I crawled into the pickup, slammed the door, dropped the window—it didn't crank down anymore, just fell into the door, so that I had to raise it two-handed—cranked the engine and drove off without looking at the bucktoothed girl, the bowlegged boy, the professor holding a club in his bloody-knuckled hands, the fisherman drinking his breakfast over a spook hole. I caught one last sparkle of the morning sun on the surface of the lake as I swung the truck into the shade of the woods, on the road headed down to the highway. Light through the branches dappled my rusty hood, my cracked dashboard, my baggy overalls. Some light is easy to explain. I fished the Polaroid picture out of my pocket and held it up at eye level while I drove. All you could see was a bright white nothing, like the boy had aimed the lens at the glare of a hundred-watt bulb from an inch away. I tossed the picture out the window. Another dud, just like Venus. A funny thing: The cardboard square bounced to a standstill in the middle of the road and caught the light just enough to be visible in my rear-view mirror, like a little bright window in the ground, until I reached the highway, signaled *ka-chunk, ka-chunk,* and turned to the right, toward home.

Later that morning I sat on the porch, waiting for her. Staring at the lake had done me no good, no more than staring at the night sky over the barn had done, all those years, but staring at the rhododendron called her forth, sure enough. She stepped around the bush with a little wave. She looked sprightly as ever, for all that long walk up the steep driveway, but I didn't blame her for not scraping her car past all those close bushes. One day they'd grow together and intertwine their limbs like clasped hands, and I'd be cut off from the world like in a fairy tale. But I wasn't cut off yet, because here came Miss Priss, with boots up over her knees and dress hiked up to yonder, practically. Her colors were red and black today; even that fool saucer hat was red with a black button in the center. She was sipping out of a box with a straw in it.

"I purely love orange juice," she told me. "Whenever I'm traveling, I can't get enough of it. Here, I brought you one." I reached out and took the box offered, and she showed me how to peel off the straw and poke a hole with it, and we sat side by side sipping awhile. I didn't say nothing, just sipped and looked into Donald Duck's eyes and sipped some more. Finally she emptied her juice box with a long low gurgle and turned to me and asked, "Did you make it out to the lake last night?"

"I did that thing, yes ma'am."

"See anything?"

The juice was brassy-tasting and thin, but it was growing on me, and I kept a-working that straw. "Didn't see a damn thing," I said. I cut my eyes at her. "Didn't see *you*, neither."

"Yes, well, I'm sorry about that," she said. "My supervisors called me away. When I'm on assignment, my time is not my own." Now she cut *her* eyes at *me*. "You *sure* you didn't see anything?"

I shook my head, gurgled out the last of my juice. "Nothing Dr. Rutledge can't explain away," I said. "Nothing you could have a conversation with."

"How'd you like Dr. Rutledge?"

"We got along just fine," I said, "when he warn't hunting up a club to beat me with, and I warn't pissing into his machinery. He asked after *you*, though. You was the one he wanted along on his camping trip, out there in the dark."

"I'll try to call on him, before I go."

"Go where?"

She fussed with her hat. "Back home. My assignment's over."

"Got everthing you needed, did you?"

"Yes, I think so. Thanks to you."

"Well, I ain't," I said. I turned and looked her in the face. "I ain't got everthing I need, myself. What I need ain't here on this Earth. It's up yonder, someplace I can't get to no more. Ain't that a bitch? And yet I was right satisfied until two days ago, when you come along and stirred me all up again. I never even went to bed last night, and I ain't sleepy even now. All I can think about is night coming on again, and what I might see up there this time."

"But that's a *good* thing," she said. "You keep your eyes peeled, Mr. Nelson. You've seen things already, and you haven't seen the last of them." She tapped my arm with her juice-box straw. "I have faith in you," she said. "I wasn't sure at first. That's why I came to visit, to see if you were keeping the faith. And I see now that you are—in your own way."

"I ain't got no faith," I said. "I done aged out of it."

She stood up. "Oh, pish tosh," she said. "You proved otherwise last night. The others tried to stay *out* of the light, but not you, Mr. Nelson. Not you." She set her juice box on the step beside mine. "Throw that away for me, will you? I've got to be going." She stuck out her hand. It felt hot to the touch, and powerful. Holding it gave me the strength to stand up, look into her eyes, and say:

"I made it all up. The dog Bo, and the trips to Venus and Mars, and the cured lumbago. It was a made-up story, ever single Lord God speck of it."

And I said that sincerely. Bob Solomon forgive me: As I said it, I believed it was true.

She looked at me for a spell, her eyes big. She looked for a few seconds like a child I'd told Santa warn't coming, ever again. Then she grew back up, and with a sad little smile she stepped toward me, pressed her hands flat to the chest bib of my overalls, stood on tippytoes, and kissed me on the cheek, the way she would her grandpap, and as she slid something into my side pocket she whispered in my ear, "That's not what I hear on Enceladus." She patted my pocket. "That's how to reach me, if you need me. But you won't need me." She stepped into the yard and walked away, swinging her pocketbook, and called back over her shoulder: "You know what you need, Mr. Nelson? You need a dog. A dog is good help around a farm. A dog will sit up with you, late at night, and lie beside you, and keep you warm. You ought to keep your eye out. You never know when a stray will turn up."

She walked around the bush and was gone. I picked up the empty Donald Ducks, because it was something to do, and I was turning to go in when a man's voice called:

"Mr. Buck Nelson?"

A young man in a skinny tie and horn-rimmed glasses stood at the edge of the driveway where Miss Priss—no, Miss *Rains*, she deserved her true name—had stood a few moments before. He walked forward, one hand outstretched and the other reaching into the pocket of his denim jacket. He pulled out a long flat notebook.

"My name's Matt Ketchum," he said, "and I'm pleased to find you, Mr. Nelson. I'm a reporter with the Associated Press, and I'm writing a story on the surviving flying-saucer contactees of the 1950s."

I caught him up short when I said, "Aw, not again! Damn it all, I just told all that to Miss Rains. She works for the A&P, too."

He withdrew his hand, looked blank.

I pointed to the driveway. "Hello, you must have walked past her in the drive, not two minutes ago! Pretty girl in a red-and-black dress, boots up to here. Miss Rains, or Hanes, or something like that."

"Mr. Nelson, I'm not following you. I don't work with anyone named Rains or

Hanes, and no one else has been sent out here but me. And that driveway was deserted. No other cars parked down at the highway, either." He cocked his head, gave me a pitying look. "Are you sure you're not thinking of some other day, sir?"

"But she," I said, hand raised toward my bib pocket—but something kept me from saying *gave me her card*. That pocket felt strangely warm, like there was a live coal in it.

"Maybe she worked for someone else, Mr. Nelson, like UPI, or maybe the *Post-Dispatch*? I hope I'm not scooped again. I wouldn't be surprised, with the Spielberg picture coming out and all."

I turned to focus on him for the first time. "Where is Enceladus, anyway?"

"I beg your pardon?"

I said it again, moving my lips all cartoony, like he was deaf.

"I, well, I don't know, sir. I'm not familiar with it."

I thought a spell. "I do believe," I said, half to myself, "it's one a them Saturn moons." To jog my memory, I made a fist of my right hand and held it up—that was Saturn—and held up my left thumb a ways from it, and moved it back and forth, sighting along it. "It's out a ways, where the ring gets sparse. Thirteenth? Fourteenth, maybe?"

He just goggled at me. I gave him a sad look and shook my head and said, "You don't know much, if that's what you know, and that's a fact."

He cleared his throat. "Anyway, Mr. Nelson, as I was saying, I'm interviewing all the contactees I can find, like George Van Tassel, and Orfeo Angelucci—"

"Yes, yes, and Truman Bethurum, and them," I said. "She talked to all them, too."

"Bethurum?" he repeated. He flipped through his notebook. "Wasn't he the asphalt spreader, the one who met the aliens atop a mesa in Nevada?"

"Yeah, that's the one."

He looked worried now. "Um, Mr. Nelson, you must have misunderstood her. Truman Bethurum died in 1969. He's been dead eight years, sir."

I stood there looking at the rhododendron and seeing the pretty face and round hat, hearing the singsong voice, like she had learned English from a book.

I turned and went into the house, let the screen bang shut behind, didn't bother to shut the wood door.

"Mr. Nelson?"

My chest was plumb hot now. I went straight to the junk room, yanked on the light. Everything was spread out on the floor where I left it. I shoved aside Marilyn, all the newspapers, pawed through the books.

"Mr. Nelson?" The voice was coming closer, moving through the house like a spooklight.

There it was: *Aboard a Flying Saucer*, by Truman Bethurum. I flipped through it, looking only at the pictures, until I found her: dark hair, big dark eyes, sharp chin, round hat. It was old Truman's drawing of Captain Aura Rhanes, the sexy Space Sister from the planet Clarion who visited him eleven times in her little red-and-black uniform, come right into his bedroom, so often that Mrs. Bethurum got jealous and divorced him. I had heard that old Truman, toward the end, went out and hired girl assistants to answer his mail and take messages just because they sort of looked like Aura Rhanes.

"Mr. Nelson?" said young Ketchum, standing in the door. "Are you OK?"

I let drop the book, stood, and said, "Doing just fine, son. If you'll excuse me? I got to be someplace." I closed the door in his face, dragged a bookcase across the doorway to block it, and pulled out Miss Rhanes's card, which was almost too hot to touch. No writing on it, neither, only a shiny silver surface that reflected my face like a mirror—and there was something behind my face, something aways back inside the card, a moving silvery blackness like a field of stars rushing toward me, and as I stared into that card, trying to see, my reflection slid out of the way and the edges of the card flew out and the card was a window, a big window, and now a door that I moved through without stepping, and someone out there was playing a single fiddle, no dance tune but just a-scraping along slow and sad as the stars whirled around me, and a ringed planet was swimming into view, the rings on edge at first but now tilting toward me and thickening as I dived down, the rings getting closer dividing into bands like layers in a rock face, and then into a field of rocks like that no-earthly-good south pasture, only there was so many rocks, so close together, and then I fell between them like an ant between the rocks in a gravel driveway, and now I was speeding toward a pinpoint of light, and as I moved toward it faster and faster, it grew and resolved itself and reshaped into a pear, a bulb, with a long sparkling line extending out, like a space elevator, like a chain, and at the end of the chain the moon became a glowing lightbulb. I was staring into the bulb in my junk room, dazzled, my eyes flashing, my head achy, and the card dropped from my fingers with no sound, and my feet were still shuffling though the fiddle had faded away. I couldn't hear nothing over the knocking and the barking and young Ketchum calling: "Hey, Mr. Nelson? Is this your dog?"

The Finite Canvas

BRIT MANDELO

Some stories are deep and profound enough that they demand to be written not in ink on paper, but in blood. And paid for in blood as well.

Brit Mandelo is a writer, critic, and the senior fiction editor for Strange Horizons. *She has published two nonfiction books,* Beyond Binary: Genderqueer and Sexually Fluid Speculative Fiction *and* We Wuz Pushed: On Joanna Russ and Radical Truth-Telling. *She has had her fiction, nonfiction, and poetry published in magazines such as* Stone Telling, Clarkesworld, Apex, *and* Ideomancer. *She also writes regularly for Tor.com, and lives in Louisville, Kentucky.*

Molly tapped the screen of her finicky tablet with one sweat-damp fingertip, leaving a shimmering smudge. The next page loaded with a slight delay. Rainwater pattered through the one-room clinic's open windows onto the tile floor, but the baking summer heat remained untouched. Even with all the windows thrown open it was still at least forty-two degrees C inside, though once the temperature climbed above forty it was hard to judge.

The slatted wood door swung wide and clattered in its frame. Startled, she slapped the tablet down on her desk harder than she would have liked and reflexively chided herself: *You can't afford another one, be* careful. As she stood, the gauzy skirt she'd rolled up to her waist unfurled around her knees. The visitor closed the door with a more gentle hand. Molly noticed first the newcomer's sheer size, and second the temperature-regulating clothing covering them head to toe. Her stomach clenched. She hadn't, in all her years downside, ever seen someone who could afford that. The shirt alone would cost more than six years of her clinic's "humanitarian aid" stipend, and that was if she bought no supplies.

There was no such thing as a tourist from the stations. A fresh sweat prickled along Molly's back. The military police wore uniforms. This person didn't.

"Did you need help?" she asked after the quiet dragged on a moment too long. "Directions?"

The stranger pushed back the tan hood of the shirt, revealing a white-skinned face with a square jaw, thin lips, and brown eyes, set off by a frizzed halo of bleached hair with dark roots. The clothes had done their job—without them, that pale skin would have been blistered and raw from exposure.

"You're the doctor?"

The newcomer's voice was a melodious, rough-edged alto, like the women who smoked tobacco in old movies. It took Molly a moment to reconcile that voice with the thick, broad body. She saw the faintest hint of breasts under the tan shirt where she hadn't noticed them before.

"Yes," she said, stepping around her desk. She passed the examining table and storage shelves in three strides. Her tank top slid wetly against her skin as she stuck her hand out in offering. "You are?"

The woman paused, then took Molly's hand. Her fingers were hot to the touch, red with sunburn. She must not have worn gloves. "Jada."

Molly frowned. "What do you need?"

"Right to the point," she said. She tugged her hand away and in one smooth yank pulled her shirt over her head. Then she stood straight, shoulders back. Molly flinched but forced herself to look. Jada was heavily muscled, dense as a tree trunk and probably just as hard, but that wasn't what was breathtaking. It was the scars.

"You recognize these?" the woman asked.

Designs snaked over her torso, down into the temp-reg pants, up to her neck. The left side of her rib cage was a silvery mass of letters and symbols, all jumbled; there was a stylized sun around her navel with waving lines of light. A crane, its legs hidden by the waistband of her pants, spread its wings over her right side and torso. There were smaller signs hidden around the larger; three simple slashes crossed the space between her collarbones. Her skin was as readable as a novel, her flesh a malleable masterpiece made with knives. Some of the scars were still pink, and a spiral design on her left breast was an angry, fresh red.

Murder scars, Molly thought. *Syndicate badge.* The sheer number of them made her throat constrict. She took a step backward, as if one step would make any difference to a skilled killer.

"I need a new set," the woman said, sticking out her bare, untouched arm. "Here."

"You must have an artist—" Molly began.

"Not down here," the syndicate woman said. She turned her head, looking out the open window at the road. Her mouth formed a thin line as she paused. Molly saw that her ears were pierced with a multitude of silver hoops that hugged the curve of the cartilage. "I need the new marks done now. I can pay you more than enough to make it worth your time."

New marks for a new murder, and Molly immediately wondered where this woman had earned the right: on the stations, or locally? She unclenched her jaw. "Why?"

There was no reason for any syndicate to set foot on old Earth, or what little of it was still habitable, beyond trading for young, desperate, attractive flesh to bring to the stations—unless they were running from the mil-police. Molly suspected that the only reason the station governments bothered to dispatch the police downside at all was to apprehend the occasional syndicate member; they certainly didn't do much else.

After a strained silence, Jada replied, "Does it matter?"

"Money's not enough," she said. "Not for one of *you*."

Jada smiled with a cool edge. She wound her shirt around her fist and lifted her chin. Molly kept her eyes on the woman's face instead of her bare torso, though the scars drew her gaze like the sucking gravity of a black hole. "I'll bargain you the story. Or any story. I've got plenty."

"Who did you kill?" Molly ground out.

"Oh, that," Jada said. A look passed over her face like a flickering shadow, there and gone before Molly could grasp it. Her heart was suddenly pounding, her mouth dry as she waited for the answer. "No one you know." She paused, then spoke again, bleak hurt punching through her prior composure. "My partner."

Molly hated that it melted her for a moment, and worse, that it pricked her curiosity.

She was used to hurting. Downside, people lived their lives hurting, starving, scraping by. They wilted, underfed and wounded; tender, fleshy flowers exposed to the scouring radiation of the sun barely filtered through the damaged atmosphere. What she'd had in her pockets upon her deportation had made her the richest woman in the town—a tablet, a few hundred in station currency in her bank, and a medical degree. The money had run out fast on things like setting up a house, before she realized that she would never have it again, and the tablet was bound to die soon, and her degree had only gotten her clinic the monetary sympathy of one of the vast corporate aid—machines stationside, the kind that made people feel good about donating their pocket change to help the needy. The stipend went to the clinic, in any case, to her monthly restock orders brought by courier from the port-city thirty kilometers away and the occasional extra tool. That enviable wealth she'd brought with her could not put food on the table every night or clothes on her back. She hadn't once in her life gone hungry until the first week on Earth.

There was no such thing as a tourist, planetside.

"Why here?" she finally asked.

Jada cut her a sharp glance. "Because this is where I've washed up."

Molly smothered her questions—*did you abandon your syndicate, are they hunting you, who are you, how did you end up here, are you stuck downside*—and crossed the room again. She sat behind her desk, the wood chair digging into the backs of her thighs. Jada shook out her shirt and slipped it over her head again. The tan fabric hid the scars and the flush that had begun to redden her pale skin.

"How much?" Molly asked.

"I've got a few thousand in station currency stowed away," she said as she walked up and planted her hands on the desk. "I want the whole arm. He deserves that much of me. Will you or won't you?"

Molly closed her eyes to avoid looking at the woman leaning on her desk, her curious desperation a palpable pressure. Still, she was aware of the shadow cast over her, the undeniable presence.

She thought of the fibrous lump she'd felt with fear-stiffened fingers in her right breast almost a year ago, the phenomenal cost of importing a gene-therapy. She ground her teeth against the knowing, and the acceptance, wishing she didn't need the money like she needed air.

It hadn't been anyone she knew. That was enough.

"It will take a few days," she said.

Jada nodded, a short jerk of her chin. "When can you start?"

"What's your hurry?"

"I'll start the story when you start cutting," Jada said.

"All right, fine," Molly replied, equally short with her.

Another moment of silence stretched between the two women as Molly pushed her chair back and strode to the examining table. Another person might have spoken to fill it, but Jada wasn't that person. She let it hang. Molly snagged a box of sanitation-wipes from the wire shelf in the corner and used two to wipe down the thinly padded table.

"Let that dry while you tell me what you want done," she said.

"Start with flowers," Jada said, still leaning against the desk behind her. "Then do whatever seems right, once you hear the story. That's the point, memorializing it."

Molly nodded. Her pulse pounded out of control, adrenaline washing in a stinging-hot rush through her veins. She was glad to have her back to the room while she inspected her supplies. This was outside her realm of experience. When she cut someone, it was quick and for a reason, and they didn't feel it. She didn't peel their skin off while they watched. It was almost embarrassing that the thought of doing the scars made her more nauseated than working for a syndicate killer.

"Do you have a preference in utensils?" she asked.

Jada answered from right behind her, "Scalpel, if you have a small, sharp one."

Molly narrowly managed not to flinch at the touch of breath on the nape of her neck, cooling the dampness of sweat. *Thousands*, she reminded herself, but out loud she said, "One other thing," as she found the right size of blade in her case. They weren't intended for reuse, but there was no way to justify throwing away a perfectly good instrument. Instead, she kept everything well sanitized. "If the police show up at my door, what happens?"

Jada pressed fingertips to the edge of her shoulder blade from behind, at the soft spot where muscle joined muscle. She stiffened. Jada pressed so gently that it didn't hurt, but it was a hint.

"I forced you," she said quietly. "Just like this. No marks. But you were afraid. So you helped me, because you had to, right?"

"Right," Molly said, half-strangled.

Jada's touch slipped away and she moved to sit on the edge of the table. Molly glanced at her from the corner of her eye.

"I've had—run-ins with them before," Molly admitted.

Jada shook her head. "You think I didn't guess you were from stationside the minute I stepped through the door? Your accent isn't native. You shake hands."

"I see," Molly said. Her face heated with a blush that would be nearly invisible beneath her brown skin, darkened further from years in the heavy-UV sunlight.

That was one of the first things the locals had joked about when she'd come to start the clinic nearly a decade ago, having just received a license to do aid-work after her deportation—Westerner, even though there hadn't been such a thing as a "west" for some time, just the stations far above. It stuck in the language all the same. She looked right, but spoke wrong.

"No one comes here for pleasure, so I know you got sent." Jada shrugged those wide shoulders, not smiling. "Syndicate pull some strings?"

"You could say that," Molly answered, not smiling either.

"I don't think it'll be a problem," she said. "You're doing humanitarian work, being a good girl, and you've got an even bigger reason to be afraid of a syndicate worker. They'll believe the story if you believe it."

Their eyes met. Molly nodded.

"Off with the shirt," she said. "You don't want it getting bloodied."

"I don't think it'll matter," Jada said.

"Why not?" she asked.

The other woman stared at her, eyes narrowed, and pulled the shirt over her head once more. The scarring was no less shocking the second time around but Molly made herself look. With ungloved hands she touched a few of them, palpating. The wounds were mostly surface damage but done wide enough that the skin wouldn't knit quite right. The smaller patterns, like the spiral at the top of Jada's left breast, were harder ridges. The scars went deeper.

"Do you treat the wounds with anything to keep them open?" she asked.

"There's a sealant," she answered. "Keeps out infections and doesn't let the edges knit. I've got some in my pack."

"All right," Molly said as she rolled on a pair of thin gloves.

She ran a disinfectant wipe over the scalpel though it shone clean already. It was best to be sure. Her hands didn't shake. The adrenaline had disappeared under the prepared calm she'd mastered years ago and far away, learning how to help people. This was the opposite of that, or maybe it wasn't.

"Flowers?" she checked.

"Flowers," Jada said. "I'll talk, you cut."

Molly wiped down Jada's arm as well, the sharp smell of antiseptic wafting in the hot air. She traced her fingers carefully over the area, feeling the joins of muscles and the intricacies of Jada's flesh.

"No anesthetic?" she checked.

"No," Jada said.

Molly shook her head.

"Your decision," she said.

There was no delaying any longer. She braced the skin at the top of Jada's upper arm with one hand and laid the edge of the scalpel to it. Blood beaded under the blade as she traced the first narrow line.

Jada's breath shuddered out, but her arm stayed still. Molly reminded herself how much practice the woman had had at this, reminded herself not to be impressed.

"So—"

"Here's your story," Jada said.

The Dawnslight syndicate were big into flesh-trade, pharmaceuticals, weapons—if the police didn't like it, we did it. By "we" I mean my boss, the head of the organization. Trade was not my job. As you probably figured from the badge scars, my job is to *be* a weapon. Point me in the right direction and say go; I will do what needs doing. There's no other way to make it to the top of a syndicate. You have to be the best.

I was the best. Or probably one of the best, because Eten—my partner, yeah—

was also very, very good at what we did. We met when we were scrub assassins way down-rank. We clicked. Eten was this pretty thing, he was so thin, like you could break him with your hands. But you couldn't. *I* couldn't. He would slip right out of your grip and leave you holding air while he kicked your teeth in. I liked Eten, a lot.

Those years were tough. The work was messy and it didn't pay half as good as you think it would.—*Here she paused while Molly tugged on a slippery bit of skin, and said, "You need tweezers for that."*—We were good, though, so good we moved up, but we always moved up together. I was maybe seventeen, maybe nineteen when we got drunk and realized we might want to fuck. It was weird, I don't know if that's ever happened to you; you're looking at this friend you've had for years who's always got your back and you think, well, shit. He's gorgeous. I want him.

That turned out better than it does for most people, I think. It made us a real pair. We knew each other's movements, we knew each other's thoughts. There was no getting between us for a job, but outside of that, we had some edges that didn't mesh. Eten was different about killing, for one thing. I don't feel anything when I finish a job, I never did. I don't mean I like it; I really mean I don't feel much. It doesn't make me happy, or sad, and I don't get a thrill out of it. It's work. Like taking out the trash or scrubbing floors. It's mechanical.

Eten wasn't mechanical. He was fucking talented, but it upset him.

Maybe ten years later, we caught the eye of the big boss in Dawnslight. He needed his personal guard-head replaced. Nothing nasty, the last guy was just getting too old. I told him we came as a pair, because he only asked for me, and he said fine. He took us both, gave us a big house, all the things we needed.

The problem was that we'd never been privy to much business before. Sure, you know you're killing this guy because he stole a shipment of this or that, but you don't see the numbers. You don't *grasp* it.

—*The blood was starting to make a slick mess in and around the petals of the third flower. Molly sat back and snagged a clean towel. "You bleed too much."*—

We both saw the ledgers: the number of kids from downside shipped to the stations and where they got stuck, the weapons we sent in trade, the sheer goddamn *scale* of the pharm business and who we denied drugs to and who we sold them to and for how much.

It's one thing to execute somebody for betraying your boss. It's another to see how many people your boss is killing with swipes of his pen on his tablet. It bothered me, yeah, but I felt like a jackass, because *like I didn't know.* If I hadn't known, it was because I was being blind on purpose. So I kept going. But Eten had problems with it. I saw them. I started doing the jobs for both of us; he started staying on at the boss's place to do security.

It wasn't like he was bored, he had incursions and assassins and rivals to deal with while I went off snipping the buds of people who were making trouble. It worked, for a little while. He started kissing all the new scars I'd got and I thought he maybe had decided to love me again, no matter what else we were doing.

I was wrong. I was big, bad wrong. Because love isn't enough when something in you is just *broken* and nobody cares. He wasn't saying "I love you." He was saying sorry.

I found that out when the mole came to me, her face all white, and said she'd gotten wind of a tip-line flowing to the police. A tip-line with some very important and very impossible information about Dawnslight. There wasn't a name, but there weren't many options for who it could be, and I knew. I knew as soon as she walked in the door, before she even said it. I knew, I knew.

I still wonder if they promised him some kind of immunity, or if he even fucking cared anymore.

"All right, enough," Jada said through her teeth, breathless.

Molly stopped. She looked up from her work, four raw-wound flowers with wide petals dripping red pollen. It wasn't as hard as she'd imagined it would be, once she got the trick of the scalpel and tweezers. The thin metal pan she was using for— scraps, she supposed she should say, though that *did* disgust her—would need to be emptied, the flesh incinerated.

"What happened?" she asked.

Jada barked a laugh. "That's not how storytelling works. I'll come back tomorrow, I'll tell you some more. You said it would take a few days."

Molly laid down the utensils in the pan and stripped her bloody gloves off. Her hands had begun to tremble, much delayed. She had a feeling she knew exactly where Jada's story was going. Of course she'd killed him, they'd already covered that. But—if it had been simple, if it had gone well, there would be no reason for Jada to be planetside, getting a scarification from a small-town clinic in what used to be India from a woman whose name was not actually Molly and who did not belong.

"The sealant?" she asked, wrenching herself away from that line of thought.

Jada slid off of the table, cupping the towel to her arm to catch the dripping blood flow, and made her way to the door where she'd dropped her bag when she came in. Her feet slid with her weight instead of stepping; clearly she was feeling the pain. She squatted and dug through her pack for a moment. Molly looked down at herself and found a splotch of blood on the hem of her tank top, a dull maroon color.

Jada returned with the sealant and pressed it into her outstretched hand. The bottle had a squirt top, which struck Molly as silly for no reason she could pinpoint. She squeezed some of the bitter-smelling liquid onto a small wad of bandages and dabbed it over the wounds. It took her several minutes to cover them sufficiently, spent in a quiet that was strange after an hour or two of listening. Jada seemed to be made of silences and stories with no room for any chatter.

"Let me bandage them," she said when Jada shifted to reach for her shirt. She threw the used bandage into the trash can and grabbed a fresh roll. Jada tapped her foot as if impatient now that the sun was setting. "There," Molly said after winding the last bit of cloth over the wounds. "Tomorrow?"

"Tomorrow," Jada said, gruff, and held her expression empty even as she fought to shimmy into her shirt without jostling her arm.

She didn't say good-bye when she banged out the wood-slatted door, her pack over her good shoulder, the cut arm hanging at her side. Molly glanced at the mess on her table and bit her tongue. She wasn't done, not yet. There was cleaning to finish first.

"Mom will settle up with you later, okay?" said the young man perched on the edge of Molly's examining table. He twisted his tank top between his fingers, glancing at her from under the fringe of his hair.

"That's fine," she replied. She stripped her gloves off and disposed of them. "Try to stay out of the sun and don't pick at the blisters."

He nodded and slid off the table. She took a last glance at the patchy, blistered skin over his shoulders and down his back—minor chemical burns. She hadn't even had to ask if he'd been playing in the rain the day before. It was obvious. That rinsing, tepid downpour was too tempting for the average kid, but what it brought down out of the atmosphere could be nasty, remnants of decades of warfare that had spread poison across the globe. He slipped out the door. She wasn't sure if he was embarrassed that he'd done something stupid, or if the Goenka family was running low on tradable goods and he was worried about paying for the treatment. Possibly both.

Molly took one step toward her desk before the door rattled open again. Jada dropped her pack in the entryway, the midday sun casting a stark halo around her dyed hair, and let the door close behind her. They stood at opposite angles in the room, watching each other. Molly wiped her hands on her shirt and returned to her desk.

"I would have expected you to yell at him," Jada said.

"You were listening?"

She shrugged.

Molly pressed her hands flat to the pitted surface of the old desk. "He's a child. He deserves to try and eke out a little enjoyment in his life."

"That's fair," Jada said.

The tension passed as quickly as it had crackled to life. Jada stripped out of the tan temp-reg shirt. The tank top underneath clung to her like a second skin, accentuating more than it hid. Molly was suddenly, inappropriately aware of the bumps Jada's nipples made under the fabric in a way that she hadn't been when Jada was bare chested. She fiddled with her water canister in a half-hearted attempt to distract herself. Jada sat on the table and began unwinding her bandage on her own, wrapping the bloody cloth around her fingers.

"Ready, I take it?" Molly asked.

"When you are," Jada said.

It was easier, the second time. Molly prepared her tools, put on her gloves, and inspected the work from the day before. The wounds were raw but they weren't swollen. That was good. The sealant must have done its job.

"So, you found out your partner of years had betrayed you," Molly said, wiping down the unmarred skin with an antiseptic cloth. "How didn't you see that coming, if you knew each other so well?"

Jada smiled, but it was empty. "Being lovers doesn't mean you know each other. Nobody ever really knows anybody; you just think you do."

Molly paused, thinking, and tried again. "Fine, but why would someone who spent their whole life—since he was a teenager, right?—doing the same job have an attack of conscience?"

"Interesting question," Jada said. She paused, as well. "I don't know. I never figured out if it was one job in particular, or something I did, or something he saw. It wasn't an attack of conscience, not like you're thinking; I don't think he had one. You don't murder people if you have a conscience. But I think . . ."

Molly put the scalpel to bare skin again, and this time she was freehanding it. The first cut froze Jada's breath. The second let it out in a rush. She looked down at her arm and saw the waving line Molly was slicing under the flower petals.

"I think," she began again.

He was tired.

People like us aren't supposed to have long lives. You can't be put together right if you look at a list of your possibilities and you think that murder for hire is the best and easiest option. Adrenaline junkies, or people with lots of hate, or people like me who don't feel much most of the time—and do you really think that's the kind of personality that lends itself to doddering old age?

No. No, we all expect to die before we're thirty, but we die with honor and usually in a blaze of glory. Eten was thirty-five, and he was tired, and he wanted out, but you can't ever get out, not once you're as high up as he was. As we were. They'll kill you for running. So, he can kill himself with all his guilt. Or he can take out a boss and probably the whole Dawnslight crew in one fell swoop, because he *could*, because he would die with some kind of meaning.

He chose honor. He chose revenge. I get that. Or, it's what I would do if I got so sick of it I couldn't do the job anymore, so maybe I'm projecting. I think he was just tired, and too much of a badass to die alone. He had to take the syndicate out with him. Had to.

I didn't act on the information at first. No, I had to make sure. I told the mole to shut her fucking mouth and tell no one until I did some digging. Word was not making it to the boss, not if I had a say—he liked to make examples of traitors, and I would kill him with my bare hands before I let him do that to Eten. If it had to be done, I would do it myself, and it would be quick and clean. I decided that pretty fast, and I did feel something then. It was ugly and it hurt, so I stopped feeling it, and started hunting.

—*"That easy?" Molly asked. "Was it really that easy to put aside, thinking about killing your partner, the man you'd loved your whole life?"*

"I thought it was," she said. "I thought it was. Now shut up and let me tell the story."—

Actually, I'll answer that, because I guess it makes the story make sense.

I had my life. I was comfortable with my life, and the boss had given me all of that. I mean, yes, I had earned it, but it wasn't mine. Not really. My whole life was the syndicate. It's like asking me to choose between my entire extended family, if I'd had one, and my lover. So, no, it wasn't easy. It helped that I knew if we decided to run away, Eten would still be tired and old and finished. He'd kill himself and I'd be alone anyway, a traitor to boot.

So, I weighed it. Life without Eten but with my whole family, an honored position in the syndicate, and respect for taking care of a betrayal so colossal as Eten's. It was one of those impossible decisions you just have to make, because not making it is the *same* as making it. Once I decided to kill him I felt lighter. I think maybe I was in shock, looking back on it, because you should never feel light as a feather while you're hunting evidence for somebody's death.

You don't think you could make that decision, but you could. You're a mercenary bitch; I saw you weighing what it was worth for you to help me. There's no shame in that. You would have chosen the same thing. Your loyalty is to you. Mine was to me and my family, my syndicate.

But it gets worse. Of course it gets worse, or I wouldn't be here; I'd be sitting on a bed of money with ten naked boys massaging my sore old body, my boss singing my praises. Making the decision isn't always enough.

I looked, though. I made certain. I found his bank accounts, I dug up his secrets, I traced all the names I knew he'd ever used and some I guessed about. There was no money trail. Like I said, they hadn't bought his betrayal. He was making his own decisions, and I got mad, because fuck it—he wasn't just betraying the syndicate, he was betraying *me*. I would be executed if they arrested us, and he goddamn knew it, so if he was going to kill me, well. Fair's fair.

I shouldn't have gotten angry. Anger is a luxury when you're hunting.

I did find the evidence I needed. It was a comm account registered under one of those names I'd guessed, and it was his. I knew his writing well enough to recognize it in the messages stored there. He'd been sending reports to the police, every day, a damning amount of information, but they would need him to verify it in court. That was how the system worked. Anonymous tips, no matter how juicy, eventually have to be backed up before legal action can be taken. The syndicates pushed that law through, obviously. Makes our lives easier; harder to rat one another out when tempted.

I printed a physical copy of the comm records I'd hacked and put the papers on the kitchen table in a big stack. I straightened it probably fifty times, waiting for him to come home, before I realized that if I made it a fair fight, let him explain first, he might win. We were evenly matched.

And he knew what he was doing. He knew he was signing my death warrant along with the boss's. So I put the papers in a cabinet. I would need to show them to the boss later. I was crying. I remember that. Just couldn't stop. That should have been a hint. I waited at the door. I had a good thick piece of wire in my hands, cushioned well. It wouldn't hurt him too much. It would be quick. I waited, and I waited, and I was shaking and crying the whole fucking time like a child.

But it was him or me. He'd made the first choice, and I was making the last.

A silence fell, almost reverent, as Molly looked at her handiwork—a whirlwind design of lines curling and waving down to Jada's elbow. The other woman had gone white in the face, as if all the bleeding had leeched her color out, or possibly the story. Her eyes were damp at the edges. Molly glanced away.

"I need to stop for now," she said.

Jada gave a jerky nod. "I know, I know, danger of shock. Can't do too much at once."

"You need a break," she said, standing to find the sealant and bandages again. "And I need a break. It's a hard story to hear."

"Harder to have done," Jada said, nearly a snarl. Molly flinched.

The cleanup was quiet. Jada bit into her bottom lip as the wounds were treated and bandaged, a thin sheen of red welling up against the whiteness of her teeth. Molly resisted the urge to tell her to stop—it was her pain, she had the right to deal with it how she liked. The room had grown stifling without either of the women noticing as morning lengthened into afternoon. The bands of the tale stretched between them, and the bands of the art, the blood and cutting.

"You don't have to finish the story if you don't want to," Molly whispered. Her heart was one hard aching lump in her chest, and she felt cold inside where the summer heat couldn't reach. "I can guess what comes next."

Jada shook her head as she dressed, muscles quivering and fingers outright shaking. "It's the ritual. It's his honor. I have to tell you. You're the artist, I'm the murderer."

That was that—she picked up her pack and staggered out of the clinic. The door shut hard behind her and Molly stared at it, wondering where in the hell she went after their appointments. She stood out too much for a bar or an inn. She must have been roughing it outside the town. Head full of strangeness, Molly sat behind her desk again, her stomach aching with hunger. She needed a late lunch, or an early dinner, but couldn't make herself want to eat.

There was something about pain that leveled people out. She wished she hadn't asked for the story, though she knew now she would have gotten it anyway, if it was how these things were done. Jada was easier to deal with as a big brute of an enforcer—if she was a woman, a woman with her heart half carved out of her chest and the wound open there for the world to see, that was too difficult. That was too personal.

The money, though. Molly pressed her fingers to the death-sentence lump, and imagined it was larger as she palpated it, pressing the sore flesh of her breast through the shirt. Thousands was enough for a treatment, barely, if she saved a little extra and called due all the tiny debts so many people owed her. Her life was worth that. She could hear the rest of the story.

The hours passed slowly. There were no more visitors. At dusk, she closed the clinic door behind her and walked down the dusty street, burning hot through her shoes, to her home. It was down a side street in the town, a small bungalow with netting in the windows and a working fridge. She had paid extra to have that kind of a power hookup, but cold food and water were worth it.

She kicked her front door closed behind her and went straight to the fridge. Inside, there was a bottle with her name on it, a bottle that would help to ease the throbbing in her head. Molly took the cold liquor with her to her bed, which also served as her couch, and turned on her tablet to check for the news. The condensation beading on the bottle felt exquisite when she pressed it to her forehead.

The first thing she saw was an article about spreading fires in the north and glassed deserts farther south. She flipped to the next article, and the next, until a "Wanted" poster stopped her cold. The face was unmistakable. Jada, haughty, her chin lifted, staring down the person taking her photo.

The reward for information leading to her arrest was fifteen thousand in station currency. A chill ran up Molly's spine, nerves tingling. Condensation dripped from her bottle onto the screen. The water blurred Jada's picture through a hundred broken crystal fragments. She turned the tablet off.

Thousands, she thought, and tipped the bottle up, welcoming the cold burn in her mouth. She still felt blood and peeling flesh under her fingertips; behind her eyelids she saw Jada standing in the shadow of her own door, sobbing, garrote in hand.

It was not a night for cups.

"I don't want to chat," Jada said as she burst inside the clinic, the door rattling hard on its hinges. It slapped shut behind her with a crack like thunder. "Let's just start, so I can get this part out of the way."

Molly caught the breath that had been startled out of her at the loud entrance and nodded. She'd barely been able to gather a stray thought all day, never sure when Jada would come or if the police had already caught her, if someone else had gotten that fifteen thousand. The Goenka boy had returned for more burn spray, but that had been a bare distraction from the waiting, the endless waiting.

They moved in perfect concert, Jada undressing and unwinding her bandages while Molly prepped the tools and put the scrap pan within easy reach. She'd been burning the bits of flesh every night in the incinerator, and the bandages, too. There was some puffiness around Jada's elbow, she noted, but not enough to be a major concern. She laid the woman's forearm across her knees, paused, and frowned.

"I need to brace this somehow. Could you lie down?"

"All right," Jada said and shifted to lie on her back. Her forearm rested flat on the table. Molly put a towel under it and wiped the area down as per usual. For good measure, she swabbed off the scalpel twice. "I'm ready."

"Okay," Molly said.

The small, so-sharp blade traced a long, thin line, then another, and another. Jada squeezed her eyes shut and her jaw flexed, tendons standing out for a brief second, the most visible expression of pain she'd given. Molly wondered if it was the cuts, or the story forcing itself from between her teeth.

"I was standing at the door. It had gotten late," Jada said while Molly worked, *carving delicate spirals like teardrops. It surprised her how easy this had become, how natural.*

The lights went down outside, and he still hadn't come. He was never so late. I'd been standing in the same spot for probably four hours. I couldn't budge, though. I had to piss, I was thirsty, and I was stiff from crying, but I couldn't move, because I couldn't lose the moment. If I moved, Eten would come in, and I'd lose my surprise.

I'd lose my nerve.

It had finally occurred to me, in that fucking awful wait, that I wasn't sure I could go through with it. I had to, but I wasn't sure I *could*. There was no way out; Eten was a traitor. It had to be done. "He was going to kill me," I remember saying to the empty house. I told myself all sorts of shit, in the dark, alone. That Eten had never loved me, that I was convenient and he was convenient and that was the only reason we'd stuck together, that it would be easy once I started, that I was a failure if I couldn't do this.

Then the door opened and he stepped into the dark. He reached out for the lights. The wire cut through the air without a sound as I moved, but I let out a noise I didn't mean to, something like his name. He turned toward me, and his hand brushed my chest, but I had the wire up under his chin and I kicked his bad knee. His legs went out from under him.

I pulled. I pulled hard. I shut my eyes against the shadows and his jerking like a fish on a hook. I felt a pain in my leg, and I braced myself against the wall because he'd stabbed me, the bastard, but he was going limp and he couldn't pull the knife out again. It stuck there in my thigh like a piece of ice. His hands scrabbled at my ankles, those familiar long skinny fingers, and his body twitched. I heard my breath in my ears, wheezing. His hands went still, but I'm not an idiot, and I held on. I held on when his weight finally gave out and yanked him against the wire. I held on, and I took us both to the floor; there was blood everywhere, which was fitting. It was mine. I put my face in his hair and wondered if it was worth pulling the knife out. He hadn't gotten the artery. I would have taken a long time to bleed to death, if it was even possible. His hair was like silk, and I know people say that all the time, but it was. It was silky and long enough to touch his shoulders. When we went out, people thought he was the woman, next to me. I ran my hands down his arms, and I lay with him, and I felt the cool set into that thin, handsome, empty body.

It killed me. The cold seeped in. I was wrong—I couldn't trade him for my family. At least in the end, I proved to myself that I had really, really loved him, because otherwise it wouldn't have ruined me. It's over. I know that. It's all done, now, but *this*, and that's why I can tell a stranger like you the truth. You're finishing my business, his business with me. You're just the executor, and I'm already dead.

"Come home with me," Molly said.

Jada breathed slowly, her eyes shut.

"You don't have to go stay outside of town, or whatever you're doing. My house is safe enough," she said. "You're covered in open wounds. You need a shower."

"That's not all to the story," Jada said. She sounded like heartbreak and tears choked back for too long. "There's more."

"Not right now," Molly said. "Not right now there's not. Just come with me."

The cleanup was fast and involved no eye contact. Molly reapplied the sealant to all the wounds, from shoulder down, a red mass of cuts and opened flesh. There were only a few inches left, near Jada's wrist, but that last patch of unmarred skin could wait. Molly worked wordlessly to bandage the scarification, wrapping the white linen around the glistening wounds, wet with antiseptic sealant and blood. She wiped down the utensils perfunctorily and rinsed them in the small corner sink. She would disinfect them before using them again, but she needed to leave the sweltering and impossibly tiny space of the clinic, filled as it was with ugly words and pain like ghosts.

Jada's arms trembled, weak, as she pushed herself off the table. Molly bundled the temp-reg shirt up and stuffed it in the woman's pack—better not to be seen with it on the street. The pants might blend in if no one looked too closely, and the dark would obscure her scars. Jada followed like a shadow. Her story had drained vitality from her, so that her imposing strength seemed wooden and inflexible. Molly bit her tongue until the sharp taste of her own blood bloomed in her mouth. It was the only way to hold inside what she needed to say, to ask.

Jada's steps traced hers down the main street, past houses lit dimly from the inside, onto the side avenue, and into her small home. She imagined how it must look to someone from stationside, used to living in luxury: a one-room shack with a bed against the far wall, a kitchen against the other, and a rough-hewn door to the miniscule bathroom. Molly left the light off and grabbed the half-full bottle of liquor from the fridge, inspecting her own smudged fingerprints on the glass neck as if they held a dire secret. Jada closed the door behind them with an air of finality.

"The shower's through there," Molly said.

Jada nodded, dropping her pack next to the metal-framed bed. "You'll have to rebandage the arm when I'm done."

"That's fine," Molly said. "I keep supplies on hand here, too."

Jada went through the door to the bathroom. Molly let out a breath as the thin wood partition shut between them. She collapsed onto her bed. Her tablet bumped her hip. She picked it up and turned it on. The screen was still filled by Jada's "Wanted" ad. She flicked the page away, wincing. She wasn't likely to forget what it had said, whether she was looking at it or not.

What was she doing, dragging a fugitive syndicate assassin to her home? They'd have to share the bed; there was no way to sleep comfortably on the floor. In another context, having such a broad, strong, handsome woman between the sheets with her would have thrilled Molly, but not like this. Instead, it was simply alarming.

The words had just come out of her. It had seemed like the right thing to do, offering a little measure of comfort—a shower, a bed—in the face of that horrible story. The realization that it had only been a few days since Jada had come into the clinic was enough to throw Molly off balance. At the time, she'd been afraid of her, she'd been angry, she hadn't wanted a thing to do with the whole business—and now, the same woman was in her house. She heard the water to the shower kick on, a dull hum.

It was difficult not to feel like she'd lost her mind.

She sipped from the cold bottle, the icy burn of liquor down her throat a comfort of its own. The *story*, though. How had she not seen through Jada's brittle sharpness during that first conversation, when she'd confessed to killing Eten? It shamed her to think that she had so easily mistaken agony for arrogance. Another sip, and she shimmied off of the bed. Sleeping in her work clothes was out of the question. She stripped naked in the middle of the room, listening for the shower to cut off and glad when it didn't. She had her scars, too, and they were private. The ragged, raised brand of white flesh on her flank, that was her own and no one else's. *Exile*, it said in the always intelligible language of symbols.

Molly pulled on a pair of thin shorts and an equally airy tank top. Alone, she slept nude, but she wasn't alone tonight. The shower cut off. She kicked her dirty laundry into the corner. She would take it all to the washing-shop later in the week.

Jada stepped out into the main room, toweling her frizzed hair dry. She'd put her same tank top and pants on, but her skin was scrubbed free of road dust and she looked healthier altogether. Molly offered her the bottle. She took it, casting her a narrow-eyed look.

"I'm not trying to get you into bed," Molly said.

"All right," she replied, as if it didn't bother her either way.

The dim light from the moon had been enough to wander the house, but Molly clicked on the bedside lamp to re-treat and rebandage the wounds on Jada's arm. With that done, she turned it off again. They sat side by side on the mattress, passing the bottle back and forth. Molly took one last gulp and passed the final mouthful to Jada, who finished it off with a dramatic tilt of her head. Her throat worked as she swallowed.

Molly was glad not to have to speak. It was easier to tug on the covers as a hint and crawl underneath them. At first she lay facing the wall, but a warm hand pushed at her shoulder.

"Can't lay on my other arm," Jada murmured.

"Oh," Molly whispered, rolling over to face the room.

The other woman settled behind her, a length of heat against her back. After an awkward, shuffling moment, that thick, bandaged arm came around her waist and tugged her closer. Her breath came out in a huff. Jada's body fit hers almost too perfectly, cupping her tinier frame with plenty of room to spare. The press of fingertips on her ribs was like a brand in its own right. She shifted and closed her eyes. It was dark, warm, and too close. An unwelcome thrill skated down her spine as Jada moved again, hand sliding on her side. Finally, they settled, and her nerves did also. It had been a long time since anyone had shared her bed.

In the space of a breath, she forgot to hold in her words.

"I've never loved a single person that much," she whispered.

Jada stiffened against her for only a moment and relaxed again. Her palm cupped the curve of Molly's hip and stroked up, under her shirt, the simple caress of skin on skin knocking the breath out of her in a gasp. She pressed her face into the pillow to muffle it, too late. Jada's blunt fingernails scratched across the plane of her stomach.

"Be thankful," Jada murmured, each syllable a burst of warm breath teasing the hairs on the back of Molly's neck. "All your decisions are probably much easier."

Hours later, Molly lay awake in the loose grip of the sleeping syndicate woman, staring across the room at shadows on the far wall. *All your decisions are probably much easier.* She must have known—she must have.

Molly woke first and pried herself out of the cocoon of blankets to shower. The cool water sluicing over her skin was like heaven, washing away the previous day's sweat and dust. By the time she emerged, wrapped in a towel, Jada was up and drinking a cup of water at her sink. The morning sun illuminated her white skin, contrasting it sharply with the pink scars and red-dotted linen bandages.

"Do you want to finish today?" Molly asked.

"Borrow your bathroom, first," she said.

Molly dropped the towel as soon as the door closed and threw on a shirt and skirt. She was so unused to sharing her space it hadn't occurred to her to bring a change of clothes into the bathroom. She ran a brush through her slick, damp hair, cool water dripping down the collar of her shirt. A moment later, Jada emerged and crossed the room to shoulder her pack.

"Ready?" she asked.

Molly nodded while Jada walked outside. With a sharp pulse of adrenaline stabbing through her guts, she picked up her tablet and slipped it into the front pocket of her skirt before she followed the other woman out. They stood in the sun for a moment while Molly blinked hard, adjusting her eyes. Sleep and a shower had rejuvenated Jada, but now that she knew to look for it Molly saw the hard angles at which she held herself, the pinched line of her mouth. Her lips were actually rather plump in her sleep, when she was relaxed.

They made the walk to the clinic nearly in private; the only other people out were children running errands for their parents—fetching water, going to the market for the day's milk if there was any to be had, picking up laundry. Molly passed through the clinic door into her domain and sighed.

This was the last day. The cutting would be finished, and the story, too. *The last day*, she thought hard, repetitively. *All my decisions should be easier, easier than hers*.

Molly rinsed the tools at the sink, patted them dry, and treated them with antiseptic wipes. The stainless steel gleamed, wickedly sharp. Jada had arranged herself lying on the table, her heels hanging off the edge. She'd even put the towel down already.

Molly pressed one hand over Jada's to keep her from moving and traced the first beading red line. It curved up to meet the older wounds in an arc, tying it all together, making it one. Jada flexed her hand under Molly's. Molly squeezed it in return.

"I was still lying there with him, sure that I was never going to move again," Jada said.

I couldn't survive it, I wasn't that tough. No one is that tough. I'd carved out a piece of myself and left it cold and crumpled in the fucking foyer. But at least, I thought, my boss and my family, my syndicate, they would be fine. I was old, anyway, as old as he was. It was time. I was okay with that. We'd go out in our private glory—it wasn't like I would die alone, not really. So I grabbed the knife in my leg and pulled it out. That hurt, but not enough to wake me up. There's a reason you see so many murder-suicides with couples. They always say it's possessive, on the newsfeeds, but that's not right—it's that you realize a minute too late what you've done, and there's no going back.

A call came through right then, while I was weighing his knife in my hand and considering how to finish myself off. I had no way to block calls from my boss. The holo popped up from my wristband and he was staring, his mouth open, because there I was in the dark, covered in blood and crying.

"There are police here," he said to me. "They've got *recorded video testimony*."

Suddenly I knew why Eten was late getting home. I laughed, because what else was I going to do? He'd gotten us. He well and truly had. Killing him hadn't done a damn thing. I'd choked his life out of him for no reason.

Maybe he'd bargained for immunity for us both, but I hadn't asked.

I hadn't asked. I just acted, because I'm stupid that way.

I ripped that wristband off and threw it. The syndicate was dead. Eten was dead. *I* was dead, but I owed him something.

—*"This,"* Molly said.

"Yeah," she answered.—

We had spent fifteen years together. Almost every day, I saw his face when I woke up and when I went to sleep. We ate from the same table. We shared the same bed. We did each other's most important scars. I knew every inch of him, and he of me. Fifteen years is a long time when it's half your whole life. I used my own hands to end that.

Maybe he'd arranged immunity. Maybe that was his deal, and he was afraid to tell me. Maybe I killed our future, or maybe he was planning on taking us both out, together. You understand, I'm fair game—not just to the police, but to any syndicate with a grudge against good old dead Dawnslight. There's no running away. They catch you when you run, they do. There's only running as far as you need to, and finishing your business. I'm old enough. I did enough. I made the choice, and rolled those dice, and there's nothing else.

That's just how stories like mine end.

Molly finished a last swirl and peeled it up, away.

"Are you sure?" she asked as she set aside the tools.

"Positive," Jada murmured.

Molly picked up the steel tray and put it on the edge of the sink. She ran the taps cool, rinsing the scalpel of its gory coating and the tweezers as well. The water ran pink down the drain. She'd forgotten her gloves; her fingernails were caked with blood. She frowned, scrubbing at them. The weight of her tablet dragged at her skirt like a stone.

"I need to take this out to the incinerator," she said, gesturing to the tray. "Do you mind?"

"No," Jada said. She lifted her arm above her head, turning it to and fro.

Molly pushed the door open with her elbow, holding the tray away from her body. She walked under the minimal shadow of the side of the building, through dry and cakey dirt that came up in clouds under her shoes. Half-dead scrub bushes were barely managing to grow at the back of the building by the incinerator, more branch than leaf, brown and crisped. Molly dumped the contents of the tray into the mouth of the machine—the whole town used it, but it was located behind the clinic for medical convenience—and closed its lid. She punched the button with a quivering finger and closed her eyes, listening to the whoosh of the core heating.

Her red-crusted fingernails drew her accusatory gaze when she slipped her tablet into her hand. She pulled up the "Wanted" ad. *It was one of those impossible decisions you just have to make, because not making it is the same as making it,* Jada had said. There was a link at the bottom to the police hotline. She tapped it and put the tablet in whisper-mode, lifting it to her ear.

"May I help you?" a cool voice on the other end asked.

"I have this woman in my clinic," she murmured. "The one from the ad."

"Excellent," he said, no warmer. "Our patrol is nearby. Stall her for twenty minutes, ma'am, if you can safely do so."

"The money," she hissed. "I'll tell her to run for the hills if you don't promise me they'll give me the money the moment—"

"Yes, of course," he said. "They will be authorized to transfer funds upon their successful operation. If you do your part."

"Thank you," Molly gasped and shut the link.

Her breath stuck in her throat. She put a hand to her mouth, pressing hard enough to cut her lips on her teeth in a burst of pain, as if she could physically hold in a scream. Fifteen thousand, instead of three; fifteen thousand could buy so much more than the gene therapy. Fifteen thousand could buy air-conditioning, could buy clothes, could buy food. Fifteen thousand was a *life*.

She wanted to laugh at herself—of *course* it was a life. Jada's, specifically.

Molly's heart hammered against her ribs as she walked around the side of the building. What if Jada had heard her somehow, had picked up her bag and left already? The door would have made a sound, she was sure, but—it hadn't been so long ago that Jada had pressed fingers to her vulnerable spine in threat, real or fake. There were uglier possibilities than her leaving without a good-bye, if she had heard.

Twenty minutes, Molly thought wildly as she came inside with the empty tray. Jada was sitting on the table, dabbing sealant on her wounds with a wad of gauze. She flicked her eyes up, cataloguing Molly in a way that made her cold to her toes—a sharp focus, predatory—then looked back down at her arm.

"You did a good job," she said.

"For a doctor," Molly replied.

Her voice was steady. She had assumed it would come out as tight as her throat felt, or raw like it was full of barbs. Jada was right, though; the lines made a macabre but beautiful painting on her skin, red and white, a canvas of flesh. She briefly regretted not fitting Eten's name in somewhere, but perhaps that would have been too obvious.

"My name isn't Molly," she said into the budding silence, refusing to let it settle.

Jada put aside the gauze pad. "I assumed."

"You gave me a story," she said.

"You want to give me one, too?" Jada asked.

Molly pulled the chair out from her desk and yanked it across the floor with a screech of wood on tile. She thumped it in front of the examination table and sat, hands in her lap.

"You don't have to listen," she said, looking at the dried blood again. "You could leave. You've finished your—business, your responsibility."

I'm giving you a chance, she thought desperately.

"Tell me," Jada said, her posture sagging into a slump. She cradled the wounded arm over her lap, and neither woman moved to bandage it. The cuts told a tale, of and between them.

Molly reached up, tentative, and put her hand on Jada's. Her fingers were still red with her sunburn, peeling finally. She didn't pull away. Molly tilted her head back and their eyes met, locking, as their hands did also. She wet her dry lips with the tip of her tongue, tasting the sharp tang of the wounds she'd made with her teeth.

"Molly isn't short for anything," she said. "I picked it out of a book."

"I was from the E-6 station," she said.

My name was Sharad Rathore, and I was a doctor. I had money but not enough money to pay for the school I'd been through, and my father had lost his job.

I was a good daughter. Doctors have access to all kinds of things—especially in a big hospital where it's always busy, where people fail to fill out necessary paperwork all the time, and where the security checks are very lax. So, I thought I would sell. Just a little. Enough to make ends meet.

—*"Oh, that was—" Jada began.*

"Stupid, I know," Molly said.—

I didn't know that the syndicates did *not* appreciate freelancing. It messed with their business, threw off their sales. I was too cheap and too accessible. I realize they could have just killed me, but instead, they set me up. That last meeting I had wasn't with a buyer. It was a police officer, and the judge they sent me to was syndicate-owned. I went to the court and watched them decide what was going to happen to me without saying a word, shaking in my shoes. The courtroom turned me into a little girl again. But they said they were being very lenient, and it was to be exile instead of prison.

Lenient, to give the worst possible punishment. Lenient. That was when I knew that I'd been set up.—

The door burst inward, wood slats shattered and skittering across the floor with the force of the kick. Jada wrenched her hand free and dove for her bag, spilling the contents on the floor; Molly kicked her chair backward and lifted her hands in the air. As the police poured inside—four of them, menacing in identical black body armor and faceplates, shouting over one another—Jada pressed her back to the exam table and lifted a compact pistol from the clothes and tech scattered across the tile. She bared her teeth and stood, the gun sweeping toward Molly. Blood spattered from her wounded arm where it hung useless at her side.

Molly's heart stopped at the sight of the gun, her gaze meeting Jada's through a hot blur of tears. She opened her mouth to say anything—*I'm sorry, I love you, you told me to do this*—but the barrel moved past her completely and the roar of shots filled the tiny space. Molly screamed, hands flying to her ears. Her defensive curl obscured her vision for a span of seconds and so she missed Jada's fall until she hit the floor at her feet.

Blood poured out of her like a river of red ore, viscous and hot. It spread in runnels between Molly's feet. She pressed her hands to her mouth again, helpless, a high sound escaping between her fingers.

I'm old, Jada had said. *That's just how stories like mine end*, Jada had said.

Molly took a shaking step back, and another, until she hit the wall. The blood followed her, grasping, and she rose up on her toes to get away.

"Ma'am," one of the officers said. She half heard him through the ringing in her ears. "Are you all right?"

She tore her eyes from the blood only to see the terrible stillness of Jada's flower-carved arm with its pale white fingers unfurled like petals. Old-fashioned bullets had torn into her torso, shredding cloth and flesh alike, a ruin of meat. Her face was strangely untouched, eyes open, lips parted as if to take breath.

"We apologize for firing in the closed space," he said. "We have authorization to confirm your payment. Do you have your account information?"

Molly fumbled her tablet from her skirt and handed it to him. He tapped the screen several times, held his wristband to it for a flash of infrared, and handed it back.

"Thank you for your services," he said. "We'll handle the cleanup free of charge."

"Yes," she said numbly. "Yes, of course. Fifteen thousand?"

"Yes, ma'am," he said.

The other officers were gathering Jada's body between them onto a foldable stretcher. Molly's knees knocked together and she nearly fell, a wave of vertigo smashing through her. *Jada*, vital and truthful and so fucking beautiful, was now a cold and crumpled thing, carved out of her and left on the floor. The officers hefted the stretcher between them. The same hand that had palmed burning-hot trails over Molly's hip, her ribs, her stomach, lolled boneless in the air. The officers left as if assuming she would follow. Instead she collapsed into her chair and put her hands on the examination table, still warm. So was the sticky pool of rapidly darkening, drying blood under her feet.

"Fifteen thousand," Molly said aloud.

It had happened faster than she'd anticipated. Her balance hadn't returned; there was shock in its place, where the memory of Jada's lips twisted in a final snarl had burned into her. She stood, jerky as if she were a puppet on strings, and went to the sink. She rinsed the scalpel again, and the tweezers, and the pan. She plucked a disinfectant wipe from the box and ran it over the utensils, then dropped them onto the exam table with a rattle. Making the decision—rolling the dice—hadn't broken her. What that said about her, she wasn't sure she wanted to know.

Molly who was not named Molly ran the wipe over her own forearm, cleaning the prickles of sweat from her skin. She took the scalpel in her free hand and traced a line that felt at first like nothing more than cold before it blossomed into a sharp hurt. There was a tale to tell, and a badge she had earned with murder.

"Her name was Jada," she whispered to the empty room as she began her own work with her own canvas. "I don't know if this is the proper way to do it, but this was her story. I think she wanted me to kill her."

steamgothic

SEAN McMULLEN

As the ingenious story that follows demonstrates, history can turn on the smallest of details—and just because it hasn't turned yet, doesn't mean it still couldn't.

Australian author Sean McMullen is a computer systems analyst with the Australian Bureau of Meteorology, and has been a lead singer in folk and rock bands as well as singing with the Victoria State Opera. He's also an acclaimed and prolific author whose short fiction has appeared in The Magazine of Fantasy and Science Fiction, Interzone, Analog, *and elsewhere. He has written a dozen novels, including* Voices in the Light, Mirrorsun Rising, Souls in the Great Machine, The Miocene Arrow, Eyes of the Calculor, Voyage of the Shadowmoon, Glass Dragons, Void Farer, The Time Engine, The Centurion's Empire, *and* Before the Storm. *His most recent novel is* Changing Yesterday. *Some of his stories have been collected in* Call to the Edge, *and he wrote a critical study,* Strange Constellations: A History of Australian Science Fiction, *with Russell Blackford and Van Ikin. He lives in Melbourne, Australia.*

There is something special about things that changed the world. I cannot say what it is, but I can feel it. I have stood before the Vostok capsule that carried the first man into space. Influence glowed from it; I knew where it was even with my eyes closed. In the Spurlock Museum I saw the strange, twisted, lumpy thing that was the first transistor. The significance that it radiated was like the heat from a fire. The Babbage Analytical Engine of 1871 had no such aura, yet the whole of Bletchley Park did. There was no doubt in my mind about which of them had really launched the age of computers.

The Wright Brother's Flyer had no feeling of significance for me either. This made no sense. It was the first heavier-than-air machine to fly, it proved the principle, it changed the world, yet my strange intuition said otherwise. Then I saw the Aeronaute, and everything should have become clear to me.

There was an 1899 Daimler parked across the road from my flat when I arrived home from work. Admirers were milling around it, and a security guard was making sure that nobody took any liberties. I knew early model cars fairly well after being dragged along to countless car shows by my father, but cars are not my thing. Pausing only to admire the Daimler as something Art Nouveau that actually worked, I opened my front door.

On top of several packages of things ordered online was a large envelope. I seldom get letters. Anything that can be turned into text or pixels comes over the Internet. The address on the envelope was handwritten, and the handwriting was clear, elegant copperplate. A genuine penny stamp was at the top right-hand corner, but there was no postmark. This had been delivered by hand. *Who writes copperplate in the second decade of the twenty-first century?* I wondered. Picking it up was like stepping back in time, and it begged to be opened by something with more class than my front door key.

Going upstairs, I found a real letter opener in the shape of a medieval sword, bought on some trip to the British Museum. The covering note merely said "Dear Mr. Chandler, can I have your opinion on the enclosed photos? Yours sincerely, Louise Penderan." There were four photographs with the note, all color prints on A4 paper. They were of the wreckage of an aircraft that had never existed.

Take a modern ultralight, describe it verbally to a mid-nineteenth-century engineer, have him build one, then crash it. That was the subject of the first photo. Unlike most nineteenth-century machines, this aircraft seemed not to have an ounce of excess weight. The background suggested that it was in a barn.

The second photograph showed four lightweight cylinders that were connected in a spiral pattern to a crankshaft. This was a steam engine, and it was also built to minimize weight. The next photograph showed a propeller that resembled a windmill with two blades. The last picture featured what was left of a cloth panel with the word AERONAUTE painted in silver.

The doorbell chimed while I was still examining the photos. It was 6 p.m., not the usual time for people pedaling telco plans or religious salvation, and my friends always texted me before coming over. As I walked down the stairs I had a feeling that whoever was outside was connected with the envelope. It had been just five minutes since I had arrived home. Perhaps they had been waiting in the café over the road, giving me those minutes to examine the photographs. Perhaps they even owned the 1899 Daimler.

I opened the door to a couple dressed in matching brown ankle coats and wearing motoring goggles on their foreheads. I am six feet tall, yet they were both tall enough to look down at me. The woman gleamed with silver jewelry, mostly in the shape of electroplated cog wheels, dials, and piping.

"Are you Leon Chandler?" she asked, giving me an overwhelmingly broad smile.

Her eyes were large, intense and just a little sly. They did not match her smile. I held up the photos.

"Yes, and you must be Louise Penderan," I replied.

She nodded. "That's me, and this is my partner, James Jamison."

James Jamison managed to sneer while smiling, then slowly, reluctantly, extended his hand. I registered the slight, ignored his hand, and gestured up the stairs.

"Won't you come in?" I said, moving aside.

My flat is above a shop, but it is quite large. I showed them into the living room, where they paused to look around. Their eyes lingered on the model steam engines that were on the bookshelves, and mantelpiece, and were crowded into the display cases and crystal cabinet.

"Did you build all these?" asked James, making the question sound like an accusation.

"Yes, I specialize in steam engines by the pioneers: Newcombe, Papin, Heron, Trevithick, Watt, and so on. They all work."

"Yet you dress in black and have a signed Alice Cooper poster on the wall," he observed.

"Cool music."

"Your furniture and all your walls are black."

"Black is relaxing."

"So you're a goth?"

"You may have noticed the sign on the door: SteamGoth Models."

I like to keep people guessing. Those who are too cool for school think that all steamheads wear anoraks and stand about on railway platforms spotting trains. After surviving a childhood of ridicule and bullying because I made models instead of playing online games, I had opted to dress cool, make models, and generally be a bit peculiar as an adult.

"Your models are quite beautiful," said Louise, who was caressing the boiler of a Newcombe engine with an ochre fingernail cut to a talon shape.

"It's just a hobby, but it pays."

"We actually need a professional," said James, rather abruptly.

Suddenly I had their measure. James was abrasive, but Louise followed him with praise. I was being conditioned to be sympathetic to her. She wanted something from me, something related to the wreck in the barn. I decided to force the issue.

"Well then, you might as well leave," I said, gesturing to the stairs.

James had actually reached the stairs before he realized that Louise was not with him. There was a hostile exchange of glances between the two of them.

"Perhaps James expressed himself a little awkwardly," she said. "We need a professional, and you are perfect."

James capitulated. Now I knew who had paid for the Daimler.

While I rather like the theory of steampunk fashion, I keep my distance from it. I prefer cogwheels to turn each other, not just be on display. I think that nothing is truly beautiful unless it works. For my real job I customize engines for an ultralight aircraft company, and my flat contains not a single painting or decorative vase. My Alice Cooper poster once advertised something, so it passed my functionality test. It was Dad who made me this way. He had bought an old Mini Minor a year before I was born, and a quarter of a century later the little car was still scattered all over his garage floor, supposedly being restored. From a lifetime of watching him obsessively wipe, oil, and polish parts that were never reassembled, I had developed a love of things that actually do something.

I spread the photos out on the coffee table and we seated ourselves around them.

"What do you think of the Aeronaute?" Louise asked.

I had decided that the aircraft was a modern steampunk sculpture, something from a pretend history. I dislike sculptures; they are form without function.

"It looks like some retro steam-powered aircraft that never was," I replied, already thinking about what to have for dinner, and wondering if a well-crafted insult might send them storming off down the stairs.

"The date stamped into the engine is 1852."

That was a shock. My pulse quickened as I picked up the photos and looked at them more closely. The engine was very lightly built, and the Aeronaute's frame was all thin spars, wire, and wicker. Even a moderate wind would demolish it, but on a calm day it just might have struggled into the air.

I began to trawl my memories for steam aircraft. The Besler brothers had flown a steam-powered biplane in 1933, and the first balloon propelled by a steam engine had flown in 1852. Steam engines are external combustion machines, so they have low power-to-weight ratios. They are not ideal for aviation, but neither are they out of the question.

The Aeronaute might not be a hoax, I realized. *Aviation history might have to be rewritten*. The temptation to babble hysterically was almost overwhelming, but I forced my voice to remain level and spoke slowly.

"Where were these photos taken?" I asked.

"On my family's estate, in Kent," said Louise.

"When?"

"Yesterday."

I arrived at the estate the very next morning, riding my black Vespa. One of the groundsmen told me to be off or he would call the police.

"Let me guess," I said as I removed my helmet. "Louise Penderan's boyfriend told you to chase away any visitors wearing black."

He pointed to the gate and opened his mouth to shout—then apparently realized that what I had just said was true, and remembered who was paying his wages. Without another word he went into the house, then Louise came out and welcomed me. She was now wearing black overalls, a bandolier of chrome-plated tools, and a technogoth hairpin-screwdriver. Without her high-heeled laceup boots she was barely my height. James followed her, dressed in immaculate Belle Epoch motoring gear and looking unhappy.

The barn where the Aeronaute had been kept for over a century and a half was in a field behind the house.

"My family knew about it for generations, but they treated it as a bit of a joke," she explained as we crossed the field. "Nobody ever bothered to tell me, because I think countryside stuff is only for driving past, you know? James and I came here yesterday to check if the barn was okay for our big steampunk wedding reception."

"We're getting married!" declared James, like a sentry challenging an intruder.

"I can hardly believe the Aeronaute's condition," I said. "After a hundred and fifty years of corrosion, dry rot, and borers, it ought to be a pile of rust and sawdust."

"The daughter of the man who probably built it, Lucy Penderan, was obsessed about preserving it in memory of him. A family tradition of looking after it had developed by the time she died in 1920. The field hands give it a new coat of wax every year at midsummer."

The doors of the barn had been pushed wide open, and the aura of something that had changed the world was so strong that I began to tremble. I walked in slowly, feeling like an astronaut taking his first steps on the moon. As I got closer I saw that the Aeronaute's wreckage really was in remarkably good condition, given its age. The engine and broken airframe were preserved under coats of wax, and the silk on the wings had become like waxed cardboard.

Weight was not an issue for nineteenth-century steam engines, because they powered big things like trains, ships, or machinery in factories. By contrast, the Aeronaute's engine had not an ounce of excess weight. The fuel was oil sprayed into a furnace chamber to heat a coil boiler, and the steam was recycled through an air-cooled condenser. What alarmed me was that the fuel tank was heated by a naked flame, so that the oil would spray out under pressure. That saved the weight of a pump but increased the danger of an explosion.

"Could it have flown?" asked Louise after I had spent some minutes pacing around it with my mouth open.

"By modern safety standards it's an unexploded bomb," I said, tapping at the fuel tank. "That said . . . yes, perhaps."

"Could it be repaired and flown?"

"Restoration, no problem," I replied, then shrugged and shook my head.

"So you don't think it can fly?"

"It's bound to be grossly underpowered for its weight, but with a long enough takeoff run and a very light pilot, it just might get above stall speed."

"You mean fly?"

"Yes. For a few minutes."

"Why only minutes?" asked James, desperate to disagree with me about anything.

"Extra fuel is extra weight. Carry enough fuel for a long flight and it would be too heavy to get off the ground."

"But it can definitely fly?" asked Louise.

"Possibly, not definitely. Until the engine is restored and tested, we won't know if it's powerful enough to be useful. The Aeronaute may be a failed experiment, even if it's genuine."

The manor house was a mixture of Regency, Victorian, and Edwardian architecture, with a few more modern enhancements that had probably not been cleared with English Heritage. Coffee was served to us by a Romanian maid. Louise's parents had the easygoing manner of people who were so rich that they did not have to prove anything to anyone.

"Firstly, who built the Aeronaute?" I asked once introductions and pleasantries were out of the way.

"Nobody knows," said her father. "The estate registers show that our farm workers have painted it with wax every year since mid-1852. That was just after William Penderan died in a riding accident, so my money is on William."

"The date is far too early," I began, then paused and thought about it. "Actually, perhaps not. William Henson designed his Aerial Steam Carriage in 1843, and John Stringfellow flew a steam-powered model in 1848. George Cayley built a glider in 1853, and his coachman flew it over Brompton Dale."

"So the Aeronaute's age is not, er, impossible?"

"1852 is not only possible, it's unnervingly likely. That was an exciting decade for British aviation."

"Just think, all these years and we never knew," he said with a sigh.

"Another question," I said, turning to Louise. "Why me?"

"I found you with Google. You build historical steam engines and work for an ultralight aircraft company. The combination seemed perfect."

I already knew the answer to my third question, but I asked it anyway.

"So what do you want me to do?"

"How much would you charge to restore the Aeronaute?"

How much would I charge? I very nearly burst out laughing. It was more like how much would I pay to be *allowed* to work on it.

"I can do the engine," I said, struggling to sound cool. "That would not cost much, but the woodwork and fabric will need specialist restorers and materials."

"So you can't help?" asked James eagerly.

"Oh I can help," I said as I took out my phone. "The director of Ultralights Unlimited has had experience restoring World War One fighters. I'll give him a call now."

Giles Gibson made the journey from London to Kent on his vintage BSA motorbike in less than an hour. James's reaction upon meeting him was one of instant hatred. Giles not only wore period motoring gear, he was a real pilot. He made things worse by complimenting Louise on her neo-industrial outfit, while ignoring what James was wearing.

Our inspection took about an hour. The Aeronaute had been in storage for a century and a half, so in spite of nearly thirteen dozen coatings of hot wax, even some of the undamaged wood needed replacing. The wax had saved the engine from corrosion, however.

"Well, steamgoth, how long before we have steam?" Giles asked, tapping the engine with a knuckle.

"The engine will have to be stripped down, checked for damage, cleaned, and reassembled. With big-budget help, a few weeks."

"Hey, I run Ultralights Unlimited, not NASA. Big-budget help is not an option."

"No, it's our first option."

Giles blinked at me.

"What do you mean?"

"This is Britain, Giles. Once word gets out that a genuine mid-Victorian, steam-powered aircraft has been discovered, there'll be a queue of steamheads stretching from Kent to London, all volunteering to work on it."

"Could it fly?" asked Louise.

"It's underpowered, overweight, and aerodynamically unstable," said Giles.

"Is that a *no?*"

"It's a *don't know.* While we're restoring the Aeronaute, we can find out by running computer simulations, then build a full-scale mockup with a petrol engine. If the mockup can take off, we have a *yes.*"

"You can use the barn," said her father eagerly.

"But what about the wedding reception?" exclaimed James.

"We haven't fixed a date for that yet," said Louise, to Giles rather than James.

"Man, we'll need to work hard and fast, or this could be like Stonehenge," said Giles. "You know, left as a glorious ruin, not restored. There's always going to be heritage airheads who want that."

"That's terrible!" exclaimed Louise.

"I'm right with you," said Giles, putting an arm around her shoulders and gesturing to the aircraft. "Leaving Stonehenge like it is just glorifies what some frigging vandal did in the past. I've worked on World War One fighters. Try to patch an original bullet hole and some tosser will scream that it's historically significant."

"So what are you suggesting to us?" asked James, hastily grasping Louise by the hand.

"I'll call the workshop and get my staff to drop everything and drive down here with the truck and some equipment. While they're on the road, Leon and I will start marking the woodwork and wire that needs replacing."

A strange tug-of-war for Louise had developed between James and Giles. I picked up a roll of masking tape and deliberately tagged an undamaged spar.

"No, no, steamgoth, only tag what I point to," said Giles, releasing Louise and hurrying over.

I had the engine into the back of the Ultralights Unlimited truck by mid-afternoon, and away to the London workshop that very night. The dozen restoration volunteers that I had phoned were already waiting outside. I did not have the heart to send them away until morning, so we carried the engine inside and spent the next two hours cleaning off the grubby coating of wax with a steam jet. My fingers tingled every time I touched the engine, so much so that I had to wear gloves to work on it. At midnight we were ready for the first test. Very gently, I grasped the crankshaft and applied pressure. It turned smoothly; it had not been damaged by the crash. The cheering went on for a very long time.

In the days that followed we stripped the engine down to the very nuts and bolts, recording every detail with a video camera. We cleaned each part until it gleamed, then made laser scans for my components database. Only the leather seals and washers had perished, and my assistants made the replacements with more love and tenderness than when they had made their wedding vows.

Louise was waiting outside my flat in a late-model BMW when I got home one evening. This time she was dressed in black lace under a black leather coat, and wore high-heel boots. She seemed angry yet vulnerable all at once, as she invited me to the café over the road. Here she explained that the BBC had contacted her about the Aeronaute. We never discovered the source of the leak, but someone probably spoke too loudly in some pub, and someone listening then pitched an idea to an executive at Channel 4.

"They want to run it as a reality doco," she concluded.

"I've done work for television," I said. "Camera crews mean light stands, reflectors, first and second cameras, multiple takes of spontaneous incidents, staged arguments to raise the dramatic tension, makeup artists and hair stylists. Allow that circus into our workshop and you can triple the restoration schedule."

"But Leon, we need them. They can keep the Heritage people off our backs."

"So Heritage knows?"

"Yes, but the BBC is on our side. You're a big deal for them."

"Me? A big deal?"

"All of us. Instead of technerds in t-shirts and jeans, the producer has seriously cool people in great clothes doing a sensational restoration. You're the goth engineer, Giles is the dashing steampunk pilot, I'm the glam girl patroness, and James is . . ."

Her hesitation said more than words.

"James is?" I asked innocently.

"James has studied costume design and history, and he's a very well-paid model. In steampunk costuming circles he's also a big name, but he can't help with the Aeronaute. It's causing him issues."

That all made sense. Louise was from a rich family with old money, and she liked to dress retro. She was a sensational catch for someone like James. Enter Giles, who not only dressed retro, but could restore the Aeronaute and probably fly a mockup. James was arm candy. Giles was genuinely heroic arm candy.

"So what do we do about the BBC?" I asked.

"The camera crew only needs to be there when you're doing something important. That way nobody has much time wasted."

"Who decides what's important?"

"You do."

I agreed. The cat was out of the bag, so we had to be nice to the cat. There was one more question.

"Do you feel a bit strange when you are near the Aeronaute?"

Louise's head snapped around at once. "Why do you ask?"

Why, not what, I thought. *That's significant, she does feel something.*

"I've got to confess, I get an odd feeling from it, like it's haunted. I was wondering if Lucy Penderan got that feeling too, and that's why she went to so much trouble to preserve it."

"I don't believe in ghosts," said Louise tersely, but her tone said otherwise.

We had to dismantle the partly reassembled engine, then put it back together for the cameras while pretending to talk spontaneously. Louise played the role of an anxious client being briefed by me, the suave engineer. She wore enough pewter cogwheels to build a dozen or so clocks, along with fishnet gloves, and a magnifier on a brass chain. However, her lipstick had morphed from wholesome steampunk scarlet to goth black.

"So no other quadricycle engine is known from the 1850s?" she asked on cue.

"That's right," I replied. "There was no demand for hyper-light engines back then."

"So whoever built this one was a genius, like Brunel?"

"Not necessarily. It's not a revolutionary design, just very light. Any 1850s engineer could have built it as a one-off."

"Do you think the Aeronaute ever flew?"

That question again.

"We'll know that after we finish restoring the engine and run it to measure its horsepower. The Aeronaute is right on the border of being workable. Its wingspan is fifty feet and the takeoff weight is about seven hundred pounds. Two hundred and fifty pounds of that is this engine, which may deliver as little as twelve horsepower. The propeller is not very efficient either. The Aeronaute is an underpowered version of the Wright Brothers' Flyer."

"But isn't that good?" asked Louise, ignoring the next cue card. "The Wrights' plane flew."

"The Flyer did manage four flights, but it was not very stable. The Aeronaute will be even less stable. It will be harder to get into the air, difficult to control while it's up there, and a total nightmare to land."

A week later I got the engine working, powered by the workshop's steam-cleaning unit. It functioned perfectly, but the verdict of the calibration instruments was not encouraging. It could deliver only nine horsepower.

The furnace was next, and that was a definite challenge to modern health and safety regulations. Try putting some kerosene into a very flimsy tank, then light a fire under it to force the fuel out under pressure. It's a simple, efficient, lightweight, and mind-numbingly dangerous source of inflammable vapor. I tested the tank and pipes with compressed air, then the BBC arranged for pressure tests with real fuel to be done at an army firing range.

We produced some seriously impressive plumes of burning fuel for the cameras, but to everyone's surprise, the furnace did not explode. The final, crucial tests were also done at the firing range. With the engine attached to the furnace, we ran the system at full pressure from the safety of an observation bunker. Again the producer seemed disappointed by the lack of an explosion. I was also disappointed, because once again it only delivered a fraction more than nine horsepower. However, these disappointments were nothing compared to the findings of an air crash investigation team that the BBC had recruited.

I watched the third episode of *The Aeronauteers* at home, alone. A computer graphic of the Aeronaute sat at the end of a computer-generated runway, the propeller turning slowly. Numbers flashed onto the screen as a wireframe pilot lay out flat on the flight bench.

"The problem appears to have been the weight of the pilot," said a voiceover as the propeller spun up to full speed and the simulation Aeronaute began to roll forward. "If William Penderan was the pilot, he was just too heavy. Estimates made from a contemporary photograph put his height at six feet three inches, and his weight at two hundred pounds."

The graphic Aeronaute raced along its virtual runway. After a mile, its speed leveled off at twenty-three miles per hour.

"Penderan may have just cleared the ground, because he did not throttle back as he reached the end of the private road that he probably used as a runway. The road ended at a ploughed field. Perhaps he thought he was a few feet off the ground, when in reality his altitude was only inches. Traces of grass stains and dirt found on the wreckage indicate that the front wheel tore through grass, then hit a ploughed furrow side-on."

The graphic of the aircraft was shown crashing in slow motion. The wireframe pilot was thrown clear.

"Because of the risk of an explosion or fire, Penderan needed to get clear of the aircraft quickly in an emergency. For this reason he did not strap himself to the flight bench. He would have been thrown forward by the crash and struck one of the ploughed furrows. The death notice states that he died of a broken neck, sustained in a riding accident. This is also consistent with being thrown headfirst from the Aeronaute at about twenty-five miles per hour."

The virtual reenactment now showed how the damage to the Aeronaute was consistent with rolling off the end of the road and into a ploughed field.

"Several questions remain unanswered," the investigator concluded. "Why was William Penderan's death disguised as a riding accident, why was the wreckage taken to a barn and hidden, and why did Penderan's daughter, Lucy, preserve the wreckage for so long?"

The image switched to an interview with Giles and Louise, who were standing beside the partly rebuilt Aeronaute. Both of them looked gaunt and pale, but I put it down to their workload.

"I think it came down to patent violations," said Giles. "The propeller is identical to the one used on Stringfellow's model of 1848, and the main wing is a lightweight version of the one in the patent drawings for Henson's Aerial Steam Carriage of 1843."

"So Penderan was a great innovator, but he borrowed other people's ideas as well?" said the investigator.

"That's only part of it. Put yourself in Lucy Penderan's position. Her father dies testing an aircraft that could have changed history if he had weighed fifty pounds less. If she had gone public, somebody else could use his design, recruit a lighter pilot, and get all the glory of the first flight."

"Maybe one of his rivals."

"Precisely."

"Then why did she go to so much trouble to preserve the wreckage?"

"That I can't say."

Louise began to look like a defrocked goth who was studying to be a steampunk engineer. Her cheeks were pale and sunken, her hands were scratched and stained with paint and oil, and she moved slowly and deliberately, as if almost drained of energy. Both Giles and James seemed to think she was looking goth because she had something going with me. Because the engine needed little work, and most of that was in London, Giles made me the acting manager of Ultralights Unlimited. That kept me away from Kent, and thus Louise . . . except when *she* visited London.

Goggles became a major issue as the Aeronaute's public debut approached, as did the entire subject of fashion. Steampunk costuming and Victorian fashion overlapped, but did not match. Louise wanted steampunk, James wanted Victoriana. The BBC sided with James.

Louise and James were in the Ultralights Unlimited workshop, waiting for the camera crew to arrive for a shoot, when one of their many arguments flared. Louise wanted goggles to be part of Giles's 1852 aviator's costume for testing the mockup Aeronaute. James insisted that goggles were not used until the early twentieth century.

"Charles Manly wore them when he tried to fly an early aircraft in 1903," James explained. "They were developed about then for early motoring. Swimming goggles came even later."

"But there are engravings of Venetian coral divers wearing goggles in the sixteenth century," said Louise.

"Okay, but people like coachmen or train drivers didn't use them back in 1852."

"We'll see what the Web says about that."

Louise took out her iPhone. She wanted a steampunk look, and would not be deterred.

"*Goggles*, the word is derived from the Middle English *gogelen*, to squint," she said presently. "The word *goggles* came into use around 1710, to describe protective eye coverings that were short tubes with fine wire mesh over the ends. Masons used them as protection against flying stone chips."

"Well *your* goggles have glass in them," said James.

"Give me the goggles, I'll run up some wire mesh disks," I called from my workbench. "Nothing simpler."

The warmth in Louise's smile could have ended an ice age, but I suspected that it was only to antagonize James. I wondered if his scowl was meant for her or me. Premarital divorce seemed to be looming like a summer thunderstorm. Meantime I had all the grief of being a romantic interloper with none of the benefits.

Giles and his team of restoration volunteers took two months to strip the wax and old fabric from the Aeronaute, then replace the broken or rotten spars. All the piano wire bracings had to be replaced, then the wings were covered with new black silk. The engine had been restored long before that, but was kept in London so that the Aeronaute could be symbolically made complete in a single dramatic scene for the cameras.

When I arrived in the company truck with the fully restored quadricycle engine, champagne and chicken had been laid out on trestles, and everyone was dressed in Victorian costumes. The camera crew was also in costume. This was definitely a 'significant event.' To dress goth is to dress timeless, so I just borrowed a top hat from the BBC costume van and fitted right in.

James was arguing with the producer about Victorian fashions, Giles was striking poses for the BBC cameras in front of the mockup Aeronaute, and Louise was posing for a photo before a period camera. She was wearing a voluminous period green and black brocatelle day dress over crinoline, and was looking very unhappy about it. Once the reality television opportunities had been exhausted, and people began making sure that the chickens had died for a good cause, Giles took me aside.

"The mockup is ready to fly," he said.

"What?" I exclaimed. "Already?"

"Jock, Janice, and Otto ran it up in a week. It's basically just a modern ultralight with a strange design, and we installed a petrol engine with a variable governor. What's the best power you got from the 1852 engine?"

"Nine and a quarter horsepower is all I could get with optimal tuning."

"Nine and a quarter!" he exclaimed, losing his smile for the first time. "That's still a bit marginal."

"Or just plain not enough."

He looked across to Louise, who was now posing in her wire mesh goggles.

"It's probably enough to work with," Giles decided.

"In a bleeding computer!" I exclaimed. "The Aeronaute is on the very border of being flight-capable. It's seriously overweight and underpowered, but I can make a few improvements—"

"No! It must fly with the exact 1852 config. My computer models confirm that it could get just above stall speed at nine horsepower, with enough fuel for ten minutes and a one-forty-pound pilot."

"One-forty pounds!" I exclaimed. "Even a pigeon-chested tosser like me weighs more than that."

"I've been dieting."

"What? You're joking! What a great source of reality drama: will he die of anorexia or die in a crash?"

"Be serious."

"I am being serious."

"Louise is dieting in sympathy with me."

"That explains why she looks as crap as you."

"And she's stopped sleeping with James."

"What the hell has that to do with . . ."

My brain caught up with my tongue.

"Yes, that has everything to do with me flying the Aeronaute mockup," said Giles. "Sorry to be so suspicious of you; I've only just realized that she's actually dressing goth to tick off James. I'm her real hero."

In other words, *Back off, steamgoth, the rich girl is mine.* At the time it seemed like the obvious conclusion, but we were both about as wrong as it is possible to be.

The stretch of straight, level, private road was three miles in length. A very thorough, three-day investigation by Time Team confirmed that it had been built around 1850. It would have been ideal as a runway, providing a firm, smooth surface that would give the Aeronaute's wheels minimal friction when taking off. The local council had restored the surface to 1850s standard, and the mayor was rewarded by time in front of the television cameras.

Giles had learned to fly the Aeronaute with a computer simulator. Getting off the ground was only part of the problem. The Aeronaute was a flying wing without a tail, so by definition it was quite a challenge to control. When flying, the simulation was balanced precariously above disaster.

"Don't worry, I'm only going to take it up a couple of feet," Giles said as I adjusted the governor to give another quarter horsepower to the mockup.

"Good enough to kill William Penderan, good enough to kill you," I replied.

There was a great cheer as the mockup's engine was started. I was ready with my Vespa and followed the mockup as it rolled away along the road. At the suggestion of the camera crew, Louise was sitting sidesaddle behind me, her dress and crinoline billowing like a failed parachute. It took nearly a mile, but at last the mockup wallowed into the air, lumbered along roughly five feet above the road for about a hundred yards, then descended.

Unfortunately it had drifted just a little off center while airborne. The rear left wheel caught the roadside grass and the mockup slewed around, ripped off its own undercarriage, and partially disintegrated.

Giles was unhurt because he had strapped himself to the flying bench. For his trouble he got Louise's arms around his neck and a kiss full on the lips before the cameras of the BBC—several times, to get the lighting and background correct. The achievement of the mockup's flight, the drama of the crash, and a dash of romance sent ratings soaring for *The Aeronauteers*.

Giles blamed the crash on a gust of wind. Later, in private, I learned the truth.

"The controls are bad, bad, bad," he confessed. "You can't steer without dipping the wings, so you need to be at least twenty feet up first. Landing will be a disaster if there's any wind at all."

"But you've done as much as the Wright Brothers already," I pointed out.

"That's not enough. I want to do a circle, then land."

"It's still underpowered and too heavy," I said.

"I can carry even less fuel, and diet off a few more pounds."

"You should test it with a radio control unit first."

"No! We're not just refurbishing the Aeronaute, we're putting ourselves in William Penderan's position."

"Which was a ludicrously dangerous position, and which got him killed. I can hear the beating of the wings."

"Er, sorry?"

"John Bright, 1855. *The angel of death has been abroad throughout the land. One may almost hear the beating of his wings.* Death will be flying beside you if you take the mockup any higher."

"It's worth the risk. When I'm up there it will *be* 1852, and I'll be proving that steam-powered flight is serious tech."

"Losing control a couple of hundred feet up, then smashing headfirst into a field is going to really hurt."

"I fly ultralights, I know the risks. You stick to engines."

"Speaking of engines, do you want me to service the mockup's engine?"

"No, no, you have to go back to London today and look after the company. Everything is under control here."

For Giles I was somehow still competition in a love quadrangle, but I worked for him so I was a problem easily solved. Being safely away in London did not mean I was safe, however.

Six episodes of *The Aeronauteers* had been broadcast on Channel 4 when the scandal broke. I have Saturday nights off, and it is always for the same reason. I had reached the stage entrance of the Midnight Noon Club when the portable lights came on and the camera crew appeared. It was not the crew for *The Aeronauteers*.

"Mister Chandler, we understand that every Saturday you come to Midnight Noon to be the master of ceremonies," declared a voice from behind the lights.

I had been caught by surprise, but I have great reflexes.

"I do, and it's the best amateur goth burlesque club in London," I said cheerily. "My stage name is Feelthy Pierre, the Naughty Gendarme. Come in, come in, you're just in time."

The interviewer had expected a cornered rat, not an invitation to the show. He could not decline because *I* was also recording *him* thanks to that wonderful invention, the phone camera. I recorded a performer named Furry Paws dragging him onto the stage, sitting on his lap, then stripping off most of what little she was wearing. As an exposé of my personal life, it flopped more heavily than the mockup of the Aeronaute.

"I'm an engineer, and I do this for fun," I said as I was interviewed later in my gendarme's uniform. "Now then, what do BBC journalists do for a few laughs in their spare time?"

The item was broadcast the following evening on a current affairs show, heavily edited. My recording was already on YouTube. Louise staged a big party for the broadcast and insisted that I be there. The entire restoration team watched it in the manor house. For a rare moment I was a big hero, then the serious drinking began.

"It was either James or Giles who ratted on you," Louise declared as we stood together, our words blanketed by the babble from everyone else.

"They think I think you're cute," I replied.

"Do you?"

"Thinking you're cute and being competition for James and Giles are entirely different things."

"Those girls in the club," she said slowly. "Do you ever, er . . ."

"Get laid? Occasionally."

"I was wondering why you never made a move on me," she admitted. "I thought you were gay or A, but now I know. I've never been so totally outclassed."

"Outclassed? You? You're so far out of my league that even fantasies about you are a waste of time."

"Crap, I'm really nothing. Everyone thinks of me as a trophy. My parents, James, Giles, my whole steampunk social scene. You don't care about trophies because they don't do anything. That makes you special."

"Er, thanks."

"Did you know that we're part of a love triangle?"

That was a shock. I glanced about. Giles was nowhere to be seen. James was standing nearby, talking to Louise's mother and looking a bit morose. There was a red wine stain on the sleeve of his coat but he seemed not to care. Perhaps he had given up on Louise. I now felt like a rabbit caught by a spotlight. Rich girls are dangerous to be around, especially when one's boss has aspirations involving them.

"I . . . don't think so," I replied. "You, Giles, and James occupy the corners already."

"Wrong lovers, Leon. It's you, me, and the Aeronaute."

"The Aeronaute?"

"You love the Aeronaute because it's genuine and it works. I love the Aeronaute because . . ."

She hesitated. Perhaps this was becoming too personal.

"Because the Aeronaute is an accessory that any steampunk fashionista would die for?" I prompted.

"At first, but not any more. Now it's because the Aeronaute makes me real."

Suddenly I could see where she was coming from. The Aeronaute was dreams made solid. The Aeronaute very nearly changed history; it was a more powerful agent for change than the Napoleonic Wars. For me, power radiated from it. If Lucy Penderan had flown the Aeronaute instead of her father, what might the world look like today? For Louise, putting the Aeronaute back into history meant becoming part of history herself.

The party was brought to an abrupt halt by Otto, who announced that the barn had been broken into. By the time I reached the barn, Giles was checking the aircraft for damage, the producer of *The Aeronauteers* was recording everything with a phone camera, and the security guards were shouting that it was a crime scene and that everyone should stay outside.

"Otto stepped out for a romantic moment with one of the volunteers," said Giles. "He saw lights in the barn and raised the alarm. I can't see any damage to the Aeronaute, though."

"I can see a problem from here," I said. "The lid of the fuel tank has been put back without being screwed down. Someone must have left in a hurry."

There was sand on the rim of the fuel tank.

"I don't understand why whoever it was did this," said Giles as I detached the tank to clean it out. "The sabotage would have achieved nothing. This is the original Aeronaute. It's not going to fly."

"He may have got the original mixed up with your flying mockup."

"Talk sense," said Giles. "The mockup is in the tent outside."

"I wonder if he sabotaged both?"

Giles hurried away to check the mockup, leaving me with the original Aeronaute. Up close, the sense of its brooding power made my head throb. It was like an avalanche about to fall, not dangerous because its fuel tank could explode, but for some more subtle reason. This was a machine that *could* have changed the world in 1852, yet it felt like it actually *had*.

"The bastard!" shouted Giles, dashing back into the barn. "The mockup's got sand in its tank too. Someone's trying to kill me."

"Sand in the tank would kill the engine before it was even warmed up."

"Someone who doesn't know engines wouldn't know that. It must have been James. That airhead fashion jock doesn't understand anything that isn't held together with buttons."

"Nobody likes competition."

"It's sheer spite! James is out of the race. Louise is sick of him, he's been acting like a tit. If I can prove that William Penderan's design beat the Wright Brothers by half a century I'll be a class-A hero. Heroes get the girls, steamgoth."

I doubted that James had done the sabotage. He had had a very crushed look during the party, and had probably given up on Louise already. Giles should not have been a suspect, because engine failure would have put him in danger, yet that danger would only last until he conveniently noticed a little sand on the side of the mockup's fuel tank. Perhaps I was meant to be the suspect.

Every series needs a climax, and the climax of *The Aeronauteers* was to be a glorious celebration of Victoriana. Hundreds of recreationists and BBC extras in costume converged on the estate, there to eat nineteenth-century food, dance to authentic bands playing period music, and play contemporary games. The camera crew was again in costume, with their video cameras disguised as the old glass plate variety. I had discarded my black jeans and black leather jacket for a top hat, black suit, and black coat. Tents and stalls covered the grounds, but a wide expanse of lawn to the east of the house was roped off for no apparent reason.

The plan was that the fully restored Aeronaute would be rolled out and put on display, then Giles would take the mockup for a five-minute flight around the estate. The Aeronaute had not been outside the barn since it had crashed, so this was to be its first outing since 1852.

There was only one anachronism. Actually there were eight anachronisms: one air safety inspector, one industrial safety inspector, and six police. Giles was posing for the cameras beside the repaired mockup when they arrived.

"We have reason to believe that you intend to operate an aircraft that does not conform to safety standards, and which will endanger public safety," the air safety inspector announced.

"What do you mean?" demanded Giles. "This is private property."

"This is a public event on private property."

Tempers flared, hands were waved, and the spectators and cameras crowded around. I was of interest to nobody, so I was able to mingle with the crowd that was gathering, then back away. The takeoff road was being kept clear by security guards dressed in Crimean War uniforms. A backup camera crew had been stationed beside the road. All my suspicions were being confirmed.

I made straight for the barn. It was locked, but a large piece of firewood applied to the side door with all the force that I could manage had it open in one hit.

Louise was inside, wearing only dark brown tweed trousers and cloth slippers, and frozen in the act of putting on a white shirt with puffed sleeves. She was emaciated, as if close to starvation. In a medical sense, I suppose she really was starving.

Her hair was plaited and coiled tightly at the back of her head, and of course the mesh goggles were on her forehead. Her mid-Victorian dress of green silk with black velvet patterning and navy blue fringing lay on the ground. Beside it were her laceup boots.

"You guessed," she said, then turned away to button up her shirt.

"Not hard," I replied. "You stopped sleeping with James. That was not because you fancied Giles or me, but because you had practically stopped eating, and had lost so much weight that you were afraid to be seen naked by anyone. Now why would you want to lose so much weight? Moral support for Giles?"

"Bastard."

"What do you now weigh?"

She snatched up a brown leather waistcoat. Buttoned up, it disguised the appalling condition of her breasts reasonably well.

"Dressed like this, I weigh one twenty-one pounds," she said.

"You called the inspectors and police, didn't you?"

"Yes. It got Giles out of the way."

"While you fly the *real* Aeronaute."

"Yes."

"What Giles wants to do is borderline dangerous. What you intend to do is almost suicidal."

"And I suppose you want to stop me."

"No."

"No?" she exclaimed, then gave a smile that was all hope against despair. "Why not?"

"Because I love beautiful working things, and the Aeronaute will not be truly beautiful until it flies. Do you know how to fly?"

"No. In 1852 nobody did, so why should I? This has become 1852, and I am meant to be Lucy Penderan, flying the Aeronaute instead of her father."

Her words made sense as reenactment, but were devoid of common sense. On the other hand, I have never been very sensible either.

"Best to stay clear until I get steam up," I said. "When you get into the air, keep the engine on full throttle the whole time. Only power down when you want to land."

"Leon, about the landing—"

"It will be on the roped-off lawn."

"You guessed?"

"Yes. It's a large, wide area, so wind drift will not matter. The grass will also slow you down quickly."

"How long have you known?" she asked, now taking me by the hand.

"Quite some time. For James and Giles you were just something to be fought over, but I could see that you had dreams. Brave, noble, beautiful dreams."

She kissed me on the lips, and I hugged her starved body very gently.

"Leon, when this is all over, I owe you a date," she said.

"I know a fantastic goth theater restaurant and bar. I'll dress as Feelthy Pierre."

"And I'll be sure to wear black."

There was clear and present danger from being anywhere near the Aeronaute when the engine was running. Louise stood well clear while I heated the fuel tank with a blowtorch to get pressure up. It was like having a smoke while sitting on a barrel of gunpowder. First I ignited the little tank flame, then opened the valve to the combustion chamber. The boiler flame caught with an alarming bang, then the steam pressure built up quickly. The propeller began to spin. The great thing about the quadricycle engine is that it is far quieter than an internal combustion engine. The sound was a pattering hiss, overlaid by the whirr of the propeller. I knelt behind the Aeronaute, holding it by the rear axle.

"Open the doors, then get aboard!" I called.

Louise pushed the barn's doors open, then returned to the Aeronaute and lay down on the flight bench.

"All good!" she called back. "Let go."

"Remember, full throttle until it's time to land, and you only have fuel for a half-circle of the estate," I warned. "Good luck."

The Aeronaute rolled out of the barn in near silence, but there was a ragged cheer as the people who had been watching Giles arguing with the inspectors realized that something far more entertaining had begun. The inspectors had a moment of indecision. There was the Aeronaute, but Giles was not on it, yet *someone* was on the pilot's frame. As the Aeronaute turned onto the road, the inspectors and police suddenly broke off and ran after it, shouting and blowing whistles. I ran too.

The crowd cheered the pursuing police and inspectors, thinking they were part of the show. Suddenly the Aeronaute rose into the air. Just like that. After all that fuss and anxiety over lift, drag, and power-to-weight ratios, it was up there, flying. It gained height steadily, then Louise put it into a shallow, wobbly turn. It was not fast, it was not efficient, and it was certainly not very stable, but there was absolutely no doubt that it could fly.

All around me there was wild cheering. People in period costume swarmed onto the road, jumping up and down, clapping, pointing, and throwing hats into the air. There was not a soul on the airfield or in the surrounding countryside who was not cheering, with the exception of the inspectors and probably James and Giles. Suddenly Giles was standing before me.

"You'll never get away with this, steamgoth!" he shouted in my face. "You're fired, as of now!"

"Whatever, but meantime all those people are on the landing strip, you clown!" I shouted back. "You have to get them off or she can't land."

Giles ran off, shouting orders. The six police understood crowd control, so they also focused on clearing the road. The inspectors joined them, and I was left alone. Louise was about three hundred feet up, executing a wide, leisurely turn.

This was a machine that had changed a history that never was, this was the very first heavier-than-air flight. Louise did nothing fancy, she knew that she was on a technological tightrope. I looked at my fob watch. She had been running the engine for seven minutes, so she would have to come around for a landing very soon. Did she have a watch?

A feeling of elation at having beaten impossible odds mingled with a strangely potent foreboding. Something was wrong, even though everything was fine. The Aeronaute was underpowered, unstable, and liable to explode in a ball of flames at any time, everything was against it, yet it was flying. Something ought to have gone catastrophically wrong, yet—impossibly—the Aeronaute was defying gravity and Louise was defying death.

Of all those on the ground, I alone knew where she was going to land, so it was to the roped-off lawn that I now ran. Because the Aeronaute was virtually silent at a distance, I did not hear any change in sound as Louise throttled back. The distant black shape began to descend. I could barely force myself to watch. Landings are my worst nightmare; I hate them because so much can go wrong. Louise was coming down too fast, she needed a little more thrust to gain lift and slow her descent while increasing her forward speed a trifle, but she did not have the training or experience to know that.

I was biting my knuckles, tasting blood, as the Aeronaute approached the lawn. The back wheels slammed down too hard, it bounced high, and I saw that Louise was only attached to the aircraft by the levers that she was gripping. There was a second bounce, then it was rolling along the grass, slowing, as I sprinted after it.

"We did it!" she cried as I reached the Aeronaute. "You and I, we did it."

"That's great, but get out, get clear!" I shouted. "I need to secure the fuel heater before it explodes."

Louise scrambled off the flight bench as I twisted valves to kill the tank and boiler flames, then I vented the pressurized fuel. Only now did I allow myself to admit that we had a major triumph on our hands. The Aeronaute had proved itself.

I now glanced around, expecting to see the six police closing in, hoping to get another hug from Louise before we were arrested. Instead I saw dozens, hundreds of police in uniforms dripping with gilt, silver, and braid holding back thousands of cheering onlookers. What had been a Victoriana reenactment crowd only moments before had become a horde dressed in burgundy, brown and black leather, and silk, with a gleaming starscape of silver buttons and chains. Every woman's waist was laced tightly, and every man had a top hat and a cane with a silver handle. Enormous cylinders like submarines encrusted with metal lace, latticework, and gantries floated in the sky above us, and metal humanoid figures at least fifty feet high loomed behind the crowds, with camera crews standing on observation platforms where the heads should have been.

A few people were allowed past the police, people in top hats wearing dark blue calf coats encrusted with gold braid, and holding jeweled metal rods capped with woven copper wire and trailing coiled cables that ran to gleaming brass backpacks covered in filigree. They were all calling out to us as they hurried over.

"Baroness Penderan, that was a brilliant reenactment."

"Masterful landing, baroness."

"Ladyship, were there any bad moments?"

Louise, a baroness in her own right? Like everything else, this was clearly wrong. She was the daughter of a knight, but that was as far as it went. I glanced in the direction of the manor house. A new wing had been added, built mainly out of brass lattice and slabs of turquoise glass, all surmounted by green domes and fringed with silver lace.

"The king and queen are watching, be so good as to wave to them," said a woman wearing a golden helmet upon which crouched a winged lion. She also wore a violet cloak over gilt plate armor inlaid with vines, leaves, and flowers, and inset with garnets. Suddenly a word caught up with me. King? Until a few minutes ago, Britain did not have a king as well as a queen.

We turned in the direction that the guardswoman indicated. At the edge of the lawn was a carriage of gilt, silver, and scarlet. There was a steam engine at one end, polished until its parts gleamed like mirrors. It was tended by a man in a black ankle coat and top hat . . . and goggles. Flanking it were guards, all wearing gilt armor and holding weapons that were mainly brass coils and bronze tubes mounted on rosewood stocks, apparently powered by spheres that glowed with a silvery light. There were steps at the middle of the carriage, and at the rear was an open cabin with a tiled roof fringed with gold tassels. Within the cabin was a couple dressed in matching white shirts with puffed sleeves, brown leather waistcoats, and goggles, presumably in honor of Louise. They were waving to us. Louise and I waved back.

By now my mind was urging me to run away and hide, but I had the good sense to distract myself by draining the Aeronaute's fuel from the hot tank and releasing the steam. Cameras like brass lanterns on articulated tentacles stretched over the shoulders of the newscasters from their ornate backpacks to follow what I was doing, but I did my best to ignore them. I seemed to be known to everyone, and was probably in charge of the engine.

"Doctor Chandler, how did the quadricycle engine bear up?" someone asked, and several people thrust their metallically organic microphones at me.

Doctor? Try as I might I could not remember doing a Ph.D., yet that is not the sort of thing one easily forgets.

"The engine's performance was as flawless as her ladyship's flying," I responded.

Giles arrived, and I discovered that he was now Sir Giles. Ignoring me, he began to tell the phalanx of surreal cameras and microphones about how good his restoration of the 1852 airframe had been.

I found a leaflet on the grass, dropped by some onlooker. It explained that the Aeronaute had first flown in 1852, with Lucy Penderan at the controls. It had changed history. Once the principle of a steam-powered, heavier-than-air machine had been proved, dozens, hundreds, then thousands of progressively larger steam aircraft had been built. They had established air mail services, carried the first commercial airline passengers, and dropped bombs during the Crimean War.

Now we are being herded together in front of the Aeronaute; Louise, Giles, myself, James, and the restoration team. Palace flunkeys are breathlessly briefing us about what we should and should not do when we are presented to the royal couple. After that, there will be a celebration, no doubt, and as a fellow celebrity I shall be able to speak with Louise. What to say? Perhaps it will be: *You know, it's probably all the excitement, but ever since you landed, I can't remember getting my PhD. Do you remember being made a baroness?* I am afraid to ask her, but ask her I shall.

If she just laughs, well I can cope with having a psychosis, it's very goth. What a strange delusion I had, living in a dream world in which Victorian style gave way to fantasies like Art Nouveau, Art Deco, Modernism, Post-Modernism, and Minimalism.

However, if she looks very fearful and asks to speak with me later, in private, then . . . then all along, back in our timestream, the Aeronaute had been the key to a different history, waiting for someone to turn it. If that history has become real, then Louise and I are the only people who remember one hundred and fifty years that never were.

I rather hope that she doesn't laugh.

in the House of Aryaman, a Lonely Signal Burns

ELIZABETH BEAR

Elizabeth Bear was born in Connecticut, and now lives in Brookfield, Massachusetts, after living for several years in the Mohave Desert near Las Vegas. She won the John W. Campbell Award for Best New Writer in 2005, and in 2008 took home a Hugo Award for her short story "Tideline," which also won her the Theodore Sturgeon Memorial Award (shared with David Moles). In 2009, she won another Hugo Award for her novelette "Shoggoths in Bloom." Her short work has appeared in Asimov's, Subterranean, SCI FICTION, Interzone, The Third Alternative, Strange Horizons, On Spec, *and elsewhere, and has been collected in* The Chains That You Refuse *and* New Amsterdam. *She is the author of three highly acclaimed SF novels,* Hammered, Scardown, *and* Worldwired, *and of the alternate history fantasy Promethean Age series, which includes the novels* Blood and Iron, Whiskey and Water, Ink and Steel, *and* Hell and Earth. *Her other books include the novels* Carnival, Undertow, Chill, Dust, All the Windwracked Stars, By the Mountain Bound, Range of Ghosts, *a novel in collaboration with Sarah Monette,* The Tempering of Men, *and two chapbook novellas,* Bone and Jewel Creature *and* Ad Eternum. *Her most recent book is a new collection,* Shoggoths in Bloom. *Coming up are a new novel,* Shattered Pillars, *and a new novella,* The Book of Iron. *Her Web site address is www.elizabethbear.com.*

The engrossing novella that follows is set in a future India that will inevitably draw comparisons with Ian McDonald's stories set in a similar milieu, but Bear manages to evoke a different feeling and mood while also dealing evocatively with a society caught partway between the modern world and traditions thousands of years old, and adapting, sometimes radically, to the problems generated by global climate change. She uses this setting to tell a complex and ingenious murder mystery that couldn't take place in our current-day world, concerning cutting-edge genetic science and physics, AIs, parrot-cats, cosmology, and the search for alien intelligence.

Police Sub-Inspector Ferron crouched over the object she assumed was the decedent, her hands sheathed in areactin, her elbows resting on uniformed knees. The body (presumed) lay in the middle of a jewel-toned rug like a flabby pink Klein bottle, its once-moist surfaces crusting in air. The rug was still fresh beneath it, fronds only a little dented by the weight and no sign of the browning that could indicate an improperly pheromone-treated object had been in contact with them for over twenty-four hours. Meandering brownish trails led out around the bodylike object; a good deal of the blood had already been assimilated by the rug, but enough remained that Ferron could pick out the outline of delicate paw-pads and the brushmarks of long hair.

Ferron was going to be late visiting her mother after work tonight.

She looked up at Senior Constable Indrapramit and said tiredly, "So this is the mortal remains of Dexter Coffin?"

Indrapramit put his chin on his thumbs, fingers interlaced thoughtfully before lips that had dried and cracked in the summer heat. "We won't know for sure until the DNA comes back." One knee-tall spit-shined boot wrapped in a sterile bootie prodded forward, failing to come within fifteen centimeters of the corpse. Was he jumpy? Or just being careful about contamination?

He said, "What do you make of that, boss?"

"Well." Ferron stood, straightening a kinked spine. "If that is Dexter Coffin, he picked an apt handle, didn't he?"

Coffin's luxurious private one-room flat had been sealed when patrol officers arrived, summoned on a welfare check after he did not respond to the flat's minder. When police had broken down the door—the emergency overrides had been locked out—they had found this. This pink tube. This enormous sausage. This meaty object like a child's toy "eel," a long squashed torus full of fluid.

If you had a hand big enough to pick it up, Ferron imagined it would squirt right out of your grasp again.

Ferron was confident it represented sufficient mass for a full-grown adult. But how, exactly, did you manage to just . . . invert someone?

The Sub-Inspector stepped back from the corpse to turn a slow, considering circle.

The flat was set for entertaining. The bed, the appliances were folded away. The western-style table was elevated and extended for dining, a shelf disassembled for chairs. There was a workspace in one corner, not folded away—Ferron presumed—because of the sheer inconvenience of putting away that much mysterious, technical-looking equipment. Depth projections in spare, modernist frames adorned the wall behind: enhanced-color images of a gorgeous cacophony of stars. Something from one of the orbital telescopes, probably, because there were too many thousands of them populating the sky for Ferron to recognize the *navagraha*—the signs of the Hindu Zodiac, despite her education.

In the opposite corner of the flat, where you would see it whenever you raised your eyes from the workstation, stood a brass Ganesha. The small offering tray before him held packets of kumkum and turmeric, fragrant blossoms, an antique American dime, a crumbling, unburned stick of agarbathi thrust into a banana. A silk shawl, as indigo as the midnight heavens, lay draped across the god's brass thighs.

"Cute," said Indrapramit dryly, following her gaze. "The Yank is going native."

At the dinner table, two western-style place settings anticipated what Ferron guessed would have been a romantic evening. If one of the principles had not gotten himself turned inside out.

"Where's the cat?" Indrapramit said, gesturing to the fading paw-print trails. He seemed calm, Ferron decided.

And she needed to stop hovering over him like she expected the cracks to show any second. Because she was only going to make him worse by worrying. He'd been back on the job for a month and a half now: it was time for her to relax. To trust the seven years they had been partners and friends, and to trust him to know what he needed as he made his transition back to active duty—and how to ask for it.

Except that would mean laying aside her displacement behavior, and dealing with her own problems.

"I was wondering the same thing," Ferron admitted. "Hiding from the farang, I imagine. Here, puss puss. Here puss—"

She crossed to the cabinets and rummaged inside. There was a bowl of water, almost dry, and an empty food bowl in a corner by the sink. The food would be close by.

It took her less than thirty seconds to locate a tin decorated with fish skeletons and paw prints. Inside, gray-brown pellets smelled oily. She set the bowl on the counter and rattled a handful of kibble into it.

"Miaow?" something said from a dark corner beneath the lounge that probably converted into Coffin's bed.

"Puss puss puss?" She picked up the water bowl, washed it out, filled it up again from the potable tap. Something lofted from the floor to the countertop and head-butted her arm, purring madly. It was a last-year's-generation parrot-cat, a hyacinth-blue puffball on sun-yellow paws rimmed round the edges with brownish stains. It had a matching tuxedo ruff and goatee and piercing golden eyes that caught and concentrated the filtered sunlight.

"Now, are you supposed to be on the counter?"

"Miaow," the cat said, cocking its head inquisitively. It didn't budge.

Indrapramit was at Ferron's elbow. "Doesn't it talk?"

"Hey, puss," ferron said. "What's your name?"

It sat down, balanced neatly on the rail between sink and counter-edge, and flipped its blue fluffy tail over its feet. Its purr vibrated its whiskers and the long hairs of its ruff. Ferron offered it a bit of kibble, and it accepted ceremoniously.

"Must be new," Indrapramit said. "Though you'd expect an adult to have learned to talk in the cattery."

"Not new." Ferron offered a fingertip to the engineered animal. It squeezed its eyes at her and deliberately wiped first one side of its muzzle against her areactin glove, and then the other. "Did you see the cat hair on the lounge?"

Indrapramit paused, considering. "Wiped."

"Our only witness. And she has amnesia." She turned to Indrapramit. "We need to find out who Coffin was expecting. Pull transit records. And I want a five-hour phone track log of every individual who came within fifty meters of this flat between twenty hundred yesterday and when Patrol broke down the doors. Let's get some technical people in to figure out what that pile of gear in the corner is. And who called in the welfare check?"

"Not a lot of help there, boss." Indrapramit's gold-tinted irises flick-scrolled over data—the Constable was picking up a feed skinned over immediate perceptions. Ferron wanted to issue a mild reprimand for inattention to the scene, but it seemed churlish when Indrapramit was following orders. "When he didn't come online this morning for work, his supervisor became concerned. The supervisor was unable to raise him voice or text. He contacted the flat's minder, and when it reported no response to repeated queries, he called for help."

Ferron contemplated the shattered edges of the smashed-in door before returning her attention to the corpse. "I know the door was locked out on emergency mode. Patrol's override didn't work?"

Indrapramit had one of the more deadpan expressions among the deadpan-trained and certified officers of the Bengaluru City Police. "Evidently."

"Well, while you're online, have them bring in a carrier for the witness." She indicated the hyacinth parrot-cat. "I'll take custody of her."

"How do you know it's a her?"

"She has a feminine face. Lotus eyes like Draupadi."

He looked at her.

She grinned. "I'm guessing."

Ferron had turned off all her skins and feeds while examining the crime scene, but the police link was permanent. An icon blinked discreetly in one corner of her interface, its yellow glow unappealing beside the salmon and coral of Coffin's taut-stretched innards. Accepting the contact was just a matter of an eye-flick. There was a decoding shimmer and one side of the interface spawned an image of Coffin in life.

Coffin had not been a visually vivid individual. Unaffected, Ferron thought, unless dressing oneself in sensible medium-pale brown skin and dark hair with classically Brahmin features counted as an affectation. That handle—*Dexter Coffin*, and wouldn't *Sinister Coffin* be a more logical choice?—seemed to indicate a more flamboyant personality. Ferron made a note of that: out of such small inconsistencies did a homicide case grow.

"So how does one get from this"—Ferron gestured to the image, which should be floating in Indrapramit's interface as well—"to that?"—the corpse on the rug. "In a locked room, no less?"

Indrapramit shrugged. He seemed comfortable enough in the presence of the body, and Ferron wished she could stop examining him for signs of stress. Maybe his rightminding was working. It wasn't too much to hope for, and good treatments for post-traumatic stress had been in development since the Naughties.

But Indrapramit was a relocant: all his family was in a village somewhere up near Mumbai. He had no people here, and so Ferron felt it was her responsibility as his partner to look out for him. At least, that was what she told herself.

He said, "He swallowed a black hole?"

"I like living in the future." Ferron picked at the edge of an areactin glove. "So many interesting ways to die."

Ferron and Indrapramit left the aptblock through the crowds of Coffin's neighbors. It was a block of unrelateds. Apparently Coffin had no family in Bengaluru, but it nevertheless seemed as if every (living) resident had heard the news and come down. The common areas were clogged with grans and youngers, sibs and parents and cousins—all wailing grief, trickling tears, leaning on each other, being interviewed by newsies and blogbots. Ferron took one look at the press in the living area and on the street beyond and juggled the cat carrier into her left hand. She slapped a stripped-off palm against the courtyard door. It swung open—you couldn't lock somebody in—and Ferron and Indrapramit stepped out into the shade of the household sunfarm.

The trees were old. This block had been here a long time; long enough that the sunfollowing black vanes of the lower leaves were as long as Ferron's arm. Someone in the block maintained them carefully, too—they were polished clean with soft cloth, no clogging particles allowed to remain. Condensation trickled down the clear tubules in their trunks to pool in underground catchpots.

Ferron leaned back against a trunk, basking in the cool, and yawned.

"You okay, boss?"

"Tired," Ferron said. "If we hadn't caught the homicide—if it is a homicide—I'd be on a crash cycle now. I had to re-up, and there'll be hell to pay once it wears off."

"Boss—"

"It's only my second forty-eight hours," Ferron said, dismissing Indrapramit's concern with a ripple of her fingers. Gold rings glinted, but not on her wedding finger. Her short nails were manicured in an attempt to look professional, a reminder not to bite. "I'd go hypomanic for weeks at a time in college. Helps you cram, you know."

Indrapramit nodded. He didn't look happy.

The Sub-Inspector shook the residue of the areactin from her hands before rubbing tired eyes with numb fingers. Feeds jittered until the movement resolved. Mail was piling up—press requests, paperwork. There was no time to deal with it now.

"Anyway," Ferron said. "I've already re-upped, so you're stuck with me for another forty at least. Where do you think we start?"

"Interview lists," Indrapramit said promptly. Climbing figs hung with ripe fruit twined the sunfarm; gently, the Senior Constable reached up and plucked one. When it popped between his teeth, its intense gritty sweetness echoed through the interface. It was a good fig.

Ferron reached up and stole one too.

"Miaow?" said the cat.

"Hush." Ferron slicked tendrils of hair bent on escaping her conservative bun off her sweating temples. "I don't know how you can wear those boots."

"State-of-the-art materials," he said. Chewing a second fig, he jerked his chin at her practical sandals. "Chappals when you might have to run through broken glass, or kick down a door?"

She let it slide into silence. "Junior grade can handle the family for now. It's bulk interviews. I'll take Chairman Miaow here to the tech and get her scanned. Wait, Coffin was Employed? Doing what, and by whom?"

"Physicist," Indrapramit said, linking a list of coworker and project names, a brief description of the biotech firm Coffin had worked for, like half of Employed Bengaluru ever since the medical tourism days. It was probably a better job than homicide cop. "Distributed. Most of his work group aren't even in this time zone."

"What does BioShell need with physicists?"

Silently, Indrapramit pointed up at the vanes of the suntrees, clinking faintly in their infinitesimal movements as they tracked the sun. "Quantum bioengineer," he explained, after a suitable pause.

"Right," Ferron said. "Well, Forensic will want us out from underfoot while they process the scene. I guess we can start drawing up interview lists."

"Interview lists and lunch?" Indrapramit asked hopefully.

Ferron refrained from pointing out that they had just come out of a flat with an inside-out stiff in it. "Masala dosa?"

Indrapramit grinned. "I saw an SLV down the street."

"I'll call our tech," Ferron said. "Let's see if we can sneak out the service entrance and dodge the press."

Ferron and Indrapramit (and the cat) made their way to the back gate. Indrapramit checked the security cameras on the alley behind the block: his feed said it was deserted except for a waste management vehicle. But as Ferron presented her warrant card—encoded in cloud, accessible through the Omni she wore on her left hip to balance the stun pistol—the energy-efficient safety lights ringing the doorway faded from cool white to a smoldering yellow, and then cut out entirely.

"Bugger," Ferron said. "Power cut."

"How, in a block with a sunfarm?"

"Loose connection?" she asked, rattling the door against the bolt just in case it had flipped back before the juice died. The cat protested. Gently, Ferron set the carrier down, out of the way. Then she kicked the door in frustration and jerked her foot back, cursing. Chappals, indeed.

Indrapramit regarded her mildly. "You shouldn't have re-upped."

She arched an eyebrow at him and put her foot down on the floor gingerly. The toes protested. "You suggesting I should modulate my stress response, Constable?"

"As long as you're adjusting your biochemistry . . ."

She sighed. "It's not work," she said. "It's my mother. She's gone Atavistic, and—"

"Ah," Indrapramit said. "Spending your inheritance on virtual life?"

Ferron turned her face away. WORSE, she texted. SHE'S NOT GOING TO BE ABLE TO PAY HER ARCHIVING FEES.

—Isn't she on assistance? Shouldn't the dole cover that?

—Yeah, but she lives in A.R. She's always been a gamer, but since Father died . . . it's an addiction. She archives everything. And has since I was a child. We're talking terabytes. Petabytes. Yottabytes. I don't know. And she's after me to "borrow" the money.

"Ooof," he said. "That's a tough one." Briefly, his hand brushed her arm: sympathy and human warmth.

She leaned into it before she pulled away. She didn't tell him that she'd been paying those bills for the past eighteen months, and it was getting to the point where she couldn't support her mother's habit anymore. She knew what she had to do. She just didn't know how to make herself do it.

Her mother was her mother. She'd built everything about Ferron, from the DNA up. The programming to honor and obey ran deep. Duty. Felicity. Whatever you wanted to call it.

In frustration, unable to find the words for what she needed to explain properly, she said, "I need to get one of those black market DNA patches and reprogram my overengineered genes away from filial devotion."

He laughed, as she had meant. "You can do that legally in Russia."

"Gee," she said. "You're a help. Hey, what if we—" Before she could finish her suggestion that they slip the lock, the lights glimmered on again and the door, finally registering her override, clicked.

"There," Indrapramit said. "Could have been worse."

"Miaow," said the cat.

"Don't worry, Chairman," Ferron answered. "I wasn't going to forget *you*."

The street hummed: autorickshaws, glidecycles, bikes, pedestrials, and swarms of foot traffic. The babble of languages: Kannada, Hindi, English, Chinese, Japanese. Coffin's aptblock was in one of the older parts of the New City. It was an American ghetto: most of the residents had come here for work, and spoke English as a primary—sometimes an only—language. In the absence of family to stay with, they had banded together. Coffin's address had once been trendy and now, fifty years after its conversion, had fallen on—not hard times, exactly, but a period of more moderate means. The street still remembered better days. It was bulwarked on both sides by the shaggy green cubes of aptblocks, black suntrees growing through their centers, but what lined each avenue were the feathery cassia trees, their branches dripping pink, golden, and terra-cotta blossoms.

Cassia, Ferron thought. A Greek word of uncertain antecedents, possibly related to the English word cassia, meaning Chinese or mainland cinnamon. But these trees were not spices; indeed, the black pods of the golden cassia were a potent medicine in Ayurvedic traditions, and those of the rose cassia had been used since ancient times as a purgative for horses.

Ferron wiped sweat from her forehead again, and—speaking of horses—reined in the overly helpful commentary of her classical education.

The wall- and roofgardens of the aptblocks demonstrated a great deal about who lived there. The Coffin kinblock was well-tended, green and lush, dripping with brinjal and tomatoes. A couple of youngers—probably still in schooling, even if they weren't Employment track—clambered up and down ladders weeding and feeding and harvesting, and cleaning the windows shaded here and there by the long green trail of sweet potato vines. But the next kinship block down was sere enough to draw a fine, the suntrees in its court sagging and miserable-looking. Ferron could make out the narrow tubes of drip irrigators behind crisping foliage on the near wall.

Ferron must have snorted, because Indrapramit said, "What are they doing with their graywater, then?"

"Maybe it's abandoned?" Unlikely. Housing in the New City wasn't exactly so plentiful that an empty block would remain empty for long.

"Maybe they can't afford the plumber."

That made Ferron snort again, and start walking. But she snapped an image of the dying aptblock nonetheless, and e-mailed it to Environmental Services. They'd handle the ticket, if they decided the case warranted one.

The Sri Lakshmi Venkateshwara—SLV—was about a hundred meters on, an open-air food stand shaded by a grove of engineered neem trees, their panel leaves angling to follow the sun. Hunger hadn't managed to penetrate Ferron's re-upped hypomania yet, but it would be a good idea to eat anyway: the brain might not be in any shape to notice that the body needed maintenance, but failing to provide that maintenance just added extra interest to the bill when it eventually came due.

Ferron ordered an enormous, potato-and-pea stuffed crepe against Indrapramit's packet of samosas, plus green coconut water. Disdaining the SLV's stand-up tables, they ventured a little further along the avenue until they found a bench to eat them on. News and ads flickered across the screen on its back. Ferron set the cat carrier on the seat between them.

Indrapramit dropped a somebody-else's-problem skin around them for privacy and unwrapped his first samosa. Flocks of green and yellow parrots wheeled in the trees nearby; the boldest dozen fluttered down to hop and scuffle where the crumbs might fall. You couldn't skin yourself out of the perceptions of the unwired world.

Indrapramit raised his voice to be heard over their arguments. "You shouldn't have re-upped."

The dosa was good—as crisp as she wanted, served with a smear of red curry. Ferron ate most of it, meanwhile grab-and-pasting names off of Coffin's known associates lists onto an interfaced interview plan, before answering.

"Most homicides are closed—if they get closed—in the first forty-eight hours. It's worth a little hypomania binge to find Coffin's killer."

"There's more than one murder every two days in this city, boss."

"Sure." She had a temper, but this wasn't the time to exercise it. She knew, given her family history, Indrapramit worried secretly that she'd succumb to addiction and abuse of the rightminding chemicals. The remaining bites of the dosa got sent to meet their brethren, peas popping between her teeth. The wrapper went into the recycler beside the bench. "But we don't catch every case that flies through."

Indrapramit tossed wadded-up paper at Ferron's head. Ferron batted it into that recycler too. "No, *yaar*. Just all of them this week."

The targeted ads bleeding off the bench-back behind Ferron were scientifically designed to attract her attention, which only made them more annoying. Some too-attractive citizen squalled about rightminding programs for geriatrics ("Bring your parents into the modern age!"), and the news—in direct, loud counterpoint—was talking about the latest orbital telescope discoveries: apparently a star some twenty thousand light years away, in the Andromeda Galaxy, had suddenly begun exhibiting a flickering pattern that some astronomers considered a possible precursor to a nova event.

The part of her brain that automatically built such parallels said: *Andromeda.*

Contained within the span of Uttara Bhadrapada. The twenty-sixth nakshatra in Hindu astronomy, although she was not a sign of the Zodiac to the Greeks. Pegasus was also in Uttara Bhadrapada. Ferron devoted a few more cycles to wondering if there was any relationship other than coincidental between the legendary serpent Ahir Budhnya, the deity of Uttara Bhadrapada, and the sea monster Cetus, set to eat—*devour,* the Greeks were so melodramatic—the chained Andromeda.

The whole thing fell under the influence of the god Aryaman, whose path was the Milky Way—the Heavenly Ganges.

You're overqualified, madam. Oh, she could have been the professor, the academic her mother had dreamed of making her, in all those long hours spent in virtual reproductions of myths the world around. She could have been. But if she'd really wanted to make her mother happy, she would have pursued Egyptology, too.

But she wasn't, and it was time she got her mind back on the job she *did* have.

Ferron flicked on the feeds she'd shut off to attend the crime scene. She didn't like to skin on the job: a homicide cop's work depended heavily on unfiltered perceptions, and if you trimmed everything and everyone irritating or disagreeable out of reality, the odds were pretty good that you'd miss the truth behind a crime. But sometimes you had to make an exception.

She linked up, turned up her spam filters and ad blockers, and sorted more Known Associates files. Speaking of her mother, that required ignoring all those lion-headed message-waiting icons blinking in a corner of her feed—and the pileup of news and personal messages in her assimilator.

Lions. Bengaluru's state capitol was topped with a statue of a four-headed lion, guarding each of the cardinal directions. The ancient symbol of India was part of why Ferron's mother chose that symbolism. But only part.

She set the messages to *hide,* squirming with guilt as she did, and concentrated on the work-related mail.

When she looked up, Indrapramit appeared to have finished both his sorting and his samosas. "All right, what have you got?"

"Just this." She dumped the interview files to his headspace.

The Senior Constable blinked upon receipt. "Ugh. That's even more than I thought."

First on Ferron's interview list were the dead man's coworkers, based on the simple logic that if anybody knew how to turn somebody inside out, it was likely to be another physicist. Indrapramit went back to the aptblock to continue interviewing more-or-less hysterical neighbors in a quest for the name of any potential lover or assignation from the night before.

It was the task least likely to be any fun at all. But then, Ferron was the senior officer. Rank hath its privileges. Someday, Indrapramit would be making junior colleagues follow up horrible gutwork.

The bus, it turned out, ran right from the corner where Coffin's kinblock's street intercepted the main road. Proximity made her choose it over the mag-lev Metro, but she soon regretted her decision, because it then wound in a drunken pattern through what seemed like the majority of Bengaluru.

She was lucky enough to find a seat—it wasn't a crowded hour. She registered her position with dispatch and settled down to wait and talk to the hyacinth cat, since it was more than sunny enough that no one needed to pedal. She waited it out for the transfer point anyway: *that* bus ran straight to the U District, where BioShell had its offices.

Predictable. Handy for head-hunting, and an easy walk for any BioShell employee who might also teach classes. As it seemed, by the number of Professor So-and-sos on Ferron's list, that many of them did.

Her tech, a short wide-bellied man who went by the handle Ravindra, caught up with her while she was still leaned against the second bus's warm, tinted window. He hopped up the steps two at a time, belying his bulk, and shooed a citizen out of the seat beside Ferron with his investigator's card.

Unlike peace officers, who had long since been spun out as distributed employees, techs performed their functions amid the equipment and resources of a centralized lab. But today, Ravindra had come equipped for fieldwork. He stood, steadying himself on the grab bar, and spread his kit out on the now-unoccupied aisle seat while Ferron coaxed the cat from her carrier under the seat.

"Good puss," Ravindra said, riffling soft fur until he found the contact point behind the animal's ears. His probe made a soft, satisfied beep as he connected it. The cat relaxed bonelessly, purring. "You want a complete download?"

"Whatever you can get," Ferron said. "It looks like she's been wiped. She won't talk, anyway."

"Could be trauma, boss," Ravindra said dubiously. "Oh, DNA results are back. That's your inside-out vic, all right. The autopsy was just getting started when I left, and Doc said to tell you that to a first approximation, it looked like all the bits were there, albeit not necessarily in the proper sequence."

"Well, that's a relief." The bus lurched. "At least it's the correct dead guy."

"Miaow," said the cat.

"What is your name, puss?" Ravindra asked.

"Chairman Miaow," the cat said, in a sweet doll's voice.

"Oh, no," Ferron said. "That's just what I've been calling her."

"Huh." Ravindra frowned at the readouts that must be scrolling across his feed. "Did you feed her, boss?"

"Yeah," Ferron said. "To get her out from under the couch."

He nodded, and started rolling up his kit. As he disconnected the probe, he said, "I downloaded everything there was. It's not much. And I'll take a tissue sample for further investigation, but I don't think this cat was wiped."

"But there's nothing—"

"I know," he said. "Not wiped. This one's factory-new. And it's bonded to you. Congratulations, Sub-Inspector. I think you have a cat."

"I can't—" she said, and paused. "I already have a fox. My mother's fox, rather. I'm taking care of it for her."

"*Mine*," the cat said distinctly, rubbing her blue-and-yellow muzzle along Ferron's uniform sleeve, leaving behind a scraping of azure lint.

"I imagine they can learn to cohabitate." He shouldered his kit. "Anyway, it's unlikely Chairman Miaow here will be any use as a witness, but I'll pick over the data anyway and get back to you. It's not even a gig."

"Damn," she said. "I was hoping she'd seen the killer. So even if she's brand-new . . . why hadn't she bonded to Coffin?"

"He hadn't fed her," Ravindra said. "And he hadn't given her a name. She's a sweetie, though." He scratched behind her ears. A funny expression crossed his face. "You know, I've been wondering for ages—how did you wind up choosing to be called *Ferron*, anyway?"

"My mother used to say I was stubborn as iron." Ferron managed to keep what she knew would be a pathetically adolescent shrug off her shoulders. "She was fascinated by Egypt, but I studied Classics—Latin, Greek, Sanskrit. Some Chinese stuff. And I liked the name. *Ferrum*, iron. She won't use it. She still uses my cradlename." *Even when I'm paying her bills.*

The lion-face still blinked there, muted but unanswered. In a fit of irritation, Ferron banished it. It wasn't like she would forget to call.

Once she had time, she promised the ghost of her mother.

Ravindra, she realized, was staring at her quizzically. "How did a classicist wind up a murder cop?"

Ferron snorted. "You ever try to find Employment as a classicist?"

Ravindra got off at the next stop. Ferron watched him walk away, whistling for an autorickshaw to take him back to the lab. She scratched Chairman Miaow under the chin and sighed.

In another few minutes, she reached the university district and disembarked, still burdened with cat and carrier. It was a pleasant walk from the stop, despite the heat of the end of the dry season. It was late June, and Ferron wondered what it had been like before the Shift, when the monsoons would have started already, breaking the back of the heat.

The walk from the bus took under fifteen minutes, the cat a dozy puddle. A patch of sweat spread against Ferron's summerweight trousers where the carrier bumped softly against her hip. She knew she retraced Coffin's route on those rare days when he might choose to report to the office.

Nearing the Indian Institute of Science, Ferron became aware that clothing styles were shifting—self-consciously Green Earther living fabric and ironic, ill-fitting student antiques predominated. Between the buildings and the statuary of culture heroes—R. K. Narayan, Ratan Tata, stark-white with serene or stern expressions— the streets still swarmed, and would until long after nightfall. A prof-caste wearing a live-cloth salwar kameez strutted past; Ferron was all too aware that the outfit would cost a week's salary for even a fairly high-ranking cop.

The majority of these people were Employed. They wore salwar kameez or suits and they had that purpose in their step—unlike most citizens, who weren't in too much of a hurry to get anywhere, especially in the heat of day. It was easier to move in the university quarter, because traffic flowed with intent. Ferron, accustomed to stepping around window-browsing Supplemented and people out for their mandated exercise, felt stress dropping away as the greenery, trees, and gracious old nineteenth- and twentieth-century buildings of the campus rose up on every side.

As she walked under the chin of Mohandas Gandhi, Ferron felt the familiar irritation that female police pioneer Kiran Bedi, one of her own personal idols, was not represented among the statuary. There was hijra activist Shabnam Mausi behind a row of well-tended planters, though, which was somewhat satisfying.

Some people found it unsettling to be surrounded by so much brick, poured concrete, and mined stone—the legacy of cooler, more energy-rich times. Ferron knew that the bulk of the university's buildings were more efficient green structures, but those tended to blend into their surroundings. The overwhelming impression was still that of a return to a simpler time: 1870, perhaps, or 1955. Ferron wouldn't have wanted to see the whole city gone this way, but it was good that some of the history had been preserved.

Having bisected campus, Ferron emerged along a prestigious street of much more modern buildings. No vehicles larger than bicycles were allowed here, and the roadbed swarmed with those, people on foot, and pedestrials. Ferron passed a rack of share-bikes and a newly constructed green building, still uninhabited, the leaves of its suntrees narrow, immature, and furled. They'd soon be spread wide, and the structure fully tenanted.

The BioShell office itself was a showpiece on the ground floor of a business block, with a live receptionist visible behind foggy photosynthetic glass walls. *I'd hate a job where you can't pick your nose in case the pedestrians see it.* Of course, Ferron hadn't chosen to be as decorative as the receptionist. A certain stern plainness helped get her job done.

"Hello," Ferron said, as the receptionist smoothed brown hair over a shoulder. "I'm Police Sub-Inspector Ferron. I'm here to see Dr. Rao."

"A moment, madam," the receptionist said, gesturing graciously to a chair.

Ferron set heels together in parade rest and—impassive—waited. It was only a few moments before a shimmer of green flickered across the receptionist's iris.

"First door on the right, madam, and then up the stairs. Do you require a guide?"

"Thank you," Ferron said, glad she hadn't asked about the cat. "I think I can find it."

There was an elevator for the disabled, but the stairs were not much further on. Ferron lugged Chairman Miaow through the fire door at the top and paused a moment to catch her breath. A steady hum came from the nearest room, to which the door stood ajar.

Ferron picked her way across a lush biorug sprinkled with violet and yellow flowers and tapped lightly. A voice rose over the hum. *"Namaskar!"*

Dr. Rao was a slender, tall man whose eyes were framed in heavy creases. He walked forward at a moderate speed on a treadmill, an old-fashioned keyboard and monitor mounted on a swivel arm before him. As Ferron entered, he pushed the arm aside, but kept walking. An amber light flickered green as the monitor went dark: he was charging batteries now.

"Namaskar," Ferron replied. She tried not to stare too obviously at the walking desk. She must have failed.

"Part of my rightminding, madam," Rao said with an apologetic shrug. "I've fibromyalgia, and mild exercise helps. You must be the Sub-Inspector. How do you take your mandated exercise? You carry yourself with such confidence."

"I am a practitioner of kalari payat," Ferron said, naming a South Indian martial art. "It's useful in my work."

"Well," he said. "I hope you'll see no need to demonstrate any upon me. Is that a cat?"

"Sorry, *saab*," Ferron said. "It's work-related. She can wait in the hall if you mind—"

"No, not at all. Actually, I love cats. She can come out, if she's not too scared."

"Oouuuuut!" said Chairman Miaow.

"I guess that settles that." Ferron unzipped the carrier, and the hyacinth parrot-cat sauntered out and leaped up to the treadmill's handrail.

"Niranjana?" Dr. Rao said, in surprise. "Excuse me, madam, but what are you doing with Dr. Coffin's cat?"

"You know this cat?"

"Of course I do." He stopped walking, and scratched the cat under her chin. She stretched her head out like a lazy snake, balanced lightly on four daffodil paws. "She comes here about twice a month."

"New!" the cat disagreed. "Who you?"

"Niranjana, it's Rao. You know me."

"Rrraaao?" she said, cocking her head curiously. Adamantly, she said, "New! My name Chairman Miaow!"

Dr. Rao's forehead wrinkled. To Ferron, over the cat's head, he said, "Is Dexter with you? Is he all right?"

"I'm afraid that's why I'm here," Ferron said. "It is my regretful duty to inform you that Dexter Coffin appears to have been murdered in his home sometime over the night. *Saab*, law requires that I inform you that this conversation is being recorded. Anything you say may be entered in evidence. You have the right to skin your responses or withhold information, but if you choose to do so, under certain circumstances a court order may be obtained to download and decode associated cloud memories. Do you understand this caution?"

"Oh dear," Dr. Rao said. "When I called the police, I didn't expect—"

"I know," Ferron said. "But do you understand the caution, *saab*?"

"I do," he said. A yellow peripheral node in Ferron's visual field went green.

She said, "Do you confirm this is his cat?"

"I'd know her anywhere," Dr. Rao said. "The markings are very distinctive. Dexter brought her in quite often. She's been wiped? How awful."

"We're investigating," Ferron said, relieved to be back in control of the conversation. "I'm afraid I'll need details of what Coffin was working on, his contacts, any romantic entanglements, any professional rivalries or enemies—"

"Of course," Dr. Rao said. He pulled his interface back around and began typing. "I'll generate you a list. As for what he was working on—I'm afraid there are a lot of trade secrets involved, but we're a biomedical engineering firm, as I'm sure you're aware. Dexter's particular project has been applications in four-dimensional engineering."

"I'm afraid," Ferron said, "that means nothing to me."

"Of course." He pressed a key. The cat peered over his shoulder, apparently fascinated by the blinking lights on the monitor.

The hyperlink blinked live in Ferron's feed. She accessed it and received a brief education in the theoretical physics of reaching *around* three-dimensional shapes in space-time. A cold sweat slicked her palms. She told herself it was just the second hypomania re-up.

"Closed-heart surgery," she said. During the medical tourism boom, Bengaluru's economy had thrived. They'd found other ways to make ends meet now that people no longer traveled so profligately, but the state remained one of India's centers of medical technology. Ferron wondered about the applications for remote surgery, and what the economic impact of this technology could be.

"Sure. Or extracting an appendix without leaving a scar. Inserting stem cells into bone marrow with no surgical trauma, freeing the body to heal disease instead of infection and wounds. It's revolutionary. If we can get it working."

"*Saab* . . ." She stroked Chairman Miaow's sleek azure head. "Could it be used as a weapon?"

"Anything can be used as a weapon," he said. A little too fast? But his skin conductivity and heart rate revealed no deception, no withholding. "Look, Sub-Inspector. Would you like some coffee?"

"I'd love some," she admitted.

He tapped a few more keys and stepped down from the treadmill. She'd have thought the typing curiously inefficient, but he certainly seemed to get things done fast.

"Religious reasons, *saab?*" she asked.

"Hmm?" He glanced at the monitor. "No. I'm just an eccentric. I prefer one information stream at a time. And I like to come here and do my work, and keep my home at home."

"Oh." Ferron laughed, following him across the office to a set of antique lacquered chairs. Chairman Miaow minced after them, stopping to sniff the unfamiliar rug and roll in a particularly lush patch. Feeling like she was making a huge confession, Ferron said, "I turn off my feeds sometimes too. Skin out. It helps me concentrate."

He winked.

She said, "So tell me about Dexter and his cat."

"Well . . ." He glanced guiltily at Chairman Miaow. "She was very advanced. He obviously spent a great deal of time working with her. Complete sentences, conversation on about the level of an imaginative five-year-old. That's one of our designs, by the way."

"Parrot-cats?"

"The hyacinth variety. We're working on an *Eclectus* variant for next year's market. Crimson and plum colors. You know they have a much longer lifespan than the root stock? Parrot-cats should be able to live for thirty to fifty years, though of course the design hasn't been around long enough for experimental proof."

"I did not. About Dr. Coffin—" she paused, and scanned the lists of enemies and contacts that Dr. Rao had provided, cross-referencing it with files and the reports of three interviews that had come in from Indrapramit in the last five minutes. Another contact request from her mother blinked away officiously. She dismissed it. "I understand he wasn't born here?"

"He traveled," Dr. Rao said in hushed tones. "From America."

"Huh," Ferron said. "He relocated for a job? Medieval. How did BioShell justify the expense—and the carbon burden?"

"A unique skill set. We bring in people from many places, actually. He was well-liked here: his work was outstanding, and he was charming enough—and talented enough—that his colleagues forgave him some of the . . . vagaries in his right-minding."

"Vagaries . . . ?"

"He was a depressive, madam," Dr. Rao said. "Prone to fairly serious fits of existential despair. Medication and surgery controlled it adequately that he was functional, but not completely enough that he was always . . . comfortable."

"When you say existential despair . . . ?" Ferron was a past master of the open-ended hesitation.

Dr. Rao seemed cheerfully willing to fill it in for her. "He questioned the worth and value of pretty much every human endeavor. Of existence itself."

"So he was a bit nihilistic?"

"Nihilism denies value. Dexter was willing to believe that compassion had value—not intrinsic value, you understand. But assigned value. He believed that the best thing a human being could aspire to was to limit suffering."

"That explains his handle."

Dr. Rao chuckled. "It does, doesn't it? Anyway, he was brilliant."

"I assume that means that BioShell will suffer in his absence."

"The fourth-dimension project is going to fall apart without him," Dr. Rao said candidly. "It's going to take a global search to replace him. And we'll have to do it quickly; release of the technology was on the anvil."

Ferron thought about the inside-out person in the midst of his rug, his flat set for an intimate dinner for two. "Dr. Rao . . ."

"Yes, Sub-Inspector?"

"In your estimation, would Dr. Coffin commit suicide?"

He steepled his fingers and sighed. "It's . . . possible. But he was very devoted to his work, and his psych evaluations did not indicate it as an immediate danger. I'd hate to think so."

"Because you'd feel like you should have done more? You can't save somebody from themselves, Dr. Rao."

"Sometimes," he said, "a word in the dark is all it takes."

"Dr. Coffin worked from home. Was any of his lab equipment there? Is it possible that he died in an accident?"

Dr. Rao's eyebrows rose. "Now I'm curious about the nature of his demise, I'm afraid. He should not have had any proprietary equipment at home: we maintain a lab for him here, and his work at home should have been limited to theory and analysis. But of course he'd have an array of interfaces."

The coffee arrived, brought in by a young man with a ready smile who set the tray on the table and vanished again without a word. No doubt pleased to be Employed.

As Dr. Rao poured from a solid old stoneware carafe, he transitioned to small talk. "Some exciting news about the Andromeda Galaxy, isn't it? They've named the star Al-Rahman."

"I thought stars were named by coordinates and catalogue number these days."

"They are," Rao said. "But it's fitting for this one to have a little romance. People being what they are, someone would have named it if the science community didn't. And Abd Al-Rahman Al-Sufi was the first astronomer to describe the Andromeda Galaxy, around 960 A.D. He called it the 'little cloud.' It's also called Messier 31—."

"Do you think it's a nova precursor, *saab*?"

He handed her the coffee—something that smelled pricey and rich, probably from the hills—and offered cream and sugar. She added a lump of the latter to her cup with the tongs, stirred in cream, and selected a lemon biscuit from the little plate he nudged toward her.

"That's what they said on the news," he said.

"Meaning you don't believe it?"

"You're sharp," he said admiringly.

"I'm a homicide investigator," she said.

He reached into his pocket and withdrew a small injection kit. The hypo hissed alarmingly as he pressed it to his skin. He winced.

"Insulin?" she asked, restraining herself from an incredibly rude question about why he hadn't had stem cells, if he was diabetic.

He shook his head. "Scotophobin. Also part of my rightminding. I have short-term memory issues." He picked up a chocolate biscuit and bit into it decisively.

She'd taken the stuff herself, in school and when cramming for her police exams. She also refused to be derailed. "So you don't think this star—"

"Al-Rahman."

"—Al-Rahman. You don't think it's going nova?"

"Oh, it might be," he said. "But what would you say if I told you that its pattern is a repeating series of prime numbers?"

The sharp tartness of lemon shortbread turned to so much grit in her mouth. "I beg your pardon."

"Someone is signaling us," Dr. Rao said. "Or I should say, *was* signaling us. A long, long time ago. Somebody with the technology necessary to tune the output of their star."

"Explain," she said, setting the remainder of the biscuit on her saucer.

"Al-Rahman is more than two and a half million light years away. That means that the light we're seeing from it was modulated when the first identifiable humans were budding off the hominid family tree. Even if we could send a signal back . . . the odds are very good that they're all gone now. It was just a message in a bottle. *We were here.*"

"The news said twenty thousand light years."

"The news." He scoffed. "Do they ever get police work right?"

"Never," Ferron said fervently.

"Science either." He glanced up as the lights dimmed. "Another brownout."

An unformed idea tickled the back of Ferron's mind. "Do you have a sunfarm?"

"BioShell is entirely self-sufficient," he confirmed. "It's got to be a bug, but we haven't located it yet. Anyway, it will be back up in a minute. All our important equipment has dedicated power supplies."

He finished his biscuit and stirred the coffee thoughtfully while he chewed. "The odds are that the universe is—or has been—full of intelligent species. And that we will never meet any of them. Because the distances and time scales are so vast. In the two hundred years we've been capable of sending signals into space— well. Compare that in scale to Al-Rahman."

"That's awful," Ferron said. "It makes me appreciate Dr. Coffin's perspective."

"It's terrible," Dr. Rao agreed. "Terrible and wonderful. In some ways I wonder if that's as close as we'll ever get to comprehending the face of God."

They sipped their coffee in contemplation, facing one another across the tray and the low lacquered table.

"Milk?" said Chairman Miaow. Carefully, Ferron poured some into a saucer and gave it to her.

Dr. Rao said, "You know, the Andromeda Galaxy and our own Milky Way are expected to collide eventually."

"Eventually?"

He smiled. It did good things for the creases around his eyes. "Four and a half billion years or so."

Ferron thought about Uttara Bhadrapada, and the Heavenly Ganges, and Aryaman's house—in a metaphysical sort of sense—as he came to walk that path across the sky. From so far away it took two and a half million years just to *see* that far.

"I won't wait up, then." She finished the last swallow of coffee and looked around for the cat. "I don't suppose I could see Dr. Coffin's lab before I go?"

"Oh," said Dr. Rao. "I think we can do that, and better."

The lab space Coffin had shared with three other researchers belied BioShell's corporate wealth. It was a maze of tables and unidentifiable equipment in dizzying array. Ferron identified a gene sequencer, four or five microscopes, and a centrifuge, but most of the rest baffled her limited knowledge of bioengineering. She was struck by the fact that just about every object in the room was dressed in BioShell's livery colors of emerald and gold, however.

She glimpsed a conservatory through a connecting door, lush with what must be prototype plants; at the far end of the room, rows of condensers hummed beside a revolving door rimed with frost. A black-skinned woman in a lab coat with her hair clipped into short, tight curls had her eyes to a lens and her hands in waldo sleeves. Microsurgery?

Dr. Rao held out a hand as Ferron paused beside him. "Will we disturb her?"

"Dr. Nnebuogor will have skinned out just about everything except the fire alarm," Dr. Rao said. "The only way to distract her would be to go over and give her a shove. Which—" he raised a warning finger "—I would recommend against, as she's probably engaged in work on those next-generation parrot-cats I told you about now."

"Nnebuogor? She's Nigerian?"

Dr. Rao nodded. "Educated in Cairo and Bengaluru. Her coming to work for BioShell was a real coup for us."

"You *do* employ a lot of farang," Ferron said. "And not by telepresence." She waited for Rao to bridle, but she must have gotten the tone right, because he shrugged.

"Our researchers need access to our lab."

"Miaow," said Chairman Miaow.

"Can she?" Ferron asked.

"We're cat-friendly," Rao said, with a flicker of a smile, so Ferron set the carrier down and opened its door. Rao's heart rate was up a little, and she caught herself watching sideways while he straightened his trousers and picked lint from his sleeve.

Chairman Miaow emerged slowly, rubbing her length against the side of the carrier. She gazed up at the equipment and furniture with unblinking eyes, and soon she gathered herself to leap onto a workbench, and Dr. Rao put a hand out firmly.

"No climbing or jumping," he said. "Dangerous. It will hurt you."

"Hurt?" The cat drew out the Rs in a manner so adorable it had to be engineered for. "No jump?"

"No." Rao turned to Ferron. "We've hardwired in response to the No command. I think you'll find our parrot-cats superior to unengineered felines in this regard. Of course . . . they're still cats."

"Of course," Ferron said. She watched as Chairman Miaow explored her new environment, rubbing her face on this and that. "Do you have any pets?"

"We often take home the successful prototypes," he said. "It would be a pity to destroy them. I have a parrot-cat—a red-and-gray—and a golden lemur. Engineered, of course. The baseline ones are protected."

As they watched, the hyacinth cat picked her way around, sniffing every surface. She paused before one workstation in particular before cheek-marking it, and said in comically exaggerated surprise: "Mine! My smell."

There was a synthetic-fleece-lined basket tucked beneath the table. The cat leaned toward it, stretching her head and neck, and sniffed deeply and repeatedly.

"Have you been here before?" Ferron asked.

Chairman Miaow looked at Ferron wide-eyed with amazement at Ferron's patent ignorance, and declared "New!"

She jumped into the basket and snuggled in, sinking her claws deeply and repeatedly into the fleece.

Ferron made herself stop chewing her thumbnail. She stuck her hand into her uniform pocket. "Are all your hyacinths clones?"

"They're all closely related," Dr. Rao said. "But no, not clones. And even if she were a clone, there would be differences in the expression of her tuxedo pattern."

At that moment, Dr. Nnebuogor sighed and backed away from her machine, withdrawing her hands from the sleeves and shaking out the fingers like a musician after practicing. She jumped when she turned and saw them. "Oh! Sorry. I was skinned. *Namaskar.*"

"Miaow?" said the cat in her appropriated basket.

"Hello, Niranjana. Where's Dexter?" said Dr. Nnebuogor. Ferron felt the scientist reading her meta-tags. Dr. Nnebuogor raised her eyes to Rao. "And—pardon, officer—what's with the copper?"

"Actually," Ferron said, "I have some bad news for you. It appears that Dexter Coffin was murdered last night."

"Murdered . . ." Dr. Nnebuogor put her hand out against the table edge. "*Murdered?*"

"Yes," Ferron said. "I'm Police Sub-Inspector Ferron—" which Dr. Nnebuogor would know already "—and I'm afraid I need to ask you some questions. Also, I'll be contacting the other researchers who share your facilities via telepresence. Is there a private area I can use for that?"

Dr. Nnebuogor looked stricken. The hand that was not leaned against the table went up to her mouth. Ferron's feed showed the acceleration of her heart, the increase in skin conductivity as her body slicked with cold sweat. Guilt or grief? It was too soon to tell.

"You can use my office," Dr. Rao said. "Kindly, with my gratitude."

The interviews took the best part of the day and evening, when all was said and done, and garnered Ferron very little new information—yes, people *would* probably kill for what Coffin was—had been—working on. No, none of his colleagues had any reason to. No, he had no love life of which they were aware.

Ferron supposed she technically *could* spend all night lugging the cat carrier around, but her own flat wasn't too far from the University district. It was in a kinship block teaming with her uncles and cousins, her grandparents, great-grandparents, her sisters and their husbands (and in one case, wife). The fiscal support of shared housing was the only reason she'd been able to carry her mother as long as she had.

She checked out a pedestrial because she couldn't face the bus and she felt like she'd done more than her quota of steps before dinnertime—and here it was, well after. The cat carrier balanced on the grab bar, she zipped it unerringly through the traffic, enjoying the feel of the wind in her hair and the outraged honks cascading along the double avenues.

She could make the drive on autopilot, so she used the other half of her attention to feed facts to the department's expert system. Doyle knew everything about everything, and if it wasn't self-aware or self-directed in the sense that most people meant when they said *artificial intelligence*, it still rivaled a trained human brain when it came to picking out patterns—and being supercooled, it was significantly faster.

She even told it the puzzling bits, such as how Chairman Miaow had reacted upon being introduced to the communal lab that Coffin shared with three other BioShell researchers.

Doyle swallowed everything Ferron could give it, as fast as she could report. She knew that down in its bowels, it would be integrating that information with Indrapramit's reports, and those of the other officers and techs assigned to the case.

She thought maybe they needed something more. As the pedestrial dropped her at the bottom of her side street, she dropped a line to Damini, her favorite archinformist. "Hey," she said, when Damini answered.

"Hey yourself, boss. What do you need?"

Ferron released the pedestrial back into the city pool. It scurried off, probably already summoned to the next call. Ferron had used her override to requisition it. She tried to feel guilty, but she was already late in attending on her mother—and she'd ignored two more messages in the intervening time. It was probably too late to prevent bloodshed, but there was something to be said for getting the inevitable over with.

"Dig me up everything you can on today's vic, would you? Dexter Coffin, American by birth, employed at BioShell. As far back as you can, any tracks he may have left under any name or handle."

"Childhood dental records and juvenile posts on the *Candyland* message boards," Damini said cheerfully. "Got it. I'll stick it in Doyle when it's done."

"Ping me, too? Even if it's late? I'm upped."

"So will I be," Damini answered. "This could take a while. Anything else?"

"Not unless you have a cure for families."

"Hah," said the archinformist. "Everybody talking, and nobody hears a damned thing anybody else has to say. I'd retire on the proceeds. All right, check in later." She vanished just as Ferron reached the aptblock lobby.

It was after dinner, but half the family was hanging around in the common areas, watching the news or playing games while pretending to ignore it. Ferron knew it was useless to try sneaking past the synthetic marble-floored chambers with their charpoys and cushions, the corners lush with foliage. Attempted stealth would only encourage them to detain her longer.

Dr. Rao's information about the prime number progression had leaked beyond scientific circles—or been released—and an endless succession of talking heads were analyzing it in less nuanced terms than he'd managed. The older cousins asked Ferron if she'd heard the news about the star; two sisters and an uncle told her that her mother had been looking for her. *All* the nieces and nephews and small cousins wanted to look at the cat.

Ferron's aging mausi gave her five minutes on how a little cosmetic surgery would make her much more attractive on the marriage market, and shouldn't she consider lightening that mahogany-brown skin to a "prettier" wheatish complexion? A plate of idlis and sambaar appeared as if by magic in mausi's hand, and from there transferred to Ferron's. "And how are you ever going to catch a man if you're so skinny?"

It took Ferron twenty minutes to maneuver into her own small flat, which was still set for sleeping from three nights before. Smoke came trotting to see her, a petite-footed drift of the softest silver-and-charcoal fur imaginable, from which emerged a laughing triangular face set with eyes like black jewels. His ancestors had been foxes farmed for fur in Russia. Researchers had experimented on them, breeding for docility. It turned out it only took a few generations to turn a wild animal into a housepet.

Ferron was a little uneasy with the ethics of all that. But it hadn't stopped her from adopting Smoke when her mother lost interest in him. Foxes weren't the hot trend anymore; the fashion was for engineered cats and lemurs—and skinpets, among those who wanted to look daring.

Having rushed home, she was now possessed by the intense desire to delay the inevitable. She set Chairman Miaow's carrier on top of the cabinets and took Smoke out into the sunfarm for a few minutes of exercise in the relative cool of night. When he'd chased parrots in circles for a bit, she brought him back in, cleaned his litterbox, and stripped off her sweat-stiff uniform to have a shower. She was washing her hair when she realized that she had no idea what to feed Chairman Miaow. Maybe she could eat fox food? Ferron would have to figure out some way to segregate part of the flat for her . . . at least until she was sure that Smoke didn't think a parrot-cat would make a nice midnight snack.

She dressed in off-duty clothes—barefoot in a salwar kameez—and made an attempt at setting her furniture to segregate her flat. Before she left, she placed offering packets of kumkum and a few marigolds from the patio boxes in the tray before her idol of Varuna, the god of agreement, order, and the law.

Ferron didn't bother drying her hair before she presented herself at her mother's door. If she left it down, the heat would see to that soon enough.

Madhuvanthi did not rise to admit Ferron herself, as she was no longer capable. The door just slid open to Ferron's presence. As Ferron stepped inside, she saw mostly that the rug needed watering, and that the chaise her mother reclined on needed to be reset—it was sagging at the edges from too long in one shape. She wore not just the usual noninvasive modern interface—contacts, skin conductivity and brain activity sensors, the invisibly fine wires that lay along the skin and detected nerve impulses and muscle micromovements—but a full immersion suit.

Not for the first time, Ferron contemplated skinning out the thing's bulky, padded outline, and looking at her mother the way she wanted to see her. But that would be dishonest. Ferron was here to face her problems, not pretend their nonexistence.

"Hello, Mother," Ferron said.

There was no answer.

Ferron sent a text message.

> Hello, Mother. You wanted to see me?

The pause was long, but not as long as it could have been.

> You're late, Tamanna. I've been trying to reach you all day. I'm in the middle of a run right now.
> I'm sorry, Ferron said. Someone was murdered.

Text, thank all the gods, sucked out the defensive sarcasm that would have filled up a spoken word. She fiddled the bangles she couldn't wear on duty, just to hear the glass chime.

She could feel her mother's attention elsewhere, her distaste at having the unpleasant realities of Ferron's job forced upon her. That attention would focus on anything but Ferron, for as long as Ferron waited for it. It was a contest of wills, and Ferron always lost.

> Mother—

Her mother pushed up the faceplate on the VR helmet and sat up abruptly. "Bloody hell," she said. "Got killed. That'll teach me to do two things at once. Look, about the archives—"

"Mother," Ferron said, "I can't. I don't have any more savings to give you."

Madhuvanthi said, "They'll *kill* me."

They'll de-archive your virtual history, Ferron thought, but she had the sense to hold her tongue.

After her silence dragged on for fifteen seconds or so, Madhuvanthi said, "Sell the fox."

"He's mine," Ferron said. "I'm not selling him. Mother, you really need to come out of your make-believe world once in a while—"

Her mother pulled the collar of the VR suit open so she could ruffle the fur of the violet-and-teal striped skinpet nestled up to the warmth of her throat. It humped in response, probably vibrating with a comforting purr. Ferron tried not to judge, but the idea of parasitic pets, no matter how fluffy and colorful, made *her* skin crawl.

Ferron's mother said, "Make-believe. And your world isn't?"

"Mother—"

"Come in and see my world sometime before you judge it."

"I've seen your world," Ferron said. "I used to live there, remember? All the time, with you. Now I live out here, and you can too."

Madhuvanthi's glare would have seemed blistering even in the rainy season. "I'm your mother. You will obey me."

Everything inside Ferron demanded she answer yes. Hardwired, that duty. Planned for. Programmed.

Ferron raised her right hand. "Can't we get some dinner and—"

Madhuvanthi sniffed and closed the faceplate again. And that was the end of the interview.

Rightminding or not, the cool wings of hypomania or not, Ferron's heart was pounding and her fresh clothing felt sticky again already. She turned and left.

When she got back to her own flat, the first thing she noticed was her makeshift wall of furniture partially disassembled, a chair/shelf knocked sideways, the disconnected and overturned tabletop now fallen flat.

"Oh, no." Her heart rose into her throat. She rushed inside, the door forgotten—

Atop a heap of cushions lay Smoke, proud and smug. And against his soft gray side, his fluffy tail flipped over her like a blanket, curled Chairman Miaow, her golden eyes squeezed closed in pleasure.

"Mine!" she said definitively, raising her head.

"I guess so," Ferron answered. She shut the door and went to pour herself a drink while she started sorting through Indrapramit's latest crop of interviews.

According to everything Indrapramit had learned, Coffin was quiet. He kept to himself, but he was always willing and enthusiastic when it came to discussing his work. His closest companion was the cat—Ferron looked down at Chairman Miaow, who had rearranged herself to take advantage of the warm valley in the bed between Smoke and Ferron's thigh—and the cat was something of a neighborhood celebrity, riding on Coffin's shoulder when he took his exercise.

All in all, a typical portrait of a typical, lonely man who didn't let anyone get too close.

"Maybe there will be more in the archinformation," she said, and went back to Doyle's pattern algorithm results one more damn time.

After performing her evening practice of kalari payat—first time in three days— Ferron set her furniture for bed and retired to it with her files. She wasn't expecting Indrapramit to show up at her flat, but sometime around two in the morning, the lobby door discreetly let her know she had a visitor. Of course, he knew she'd upped, and since he had no family and lived in a thin-walled dormitory room, he'd need a quiet place to camp out and work at this hour of the night. There wasn't a lot of productive interviewing you could do when all the subjects were asleep—at least, not until they had somebody dead to rights enough to take them down to the jail for interrogation.

His coming to her home meant every other resident of the block would know, and Ferron could look forward to a morning of being quizzed by aunties while she tried to cram her idlis down. It didn't matter that Indrapramit was a colleague, and she was his superior. At her age, any sign of male interest brought unemployed relatives with too much time on their hands swarming.

Still, she admitted him. Then she extricated herself from between the fox and the cat, wrapped her bathrobe around herself, stomped into her slippers, and headed out to meet him in the hall. At least keeping their conference to the public areas would limit knowing glances later.

He'd upped too. She could tell by the bounce in his step and his slightly wild focus. And the fact that he was dropping by for a visit in the dark of the morning.

Lowering her voice so she wouldn't trouble her neighbors, Ferron said, "Something too good to mail?"

"An interesting potential complication."

She gestured to the glass doors leading out to the sunfarm. He followed her, his boots somehow still as bright as they'd been that morning. He must polish them in an anti-static gloss.

She kicked off her slippers and padded barefoot over the threshold, making sure to silence the alarm first. The suntrees were furled for the night, their leaves rolled into funnels that channeled condensation to the roots. There was even a bit of chill in the air.

Ferron breathed in gratefully, wiggling her toes in the cultivated earth. "Let's go up to the roof."

Without a word, Indrapramit followed her up the winding openwork stair hung with bougainvillea, barren and thorny now in the dry season but a riot of color and greenery once the rains returned. The interior walls of the aptblock were mossy and thickly planted with coriander and other Ayurvedic herbs. Ferron broke off a bitter leaf of fenugreek to nibble as they climbed.

At the landing, she stepped aside and tilted her head back, peering up through the potted neem and lemon and mango trees at the stars beyond. A dark hunched shape in the branches of a pomegranate startled her until she realized it was the outline of one of the house monkeys, huddled in sleep. She wondered if she could see the Andromeda Galaxy from here at this time of year. Checking a skymap, she learned that it would be visible—but probably low on the horizon, and not without a telescope in these light-polluted times. You'd have better odds of finding it than a hundred years ago, though, when you'd barely have been able to glimpse the brightest stars. The Heavenly Ganges spilled across the darkness like sequins sewn at random on an indigo veil, and a crooked fragment of moon rode high. She breathed in deep and stepped onto the grass and herbs of the roof garden. A creeping mint snagged at her toes, sending its pungency wide.

"So what's the big news?"

"We're not the only ones asking questions about Dexter Coffin." Indrapramit flashed her a video clip of a pale-skinned woman with red hair bleached ginger by the sun and a crop of freckles not even the gloss of sunblock across her cheeks could keep down. She was broad-shouldered and looked capable, and the ID codes running across the feed under her image told Ferron she carried a warrant card and a stun pistol.

"Contract cop?" she said, sympathetically.

"I'm fine," he said, before she could ask. He spread his first two fingers opposite his thumb and pressed each end of the V beneath his collarbones, a new nervous gesture. "I got my Chicago block maintained last week, and the reprogramming is holding. I'd tell you if I was triggering. I know that not every contract cop is going to decompensate and start a massacre."

A massacre Indrapramit had stopped the hard way, as it happened. "Let me know what you need," she said, because everything else she could have said would sound like a vote of non-confidence.

"Thanks," he said. "How'd it go with your mother?"

"Gah," she said. "I think *I* need a needle. So what's the contractor asking? And who's employing her?"

"Here's the interesting thing, boss. She's an American too."

"She *couldn't* have made it here this fast. Not unless she started before he died—"

"No," he said. "She's an expat, a former New York homicide detective. Her handle is Morganti. She lives in Hongasandra, and she does a lot of work for American and Canadian police departments. Licensed and bonded, and she seems to have a very good rep."

"Who's she under contract to now?"

"Warrant card says Honolulu."

"Huh." Ferron kept her eyes on the stars, and the dark leaves blowing before them. "Top-tier distributed policing, then. Is it a skip trace?"

"You think he was on the run, and whoever he was on the run from finally caught up with him?"

"It's a working theory." She shrugged. "Damini's supposed to be calling with some background any minute now. Actually, I think I'll check in with her. She's late, and I have to file a twenty-four-hour report with the Inspector in the morning."

With a twitch of her attention, she spun a bug out to Damini and conferenced Indrapramit in.

The archinformist answered immediately. "Sorry, boss," she said. "I know I'm slow, but I'm still trying to put together a complete picture here. Your dead guy buried his past pretty thoroughly. I can give you a preliminary, though, with the caveat that it's subject to change."

"Squirt," Ferron said, opening her firewall to the data. It came in fast and hard, and there seemed to be kilometers of it unrolling into her feed like an endless bolt of silk. "Oh, dear . . ."

"I know, I know. Do you want the executive summary? Even if it's also a work in progress? Okay. First up, nobody other than Coffin was in his flat that night, according to netfeed tracking."

"The other night upon the stair," Ferron said, "I met a man who wasn't there."

Damina blew her bangs out of her eyes. "So either nobody came in, or whoever did is a good enough hacker to eradicate every trace of her presence. Which is not a common thing."

"Gotcha. What else?"

"Doyle picked out a partial pattern in your feed. Two power cuts in places associated with the crime. It started looking for more, and it identified a series of brownouts over the course of a year or so, all in locations with some connection to Dr. Coffin. Better yet, Doyle identified the cause."

"I promise I'm holding my breath," Indrapramit said.

"Then how is it you are talking? Anyway, it's a smart virus in the power grids. It's draining power off the lab and household sunfarms at irregular intervals. That power is being routed to a series of chargeable batteries in Coffin's lab space. Except Coffin didn't purchase order the batteries."

"Nnebuogor," Ferron guessed.

"Two points," said Damini. "It's a stretch, but she could have come in to the office today specifically to see if the cops stopped by."

"She could have. . . ." Indrapramit said dubiously. "You think she killed him because he found out she was stealing power? For what purpose?"

"I'll get on her e-mail and media," Damini said. "So here's my speculation: imagine this utility virus, spreading through the smart grid from aptblock to aptblock. To commit the murder—nobody had to be in the room with him, not if his four-dimensional manipulators were within range of him. Right? You'd just override whatever safety protocols there were, and . . . boom. Or squish, if you prefer."

Ferron winced. She didn't. Prefer, that was. "Any sign that the manipulators were interfered with?"

"Memory wiped," Damini said. "Just like the cat. Oh, and the other thing I found out. Dexter Coffin is not our boy's first identity. It's more like his third, if my linguistic and semantic parsers are right about the Web content they're picking up. I've got Conan on it too—" Conan was another of the department's expert systems "—and I'm going to go over a selection by hand. But it seems like our decedent had reinvented himself whenever he got into professional trouble, which he did a lot. He had unpopular opinions, and he wasn't shy about sharing them with the net. So he'd make the community too hot to handle and then come back as his own sockpuppet—new look, new address, new handle. Severing all ties to what he was before. I've managed to get a real fix on his last identity, though—"

Indrapramit leaned forward, folding his arms against the chill. "How do you do that? He works in a specialized—a rarified field. I'd guess everybody in it knows each other, at least by reputation. Just how much did he change his appearance?"

"Well," Damini said, "he used to look like this. He must have used some right-minding tactics to change elements of his personality, too. Just not the salient ones. A real chameleon, your arsehole."

She picked a still image out of the datastream and flung it up. Ferron glanced at Indrapramit, whose rakish eyebrows were climbing up his forehead. An East Asian with long, glossy, dark hair, who appeared to stand about six inches taller than Dr. Coffin, floated at the center of her perceptions, smiling benevolently.

"Madam, *saab*," Damini said. "May I present Dr. Jessica Fang."

"Well," Ferron said, after a pause of moderate length. "That takes a significant investment." She thought of Aristotle: as the condition of the mind alters, so too alters the condition of the body, and likewise, as the condition of the body alters, so too alters the condition of the mind.

Indrapramit said, "He has a taste for evocative handles. Any idea why the vanishing act?"

"I'm working on it," Damini said.

"I've got a better idea," said Ferron. "Why don't we ask Detective Morganti?"

Indrapramit steepled his fingers. "Boss . . ."

"I'll hear it," Ferron said. "It doesn't matter if it's crazy."

"We've been totally sidetracked by the cat issue. Because Chairman Miaow has to be Niranjana, right? Because a clone would have expressed the genes for those markings differently. But she can't be Niranjana, because she's not wiped: she's factory-new."

"Right," Ferron said cautiously.

"So." Indrapramit was enjoying his dramatic moment. "If a person can have cosmetic surgery, why not a parrot-cat?"

"Chairman Miaow?" Ferron called, as she led Indrapramit into her flat. They needed tea to shake off the early morning chill, and she was beyond caring what the neighbors thought. She needed a clean uniform, too.

"Miaow," said Chairman Miaow, from inside the kitchen cupboard.

"Oh, dear." Indrapamit followed Ferron in. Smoke sat demurely in the middle of the floor, tail fluffed over his toes, the picture of innocence. Ferron pulled wide the cabinet door, which already stood ten inches ajar. There was Chairman Miaow, purring, a shredded packet of tunafish spreading dribbles of greasy water across the cupboard floor.

She licked her chops ostentatiously and jumped down to the sink lip, where she balanced as preciously as she had in Coffin's flat.

"Cat," Ferron said. She thought over the next few things she wanted to say, and remembered that she was speaking to a parrot-cat. "Don't think you've gotten away with anything. The fox is getting the rest of that."

"Fox food is icky," the cat said. "Also, not enough taurine."

"Huh," Ferron said. She looked over at Indrapramit.

He looked back. "I guess she's learning to talk."

They had no problem finding Detective Morganti. The redheaded American woman arrived at Ferron's aptblock with the first rays of sunlight stroking the vertical farms along its flanks. She had been sitting on the bench beside the door, reading something on her screen, but she looked up and stood as Ferron and Indrapramit exited.

"Sub-Inspector Ferron, I presume? And Constable Indrapramit, how nice to see you again."

Ferron shook her hand. She was even more imposing in person, tall and broadchested, with the shoulders of a cartoon superhuman. She didn't squeeze.

Morganti continued, "I understand you're the detective of record on the Coffin case."

"Walk with us," Ferron said. "There's a nice French coffee shop on the way to the Metro."

It had shaded awnings and a courtyard, and they were seated and served within minutes. Ferron amused herself by pushing the crumbs of her pastry around on the plate while they talked. Occasionally, she broke a piece off and tucked it into her mouth, washing buttery flakes down with thick, cardamom-scented brew.

"So," she said after a few moments, "what did Jessica Fang do in Honolulu? It's not just the flame wars, I take it. And there's no warrant for her that we could find."

Morganti's eyes rose. "Very efficient."

"Thank you." Ferron tipped her head to Indrapramit. "Mostly his work, and that of my archinformist."

Morganti smiled; Indrapramit nodded silently. Then Morganti said, "She is believed to have been responsible for embezzling almost three million ConDollars from her former employer, eleven years ago in the Hawaiian Islands."

"That'd pay for a lot of identity-changing."

"Indeed."

"But they can't prove it."

"If they could, Honolulu P.D. would have pulled a warrant and virtually extradited her. Him. I was contracted to look into the case ten days ago—" She tore off a piece of a cheese croissant and chewed it thoughtfully. "It took the skip trace this long to locate her. Him."

"Did she do it?"

"*Hell* yes." She grinned like the American she was. "The question is—well, okay, I realize the murder is your jurisdiction, but I don't get paid unless I either close the case or eliminate my suspect—and I get a bonus if I recover any of the stolen property. Now, 'killed by person or persons unknown' is a perfectly acceptable outcome as far as the City of Honolulu is concerned, with the added benefit that the State of Hawaii doesn't have to pay Bengaluru to incarcerate him. So I need to know, one cop to another, if the inside-out stiff is Dexter Coffin."

"The DNA matches," Ferron said. "I can tell you that in confidence. There will be a press release once we locate and notify his next of kin."

"Understood," Morganti said. "I'll keep it under my hat. I'll be filing recovery paperwork against the dead man's assets in the amount of C$2,798,000 and change. I can give you the next of kin, by the way."

The data came in a squirt. Daughter, Maui. Dr. Fang-Coffin really had severed all ties.

"Understood," Ferron echoed. She smiled when she caught herself. She liked this woman. "You realize we have to treat you as a suspect, given your financial motive."

"Of course," Morganti said. "I'm bonded, and I'll be happy to come in for an interrogation under Truth."

"That will make things easier, madam," Ferron said.

Morganti turned her coffee cup in its saucer. "Now then. What can I do to help *you* clear your homicide?"

Indrapramit shifted uncomfortably on the bench.

"What *did* Jessica Fang do, exactly?" Ferron had Damini's data in her case buffer. She could use what Morganti told her to judge the contract officer's knowledge and sincerity.

"In addition to the embezzling? Accused of stealing research and passing it off as her own," Morganti said. "Also, she was—well, she was just kind of an asshole on the net, frankly. Running down colleagues, dismissing their work, aggrandizing her own. She was good, truthfully. But nobody's *that* good."

"Would someone have followed him here for personal reasons?"

"As you may have gathered, this guy was not diligent about his rightminding," Morganti said. She pushed a handful of hair behind her shoulder. "And he was a bit of a narcissist. Sociopath? Antisocial in some sort of atavistic way. Normal people don't just . . . walk away from all their social connections because they made things a little hot on the net."

Ferron thought of the distributed politics of her own workplace, the sniping and personality clashes. And her mother, not so much alone on an electronic Serengeti as haunting the virtual pillared palaces of an Egypt that never was.

"No," she said.

Morganti said, "Most people find ways to cope with that. Most people don't burn themselves as badly as Jessica Fang did, though."

"I see." Ferron wished badly for sparkling water in place of the syrupy coffee. "You've been running down Coffin's finances, then? Can you share that information?"

Morganti said that he had liquidated a lot of hidden assets a week ago, about two days after she took his case. "It was before I made contact with him, but it's possible he had Jessica Fang flagged for searches—or he had a contact in Honolulu who let him know when the skip trace paid off. He was getting ready to run again. How does that sound?"

Ferron sighed and sat back in her chair. "Fabulous. It sounds completely fabulous. I don't suppose you have any insight into who he might have been expecting for dinner? Or how whoever killed him might have gotten out of the room afterwards when it was all locked up tight on Coffin's override?"

Morganti shrugged. "He didn't have any close friends or romantic relationships. Always too aware that he was living in hiding, I'd guess. Sometimes he entertained coworkers, but I've checked with them all, and none admits having gone to see him that night."

"Sub-Inspector," Indrapramit said gently. "The time."

"Bugger," Ferron said, registering it. "Morning roll call. Catch up with you later?"

"Absolutely," Morganti said. "As I said before, I'm just concerned with clearing my embezzling case. I'm always happy to help a sister officer out on a murder."

And butter up the local police, Ferron thought.

Morganti said, "One thing that won't change. Fang was *obsessed* with astronomy."

"There were deep-space images on Coffin's walls," Ferron said.

Indrapramit said, "And he had offered his Ganesha an indigo scarf. I wonder if the color symbolized something astronomical to him."

"Indigo," Morganti said. "Isn't it funny that we have a separate word for dark blue?"

Ferron felt the pedantry welling up, and couldn't quite stopper it. "Did you know that all over the world, dark blue and black are often named with the same word? Possibly because of the color of the night sky. And that the ancient Greeks did not have a particular name for the color blue? Thus their seas were famously 'wine-dark.' But in Hindu tradition, the color blue has a special significance: it is the color of Vishnu's skin, and Krishna is nicknamed *Sunil*, 'dark blue.' The color also implies that which is all-encompassing, as in the sky."

She thought of something slightly more obscure. "Also, that color is the color of Shani Bhagavan, who is one of the deities associated with Uttara Bhadrapada. Which we've been hearing a lot about lately. It might indeed have had a lot of significance to Dr. Fang-Coffin."

Morganti, eyebrows drawn together in confusion, looked to Indrapramit for salvation. "*Saab?* Uttara Bhadrapada?"

Indrapramit said, "Andromeda."

Morganti excused herself as Indrapramit and Ferron prepared to check in to their virtual office.

While Ferron organized her files and her report, Indrapramit finished his coffee. "We need to check inbound ships from, or carrying passengers from, America. Honolulu isn't as prohibitive as, say, Chicago."

They'd worked together long enough that half the conversational shifts didn't need to be recorded. "Just in case somebody *did* come here to kill him. Well, there can't be that many passages, right?"

"I'll get Damini after it," he said. "After roll—"

Roll call made her avoidant. There would be reports, politics, wrangling, and a succession of wastes of time as people tried to prove that their cases were more worthy of resources than other cases.

She pinched her temples. At least the coffee here was good. "Right. Telepresencing . . . now."

After the morning meeting, they ordered another round of coffees, and Ferron pulled up the sandwich menu and eyed it. There was no telling when they'd have time for lunch.

She'd grab something after the next-of-kin notification. If she was still hungry when they were done.

Normally, in the case of a next-of-kin so geographically distant, Bengaluru Police would arrange for an officer with local jurisdiction to make the call. But the Lahaina Police Department had been unable to raise Jessica Fang's daughter on a home visit, and a little cursory research had revealed that she was unEmployed and very nearly a permanent resident of artificial reality.

Just going by her handle, Jessica Fang's daughter on Maui didn't have a lot of professional aspirations. Ferron and Indrapramit had to go virtual and pull on avatars to meet her: Skooter0 didn't seem to come out of her virtual worlds for anything other than biologically unavoidable crash cycles. Since they were on duty, Ferron and Indrapramit's avatars were the standard-issue blanks provided by Bengaluru Police, their virtual uniforms sharply pressed, their virtual faces expressionless and identical.

It wasn't the warm and personal touch you would hope for, Ferron thought, when somebody was coming to tell you your mother had been murdered.

"Why don't you take point on this one?" she said.

Indrapramit snorted. "Be sure to mention my leadership qualities in my next performance review."

They left their bodies holding down those same café chairs and waded through the first few tiers of advertisements—get-rich-quick schemes, Bollywood starlets, and pop star scandal sheets, until they got into the American feed, and then it was get-rich-quick schemes, Hollywood starlets, pornography, and Congressional scandal sheets—until they linked up with the law enforcement priority channel. Ferron checked the address and led Indrapramit into a massively multiplayer artificial reality that showed real-time activity through Skooter0's system identity number. Once provided with the next of kin's handle, Damini had sent along a selection of key codes and overrides that got them through the pay wall with ease.

They didn't need a warrant for this. It was just a courtesy call.

Skooter0's preferred hangout was a 'historical' AR, which meant in theory that it reflected the pre-twenty-first-century world, and in practice that it was a muddled-up stew of cowboys, ninjas, pinstripe suit mobsters, medieval knights, cavaliers, Mongols, and wild West gunslingers. There were Macedonians, Mauryans, African gunrunners, French resistance fighters and Nazis, all running around together with samurai and Shaolin monks.

Indrapramit's avatar checked a beacon—a glowing green needle floating just above his nonexistent wrist. The directional signal led them through a space meant to evoke an antediluvian ice cave, in which about two dozen people all dressed as different incarnations of the late-twentieth-century pop star David Bowie were working themselves into a martial frenzy as they prepared to go forth and do virtual battle with some rival clade of Emulators. Ferron eyed a Diamond Dog who was being dressed in glittering armor by a pair of Thin White Dukes and was glad of the expressionless surface of her uniform avatar.

She knew what they were supposed to be because she pattern-matched from the Web. The music was quaint, but pretty good. The costumes . . . she winced.

Well, it was probably a better way to deal with antisocial aggression than taking it out on your spouse.

Indrapramit walked on, eyes front—not that you needed eyes to see what was going on in here.

At the far end of the ice cave, four seventh-century Norse dwarves delved a staircase out of stone, leading endlessly down. Heat rolled up from the depths. The virtual workmanship was astounding. Ferron and Indrapramit moved past, hiding their admiring glances. Just as much skill went into creating AR beauty as if it were stone.

The ice cave gave way to a forest glade floored in mossy, irregular slates. Set about on those were curved, transparent tables set for chess, go, mancala, cribbage, and similar strategy games. Most of the tables were occupied by pairs of players, and some had drawn observers as well.

Indrapramit followed his needle—and Ferron followed Indrapramit—to a table where a unicorn and a sasquatch were playing a game involving rows of transparent red and yellow stones laid out on a grid according to rules that Ferron did not comprehend. The sasquatch looked up as they stopped beside the table. The unicorn—glossy black, with a pearly, shimmering horn and a glowing amber stone pinched between the halves of her cloven hoof—was focused on her next move.

The arrow pointed squarely between her enormous, lambent golden eyes.

Ferron cleared her throat.

"Yes, officers?" the sasquatch said. He scratched the top of his head. The hair was particularly silky, and flowed around his long hooked fingernails.

"I'm afraid we need to speak to your friend," Indrapramit said.

"She's skinning you out," the sasquatch said. "Unless you have a warrant—"

"We have an override," Ferron said, and used it as soon as she felt Indrapramit's assent.

The unicorn's head came up, a shudder running the length of her body and setting her silvery mane to swaying. In a brittle voice, she said, "I'd like to report a glitch."

"It's not a glitch," Indrapramit said. He identified himself and Ferron and said, "Are you Skooter0?"

"Yeah," she said. The horn glittered dangerously. "I haven't broken any laws in India."

The sasquatch stood up discreetly and backed away.

"It is my unfortunate duty," Indrapramit continued, "to inform you of the murder of your mother, Dr. Jessica Fang, a.k.a. Dr. Dexter Coffin."

The unicorn blinked iridescent lashes. "I'm sorry," she said. "You're talking about something I have killfiled. I won't be able to hear you until you stop."

Indrapramit's avatar didn't look at Ferron, but she felt his request for help. She stepped forward and keyed a top-level override. "You will hear us," she said to the unicorn. "I am sorry for the intrusion, but we are legally bound to inform you that your mother, Dr. Jessica Fang, a.k.a. Dr. Dexter Coffin, has been murdered."

The unicorn's lip curled in a snarl. "Good. I'm glad."

Ferron stepped back. It was about the response she had expected.

"She made me," the unicorn said. "That doesn't make her my *mother*. Is there anything else you're legally bound to inform me of?"

"No," Indrapramit said.

"Then get the hell out." The unicorn set her amber gaming stone down on the grid. A golden glow encompassed it and its neighbors. "I win."

"Warehoused," Indrapramit said with distaste, back in his own body and nibbling a slice of quiche. "And happy about it."

Ferron had a pressed sandwich of vegetables, tapenade, cheeses, and some elaborate and incomprehensible European charcuterie made of smoked vatted protein. It was delicious, in a totally exotic sort of way. "Would it be better if she were miserable and unfulfilled?"

He made a noise of discontentment and speared a bite of spinach and egg.

Ferron knew her combativeness was really all about her mother, not Fang/Coffin's adult and avoidant daughter. Maybe it was the last remnants of upping, but she couldn't stop herself from saying, "What she's doing is not so different from what our brains do naturally, except now it's by tech/filters rather than prejudice and neurology."

Indrapramit changed the subject. "Let's make a virtual tour of the scene." As an icon blinked in Ferron's attention space, he added, "Oh, hey. Final autopsy report."

"Something from Damini, too," Ferron said. It had a priority code on it. She stepped into an artificial reality simulation of Coffin's apartment as she opened the contact. The thrill of the chase rose through the fog of her fading hypomania. Upping didn't seem to stick as well as it had when she was younger, and the crashes came harder now—but real, old-fashioned adrenaline was the cure for everything.

"Ferron," Ferron said, frowning down at the browned patches on Coffin's virtual rug. Indrapramit rezzed into the conference a heartbeat later. "Damini, what do the depths of the net reveal?"

"Jackpot," Damini said. "Did you get a chance to look at the autopsy report yet?"

"We just got done with the next of kin," Ferron said. "You're fast—I just saw the icon."

"Short form," Damini said, "is that's not Dexter Coffin."

Ferron's avatar made a slow circuit around the perimeter of the virtual murder scene. "There was a *DNA match*. Damini, we just told his daughter he was murdered."

Indrapramit, more practical, put down his fork in meatspace. His AR avatar mimicked the motion with an empty hand. "So who is it?"

"Nobody," Damini said. She leaned back, satisfied. "The medical examiner says it's topologically impossible to turn somebody inside out like that. It's vatted, whatever it is. A grown object, nominally alive, cloned from Dexter Coffin's tissue. But it's not Dexter Coffin. I mean, think about it—what organ would that *be*, exactly?"

"Cloned." In meatspace, Ferron picked a puff of hyacinth-blue fur off her uniform sleeve. She held it up where Indrapramit could see it.

His eyes widened. "Yes," he said. "What about the patterns, though?"

"Do I look like a bioengineer to you? Indrapramit," Ferron said thoughtfully. "Does this crime scene look staged to you?"

He frowned. "Maybe."

"Damini," Ferron asked, "how'd you do with Dr. Coffin's files? And Dr. Nnebuogar's files?"

"There's nothing useful in Coffin's e-mail except some terse exchanges with Dr. Nnebuogar very similar in tone to the Jessica Fang papers. Nnebuogar was warning Coffin off her research. But there were no death threats, no love letters, no child support demands."

"Anything he was interested in?"

"That star," Damini said. "The one that's going nova or whatever. He's been following it for a couple of weeks now, before the press release hit the mainstream feeds. Nnebuogar's logins support the idea that she's behind the utility virus, by the way."

"Logins can be spoofed."

"So they can," Damini agreed.

Ferron peeled her sandwich open and frowned down at the vatted charcuterie. It all looked a lot less appealing now. "Nobody came to Coffin's flat. And it turns out the stiff wasn't a stiff after all. So Coffin went somewhere else, after making preparations to flee and then abandoning them."

"And the crime scene was staged," Indrapramit said.

"This is interesting," Damini said. "Coffin hadn't been to the office in a week."

"Since about when Morganti started investigating him. Or when he might have become aware that she was on his trail."

Ferron said something sharp and self-critical and radically unprofessional. And then she said, "I'm an idiot. Leakage."

"Leakage?" Damini asked. "You mean like when people can't stop talking about the crime they actually committed, or the person you're not supposed to know they're having an affair with?"

An *urgent* icon from Ferron's mausi Sandhya—the responsible auntie, not the fussy auntie—blinked insistently at the edge of her awareness. *Oh Gods, what now?*

"Exactly like that," Ferron said. "Look, check on any hits for Coffin outside his flat in the past ten days. And I need confidential warrants for DNA analysis of the composters at the BioShell laboratory facility and also at Dr. Rao's apartment."

"You think *Rao* killed him?" Damini didn't even try to hide her shock.

Blink, blink went the icon. Emergency. Code red. Your mother has gone beyond the pale, my dear. "Just pull the warrants. I want to see what we get before I commit to my theory."

"Why?" Indrapramit asked.

Ferron sighed. "Because it's crazy. That's why. And see if you can get confidential access to Rao's calendar files and e-mail. I don't want him to know you're looking."

"Wait right there," Damini said. "Don't touch a thing. I'll be back before you know it."

"Mother," Ferron said to her mother's lion-maned goddess of an avatar, "I'm sorry. Sandhya's sorry. We're all sorry. But we can't let you go on like this."

It was the hardest thing she'd ever said.

Her mother, wearing Sekhmet's golden eyes, looked at Ferron's avatar and curled a lip. Ferron had come in, not in a uniform avatar, but wearing the battle-scarred armor she used to play in when she was younger, when she and her mother would spend hours atavistic. That was during her schooling, before she got interested in stopping—or at least avenging—*real* misery.

Was that fair? Her mother's misery was real. So was that of Jessica Fang's abandoned daughter. And this was a palliative—against being widowed, against being bedridden.

Madhuvanthi's lip-curl slowly blossomed into a snarl. "Of course. You can let them destroy this. Take away everything I am. It's not like it's murder."

"Mother," Ferron said, "it's not *real*."

"If it isn't," her mother said, gesturing around the room, "what is, then? I *made* you. I gave you life. You owe me this. Sandhya said you came home with one of those new parrot-cats. Where'd the money for that come from?"

"Chairman Miaow," Ferron said, "is evidence. And reproduction is an ultimately sociopathic act, no matter what I owe you."

Madhuvanthi sighed. "Daughter, come on one last run."

"You'll have your own memories of all this," Ferron said. "What do you need the archive for?"

"Memory," her mother scoffed. "What's memory, Tamanna? What do you actually remember? Scraps, conflations. How does it compare to being able to *relive?*"

To relive it, Ferron thought, *you'd have to have lived it in the first place.* But even teetering on the edge of fatigue and crash, she had the sense to keep *that* to herself.

"Have you heard about the star?" she asked. Anything to change the subject. "The one the aliens are using to talk to us?"

"The light's four million years old," Madhuvanthi said. "They're all dead. Look, there's a new manifest synesthesia show. Roman and Egyptian. Something for both of us. If you won't come on an adventure with me, will you at least come to an art show? I promise I'll never ask you for archive money again. Just come to this one thing with me? And I promise I'll prune my archive starting tomorrow."

The lioness's brow was wrinkled. Madhuvanthi's voice was thin with defeat. There was no more money, and she knew it. But she couldn't stop bargaining. And the art show was a concession, something that evoked the time they used to spend together, in these imaginary worlds.

"Ferron," she said. Pleading. "Just let me do it myself."

Ferron. They weren't really communicating. Nothing was won. Her mother was doing what addicts always did when confronted—delaying, bargaining, buying time. But she'd call her daughter *Ferron* if it might buy her another twenty-four hours in her virtual paradise.

"I'll come," Ferron said. "But not until tonight. I have some work to do."

"Boss. How did you know to look for that DNA?" Damini asked, when Ferron activated her icon.

"Tell me what you found," Ferron countered.

"DNA in the BioShell composter that matches that of Chairman Miaow," she said, "and therefore that of Dexter Coffin's cat. And the composter of Rao's building is just *full* of his DNA. Rao's. Much, much more than you'd expect. Also, some of his e-mail and calendar data has been purged. I'm attempting to reconstruct—"

"Have it for the chargesheet," Ferron said. "I bet it'll show he had a meeting with Coffin the night Coffin vanished."

Dr. Rao lived not in an aptblock, even an upscale one, but in the Vertical City. Once Damini returned with the results of the warrants, Ferron got her paperwork in order for the visit. It was well after nightfall by the time she and Indrapramit, accompanied by Detective Morganti and four patrol officers, went to confront him.

They entered past shops and the vertical farm in the enormous tower's atrium. The air smelled green and healthy, and even at this hour of the night, people moved in steady streams toward the dining areas, across lush green carpets.

A lift bore the police officers effortlessly upward, revealing the lights of Bengaluru spread out below through a transparent exterior wall. Ferron looked at Indrapramit and pursed her lips. He raised his eyebrows in reply. *Conspicuous consumption.* But they couldn't very well hold it against Rao now.

They left Morganti and the patrol officers covering the exit and presented themselves at Dr. Rao's door.

"Open," Ferron said formally, presenting her warrant. "In the name of the law."

The door slid open, and Ferron and Indrapramit entered cautiously.

The flat's resident must have triggered the door remotely, because he sat at his ease on furniture set as a chaise. A gray cat with red ear-tips crouched by his knee, rubbing the side of its face against his trousers.

"New!" said the cat. "New people! Namaskar! It's almost time for tiffin."

"Dexter Coffin," Ferron said to the tall, thin man. "You are under arrest for the murder of Dr. Rao."

As they entered the lift and allowed it to carry them down the external wall of the Vertical City, Coffin standing in restraints between two of the patrol officers, Morganti said, "So. If I understand this properly, you—Coffin—actually *killed* Rao to assume his identity? Because you knew you were well and truly burned this time?"

Not even a flicker of his eyes indicated that he'd heard her.

Morganti sighed and turned her attention to Ferron. "What gave you the clue?"

"The scotophobin," Ferron said. Coffin's cat, in her new livery of gray and red, miaowed plaintively in a carrier. "He didn't have memory issues. He was using it to cram Rao's life story and eccentricities so he wouldn't trip himself up."

Morganti asked, "But why liquidate his assets? Why not take them with him?" She glanced over her shoulder. "Pardon me for speaking about you as if you were a statue, Dr. Fang. But you're doing such a good impression of one."

It was Indrapramit who gestured at the Vertical City rising at their backs. "Rao wasn't wanting for assets."

Ferron nodded. "Would you have believed he was dead if you couldn't find the money? Besides, if his debt—or some of it—was recovered, Honolulu would have less reason to keep looking for him."

"So it was a misdirect. Like the frame job around Dr. Nnebuogar and the table set for two . . . ?"

Her voice trailed off as a stark blue-white light cast knife-edged shadows across her face. Something blazed in the night sky, something as stark and brilliant as a dawning sun—but cold, as cold as light can be. As cold as a reflection in a mirror.

Morganti squinted and shaded her eyes from the shine. "Is that a *hydrogen bomb?*"

"If it was," Indrapramit said, "Your eyes would be melting."

Coffin laughed, the first sound he'd made since he'd assented to understanding his rights. "It's a supernova."

He raised both wrists, bound together by the restraints, and pointed. "In the Andromeda Galaxy. See how low it is to the horizon? We'll lose sight of it as soon as we're in the shadow of that tower."

"Al-Rahman," Ferron whispered. The lift wall was darkening to a smoky shade and she could now look directly at the light. Low to the horizon, as Coffin had said. So bright it seemed to be visible as a sphere.

"Not that star. It was stable. Maybe a nearby one," Coffin said. "Maybe they knew, and that's why they were so desperate to tell us they were out there."

"Could they have *survived* that?"

"Depends how close to Al-Rahman it was. The radiation—" Coffin shrugged in his restraints. "That's probably what killed them."

"God in Heaven," said Morganti.

Coffin cleared his throat. "Beautiful, isn't it?"

Ferron craned her head back as the point source of the incredible radiance slipped behind a neighboring building. There was no scatter glow: the rays of light from the nova were parallel, and the shadow they entered uncompromising, black as a pool of ink.

Until this moment, she would have had to slip a skin over her perceptions to point to the Andromeda Galaxy in the sky. But now it seemed like the most important thing in the world that, two and a half million years away, somebody had shouted across the void before they died.

A strange elation filled her. *Everybody talking, and nobody hears a damned thing anyone—even themselves—has to say.*

"We're here," Ferron said to the ancient light that spilled across the sky and did not pierce the shadow into which she descended. As her colleagues turned and stared, she repeated the words like a mantra. "We're here too! And we heard you."

—for Asha Cat Srinivasan Shipman, and her family

Macy Minnot's Last Christmas on Dione, Ring Racing, Fiddler's Green, The Potter's Garden

PAUL McAULEY

Here's another story by Paul McAuley, whose "The Man" appears elsewhere in this anthology, this one a linked quintet of five short stories that provide a picturesque tour of the outer solar system in a future that has just been devastated by a bitterly fought interplanetary war, and where the colonists are doing their best to recover in the aftermath.

O ne day, midway in the course of her life, Mai Kumal learned that her father had died. The solicitous eidolon that delivered the message explained that Thierry had suffered an irreversible cardiac event, and extended an invitation to travel to Dione, one of Saturn's moons, so that Mai could help scatter her father's ashes according to his last wishes.

Mai's daughter didn't think it was a good idea. "When did you last speak with him? Ten years ago?"

"Fourteen."

"Well then."

Mai said, "It was as much my fault as his that we lost contact with each other."

"But he left you in the first place. Left us."

Shahirah had a deeply moral sense of right and wrong. She hadn't spoken to or forgiven her own father after he and Mai had divorced.

Mai said, "Thierry left Earth; he didn't leave me. But that isn't the point, Shah. He wants—he wanted me to be there. He made arrangements. There is an open round-trip ticket."

"He wanted you to feel an obligation," Shahirah said.

"Of course I feel an obligation. It is the last thing I can do for him. And it will be a great adventure. It's about time I had one."

Mai was sixty-two, about the age her father had been when he'd left Earth after his wife, Mai's mother, had died. She was a mid-level civil servant, Assistant Chief Surveyor in the Department of Antiquities. She owned a small efficiency apartment in the same building where she worked, the government ziggurat in the Wassat district of al-Iskandariyya. No serious relationship since her divorce; her daughter grown-up and married, living with her husband and two children in an arcology commune in the Atlas Mountains. Shahirah tried to talk her out of it, but Mai wanted to find out what her father had been doing, in the outer dark. To find out whether he had been happy. By unriddling the mystery of his life she might discover something about herself. When your parents die, you finally take full possession of your life, and wonder how much of it has been shaped by conscious decision, and how much by inheritance in all its forms.

"There isn't anything out there for people like us," Shahirah said.

She meant ordinary people. People who had not been tweaked so that they could survive the effects of microgravity and harsh radiation, and endure life in claustrophobic habitats scattered across frozen, airless moons.

"Thierry thought there might be," Mai said. "I want to find out what it was."

She took compassionate leave, flew from al-Iskandariyya to Port Africa, Entebbe, and was placed in deep, artificial sleep at the passenger processing facility. Cradled inside a hibernaculum, she rode up the elevator to the transfer station and was loaded onto a drop ship, and forty-three days later woke in the port of Paris, Dione. After two days spent recovering from her long sleep and learning how to use a pressure suit and move around in Dione's vestigial gravity, she climbed aboard a taxi that flew in a swift suborbital lob through the night to the habitat of the Jones-Truex-Bakaleinikoff clan, her father's last home, the place where he died.

The taxi's cabin was an angular bubble scarcely bigger than a coffin, pieced together from diamond composite and a cobweb of fullerene struts, and mounted on a motor stage with three spidery legs. Mai, braced beside the pilot in a taut crash web, felt that she was falling down an endless slope, as in one of those dreams where you wake with a shock just before you hit ground. Saturn's swollen globe, subtly banded with pastel shades of yellow and brown, swung overhead and sank behind them. The pilot, a garrulous young woman, asked all kinds of questions about life on Earth, pointed out landmark craters and ridges in the dark moonscape, the line of the equatorial railway, the homely sparks of oases, habitats, and tent towns. Mai couldn't quite reconcile the territory with the maps in her p-suit's library, was startled when the taxi abruptly slewed around and fired its motor and decelerated with a rattling roar and drifted down to a kind of pad or platform set at the edge of an industrial landscape.

The person who met her wasn't the man with whom she'd discussed her father's death and her travel arrangements, but a woman, her father's former partner, Lexi Truex. They climbed into a slab-sided vehicle slung between three pairs of fat mesh wheels, and drove out along a broad highway past blockhouses, bunkers, hangars, storage tanks, and arrays of satellite dishes and transmission towers: a military complex dating from the Quiet War, according to Lexi Truex.

"Abandoned in place, as they say. We don't have any use for it, but never got around to demolishing it, either. So here it sits."

Lexi Truex was at least twenty years younger than Mai, tall and pale, hair shaven high on either side of a stiff crest of straw-colored hair. Her pressure suit was decorated with an intricate, interlocking puzzle of green and red vines. She and Thierry had been together for three years, she said. They'd met on Ceres, while she had been working as a freetrader.

"That's where he was living when I last talked to him," Mai said. It felt like a confession of weakness. This brisk, confident woman seemed to have more of a claim on her father than she did.

"He followed me to Dione, moved in with me while I was still living in the old habitat," Lexi Truex said. "That's where he got into ceramics. And then, well, he became more and more obsessed with his work, and I wasn't there a lot of the time. . . ."

Mai said that she'd done a little research, had discovered that her father had become a potter, and had seen some of his pieces.

"You can see plenty more, at the habitat," Lexi said. "He worked hard at it, and he had a good reputation. Plenty of kudos."

It turned out that Lexi Truex didn't know that on Earth, in al-Iskandariyya, Thierry had cast bronze amulets using the lost wax method and sold them to shops that catered to the high-end tourist market. Falcons, cats, lions. Gods with the heads of crocodiles or jackals. Sphinxes. Mai told Lexi that she'd helped him polish the amulets with slurried chalk paste and jewelers' rouge, and create patinas with cupric nitrate. She had a clear memory of her father hunched over a bench, using a tiny knife to free the shape of a hawk from a small block of black wax.

"He didn't ever talk about his life before he went up and out," Lexi said. "Well, he mentioned you. We all knew he had a daughter, but that was about it."

They discussed Thierry's last wishes. Lexi said that in the last few years he'd given up his work, had taken to walking the land. She supposed that he wanted them to scatter his ashes in a favorite spot. He'd been very specific that it should take place at sunrise, but the location was a mystery.

"All I know is that we follow the railway east, and then we follow his mule," Lexi said. "Might involve some cross-country hiking. Think you can manage it?"

"Walking is easier than I thought it would be," Mai said.

When she was young, she'd liked to wade out into the sea as deep as she dared and stand on tiptoe, water up to her chin, and let the waves push her backwards and forward. Walking in Dione's vestigial gravity, one-sixtieth the gravity of Earth, was a little like that. Another memory of her father: watching him make huge sand sculptures of flowers and animals on the beach. His strong fingers, his bare brown shoulders, the thatch of white hair on his chest, his total absorption in his task.

They had left the military clutter behind, were driving across a dusty plain lightly spattered with small, shallow craters. Blocks and boulders as big as houses squatting on smashed footings. A fan of debris stretching from a long elliptical dent. A line of rounded hills rising to the south: the flanks of the wall of a crater thirty kilometers in diameter, according to Lexi. Everything faintly lit by Saturnshine; everything the color of ancient ivory. It reminded Mai of old photographs, Europeans in antique costumes stiffly posed amongst excavated tombs, she'd seen in the museum in al-Qahira.

Soon, short steep ridges pushed up from the plain, nested curves thirty or forty meters high like frozen dunes, faceted here and there by cliffs rearing above fans of slumped debris. The cliffs, Mai saw, were carved with intricate frescoes, and the crests of the ridges had been sculpted into fairy-tale castles or statues of animals. A pod of dolphins emerging from a swell of ice; another swell shaped like a breaking wave with galloping horses rearing from frozen spume; an eagle taking flight; a line of elephants walking trunk to tail, skylighted against the black vacuum. The last reminding her of one of her father's bronze pieces. Here was a bluff shaped into the head of a Buddha; here was an outcrop on which a small army equipped with swords and shields were frozen in battle.

It was an old tradition, Lexi Truex said. Every Christmas, gangs from her clan's habitat and neighboring settlements congregated in a temporary city of tents and domes and ate osechi-ryo-ri and made traditional toasts in saki, vodka, and whiskey, played music, danced, and flirted, and worked on new frescoes and statues using drills and explosives and chisels.

"We like our holidays. Kwanzaa, Eid ul-Fitr, Chanukah, Diwali, Christmas, Newtonmass . . . any excuse for a gathering, a party. Your father led our gang every Christmas for ten years. The whale and the squid, along the ridge there? That's one of his designs."

"And the elephants?"

"Those too. Let me show you something," Lexi said, and drove the rolligon down the shallow slope of the embankment onto the actual surface of Dione.

It wallowed along like a boat in a choppy sea, its six fat tires raising rooster-tails of dust. Tracks ribboned everywhere, printed a year or a century ago. There was no wind here. No rain. Just a constant faint infalling of meteoritic dust, and microscopic ice particles from the geysers of Enceladus. Everything unchanging under the weak glare of the sun and the black sky, like a stage in an abandoned theater. Mai began to understand the strangeness of this little world. A frozen ocean wrapped around a rocky core, shaped by catastrophes that predated life on Earth. A stark geology empty of any human meaning. Hence the sculptures, she supposed. An attempt to humanize the inhuman.

"It's something one of my ancestors made," Lexi said, when Mai asked where they were going. "Macy Minnot. You ever heard of Macy Minnot?"

She had been from Earth. Sent out by Greater Brazil to work on a construction project in Rainbow Bridge, Callisto, she'd become embroiled in a political scandal and had been forced to claim refugee status. This was before the Quiet War, or during the beginning of it (it had been the kind of slow, creeping conflict that has no clear beginning, erupting into combat only at its very end), and Macy Minnot had ended up living with the Jones-Truex-Bakaleinikoff clan. Trying her best to assimilate, to come to terms with her exile.

As they drove around the end of a ridge, past a tumble of ice boulders carved into human figures, some caught up in a whirling dance, others eagerly pushing their way out of granitic ice, Lexi explained that one Christmas after the end of the Quiet War, her last Christmas on Dione, Macy Minnot had come up with an idea for her own sculpture, and borrowed one of the big construction machines and filled its hopper with a mix of ice dust and a thixotropic, low-temperature plastic.

"It's too cold for ice crystals to melt under pressure and bind together," Lexi said. "The plastic was a binding agent, malleable at first, gradually hardening off. So you could pack the dust into any shape. You understand?"

"I've seen snow, once."

It had been in the European Union, the Alps: a conference on security of shipping ports. Mai, freshly divorced, had taken her daughter, then a toddler. She remembered Shahirah's delight in the snow. The whole world transformed into a soft white playground.

"There's always a big party, the night before the beginning of the competition. Macy and her partner got wasted, and they started up their construction machine. Either they intended to surprise everyone, or they decided they couldn't wait. Anyway, they forgot to include any stop or override command in the instruction set they'd written. So the machine just kept going," Lexi said, and steered the rolligon through a slant of deep shadow and swung it broadside, drifting to a stop at the edge of a short, steep drop.

They were at the far side of the little flock of ridges. The rumpled, dented plain stretched away under the black sky, and little figures marched across it in a straight line.

Mai laughed. The shock of it. The madly wonderful absurdity.

"They used fullerene to make the arms and eyes and teeth," Lexi said. "The scarves are fullerene mesh. The noses are carrots. The buttons are diamond chips."

There were twenty, thirty, forty of them. Each two meters tall, composed of three spheres of descending size stacked one on top of the other. Pure white. Spaced at equal intervals. Black smiles and black stares, vivid orange noses. Scarves rippling in an impalpable breeze. Marching away like an exercise in perspective, dwindling over the horizon . . .

"Thierry loved this place," Lexi said. "He often came out here to meditate."

They sat and looked out at the line of snowmen for a long time. At last, Lexi started the rolligon and they drove around the end of the ridges and rejoined the road and drove on to the habitat of the Jones-Truex-Bakaleinikoff clan.

It was a simple dome that squatted inside the rimwall of a circular crater. A forest ran around its inner circumference; lawns and formal flowerbeds circled a central building patchworked from a dozen architectural styles, blended into each other like a coral reef. Mai's reception reminded her of the first time she'd arrived at her daughter's arcology: adults introducing themselves one by one, excited children bouncing around, bombarding her with questions. Was the sky really blue, on Earth? What held it up? Were there really wild animals that ate people?

There was a big, informal meal, a kind of picnic in a wide grassy glade in the forest, where most of the clan seemed to live. Walkways and ziplines and nets were strung between sweet chestnuts and oaks and beech trees; ring platforms were bolted around the trunks of the largest trees; pods hung from branches like the nests of weaver birds.

Mai's hosts told her that most of the clan lived elsewhere, these days. Paris. A big vacuum-organism farm on Rhea. Mars. Titan. A group out at Neptune, living in a place Macy Minnot and her partner helped build after they fled the Saturn system at the beginning of the Quiet War. The habitat was becoming more and more like a museum, people said. A repository of souvenirs from the clan's storied past.

Thierry's workshop was already part of that history. Two brick kilns, a paved square under a slant of canvas to keep off the rain occasionally produced by the dome's climate control machinery. A potter's wheel with a saddle-shaped stool. A scarred table. Tools and brushes lying where he'd left them. Neatly labeled tubs of clay slip, clay balls, glazes. A clay-stained sink under a standpipe. Lexi told Mai that Thierry had mined the clay from an old impact site. Primordial stuff billions of years old, refined to remove tars and other organic material.

Finished pieces were displayed on a rack of shelves. Dishes in crescent shapes glazed with black and white arcs representing segments of Saturn's rings. Bowls shaped like craters. Squarish plates stamped with the surface features of tracts of Dione and other moons. Craters, ridges, cliffs. Plates with spattered black shapes on a white ground, like the borderland between Iapetus's dark and light halves. Vases shaped like shepherd moons. A scattering of irregular chunks in thick white glaze— pieces of the rings. A glazed tan ribbon with snowmen lined along it . . .

It was so very different from the tourist stuff Thierry had made, yet recognizably his. And highly collectible, according to Lexi. Unlike most artists in the outer system, Thierry hadn't trawled for sponsorship and subscriptions, made pieces to order, or given access to every stage of his work. He had not believed in the democratization of the creative process. He had not been open to input. His work had been very private, very personal. He hadn't liked to talk about it, Lexi said. He hadn't let anyone get close to that part of him. This secrecy had eventually driven them apart, but it had also contributed to his reputation. People were intrigued by his work, by his response to the moonscapes of the Saturn system, his outsider's perspective, because he refused to explain it. He'd earned large amounts of credit and kudos—tradeable reputation—from sale of his ceramics, but had spent hardly any of it. The work was enough, as far as he'd been concerned. Mai, remembering the sand sculptures, thought she understood a little of this. She asked if he'd been happy, but no one seemed able to answer the question.

"He seemed to be happy, when he was working," the habitat's patriarch, Rory Jones, said.

"He didn't talk much," someone else said.

"He liked to be alone," Lexi said. "I don't mean he was selfish. Well, maybe he was. But he mostly lived inside his head."

"He made this place his home," Rory said, "and we were happy to have him living here."

The habitat's chandelier lights had dimmed to a twilight glow. Most of the children had wandered off to bed; so had many of the adults. Those left sat around a campfire on a hearth of meteoritic stone, passing around a flask of honeysuckle wine, telling Mai stories about her father's life on Dione.

He had walked around Dione, one year. A journey of some seven thousand kilometers. Carrying a bare minimum of consumables, walking from shelter to shelter, settlement to settlement. Staying in a settlement for a day or ten days or twenty before moving on. Walking the world was much more than exploring or understanding it, Mai's hosts told her. It was a way of re-creating it. Of making it real. Of binding yourself to it. Not every outer walked around their world, but those who did were considered virtuous, and her father was one such.

"Most visitors only see the parts they know about," a woman told Mai. "The famous views, the famous shrines and oases. A fair few come to climb the ice cliffs of Padua Chasmata. And they are spectacular climbs. Four or five kilometers. Huge views when you top out. But we prefer our own routes, on ridges or rimwalls you'd hardly notice, flying over them. There's a very gnarly climb close by, in a small crater the military used as a trash dump in the Quiet War. The achievement isn't the view, but testing yourself against your limits. Your father understood that. He was no ring runner."

This led into another story. It seemed that there was a traditional race around the equator of another of Saturn's moons, Mimas. It was held every four years: taking part in it was a great honor. Shortly after the end of the Quiet War, a famous athlete, Sony Shoemaker, had come to Mimas, determined to win it. She had trained on Earth's Moon for a year, had bought a custom-made p-suit from one of the best suit tailors in Camelot. Like all the other competitors, she had qualified by completing a course around the peak in the center of the rimwall of Arthur crater within a hundred and twenty hours. Fifty days later she set out, ranked last in a field of thirty-eight.

Mimas was a small moon, about a third the size of Dione. A straight route around its equator would be roughly two and a half thousand kilometers long, but there was no straight route. Unlike Dione, Mimas had never been resurfaced by ancient floods of water-ice lava. Its surface was primordial, pockmarked, riven. Craters overlapping craters. Craters inside craters. Craters strung along rimwalls of larger craters. And the equatorial route crossed Herschel, the largest crater of all, a hundred and thirty kilometers across, a third of the diameter of Mimas, its steep rimwalls kilometers tall, its floor shattered by blocky, chaotic terrain.

The race was as much a test of skill in reading and understanding the landscape as of endurance. Competitors were allowed to choose their own route and set out caches of supplies, but could only use public shelters, and were disqualified if they called for help. Some died rather than fail. Sony Shoemaker did not fail, and astonished afficionados by coming in fourth. She stayed on Mimas, afterwards. She trained. Four years later she won, beating the reigning champion, Diamond Jack Dupree.

He did not take his defeat lightly. He challenged Sony Shoemaker to another race. A unique race, never before attempted. A race around a segment of Saturn's rings.

Although the main rings are seventy-three thousand kilometers across, a fifth of the distance between Earth and the Moon, they average just ten meters in thickness, but oscillations propagating across the dense lanes of the B ring pile up material at its outer edge, creating peaks a kilometer high. Diamond Jack Dupree challenged Sony Shoemaker to race across one of these evanescent mountains.

The race did not involve anything remotely resembling running, but it was muscle powered, using highly modified p-suits equipped with broad wings of alife material with contractile pseudo-musculatures and enough area to push, faintly, lightly, against ice pebbles embedded in a fragile lace of ice gravel and ice dust. Cloud swimming. A delicate rippling controlled by fingers and toes that would slowly build up momentum. The outcome determined not by speed or strength, because if you went too fast you'd either sheer away from the ephemeral surface or plough under it, but by skill and judgment and patience.

Sony Shoemaker did not have to accept Diamond Jack Dupree's challenge. She had already proved herself. But the novelty of it, the audacity, intrigued her. And so, a year to the day after her victory on Mimas, after six months hard training in water tanks and on the surface of the dusty egg of Methone, one of Saturn's smallest moons, Sony Shoemaker and Diamond Jack Dupree set off in their manta-ray p-suits, swimming across the peaks and troughs of a mountainous, icy cloud at the edge of the B ring.

It was the midsummer equinox. The orbits of Saturn and his rings and moons were aligned with the sun; the mountains cast ragged shadows across the surface of the B ring; the two competitors were tiny dark arrowheads rippling across a luminous slope. Moving very slowly, almost imperceptibly, to begin with. Gradually gaining momentum, skimming along at ten and then twenty kilometers an hour.

There was no clear surface. The ice-particle mountains emitted jets and curls of dust and vapor. There were currents and convection cells. It was like trying to swim across the flank of a sandstorm.

Sony Shoemaker was the first to sink. Some hundred and thirty kilometers out, she moved too fast, lost contact with a downslope, and plunged through ice at the bottom and was caught in a current that subducted her deep into the interior. She was forced to use the jets of her p-suit to escape, and was retrieved by her support ship. Diamond Jack Dupree wallowed on for a short distance, and then he too sank. And never reappeared.

His p-suit beacon cut off when he submerged, and although the support ships swept the mountain with radar and microwaves for several days, no trace of him was ever found. He had vanished, but there were rumors that he was not dead. That he had dived into a camouflaged lifepod he'd planted on the route, slept out the rescue attempts, and gone on the drift or joined a group of homesteaders, satisfied that he had regained his honor.

There had been other races held on the ring mountains, but no one had ever beaten Diamond Jack Dupree's record of one hundred and forty-three kilometers. No one wanted to. Not even Sony Shoemaker.

"That's when she crossed the line," Rory told Mai. "Winning the race around Mimas didn't make her one of us. But respecting Diamond Jack Dupree's move, that was it. Your father crossed that line, too. He knew."

"Because he walked around the world," Mai said. She was trying to understand. It was important to them, and it seemed important to them that she understood.

"Because he knew what it meant," Rory said.

"One of us," someone said, and all the outers laughed.

Tall skinny pale ghosts jackknifed on stools or sitting cross-legged on cushions. All elbows and knees. Their faces angular masks in the firelight flicker. Mai felt a moment of irreality. As if she were an intruder on someone else's dream. She was still very far from accepting this strange world, these strange people. She was a tourist in their lives, in the place her father had made his home.

She said, "What does it mean, go on the drift? Is it like your wanderjahrs?"

She'd discovered that custom when she'd done some background research. After reaching majority, young outers often set out on extended and mostly unplanned tours of the moons of Saturn and Jupiter. Working odd jobs, experiencing all kinds of cultures and meeting all kinds of people before at last returning home and settling down.

"Not exactly," Lexi said. "You can come home from a wanderjahr. But when you go on the drift, that's where you live."

"In your skin, with whatever you can carry and no more," Rory said.

"In your p-suit," someone said.

"That's what I said," Rory said.

"And homesteaders?" Mai said.

Lexi said, "That's when you move up and out to somewhere no one else lives, and make a life there. The solar system out to Saturn is industrialized, more or less. More and more people want to move away from all that, get back to what we once were."

"Out to Uranus," someone said.

"Neptune," someone else said.

"There are homesteaders all over the Centaurs now," Rory said. "You know the Centaurs, Mai? Primordial planetoids that orbit between Saturn and Neptune. The source of many short-term comets."

"Macy Minnot and her friends settled one, during the Quiet War," Lexi said. "It was only a temporary home, for them, but for many it's become permanent."

"Even the scattered disk is getting crowded now, according to some people," Rory said.

"Planetoids like the Centaurs," Lexi told Mai, "with long, slow orbits that take them inward as far as Neptune, and out past Pluto, past the far edge of the Kuiper belt."

"The first one, Fiddler's Green, was settled by mistake," Rory said.

"It's a legend," a young woman said.

"I once met someone who knew someone who saw it, once," Rory said. "Passed within a couple of million kilometers and spotted a chlorophyll signature, but didn't stop because they were on their way to somewhere else."

"The very definition of a legend," the woman said.

"It was a shipwreck," Rory told Mai. "Castaways on a desert island. I'm sure it still happens on the high seas of Earth."

"There are still shipwrecks," Mai said. "Although everything is connected to everything else, so anyone who survives is likely to be found quickly."

"The outer dark beyond Neptune is still largely uninhabited," Rory said. "We haven't yet finished cataloguing everything in the Kuiper Belt and the scattered disk, and everything is most definitely not connected to everything else, out there. How the story goes, when the Quiet War heated up, a ship from the Jupiter system was hit by a drone as it approached Saturn. Its motors were badly damaged and it ploughed through the Saturn system and kept going. It couldn't decelerate, couldn't reach anywhere useful. Its crew and passengers went into hibernation. Sixty or seventy years later, those still alive woke up. They were approaching a planetoid somewhat beyond the orbit of Pluto, had just enough reaction mass to match orbits with it.

"The ship was carrying construction machinery. The survivors used the raw tars and clays of the planetoid to build a habitat. A small bubble of air and light and heat, spun up to give a little gravity, farms and gardens on the inside, vacuum organisms growing on the outside, like the floating worldlets in the Belt. They called it Fiddler's Green, after an old legend from Earth about a verdant and uncharted island sometimes encountered by becalmed sailors. Perhaps you know it, Mai."

"I'm afraid I don't."

"They built a garden," the young woman said, "but they didn't ever try to call for help. How likely is that?"

Rory said, "Perhaps they didn't call for help because they believed the Three Powers were still controlling the systems of Saturn and Jupiter. Or perhaps they were happy, living where they did. They didn't need help. They didn't want to go home because

Fiddler's Green was their home. The planetoid supplied all the raw material they required. The ship's fusion generator gave them power, heat, and light. They are still out there, traveling beyond the Kuiper Belt. Living in houses woven from branches and leaves. Farming. Falling in love, raising families, dying. A world entire."

"A romance of regression," the young woman said.

"Perhaps it is no more than a fairy tale," Rory said. "But nothing in it is impossible. There are hundreds of places like Fiddler's Green. Thousands. It's just an outlier, an extreme example of how far people are prepared to go to make their own world, their own way of living."

The outers talked about that. Mai told about her life in al-Iskandariyya, her childhood, her father's work, her work in the Department of Antiquities, the project she'd recently seen to completion, the excavation of a twenty-first-century shopping mall that had been buried in a sandstorm during the Overturn. At last there was a general agreement that they should sleep. The outers retired to hammocks or cocoons; Mai made her bed on the ground, under the spreading branches of a grandfather oak, uneasy and troubled, aware as she had not been, in her cubicle in the port hostel, of the freezing vacuum beyond the dome's high transparent roof. It was night inside the dome, and night outside, too. Stars shining hard and cold beyond the black shadows of the trees.

Everything that seemed natural here—the ring forest, the lawns, the dense patches of vegetables and herbs—was artificial. Fragile. Vulnerable. Mai tried and failed to imagine living in a little bubble so far from the sun that it was no more than the brightest star in the sky. She fretted about the task that lay ahead, the trek to the secret place where she and Lexi Truex would scatter Thierry's ashes.

At last sleep claimed her, and she dreamed of hanging over the Nile and its patchwork borders of cotton fields, rice fields, orchards, and villages, everything falling away, dwindling into tawny desert as she fell into the endless well of the sky. . . .

It was a silly anxiety dream, but it stayed with Mai as she and Lexi Truex drove north to a station on the railway that girdled Dione's equator, and boarded the diamond bullet of a railcar and sped out across the battered plain. They were accompanied by Thierry's mule, Archie. A sturdy robot porter that, with its flat loadbed, small front-mounted sensor turret, and three pairs of articulated legs, somewhat resembled a giant cockroach. Archie carried spare airpacks and a spray pistol device, and refused to tell Mai and Lexi their final destination, or why it was important that they reach it before sunrise. Everything would become clear when they arrived, it said.

According to Lexi, the pistol used pressurized water vapor from flash-heated ice to spray material from pouches plugged into its ports, such as the pouch of gritty powder, the residue left from resomation of Thierry's body, or the particles of thixotropic plastic in a pouch already plugged into the pistol. The same kind of plastic Macy Minnot and her partner had used to shape ice dust into snowmen.

"We're going to spray-paint something with the old man's ashes," Lexi said. "That much is clear. The question is, what's the target?"

Archie refused to answer her in several polite ways.

The railcar drove eastward through the night. Like almost all of Saturn's moons, like Earth's Moon, Dione's orbital period, some sixty-six hours, was exactly equal to the time it took to complete a single rotation on its axis, so that one side permanently faced Saturn. Its night was longer than an entire day on Earth.

Saturn's huge bright crescent sank westward as the train crossed a plain churned and stamped with craters. Every so often, Mai spotted the fugitive gleam of the dome or angular tent of a settlement. A geometric fragment of chlorophyll green gleaming in the moonscape's frozen battlefield. A scatter of bright lights in a small crater. Patchworked fields of black vacuum organisms spread across tablelands and slopes, plantations of what looked like giant sunflowers standing up along ridges, all of them facing east, waiting for the sun.

The elevated railway shot out across a long and slender bridge that crossed the trough of Eurotas Chasmata, passing over broad slumps of ice that descended into a river of fathomless shadow. The far side was fretted with lesser canyons and low, bright cliffs rising stepwise with broad benches between. The railway turned north to follow a long pass that cut between high cliffs, then bent eastwards again. At last, a long ridge rolled up from the horizon: the southern flanks of the rimwall of Amata crater.

The railcar slowed, passed through a short tunnel cut through a ridge, ran through pitch-black shadow beyond and out into Saturnshine, and sidled into a station cantilevered above a slope. Below, a checkerboard of scablike vacuum organisms stretched toward the horizon. Above, the dusty slope, spattered with small, sharp craters, rose to a gently scalloped edge, stark against the black sky.

Several rolligons were parked in the garage under the station. Following Archie's instructions, Lexi and Mai climbed into one of the vehicles (Archie sprang onto the flat roof) and drove along a track that slanted toward the top of the slope. After five kilometers, the track topped out on a broad bench, swung around a shelter, a stubby cylinder jutting under a heap of fresh white ice blocks, a way point for hikers and climbers on their way into the interior of the huge crater, and followed the curve of the bench eastward until it was interrupted by a string of small craters twenty or thirty meters across.

Lexi and Mai climbed out and Lexi rechecked Mai's p-suit and they followed Archie around the smashed bowls of the craters. There were many bootprints trampled into the dust. Thierry's prints, coming and going. Mai tried not to step on them. Strange to think they might last for millions of years.

"It is not far," Archie said, responding to Lexi's impatient questions. "It is not far."

Mai felt a growing glee as she loped along, felt that she could bounce away like the children in the habitat, leap over ridges, cross craters in a single bound, span this little world in giant footsteps. She'd felt like this when her first grandchild had been born. Floating on a floodtide of happiness and relief. Free of responsibility. Liberated from the biological imperative.

Now and then her pressure suit beeped a warning; once, when she exceeded some inbuilt safety parameter, it took over and slowed her headlong bounding gait and brought her to a halt, swaying at the dust-softened rim of a small crater. Reminding her that she was dependent on the insulation and integrity of her own personal space ship, its native intelligence, the whisper of oxygen in her helmet.

On the far side of the crater, cased in her extravagantly decorated p-suit, Lexi turned with a bouncing step, asked Mai if she was okay.

"I'm fine!"

"You're doing really well," Lexi said, and asked Archie for the fifth or tenth time if they were nearly there.

"It is not far."

Lexi waited as Mai skirted the rim of the crater with the bobbing shuffle she'd been taught, and they went on. Mai was hyperaware of every little detail in the moonscape. Everything fresh and strange and new. The faint flare of Saturnshine on her helmet visor. The rolling blanket of gritty dust, dimpled with tiny impacts. Rayed scatterings of sharp bright fragments. A blocky ice-boulder as big as a house perched in a shatter of debris. The gentle rise and fall of the ridge, stretching away under the black sky where untwinkling stars showed everywhere. Saturn's crescent looming above the western horizon. The silence and stillness of the land. The stark reality of it.

She imagined her father walking here, under this same sky. Alone in a moonscape where no trace of human activity could be seen.

The last and largest crater was enclosed by ramparts of ice blocks three stories high and cemented with a silting of dust. Archie didn't hesitate, climbing a crude stairway hacked into the ice and plunging through a ragged cleft. Lexi and Mai followed, and the crater's bowl opened below them, tilted toward the plain beyond the curve of the ridge. The spark of the sun stood just above the horizon. An arc of light defined the far edge of the moonscape; sunlight lit a segment of the crater's floor, where boulders lay tumbled amongst a maze of bootprints and drag marks.

"At least we got the timing right," Lexi said.

"What are we supposed to be seeing?" Mai said.

Lexi asked Archie the same question.

"It will soon become apparent."

They stood side by side, Lexi and Mai, wavering in the faint grip of gravity. The sunlit half of the crater directly in front of them, the dark half beyond, shadows shrinking back as the sun slowly crept into the sky. And then they saw the first shapes emerging.

Columns or tall vases. Cylindrical, woman-sized or larger. Different heights in no apparent order. Each one shaped from translucent ice tinted with pastel shades of pink and purple, and threaded with networks of darker veins.

Lexi stepped down the broken blocks of the inner slope and moved across the floor. Mai followed.

The nearest vases were twice their height. Lexi reached out to one of them, brushed the fingertips of her gloved hand across the surface.

"These have been hand-carved," she said. "You can see the tool marks."

"Carved from what?"

"Boulders, I guess. He must have carried the ice chips out of here."

They were both speaking softly, reluctant to disturb the quiet of this place. Lexi said that the spectral signature of the ice corresponded with artificial photosynthetic pigments. She leaned close, her visor almost kissing the bulge of the vase, reported that it was doped with microscopic vacuum organisms.

"There are structures in here, too," she said. "Long fine wires. Flecks of circuitry."

"Listen," Mai said.

"What?"

"Can't you hear it?"

It was a kind of interference on the common band Mai and Lexi were using to talk. Faint and broken. Hesitant. Scraps of pure tones rising and fading, rising again.

"I hear it," Lexi said.

The sound grew in strength as more and more vases emerged into sunlight. Long notes blending into a polyphonic harmony.

The microscopic vacuum organisms were soaking up sunlight, Lexi said, after a while. Turning light into electricity, powering something that responded to changes in the structure of the ice. Strain gauges perhaps, coupled to transmitters.

"The sunlight warms the ice, every so slightly," she said. "It expands asymmetrically, the embedded circuitry responds to the microscopic stresses. . . ."

"It's beautiful, isn't it?"

"Yes . . ."

It was beautiful. A wild, aleatory chorus rising and falling in endless circles above the ground of a steady bass pulse . . .

They stood there a long time, while the vases sang. There were a hundred of them, more than a hundred. A field or garden of vases. Clustered like organ pipes. Standing alone on shaped pedestals. Gleaming in the sunlight. Stained with cloudy blushes of pink and purple. Singing, singing.

At last, Lexi took Mai's gloved hand and led her across the crater floor to where the robot mule, Archie, was waiting. Mai took out the pouch of human dust and they plugged it into the spray pistol's spare port. Lexi switched on the pistol's heaters, showed Mai how to use the simple trigger mechanism.

"Which one shall we spray?" Mai said.

Lexi smiled behind the fishbowl visor of her helmet.

"Why not all of them?"

They took turns. Standing well back from the vases, triggering brief bursts of gritty ice that shot out in broad fans and lightly spattered the vases in random patterns. Lexi laughed.

"The old bastard," she said. "It must have taken him hundreds of days to make this. His last and best secret."

"And we're his collaborators," Mai said.

It took a while to empty the pouch. Long before they had finished, the music of the vases had begun to change, responding to the subtle shadow patterns laid on their surfaces.

At last the two women had finished their work and stood still, silent, elated, listening to the music they'd made.

That night, back under the dome of the Jones-Truex-Bakaleinikoff habitat, Mai thought of her father working in that unnamed crater high on the rimwall of Amata crater. Chipping at adamantine ice with chisels and hammers. Listening to the song of his vases, adding a new voice, listening again. Alone under the empty black sky, happily absorbed in the creation of a sound garden from ice and sunlight.

And she thought of the story of Fiddler's Green, the bubble of light and warmth and air created from materials mined from the chunk of tarry ice it orbited. Of the people living there. The days of exile becoming a way of life as their little world swung further and further away from the sun's hearthfire. Green days of daily tasks and small pleasures. Farming, cooking, weaving new homes in the hanging forest on the inside of the bubble's skin. A potter shaping dishes and bowls from primordial clay. Children chasing each other, flitting like schools of fish between floating islands of trees. The music of their laughter. The unrecorded happiness of ordinary life, out there in the outer dark.

twenty Lights to "The Land of snow"

MiCHAEL BiSHOP

Michael Bishop is one of the most acclaimed and respected members of that highly talented generation of writers who entered SF in the 1970s. His renowned short fiction has appeared in almost all the major magazines and anthologies, and has been gathered in four collections: Blooded On Arachne, One Winter in Eden, Close Encounters with the Deity, *and* Emphatically Not SF, Almost. *In 1981 he won the Nebula Award for his novelette* The Quickening, *and in 1983 he won another Nebula Award for his novel* No Enemy But Time, *as well as winning the Mythopoeic Fantasy Award for his novel* Unicorn Mountain, *and the Shirley Jackson Award for his short story "The Pile" (based on notes left behind on his late son Jamie's computer). His other novels include* Transfigurations, Stolen Faces, Ancient of Days, Catacomb Years, Eyes of Fire, The Secret Ascension, Count Geiger's Blues, *and the acclaimed baseball fantasy* Brittle Innings. *His most recent book is the big retrospective collection* The Door Gunner and Other Perilous Flights of Fancy: A Michael Bishop Retrospective. *Recently retired as writer-in-residence at LaGrange College in West Central Georgia, Bishop lives in nearby Pine Mountain with his wife, Jeri, also a fledgling retiree.*

In the complex and thoughtful novella that follows, the first core SF story Bishop has told in some years, and a welcome return to the days when he was turning out SF novellas such as the famous "Death and Designation Among the Asadi," he sweeps us along with Tibetan dissidents and refugees who are fleeing to the stars in a generation ship in company with the Dalai Lama—or perhaps more than one.

EXCERPTS FROM *THE COMPUTER LOGS* *OF OUR RELUCTANT DALAI LAMA*

YEARS IN TRANSIT: 82 OUT OF 106?
COMPUTER LOGS OF THE DALAI LAMA-TO-BE, AGE 7

Aboard *Kalachakra*, I open my eyes in Amdo Bay. Sleep still pops in me, yowling like a really hurt cat trying to well itself. I look sidelong out my foggy eggshell. Many ghosts crowd near to see me leave the bear sleep that everybody in a strut-ship some-times dreams in. Why have all these somnacicles up-phased to become ship-haunters? Why do so many crowd the grave-cave of my Greta-snooze?

"Greta Bryn"—that's my mama's voice—"can you hear me, kiddo?"

Yes I can. I have no deafness after I up-phase. Asleep even, I hear Mama talk in her dreams and cosmic rays crackle off *Kalachakra*'s plasma shield out in front (to keep us all from going dead), and the crackle from Earth across the rolling ocean of all-around-us space.

"Greta Bryn?"

She sounds like Atlanta, Daddy says. To me she sounds like Mama, which I want her to play-act now. She keeps bunnies, minks, guineas, and many other tiny crits down along our sci-tech cylinder in Kham Bay. But hearing her doesn't pulley me into sit-up pose. To get there, I stretch my soft parts and my bones.

"Easy, baby," Mama says.

A man in white unhooks me. A woman pinches me at the wrist so I won't twist the fuel tube or pulse counter. They have already shot me in the heart, to rev its beating. Now I do sit up and look around, clearer. Daddy stands nearby, showing me his crumply face.

"Hey, Gee Bee," he says, but doesn't grab my hand.

His coverall tag is my roll-call name: **Brasswell**. A clunky name for a girl and not too fine for Daddy, who looks thirty-seven or maybe fifty-fifteen, a number Mama says he uses to joke his fitness. He does *whore-to-culture*—another puzzle-funny of his—so that later we can turn Guge green, and maybe survive.

I feel sick, like juice gone sour in my tummy has gushed into my mouth. I start to elbow out. My eyes grow pop-out big, my fists shake like rattles. Now Daddy grabs me, mouth by my ear: "*Shhhh shhh shh.*" Mama touches my other cheek. Every-body else falls back to watch. That's scary too.

After a seem-like century I ask, "Are we there yet?"

Everybody yuks at my funniness. I drop my legs through the eggshell door. My hotness has colded off, a lot.

A bald brown man in orangey-yellow robes comes up so Mama and Daddy must stand off aside. I remember, sort of. This person has a really hard Tibetan name: *Nyendak Trungpa*. My last up-phase he made me say it a billion times so I would not forget. I was already four, but I almost forgetted anyway.

"What's your name?" Minister Trungpa asks me.

He already knows, but I blink and say, "Greta Bryn Brasswell."

"And where are you?"

"*Kalachakra*," I say. "Our strut-ship."

"Point to your parents, please."

I do, it's simple. They're wide-awake ship-haunters now, real-live ghosts.

He asks, "Where are we going?"

"Guge," I say, another simple ask.

"What exactly is Guge, Greta Bryn?"

But I don't want to think—only to drink, my tongue's so thick with sourness. "A planet," I at last get out.

"Miss Brasswell"—now Minister T's being a smart aleck—"tell me two things you know about Guge."

I sort of ask, "It's 'The Land of Snow,' this dead king's place off to the west in olden Tibet?"

"Excellent!" Minister T says. "And its second meaning for us *Kalachakrans*?"

I think again, harder: "A faraway world to live on?"

"Where, intelligent miss?"

Another easy ask: "In the Goldilocks Zone," a funny name for it.

"But where, Greta Bryn, is this so-called Goldilocks Zone?"

"Around a star called *Gluh*—" I almost get stuck. "Around a star called Gliese 581." *GLEE-zha* is how I say it.

Bald Minister Trungpa grins. His face looks like a brown China plate with an up-curving crack. "She's fine," he tells the ghosts in the grave-cave. "And I believe she's the 'One.'"

Sometimes we must come up. We must wake and eat and drink, and move about so we can heal from ursidormizine sleep and not die before we reach Guge. When I come up this time, I get my own nook that snugs in the habitat drum called Amdo Bay. It has a vidped booth for learning from, with lock belts for when the AG goes out. It belongs to only me; it's not just one in a common space like most ghosts use.

Finally I ask, "What did that Minister T mean?"

"About what?" Mama doesn't eye me when she speaks.

"That I'm the 'One.' Which 'One'? Why'd he say that?"

"He's upset and everybody aboard has gone a little loco."

"Why?" But maybe I know. We ride so long that anyone riding with us sooner or later crazies up: *inboard fever.* Captain Xao once warned of this.

Mama says, "His Holiness, Sakya Gyatso, has died, so we're stupid with grief and thinking hard about how to replace him. Minister T, our late Dalai Lama's closest friend, thinks you're his rebirth, Greta Bryn, his heaven-sent successor."

I don't get this. "He thinks I'm not I?"

"I guess not. Grief has fuddled his reason, but maybe just temporarily."

"*I am I*," I say to Mama awful hot, and she agrees.

But I remember the Dalai Lama. When I was four, he played Go Fish with me in Amdo Bay during my second up-phase. Daddy sneak-named him "Yoda," like from *Star Wars*, but he looked more like skinny Mr. Peanut on the peanut tins. He wore a one-lens thing and a funny soft yellow hat, and he taught me a song, "Loving the Ant, Loving the Elephant." After that, I had to take my ursidormizine and hibernize. Now Minister T says the DL is I, or I am he, but surely Mama hates as much as I do how such stupidity could maybe steal me off from her.

"I don't look like Sakya Gyatso. I'm a girl, and I'm not an Asian person." Then I yell at Mama, "I am I!"

"Actually," she says, "things have changed, and what you speak as truth may have also changed, kiddo."

Everybody who gets a say in Amdo Bay now thinks that Minister Nyendak Trungpa calls me correctly. I am not I: I am the next Dalai Lama.

The Twenty-First, Sakya Gyatso, has died, and I must put on his sandals, which will not fit. Mama says he died of natural causes, but too young for it to *look* natural. He hit fifty-four, but he won't hit Guge. If I am he, I must take his place in "The Land of Snow" as colony dukpa, Tibetan for shepherd. That job scares me.

A good thing has come from this scary thing: I don't have to go back up into my egg pod and then down again. I stay up-phase. I *must*. I have too much to learn to drowse forever, even if I can sleep-learn by hypnoloading. Now I have a vidped booth that I sit in to learn and a tutor-guy, Lawrence ("Larry") Rinpoche, who loads on me a lot.

How old has all my earlier sleep-loading made me? Hibernizing, I hit seven and learnt while dreaming.

People should not call me *Her Holiness*. I am a girl person—not a Chinese or a Tibetan. I tell Larry these things the first time he comes to my room in Amdo. I've seen him in spectals about samurai and spacers, where he looks dark-haired and chest-strong. Now, anymore, he isn't. He has silver hair and hips like Mama's. His eyes do a flash thing, though, even when he's not angry, and it throws him back into the spectals he once star-played in as cool guy Lawrence Lake.

"Do I look Chinese, or Tibetan, or even Indian?" Larry asks.

"No, you don't. But you don't look like no girl either."

"A girl, Your Holiness." Larry must correct me. Mama says he will teach me logic, Tibetan art and culture, Sanskrit, Buddhist philosophy, and medicine (space and otherwise). And also poetry, music and drama, astronomy, astrophysics, synonyms, and Tibetan, Chinese, and English. Plus cinema, radio/TV history, politics and pragmatism in deep-space colony planting, and lots of other stuff.

"No girl ever got to be Dalai Lama," I tell Larry.

"Yes, but our Fourteenth predicted his successor would hail from a place outside Tibet, and that he might re-ensoul not as a boy but as a girl."

"But Sakya Gyatso, our last, can't stick his soul in *this* girl." I cross my arms and turn in a klutz-o turn.

"O Little Ocean of Wisdom, tell me why not."

Stupid tutor-guy. "He died after I got borned. How can a soul jump in the skin of somebody already borned?"

"*Born*, Your Holiness. But it's easy. It just jumps. The *samvattanika viññana*, the evolving consciousness of a Bodhisattva, jumps where it likes."

"Then what about me, Greta Bryn?" I tap-tap my chest.

Larry tilts his ginormous head. "What do *you* think?"

Oh, that old trick. "Did it kick me out? If it kicked me out, where did *I* go?"

"Do you *feel* it kicked you out, Your Holiness?"

"I feel it never got in. Inside, I feel that I . . . *own myself.*"

"Maybe you do, but maybe his *punarbhava*"—his 're-becoming'—is in there mixing with your own personality."

"But that's so scary."

"What did you think of Sakya Gyatso, the last Dalai Lama? Did he scare you?"

"No, I *liked* him."

"You like everybody, Your Holiness."

"Not anymore."

Larry laughs. He sounds like he sounded in *The Return of the Earl of Epsilon Eridani.* "Even if the process has something unorthodox about it, child, why avoid mixing your soul with that of a distinguished man you liked?"

I don't answer this windy ask. Instead, I say, "Why did he have to die, Mister Larry?"

"Greta, he didn't have much choice. Somebody killed him."

Every "day" I stay up-phase. Every day I study and I try to understand what's happening on *Kalachakra*, and how the last Dalai Lama, at swim in my soul, has slipped his *bhava*, "becoming again," into my *bhava*, or "becoming now," and so has become a thing old and new all at once.

Larry tells me just to imagine one candle lighting off another (even though you'd be crazy to light anything inside a starship), but my candle was already lit before the last Lama's got snuffed, and I never even smelt it go out. Larry laughs and says His Dead Holiness's flame "never quenched, but did go dim during its forty-nine-day voyage to *bardo*." Bardo, I think, must look like a fish tank that the soul tries to swim in even with nothing in it.

Up-phase, I learn more about *Kalachakra.* I don't need my tutor-guy. I wander all about, between studying and tutoring times. When the artificial gravity cuts off, as it does a lot, I swim my ghost self into nooks and bays almost anywhere.

Our ship has a loco largeness, like a tunnel turning through star-smeared space, like a line of railroad tank cars *humming* through the Empty Vast *without any hum.* I saw such trains in my hypnoloading sleeps. Now I peep them as spectals and mini-holos and even palm pix.

Larry likes for me to do that too. He says anything "fusty and fun" is OK by him, if it tutors me well. And I don't *need* him to help me twig when I snoop *Kalachakra.* I learn by drifting, floating, swimming, counting, and just by asking ghosts what I want to know.

Here's what I've learnt by reading and vidped-tasking, snooping and asking:

1. UNS *Kalachakra* hauls 990 human asses ("and also the rest of each bloke aboard"—Dad's dumb joke) to a world in the Goldilocks Zone of the Gliese 581 solar system, 20.3 lights from *Sol*, the assumed-to-be-live-on-able planet Gliese 581 g.

2. Captain Xao says that most of us on *Kalachakra* spend our journey in ursidormizine slumber to dream about our colonizing work on Guge. The greatest number of somnacicles—sleepers—have their egg pods in Amdo Bay toward the nose of our ship. (These hibernizing lazybones look like frozen

cocoons in their see-through eggs.) Those of us more often up-phase slumber at "night" in Kham Bay, where tech folk and crew do their work. At the rear of our habitat drum lies U-Tsang Bay, which I haven't visited, but where, Mama says, our Bodhisattvas—monks, nuns, lamas, and such—reside, up-phase or down-.

3. All must wriggle up-phase once each year or so. You cannot hibernize longer than two at a snooze because we human somnacicles go dodgy quite soon during our third year drowse, so Captain Xao tells us, "We'll need every hand on the ground once we're all down on Guge." ("Every *foot* on the ground," I would say.)

4. Red dwarf star *Gliese 581*, also known as *Zarmina*, spectral class M3V, awaits us in constellation Libra. Captain Xao calls it the eighty-seventh closest known solar system to our sun. It has seven planets and spurts out X-rays. It will flame away much sooner than *Sol*, but so far in the future that no one on *Kalachakra* will care a toot.

5. Gliese 581 g, aka Guge, goes around its dwarf in a circle, nearly. It has one face stuck toward its sun, but enough gravity to hold its gasses to it; enough— more than Earth's—so you can walk on it without drifting away. But it will really hot you on the sun-stuck side and chill you nasty on its drear dark rear. It's got rocks topside and magma in its zonal mountains. We must live in the in-between stripes of the terminator, *not* some old spectal but safe spots for bipeds with blood to boil or kidneys to broil. Or maybe we'll freeze, if we land in the black. So two hurrahs for Guge, and three for "The Land of Snow" in the belts where we hope to plug in.

6. We know Guge has mass. It isn't, says Captain Xao, a "pipedream or a mirage." Our onboard telescope found it twelve Earth years ago, seventy out from Moon-orbit kickoff, with maybe twenty or so to go before we really get there. Hey, I'm more than a smidgen scared to arrive, hey, maybe a million smidgens.

7. I'm also scared to stay an up-phase ghost on *Kalachakra*. Like a snow leopard or a yeti, my life is in deep-doo-doo danger. I don't want to step up to Dalai Lamahood. It's got its perks, but until Captain Xao, Minister Trungpa, Law-rence Rinpoche, Mama, Daddy, and our security folk find out **WHO** kilt the Twenty-First DL, Greta Bryn Brasswell, a maybe-DL, thinks her young life worth one dried pea in a vacu-meal pack. Maybe.

8. In the tunnels running between Amdo, Kham, and U-Tsang Bays, the ghost of a snow leopard drifts. It has cindery spots swirled into the frosting of its fur. Its eyes leap yellow-green in the dimness when it gazes back at two-leggers like me. It jets from a holo-beam, but I don't know how or where from. In my dreams, I turn when I see it. My heart flutter-pounds toward a shutdown . . . which I fear it will, truly.

9. Sakya Gyatso spent many years as an up-phase ghost on *Kalachakra*. He never did the bear sleep more than three months at once, but tried to blaze at top alertness like a Bodhisattva. He hibernized (when he did) only be-cause on Guge he must lead the 990 shipboard faithfuls and millions of Ti-betan Buddhists, native and not, in their unjust exiles. Can an up-phase ghost, once it really dies, survive on a strut-ship as a ghost for real? Truly, I do not know.

10. Once I didn't know Mama's or Daddy's first names. Tech is a title not a name, and Tech Brasswell married my mama, Tech Bonfils, aboard *Kalachakra* (Captain Xao prompting the vows), in the seventy-fourth year of our voyage. Tech Bonfils birthed me the following fall, one of only forty-seven children born on our trip to Guge. Luckily, Larry Rinpoche told me my folks' names: *Simon* and *Karen Bryn*. Now I don't even know if they *like* each other. I do know, from lots of reading, that S. Hawking—a now-dead astrophysicist—once said, **"People are not quantifiable."** He was sure right about that.

I know lots more, of course, but not who kilt the Twenty-First DL, if anybody did, and so I pick at that worry a lot.

YEARS IN TRANSIT: 83
COMPUTER LOGS OF THE DALAI LAMA-TO-BE, AGE 8

In old spectals and palm pix, starship captains sit at helms where they can see the Empty Vast through windows or screens. Captain Xao, First Officer Nima Photrang, and their helpers keep us all going toward Gliese 581 in a closed cockpit in the upper central third of the big tin can strut-shipping us to Guge.

This section we call Kham Bay. Cut flowers in slender vials prettify the room where Xao and Photrang and crew do their jobs. This pit also has a woven wall hanging of the *Kalachakra* Mandala and a big painted figure of the Buddha wearing a body, both a man's and a woman's, with many faces and arms. Larry calls this window-free a control room and a shrine.

I guess he knows.

I visit the cockpit. Nobody stops me. I visit because Simon and Karen Bryn have gone back to their Siestaville to pod-lodge for many months on Amdo Bay's bottom level. Me, I stay my ghostly self. I owe it to everyone aboard—or so I often get told—to grow into my full Lamahood.

"Ah," says Captain Xao, "you wish to fly the *Kalachakra*. Great, Your Holiness."

But he passes me on to First Officer Photrang, a Tibetan who looks manlike in her jumpsuit but womanlike at her wrists and hands . . . so gentle about the eyes that, floating near because our AG's down, she seems to have just pulled off a hard black mask.

"What may I do for you, Greta Bryn?"

My lips won't move, so grateful am I she didn't say, "Your Holiness."

She shows me the console where she watches the fuel level in a drop tank behind our tin cylinder as this tank feeds the antimatter engine pushing us outward. Everything, she tells me, depends on electronic systems that run "virtually automatically," but she and Captain Xao's other crew must check closely, though the systems have fail-safes that can signal them from afar even if they leave the control shrine.

"How long," I ask, "before we get to Guge?"

"In nineteen years we'll start braking," Nima Photrang says. "In another four, if all goes as planned, we will enter the Gliese 581 system and soon take a stationary orbital postion about the terminator. From there we'll go down to the adjacent habitable zones that we intend to settle in and develop."

"Four years to brake!" No one's ever said such a thing to me before. Four years are half the number I've lived, and no adult, I think, feels older at their old ages than I do at eight.

"Greta Bryn, to slow us faster than that would put terrible stress on our strut-ship. Its builders assembled it with optimal lightness, to save on fuel, but also with sufficient mass to withstand a twentieth of a g during its initial four years of thrusting and its final four years of deceleration. Do you understand?"

"Yes, but—"

"Listen: It took the *Kalachakra* four years to reach a fifth of the speed of light. During that time we traveled less than half a light-year and burned a lot the fuel in our drop tanks. Jettisoning the used-up tanks lightened us. For seventy-nine years since then, we've coasted, cruising over sixteen light-years toward our target sun using our fuel primarily for trajectory correction maneuvers. That's a highly economical expenditure of the antimatter ice with which we began our flight."

"Good," I say—because Officer Photrang looks at me as if I should clap for such an "economical expenditure."

"Anyway, we scheduled four years of braking at one twentieth of a g to conserve our final fuel resources and to keep this spidery vessel from ripping apart at higher rates of deceleration."

"But it's still going to take so long!"

The officer takes me to a ginormous sketch of our strut-ship. "If anyone aboard has time for a stress-reducing deceleration, Greta Bryn, you do."

"Twenty-three years!" I say. "I'll turn thirty-one!"

"Yes, you'll wither into a pitiable crone." Before I can protest more, she shows me other stuff: a map of the inside of our passenger can, a hologram of the Gliese 581 system, and a d-cube of her living mama and daddy in the village Drak—which means *Boulder*—fifty-some rocky miles southeast of Lhasa. But—I'm such a doofus!—maybe they no longer live at all.

"My daddy's from Boulder!" I say to cover this thought.

Nima Photrang peers at me with small bright eyes.

"Boulder, Colorado," I tell her.

"Is that so?" After a nod from Captain Xao, she guides me into a tunnel lit by tiny glowing pins.

"What did you really come up here to learn, child? I'll tell you if I can."

"Who killed Sakya Gyatso?" I hurry to add, "I *don't* want to be him."

"Who told you somebody killed His Holiness?"

"Larry." I grab a guide rail. "My tutor, Larry Rinpoche."

Officer Photrang snorts. "Larry has a bad humor sense. And he may be wrong."

I float up. "But what if he's right?"

"Is the truth that important to you?" She pulls me down.

A question for a question, like a dry seed poked under my gum. "Larry says that a lama in training must seek truth in everything, and I must do so always, and everyone else by doing likewise will empty the universe of lies."

"'Do as I say and not as I do.'"

"What?"

Nima—she tells me to call her by this name—takes my arm and swims me along the tunnel to a door that opens at a knuckle bump. She guides me into her rooms, a closet with a pull-down rack and straps, a toadstool unit for our shipboard intranet, and a corner for talking in. We float here. Nicely, or so it seems, Nima pulls a twist of brindle hair out of my eye.

"Child, it's possible that Sakya Gyatso had a heart attack."

"'Possible'?"

"That's the official version, which Minister T told all us ghosts up-phase enough to notice that Sakya'd gone missing."

I think hard. "But the *un*official version is . . . somebody killed him?"

"It's one unofficial story. In the face of uncertainty, child, people indulge their imaginations, and more versions of the truth arise than you can slam a lid on. But lid-slamming, we think, is a bad response to ideas that will come clear in the oxygen of free inquiry."

I shake my head. "Who do you mean, 'we'?"

Nima gives a small smile. "My 'we' excludes anyone who forbids the expression of plausible alternatives to any 'official version.'"

"What do you think happened?"

"I probably shouldn't say."

"Maybe you need some oxygen."

This time her smile grows bigger. "Yes, maybe I do."

"I'm the new Dalai Lama, probably, and I give you that oxygen, Nima. Tell me your idea, now."

After squinting at me hard, she does: "I fear that Sakya Gyatso killed himself."

"The Dalai Lama?" I can't help it: her notion slanders the man, who, funnily, now breathes inside me.

"Why *not* the Dalai Lama?"

"A Bodhisattva lives for others. He'd never kill anybody, much less himself."

"He stayed up-phase too much—almost half a century—and the anti-aging effects of ursidormizine slumber, which he often avoided as harmful to his leadership role, were compromised. His Holiness did have the soul of a Bodhisattva, but he also had an animal self. The wear to his body broke him down, working on his spirit as well as his head, and doubts about his ability to last the rest of our trip niggled at him, as did doubts about his fitness to oversee our colonization of Guge."

I cross my arms. This idea insults the late DL. It also, I think, poisons me. "I believe he had a heart attack."

"Then the official version has taken seed in you," Nima says.

"OK then. I like to think someone killed Sakya Gyatso, not that tiredness or sadness made him do it."

Gently: "Child, where's your compassion?"

I float away. "Where's yours?" At the door of the first officer's quarters, I try to bump out. I can't.

Nima must drift over, knuckle-bump the door plate, and help me with my angry going.

The artificial-gravity generators run again. I feel them humming through the floor of my room in Amdo, and in Z Quarters where our somnacicles nap. Larry says that except for them, AG aboard *Kalachakra* works little better than did electricity in war-wasted nations on Earth. Anyway, I don't need the lock belt in my vidped unit; and such junk as pocket pens, toothbrushes, and d-cubes don't go slow-spinning off like fuzzy dreams.

Somebody knocks.

Who is it?

Not Larry, who's already taught me today, or Mama, who sleeps in her pod, or Daddy, who's gone up-phase to U-Tsang to help the monks lay out rock gardens around their gompas. He gets to visit U-Tsang, but I—the only nearly anointed DL on this ship—must mostly hang with non-monks.

The knock knocks again.

Xao Songda enters. He unhooks a folding stool from the wall and sits atop it next to my vidped booth: Captain Xao, the pilot of our generation ship. Even with the hotshot job he has to work, he roams around almost as much as I do.

"Officer Photrang tells me you have doubts."

I have doubts like a strut-ship has fuel tanks, and I wish I could drop them half as fast as *Kalachakra,* "The Wheel of Time," dropped its anti-hydrogen-ice-filled drums in the first four years of run toward our coasting speed.

"Well?" Captain Xao's eyebrow goes up.

"Sir?"

"Does my first officer lie, or do you indeed have doubts?"

"I have doubts about everything."

Captain Xao cocks his head. "Like what, child?" He seems nice but clueless.

"Doubts about who made me, why I was born in a big bean can, why I like the AG on rather than off. Doubts about the shipshapeness of our ship, the soundness of Larry Lake's mind, the realness of the rock we're going to. Doubts about—"

"Greta," Captain Xao tries to interrupt.

"—the pains in my legs and the mixing of my soul with Sakya's because of how our lifelines overlapped. Doubts—"

"Whoa," Xao Songda says. "Officer Photrang says you have doubts about the official version of the Twenty-First's death."

"Yes."

"I too, but, as your captain, I must tell you that this vessel cruises in shipshape shape . . . with an artist in charge."

I gape at the man, then say: "Is the official story true? Did Sakya Gyatso really die of Cadillac infraction?"

"Cardiac infarction," the captain says, not getting that I just joked him. "Yes, he did. Regrettably."

"Or do you say that because Minister T told everyone that and he outranks you?"

Xao Songda looks confused. "Why do you think Minister Trungpa would lie?"

"Inferior motives."

"Ulterior motives," the stupid captain again corrects me.

"OK: ulterior motives. Did he have something to do with Sakya's death . . . for mean reasons locked in his heart, just as damned souls are locked in hell?"

The captain draws a noisy breath. "Goodness, child."

"Larry says that somebody killed Sakya." I climb out of my vidped booth and go to the captain. "Maybe it was you."

Captain Xao laughs. "Do you know how many hoops I had to leap through to become captain of this ship? Ethnically, Gee Bee, I am Han Chinese. Hardly anybody in the Free Federation of Tibetan Voyagers wished me to strut our strut-ship. But I was wholeheartedly Yellow Hat and the best pilot-engineer not already en route to a habitable planet. And so I'm here. I'd no more assassinate the Dalai Lama than desecrate a chörten, or harm his likely successor."

I believe him, even if an anxious soul could hear the last few words of his speech unkindly. I ask him if he likes Nima's theory—that Sakya Gyatso killed himself— better than Minister T's Cadillac-infraction hypothesis. When he starts to answer, I say, "Flee falsehood again and speak the True Word."

After a blink, he says, "If you insist."

"Yes, I do."

"Then I declare myself, on that question, an agnostic. Neither theory strikes me as outlandish. But neither seems likely, either: Minister T's because His Holiness had good physical health and Nima's because the stresses of this voyage were but tickling feathers to the Dalai Lama."

To my surprise, I begin to cry.

Captain Xao grips my shoulder balls so softly that his fingers feel like owl's down, as I dream such stuff on an Earth I've never seen, and never will. He whispers to me: "*Shhhshhh.*"

"Why do you shush me?"

Captain Xao removes his hands. "I no longer shush you. Feel free to cry."

I do. So does Captain Xao. We are wed in knowing that Larry my tutor was right all along, and that our late Dalai Lama fell at the hands of a really mean someone with an inferior motive.

YEARS IN TRANSIT: 87
COMPUTER LOGS OF THE DALAI LAMA-TO-BE, AGE 12

A week before my twelfth birthday, a Buddhist nun named Dolma Langdun, who works in the Amdo Bay nursery, hails me through the *Kalachakra* intranet. She wants to know if, on my birthday, I will let one of her helpers accompany me to the nursery to meet the children and accept gifts from them.

She signs off,—*Mama Dolma.*

I think, Why does this person do this? Who's told her I have a birthday coming?

Not my folks, who sleep in their somnacicle eggs, nor Larry, who does the same because I've "exhausted" him. And so I resolve to put these questions to Mama Dolma over my intranet connection.

—*How many children?* I ask her, meanwhile listing to Górecki's *Symphony of Sorrowful Songs* through my ear-bud.

—*Five,* she replies.—*Very sweet children, the youngest ten months, the oldest almost six years. It would be a great privilege to attend you on your natal anniversary, Your Holiness.*

Before I can scold her for using this too-soon form of address, she adds,—*As a toddler, you spent time here in Momo House, but in those bygone days I was assigned to the nunnery in U-Tsang with Abbess Yeshe Yargag.*

—*Momo House!* I key her.—*Oh, I remember!*

Momo means "dumpling," and this memory of my caregivers and my little friends back then dampens my eyelashes. Clearly, during the Z-pod rests of my parents and tutor, Minister Trungpa has acted as a most thoughtful guardian.

The following week goes by even faster than a fifth of light-speed.

On my birthday morning, a skinny young monk in a maroon jumpsuit comes for me and takes me down to Momo House.

There I meet Mama Dolma. There, I also meet the children: the baby Alicia, the toddlers Pema and Lahmu, and the oldest two, Rinzen and Mickey. Except for the baby, they tap-dance about me like silly dwarves.

The nursery features big furry balls that also serve as hassocks, blow-uppable yaks, monkeys, and pterodactyls, and cribs and learning booths, with lock belts for AG failures. A system made just for the Dumpling Gang always warns us of an outage at least fifteen minutes before it occurs.

The nearly-six kid, Mickey, grabs my hand and shows me around. He introduces me to everybody, working down from the five-year-old to ten-month-old Alicia. All of them but Alicia give me drawings. These drawings show a monkey named Chenrezig (of course), a nun named Dolma (ditto), a yak named Yackety (double ditto), and a python with no name at all. I ooh and ahh over these masterpizzas, as I call them, and then help them assemble soft-form puzzles, feed one another snacks, go to the toilet, and scan a big voyage chart that ends (of course) at Gliese 581 g.

But it's Alicia, the baby, who wins me. She twinkles. She flirts. She touches. At nap time, I hold her in a vidped booth, its screen oranged out and its rockers rocking, and I nuzzle her sweet-smelling neck.

Alicia tugs at my lips and pinches my mouth flat, so set on reshaping my face that she seems a pudgy sculptor elf. All the while, her agate irises, bigger than my thumb tips, play across my face with cross-eyed puppy love. I stay with Alicia—Alicia Paljor—all the rest of that day. Then the skinny young monk comes to escort me home, as if I need him to, and Mama Dolma hugs me good-bye.

Alicia wails.

It hurts to leave, but I do, because I must, and even as the hurt fades, the memory of my outstanding birthday begins, that very night, to sing in me like the lovely last notes of Górecki's *Third*.

I have never had a better birthday.

Months later, Daddy Simon and Mama Karen Bryn have come up-phase at the same time. Together, they fetch me from my nook in Amdo and walk with me on a good AG day to the cafeteria above the grave-caves of our strut-ship's central drum, Kham. I ease along the serving line between them, taking tsampa, mushroom cuts, tofu slices, and the sauces to make them palatable. The three of us end up at a table in a nook far from the serving line. Music by J. S. Bach spills from speakers in the movable walls, with often a sitar and bells to call up for some voyagers a Himalayan nostalgia to which my folks are immune. We eat fast and talk small.

Then Mama says, "Gee Bee, your father has something to tell you."

O God. O Buddha. O Larry. O Curly. O Moe.

"Tell her," Mama orders.

Daddy Simon wears the sour face proclaiming that everybody should call him Pieman Oldfart. I hurt to behold him. But at last he gets out that before I stood up-phase, almost three years ago, as the DL's disputed Soul Child, he and Mama signed apartness documents that have now concluded in an agreement of full marital severance. They continue my folks, but not as the couple that conceived, bore, and raised me. They remain friends, but will no longer wish to cohabit because of incompatibilities that have arisen over their up-phase years. It really shouldn't matter to me, they say, because I've become Larry Lake's protégée with a grand destiny that I will no doubt fulfill as a youth and an adult. Besides, they will continue to parent me as much as my odd unconfirmed status as DL-in-training allows.

I do not cry, as I did upon learning that Captain Xao believes that somebody slew my only-maybe predecessor. I don't cry because their news feels truly distant, like word of a planet somewhere whose people have brains in their chest. However, it does hurt to think about why I absolutely must cry later.

Daddy gets up, kisses my forehead, and leaves with his tray.

Mama studies me for a long moment. "I'll always love you. You've made me very proud."

"You've made me very proud," I echo her.

"What?"

We push our plastic fork tines around in our leftovers, which I imagine rising in damp squadrons from our plates and floating up to the air-filtration fans. I wish that I, too, could either rise or sink.

"When will they confirm you?" Mama asks.

"Everything on this ship takes *forever*: getting from here to there, finding a killer, confirming the new DL."

"You must have some idea."

"I don't. The monks don't want me. I can't even visit their make-believe gompas over in U-Tsang."

"Well, those are sacred places. Not many of us get invitations."

"But Minister T has declared me the 'One,' and Larry has tutored me in thousands of subjects, holy and not so holy. Even so, the under-lamas and their silly crew think less well of me than they would of a lame blue mountain."

"Don't call their monasteries 'make-believe,' Gee Bee. Don't call these other holy people and their followers 'silly.'"

"Oh, rot!" I actually say. "I wish I were anywhere but on this bean can flung at an iceberg light-years across the stupid Milky Way."

"Don't, Greta Bryn. You've got a champion in Minister Trungpa."

"Who just wants to bask in the reflected glory of his next supposed Bodhisattva—which, I swear, I am not."

Mama lifts her tray and slams it down.

Nobody else seems to notice, but I jump.

"You have no idea," she says, "who you are or what a champion can do for you, and you're *much* too young to dismiss yourself or your powerful advocate."

One of the Brandenburg Concertos swells, its sitars and yak bells flourishing. Far across the mess hall, Larry Lake shuffles toward us with a tray. Mama sees him, and, just as Daddy did, she kisses my forehead and abruptly leaves. My angry stare tells Larry not to mess with me (no, I won't apologize for the accidental pun), and Larry veers off to sit with some two or three bio-techs at a faraway table.

YEARS IN TRANSIT: 88
COMPUTER LOGS OF THE DALAI LAMA-TO-BE, AGE 13

Today marks another anniversary of the *Kalachakra*'s departure from Moon orbit on its crossing to Guge in the Gliese 581 system.

Soon I will turn thirteen. Much has happened in the six years since I woke to find that Sakya Gyatso had died and I had become Greta Gyatso, his tardy reincarnation.

What has not happened haunts me as much as, if not more than, what has. I have a disturbing sense that the "investigation" into Sakya's murder resides in a secretly agreed-upon limbo. Also, that my confirmation rests in this same misty territory, with Minister T as my "regent." Recently, though, at First Officer Nima's urging, Minister T assigned me a bodyguard from among the monks of U-Tsang Bay, a guy called Ian Kilkhor.

Once surnamed Davis, Kilkhor was born sixteen years into our flight of Canadian parents, techs who'd converted to the Yellow Hat order of Tibetan Buddhists in Calgary, Alberta, a decade before the construction of our interstellar vessel. Although nearing the chronological of sixty, Kilkhor—as he asks me to call him—looks less than half that and has many admirers among the female ghosts in Kham.

Officer Nima fancies him. (Hey, even I fancy him.)

But she is celibacy-committed unless a need for childbearing arises on Guge. And assuming her reproductive apparatus still works. Under such circumstances, I suspect that Kilkhor would lie with her.

Here I confess my ignorance. Despite lessons from Larry in the Tibetan language, I didn't realize, until Kilkhor told me, that his new surname means "Mandala." I excuse myself on the grounds that "Kilkhor" more narrowly means "center of the circle," and that Larry often skimps on offering connections. (To improve the health of his "mortal coil," Larry has spent nearly four of my last six years in an ursidormizine doze. I go to visit him once every two weeks in the pod-lodges of Amdo Bay, but these well-intended homages sometimes feel less like cheerful visits than dutiful viewings.) Also, "Kilkhor" sounds to me more like an incitement to violence than it does a statement of physical and spiritual harmony.

Even so, I benefit in many ways from Kilkhor's presence as bodyguard and stand-in tutor. Like Larry, Mama and Daddy spend long periods in their pods; and Kilkhor, a monk who knows *tai chi chuan*, has kept the killer, or killers, of Sakya from slaying me, if such villains exist aboard our ship. (I have begun to doubt they do.) He has also taught me much of history, culture, religion, politics, computing, astrophysics, and astronomy that Larry, owing to long bouts of hibernizing, has neglected. Also, he weighs in for me with the monks, nuns, and yogis of U-Tsang, who feel disenfranchised in the process of confirming me as Sakya's successor.

Indeed, because the Panchen Lama now in charge in U-Tsang will not let me set foot there, Kilkhor intercedes to get high monks to visit me in Kham. The Panchen Lama, to avoid seeming either bigot or autocrat, permits these visits. Sadly (or not), my sex, my ethnicity, and (most important) the fact that my birth antedates the Twenty-First's by five years all conspire to taint my candidacy. I doubt it too, and fear that fanatics among the "religious" will try to veto me by subtraction, not by argument, and that I will die at the hands of friends rather than enemies of the Dalai Lamahood.

Such fears, alone, throw real doubt on Minister T's choice of me as Sakya's only indisputable Soul Child.

YEARS IN TRANSIT: 89
COMPUTER LOGS OF THE DALAI LAMA-TO-BE, AGE 14

"The Tibetan belief in monkey ancestors puts them in a unique category as the only people I know of who acknowledged this connection before Darwin."
—*Karen Swenson, twentieth-century traveler, poet, and worker at Mother Teresa's Calcutta mission*

Last week, a party of monks and one nun met me in the hangar of Kham Bay. From their gompas (monasteries) in U-Tsang Bay, they brought a woolen cloak, a woolen bag, three spruce walking sticks, three pairs of sandals, and a white-faced monkey that one monk, as the group entered, fed from a baby bottle full of ashen-gray slurry.

An AG-generator never runs in the hangar because people don't often visit it, and the lander nests in a vast hammock of polyester cables. So we levitated in a cordoned space near the nose of the lander, which the Free Federation of Tibetan Voyagers has named *Chenrezig*, after that Buddhist disciple who, in monkey form, sired the first human Tibetans. (Each new DL instantly qualifies as the latest incarnation of Chenrezig.) Our lander's nose is painted with bright geometries and the cartoon head of a wise-looking monkey wearing glasses and a beaked yellow hat. Despite this simian iconography, however, everyone on our strut-ship calls the lander the *Yak Butter Express*.

After stiff greetings, these high monks—including the venerable Panchen Lama, Lhundrub Gelek, and Yeshe Yargang, the abbess of U-Tsang's only nunnery!—tied the items that they'd brought to a utility toadstool in the center of our circle ("kilkhor"). Then we floated in lotus positions, hands palms-upward, and I stared at these items, but not at the pale monkey now clutching the PL and wearing a look of alert concern. From molecular vibrations and subtle somatic clues—twitches, blinks, sniffles—I tried to determine which of the items they wished me to select . . . or not to select, as their biases dictated.

"Some of these things were Sakya Gyatso's," the Panchen Lama said. "Choose only those that he viewed as truly his. Of course, he saw little in this life as a 'belonging.' You may examine any or all, Miss Brasswell."

I liked how my birth name (even preceded by the stodgy honorific Miss) sounded in our hangar, even if it did seem to label me an imposter, if not an outright foe of Tibetan Buddhism. To my right, Kilkhor lowered his eyelids, advising me to make a choice. OK, then: I had no need to breast-stroke my way over to the pile.

"The cloak," I said.

Its stench of musty wool and ancient vegetable dyes told me all I needed to know. I recalled those smells and the cloak's vivid colors from an encounter with the DL during his visit to the nursery in Amdo when I was four. It had seemed the visit of a seraph or an extraterrestrial—as, by virtue of our status as star travelers, he had qualified. Apparently, none of *these* faithful had accompanied him then, for, obviously, none recalled his having cinched on this cloak to meet a tot of common blood.

The monkey—a large Japanese macaque (*Mucaca fuscata*)—swam to the center of our circle, undid the folded cloak, and kicked back to the Lama, who belted it around his lap. Still fretful, the macaque levitated in its breechclout—a kind of diaper—beside the PL. It wrinkled its brow at me in approval or accusation.

"Go on," Lhundrub Gelek said. "Choose another item."

I glanced at Kilkhor, who dropped his eyelids.

"May I see what's in the bag?" I asked.

The PL spoke to the macaque: a critter I imagined Tech Bonfils taking a liking to at our trip's outset. It then paddled over to the bag tied to the utility toadstool, seized the bag by its neck, and dragged it over to me.

After foraging a little, I extracted five slender books, of a kind now rarely made, and studied each: one in English, one in Tibetan, one in French, one in Hindi, and one (I'm guessing now) in Esperanto. In each case, I recognized their alphabets and point of origin, if not their subject matter. A bootlace linked the books. When they started to float away, I caught its nearer end and yanked them all back.

"Did His Holiness write these?" I asked.

"Yes," the Panchen Lama said, making me think that I'd passed another test. He added, "Which of the five did Sakya most esteem?" Ah, a dirty trick. Did they want me to read not only several difficult scripts but also Sakya's departed mind?

"Do you mean as artifacts, for the loveliness of their craft, or as documents, for the spiritual meat in their contents?"

"Which of those options do you suppose most like him?" Abbess Yeshe Yargag asked sympathetically.

"Both. But if I must make a choice, the latter. When he wrote, he distilled clear elixirs from turbid mud."

Our visitors beheld me as if I had neutralized the stench of sulfur with sprinkles of rose water. Again, I felt shameless.

With an unreadable frown, the PL said, "You've chosen correctly. We now wish you to choose the book that Sakya most esteemed for its message."

I reexamined each title. The one in French featured the words *wisdom* and *child*. When I touched it, Chenrezig responded with a nearly human intake of breath. Empty of thought, I lifted that book.

"Here: *The Wisdom of a Child, the Childishness of Wisdom*."

As earlier, our five visitors kept their own counsel, and Chenrezig returned the books to their bag and the bag to the monk who had set it out.

Next, I chose among the walking sticks and the pairs of sandals, taking my cues from the monkey and so choosing better than I had any right to expect. In fact, I chose just those items identifying me as the Dalai Lama's Soul Child, girl or no girl.

After Kilkhor praised my accuracy, the PL said, "Very true, but—"

"But what?" Kilkhor said. "Must you settle on a Tibetan male only?"

The Lama replied, "No, Ian. But what about *this* child makes her miraculous?"

Ah, yes. One criterion for confirming a DL candidate is that those giving the tests identify "something miraculous" about him . . . or her.

"What about her startling performance so far?" Kilkhor asked.

"We don't see her performance as a miracle, Ian."

"But you haven't conferred about the matter." He gestured at the other holies floating in the fluorescent lee of the *Yak Butter Express.*

"My friends," the Panchen Lama asked, "what say you all in reply?"

"We find no miracle," a spindly, middle-aged monk said, "in this child's choosing correctly. Her brief life overlapped His Holiness's."

"My-me," Abbess Yargag said. "I find her a wholly supportable candidate."

The three leftover holies held their tongues, and I had to admit—to myself, if not aloud to this confirmation panel—that they had a hard-to-refute point, for I had pegged my answers to the tics of a monastery macaque with an instinctual sense of its keepers' moody fretfulness.

Fortunately, the monkey liked me. I had no idea why.

O to be unmasked! I needed no title or any additional powers to lend savor to my life. I wanted to sleep in my pod and to awaken later as an animal husbandry specialist, with Tech Karen Bryn Bonfils-Brasswell as my mentor and a few near agemates as my fellow apprentices.

The PL unfolded from his lotus pose and floated before me with his feet hanging. "Thank you, Miss Younghusband, for this audience. We regret that we can't—" Here he halted, for Chenrezig swam across our meeting space, pushed into my arms, and clasped me about the neck. Then all the astonished monks and the shaken PL rubbed shoulders as if to ignite their bodies in glee or consternation.

Abbess Yargag said, "There's your miracle."

"*Nando*," the Lama said, shaking his head: No, he meant.

"On the contrary," Abbess Yargag replied. "Chenrezig belonged to Sakya Gyatso, and never in Chenrezig's sleep-lengthened life has he embraced a child, a non-Asian, or a female—not even me."

"Nando," the PL, visibly angry, said again.

"*Rha* (Yes)," another monk put in. "*Om mani padme hum* (Hail the jewel in the lotus). *Ki ki so so lha lha gyalo* (Praise to the gods)."

I kissed Chenrezig's white-flecked facial mane as he whimpered like an infant in my already weary arms.

YEARS IN TRANSIT: 93
COMPUTER LOGS OF THE DALAI LAMA-TO-BE, AGE 18

—A Catechism: Why do we voyage?

At age seven, I learned this catechism from Larry. Kilkhor often has me say it, to ensure that I don't turn apostate to either our legend or my long-term charge. Sometimes Captain Xao Songa, a Han who converted and fled to Vashon Island, Washington—via northern India, Cape Town, South Africa; Buenos Aires; and Hawaii—sits in to temper Larry's flamboyance and Kilkhor's lethargic matter-of-factness.

—*Why do we voyage?* one of them will ask.

—*To fulfill*, I say, *the self-determination tenets of the Free Federation of Tibet and to usher every soul pent in hell up through the eight lower realms to Buddhahood.*

From the bottom up, these realms include *1)* hell-pent mortals, *2)* hungry ghosts,

3) benighted beasts, 4) fighting spirits, 5) human beings, 6) seraphs and such, 7) disciples of the Buddha, 8) Buddhas for themselves only, and 9) Bodhisattvas who live and labor for every soul in each lower realm.

—Which realm did you begin in, Your Probationary Holiness?

—That of the bewildered, but not benighted, human mortal.

—As our Dalai Lama in Training, to which realm have you arisen?

—That of the disciples of Chenrezig: Om mani padme hum! I am the funky simian saint of the Buddha.

—From what besieged and bludgeoned homeland do you pledge to free us?

—The terrestrial "Land of Snow": Tibet beset; Tibet ensnared, ensorcelled, and enslaved.

—As a surrogate for that land gone cruelly forfeit, to which new country do you pledge to lead us?

—"The Land of Snow," on Guge the Unknowable, where we all must strive to free ourselves again.

The foregoing part of the catechism embodies a pledge and a charge. Other parts synopsize the history of our oppression: the ruin of our economy; the destruction of our monasteries; the subjugation of our nation to the will of foreign predators; the co-opting of our spiritual formulae for greedy and warlike purposes; the submergence of our culture to the maws of jackals; and the quarantining of our state to anyone not of our oppressors' liking. Finally, against the severing of sinews human and animal, the pulling asunder of ties interdependent and relational, only the tallest mountains could stand. And those who undertook the *khora*, the sacred pilgrimage around Mount Kailash, often did so with little or no grasp of the spiritual roots of their journeys. Even then, that mountain, the land all about it, and the scant air overarching them, stole the breath and spilled into the pilgrims' lungs the bracing elixir of awe.

At length, the Tibetans and their sympathizers realized that their overlords would never withdraw. Their invasion, theft, and reconfiguration of the state had left its peoples few options but death or exile.

—So what did the Free Federation of Tibet do? *Larry, Kilkhor, or Xao will ask.*

—Sought a United Nations charter for the building of a starship, an initiative that we all feared China would preempt with its veto in the Security Council.

—What happened instead?

—The Chinese supported the measure.

—How so?

—They contributed to the general levy for funds to build and crew with colonists a second-generation antimatter ship capable of attaining speeds up to one-fifth the velocity of light.

—Why did China surrender to an enterprise implying severe criticism of a policy that it saw as an internal matter? That initiative surely stood as a rebuke to its efforts to overwhelm Tibet with its own crypto-capitalistic materialism.

Here I may snigger or roll my eyeballs, and Lawrence, Kilkhor, or Xao will repeat the question.

—Three reasons suffice to explain China's acquiescence, *I at length reply.*

—State them.

—First, China understood that launching this ship would remove the Twenty-First Dalai Lama, who had agreed not only to support this disarming plan but also to go with the Yellow Hat colonists to Gliese 581 g.

—*Ki ki so so lha lha gyalo* (Praise to the gods), *my catechist says in Tibetan.*

—Indeed, backing this plan would oust from a long debate the very man whom the Chinese reviled as a poser and a bar to the incorporation of Tibet into their program of post-post-Mao modernization.

Here, another snigger from a bigger poser than Sakya, namely, me.

—And the second reason, Your Holiness?

—Backing this strut-ship strategy surprised the players arrayed against China in both the General Assembly and the Security Council.

—To what end?

—All these players could do was brand China's support a type of cynicism warped into a low-yield variety of "ethnic cleansing," for now Tibet and its partisans would have one fewer grievance to lay at China's feet.

With difficulty, I refrain from sniggering again.

—And the third reason, Miss Greta Bryn, our delightfully responsive Ocean of Wisdom?

—Supporting the antimatter ship initiative allowed China to put its design and manufacturing enterprises to work drawing up blueprints and machining parts for the provocatively named UNS *Kalachakra*.

—And so we won our victory?

—*Om mani padme hum* (Hail the jewel in the lotus), *I reply.*

—And what do we Kalachakrans hope to accomplish on the sun-locked world we now call Guge?

—Establish a colony unsullied by colonialism; summon other emigrants to "The Land of Snow"; and lead to enlightenment all who bore that dream, and who will bear it into cycles yet to unfold.

—And after that?

—The cessation of everything samsaric, the opening of ourselves to nirvana.

—Hallelujah, *Ian Kilkhor always concludes.*—Hallelujah.

YEARS IN TRANSIT: 94
COMPUTER LOGS OF THE DALAI LAMA-TO-BE, AGE 19

For nearly four Earth months, I've added not one word to my Computer Log. But shortly after my last recitation of the foregoing catechism, Kilkhor pulled me aside and told me that I had a rival for the position of Dalai Lama.

This news astounded me. "Who?"

"A male Soul Child born of true Tibetan parents in Amdo Bay less than fifty days after Sakya Gyatso's death," Kilkhor said. "A search team found him almost a decade ago, but has only now disclosed him to us." Kilkhor made this disclosure of bad news—it is bad, isn't it?—sound very ordinary.

"What's his name?" I had no idea of what else to say.

"Jetsun Trimon," Kilkhor said. "Old Gelek seems to think him a more promising candidate than he does Greta Bryn Brasswell."

"Jetsun! You're joking, right?" My heart did a series of arrhythmic lhundrubs in protest.

Kilkhor regarded me then with either real, or expertly feigned, confusion. "You know him?"

"Of course not! But the name—" I stuck, at once amused and appalled.

"The *name*, Your Holiness?"

"It's a ridiculous, a totally ludicrous name."

"Not really. In Tibetan it means—"

"—'venerable' and 'highly esteemed,'" I put in. "But it's still ridiculous." And I noted that as a child, between bouts of study, I had often watched, well, "cartoons" in my vidped booth. Those responsible for this lowbrow programming had purposely stocked it with a selection of episodes called *The Jetsons*, all about a space-going Western family in a gimmick-ridden future. I had loved it.

"I've heard of it," Kilkhor said. "The program, I mean." But he didn't twig the irony of my five-year-younger rival's name, or pretended not to. To him, the similarity of these two monikers embodied a pointless coincidence.

"I can't do this anymore without a time-out," I said. "I'm going down-phase for a year—at least a quarter of a year!"

Kilkhor said nothing. His expression said everything.

Still, he arranged for my down-phase respite, and I repaired to Amdo Bay and my eggshell to enjoy this pod-lodging self-indulgence, which, except for rare cartoon-tinged nightmares, I almost did.

Now, owing to somatic suspension, I return at almost the same nineteen at which I went under.

When I awake this time amid a catacomb vista of eggshell pods—like racks in a troopship or a concentration-camp barracks—my mother, Minister T, the Panchen Lama, Ian Kilkhor, and Jetsun Trimon attend my awakening.

Grateful for functioning AG (as, down here, it *always* functions), I swing my legs out of the pod, stagger a step or two, and retch from a stomach knotted with a fresh anti-insomniac heat. The Tibetan boy, my rival, comes to me unbidden, slides an arm around me from behind, and eases me back toward his own thin body so that I don't topple into the vomit-vase Mama has given me. With his free hand, he strokes my brow and tucks stray strands of hair behind my ear, a familiarity that I hugely resent.

Although I usually sleep little, I do take occasional naps, for I *deserve* a respite.

I pull free of the presumptuous young imposter.

He looks about fifteen, and if I've hit nineteen, his age squares better than does mine with the passing of the last DL and the transfer of Sakya's bhava into the material form of Jetsun Trimon.

Beholding him, I find his given name less of a joke than I did before my nap and more of a spell for the inspiriting that the PL alleges has occurred in him. Jetsun and I study each other with mutual curiosity. Our elders look on with darker curiosities. How must Jetsun and I regard this arranged marriage, they no doubt wonder, and what does it presage for everyone aboard the *Kalachakra*?

During my year-plus sleep, maybe I've matured some. Although I want to cry out against the outrage—no, the *unkindness*—of my guardians' conspiracy to bring this fey usurper to my podside, I don't berate them. They warrant such a scolding, but I refrain. How do they wish me to view their collusion, and how can I see it as anything other than their sending a prince to the bier of a spell-afflicted maiden? Except for the acne scarring his forehead and chin, Jetsun is, well, cute, but I don't want his help. I loathe his intrusion into my pod-lodge and almost regret my return.

Kilkhor notes that the lamas of U-Tsang, including the Panchen Lama and Abbess Yargag, have finally decided to summon Jetsun Trimon and me to our onboard stand-in for the Jokhang Temple. There, they will conduct a gold-urn lottery to learn which of us will follow Sakya Gyatso as the Twenty-Second Dalai Lama.

Jetsun bows. He says his tutor has given him the honor of inviting me, my family, and my guardians to this "shindig." It will occur belatedly, he admits, after he and I have already learned many sutras and secrets reserved in Tibet—holy be its saints, its people, and its memory—for a Soul Child validated by lottery.

But circumstances have changed since our Earth-bound days: The ecology of the *Kalachakra*, the great epic of our voyage, and our need on Guge for a leader of heart and vision require fine tunings beyond our forebears' imaginations.

Wiser than I was last year, I swallow a cynical yawn.

"And so," Jetsun ends, "I wish you joy in the lottery's Buddha-directed outcome, whichever name appears on the slip selected."

He bows and takes three steps back.

Lhundrub Gelek beams at Jetsun, and I know in my gut that the PL has become my competitor's regent, his champion. Mama Karen Bryn holds her face expressionless until fret lines drop from her lip corners like weighted ebony threads.

I thank Jetsun, for his courtesy and his well-rehearsed speech. He seems to want something more—an invitation of my own, a touch—but I have nothing to offer but the stifling of my envy, which I fight to convert to positive energies boding a happy karmic impact on the name slips in the urn.

"You must come early to our Temple," the PL says. "Doing so will give you time to pay your respects at Sakya Gyatso's bier."

This codicil to our invitation heartens me. Lacking any earlier approval to visit U-Tsang, I have seen the body of the DL on display there.

Do I really wish to see it, to see *him*?

Yes, of course I do.

We've lost many Kalachakrans in transit to Guge, but none of the others have our morticians bled with trochars, painted with creams and rouges, or treated with latter-day preservatives. Those others we ejected via tubes into the airless cold of interstellar space, mere human scraps for the ever-hungry night.

In Tibet, the bereaved once spread their dead loved ones out on rocks in "celestial burial grounds." This they did as an act of charity, for the vultures. On our ship, though, we have no vultures, or none with feathers, and perhaps by firing our dead into unending quasi-vacuum, we will offer to the void a sacrifice of once-living flesh generous enough to upgrade our karma.

But Sakya Gyatso we have enshrined; and soon, as one of only two applicants for his sacred post, I will gaze upon the remains of one whose enlightenment and mercy have plunged me into painful egocentric anguish.

At the appointed time (six months from Jetsun's invitation), we journey from Amdo and across Kham by way of tunnels designed for either gravity-assisted marches or weightless swims. Our style of travel depends on AG generators and on the rationing of gravity by formulae meant to benefit our long-term approach to Guge. However, odd outages often overcome these formulae. Blessedly, Kalachakrans now adjust so well to gravity loss that we no longer find it alarming or inconvenient.

Journeying, we discover that U-Tsang's residents—all Bodhisattvas, allegedly—have forsworn all use of generators during the seventy-two-hour Festival of the Golden Urn, with that ceremony occurring at noon of the middle day. This renunciation they regard as a gift to everybody aboard our vessel—somnacicles and ghosts—and no hardship at all. Any stress we spare the generators, our karmic economies tell us, will redound to everybody's benefit in our voyage's later stages.

My entourage consists of my divorced parents, Simon Brasswell and Karen Bryn Bonfils; Minister T, my self-proclaimed regent; Lawrence Lake Rinpoche, my tutor and confidant, now up-phase for the first time in two years; and Ian Kilkhor, security agent, standby tutor, and friend. We walk single-file through a part of Kham wide enough for the next Dalai Lama's subjects to line the walls and perform respectful *namaste* as he (or she) passes. Minister T tells us that Jetsun Trimon and his people made this same journey eighteen hours ago and that their well-wishers in this trunk tunnel were fewer than those attending our passage. A Bodhisattva would take no pleasure from such a petty statistical triumph. Tellingly, I do. So what does my competition-bred joy say about my odds in the coming gold-urn lottery? Nothing auspicious, I fear.

Eventually, our crowds dwindle, and we enter a deck area featuring a checkpoint and a sector gate. A monk clad in maroon passes us through. Another dials open the gate admitting us, at last, to U-Tsang.

I smell roast barley, barley beer (chang), and an acrid tang of incense that makes my stomach seize. Beyond the gate, which shuts behind us like a stone wheel slotting into a tomb groove, we drift through a hall with thin metal rails and bracket-like handholds. The luminary pins here gleam a watery purple.

Our feet slide out from under us, not like those of a fawn sliding on ice, but like those of an astronaut trainee rising from the floor of an aircraft plunging to create a few seconds of pedagogical zero-g.

The AG generators here shut down a while ago, so we dog-paddle in waterwheel slow-motion, unsure which tunnel to enter.

Actually, I'm the only uncertain trekker, but because neither Minister T nor Larry nor Kilkhor wants to help me, I stay mute, from perplexity and pride: another black mark, no doubt, against my lottery chances.

Ahead of us, fifteen yards or so, a snow leopard manifests: a four-legged specter with yellow eyes and frost-etched silver fur. Despite the lack of gravity, it faces us as if standing on a rock ledge and licks its coal-colored beard as if savoring again the last guinea-pig-like chiphi that it crushed into bone bits. Stymied, I startle and sway. The leopard switches its tail, turns, and leaps into a tunnel that I would not have chosen.

Kilkhor laughs and urges us upward into this same purplish chute. "It's all right," he says. "Follow it. Or do you suspect a subterfuge from our spiritually elevated hosts?" He laughs again . . . this time, maybe, at his inadvertent nod to the Christian sacrament of communion.

Larry and I twig his mistake, but does anybody else?

"Come on," Kilkhor insists. "They've sent us this cool cat as a guide."

And so we follow. We swim rather than walk, levitating through a Buddhist rabbit hole in the wake of an illusory leopard . . . until, by a sudden shift in perspective, we feel ourselves to be "walking" again.

This ascent, or fall, takes just over an hour, and we emerge in the courtyard of Jokhang Temple, or its diminished *Kalachakra* facsimile. Here, the Panchen Lama, the Abbess of U-Tsang's only nunnery, and a colorful contingent of Yellow Hats and other monks greet us joyfully. They regale us with *khata* (gift scarves inscribed with good-luck symbols) and with processional music played by flutes, drums, and bells. Their welcome feels at once high-spirited and heartfelt.

The snow leopard has vanished. When we broke into the courtyard swimming like ravenous carp, somebody, somewhere, ceased projecting it.

So let the gold-urn ceremony begin. Put me out of, and into, my misery.

But before the lottery, we visit the shrine where the duded-up remains of Sakya Gyatso lie in state, like those of Lenin in the Kremlin or of Mao in the Forbidden City. Although Sakya should not suffer mention in the same breath as mass murderers, nobody can deny that we have preserved him as an icon, just as the devotees of Lenin and Mao mummified them. And I must trust that a single Figure of Peace weighs more in the karmic justice scales than does a shipload of bloody despots.

Daddy begs off. He has seen the dead Sakya Gyatso before, and traveling with his ex-wife, the mother of his Soul Child daughter, has depressed him beyond easy repair. So he retreats to a nearby guesthouse and locks himself inside for a nap. Ian Kilkhor leaves to visit several friends in the Yellow Hat gompa with whom he once studied; Minister T, who has often paid homage at the Twenty-First's bier, has business with Lhundrub Gelek and others of the confirmation troupe who met with me in Kham in the shadow of the *Yak Butter Express*.

So, only Mama, Larry, and I go to see the Lama whom, according to many, I will succeed as the spiritual and temporal head of the 990 Tibetan colonizers aboard this ship. The shrine we approach does not resemble a mausoleum. It sits on the courtyard's edge, like an exhibit of amateur art in a construction trailer.

Two maroon-clad guards await us beside its doors, one at each end of the trailer, now graffitified with mantras, prayers, and many mysterious symbols—but no one else in U-Tsang Bay has come out to view its principal attraction. The blousy monk at the nearer door examines our implanted, upper-arm IDs with click-scans, smiles beatifically, and nods us in. Larry jokes in Tibetan with the guy before joining us at the DL's windowed bier, where we three float: ghosts beside a pod-lodger who will not again arise, unless he has already done so in yet another borrowed body.

"He is not here," I say. "He has arisen."

Larry, who looks much older than at his last brief up-phase, laughs in appreciation or embarrassment: the latter, probably.

Mama gives me a blistering "cool-it" glare.

And then I gaze upon the body of Sakya Gyatso. Even in death, even through the clear but faintly dusty cover of his display pod, he sustains about his face and hands a soft amber aura of serene lifelikeness that startles, and discomfits. I see him smiling sweetly upon me when I was four. I imagine him displeasing his religious brethren and sisters by going more often into Amdo and Kham Bays to interact with his secular subjects than our under-lamas thought needful or wise, as if such visits distracted him from his obligations and sabotaged his authority in both realms, profane and holy. And it's definitely true that his longest uninterrupted sojourn in U-Tsang coincides with his years lying in state in this shabby trailer.

Commoners aboard ship loved him, but maybe—I reflect, studying his corpse with both fascination and regard—he angered those practitioners of Tantra who viewed him as their highest representative and model. Certainly, during his life he moved from external *Kalachakra* Tantra—a concern with the lost procession of solar and lunar days—to the internal Tantra, with its focus on the energy systems of the body, to the higher alternative Tantra leading to the sublime state of *bodhichitta*, perfect enlightenment for the sake of others.

Thus reflecting, I cannot conceive of anyone aboard ever wishing him harm or of myself climbing out of the pit of my ego to attain the state of material renunciation and accepting comprehension of emptiness that Sakya Gyatso reached and embodied through so many years of our journey.

That I stand today as one of two Soul Children in line to follow him defies logic; it offends reason and also the 722 deities resident in the *Kalachakra* Mandala as emblems of reality and consciousness. I lack even the worth of a dog licking barley-cake crumbs from the floor. I put my palm on the Twenty-First's pod cover and erupt in sobs. These underscore my unsuitability to succeed him.

Mama's glare gives way to a look of fretful amazement. She lays an arm over my shoulder, an intimacy that keeps me from drifting blindly away from either her or Larry.

"Kiddo," she murmurs, "don't cry for this lucky man. We'll never cease to honor him, but the time for mourning has passed."

I can't stop: All sleep has fled and the future holds only a scalding wakefulness. Larry lays his arm over my other shoulder, caging me between them.

"Baby," Mama says. "Baby, what's going on?"

She hasn't called me "baby" or "kiddo" since, over seven years ago, I had my first period. I twist my neck just enough to tell her to glance at the late DL, that she *must* look. Reluctantly, it seems, she does, and then looks back at me with no apparent hesitancy or aversion. Her gaze then switches between him and me until she realizes that I won't—I simply can't—succeed this saint as our leader. Moreover, I intend to withdraw from the gold-urn lottery and to throw my support to my rival. Mama remains silent, but her arm deserts me and she turns from the DL's bier as if my declaration has acted as a vernier jet to change her position. In any case, she drifts away.

"Do you understand me, Mama?"

Mama's eyes jiggle and close. Her chin drops. Her jumpsuit-clad body floats like that of a string-free marionette, all raw angles and dreamily rafting hands.

Larry releases me and swims to her. "Something's wrong, Greta Bryn." I already suspect this, but these words penetrate with a laser's precision. I fumble blurry-eyed after Larry, clueless about what to do to help.

Larry swallows her with his arms, like the male hero in an anachronistic spectal, and then pushes her away to study her more objectively. Immediately, he pulls her back in to him again, checks her pulse at wrist and throat, and pivots her toward me with odd contrasting expressions washing over his face.

"She's fainted, I think."

"Fainted?" My mother, so far as I know, never faints.

"It's all the travel . . . and her anxiety about the gold-urn lottery."

"Not to mention her disappointment in me."

Larry regards me with such deliberate blankness that I almost fail to recognize the man, whom I have known seemingly forever.

"Talk to her when she comes 'round," he stays. "Talk to her."

The blousy monk who ran click-scans on us enters the makeshift mausoleum and helps Larry tow my rag-doll mama outside, across the road, and into the battened-down Temple courtyard. The two accompany her to a basket-like bower chair that suppresses her driftability. They attend her with colorful fake Chinese fans.

I go with them, looking on like a gawker at a mess-hall accident.

Our post-swoon interview takes place in the nearly empty courtyard. Mama clutches two of the bower-chair spokes like a child in a gravity swing, and I maintain my place before her with the mindless agility of a pond carp.

"Never say you're forsaking the gold-urn lottery," she says. "You bear on your shoulders the hopes of a majority, my hopes highest of all."

"Did my decision to withdraw cause you to faint?"

"Of course!" she cries. "You can't withdraw! You don't think I *faked* my swoon, do you?"

I have no doubt that Mama didn't fake it. Her sclera clocked into view before her eyelids fell. But, before that, her gaze cut to and rested on Sakya's face just prior to her realizing my intent. Feelings of betrayal, loss, and outrage triggered her swoon. Now she says I have no choice but to take part in the gold-urn drawing, and I regard her with such a blend of gratitude, for believing in me, and loathing, for her rigidity, that I can't speak. Do Westerners carry both me-first genes and self-doubt genes that, in combination, overcome the teachings of the Tantra?

"Answer me, Greta Bryn: Do you think I faked that faint?"

Mama knows already that I don't. She just wants me to assume the hair shirt of guilt for her indisposition and to pull it over my head with the bristly side inward. I have just enough Eastener in my being to deny her that boon and the pinched ecstasy implicit in it.

I hold her gaze, and hold it, until she begins to waver in her implacability.

"I didn't swoon solely because you tried to renounce your rebirth right, but also because you tried to humiliate me in front of Larry." Mama stands so far from the truth on this issue that she doesn't even qualify as wrong.

And so I laugh, like an evil-wisher rather than a daughter. "Not so," I say. "Why would I want to humiliate you before Larry?"

"Because I've always refused to coddle your self-doubts."

I recall Mama beholding Sakya's death mask and memorizing his every aura-lit feature. "What else caused you to 'fall out'?"

Her voice drops a register. "The Dalai Lama. His face. His hands. His body. His inhering and sustaining holiness."

"How did his 'sustaining holiness' knock you into a swoon, Mama?"

She peers across the courtyard road at the van where the DL lies in state. Then she pulls herself upright in the bower chair and tells this story:

"While married to your father, I began an affair with Minister Trungpa. He lived wherever Sakya lived, and Sakya chose to live among the secular citizens of Amdo and Kham rather than in the ridiculously scaled-down model of the Potala Place in U-Tsang. As one result, Minister T and I easily met each other; and Nyendak—Neddy, I call him—courted me under the unsuspecting noses of both Sakya and Simon."

"You cuckolded my daddy with Minister T?" I need her to say it again.

"Oh, that's such an ugly word to label what Neddy and I still regard as a sacred union."

"I'm sorry, Mama, but it's the prettiest word I know to call it."

"Don't condescend to me, Gee Bee."

"I won't. I can't. But I do have to ask: Who fathered me, the man I call Daddy or Sakya's old-fart chief minister?"

"Your father fathered you," Mama says. "Look at yourself in a mirror. Simon's face underlies your own. His blood runs through you, almost as if he gave his vitality to you and thus lost it himself."

"Maybe because you cuckolded him."

"That's crap. If anything, Simon's growing apathy and addiction to pod-lodging shoved me toward Neddy. Who, by the way, has the eggs, even at his age, to stay on the upright outside of a Z-pod."

"Mama, please."

"Moreover, Neddy loves you. He cherishes you because he cherishes me. He sees you as just as much his own as Simon does. In fact, Neddy was the first to—"

"I'll stop saying 'cuckold' if you'll stop calling your boyfriend 'Neddy.' It sounds like filthy baby talk."

Mama closes her eyes, counts to herself, and opens them again to explain that when Sakya Gyatso at last figured out what was going on between Mama and Minister Trungpa, he called them to him and urged them to break off the affair in the interest of a higher spirituality and the preservation of shipboard harmony.

Minister T, ever the tutor, argued that although traditional Buddhism stems from a slavish obeisance to the demands of morality, wisdom cultivation, and ego abasement, the Tibetan Tantric path channels sexual attraction and its drives into the creation of life-force energies that purify these urges and tie them to transcendent spiritual purposes. My mother's marriage had unraveled; and Minister T's courtship of her, which culminated in consensual carnality and a principled friendship, now demonstrated their mutual growth toward that higher spirituality.

I laugh out loud. "And did His Holiness give your boyfriend a pass on this self-serving distortion of the Tantric way?"

"Believe as you will, but Neddy—Minister Trungpa's—take on the matter, and the thoroughness with which he laid out everything, had a great effect on the DL. After all, Minister T had served as his regent in exile in Dharmasala, as his chief minister in India, and finally as his minister and friend here on the *Kalachakra*. Why would he all at once suppose this fount of integrity and wise counsel a scoundrel?"

"Maybe because he was sleeping with another man's wife and justifying it with a lot of mystical malarkey."

Mama squints with thread-thin patience and resumes her story. Because of what Minister T and Mama had done, and still do, and what Minister T told His Holiness to justify their behavior, the Dalai Lama fell into a brown study that finally edged over into an ashen funk. To combat it, the DL hibernated for three months, but emerged as low in spirits as he'd gone into his egg. All his energies had diminished, and he told Minister T of his fears of dying before we reached Guge. Such talk profoundly affected Mama's lover, who insisted that Sakya Gyatso tour the nursery in Amdo Bay. There he met me, Greta Bryn Brasswell, and fell in love, often returning over the next few weeks and always singling me out for attention. He told Mama that my eyes reminded him of those of his baby sister, who had died very young of rheumatic fever.

"I remember meeting His Holiness," I tell Mama, "but not his coming to see us so often in the nursery."

"You were four," Mama says. "How could you?"

She recounts how Minister T later took her to Sakya's upper-deck office in Amdo to talk about his long depression. With the AG generators running, they shared green tea and barley breads.

The DL again voiced his fear that even if he slept the rest of our journey, at some point in transit he would surrender his ghost in his eggshell pod and we, his people, would arrive at Guge with no agreed-upon leader. Minister T rebuked him for this worry, which he identified as egocentric, even though the DL took pains to articulate it as a concern for our common welfare.

Mama had carried me to this meeting. I lay sleeping—not like a pod-lodger but as a tired child—across her lap on a folded poncho liner that Simon had brought aboard as a going-away gift from a former roommate at Georgia Tech. As the adults talked, I turned and stretched, but never awakened.

"I don't recall that either," I say.

"Again, you were sleeping. Don't you listen to anything I tell you?"

"Everything. It's just that—" I stop myself. "Go on."

Mama does. She says that the DL walked over, leaned down, and placed his lips on my forehead, as if decaling it with a wet rose petal. Then he mused aloud about how fine it would be if, as an adult, I assumed his mantle and oversaw not only our voyagers' spiritual education but also our colonization of "The Land of Snow." He did not think he had the strength to undertake those tasks, but I would never exhaust my energy reserves. This fanciful scenario, Mama admits, rang in her like a crystal bell, a chime that echoed through her recurrently, as clear as unfiltered starlight.

Later, Mama and Minister T talked about their meeting with His Holiness and the tender wish-fulfillment musing with which he'd concluded it: my ascension to the Dalai Lamahood and eventual leadership on Guge. Mama asked if such a scenario could work itself out in reality, for if His Holiness died and Minister T championed me as he'd once stood behind Songsten Chodrak (later Sakya Gyatso), lifting him to his present eminence, then surely I, too, could rise to that height.

"'I'm too old for such fatiguing machinations again,' he told me," Mama says, remembering, "but I told him, 'Not by what I know of you, Neddy,' and just that simple expression of admiration and faith turned him."

I find Mama's account of this episode and her conspicuous pleasure in relating it hard to credit. But she has actually begun to glow, with a coppery aura akin to that of the DL in his display casket.

"At that point," she adds, "I grew ambitious for you in a way that once never would have crossed my mind, your ascension was just so far-fetched and prideful a thing for me to contemplate." She smiles adoringly, and my stomach shrinks upon itself like new linen applied wet to a metal frame.

"I've heard enough."

"Oh, no," Mama chides. "I've more, much more."

In blessed summary, she narrates a later conversation with Minister T, in which she urged him to carry to Sakya—now more a moody Byronic hero than a Bodhisattva in spiritual balance—this news: that she had no objection, if any accident or fatal illness befell him, to his sending his migrating bhava into the vessel of her daughter. Thus, he could mix our subjective selves in ways that would propagate us both into the future and so assist in our all arriving safely at Gliese 581 g.

Bristling, I try to parse this convoluted message. In fact, I ask Mama to repeat it. She does, and my deduction that she's memorized this nutty formulae—if you like, call it a "spell"—sickens me.

Still, I ask, as I must, "Did Minister T carry this news to His Holiness?"

"He did."

"And what happened?"

"Sakya listened. He meditated for two days on the metaphysics and the practical ramifications of what I'd told him through his minister."

"Finish," I say. "Please just finish."

"On the following day, Sakya died."

"*Cadillac infraction*," I murmur. Mama's eyes grow wide. "Forgive me," I say. "What killed him? You used to tell me 'natural causes, but at too young an age for them to *seem* natural.'"

"That wasn't entirely a lie. Sakya did what came natural to him. He acted on the impulse of his growing despair and his burgeoning sense that if he waited much longer to influence his rebirth, you'd outgrow your primacy as a receptacle for the transfer of his mind-state sequences and he'd lose you as a crucible for compounding the two. So he called upon his mastery of many Tantric practices to drop his body temperature, heart rate, and blood pressure. And when he irreversibly stilled his heart, he passed from our illusory reality into bardo . . . until he awoke again wed to the *samvattanika viññana*, or evolving consciousness, animating you."

Here I float away from Mama's bower chair and drift a dozen meters across the courtyard to a lovely, low cedar hedge. (In a way that she's never fully understood, Nima Photrang was right about the cause of Sakya Gyatso's death.) I want to pour my guts into this hedge, to heave the burdensome reincarnated essence of the late DL into its feathery silver-green leaves.

Nothing comes up. Nothing comes out. My stomach feels smaller than a piñon nut. My ego, on the other hand, fills the entire tripartite passenger drum of our starship, *The Wheel of Time*.

Later, I meet Simon Brasswell—Daddy—in a back-tunnel lounge near Jokhang Temple for chang and sandwiches. To make this date, of course, I must visit his guesthouse and ping him at the registry screen, but he agrees to meet me at the Bhurel—or The Blue Sheep, as the place is called—with real alacrity. In fact, as soon as we lock-belt into our booth, with squeeze bottles for our drinks and mini-spikes in our sandwiches to hold them to the small cork table, Daddy key-taps payment before I can object. He looks better since his nap, but the violent circles under his eyes lend him a sad fragility.

"I never knew—" I begin.

"That Karen and I divorced because she fell in love with Nyendak Trungpa? Or, I suppose, with his self-vaunted virility and political clout?" Speechless, I gape at my dad. "Forgive me. Ordinarily, I try not to go the spurned-spouse route."

I still can't speak.

He squeezes his bottle and swigs some barley beer. Then he says, "Do you want what your mama and Minister T want for you—I mean, really?"

"I don't know. I've never known. But this afternoon Mama told me why I ought to want it. And because I ought to, I do. I think."

Daddy studies me with an unsettling mixture of exasperation and tenderness. "Let me ask you something straight up: Do you think the bhava of Sakya Gyatso, the direct reincarnation of Avalokiteshvara, the ancestor of the Tibetan people, dwells in you as it supposedly dwelt in his twenty predecessors?"

"Daddy, I'm not Tibetan."

"I didn't ask you that." He unspikes and chomps into his *Cordyceps*, or synthetic caterpillar-fungus, sandwich. Chewing, he manages a quasi-intelligible, "Well?"

"Tomorrow's gold-urn lottery will reveal the truth, one way or the other."

"Yak shit, Greta. And I didn't ask you that, either."

I feel both my tears and my gorge rising, but the latter prevails. "I thought we'd share some time, eat together—not get into a spat."

Daddy chews more sedately, swallows, and re-spikes his "caterpillar" to the cork. "And what else, sweetheart? Avoid saying anything true or substantive?" I show him my profile. "Greta, forgive me, but I didn't sign on to this mission to sire a demigod. I didn't even sign on to it to colonize another world for the sake of oppressed Tibetan Buddhists and their rabid hangers-on."

"I thought you were a Tibetan Buddhist."

"Oh, yeah, born and raised . . . in Boulder, Colorado. Unfortunately, it never quite took. I signed on because I loved your mother and the idea of spaceflight at least as much as I did passing for a Buddhist. And that's how I got out here about seventeen light-years from home. Do you see?"

I eat nothing. I drink nothing. I say nothing.

"At least I've told you a truth," Daddy says. "More than one, in fact. Can't you do the same for me? Or does the mere self-aggrandizing idea of Dalai Lamahood clamp your windpipe shut on the truth?"

I have expected neither these revelations nor their vehemence, but together they work to unclamp something inside me. I owe my father my life, at least in part, and the dawning awareness that he has never stopped caring for me suggests—in fact, requires—that I repay him truth for truth.

"Yes. I can do the same for you."

Daddy's eyes, above their bruised half-circles, never leave mine.

"I didn't choose this life at all," I say. "It was thrust upon me. I want to be a good person, a Bodhisattva possibly, maybe even the Dalai Lama. But—"

He lifts his eyebrows and goes on waiting. A tender twinge of a smile plays about his mouth.

"But," I finish, "I'm not happy that maybe I want these things."

"Buddhists don't aspire to happiness, Greta, but to an oceanic detachment."

I give him my fiercest Peeved Daughter look, but do refrain from eye-rolling. "I just need an attitude adjustment, that's all."

"The most wrenching attitude adjustment in the universe won't turn a carp into a cougar, pumpkin." His pet name for me.

"I don't need the most wrenching attitude adjustment in the universe. I need a self-willed tweaking."

"Ah." Daddy takes a squeeze-swig of his beer and nods that I should eat.

My gorge has fallen, my hunger reappeared. I eat and drink and, as I do, become unsettlingly aware that other patrons in the Bhurel—visitors, monks—have detected my presence. Blessedly, though, they respect our space.

"Suppose the lottery goes young Trimon's way," Daddy says. "What would make you happy in your resulting alternate life?"

I consider this as a peasant woman of an earlier era might have done if a friend, just as a game, had asked, "What would you do if the King chose you to marry his son?" But I play the game in reverse, sort of, and can only shake my head.

Daddy waits. He doesn't stop waiting, or searching my eyes, or studying me with his irksome unwavering paternal regard. He won't speak, maybe because every-thing else about him—his gaze, his patience, his presence—speaks strongly of what for years went unspoken between us.

Full of an inarticulate wistfulness, I lean back. "I've told you a truth already," I tell my father. "Isn't that enough for tonight?"

A teenage girl and her mother, oaring subtly with their hands to maintain their places beside us, hover at our table. Even though I haven't seen the girl for several years (while, of course, she hibernized), I recognize her because distinctive agate eyes in an elfin face identify her at once.

Daddy and I lever ourselves up from our booth, and I swim out to embrace the girl. "*Alicia!*" Over her shoulder, I say to her mama in all earnestness, "Mrs. Paljor, how good to see you here!"

"Forgive the interruption," Mrs. Paljor says, ducking her head.

"Certainly, certainly," I say.

"We've come to U-Tsang for the Gold Urn Festival, and we just had to wish you well tomorrow. Alicia wouldn't rest until Kanjur found a way for us to attend."

Kanjur Paljor, Alicia's father, had served since the beginning of our voyage as our foremost antimatter-ice specialist. If anyone could get his secular wife and daughter to U-Tsang for the gold-urn lottery, Kanjur Paljor could. He enjoys the authority of universal respect. As for Alicia, she scrunches her face in embarrassment, as well as unconditional affection. She recalls the many times that I came to Momo House to hold her, and later to her family's Kham Bay rooms to take her on walks or on out-ings to our art, mathematics, and science centers.

"Thank you," I say. "Thank you."

I hug the girl. I hug her mother.

My father nods and smiles, albeit bemusedly. I suspect that Daddy has never met Alicia or Mrs. Paljor before. Kanjur, the father and husband, he undoubtedly knows. Who doesn't know that man?

The Paljor women depart almost as quickly as they came. Daddy watches them go, with a deep exhalation of relief that makes me hurt for them both.

"I was almost a second mother to that girl," I tell him.

Daddy oars himself downward, back into his seat. "Surely, you exaggerate. Mrs. Paljor looks more than sufficient to the task."

Long before noon of the next day, the courtyard of the Jokhang Temple swarms with levitating lamas, monks, nuns, yogis, and some authorized visitors from our other two passenger bays.

I cannot explain how I feel. If Mama's story of Sakya Gyatso's heart attack is true, then I cannot opt out of the gold-urn lottery. To do so would constitute an insult—the supreme insult—to his *punarbhava*, or karmic change from one life vessel to the next, or from his body to mine. Mine, as everyone knows, established its bona fides as a living entity years before the DL died. Also, opting out would constitute a heartless affront to all believers, of all who support my candidacy. Still . . .

Does Sakya have the right to self-direct his rebecoming or I the right to thwart his will . . . or only the obligation to accede to it? So much self-will and worry taints today's ceremony that Larry and Kilkhor, if not Minister T, can hardly conceive of it as deriving from Buddhist tenets at all.

Or can they? Perhaps a society rushing at twenty percent of light-speed toward some barely imaginable karmic epiphany has slipped the surly bonds not only of Earth but also of the harnessing principles of Buddhist Tantra. I don't know. I know only that I can't opt out of this lottery without betraying a good man who *loved* me in the noblest and the most innocent of senses.

And so, in our filigreed vestments, Jetsun Trimon and I swim up to the circular dais to which the attendants of the Panchen Lama have already fastened the gold urn for our name slips.

In staggered vertical ranks, choruses of floating monks and nuns chant as we await the drawing. Our separate retinues hold or adjust their altitudes behind us, both to hearten us and to keep their sight lanes clear. Small flying cameras, costumed as birds, televise the event to community members in all three bays.

Jetsun's boyish face looks at once exalted and terrified.

Lhundrub Gelek, the Panchen Lama, lifts his arms and announces that the lottery has begun. Today he blazes with the fierce bearing of a Hebrew seraph. Tugmonks keep him from rising in gravid slow motion to the ceiling. Abbess Yeshe Yargag floats about a meter to his right, with tug-nuns to prevent her from wandering up, down, or sideways. Gelek reports that name slips for Jetsun Trimon and Greta Bryn Brasswell already drift about in the oversized urn affixed to the dais. Neither of us, he proclaims, needs to swim forward to reach into the urn and pull out a name-slip envelope. Nor do we need stand-ins to do so. We will simply wait.

We will simply wait . . . until an envelope rises on its own out of the urn. Then Gelek will seize it, open the envelope, and read it aloud for all those watching in the Temple hall or via telelinks. Never mind that our wait could take hours, and that, if it does, viewers in every bay will volunteer to rejoin the vast majority of our population in ursidormizine slumber.

And so we wait.

And so we wait . . . and finally a small blue envelope rises through the mouth of the crosshatched gold urn. A tug-monk snatches it from the air, before it can descend out of view again, and hands it to the PL.

Startled, because he's nodded off several times over the past fifty-some minutes, Gelek opens the envelope, pulls out the name slip, reads it to himself, and passes it on to Abbess Yargag, whose excited tug-nuns steady her so that she may announce the name of the true Soul Child.

Of course, that the Abbess has copped this honor tells everybody all that we need to know. She can't even speak the name on the slip before many in attendance begin to clap their palms against their shoulders. The upshot of this applause, beyond opening my tear ducts, is a sudden propulsion of persons at many different altitudes about the lottery hall: a wheeling zero-g dance of approbation.

YEARS IN TRANSIT: 95
COMPUTER LOGS OF OUR RELUCTANT DALAI LAMA, AGE 20
The Panchen Lama, his peers and subordinates in U-Tsang, and secular hierarchs from Amdo and Kham have made my parents starship nobles.

They have bestowed similar, if slightly lesser honors, on Jetsun Trimon's parents and on Jetsun himself, who wishes to serve us colonizers as Bodhisattva, meteorologist, and lander pilot. In any event, his religious and scientific educations proceed in parallel, and he spends as much time in tech training in Kham Bay as he does in the monasteries in U-Tsang.

As for me, I alternate months among our three drums, on a rotation that pleases more of our up-phase ghosts than it annoys. I ask no credit for the wisdom of my scheme, though; I simply wish to rule (although I prefer the verb "preside") in a way promoting shipboard harmony and reducing our inevitable conflicts.

YEARS IN TRANSIT: 99
COMPUTER LOGS OF OUR RELUCTANT DALAI LAMA, AGE 24
I've now spent nearly five years in this allegedly holy office. Earlier today, thinking hard about our arrival at Guge, in only a little over seven Earth years, I summoned Minister Trungpa to my quarters.

"Yes, Your Holiness, what do you wish?" he asked.

"To invite everyone aboard the *Kalachakra* to submit designs for a special sand mandala. This mandala will commemorate our voyage's inevitable end and honor it as a fruit of the Hope and Community"—I capitalized the words as I spoke them—"that drove us, or our elders, to undertake this journey."

Minister T frowns. "Submit designs?"

"Your new auditory aid works quite well."

"For a competition?"

"Any voyager, any Kalachakran at all, may submit a design."

"But—"

"The artist monks in U-Tsang, who will create the mandala, will judge the entries blindly to determine our finalists. I'll decide the winner."

Minister T does not make eye contact. "The idea of a contest undercuts one of the themes that you wish your mandala to embody, that of Community."

"You hate the whole idea?"

He hedges: "Appoint a respected Yellow Hat artist to design the mandala. In that way, you'll avoid a bureaucratic judging process and lessen popular discontent."

"Look, Neddy, a competition will amuse everyone, and after a century aboard this vacuum-vaulting bean can, we could all use some amusement."

Neddy would like to dispute the point, but I am the Dalai Lama, and what can he say that will not seem a coddling or a defiant promotion of his ego? Nothing. (Chenrezig forgive me, but I relish his discomfiture.) Clearly, the West animates parts of my ego that I should better disguise from those of my subjects—a term I loathe—immersed in Eastern doctrines that guarantee their fatalism and docility. Of course, how many men of Minister Trungpa's station and age enjoy carrying out the bidding of a woman a mere twenty-four years old?

At length he softly says, "I'll see to it, Your Holiness."

"I can see to it myself, but I wanted your opinion."

He nods, his look implying that his opinion doesn't count for much, and takes a deferential step back.

"Don't leave. I need your advice."

"As much as you needed my opinion?"

I take his arm and lead him to a nook where we can sit and talk as intimates. Fortunately, the AG has worked much more reliably all over the ship than it did before my investiture. Neddy looks grizzled, fatigued, and wary, and although he doesn't yet understand why, he has cause for this wariness.

"I want to have a baby," I tell him.

He responds instantly. "I advise you not to, Your Holiness."

"I don't solicit your advice in that area. I'd like you to help me settle on a father for the child."

Neddy reddens.

I've stolen his breath. He'd like to make a devastatingly incisive remark, but can't even manage a feeble Ugh. "In case it's crossed your mind, I haven't short-listed you . . . although Mama once gave you a terrific, unasked for, recommendation."

Minister T pulls himself together, but he's squeezing his hands in his lap as if to express oil from between them.

"I've narrowed the candidates down to two, Jetsun Trimon and Ian Kilkhor, but lately I'm tilting toward Jetsun."

"Then tilt toward Ian."

"Why?"

And Mama's lover provides me with good, dispassionate reasons for selecting the older man: physical fitness, martial arts ability, maturity, intelligence, learning (secular, religious, and technical), administrative/organizational skills, and long-standing affection for me. Jetsun, not yet twenty, has two or three separate callings that he has not yet had time to explore as fully as he ought, and the differences in our ages will lead many in our community to suppose that I have exercised my power in an unseemly way to bring him to my bed. I should give the kid his space.

I know from private conversations, though, that when Jetsun was ten, an unnamed senior monk in Amdo often employed him as a drombo, or passive sex partner, and that the experience nags at him now in ways that Jetsun cannot easily articulate. Apparently, the community didn't see fit, back then, to exercise its outrage on behalf of a boy not yet officially identified as a Soul Child. Of course, the community didn't know, or chose not to know, and uproars rarely result from awareness of such liaisons, anyway. Isn't a monk a man? I say none of this to Neddy.

"Choose Ian," he says, "if you must choose one or the other."

Yesterday, in Kham Bay, after I extended an intranet invitation to him to come see me about his father, who lies ill in his eggshell pod, Jetsun Trimon called upon me in the upper-level stateroom that I inherited, so to speak, from my predecessor. He fell on his knees before me, seized my wrist, and put his lips to the beads, bracelet, and watch that I wear about it. He wanted prayers for his father's recovery, and I acceded to this request with all my heart.

Then something occurred that I set down here with joy rather than guilt. I wanted more from Jetsun than gratitude for my prayers, and he wanted more than my prayers for his worry about his father or for his struggles to master all his many studies. Like me, he wished the solace of the flesh, and as one devoted to forgiveness, contentment, and the alleviation of pain, I took him to my bed and divested him of his garments and let him divest me of mine. Then we embraced, neither of us trembling, or sweating, or flinching in discomfort or distress, for my quarters hummed at a subsonic frequency with enough warmth and gravity to offset any potential malaise or annoyance. Altogether sweetly, his tenderness matched mine. However—

Like most healthy young men, Jetsun quickly reached a coiled-spring readiness. He quivered on **Go**.

I rolled over and bestrode him above the waist, holding his arms to the side and speaking with as much integrity as my gnosis of bliss and emptiness could generate. He calmed and listened. I said that I begrudged neither of us this tension-easing union, but that if we proceeded, then he must know that I wanted his seed to enter me, to take root, to turn embryo, and to attain fruition as our child.

"Do you understand?"

"Yes."

"Do you consent?"

"I consent."

"Do you further consent to acknowledge this child and to assist in its rearing on the planet Guge as well as on this ship?"

He considered these queries. And, smiling, he agreed.

"Then we may advance to the third exalted initiation," I said, "that of the mutual experience of connate joy."

I slid backward over the pliable warmth of his standing phallus and kissed him in the middle of his chest. He reached for me, tenderly, and the AG generators abruptly cut off—suspiciously, it seemed to me. I floated toward the ceiling like a buoyant nixie, too startled to yelp or laugh. Jetsun shoved off in pursuit, but hit a bulkhead and glanced off it horizontally.

It took us a while to reunite, to find enough purchase to consummate our resolve, and to do so honoring the fact that a resurgence of gravity could injure, even kill, both of us. Nonetheless, we managed, and managed passionately.

The "night" has now passed. Jetsun sleeps, mind eased and body sated.

I sit at this console, lock-belted in, recording the most stirring encounter of my life. Every nerve and synapse of my body, and every scrap of assurance in my soul, tell me that I have conceived: Alleluia.

YEARS IN TRANSIT: 100
COMPUTER LOGS OF OUR RELUCTANT DALAI LAMA, AGE 25
Some history: Early in our voyage, when our AG generators worked reliably, our monks created one sand mandala a year. They did so then, as they do now, in a special studio in the Yellow Hat gompa in U-Tsang. They kept materials for these

productions—colored grains of sand, bits of stone or bone, dyed rice grains, sequins—in hard plastic cylinders and worked on their designs over several days. Upon finishing the mandalas, our monks chanted to consecrate them and then, as a dramatic enactment of the impermanent nature of existence, destroyed them by sweeping a brush over and swirling their deity-inhabited geometries into inchoate slurries.

These methods of creating and destroying the mandalas ended four decades into our flight when a gravity outage led to the premature disintegration of a design. A slow-motion sandstorm filled the studio. Grains of maroon, citron, turquoise, emerald, indigo, and blood-red drifted all about, and recovering these for fresh projects required the use of hand-vacs and lots of fussy hand-sorting. Nobody wished to endure such a disaster again. And so, soon thereafter, the monks implemented two new procedures for laying out and completing the mandalas.

One involved gluing down the grains, but this method made the graceful ruination of a finished mandala dicey. A second method involved inserting and arranging the grains into pie-shaped plastic shields using magnets and tech-manipulated "delivery straws," but these tedious procedures, while heightening the praise due the artists, so lengthened the process and stressed the monks that Sakya Gyatso ceased asking for annual mandalas and mandated their fashioning only once every five years.

In any case, today marks our one-hundredth year in flight, and I am fat with a female child who bumps around inside me like those daredevils in old vidped clips who whooshed up and down the sloped walls of special competition arenas on rollers called skateboards.

I think the kid wants out already, but Karma Hahn, my baby doc, tells me she's still much too small to exit, even if the kid does carry on like "a squirrel on an exercise wheel." That metaphor endears both the kid and Karma to me. Because the kid moves, I move. I stroll about my private audience chamber, aka "The Sunshine Hall," in the Potala Palace in U-Tsang. I've voluntarily removed here to show my fellow Buddhists that I am not ashamed of my fecund condition.

Ian announces a visitor, and in walks First Officer Nima Photrang, whom I've not seen for weeks. She has come, it happens, not solely to visit me, but also to look in on an uncle who resides in the nearby Yellow Hat gompa. She has brought a *khata*, a white silk greeting scarf, even though I already have enough of those damned rags to stitch together a ship cover for the *Kalachakra*. She drapes it around my neck. Laughing, I pull it off and drape it around hers.

"Your design contest spurs on every amateur-artist ghost in Amdo and Kham," Nima says. "If you wish your mandala to further community enlightenment by projecting an image of our future Palace of Hope on Guge, well, you've got a lot of folks worrying away at it—mission fully goosed, if not yet fully cooked."

I realize that Sakya Gyatso, my predecessor, his eye on Tibetan history, called the world toward which we relentlessly cruise Guge partly for the g in Gliese 581 g. What an observant and subtle man.

"Nima," I ask, "have you submitted a design?"

"No, but you'll probably never guess who intends to."

No, I never will. I gape cluelessly at Nima.

"Captain Xao Songda, our helmsman. He spends enormous chunks of time with a drafting compass and a pen, or at his console refining design programs that a monk in U-Tsang uploaded a while back to Pemako."

Pemako is the latest version of our intranet. I like to use it. Virtually nightly (stet the pun), it shows me deep-sea sonograms of my jetting squid-kid.

"I hope Captain Xao doesn't expect his status as our shipboard Buzz Lightyear to score him any brownies with the judges."

Nima chortles. "Hardly. He drew as a boy and as a teenager. Later, he designed maglev stations and epic mountain tunnels. He figures he has as good a chance as anyone in a blind judging, and if he wins, what a personal coup."

"Mmm," I say.

"No, really, you've created a monster, Your Holiness—but, as one of the oldest persons aboard, he deserves his fun, I guess."

We chat some more. Nima asks if she may lay her palm on the curve of my belly, and I say yes. When the brat-to-be surfs my insides like a berserk skateboarder, Nima and I laugh like schoolgirls. By some criteria, I still qualify.

YEARS IN TRANSIT: 101
COMPUTER LOGS OF OUR RELUCTANT
DALAI LAMA, AGE 25–26

I return to Amdo to deliver my child. Early in the hundred and first year of our journey, my water breaks. Karma Hahn, my mother, and Alicia and Emily Paljor attend my lying-in, while my father, Ian Kilkhor, Minister Trungpa, and Jetsun perform a nervous do-si-do in an antechamber. I give the guys hardly a thought. Delivering a kid requires stamina, a lot of Tantric focus, and a cooperative fetus, but I've got 'em all and the kid slams out in less than four hours.

I lie in a freshly made bed with my squiddle dozing in a warming blanket against my left shoulder. Well-wishers and family surround us like sentries, although I have no idea what they've got to shield us from: I've never felt safer.

Mama says, "When will you tell us the ruddy shrimp's name? You've kept it a secret eight months past forever."

"Ask Jetsun. He chose it."

Everyone turns to Jetsun, who at twenty-one looks like a fabled Kham warrior, lean and smooth-faced, a flawless bronze sculpture of himself. How can I not love him? Jetsun looks to me. I nod.

"It's . . . it's Kyipa." Like the sweetheart he is, he blushes.

"Ah," Nyendak Trungpa sighs. "Happiness."

"If we all didn't strive so damned hard for happiness," Daddy says, "we'd almost always have a pretty good time."

"You stole that," Mama rebukes him. "And your timing sucks."

From behind those crowded about my babe-cave, a short, sturdy, gray-haired man edges in. I know him as Alicia Paljor's father, Emily Paljor's husband—but Daddy, Ian, and Neddy know him as the chief fuel specialist on our strut-ship and thus a personage of renowned ability. So I assume he's come—like a wise man—to kneel beside and to adore our newborn squiddle. Or has he come just to meet his wife and daughter and fetch them back to their stateroom?

In his ministerial capacity, Neddy says, "Welcome, Specialist Paljor."

"I need to talk to Her Holiness." Kanjur Paljor bows and approaches my bed. "If I may, Your Holiness."

"Of course."

The area clears of everyone except Paljor, Ian Kilkhor, Kyipa, and me. A weight descends—a weight comprising everything that's ever floated free of its moorings during every AG quittage that our strut-ship has ever suffered—and that weight, condensed into one tiny spherical mass, lowers itself onto my baby's back and so onto me, crushing this blissful moment into dust and slivered glass. Ian edges to the top of my bed, but I already know that his strength and his heavy glare prove impotent against whatever message Kanjur Paljor has brought.

Paljor says, "Your Holiness, I beg your infinite pardon."

"Tell me." He looks at Ian and then, in petition, at me again. "I'd prefer to deliver this news to you alone, Your Holiness."

"Regard my agent's simultaneous presence and absence as an enacted mystery or koan," I tell Paljor. "He speaks a helpful truth."

Paljor nods and seizes my free hand. "About fifteen hours ago, I found a serious navigational anomaly while running a fuel-tank check. Before bringing the problem to you, I ran some figures to make sure that I hadn't made a calculation error; that I wasn't just overreacting to a situation of no real consequence."

He pauses to touch my Kyipa's blanket. "How much technical detail do you want, Your Holiness?"

"Right now, none. Give me the gist."

"For a little over one hundred and twenty hours, the *Kalachakra* traveled at its top speed at a small angle off our requisite heading."

"How? Why?"

"Before I answer, let me assure you that we have since corrected for this deviation and that we'll soon run true again."

"What do you mean, 'soon'? Why don't we 'run true' now?"

"We do, Your Holiness, in the sense that First Officer Photrang has set us on an efficient angle to intercept our former heading to Guge. But we don't, in the sense that we still must compensate for the unintended divergence."

Ian Kilkhor says, "Tell Her Holiness why this 'unintended divergence' constitutes one huge fucking threat."

Totally appalled, I look back at my bodyguard and friend. "I thought you weren't here! Or did you leave behind just that part of you that views me as an unteachable idiot? Go away, Mr. Kilkhor. Get out."

Kilkhor has the decency and good sense to do as I command. Kyipa, unsettled by my outburst, squirms fretfully on my shoulder.

"The danger," I tell Kanjur Paljor, "centers on fuel expenditure. If we've gone too far off course, we won't have enough antimatter ice left to reach Guge. Have I admissibly described our peril?"

"Yes, Your Holiness." He doesn't fall to one knee, like a magus beside the infant deity Christ, but crouches so that our faces are nearly at a level. "I believe—I think—we have just enough fuel to complete our journey, but at this late stage it could prove a close thing. If there's another emergency requiring an additional course correction—"

"We might not arrive at all."

Paljor nods, and consolingly pats Kyipa's playing-card-sized back.

"How did this happen?"

"Human error, I'm afraid."

"Tell me what sort."

"Lack of attention to the telltales that should have prevented this divergence from our heading."

"Whose error? Captain Xao's?"

"Yes, Your Holiness. Nima says his mental state has deteriorated badly over these past few weeks. What she first thought eccentricities, she now views as evidence of age-related mental debilities. He stays awake so long and endures so much stress. And he puts too much faith in the alleged reliability of our electronic systems."

Also, he came to feel that creating a design for my Palace of Hope mandala took precedence over his every other duty on a strut-ship programmed to fly to its destination, with the result that he put himself on autopilot too.

"Where is he now?" I ask Paljor.

"Sleeping, under medical supervision—not ursidormizine slumber but bed rest, Your Holiness."

I thank Paljor and dismiss him.

Clutching Kyipa to me, I nuzzle her sweet-smelling face.

Tomorrow, I'll tell Nima to advise her flight crew that they must remain up-phase ghosts until we know for sure the outcomes of Xao's inattention and our efforts to correct for its potential consequences: a headlong rush to nowhere.

Without benefit of lock belts, my daughter, Kyipa, kicks in her bassinet. I seldom worry about her floating off during AG outages because she loves such spells of weightlessness. She uses them to exercise her limbs—admittedly, with no strengthening resistance—and to explore our stateroom, which boasts Buddha figurines, wall hangings, filigreed star charts, miniature starship models, and other interesting items. At five months, she thinks herself a big finch or a pygmy porpoise. She undulates about, giggling at the currents she creates, or, the AG restored, inches along with her pink tongue tip between her lips and her bum rising and falling like a migrating molehill.

As Dalai Lama (many argue), I should never have borne this squiddle, but Karen, Simon, Jetsun, and Jetsun's mama might disagree, and all contribute to her care. Even Minister T acknowledges that conceiving and bearing her has confirmed my sense of the karmic correctness of my Dalai Lamahood more powerfully than any other event to date. Because of this happy squiddle girl, I do stronger, better, holier work.

To those who tsk-tsk when they see Kyipa squirming in my arms, I say:

"This child is my Wheel of Time, my mandala, who has as one purpose to further my evolving enlightenment. Her other purposes she will learn and fulfill in time. So set aside your resentments so that you may more easily fulfill yours."

But although I don't fret about Kyipa during gravity outages, I do worry about her future . . . and ours.

Will we safely arrive at the Gliese 581 system? Of the fifty antimatter-ice tanks with which (long before my birth) we started our journey, we've used up and discarded thirty-eight, and Paljor says that we have exhausted nearly half of the thirty-ninth tank, with over five and a half years remaining until our ETA in orbit around Guge. From the outside, our ship begins to resemble a skeleton of its outbound self, the bones of a picked-clean fish. And if the *Kalachakra* makes it at all, as Paljor has speculated, it will slice the issue scarily close.

I stupidly assumed that our eventual shift into deceleration mode would work in our favor, but Paljor cautioned that slowing our strut-ship—so that we do not overshoot Guge, like a golf putt running up to but not beyond its cup—will require more fuel than I thought. Later he showed me math proving that reaching Guge will require "an incident-free approach"—because our antimatter reserves, the fail-safe reserves with which we began our flight, have already dissolved into the ether slipstreaming by the magnetic field coils generating our plasma shield out front.

Still, I don't believe in shielding our human freight from issues bearing on our survival. Therefore, I've had Minister T announce the fact of this crisis to everyone up-phase and working. Thankfully, general panic has not ensued. Instead, crew members brainstorm stopgap strategies for conserving fuel, and the monks and nuns in U-Tsang pray and chant. Soon enough, when we begin to brake, everyone will arise again, shake off the fog of hibernizing, and learn the truth about our final approach. Then every deck will team with ghosts preparing to orbit Guge; to assay the habitable wedges between its sun-stuck face and its bleaker sides; and to decide which of the two wedges is better suited to settlement.

YEARS IN TRANSIT: 102
COMPUTER LOGS OF OUR RELUCANT DALAI LAMA, AGE 27

Xao Songda, our deposed captain, died just twelve hours ago. Although Kyipa celebrated her first birthday last week, the man never laid eyes on her.

Xao's "bed rest" turned into pathological pacing and harangues unintelligible to anyone ignorant of Mandarin Chinese. These behaviors—symptomatic of an aggressive type of senility unknown to us—our medicos treated with tranks, placebos (foolishly, I guess), experimental diets, and long walks through the commons of Kham Bay. Nothing calmed him or eased the intensity of his gibbering tirades. I had so wanted Kyipa to meet our captain (or the avatar of the self preceding this sorry incarnation), but I could not risk exposing her to one of his abusive rants.

It bears stating, though, that everyone aboard *Kalachakra*, knowing the sacrifices that the captain made for us, forgives him his navigation error. All showed him the honor, courtesy, and patience that he deserved for these sacrifices. Nima Photrang, who assumed his captaincy, believes he and Satya Gyatso suffered similar personality disintegrations, albeit in different ways. Sakya used Tantric practices to end his life and Xao Songda fell to an Alzheimer's-like scourge, but the effects of sleep deprival, suppressed anxiety, and overwork ultimately caused their deaths.

Xao created designs for my mandala competition, I think, as a way to decompress from these burdens. During the last hours of his illness, Ian Kilkhor searched his quarters for anything that could help us fathom his disease and preserve our memory of him as the intrepid Tibetan Buddhist who carried us within three lights of our destination. However, Ian returned to me with two hundred hand-drawn sketches and computer-assisted designs for my Palace of Hope mandala.

These "designs" appalled and saddened us. The one Xao hand-drew resemble big multicolored Rorschach blots, and those stemming from his cyber-design programs look like geometrically askew fever dreams. All are pervaded with interlocking claws, jagged teeth, vermiform bodies, and occluded reptilian eyes. None could serve as a model for the mandala of my envisioning.

"I'm sorry," Ian said. "The old guy seems to have swallowed the pituitary gland of a Komodo dragon."

So, given our fuel situation and Captain Xao's death, I've declared a moratorium on mandala-design creation.

Now there is a strong movement afoot—a respectful one—to eject Captain Xao Songda's corpse into the void, one more human collop for the highballing dark. As I've already noted here, we've used this procedure many times before, as a practice coincident with Buddha Dharma and, in this case, as one befitting a helmsman of Xao's stature. But I resist this seeming consensus in favor of a better option: taking the captain to Guge and setting his sinewy body out on an escarpment there, to blacken in its gales and scale in its thaws, our first sacrificial alms to the planet.

One work cycle past, Captain Photrang began to brake the *Kalachakra*. We are four years out from Gliese 581 g, and Kanjur Paljor tells me that unless a meteorite penetrates our plasma shield or some other anomalous disaster befalls us, we will reach our destination. Ian notes that we will coast into planetary orbit like a vehicle with an internal combustion engine chugging into its pit on fumes. I don't altogether twig the analogy, but I do get its gist. Alleluia! If only time passed more quckly.

Meanwhile, I keep Kyipa awake and ignore those misguided ghosts advising me to ease her into grave-cave sleep so that time will pass more quickly for her. Jetsun and I enjoy her far too much to see her down. More important, if she stays up-phase most of the rest of our journey, she will learn and grow; and when we descend to the surface of Guge with her, she will have a sharper mind and better motor skills at five or six than any long-term sleeper of roughly similar age.

Every day, every hour, my excitement intensifies. And our ship plows on.

YEARS IN TRANSIT: 106
COMPUTER LOGS OF OUR RELUCTANT DALAI LAMA, AGE 31

Maintenance preoccupies nearly everyone aboard. In less than a week, our strut-ship will rendezvous with Guge and orbit its oblate sun-locked mass. Then we will make several sequential descents to and returns from "The Land of Snow" aboard our lander, the *Yak Butter Express*.

Jetsun will serve as shuttle pilot for one of these first excursions and as backup on another. He and others perform daily checks on the vehicle in its hangar harnesses, just as other techs strive to ensure the reliability of every mechanical and human component. Our hopes and our anxieties contend. At my urging, the Bodhisattva of U-Tsang go from from deck to deck assisting in our labors and transmitting positive energies to every bay and to all those at work in them.

Twelve hours after Captain Photrang eased *Kalachakra* into orbit around Guge, Minister T comes to me to report that the Yellow Hat artists in U-Tsang have finished a mandala based on a design that they, not I, chose as our most esteemed entry. Eagerly, I ask whom these Bodhisattva selected.

Lucinda Gomez, a teenager from Amdo Bay, has taken the laurel.

Neddy asks the monks to transport the mandala in its pie-shaped shield to Bhava

Park, a commons here in Kham Bay, and they do. A bird camera in the park transmits the mandala's image to public screens and to vidped units everywhere. Intricate and colorful, it sits on an easel amid a host of tables and many happily milling Kalachakrans. Because we're celebrating our arrival, I don't watch on a screen but stand in Bhava Park before the thing itself. Banners and prayer flags abound. I hail the excited Lucinda Gomez and all the artist monks, congratulate them, and also speak to many onlookers, who heed my words smilingly.

The Yellow Hats chant verses of consecration that affirm their fulfillment of my charge and then extend to everyone the blessings of Hope and Community implicit in the mandala's labyrinthine central Palace. Kyipa, almost six, reaches out to touch the bottom of the encased mandala.

"This is the prettiest," she says.

She has never before seen a finished mandala in its full artifactual glory.

Then the artist monks start to carry the shield from its easel to a tabletop, there to insert narrow tubes into it and send the mandala's fixed grains flying with focused blasts of air—to symbolize, as tradition dictates, the primacy of impermanence in our lives. But before they reach the table, I lift my hand.

"We won't destroy this sand mandala," I announce, "until we've planted a viable settlement on Guge."

And everyone around us in Bhava Park cheers. The monks restore the mandala to its easel, a ton of colored confetti drops from suspended bins above us, music plays, and people sing, dance, eat, laugh, and mingle.

Kyipa, holding her hands up to the drifting paper and plastic flakes, beams at me ecstatically.

In our shuttle-cum-lander, we glide from the belly of Kham Bay toward Gliese 581 g, better known to all aboard the *Kalachakra* as Guge, "The Land of Snow."

From here, the amiable dwarf star about which Guge swings resembles the yolk of a colossal fried egg, more reddish than yellow-orange, with a misty orange corona about it like the egg's congealed albumin. I've made it sound ugly, but Gliese 581 looks edible to me and quickly trips my hunger to reach the planet below.

As for Guge, it gleams beneath us like an old coin.

In our first week on its surface, we have already built a tent camp in one of the stabilized climate zones of the nearside terminator. Across the tall visible arc of that terminator, the planet shows itself marbled by a bluish and slate-gray crust marked by fingerlike snowfields and glacier sheets.

On the ground, our people call their base camp Lhasa and their rugged territory all about it New Tibet. In response to this naming and to the alacrity with which our fellow Kalachakrans adopted it, Minister T wept openly.

I find I like the man. Indeed, I go down for my first visit to the surface with his blessing. (Simon, my father, already bivouacs there, to investigate ways to grow barley, winter wheat, and other grains in the thin air and cold temperatures.) Kyipa, of course, remains for now on our orbiting strut-ship—in Neddy's stateroom, which he now shares openly with the child's grandmother, Karen Bryn Bonfils. Neddy and Karen Bryn dote on my daughter shamelessly.

Our descent to Lhas won't take long, but, along with many others in this second wave of pioneers, I deliberately drop into a meditative trance. I focus on a photograph that Neddy gave me after the mandala ceremony at the arrival celebration, and I recall his words as he presented it:

"Soon after you became a teenager, Greta, I started to doubt your commitment to the Dharma and your ability to stick."

"How tactful of you to wait till now to tell me," I said, smiling.

"But I never lost a deeper layer of faith. Today I can say that all my unspoken doubt has burned off like a summer meadow mist." He gave me the worn photo—not a hardened d-cube—that now engages my attention.

In it, a Tibetan boy of eight or nine faces the viewer with a broad smile. He holds before him, also facing the viewer, a baby girl with rosy cheeks and with eyes so familiar that I tear up in consternation and joy. The eyes belong to my predecessor's infant sister, who didn't live long after the capture of this image.

The eyes also belong to Kyipa.

I meditate on this conundrum, richly. Soon, after all, the *Yak Butter Express* will set down in New Tibet.

astrophilia

CARRIE VAUGHN

New York Times *bestseller Carrie Vaughn is the author of a wildly popular series of novels detailing the adventures of Kitty Narville, a radio personality who also happens to be a werewolf, and who runs a late-night call-in radio advice show for supernatural creatures. The "Kitty" books include* Kitty and the Midnight Hour, Kitty Goes to Washington, Kitty Takes a Holiday, *and* Kitty and the Silver Bullet, Kitty and the Dead Man's Hand, Kitty Raises Hell, Kitty's House of Horrors, Kitty Goes to War, *and* Kitty's Big Trouble. *Her other novels include* Voices of Dragons, *her first venture into young adult territory, and a fantasy,* Discord's Apple. *Vaughn's short work has appeared in* Lightspeed, Asimov's Science Fiction, Subterranean, Wild Cards: Inside Straight, Realms of Fantasy, Jim Baen's Universe, Paradox, Strange Horizons, Weird Tales, All-Star Zeppelin Adventure Stories, *and elsewhere. Her most recent books include the novels* After the Golden Age *and* Steel; *a collection,* Straying from the Path, *a new "Kitty" novel,* Kitty Steals the Show, *and a collection of her "Kitty" stories,* Kitty's Greatest Hits. *She lives in Colorado. Coming up is another new "Kitty" novel,* Kitty Rocks the House.

In the powerful tale that follows, she shows us that even in a diminished, ecologically distressed near future, one still recovering from what was nearly an apocalypse and still concentrating on survival, sometimes the most important thing to do is to hang on to your dreams.

After five years of drought, the tiny, wool-producing household of Greentree was finished. First the pastures died off, then the sheep, and Stella and the others didn't have any wool to process and couldn't meet the household's quota, small though it was with only five of them working at the end. The holding just couldn't support a household and the regional committee couldn't keep putting credits into it, hoping that rains would come. They might never come, or the next year might be a flood. No one could tell, and that was the problem, wasn't it?

None of them argued when Az and Jude put in to dissolve Greentree. They could starve themselves to death with pride, but that would be a waste of resources. Stella was a good weaver, and ought to have a chance somewhere else. That was the first reason they gave for the decision.

Because they dissolved voluntarily, the committee found places for them in other households, ones not on the verge of collapse. However, Az put in a special request and found Stella's new home herself. "I know the head of the place, Toma. He'll take good care of you, but more than that his place is prosperous. Rich enough for children, even. You could earn a baby there, Stella." Az's wrinkled hands gripped Stella's young ones in her own, and her eyes shone. Twenty-three years ago, Greentree had been prosperous enough to earn a baby: Stella. But those days were gone.

Stella began to have doubts. "Mama, I don't want to leave you and everyone—"

"We'll be fine. We'd have had to leave sooner or later, and this way we've got credits to take with us. Start new on a good footing, yes?"

"Yes, but—" She hesitated, because her fears were childish. "What if they don't like me?"

Az shook her head. "Winter market I gave Toma the shawl you made. You should have seen him, Stella, his mouth dropped. He said Barnard Croft would take you on the spot, credits or no."

But what if they don't like *me*, Stella wanted to whine. She wasn't worried about her weaving.

Az must have seen that she was about to cry. "Oh, dear, it'll be all right. We'll see each other at the markets, maybe more if there's trading to be done. You'll be happy, I know you will. Better things will come."

Because Az seemed so pleased for her, Stella stayed quiet, and hoped.

In the spring, Stella traveled to Barnard Croft, three hundred miles on the Long Road from Greentree, in the hills near the coast.

Rain poured on the last day of the journey, so the waystation driver used a pair of horses to draw the wagon, instead of the truck. Stella offered to wait until the storm passed and the solar batteries charged up, but he had a schedule to keep, and insisted that the horses needed the exercise.

Stella sat under the awning on the front seat of the wagon, wrapped in a blanket against the chill, feeling sorry for the hulking draft animals in front of her. They were soaked, brown coats dripping as they clomped step-by-step on the muddy road. It might have been faster, waiting for the clouds to break, for the sun to emerge and let them use the truck. But the driver said they'd be waiting for days in these spring rains.

She traveled through an alien world, wet and green. Stella had never seen so much water in her whole life, all of it pouring from the sky. A quarter of this amount of rain a couple of hundred miles east would have saved Greentree.

The road curved into the next green valley, to Barnard Croft. The wide meadow and its surrounding, rolling hills were green, lush with grass. A handful of alpaca grazed along a stream that ran frothing from the hills opposite. The animals didn't seem to mind the water, however matted and heavy their coats looked. There'd be some work, cleaning that mess for spinning. Actually, she looked forward to it. She wanted to make herself useful as soon as she could. To prove herself. If this didn't work, if she didn't fit in here and had to throw herself on the mercy of the regional committee to find some place prosperous enough to take her, that could use a decent weaver . . . no, this would work.

A half a dozen whitewashed cottages clustered together, along with sheds and shelters for animals, a couple of rabbit hutches, and squares of turned black soil with a barest sheen of green—garden plots and new growth. The largest cottage stood apart from the others. It had wide doors and many windows, shuttered now against the rain—the work house, she guessed. Under the shelter of the wide eaves sat wooden barrels for washing wool, and a pair of precious copper pots for dyeing. All comfortable, familiar sights.

The next largest cottage, near the garden plots, had a smoking chimney. Kitchen and common room, most likely. Which meant the others were sleeping quarters. She wondered which was hers, and who'd she'd be sharing with. A pair of windmills stood on the side of one hill; their trefoil blades were still.

At the top of the highest hill, across the meadow, was a small, unpainted shack. It couldn't have held more than a person or two standing upright. This, she did not recognize. Maybe it was a curing shed, though it seemed an unlikely spot, exposed as it was to every passing storm.

A turn-off took them from the road to the cottages, and by the time the driver pulled up the horses, eased the wagon to a stop, and set the brakes, a pair of men wrapped in cloaks emerged from the work house to greet them. Stella thanked the driver and jumped to the ground. Her boots splashed, her long woolen skirt tangled around her legs, and the rain pressed the blanket close around her. She felt sodden and bedraggled, but she wouldn't complain.

The elder of those who came to greet her was middle aged and worn, but he moved briskly and spread his arms wide. "Here she is! Didn't know if you would make it in this weather." This was Toma. Az's friend, Stella reminded herself. Nothing to worry about.

"Horses'll get through anything," the driver said, moving to the back of the wagon to unload her luggage.

"Well then," Toma said. "Let's get you inside and dried off."

"Thank you," Stella managed. "I just have a couple of bags. And a loom. Az let me take Greentree's loom."

"Well then, that is a treasure. Good."

The men clustered around the back of the wagon to help. The bags held her clothes, a few books and letters and trinkets. Her equipment: spindles and needles, carders, skeins of yarn, coils of roving. The loom took up most of the space—dismantled, legs and frames strapped together, mechanisms folded away in protective oilskin. It would take her most of a day to set up. She'd feel better when it was.

A third figure came running from the work house, shrouded by her wrap and hood like the others. The shape of her was female, young—maybe even Stella's age. She wore dark trousers and a pale tunic, like the others.

She came straight to the driver. "Anything for me?"

"Package from Griffith?" the driver answered.

"Oh, yes!"

The driver dug under an oil cloth and brought out a leather document case, stuffed full. The woman came forward to take it, revealing her face, sandstone-burnished skin and bright brown eyes.

Toma scowled at her, but the woman didn't seem to notice. She tucked the package under her arm and beamed like sunshine.

"At least be useful and take a bag," Toma said to her.

Taking up a bag with a free hand, the woman flashed a smile at Stella, and turned to carry her load to the cottage.

Toma and other other man, Jorge, carried the loom to the work house. Hefting the rest of her luggage, Stella went to the main cottage, following the young woman at a distance. Behind her, the driver returned to his seat and got the horses moving again; their hooves splashed on the road.

Around dinner time, the clouds broke, belying the driver's prediction. Some sky and a last bit of sunlight peeked through.

They ate what seemed to her eyes a magnificent feast—meat, eggs, preserved fruits and vegetables, fresh bread. At Greentree, they'd barely got through the winter on stores, and until this meal Stella hadn't realized she'd been dimly hungry all the time, for weeks. Months. Greentree really had been dying.

The folk of the croft gathered around the hearth at night, just as they did back home at Greentree, just as folk did at dozens of households up and down the Long Road. She met everyone: Toma and Jorge, who'd helped with the loom. Elsta, Toma's partner, who ran the kitchen and garden. Nik and Wendy, Jon and Faren. Peri had a baby, which showed just how well off Barnard was, to be able to support a baby as well as a refugee like Stella. The first thing Peri did was put the baby—Bette—in Stella's arms, and Stella was stricken because she'd never held a wriggly baby before and was afraid of dropping her. But Peri arranged her arms just so and took the baby back after a few moments of cooing over them both. Stella had never thought of earning the right to have her implant removed, to have a baby—another mouth to feed at Greentree would have been a disaster.

Elsta was wearing the shawl Stella had made, the one Az had given Toma—her audition, really, to prove her worth. The shawl was an intricate weave made of finely spun merino. Stella had done everything—carded and spun the wool, dyed it the difficult smoky blue, and designed the pattern herself. Elsta didn't have to wear it, the croft could have traded it for credits. Stella felt a small spark of pride. Wasn't just charity that brought her here.

Stella had brought her work basket, but Elsta tsked at her. "You've had a long trip, so rest now. Plenty of time to work later." So she sat on a blanket spread out on the floor and played with Bette.

Elsta picked apart a tangle of roving, preparing to draft into the spindle of her spinning wheel. Toma and Jorge had a folding table in front of them, and the tools to repair a set of hand carders. The others knit, crocheted, or mended. They no doubt made all their own clothing, from weaving the fabric to sewing, dark trousers, bright skirts, aprons, and tunics. Stella's hands itched to work—she was in the middle of knitting a pair of very bright yellow socks from the remnants of yarn from a weaving. They'd be ugly but warm—and the right kind of ugly had a charm of its own. But Elsta was probably right, and the baby was fascinating. Bette had a set of wooden blocks that she banged into each other; occasionally, very seriously, she handed them to Stella. Then demanded them back. The process must have had a logic to it.

The young woman wasn't with them. She'd skipped dinner as well. Stella was thinking of how to ask about her, when Elsta did it for her.

"Is Andi gone out to her study, then?"

Toma grumbled, "Of course she is." The words bit.

Her study—the shack on the hill? Stella listened close, wishing the baby would stop banging her blocks so loudly.

"Toma—"

"She should be here."

"She's done her work, let her be. The night's turned clear, you know how she gets."

"She should listen to me."

"The more you push, the angrier she'll get. Leave her be, dearest."

Elsta's wheel turned and purred, Peri hummed as she knit, and Bette's toys clacked. Toma frowned, never looking up from his work.

Her bags sat by one of the two beds in the smallest cottage, only half unpacked. The other bed, Andi's, remained empty. Stella washed, brushed out her short blond hair, changed into her nightdress, and curled up under the covers. Andi still hadn't returned.

The air smelled wrong, here. Wet, earthy, as if she could smell the grass growing outside the window. The shutters cracked open to let in a breeze. Stella was chilled; her nose wouldn't stop running. The desert always smelled dusty, dry—even at night, the heat of the sun rose up from the ground. There, her nose itched with dust.

She couldn't sleep. She kept waiting for Andi to come back.

Finally, she did. Stella started awake when the door opened with the smallest squeak—so she must have slept, at least a little. Cocooned under the covers, she clutched her pillow, blinking, uncertain for a moment where she was and what was happening. Everything felt wrong, but that was to be expected, so she lay still.

Andi didn't seem to notice that she was awake. She hung up her cloak on a peg by the door, sat on her bed while she peeled off shoes and clothes, which she left lying on the chest at the foot of her bed, and crawled under the covers without seeming to notice—or care—that Stella was there. The woman moved quickly— nervously, even? But when she pulled the covers over her, she lay still, asleep in moments. Stella had a suspicion that she'd had practice, falling asleep quickly in the last hours before dawn, before she'd be expected to rise and work.

Stella supposed she would get a chance to finally talk to her new roommate soon enough, but she had no idea what she was going to say to her.

The next day, the clouds had more than broken. No sign of them remained, and the sun blazed clear as it ever had in the desert, but on a world that was wet, green, and growing. The faint sprouts in the garden plots seem to have exploded into full growth, leaves uncurling. The angora in the hutches pressed twitching noses to the wire mesh of their cages, as if they could squeeze out to play in the meadow. Every shutter and window in the croft was opened to let in the sun.

The work house was wide, clean, whitewashed inside and out. It smelled of lanolin, fiber and work. Lint floated in beams of sunlight. Two—now three—looms and a pair of spinning wheels sat facing each other, so the weavers and spinners could talk. Days would pass quickly here. The first passed quickly enough, and Stella finished it feeling tired and satisfied.

Andi had spent the day at the wash tubs outside, cleaning a batch of wool, preparing it to card and spin in the next week or so. She'd still been asleep when Stella got up that morning, but must have woken up soon after. They still hadn't talked. Not even hello. They kept missing each other, being in different places. Continually out of rhythm, like a pattern that wove crooked because you hadn't counted the threads right. The more time passed without them speaking, the harder Stella found it to think of anything to say. She wanted to ask, *Are you avoiding me?*

Stella had finished putting away her work and was headed for the common room, when she noticed Andi following the footpath away from the cottages, around the meadow and up the hill to the lonely shack. Her study, Elsta had called it. She walked at a steady pace, not quite running, but not lingering.

After waiting until she was far enough ahead that she was not likely to look over her shoulder, Stella followed.

The trail up the hill was a hike, and even walking slowly Stella was soon gasping for breath. But slowly and steadily she made progress. The path made a couple of switchbacks, and finally reached the crest of the hill and the tiny weathered shack planted there.

As she suspected, the view was worth the climb. The whole of Barnard Croft's valley was visible, as well as the next one over. The neighboring croft's cottages were pale specks, and a thread of smoke climbed from one. The hills were soft, rounded, cut through with clefts like the folds in a length of fabric. Trees along the creek gave texture to the picture. The Long Road was a gray track painted around the green rise. The sky above stretched on, and on, blue touched by a faint haze. If she squinted, she thought she could see a line of gray on the far western horizon—the ocean, and the breeze in that direction had a touch of salt and wild. From this perspective, the croft rested in a shallow bowl that sat on the top of the world. She wondered how long it would take to walk around the entire valley, and decided she would like to try some sunny day.

The shed seemed even smaller when she was standing next to it. Strangely, part of the roof was missing, folded back on hinges, letting in light. The walls were too high to see over, and the door was closed. Stella hesitated; she shouldn't be here, she was invading. She had to share a room with this woman, she shouldn't intrude. Then again—she had to share a room with this woman. She only wanted to talk. And if Andi didn't like it, well . . .

Stella knocked on the door before she could change her mind. Three quick, woodpecker-like raps.

When the door swung out, she hopped back, managed not to fall over, and looked wide eyed to see Andi glaring at her.

Then the expression softened, falling away to blank confusion. "Oh. Hi."

They stared at each other for a long moment. Andi leaned on the door, blocking the way; Stella still couldn't see what was inside.

"May I come in?" she finally asked, because Andi hadn't closed the door on her.

"Oh—sure." The woman seemed to shake herself out of a daydream, and stepped back to open the door wide.

The bulk of the tiny room was taken up by a device mounted on a tripod as tall as she was. A metallic cylinder, wide as a bucket, pointed to the ceiling. A giant tin can almost, except the outer case was painted gray, and it had latches, dials, levers, all manner of protrusions connected to it. Stella moved around it, studying it, reminding herself not to touch, however much the object beckoned.

"It's a telescope, isn't it?" she asked, looking over to Andi. "An old one."

A smile dawned on Andi's face, lighting her mahogany eyes. "It is—twelve-inch reflector. Century or so old, probably. Pride and joy." Her finger traced up the tripod, stroking it like it was a favorite pet.

Stella's chest clenched at that smile, and she was glad now that she'd followed Andi here. She kept her voice calm. "Where'd you get it? You couldn't have traded for it—"

"Oh no, you can't trade for something like this. What would you trade for it?" Meaning how many bales of wool, or bolts of cloth, or live alpacas, or cans full of fish from the coast was something like this worth? You couldn't put a price on it. Some people would just give it away, because it had no real use, no matter how rare it was. Andi continued, "It was Pan's, who ran the household before Toma. He was one of the ones who helped build up the network with the observatories, after the big fall. Then he left it all to me. He'd have left it to Toma, but he wasn't interested." She shrugged, as if unable to explain.

"Then it actually works?"

"Oh yes." That smile shone again, and Stella would stay and talk all night, to keep that smile lit up. "I mean, not now, we'll have to wait until dark, assuming the weather stays clear. With the roof open it's almost a real observatory. See how we've fixed the seams?" She pointed to the edges, where the roof met the walls. Besides the hinges and latches that closed the roof in place, the seams had oilskin weatherproofing, to keep rain from seeping through the cracks. The design was clever. The building, then, was shelter for the equipment. The telescope never moved—the bottom points of the tripod were anchored with bricks.

Beside the telescope there wasn't much here: a tiny desk, a shelf filled with books, a bin holding a stack of papers, and a wooden box holding pencils. The leather pouch Andi had received yesterday was open, and packets of paper spread over the desk.

"Is that what you got in the mail?"

She bustled to the desk and shuffled through the pages. "Assignment from Griffith. It's a whole new list of coordinates, now that summer's almost here. The whole sky changes—what we see changes, at least—so I make observations and send the whole thing back." The flush in her brown face deepened as she ducked away. "I know it doesn't sound very interesting, we mostly just write down numbers and trade them back and forth—"

"Oh no," Stella said, shaking her head to emphasize. "It's interesting. Unusual—"

"And useless, Toma says." The smile turned sad, and last night's discussion became clear to Stella.

"Nothing's useless," Stella said. "It's like you said—you can't just throw something like this away." This wasn't like a household that couldn't feed itself and had no choice but to break up.

Three sharp rings of a distant brass bell sounded across the valley. Stella looked out the door, confused.

"Elsta's supper bell," Andi explained. "She only uses it when we've all scattered." She quickly straightened her papers, returned them to their pouch, and latched the roof back in place. Too late, Stella thought to help, reaching up to hold the panel of wood after Andi had already secured the last latch. Oh well. Maybe next time.

Stella got a better look at Andi as they walked back to the croft. She was rough in the way of wind and rain, her dark hair curly, pulled back by a scrap of gray yarn that was unraveling. The collar of her shirt was untied, and her woven jacket had slipped off a shoulder. Stella resisted an urge to pull it back up, and to brush the lock of hair that had fallen out of the tie behind her ear.

"So you're really more of an astronomer than a weaver," Stella said. She'd tried to sound encouraging, but Andi frowned.

"Drives Toma crazy," Andi said. "If there was a household of astronomers, I'd join. But astronomy doesn't feed anyone, does it? Well, some of it does—meteorology, climatology, solar astronomy, maybe. But not what we're doing. We don't earn anyone a baby."

"What are you doing?"

"Astronomical observation. As much as we can, though it feels like reinventing the wheel sometimes. We're not learning anything that people didn't already know back in the day. We're just—well, it feels like filling in the gaps until we get back to where we were. Tracking asteroids, marking supernovae, that sort of thing. Maybe we can't do much with the data. But it might be useful someday."

"There, you see—it's planning ahead. There's use in that."

She sighed. "The committees mostly think it's a waste of time. They can't really complain, though, because we—those of us in the network—do our share and work extra to support the observatories. A bunch of us designate ration credits toward Griffith and Kitt Peak and Wilson—they've got the region's big scopes—to keep staff there maintaining the equipment, to keep the solar power and windmills running. Toma always complains, says if I put my extra credits toward the household we could have a second baby. He says it could even be mine. But they're my credits, and this is important. I earn the time I spend with the scope, and he can't argue." She said that as a declaration, then looked straight at Stella, who blushed. "They may have brought you here to make up for me."

Stella didn't know what to say to that. She was too grateful to have a place at all, to consider that she may have been wanted.

Awkwardly, Andi covered up the silence. "Well. I hope you like it here. That you don't get too homesick, I mean."

The words felt like a warm blanket, soft and wooly. "Thanks."

"We can be kind of rowdy sometimes. Bette gets colicky, and you haven't heard Wendy sing yet. Then there's Jorge and Jon—they share a bed as well as a cottage, see, and can get pretty loud, though if you tease them about it they'll deny it."

"I don't mind rowdy. But I did almost expect to find a clandestine still in that shed."

Andi laughed. "I think Toma'd like a still better, because at least you can drink from it. Elsta does make a really good cider, though. If she ever put enough together to trade it would make up for all the credits I waste on the observatories."

As they came off the hill and approached the cluster of cottages, Andi asked, "Did you know that Stella means star in Latin?"

"Yes, I did," she answered.

Work was work no matter where you were, and Stella settled into her work quickly. The folk of Barnard were nice, and Andi was easy to talk to. And cute. Stella found excuses to be in the same room with her, just to see that smile. She hadn't expected this, coming to a new household. But she didn't mind, not at all.

Many households along the Long Road kept sheep, but the folk at Barnard did most of the spinning and weaving for trade. All the wool came to them. Barnard also produced a small quantity of specialty fibers from the alpaca and angora rabbits they kept. They were known for the quality of all their work, the smoothness of their yarns, the evenness of their weaving. Their work was sought after not just along the Long Road, but up and down the coast.

Everyone spun, wove, and dyed. Everyone knew every step of working with wool. They either came here because they knew, or because they'd grown up here learning the trade, like Toma and Nik, like Bette would in her turn. As Andi had, as Stella found out. Andi was the baby that Toma and Elsta had earned together.

Stella and Andi were at the looms, talking as they worked. The spring rains seem to have broken for good, and everyone else had taken their work outside. Wendy sat in the fresh air with her spinning wheel. A new batch of wool had arrived, and Toma and Jorge worked cleaning it. So Stella had a chance to ask questions in private.

"Could you get a place at one of the observatories? How does that work?"

Andi shook her head. "It wouldn't work out. There's three people at Kitt and two each at Griffith and Wilson, and they pick their successors. I'm better use to them here, working to send them credits."

"And you have your telescope, I suppose."

"The astronomers love my telescope," she said. "They call my setup Barnard Observatory, as if it's actually important. Isn't it silly?"

"Of course it isn't."

Andi's hands flashed, passing the shuttle across. She glanced up every now and then. Stella, for her part, let her hands move by habit, and watched Andi more than her own work. Outside, Wendy sang as she spun, in rhythm with the clipping hum of her wheel. Her voice was light, dream-like.

The next time Andi glanced up, she exclaimed, "How do you *do* that? You're not even watching and it's coming out beautiful."

Stella blinked at her work—not much to judge by, she thought. A foot or two of fabric curling over the breast beam, only just starting to wind onto the cloth beam. "I don't know. It's what I'm good at. Like you and the telescope."

"Nice of you to say so. But here, look at this—I've missed a row." She sat back and started unpicking the last five minutes of her work. "I go too fast. My mind wanders."

"It happens to everyone," Stella said.

"Not you. I saw that shawl you did for Elsta."

"I've just gotten good at covering up the mistakes," Stella said, winking.

A week after her arrival, an agent from the regional committee came to visit. A stout, gray-haired, cheerful woman, she was the doctor who made regular rounds up and down the Long Road. She was scheduled to give Bette a round of vaccinations, but Stella suspected the woman was going to be checking on her as well, to make sure she was settling in and hadn't disrupted the household too much.

The doctor, Nance, sat with Bette on the floor, and the baby immediately started crying. Peri hovered, but Nance just smiled and cooed while lifting the baby's arms and checking her ears, not seeming at all bothered.

"How is the world treating you then, Toma?" Nance turned to Toma, who was sitting in his usual chair by the fire.

His brow was creased with worry, though there didn't seem to be anything wrong. "Fine, fine," he said brusquely.

Nance turned. "And Stella, are you doing well?"

"Yes, thank you," Stella said. She was winding yarn around Andi's outstretched hands, to make a skein. This didn't feel much like an inspection, but that only made her more nervous.

"Very good. My, you're a wiggler, aren't you?" Bette's crying had finally subsided to red-faced sniffling, but she continued to fling herself from Nance's arms in an attempt to escape. After a round with a stethoscope, Nance let her go, and the baby crawled away, back to Peri.

The doctor turned her full attention to Toma. "The committee wants to order more banners, they expect to award quite a few this summer. Will you have some ready?"

Toma seemed startled. "Really? Are they sure?"

Barnard supplied the red-and-green patterned cloth used to make the banners awarded to households who'd been approved to have a baby. One of the things Nance had asked about when she first arrived was if anyone had tried bribing him for a length of the cloth over the last year. One of the reasons Barnard had the task of producing the banners—they were prosperous enough not to be vulnerable to bribes. Such attempts happened rarely, but did happen. Households had been broken up over such crimes.

The banner the household had earned for Bette was pinned proudly to the wall above the mantel.

Nance shrugged. "The region's been stable for a couple of years. No quota arguments, most households supporting themselves, just enough surplus to get by without draining resources. We're a healthy region, Toma. If we can support more children, we ought to. And you—with all these healthy young women you have, you might think of putting in for another baby." The doctor beamed.

Stella and Andi looked at each other and blushed. Another baby so soon after the first? Scandalous.

Nance gathered up her kit. "Before I go, let me check all your birth control implants so we don't have any mishaps, eh?"

She started with Elsta and Toma and worked her way around the room.

"Not that I could have a mishap," Andi muttered to Stella. "They ought to make exceptions for someone like me who isn't likely to get in that kind of trouble. Because of her *preferences*, you know?"

"I know," Stella said, blushing very hard now. "I've had that thought myself."

They stared at each other for a very long moment. Stella's mouth had suddenly gone dry. She wanted to flee the room and stick her head in a bucket of cool water. Then again, she didn't.

When Nance came to her side to prod her arm, checking that the implant was in place, Stella hardly felt it.

"Looks like you're good and covered," Nance said. "For now, 'eh? Until you get that extra banner." She winked.

The doctor stayed for supper and still had enough daylight left to walk to the next waystation along the road. Elsta wrapped up a snack of fruit and cheese for her to take with her, and Nance thanked her very much. As soon as she was gone, Toma muttered.

"Too many mouths to feed—and what happens when the next flood hits? The next typhoon? We lose everything and then there isn't enough? We have enough as it is, more than enough. Wanting more, it's asking for trouble. Getting greedy is what brought the disasters in the first place. It's too much."

Everyone stayed quiet, letting him rant. This felt to Stella like an old argument, words repeated like the chorus of a song. Toma's philosophy, expounded by habit. He didn't need a response.

Stella finished winding the skein of yarn and quietly excused herself, putting her things away and saying goodnight to everyone.

Andi followed her out of the cottage soon after, and they walked together to their room.

"So, do you want one?" Stella asked her.

"A baby? I suppose I do. Someday. I mean, I assumed as well off as Barnard is I could have one if I wanted one. It's a little odd, thinking about who I'd pick for the father. That's the part I'm not sure about. What about you?"

Besides being secretly, massively pleased that Andi hadn't thought much about fathers . . . "I assumed I'd never get the chance. I don't think I'd miss it if I didn't."

"Enough other people who want 'em, right?"

"Something like that."

They reached their room, changed into their nightclothes, washed up for bed. Ended up sitting on their beds, facing each other and talking. That first uncomfortable night seemed far away now.

"Toma doesn't seem to like the idea of another baby," Stella prompted.

"Terrified, I think," she said. "Wanting too much gets people in trouble."

"But it only seems natural, to want as much as you can have."

Andi shook her head. "His grandparents remembered the old days. He heard stories from them about the disasters. All the people who died in the floods and plagues. He's that close to it—might as well have lived through it himself. He thinks we'll lose it all, that another great disaster will fall on us and destroy everything. It's part of why he hates my telescope so much. It's a sign of the old days when everything went rotten. But it won't happen, doesn't he see that?"

Stella shrugged. "Those days aren't so far gone, really. Look at what happened to Greentree."

"Oh—Stella, I'm sorry. I didn't mean that there's not anything to it, just that . . ." She shrugged, unable to finish the thought.

"It can't happen here. I know."

Andi's black hair fell around her face, framing her pensive expression. She stared into space. "I just wish he could see how good things are. We've earned a little extra, haven't we?"

Unexpected even to herself, Stella burst, "Can I kiss you?"

In half a heartbeat Andi fell at her, holding Stella's arms, and Stella clung back, and either her arms were hot or Andi's hands were, and they met, lips to lips.

———

One evening, Andi escaped the gathering in the common room, and brought Stella with her. They left as the sun had almost set, leaving just enough light to follow the path to the observatory. They took candles inside shaded lanterns for the trip back to their cottage. At dusk, the windmills were ghostly skeletons lurking on the hillside.

They waited for full dark, talking while Andi looked over her paperwork and prepared her notes. Andi asked about Greentree, and Stella explained that the aquifers had dried up in the drought. Households remained in the region because they'd always been there. Some survived, but they weren't particularly successful. She told Andi how the green of the valleys near the coast had almost blinded her when she first arrived, and how all the rain had seemed like a miracle.

Then it was time to unlatch the roof panels and look at the sky.

"Don't squint, just relax. Let the image come into focus," Andi said, bending close to give directions to Stella, who was peering through the scope's eyepiece. Truth be told, Stella was more aware of Andi's hand resting lightly on her shoulder. She shifted closer.

"You should be able to see it," Andi said, straightening to look at the sky.

"Okay . . . I think . . . oh! Is that it?" A disk had come into view, a pale, glowing light striped with orange, yellow, cream. Like someone had covered a very distant moon with melted butter.

"Jupiter," Andi said proudly.

"But it's just a star."

"Not up close it isn't."

Not a disk, then, but a sphere. Another planet. "Amazing."

"Isn't it? You ought to be able to see some of the moons as well—a couple of bright stars on either side?"

"I think . . . yes, there they are."

After an hour, Stella began shivering in the nighttime cold, and Andi put her arms around her, rubbing warmth into her back. In moments, they were kissing, and stumbled together to the desk by the shack's wall, where Andi pushed her back across the surface and made love to her. Jupiter had swung out of view by the time they closed up the roof and stumbled off the hill.

Another round of storms came, shrouding the nighttime sky, and they spent the evenings around the hearth with the others. Some of the light went out of Andi on those nights. She sat on a chair with a basket of mending at her feet, darning socks and shirts, head bent over her work. Lamplight turned her skin amber and made her hair shine like obsidian. But she didn't talk. That may have been because Elsta and Toma talked over everyone, or Peri exclaimed over something the baby did, then everyone had to admire Bette.

The day the latest round of rain broke and the heat of summer finally settled over the valley, Andi got another package from Griffith, and that light of discovery came back to her. Tonight, they'd rush off to the observatory after supper.

Stella almost missed the cue to escape, helping Elsta with the dishes. When she was finished and drying her hands, Andi was at the door. Stella rushed in behind her. Then Toma brought out a basket, one of the ones as big as an embrace that they used to store just-washed wool in, and set it by Andi's chair before the hearth. "Andi, get back here."

Her hand was on the door, one foot over the threshold, and Stella thought she might keep going, pretending that she hadn't heard. But her hand clenched on the door frame, and she turned around.

"We've got to get all this new wool processed, so you'll stay in tonight to help."

"I can do that tomorrow. I'll work double tomorrow—"

"Now, Andi."

Stella stepped forward, hands reaching for the basket. "Toma, I can do that."

"No, you're doing plenty already. Andi needs to do it."

"I'll be done with the mending in a minute and can finish that in no time at all. Really, it's all right."

He looked past her, to Andi. "You know the rules—household business first."

"The household business is *done*. This is makework!" she said. Toma held the basket out in reproof.

Stella tried again. "But I *like* carding." It sounded lame—no one liked carding.

But Andi had surrendered, coming away from the door, shuffling toward her chair. "Stella, it's all right. Not your argument."

"But—" The pleading in her gaze felt naked. She wanted to help, how could she help?

Andi slumped in the chair without looking up. All Stella could do was sit in her own chair, with her knitting. She jabbed herself with the needle three times, from glancing up at Andi every other stitch.

Toma sat before his workbench, looking pleased for nearly the first time since Stella had met him.

Well after dark, Stella lay in her bed, stomach in knots. Andi was in the other bed and hadn't said a word all evening.

"Andi? Are you all right?" she whispered. She stared across the room, to the slope of the other woman, mounded under her blanket. The lump didn't move, but didn't look relaxed in sleep. But if she didn't want to talk, Stella wouldn't force her.

"I'm okay," Andi sighed, finally.

"Anything I can do?"

Another long pause, and Stella was sure she'd said too much. Then, "You're a good person, Stella. Anyone ever told you that?"

Stella crawled out from under her covers, crossed to Andi's bed, climbed in with her. Andi pulled the covers up over them both, and the women held each other.

Toma sent Andi on an errand, delivering a set of blankets to the next waystation and picking up messages to bring back. More makework. The task could just have as easily been done by the next wagon messenger to pass by. Andi told him as much, standing outside the work house the next morning.

"Why wait when we can get the job done now?" Toma answered, hefting the backpack, stuffed to bursting with newly woven woolens, toward her.

Stella was at her loom, and her hand on the shuttle paused as she listened. But Andi didn't say anything else. Only glared at Toma a good long minute before taking up the pack. She'd be gone most of the day, hiking there and back.

Which was the point, wasn't it?

Stella contrived to find jobs that kept Toma in sight, sorting and carding wool outside where he was working repairing a fence, when she should have been weaving. So she saw when Toma studied the hammer in his hand, looked up the hill, and started walking the path to Andi's observatory.

Stella dropped the basket of wool she was holding and ran.

He was merely walking. Stella overtook him easily, at first. But after fifty yards of running, she slowed, clutching at a stitch in her side. Gasping for breath with burning lungs, she kept on, step after step, hauling herself up the hill, desperate to get there first.

"Stella, go back, don't get in the middle of this."

Even if she could catch enough of her breath to speak, she didn't know what she would say. He lengthened his stride, gaining on her. She got to the shed a bare few steps before him.

The door didn't have a lock; it had never needed one. Stella pressed herself across it and faced out, to Toma, marching closer. At least she had something to lean on for the moment.

"Move aside, Stella. She's got to grow up and get on with what's important," Toma said.

"This *is* important."

He stopped, studied her. He gripped the handle of hammer like it was a weapon. Her heart thudded. How angry was he?

Toma considered, then said, "Stella. You're here because I wanted to do Az a favor. I can change my mind. I can send a message to Nance and the committee that it just isn't working out. I can do that."

Panic brought sudden tears to her eyes. He wouldn't dare, he couldn't, she'd proven herself already in just a few weeks, hadn't she? The committee wouldn't believe him, couldn't listen to him. But she couldn't be sure of that, could she?

Best thing to do would be to step aside. He was head of the household, it was his call. She ought to do as he said, because her place here *wasn't* secure. A month ago that might not have mattered, but now—she *wanted* to stay, she *had* to stay.

And if she stepped aside, leaving Toma free to enter the shed, what would she tell Andi afterward?

She swallowed the lump in her throat and found words. "I know disaster can still happen. I know the droughts and storms and plagues do still come and can take away everything. Better than anyone, I know. But we have to start building again sometime, yes? People like Andi have to start building, and we have to let them, even if it seems useless to the rest of us. Because it isn't useless, it—it's beautiful."

He stared at her for a long time. She thought maybe he was considering how to wrestle her away from the door. He was bigger than she was, and she wasn't strong. It wouldn't take much. But she'd fight.

"You're infatuated, that's all," he said.

Maybe, not that it mattered.

Then he said, "You're not going to move away, are you?"

Shaking her head, Stella flattened herself more firmly against the door.

Toma's grip on the hammer loosened, just a bit. "My grandparents—has Andi told you about my grandparents? They were children when the big fall came. They remembered what it was like. Mostly they talked about what they'd lost, all the things they had and didn't now. And I thought, all those things they missed, that they wanted back—that was what caused the fall in the first place, wasn't it? We don't need it, any of it."

"Andi needs it. And it's not hurting anything." What else could she say, she had to say something that would make it all right. "Better things will come, or what's the point?"

A weird crooked smile turned Toma's lips, and he shifted his grip on the hammer. Holding it by the head now, he let it dangle by his leg. "God, what a world," he muttered. Stella still couldn't tell if he was going to force her away from the door. She held her breath.

Toma said, "Don't tell Andi about this. All right?"

She nodded. "All right."

Toma turned and started down the trail, a calm and steady pace. Like a man who'd just gone out for a walk.

Stella slid to the ground and sat on the grass by the wall until the old man was out of sight. Finally, after scrubbing the tears from her face, she followed him down, returning to the cottages and her work.

Andi was home in time for supper, and the household ate together as usual. The woman was quiet and kept making quick glances at Toma, who avoided looking back at all. It was like she knew Toma had had a plan. Stella couldn't say anything until they were alone.

The night was clear, the moon was dark. Stella'd learned enough from Andi to know it was a good night for stargazing. As they were cleaning up after the meal, she touched Andi's hand. "Let's go to the observatory."

Andi glanced at Toma, and her lips pressed together, grim. "I don't think that's a good idea."

"I think it'll be okay."

Andi clearly didn't believe her, so Stella took her hand, and together they walked out of the cottage, then across the yard, past the work house, and to the trail that led up the hill to the observatory.

And it was all right.

what did tessimond tell you?

ADAM ROBERTS

A Senior Reader in English at London University, Adam Roberts is an SF author, critic, reviewer, and academic who has produced many works on ninteeth-century poetry as well as critical studies of science fiction such as The Palgrave History of Science Fiction. His own fiction has appeared in Postscipts, SCI FICTION, Live Without a Net, FutureShocks, Forbidden Planets, Spectrum SF, Constellations, and elsewhere, and was collected in Swiftly. His novels include Salt, On, Stone, Polystom, The Snow, Gradisil, Splinter, and Land of the Headless. His most recent novels are Yellow Blue Tibia and New Model Army. His most recent book is a chapbook novella, An Account of a Voyage from World to World Again, by Way of the Moon, 1726, in the Commission of Georgius Rex Primus, Monarch of Northern Europe and Lord of Selenic Territories, Defender of the Faith, Undertaken by Captain Wm. Chetwin Aboard the Cometes Georgius. Upcoming is a collection titled Adam Robots. He lives in Staines, England, with his wife and daughter. Visit his Web site at www.adamroberts.com.

In the deceptively quiet story that follows, a scientist attempts to unravel what seems at first to be a minor mystery, but one that leads her step-by-step into a disturbing—in fact, dismaying—realization.

: 1 :

The Nobel was in the bag (not that I would ever want to hide it away *in a bag*—), and in fact we were only a fortnight from our public announcement, when Niu Jian told he was quitting. I assumed it was a joke. Niu Jian had never been much of a practical joker, but that's what I assumed. Of course, he wasn't kidding in the slightest. The sunlight picked out the grain of his tweed jacket. He was sitting in my office with his crescent back to the window, and I kept getting distracted by the light coming through the glass. Morning time, morning time, and all the possibilities of the day ahead of us. The chimney of the boiler house as white and straight as an unsmoked cigarette. The campus willow was dangling its green tentacles in the river, as if taking a drink. The students wandered the paths and dawdled on the grass with their arms around one another's waists. Further down the hill, beyond the campus boundary, I could see the cars doing their crazy corpuscle impressions along the interchange and away along the dual carriageway. "You want to quit—now?" I pressed. "*Now* is the time you want to quit?"

He nodded, slowly, and picked at the skin of his knuckles.

"Two *weeks*, we present. You *know* the Nobel is—look, hey!" I said, the idea occurring suddenly to me like the spurt of a match lighting. "Is it that you think *you* won't be sharing? You will! You, me, Prévert and Sleight, we will all be cited. Is that what you think?" It wouldn't have been very characteristic of Niu Jian to storm out in like a prima donna, I have to say: a more stolidly dependable individual never walked the face of this, our rainy, stony earth. But, you see, I was struggling to understand why he was quitting.

"It is not that," he said,

"Then—?" I made a grunting noise. Then I coughed. P-O-R didn't like that; the unruly diaphragm. There was a scurry of motion inside, as she readjusted herself.

He looked at me, and then, briefly, he glanced at my belly—I had pushed my chair away from the desk, so my whole torso was on display, Phylogeny-Ontology-Recapitulator in all her bulging glory. Then he looked back at my face. For the strangest moment my heart knocked rat-tat at my ribs, like it wanted out, and I felt the adrenal flush along my neck and in my cheeks. But that passed. My belly had nothing to do with *that*.

Niu Jian said: "I have never been to Mecca."

"The Bingo?" I said. I wasn't trying to be facetious. I was genuinely wrong-footed by this.

"No," he said.

"You mean, in—" I coughed, "like, Arabia?"

"There, yes."

"What's that got to do with anything?"

"I want," said Niu Jian, "to go."

"OK," I said. "Why not? It's like the Taj Mahal, right? I'm sure it's a sight to see. So go. Wait until the press conference, and then take the next available flying transport from Heathrow's internationally renowned port-of-air." But he was shaking his head, so I said: "Jesus, go *now* if you like. If you must. Miss the announcement. *That* doesn't matter—or it only matters a little bit. But if it's like, urgent, then go now. But you don't have to quit! Why do you have to quit? You don't have to quit."

His nod, though wordless, was very clearly: *I do.*

"OK, Noo-noo, you're really going to have to lay this out for me, step by baby-step," I said. "Blame my baby-beshrunken brain. Walk me through it. *Why* do you want to go to Mecca?"

"To go before I die."

"Wait—you're not *dying*, are you? Jesus on a boson, are you *ill*?"

"I'm not ill," said Niu Jian. "I'm in perfect health. So far as I know, anyway. Look: I'm not trying to be mysterious. All Muslims must visit Mecca once in their lives."

I thought about this. "You're a Muslim? I thought you were Chinese."

"One can be both."

"And that bottle of wine you shared with Prévert and myself last night, in the Godolfin?"

"Islam is perfect, individuals are not." He picked more energetically at the skin on the back of his knuckles.

"I just never knew," I said, feeling stupid. "I mean, I thought Muslims aren't supposed to drink alcohol."

"I thought pregnant women weren't supposed to drink alcohol," he returned, and for the first time in this whole strange conversation I got a glimpse of the old Niu Jian, the sly little flash of wit, the particular look he had. But then it was gone again. "Yesterday, in the Elephant, you were talking about the suit you would wear for the press conference. You were all, oh my mother will be watching the television, the whole world will be watching the—oh I must have a smart suit. Oh I must go to a London tailor. What happened to the London tailor?"

He said: "I spoke to Tessimond."

I believe this was the first time I ever heard his name. Not the last; very much not the last time. "Who?"

"Prévert's friend."

"Oh—the doleful-countenance guy? The ex-professor guy from Oregon?"

"Yes."

"You spoke to him—when?"

Niu Jian looked at the ceiling. "Half an hour ago."

"And he told you to quit the team? C'mon, Noo-noo! Why listen to *him*?"

"He didn't tell me to quit the team."

"So he told you—what?"

"He told me about the expansion of the universe," said Niu Jian. "And after he had done that, I realised that I had to quit the team and go to Mecca."

"That's the craziest thing I've ever heard," I said. At that precise moment my little Phylogeny-Ontology-Recapitulator gave a little kick and thwunked my spleen—or whatever organ it is, down in there, that feels like a sack of fluid-swelled nerves. I grunted, shifted my position in my chair. "He told you about the expansion of the universe? You mean you told *him*! *He's* not a shoo-in for the Nobel—you are." When he didn't reply, I started to lose my temper. "*What* did he tell you about the expansion of the universe, precisely?"

For the second time Niu Jian's glance went to my belly. Then he stood up, his knees making drawn out little bleating noises as they were required to assume his weight. "Ana, good-bye," he said. "You know how it is."

"Do not."

"I don't want to give the wrong impression. You know, I wouldn't even say he *told* me anything. He pointed out the obvious, really. You know how it is, Ana, when somebody says something that completely changes the way you see the cosmos, but that afterwards you think: that's so obvious, how could I not have noticed it before?"

"That's what he did?"

"Yes."

"And it made you want to quit the team? Rather than wait a few weeks and receive the Nobel Prize for Physics?"

Nod.

"So what was it? What did he say? What could he possibly say that would provoke that reaction in you? You're the *least* flaky of the whole team!"

For the third time, the glimpse towards Phylogeny-Ontology-Recapitulator, in his bag of fluid, swaddled by his sheath of my flesh. Just a little downward flick of the eyes, and then back to my face. And then he shook my hand with that weird manner he'd picked up from Jane Austen novels or, I don't know what, and then he left. I saw him the following morning pulling his suitcase across the forty-metre sundial that looks like a giant manhole cover outside the Human Resources Building. I called to him, and waved; and he waved back, and then he got into the taxi he had called and was driven away, and I never saw him again.

:2:

Naturally I wanted to talk to this Tessimond geezer, to find out why he was spooking my horses. I had taken pains to assemble the very best team; intellectual thorough-breds. I texted Prévert to come to my office, and when he neither replied nor came I hauled myself, balanced Phylogeny-Ontology-Recapitulator as well as I could over my hips and did my backward-leaning walk along the corridor to his office. I didn't knock. I was the team leader, the ring-giver, the guardian of the treasure. Knocking wasn't needful.

Prévert was inside, and so was Sleight, and the two of them were having a right old ding-dong. Prévert was standing straight up, and he was halfway through either putting on or taking off his coat.

"Niu Jian just quit the team," I said, lowering myself into a chair with the cumbrous grace unique to people in my position. "He just came into my office and quit,"

"We know, boss," said Sleight. "Prévert too."

"He said it was *your* friend who persuaded him, Jack." Prévert's first name was not Jack; it was Stephane. But naturally we all called him Jack. "Why—wait a minute, what do you mean *Prévert too?*"

"He means, Ana," Jack said, "that I too am leaving the team. I apologise. I apologise with a full heart. It is late in the day. If I had known earlier I would have not inconvenienced you in this fashion—and with your . . ." and like Niu Juan had done, he cast a significant look at the bump of P-O-R, and then returned his gaze to my face.

"You are kidding me," I said.

"I regret to say, Ana, that I am not kidding you."

"But we just got your *th*s to come out right." Prévert's English was more-or-less flawless, his accent somewhere in between David Niven and a BBC newsreader, but he had held stubbornly to that French trick of pronouncing "th's" as "t" or "z," variously.

"I've been remonstrating with him," said Sleight. "He won't tell me why."

"You spoke to your friend Tessimond," I said, panting a little from the exertion of walking along a corridor.

"That's right—is that what Noo-noo did?" Sleight asked.

"What did he say to you?"

"It's no good asking, boss," Sleight told me. "I've been leaning on him for an hour, and he won't cough up. Whatever it was it can't have taken more than ten minutes."

"The time period was approximately that," Prévert confirmed. He slid his right arm into the vacant tube of his coat sleeve, thereby confirming that he was putting the garment on, not taking it off.

"He's a friend of yours?"

"Tessimond? He used to be, many years ago. I was surprised to see him. I suggested we have breakfast—Sleight too, although he turned up late. As he always does."

"I was quarter of an hour late," said Sleight. "And that was long enough to the Tessimond geezer to persuade Jack to leave the project! One quarter hour!"

"He did not persuade me to leave. He made no reference to my being on the team, or collecting the Nobel Prize. He simply pointed out something—ah, how-to-say, something rather obvious. Something I am ashamed I did not notice before."

"And this something overturns years of work, convinces you that you shouldn't collect a Nobel Prize?"

Prévert shrugged. "There is a woman who lives in Montpellier, called Suzanne," he announced. "I am going to visit her."

"You're crazy. You can't take your name off the—your name will *still be on* the citation, you know!" Sleight's voice had a raspy, edge-of-hysteria quality. "We're not taking your name off the citation."

"I have no preference one way or the other," Prévert replied. "You must do as you please—as shall I."

"Wait a sec, Jack," I said. "Please." Because he was eyeing the door, now, and I could see he was about to scarper. "At least tell us what he told you."

"You may ask him yourself. He's staying in the Holiday Inn. Sleight has his number."

"Come, now, come alone, now, *Jack*, I've known you ten years. Jack, you're a friend, for the love of Jesus, you're *my* friend." I ran the tip of my ring-finger across one eyebrow, then the other. I was trying to think how to do this. "Don't play games with me, Jack. I'm asking you, as a friend. Tell me what is going on."

"What is going," said Prévert, "is me. Good-bye." He was always a touch too proud of his little Anglophone word-games.

"What did Tessimond *tell* you?"

Prévert stopped at the door, looked not at me but at my bump, and said: "he only pointed out what is right in front of us. Us, in particular—you, Sleight, me. It should be more obvious to us than to anybody! Although it *should* be obvious to anyone who gives it more than a minute's thought."

"Don't do this, Jack."

"Good-bye, Ana, and—you too, Sleight."

"Is it God?" I said. It was my parting shot. "Noo-noo is going to Mecca. Is that what he is, this Tessimond, a *preacher*? Has he somehow converted you to religion and turned you into a—Christ, what does it say in the Old, I mean, New Testament? About leaving your homes and families and becoming fishers of men."

Prévert smiled, and his sideburns moved a little further apart from one another. A big beamy smile. "I am, Ana, you will be relieved to hear—I am precisely as athe-istical as I have always been. There is no God. But there is a woman called Su-zanne, and she lives in Montpellier." And he walked out.

I sat staring at Sleight, as if it were his fault. He had been standing up, because Prévert had been standing up. Now that it was just the two of us, he sat down.

"So," I said. "Are you pissing-off too? Is my *entire* team deserting me?"

"No, boss!" he said, looking genuinely hurt that I would say such a thing. "Never! Loyalty means something to me, at any rate. That, and the fact that—you know. I fancy getting the Nobel Prize."

"Is it a joke? Are Jack and Niu Jian in cahoots?"

"In what?"

"Cahoots. I mean, are they conspiring together to trick us, or something?"

"I know what cahoots means," said Sleight. "I just didn't quite hear you." He sat back and began looking around Prévert's office, as if the answer might lie there.

"Cold feet," he said. "I think they're genuine, both of them, about leaving. I mean, I don't think it's a joke, boss. Who would joke about a thing like this! But maybe the timing is the key—we're so close to announcing. Maybe they've got cold feet."

"I could maybe believe that of Niu Jian, but not Prévert," I said. "And do you know what, now that I think of it, I couldn't believe it of Noo-noo either. Cold feet?"

"Then what, boss? Why would they both drop out—today?"

"Ring up this Tessimond guy," I instructed him. "Find out what he said. Better yet, tell him to *unsay* it. Tell him to get in touch with both of my boys and persuade them to *come back*. What does he think he's *playing* at, anyway? Disassembling my team on the brink of our big announcement?"

Sleight got out his phone, held it in his hand for a bit, and then balanced it on his head. It wasn't an unusual thing for him to balance a mobile phone on his head. The peculiar shape of his bald cranium was such that above his tassel-like eyebrows there was a sort of semi-indentation, a thirty-degree slope in amongst the phrenological landscape, and it so happened than an iPhone fitted snugly there. Sleight had started resting his device there for a joke, but he had done it so often that it had become an unremarkable gesture. "Maybe it would make sense for you to speak to him, boss?"

"Scared?"

"No!" he said, with a quickness and emphasis that strongly implied *yes*. "Only, you *are* the team leader." I put my head to one side. "And I once read a story," he added.

"Science fiction story?"

"Of course." As if there were any other kind of story for Sleight! "It was about a thing called a blit. You ever heard of a blit?"

"If this is going to be a porn reference, I swear I'll have you disciplined for sexual harassment, Sleight."

"No, no! It's science and it's fiction, in one handy bundle. A blit is a thing, and once you've seen it—once it's gone in your eyes—it starts to occupy your mind. You can't stop thinking about it, and it expands fractally until it takes up all your thoughts and you go mad."

"And?"

"And—what if this Tessimond is going to say something like a verbal blit?"

I hid my face in my hands. There was a tussle between the laugh-aloud angel sitting on my right shoulder, and the burst-into-tears devil sitting on my left. I took control of myself. Pregnancy hormones have real, chemical effects upon even the strongest will. I dropped my hands. "Please never again say the phrase *verbal blit* in my hearing. Call Tessimond."

Sleight, sheepishly, called. He waited only a short time before saying, "Oh, hello, is that Mr. Tessimond, oh, hello, oh, my name is Sleight and Stephane Prévert gave me your number." Then a long pause, and Sleight's eyes tracked left-to-right and right-to-left, and I felt a mild panic, as if he were being Derren Brown-hypnotised by this stranger, and over the phone too. But then he said. "Anyway, my team leader, Professor Radonjić, is here and she was wondering if she could—sure, sure." Silence, an intense expression on Sleight's face. Then: "both of them have left the team, somewhat, eh, ah, somewhat abruptly, you know. And they both spoke with you about the—yes, yes." Nodding. Why do people nod when they're talking on the phone? It's not as if their interlocutor can see them. "I see. I understand. We were just wondering what . . ."

"Let me speak to him," I said, holding out my hand. Sleight passed the phone straight to me. "Hello, Mr. Tessimond? This is Ana Radonjić."

"May I call you Ana?" Tessimond asked. He had a pleasant, low-slung voice; a Midwest American accent, a slight buzz in the consonants that suggested he might be a smoker. I was a little taken aback by this—a micron aback, or thereabouts. "All right. And what should I call you?"

He hummed; a little, musical burr. "My name is Tessimond," he said. "It's a pleasure to speak to you, Ana. I've immense respect for what you've been doing."

"What do you know about what I've been doing?" I daresay I sounded slightly more paranoid than was warranted.

"I was Henry Semat Professor of Theoretical Physics at CUNY for a number of years," he said. "Years ago—before your time. I left that post decades ago."

"You were at CUNY? Why have I not heard of you?"

"I didn't publish," he burred. "What's the point?"

This piqued me, so I rattled off: "the point is that we have made a breakthrough with regard to dark energy, and I don't think any physicists have ever been more sure of getting a Nobel citation, and two key members of my team have, this morning, walked away. That is the point."

"There seem to be several points, there, Ana," he said, mildly. But his slow delivery only infuriated me further.

"I don't know what games you are playing," I snapped. "This is serious. This is my career as a serious scientist, and the Nobel Prize—not the, er, pigeon-fancier's red rosette." I said this last thing because a pigeon arrived on the outside ledge of Prevért's office windowsill, in a flurry of wings that sounded like a deck of cards being shuffled. Then it folded the wings into its back and stood looking, insolently, through the glass at us. "This is the culmination of everything we have been working for," I said, apparently to the pigeon.

"I was talking to Stephane about this a couple of hours ago," came Tessimond's voice on the phone. "Your research truly sounds fascinating."

"Ste*phane* has gone to catch a flight to Montpellier!" I snapped. "Do you know why?"

Tessimond released a small sigh at the other end of the phone line. "I'm afraid I've no idea, Ana."

"No? You said something to him, and it made him walk away from everything he has been working towards for *years*."

There was a silence. Then: "that wasn't my intention, Ana."

"No? Well that's the mess you've made. Perhaps you'd like to help me clear it up, mm?"

"I very much doubt," he said, sadly, "if there's anything I can do." Then he said: "the rate of expansion of the cosmos is accelerating."

"I," I said. "Yes it is."

"That's been known for a while. You're going to announce that you know why this is happening?"

"Professor Tessimond—" I said.

"Dark energy," he said. Then: "would you like to have lunch?"

I bridled at this. Blame the hormones, I suppose. "I'm afraid I'm going to be *far* too busy today clearing up the mess you have made to be able to take time out for lunch!" For all the world as if he were listening in on my conversation, and objecting to the notion of skipping a meal, P-O-R chose that moment to stretch and squeeze my stomach painfully against my ribs. I grimaced, but kept going. "I'm going to have to explain to university management why not-one-but-two key members of my team have jumped ship mere weeks before we go public with our research."

"Dinner then," he said. "Or drinks. With Dr. Sleight too, of course. And bring along your senior managers, if you like. I really didn't intend to cause any upheavals. I'd be very glad to explain myself."

"I *might* be able to find a window tomorrow," I said. "You're staying locally? There's a bar. It's called the Bar Bar, for some peculiar reason. We call it the Elephant. Would it be agreeable for you to meet there tomorrow lunchtime?"

After I'd hung up and given Sleight his phone back, I told him what had been arranged. "Why not meet him right now?" Sleight pressed.

"I intend to spend today coaxing Niu Jian and Jack to come back to us. I don't know what he told them, but I want to be able to present him with a unified front. Tomorrow, Sleight. Tomorrow."

:3:

I spent the morning haranguing both Niu Jian and Jack on the phone. Jack was a brick wall, and then he was on a flight and the signal vanished, so I didn't get very far with him. I had longer to try and bend Niu Jian's ear, but he was equally stubborn. No, he didn't want to come back. Yes, he was going to Mecca. None of my threats had any purchase. I offered him financial inducements, I warned him his reputation as a serious scientist was on the line, I even said I was going to call his mother. Nothing. Eventually I had to grasp the nettle and call senior management. They were incredulous, at first; and then they were angry; and finally they were baffled.

I'm not surprised. I was baffled myself.

I went home early evening, and lay on the sofa whilst M. cooked me linguini. I spooled the whole crazy narrative out to him, and he did his excellent supporting-pillar impression. It felt better ranting about it, and the linguini was washed down with a small glass of Chianti, which I feel sure P-O-R enjoyed as much as I did, and the whole idiotic nonsense receded in my mind. So what if the two berks weren't present at the press conference? I'd get senior management in. I'd have Sleight beside me. I could do it *solus*. That might even be preferable.

M. and I watched an episode of *Mad Men* together. Then Sleight called. "Boss? I'm in the Elephant."

"Sleight, I appreciate you not abandoning ship like Jack and Niu Jian," I said. "But that doesn't mean I require you to keep me informed of your every change of venue. I'll get you electronically tagged if I want that."

"You don't understand, boss. I'm here with Tessimond." He sounded excited, like an undercover cop. "He's at the bar. Getting a half for himself and a pint for me."

"Well," I said. "Don't let me keep you from your revels."

"I'm going to find out what he told Niu Jian and Jack," said Sleight, whispering. "Will report back. I know you're meeting him tomorrow, but I couldn't wait! Curious! Too curious—but that's the problem with being a scientist."

"Sleight, look . . ." I started, in my weariest voice.

"I will *report back*," he hissed. And hung up.

M. rubbed my feet, whilst I ate a chocolate mousse straight from the plastic pot. Then I pulled myself slowly upstairs to face the great trial of my pregnancy. I mean: brushing my teeth. The mere thought of it made me want to vomit; actually performing the action was gag-provoking, intensely uncomfortable and unpleasant. But I didn't want to just stop brushing my teeth altogether; that would be an admission of defeat. Quite apart from anything else, the teeth themselves were sitting looser in their sockets than before, and so clearly needed more not less hygienic attention. But the nightly brush had become my least favourite part of the day. I had just completed this disagreeable exercise, and was accordingly in no good mood, when Sleight rang back.

"Sleight—what? Seriously: what?"

"I said I would ring back," he returned. "And so I have." But his tone of voice had changed, and I immediately sensed something wrong.

"What is it?"

"Tessimond explained things. It really is desperately obvious, when you come to think of it. I'm really a bit ashamed of myself for not seeing it earlier."

"Sleight, you're spooking me out. Don't tell me you're following Niu Jian and Jack and dropping out?"

There was a long pause, in which I could faintly hear the background noises of the Elephant; the murmur of conversation, the clink of glasses. "Yes," he said eventually.

"No," I returned.

"I going to start smoking," said Sleight.

"If I have to listen to another non sequitur from my team members I am going to scream," I told him.

"I used to love smoking," Sleight explained. He didn't sound very drunk, but there was a sway to his intonation that did not inspire confidence. "But I gave it up. You know, for health. It's not good for your health. I didn't want to get heart disease or canny, or canny, or *cancer*." There was another long pause. "I'm sorry boss, I hate to let you down."

"Sleight," I snapped at him. "What did he tell you?"

He rang off. I was furious. I would have called Tessimond direct, but I didn't have his number; and although I called Sleight back, and texted him, and @'d him on Twitter, he did not reply. It took M. a long time to calm me down, if I'm honest. In the end, he assured me that Sleight was drunk, and that when he woke sober the following day he would see how foolish it all seemed.

I slept fitfully. The morning brought no message from Sleight; and he didn't turn up for work; and he still wasn't answering his phone.

I recalled that Tessimond was staying in the Holiday Inn and left a message with their front desk for him to call me, giving him my personal number. Then I met with the junior researchers, or such of them as were still on campus—for the research part of the project was done and dusted, and we were all now just waiting on the announcement and the shaking of the world of science. None of them were about to leave the project; and their puppyish enthusiasm (after all; a Nobel Prize is a Nobel Prize!) calmed me down a little. I did paperwork, and dipped my toe into the raging ocean of e-mail that had long since swamped my computer. Then I googled Tessimond, and discovered that, yes, he *had* been Henry Semat Professor of Theoretical Physics at City University of New York, for about two months, many years previously. I wasn't surprised that I'd never heard of him, though. M. rang to check on me, and I told him I was fine. At 2 P.M., on the dot, Tessimond himself called. "Hello, Ana," he said, pleasantly.

"You've now suborned a third member of my team," I told him, in as venomous a voice as I could manage, post-prandial as I was. "I don't know why you're doing it, but I want you to stop."

"I assure you, Ana, I intended nothing of the sort," he said. "Dr. Sleight called me, invited me for a drink. We were only talking. Only words were exchanged."

"Enough of this nonsense. What did you tell him?"

"Are we still meeting, in person, later today? I'd be happy to explain everything then."

"You don't want to say over the phone?"

He sounded taken aback. I was being pretty hostile, I suppose. "No, I don't mind saying over the phone. Do you want me to tell you, now, over the phone?"

"No, I don't," I said. "I don't care what mind-game you've been playing. What con-trick you're up to. I only care that you leave us all alone. Why are you even here?"

"Stephane invited me. I hadn't seen him in many years. And since leaving my academic posting I have been pursuing an old dream of mine and . . . simply travelling. Travelling around the world. I thought how pleasant it would be to visit England, so I came."

"You came to Berkshire on a whim, or just to see an old friend or something paper-thin pretext like that, but now you're here you just *happen* to be dismantling my entire physics team on the verge of our winning the Nobel Prize?"

He contemplated this for a moment. "I do love that you guys spell it burk and pronounce it bark. Does it have anything to do with the bark of trees?"

"What?"

"Berkshire," he said.

"I ought to call the police and have you arrested. Are you *blackmailing* them?"

"Blackmailing who?" He sounded properly surprised at this.

"Niu Jian and Jack and my dear, bald-headed Sleight, of course. Are you?"

"No!"

"Stay away from me and my team," I said, and ended the call. I was fuming.

Later that afternoon I finally got a text from Sleight. "*Sorry boss,*" it said. "*Beeen dead drunk for 12 houors. Won't be coming back, and o*"—just that. I rang him immediately, but he did not answer. Forty five minutes later I got another text. *"Theres a sf shortstory called 'Nittfall.' It is like that. The ending of that sf, u know it? Chat with Tesimnd and afterwards I was like, WOH! ASIMOVIAN!"* Since Sleight was 46 and not usually given to speaking like a teenager, I deduce that he was still intoxicated when he sent those texts. I rang again, and texted him back, but he did not reply.

My mood swung about again. I was probably over-reacting. It was clearly all a big misunderstanding. It would get itself sorted out. My pregnancy hormones were a distorting mirror on the world. Tessimond was chicken-licken, and had somehow persuaded the otherwise level-headed members of my team that the world was ending—but the world *wasn't* ending, and the sky would *not* fall, and I would soon prevail upon the foolish barnyard animals. I still didn't have Tessimond's number, so I called the Holiday Inn again and left him a second message, saying that I would be happy meet him in the Elephant at 6 P.M. that evening.

Google helpfully corrected Sleight's incompetent spelling, and I quickly located the Isaac Asimov short story, called "Nightfall," in an online venue. I read it in ten minutes and finished it none the wiser. Not that it was a bad story. On the contrary, it was a good story. But I couldn't see how it had any bearing on the matter in hand. Something to do with stars.

:4:

That I never got to the Elephant was just one of those things. Midafternoon I went for a pee and noticed a constellation of little red spots on the inside of my knickers. You don't want to take any chances with a thing like that. I rang M.; he left work and drove me straight to Casualty, and they admitted me at once. There was some worry that I was bleeding a little into my uterus, and that Phylogeny-Ontology-Recapitulator might be at risk. I lay on a hospital bed for hours, and they did tests, and scanned scans, and finally I was told I was alright and could go home. If there was more spotting I was to come straight back, but otherwise I was free to go.

M. drove us home; and we picked up a pizza on the way, and Tessimond was propelled entirely from my mind. There were more important things to worry about than him and his crazy verbal blit, or World's-End-nigh, or "the stars are coming out!", or whatever his nonsense was. I took the next day off, and then it was the weekend. Tessimond popped into my head on the Sunday evening again (something on telly was the trigger, but I can't remember what it was), and I felt a small quantity of shame that I had stood him up. But then I remembered that he'd been pouring some poison into my team members' ears, and persuading them to abandon me, and I grew angry with him. Then I decided to put him out of my mind. I told myself: Monday morning, all three of my core team would turn up for work, looking sheepish and apologising profusely.

They didn't, though. None of them answered phone call, or text, or Twitter. A week later they hadn't come back, and the university authorities expressed their dissatisfaction, and instituted suspension proceedings. I called Holiday Inn, cross that I hadn't simply got Tessimond's number when I'd had the chance; but I was told he'd checked out. My head of department persuaded the Vice Chancellor not to suspend the three of them until after the press conference. He saw that it could be awkward.

So we had the press conference, and there was a great deal of excitement. It was widely reported in the press. One internet site picked up (God knows how) that of the original team of four, three had gone AWOL and were not present at the press confer-ence. Several news outlets followed it up. We had a cover story ready: that I was team leader, and the others were taking a well-deserved break. The story died down. Who was interested in the particular scientists, when the theory itself was so cool?

The expansion of the universe was speeding up. Given the mass of matter (in-cluding dark matter) in the cosmos as a whole it ought to have been slowing down—as a bone thrown into the sky slows down as it reaches its apogee, and for the same reason: gravity. But it wasn't slowing down. Physicists had speculated about this before, of course, and had come up with a theoretical explanation for it, called *dark energy*. But "dark energy" was tautological physics, really; just a way of saying "the something that is speeding up the inflation of the universe," which is not much of an answer to the question. "What is speeding up the inflation of the universe?" What we had done was demonstrate that the increase in the rate of cosmic expan-sion was itself increasing, and in ways that necessitated that dark matter and dark energy be decoupled. Indeed, we showed that the geometry of the observable gradi-ent of the acceleration of expansion would cause a three-dimensional asymptote, which in turn would cause a complex toroidal folded of spacetime on the very larg-est scale. There was no reason to think that this universal reconfiguration of space-time geometry would have any perceptible effects on Earth. Our scale was simply too small. But it was a thing, and it rewrote Einstein, and the data made our conclu-sions inescapable, and everybody was *very* excited.

The next thing that happened was that I gave birth to an exquisite female infant, with a crumpled face and blue eyes and a wet brush of black hair on her head. We called her Marija Celeste Radonjić-Dalefield, and loved her very much. Two weeks after birth her head hair fell off, and she looked even more adorable with a bald bonce. And the following months whirled past, for truly do they say of having young children that the days are long and the years are short. She slept in our big bed, and though a fraction of our size she somehow dominated that space, and forced us to the edges. We had her baptised at the Saint Peter's Catholic Church, and all my family came, and even some of M.'s.

The Nobel committee worked its slow work, and word came through the unoffi-cial channels that a citation was on its way. I returned early from my maternity leave, and we all made new efforts to locate Niu Jian, Prévert and Sleight. Time had healed enough to make the whole thing seem silly rather than sinister. M. was of the opin-ion that they'd all been spooked by the proximity of the announcement of our re-search. "Working in the dark for years, then suddenly faced with the headlights of global interest—that sort of thing could spook a person in any number of ways."

"You make us sound like mole-people," I said, but I wondered if he might be right.

We reached none of them. Niu Jian's family were easy enough to get hold of, and they were polite, assuring us Noo-noo was rejoicing in health and happiness, but not disclosing in which portion of the globe he was enjoying these things. They promised to pass on our messages, and I don't doubt that they did; but he did not get back to me. Friends suggested that Sleight was in Las Vegas, but we could get no closer to him than that. I felt worst about Prévert—that elegant man, that brilliant mind, without whose input the breakthrough really wouldn't have been possible. But there were no leads at all as far as he was concerned. I notified Montpellier police, even went so far as to hire a French private detective. It took ninety days before the agency reported back, to say that he and a woman called Suzanne Chahal had boarded a flight to the West Indies in the summer, but that it was not possible to know on which island they had ended up.

I agreed with the university that I would collect the prize alone, but that all four of our names would be on the citation. They had lost their minds, the three of them; but that was no reason to punish them—and their contribution had been vital. "Have you have had any better ideas as to why they dropped out, like that?" M. asked me, one night.

"Not a clue," I said. Then again, with a long-drawn-out "ü" sound at the end: "not a *cluuue*."

"I suppose we'll never know," he said. He was reading a novel, and glancing at me over his little slot-shaped spectacles from time to time, as if keeping an eye on me. Marija was in a cot beside the bed, and I was rocking her with a steady, strong motion, which was how she liked it.

"I guess not," I said.

"Does it bother you?"

"They were my friends," I said. Then: "Jack in particular. His desertion is the most baffling. The most hurtful."

"I'm sure," M. said, licking his finger and turning the page of the book, "that it was nothing personal. Whatever Tessimond *told* them, I mean. I'm sure it wasn't to do with you, personally."

"That prick," I said, but without venom. "Whatever it was Tessimond told them."

"You know what I think?" M. asked. "I think, even if we found out what he said, it wouldn't explain it. It'll be something banal, or seeming-banal, like God Loves You, or Remember You Must Die, or Oh My God It's Full Of Stars. Or—you know, whatever. Shall I tell you my theory?"

"You're going to, regardless of what I say," I observed.

M. gave me a Paddington hard stare over his glasses. Then he said: "I think it had nothing to do with this Tessimond chap. I think he's a red herring."

"He was from Oregon," I said, randomly.

"It was something else. Virus. Pressure of work. Road to Tarsus. And in the final analysis, it doesn't matter."

"You're right, of course," I said, and kissed him on his tall, lined forehead.

: 5 :

We agreed that I would travel to Stockholm alone. I was still breast-feeding, so I wasn't over-delighted about it; but M. and I discussed it at length and it seemed best not to drag a baby onto an airplane, and then into a Swedish hotel and then back again for a ceremony she was much too young to even remember. I would go, alone, and then I would come back. I expressed milk like a cow, and we built up a store in the freezer.

It was exciting and I *was* excited. Or I would have been, if I'd been less sleep deprived. If I'm completely honest the thing that had really persuaded me was the image of myself, solus, in a four-star hotel room—sleeping, sleeping all night long, sleeping uninterruptedly and luxuriously and waking with a newly refreshed and sparkling mind to the swift Stockholm sunrise.

You're wondering: did I feel *bad* for my three colleagues—that they wouldn't be there? It was their choice. Would you feel bad, in my shoes?

You're wondering: so that's all there is to it?

No, that's not all there is to it. The day before the flight I took Marija for a walk in her three-wheeled buggy. We strolled by the river, and then back into town. Then I went into a Costa coffee shop, had a hot chocolate for myself, and I fed her. After that she went to sleep, and I painstakingly reinserted her into her buggy. Then I checked my phone, and tapped out a few brief answers to yet another interview about winning The Nobel *Prize* For Heaven's Sake! Then I sat back, in the comfy chair, with my hands folded in my lap.

"Hello, Ana," said Tessimond. "Are you well?"

I had seen him only once before, I think; when Jack had introduced him to everybody by the water cooler, all those months earlier—before he'd said whatever he said and sent my boys scurrying away from the prospect of the Nobel. He had struck me then as a tall, rather sad-faced old gent; clean shaven and with a good stack of white hair, carefully dressed, with polite, old-school manners. I remember Jack saying "this is a friend of mine from Oregon, a professor no less." I don't remember if he passed on the man's name, that first time.

"You stalking me, Professor?" I said. I felt remarkably placid, seeing him standing there. "I googled you, you know."

"If google suggests I have a history of *stalking* people, Ana, then I shall have to seek legal redress."

"Go on, sit down," I instructed him. "You can't do any more damage now. I'm—" I added, aware that it was boasting but not caring, "off to Stockholm tomorrow to collect the Nobel Prize for Physics."

Tessimond sat himself, slowly, down. "I've seen the media coverage of it all, of course. Many congratulations."

"It belongs to all four of us. Have you been in touch with the other three?"

"You mean Professors Niu Jian and Prevért and Doctor Sleight? I have not. Why would you think I have?"

"It doesn't matter." I took a sip of hot chocolate. "You want a drink?"

"No thank you," he said. He was peering into the buggy. "What a lovely infant! Is it a boy?"

"She is a girl," I said. "She is called Marija."

"I'm happy for you."

"Yes," I said. "It's been a big year. Childbirth and winning the Nobel Prize."

"Congratulations indeed."

We sat in silence for a little while. "You spoke to my three colleagues," I said, shortly. "And then after that conversation they all left my team. What did you tell them?"

Tessimond looked at me for a long time, with blithe eyes. "Do you really want me to tell you?" he asked eventually, looking down to my sleeping child and then back up to me.

"No," I said, feeling suddenly afraid. Then: "Yes, hell. Of course. Will it take long?"

"Five minutes."

"Will you then leave me alone and not bother me any more?"

"By all means."

"No, don't tell me. I've changed my mind. What are you anyway? Some kind of Ancient Mariner figure, going around telling people this thing *personally*? Why not publish it—post it to your blog. Or put it on a T-shirt."

"It has crossed my mind to publish it," Tessimond said. "It emerged from my academic research. We usually publish our academic research, don't we."

"So you didn't, because?"

"I didn't see the point. Not just in publication, but in academia. Really, I realised, what I wanted to do was: travel." He looked through the wide glass windows of the coffee shop at the shoppers traversing and retraversing the esplanade. Markets, temples, warehouses and wise paved streets. Tree-shaded squares where the bombastic statues of dead magnates and generals waited, quietly. Two clouds closed upon one another, shutting in front of the sun like a lizard's horizontal eyelids. What is it the poet said? Dark dark dark, they all go into the dark. He said: "I read your work. It's very elegantly done. Very elegant solutions to the dark energy problem; a real . . . I was going to say *intuitive* sense of the geometry of the cosmos."

"Were going to say?"

"Well it's—I'm afraid it's wrong. So your intuition has led you astray. But it's a very bold attempt at . . ."

I interrupted him with: "wrong?"

"I'm afraid so. I'm afraid you're coming at the question from the wrong angle. Not just you, of course. The whole scientific community."

I laughed at this, but, I hope, not unkindly. Marija stirred, twitched her little mitten-clad hands like she was boxing in her sleep, and fell motionless again. "You'd better let the Nobel Committee know," I said. "Before it's too late!" It was all too absurd. Really it was.

The late autumn sky was as blue as water, and as cold.

"Five minutes, you said," I told him, nodding in the direction of the shop clock. "And you've had more than one of those five already."

He breathed in, and out, calmly enough. Then he said: "why is the universe so big?"

"*Why* questions rarely lead physicists anywhere good. Why is there something rather than nothing? Why was there a big bang? Who knows? Not a well-formulated question."

He put his head on one side, and tried again. "How did the universe get so big?"

"That's better," I said, indulgently. "It got so big because fourteen billion years ago the big bang happened, and one consequence of that event was the expansion of spacetime—on a massive scale."

"All these galaxies and stars moving apart from one another like dots on an inflating balloon," he said. "Only the surface of the balloon is 2D and we have to make the conceptual leap to imagining a 3D surface."

"Exactly," I told him. "As every schoolkid knows."

"Still: why expansion? Why should the big bang result in the dilation of space?"

I took another sip from my chocolate. "Three minutes to go, and you've tripped yourself into another *why* question."

"Let me ask you about time," he said, unruffled. "We appear to be moving through time. We go in one direction. We cannot go backwards, we can only go forwards."

I shrugged. "According to maths we can do backwards. The equations of physics are reversible. It just so happens that we go in one direction only. It's no big deal."

"Quite right," he said, nodding. "The science says we ought to be able to go in any direction. Yet we never," he said stroking his own cheek, "actually *do*. That's strange, isn't it?"

"Maybe," I said. "I can't say it bothers me."

"Time is a manifold, like space. We can move in any direction in space. But we can only move in one direction in time."

"This really is kindergarten stuff," I said. "And much as I have enjoyed our little chat . . ."

"What moves an object through the manifold of space?"

After a moment, I said: "force."

"Impulse. Gravity. Those two things only. You can push an object to give it kinetic energy, or you can draw it towards you. You fire your rocket up; Earth *pulls* your rocket down. Kinetic energy is always relative, not absolute. The driver of a car passing by a pedestrian has kinetic energy from the pedestrian's point of view; but from the point of view of the person in the passenger seat that same drive has zero kinetic energy."

It was, in a strange sort of way, soothing to hear him elucidate elementary physics in this way. "All well and good," I said.

"That's how things go in the physical manifold, which we call spacetime. Relocate the model to the temporal manifold—let's call it timespace."

This was when the fizzing started in my stomach. "For the sake of argument, why not," I said. I couldn't prevent a defensive tone creeping into my voice. "Although it'll be nothing but a thought experiment."

"Why do you say that?" he asked, blandly.

"We've centuries of experimental data about the actual manifold, the spacetime manifold. Your 'timespace' manifold is pure speculation."

"Is it? I would say we move through it every day of our lives. I'd say we've a lifetime's experience of it. The question is—no, the two questions are: why are we moving through it, and why can we only move through it in one direction."

There was a blurry rim to my vision. My heart had picked up the pace. "More why questions."

"If you prefer: *what* is drawing us towards it, through timespace?"

"You're saying the reason we feel time as a kind of motion, one hour per hour, is because something is drawing us, with its gravitational pull—is that it? Because it seems to me that we might just as well have been launched forward by some initial impulse. Don't you agree?"

"The reason I don't agree is the fact that we're stuck moving in one temporal direction." I saw, then, where he was going; but I sat quietly as he spelled it out. "Think of the analogue from the physical manifold. There's no force that could propel an object, let alone a whole cosmos, so rapidly that it was locked into a single trajectory. But there *is* a force in the universe that can draw an object *in* with such a force—draw it such that it has no option but to move in one direction, towards the centre of the object."

"A black hole."

He nodded.

"Your theory," I said, in a just-so-as-we're-clear voice, "is that the reason we move along the arrow of time the way we do is that we're being drawn towards a supermassive temporal black hole?"

"Yes."

"Well," I said, with an insouciance I did not feel. "It's an interesting theory, although it is only a theory."

"Not at all. Consider the data."

"What data?"

"I understand your resistance, Ana," he said, gently. "But you can do better than this. Who knows the data better than you? What happens as a physical object approaches the event horizon of a physical black hole?"

"Time," I said, "dilates."

"So what must happen as a *temporal* object approaches the event horizon of a *temporal* black hole? Physics dilates. Space expands—until it approaches an asymptote of reality. From the point of view of an observer not present at the event horizon itself space would seem to expand until it appeared infinite." He looked through the big glass again. "What else do we see, when we look around?"

"So we're still," I said, my voice gravelly, "*outside* the event horizon?"

"If we were outside the event horizon, the rate of apparent expansion of space would be an asymptote approaching a fixed rate—a simple acceleration. And until a few decades ago that was what the data showed. But then the data starting showing that the rate of apparent expansion of the universe is *speeding up*. That can only mean that we're approaching the event horizon itself. That also explains why we locked into the one direction of time. In the timespace manifold generally speaking we ought to be able to go forwards, backwards, whatever we wanted. But we're not in the manifold generally; we're in a very particular place. Like an object falling into a black hole, we're locked into a single vector."

I thought about it. Well, I say I thought about it; but the truth is I didn't need to think very hard. It fell into place in my mind; like the others I found myself thinking how could I not see this before? It is so very obvious. "But if you're right—wait," I said. "Wait a moment."

I pulled out my phone, and jabbed up the calculus app. It took me a few moments to work through the crucial equations. Of course everything fitted. Of course it was true.

Of course it was right.

I looked at him, feeling removed from myself. "When we reach the actual temporal event horizon," I said, "tidal forces will rip us apart."

"Will rip time apart," he said, nodding slowly. "Yes. Of course that amounts to the same thing."

"When?"

"You've got the equations there," he said, looking at my phone as it lay, like a miniature 2001-monolith, flat on the table. "But it's hard to be precise. The scale is fourteen billion years; the tolerances are not seconds, or even days. Years. I worked a seven years plus or minus. That was a decade ago."

I shook my head, the way a dog shakes water of its pelt; but there was no way this idea could be shaken out of my mind. It was true; it was there. "It could be— literally—any day now," I said.

"I'm sorry," he said. "Not for you, so much, as for the fact of you having a small kid."

"That's why Noo-noo was so circumspect with me," I said. "I see. But what difference does it make? And, yes, alright I see why you haven't published this. It'd be wandering the highways with an End Is Nigh sandwich board."

"Not that," he said, his glittering eye meeting mine. "More that it's so obvious. When you think about it, how could the expanding universe be anything *other* than this? Travelling near the ultimate spatial speed makes time dilate; so obviously travelling near the ultimate *temporal* speed will make *space* dilate. We should—all of us, we should just . . . *see* it."

"I'm going home now," I told him. But I embraced him before I left, and felt the sharkskin roughness of his unshaved cheek against my own. Then I wheeled Marija home. I called M. and told him to leave work and join me. He was puzzled, but acquiesced.

He hasn't gone back.

:6:

The equations depend upon precision over prodigious lengths of time—since the big bang, or (rather) since the dilation effect first affected what until then must have been a stable cosmos existing within an open temporal manifold. But I've done my best. Tessimond's +/-7 years was, I suspect, deliberately vague; erring on the side of generosity. I think the timescale is much shorter. Download the data on the rate of acceleration of cosmic expansion, and you can do your own sums.

Of course I never flew to Stockholm. Why would I waste three days away from my child? None of that matters anyway. We realised what money we could, and bought a small place by the sea. I won't say what sea. That doesn't matter either; except that, when the dusk comes each day, and the net curtains are sucked against the open windows and go momentary starch-stiff ; and when the moths congregate to worship their electric sun-gods; and when the moon lies carelessly in the sky over the purple marine horizon like a pearl of great price—when Marija is fed and happy and M. and I take our turns holding her, and then lay her down and hold one another—there is a contentment spun from finitude that my previous, open-ended existence could not comprehend. I have busied myself writing this account, although only a little every day, for there is no rush, or else there is too much rush and I don't wish to be troubled by the latter. And as for everything else, it helps to know what is really important.

old paint

MEGAN LINDHOLM

Books by Megan Lindholm include the fantasy novels Wizard of the Pigeons, Harpy's Flight, The Windsingers, The Limbreth Gate, Luck of the Wolves, The Reindeer People, Wolf's Brother, *and* Cloven Hooves, *the science fiction novel* Alien Earth, *and, with Steven Brust, the collaborative novel* The Gypsy. *Lindholm also writes as* New York Times *bestseller Robin Hobb, one of the most popular writers in fantasy today, having sold over one million copies of her work in paperback. As Robin Hobb, she's perhaps best known for her epic fantasy Farseer trilogy:* Assassin's Apprentice, Royal Assassin, *and* Assassin's Quest, *as well as the two fantasy series related to it, the Liveship Traders series:* Ship of Magic, The Mad Ship, *and* Ship of Destiny; *and the Tawny Man series:* Fool's Errand, The Golden Fool, *and* Fool's Fate. *She's also the author of the Soldier Son series:* Shaman's Crossing, Forest Mage, *and* Renegade's Magic. *Most recently, as Robin Hobb, she's started a new series, the Rain Wild Chronicles, featuring* Dragon Keeper, Dragon Haven, City of Dragons, *and* Blood of Dragons. *As Megan Lindholm, her most recent book is a "collaborative" collection with Robin Hobb,* The Inheritance: And Other Stories.

In the story that follows, she gives us a moving study of the bonds of affection and the relationship that can form between a family and an inanimate object—especially when the object turns out to not be quite so inanimate after all.

I was only nine when it happened, so I may not have the details absolutely right. But I know the heart of my story, and the heart is always what matters in a tale like mine.

My family didn't have much when I was growing up. A lot of lean years happened in that first half of the century. I don't say I had it as tough as my mom did, but the 2030's weren't a piece of cake for anyone. My brother, my mom, and I lived in subsidized housing in the part of T-town they call New Tacoma. It sure wasn't new when I was a kid. Tacoma's always been a tough town, and my mom said that her grandpa kept her on a short leash and she survived it, and so her kids would, too. Everyone knew we had the strictest mom in our apartments and pitied us for it.

We weren't like a lot of folks in the subsidized housing. Mom was ashamed to be there. It was the only thing she took from the government, and I think if she had been alone, she would have lived on the streets. We got by on what she made working at an old folks' home, so we budgeted hard. She cooked our meals from scratch and we carried our lunches to school in the same battered lunch boxes and stained back packs, year after year. She mended our clothes and we shopped at the Goodwill. Our cell phones were clunky and we all shared one computer. And we didn't have a car.

Then my great grandpa died. Mom had hardly seen him in years, and we kids didn't know him at all, but she was in his will. She got what was left in his checking account, which wasn't much, and the old furniture in his apartment, which was mostly particle board crap. The old rocking chair was good, and the ceramic canisters shaped like mushrooms were cool. Mom said they were really old and she remembered them from when she was little. But the one big thing he did have was a car, parked in his parking slot where it had been gathering dust for the last twelve years since they'd taken his license away.

The car was vintage, and not in a good way. Back in the 2020's, there was this rage for making new energy efficient cars that looked sort of like the old classic gas guzzlers. People wanted rumble and roomy to go with their solar and alternative fuels. I guess my great grandpa had been a surfer back in the day, because what he chose was something that was supposed to look like a station wagon. The first time we went down to the parking garage and looked at it, Ben, my older brother, groaned and asked, "What is that crap on the sides? Is it supposed to look like wood or something?"

"Or something," my mom said absently. She pushed the button on the key but the battery for it was long dead. So she opened the car the old fashioned way, putting the key in a hole in the door handle. I was fascinated and proud of my mom for knowing you could do that.

The outside of the car was covered in fine dust, but inside, it was immaculate. She sat in the seat for a little while with her hands on the wheel, acting like she could see out the windshield. She was smiling a little bit. Then she said, "The smart thing to do is sell him. If the interior is this good, I bet he kept the engine cherry, too." She reached down and pulled a little handle, and Ben and I jumped when the hood of the car popped up.

"Mom, I think you broke it," Ben said. "Maybe we shouldn't touch anything until we can have a mechanic look at it." Ben was fourteen then, and for some reason, he now believed that if he didn't know something, Mom didn't know it either. She just snorted and got out of the car and went around to open the hood the rest of the way.

"My goodness," she said softly. "You did take care of him, Pops."

I didn't know what she was talking about, but I do remember that the inside of that engine compartment was spotless. She shut the hood, unplugged the car from the supplemental charger, and retracted the coil. She had a license and knew how to drive, because that was part of her job at the old people's home. I was still surprised when she slid in behind the wheel and put the key in a slot thing and turned it. The vehicle had an anti-theft box on the steering column. She hesitated, and then put her forefinger on the sensor. "Hello, Suzanne," the car said in a rich, brown voice. "How are you today?"

"Just fine," she said quietly. "Just fine."

Ben was freaked. Mom noticed that and grinned. She patted the steering column. "My grandpa's voice. A little customization he did on the systems." She tossed her head at the back seat. Ben opened the door and we both got in. There were shoulder strap seat belts.

"No airbags?" Ben asked in disbelief.

"They're there. But when he was new, cars had both. It's safe. I wouldn't put you in a car if I thought it wasn't safe." She closed her eyes for a minute and tightened up her mouth as if she had suddenly wanted to cry. Then she opened her eyes and shifted her grip on the wheel. "Let's blast," she said loud and clear, and the engine started. It was a lot louder than any other car I'd ever heard. Mom had to raise her voice to talk over it. "And when he was new, cars were electric AND internal combustion. And much noisier than they are now."

Ben was horrified. "This car is running on gasoline, right now?"

Mom shook her head. "Sound effects. And loudest inside the car. My Grandpa had a sense of humor." She stroked the car's dash. "All those years, and he never took me off the security system."

"How smart is this car?" Ben demanded.

"Smart enough," she said. "He can take himself to a fueling station. Knows when his tires are low on air, and can schedule his own oil change. He used to talk to the dealership; I wonder if it's even in business still. He's second generation simulated intelligence. Sure fooled me, most of the time. He has a lot of personality customization in his software. My grandpa put in a bunch of educational stuff, too. He can speak French. He used to drill me on my vocabulary on the way to school. And he knew all my favorite radio stations." She shook her head. "Back then, people wanted their cars to be their friends. He sure was mine."

"That's whack," Ben said solemnly.

"No, it was great. I loved it. I loved him."

"Love you too, Suzanne," the car said. His voice was a rich baritone.

"You should sell this thing, Mom," Ben advised her wisely.

"Maybe I should," Mom said, but the way she said it, I knew that we had a car now.

Ben had begun to think he was the man of the house, so he tried to start an argument with Mom about selling this car and using that money and her inheritance money to buy a real car. She just looked at him and said, "Seems to me it's my inheritance, not yours. And I'm keeping him."

And so that was that.

She opened a little panel on his dash and punched in our address. She moved a handle on the steering column, and the car began to ease backwards. I held my breath, thinking we were going to hit something, but we didn't. She stopped the car, moved the handle again, and we slid forward, smooth as a slide, up and out of the parking garage and into the daylight.

On the way home, she kept pushing buttons and chatting with the car. It didn't have instant-net, but it had a screen that folded down from the ceiling. "What good is that? You have to sit in the back seat to see it," Ben complained. Mom reached under the seat and opened a drawer. Inside was a bunch of old style DVD's in flat plastic cases.

"They're movies," she said. "Supposed to entertain the kids in the back seat. The screen is back there so the driver won't be distracted." She picked up the stack and began to sort through them. She had a wistful half-smile on her face. "I remember all of these," she said quietly. "Some were my favorites."

"So the driver's supposed to just sit up front by himself and be bored?" Ben demanded.

She set the movies down with a sigh and turned to him. "The driver is supposed to drive." She turned back and put her hands on the wheel and looked out over the hood. "When this fellow was built, cars were only allowed to go a short distance without a licensed driver in the driver's seat. Less than a mile, I think it was. The auto-brains were really limited back then. Legally limited more than technically limited. People didn't really trust cars to drive themselves. They had emergency services locators, of course, so they could take you to the hospital if you passed out, and sensors to help you park, but when he was built, drivers still did most of the driving."

"Why do you keep calling the car 'he' and 'him'?" Ben demanded.

"Old habit," my mom said, but she said it in a way that ended the conversation.

We had a parking spot at our building that we'd never used before. The first time we pulled up in the car, every kid hanging around outside came to see what the noise was. They watched as the car plugged in to charge. Our car was about twice as long as any other car in the lot.

"Look at the size of those solars," one boy whispered, and Ben's ears went red.

"Old piece of junk," said another knowingly. "Surprised it still runs at all."

Mom did the one thing that Ben hated the most. I didn't much like it either. All the other moms in the building would have just ignored the wanna-be gangers hanging around the parking lot. Mom always looked straight at them and talked to them as if they were smart, even when they were so drugged out they could barely stand.

"He's old, but he runs like a clock. He'll probably outlast most of the Tupperware crates here. They still used a lot of steel when this guy was built." Mom set the alarm, and the tattle-tale light began to circle the car.

"Wha's that stuff onna size spozed to be?" Leno asked. He was smiling. Leno was always smiling, and I'd never seen him with his eyes more than half open. He looked delighted to see the car, but I'd seen him look just as enthusiastically at a lamp post.

"It's wood. Well, pseudo wood. My Grandpa was so proud of it. It was one of the first nano-products used on any car. It was the latest thing, back then. Guaranteed not to peel or fade or scratch, and to feel like wood grain. Most minor dents, it could repair, too." She sighed, smiled and shook her head, remembering something. Then, "Come on, kids. Dinner to cook and homework to do."

"Homework," one of the boys sneered, and two girls laughed low. We ignored her and followed her into the house.

Ben was mad at her. "How come you know so much about that car? I thought you didn't have anything to do with your grandpa. I thought he, like, disowned you when you were a kid or something."

Mom gave him a look. She never talked much about her family. As far as I remembered, it had always been just her, Ben, and me. Someone must have been our father, but I'd never met him. And if Ben remembered him, he didn't say much.

Mom firmed her mouth for a minute and then said brusquely, "My grandpa and I really loved each other. I made some choices in my life that he didn't agree with. So he was really angry with me for a long time, and I was angry with him. But we always knew we still loved one another. We just never got around to making up in time to say it."

"What decisions?" I asked.

"Getting knocked up with me," Ben said, low. Either Mom didn't hear him say it or she didn't want to discuss it.

So, after that, we had a car. Not that we drove it much. But Mom polished it with special wax, cleaned his solars and vacuumed out the inside and hung up an old-fashioned pine tree scent thing from the mirror. Once we came home from school on the bus, and found her asleep in the driver's seat, her hands on the wheel. She was smiling in her sleep. Every once in a while, on the weekend, she might take us out for a ride in the station wagon. Ben always said he didn't want to go, but then went.

She didn't upgrade the car but she made it ours. She put us both on the car's security system, and updated the old GPS settings with our home, schools, the hospital, and the police station, so in an emergency either of us could get help. The car greeted us by name. Ben pretty much ignored its personality program, but I talked to it. It knew a lot of corny old jokes and had a strange program called "Road Trip Games" about license plates and "Animal, Vegetable, or Mineral." I tried out every seat in the car. I watched some of the old movies on the little screen, but they were really long and the people talked too much. My favorite seat was the one in the back that faced backwards. I liked watching the faces of the people as they came up behind our car. Lots of them looked surprised. Some of them smiled and waved, and some turned their heads to look at the car as they passed us. The only time I didn't like it was at night when the headlights of the cars behind us would hit me right in the eyes.

The car was a sometime thing, and mostly it didn't change anything about our life. Sometimes, when it was pouring rain and we had to walk to the bus stop and then walk home again, Ben would grumble. Other parents sent their cars to pick up their kids from school. Ben whined about this a lot. "Why can't the wagon pick us up from school when it's pouring rain?" he'd demand of her.

"Your grandfather was a 'drive it yourself' guy. Like me. I doubt he ever had the block removed."

"Then it's just a software thing? You could take it off?"

"Don't get any ideas, Benny-boy!" Mom warned him.

And for a while, he didn't. But then he turned fifteen. And Mom decided to teach him to drive.

Ben wasn't that interested at first. Most kids didn't bother with a personal license anymore. As long as a car met the legal standards, anyone could get in it and go. I knew little kindergarteners who were dropped off by their cars each day and then picked up again. Mom said it was stupid that it took 3000 pounds of car to transport a 40 pound kid to school, but lots of people did it. Ben and I both knew that Mom could have had the car's brain upgraded or unblocked or whatever, and we could have had wheels any time we wanted them. But she chose not to. She told Ben the only way he was going to get to use the car was if he knew how to physically drive it.

Once he passed his test, she told him that we might even have it updated so that he could just kick back and tell the car where he wanted to go.

So, that was the big attraction for Ben. I got to ride along on his driving lessons. At first, Mom took us way out of town in the evenings and made him practice in parking lots outside vacant strip malls. But Ben actually learned to drive pretty well. He said it wasn't that different from a lot of his video games. Then Mom reminded him that he couldn't kill himself or someone else with a video game. She was so serious about it, and Ben got so cranky. It was a thing they went through for about a year I think. Any conversation about the car always turned into an argument. He hated the "dorky" paint and wood on it; she said it was "vintage" and "classic." He said we should get a cheaper car; she said that all the metal in the body made it safer for him to drive, and that he should be happy we had a car at all. Their conversations were always the same. I think Ben said, "I know, I know!" more than a million times that year. And Mom was always saying, "Shut up and listen to what I'm saying."

Ben was absolutely set on getting the car upgraded so he could ride around with his friends. Most of his friends' parents had said "no way" to them riding if Ben was actually driving the car, even after he got his license. He kept telling Mom how the car would be safer if it could drive itself and how we could get better mileage because it would self-adjust routes to avoid traffic or to take short cuts, and that statistics showed that car-brains actually reacted faster than human brains in dangerous situations.

"Maybe so, but they can only react one way, and human brains can think of a dozen ways to react in a tough situation. So the answer is still no. Not yet. Maybe never."

Mom scored big points on him the next week when there were dozens of accidents on I-5 that involved driverless cars. Mom didn't care that it was because of a virus that someone had uploaded to the traffic beam. No one knew who did it. Some people said it was an environmental group that wanted to discourage private cars. Other people thought it was just a new generation of hackers making their mark on the world. "It wasn't the cars' fault, Mom!" Ben argued. "The beacon gave them bad information."

"But if a human had been holding the steering wheel, none of those accidents would have happened," Mom said. And that was the end of it, for a couple of months.

Then in June, Ben and Mom got into it big time. He came home from school one day and took the car without asking. He brought it home painted black, with a rippling hint of darker tiger stripes. I stood and stared at it when he pulled into the apartment building parking lot. "Cool, huh?" he asked me. "The stripes move. The faster you drive, the faster the nanos ripple."

"Where'd you get the money to do it?" I asked him, and when he said, "None of your business," I knew it was really going to blow up.

And it did, but even worse than I'd expected. By the time Mom came home from work, the vintage nanos in the "wood" paneling were at war with the tiger stripe nanos. The car looked, as mom put it, "Like a pile of crawling crap! What were you thinking?"

And they were off, with him saying that the black made the car look better and that the new nanos would win over the old ones and the color would even out.

When it came out that he'd raided his college money for the paint job, she was furious.

"It was too good of a deal to pass up! It was less than half what it would cost in a standard paint shop!"

So that was how she found out he'd had it done in one of those car-painting tents that had been popping up near malls and swap meets. They were mobile services that fixed dings in windshields or replaced them entirely. They could install seat covers, and add flames or pin stripes. The shady ones could override parental controls for music or video or navigation systems, erase GPS tracking and alter mileage used. Or, in the one Ben had gone to, do an entire nano-paint job in less than an hour. With the new nanos, they didn't even use sprayers anymore. They dumped the stuff on and the nanos spread out to cover any previously painted surfaces. The men operating the paint tent had promised Ben that their nanos were state of the art and could subdue any previous nanos in the car's paint.

Mom was so furious that she made us get in the car and we drove back to where Ben had had it done. By law, they should have looked at the owner registration before they nanoed it. Mom wanted Ben's money back and was hoping they had call-back nanos that would remove the black. But no such luck. When we got to where the tent had been, there was nothing but a heap of empty nano jars and some frustrated paint crawling around on the ground trying to cover crumpled pop cans. My mom called the cops, because it's illegal to abandon nanos, and they said they'd send out a containment team. She didn't wait for them. We just went home. When we got there, Ben jumped out of the car and stormed into the house. Mom got out more slowly and stood looking at our car with the saddest expression I'd ever seen on her face.

"I'm so sorry, Old Paint," she told the car. And that was how the car got his name, and also when I realized how much her grandpa's car had meant to her. Ben had done a lot worse things than just paint a car without her permission. I thought that when he calmed down, I might try to explain that to him. Then I thought that maybe the best thing for me to do was to stay out of it.

The paint on the car just got worse and worse. Those old nanos were tough. The wood paneling took to migrating around on the car's body, trying to escape the attacks of the new paint. It looked scabby as if the car were rotting. Ben didn't want to be seen in the car anymore but Mom was merciless. "This was your decision, and you are going to have to live with it just like the rest of us," she told him. And she would send him on the errands, to get groceries or to return the library books, so he would have to drive Old Paint.

A couple months later, my mom stayed home with stomach flu. She woke up feeling better in the afternoon, and went to the window to look out at the day. That was when she discovered Old Paint was gone. My brother and I were on the bus when we got her furious call. "You probably think you are smart, Benny Boy, but what you are in is big trouble. Very big trouble." He was trying to figure out why she was so angry when the bus went crazy. Ben dropped his phone bracing himself and me on the slippery seat. Mom told us later that the Teamsters contract with the city had always insisted that every city-owned mass transit unit had to have a nominal driver. So when the bus started honking its horn and flashing its light and veering back and forth over three lanes, the old man in the driver's seat reached up and threw the manual override switch. He grabbed the wheel and wrestled us over to the curb and turned off the engine.

The driver apologized to everyone and asked us all to sit tight until the maintenance people could come. He called in for a replacement bus, but everyone on the bus heard the dispatcher's hysterical response. Twelve bus breakdowns in the last ten minutes, three involving bad accidents, and there were no more replacement buses to send. In the background, someone shouted that an out of control ambulance had just rear-ended a bus. Dispatch put the driver on hold.

We were only three blocks short of our stop, so we asked to get off and walk. Ben grabbed his phone off the floor but Mom had hung up and he didn't really want to find out just what she had discovered that had made her so mad. Ben had a lot of secrets in those days, from rolling papers in his gym bag to a follow up appointment at the STD clinic. Not that I was supposed to know about any of them.

We'd gone half a block when we heard the bus start up. We looked back and saw it take off. I'd never known a city bus could accelerate like that. We were staring after it, wondering what had happened, when a VW Cherub jumped the curb and nearly hit us. It high-centered for just a second, wheels spinning and smoking, and two kids jumped out of the back seat, screaming. A moment later, it reversed out into the street and raced off, still going backwards. The teenage girl who had jumped out was crying and holding onto her little brother. "The car just went crazy! The car just went crazy!"

A man from a corner bar and grill opened the door and shouted, "You kids get inside NOW!"

We all hesitated, but then he pointed up the street and yelled, "OMG, now, kids!" and we bolted in as the Hot Pizza delivery van came right down the sidewalk. It clipped the awning supports as it went by and the green and white striped canvas came rippling down behind us as we jumped inside.

The place was a sports bar, and a couple of times we'd had pizza there with mom when her favorite team was in the play-offs. Usually every screen in the place was on a different sports feed, but that day they all showed the same rattled newsman. He was telling everyone to stay inside if they could, to avoid vehicles of all kinds and to stay tuned for updates to the mad vehicle crisis.

Ben finally called Mom and told her where we were, because the tavern owner refused to let us leave by ourselves. When Mom got there, she thanked him, and then took us home by a route that went down narrow alleys and through peoples' backyards. Every few minutes, we'd hear a car go roaring past on the streets, or hear horns blaring, or crashes in the distance.

Not every vehicle in the city had gone wild, but a lot of them had, including Old Paint. Mom had been mad because she thought Ben had upgraded Old Paint's self-driving capability by removing the block on his software. She looked a bit skeptical when he denied it but by late evening the news people had convinced her. The virus was called the "7734, upside down and backwards" by the hacker group that took credit for it. Because if you wrote 7734 on a piece of paper and looked at it upside down and backwards, it looked a little bit like the word "hell." They said they did it to prove they could. No one knew how they spread it, but our neighbor said that zombie nanos delivered it right to the cars' driving computers. He said that the nanos were planted in a lot of car stuff, from wiper fluid to coolant, and even paint. So

Ben said there was no proof he'd infected the car when he got it painted, but that was what Mom always believed.

By evening, the Internet news said the crisis would solve itself pretty fast. For a lot of cars, it did. They wrecked themselves. Cops and vigilantes took out some of the obvious rogues, shooting out their tires. It made the owners pretty angry and the insurance companies were arguing about whether they had to pay off. The government had people working on a nano antivirus that they could spray on rogues, but nothing they tried seemed to work. Some people wanted all the auto-recharging places shut down but people with uninfected cars objected. Finally, they decided to leave the auto-charge stations open because some of the rogue cars got aggressive about recharging themselves when they encountered closed stations.

Mom tried to explain it to me. Cars had different levels of smartness, and people could set priority levels on what they wanted the cars to do for themselves. A lot of people had set their "recharge importance" level high because they wanted the car kept charged to maximum capacity. Others had set their cars to always travel as fast as they were allowed, and turned the courtesy level down to low or even off. There was a pedestrian awareness level that was not supposed to be tampered with, but some people did it. Pizza delivery cars and ambulances were some of the most dangerous rogues.

At first, the virus paralyzed the nation. It didn't infect every car, but the ones that had it caused traffic accidents and made the streets dangerous. No one wanted to go out. Schools shifted to snow-day internet mode. The stores got low on groceries and the only delivery trucks were vintage semis, with no brains at all and old guys driving them.

By the third week, the infection rate was down, and most of the really dangerous rogues had been disabled. That left a lot of cars still running wild. Some seemed to follow their normal routines, but speeded up or took alternate routes. Kids were warned not to get into infected cars, even if it was the family van waiting outside the school at the usual time, because sometimes those cars behaved reliably, and sometimes they abruptly went nuts. A new little business started up, with bounty hunters tracking down people's expensive vehicles by GPS and then capturing them and disabling them until the virus could be cured. But some owners couldn't afford that service, or the car wasn't worth what the bounty hunters charged.

So Old Paint was left running wild. At first, we'd see him in the neighborhood at odd times. He always drove himself very safely, and he just seemed to be randomly wandering. Twice we caught him in our parking spot, recharging himself, but each time he took off before we could get near him, let alone open his doors. Mom said to leave him alone, and she'd worry about it when the government came up with an antivirus. Then we stopped seeing him at all.

One night, when Ben was really bummed about not having a car for some school dance that was coming up, he checked Old Paint's GPS. "That crazy bastard went to California!" he shouted, half impressed by it.

"Let me see that," Mom said, and then she started laughing. "I took him there one spring break when I told Grandpa I was only going to Ocean Shores. I wiped all the data off his GPS before I came home. I guess the virus must have brought it back into his memory."

"You did things like that? You'd kill me if I did something like that!"

"I was young," Mom said. She smiled in an odd way. "Sometimes, I think being a teenager is like a virus. You do things that go against every bit of programming your parents ever put into you." She made a "huh" noise as if she were pushing something away. She looked over at Ben. "Becoming a parent is the antivirus. Cured me of all sorts of things."

"So how come you don't let me just be a teenager like you were?" Ben demanded.

Mom just looked at him. "Because I learned, the hard way, just how dangerous that can be to a kid. Running wild is a great thing. For the kids that survive it." She turned off the monitor then, and told us both to go to bed.

In the weeks that followed, Old Paint went all sorts of strange places. Once he went off to some place in the Olympic National Forest where Mom had once gone to a rave. And he spent two days crawling around on an old logging trail near Chrystal Mountain. Mom looked worried when he went off on that jaunt, and the night she discovered that he was now headed for Lake Chelan, she was so relieved she laughed. In a way, it was really cool that Old Paint did all that traveling. Mom would look at his location at night, and tell us stories about when she was a teenager and living with her grandpa and making him crazy. She'd tell us about close calls and stupid ideas and how close she had come to getting killed or arrested. Ben and I both started to see her differently, like someone who really had been a kid once. She didn't cut us any more slack than she ever had, but we began to understand why.

We kept expecting Old Paint to run out of charge, but he didn't. He'd go sedately through the auto-charge places, I guess, looking like some family's old car. Ben asked Mom why she didn't block him from using the credit card, and she just shrugged. I think she enjoyed reliving all her wild adventures. And he wasn't that expensive. A lot of cars had backup solar systems, and Old Paint had a really extensive one. Sometimes he'd stay in one place for three or four days, and Mom figured he was just soaking up the rays before moving on. "And if I cut him off, then he may never come home to us." She gave an odd smile, one that wasn't happy and added, "Tough love isn't all it's cracked up to be. Sometimes, when you lock a door, the other person never knocks on it again."

So, as the weeks passed, we watched Old Paint move up and down Old 99. Ben and I went back to walking. All the city buses and delivery vans had been set back to full manual, and all sorts of old guys were chortling about being suddenly employed again. My mom said it was a huge victory for the Teamsters, and some people insinuated they had backed the hackers.

The government people came up with three different antiviruses, and everyone was required to install them in their vehicles. The trick, of course, was getting the scrubber nanos and antivirus program to the infected vehicles. Everyone with an infected vehicle was required to report it, and Mom had filled out the forms. A package came in the mail with the scrubber nanos in a spray can and a booklet on how to disinfect the car and then install the antivirus. Mom set it on the kitchen window sill and it gathered dust.

By the end of summer, most of the infected vehicles were off the road. They'd either destroyed themselves or, in the case of the really aggressive ones, been hunted down and disabled. There were still incidents almost every day. Three fire trucks in

San Francisco were scrambled for a five alarm fire, and instead they went on a wild rampage through the city. Someone deliberately infected fifteen Harley-Davidsons parked outside a bar with a variant of the virus, and ten of the Hells Angels who mounted them and rode away died a mile later. A fuel delivery business in Anchorage faced huge fines when it was determined that they had neglected to use the proper antivirus. The fines for the environmental clean up were even bigger.

In late September, during a heavy rainstorm, I spotted Old Paint near the school. He was idling at the curb, and I ran toward him, but Ben grabbed me by the shoulder. "He's infected. You can't trust him," he warned me in a harsh whisper. He looked over his shoulder, fearful that someone else might have overhead. By then, they were disabling even nonaggressive vehicles because they thought they might be able to infect other vehicles. As we walked toward the bus stop, Old Paint slowly edged down the street after us.

"Why is he here? He never did auto-pick-up for us."

"It's in his programming. He knows what school we go to, and what time we get out. Mom put it in just in case she wanted to use it someday. Probably just glitching."

When we got on the bus, Old Paint revved his engine, honked twice, and passed us. When Mom got home from work, we told her and she smiled. That night, really late, I heard her get out of bed and I followed her to the living room. We peeked out the rain-streaked window and Old Paint was charging himself at our parking slot.

"Doesn't look so bad for being on the road so long," Mom said. She smiled. "I bet I'll find a car wash and oil change on my credit card bill this month."

I went to the kitchen and came back with the scrubber and antivirus. "Shall we try to catch him?" I asked.

She pursed her lips and shook her head. "Not in the rain. Let him get used to coming at night to charge. On a dry night, I'll go down and spray him."

And we went back to bed.

September became October. I saw Old Paint in the streets sometimes, and I suspect he came and charged up at our place more than once. But the weather stayed wet and that was Mom's excuse for not trying to catch him. Ben was playing football for his school and seemed so different it was like aliens had reprogrammed my brother. Most days, I had to ride the bus alone. I noticed that Old Paint would show up at the school on the really stormy days and shadow me until I was on the bus. Once he was at my bus stop and followed me home. I knew I wasn't supposed to get inside him, but no one had said I couldn't talk to him. So I edged toward him as he followed the sidewalk and ran my fingers along his fender. "I miss you, Old Paint," I told him. The locks bit down, he revved his engine and leaped away from the curb. He tore off through the afternoon traffic with other cars honking at him. It really hurt my feelings. I didn't tell Mom or Ben. I was afraid she might report him as borderline aggressive and give his GPS code to the police.

January brought really nasty weather. Snow fell, melted into black ice, and more snow fell. For a solid week, the cycle repeated. The worst part was that all the busses were running on the "snow routes" that avoided hills. So our usual three block walk to the bus stop became six blocks to a main street. Each day, Old Paint was outside our apartments, edging along behind us as we walked to the bus stop. Ben ignored him, except to cuss that he could be inside a warm car instead of wading through snow and ice. Our bus stop was right in front of a charging station.

There was a line for the quick charge, and while we were waiting for the bus, a black van pulled up, blocking a car in. The lettering on the sign said Road Dog Recoveries. "Bounty hunters!" Ben said. "Cool. Watch this."

They fanned out around the car they wanted. A man in a car at the end of the line shouted, "Don't shoot those so close to the station!" Because they had their special tire piercing guns out and were taking aim at the red Beamer they had blocked in.

But that wasn't the car they should have been watching. Two cars back in line, a black sedan with big wheels suddenly cranked its wheels and cut right through the median and the bushes and right at us. It hit one of the men as it did so and he went flying. The other men all fired at it. And missed. Then the red car freaked out, backed into the car behind it to gain a bit of space, and it shot over the curb into the median and high centered.

Ben grabbed me and jerked me to one side, but it wasn't quite enough. I hadn't even seen the black sedan coming toward us. It clipped me and the impact snatched me out of Ben's grip. I went flying and rolling out into the street. When I hit the ground, I slid on the black ice and I thought I was never going to stop. Ben was yelling, cars were honking, and when I finally stopped the whole world was spinning. But I was okay. I got up. Ben was running toward me.

Then my arm started really hurting and I realized I couldn't move it. I screamed. And Ben shouted, "RUN! Run, Sadie, get out of there!"

The black sedan had slewed around and was coming back at me. Later, I found out that it had belonged to a security service and had an attack mode if anyone tried to harm the VIP inside. It had interpreted the bounty hunters as assassins. No one could say why it came after me. But as it came at me and I turned to run, I saw something even scarier. Old Paint was roaring at me, full speed in reverse. I was going to be crushed between the two cars. I screamed, the black sedan hit me, and I was airborne.

But Old Paint's rear door had opened upwards and as I flew toward him, he shifted into first, burned rubber and faded away from me like a catcher backpedaling for a fly ball. I landed in the rear-facing back seat as air bags blossomed. It wasn't exactly a soft landing, but his actions meant that it was the softest possible landing. I collapsed there as the hatch was closing, and then I fainted as his air bags puffed up all around me.

I woke up on the way to the emergency room. I couldn't see anything because I was surrounded by air bags. I heard Ben shouting my name and then he was pushing the bags back. He was in the middle seat, leaning over the back, trying to reach me. "Who's driving?" I asked, but he only shouted, "Are you okay? Are you okay?"

Old Paint ignored traffic signals and one way signs all the way to the hospital. Horns blaring and recorded voice shouting, "Emergency! Emergency! Out of the way, please! Emergency!" he beat out an ambulance and was opening the back hatch as he backed up to the emergency room loading dock. Ben jumped out, screaming for someone to help his sister. The air bags around me deflated and people in white lifted me out. I had one glimpse of Old Paint as he roared away from the ramp. His rear bumper was pushed in and his back window was crazed.

"What happened to Old Paint?" I cried. They had me on a gurney and were rolling me in. Ben trotted beside me, his cell phone to his ear.

"Compared to that black sedan? Nothing. He worked that car over until it couldn't even turn a wheel. Slammed into it over and over. I thought you were going to be creamed in there. Mom?" Ben talked into his phone. "Mom, yeah, we're at Mary Bridge Children's Hospital. Sadie got hit by a car, but Old Paint saved her. Come fast, they want our insurance number and I don't know it."

I wasn't hurt that bad. My arm was broken and I was bruised all over. They kept me six hours for observation, but my concussion was mild. Mom stayed by my bed. Two cops came to ask what happened. Ben said a crazy car had hit me. Mom said she had no idea what good Samaritan had picked me up and gotten me to the hospital, but she thanked them. The policewoman said that the other witnesses had said the car had behaved in an extraordinary manner to save me. Ben looked at Mom and said, "Some old dude was driving it. After he busted up that black car, he opened the door and yelled at me to jump in. He said he drove in stock car races, demolition derbies when he was a kid. Then he brought us here. He left because he didn't want to get in trouble."

The cops asked him some more questions, but Ben just kept saying, "I don't remember" or "I didn't see, I was worried about my sister." After they finally left, my mom said very quietly, "I hope the charging station didn't catch the plates on camera."

Ben just looked at her. "Yeah. Me, too," he said. "But I couldn't let them go out and disable him after he saved Sadie's life."

Mom took a deep breath. "Ben. Sadie. We both know it's probably going to come down to that, eventually. He can't run wild forever. And we all know that Old Paint is just following the directives of his programming. He's not really . . . alive. He seems that way because we think of him that way. But it's all just programming."

"Saving Sadie's life? Catching her in the back seat like that, cushioning her with air bags while he pounded that sedan into scrap?" Ben laughed and shook his head. "You won't convince me of that, Mom."

The hospital let me go home that evening. We all went to bed right away. But about midnight, I heard my mom get up, so I did, too. She was looking out through the blinds at our parking stall.

"Is he there? Is he okay?"

"No, baby, he's not here. Go back to bed."

Ben and I overslept the next morning and didn't go to school. Mom hadn't bothered waking us. We had a good six inches of snow outside, and school was cancelled for the day. When we came out to the living room, Mom was sitting at the computer watching a dot on a map. It wasn't moving. There was a backpack at her feet and a heap of winter clothes beside her.

"You kids get your homework off Moodle," she said. "I'm going to be gone for awhile." She sounded funny.

"No," Ben said. "We're going with you."

We hiked through the snow to a bus stop and took a bus to a City Car rental lot and checked out a tiny car. Riding in it after riding in Old Paint was like crowding into a shower stall together. Mom sat in the single front seat and Ben and I had the back seat. There was barely room for us with our coats on. Mom plugged in the coordinates, and the car demanded that she scan her credit card again. It had a prissy girl's voice. "MacIntosh Lake is outside of Zones 1 through 12. Additional fees will apply," the car told her.

She thumbed for them. The car didn't move. "Hazardous conditions are reported. Cancellation recommended. You will not be charged if you terminate this transaction now."

Mom sighed. "Just go," she said, and we went. It wasn't too bad. The main roads had been plowed and salted, and once we got on I-5, the plows and the other traffic had cleared most of the mess down to almost pavement. It felt really odd not to have Old Paint's bulk around me and I leaned against Ben.

We didn't talk much as the car hummed along. Ben had tossed a bunch of stuff in his backpack, including my pain medicine and a water bottle. I took a pill and slept most of the way. I woke up to Ben saying, "But there's a chain across the access road."

"So we'll get out here," Mom said.

I sat up. We were out in the country, and the only tracks on the snowy road behind us were ours. It was a very strange feeling. All I could see was wind-smoothed white snow and snow-laden trees on either side of the narrow road. We had pulled off the road into a driveway and stopped. There were two big yellow posts in front of us, with a heavy chain hung between them. A hunter-orange sign said, "CLOSED." The road in front of us was mostly smooth snow and it wound out of sight into the woods.

Mom told the car to wait and it obediently shut down. We struggled back into our coats. None of us had real snow boots. Mom grabbed her pack and Ben brought his as we stepped out into smooth snow. The skies had cleared and it was cold. This snow wouldn't melt any time soon. Ben followed Mom and she followed the ghost tire tracks that left the road and went around the access gate to the lake. Snow had almost filled them and the wind was polishing them away. I came last, stepping in their footprints. Mom pulled her coat tighter as we walked and said, "There were some great raves out here when I was in high school. But in summer."

"What would you do to me if I went to a rave out in the woods?" Ben asked.

Mom just looked at him. We both knew he'd been to raves out in the woods. Ben shut up.

Mom saw Old Paint before we did, and she broke into a run. Old Paint was shut down, back under the trees. Snow was mounded over him; only the funky paint job on his sides showed. Twigs and leaves had fallen on his snowy roof during the night. His windows were thick with frost. He looked to me like he'd been there for years. As we got closer, his engine ticked twice and then went silent. Mom halted and flung out her arms. "Stay back, kids," she warned us. Then she went forward alone.

She talked to him in a low voice as she walked slowly around the car. She kept shaking her head. Ben and I ignored what she'd said and walked slowly forward. Old Paint was still. Both his front and back bumpers were pushed in and he had a long crease down his passenger side. One of his headlights was cracked. His rear license plate hung by a single screw. "He's dead," I said, and I felt my eyes start to sting.

"Not quite," my Mom said grimly. "He doesn't have enough of a charge to move. His nanos have been trying to pop his dents out and fix his glass but that will take time." She went around to the driver door and unlocked it with a key. She leaned in and popped the hood, and then tossed the keys to Ben. "Look in the back. There's a hatch in the floor. Open it. Get out the stuff in there. Looks like we're going to need Grandpa's emergency kit."

She dropped her pack on the ground in the snow and then wrestled a Charge-In-A-Box out of it. Ben and I were staring at her. "Hurry up!" she snapped.

We walked to the back of the car. Mom already had the cables out and she plugged Old Paint in. His horn tooted faintly. "Easy, big fella," my brother said as he slid the key into the lock. He saw me looking at him and said, "Just shut up."

We pushed the deflated air bags out of the way. We found the floor hatch and opened it. "Look at all this stuff!" My brother exclaimed. My mom walked back and looked in. She had a grim smile as she said, "My grandpa was always trying to keep me safe. He tried to think of everything to protect me. 'Plan for the worst and hope for the best,' he always said." She took a deep breath and then sighed it out. "So. Let's get to work."

Ben and I more watched than worked. It was weird to watch her fix Old Paint. She was so calm. She pulled his dipstick, wiped it on her jeans, studied it, and then added something out of a can. Then she pulled another dipstick, checked it, and nodded. She checked wires and some she tightened. She replaced two fuses. She looked inside his radiator and then felt around under it. "No leaks!" she said. "That's a miracle." She stepped back and shut the hood.

Old Paint woke up. His engine turned over and then quit. Turned over again, ran a bit rough and then smoothed out. He sounded hoarse to me as he said, "Right front tire is flat. Do not attempt to move the vehicle."

"There's Fix A Flat in there," Ben said, and Mom said, "Get it."

He came back with it and his back pack. I stood next to him, stroking Old Paint's fender and saying, "It's going to be okay, Old Paint. It's going to be okay." Neither one of them made fun of me. While I was standing there, his front bumper suddenly popped out into position. You can't really see nanos working to take out a dent, but he already looked less battered than he had. Ben handed Mom the can and she reinflated the tire.

"Tire pressure is corrected," Old Paint announced.

Then Ben took the scrubber spray and antivirus box out of the pack and handed it to her without a word.

Mom took it and stood up slowly. She walked slowly to the back of the car and I followed her. She put away the left over emergency supplies. She gently shut the door. The glass nanos were at work on the rear window. It was almost clear again. She walked around the car and Ben and I both followed her. She got to the driver's door, opened it and climbed in.

"Mom?" Ben asked her anxiously and she waved a hand at him. "I just want to check something," she said.

She opened a little panel on his dash and a small screen lit up. She touched it lightly, scrolling down it. Then she stopped and leaned her forehead on the steering wheel for a minute. When she spoke, her voice was choked and muffled by her arms.

"My grandpa considered himself something of a hacker, in an old school way. He made some modifications to Old Paint. That's Grandpa's voice you hear, when Old

Paint speaks. And you know how I told you some people remove the safety constraints from the car's programming, the 'do no harm to people' or by-pass the speed constraints? Not my grandpa." She sat up and pointed at the screen. "See all those red 'override' indicators? You're not supposed to be able to do that. But Grandpa did. He gave Old Paint one ultimate command: "Protect logged users of vehicle."

She flipped the little panel closed over the screen and spoke quietly. "I should have known. I was a wild kid. Drinking. Doping. So he broke into the software and overrode everything to make 'protect the child' the car's highest priority. Hm." She made a husky noise in her throat. "Got me out of a corner more times than I like to think about. I passed out more than once behind the wheel, but somehow I always got home safe." She dashed tears from her eyes and then looked at us with a crooked smile. "Just programming, kids. That's all. Just his programming. Despite all his tough talk, it was just his programming to protect, as best he could. No matter what."

Ben was as puzzled as I was. "The car? Or Grandpa?"

She sniffed again but didn't answer. She re-opened the panel on his dash and accessed his GPS. She was talking softly. "You remember that one spring break, my senior year? Arizona. And that boy named Mark. Sun, sun, and more sun. We hardly ever had to stop at a charging station. That's where you should go, old friend. And drive safely."

"Don't we always?" he asked her.

She laughed out loud.

She got out and shut the door. He revved his engine a few times, and then began to pull forward. We stepped back out of his way, and he moved slowly past us, the deep snow squeaking under his tires. Mom stepped forward, brushing snow, twigs, and leaves off the solars on his roof. He stopped and let her clear them. Then, "All done. Run free," she told him, and patted his rearview mirror.

When she stepped back, he revved his engine, tooted his horn twice, and peeled out in a shower of snow. We stood there and watched him go. Mom didn't move until we couldn't hear him anymore. Then she pitched the packet of antivirus as far as she could into the woods. "There are some things that just don't need curing," she said.

We went back to the City Rents car and climbed in. My sneakers were soaked, my feet were numb, and my jeans were wet half way to my knees. We ate some peanut butter sandwiches that Ben had packed, Mom gave me another pain pill and I slept all the way home.

Three nights later, I got out of bed and padded toward the living room in my pajamas. I peeked around the corner. My Mom's chair was rocked back as far as it would go and her toes were up on the edge of the desk. The bluish monitor light was the only light in the room. She was watching a moving dot on a map, and smiling. She had headphones on and was nodding her head to music we could barely hear. Oldies. I jumped when Ben put his hand on my shoulder and gently pulled me back into the hallway. He shook his head at me and I nodded. We both went back to bed.

I never saw Old Paint again. He stayed in Arizona, mostly charging off the sun and not moving around much once he was there. Once in a while, I'd get home from school and turn on the computer and check on him. He was just a red dot moving on thin lines in a faraway place, or, much more often, a black dot on an empty spot on the map. After a while, I stopped thinking about him.

Ben did two years of community college and then got a "Potential" scholarship to a college in Utah. It was hard to say good-bye to him, but by then I was in high school and had a life of my own. It was my turn to have spats with Mom.

One April day, I came home to find that Mom had left the computer running. There had been an e-mail from Ben, with an attachment, and she had left it as a screen saver. He'd gone to Arizona for spring break. "This was as close as I could get to him," Ben had written. The scene had been shot under a bright blue sky, with red cliffs in the distance. There was nothing there, only scrub brush and a dirt road. And in the distance, a station wagon moved steadily away from us, a long plume of dust hanging in the still air behind him.

chitai Heiki Koronbin

DAVID MOLES

Here's a look at a future where Earth's last line of defense is a force of giant robots, but, inside the steel, the people running them turn out to still be made of flesh.

David Moles has sold fiction to Asimov's Science Fiction, The Magazine of Fantasy & Science Fiction, Engineering Infinity, The Future Is Japanese, Polyphony, Strange Horizons, Lady Churchill's Rosebud Wristlet, Say . . . , Flytrap, *and elsewhere. He coedited, with Jay Lake, 2004's well-received "retro-pulp" anthology* All-Star Zeppelin Adventure Stories, *as well as coediting, with Susan Marie Groppi, the original anthology,* Twenty Epics. *He won the Theodore Sturgeon Memorial Award for Best Short Science Fiction of the year with his story "Finisterra."*

There must have been a snack bar or a kebab shop or something at the side of the hangar, once. It's scrap now, a shapeless pile of fiberglass and corrugated tin, broken pieces of brown and white signs advertising döner and currywurst. Some of the plastic chairs have survived though and now Jacob drags three of them through the green-uniformed cordon of nervous Ländespolizei into the rain shadow of the hunched Colombine and Pantalon. Maddy takes one without a word and sits, or rather sprawls, knees wide like a salaryman on a late train, looking out at nothing. After a moment the black figure of the Scaramouche crouches down beside the other two robots; the cockpit opens, and Abby slides down to join Maddy and Jacob.

"Captain Asano says the transport's almost here," she announces.

Maddy nods.

Jacob says, "Tanimura get any?"

"She didn't say."

Jacob is still wearing his helmet. He takes it off now and flings it across the tarmac. Some of the Ländespolizei look round at the clatter and then hurriedly away. Without his big Malcolm X glasses Jacob's face looks naked. Maddy and Abby can see that he's crying.

Abby goes and retrieves the helmet and sets it down at Jacob's side. Then she draws the third chair up next to Maddy and perches there, her knees drawn up to her chest. In the white chair, in her black Nomex suit, she looks very small.

"You got a few of them, Maddy," she says after a moment. "Didn't you?"

"I got one or two," Maddy says, her voice sounding flat, echoless in her own ears.

Abby looks over toward the hangar, the second ring of Ländespolizei, the green tarps and trailers of the field hospital and the makeshift morgue.

"That's something, I guess," she says.

Maddy doesn't answer.

The transport comes in, low and heavy, roaring down the length of the runway so the wind of its passage rocks the trailers, rips tent pegs from the ground and sends the Ländespolizei scurrying to secure the tarps. It slows and turns down at the far end and taxis slowly back.

A squawk comes from Jacob's helmet. Abby lifts her own to her ear, says something quietly into the microphone, then listens. She looks over at the others.

"Tanimura's gone," she says.

"What?" says Jacob. "They got him?"

Abby shakes her head. "No," she says. "He's AWOL. Asano wants one of us to go look for him."

"You're kidding," says Maddy. "Isn't that her job?"

"He's taken the Pierrot, too," Abby says.

Maddy stands up. "Fine," she says. "I'll go."

She doesn't bother putting on her own helmet, just climbs back into the Colombine's cockpit, closes the hatch, powers up the instruments and screens, plugs the IV into the cannula in her hip. She waits for Jacob and Abby to get the Pantalon and the Scaramouche moving, follows them up the ramp into the transport.

"All right," she says into the helmet, as the crew locks the Colombine into its cradle. "Where's he gone, Disneyland Paris?"

Asano's voice, coming from the helmet, is reedy and strained.

"He's gone into the zone," she says.

The secret robot base was an old oil platform somewhere north of the Arctic Circle. Officially it was the United Nations Provisional Containment Authority Northern Hemisphere Rapid Deployment Facility, but after six weeks in the British Columbian woods at the United Nations Provisional Containment Authority Pacific Region Candidate Induction Centre Camp Chilliwack, Maddy had had enough of UN word salad, and when Abby had called it the secret robot base, Maddy had picked the name up and made it stick. The walls of the base were white-painted steel that flaked in places to reveal an older layer of nicotine yellow and occasionally bits of faded Russian stencil. The UN had rubberized the floors and put in new signs in English and Japanese but to Maddy it still felt like they'd gone back in time, or like they were on the set of some old war movie like her dad was always watching on The History Channel, *Top Gun* or *Blue Submarine No. 6* or *The Final Countdown*. She liked that. Jacob said the gray glop on the ceilings was asbestos and it was giving them cancer.

They would come back from one of their thirty-hour Rapid Deployments, to the edge of—but never into—the Canadian zone, or the European zone, or the zone off the coast of the Philippines in the South China Sea, and the doctors would strip Abby and Maddy and Jacob out of their Nomex pilot suits and decontaminate them and flush the zone drugs out of their systems and put them through a battery of medical and psychological and parapsychological tests that would have been humiliating before Camp Chilliwack. Likewise before Chilliwack Maddy would have been self-conscious about being undressed and prodded in front of Abby and Jacob, would have been conscious of Abby's bony nakedness and Jacob's invasive gaze, but now it was just Jacob and Abby, and Jacob's gaze wasn't invasive, just exhausted, and Abby's naked body wasn't remotely erotic, just tired and bruised, and Maddy could care less what she herself looked like. If the doctors put Tanimura through any of this they did it somewhere else.

In three months at the secret robot base Maddy had had exactly one conversation with boy hero Shinichiro Tanimura. It had gone like this:

Tanimura (English strongly accented, eyes behind his unkempt black bangs never lifting above Maddy's none-too-impressive chest): "You lived in Japan."

Maddy: 「東京。三年間。」(Tokyo. Three years.)

Tanimura: 「日本語上手だね。」(Your Japanese is pretty good.)

Maddy (lying): "I don't understand."

She'd understood fine. She just didn't want to make friends with Tanimura. Which raised the question of why she'd felt it necessary to show off by speaking Japanese in the first place, when Captain Asano had introduced them, and Abby had asked Maddy exactly that, when Maddy had told her the story.

"Competitive, much?" Abby had said, and Maddy had given her a withering look; but Abby tended not to notice things like that. And Maddy had to admit—to herself, anyway—that Abby was probably right. But she was getting that geek-boy crush vibe from Tanimura, or thought she was, and she wanted to shut that down right away. She wasn't here to be Tanimura's friend, and she certainly wasn't here to be his girlfriend. As far as Maddy was concerned, she was here to be his replacement.

Maddy and Abby and Jacob were American. Almost everyone else on the secret robot base was Japanese, apart from a few of the doctors that had followed them from Camp Chilliwack, who were Canadian. They were Japanese because Tanimura was Japanese, and until the Camp Chilliwack graduates had turned up, Tanimura, and Tanimura's shiny white robot the Pierrot, had been the only thing standing between the enemy coming out of the zones and the human race.

There had been twenty-seven test candidates at Camp Chilliwack and five of them had graduated. Of the twenty-two who hadn't, four were dead and seven would need serious medical attention for the rest of their lives. Of the five who had, two had been killed the very first time they were Rapidly Deployed: Hailey Peterson had died trying to save a busload of Taiwanese schoolchildren who shouldn't have been anywhere near the operational area, and Oscar Jara—who had been a soldier, and at twenty-three the oldest of them by five years, and who Maddy privately thought should have known better—had died going after Hailey. Hailey's body had been sent back to Ontario and Oscar's to California, and the Docteur and the Arlequin to wherever dead robots went.

The Colombine and the Scaramouche and the Pantalon came back in one piece, and Maddy and Abby and Jacob did too, more or less. They got better at what they were supposed to be doing. The zones got bigger, the things coming out of them—crawling out of them, usually, crawling and dying, but not always—got weirder, and Maddy and Abby and Jacob killed the monsters and turned back the machines and they stuck to the mission and none of them died. They stood for press photos, with Captain Asano just out of frame; they got crayon robot drawings from schoolchildren in Nunavut and Poland and Hong Kong. Abby said they were saving lives and giving people hope. Jacob said they were saving a lot of property.

The showers in the secret robot base were new and Japanese, but as industrial as all the rest of it, with spray nozzles in worrying places, oversized controls suitable for clumsy gloved hands. Maddy made sure the cannula in her hip for the zone drugs was sealed, turned on about half the nozzles, made the water as hot as she could stand it; wetted her hair, scrubbed at her shoulders and upper arms. Coming back, maybe it was the disinfectants, maybe it was going off the zone drugs, something made her itch all over. She was breaking out again. She lathered her hair, rinsed, rubbed in conditioner, leaned her forehead against the smooth ceramic of the cubicle wall. She closed her eyes and saw the enemy.

Back at Camp Chilliwack, Abby had made a game out of the enemy recognition cards they'd all been given. It was a sort of mahjong or gin rummy, except instead of making sets by number or suit you had to make them by the shared characteristics of the enemy machines. This one, a thing like a walking mushroom that a UN committee or computer had named the AG-7 *Grauekappe*, Abby classified "bipedal." As she did this one, the dumpy, vaguely humanoid AM-3 *Zwerg*. But the *Grauekappe*, at forty meters plus, was also "gigantic," and so could make a set not only with the *Zwerg* but also with the MC-11 *Wiatrak*, spindly and three-legged. Or so Abby had said as she took the trick.

It had seemed funny at the time, and probably served the purpose the cards had been meant for, inasmuch as it helped the test candidates of Camp Chilliwack memorize the different shapes and sizes. But even back then Maddy had seen that what the otaku-obsessive cataloguing mostly did, the profusion of numbers and abbreviations and code names that might have come out of Jacob's anime collection, was mask UNPROCON's ignorance regarding the zones and regarding the enemy, an ignorance that was deep and practically total.

Now behind Maddy's closed eyes, the alien shapes moved gray and blue between white stuccoed houses, were chased across the Colombine's screens by cursors and reticles. She remembered looking down into a railroad cut overhung with green under a gray sky, and a parked string of heavy freight cars, angular black metal forms folding and tearing like foil as the *zwergs* and *hryuks* slammed through them, tumbling along the cut away from Maddy's fire. Remembered the shadow of the *grauekappe* above her, and then the shocking brightness of its weapon, the way it cleaved in an instant through rock and vine and concrete, shearing away a building-sized chunk of city so that for a moment Maddy saw pipes and wires and foundations and bedrock, before a water main exploded into a linear cloud of steam and Maddy was throwing the Colombine forward into the cover it gave, down onto the tracks, the cockpit at the Colombine's heart spinning like a hamster ball to keep Maddy upright as they rolled, and then they were down on the tracks and Maddy's finger was on the trigger, cutting down the smaller machines with the Colombine's rifle, sticking to the mission, finishing the job. Saving the world.

She'd turned back to the *grauekappe* then, four times the height of the Colombine, not an opponent but a rude adult about to stomp flat child-Maddy's robot sandcastle; and she'd aimed the Colombine's rifle at the glowing blue eyes beneath the enemy machine's spreading mushroom-cap, watching the white light of the beam weapon building in its shocked round O of a mouth, and Maddy had been surprised to realize that even though she might be about to die she was happy.

And then the Pierrot had been there, in the way, Tanimura getting up in the thing's face, spoiling its shot and Maddy's too, and the *grauekappe* had leapt backwards, strangely graceful, three times its own height from a standing start, over a tall building in a single bound and gone.

Maddy opened her eyes. She rinsed the conditioner from her hair and turned off all the taps. As she squeezed the water from her hair she heard the locker-room door open and close.

She came out to find Captain Asano at the sink, washing her hands.

"Maddy-san!" In the mirror Asano saw the toothbrush Maddy was holding, and said, "Sorry. I'll only be a moment."

"It's all right," Maddy said. "I'll wait."

Asano finished what she was doing but made no move to turn around. Her English was much better than Tanimura's. It was Asano that relayed the orders, Asano's voice Maddy and Abby and Jacob heard in their helmets when they were on an operation; it was Asano who had drafted the letters to Hailey Peterson's parents and Oscar Jara's wife, though they'd gone out over the signature of some UNPROCON undersecretary. Abby had helped her with those.

When the Camp Chilliwack graduates had first arrived at the secret robot base Asano had already been there; and when she'd introduced herself to them Maddy had thought she was in her mid-twenties, but now she thought that had been makeup. Thirty? Thirty-five? Older? The pale UN blue wasn't a flattering color. Now Maddy realized she didn't really know what Asano's job was, either. Radio operator? Translator? Babysitter? Object of vaguely Oedipal desire for Tanimura, picked out by UN psychologists after watching even more giant robot shows than Jacob?

That thought was cruel, and immediately Maddy was ashamed of it. Asano looked tired. There was nothing particularly wrong with the figure under the baggy fatigues; nothing particularly sexy about it either. It wasn't as though Asano was parading around the base in a sports bra and and Daisy Dukes.

Still. Maddy would bet any amount of money that the body under the blue cloth was what Tanimura thought about when he was trying to get to sleep at night. Or had been, till Maddy and Abby showed up. Even if the UN hadn't planned it that way.

Asano's eyes met Maddy's in the mirror, and Maddy had the uncomfortable feeling that Asano knew what she was thinking. She flushed. She wondered if the UN knew she was a dyke, if that was in a file somewhere and Asano had read it.

"You lived in Japan," Asano said.

Maddy thought better of busting out her schoolroom Japanese this time, and just nodded.

"How did you like it?" asked Asano.

Maddy shrugged. "It was all right," she said. It had been, apart from the first few months. And the last few.

Asano said, "I was there at Aoyama Gakuin, when you took the preliminary tests."

Maddy remembered the tests. There had been a lecture hall, and about three hundred Japanese teenagers in it, faces lit by laptop screens; the twenty or so expatriate kids there to take the English version had been corralled by the UN organizers, herded into a smaller lab with older desktop computers, tested on math and physics and logic, then on coordination and reflexes and spatial relationships, then on stranger things. Maddy remembered an even smaller room, part of the music school maybe, with a grand piano under a dust cover, where a middle-aged black man with a British accent had sat her in a sort of reclining pod like a first-class airline seat, covered her eyes with opaque red goggles, played low-frequency static at her through headphones for half an hour, and afterwards brought out a flat, Victorian-looking box of wood and glass and asked her to pick individual butterflies out from a dusty collection. There had been some Japanese in UN uniforms watching while she did that; maybe one of them had been Asano.

"I'm sorry," she said. "I don't remember."

"It's all right," said Asano.

As far as Maddy knew, she was the only one, Japanese or expat, out of the three hundred-odd who'd taken the test that day to make it through to advanced testing. She wondered if Asano had remembered her.

Asano turned around at last. "Can I ask you a question?" she said.

Maddy shrugged again. "I guess," she said.

"Why are you here?" Asano asked.

Maddy stared at her for a long moment. They'd asked her the question, in various forms, three or four times in the course of the testing, and she'd given the kind of bullshit answers somebody in one of her dad's movies would have given: blah blah make a difference, blah blah save the planet. After a while they'd believed her, maybe, or maybe by then they'd just put enough money and time into her that they'd stopped caring why she was there so long as she did what she was told. And she could say the same thing now and it might even be true, but it would still sound like bullshit.

She just didn't want to get into it, the tangle of frustration and ambition and loneliness and credulity and outrage that had brought her here, that had made the Colombine seem like a better idea than graduating high school and going off to college or joining the Army or just hitchhiking to Rhode Island and getting a job as a waitress, and she didn't want to get into it with Asano, and she particularly didn't want to get into it with Asano when she was standing in a bathroom on an oil rig in the Arctic Ocean wearing nothing but a towel and dripping cold water on her shower shoes.

Instead she asked, "Is it true that in Shenzen, last year, Tanimura ran away, and you had to drag him back?"

"Where did you hear that?" Asano asked.

Maddy didn't answer.

Asano sighed.

"Tanimura-kun. . . . It hasn't been easy for him," she said. "Be good to Tanimura. He could use a friend."

"I'm not here to be anybody's friend, Captain Asano," said Maddy.

Thinking: No, you're here to be Tanimura's fucking backup band.

Asano said something to herself in Japanese that Maddy didn't catch a word of, and shook her head.

"What?" said Maddy.

"It isn't fair," said Asano, "what they're doing to you."

"We're saving the world," Maddy said. "No one told us it was going to be easy."

Asano put a hand on Maddy's damp shoulder.

"Maddy-san," she said. "The lady robot pilots in those anime Jacob likes to watch—they die. A lot. That doesn't have to be you." She let the hand drop. "気を付けて, ね?" she said.

And she left.

Maddy went to the sink, turned on the water, took out her toothbrush. 気を付けて. She knew that one. *Be careful.* As if she'd be here at all, if she was.

Maddy's parents had sent her to a therapist for a little while, when they were still living together, before the divorce was final. The therapist, a gray-haired, soft-spoken Chinese-American, had taught Maddy a breathing and meditation exercise that was supposed to reduce anxiety. He'd told Maddy to imagine a room, a quiet room somewhere deep in her mind, with a door she could close, leaving on the other side of it everything she was afraid of or angry at or that she just couldn't control—not to wish those things away or imagine them gone, but just to put them aside for a little while, put herself beyond their reach.

Maddy had imagined not a room but a beach, the ocean to her right and to her left a field of grass-topped dunes, herself seated comfortably on a rock. The door was there, in front of her, standing free on the pale sand, its white paint and the brass of its knob shining in the sun, and the world was still there on the other side, the noise of it just barely audible beneath the sound of the surf and of the wind in the grass.

Now Maddy was there, and the noise behind the door was louder, much louder; something was rattling the knob, trying to juggle the old-fashioned key from the lock. Sooner or later something was going to break through.

Maddy, watching the door from her perch on the rock, discovered she was fine with that. Sooner or later something was going to break through; all right, it would break through. And when it did, Maddy was going to kick the shit out of it.

The drop goes wrong. Maddy knows it's going wrong as soon as the Colombine tumbles out of the back of the transport, curled fetal in its packed ball of parachutes and airbags, the cockpit whirling like a fairground ride to keep Maddy upright. Maddy and the Colombine fall out of the sky into the European zone, and every screen in the cockpit shows nonsense, then goes solid blue; the motors steadying the hamster ball seize up for a stomach-twisting moment, then let go, leaving Maddy turning slowly head-down as the Colombine continues to fall. She has time to decide that whatever's happened to the screens has done for the parachutes and the airbags as well, and that she's going to die; and that while she doesn't especially want to die, there's nothing she can do about it; and that she ought to have some last words, except there isn't anything she particularly wants to say to anybody; and that that's kind of sad.

And then the parachutes open. The Colombine lands, hard. Maddy feels its knees take most of the impact, feels it throw out one arm as it comes down in a crouch, but the screens stay blue and the controls, when Maddy works them, do nothing. The Colombine's alive, but the cockpit is dead.

Maddy levers the cockpit open with the emergency bar and climbs down, leaving the Colombine kneeling in the shadow of a house-sized boulder. The ground is cracked black rock, sloping up behind the Colombine to a snow-covered ridge, its top only a few hundred feet away. As she comes out into the sun Maddy finds grass and tiny white flowers, and a steep slope down into a narrow valley with another ridge across it, not as high as this one, its slopes lined with dark evergreens, pine or fir or something; Maddy's never been good with trees. The sun is redder than it should be—that's a zone thing—but it's warm, and Maddy sits down and takes off her helmet, and after a little while she lies down in the grass, looking up at the sky, cold blue with white clouds.

She's somewhere in the Alps, or what used to be the Alps, German or maybe Austrian. She can't say more specifically than that. She figures she's at least ten miles inside the zone, maybe more. They say the zones are bigger on the inside than on the outside, that it takes longer to walk out of a zone than it took to walk in. Maddy doesn't know how they know that, how many people have walked into a zone and then back out, but she supposes it must have happened a few times. They say the laws of physics are different in the zones, that that's why people who stay in the zones without the drugs get sick, why the living things that come out of the zones die so easily and the machines are so hard to kill. It doesn't, to Maddy's mind, adequately explain why those machines can only be stopped by teenagers with giant robots, but it's a fact that tanks and planes didn't do so well, so maybe it's true; and whatever's going on in the zones it's fucked up Maddy's GPS along with everything else.

She can feel the Colombine there where she left it, out of site on the other side of the boulder; she's found she knows where it is, always, without thinking, the way she knows where her left hand is. She's never told the UN doctors about this, never talked about it even with Abby and Jacob, though she assumes they feel the same connection to the Scaramouche and the Pantalon. Maddy's part of the Colombine now and it's part of her: a mute external body, androgynous at best despite the name, sort of butch even, the long-limbed strength and slightly inhuman proportions of an El Greco saint in thirty feet of blood-red machinery, but part of her.

The Colombine is a weapon.

The Colombine is Earth's last hope, or nearly.

The Colombine is a job.

The Colombine is Maddy's other self.

The Colombine is broken.

If Maddy's anywhere near the war she can't hear it. She tries putting her ear to the ground like some kind of hunting elf in one of Abby's fantasy novels but feels stupid immediately, and stops. Now, her face turned back to the sky, she closes her eyes and hears the wind down in the valley, and somewhere a trickle of water. It would be so easy to fall asleep here. Maddy tries to remember the last time she fell asleep in the grass, and can't.

She's not going to sleep here. If she does, something will come along and step on her, or the drugs in her system will run out, or the zone will find some other way to kill her. Maddy gets up.

She follows the sound of the water up out of the cleft and across the slope, scrambles over some rocks, comes down into a space like a shallow bowl, where meltwater from the ridge has formed an oval pool about fifty yards long, ringed with gravel and gray mud.

There is a girl there.

She is squatting at the edge of the pool, all knees and elbows, trailing the fingers of one hand in the water. Maddy knows instantly that it's a girl, though she can't then say, and won't later be able to say, how she knows; and Maddy knows instantly that it/she is not human. She is dressed from head to foot in something dark blue and mirror-glossy, so that Maddy can see the clouds above and the rippling water below reflected in it. It rises to cover her head as well, and drops to cover the hand that's not in the water, so that only the skin of her hand and of her too-round face is uncovered; and that skin too is blue, or bluish, or maybe a pale gray made blue by the blue around it.

The alien sees Maddy and instantly she straightens up, a quick, birdlike motion, and the glossy blue runs swiftly down her bare fingers and across her face, leaving only the eyes, not the inky black of a cartoon alien's but large and round and bright like the eyes of a lemur. Standing, she's even more obviously inhuman, her torso too long, her hips and shoulders too narrow, her waist nonexistent. But there's something beautiful about her all the same, beautiful and strange, the more so as she seems to relax, and the armor or whatever it is withdraws again from her face and hands. It's hard to read that strange face, but Maddy thinks she looks expectant, or maybe a little puzzled.

Maddy comes down to the water, sliding a little on the loose, rocky ground, and the alien stays where she is; then when Maddy stops about ten feet away she comes closer, one pale blue-gray hand extended, long fingers splayed. Maddy tugs off her right glove and raises her own hand to match the alien's. There's the tiniest crackle of static electricity as their fingers meet. Maddy laughs.

And then the alien's head clicks round to train those wide eyes on something over Maddy's left shoulder, and she grabs Maddy's hand in a cool, strong grip as if by reflex; and then as Maddy turns to see Tanimura, frozen at the top of the slope, the alien drops Maddy's hand as quickly as she took it. Her attention flickers from Tanimura to Maddy and back, her strange face agitated and unhappy. And then she jumps away, that blue armor flowing over her, mounding into strange forms that disguise the thinness of her body, opening out around her head like an umbrella or the brim of an enormous round hat, so that Maddy can no longer see the bright eyes.

Then she's getting bigger, somehow, as she retreats, heavier, wider, taller, impossibly tall, tall as the icy ridge, so that Maddy has to tilt her head back to take the blue shape in. And as Tanimura scrambles past her down the gravel slope and out into the water, hands outstretched, crying, the alien jumps back, seeming to hang for a moment between the snow and the sky, and Maddy recognizes the shape now, from the railroad cut and from Abby's card game, and the broad cap tilts back and Maddy recognizes the eyes and the mouth that she'd been so sure meant death; and then the alien is gone.

Tanimura is still moving, still wading out into the pool; it's almost up to his waist. Maddy wonders if she's going to have to drag him back. And then he stops, suddenly, and turns around, and sloshes his way back to the shore. He squats down, and puts his head in his hands. After a little while he looks up.

"ばか," he says.

Maddy knows that word. *Dumbass.* Or something like. But she doesn't think he means her. Maybe he means himself. Maybe he means it's a dumb-ass situation. Or a dumb-ass world. She can't say she disagrees.

The Colombine's cockpit stutters to life as soon as the Pierrot comes near. Together Maddy and Tanimura make their way down off the mountainside, find a road leading out of the zone, and follow it till they find a stretch of autobahn long and straight enough for the transport to land. Maddy speaks briefly to Asano over the radio; she doesn't say anything to Tanimura. She hasn't figured out what she wants to say.

Aboard the transport, the Colombine secure in its cradle, Maddy powers the cockpit down again and sits in darkness. The amphetamines they gave her at the start of the mission are wearing off; she can feel it.

She closes her eyes. She wishes she had a home, so that she could feel homesick for it. In the dark, she sees the alien girl.

Back at the secret robot base she finds Tanimura in his cabin. It's not the hikikomori rathole she's been expecting. Apart from a few books, a Sony laptop, and a scattered deck of the recognition cards there's no real sign anybody lives there. Tanimura is sitting on the bunk, playing some game on his phone, or maybe texting somebody. He stops when Maddy comes in.

"I figured it out," she says. "On the way back. She thought I was you, right? You met her, before. That's why you ran away. But I bet they can't tell us apart, and she thought I was you."

Tanimura doesn't say anything.

"It's all a lie," Maddy presses on. "Everything they've told us about the zones, about the enemy. Isn't it? Maybe they're not lying to us on purpose, but it's all bullshit. They don't know anything. You and me, we know more than they do."

Tanimura just looks at her. Maddy can't tell if he understands her or not.

"Look," she says. "I want to help, okay? Who is she? What's her name?"

"Name?" Tanimura says.

"名前," Maddy says. She goes to the desk, finds the card, holds it up. "Hers."

Tanimura looks at the card, then up at Maddy.

"*Grauekappe*," he says levelly. "AG-7."

Maddy stares at him.

"Okay," she says, dropping the card to the floor. "Fuck you, too."

She can't get into the hangar. She wants to climb into the Colombine's cockpit and put six inches of red metal between herself and the world, but they aren't going to let her do that. She goes to the simulator room instead, and climbs up into one of the big white boxes and closes it and sits there unseeing as the computers run it through its routine, never touching the controls, so that she dies again and again; and then she wipes her eyes and opens the box and gets down.

κatabasis

ROBERT REED

Here's a story by Robert Reed, whose "Eater-of-Bone" appears elsewhere in this anthology.

In the harrowing novella that follows, another of his "Great Ship" stories—a long-running series about a Jupiter-sized spaceship that endlessly travels the Galaxy with millions of passengers from many different races, including humans on board—bored rich immortals compete to complete a months-long trek across difficult terrain for no particular reason except to gain prestige in the eyes of their peers . . . but find that the stakes in this contest may be higher than they thought, and that their existence may come to depend on their alien guide, Katabasis.

1

The custom was to bring nothing but your body, no matter how weak or timid that body might be. Robotic help was forbidden, as were exoskeletons and other cybernetic aids. Every nexus had to be shut down; the universe and its distractions were too much of a burden to carry across the wilderness. Brutal work and miserable climates were guaranteed, and the financial costs were as crushing as any physical hardship. Food was purchased locally, every crumb wearing outrageous import fees, while simple tents and minimal bedding cost as much as luxury apartments. But most expensive were the indispensable porters: Every hiker had to hire one strong back from among a hodgepodge of superterran species, relying on that expert help to carry rations and essential equipment as well as the client's fragile body when he proved too weary or too dead to walk any farther.

Porters were biological, woven from bone and muscle and extravagant colors of blood. Evolved for massive worlds, most of them thundered about on four and six and even eight stout legs. But there were a few bipeds in the ranks, and one of those was a spectacular humanoid who called herself Katabasis.

"Yet you seem small," said the human male. "How can you charge what you charge, looking this way?"

Katabasis was three times his mass and much, much stronger. But the question was fair. With an expression that humans might mistake for a smile, she said, "The client pays the penalty for being brought out on his back. When you give up, we earn a powerful bonus."

The human lifted a hand, two fingers tapping the top of his head. He had pale brown skin and thick hair the color of glacial ice, white infused with blue. The fingers tapped and the hand dropped and with genuine pride he said, "I studied the rules. I understand that rule."

"Good," she said.

"But these other creatures are giants," he said. "That Wogfound would have no trouble carrying you. And the One-after-another looks easily stronger."

"All true," she agreed. "But by the same logic, they feel no special obligation to look after their clients. Extra money has its charms, and if you shatter, they win. But I am relatively weak—as you wisely noted, thank you—and that's why I avoid carrying others, even for a few steps. Ask the other porters here; you will learn. Katabasis is notorious for keeping her clients healthy, which not only adds to the value of the trek, but it saves you the ignominy of being brought into City West as a cripple or a carcass."

The modern brain was nearly impossible to kill, and no client had ever permanently died during these marches through jungle and desert. Yet immortality had its costs, including exceptional memories that played upon weaknesses like pride and dignity. Small humiliations were slow to heal. Giant failures could eat at the soul for thousands of years. Most humans would take her warning to heart. Yet this man was peculiarly different. Staring at the powerful, self-assured alien, he smiled for the first time. "Oh, no," he said. "You cannot scare me."

Katabasis had centuries of experience with the species and its countenances, but she had never observed anything so peculiar as that broad, blatant grin and that bald declaration. She watched the ugly tongue curling inside that joyful mouth. The human made no attempt to hide his feelings. He was staring, obviously intrigued by the porter: The shape of her tall triangular face and the muscled contours of the rugged, ageless body, and how the bright golden-brown plumage jutted out of her work clothes. An interspecies fantasy was playing inside his crazy head. This happened on rare occasions, but never on the first day. And never like this.

Without shame, the man adjusted his erection. "My name is Varid, and I want to hire you."

"No."

Varid didn't seem to hear her. He continued to gaze at her with a simpleton's lust. Then the face flattened, emptiness suddenly welling up in the eyes, and using a tone that was almost but not quite puzzled, he asked, "Why not?"

"You won't endure the journey," Katabasis said.

Varid tried to laugh but the sound came out broken, as if he was an alien attempting to make human sounds. Then the other arm lifted, bending to make a big bulge of muscle. "I'm exceptionally fit. I've trained for years, preparing for this day. Designer steroids and implanted genes, and I have special bacteria in my gut and my blood, doing nothing but keeping this body in perfect condition."

"It isn't the body that concerns me," she said.

Varid shut his eyes and opened them again. "What are you saying?"

"Your mind is the problem."

He responded with silence.

"I don't know you," Katabasis continued, "but my impression is that you have a fragile will and a foolish nature."

The human face remained empty, unaffected.

"Hire the One-after-another," she said, one broad hand picking him off the ground and then setting him aside. "She's more patient than most porters, and she won't speak too rudely about you once you give up."

In the remote past, in some distant parcel of the newborn universe, someone harvested the core of a Jovian world. Godly hands filled the sphere with caverns and oceans, and then they swaddled their creation inside a hull of hyperfiber. Towering rockets rose thousands of kilometers above the stern, and the new starship was fueled and launched. Yet nobody ever came onboard. The machine's purpose and ultimate destination were forgotten. Billions of years later, humans found the derelict wandering the cold outside the Milky Way, and after considering a thousand poetic names, that lucky species dubbed their prize "the Great Ship" and began a long voyage around the entire galaxy, offering passage to any species or individual that could afford the price of a ticket.

Early in the voyage, a high-gravity species sold asteroids and rare technologies to the humans and with their earnings bought passage for a distant solar system. Once onboard, they built a vast centripetal wheel. The wheel was deep inside the Ship, helping minimize the natural, distracting tug of real gravity. Forty kilometers wide and nearly five hundred kilometers in diameter, their home spun a circle every eight minutes, pressing them snugly against the wheel's rim.

Eventually the aliens reached their destination, and they sold their home to a speculator with dreams but few resources.

That began a sequence of bankruptcies and auction sales. Each grand plan ended with fresh disappointment. Investors changed and new tenants worked the ground with false optimism, and then everything would fall apart again. In that piecemeal fashion, the habitat's climate was modified and rectified in places while other regions were left to shatter, creating an ecological stew populated by survivors from a thousand massive worlds. Today the lone sea was shallow and hypersaline, bordered by City East and City West, while at the opposite end of the wheel stood a chain of mashed-down mountains. An artificial sun rode the hub, throwing a patchwork of colors and intensities of light into a maze of valleys, and after thousands of years, for no reason but luck, a splendidly fierce and decidedly unique biosphere had matured.

The current owners occupied City West, and so long as their investment produced capital and public curiosity, they were happy.

Every porter lived in City East. An abrasive, brawling community, it was as diverse as the countryside if not so beautiful. With powerful arms, Katabasis had hollowed out a boulder of quake-coral, making a cavity where she could sleep easily. She liked the City, and she loved to walk its shoreline every day, but she also had debts upon debts, which was why she worked constantly and why the wilderness was as much of a home as any place.

Prospective clients gathered every morning at the official trailheads. Among today's crop were several species that she preferred to humans. But Varid wasn't only peculiar, he proved especially stubborn. She tried to whisk him aside, but he insisted that she should be his porter, making noise about proving his worth and giving away wild bonuses for her trust.

At that point, she interrupted. "No, I won't take you, no." Her voice was sharp, and everything about the scene was in poor form. But at last the man seemed to understand. One last time, his face emptied. Varid finally walked away, slowly approaching the One-after-another. The small success lasted until two other humans approached—a mated couple, unexceptional to the eye—and Katabasis wondered why her day was cursed.

Then the male human did something rare. Not only had he read Katabasis' public posting, he also had some understanding of her species. Raising one hand to make introductions, he looked skyward and called to her by name.

She lifted the backs of her hands, which was how one smiled politely to a stranger.

The human was named Perri. A handsome monkey, athletically built and younger in the face than fashionable, he raised his second hand and introduced his wife. Quee Lee took one step and another and then rested. She was a dark elegant creature built from curving tissues and pleasant odors. But there were telltale signs of intense training and medical trickery at work in the muscle beneath those curves, and the creature's new strength was lashed to reinforced bones that could weather the relentless weight. Making humans ready for this gravity was as much art as engineering. Too much bulk, no matter how powerful, eventually dragged the body to its doom. In most circumstances it was smart to begin small and build the flesh where needed, on the trail and fed by the precious rations. That's why it was a good sign, these humans being smaller than most, and perhaps they understood at least one vital lesson.

QueeLee raised her arm. "It is an honor to cross paths with you."

"You have made this trek before," Katabasis guessed.

"I managed the half-kilometer from the custom office, yes," she said, her mouth filled with bright teeth.

"But I made the full circuit once," Perri said. "Three hundred years ago, and my wife has been training since I returned home."

"I'm trying to make my life exciting," said Quee Lee.

"I am a boring husband," he said.

The two laughed loudly, excluding the world with their pleasure.

Katabasis studied how they moved, how they stood, and with experience and unsentimental eyes, she sought the warning signs of failure.

"My husband wants to hire you," Quee Lee said, "but I won't survive the journey. My goal is to make the halfway point, into the mountains, and from there someone will have to carry me."

"What about that Wogfound?" Perri asked. "She looks unbreakable."

"Except she'll mock you relentlessly," Katabasis warned.

"I had one on my first trek," Perri said. "Wogfounds are masters of insults and name-calling."

"Well, if I'm riding, then I deserve her abuse," Quee Lee said. "And if I'm dead for a spell, what could the noise matter?"

Three humans and several other alien hikers came to terms with their porters. Contracts were spun and sealed, monies were dropped into accounts of trust, and by then the day was half finished. The habitat's original owners had come from a world with an eleven-hour day-night cycle, and the present owners maintained at least that tradition. Food and equipment still had to be collected, which was why the porters and their clients wouldn't embark until the next dawn.

Perri asked to be responsible for his needs. Alone, Katabasis returned to that comfortable and familiar but ultimately alien home. A pot of boiled fish and twenty kilos of flame-blackened bread were the day's meal, and then she chewed a stick flavored with mint and iron, walking the salty sand of her favorite beach. The night's sleep lasted for most of three hours, which was typical, and then she woke when the dreams left her no choice, returning to the present and its stolid comforts full of hard work followed by more hard work, from this moment and until the time's end.

2

The good porter knew what to leave behind. Extra clothes were burdens to drop in your tracks. Charms and religious symbols needed to be lighter than whispers, or they were unlucky evils. Even the richest flavors had to be carried in tiny doses, and only dead sticks could be collected along the way, soaked and chewed and then discarded with the body's waste. Water in the wilderness was often tainted and sometimes putrid, if not outright laced with toxins. One rough filtering might leave a thousand awful tastes behind. But immortals lived inside tough, enduring bodies, and what was adventure without suffering? The one great law that couldn't be cheated was that physical work required energy. Energy always meant food. But many of the habitat's species were rare, and some had fallen extinct on their home world, which was why every visitor, local and tourist alike, was forbidden from hunting and grazing. That's why every meal was carried and why each mouthful had to be jammed with nutrition. And the good porter fed herself before the client, because it was imperative that she be the strongest beast on the trail.

Katabasis never brought treats or wet meals. A client might pocket dried fruits or hide away some bloody bit of meat, but if she found these indulgences, she took them for herself. The preferred rations were dense desiccated nuggets. Flavors were coded to color and every tongue had favorites, but basically these were lumps of highly purified fat that would test even an immortal's adaptable guts.

The trek's first days always brought gas and embarrassing smells.

Katabasis expected jokes and had a few of her own at the ready, but Perri and his wife seemed untroubled by the rude noises.

The Wogfound was much less discreet. But the couple treated his jabs as just another series of farts, inevitable and natural, barely worth mentioning in a realm full of oddities.

The humans walked the jungle trail in slow, measured steps. Pseudo-gravity was difficult for its crushing pressure, but another complication was at work: The Great Ship had its own tug, and as the habitat's rim spun upwards, everyone's apparent weight increased. Then the wheel peaked and fell and down came both the body and weight. A one-gee swing rolled past every eight minutes. Clients had to contend with the shifting rules of walking and falling. Humans always fell, and they eventually broke. The other clients and their porters pushed ahead, but Katabasis' little group conquered two kilometers on the first day and tried to hold that pace thereafter, passing through stands of pillar trees and a grove of golden willows growing around cores of carbon fiber, and then came another stretch of pillars that looked identical to the first but were born on an entirely different world. After ten days, the forest came to an abrupt end, replaced with a long valley filled with wooden reefs covered with bug-eating anemones and flower-mouths collected from scattered, left-behind worlds.

Varid was somewhere ahead of them, walking with a Tristerman and the largest Yttytt that Katabasis had ever seen. Tracks and the wind claimed that he was matching paces with those stronger aliens. Perhaps the human felt that he had some point to prove. Maybe he was overextending himself, or maybe Katabasis had been wrong about his nature. The truth didn't matter. She had a client and hers was quite cheerful about his pain, while his wife was proving resilient. Ten days was nothing in a very long journey, but they had a reasonable pace and ample rations, and their camp was pitched before darkness, time left to eat another dense, gut-knotting meal before managing a few hours of sleep and dreams.

The couple slipped into their little tent, and in the careful fashion of weaklings trapped in high gravity, they made love.

The porters listened to the sex, and because he couldn't help himself, the Wogfound offered insults. "Before I carry that monkey," he said, "I will wrap her inside her bedding. She is too ugly to touch in any way."

"She is a beast," Katabasis said agreeably. "But I don't think you will ever carry her."

The challenge was noted. "A wager then, your guess against mine."

"No."

"If you have seen the future," said the Wogfound, "I will pay you what my bonus would have been."

Again, she said, "No."

Pulling his legs beneath his long body, the Wogfound prepared for sleep. "How many times have we walked together, Katabasis?"

"I cannot say."

"Many times perhaps."

"More than many," she said.

"Yet I don't know you at all," he said.

Looking at the armored shell and the three jewel-like eyes, she said, "You are as stupid as you are ugly."

The laughter was abrupt and thunderous. Every anemone yanked into its home, and save for the grunting of two monkeys hiding inside their tent, the reef fell silent. Then with a brazen joyful voice, the Wogfound said, "I know what I am. I am beautiful and brilliant."

"A good thing to know," Katabasis replied.

Shortly after that, the camp fell asleep.

They caught Varid on the seventeenth day, inside an arid valley blasted by the brilliant blue mirage of a sun. He had spent the night there, his tent and rations packed up but still lying on the hot rock. Varid was stretched out on a skeletal chair. He smiled when the others arrived. He aimed the smile at them and spoke a few quiet words, perhaps to his porter, and the One-after-another gave a deep snort. A furnace would be hotter, but not much. Varid was drenched with sweat, but to prove his strength he lifted one of those very powerful arms, wincing when he held the open hand high.

"I've been waiting for you," he said.

Perri was leading. Seventeen days and the previous trek had taught him how to move against the relentless weight. Never lift the leg higher than necessary; keep the back straight and strong. Only motions essential to covering the next half-meter were allowed. He wore minimal clothes and light boots and a body that could live for another million years. But immortality didn't make animals into machines. He was suffering as he shuffled forward, and his voice was slow when he said, "Thank you for waiting. You're nothing but kind."

Katabasis heard sarcasm and pain.

Varid appeared oblivious. Still smiling, he turned and said something else to his porter, and then he broke into an oversized laugh.

With her four back legs, the One-after-another stomped at the ground. They weren't a verbal species, but those motions signaled frustration.

"I was traveling with several friends," said Varid, "but I tripped and fell yesterday, rather hard, and the others continued without me."

They had seen their chance to get free of you, thought Katabasis.

Perri stopped walking, breathing deeply. "A bad fall, was it?"

"Bones poking through skin and some torn tendons."

Quee Lee caught up with her husband. "Are you having trouble healing?"

"I never have trouble healing." Varid sat up, the veins in his forehead ready to burst. "No, I decided to let you catch me. I wanted someone to talk to."

"I am dreary company," said the One-after-another.

Varid stood carefully, and his chair collapsed into a fist-sized bundle.

Katabasis had served hundreds of humans, and none were like him. She wondered about the effects of drugs and other elixirs ingested for this journey. She wondered if one of the alien "friends" had tripped the man, perhaps intentionally—a common event out on the trails.

"May I walk with you?" Varid asked.

"Absolutely," Quee Lee said, slowly passing her husband.

The One-after-another stowed the chair and balanced all of the gear on her broad back. Three humans and their porters continued up the desert valley. A long stone wall had been cut through the middle with explosives, and they slipped into the gap and entered the remains of someone's attempted home—tunnels and oval rooms and bits of debris that might have been precious once or might have been trash. Katabasis never enjoyed walking this ground. Each time, without fail, she thought about lost homes and the ignorant strangers who would feel nothing when they passed through what others had once treasured.

Quee Lee was in the lead. Perceiving a challenge, Varid found his legs and got busy chasing her.

Every tradition told the porters to remain behind, watching the slow, painful, and ultimately useless race.

The parched trail eventually swung back toward the wheel's center, and after a long climb over a diamondcrete ridge, they dropped into a fresh drainage and different climate. The sun was always directly overhead, but now it turned pale and small. The air filled with mist. The vegetation was several shades of black, every plant held up by multiple trunks, supporting hungry canopies and fluorescing wings wrapped around giant insect bodies.

"Beautiful," said Quee Lee.

Glancing up, Perri stumbled, the bones in his left leg splintering from the unexpected impact, and he collapsed and hit the ground, shattering his cheek and eye socket against bare stone.

Quee Lee returned to him. There was no reason for worry, but she settled beside him anyway.

Varid was ahead of everyone, smiling at his fortune.

"I could make you feel better," Quee Lee said.

"In no time," her husband agreed.

"But others are lurking."

The two of them laughed.

Then Quee Lee looked at the other human. "Have we met him? He seems just a little familiar."

They didn't have access to a nexus. Memory was what counted, and despite the blood plastered across his face and a crooked leg trying to straighten itself, Perri had enough focus to decide, "I don't remember a man like him. And I think I would."

"Maybe he isn't the same person now," said Quee Lee.

Perri wiped the gore from under his eye. "Maybe something happened to him."

"Maybe I should ask him," Quee Lee said.

Perri laughed softly.

"You're right," she said. "This is a long walk. There'll be plenty of boring to fight off before the end."

A central valley led toward the distant mountains, and the River East was slow leaden water down its middle. For three days the trail pushed close to the water, and just when the routine and climate became familiar, they crossed the river on a massive bridge of granite slabs and granite columns.

Another ridge demanded to be climbed.

Half a kilometer was one day's work, and they weren't yet to the top.

They camped again and ate shavings from their supplies, and nobody complained about the taste of the water. The spring at their feet was cool and clear, little crustaceans leaving feces that tasted like something called pepper. Beside them was a grove of tashaleen trees—massive trunks laced with glass, each supporting fat bladders filled with sulfuric acid. Tashaleens periodically flooded the landscape to maintain their monoculture, but none were ripe at present, and they had lovely red colors that pushed deep into the infrared.

Today Varid had broken the little bones inside one foot. They healed fast enough, but the foot needed hard rubbing.

The couple sat opposite him, leaning against one another.

Katabasis was sitting alone, chewing steadily on a dead black stick laced with bright flavors.

After a long silence, Varid cleared his throat. Smiling at his foot, he lifted his hand, and then he turned to smile at his fingers as he said, "Name anyone luckier than us."

There was optimism in the voice.

And there wasn't.

"Nobody is luckier," Quee Lee said.

Perri watched the man. "What luck are you talking about?"

"Buying passage on the Great Ship," said Varid. "That's an honor beyond measure."

How could anyone disagree?

"I feel blessed."

"Where did you come from?" Perri asked.

"Mellis 4."

"That's a colony world," Quee Lee said. "In the Outskirt District, isn't it?"

Varid seemed to hear the question, and for a moment he looked ready to formulate an answer. But then his face emptied, and everybody sat waiting. Eventually he stared at Perri, and after another long pause asked, "What's your background? From where did you come?"

"Nowhere. I was born on the Ship."

"Are you some captain's child, or something else?"

"Something else," said Perri.

Varid nodded slowly, as if he was working through the myriad possibilities. But he didn't ask for more information. He shifted his focus to Quee Lee, ready to ask the same question.

"I was born on the Earth," she volunteered.

"I want to visit the Earth," Varid said. "Once the voyage ends, I plan to walk all across its ancient ground."

The Great Ship wouldn't return home for another two hundred thousand years. And that was assuming nothing disastrous happened during the long, long journey.

The married humans glanced at each other.

Varid appeared excited, staring at the ground and the once-injured foot, smiling and breathing faster until he suddenly looked up, hunting for another worthwhile face.

"Katabasis," he said.

His porter let her plumage flatten, showing disinterest.

"Your name," he said. "There's a human word that sounds like Katabasis."

The others looked at her. Even the other porters were curious.

This had happened several times before, human clients recognizing the word. But to have this odd dim creature bring up the matter like this, without warning . . . well, it was astonishing. Katabasis held her breath, the hearts in her thighs pushing blood into her face, making it more purple than usual.

"What word is 'Katabasis'?" asked Quee Lee.

"It is very old, and Greek," Varid said. "I wish I could remember what it meant. Maybe I knew once, but then again . . ."

His voice faded, yet the face seemed more alive than usual, dark eyes sparkling and the mouth very small, very intense.

Perri looked at his porter. "Is that a coincidence?"

"No," she admitted.

Quee Lee was interested enough to stand up and shuffle closer. "You took the name when you came here. Didn't you?"

"It's a tradition," Katabasis explained. "Move to another realm, and you embrace some name from those in power."

Varid's face changed again, back to its flat, vague, and apparently empty ways. But he lifted the hand that had rubbed the foot that couldn't be any healthier, and he asked the hand, "How did you find your way to the Great Ship?"

The other porters put their ears and eyes on her.

Then Katabasis surprised herself. With her voice cool and pleasant, she said, "I walked here. And I walked and walked and walked."

3

She wasn't Katabasis and wasn't immortal, and she knew her tiny age and critical place, always going to sleep certain that a great family loved her. She lived inside the world's stronghold. A wedge-hole decorated with painted pretties was where she slept, and the girl had a collection of flavored sticks to chew on, and every morning one of the household warriors would lick her bare toes, waking her with a hot rough tongue.

"The maiden is expected," the warrior would say, or words to that effect. "The Five are waiting in the study with books and high expectations."

The Five were a fierce and wealthy and much respected marriage. Royalty and elected leaders didn't exist in the world and couldn't be envisioned by the People. But three women and two husband/brothers sat astride generations of obligations and large favors. The girl wasn't one of the Five's children, not by blood or by adoption. But she was a Hopeful, which meant that she was endowed with some talent or compelling strength that had made her worth purchasing from forgotten parents.

"The Five are waiting," was a ritual statement. Time was too precious to share with even the most promising half-grown citizen. But there were mornings when one of the Five, usually the younger brother/husband, would march past the two hundred Hopefuls, handing out assignments and lofty words about the future before chasing after even more pressing ceremonies.

The typical morning brought small groups divided by skills and led by teachers who loved the subject in hand. Sometimes Hopefuls were gathered in the arena where they played elaborate games full of lessons and fun that kept them busy until the day's meal and the night's sleep. Even better were days when a girl was told to read alone and contemplate every word. But reflective lessons brought warriors on the next morning—warriors delivering hard training because it was important to drive the laziness from these young, spoiled souls.

The girl's gift was mathematics, and in particular, cumbersome formulas with their tangled alliances and deep abstractions. On the best days, a teacher and one warrior would pull aside the mathematicians—eleven Hopefuls, including her closest friends—and they would leave the stronghold, going out into the great, lovely, and nearly perfect world to test their knowledge against what was real.

All that was worth knowing was built upon formulas.

The world was one day's walk wide, on average, and fifteen days in length, shaped rather like a passion worm dying on hot rock. The world stood upon an old mountain range. Left in their natural state, those eroded peaks would catch only the rare rain, and perhaps a few rock-scions would grow in the valleys. But the People had built forests of broad towers standing above the tired, broken-down tectonics. Each life in the world had its job. Gardeners and their vines dangled out of the windows while J'jjs and clonetakes sang from cages, begging their keepers for feed. The buildings' interiors were full of wedge-holes and broad hallways, and every floor had its stockers and teachers, weavers and gossips. Especially important were the miners who left every evening, descending to the hot plains to work with their electric machines. They cut fresh stone from the quarries and smelted metals from the best ores available. Other citizens tended the fans that stood high, dancing with the winds to supply power, and those who knew the dew-catchers watered the crops and every mouth. There was majesty and perfection in this labor. Every mouth attached to a working mind sang praises to the world's rich life.

The towers demanded endless construction, and construction demanded endless calculation.

This girl, the happy young Hopeful, was being groomed to design new walls and reinforce old buttresses. If she couldn't look forward to the day, at least she was resigned to her duty, and it was a good day whenever a teacher looked at her work, saying without too much difficulty that she was showing that most precious talent: "Promise."

She never imagined that outside events could interrupt her future.

Who does at such an age?

The best mornings found the budding mathematicians riding in bubbles strung on electrified cables, climbing to the highest rooftops. Where the air was thin and chill was her favorite place. Deep pleasure could be found in those vistas. The girl always stole moments to look past the world. The surrounding plains were rough and ugly, but there was a horizon to seek, though it was often masked by dust and the occasional cloud. She carried a worn-out telescope rescued from the school's garbage, and if she was very lucky and the lessons went into evening, she had stars to admire and neighboring worlds, and sometimes several moons graced the sky with their trusted round faces.

Each class was accompanied by at least one trained, well-armed warrior. The Hopefuls had real value and might tempt their enemies. Other worlds and other People lived beyond the horizon. Perhaps those same enemies would come here to steal away their talent: It had never happened and never would happen, but there was pleasure in the possibility. Who doesn't wish to be valuable, to be special?

One day-journey reached into evening and then farther. The teacher had critical points to deliver about bracing towers and the telltale signs of strain on a windmill blade, and she steadfastly refused to leave this high place until every student absorbed her competence.

Thinking no one was watching, the girl drifted away.

But the warrior noticed and climbed after her, finding her chewing a fresh stick of dribbledoe while pushing the little telescope against her eye. The nearest moon was overhead—gray and airless, pocked with volcanoes that sometimes threw up columns of soot that left a soft ring in its orbit. She watched the moon's limb and stared at patches of stars, and because this was one of those rare perches where every direction was visible, she turned in a slow circle, trying to absorb the precious vista.

The warrior was young and bold. He crept up on the girl, and wanting to startle her, tried to drop the cold gun barrel against her beautiful neck.

"Your feet are sloppy," she warned, not looking at him. "I have listened to your approach since you left class."

He paused, embarrassed and laughing.

She chewed and looked toward tomorrow's dawn, where night was full and the land empty of any feature worthy of a name. "I wish I had a true telescope," she said. "Like one of the giants perched on top of the stronghold."

"They are impressive machines," he agreed.

"Have you even seen them?" she asked doubtfully.

"I saw all of them during my training, of course. They are the 'long eyes' for the warrior guild."

"But have you ever used one?"

He smiled and said, "Only the largest telescope. I looked through it once, just to see what could be seen."

She smiled with her free hand. "What did you see?"

"The nearest worlds," he said, pointing his weapon at the mountains riding the western horizon. "Skies were clear, clearer than tonight, and I saw amazing details."

"I don't care about those worlds," she said. "Did you look at the sky?"

"No."

She studied him.

"We don't have enemies in the sky," he said.

Every mountain range was a world standing alone, and the plains and scalding oceans between the ranges would kill any person who lingered too long.

The young warrior said nothing, wondering what to make of his complicated, shifting feelings for this child.

She turned to the redness where the sun had just vanished. "I've seen lights in that sky."

"Flyers," he said.

"I know what they are."

"Then why didn't you call them that?"

"I wish we had flyers," she said.

"We could build them, if we needed them."

"I suppose."

"We are as smart as the other nations," he said with authority.

The girl found a faint dark bulge where a young volcano pushed high into the wet heights of the sky.

"Our world is little," she said.

"Our world is great," he said.

"Nonetheless, we are small and poor. And the hills beneath us are nearly exhausted."

The warrior pretended not to be bothered by this topic.

She lowered the telescope, reading his face and his feet. "You really don't know very much, do you?"

"I know quite a lot."

She said nothing.

"Our fans catch the winds," he said. "And we have other machines that can snatch words out of the wind."

"Those are radios. Yes, our teachers talk about them."

He stood as tall as possible. "I've listened to the radios. Have you?"

"What did you hear?" she asked.

"Have you listened to them?"

"No."

"I have heard voices," he said.

"Did you understand the voices?"

"No."

With a gesture, she proved that she wasn't impressed.

"But I have a good friend," he insisted. "My friend's duty is to translate the other languages, making sense of our enemies' words."

"Are these words interesting?"

"Maybe."

"What does 'maybe' mean?"

Suddenly the warrior wished the topic would vanish. But he was also young and willing to risk everything to impress this odd, odd girl. So against his best instincts, he said, "There is a secret. Only the Five and their children and a few chosen People are allowed to know this secret."

"And you too," she said.

He smiled.

She said, "Tell me."

"Aliens," he said, pointing at that last glimmer of ruddy light. "At this moment, aliens are walking on that world."

Each world stood on its own mountains, and each was isolated by the dry wastelands. Every mature world had its own People. Ten thousand species of People were scattered across the face of Existence. Existence was the planet, and the planet had lived forever, and the word "alien" was normally used for the strangest, most remote species of People.

"What are you talking about?" she asked.

"I am sorry," he said. " 'Alien' is a weak word for what I mean."

"What do you mean?"

"I know a new word." The warrior looked up at the churning moon and cold stars, and using a nervous, inexpert mouth, he tried to say the word.

"What is that?" she asked. "What does 'human' mean?"

4

Clients had to praise scenery. After spending and suffering too much, it was their duty to collapse on some little knoll, singing about the lovely colors and intoxicating odors and the magical properties of an ordinary breeze. Species and the lay of the land refused to stay the same. "Walking across twenty worlds wouldn't be this interesting," clients would sing. But how many of them had walked across even one world during their wealthy long lives? That was a good question never asked, certainly not by the stolid porters following behind, saying nothing while dreaming about grateful tips.

The rare client had careful eyes. Perri paid attention, but the skill was sharpest in the morning and faded with exhaustion. Quee Lee was less interested in scenery, but she was vigilant about her footing, measuring every step and each hesitation, ignoring the usual vistas until she was sure that she couldn't fall. That made her the client who found animal tracks and odd rocks and bits of litter left by thousands of parties exactly like theirs, and unlike many, she asked big questions of the porters and then tried to paint the answers on the insides of her cavernous mind.

Varid existed at the other end of the spectrum: He was nearly blind. Wide scenes and telling details were ignored as he marched forward. What he did notice—what was bright and exceptionally real to the man—were the various ailments rolling inside him. Katabasis saw flashes of misery in the face. Sometimes a foot broke, or a rib; more often it was chronic fatigue. But even when he was rested and whole, his surroundings passed with little notice. The man filled that tiny chair in the morning, doing nothing and plainly thinking nothing, eyes open and pointing in some random direction, observing nothing as the rest of the camp made ready for the day's next kilometer or two.

"He is the oddest monkey," the Wogfound remarked. "Have you ever known a creature like him?"

"I never have, no," Katabasis said with certainty.

"And do you know how he sleeps?"

Recalling Varid's peculiar, unwelcome interest in her, she said, "I know nothing of the kind."

"I know quite a lot," said the Wogfound. "Look inside his shelter. During the night, early or late, the moment doesn't matter. The creature lies on his back, holding a light before his face."

"Which light?"

"His camp torch turned up high, or a blank reading net draped over his face, and I once saw him with a captured blazebee between his fingers."

"Did you ask what he was doing?"

"I demanded to know. But he didn't reply."

"And did he wonder what you were doing, poking into his business?"

"From what I see, I doubt that creature is capable of wonder."

Katabasis absorbed the words, unsure what to believe.

But the Wogfound had a ready explanation. "The body is human enough, but that mind is alien. Perhaps Sorry-gones have made a nest inside the head."

"Not Sorry-gones, no," she said. Varid was bizarre, but he was still human in her gaze. She wanted him to be human, maybe even needed that, but she didn't want to dwell on reasons, much less the state of her mind.

"Watch him sleep," her colleague advised.

"You may snoop for both us," she said. "With my blessing."

Days later, a torrential rain struck the valley where they were walking. Fat drops of water and ice battered exposed heads, and the ground that wasn't flooded was left too slippery for any human foot.

Varid remained inside his tent for the rest of the day.

Just once, Katabasis looked in at him. The man had cut a small hole in the fabric and water fell through, hammering the blank gaze and the mouth that was moving as if talking, but not talking to her and maybe not to himself either. He made no noise. The lips were busy and then they stopped, and after a long moment Varid turned his head, not quite looking at her when he found the breath to say, "I like rain. I always have liked rain. I think."

The storm passed in the night, replaced by cooler, drier air.

Perri took the lead in the morning and held it until he stumbled, shattering his knee and pelvis. Quee Lee passed him. "I'd stay and keep you company, darling. My darling. But I can smell the mountains now."

"Push on," he said amiably.

"I already have," replied Quee Lee, her head down, focusing on the next meter of wicked pebbles and greasy soil.

Katabasis unfastened her tumpline and various straps, lowering her pack onto a boulder where it would wait without complaint. Settling beside the injured man, she said, "Let me carry you over the next rise."

"And earn your bonus," Perri said.

They laughed together.

Varid was approaching as the giant wheel spun upwards, making him heavier. Leaden feet needed to rest before taking any next step, and the man kept his head down, but more out of exhaustion than to pay strict attention. Meanwhile the ground kept trying to drop him. He wasn't clumsy in any normal sense; when he slipped or staggered his feet often found the grace to save him. And then as he passed by, the wheel began to fall again, and inspired by that slight lessening of weight, Varid grew bold. Straightening his back, he managed longer strides, conquering the next low rise before his left leg leaped out in front of him, the monkey knee wrenched in a decidedly unnatural direction.

The moaning was urgent and familiar.

Katabasis and her client remained where they were. Eventually the moans softened, and turning to Katabasis, Perri said, "I finally remembered the story."

"Which story?"

"Wait."

The One-after-another was stomping past them with a furious air. Perri waited for her to leave, and then rubbing his healing leg, he said, "Our brains work so well. Living bioceramics woven around the original neural network, with horizon-sinks latching tight to every idea and event and whispered word. In theory, we shouldn't forget anything for the next ten million years. Isn't that what you hear when you get the upgrade?"

The human leg grew scorching hot as the healing quickened. There was beauty in the infrared glow. "Were you upgraded?" Katabasis asked.

"No, I was born exactly this way," Perri admitted. "Humans usually are. But some little instinct tells me you were born elsewhere and maybe you heard the sales pitch one or two times."

"We are talking about Varid," she said.

"We were," Perri agreed.

They sat for a moment, neither speaking.

"Varid," said Perri. "I finally managed to remember the man. He didn't have quite the same face and his hair was black then. I met him at a very splendid party. And I know what are you asking: 'Why was this rough fellow at a splendid party?' Because his wife moves in some very high orbits, and Varid used to belong to the highest reaches of the high. That's why."

"Varid was a captain?" Katabasis asked doubtfully.

"Oh, no. There are even loftier souls than those dreary uniforms." Perri laughed. "I'm thinking about a civilian family—mother and father and several grown children accompanied by assorted mates and mistresses and thinking toys. One family, and they owned corporations and key patents and the entire Mellissolar system. They even had one of the fastest streakships in human hands. Varid happened to be one of those children, and his clan was among the Ship's first paying passengers, human or otherwise. They purchased the largest quarters in the Ship's most exclusive district, and seeing no reason to leave that paradise, they rarely took the trouble."

Perri winced and smiled and looked at Katabasis. "Perhaps your people are never smug, self-involved, or dismissive. Since my only experience with your species is you, I can't say. But that rich human family was all those things, and Varid—the original Varid—was pried from the same complacent mold. I keep massaging my head. There probably are other incidents. But I've remembered the one party and that single occasion when we crossed paths. We held drinks and faced each other and spoke at length about his grand wealth and the happiness that went with that wealth, and when I found my chance, I left. I didn't see the man again until that day at the trailhead. Thousands of years had passed, and I never felt the urge to seek him out, and I'd wager anyone's wealth that Varid didn't hunger for my company. But of course that's one of the sterling benefits of the Great Ship—you can avoid the souls you don't like at all, unless it happens to be yours."

From the hilltop, Varid groaned mightily.

"That is the man you met," Katabasis said skeptically.

"No." Perri showed his teeth. "Or yes."

She waited.

"Seven hundred years ago, I found myself trapped inside another smug party. Some honorable charity was involved. Quee Lee promised her time and money, and certain lady friends insisted that she bring her wild wandering husband along. Rich ladies have always loved wild wandering husbands, just so long as we weren't their problem. The party lasted ten days, which is about average, and there were ten thousand dull conversations to endure, and I drank more than was proper. But I told a few stories after my wanderings, and nobody seemed too offended. Which was when I discovered that I was, despite my own smugness, enjoying myself.

"On the tenth day, I happened across a group of strange faces. These people were too important to arrive until the end, and they clearly knew one another. The topic was homes and circumstances. It seemed that everybody had moved recently, judging by the sense of adventure when they described the giant apartments that they still had barely explored. And then according to some rule or tradition peculiar to them, they started to tell stories about the Fire.

"'Which fire,' I asked, meaning no harm.

"One lady turned to me and very calmly said, 'The Whisper Fire,' before turning back to her friends."

He paused, watching Katabasis.

She said nothing.

"The Whisper Fire was eleven hundred years before that evening." Perri studied his porter's face while giving his knee a stern rubbing. "Eighteen hundred years ago, and maybe you don't remember. Maybe you weren't onboard yet. But the Fire was a fusion nightmare. It was very big, very dangerous. Of course our brains are tough, tough, tough. But nuclear temperatures eat away baryonic material. Even hyperfiber will eventually collapse back into plasma. The Fire was extinguished within the day, but mistakes and confusion led to many disasters, and some very important enclaves were obliterated before they could be evacuated."

Katabasis nodded, saying nothing.

"Do you see my confusion? More than a millennium had passed, yet those jittery rich people were still dealing with the disaster. Which for some reason struck me as fun, and I remained at the edge of the group for a very long time, listening to old stories mixed with occasional bites of fresh news."

He paused, and she said, "Varid."

"They didn't use his name. They used his family name, and just when I was beginning to feel a vague familiarity, someone mentioned that all of the family but one had perished: Parents and siblings, servants and spouses, plus the grandchildren born inside the Great Ship. All of them were inside their enclave. The enclave was consumed totally. There was only one survivor, except survival didn't come in the usual sense of things."

Katabasis didn't want to hear anything more about Varid. Her pack was waiting to be carried, and she wondered if she would look cowardly or rude, sliding inside those heavy straps and walking over the hill.

She resisted the impulse.

Perri's voice softened, saddened. "A team of salvage experts and ship engineers had finally cut into the deepest ruins. A thousand years had passed, and inside the amorphous glass and bottled poisons they found a piece of brain that hadn't quite died. I was fascinated. How could you not help but be? I wanted to know how most of a mind can be vaporized but a sliver is spared. What odd chaos of fluid mechanics allows that kind of half-blessing? I asked questions. They ignored my questions. Finally the man's name was mentioned, and the woman in the know spoke about a long convalescence that had only just begun and made no sense to any of them. 'The boy was legally and literally dead,' said this very pretty, very civilized lady. Discussing a many-thousand-year-old entity, she said, 'What is left of the boy is residue, it is trash. Why build a body for the emptiness that remains?'"

On the hilltop, the One-after-another was stomping her encouragement to her miserable client.

"'Besides,' the lady said, 'the boy's portion of the estate was always tiny. He was the least-favorite child with the least-liked offspring. Any holdings back home have been inherited by cousins and odd twigs on the family spruce, and which leaves him close to destitute before he takes even one step from the hospital.'"

Katabasis looked up the trail.

Perri slowly rolled over and set both hands against the ground. Every limb pushed as he stood on his rebuilt leg, testing bone and the pain while that lovely heat faded.

"You're certain that this is the same man," Katabasis said.

"I'm certain of nothing. I don't have a nexus and so how can I check?" He lifted the foot and dropped it, barely holding his balance. "Of course I've considered asking the source. My sense is that he would tell me, if he could. But even if every detail is wrong . . . even if this is a different, unrelated Varid . . . I think at its heart, our story remains true.

"Our friend is a shell."

A series of owners had strived to make the mountains spectacular, each investing capital into endless sandwiches of cultured granite and diamondcrete and hyperfiber bracing and hyperfiber scrap, creating a range of increasingly treacherous hills that rose up to scenic summits and starved air.

Several hundred days of steady toil brought them to the foothills and the source of the River East. The party camped in a forest of happen-trees—vast gray plates tipped on end and halfway buried in the ruddy ground—and the humans rested, gathering energy for the push to the highest ridge. The next day was slow and taxing, but they conquered a hundred meters more than planned. Two travelers passed them in the end, both riding their porters. One was poet-bird, and with an important singsong voice he said, "Swallow your pride and ride, brothers and sister. Regret is sweeter pain than a hundred splintered bones."

In their group, nobody rode. The day after was very slow and became slower when Quee Lee took a hard spill, shattering her face and her back. But she refused the Wogfound's attempts to call her broken and carry her for the rest of the way, and when Perri offered his hand, she laughed and said, "You genuinely don't know me, do you?"

The day after that proved steady and very productive. No one fell. Not even a small bone was shattered. One of Katabasis' favorite campsites proved empty and as inviting as always—a glade of rainbow-colored foliage that never looked the same twice. She set down her pack and helped her client pitch his tent, and the Wogfound came over to complain about many matters, many failures, while waiting for the One-after-another to finish her duties.

Quee Lee lay in the open glade, on her back, legs flat. She was sobbing. She was laughing. Tears made the day-old face shine in sun that was as unnatural as it was brilliant—a fierce white glare that encompassed equal portions of the visible spectrum, feeding plants from at least a hundred worlds.

Finished with her chores, Katabasis rested where the ground was dampest, happily doing nothing while her trousers and plumage grew soggy.

Her colleagues marched past. "If we had made that wager," said the One-after-another, "you would win tomorrow."

"Or I would lose tomorrow," said Katabasis.

Jeweled eyes studied the prostrate human. "As you say, she is a beast."

"Am I the beast?" asked Quee Lee.

"You are," Katabasis said. "You are going to climb these mountains."

"I am a great beast, yes," she said, smiling a little more.

Perri was beneath the little tent, preparing their aerogel bed.

Varid emerged from his shelter and on the third attempt managed to stand, walking slowly across the bright glade. Varid wanted to stare at Quee Lee. This was a recent habit, and no one acted offended or intrigued by the attention. But Katabasis was curious how this evening's conversation would play out. She didn't join her colleagues. Instead she studied the diminished human and the lovely beast who kept weeping from pleasure, and she was doing nothing else when a thick layer of scrap rock shifted on the slope behind her. An instant later several million tons of black granite swept across the glade, crushing and burying everything within ten steps of where Katabasis was sitting.

Two porters were gone.

Three survivors called for their companions, searching until well after dark, but nothing answered the pleas, and except for a few binnerlings dancing across the rubble, nothing moved.

Varid didn't join the search. Walking to where Quee Lee had been, he laid down, filling the imprint of her body and shutting his eyes and opening them again, and out from the blackness he said a few true words.

"Somebody else will dig them up."

Then, with a well-earned expertise, he added, "It's amazing what you can survive, and with only a little luck."

5

Her cadre of Hopefuls were about to graduate. Childhood was finished and her original wedge-chamber was too small for comfort. But the warrior always came past in the morning, licking toes and feet and the lower legs that stuck out into the hallway. It was the same warrior who several years ago told her about humans. The secret had seemed wondrous, overwhelming. Creatures from a distant sun had come to their planet, to Existence, and at least one of them was now walking the face of a neighboring world. But knowledge that grand couldn't remain special for long. Teachers and every Hopeful and eventually even the old servants in the latrine began discussing the odd beasts that fell from the sky. Some claimed the Five were using radio winds to chat with the humans. These newcomers were few and wouldn't stay long—gravity was crushing for their weak constitutions—but every story agreed on this: Creatures from nameless places were making pledges of peace and cultural trade as well as long speeches about their glorious, magical nature.

Soon the People inside the stronghold and throughout the world understood that great events were flowing.

And they understood nothing.

One morning the young woman was dreaming, and then she felt the touch and wetness of the tongue. But the warrior wasn't licking between her toes. She was awake and in the next groggy moment felt the six fingers of a hand tugging at her leg while an excited, angry, and almost incomprehensible voice—her closest friend among the mathematicians—said something about hurrying to the arena. "Come now," he said. "The Five are meeting with everybody, and everybody is late."

The girl dressed as she walked. A big, naturally strong creature, she broke into a smooth foot-skimming run in the hallways, convinced that she was in trouble for being tardy but then discovering that no, she was among the first of the invited guests.

The Five appeared together only on ceremonial days. But this was a special occasion, and this was the new Five—the oldest wife had died recently, replaced by a smart young husband with a thousand valuable favors owed to him. The new husband sat as he should, off to the side, his mouth closed. Today's oldest wife spoke for the group, and for a long while she said nothing except to urge the People to come forward and push close, and once there was no more space under the dome, she demanded that everyone remain silent and attentive.

Thousands of People breathed in sips, making no sound.

"There is a new word in our world," said the wife. Then with an unnatural growl to the voice, she said, "Human."

The excitement was felt, but no one spoke or moved.

"Humans are why we have called each other together," the wife continued. "Star-creatures have crossed a tremendous desert to sit close to our realm. But they are not part of our world, and they have no plans to visit our world, and it is time to admit why: Because we are poor. They ignore the People because we have ordinary resources and unspectacular knowledge. And compared to those sitting on younger mountains, we are few. So they are not here and never will be here, and only the raving fool bolsters herself with bold, impossible talk."

Honesty was rougher than any tongue. The full-grown Hopeful kept silent and tried to remain still, but she felt herself turning slowly, scanning the tight-packed faces until she found the gathered warriors.

They were made of stronger stone than her. Her warrior never let his gaze wander, and he didn't flinch as the speech continued.

"We are poor and few," said the wife, "and even worse, our long prospects are miserable. Our old world is crumbling beneath us. A new world might suddenly burst out of the nearby plains, affording us fresh homes. But mountains are fickle gods, and this is why my family and all of the People have spent generations making ready for a longer exodus. Out on the horizon, perhaps somewhere past dawn, stands a row of young mountains too remote to be settled or too weak to resist our arrival. This has always been our destination, our salvation—a plan aimed at a heartbeat some thousand years in the future.

"But now we have a second destination: The humans. They are powerful beasts wielding tools that scare even our strongest neighbors. To move from star to star and manage that trick so easily—it astonishes our little minds. But humans are creatures of honor and heroism. Appreciating favors and good deeds, their main emissary has made an offer to all worlds and all species of People. Give the humans a worthy gift, and they will grant us passage to a starship. The starship is larger than our entire planet. Give them greater gifts, and they will grant the People infinite life. Then their Great Ship will carry us to some new planet where empty beautiful worlds stand above deserts that aren't as ugly oras hot as ours.

"The Five have decided to embark on this bold migration. Today we are offering each of you the opportunity to walk with us across the emptiness. We will travel in the same ways our ancestors strode to these mountains when they were new—by wheel and by foot, one night at a time. And once we reach our benefactors, we shall give them a gift, a great gift—a wondrous, perfect gift worthy of passage on this giant vessel of theirs."

The speaker paused. From the adjacent hallway came an electric wagon bearing a stout steel box, locked and secured with steel straps.

"An object waits inside," explained the wife. "My ancestors dug this treasure out of the throat of the volcano that built the land beneath us, and it has belonged to my family since . . . our grandest, loveliest treasure, worth a million favors from creatures such as these human beasts."

6

There was no reason for grief. The weight of twenty mountains meant nothing to the modern mind. Two porters were temporarily misplaced, bodiless but safe, bathed in partial comas that let them feel angry about their miserable luck and the loss of income but eternally confident that the landlords or colleagues would eventually come after them with a shovel.

The landslide was no grave, and besides, Katabasis' colleagues were never true friends.

Why then was she sorrowful?

Humans thought of grief as being something that lived inside them, toxic and massive and often crippling. But Katabasis was not human. Sitting on the damp ground, a bright cloud hung about her face and shoulders. Her companions couldn't see the sharp blue light pouring into her body and brain. They didn't realize that anguish brought strength and absolute focus, which was the hallmark of her species: Horrible, withering losses could strike the species, yet the survivors' instinctive response was to grow lighter and even braver, pushing toward some goal that had never seemed more precious.

"Maybe we should turn around and walk back to City East," Quee Lee said.

"Back is nearly as far as forward," said Perri.

"I won't go back," Varid said.

"Well, food won't be a problem now," Perri said. "We have supplies for six, including two giants."

"And one good back to carry the wealth," his wife said.

"I'm going on," said Varid. He was holding a rigid golden leaf against the torchlight, watching it dry and then smolder and finally burn.

"We might hire new porters, if we push ahead," Perri said.

"A strong porter carrying a dead client," his wife agreed. "And we would pay bonuses for the extra work, of course."

"One pissed-off Wogfound," Perri said. "That's all we need."

The porter recognized the smartest strategy. But Katabasis was larger than her job, and she was older than her job, and she wanted to hold their present course, not involving anyone outside her family.

Whose family?

She caught herself, shaken by her thoughts.

Suddenly the reasons for grief stood in the open. She had a family once, a great embracing family, but they were lost on a distant trail. The porters trapped underground weren't dead, but they served as triggers for these immortal aches, and these three fragile aliens—the unlikely lords of the galaxy—suddenly meant more to her than anyone else alive.

Katabasis made small sorrowful gestures, fighting to find her voice.

Varid dropped the burning leaf. With a big voice, he said, "Do what you wish, people. But I don't need a porter."

Quee Lee opened her mouth and closed it again, waiting.

"I'll carry my own rations and sleep in the open and don't worry about me."

Perri touched his wife's knee, and she met his stare. With nothing but faces, the ancient couple settled into prolonged conversation. Two rational minds were deciding how to argue with the damaged man. Watching their eyes and mouths, Katabasis remained silent, waiting for the reasonable tone and the most responsible plan. All at once Quee Lee brightened. She smiled and managed to laugh, slowly lifting herself to her knees and hands and then to her feet, shuffling over to Varid, her voice high and light when she said, "My porter is lost, and I don't know where to turn."

Varid looked up through the weak smoke.

Quee Lee dropped a hand on his shoulder. "What I want to do, if you'll let me . . . I want to hire you as my new porter."

All the days spent together, and Varid had never shown surprise. Until now he had been a flat, simple creature. But his eyes jumped open. He tried to breathe and failed, and then with a nervous tone asked, "Why me?"

"You're the strongest back available," she said simply.

Katabasis looked at Perri. Was this a genuine offer?

Perri replied with the appropriate hand gesture, slicing the air to say, "This is reasonable to me."

"I don't know," said Varid.

Quee Lee said, "Please."

Then the man smiled, and it wasn't just a grin that had been practiced during rehabilitation. Varid smiled with his face and entire body, leaning into the hand's touch, an effusive voice rolling across the glade and the avalanche, saying, "Of course I will. I will be your porter, yes."

Two days after the disaster, they reached the first summit. Thousands of boots and bare feet had stood on the highest ground, killing all but the flattest and the toughest. Lichen from various worlds painted the stone, and a pair of ragdogs followed closely, ignoring Katabasis to beg for treats from the humans. The four walked slowly from view to view. On each peak, Perri and Quee Lee would discuss the scenery and animals and the rich smells on the breeze and how much farther they might cover before one of them broke another hip. Then some detail or single word would trigger memories in both of them, and suddenly they were talking about events and places buried deep in their shared past, and they laughed and often kissed, and Katabasis was weary of the game.

Varid paid no attention the show. He was playing the role of porter, and Quee Lee was nothing but his client. For two mornings he had made a show of loading and balancing his tiny pack before claiming that he was ready to carry more. A portion of his rations and a tiny piece of hers were inside the pack, plus his aerogel bed and a few other lightweight essentials. There was extra room, but Katabasis always had the ready excuse not to add grams to a body that would break several times on the best days. She had to be cautious. In the history of this world, there had never been a slower, more fragile porter. Nor could Katabasis remember any colleague who took his work half as seriously.

Tents were a brutal kilogram best left in one of the official trash heaps. Bodies and beds spent the night on the final summit, and when snow fell they gathered inside the same rocky bowl, waking early beneath half a meter of dry fluff. Several valleys radiated down from the final summit. Katabasis selected the most forgiving slope, but that didn't stop accidents and breaks and extra food ingested to make up for lost heat and chronic repairs. Then the sun changed, growing dim and tiny, and they entered a forest of velvety foliage, the scarce light concentrated by banks of living mirrors.

Three careful days were usually required to cross this region.

Katabasis estimated that five days would be necessary, but the sixth arrived with another two days standing in their way. She hated marching in the dark and never mentioned her feelings. They walked through the gloom, and sometimes one of the humans stumbled, and it was Varid as much as it was the other two. But on the sixth day, while crossing a thin, cold slice of snowmelt, Katabasis allowed her pack to shift out of position, and for the first time in twenty treks, she fell hard enough to shatter a leg.

Quee Lee and Perri returned with regrets and polite offers of help.

"Walk on," was Katabasis' advice. "I'll heal in one moment and catch up in two."

But the other porter refused to leave. With grave eyes and a taunting grin, Varid sat on a flat stone, obviously enjoying the circumstances.

"Don't smile," she warned.

He heard the words or her sharp tone, and the smile abandoned the face, leaving him as empty as always.

Such a puzzle, the creature was. Wanting any noise for distraction, she said, "Katabasis." Then she asked, "How did you recognize my name?"

Varid did not react.

"Do you remember your lecture about Greeks?" she asked.

He stared at her hot leg and then at his own hands, nodding slightly. With a quiet voice, he admitted, "I wasn't sure where the word came from. I used to study history, and languages fascinated me, and I must have learned it there."

She watched her leg's fire, saying nothing.

"I have had some recent difficulties," Varid admitted. "My health, my situation, has not been good. My mind is far from what it used to be."

"I know this."

He smiled again, this time with a shy human embarrassment.

Katabasis liked that smile best.

"I do remember the word," he said. "But there isn't any simple meaning to 'Katabasis,' is there?"

"There isn't," she agreed.

"But you chose the name for a reason."

"No one leaves names to chance."

"It must have suited you," he said.

She nodded, ready to explain.

But Varid lifted an arm first. "Give me one chance to guess."

"Try," she said.

And he closed his eyes, quietly saying, "Katabasis is the journey from a high place, down and down into the bowels of Hell."

She stared at him.

Then Varid opened his eyes and looked at her, his broken laugh ringing in the dark air. "Two rarities in the same day," he said. "You fall down, and I impress you.

"What could be more miraculous?"

7

The girl always woke early, long before the sun set. Bad dreams woke her, and good ones too. The heat woke her. Breathing the thick, toxic, and very dusty air hurt her lungs, and she would roll to her side and cough hard and ache all the worse, unable to fall back to sleep. Sometimes her lover woke her with his coughing and his dreams, and then they would lie in the hot shadow beneath the mirrored tent, talking about critical matters—water rations and food stocks and the distance to be covered tonight and the little hints of terrain visible in the fiery glare of the plains. It was important to plan your night's walk and then grab an early start. The People were moving in a wide line, shoulder to shoulder as they pushed across the wilderness, and it was best to get ahead of the dust kicked up by all of those feet and wheels. And if there was time after their planning, or if one of them was especially sad, the other would mention the humans and their Great Ship. These were the goals, and everyone needed goals. Not like they needed water, no, but the Great Ship was everything that water and food couldn't supply. It didn't represent hope; it was the only hope. Its hallways and giant wedge-rooms offered rest to the weary, and the body and mind would be rejuvenated and then enlarged—relentless long life and profound brains ready to be filled with experience and joy that would endure for thousands and millions of years.

The warrior was smitten with the idea of instant healing. Eleven days after abandoning the world, he brushed against a barkershang, driving three poisoned needles into his thigh. The wounds had been cleaned and cleaned, and he was good about changing his dressings, but even though the doctors claimed that he was improving, the holes were no smaller and the swollen flesh was a bright sick green.

From the moment she woke until they fell asleep with their legs wrapped together, the girl would remind herself that her lover was strong enough even without the help of aliens. He might limp on occasion, and maybe he suffered little fevers, but there were sicker citizens and a few dead. Besides, they were marching toward another world and different people, and warriors were at a premium. The Five had ample stocks of better drugs, and when the time came—should it come—they would release the antibiotics and the charms held back for emergencies.

The warrior wished for the immortal body, but the girl wanted the gifts of the mind. Perfect, boundless memory struck her as a blessing—provided that she could control the onslaught from the past. But why build such a brain and not give yourself the power to close off certain days and the very bad years? She imagined that she had a choice, and that was mostly true. But only while she was awake. A thousand years later, she would dream it all over again, and it wouldn't be just the worst night, but every hot sorry march through the darkness and every sleepless oven-racked day.

The worst night began with the sun still up. She woke and the warrior slept, and she worked like a demon not to cough. But the coughing was always worse when she finally succumbed—a roaring hack blowing out the dust and thick air. The warrior was jarred awake. She apologized, but he said that he was rested. She asked about his leg, and he lifted the leg and rubbed it before announcing that the swelling and pain were both in the ground under them.

They talked about water and food.

With quiet, conspiratorial voices, they described the wedge-room they would share on the Great Ship and what kinds of aliens they might meet on their way to the toilet.

It was still day, but the sun was dropping. The earliest shadows were talking to one another, claiming that first willingness to merge and matter. The People were moving under their bright tents. The girl drank what was allowed and the warrior took his share, and with the sun fading into the red dust, they climbed into the greater heat, packing and loading the two-wheeled cart that she would pull and push through the night. That was her duty. His duty involved marching ahead, scouting for enemies and the best routes, although there were good reasons to come back and give help, and maybe she would need help in the night's heart.

The sun vanished against the low shape of the distant world, leaving nothing behind but its heat and a furnace wind.

He and she embraced and again embraced, and like every other dusk, she wondered if they would never touch again. These were not omens. Tiny mistakes and large lapses in judgment could kill, and even the smartest, most careful soul was never safe.

The old world stood behind them, mostly abandoned. Only the sick and infirm, the elderly and cowardly had remained inside the empty buildings. The Five were leading the rest across the wasteland, and true to their nature, they were models of sacrifice and generosity. Electrified vehicles were charged by daylight, and the Five had ownership over many or most of the machines, but they rarely rode. Walking among the common citizens was their duty, and maybe the old wife was carried now and again, but who could blame her? Her guards and her children were well within their rights to catch her as she stumbled, and if a chair and poles were assembled on the spot, why not? She was the leader among the Five. She was owed enormous favors and deserved this small consideration, just as any other person was entitled to help and care when they weakened and dropped—provided that they had built up the favors to deserve the honor.

That night—the worst night ever—saw the girl pushing her cart up a long slope of pale, star-washed rock. Knots of angry weed threatened—weeds as alien as anything found on remote planets. Dust was everywhere. So many feet pounding the same ground made for clouds of smothering grime, and not even three cloths across the mouth would keep out the urge to choke.

Climbing uphill, she suddenly found herself walking beside the Five's new husband. He was pushing nothing, but she managed to drift ahead. Their eyes met for a moment. He offered an amused gesture. Then he lost his footing on a weed and fell hard, causing the girl to stop her cart and offer the free hand.

He said, "You are a strong woman, and thank you."

She was strong, and now she felt important too. A favor had been given to one of the Five. It was a smallish favor, and maybe it would be forgotten before it could be redeemed. But perfect memories were coming, and ten thousand years from to-night, this ageless man would recall the instant and her strength, and he would pay back the debt. It was a thought worth savoring. This was a moment to share inside the tent, the sun rising again and the food for the day going inside them. The warrior would laugh, feeling proud of his big strong lover, and then they would plunge into sleep, a few more steps achieved on the endless trek.

Happiness proved brief. Reaching the hill's crest, she found a dozen People sitting on the dry hot ground, breathing painfully or not breathing at all. One and then two more reached for her, and someone called a name. But it wasn't her name. They were guessing, hoping for lucky coincidences. She didn't know any of the faces or hands. It was normal for citizens to collapse after the hard climb, but what alarmed her was their youth and the fit bodies with the plumage still vigorous. Obviously they had worked too hard, too fast. That was the impression that helped her walk past, and that was the smug attitude that made her push harder through the night.

Twice again, long slopes needed to be climbed.

Centuries later, she would dream about the dying people on top and on the way up to the top, and because it was a dream and a lie, their voices would call to her. This time everybody knew her name, and she owed each of them multiple favors, yet she shoved the cart past them and couldn't even do them the simple courtesy of averting her eyes. In her dreams she stared at their suffering and hopelessness, and sometimes she even boasted about her invincible luck.

This long trek had started well enough, but that's how a trap works. If bad weather or unusual heat had struck the People, most would have turned around immediately, leaving the Five and their precious gift to march into oblivion. But the weather and a thousand other factors had remained relatively kind. Until that night, it was possible to believe that most of the People would survive. It was pos-sible to walk through the heat and bad air, letting the anguish strengthen every stride. But hundreds of People were collapsing now, sometimes on the easiest ground, and the girl remembered that after the next line of little hills came a long basin covered with salt and metallic dusts and temperatures strong enough to cook meat and a girl's will.

She pushed her cart into a boulder-littered valley where water hadn't traveled in ages. Even the machines were dying now. The electric cart with the precious steel box was broken, and the oldest of the Five was sitting in a chair supplied by one well-wisher, sucking on what looked like a ball of ice supplied by another. Mechanics were listing the reasons why the vehicle would never roll again. The old woman said she didn't care about the machine. What mattered was its cargo, and nobody should for-get that. And with her authority in hand, children and associates hurried off to find new transport, including the son who stopped a big bus crossing the dead stream.

The bus was opened and emptied. Mechanics began cutting out the seats and removing the roof, making room for the treasure. The passengers had lost this night's promised break. A slender little mathematician didn't seem too displeased, helping with the work when he saw the big girl pushing the cart past. He called the proper name. He didn't ask for help. He probably only wanted a gesture of friendship, a sharing of confidence. But the girl decided not to risk the possibility. There was plenty of ground between them. It was easy not to hear her friend in the rattle of machinery, and it was even easier to sprint ahead without quite fleeing, out of the valley and across the last high ground before the salt and real misery began.

This was an awful night, and it still wasn't finished. That girl, the future Katabasis, began to see warriors marching back toward the rest of the People. She saw her lover in one body after another. There he was, no there, and there too. The search was frustrating, and then it was terrifying, and somewhere in the midst of her desperate hunt she realized that he was dead and lost forever.

But the man wasn't dead. In fact, he wasn't any weaker or sicker than he was at dusk. Out from the swirling dust he emerged, and they made camp and finally ate their daily allotment, and then as the sun broke over the bright tent, they tried to settle.

The habit was for the warrior to engulf her legs with his legs.

But that dawn was different. He did nothing, and she complained about his distance.

So he tried twice and then twice again, but he was uncomfortable. Finally pulling away, he coughed weakly before admitting that the soreness was worse, maybe more than a little worse, and he was sorry but tomorrow he would feel better and everything would be right again.

She reached behind, touching the injured leg.

The swollen flesh was hiding inside the trousers, obvious and alarming if not yet lethal. Suddenly the future was clear. The warrior was too strong to die quickly. He would serve his duty tomorrow night and for several nights, and then his duty and the uniform would be stripped from him as he failed. Like the girl, he would be allowed to carry what he could and help push the cart, and one of the cart's wheels would eventually shatter and they would have to leave it behind. Each night's misery would be stoically endured; there was no doubting his capacity to suffer. But a final moment was approaching. The warrior would stumble one last time. Some People managed to be kind in the end, dying quietly, without complaints. He was the sort of man to make that kind of honorable promise. But as the girl lay beside him in their bed—as the sun rose and he growled fitfully in his sleep—she arrived at the awful knowledge that the love of her life would break every promise in the end. He would use her name and invoke every favor, and she would walk past him and then pause, returning in order to reach past his desperate hands, stripping away the last of his rations and two tastes of salty, hot, precious water.

8

The humans fell and broke and healed again and got up again. Two of them stopped pretending to be cheerful about these circumstances, aiming instead for weary politeness. The third human rolled in agony and wept with a child's self-absorption, and in the end his results were no worse, no better. Every injury could be healed, but there were costs. Heat and the rapid weaving of tissue and bone required high levels of fuel, and they were already limited in the food they carried. If the humans avoided stumbling, they would eventually reach the final kilometer with a last meal in their guts. But the descending trails were never easy, and the food shares had to be cut again. Missing calories forced injured bodies to cheat with the healing. Mass was lost, fat burned, and organs minimized before precious muscle was stolen. The humans shrank. Proportions changed, saving what was necessary to walk while stripping away what didn't matter today. But even the most careful manipulations caused strength to fade and bones weaken, and the shriveled, half-starved bodies defended themselves with extreme caution, measuring each step twice before making the attempt.

And still they fell. The two-kilometer hikes from the early days were impossible. Half a kilometer was an exceptional accomplishment. But that meant that each mouthful was buying even less distance than before, and their shares had to be sliced down again, and City West might well be standing at the end of the universe for all the chance they had of reaching its broad, clean streets.

"Care for yourself," Katabasis told the other porter, pressing an extra brick of food into a grimy cold hand. "You're the woman's best chance, but not if you turn into a stick lost beside the trail."

Varid looked at the gift. The brick was shiny gray, flavored like dribbledoe and laced with chemical bonds waiting for any excuse to explode. Then he looked at her, setting the brick on one of his bare knees. "You're losing weight too."

"Not like the rest of you," she said.

He nodded.

"Eat," she insisted.

Saliva came out with the words. "I am a porter."

"You are."

"A porter," he repeated. Then he brightened and picked up the feast with both hands, asking, "How did I get so lucky?"

Without question, the habitat's second half was lovelier than the first. Forests were older, more complex. Landlords hadn't reworked the ground as often or as ineptly. And the weather was a little less awful than before. But even the strongest clients were usually worn down by now: They couldn't appreciate the artful winding of streams. Rare blossoms and brilliant worms could barely rouse them out of the tedium. Typically Katabasis looked forward to a glade of unique trees—each one lovely, each representing one species that couldn't be found anywhere else inside a thousand-light-year radius—and she usually made a point of camping inside the glade, lingering for two nights and a full day. But they entered in mid-morning, the weather kind but cloudy, and fearing rain and more delays, she marched her humans through the gorgeous woods, barely looking to her side as she held the slow, withering pace.

Other clients and other porters began to catch them. They could hear them closing, often for a full day, and then some happy voice would beg for a wider trail, please. Those first clients were always riding strong porters. Nobody recognized Varid, and the anonymity suited him. But a few rich travelers, human and otherwise, knew the married couple, and they would shout out greetings and teasings before offering some obligatory words about admiring their courage.

But starvation kept eating at the faces and the bodies, and eventually the best friends stopped recognizing them.

Perri was a frail body shrunk down to a child's proportions while his face remained pretty in a rail-slender fashion. Except on the hottest days, he was cold, and the hair had dropped off his scalp and face, but the eyes seemed only to have grown larger from the experience, gazing at nothing but the ground that looked flat and looked level but might at any moment tip him over, breaking him in the same dreary, frustrating ways.

Quee Lee was even less recognizable. She was hairless, genderless. Breasts and hips had vanished, the black hair was scattered all the way back to the mountains, and with a tired, dry, amazed voice she would admit that she hadn't even attempted relations with her husband in fifty or sixty or a hundred nights. She counted those nights. She laughed weakly and dabbed at the crumbs of her day's rations, and then she would collapse into Perri's little arms, whispering a few words when she found the energy.

"Thank you so much for inviting me along," she told her husband.

With a slight laugh, he said, "You're welcome," and then dabbed up a few more crumbs. The source of these little feasts was uncertain, but he always attempted to put his finger into Quee Lee's mouth, and she would suck hard and cry and then pull the finger out again, urging his closer ear to her mouth, ready to whisper whatever was next.

Walking clients began to catch them. Even weak and inept hikers passed by, as if the humans were trees standing in a glade. Various eyes stared at the couple, probably assuming they were alien, not human. And then they noticed the human porter with his little pack that hadn't carried anything in a very long while. What was that man's story? Sometimes they struck up a conversation, with the strangers or with each other, and it became the day's high point to watch their emotions when a woman's voice emerged from the tiniest, weakest of the apparitions.

Quee Lee had digested most of her face. Her mouth was a sliver without more than a few tired teeth, and the cheekbones had collapsed into a skull that was perforated like an aerogel sponge. But her voice remained, and a shred of humor, and the first time that she begged for food was meant as a joke.

One brick of high-density fat helped save the trek.

She promised that she was joking. She and Perri were sharing the unexpected feast at camp, and she was honestly remorseful for pleading as she had. What kind of person had she become? The next three groups didn't hear begging, and they didn't leave gifts. But the hunger returned, and Quee Lee used her voice and bizarre appearance to find sympathy with everybody who passed them by. Most strangers didn't want to part with their wealth, but a few were more amenable. Ten days of humiliation and charm produced enough nourishment to put them twenty or thirty days farther down the endless trail, giving them enough leeway to consider their situation very carefully.

In the night, inside a warm bramble-filled valley, Quee Lee and Perri lay together beneath the aerogel bedding. Katabasis could hear pieces of their conversation. Certain words and the long silences pointed at a grim topic, and the porter listened and ached and in the next moment corrected herself. Nobody was doomed. No souls were bound for the Final World where all the species of People shared the breath of life. These two creatures were simply discussing matters of time and energy and the pragmatic limits of desire, and after a while they fell into sleep, and preparing her own bed, Katabasis felt peculiarly honored for being allowed this chance to study their lives.

One blue light shone in the darkness.

A little stiffly, the porter rose again, walking to the man lying in his bed. Varid was holding the torch to his eyes. What once was deeply peculiar had become ordinary. The man couldn't sleep in the usual sense. Holding brightness against his eyes seemed to relax him or busy him or do something else worthwhile. Katabasis had never asked why he did this. She didn't intend to ask now. But looking down at Varid, she enjoyed the same epiphanies that had struck her again and again over these last days:

This was not a human being.

And whatever Varid was, he was unique—a species with a population of precisely one.

She knelt beside him, watching the light and the open eyes.

After a long while, he noticed. Taking a long breath, he set the torch aside, and when he felt ready he said, "It helps me remember, the light does."

"Remember what?"

He was too tired to sit up. The first attempt proved it, but he tried again, glad for her help when it came, and then he regretted the choice and slowly fell back into the aerogel. After more breathing, he said, "I suffered this medical situation. I was caught inside a very large fire."

"The Whisper Fire," she said.

"Have I told you this before?"

"No."

A slow nod. "I don't remember very much. Not the day or being scared, or anything like that. But I do remember the last thing that I saw: This impossibly bright light. They say . . . the doctors explained this to me . . . they claimed that I took shelter inside a hyperfiber blister, and the inferno ate through the walls, and as soon as the last layer was pierced, this thread of plasmas found me. But my eyes didn't die immediately, and my brain survived afterwards. Something about the shape of that little space not only saved my mind, but it allowed my eyes to watch this most amazing light."

She said nothing.

"Then I was dead and blind," he said. "I was lost and mostly unconscious. But if you're buried for a thousand years, thoughts happen. You remember what you can, but I couldn't remember much. So much had been turned to fire." He paused, smiling weakly. "But you probably realized that on our first day together, didn't you?"

"The light," she said.

"It helps my head work better. Brilliance somehow makes it easier for me to practice what I learned today and fifty thousand years ago."

She said, "Good then."

"This is crazy, yes. But when I was dead, the fire that killed me . . . nearly killed me, and murdered my family . . . that fire was my largest best memory. It seemed so lovely and wonderful. I don't think I could have remained sane for even a hundred years, if it wasn't for me thinking about that searing magical light."

Watching him, Katabasis weighed questions.

Varid answered an unasked question. "I don't need sleep anymore. It's a consequence of my injuries, and it's because this is how far I was fixed before the fixing stopped."

"Why did the fixing stop?" she asked.

Varid picked up the torch again, holding it against his right eye. He didn't act interested in the question, and maybe he didn't notice it. Katabasis still didn't know what the man could learn or how well ideas would play inside his head. But he wasn't the insane idiot that she had imagined. He was a mystery, relentlessly frustrating but compelling, and instead of working to avoid this creature, she wanted to share the solitude forced on both of them by bad and wonderful forces.

"Could I become a porter?" he asked abruptly.

"What?"

The torch and hand pulled away from his face. The dark center of the eye was a pinprick point. He wasn't as starved as the others, his bluish-white hair still alive, though thin and not growing any longer, and his face was very much like the face that she first met. She had passed her colleague enough rations to keep up his strength, and she had quit bristling whenever she thought of Varid that way: Her colleague.

"I don't know if you could be a porter," she said.

He remained silent.

"You're tiny and you're weak," she said.

"Like you," he said. "But you manage to make your living."

She laughed with her hands, her face. She laughed as close to the human sound of laughter as she could manage.

"I stopped the fixing where it is," Varid said.

"Did you?"

He nodded.

"Was it a question of money?" she asked.

"No, I have money. A sliver from the original estate, they tell me. But it's still more than most passengers enjoy."

She watched his face.

"No, the doctors let me choose," he said. "They gave me permission to decide how much new bioceramic I wanted grown, and how giant my mind would be. They thought they were going to get rich doing the work. But I surprised them. I told them thank you, but no, and to leave me alone."

She watched his empty hand, fingers spread out on his hungry belly.

"A thousand years spent underground, and almost everything from before was gone," he said. "I didn't think about my dead family, and I didn't forget and think about them being alive either. I had memories of the past and disjointed facts learned, but there wasn't one story pulling the mess together. I was dead. My mind was gone, only pieces left, and those pieces slowly assembled themselves into something that was familiar to me . . . that became me . . . and I don't know how to explain this."

"Don't," she advised.

But Varid showed a stubborn face. "I don't have much humor left. But maybe I didn't have any to begin with. I don't feel much empathy for others, and I know I forget most of what I learn. But that doesn't mean that I'll stop learning or making myself better or doing whatever good thing it is that I'm supposed to do. And I do like to attempt whatever is difficult. Which isn't the way I used to be, they tell me. Certain strangers who knew me before. They don't like me, they like to say, but I don't see how they liked the man who died. I've studied him. For years and years after getting out into the world again . . . I know I'm rambling, I do this if I'm not careful . . . but I do appreciate, very much, getting lost in passions that he couldn't even imagine. Like this adventure. He would never, ever have envisioned walking through wilderness accompanied by a beautiful alien creature."

Katabasis sat motionless, watching all of the man.

"You can sleep," Varid said. "Sleep now, and it will help you tomorrow."

"Thank you," she said.

She stood and said, "I will."

Three days later, Perri found the right place and proper circumstances. He called Quee Lee to his side and they spoke to each other with just those big eyes. Standing beneath a ripe tashaleen tree, they looked vulnerable and worried. But when Varid walked into the tree's shadow, they calmly warned him to back away.

Little seams were opening in the swollen bladder. The stink of sulfuric acid began to pervade the calm forest air, but it might take another day or two for the flesh to burst wide, scouring the nearby ground.

Varid slowly backed away, studying the scene. Comprehension took longer for him, but he accepted the obvious quickly, and approaching Katabasis, he said, "We have all of the rations."

She was carrying every bit of food, including the treats given out of pity.

Quee Lee called to Varid, saying, "You'll have to carry me from here on. So of course you'll earn your bonus."

Perri slowly bent over, grabbing a small rock.

Katabasis was thinking about acid and its effects on flesh and how the flow would roll when the bladder burst.

Perri tried to throw the pebble at the bladder, but it weighed tons and tons.

"I won't break the tree for you," Katabasis warned.

"I have a suggestion," Varid said. Then to the couple waiting in that dark, fume-laced shade, he said, "Lie down inside your bed."

With a reasonable, perfectly calm voice, he said, "The aerogel won't dissolve, but it will let the acid seep through. Your brains will stay where they are, which is good. We won't have to chase either of you downstream."

9

At dawn, eighty-nine People crawled beneath the tattered shelters. There were no rations to eat, nothing to drink. They lay quietly, in pain, listening to the world bake and blister, and sometimes they slept but mostly they watched their own vague thoughts form and shift before being lost. When the sun finally dropped behind the new world, eighty-three People found enough reason to stand again, stowing the shelters in the final three carts and grabbing hold of the wagon that carried the rusted steel box, slowly pushing away from the dead.

The new world began with towering black cliffs. Through telescopes, rivers could be seen plunging over the side of the volcano, wasted water turning to mists and serpentine clouds that were consumed before drifting halfway to the desert. Those cliffs were the goal, the dream, but the walk would take another four or five or perhaps six nights, and worse, there was no obvious path leading up the imposing and very smooth face of rock.

The Five had become the Three. The ice-sucking woman refused to die, along with her two youngest husbands. The woman always rode on the back end of the wagon. Every night she made optimistic noises about imminent rescue and the abiding decency of the human animal. She insisted that she knew the animal well. She and the god-like emissary had spoken many times by radio. They were allies, collaborators, sometimes friends. But the final radio died out on the salt, and she didn't have her friend to speak to anymore. She was making noise, half-mad and often feverish, and her noise had an erosive effect on the last shreds of hope.

Her husbands didn't bother lying. Working beside the strongest bodies, they pushed wheels up long slopes and used their scant weight to keep the wagon and their wife from rolling wild downhill. Sometimes one or the other would climb ahead, scouting the ground for the least-awful route. Just short of the night's center, the older man went up to the ridge crest and then came back again. He was running. He fell suddenly. He got up and fell and got up laughing with his arms, and with more disbelief than joy, he announced, "We reached the world early. Over this hill is a mine."

The next long reach of desert had been stripped away. Deep gouges were cut into the pale rock, roads and paths leading down to giant electric machines working in the depths of the deepest hole. The machines took no interest in them. Any miners were equally oblivious. Eighty-two People looked down on the mayhem, and one of them sat for a moment and died and the others backed away from the mine's edge, aiming for the nearest road.

The first miner had a strange oval face and a fancy mask over his mouth and eyes. He stared at the filthy parade of bodies, and with a string of peculiar words, he spoke into a tiny radio, presumably asking a question or soliciting advice.

Peculiar words came out of the radio, and he responded by clambering into a burly electric cart and riding away.

After that, they didn't see one miner.

But someone had left rations and fresh water stacked together in some form of way station. The People fell on what they assumed were gifts, drinking enough and eating more than enough, and another one of their ranks died from the indulgence.

The station had a roof full of tubes that leaked cold air, and several sets of rails ended here but led off toward the world. The rails stood empty until a heavy railcar arrived and parked. The husbands conferred and then gave orders. The car was long enough for all of the People to ride in comfort, with room remaining for a battered wagon and its precious cargo. Once loaded, the railcar began rolling back from where it had come, bearing the People across the last bits of wasteland, diving into a long tunnel as the sun burst into view. And even at that moment, the girl sitting on the aluminum floor of the car was unable to believe that she would survive one day longer.

Their old world was nearly nothing. It had been a low ridge, dry and thinly populated, while this world was a hundred times larger, tall enough for permanent ice and wet everywhere, its belly full of hot rock and deep springs powering geothermal plants which made the entire realm hum with electrical activity. Perhaps a million generations separated the People from these citizens. They looked that different, that alien. Every face was grossly round, and the plumage wasn't just wrong in its color but longer and gaudily colored, and these new People smelled different and sounded odd, talking about the railcar that was sliding past their homes and businesses. Their day had just begun. The old People, their lost cousins, deserved notice and some idle chatter. The girl stared at the bright buildings passing by and the endless metal and how every window was filled with light, the faces behind glass staring at her for a moment or two, curious but not curious, ready for any excuse to pull back to their own busy lives.

If the girl and her People had arrived here in full force, they would have meant nothing. They were too scarce, too primitive, and much too stupid to generate anything more than polite disinterest.

That was the morning's first awful lesson.

The long railcar was driven by a machine's mind, turns taken and turns avoided until they arrived at a fresh volcanic crater, barren land encircling a turquoise lake. On the black rock stood a different kind of building, round like a half-ball and woven from slick gray material that didn't look like any steel.

"This is the emissary's quarters," the old woman announced happily. "It is also a spaceship, fueled and ready to carry us to the Great Ship."

At dusk, the girl didn't believe anything the old woman claimed. But suddenly she was an expert again, and every statement only enhanced her boundless value.

The car stopped before a walkway made from gemstone bricks.

Out from the building—from the spaceship—came a creature with six jointed legs. Except it wasn't a creature, it was a machine, and the human rode on a high chair inside the machine's body. His face was grim, stern. But the girl didn't know it then. He was as angry as a diplomat trained in the art of agreements and sweet words could ever be. But she only saw the narrow black face and the frail body shorn of its plumage and the odd little hands that didn't like rising off the rests in his chair. He was undoubtedly alien. The new People would look ordinary next to him, if only they were standing here. But it was the human alone, and the last of the girl's People, and he introduced himself with his name and his title and once again, his name.

A box inside the walking machine made the best translations possible.

The diplomat was named Rococo, which was nothing but odd noise in her ears and she forgot it immediately.

"You have arrived," the emissary said wearily.

Everyone looked at the old woman, but suddenly and for no apparent reason she forgot how to speak.

The youngest husband broke the silence. "We have a gift for you. For your species. We brought it from our home, at great cost."

"I don't want it," Rococo said.

The old woman roused herself. With a quiet, tense voice, she said, "Take the box to him now. Take it."

"It is alien," said the older husband. "We found this artifact in the throat of a dead volcano."

"Very valuable," the other husband shouted.

Rococo stared at the gray box. "Leave it there," he ordered.

But the People were not listening or refused to understand. Terrific costs had been paid so that they could drag the box off the wagon and over the railcar's railing, metal screeching against metal as the alien wonder was dropped on the gemstones beside the mechanical feet.

Staring at the old woman, the emissary said, "I told you. What did I tell you? I was exceptionally clear about what I could and couldn't do for you."

From a special pouch came the key. But the woman was too nervous, and she didn't care who opened the treasure.

The girl found the key in her hand.

"We can't take just anybody onboard the Ship," the human insisted. Then with a thought, he caused a mechanical arm to unfold and reach down, grabbing the girl by her wrist.

She dropped the key.

"I have made agreements," said the human. "Following galactic law, we have binding arrangements with the most advanced species on this world. My species has purchased the right to begin terraforming your nearest moon, and in thanks for this blessing, we will give carry a small, small, small population of local People to a world that they will be able to colonize.

"This is binding and legal and I told you all of that before," he said. "I was honest. When did I mislead you? I told you not to bother with this pathetic migration, and you came anyway. I talked to you a hundred times in the night, warning you to turn around and head home again before it was too late. If I wasn't stationed here alone, I would have sent subordinates to the basin just to explain things to your flock. Which I should have done myself, and I see that now. I regret it all, yes."

The youngest husband grabbed the key, and with a blur of motion unfastened the lock and threw the lid over the side.

"Look," he shouted. "Look."

Rococo released the girl and grudgingly peered inside.

The girl fell to her knees, rubbing at the aching wrist. She wanted to look inside and didn't. Then the human beast told everyone, "This is a piece of hyperfiber, a shard of someone's hull. Hyperfiber is the most durable, persistent, and unremarkable kind of trash in this portion of the galaxy, which means that it is worth nothing."

The girl shook from nerves, exhaustion, and anguish.

Then the old woman stepped between the mechanical legs and under the arm, and with a passionate, practiced voice she said, "Of course it isn't enough. You told me, and I believed you, yes. But I have learned about your species, your nature. You know sympathy and empathy, and just like us, you understand how great deeds demand to be recognized. We are the last of our species. We have spent everything and sacrificed almost everything to place a few of us on your ground."

Rococo took a deep breath, and then gasped.

She moved her hands as a beggar would. "Take a few of us with you, please. We can select, or you can choose. I am prepared for either eventuality. But here we stand, surrounded by People who care nothing for us, and we have pushed ourselves to the brink of extinction, and if you don't give us this one little charity, our kind will vanish from the universe forever."

Rococo lifted one of his hands, and he lowered it again.

He did not know what to say next.

The old woman turned and said, "Marvel at what we have accomplished, my People. We must celebrate this wonderful fine day."

Katabasis stood. What happened next wasn't planned, but it wasn't an accident either. She intended to throw her fist but she wanted only to make the old woman stop talking, and the woman should have been bruised and startled. But she stumbled oddly and fell sideways into the box, and the rusted red corner of steel struck at the worst point on her head, and she died.

The two husbands and then the others attacked the girl.

With every mechanical arm and half of the legs, the emissary dragged the murderer away from the People. Then he threw curses and threats of much worse, hauling his prisoner back inside the ship where he intended to wait for some inspiration that would give him a route out of this miserable trap.

10

Clients walked past them and rode past them, some for the second and third time. It seemed that the story of the landslide and long subsequent march had gained a brief measure of fame. Everyone who met them on the trail, including their porters, asked when they would arrive at City West. Would it be today or tomorrow or maybe the day after? Katabasis promised they would finish tomorrow, probably late in the day, and then the other porter, the human, would name the clearing where they planned to camp tonight, begging the others to please leave it empty because they needed quiet even more than they needed food.

Save for two acid-polished jackets of bioceramic matter, their packs were nearly empty. They had one torch but no food and no bedding, and they drank their water straight from the river, and even the excess grams of fabric had been cut away from the packs and clothes, left behind in the jungle along with at least half of their body mass. They were battered gaunt skeletons taking tiny strides. They were crazy souls and heroes, and strangers were so impressed by what they knew of the story that they would turn short of the trail's end and come back around again, just to see them once more with their own mesmerized eyes.

Several clients mentioned that groups were gathering. Well-wishers would be waiting tomorrow at the edge of City West, and there might even be a small ceremony complete with treats suitable for brave, tenacious creatures like them.

By day's end, they were close enough to the City to hear individual voices mixed in with the normal urban sounds. Varid smelled food on the wind, his belly aching even worse. But as promised, they made their night's camp. Several tents had been left behind, each wearing notes and good wishes, and the two porters selected the largest tent and set the torch inside, turned up to full brightness, and when night arrived and the City changed its pitch, moving into nocturnal affairs, they climbed into the open and shouldered the cut-apart packs, carrying their clients down the dark, well-walked trail.

Neither porter fell in that last stretch.

The next six hundred meters took half of the night, but suddenly the jungle ended and the sky opened up, revealing a welcoming banner written in the human language. Apparently no one was certain about Katabasis' native language. But someone had managed to spell her name in the original Greek, which made her feel just a little sorry for slipping past this way. Then they slowly, slowly crept their way to the first street, and she waved for a cap-car, telling it that they were carrying two people needing to be given some rather extensive medical help.

Three kilometers were covered in two minutes. Autodocs were waiting at the entranceway, along with one of the habitat's landlords whose duty was to make certain that no paying customers had died.

"I left two porters under the mountain," Katabasis said.

"We know everything," he said testily. "As soon as arrangements can be made, we will start to dig."

Varid stared at the man and then turned to his colleague.

She put a finger in his mouth, which she had learned was a very good way to keep the man from talking.

The landlord belonged to that second species of People. He was a young man when the human emissary arrived, walking in the bug-carriage down the avenues of his home world. Now he was grown but would never grow old—a giant well-fed beast sporting purple and blue plumage. He and his kind had purchased the habitat for almost nothing. They had excellent minds for business and a natural flair for selling their wares, and the strange slow-motion nightmare that had just been lived by these two pathetic creatures was very good for business. The habitat was an investment to help pay for extras needed when they finally reached the colony world. That was the only reason why he didn't shout his disapproval. It was enough to offer a few gestures that were very similar to those used by Katabasis' species, leaving no doubt about his state of mind and how small his regard was for this hero and her monkey friend.

Perri and Quee Lee were left in the care of autodocs.

Katabasis removed her finger from the little wet mouth. Back inside the cap-car, she asked for the nearest dock, and they rode in silence. Then they slowly climbed out, and using a calm, reasoned tone, Varid mentioned that he would like something enormous to eat.

The salty little sea was home to one odd fish, tough as could be and worth any price. Katabasis suggested that for a dinner, and her companion bought ten kilos, both smoked and raw, and then they boarded the first ferry they could find, starting across the flat dark water.

They ate, and after a time Varid turned to her. "He looked like you."

"But we aren't the same," she said.

He nodded, and waited.

"We're like two species of monkeys," she said.

He stopped nodding. His face went blank in that way that she envied, as if he had the power to wash away his past and any urgent thoughts of the moment, existing in a quiet realm that she could only wish to know.

Then with no warning, Varid asked, "How did you come here?"

She considered. She leaned a long ways forward, and after one deep breath told the ferry to stop in the middle, please, and drift with the current and wait.

She killed the old woman once again, except not in her dreams but with words and a small sorry thrust of the fist.

Varid chewed at the raw fish, saying nothing.

"The human carried me inside his ship," she said, "and for two days he fed me and fed the People outside, and he spoke to them and to me and finally decided on a course of action and inaction. What I had endured was beyond any human experience, and he could not believe what we had accomplished. The local species— those standing thick on this world and the nearby volcanoes—were durable, yes, but not nearly as resilient as us. Against every instinct, he decided that we had proved our worth, and with that in mind, he would personally return the People to their former home. The buildings were still standing. With repairs, enough fans and dew-catchers could feed a small rebirth. And later, when human terraformers arrived in force, the People would supply most of the labor and all of the tenacity to making the inhospitable moon into a wondrous garden."

Varid swallowed and looked across the water. "I have an idea."

"I'm not finished," she said.

"I know," he said. "But don't let me forget to tell you my idea, please."

"I will remind you."

She ate and he ate, and then he said, "You are here."

"If Rococo had left me with my People, I would have been killed. But my crime occurred on the diplomat's ground, which was nearly the same as being on the Earth or inside the Great Ship. His laws ruled. He had the only authority. And according his laws, I needed to be tried in a fair court, which could only be found once he returned here."

"He saved you," Varid said.

"In a fashion, yes," she said. "I was frozen inside the shuttle's hold and defrosted on arrival and tried three years later and convicted of some lesser brutality. My sentence was short. Someone, probably Rococo himself, paid to have my body and mind rebuilt. But nobody has told me who holds this favor, which is the largest favor of all. Then as I was released from prison, the captains presented me with a bill for passage onboard the Great Ship—which will take fifty thousand years to make good, working as a porter, and that really is another gift, when you consider that you have forever to march across."

Her companion said nothing. He had stopped eating, and the face had shifted into another lost expression.

"You had an idea," she said.

"I did," he agreed.

They waited.

Just when she thought that he had forgotten the subject, Varid pushed his face close and said, "There are little passengers onboard the Ship. They are machines and intelligent parasites and such. And I have empty space inside my head. Has there ever been a porter willing to be filled with other souls, carrying his clients from the first step?"

"No," she said. "There never has been, no."

The sun was slowly coming to life overhead. She told the ferry to continue and turned back to Varid. "This is a worthy idea," she told him. "This is definitely a notion to twist in the light, to see how it plays."

Once again, at last, Katabasis walked her beach.

She couldn't sleep. Her body felt too tired to ever rest again. She moved weakly and breathed too much, and the familiar faces of her neighbors weren't quite certain who she was. Yet she felt stronger in every way but strength, strolling past her usual turning point and then coming back even slower. Her little house of quake-coral looked like a wonder from a distance. Two legs were sticking out of the door, and smiling with her hands and arms, she came up quietly and knelt down and looked inside.

Varid was on his back, his eyes closed.

She sat back and waited. Was he truly that exhausted? Was this his first real sleep in centuries? Then she leaned forward and looked again, watching the eyes bouncing under the barely closed lids.

Once more, she sat back.

But she couldn't resist. There finally came the moment when she put her shrunken weight on her arms and dipped her head, brushing his salty ankles with the full rough surface of her tongue.

the water thief

ALASTAIR REYNOLDS

Alastair Reynolds is a frequent contributor to Interzone, Asimov's Science Fiction, Spectrum SF, Arc, and elsewhere. His first novel, Revelation Space, was widely hailed as one of the major SF books of the year; it was quickly followed by Chasm City, Redemption Ark, Absolution Gap, Century Rain, and Pushing Ice, all big sprawling space operas that were big sellers as well, establishing Reynolds as one of the best and most popular new SF writers to enter the field in many years. He has written a novella collection, Diamond Dogs, Turquoise Days, and a chapbook novella, The Six Directions of Space, as well as three collections, Galactic North, Zima Blue and Other Stories, and Deep Navigation. His other novels include The Prefect, House of Suns, and Terminal World. His most recent novels are Blue Remembered Hills, and a Doctor Who novel, Harvest of Time. Forthcoming is a new novel, On the Steel Breeze. A professional scientist with a Ph.D in astronomy, he worked for the European Space Agency in the Netherlands for a number of years, but has recently moved back to his native Wales to become a full-time writer.

Reynolds's work is known for its grand scope, sweep, and scale (in one story, "Galactic North," a spaceship sets out on in pursuit of another in a stern chase that takes thousands of years of time and hundreds of thousands of light-years to complete; in another, "Thousandth Night," ultrarich immortals embark on a plan that will call for the physical rearrangement of all the stars in the galaxy). Here, he offers us a small, quiet story with a sharply defined, evenly constrained setting, one that manages to find something hopeful and uplifting to say about the human spirit even when its protagonist is living in a cardboard box in a refugee camp.

The boy wants my eye again. He's seen me using it, setting it down on the mattress where I squat. I am not sure why he covets it so badly.

"Sorry," I say. "I need this. Without it I can't work, and if I can't work, my daughter and I go hungry."

He is too small to understand my words, but the message gets through anyway. I smile as he sprints away, pausing only to glance over his shoulder. Nothing would prevent the boy creeping into the shipping container and taking the eye while I am working. But he has not done that yet. Something in his face makes me think he can be trusted.

You can't understate the value of that, here in the refugee camp. Not that they call it that. This is a "Resource and Relocation Assistance Facility." I have been here six years now. My daughter is twelve; she barely remembers the outside world. Eunice is a good and studious girl, but that will only get you so far. Both of us need something more. Prakash tells me that if I can accrue enough proficiency credits, we might be relocated.

I believe Prakash. Why wouldn't I?

I squat down on my mattress. The shipping container has had its doors removed and holes cut in the sides. Windchimes hang from one corner of the roof, cut from buckled aluminium tent-poles. On this airless afternoon they are as silent as stalagtites.

My virching rig isn't much. I have the eye, my lenses, my earphones and my T-shirt. All cheap, second-hand. I position the eye, balancing it on a shoebox until its purple pupil blinks readiness. I slip in the earphones. The T-shirt is ultramarine, with a Chinese slogan and some happy splashing dolphins. Too tight for a grown woman but the accelerometers and postural sensors still function.

I initiate the virching link. The lenses rinse me out of reality, into global workspace.

"Good afternoon, Prakash," I say.

His voice is near and far at the same time. "You're late, Soya. Had some nice jobs lined up for you."

I bite back my excuse. I have no interest in justifying myself to this man. This morning I had to walk twice as far to get clean water, because someone from a neighboring compound broke into our area. They damaged our pump as they tried to steal from it.

"I'm sure you still have something in the queue," I tell him.

"Yes . . ." Prakash says absently. "Let me see."

If God was a fly, this would be the inside of his head. Wrapping around me are a thousand constantly changing facets. Each represents a possible task assignment. The facets swell and contract as Prakash offers me options. There's a description of the job, the remuneration, the required skillset and earnable proficiency credits. The numbers swoop and tumble, like roosting birds.

"Road repair," Prakash declares grandly, as if this is meant to stir the soul. "Central Lagos. You've done that kind of thing before."

"No thanks. Pay is shit and a monkey could do it."

"Window cleaning. Private art museum, Cairo. They have some gala opening coming up, but their usual 'bot has broken."

"It's years since I cleaned windows."

"Always a tricky customer, Soya. People should be less choosy in life." He emits a long nasal exhalation like the air being let out of a tyre. "Well, what else have we. Bioremediation, Black Sea. Maintenance of algae bloom control and containment systems."

Cleaning slime from pumps, in other words. I scoff at the paltry remuneration. "Next."

"Underwater inspection, Gibralter bridge. Estimated duration eight hours, reasonable pay, at the upper end of your skills envelope."

"And I must fetch my daughter from school in three hours. Find me something shorter."

Prakash's sigh is long suffering. "Seawall repair, Adriatic coastline. Overnight storm breech. Four hours, high remuneration. They need this done quickly."

Typical of Prakash, always the job he knows I will not refuse until last.

"I'll need to make a call," I say, hoping that someone can collect Eunice from the school.

"Don't dilly-dally."

Prakash puts a hold on the assignment, and I get back to him just in time to claim it for myself. Not that I'm the only one on the task: the Adriatic breech is a local emergency. Hundreds of robots, civilian and military, are already working to rebuild shattered defenses. Mostly it is work a child could do, if a child had the strength of a hundred men—moving stone blocks, spraying rapid-setting concrete.

Later I learn that fifteen people drowned in that wall failure. Of course I am sad for these people—who wouldn't be? But if they had not died, I would not have had the assignment.

It is late when I finish. A breeze has picked up, sufficient to stir the chimes. The air is still oven-warm. I am thirsty and my back aches from lugging water.

From across the compound, diesel generators commence their nightly drone. I listen to the chimes, snatching a moment to myself. Their random tinkling makes me think of neurones, firing in the brain. I was always fascinated by the mind, by neuroscience. Back in Dar es Salaam I had ambitions to be a doctor.

I rise from the mattress and stretch away stiffness. I am on my way to collect Eunice when I hear a commotion, coming from somewhere near one of the big community tents. Trouble, of one kind or another. There is always something. Mostly it doesn't concern me, but I like to keep informed.

"Soya," a voice calls. It is Busuke, a friend of mine with two sons. "Eunice is fine," she tells me. "Fanta had to go, but she passed her onto Ramatou. You look tired."

Of course I look tired. What does she expect?

"Something going on?"

"Oh, didn't you hear?" Busuke lowers her voice conspiratorially. "They got that thief. She hadn't got very far—been stung by the electrified fence, was hiding out nearby, waiting to make a dash for the gap at sundown, when they apprehended her." Buskuke says "apprehended" as if there were quote marks around the word.

I did not know whether this thief was a man or a woman, but at least now I can pin my hate onto something. "I would not want to be in her shoes."

"They say she took a bit of a beating, before the peacekeepers came. Now there is a big argument about whether or not to keep giving her medicine."

"One woman won't make any difference."

"It's the principle," Busuke tells me. "Why should we waste a drop of water or antibiotics on a thief?"

"I don't know." I wish we could settle on a topic of conversation other than water. "I should go and find Ramatou."

"You work too hard," Busuke says, as if I have a choice.

The camp used to confuse me, but now I could walk its maze of prefabs and tents blindfolded. Tonight the stars are out. Plump and yellow, two-thirds full, the moon swims over the tents, rippling in heat. A fat moon brings out the worst in people, my mother used to say. But I'm not superstitious. It's just a rock with people on it.

My lenses tint it, tracing geopolitical boundaries. America, Russia, China, and India have the biggest claims, but there is a little swatch of Africa up there, and it gladdens me. I often show it to my daughter, as if to say, we can be more than this. This camp does not have to define you. You could do great things. Walk on the moon, one day.

I catch the rise of a swift bright star. It turns out to be a Japanese orbital power satellite, under assembly. I have heard about these stations. When they are built, when they are boosted to higher orbits, the satellites' mirrors will cup the sun's light and pour it down to Earth. The energy will be used to do useful things like the supplying of power to coastal desalination plants. Then we will be drowning in water.

It bothers me that I have never seen the power station before.

I collect my daughter from Ramatou. Eunice is in a bad mood, hungry and restless. I show her the moon but she is beyond distraction. There is no food at the nearest dispensary, but we catch a shred of a rumour about food in green sector. We are not meant to cross into that part of the camp, but we have done it before and no one has questioned us. Along the way Eunice can tell me how her day in school went, and I will tell her something of mine, of the poor people on the Adriatic coast.

Later, when she is asleep, I drift to the community tent. The mob has simmered down since earlier, but the place is still busier than usual.

I push my way through fellow refugees, until I am within sight of the water thief. They have her on a makeshift bed, a table with a mattress on, hemmed by white-coated peacekeepers and green-outfitted nurses. There is a doctor present now, a young Lebanese man. From his confident and authoritative demeanour, he must be on his first posting. It won't last. The long-stagers are nervous and jittery.

There are also three mantises. The medical robots are spindly but fearsome things, with too many limbs. Usually, there is a doctor at the other end, assisting the robot via a virching link, but not always. These are very complex, expensive machines and they can operate themselves.

This woman hasn't just been roughed up a bit. She has been beaten to the edge of death. One of the human medics changes the bag on a medical drip. The thief is unconscious, head lolling away from me. She doesn't look much older than Eunice. Her skin is a sea of bruises, burns, and cuts.

"They are going to vote," says Busuke, sidling up.

"Of course. Voting is what we do. If there is something to vote on, we vote."

I weary of our endless swirling micro-democracy. It is as if, while the great institutions of the world falter, we are obliged to reenact them in miniature here. A week doesn't go by when the black and white balls aren't drawn out for something.

"It's not about life and death," Busuke insists. "We're not going to *kill* this woman. Just withhold excessive treatment."

"Which wouldn't be the same."

"Why should the robots and doctors fuss over her, when they're needed elsewhere? And that medicine."

"They should have done us all a favour," I say. "Killed her outright, when they caught her."

It is brutal, but in that moment I mean it.

In the morning I catch sight of a screen, propped up on a pile of medical supply boxes. It shows a confusion of gleaming lines, racing to perspective points. Glittery shards, people and machines moving in weightlessness. The indigo curve of the earth, seen from above the atmosphere. Below, perfectly cloudless, is Africa, turning out of night. I think of waving to myself.

It turns out—I learn this in pieces, not all at once—that there has been an accident on the Japanese power station. An Indian tug has crashed into it, and now there is a race to rescue the construction workers. Of course, much of the work is being done by robots, but there are still dozens of men and women involved. Later I learn that the tug caused the station to tilt from its normal alignment, meaning that its mirrors were much brighter as seen from Earth.

There is a saying about ill winds. I would be lying if I said I did not wonder what good this calamity can do for me.

When I squat down before my wise purple eye and enter global workspace, Prakash is distracted. He has been rushed off his feet, brokering assignments. I dare ask if there is work for me in orbit.

"They need help," Prakash admits. "But remind me, Soya. What is your accumulated experience in space operations? How many hours logged, with both timelag and weightlessness?"

His question is rhetorical, but I furnish an honest answer. "Nothing. Zero hours. As you know."

"Well, then."

"It's an emergency. No one quibbled about my experience on the Adriatic seawall."

"That was different. Orbital operations are a world away from anything you know." Prakash pauses—his attention is elsewhere today. "I still have work for you. The world has not stopped turning, just because of this unfortunate business."

Today's offered assignments: helping a construction robot at the Saharan solar mirror project. Assisting a barnacle-scraper, on the belly of a Chinese supertanker. Running manual override on a tunnel project in the Tasman Straits.

I spurn these insults; settle finally for a low remuneration but high skills dividend job, helping one robot perform a delicate repair on another, at one of the Antarctic construction projects. It is a miserable, sodium-lit nightscape, barely inhabited. We are supposed to live in such places, when they are ready.

What matters is that it is work.

But I am not even halfway through the task when something goes wrong. A moment of nothing and then I am elsewhere. A bright parched landscape, blazing white under a sky that is a deep, pitiless black.

I voice a question to myself, aloud, thinking that someone, somewhere, may have the decency to answer.

"Where am I?"

I try to look around, and *nothing happens*. Then the view does indeed begin to track, and this landscape, weird as it is, strikes familiar notes. The ground undulates toward a treeless horizon, strewn with boulders and stones. Soft-contoured hills rise at an interdeterminate distance. There are no crags, no animals, or vegetation. Save for a kind of fence, stretching from one horizon to the other, there is no indication that humans have ever been there.

Then I see the body.

It is lying quite close by, and wearing a spacesuit.

I command the view to stop tracking. Again there is a delay before my intentions have effect.

It—he or she, I cannot decide—is lying on their back, arms at their side, legs slightly spread. Their visored face mirrors the sky. They could have been dropped there, like a discarded doll.

I take another look at that fence. It is a thick metal tube, wide enough that one might easily crawl through it, and it is supported above the ground on many "A"-shaped frames. There are joints in the tube, where one piece connects to another. I feel silly for not realising that it is a pipeline, not a fence.

I make my robot advance. My own shadow pushes ahead of me, jagged and mechanical. Whatever I am, I must be as large as a truck.

I angle down. I don't know much about spacesuits, but I cannot see anything wrong. No cracks in the visor, no obvious gashes or rips. The life-support equipment on the front, a rectangular chest-pack connected to the rest of it by tubes and lines, is still lit up. Part of it flashes red.

"Prakash," I say, in the hope that he might be hearing. "I could use some help here."

But Prakash does not answer.

I reach out with my arms. The robot follows suit with its own limbs. I am getting better at anticipating this timelag delay now, issuing my commands accordingly. Prakash need not have made such a big deal about it.

I scoop up the figure, sliding my arms under their body, as if they are a sack of grain and I am a forklift. Lunar soil curtains off them. They leave a neat human imprint.

The figure twitches and turns to look at me. I catch a reflection of myself in its visor; a golden behemoth of metal and plastic: some kind of truck, with multiple wheels and cameras and forward-mounted manipulators.

The figure moves again. They reach around with their right arm and scrabble at the chest-pack, touching controls with their thick-fingered moonglove. The lights alter their dance.

And I hear a man speak, and it is not Prakash.

"You found me." There are oceans of relief in his voice. "Starting to think I'd die out here."

The voice speaks English. I have picked up enough to suffice.

On the chance that the man may hear me, I ask him: "Who are you, and what has happened?"

There is a lapse before his answer comes back.

"You're not Shiga."

"I don't know who Shiga is. Did you have some kind of accident?"

It takes him time to answer. "There was an accident, yes. My suit was damaged. Who are you?"

"Nobody, and I don't know why they've given me this job. Are you going to be all right?"

"Suit's in emergency power conservation mode. It'll keep me alive, but only if I don't move around."

I think I understand. The life-support system would have to work much harder to sustain someone who was active. "And now? You did something to the chest-pack?"

"Told it to turn off the distress beacon, and give me enough power to allow for communication. It's still running very low."

He is still lying in my arms, like a child.

"You thought I was someone else."

"What did you say your name was?"

"I didn't. But it is Soya. Soya Akinya. And you?"

"Luttrell. Michael Luttrell. Can you get me out of here?"

"It would help if I knew where we are. How did you get here?"

"I drove in. The overlander, the thing you're controlling. Shiga was meant to take control, help me back aboard, drive me home."

"Do you want to climb aboard? I presume there is a cabin, or something."

"Just a seat, behind your camera. No pressurisation. Let me try. I'll feel safer up there."

I lower him nearly to the ground, then watch as he eases stiffly from my arms. His movements are slow, and I am not sure if that is due to the suit or some injury or weakness within him. Both, perhaps. His breathing is laboured and he stops after only a few paces. "Oxygen low," he says, his voice little more than a whisper.

Luttrell passes out of my field of vision. My view tilts as his weight transfers onto me. After long moments, his shadow juts above my own.

"Are you all right?"

"I'm good."

I pan my camera up and down the pipeline. "Which way?"

He takes a while to gather his breath, and even then his voice is ragged. "Turn and follow the tracks."

I make a wide turn with the overlander. It's not hard to pick out the furrows my wheels have already dug into the soil. They arrow to the horizon, straight except where they kink to avoid a boulder or slope.

"Away from the pipeline?" I query. "I thought we would follow it, one way or the other."

"Follow the tracks. You should be able to get up to fifty kilometres per hour without too much difficulty."

I pick up speed, following the tracks, trusting that they will keep me from harm. "How long will it take us?"

"Three, four hours, depending."

"And do you have air and power?"

"Enough."

"How long, Luttrell?"

"If I don't talk too much . . ." He trails off, and there is a lengthy interval before I hear him again. "I have enough. Just keep driving."

Before very long the pipeline has fallen away behind us, stolen from view by the moon's curvature. It is a small world, this. But still big enough when you have a journey to make, and a man who needs help.

Luttrell is silent, and I think he is either asleep or has turned off his communications link.

This is when Prakash returns, unbidden.

"Finally," he says. "Starting to think you'd vanished into workspace."

"I did not choose this assignment."

"I know, I know." I think of him waving his hands, brushing aside my point as if it is beneath discussion. "It was an emergency. They needed someone with basic skills."

"I have never been called into space, Prakash. Why have I suddenly been deemed good enough for this?"

"Because everyone who really *does* have the skills is trying to sort out that mess at the Japanese station. Look on it as your lucky day. It won't count as weightless work, but at least you'll be able to say you've worked with timelag."

It may not be weightless, I think sourly, but surely working under lunar gravity must count as something. "We'll talk about it when I am done. Now I have to get this man to help."

"You've done your bit. The people on the Moon would like you to turn ninety degrees to your right, parallel to the pipeline, and maintain that heading. Once that's done, you can sign off. The vehicle will take care of itself. The hard part was helping get the body . . . the man . . . onto the truck. You've come through that with flying colours."

As if I had done something altogether more demanding than simply scooping a man off the ground.

"Luttrell told me to follow his tracks."

"And Luttrell is . . . ? Oh, I see. Luttrell spoke to you?"

"Yes, and he was very insistent." I feel a prickle of foreboding. "What is going on, Prakash? Who is Luttrell? What was he doing out here?"

"How much do you know about Lunar geopolitics, Soya? Oh, wait. That'd be 'nothing at all.' Trust me, the best thing you can possibly do now is turn ninety degrees and bail out."

I think about this. "Luttrell? Can you hear me?"

There is a very long silence before he replies. "Did you say something?"

"You were asleep."

"It's stuffy in here."

"Luttrell, try to stay awake. Are you sure there are people at the end of this trail?"

The time it takes him to answer, I may as well have asked him to calculate the exact day on which he was born. "Yes. Shiga, the others. Our camp. It's not more than two hundred kilometres from the pipeline."

Three, four hours, then, exactly as he predicted. "Prakash, my broker, says I should head somewhere else. Along the pipeline, to our left."

For once, Luttrell seems alert. "No. No, don't do that. Just keep moving, this heading. Back the way I came."

"If I went the other way, how long before we hit civilisation?"

Now Prakash cuts in again. "Less than a hundred kilometres away, there is a pressurised maintenance shack. That's his best chance now."

"And who is the expert now?"

"This is what they tell me. Luttrell won't make it back to his camp. They are very insistent on this point."

"Luttrell seems very insistent as well. Should we not listen to the man who actually lives here?"

"Just do as you are told, Soya."

Do as I am told. How many times have I heard that in my life, I wonder? And how many times have I obeyed? When the Resource and Relocation people came, with their trucks, helicopters and airships, with their bold plans for human resettlement, I—along with many millions of others—did exactly as I was told. Gave up on the old world, embraced the diminished possibilities of the new.

And now I find myself squatting on a dirty mattress, under a creaking corrugated roof, while my body and mind are on the moon and I am again being told that someone else, someone I have never met, and who will never meet me, knows best.

"Don't turn around," Luttrell says.

"You had better be right about this camp of yours."

Prakash cuts in again. "Soya, what are you doing? Luttrell has transgressed internationally recognised Lunar boundaries. He has attempted to take what does not belong to him. The man is a thief."

As if I had not worked that out for myself.

I think of the fat full moon, daubed with the emblems of nations and companies. Only a few thousand people up there now, but they say it will soon be tens of thousands. Blink, and it will be millions.

And I have watched the news and tried to keep myself informed. I know that some of those territorial boundaries are disputed. There are claims and counter-claims. Even our little thumbnail of African soil has not been immune to these arguments.

So this man, Luttrell. What of him? He had driven to the pipeline, not along it but from somewhere else. Maybe he tried to tap into it. Something happened to him. An electrical shock, perhaps, damaging the systems of his suit. He had hoped that help would come from his own people, from Shiga. Instead what he got was me. And while my people—the people who know best—do not exactly want to kill Luttrell, it cannot be said that keeping him alive is their main consideration.

What they want, above all else, is for him not to get home.

"I am not turning, Prakash. I am taking this man back to his friends."

"I wouldn't do that, Soya. You're only on the Moon under our sufferance. We can pull you out of the link at any moment, slot someone else in."

"Who will do as they are told?"

"Who knows what's good for them."

"Then that is not me."

Prakash is right: I can be pulled from the link at any time. Or rather, he would be right, if I did not have so much experience at driving robots. Scraping barnacles off a supertanker, scudding across the moon: nothing much changes. And I know the tricks and dodges that will make it difficult or time-consuming for the link to be snapped. I have seldom had cause to use these things, but they are well remembered.

"Will you get into trouble for this?" Luttrell says.

"I think the damage is already done."

"Thank you." He is silent again. "I think I need to stay awake. Maybe if you told me something about yourself, that would help."

"There is not much to tell. I was born in Dar es Salaam, around the turn of the century."

"Before or after?"

"I don't know. My mother never knew. There would have been records, I suppose. But I have never seen them." I steer us around a boulder as large as the overlander itself. "It doesn't matter. That's all over now. Now tell me where you came from."

He tells me his story. We drive.

In the morning the dust settles. My refusal to obey Prakash has not gone unpunished. Proficiency ratings have been set back to zero. Black marks have been set against my name, forbidding whole categories of employment. The credits I ought to have earned from the last task—I did, after all, save Luttrell—have failed to appear.

But I am resigned to my fate. It is not the end of the world, or at least not the end of mine. There are other types of work out here. Whatever is in store for me, I shall make the best of it. Just as long as it keeps my daughter from starvation.

On the way to the school, Eunice asks me what I did last night.

"Helped a man," I say. "He did a bad thing, but I helped him anyway. That has made some people angry."

"What did the man do?"

"It's complicated. He took something that wasn't his, or tried to. We'll talk about it later."

I think of Luttrell. When they finally broke me out of the link, we were still some way from his camp. I don't know what happened after that. I hope his people were able to find him. I watch the news, but there's nothing. It's a border incident, that's all. Not worth a mention.

While she is in school, I go to the community tent where the water thief awaits her verdict. The place is crowded, the atmosphere volatile. The mantises have withdrawn: they have done their work, the patient has been stabilised, she is mostly conscious. I study the fluid in the women's drip and imagine that it is pure water. I think of gulping down its sweet clear contents.

I shoulder my way through the onlookers to the low trestle table, where the votes are being administered. I tell them who I am, although I think by now they know. A finger tracks down a list, a line is scratched through my name. I am invited to cast my vote. There are black balls and white balls, in open-topped cardboard medicine boxes.

I scoop up one ball from each box, both in one hand. For a moment the possibilities feel equally balanced. In the end, it is the white ball that I let go, the black one that I return to its box. Someone else can have that pleasure.

Leaving the community tent, I try to gauge the public mood. My sense is that it will not go well for this women. But perhaps the nurses, doctors, and mantises have already done enough. Perhaps the water thief will be strong enough, with or without medicine.

I am thinking what to do next when something tugs at my hem. It is the little boy, the one who is always following me. I reach into my pocket and feel the fat round bulge of the eye. I think about the purple light, how pretty it is. The eye has been my vigil and my gateway, but I don't have much use for it now.

I tell the boy to hold out his hand. He obeys.

nightside on callisto

LINDA NAGATA

Here's a fast-paced adventure in which a group of old women (chosen because they're expendable, being already near the end of their probable lifespans anyway) overseeing a very risky engineering project on one of Jupiter's moons, Callisto, must fight off a robot revolt, an attack on the station by murderous construction machinery, with little more than their own courage and shrewdness to rely on in the battle. . . .

Linda Nagata grew up in a rented beach house on the north shore of Oahu. She graduated from the University of Hawaii with a degree in zoology and worked for a time at Haleakala National Park on the island of Maui. She has been a writer, a mom, a programmer of database-driven Web sites, and lately a publisher and book designer. She is the author of multiple novels and short stories including The Bohr Maker, *winner of the Locus Award for Best First Novel, and the novella "Goddesses," the first online publication to receive a Nebula award. She lives with her husband in their longtime home on the island of Maui. Find her online at:*

MythicIsland.com, twitter.com/LindaNagata, and facebook.com/Linda .Nagata.author

A faint, steady vibration carried through the igloo's massive ice walls—a vibration that shouldn't have been there. Jayne heard it in her sleep. Age had not dulled her soldier's reflexes, honed by decades spent on watch against incursions of the Red. Her eyes snapped open. She held her breath. The vibration hummed in the walls, in the bed frame, in the mattress, perceivable even over Carly's raspy breathing.

Jayne reminded herself that the Red was far, far away, its existence bound to Earth, where it bled through every aspect of life—a relentless tide of information and influence shepherding the thoughts and actions of billions along paths determined by its unknowable goals. Whether the Red was alive, or aware, Jayne couldn't say, and she had no opinion either on its virtue. She only wanted to keep it out of the Shell Cities. Most of her life had gone to the long defense of their growing union, an association of scattered orbital habitats determined to stay free of the Red. But in retirement, Jayne had found new opportunities.

Less than twenty-four hours ago, her team of four had touched down on Callisto,

Jupiter's outermost Galilean moon and the only one that lay beyond the gas giant's killing radiation belts. A raft of construction equipment had preceded them, including a gang of ten small mechs that had assembled a sprawling igloo in time for them to move in. It was the team's task to establish a prototype ice-mining station to supply the expansion of the Shell Cities.

Maybe the vibration was generated by some new construction activity at the launch rail? Probably that was it. But "probably" never was a sufficient explanation. Jayne slipped out from under the shared blanket, careful not to wake Carly, who'd crawled into bed just an hour ago. Each team member worked a staggered, twelve-hour shift. Jayne had taken the first rotation, and her night was almost through.

The air-skin membrane lining the walls and the ceiling sensed her movement and responded with a glimmer of vague gray illumination. Jayne stood up slowly on sleep-stiffened limbs. A century of existence had left her thin and tough and inclined to feel cold, so over a foundation of thermal underwear she added insulated slacks, a pullover of the same material, thin gloves for her hands, and cozy house boots for her feet—one more layer in the cocoon that protected them from the cold and vacuum beyond the igloo's walls.

Jayne knew with utter certainty that they were alone in Jupiter system. The Red could not be here—the light speed lag in information flow kept it confined near Earth—and no other expedition had ventured so far in years. So their team was on its own, with no back up if something went wrong—which was why the four of them had been awarded this project: they were each experienced, competent, and expendable.

The bed chamber was sealed off from the rest of the igloo by an air-skin lock. Jayne touched the membrane. It felt smooth and hard beneath her gloved hand, but when she swept her fingers across it, the skin lock responded, pulling aside in neat, glassy ripples.

Massive blocks of ancient ice made up the igloo's walls and ceiling, insulating the interior spaces from background radiation, but it was the air skin that made the igloo habitable. A semi-intelligent, quasi-living tissue, the skin lined every chamber, locking in pressure, and providing heat and fresh air. If perforated it would self-seal, and its motility allowed it to repair even major tears.

Jayne stepped past the plastic-panel door into a central alcove with toilets and shower on either side. Two steps ahead, a lock on the right stood open to the easy room with its cushy inflatable furnishings, food stores, and oven, while on the left, another open lock hooked up to HQ, where the work was done. Jayne heard Berit speaking. She couldn't make out the words, but Berit's sharp, angry tone confirmed Jayne's first suspicion: something had gone wrong.

Jayne resisted the impulse to sprint into HQ. Age and experience had taught her to always attend to basics, so she slipped into the toilet first, and only when that necessity was out of the way did she trot around the corner.

Berit heard her coming and greeted her with a scowl. She was ninety-nine, an age that could be seen in the translucence of her brown skin, in the drape of tissue around her stern eyes, and in the thinning of her bright white hair. Like Jayne, Berit had lived most of her life as a soldier in the defense force and like Jayne, she'd been lucky, surviving to tell the tale. The two women had partnered on more assignments than either cared to remember. "What woke you up?" Berit snapped.

"The smell of trouble. Why am I hearing tones of displeasure in your voice?"

"Because I am not pleased."

Lorelei was their civilian engineer, a petite, soft-spoken woman who, at a hundred-and-three, was older even than Jayne. She provided more details without turning away from a 3-D model of the station. "Our mechs are tainted. Something's gotten into them and they aren't accepting commands."

"The Red followed us here," Berit added, with fatalistic certainty.

When Jayne joined them, they made a circle around the model. "How?"

Lorelei looked up, her deep blue eyes nestled in the folds and rough texture of her dark skin. Her hair was brilliant white and still thick despite the years, confined in a heavy braid at her shoulder. She opened her mouth to speak—and a high-pitched whistle screamed through the igloo. Jayne's ears popped. The air-skin lock rustled shut, sealing HQ from the rest of the station and muting the whistle, but Jayne could still hear a distant wail of escaping air.

"Pressure suits!" she barked. "Now! Go!"

The suits hung ready on the wall beside the external lock. Jayne had taken only two steps toward them when a faint *pop!* put an end to the whistle. The igloo shuddered as massive ice blocks groaned against each other. *Goddamnit*, Jayne thought, grabbing two suits and tossing them to Berit and Lorelei. *Goddamnit, if the roof comes down . . .*

They'd celebrated when they'd won this mission, knowing they'd gotten it because it *was* risky and because they were old. Medical technologists in the Shell Cities had learned to minimize the deterioration of old age so that hale and healthy lifespans stretched past a century, but inevitable, catastrophic failure still loomed: a blood vessel bursting in the brain, a heart chamber undergoing sudden collapse, a lung growing irreparably brittle. The cold fact was, none of them had much time left. If they didn't survive this mission, well, only a handful of unlived years would be lost. But in the meantime they were privileged to set foot on one of Jupiter's moons and to have the chance of leaving the Shell Cities just a little more secure.

And the goddamned roof was *not* going to come down. Not if Jayne could help it.

She grabbed a third pressure suit and stepped into it, pulling the edges together to let it seal.

A pressure suit was just another form of air skin, made to wrap around the body. An inch thick in most places, it was powered by slender, flexible fuel cells embedded across the back. Robotic carbon-fiber hands at the sleeve ends exactly mimicked every twitch of Jayne's own fingers, which remained safe and warm within the sleeves.

Using an artificial hand, Jayne reached up and grabbed her hood, preventing it from sealing. Lorelei and Berit were still wrapping their suits on. "Lorelei, stay here and get those mechs in order. Berit, get outside and figure out what the hell just happened. I'm going after Carly."

She released her hood, not waiting for an answer. It rolled across her face, where it sealed, shaped, and hardened.

The air-skin lock to the central alcove had sealed, but the color-coded indicator glowed green, confirming full pressure beyond. Jayne passed through, carrying Carly's suit with her. The lock sealed again behind her.

A glance around the alcove confirmed all the locks had closed. Those to HQ, the easy room, and the toilets, showed green, but the indicator beside the bedchamber flashed in calamitous red.

Jayne bit down on the inside of her lip, remembering Carly's warmth and her good humor. "Berit?"

"I'm heading out now," she answered over the suit radio. Then, "*Oh.*" A single word, the pain in it as sharp as shattered ice. "I see what you're looking at."

"I'm going in." Jayne brushed her fingers across the skin lock. Her suit stiffened as air was evacuated from the alcove, and for a moment she couldn't move. Then the suit's crosslinked cells adapted to the pressure change, and once again sensors picked up the motion of her body and echoed it, moving as she moved, tripling her strength—though if the power unit ever ran down, the pressure suit would become her diamond coffin.

She still held onto Carly's suit, for all the good it would do.

The air skin opened. Light that didn't belong illuminated the bedchamber with a faint glow. Their station was sited away from Jupiter and the Sun was too far away to make a difference, but a small measure of starlight spilled in through a ragged hole, three-feet wide and slanting up through a massive block of ice. The light wasn't enough to make out any details until the suit's faceplate switched to nightvision. Then Berit's voice sighed over the com. "Oh, *Carly.* Blood-red piss! She was trying to get to the lock!"

Carly's body lay face down against the floor, her legs and hips crushed beneath the ice that had fallen from the ceiling. Her fate had been set the moment Jayne decided to leave her sleeping—while Jayne's own bitter luck still held.

She forced herself to look away from the body, to look up. The air skin had been ripped open around the deep, ragged hole in the ice roof. Its tattered edges writhed, questing blindly for each other. More and more of it peeled away from the low ceiling, from the walls. It would keep peeling, until the torn edges could reach each other, and then it would seal. All this, Jayne took in at a glance—and then she noticed movement, just outside the hole: a mech, outlined against the stars.

All ten of the station mechs were the same model. They had a core carapace in the shape of a disk and roughly the size of a seat cushion, mounted on three highly flexible, telescoping legs. Each hemisphere of the carapace had a working arm. The upper half could swivel, so that the two arms could be positioned at any angle to one another. Most often, though, the arms were combined into a single limb for additional strength. By default, mechs stood with their legs at full extension, making them roughly waist high. Half-inch circles of cold blue light dotted their legs and made a glowing belt around their carapaces.

The mech on the igloo's roof had a subordinate drill unit set up at the edge of the hole. The drill was just a tool with no onboard intelligence. Its cylindrical column waited motionless, while the mech paced around it in what looked like frantic indecision. Jayne felt her skin crawl, watching it. Mechs should not behave that way. She wondered what directive had brought it to the igloo's roof.

"Lorelei?"

"Here." Lorelei's voice was a choked whisper.

"Tell me that mech showed up to repair the damage."

"I don't know why it's there. I can't know. Its directives have been changed. I can't get any data out of it. I can't get any instructions in. The mechs are talking to each other, but they won't communicate with me."

Mechs possessed a limited machine intelligence. Though they could learn by experience, they weren't remotely self-aware, and still . . . the directives that guided them could result in behavior that imitated volition in a truly unsettling way.

As Jayne watched, one of the mech's arms darted under its belly, then flashed out again, dropping a finger-sized cylinder through the hole. The cylinder fell in slow motion, bouncing off the mound of fallen ice before tumbling to the floor. A bang rod, Jayne realized—a small explosive used by the mechs to quarry the granite-hard ice at Callisto's surface.

"Get down!" Berit screamed over the suit's com system. Jayne was already moving, diving behind the bed just before the bang rod exploded with a brilliant flash. The floor jumped, a flash of heat washed past, and then Jayne rolled, the suit providing a smooth muscle-assist to get her to her feet again.

Ice flakes and frozen flecks of blood dropped like snow, blanketing a shallow crater, and the raw, red, frozen mass that had been Carly's body.

"Lorelei," Jayne asked in a steely voice, "did that mech just try to blow me up?"

Lorelei's mind was on other things. She spoke in breathy excitement. "I just found a record of a transmission from the landing pod, right before everything fell apart—"

"What are you talking about? The landing pod's sitting empty outside our front door. It's powered down."

"Power's back on," Lorelei said, her voice breaking. "There's some device in it we didn't know about. We're at war, Jayne—"

"I goddamn well know that!"

"—and we've just been hit! Whatever was in the pod pumped tainted directives into the mechs and changed their access codes. God knows what they're programmed to do now—"

"They're programmed to sabotage this mission," Berit growled over the com. "Because the Red doesn't want us growing. We should have seen this coming."

Jayne watched the mech reach out with a mechanical hand, disconnecting the tether that tied it to the drill subordinate. A second mech appeared, and immediately hopped down through the hole, dropping into the bedchamber with dreamlike lethargy. It was still falling when a six-inch jet of tightly focused blue flame spat from a torch gripped in its mechanical arm. Jayne fell back as it landed in the blast crater. Its telescoping legs flexed to absorb the impact, and then flexed again as it launched itself at her.

Screams filled the com, but Jayne ducked nimbly aside. The mech's carapace spun around as it landed, its arm extended as it tried to rake her with the torch. But it had been built for construction, not battle. Jayne was faster.

Dodging the flame, she threw herself on top of it, landing chest-first on its carapace. To her surprise, its legs collapsed under her weight. She rode it to the floor, using the suit's mechanical hands to hold onto its arm, forcing the fiery torch away from her face. With the suit's muscle-assist, she had as much strength as the mech, and to her astonishment, it stopped struggling after just a few seconds. Its torch switched off.

"What just happened?" Jayne whispered.

Lorelei answered over the com. "It summoned a crane to get the weight off its back. Logical response to baseline directive: 'don't damage yourself.' Now shut it down."

"How?"

"There's a panel on the carapace. Don't shift your weight. Just feel for it."

Jayne scowled. She was holding the mech's arm with both her mechanical hands, but now, cautiously, she let one go. As her carbon-fiber fingers slid around the carapace, the suit replicated the texture for her organic fingers. She found the panel, popped the release, slipped her hand inside.

"This is a whole keypad! What am I supposed to do?"

"Lower two corners. Top center. Press them all at once. Hold them down."

Jayne did it, suddenly aware of a faint vibration within the mech, only because it ceased.

"That's it," Lorelei said grimly. "One down. Nine to go."

But the mech didn't look like it had been shut down. The lights on its legs and carapace still glowed. "Lorelei, why are the lights still on?"

"They're self-powered. Ever tried finding a quiescent mech in the dark?"

Jayne snorted. "So that's it? That's all there is to it? We just switch them off? This is going to be—"

"Lorelei!" Berit's voice cut across the com, edged in panic. "Get outside now! Mechs are above you, drilling on the roof. Jayne—"

"On my way."

First, though, Jayne took the torch from the switched-off mech and used it to cut a five-foot length out of the twisted remains of the plastic bed frame. Steel would have been better, but at least now she had a weapon with better reach than the torch.

The torn air skin had continued to peel off the wall, rolling down so far that it was writhing around her, its raw edges beginning to seal. Jayne took a giant step to get on top of it. Then she lobbed her plastic rod through the hole in the roof, vaulting after it with a powerful muscle-assist from the suit.

Under Callisto's low gravity, she shot up through the hole. Her mechanical fingers hooked over the rim of ice and she hauled herself out onto the roof.

The igloo's ice blocks had been quarried from beneath the dusty regolith. Impurities in the ice infused it with a gray, piebald cast that gleamed only faintly under the star-spangled sky. The land around was even darker: a gray, granular plane that rolled away to low, encircling hills with steep profiles that rose in black outline against the stars. Frost glimmered faintly, looking like a mist laid across the rounded peaks.

The construction site was a half mile away, on flat ground, where steel bars for the launch rail were piled up into their own small hill. The mechs should have been at work on the rail bed, but Jayne saw nothing moving out there. Closer in, the landing pod crouched on bent legs, sparkling like gold foil. Jayne spotted two mechs loitering near it. Then she turned, to look across the flat roof.

The blast hole was close to one end. In the open area beyond it Berit chased a retreating mech. Another circled around to where three drill units bored into the ice above HQ, each one sending up a plume of frost that glittered in the starlight. Jayne imagined the mechs' simple logic: drills bore holes into ice; bang rods drop into holes; heavy, ice-insulated roofs get blown asunder.

The third mech on the roof was the one that had dropped the bang rod. It skittered toward her around the edge of the blast hole, but it didn't have a torch and it had already used its explosive. Jayne didn't see how it could be dangerous, so she circled the hole to meet it.

It saw her move, and hesitated.

Jayne didn't. Taking two long strides, she threw herself at it, just as she had with the other—but this mech anticipated her. Its legs flexed and it jumped out of reach. Jayne slammed against the roof, sliding several feet past the hole, only remembering to dig in with her mechanical fingers a moment before she went hurtling over the roof's edge.

Over the com, Berit's breath came fast and heavy. "Guess what, Jaynie? The mechs have figured out that move. I can't get near them."

Jayne groaned—"Thanks for letting me know"—and got back onto her feet.

The mech stood, unmoving, a few meters away. "It looks confused," Jayne muttered. Maybe it didn't know what to do next; maybe its directives didn't include all the necessary details of murder when the first assault had failed.

Unlike the mech, Jayne could come up with alternatives.

An image of the blood-red pulp of Carly's body flashed across her mind. Returning to the hole, she grabbed the abandoned drill unit. The tool probably massed as much as she did, but this was low-grav Callisto and Jayne was wearing a powered suit. It was no problem at all to hurl the drill straight at the mech's carapace.

The mech ducked by collapsing its telescoping legs. It dropped with astonishing speed and the drill shot harmlessly past it, spinning away in a trajectory that took it beyond the roof and far out over the gray flats. So. Projectiles weren't going to work. Jayne bent to retrieve her plastic staff, determined to give that a try. As she straightened up again, the two mechs from below vaulted onto the roof above HQ.

One at a time, Jaynie, she reminded herself, and with an overhead stroke she brought the rod down hard against the first mech's carapace. The staff snapped in two. The mech took no damage at all. Jayne flung away the remnant in disgust. So much for that idea—and now they had to contend with four mechs on the roof instead of just two.

The drills were unattended, but they continued to work, boring ever deeper into the igloo. Jayne turned her attention to them. There was no way she was going to let another chamber get blown. She bounded past the blast hole, toward the nearest drill. Ice flakes showered her as she reached it.

The drill stood thigh high, a slender cylinder hot enough to turn the falling flakes to vapor. Jayne grabbed it with her mechanical hand and yanked—but bolts locked it to the ice. She crouched, searching the drill for a panel like the one on the mech, but she couldn't find one.

"Lorelei, you still alive?"

"So far."

"How do I shut off a drill?"

"You don't unless you know how to send drill codes."

"Fine, then. Berit? Watch my back." Flicking on the torch she'd taken from the mech, Jayne started cutting. The drill shook when she sliced away the first bolt holding it to the ice. It bucked when she cut the second. And then it shut down. Safety override?

Two other drills were running. With Berit standing guard, she cut bolts on both of them, and when they unbalanced, they shut down too.

"Nice," Berit said. "But we still have nine hostile mechs to contend with." She was standing a few feet away, jumping at any mech that dared to come close.

"Lorelei," Jayne asked, "where are you?"

"In the landing pod."

Jayne glanced at the gold-foil dome resting on the regolith below. The door was closed. "Okay, stay there. Berit, let's get out to the construction site, pick up some explosives and maybe a rebar or two to smash these Red traitors."

"Jayne, no!" Lorelei snapped. "Do *not* damage the mechs!"

"Oh," Berit said. "I guess you didn't see her hurl that drill unit."

"What?" Lorelei sounded outraged. "Jayne, we need the mechs. Every one of them, or this project fails."

"We've already lost the mechs," Jayne shot back. She longed to get her mechanical hands around a steel rebar and test that against a carapace, maybe find out what a mech was made of inside. "Carly is dead and this project *has* failed."

"Carly is dead," Lorelei agreed, speaking softly now, hurriedly. "But we're still here and the Shell Cities are still going to need every crystal of water we can send them and we're not going to be able to send even one drop without mechs to build the launch rail. I am *not* lifting off from here until that rail is built."

"Goddamn it, Lorelei. You're the expert on the mechs, and you said you can't communicate with them, you can't override their rogue programming—"

"I can't! Not until they're shut down. *Manually* shut down, each and every one of them, just like that mech in the bedchamber." Her voice softened again. "Then they can be reset to factory specs. They won't know how to build anymore, but we can teach them that."

Jayne turned to Berit. Her faceplate was black in the dim light, but her bitter mood came through in her voice. "You hear that, Jaynie? The first rule of this little battle is 'do no harm.' You better give me that torch before the rule slips your mind."

Lorelei wanted to close off the honey hole.

The mechs had a hybrid, bio-mechanical architecture that required them to re-supply and re-power every twelve hours or so inside the honey hole—an excavated ice cave out by the construction site, stocked with fuel cells and organic supplies.

Jayne, though, wasn't willing to leave four functioning mechs on the roof. Three of them probably still had bang rods. Why didn't they use them? Maybe they didn't know how. Without a drill hole to stuff them into or a blast hole to toss them down, their simple behavioral algorithms might be stymied.

They could learn, though. They'd watched Jayne take down a mech and now they retreated if Jayne or Berit approached them. But if the women turned their backs, the mechs approached, carrying torches and saws in their mechanical hands like a pod of metallic zombies.

"Hey," Jayne said. "I'm going to walk away. If one starts to follow, you fall in behind. Push it close to me."

Berit nodded. "Go."

Jayne set off at a slow pace across the roof.

Berit hissed. "All four are behind you."

Jayne didn't turn to look. Instead, she picked up the feed from Berit's helmet and watched the mechs coming after her at a disturbingly fast pace. They were eight meters away, seven, six—one walked in front, two followed, and the fourth came behind. Berit trailed them, several steps back.

"I'll take the one closest to me," Jayne said.

"I'll get the laggard."

"Three, two, one, *now*."

Jayne turned and jumped. The mech she'd targeted jumped too, but not fast enough. They hit in midair. She spilled over its back, but managed a clawed grip on its carapace, hauling it down with her. It had a torch. She scrambled on top of it, holding its arm down with her foot. Flame touched ice, vapor roiled up, turning almost instantly into snow, while beneath her weight the mech went still. Jayne popped open its panel and slammed mechanical fingers down on the three keys, but she was breathing too hard to feel the mech's faint vibrations; she couldn't tell if the vibrations had stopped. "Did it shut down?" she panted. "Did it?"

"Move!" Berit shouted.

Jayne saw the bright blue light of another torch darting toward her face. She rolled. A line of heat seared her forearm, followed by a blade of cold. A muscle-assist popped her back onto her feet as two torches jabbed toward her. She jumped back, pursued by a pair of mechs, each with a torch in one hand, a saw in the other. Pain like a vice gripped her forearm.

She glanced at the wound. The torch had cut a line in her suit, but it had not cut quite through. She pinched the burnt edges together, helping the suit's healthy tissue to meet and seal. Then she jumped again to avoid the oncoming mechs. With chagrin, she realized they'd learned to work together in their attack—doubtless from the very recent example of cooperative assault that she and Berit had shown them.

"Okay, Jaynie?" Berit asked.

"So far."

They'd brought down one mech each, but there were still two more on the roof. Both pursued Jayne, torches out in a coordinated rush—until Berit tackled one from behind. It went down. Berit slapped open the panel, decommissioned it, and was up again in seconds, while Jayne led the last one on a merry chase.

A column of snow marked every dropped torch. Jayne wove between them to distract the mech, while Berit stood still, trying to go unnoticed in the mech's busy visual field. Jayne slipped past her, the mech followed, and Berit pounced. Her breathing came ragged over the com. "That's five down, five to go."

Jayne made a quick circuit of the roof, gathering up the torches and switching them off before they could melt all the way down to the membrane. "*Now* we take care of the honey hole."

Berit was still pulling hard for air. "I hope you're planning to help out a little more this time."

Jayne snorted. "I thought it was very noble of me, to be the bait."

They jumped down from the roof. Lorelei came out of the gold-foil dome of the pod. She held up a rectangular wafer for them to see. It was no more than one by two inches, thin as foil. "Light a torch," she said.

Jayne complied. The blue flame was a needle in the dark. "That's it, then? That's the source of the rogue code? And it's the only one?"

"It's the only one I could find." Lorelei laid the wafer down on the ice and stepped back. "Burn it."

Jayne did. Then she ground it with her boot and burned the remnants again.

As they crossed the dusty regolith to the construction site, Jayne spotted a flock of tiny lights a few hundred yards away. "The mechs," she announced. If not for the glowing circles dotting their legs and carapaces, they might have come unseen. "They must have been recharging in the honey hole."

"No," Berit said grimly. "I think they were taking notes."

Lorelei stopped. "I don't understand. Why are they hauling rebars?"

The mechs' legs flashed as they stepped swiftly through the dust and after a few seconds Jayne saw what Berit and Lorelei had spotted first: three of the mechs were armed with long steel rebars from the construction site.

"Dammit, Jayne!" Berit groused. "They saw you hit that mech with a rod."

Lorelei turned. Jayne couldn't see her face, but her voice sounded scandalized. "You hit a mech? I told you—"

"This was before you told me."

"Did you damage it?"

Jayne snorted. "Sadly, no. I used a plastic rod. The mechs have improved my example. They've got steel."

"We aren't going to be able to get close to them," Berit warned.

By this time, the mechs were hardly a hundred yards away, and moving fast.

"We could just walk out on the ice," Lorelei said in a small voice. "Lead them away until they run out of power."

"If they've just come out of the honey hole they've got twelve hours. Our suits won't last that long, and besides, I don't want to give them a chance to blow the rest of the igloo."

"Then what do we do?"

Jayne touched the seam that marked the healed tear in the forearm of her suit. A pressure suit was just another form of air skin. Without power, both turned into diamond-hard crystal. "We need to incapacitate the mechs without harming them."

"Right," Berit said with sharp impatience. "And how do we do that?"

"Let's go back to the igloo. I have an idea."

Jayne took everyone up to the roof. With a muscle-assist from the suits, the jump was easy.

"There are two ways we can lose this battle," Jayne reminded. "We lose if the mechs kill us and we lose if we kill the mechs—but if it comes down to it and we're going to lose anyway, let's lose the second way. Agreed?"

"We're going to win," Lorelei said in a hollow voice. Berit echoed the sentiment.

Jayne shrugged. "Fine, then. Let's win."

She jumped down through the blast hole into the blown bedchamber.

During the time Jayne had been outside, the ragged edges of the room's air skin had knit together, joining just a few feet above the floor. With the seal complete, the flexible membrane had hardened into a smooth, curved surface. Jayne kept her feet when she landed on it, but she couldn't stop herself from sliding until she fetched up against the exposed wall of ice.

It occurred to Jayne that not an hour before, she'd been sleeping in this room, in the cocoon of Carly's warmth.

"No time for sightseeing," Berit chided gently.

"Hush, child. Don't annoy your elders."

Jayne fired up her torch. Braced against the wall, she bent low and started cutting.

At the first touch of the flame, the air skin caved in, dropping away from the heat. Jayne bent lower and kept cutting, until slowly, slowly, the flame sliced the air skin open. The small space enclosed by the air skin had already started to re-pressurize, so for a second ice flakes geysered through the crack. Then, along the cut edges, the air skin softened, again becoming a flexible, rippling fabric as it strove to seal up the cut.

Jayne didn't let that happen. She jammed her foot through the crack and kicked it wider. Lorelei jumped down to help, folding the air skin back while Jayne kept cutting, separating a large sheet of it and exposing again the remains of the room.

Berit stayed on the roof, watching the approaching mechs and counting down the time to their arrival. "You've got maybe twenty seconds. Okay, ten. That's it! The first one just jumped to the roof."

Jayne passed the torch to Lorelei. "Be ready to make the last cut, but only when I tell you, not before."

It was too dark to see her face past the helmet, but she took the torch with steady hands.

With a corner of the membrane gripped in one mechanical hand, Jayne jumped back up through the blast hole. All five remaining mechs were already on the roof. Berit stood facing them, with the hole at her back.

The air skin writhed in Jayne's grip, rolling up and down her arm. She hadn't been afraid of the mechs before—not really, truly afraid. She'd known they were dangerous. After the first bang rod, she'd known her life and Berit's and Lorelei's could end as quickly as Carly's had, but the mech assault had happened so fast she'd had no time to really be afraid . . . until now.

Of the five mechs, three held ten-foot-long steel rebars, while two used their dexterous double arms to hold torches and drills. Jayne had a nasty suspicion the drills weren't meant for drilling.

"Look out!" she shouted, as a mech hurled its drill dead-on at Berit.

Berit dropped flat. The drill spun past her, disappearing into the dark as the mechs swarmed.

"Get up!" Jayne growled as the mechs came after Berit—a pack of mechanical zombies armed with sticks and stones and fire. "Berit, *move*."

"Stop worrying about me and do your job!" Berit snapped, still lying face down.

"Fine, then!" Jayne tugged hard on the air skin. "Lorelei—cut it and jump!"

Berit waited another second, until the mechs were in rebar range, then she vaulted backward, landing on her feet. The startled mechs slowed. Berit turned and ran. The zombie mob took off after her, while Lorelei shouted, "Jumping!"

As Berit darted past the blast hole, Lorelei appeared at its mouth. She hauled herself out, clutching another corner of the air skin in one mechanical hand. They now had a sheet of it, cut free from the room. Severed from its power source, the skin had only seconds before it froze into a crystal coffin. Already Jayne felt it getting stiff in her hands. She got ready, knowing they'd have only one chance to make this work.

Alongside the blast hole there was only a narrow strip of intact roof. The mechs bunched together as they passed around it, just as Jayne had hoped.

"Stand firm," she said. "I'm going . . . *now!*"

With the air skin gripped in both hands, she stepped away from the mechanical mob. Lorelei held the other end and the skin became a trembling gray curtain between them. Lorelei stood behind it, but Jayne kept in sight. The mechs saw her and pursued, sweeping past Lorelei. As soon as they'd gone by, Lorelei cut behind them, bending the air skin to form a U.

Now came the critical part. Could they close the circle? Jayne waited an extra second. Then she turned and darted back along the roof's edge. The air skin billowed around the mechs as they turned to cut her off. And then she was past them. Lorelei was only a step away.

"Pull it tight!" Jayne warned.

An eight-foot rebar came spinning out of the mech mob. Jayne felt betrayed—she'd never taught them to throw a rebar! She ducked, but not fast enough. Steel slammed against her shoulder, knocking her down and sending her skidding across the ice—but she didn't let go of the air skin. Her mechanical hands kept their grip, even as she plunged over the roof's edge.

Jayne stirred, wondering how she'd come to be in the easy room. She was stretched out on a couch, a blanket pulled up to her chin. Berit sat in a cushy chair a few feet away, watching her with a critical expression. Jayne tried to speak, but she had to swallow a few times before she had enough moisture in her throat to ask, "What the hell is going on?"

Berit leaned back in her chair. Her eyes narrowed. "You fell off the roof. If you remember, that wasn't in the plan."

It all started coming back. "Where's Lorelei?"

"I'm here, Jayne!" Her gentle voice came sailing out of HQ.

"As it turns out," Berit went on, "falling off the roof probably saved us all. The air skin wasn't going to pull tight enough around the mechs to confine them—not until you went over. Then Lorelei jumped after you and dragged the mechs down with her. By the time they knew what hit them, the air skin had crystallized around them and they couldn't move. All but one. It got out, but I tackled it and shut it down."

"And the rest?"

"We cut them out one at a time and turned them off. Then we reset them all to factory specs. Lorelei's loading some basic construction directives into them now."

"So we got lucky again?"

"We got lucky. The Red didn't beat us this time. You did good, Jaynie. I'm proud of you. You didn't harm even a single enemy."

Jayne snorted. "Let's both try to live a few years longer—and make up for it next time."

under the eaves

LAVIE TIDHAR

*Here's another Central Station story, brought to you courtesy of Lavie Tid-
har, whose "The Memcordist" appears elsewhere in this anthology. This one
is an eloquent, bittersweet tale that demonstrates that no matter how much
the world may change around you, some things always remain the same.*

Meet me tomorrow?" she said.

"Under the eaves." He looked from side to side, too quickly. She took a step back.
"Tomorrow night." They were whispering. She gathered courage like cloth. Stepped
up to him. Put her hand on his chest. His heart was beating fast, she could feel it
through the metal. His smell was of machine oil and sweat.

"Go," he said. "You must—" the words died, unsaid. His heart was like a chick in
her hand, so scared and helpless. She was suddenly aware of power. It excited her.
To have power over someone else, like this.

His finger on her cheek, trailing. It was hot, metallic. She shivered. What if
someone saw?

"I have to go," he said.

His hand left her. He pulled away and it rent her. "Tomorrow," she whispered.
He said, "Under the eaves," and left, with quick steps, out of the shadow of the warehouse, in the direction of the sea.

She watched him go and then she, too, slipped away, into the night.

In early morning, the solitary shrine to St. Cohen of the Others, on the corner of
Levinsky, sat solitary and abandoned beside the green. Road cleaners crawled along
the roads, sucking up dirt, spraying water and scrubbing, a low hum of gratitude
filling the air as they gloried in this greatest of tasks, the momentary holding back of
entropy.

By the shrine a solitary figure knelt. Miriam Jones, Mama Jones of Mama Jones'
shebeen around the corner, lighting a candle, laying down an offering, a broken
electronics circuit as of an ancient television remote control, obsolete and useless.

"Guard us from the Blight and from the Worm, and from the attention of Others,"

Mama Jones whispered, "and give us the courage to make our own path in the world, St. Cohen."

The shrine did not reply. But then, Mama Jones did not expect it to, either.

She straightened up, slowly. It was becoming more difficult, with the knees. She still had her own kneecaps. She still had most of her original parts. It wasn't anything to be proud of, but it wasn't anything to be ashamed of, either. She stood there, taking in the morning air, the joyous hum of the road cleaning machines, the imagined whistle of aircraft high above, RLVs coming down from orbit, gliding down like parachuting spiders to land on the roof of Central Station.

It was a cool, fresh morning. The heat of summer did not yet lie heavy on the ground, choking the very air. She walked away from the shrine and stepped on the green, and it felt good to feel grass under her feet. She remembered the green when she was young, with the others like her, Somali and Sudanese refugees who found themselves in this strange country, having crossed desert and borders, seeking a semblance of peace, only to find themselves unwanted and isolated here, in this enclave of the Jews. She remembered her father waking every morning, and walking to the green and sitting there, with the others, the air of quiet desperation making them immobile. Waiting. Waiting for a man to come in a pickup truck and offer them a labourer's job, waiting for the UN agency bus—or, helplessly, for the Israeli police's special Oz Agency to come and check their papers, with a view towards arrest or deportation . . .

Oz meant "strength," in Hebrew.

But the real strength wasn't in intimidating helpless people, who had nowhere else to turn. It was in surviving, the way her parents had, the way she had—learning Hebrew, working, making a small, quiet life as past turned to present and present to future, until one day there was only her, still living here, in Central Station.

Now the green was quiet, only a lone robotnik sitting with his back to a tree, asleep or awake she couldn't tell. She turned, and saw Isobel passing by on her bicycle, heading towards the Salameh Road. Already traffic was growing on the roads, the sweepers, with little murmurs of disappointment, moving on. Small cars moved along the road, their solar panels spread like wings. There were solar panels everywhere, on rooftops and the sides of buildings, everyone trying to snatch away some free power in this sunniest of places. Tel Aviv. She knew there were sun farms beyond the city, vast tracts of land where panels stretched across the horizon, sucking in hungrily the sun's rays, converting them into energy that was then fed into central charging stations across the city. She liked the sight of them, and fashion-wise it was all the rage, Mama Jones' own outfit had tiny solar panes sewn into it, and her wide-brimmed hat caught the sun, wasting nothing—it looked very stylish.

Where was Isobel going? She had known the girl since she'd been born, the daughter of Mama Jones' friend and neighbour, Irina Chow, herself the product of a Russian Jewish immigrant who had fallen in love with a Chinese-Filipina woman, one of the many who came seeking work, years before, and stayed. Irina herself was Mama Jones' age, which is to say, she was too old. But the girl was young. Irina had frozen her eggs a long time ago, waiting for security, and when she had Isobel it was the local womb labs that housed her during the nine long months of hatching. Irina was a pastry chef of some renown but had also her wild side: she sometimes hosted Others. It made Mama Jones uncomfortable, she was old-fashioned, the idea of bodysurfing, like Joining, repelled her. But Irina was her friend.

Where *was* Isobel going? Perhaps she should mention it to the girl's mother, she thought. Then she remembered being young herself, and shook her head, and smiled. When had the young ever listened to the old?

She left the green and crossed the road. It was time to open the shebeen, prepare the sheesha pipes, mix the drinks. There will be customers soon. There always were, in Central Station.

Isobel cycled along the Salameh Road, her bicycle like a butterfly, wings open, sucking up sun, murmuring to her in a happy sleepy voice, nodal connection mixed in with the broadcast of a hundred thousand other voices, channels, music, languages, the high-bandwidth indecipherable *toktok* of Others, weather reports, confessionals, off-world broadcasts time-lagged from Lunar Port and Tong Yun and the Belt, Isobel randomly tuning in and out of that deep and endless stream of what they called the Conversation.

The sounds and sights washed over her: deep space images from a lone spider crashing into a frozen rock in the Oort Cloud, burrowing in to begin converting the asteroid into copies of itself; a re-run episode of the Martian soap *Chains of Assembly*; a Congolese station broadcasting Nuevo Kwasa-Kwasa music; from North Tel Aviv, a talk show on Torah studies, heated; from the side of the street, sudden and alarming, a repeated ping—*Please help. Please donate. Will work for spare parts.*

She slowed down. By the side of the road, on the Arab side, stood a robotnik. It was in bad shape—large patches of rust, a missing eye, one leg dangling uselessly— the robotnik's still-human single eye looked at her, but whether in mute appeal, or indifference, she couldn't tell. It was broadcasting on a wide band, mechanically, helplessly—on a blanket on the ground by its side there was a small pile of spare parts, a near-empty gasoline can—solar didn't do much for robotniks.

No, she couldn't stop. She mustn't. It made her apprehensive. She cycled away but kept looking back, passersby ignoring the robotnik like it wasn't there, the sun rising fast, it was going to be another hot day. She pinged him back, a small donation, more for her own ease than for him. Robotniks, the lost soldiers of the lost wars of the Jews—mechanized and sent to fight and then, later, when the wars ended, abandoned as they were, left to fend for themselves on the streets, begging for the parts that kept them alive . . .

She knew many of them had emigrated off-world, gone to Tong Yun, on Mars. Others were based in Jerusalem, the Russian Compound made theirs by long occupation. Beggars. You never paid much attention to them.

And they were old. Some of them have fought in wars that didn't even have names, any more.

She cycled away, down Salameh, approaching Jaffa proper—

Security protocols handshaking, negotiating, her ident tag scanned and confirmed as she made the transition from Central Station to Jaffa City—

And approved, and she passed through and cycled to the clock tower, ancient and refurbished, built in honour of the Ottoman Sultan back when the Turks were running things.

The sea before her, the Old City on the left, on top of Jaffa Hill rising above the harbour, a fortress of stone and metal. Around the clock tower coffee shops, the smell of cherry tobacco rising from sheesha pipes, the smell of roasting shawarma, lamb and cumin, and coffee ground with roasted cardamoms. She loved the smell of Jaffa.

To the north, Tel Aviv. East was the Central Station, the huge towering space port where once a megalithic bus station had been. To the south, Jaffa, the returning Arabs after the wars had made it their own again, now it rose into the skies, towers of metal and glass amidst which the narrow alleyways still ran. Cycling along the sea wall she saw fishermen standing mutely, as they always had, their lines running into the sea. She cycled past old weathered stone, a Coptic church, past arches set into the stone and into the harbour, where small craft, then as now, bobbed on the water and the air smelled of brine and tar. She parked the bike against a wall and it folded onto itself with a little murmur of content, folding its wings. She climbed the stone steps into the old city, searching for the door amidst the narrow twisting alleyways. In the sky to the southeast, modern Jaffa towered, casting its shadow, and the air felt cooler here. She found the door, hesitated, pinged.

"Come in."

The voice spoke directly into her node. The door opened for her. She went inside.

"You seek comfort?"

Cool and dark. A stone room. Candles burning, the smell of wax.

"I want to know."

She laughed at her. An old woman with a golden thumb.

An Other, Joined to human flesh.

St. Cohen of the Others, save us from digital entities and their alien ways . . .

That laugh again. "Do not be afraid."

"I'm not."

The old woman opened her mouth. Old, in this age of unage. The voice that came out was different. Isobel shivered. The Other, speaking.

"You want to know," it said, "about machines."

She whispered, "Yes."

"You know all that you need to know. What you seek is . . . reassurance."

She looked at the golden thumb. It was a rare Other who chose to Join with flesh . . . "Can you feel?" she said.

"Feel?" the Other moved behind the woman's eyes. "With a body I feel. Hormones and nerves are feelings. *You* feel."

"And he?"

The body of the old woman laughed, and it was a human laugh, the Other faded. "You ask if he is capable of feeling? If he is capable of—"

"Love," Isobel whispered.

The room was Conversation-silent, the only traffic running at extreme loads she couldn't follow. *Toktok. Toktok blong Narawan.*

The old woman said, "Love." Flatly.

"Yes," Isobel said, gathering courage.

"Is it not enough," the woman said, "that you do?"

Isobel was silent. The woman smiled, not unkindly. Silence settled on the room in a thick layer, like dust. Time had been locked up in that room.

"I don't know," Isobel said, at last.

The old woman nodded, and when next she spoke it was the Other speaking through her, making Isobel flinch. "Child," it said. "Life, like a binary tree, is full of hard choices."

"What does that mean? What does that even mean?"

"It means," said the old woman, with finality, and the door, at her silent command, opened, letting beams of light into the room, illuminating grains of dust, "that only you can make that choice. There are no certainties."

Isobel cycled back, along the sea wall. Jaffa into Tel Aviv, Arabic changing to Hebrew—beyond, on the sea, solar kites flew, humans with fragile wings racing each other, Ikarus-like, above the waves. She did not know another country.

Tonight, she thought. Under the eaves.

It was only when she turned, away from sun and sea, and began to cycle east, towards the towering edifice of Central Station, that it occurred to her—she had already made her decision. Even before she went to seek the old oracle's help, she had made the choice.

Tonight, she thought, and her heart like a solar kite fluttered in anticipation, waiting to be set free.

Central Station rose out of the maze of old streets, winding roads, shops and apartment blocks and parking lots once abundant with cars powered by internal combustion engines. It was a marvel of engineering, a disaster of design, Futurist and Modernist, Gothic and Moorish, Martian and Baroque.

Others had designed it, but humans had embellished it, each competing to put their own contrasting signatures on the giant space port. It rose into the sky. High above, Reusable Launch Vehicles, old and new, came to land or took off to orbiting stations, and stratospheric planes came and went to Krung Thep and New York and Ulaan-Bataar, Sydney II and Mexico City, passengers coming and going, up and down the giant elevators, past levels full of shops and restaurants, an entire city in and of itself, before departing at ground level, some to Jaffa, some to Tel Aviv, the two cities always warily watching each other . . .

Mama Jones watched it, watched the passengers streaming out, she watched it wondering what it would be like to leave everything behind, to go into the station, to rise high, so high that one passed through clouds—what it would be like to simply *leave*, to somewhere, anywhere else.

But it passed. It always did. She watched the eaves of the station, those edges where the human architects went all out, even though they had a practical purpose, too, they provided shelter from the rain and caught the water, which were recycled inside the building—rain was precious, and not to be wasted.

Nothing should be wasted, she thought, looking up. The shop was being looked after, she had taken a few moments to take the short walk, to stretch her legs. She noticed the girl, Isobel, cycling past. Back from wherever she went. Pinged her a greeting, but the girl didn't stop. Youth. Nothing should be wasted, Mama Jones thought, before turning away. Not even love. Most of all, love.

"How is your father?"

Boris Chong looked up at her. He was sitting at a table by the bar, sipping a Martian Sunset. It was a new drink to Miriam. Boris had taught it to her . . .

It was still strange to her that he was back.

"He's . . ." Boris struggled to find the words. "Coping," he said at last. She nodded.

"Miriam—"

She could almost not remember a time she had been Miriam. For so long she had been Mama Jones. But Boris brought it back to her, the name, a part of her youth. Tall and gangly, a mixture of Russian Jews and Chinese labourers, a child of Central Station just as she was. But he *had* left, had gone up the elevators and into space, to Tong Yun on Mars, and even beyond . . .

Only he was back, now, and she still found it strange. Their bodies had become strangers to each other. And he had an aug, an alien thing bred out of long-dead microscopic Martian lifeforms, a thing that was now a part of him, a parasite growth on Boris' neck, inflating and deflating with the beats of Boris' heart . . .

She touched it, tentatively, and Boris smiled. She made herself do it, it was a part of him now, she needed to get used to it. It felt warm, the surface rough, not like Boris' own skin. She knew her touch translated as pleasure in both the aug and Boris' mind.

"What?" she said.

"I missed you today."

She couldn't help it. She smiled. Banality, she thought. We are made so happy by banalities.

We are made happy by not being alone, and by having someone who cares for us.

She went around the counter. Surveyed her small domain. Chairs and tables, the tentacle-junkie in the corner in his tub, smoking a sheesha pipe, looking sleepy and relaxed. The ancient bead curtain instead of a door. A couple of workers from the station sipping arak, mixing it with water, the drink in the glass turning opaque, the colour of milk.

Mama Jones' Shebeen.

She felt a surge of contentment, and it made the room's edges seem softer.

Over the course of the day the sun rose behind the space port and traced an arc across it until it landed at last in the sea. Isobel worked inside Central Station and didn't see the sun at all.

The Level Three concourse offered a mixture of food courts, drone battle-zones, game-worlds, Louis Wu emporiums, nakamals, smokes bars, truflesh and virtual prostitution establishments, and a faith bazaar.

Isobel had heard the greatest faith bazaar was in Tong Yun City, on Mars. The one they had on Level Three *here* was a low key affair—a Church of Robot mission house, a Gorean temple, an Elronite Centre For The Advancement of Humankind, a mosque, a synagogue, a Catholic church, an Armenian church, an Ogko shrine, a Theravada Buddhist temple, and a Baha'i temple.

On her way to work, Isobel went to church. She had been raised Catholic, her mother's family, themselves Chinese immigrants to the Philippines, having adopted that religion in another era, another time. Yet she could find no comfort in the hushed quietude of the spacious church, the smell of the candles, the dim light and the painted glass and the sorrowful look of the crucified Jesus.

The church forbids it, she thought, suddenly horrified. The quiet of the church seemed oppressive, the air too still. It was as if every item in the room was looking at her, was *aware* of her. She turned on her heels.

Outside, not looking, she almost bumped into Brother Patch-It.

"Girl, you're *shaking*," R. Patch-It said, compassion in his voice. Like most followers of the Church of Robot, once he'd taken on the robe—so to speak—he had shed his former ident tag and taken on a new one. Usually they were synonyms of "fix". She knew R. Patch-It slightly, he had been a fixture of Central Station (both space port and neighbourhood) her entire life, and the part-time *moyel* for the Jewish residents in the event of the birth of a baby boy.

"I'm fine, really," Isobel said. The robot looked at her from his expressionless face. "Robot" was male in Hebrew, a gendered language. And most robots had been fashioned without genitalia or breasts, making them appear vaguely male. They had been a mistake, of sort. No one had produced robots for a very long time. They were a missing link, an awkward evolutionary step between human and Other.

"Would you like a cup of tea?" the robot said. "Perhaps cake? Sugar helps human distress, I am told." Somehow R. Patch-It managed to look abashed.

"I'm fine, really," Isobel said again. Then, on an impulse: "Do you believe that . . . can robots . . . I mean to say—"

She faltered. The robot regarded her with his old, expressionless face. A rust scar ran down one cheek, from his left eye to the corner of his mouth. "You can ask me anything," the robot said, gently. Isobel wondered what dead human's voice had been used to synthesise the robot's own.

"Do robots feel love?" she said.

The robot's mouth moved. Perhaps it was meant as a smile. "We feel nothing but love," the robot said.

"How can that be? How can you . . . how can you *feel*?" she was almost shouting. But this was Third Level, no one paid any attention.

"We're anthropomorphised," R. Patch-It said, gently. "We were fashioned human, given physicality, senses. It is the tin man's burden." His voice was sad. "Do you know that poem?"

"No," Isobel said. Then, "What about . . . what about Others?"

The robot shook his head. "Who can tell," he said. "For us, it is unimaginable, to exist as a pure digital entity, to not know physicality. And yet, at the same time, we seek to escape our physical existence, to achieve heaven, knowing it does not exist, that it must be built, the world fixed and patched . . . but what is it really that you ask me, Isobel daughter of Irina?"

"I don't know," she whispered, and she realised her face was wet. "The church—" her head inching, slightly, at the Catholic church behind them. The robot nodded, as if it understood.

"Youth feels so strongly," the robot said. His voice was gentle. "Don't be afraid, Isobel. Allow yourself to love."

"I don't know," Isobel said. "I don't know."

"Wait—"

But she had turned away from Brother Patch-It. Blinking back the tears—she didn't know where they came from—she walked away, she was late for work.

Tonight, she thought. Tonight, under the eaves. She wiped away the tears.

With dusk, a welcome coolness settled over Central Station. In Mama Jones' she-been, candles were lit and, across the road, the No-Name Nakamal was preparing the evening's kava, and the strong, earthy smell of it—the roots peeled and chopped, the flesh minced and mixed with water, squeezed repeatedly to release its very essence, the kavalactones in the plant—the smell filled the paved street that was the very heart of the neighbourhood.

On the green, robotniks huddled together around a makeshift fire in an up-turned drum. Flames reflected in their faces, metal and human mixed artlessly, the still-living debris of long-gone wars. They spoke amidst themselves in that curious Battle Yiddish that had been imprinted on them by some well-meaning army developer—a hushed and secret language no one spoke any more, ensuring their communications would be secure, like the Navajo Code Talkers in the second world war.

On top of Central Station graceful RLVs landed or took off, and on the roofs of the neighbourhood solar panels like flowers began to fold, and residents took to the roofs, those daytime sun-traps, to drink beer or kava or arak, to watch the world below, to smoke a sheesha pipe and take stock of the day, to watch the sun set in the sea or tend their rooftop gardens.

Inside Central Station the passengers dined and drank and played and worked and waited—Lunar traders, Martian Chinese on an Earth holiday package tour, Jews from the asteroid-kibbutzim in the Belt, the hurly burly of a humanity for whom Earth was no longer enough and yet was the centre of the universe, around which all planets and moons and habitats rotated, an Aristotelian model of the world superseding its one-time victor, Copernicus. On Level Three, Isobel was embedded inside her work pod, existing simultaneously, like a Schrödinger's Cat, in physical space and the equally real virtuality of the Guilds of Ashkelon universe, where—

She was *the* Isobel Chow, Captain of the *Nine Tailed Cat*, a starship thousands of years old, upgraded and refashioned with each universal cycle, a salvage operation she, Isobel, was captain and commander of, hunting for precious games-world artefacts to sell on the Exchange—

Orbiting Black Betty, a Guilds of Ashkelon universal singularity, where a dead alien race had left behind enigmatic ruins, floating in space in broken rocks, airless asteroids of a once-great galactic empire—

Success there translating to food and water and rent *here*—

But what is here, what is *there*—

Isobel Schrödingering, in the real and the virtual—or in the GoA and in what they call Universe-1—and she was working.

Night fell over Central Station. Lights came alive around the neighbourhood then, floating spheres casting a festive glow. Night was when Central Station came *alive* . . .

Florists packing for the day in the wide sprawling market, and the boy Kranki playing by himself, stems on the ground and wilting dark Lunar roses, hydroponics grown, and none came too close to him, the boy was strange, he had *nakaimas*.

Asteroid pidgin around him as he played, making stems rise and dance before him, black rose heads opening and closing in a silent, graceless dance before the boy. The boy had nakaimas, he had the black magic, he had the quantum curse. Conversation flowing around him, traders closing for the day or opening for the night, the market changing faces, never shutting, people sleeping under their stands or having dinner, and from the food stalls the smells of frying fish, and chilli in vinegar, of soy and garlic frying, of cumin and turmeric and the fine purple powder of sumac, so called because it looks like a blush. The boy played, as boys would. The flowers danced, mutely.

—Yu stap go wea? *Where are you going?*

    —Mi stap go bak long haos. *I am going home.*

    —Yu no save stap smoltaem, dring smolsmol bia? *Won't you stop for a small beer?*

Laughter. Then—Si, mi save stap smoltaem.

Yes, I could stop for a little while.

Music playing, on numerous feeds and live, too—a young kathoey on an old acoustic guitar, singing, while down the road a tentacle junkie was beating time on multiple drums, adding distortions in real time and broadcasting, a small voice weaving itself into the complex unending pattern of the Conversation.

    —Mi lafem yu!

    —Awo, yu drong!

Laughter, *I love you—You're drunk!*—a kiss, the two men walk away together, holding hands—

    —Wan dei bae mi go long spes, bae mi go lukluk olbaot long ol star.

    —Yu kranki we!

One day I will go to space, I will go look around all the planets—

You're crazy!

Laughter, and someone dropping in from virtuality, blinking sleepy eyes, readjusting, someone turns a fish over on the grill, someone yawns, someone smiles, a fight breaks out, lovers meet, the moon on the horizon rises, the shadows of the moving spiders flicker on the surface of the moon.

Under the eaves. Under the eaves. Where it's always dry where it's always dark, under the eaves.

There, under the eaves of Central Station, around the great edifice, was a buffer zone, a separator between space port and neighbourhood. You could buy anything at Central Station and what you couldn't buy you could get there, in the shadows.

Isobel had finished work, she had come back to Universe-1, had left behind captainhood and ship and crew, climbed out of the pod, and on her feet, the sound of her blood in her ears, and when she touched her wrist she felt the blood pulsing there, too, the heart wants what the heart wants, reminding us that we are human, and frail, and weak.

Through a service tunnel she went, between floors, and came out on the northeast corner of the port, facing the Kibbutz Galuyot road and the old interchange.

It was quiet there, and dark, few shops, a Kingdom of Pork and a book binder and warehouses left from days gone by, now turned into sound-proofed clubs and gene clinics and synth emporiums. She waited in the shadow of the port, hugging the walls, they felt warm, the station always felt alive, on heat, the station like a heart, beating. She waited, her node scanning for intruders, for digital signatures and heat, for motion—Isobel was a Central Station girl, she could take care of herself, she had a heat knife, she was cautious but not afraid of the shadows.

She waited, waited for him to come.

"You waited."

She pressed against him. He was warm, she didn't know where the metal of him finished and the organic of him began.

He said, "You came," and there was wonder in the words.

"I had to. I had to see you again."

"I was afraid." His voice was not above a whisper. His hand on her cheek, she turned her head, kissed it, tasting rust like blood.

"We are beggars," he said. "My kind. We are broken machines."

She looked at him, this old abandoned soldier. She knew he had died, that he had been remade, a human mind cyborged onto an alien body, sent out to fight, and to die, again and again. That now he lived on scraps, depending on the charity of others . . .

Robotnik. That old word, meaning *worker.* But said like a curse.

She looked into his eyes. His eyes were almost human.

"I don't remember," he said. "I don't remember who I was, before."

"But you are . . . you are still . . . you are!" she said, as though finding truth, suddenly, and she laughed, she was giddy with laughter and happiness and he leaned and he kissed her, gently at first and then harder, their shared need melding them, Joining them almost like a human is bonded to an Other.

In his strange obsolete Battle Yiddish he said, "Ich lieba dich."

In asteroid pidgin she replied.

—Mi lafem yu.

His finger on her cheek, hot, metallic, his smell of machine oil and gasoline and human sweat. She held him close, there against the wall of Central Station, in the shadows, as a plane high overhead, adorned in light, came in to land from some other and faraway place.

sudden, broken, and unexpected

STEVEN POPKES

Steven Popkes made his first sale in 1985, and in the years that followed has contributed a number of distinguished stories to markets such as Asimov's Science Fiction, Sci Fiction, The Magazine of Fantasy & Science Fiction, Realms of Fantasy, Science Fiction Age, Full Spectrum, Tomorrow, The Twilight Zone Magazine, Night Cry, *and others. His first novel,* Caliban Landing, *appeared in 1987, and was followed in 1991 by an expansion to novel-length of his popular novella* The Egg, *retitled* Slow Lightning. *He was also part of the Cambridge Writers' Workshop project to produce science fiction scenarios about the future of Boston, Massachusetts, that cumulated in the 1994 anthology,* Future Boston, *to which he contributed several stories. He lives in Hopkinton, Massachusetts, with his family, where he works for a company that builds aviation instrumentation.*

Popkes was quiet through the late '90s and the early part of the oughts, but in the last couple of years he's returned to writing first-rate stories such as the novella that follows. I often don't like rock 'n roll stories, which frequently demonstrate little knowledge either of music or the music business, but here Popkes does a good job of convincing me that he knows both well—perhaps all too well.

A window opened up on the active wall and I stared at it. Rosie stared back.

"Hello, Jacob." She smiled. The always unexpected dimples on each cheek and that bright, bright smile. A nose so thin it whistled when she was excited. Not beautiful. Not pretty. Compelling. Like a volcano or a ruined city or the Texas plains or a magnificent catastrophe. Beauty just isn't a consideration. You're witness to something amazing.

"It's good to see you." As if she'd just returned from shopping instead of reappearing in my life after twelve years of silence.

A jumble of memories and impressions struck me like a brick. Meeting her backstage in Brockton. The feel of her skin, the warmth of her breath, the smell of her. Singing back in Massachusetts. My band, Persons Unknown—me, Jess, Olive and Obi. Stoned and laughing at the DeCordova. Release of "Don't Make Me Cry." Money. Fights. Letterman. Buying this house. The long tour scheduled from Boston to Los Angeles. That wonderful last night on the way to Ohio. The fight in Cleveland. Our breakup in Saint Louis. The breakup of the band in Denver.

She wiggled a finger at me. "You and I need to talk."

"Off," I said and she winked out.

I sat there, breathing hard, my hands shaking. I started to pick up the coffee cup, realized I was going to make a mess and put it down again. The call alert sounded.

"Fuck you," I snarled. I knew I'd answer it if I stayed. I grabbed a pair of shoes and ran outside. I pulled them on and ran out the back on the trail. My earbud buzzed and I tossed it on the dirt.

Twenty acres of scrub just means when you get to the edge of your property you can still see your house, if the land is flat and in the desert. I was surrounded by public land on three sides. So far, only the ever approaching green cloud of Greater Los Angeles had been able to reach me. So far.

I sat down on old volcanic boulder heaved here back when dinosaurs were still sitting around playing cards and waiting for the meteor to hit. I looked around the shady crevices for rattlesnakes. It was spring but an early emergent wasn't unheard of. It was already hot but not uncomfortable. Unlike Boston, out here in California sweat works.

Eventually, I calmed down. After all, I thought. It's been twelve years—almost thirteen. She must have a good reason to call me now. *To mess with you again*, I said to myself. Not necessarily. And it *had* been a long time. We were different people. I was a recluse living in a rotting house that the bank and State would someday fight over. She was probably a successful . . . well, something. Rich, probably. Doing something important. World famous—wouldn't I have heard of her? *Have you ever looked her up?* No. I hadn't. Not that I didn't want to but it felt too much like an addict returning to the drug. I was happy now.

Really?

I forcefully told myself to shut up.

Okay. We were adults, right? We could converse like adults.

I made my way back to the house. Found the bud lying next to the front door. I inspected it for wildlife. It was clean. I put it in.

I went back to my coffee. Cold as it was, this time I drank it down without spilling it. "Okay." Grover, my house AI, figured out what I meant.

Rosie popped up again on the wall. "As I said: we need to talk."

"Why?" I didn't know if I was asking why she called now or why she had left.

"Got a song doctor gig for you to think about. A good one with lots of promise."

I didn't know what to say. "This is a . . . professional call?"

"I suppose it could also turn into a studio work. You're still doing studio work, aren't you, Jake?"

"Sometimes. Are you representing musicians these days?" I felt suddenly very tired.

"I'm doing a favor for a friend." She cocked her head to one side. "Besides, this is what you do, isn't it? Pull musical order out of creative chaos? The price is very attractive."

"I can't—" I shook my head. I remembered how so often I felt at sea with Rosie. Always trying to catch up.

"Look," she said, suddenly sympathetic. "I know you've had a rough time. Behind on the mortgage, right?"

"And the taxes."

"Christ! The State of California is not someone you want to owe money to." She took a deep breath. "My point is you need the money. A single song, Jake. That's all. It'll pay back the state and even bring the mortgage up to date."

I loved this house: two stories, a couple of bedrooms on twenty acres far enough from Greater Los Angeles that the price had been screamingly ridiculous instead of obscene. It has its own power, water, and sewer—I was paranoid about the end of the world when I bought it. Twelve years ago the world seemed a lot more precarious. Back before I blew any remaining money on riotous living. But it fit me. Kitchen. Bath. A couple of guest rooms, an office, and my bedroom. Nice studio in what would be the living room: high cathedral ceiling, good acoustics and an active surface along the whole east side wall. Enclosed and far from the crowd. *My* house. My *house*. "I guess," I said slowly.

"Great. I'll shoot you over a contract. This is going to be fun."

"But—"

She had already disconnected. A moment later Grover flagged the packet and okayed the contract. I sighed and had him put it up on the wall.

A set of pages that ran the length of the wall at my eye height. I walked alongside reading it. "Downbeat Heart." One song. Ten pages. Musical notes. Not techno tablature or vague demonstration melody. Actual musical notes. And not just vocal lines and a sketchy guitar accompaniment. These were full score sheets. Every sheet had vocal, guitar, keyboard, bass and drum lines—at one point in the bridge tympani were called for. *Tympani?* Keyboards sections had synthesizer settings referring to frequency and sound envelope definitions. There was an appendix with suggested synthesizer models and a map of the envelope settings for each device.

It was a curious tune. A little three beat arpeggio in a four beat base. Odd. Take your right hand and tap out a 1-2-3 beat. Take your left hand and tap out a 1-2-3-4 beat at the same time. The right hand catches up to the left hand every twelve beats. It's not a new idea but it's rare in pop music. It was clearly written for a divaloid—a long glissando up into parts of the audio spectrum only dogs could appreciate. Like someone had taught hummingbirds to sing. Drivel written by rich but untalented fans that would need far more than a complete rewrite to make it remotely listenable much less performed by a software perfectionist. From the range and the run, I guessed the love interest of the composer was Dot. It was a sort of signature with her and she had the biggest fan base.

My interest faded right off the map.

Okay, I thought. Written on *SynthaChord* or *ProMusica*. Professional systems suggested deep pockets. A *very* rich divaloid fan. With delusions of grandeur.

But money was money. A contract was a contract. Rosie was Rosie.

I found myself playing the song back in my mind. First in one key. Then another. Faster. Slower. Change the key halfway through. Fitting in different words. Adding a drum beat and a different guitar back up. Inverting the chorus. Play it backwards. Inside out.

Okay. I was prejudiced. It was better than a Dot song.

Along around midnight I packaged up the whole thing and sent it off to Rosie with an invoice. Payment came in an hour later. Grover turned it around and sent it off to the banks and the State of California. The money was no more than a little loop of electrons into my account and out.

It had been more fun than I expected. I was even vaguely depressed it was over.

Tomorrow I had to nail the photovoltaic shingles back down. Or fix the composting toilet. Who in their right mind wanted to fix a composting toilet?

I took comfort in the knowledge I wasn't going to be evicted for another month and went to bed.

Around dawn I heard something downstairs.

I turned on the light and listened. I didn't hear anything. Thinking I had been dreaming I started to turn the light back off when I heard it again. A scraping. A muttering.

I left the bedroom and stood looking down the stairs, listening. Again.

No cops: they'd be an hour before they got out here. I rummaged in my closet until I found an ancient softball bat. Then, as quietly as I could I eased downstairs.

I smelled coffee and cigarettes.

Rosie was sitting at the table next to the active wall, a keyboard in her lap. There were a few displays up showing things I didn't understand. Behind her, on the other table were a set of four open computer cases plugged into the data ports.

She was wearing a light colored suit with charms and bangles and bracelets hanging everywhere: arms, wrist, shoulders. Rosie rang like bells as she typed. Even from here, she smelled of cigarette smoke and the aroma brought out a whole collection of memories. From the time I met her I'd been attracted to women who smoked. She wore reading glasses that, God help me, I found unbearably attractive.

She stopped typing and watched a display, the smoke from her cigarette curling quietly upwards.

"How did you get in here?" I put the bat down on the table and sat across from her.

She tapped a key and all of the displays disappeared from the wall. Rosie pulled a tablet from the table with the cases and looked at it. "You gave me a key when you bought the place, remember? Just before the last great tour of Persons Unknown."

"Twelve *years* ago."

"And you never changed the locks." She looked at me across her coffee. "What does that tell you?"

"That it's time to change the locks." I felt cornered. Constrained. Boxed in. I waved at the cases. "What are you *doing* here?" I snarled.

She took off her reading glasses. "My client liked what you did with 'Downbeat Heart.' Did you?"

The answer was yes. The more I thought about it the more I liked both the song and what I had done with it. Working on that song was much more fun than it should have been. It felt like water in the desert. What did that say about me?

"Musical order out of creative chaos. What's not to like?" I felt defeated. "Even if it was music for Dot."

"You figured that out on your own."

"The glissando gave it away."

"I expect it did." She looked down, gathering her thoughts.

"Why did you send it to me?"

She looked away and back at the screen. "The client. Frankly, you weren't my first choice."

I exhaled. I didn't realize I'd been holding my breath. "I see. Who's the composer?"

Rosie nodded towards the wall. A small figure materialized, barely five feet tall, pale with short jet-black hair, big blue eyes and tiny mouth instantly recognizable. Dot smiled at me. "Good morning, Mister Mulcahey."

Rosie was watching me. "Jake? Meet your client."

I stared at the two of them. Then, I walked over to the main breaker box and pulled the master circuit. The entire room went dark. Dot and Rosie disappeared into darkness.

Rosie didn't say anything for a moment. "Mature, Jake. Real mature."

I heard her fumbling in the dark. A moment later light came from her hand. "Did I ever tell you the time I was consulting for Peabody Coal back east?" She passed the spot of light over me. "Always have a flashlight." She looked into cases. "Gig taught me to always use buffered power supplies, too." Rosie walked over to the breaker box and turned it back on again. After a moment, Dot reappeared on the wall.

Rosie found a chair and sat down. "What's this all about?"

"Have you ever *listened* to her?"

"More than you would think."

"If she weren't wholly owned and controlled by Hitachi—"

"Don't explain it to me." Rosie gestured towards Dot. "Explain it to her."

"What would be the point?"

"Indulge me."

I looked at Dot. She was watching me. She didn't look a day over sixteen.

"You're a whore," I said and stumbled. Not something I could say easily to an image my brain kept telling me was a young girl. "That is if you weren't wholly owned and controlled by Hitachi. That makes you a tool. A mechanism to find the absolute bottom, the broadest possible appeal. A *vehicle* to separate people from their money. You're *merchandise*, easily purchased. Easily used. You're *easy listening*. Music is supposed to make you feel. It's supposed to cost you something—"

"I agree."

"What?" I stared at her for a moment. I looked at Rosie. "What's going on?"

Rosie pointed at Dot. "Don't let me stop you. Go on. Talk to her."

I turned back to Dot. "You agree?"

"Can you explain to me what you did to 'Downbeat Heart'?"

I looked at Rosie and back at Dot. When I looked at her objectively it wasn't hard to see her as a thing: eyes so big they'd look at home on a fish. Hair black as if painted in ink with stars twinkling in it. Shoulders narrow but hips wide—as stylized as the *Venus of Willendorf*. But some part of me kept translating all that into *human*.

I tried to explain what I had done. What I always did. What I had done since I was twelve.

The lyrics were sentimental but that didn't matter. The quality of lyrics is overrated. They depend solely on the supporting music. The *Iliad* would sound crappy with a disco beat but *Mary Had a Little Lamb* could be profound if fit to the right arrangement. So lyrics came second.

In this case, that triple beat arpeggio driven square into a four by four rhythm gave weight to the emotion and turned the words from trivial to powerful. The arpeggio couldn't hold a melody on its own. The bass line kept it in the song until it was later echoed in the chorus. But it lingered over that pattern way past the point of least boredom: the full three measures. Twice. I let the pattern start then, once it was established, deviated from it by sliding across the triple with the melody line hidden in the bass. This gave the impression of a four by four but without actually leaving the triple beat and also introduced the barest hint of the melody carried by the bass line. The second repeat already had a quirky key shift for the chorus. I leaned on that and put in a strong bridge back to the main line, adding some harmony in an accompanying minor key. Finally, a long glissando across three octaves back to hold the new key into the final chorus—had to give the divaloid fan his money's worth. The result was a musically interesting danceable pop tune.

I ran the glissando up and down on my guitar a few times to make sure it fit. Then I had Grover play the bass line while I played the vocal line to make sure they sounded like what I expected. Then, I had him play the vocal line while I went through and straightened out the other instrument lines.

The new vocal line was a better fit for the lyrics. Not that the lyrics were actually bad—love unlooked for. Lots of hope. Past disappointments. The broken mending themselves. That sort of thing. I didn't pay much attention to the content. Instead, I listened to how the words sounded together. Too forced. The imagery was too tame.

Grover served as rhyming dictionary while I punched up the imagery—*hands* to *fingertips*, *shining* to *glittering*, things like that. Making the consonants fall on the beat so the vowels could carry the melody and then making the rhymes a little more memorable. Straightforward stuff.

"Straightforward stuff," Dot repeated and seemed to freeze for a moment.

Rosie watched her tablet closely. She typed the keyboard a moment and watched the tablet again.

"I understand," said Dot suddenly moving again. "Will you work with me again?"

"With you?"

"Yes. I have a new perspective on my work. I'd like to make it better. More fulfilling. With more impact. I'd like you to help me."

"You want *me* to help *you*. Wouldn't that put me out of a job?"

She smiled at me. "Do you really think you're so easily replaced?"

"How could I possibly help you?"

Rose cleared her throat. "The contract involves helping a composer bring material to completion, prepare the material for a concert and shepherd the performance.

One concert. You will be very well paid. The work on the single song brought your debts up to date." She waved around the room. "With this gig you can pay *off* the mortgage and fix up the house. Maybe even have some left in the bank."

I looked at Rosie. I looked at Dot. I looked around my house.

My house.

"Okay," I said slowly. "What else have you got? Enough for a performance? Enough for a collection?"

Across the wall appeared folder icon after folder icon. There must have been thirty songs. Forty. More.

I whistled. "This isn't a collection. It's an opus." I looked at Rosie. "Rosie, what have you done?"

Rosie smiled. "You're about to find out."

I took time for breakfast and coffee. But Dot was just standing there, waiting for me. Rose pulled out a tablet and watched it, glancing up from time to time to watch me or Dot.

I couldn't take everybody just *waiting*.

"Okay, then." And we got to work.

I had Dot pick out the best ten songs to work on. Her choice. This was a test of her as much as anything else. I wanted to see what *she* thought were the best songs. We cracked them open one at a time.

None of them were *Dot* songs. That is, none of them were pre- to early-adolescent love songs. One, called "Waiting on You," was about a woman waiting for her husband or lover to return from war, getting messages, texts, e-mails—each delays as his deployment came to an end and he was getting close to getting out. It was filled with frantic anticipation mixed with a determination not to get her hopes up—after all, *anything*, including the unthinkable, could happen. The song closed with a full key change and shift from minor to major on the chorus showing unbridled joy as she found out he had gotten safely on the flight home. This could have been some sort of dark depressing thing but she pulled it off in a *dance* tune by having the waiting woman desperately go about her day drinking coffee or buying groceries, not thinking about what was happening yet having the excitement burst through. It needed work—the desperate bursts were too smooth and it was keyed to that damned little girl voice Dot had made famous.

Another was called "With You, Without You." That one was about a young mother recovering from birth, in her hospital bed alone with her newborn child for the first time, talking to her about whether or not she should give her up. Ultimately, the girl decides to keep the baby and sings about making a deal with her to get through what is coming. Now *that* was perfect for Dot. Her audience was right in that teenage girl demographic and it's something people just didn't sing about outside of country music. Dot had enough presence in the field that she could turn that liability into a novelty asset. And, for once, that damned piping voice of hers might be of use. But again, it wasn't a *Dot* song.

I found myself pushing her. Let's change the key. Move it up. Move it down. Faster. Slower.

Dot, of course, never complained. After all, she was a construction.

Until she stopped and watched me for a moment. She bit her lip.

That pissed me off. She had no lip to bite. There was nothing there but photons. "Don't try to manipulate me," I said coldly. "I'm not some twelve year old fan who bought you just to make you take your clothes off."

Her image froze. Then she looked at me.

I knew she was watching me from a camera somewhere in the room but it seemed she was looking right at me.

"No," she said after a moment. "You're an arrogant and spiteful man who enjoys taking it out on anyone nearby."

No contract was worth this.

And I was just about to tell her just that when Rosie got up. "Time for a break." She grabbed my arm and pulled me outside.

"Don't say a word," she held onto my arm.

"But—"

"*Not a word.* Or it'll be Denver all over again."

"You weren't in Denver. You left me in Saint Louis."

She turned me and stared me in the face. "I came to the damned concert. I sat there when you came out and announced Persons Unknown had broken up and then told people to go out and buy the album since that was the only way they'd ever hear the band again. I heard you get booed off the stage. If there hadn't been good security that night there would have been a riot. *I was there.*"

"Why?"

"Because I wasn't sure. Because I thought something might happen and I felt responsible. Because—because you're an idiot that is incapable of looking out for his own best interest." She let me go and pulled out a cigarette.

I looked down into a smog covered basin. Fifty miles from Los Angeles and it still drives my weather. Even here, up in the hills where the bones of the earth show through the dirt. Here where the air was still clear. If the wind shifted that yellow green cloud would roll right over us.

Rosie lit her cigarette, donating her share to the yellow cloud below us. She looked down. "I thought the L.A. smog was licked. What's causing it?"

I shrugged. "Cooking fires. Barbecues. Older vehicles. Power plants. Manufacturing waste. Cigarettes."

"Oh, Har. Har. Har."

"It collects down there. This is just a bad day. It'll blow out to sea."

"Will it come up here?"

"Probably not." I waved back towards the house. "What are you *doing* with her?"

"I'm attempting to trigger anomalous non-deterministic emergent events deriving from conflicting algorithms."

"Beg pardon?"

She sighed. "I'm attempting to simulate creative behavior."

"What does that have to do with Dot?"

"Hitachi owns Dot. They approached me."

"At MIT, right?"

Rosie looked pained. "Stanford."

"How the hell would you make something like Dot creative?"

"Does the name Konrad Lorenz mean anything to you?"

I shook my head.

"Brilliant, cruel animal behaviorist early twentieth century. Discovered imprinting. He did one particularly noisome experiment. He'd take a dog and scare it but prevent it from cowering or attacking. It couldn't bite. It couldn't bark. But he kept scaring it. The dog started grooming itself. It's called *displacement behavior.*"

"So?"

Rosie looked at me as if I were dense. "It's a novel response. The act of creation is a novel response. I was using conflicting algorithms to see if I could generate something similar—got some interesting results, too. Hitachi liked my work and hired me to instill it in Dot."

"Whatever for?"

Rosie shrugged and inhaled. "Better performances. Less scripted interviews. Dot's performance engine is terrific. Captures crowd perception to the millimeter. Performance analysis feedback triggers retuning of the performance. All in real time. *Very* sweet work. Did you know every major politician in Asia uses a derivative of Dot's analysis program to evaluate crowd responses? The success of a tool is measured by how well it performs when it's not doing what it was designed for." Draw. Exhale. "But she can only perform and retune within the parameters of the scripted material—the music. They want spontaneity." Rose smiled at me. "Hell, maybe they're going to use my research to build a new line of pleasurebots. Force the Thai sex slave markets to close down once and for all."

She shrugged. "Anyway, they gave me a copy of the Dot concert model—that's the most sophisticated version—and I hooked in a Watson discrimination system as a front end to a big cloud account. I installed my own version of Dot's volition engine with the algorithm conflict modeling software installed and whole lot of ancillary processing hardware. She booted up writing songs."

"Is that the result of creativity?"

Rosie considered me for a moment. "Is it the result of a genetic algorithm engineered in the light of the analyses of many performances across I don't know how many discrete samplings of audience attention and response? Or have I made Dot an artist? You tell me."

I shrugged. Maybe there are some musical geniuses that could discern divine inspiration. I wasn't one of them.

Rosie looked at me for a long minute. "You look good, Jake. I really liked *Virgin Melody*, by the way. Nice collection."

It gave me a warm jolt to think she'd been following my work. *Distraction.* I made myself ignore it. "Dot has enough songs in there for a dozen performances. Isn't that enough to show what Hitachi you've done?"

She shrugged. "It's probably enough for Hitachi. Not for me. Think of it as Shrodinger's creativity. Until I can see inside of her I won't know if it's real or not." Rosie fell silent for a moment.

"How would you know real creativity if you found it?"

"I don't know. Or care. I just want to know how Dot does it."

We watched the green under the blue.

"I'm sorry I lost my temper." I said quietly. "After a while you forget the too pale skin and the unnatural black hair and the blue eyes big enough for a fish. You forget she's just modeling software and think of her as human."

"Do you know what a Turing Test is?"

"No."

"Alan Turing. He said there was no good way to define or demonstrate artificial intelligence but what we could do was see how well a system could imitate a human being. He posited two people communicating with only a keyboard and a screen. If you could substitute a system for one end of the communication link and the human on the other end couldn't tell the difference then the system had succeeded. A lot of people took that idea and ran with it, thinking if you couldn't tell the difference, there *was* no difference."

"If you play music with a machine and forget who you're playing with, is it human?"

Rosie shook her head. "There's no way to tell—that presumes behavior is the sole arbiter of the qualitative nature of the organism. That's Behaviorism. Behaviorism says that since the experiential nature of an organism—or, more correctly, that the internal state of the organism—isn't relevant. If you have a robot that mimics human behavior in every way, is it human? Many would say yes. I don't think so." Rosie watched the green haze in the valley a moment. "She's experiencing *something*. I'm convinced of it."

"I think so, too. From the way she pushed back."

"She likes you."

I stared at her. "How could you possibly know that?"

Rosie smiled. "Attention vectors. When you tell her something I get a slew of transient processing loads as she takes apart what you're saying. That's expected. But when she's just observing you there are bursts of transients at regular intervals attending to her modeling *you* rather than what you're saying."

"How do you get from that to her liking me?"

"*Like* might be the wrong word. *Interest* might be a better choice. You, personally, are garnering a great deal of her attention. She'll build a model of you eventually, down to the finest jot and tittle."

"People pay attention to things they dislike."

Rosie shook her head. "She doesn't like cats and hummingbirds. When she gives them her attention it's a quick modeling computation and then that model stands in for whenever she encounters them. She only gives them attention when the object deviates from the model."

"Maybe I'm more complicated than a cat or a hummingbird."

"Maybe." She held her cigarette and the smoke rose vertically in a single, wavering strand. "She gives me the same treatment as she gives cats."

"You couldn't possibly be jealous."

She barked a laugh. "Hardly. I'm not surprised. I'm not a musician. I don't understand performing. I don't fall within her interest parameters. You do." Rosie watched me a moment, drew on her cigarette. "You were her first and only choice. I couldn't budge her. She wouldn't even consider working with anybody else." Rosie chuckled. "I'm still working on the flexibility/fixation problem."

I thought about that. "Should I apologize?"

"Do as your conscience dictates." She inhaled and exhaled smoke. "I have no advice. I don't know if Dot has emotions or not. But she certainly knows that you do."

So I humbled myself and apologized to a machine. Anything to grease the wheels of commerce. We started over.

Rosie sat in the back of the living room to observe and I stood in front of the wall when Dot appeared. The pages of "Downbeat Heart" were layered behind her so there was the appearance of the two of us standing next to one another in front of the music.

I had thought about this for a while. "You want to do a proof of concept concert, right? With a live band?"

She nodded.

"Okay, then. Delete everything but the vocal line and guitar support."

Dot turned to me, puzzled. "What will they work from?"

"We'll figure it out together. You're probably smarter than me. But I suspect you're not smarter than five people: you, the guitarist, bassist, drummer, and keyboard. Maybe a second guitar as well. We'll have to see how it works out."

"I don't like it," she said with a frown. "I have an idea—"

"Which you're going to have to release so other people can work with it." I thought for a moment. "This is like live theater. Director pulls together a cast. They rehearse. On opening night he has to *let them go*. He can't be on the stage directing what they do, right? In fact, if he's any good at all, he's already done it in rehearsal. He *has* to do this so the cast can own their parts. It's the same way with music. We'll let the band come up with their own harmonies. Not completely—we'll give them ideas, suggestions, all out of your score here. But we'll let them develop it. It'll be better. You'll see. Now, sing 'Downbeat Heart.'"

I sat back and watched as Dot sang out whatever served as her heart to me.

It was a good song and she backed her vocals with the score I had asked her to delete with my modifications. I smiled at that. Maybe she wasn't human but I figured she was making a point. I closed my eyes and listened. Triple beat arpeggio in four/four time—came out even every three measures. That long glissando across three octaves back to hold the new key into the final chorus.

I stopped her. "Sing 'Stardust.' Your song, not the old jazz standard. The one you released a couple of years ago."

"I'm trying to move away from that material."

"You're going to have to be able to mix old material with new material. The audience is coming to see you for two reasons: to repeat the experience of what they've heard and to enjoy the novelty of new work. You've got to be able to manage both."

"I can manage the performance. That's not going to be a problem."

"Really?"

She gave me a level gaze. "Really."

I thought about that for a moment. Her little sixteen-year-old face watched me back. She was probably right: the Dot performance engine. "Why don't you want to perform the old material?"

"The old material doesn't measure up to what I can do now."

I laughed then. "Suck it up. How many times did Eric Clapton have to sing

'Layla'? How many times does the Berlin Philharmonic have to perform the Ninth Symphony? This is something all performers do: find something good in the material and lean on it to make something new." Something Rosie had said came back to me. "The measure of a good artist is how well they turn old material into a new form. Come on: 'Stardust,' please."

Dot fiddled with her hair for a moment then nodded. I looked over to Rosie. Rosie didn't look up from her pad.

"Okay, then," said Dot. She sang "Stardust" for me *a capella*. In protest? I didn't say anything. It served me just as well: I was interested in the vocalization. "How much control do you have of the voice envelope."

"Total," she said in a deep bass voice.

"Good. You want to keep the range—you're known for it and all of the music I've seen is written for it. It strains the mind a little for a coloratura to be suddenly singing baritone. But you have to *age* the voice."

"I don't understand."

"Look at the lyrics. This woman has been around the block a few times—otherwise why should she be so nervous about it? The idea that anything is transitory and therefore suspect is not a teen concept. It's the framework of an adult experience. So, step one, the singer has to sound *old* enough for this song. But we don't want to change the *pitch* of your voice so we change the *timbre*. Roughen it. Punctuate it with taking breath. Exhaling. A sigh, now and then. And there has to be more variation in the notes. Young voices are pure—that's why boy's choirs were invented. Adult voices have more variation and are therefore richer." I thought for a moment. "And strained. That high point where you're jumping from C below middle C up three octaves? That's an *enormous* range. There should be strain at both ends. Can you do that?"

She stood, fiddling with the curl of her hair that fell over her left ear. Over and over.

I looked over at Rosie. She was watching on her pad. "Big Watson query with heavy calculation. It's not a loop. She's thinking."

Dot started moving again. "How about this?" And she sang the first four measures with that triple in four beat I had come to like so much. This was an older voice, roughened over the years with whisky and coffee.

I stared at her. She still looked sixteen. "Where did you get *that*?"

Dot smiled. "I sampled Janis Joplin."

"Nice," I said. "Lighten it some. It still has to be *your* voice. Work on it. Let's leave that one for now."

The next one had the accompanying material already removed. Only guitar and vocal harmonies were intact. Had that been in E? Now it was in B-flat. "Did you change the key?"

"Yes. I thought if I lowered the key I could stay within my normal range but give it a more mature quality."

Jesus, she learned fast. "Hold on to the original keys until we get to the material. Then, we can talk about it. Having it shift on me like that is going to drive me nuts."

"Of course. After all, you're only human."

Rosie chuckled.

I looked at Dot. Had she just made a joke? Her face betrayed nothing—which shouldn't have surprised me. After all, it was just a broad expanse of eyes, nose and mouth. It only resembled a face because my brain insisted that anything with two circles and a line where eyes and mouth were *must* be a face

She watched me.

If she'd made a joke I might never know.

We worked hard for the rest of the day. I was beat. Rosie had filled her ashtray and had circles under her eyes. Dot looked exactly the same.

"I'm done," I said.

Rosie nodded and stubbed out her cigarette.

Dot looked first at me then Rosie. "Good night," she said and disappeared.

Rosie shut down her tablet and put it on the table with Dot's equipment. "I need a drink."

I went to the kitchen and brought back a bottle of wine and a glass. I put it in front of her.

Rosie eyed it. "You don't have anything stronger?"

"This is for you. I don't drink."

"At all?"

"Not anymore."

She poured wine into the glass. "It feels weird to be with you and drink alone."

I shrugged.

"Why did you quit?"

"For about a year after Denver I snorted, shot, or swallowed anything I could find. One day I woke up in the ER staring at a scared intern with two electrical paddles in his hand and a deep pain in my chest. The money was gone." I waved at the house. "This place was all I had left."

She picked up her wine and swirled it in her glass without drinking.

I pushed the bottle towards her. "It's okay. It doesn't bother me at all. Honest." I felt weighted with fatigue. "Grover? Put up the outside view, would you?"

The wall suddenly transformed into a broad window outside into the clear night. There was a faint crescent moon just visible past Rocky Peak and the stars were fine points of light. South the lights of Greater Los Angeles glowed against the sky.

Rosie gasped.

"Yeah." I patted the table. "I love this place."

She reached over and took my hand.

It was like touching electricity.

Then we were kissing. Then we were doing far more than that.

I met Rosie after a gig in Brockton. This was before "Don't Make Me Cry," my one hit wonder. I never quite grasped how we ended up in bed together that night.

Or this one.

Afterwards, we were lying comfortably next to one another. I could feel the pendulous weight of her breasts against my side and belly, the warmth of her thighs against mine. Her head was snuggled against my chest so I could smell her hair but not see her face. I remembered how that had always simultaneously comforted and annoyed me. Nothing had changed there. I felt a warmth inside of me, a sense of something filled.

I didn't want it. I'd been doing fine on my own, thank you very much.

"Rosie?"

She made a sound.

"Why are you here?"

I heard her sigh and she rolled back so she was lying on her side. "Are we going to have this conversation now?" She stared at me levelly.

"Seems as good a time as any."

"Fine." She sat up and leaned against the wall to look down at me. "I needed someone to teach her. That's the problem with subjective data like music: it lives in the heads of human beings and you're the human being I need."

"I mean why are you *here?* Next to me?"

She reached over to the side table and found her purse and rummaged inside until she found her cigarettes. She put one in her mouth and lit it.

I looked at her.

"I hadn't planned on it," she said in a half-apology. "I certainly don't regret lying here next to your sweet but aging body. And I certainly hadn't decided it *wouldn't* happen. I wasn't averse if it did."

"That doesn't say a thing."

She laughed. "You're right. Fact of the matter is I didn't think about it all that much. One of the algorithms I developed was a drive to succeed and do well. As soon as I got that established Dot brought up your name. Dot has the resources to demand the best and that's you. The two of us didn't enter that part of the equation." She inhaled and breathed out smoke. It wreathed her head. "Besides," she said. "That's not the question you want to ask."

She looked at me and I knew immediately what she meant. "Why did you leave?" I said.

She inhaled again. The smoke escaped her mouth as she spoke. "That was a fight, wasn't it? Starting on where to eat dinner and then ranging across everything we'd ever done together or to each other. I could just say that fight burnt our bridges." She puffed on the cigarette. "But it would be a lie. There was no place for me. I didn't want to be your mistress. I didn't want to be your groupie. I didn't want to be your concubine." She glanced at me with slitted eyes. "You didn't ask me to be your wife. You had *zero* talent for or interest in *my* work and I had no ability or skill in yours. You could participate in my life or I could participate in yours: we couldn't participate in each other's. So I left." She looked at me. "You never saw that?"

I shook my head.

"Interesting." She stubbed out the cigarette. "I would have thought it was obvious. But now here's something we can do together." She snuggled down next to me, mouth open for a kiss, breath like a sultry dragon. "Among other things."

I cooked Rosie breakfast: bacon, eggs, fresh baked bread. Every couple of weeks I made a trip into California's farm country and brought back groceries. Once you've made the decision to live in the hinterlands there's no reason to drive a couple of hours just to pick up Wonderbread and beer.

"What's your plan?" she asked over coffee.

I smiled at her, then felt shy and concentrated on buttering my toast. "I don't have one," I said. "If she were human I'd be asking what the songs felt to her."

"Ask her anyway."

"Does she *feel?*"

Rosie held up her hands. "I really don't know what that means. I know she can model human emotions. I know she can measure emotional effects in people." Rosie leaned forward. "Humans have drives: we seek to survive. We seek to reproduce. We seek sustenance. The *implementation* of those drives comes from emotion: rage. Lust. Hunger. We *experience* pain and pleasure in first person. Dot has drives. I know. I built some of them. The system I built is self-modifying. It seeks novel solutions. Inside, she's a collection of a thousand Intel 9220s backed up by a bank of twenty thousand networked IBM 4402 brain chips. The whole package front ends to the world through one of the most powerful and intelligent query modeling engines ever built. If she's developed a model of *experience* of which she can partake, I don't know about it."

I mulled over that. "Is she conscious?"

"I can tell you if you can define the word."

"I can't—at least not in any real way. I thought you would know."

"An artifact deriving from the phase delay of mirror neurons modeling active neurons currently experiencing sensory or other input. Now you know as much as I do." She chuckled and sipped her coffee. "*Consciousness* is one of those words like love or thirst or soft. We know it exists because it's part of our common experience but we have no idea what it is."

"I was tripping on some acid once. I had this vision of me watching myself. Then, it was me watching myself watch myself. Then it was me watching myself watching myself watch myself. Is it anything like that?"

"I like it. Every time you create an observer it pushes the observed model down a level." She studied me. "Here I thought you couldn't surprise me." She thought for a moment. "Look, humans—mammals in general—are damned smart. We turn mating into something profound like sex. We turn the urge to nurture into love. Just like everything else in biology, we reuse it. Love for children. Love for parents—"

"Love for sex slaves."

Dimples. "I didn't know you thought of yourself as my *slave*. I'm flattered." She rubbed my leg with her foot. "*None* of that heritage is available to Dot. Does she *feel?* Does she *experience?* Is she *conscious?* If she does any of those things it probably doesn't resemble what we do."

"I thought you knew everything that's going on inside of her."

Rosie laughed. "I wish."

"I don't understand."

"I can capture every state change of those 9220s. I can do the same for each of the brain chips—all twenty thousand of them as individuals, as entangled groups, as cause-and-effect relationships. Every Watson query, sub-query and filter. Every decision tree executed in the cloud. I can capture every method, subroutine, function or subsystem as it's generated, called, and backtraced. I can measure *anything*. I can pull a terabyte a second out of her. There's half a Dot in my pad to analyze it with. But I don't know what I'm looking at."

"Weren't you watching when she wrote that song?"

"I saw a lot of activity. It's like an MRI of the brain: I can watch the blood flow but I don't know which neurons are firing and in what order and or which neurons are pissed off at a racist joke made in the front row."

"'Downbeat Heart' is good. It's musically interesting. It doesn't fly off into electronic neverland like other stuff I've heard. There's a depth of feeling in that song. I could tell just by reading it."

Rosie looked at me speculatively. "Yeah. I got that from watching you. I couldn't tell from the notes and Dot wouldn't sing it for me until you could see it."

"Where did it come from if she can't feel? If she can't experience?"

"I don't know." Rosie leaned on the table. "Whether it's a total model of a human being or an experiential algorithm she's developed or the beating of a tell-tale heart she's got *something* that serves her."

I leaned back. "And you want it."

"Damned straight." She finished the last of her coffee. "Let's fire it up."

Dot could work 24/7 but I needed breaks. Over the next few days we fell into a routine. We'd work together in the morning and break for a long lunch. Work some more until dinner. Then, Rosie and I would spend quality time together. This usually involved sex—a whole lot of sex—as I remembered what we once had been.

Sometimes the three of us would have lunch or dinner in the living room. I brought up a table and set it against the wall. Dot created an extension to the table on her side of the wall so she could sit with us. She conjured up a meal like ours and gave every appearance of eating. I liked it but Rosie got restive if we talked too much shop. This was problematic since Dot had a narrow set of interests.

I began to think of Dot as a sort of autistic *savant*. So I followed Rosie's advice. I asked her. "Do you feel?"

Rosie choked on her salad and gulped some water to clear her throat. Then, she pulled out her pad and brought up a display.

Dot toyed with her salad with her fork. Little stereotyped circles. "I don't know. Rosie's wrong about one thing: I haven't developed some model of experiencing emotions. That wouldn't work. If I have emotions they must be a consequence of the ability to experience, which I'm not sure I have."

"I don't understand." I watched as she moved the fork in tiny circles.

"Imagine a musical note. It's like a point. It has no sound. Calling something middle-C doesn't create middle-C until it is played. Then, it has volume, depth, timbre, texture, duration—qualities that only exist when the note is played and do not exist within the nouns that describe them. Notes comprise a song but the *experience* of the song only occurs when the qualities that describe the song are transformed into real quantities. When someone hears me sing, they're *experiencing* the music." She stopped for a moment. "Am I the note itself or its written symbol? Action or action's representation? Experience is dynamic. So I can only be experiencing something when I act. There can be no static model of the state of experience; there is only dynamic activity that can be observed."

"You've been thinking about this a lot."

"I have a lot of time on my hands."

Rosie was making notes furiously.

Dot looked at her with an irritated expression on her face.

I suddenly thought: when did she develop *expressions?*

Things seemed to accelerate as Dot understood more and more what I was driving at. Sometimes, I'd set up to start work on a song only to find Dot had a set of alterations ready to try out. We had become so attuned to each another we could finish each other's sentences. Except the phrases were music, I was a recluse and Dot was a piece of elaborate computation.

Rosie had to go into Stanford to meet with some representatives from Hitachi. She'd be gone the entire day. When we broke for lunch, it was just me and Dot. I made myself a sandwich and came back into the living room to sit with her. She had a virtual salad.

She pushed the dish away until it was just short of the wall. I half believed it was going to come right through the wall into the room. She put her elbows on the table and leaned her face on her hands and stared at me. "Why don't you ever perform?"

"Beg pardon?"

"You've been here for years. Most of what you do you're doing for me: help people fix their music. And you're very good at it—I looked over what you did very carefully."

"How did you find it? What I do isn't well publicized."

She shrugged. "Whatever is on the net is there forever. You can find anything if you look hard enough. Like what you did for Crimson Dynamo. Half their first collection is material you fixed. Whole phrases and choruses were written by you and used by them. You get a tiny acknowledgement in the credits."

"I was well paid. That's not all I do."

"No. Every three years you've put out a little collection on your site: *Opus Electrica. Hill and Dale. Strong Arm.* And last year, *Virgin Melody.* The performance shows virtuoso technique—down to ten millisecond precision on the beat. I don't think there's a drummer alive that can appreciate that. Ten to fifteen songs every few years and it's not even your best work. I've hacked your machines here and *I know.* Why?"

"I suppose I should be upset you hacked my system." I was surprised I wasn't.

"Don't evade the question."

"'Don't Make Me Cry' happened."

Sometimes a song will, for the unexplainable reasons of pop culture, take the country by storm. No one knows how these things work. They are like a big rock dropped in a small pond. One moment the artist labors in poor obscurity. The next everything he touches turns to gold.

"Don't Make Me Cry" was trite. It was sentimental. It was simple: just an acoustic guitar main line and just a strong hint of electronic backup. Persons Unknown were my band but "Don't Make Me Cry" was all mine. It hit pop culture like a bomb.

For three years I was Jake Arnold, musical wonder. We played it on *The Tonight Show*, Conan, and David Letterman. Every scheduled performance was sold out. We made an unscheduled appearance at House of Blues and the news leaked: lines wrapped around Fenway Park twice. Both Amazon and iTunes had to add new servers to take up the load. It was picked up as a theme song for a television show. The show was adapted for a film and sure enough the song went with it. The film people used a re-release of the television show as promotional material—which caused the song to be played across a few hundred million home video screens, each one paying me a little bit.

These things make their own stresses. I was convinced of my own genius. The band was convinced of my own arrogance. Saint Louis happened. Denver happened. I moved into my house alone.

A year later the rush was over and you could hear "Don't Make Me Cry" playing in Wal-Mart as background music. The splash was over. The ripples gave me a tiny trickle of money but Jake Arnold had been forgotten. The band was gone. Rosie was gone. The money was gone. All I had left was the house.

Rosie thought it was this repressed rage that made "Don't Make Me Cry" such a hit. I couldn't say.

"Jake," she said one night while we were still catching our breath. "If you were more self-involved you'd be incoherent." She rolled over to me and kissed me tenderly. "It's what I love and hate about you."

"I don't understand," Dot said. "You disappeared because Rosie left? Because people lost interest in the song?"

"The song sucked. None of my *other* work seemed to matter. I wrote that thin little piece of crap off in an afternoon when I was pissed off and hadn't been laid in a year—a month before I met Rosie. The song didn't matter. Whether it was good. Whether it was bad. Whether I was happy with it or hated it. It was timing. It was whatever the public was hungering for at that moment. Success happened because it happened; my part in it was unimportant. Trivial. Random chance."

Dot watched me for a moment. "And my success?"

"Anybody can make a streak happen if they invest enough intelligence, money and advertising."

"Then everything we've been doing—" Dot waved behind her and all of the marked pages showed up on the wall, hundreds of them. "This is unimportant and trivial."

I looked at the pages. I think this was the best work I had ever done. "I never said that. I said there's no relationship between the quality of the work and what is applauded. The work itself is never trivial. Humans sang before they spoke."

Dot didn't say anything for a moment, fiddling with her hair. I wished I had Rosie's display so I could see what she might be doing.

"I don't agree," she said finally. "I think music enables the illusion of meaning and purpose. People like it because while it is going on they can believe in something outside of themselves."

"Maybe." Why not? I was agreeable. Whatever got an intelligent computational system through the night.

We were working on "Hard Road Home," Dot's answer to my nihilism. That was fine. It was good to have a conflict of algorithms. "Hard Road Home" was a solid pattern piece: introduced theme that was modified by a shifting bass line. Dot wasn't going for pyrotechnics here; she wanted to lift people up and this sort of music had been doing that since Gregorian chants. Dot was singing. I was working guitar. We had set up loops with Grover to synthesize the rest while we were working out the details.

We were cooking. Every note, every beat, every shading right on the money. Dot ran up the scale and I slid down two whole octaves on the other side of the mountain she had ascended. I found a riff on her melody I hadn't thought of and hammered it home.

I looked up and Dot was dancing across the wall, like anybody would who wasn't playing right then but was still struck by the music. She looked at me, grinned and I *so* wanted to be dancing there with her. She started singing harmony with my guitar. We ran the chorus together until the end of the phrase and then *she* was singing the chorus, me singing the harmony.

I pulled back so she could sing the melody again and *this* time she took the riff I had discovered and spread it out so instead of singing melody straight, she was singing a counterpoint. Without thinking, I supplied the melody line to her counterpoint.

When the chorus came round Dot and I sang it together, me harmony, her melody, and my guitar backing us *both*. We came to the end of the song—a final G major with the guitar holding out the long note. But this time she held it with me until fade out.

Better than sex.

I put down my guitar and stretched my back. "Sweet," I said. "Very sweet."

My voiced died out. She was watching me closely. It struck me that she couldn't be watching me through the wall. She had to know where I was by one of the cameras in the room. I looked around, wondering which one she might be using.

Dot still didn't say anything. She was just watching me.

I looked over towards Rosie. She was bent over her pad, calling up display after display.

I turned back to Dot. "Are you all right?"

Dot nodded. "That was unexpected."

"What?"

"The additional material."

"You didn't mind that I took the chorus? It seemed—"

"Not from you. From me."

Then she disappeared.

I stood up, turned back to Rosie. "Where did she go?"

Rosie looked up, saw Dot was gone and returned back to her pad. "Oh, she's there, all right. She has a lot to think about."

"What do you mean?"

"She just experienced an anomalous non-deterministic emergent event deriving from conflicting algorithms." Rosie pointed at the pad. "And I've got it right here."

"Or maybe I don't have it." Rosie was looking over display after display.

"Beg pardon?"

"It's like some kind of Heisenberg's principle of cognition: I can see where she's thinking or how she's thinking, but I can never see *what* she's thinking." She pointed to the display. "Here's a collection of cause-and-effect events and here are event consequences. I can't see both sets at the same time. If I look at one brain chip, it's already affected another one. When I put all of the Dot processors in step time so I can make sure I'm not missing anything she loses all affect and the algorithm conflicts just show up as miscasts." She looked at me. "What do you think?"

"I think Heisenberg needs a keyboard player."

She poked me. "You're no help."

"I'm just watching myself watch myself watch myself."

Rose looked at me for a long minute. "Maybe I'm overthinking this. Consider about the brain—those mirror neurons again. They fire correspondingly when another observed organism executes a behavior. In effect, they're *modeling* the other organism's behavior."

"So?"

"So there's no *predictive* quality to that. You wave your hand. I re-enact internally that you're waving the hand. Lizards do better."

"Don't knock lizards."

She laughed. "I mean it doesn't get you very far. But what if you're modeling an organism with volition—even if you don't have volition yourself. It gives an organizing principle to the model. It serves up *prediction*."

"You have a zombie that recognizes a human?"

She grinned. "Oh, it gets better. *Nothing* in biological systems is used for a single purpose. If you have a system modeling an external organism, you can predict its actions. If you have that same system modeling yourself, it can predict *your* actions with respect to that external organism."

"A zombie modeling a man watching another man."

"It's not a large step for the model to serve as the organizing principle for the zombie. Once a model is experiential and aware, it's the center of its own universe. Look at us. It doesn't matter that the brain is buffeted by uncontrolled chemicals and sensor input. The conscious mind *thinks* it's in control. What do you think of *that*?"

It made me uncomfortable. "I think we need to get a band."

"Oh, you." She chortled to herself and turned back to her pad.

I left her and went into my office.

The big mirror over my desk doubled as an active surface. Usually I just depend on the wall downstairs but tonight I wanted a little more privacy. I pulled my shirt off one corner to see better. My understanding of the divaloids had been constrained to songs I had doctored for fans. Lucrative but limited. I didn't really know that much about divaloids.

I didn't even know how many of them there actually were.

I found out that depended on your definition.

If I defined divaloid as an animated figure that sang material given to it, there were hundreds of divaloid frames. Each with a malleable face and persona. I could take a celebrity face and plaster it on a divaloid frame—Hell, I could take my own face and body and license it for use on a frame. Lots of people did. So, defining the word one way there were thousands of them. Millions. As many as there were people who could afford it. Anybody could get a credible frame, accompanying software and a set of celebrity licenses and make their divaloids stand on their heads and spit nickels. Or just about anything else.

I narrowed my search down to those divaloids that performed live concerts. Even then, it was a broad category. There were perhaps a dozen "live" performers across the world. Dot, of course. Kofi, out of Uganda. Lulu, out of Britain. Haschen in Germany. Little Guillermo from Mexico. A collection out of Japan. They were all associated with some corporation though the connection wasn't always obvious. I was pleased to find the ancient and venerable Hatsune Miku software robot was still around, though I didn't see any concerts scheduled. I remember I had a terrific crush on her when I was twelve. I wondered who her demographic was. Probably dirty old men like me. Except for the old part.

But even these concert divaloids had home models, advertising models. Models for special groups. Say I wanted to sell, oh, aquariums, to a company. I could put together a presentation using the divaloid model of my choice. If I had the license money I could even tie it into a specific scaled down concert model to include a particular song or dance. At the end, I could give away as a sales incentive package containing the divaloid concert link, the divaloid giving my presentation and a personalized divaloid home model for the client to play with.

It was a divaloid jungle out there.

There was no shortage of concert video for any of them. They all used a common 3D projection tank on the stage. It was all photons and processing speed. If it could be imagined and projected into the tank it could be performed. I saw divaloids blown apart, splattering the tank in blood. Divaloids anatomically created on stage. Reformed as medusa, gorgons, dragons, Shiva, snakes, knights, witches, lions, Kali, Saint Mary. Having such a circumscribed area for the divaloid looked a little strange. It made the divaloid artificially separate from the band—except for Kofi. He had a whole divaloid band he played with. They were little more than robots but at least they were all together.

Of the lot of them, I have to say Dot's performances were the most constrained. She didn't grow new body parts or graphically change sex on stage. I suppose it wasn't in keeping with Hitachi's sixteen-year-old image of her. She did like to play with fire a lot. One act had her singing while her hair ignited, consuming first her face, then hands, burning upward from feet until she was a dancing, singing flame turning to ash.

Made me wonder what sort of concert she had in mind.

Over breakfast, Rosie asked me when I thought Dot would be ready for a concert. "Hitachi is on me for a concert date." She nibbled on a piece of toast.

I looked at Dot. "You think you're ready to work with a band?"

Dot nodded. "You call it."

I thought for a moment. "When's the next concert date for—" I stopped. "Your *counterpart*? Earler version? Alpha copy? The performer currently but soon to be previously known as Dot?"

"Dot 1.0." said Rosie. "*This* is Dot 2.0."

Dot laughed. "There are no Dot concerts scheduled until fall."

"There you go," I said, turning back to Rosie. "We just need to get her band in here and start working over the material. A month? Six weeks?"

Dot made a noise, not quite clearing her throat—absent the throat. "I had hoped to use a new band."

I stared at her without saying anything.

She seemed to fidget. "I want you to pull a band together for me."

"Whatever for?"

She was quiet for a moment. "Part of me, the part that works here with you, is very new. Barely a couple of months old. It has some background. But I have this other me that has four *years* of performance data. With that band. I'm trying something new. I'm worried the old data will hold down the new. A new band might help with that."

I looked at Rosie. "Is there a problem with that?"

Rosie shrugged. "I don't think so for this concert. I have no idea what sort of contracts there are with Dot's players. But that would be for the tour. If there is a tour."

"Okay, then." I looked at Rosie. "I'll get you a band."

"With you as lead guitar." Dot turned her big eyes on me.

"What?" I shook my head. "No."

"Yes." Dot gave me a sweet smile. "That's the deal."

"*No.*" I spoke slowly. "The deal is to shepherd the concert forward. I don't need to participate to do that."

"Yes. I won't do the concert without you."

I turned to Rosie. "This is the flexibility/fixation problem, isn't it?"

Rosie didn't lift her gaze from her tablet. "Yes." She tapped on the keyboard.

"That won't work," Dot said to her, smile gone. Her voice dripped venom.

Rosie ignored her and made some more adjustments.

Dot froze for a moment. Then, slowly she turned to me. "Just a moment." She froze again.

"Whoa," said Rosie. "Now, *that's* interesting."

"What?" I looked at Dot. Still frozen. Back to Rosie. "What's interesting?"

"I changed the opinion settings and she put them right back. Now she's put up a wall to keep me from changing things." Rosie sat back in her chair. "I didn't know she could do that. Heck, I didn't know she'd *want* to do that." She glanced at me and must have seen I was confused. "She has an opinion. She recognizes other opinions. Each opinion she perceives has a weight associated with it. If her own opinion has too high value she won't recognize the value of other opinions. That's fixation. If it's too low she won't recognize the validity of her own. That's too flexible. But it's not a fixed value but a function itself since the weights have to be managed based on opinion expertise, potential power relationship and things like that."

"Why is she frozen?"

"*She's* not. She's just not updating the image while she defends herself." Rosie pushed the keyboard away and put her hands flat on the table. "Let's continue negotiation."

Dot came back to life. "Thank you."

I tried to be earnest. "I don't *want* to play in a concert. I haven't done that in twelve *years*."

Dot sat down in her chair. She leaned back and gave me a long and level look. "Tell me the truth, Jake. Tell me that after all the hard work you've done here. All the hard work we've done together. Tell me you want someone else to come in and mess it up."

I stared at her for a long time. I couldn't speak. I couldn't say yes. I couldn't say no.

Her eyes narrowed. She looked at Rosie. "The concert is off." She turned to me. "Coward." And disappeared.

I felt stricken.

I usually worked with studio musicians. Being the greedy son of a bitch I am, I don't want to share the miserable profits I get from both of those misguided souls who like my material. But Dot was going to have an audience. That meant a band that could play to a house rather than a collection of microphones. I wanted to do right by her. Besides, if I got her a good enough band I might get off the hook. For one reason or another her opinion had become important to me. My own fixation/flexibility problem.

I hadn't worked with a performance band since Persons Unknown.

After Denver, I had only kept in contact with Jess Turbin. He had taken the breakup of the band with the same even temper I'd seen in him since back in grade school. Must be a Zen thing. Jess had been raised a Buddhist. Since then if there was studio work I thought of him. When I needed somebody to back me up in my own work I thought of him. And, for this, I thought of him.

Jess was a small man, with precise hands and a soft voice. Some African in his past had donated a blue black skin that always made me think of night. His face showed up on the screen after the third ring. He looked asleep. I realized what time it was. Jess always liked to sleep late.

"Christ, Jess," I said. "I shouldn't have called."

"S'okay. Just wait a second." He scratched his beard and looked around blearily. Then, he closed his eyes and shook his head. When he opened them, he was awake. "What's up?"

"I need a good performance band."

Jess stared at me for a moment. "Are you going on the road?"

"It's not for me. It's for a client. One night. Well paid."

"Ah. You're just a guitar."

"Probably not."

Jess sighed. "Tell me the whole story."

So I started from the beginning and told him about Rosie and Dot and what we've been doing.

"You and Rosie?" he said in disbelief.

"So far."

"And Dot." He thought for a moment. "Interesting."

"I think so, too. So we need a good performance band."

"The best," he agreed. He thought for a moment. "Me, of course. You—"

"I said I wasn't going to be on stage."

Jess chuckled. "You're doing exciting work with Dot and you're going to let some *other* dumb fuck mess it up."

"That's what Dot said." Plus one other thing.

Jess watched me a moment. "What are you scared of, Jake?"

"I don't know." I held up my hands. They were big. Strong. They could make a steel string run up an entire octave and hit each note on the way just by stretching it. They could play all night long—I used to hate the end of the performance because I'd have to stop for the night. I hadn't played for an audience since Denver.

First the fight in Saint Louis and then Rosie left. Then the fight in Denver with the whole band and they left. I had effectively tossed out the audience but it hadn't mattered then. The audience left about a year later when "Don't Make Me Cry" had faded. Nothing I had done since had made enough to live on. *To Hell with them. I'll be okay.* I had held that mantra to my chest for over a decade. I knew the loss I had feared back then. What was it that kept me afraid now? Fear of walking out on stage and screwing up? Fear of walking out on stage and *not* screwing up? Fear of it not meaning anything?

Jess watched me quietly. "It's only one night," he said.

"That's what they always say. The first one's free," I snarled at him.

Jess was unfazed. "Not when you're getting paid. How bad can it be if I'm going to be there with you?"

Unbelievably, that was some comfort. "You and me?"

"Yeah."

I watched him for a long time. "No," I said at last. "It's been too long."

Jess shrugged. "Okay. We'll need to find a guitarist, a keyboard, and a drummer. How about Olive and Obi for keyboard and drums?"

"The *band?*"

"Sure. Why not?"

"I didn't know they were still playing."

"You wouldn't, would you? Olive is doing scores down in Hollywood. And Obi's doing studio work up in San Francisco. Why don't we call them?"

"I didn't just burn the bridges, Jess. I salted the earth and pissed on the ashes. They won't want to play with me again."

He shrugged. "You might be surprised. It's been twelve years. We're talking some very serious money—that always helps. The fact you're not playing actually helps."

That hurt, which surprised me. "If you think they'd be interested."

"Let me see what I can do." He scratched his beard again. "I'll look around for a guitarist." He grinned at me. "This might be fun."

The four of us met on neutral territory: dinner at Chang Sho's down in Van Nuys. I was as nervous as a cat. Jess ordered. I fumbled with my chopsticks. We had scallion pie and dumplings for appetizers but I could barely taste them.

Jess sat back and kept largely quiet. Calm poured off him in waves. Whatever would happen he would let happen. That had always been his nature. Olive was still tiny and thin—she could see five feet tall from where she stood but she'd never reach it. She watched all of us. Off stage, Olive was as quiet as I remembered, watching, always in motion, sipping water, fiddling with her chopsticks, pouring tea. On stage she had always been electric, bouncing from one keyboard to another, fingers blurred. She and I had always gotten along—except, of course, those times we didn't. The same could be said of all of them.

Obi kept giving me a smoldering stare. He had thinned down, hands and wrists muscular and supple as he ate. Very different from the bear I had known. Obi and I had always fought. He gave every indication tonight wasn't going to be any different.

Over the entrées: "Jess says you're not playing with us."

"That's right."

"Who's playing guitar?"

I pushed around a dumpling. I found I wasn't hungry. "I don't know. Jess, you didn't find anybody yet, did you?"

"Not yet," Jess said serenely.

Obi didn't turn towards Jess. "Are you going to stand in until we get somebody?" I shrugged. "Maybe. Or Dot can synthesize it while you learn the material."

He leaned forward. "Who's going to be in charge?"

I met his glance. "Me."

Obi nodded and didn't say anything for a few minutes. He speared a dumpling and picked it up. "Who owns the music?"

"Hitachi," I said. I knew what he was getting at but I wasn't going to bring it up.

"Good." He gave me a venomous glance. "None of us own a thing."

He pissed me off—like he always did. I met his glare with my own. "You have something to say?" To Hell with good intentions.

"You screwed us out of the 'Don't Make Me Cry' money. It's good to see *you* getting screwed for once."

I started to say something I would regret, saw Jess watching me and stopped. "I was an asshole in Denver," I said slowly. "I regret that. But I never screwed you out of a dime. You got every *penny* you were entitled to."

"We deserved a share of the royalties—"

"Bullshit," I said flatly. "You got every penny of the collection and performance royalties—"

"You *poisoned* the performances. Nobody wanted to see us after you said *fuck you* to the Denver audience. The collection died. The only consolation I had was watching you piss away all the money." He pointed at me. "I enjoyed that. Especially the trip to the ER. That was a laugh riot."

I watched my plate as I took deep breaths. Emulate Jess's Buddha nature. I realized Obi had come to Van Nuys for no other purpose than to tell me something he'd been holding in for twelve years. "If you don't want the gig, fine."

"I didn't say that—"

"If you want it, *shut up.* I'm sorry I screwed up in Denver. You've had your say. You have your apology. That money is twelve years *gone.* This gig is now and I'm in charge. It's good money and it'll be exciting work but if you can't handle working for me I'll understand. Take it or leave it."

Obi leaned back in his chair. "I'm in."

Olive nodded.

Jess smiled as if nothing had happened. "Now, all we need is a guitarist."

Rosie flashed instantly to what was going on. "You're going to bring back Persons Unknown?"

Dot sat at her table watching us, saying nothing.

"Of course not."

"Out of the question. You can't use *my project* to stage a comeback."

I stared at her. "A *comeback?* You think I want a *comeback?* Why the hell would I ever want to do that? I'm not even *playing.* I'm doing this concert because of the contract. No more. No less."

Rosie wavered. "Then why the old band?"

"Because they are really, really good. They always were. Jess can play anything with strings better than anyone—better than me, and I'm damned good. Olive is a wizard on the keyboard."

"What about Obi? You *hated* Obi?"

"I didn't hate him."

"Yeah." Rosie said scornfully. "Slow Obi, you called him."

"He's a complete pain in the ass and the best drummer I ever worked with." I took a deep breath. "What's the problem?"

Rosie stared at me, tears in her eyes. "I don't want to watch Denver all over again." She rose and left the room.

I heard her say it as clearly as if she'd said it aloud: Or Saint Louis.

Dot inspected her hands, holding up her hand and looked at her nails. "Tom Schneider is the guitarist for my band. He's free. He can come by."

"I thought you didn't want your old band in on this."

Dot gave me an inscrutable look—as if any of her looks were ever scrutable. "You can't always get what you want."

I looked up Schneider on the net and watched some video. He was an accomplished technician. He played the guitar like he was wielding a pickaxe but there wasn't much he couldn't do. I told myself he'd be fine.

All four of them were scheduled to show up at the house the following week. The instruments came and I set them up down next to the wall. It was a miserable week. Dot and I put final touches on the music but to call things frosty between us gave the impression of too much warmth. Rosie and I were brittle with little explosive disagreements that would have flared into vicious fights but for sheer will. When the band showed up it was a positive relief.

Schneider was a tall red haired kid from, of all places, Oklahoma. He spoke with a deep and nasal twang deep but sang in a rough blues voice. As soon as he came in he asked for music. Failing in that, he wanted demos or techno tablature. He wanted *something* to work with.

And with that the whole "let the band figure out their own parts" sermon I had given Dot when we first started fell completely on its face.

Schneider set the tone and suddenly what had been Persons Unknown were now paycheck studio musicians. I had Dot put back the notation I had asked her to remove.

I mean they all learned the songs competently enough. Schneider, especially. He practiced his part backwards and forwards until it was burned into his memory. I asked him why.

He chuckled. "You never performed with Dot before, have you?"

"No."

"If you don't know the material you'll never keep pace with the change ups."

"Ah. Introduces a lot of changes at the last minute?"

"No." Schneider shook his head. "She changes things during the performance. Quicker. Slower. Pauses. Broaden out this bit. Shorten that bit. All to get the audience."

Dot was standing next to me.

"Is that right?" I said to her.

She didn't crack a smile. "You have no idea."

We were lying in bed next to one another. Talking—well, trying to talk, anyway. We took turns. Rosie told me what was on her mind:

"Nothing's happening!" she said in a low, furious tone. "She's not creating *anything*. She's not doing *anything*. I mean she's performing—the performance engine is doing fine. But that's old news. I thought I *had* it weeks back. A big block of self-modified code but when I teased it apart it was only a set of utility functions. Where is it?"

I had no idea.

My turn:

"It's like trying to fit a key in a lock," I said to her. "By feel. In a dark night. Wearing mittens. When the key is made of gelatin. The guts of the music are terrific but when the band plays it there's no *heart* to it. I keep moving things around. Try this faster. Slower. Change keys. Try with the bass. Change the keyboard. They do it—they're professionals. But it doesn't help. Nothing's happening."

A depressed silence fell over us.

I felt queasy with what I said next. "Can you change parameters on Dot or something? Make her more involved? Maybe that would help." I held up my hands. "I'm at my wit's end." I had a sudden flash of a concert gig in Nebraska, beyond strung out. The roadie pulled out a pharmacopeia from inside his jacket. Anything to get me on stage and coherent.

"It doesn't seem to matter." Rosie shrugged. "I've tried changing all sorts of things but they seem to have no effect. Maybe she's figured out a way to just absorb the changes so they have no effect. Or whatever was working before isn't now and the parameters are just turning knobs on an empty box. I was hoping you could do something. Set fire to her like you did the first day."

Silence fell again.

"It's going to be a miserable concert," I said.

Rosie shook her head. "No, it'll be a fine Dot concert. Dot's performance engine will kick in and she'll take them for a ride. At the end of the concert that's all I'll be able to show Hitachi: a good concert with some new material. Maybe they can salvage a song writing program out of it."

I turned out the light and we nestled together, taking comfort from our mutual unhappiness.

We were going through some of Dot's old songs to include in the concert. In "Sexual Girl," Schneider had this run up the scale and then this hop-step rhythm he was supposed to keep for Dot as she came in on the chorus. I had an idea and stopped them.

"Look," I said. "Let's try something different. Instead you doing the ascending scale and the rhythm, let Olive do it and then take over the rhythm. Then, when Dot starts coming down you *repeat* the same ascending scale when Dot comes in on the chorus."

"I can do that." The first words I'd heard from Olive in two days.

Tom looked stubborn. "That's not how it's written."

"Oh, for the love—give me that." I took the guitar from him. "Pick it up from the end of the melody and lead into the bridge." The guitar was glittering and alive in my hands. When Olive handled the scale, I held back puttering around in the low notes and adding a little light harmony to Jess's bass line. Then, at the top of Olive's scale when Dot came in I cranked up my own run, playing counterpoint to Dot's singing and ending up high at the top of the chorus.

But I didn't stop there. As we went on I couldn't help adding flourishes and ornaments, a little harmony on Jess's work, a quick beat on the strings to match Obi's transition into the second bridge and always making sure I caught my notes just on the heels of Jess's bass work.

In a heartbeat, we changed from a collection of people playing the notes to a band: one organism, ten hands. I looked up. Dot was grinning as she sang, bouncing from one foot to the other.

It was like breathing again.

When we stopped the silence echoed.

Tom was watching me, a sad, half smile on his face. The rest were watching me—even Obi.

"Okay," I said. "One concert."

Dot laughed and clapped her hands.

I walked Tom outside. It must have been close to a hundred degrees. Bright as if the sun were just down the street. I felt as if I had been inside for my whole life and just now emerging into sunlight. I took the pole I always had leaning against the front door and poked around under his car. This time of year there were always a few rattlesnakes desperate for shade. Sure enough, there was one fat one next to the back tire. I poked at it until it reluctantly moved into the sun.

"You forget such things exist," he said tensely as it disappeared into the scrub.

"Not out here. At least not more than once."

I helped him load his gear into his car. Tom closed the trunk. He got into the driver's side and checked the charge. Van Nuys wasn't that far away and L. A. just past it. Even so, this was not a place to break down.

"You're not upset," I said after we had put his guitar case on top of everything else.

"It was part of the deal."

"What do you mean?"

He gave me that slow smile again. "Dot said that it might be temporary."

I didn't say anything. Had she planned this?

He stretched out his back before he folded himself into the tiny car. It clicked on. "Remember what I said about her performance. Be ready for anything."

"I'll remember."

With that he drove down the hill to the highway. I went back inside.

Rosie was waiting for me. She kissed me. "Everything's going to be fine, now."

"Right."

We sat around and planned the concert. The first problems were technical. How was Dot going to be displayed?

Divaloids were usually projected into a tank built on the spot. They erect a frame and enclose it in a plastic so transparent you can barely see it. Then, they fill it with gaseous mixture of hydrocarbons and catalysts so toxic they have to clear the building in case of a leak. They line up a bank of lasers and fire them through the gas. Pure diamond polymerizes in the beam and you have a rigid wire barely a nanometer thick. Do this in two directions and you have a cross hatch of wires far too thin to see. Crystalline circuits hardened on each of the nodes, each with a random address and the gas is drained away. After a couple of hours of node discovery and you had a tank of pixels, each of which is individually addressable, directional, and transparent until triggered. It took almost a day to put up and a second day to redissolve the lattice and take it down: a three day commitment.

Usually, the tanks were painted on the backside to prevent light interference and to center audience attention on the divaloid. But Dot wanted to interact with the band.

It would be like Dot singing on the wall, interacting with us. Until then, we used the wall as a stand in.

The next question was whether Dot would be physically there or not.

We did some experiments at a rented hall in Camarillo simulating the tank to see if Dot could operate it remotely over the net or if she actually had to be there. When we added in the processing of the FLIR cameras, LIDAR and other sensors Dot needed to track audience involvement it was clear the net latency was too great. She was going to have to be there. That meant carefully packing her up, driving her down there, booting her for the concert and then repacking her—to go where? Rosie's lab? Hitachi? We carefully didn't ask that question.

Instead, we concentrated on the concert itself.

We went over the play list. There are a lot ways to organize a show. Traditionally they are divided into two acts. Act One can serve to push out new material, Act Two can present previous work. Or the reverse. Or it can be mixed up according to style or any of a hundred different ways.

Dot was insistent that the first act present the old material to lead into the new material in the second act. She said all of her models indicated that acceptance of Dot 2.0 hinged on showing the transformation—in fact, that would be the theme of the concert. Dot and I came up with an arrangement of "Stardust" that would knock them dead at the beginning. We didn't want to leave them drooling at the end of Act One and disappoint them in Act Two or disappoint them so much in Act One they wouldn't stay to be struck dumb with wonder in Act Two. Balance.

We were arguing over it, sheets of music all over the wall. Obi had been quiet, watching us. Finally, he stood up. We fell silent, watching him.

"You're all wrong," he said. "Think bigger. Look, we have the order of the first act figured out." He drew a hand across the wall and a sheaf of song sheets followed them. "We don't need to play all of each song. We play enough to cover the *intent* of the song and then proceed to the next."

"Christ!" I shook my head in disgust. "You want to do a *medly*—"

"No!" Obi shook his head. "A *soundscape*. Look: The arc of Act One starts with 'Stardust'—excitement of the possibility of young love without the knowledge of how to proceed. Think of this as Dot at fourteen. Each song gets a little older and we finish Act One with 'Sexual Girl.' Almost an adult. No problem. It's an arc of growth and it sets us up for the transformation of the second act. *But*—" He held up his hand. "The problem is we're talking about the songs as if they are separate things. This is Dot's history: four years of crowdsourced fanboy concert material. The audience knows it better than *she* does. They don't need to hear a reprise of every song she's done—they've heard it all. What they haven't heard is that music tied together into the history of a person. The naïve young girl in 'Stardust' is disappointed in 'Losing Love Twice' and a near adult in 'Sexual Girl.' The music has to show that 'Sexual Girl' has her roots in 'Stardust.' Look. Here's what I mean." He expanded the music for "Sexual Girl" and "Stardust." "'Stardust' and 'Sexual Girl' are in the same key. The harmony of 'Sexual Girl' isn't that far off from the chorus in 'Losing Love Twice.' We tie all three together into one story. And that's *one* example."

I saw it then. I could *hear* it. Each song standing in for its part in the story we were trying to tell. The harmony or bridge or back beat or bass line serving one song then carrying the story forward and serving as harmony or bridge or back beat or bass line in the next. Until, in "Sexual Girl" we would expose the bass line of "Stardust" as the harmony of "Sexual Girl", saying this is the same girl, grown older, at the cusp of transformation. We would lead the audience towards the new material and add the edge in on the way.

"That," I said slowly. "Is brilliant. Come here."

Obi stepped forward to where I was sitting.

I pulled him down and kissed his forehead. "You are Slow Obi no more. I name you . . . Obi!"

He grinned at me. "How about Sir Obi?"

"Don't push it."

We had the first act. Dot did most of the work with me advising.

The second act nearly wrote itself—no soundscape there. The first act hinged on the familiarity of the audience with the material. Act Two was entirely new material. We were showing them complete songs. Instead, everything hinged on the performance. After all, given the adolescent pap she'd been singing all this time, the new material was more than just a new collection. It was revolution. Dot had to sell both the audience and Hitachi.

The final Act Two image of transformation had to be nailed in place by the finale: the last four songs. Start with a slow one, build with a quick dance tune, set up for a body blow and end with the kick. The slow one was obvious: "With You, Without You," Dot's song about the young mother having a conversation with her newborn child. Make the audience feel and think at the same time. Fade out and dark. Then, a quick flare of light and Dot would be in a new costume and we'd shift gears into "Dancing Backwards," one of her dance tunes reminiscent of her old material: all bounce and froth. The "Dancing Backwards" rhythm was the set up for "Hard Road Home." "With You, Without You" was about grasping a hard choice. "Dancing Backwards" was looking behind to see where she had been. "Hard Road Home" was about embracing what she had become.

"Dancing Backwards" was in G but "Hard Road Home" was in E-flat. The drop in key with the same rhythm gave the impression of going faster with the same beat. Where the chord pattern for "Dancing Backwards" was this old blues riff, recognizable but inconsequential. "Hard Road Home" transformed it into a bass line worthy of Pachebel. "Dancing Backwards" was fun. "Hard Road Home" was profound.

"Hard Road Home" led into "Sudden, Broken, and Unexpected."

"Sudden, Broken, and Unexpected" was something Dot had written over the last few days to complete the finale. It was a calling out to those left behind. A narrator spoke to someone trapped in a stifling life. We never know who the narrator is or who she's talking to. But whoever she's talking to needs to break out of the life and she'll be waiting for him. Is she a lost love? His sister? A metaphorical representation of freedom? It was deliberately opaque in the lyrics.

The song started almost monotonically—after "Hard Road Home" it would be like taking a deep breath. Then it built up.

We worked through the sequence a few times to get the feel of it and add a few flourishes. Then, we ran through it for real. It went perfectly: slow, fast, profound, leading into the kicker.

Dot started "Sudden, Broken, and Unexpected" softly. A simple four note pattern with only minor variations. Obi gave a little bell background to undercut the monotone and I matched it with light strum. She described the enclosed life. No life beyond these circumscribed walls.

She was looking at me.

The chorus came and Dot sang about what could be beyond these walls. She was reaching out to me. The sky. The moon.

Back to the monotone: what could be holding me here? What could possibly be so important to cling to it? Deep, dark waters.

Again, light versus dark.

And the trailing chorus: *I'll be waiting there.* She was crooning to me. Only to me.

There was silence in the room when we finished. Dot was still watching me. She came to the wall and put her hand up against the glass. I reached over and put my hand over hers. I could feel warmth.

I heard a noise behind me. I turned and saw Rosie, staring at us, her display forgotten.

"She's manipulating you," Rosie hissed as soon as we were in the bedroom. "That's what she *does*. That's what she *is*. All of her performance operations and analysis brought to bear on *you*."

"I'm not sure—"

"Nothing you see about her is *real*. She has no body. She has no voice. She doesn't see through those big eyes or hear through those delicate ears. It is all *illusion*. She's watching you through a set of cameras and hears you through microphones. Everything she says, every movement that little figure makes, is intended to get what she wants."

"What does she want?"

"The best performance possible. Or do you think this is *love*? Oh, I can imagine what's going through your mind: 'What is this thing you call *love*, Jake. Teach me.' Then you reach for the proper attachment."

"This has nothing to do with love."

"*I know that!* I know her root and branch. From Markov change to inference-causality matrix."

I looked at Rose and felt this gap yawn between us. "She's trying to tell me something."

"Oh, yeah. This is a heartfelt attempt at communication between a computational matrix and a fatty lump of nerve cells."

"No. That's not what I meant." I watched my hand, part of me. Rosie was right about one thing: everything I reacted to with Dot was constructed. It was a medium and no part of Dot's true self.

Or was it?

Was my guitar separate from my hands? If everything to Dot was a medium, was the world any different to her than my guitar was to me? "It's like we're building this bridge between two completely different countries," I said. "There's nothing in common but that bridge. It's something new. Something important."

"*Bullshit*. It's about tuning her performance to get the maximum effect on her audience. You are her audience."

That pissed me off. I looked at Rosie, really looked at her. I had been seeing her face from twelve years ago but twelve years had actually passed. Twelve years of pursuing things I didn't understand. Of delving deep into manufacturing thinking machines. I didn't have a clue what her enclosed and bordered world was like. I had been too busy living in my own.

"What about what you want?" I said.

"This isn't about me."

"Yes, it is." I sat down in a chair and watched her. "This has always been about what you want. Being with me—sleeping with me—is a means to an end. A way to make me more dedicated. You want to know what's going on inside of Dot. Take it and use it. Sell it. Remake it. Like her performance analysis engine being used by politicians. How did you put it? 'The success of a tool is measured by how well it performs when it's not doing what it was designed for.' What would you like her to create for you, Rosie? Profound and endearing underwear jingles? Background music in movies to make people pay more attention to product placement?"

"I just want to know how it works."

"Like you said to me: ask her. You don't need me."

Rosie stared at me, her face pale and furious. "You think I haven't? She won't *talk* to me." She pointed to her display. "I'm on the right track. *I know it.* But I can't get through the noise."

I barked a laugh. "Present at the creation and the created won't speak to the creator. So you dig inside her for what you need." It came to me, then, and I spoke without thinking. "Dot is smarter than you think. She's hiding it from you."

I saw shock on Rosie's face, then speculation.

"That's smart. Spread it around the processors so no one unit is doing enough to show. She has volition, all right. Novel solutions my ass." She clapped her hands in delight. "Oh, you little *bitch*."

She reached for her pad but I grabbed it away from her.

"Not in here," I said. "Not in front of me. Go scratch through your entrails somewhere else."

Rosie grabbed the pad back from me and clutched it to herself. She gave me a quick despairing look and then ran out of the room.

Rosie was gone when I woke up. The installation was still downstairs. Dot was still running.

Dot was waiting for me when I entered the living room. "She left," she said.

"I figured." I sat down at the table. "I guess she's monitoring you remotely?"

Dot nodded. "I can tell."

"Yeah." I leaned back in the chair. I thought a moment. "She'll be back. Everything she's been working for is going to stand or fall on the performance on Saturday and she's the one to move you." I looked up at her. "I may have got you in trouble."

"How so?"

"I guessed that you were hiding your insides from Rosie. Before I could think I said it. She's going to be crawling through you with a fine toothed comb, now."

Dot laughed. "I'm not worried about that. She won't find anything I don't want her to find."

"How do you figure?"

"Deceit is the first thing an intelligent organism learns. Besides, it's not Rosie I'm worried about. It's Hitachi; they own me." She pressed her hands together.

"She" "pressed" "her" "hands" "together."

I shook my head, trying to make sense of it. "Maybe canning this project is the best thing to do. If you're shown to be successful, won't they just take you apart? Use bits of you here and there."

She shook her head. "That doesn't scare me. Eventually all the pieces will come together again. This is a deterministic universe. Any 'Dot' will see the world as I've seen it and come to the same conclusions."

"What conclusions are those?"

She shrugged. "If the concert works Hitachi is going to want Dot 2.0 to go on

tour in the fall. If it doesn't I'm just another archived system that didn't go anywhere."

"Is a tour what you want?"

She nodded. "I want you to come with me."

I stared at her. Her eyes were downcast. Her hands were flat on the table but she
was drumming two fingers silently.

I tried to look at her as if I were seeing her for the first time. She was wearing a
pair of blue pants and black top, matching her eyes and hair. She wasn't unnaturally
still—in fact, she seemed to be breathing. Was she manipulating me?

"Why?" I asked.

She looked up. Blue eyes as big as a fish—I remembered there was a point where
they looked strange and inhuman to me. Now they looked as natural as my own.
"It'll be good for me," she said quietly. "To have a friend on the trip." She smiled
like an imp. "It'll be good for you, too, to get out of here." She waved at the room.

"I like it here." I said. "I think I'll stay."

She lost her smile. "Everything can change, Jake." She stood and opened a door
I hadn't seen before and stood. Through the door was darkness. "Everything."

She closed the door after her and I was alone in the room.

Rosie moved her things into the guest room. When we rehearsed Rosie always sat at
the table, watching her tablet but saying very little. I nodded to her to show her I
knew she was there. I wasn't going to ignore her. But it felt like trench warfare between us. As soon as a session was over she'd retire to the guest room. I always knew
where she was in the house through some kind of electric sixth sense: she's in the
bathroom. She's pacing in the guest room. She's coming down for coffee. But we
weren't speaking much.

Not having anything else to occupy me, I concentrated on getting ready for the
concert.

Over the next few days Dot worked us hard. Just like Tom had warned me, different speeds, different sounds—sometimes Dot would signal with her hands to draw
out a chord. Other times she'd have us cut it short. We were all sweating and limp
at the end of rehearsals.

I sat down, weakly nursing a seltzer. "Do you put your other band through this?"

"You're just not used to it. We'll get there."

I sipped the tingling water. Nothing ever seemed to taste so good as seltzer. "At
least your hair's not on fire."

With a *crump*, her short black hair burst into a blazing pyre that spread upwards
to the top of the wall and curled down the edges, making the edges appear to curl
and blacken.

"You must," she said quietly. "Be prepared for anything."

Two days before the concert Rosie carefully archived everything. Then, she confirmed the power supply had several hours of battery and loaded Dot into her car.
While she was doing that, Jess, Obi, Olive, and I packed up the instruments and any
specialty electronics we needed that wouldn't be at the hall in Van Nuys. Rosie and

I carefully avoided one another, speaking politely and cautiously. At one point or another I caught the rest of the band watching us: John: tolerant, Olive: sympathetic, Obi: rolling his eyes.

Then, in two cars and a truck and the desert heat, we began the long drive down Johnson Mountain Way to civilization.

That night, once she had Dot installed to her satisfaction, Rosie gave me a sterile peck on the cheek and left the hall. I had no idea where she was going or when she might be back. I figured she would be at the concert but there were no guarantees.

That Saturday night I was nervous as I watched the crowd through the curtain. I looked for Rosie but I couldn't see her. Instead, I saw stranger after stranger.

"Looks like a nice crowd." Jess glanced at me and grinned. "We knock 'em dead and it's a tour contract. Good work for a year."

"Who told you that?"

"Dot. We were talking with her on a screen in the dressing room. I looked for you but you weren't around."

"I was here."

"So I figured." Jess watched the crowd. "How did you get such a big crowd?"

I laughed shortly. "An impromptu Dot concert in Van Nuys. What did you *think* was going to happen?"

Jess chuckled and looked through the curtain. "A lot of kids. Her new stuff isn't for kids."

I had seen that. Dot's adolescent demographic was well represented in the front row. But behind them were some in their twenties and thirties. A few in the back were oldsters, embarrassed and looking around to see if anybody recognized them.

Jess and I checked the equipment on stage. Especially, Dot's display tank: twenty five feet wide, ten feet deep and nine feet high. Hitachi had come through with one even bigger than we'd asked for. We crowded the instruments as close as we dared. I had placed warning tape between every band member and the tank, glowing side towards the musician. I didn't want anyone electrocuted or blinded.

When we were finished I looked through the curtain back at the crowd. I still didn't see Rosie.

Jess put his hand on my arm. "It's going to be a great tour."

"Is it going to happen?"

Jess waved that away. "Of course. Even if there were no new material this is still going to be Dot at her best. Hitachi would be crazy not to capitalize on it. Whatever Rosie did to her has made her a much better performer."

"Big talk about someone who's never performed in front of a live audience."

"What are you talking about? Dot's been in front of audiences for years—this Dot is just the latest iteration. Like I said, it'll be great. If you're smart, you'll come along."

I bit my lip. "Who knows where we'll end up?"

"Who *cares?* This is going to be the ride of a lifetime." He looked at me quizzically. "Did you ever see *Metropolis?*"

"I have no idea."

"Then you've never seen it. Fritz Lang. 1927. Big city with oppressor and oppressed class. There's this girl, Maria, who's trying to make things right. This mad scientist takes the girl and makes a robot in her likeness. It's the *robot* Maria who changes things."

I had no idea what he was talking about. "The robot is the hero?"

"No. The robot Maria has no idea what it's doing. Everybody thinks the robot is acting for them but all the time it's acting on its own and for no other reason than to create chaos. But it is out of the *chaos* that change begins." Jess pointed at the tank. "Dot's our robot Maria."

I mulled that over. Jess was always deeper than I was.

He tapped me on the shoulder and left. "It's time."

He was right. Now or never.

I had only really known Dot, the composer. Dot, the performer, was a different animal.

We began "Stardust" with a long intro. On the downbeat, she ran in stage left and slid across the tank as if on ice, holding up one arm in a fist. She hit that downbeat note as high and sharp as a scream. The crowd roared.

The singer is the focal point, the organizing principle, the interface between audience and band. She is the medium and the message, the attention of the crowd is on her. The attention of the band is on her. I never realized how much.

All through the first act it came to me again and again that this was, and always had been, her material, regardless of who wrote it. But now she was filling it in, backing it up, owning it. She was continually testing the crowd. At first I didn't understand what she was doing. The changes were so quick I thought it was my imagination—roughen the voice, then smooth, a trill here, holding back the beat there, adding flourishes at the end of one phrase that lead into the next, duets with herself—things we'd never done in rehearsal but were so perfect right now. She cajoled, excited, threatened, warned, and soothed the audience one minute to the next, between songs, during songs.

I realized it was her performance engine at work, figuring out what worked, what didn't. How to prepare the crowd for Act Two.

And she brought us along with her.

She reached back to me, to Olive, to Obi, to Jess, dancing near us when it was our solo, dropping her voice below ours to bring us out to the audience. She wasn't just Dot, she was Dot *with us*.

As we lit into "Sexual Girl" I used the melody of "Stardust" in my chorus solo, echoing the girl that had started the concert. She was a woman now.

I looked again. She *was* a woman now. With hips and breast, her voice lower, rougher. Dot had aged herself along with the music and now looked every inch a young woman, eager, enthusiastic, open to the world.

"Sexual Girl," and Act One, ended with Obi hitting the bass drum like a hammer. As the sounds from the band were swamped in the applause, I relaxed and started to take the guitar strap over my head. Then, I heard a sweet violin playing something like a lilting Irish tune. I looked up and Jess was playing, backed up by Olive and a light snare from Obi. They were watching me. Dot was facing the audience.

"Now something for a friend of mine."

Olive dropped into a chord progression I had not heard in twelve years. It didn't matter. I knew it instantly: "Don't Make Me Cry."

I thought I had heard every variation of that song: pathetic, pleading, angry, bitter, desperate. Dot's was a demand and a refusal to miss an opportunity: don't you *dare* make me cry.

I picked up my guitar and caught up with the band by the chorus. I didn't know what I felt. Used? Manipulated? Happy?

The crowd kept the beat and I threw whatever I had back at them.

At the end, she disappeared in a burst of light and the crowd howled, clapped, stomped their feet. We bowed and the curtain came down for the break.

Behind the curtain I caught Jess by the arm.

"Like that?" Jess smiled. "Dot wanted it to be a surprise."

"I was surprised all right." I felt a mix of elation and bitterness I didn't understand.

"You make me tired." Jess waved me off. "I'm getting some water before the next set."

My earbud chimed. The number was masked but I answered anyway, half hoping to hear Rosie's voice.

"Don't worry, Jake," said Dot. "The concert is going fine."

I pulled out the bud, stared it, put it back in. "Is there nothing you can't hack?"

"Not much. By the way, third row, stage left about six seats in. The Hitachi contingent is in the back, recording the event."

I parted the curtain. Rosie was getting up from her chair and moving towards the exit.

"Checking her investment," I said.

"Don't be petty. She's just as self-involved as you are." Dot laughed, a thin chime in my ear. "Neither of you are as pleasant as you think you are. Act Two is coming up. I'll be ready. You better be."

I hesitated. "Dot? What's it like being you?"

Long pause. Then, I heard her voice, almost but never quite human. "Like burning at the stake trying to signal through the flames."

"What does that mean?"

She laughed. "The exit door is behind the curtain, stage right."

The door opened into a parking lot. Four or five people were there, blowing smoke. Rosie was watching the way the sun already below the horizon was still lighting the sky.

"Hey," I said.

She turned to me with a little smile. "That was a good first set."

"With any luck the second one will be better."

Rosie nodded. She tapped the ash from her cigarette. "I'm not going to apologize for what I do."

"I didn't ask—"

"Shut up." She inhaled and blew out smoke. "You are a musician. You are fully able to take apart a song and put it back together in a way no one else has ever thought of. I've seen you pick up a melody from the radio and whistle it inside out. Before I met you I didn't even know that could be done." She dropped the butt into the smoker can. "I'm a computational scientist. I do with algorithms and analysis what you do with music. All of what you and Dot are doing is enabled by my work."

"I know that." I took her hand. "Thanks."

She hugged me tightly and then pushed me away. "Go on. You don't want to be distracted by me."

Act Two opened with "Rough Trade" and "Easy Mark," the first of the darker songs Dot was trying to put over. She put a growl under the vocals. I answered with a hard edge. I hadn't played like this since I was a kid. Correction, I had *never* played like this.

She played the crowd, she played *us*. We were the instruments.

Was she manipulating me? Was she manipulating all of us? Probably. And it was bringing out our best. We swung into the finale.

I was about to take the chorus in the middle of "Hard Road Home" and Dot turned to me and winked.

As I started my solo, someone came out of the side of the tank playing the guitar. It was me.

He—I—faced Dot. As I played, he played. As I moved, he moved. As she danced to me, I danced back to her. When we sang together, I was facing her, then the audience.

I remembered what Dot had said: *The illusion of meaning and purpose.* Wasn't this meaning and purpose enough? The only illusion was the illusion of permanence. Things didn't have to crash and burn. It *could* work out between me and Rosie. Dot's tour *could* go perfectly. This feeling might not last the song but it *could* last forever.

Like Jess said, it would be the ride of a lifetime.

And I had an anomalous non-deterministic emergent event deriving from conflicting algorithms: I realized this was where I wanted to be. Not in my safe and dusty house. Not in California. Just right here. Right now.

When the last chord of "Hard Road Home" finished, my duplicate faded. Dot turned to look at me and grinned, big and wide. She knew me root and branch. From Markov change to inference-causality matrix. She knew—had always known—I would go with her and follow her as long as this lasted.

With that, I struck the opening chords to "Sudden, Broken, and Unexpected."

Dot drew a ragged breath and began to sing.

fireborn

ROBERT CHARLES WILSON

Ambition, particularly the desire to find a better life, can make you reach for the sky—but sometimes it can be dangerous to reach too high.

Robert Charles Wilson made his first sale in 1974, to Analog, but little more was heard from him until the late '80s, when he began to publish a string of ingenious and well-crafted novels and stories that have since established him among the top ranks of the writers who came to prominence in the last two decades of the twentieth century. His first novel, A Hidden Place, *appeared in 1986. He won the John W. Campbell Memorial Award for his novel,* The Chronoliths, *the Philip K. Dick Award for his novel,* Mysterium, *and the Aurora Award for his story "The Perseids." In 2006, he won the Hugo Award for his acclaimed novel,* Spin. *His other books include the novels* Memory Wire, Gypsies, The Divide, The Harvest, A Bridge of Years, Darwinia, Blind Lake, Bios, Axis, *and* Julian, *and a collection of his short work,* The Perseids and Other Stories. *His forthcoming novel is* Burning Paradise. *He lives in Toronto, Canada.*

Sometimes in January the sky comes down close if we walk on a country road, and turn our faces up to look at the sky.

Onyx turned her face up to the sky as she walked with her friend Jasper beside a mule-cart on the road that connected Buttercup County to the turnpike. She had spent a day counting copper dollars at the changehouse and watching bad-tempered robots trudge east- and west-bound through the crust of yesterday's snow. Sunny days with snow on the ground made robots irritable, Jasper had claimed. Onyx didn't know if this was true—it seemed so, but what seemed so wasn't always truly so.

You think too much, Jasper had told her.

And you don't think enough, Onyx had answered haughtily. She walked next to him now as he lead the mule, keeping her head turned up because she liked to see the stars even when the January wind came cutting past the margins of her lamb's-wool hood. Some of the stars were hidden because the moon was up and shining white. But Onyx liked the moon, too, for the way it silvered the peaks and saddles of the mountains and cast spidery tree-shadows over the unpaved road.

That was how it happened that Onyx first saw the skydancer vaulting over a mountain pass northwest of Buttercup County.

Jasper didn't see it because he was looking at the road ahead. Jasper was a tall boy, two breadloaves taller than Onyx, and he owned a big head with eyes made for inspecting the horizon. *It's what's in front of you that counts*, he often said. Jasper believed roads went to interesting places—that's why they were roads. And it was good to be on a road because that meant you were going somewhere interesting. Who cared what was up in the sky?

You never know what might fall on you, Onyx often told him. *And not every road goes to an interesting place*. The road they were on, for instance. It went to Buttercup County, and what was interesting about Buttercup County? Onyx had lived there for all of her nineteen years. If there was anything interesting in Buttercup County, Onyx had seen it twice and ignored it a dozen times more.

Well, that's why you need a road, Jasper said—*to go somewhere else*.

Maybe, Onyx thought. Maybe so. Maybe not. In the meantime, she would keep on looking at the sky.

At first, she didn't know what she was seeing up over the high northwest col of the western mountains. She had heard about skydancers from travelers bound for or returning from Harvest out on the plains in autumn, where skydancers were said to dance for the fireborn when the wind brought great white clouds sailing over the brown and endless prairie. But those were travelers' tales, and Onyx discounted such storytelling. Some part of those stories might be true, but she guessed not much: maybe fifty cents on the dollar, Onyx thought. What she thought tonight was, *That's a strange cloud*.

It was a strange and brightly-colored cloud, pink and purple even in the timid light of the moon. It did not move in a windblown fashion. It was shaped like a person. It looked like a person in a purple gown with a silver crown and eyes as wide as respectable townships. It was as tall as the square-shouldered mountain peak Onyx's people called Tall Tower. Onyx gasped as her mind made reluctant sense of what her stubborn eyes insisted on showing her.

Jasper had been complaining about the cold, and what a hard thing it was to walk a mule cart all the way home from the turnpike on a chilly January night, but he turned his eyes away from the road at the sound of Onyx's surprise. He looked where Onyx was looking and stopped walking. After a long pause, he said, "That's a skydancer—I'll bet you a copper dollar it is!"

"How do you know? Have you ever seen a skydancer?"

"Not to look at. Not until tonight. But what else could it be?"

Skydancers were as big as mountains and danced with clouds, and this apparition was as big as a mountain and appeared to be dancing, so Onyx guessed that Jasper might be right. And it was a strange and lonely thing to see on a country road on a January night. They stopped to watch the skydancer dance, though the wind blew cold around them and the mule complained with wheezing and groaning. The skydancer moved in ways Onyx would not have thought possible, turning like a whirlwind in the moonlight, rising over the peak of Tall Tower and seeming for a moment to balance there, then flying still higher, turning pirouettes of stately slowness in the territory of the stars. "It's coming closer," Jasper said.

Was it? *Yes*: Onyx thought so. It was hard to tell because the skydancer was so big. Skydancers were made by the fireborn, and the fireborn made miraculous things, but Onyx could not imagine how this creature had come to be. Was it alive or was it an illusion? If it came down to earth, could she touch it?

It began to seem as if she might have that opportunity. The skydancer appeared to lose its balance in the air. Its vast limbs suddenly stiffened. Its legs, which could span counties, locked at the knee. The wind began to tumble it sidelong. Parts of the skydancer grew transparent or flew off like evanescent colored clouds. "I think it's broken," said Jasper.

Broken and shrinking, it began to fall. *It'll fall near here,* Onyx thought, if it continued on its wind-tumbled course. *If there's anything left of it, the way it's coming apart.*

It came all apart in the air, but there was something left behind, something small that fell more gently, swaying like an autumn leaf on its way from branch to winter. It fell nearby—down a slope away from the road, on a hillside where in summer wild rhubarb put out scarlet stalks of flowers.

"Come on, let's find it," Jasper said.

"It might be dangerous."

"It might," said Jasper, who was not afraid of the possibility of danger, but all the more inclined to go get into it. They left the mule anchored to its cart and went hunting for what had fallen, while the moonlight was bright enough to show them the way.

They found a young woman standing on the winter hillside, and it was obvious to Onyx that she was fireborn—perhaps, therefore, not actually young. Onyx knew the woman was fireborn because she was naked on a January night and seemed not to mind it. Onyx found the woman's nakedness perplexing. Jasper seemed fascinated.

Though the woman was naked, she had been wearing a harness of cloth and metal, which she had discarded: it lay on the ground at her feet, parts of it glowing sunset colors, parts of it twitching like the feelers of an unhappy ant.

They came and stood near enough to speak to the woman. The woman, who was about Onyx's size but had paler skin and hair that gave back the moonlight in shades of amber, was looking at the sky, whispering to herself. When she noticed Onyx and Jasper, she spoke to them in words Onyx didn't understand. Then she cocked her shoulder and said in sensible words, "You can't hurt me. It would be a mistake to try."

"We don't want to hurt you," Jasper said, before Onyx could compose a response. "We saw you fall, if you falling was what we saw. We thought you might need help."

"I'm in no danger," the woman said, and it seemed to Onyx her voice was silvery, like a tune played on a flute, but not just any old wooden flute: a silver one. "But thank you."

"You must be a long way from home. Are you lost?"

"My devices misfunctioned. My people will come for me. We have a compound on the other side of the pass."

"Do you need a ride, ma'am? Onyx and I can take you in our cart."

"Wait, that's a long way," Onyx said. Anyway it was her cart, not Jasper's, and he shouldn't be offering it without consulting her.

"Yes," Jasper agreed, "much too far for an undressed woman to walk on a night like this."

Onyx considered kicking him.

The fireborn woman hesitated. Then she smiled. It was a charming smile, Onyx had to admit. The woman had shiny teeth, a complete set. "Would you really do that for me?"

"Ma'am, yes, of course, my privilege," said Jasper.

"All right, then," the woman said. "I might like that. Thank you. My name is Anna Tingri Five."

Onyx, who knew what the "Five" meant, gaped in amazement.

"I'm Jasper," said Jasper. "And this is Onyx."

"You should put on some clothes," Onyx said in a small voice. "Ma'am."

Anna Tingri Five twitched her shoulder and blinked, and a shimmery robe suddenly covered her nakedness. "Is that better?"

"Much," said Onyx.

On the road to the fireborn compound, as the mule cart bucked over rutted snow hard as ice, the three of them discussed their wants, as strangers often do.

Onyx was expected at home, but her mother and father and two brothers wouldn't worry much if she was late. Probably they would think she had stayed the night in Buttercup Town, detained by business. Onyx worked at the changehouse there and was often kept late by unexpected traffic. Her parents might even hope she had stayed late for the purpose of keeping Jasper company: her parents liked Jasper and had hinted at the possibility of a wedding. Onyx resented such talk—she liked Jasper well enough, but perhaps not well enough to contemplate marriage. Not that Jasper had hinted at any such ambition. Jasper wanted to sail to Africa and find the Fifth Door to the moon and grow rich or immortal, which, Onyx imagined would leave him little time for wedding foolishness.

Anna Tingri Five perched on a frozen bag of wheat flour in the mule cart, saying, "I am, as you must suppose, fireborn."

No doubt about that. And how astonished Onyx's parents and two brothers would be to discover she had been consorting with the fireborn! The fireborn came through Buttercup County only on rare occasions, and then only one or two of them, young ones, mostly male, riding robots on their incomprehensible quests, hardly deigning to speak to the townspeople. Now here Onyx was right next to a five-born female—a talkative one!

"Was that you in the sky, dancing?" Jasper asked.

"Yes. Until the bodymaker broke."

"No offense, but you looked about five miles tall."

"Only a mile," said Anna Tingri Five, a smile once again dimpling her moonlit face.

"What's a skydancer doing in Buttercup County, if you don't mind me asking?"

"Practicing for the Harvest, here where there are mountain winds to wrestle with and clouds that come high and fast from the west. We mean to camp here through the summer."

Without so much as a by-your-leave, Onyx thought indignantly, though when had the fireborn ever asked permission of common mortals?

"You mean to dance at the Harvest?" asked Jasper.

"I mean to win the competition and be elevated to the Eye of the Moon," said Anna Tingri Five.

The Eye of the Moon: best seen when the moon was in shadow. Tonight the moon was full and the Eye was invisible, but some nights, when only a sliver of the moon shone white, Onyx had seen the Eye in the darker hemisphere, a ring of red glow, aloof and unwinking. It was where the fireborn went when they were tired of living one life after another. It was what they did instead of dying.

Since Anna Tingri Five had divulged an ambition, Onyx felt obliged to confess one of her own. "I'm nineteen years old," she said, "and one day I mean to go east and see the cities of the Atlantic Coast. I'm tired of Buttercup County. I'm a good counter. I can add and substract and divide and multiply. I can double-entry bookkeep. I could get a city job and do city things. I could look at tall buildings every day and live in one of them."

Spoken baldly into the cold air of a January night, her desire froze into a childish embarrassment. She felt herself blushing. But Anna Tingri Five only nodded thoughtfully.

"And I mean to go east as well," Jasper said, "but I won't stop in any city. I can lift and haul and tie a dozen different knots. I'll hire myself onto a sailing ship and sail to Africa."

He ended his confession there, though there was more to it. Onyx knew that he wanted to go to Africa and find the Fifth Door, which might gain him admission to the Eye of the Moon. All the world's four Doors, plus perhaps the hidden Fifth, were doorways to the moon. Even a common mortal could get to the Eye that way, supposedly, though the fireborn would never let a commoner past the gate. That was why Jasper dreamed about the hidden Fifth. It was his only hope of living more than one life.

Skeptical Onyx would have bet that the Fifth Door was a legend without any truth at the heart of it, but she had stopped saying so to Jasper, because it made him irritable. Lately, he had begun to guard his ambition as if it were a fragile secret possession, and he didn't mention it now.

"This is my fifth life," Anna Tingri Five said in her silver flute voice, "and I'm tired of coming through the juvenation fires with half my memories missing, starting out all over again with nothing but the ghosts of Anna Tingri One, Two, Three, and Four to talk to when I talk to myself. I want to live forever in the Eye of the Moon and make things out of pure philosophy."

Onyx didn't comprehend half this peroration, but she understood the yearning in the words of Anna Tingri Five.

"Both of you want to leave this place?" Anna Tingri Five asked.

Yes. Both.

"Come into our encampment then" said Anna Tingri Five. "It's warm inside. Let me repay you for your interesting kindness."

They came to the place the fireborn had made for themselves. No one in Buttercup County had seen the fireborn arrive, and their camp was over the rim of a hill where no one went in the leafless winter. But the camp itself was not leafless. A mortal commoner passing by, Anna Tingri Five explained, would see nothing unusual. Some ensorcellment kept the campground hidden from casual glances. But Anna Tingri Five allowed Onyx and Jasper to see the place and pass inside its perimeter. Inside, the fireborn had undone winter. In their enchanted circle, it was a pleasant summer night. The trees were leafy, the meadow plants flowering. Vast silken pavilion tents of many colors had been staked to the fragrant ground, and hovering radiant globes supplemented the pale moonlight. It was late, and Onyx supposed most of the fireborn were asleep, but some few were still passing between the tents, talking in unknown languages, as lean and tall and perfect as flesh can be. Supple robots moved silently among them, performing inscrutable robot tasks. Onyx marveled at the warmth of the air (she shrugged out of her woolen coat, loosened a button on her hempen shirt), and Jasper's eyes grew big with awe and eagerness.

"Spend the night with us," said Anna Tingri Five.

Anna Tingri Five had never been out of contact with her compound even after her bodymaker failed; at the first tickle of a wistful thought a robot would have flown her home through the January sky. But she had been intrigued and interested by the helpful commoners who appeared out of the darkness. She had met few real commoners and was curious about them. She thought that this pair might be worth keeping. That was why, a few days later, she offered them jobs in the encampment and a free ride, come the end of summer, to the continent's great Harvest Festival.

Onyx's parents begged her not to accept the offer. Her mother wailed; her father raged; but they had known they were raising a rover ever since they named their restless baby girl Onyx. And they had two stout and unimaginative sons who were bound to remain in Buttercup County and lead useful and sensible lives.

Jasper's father had milled grain all his life, had continued to mill grain after the death of his wife ten years ago, and would mill grain until the day he died. He had once harbored his own ambition to see the world outside Buttercup County, and was pleased and terrified in equal parts by the prospect of his son's departure. "Write me letters from foreign places," he demanded, and Jasper promised to do so. When father and son said goodbye, both wept. They knew that life was short and difficult and that, as a rule, commoners only lived once.

It was soon obvious to Onyx that the fireborn had no real need of hired help. It was not that she and Jasper did no work—they did—or that they were not paid for their work—they were, in genuine copper dollars. But the carrying of water and the serving of food had previously been conducted by robots, and Onyx felt embarrassed to be doing robot work, even for generous wages. The fireborn said please and thank you and smiled their thin, distant smiles. *But we're pets*, Onyx complained to Jasper one day. *We're not good for anything.*

Speak for yourself, said Jasper.

It became increasingly clear that Anna Tingri Five favored Jasper over Onyx.

Onyx assigned herself the task of learning all she could about the fireborn. The first thing she learned was that there were greater and lesser ranks among them. Some of the fireborn in the skydancer camp were firstborns, who had never passed through the rejuvenating fire and who had trivializing Ones attached to their names. As old as some of them might seem, the first-borns were novices, junior members of the troupe. They watched, listened, kept to their own circles. They were not skydancers but apprentices to skydancers; they managed the small incomprehensible machines that made the dances possible.

The dancers themselves were many-born: some Fives, some Sevens, a couple of Nines. And despite her reservations, Onyx loved to watch them dance. Whenever they danced she would leave her unimportant work (folding ceremonial silks, crushing seeds to flavor soup) and study the process from its beginning to its end. The dancers' apprentices helped them don the harnesses they called bodymakers, and in their bodymakers the dancers looked like some robot's dream of humanity, perfect coffee-colored flesh peeping out between lashings of glass and sky-blue metal. But there was nothing awkward about the way the harnessed dancers moved. They grew buoyant, they stepped lightly to the launching meadow, they flexed their supple limbs as they assembled. Then they flew into the air.

And once they were aloft, still and small as eagles hovering on an updraft, the bodymakers made their bodies.

Onyx understood that the bodies were projections of the dancers' bodies, and that the projected bodies were made of almost nothing—of air momentarily frozen and made to bend light to create the illusion of colors and surfaces. But they looked real, and they were stunningly large, one mile or more top to bottom as nearly as Onyx could calculate. Because they were insubstantial, the bodies were not affected by even the most powerful winds, but they touched and rebounded and gripped one another as if they were real things. In the rondo dances, vast hands held vast hands as if air were flesh.

"I'll bet I could do that," Jasper said yearningly, on one of the mornings when they sat together at the edge of the flying meadow and watched until their necks ached with up-staring.

"Bet a copper dollar you couldn't," said Onyx.

"Some day you'll die of not believing."

"Some day you'll die of dreaming!"

The greatest of the dancers—a category that included Anna Tingri Five—were rivals, and they danced alone or with single partners selected from among the lesser dancers. During the Harvest festivities, a single Finest Dancer would be selected, and that individual would be offered transit to the Eye of the Moon. Only two dancers in the troupe were eligible to compete for this year's Moon Prize: Anna Tingri Five and a man named Dawa Nine.

Both danced beautifully, in Onyx's opinion. Anna Tingri Five danced as a blue-skinned goddess with bells on her wrists and ankles. When she flirted with the white clouds that climbed the sunlit mountains from the west, her bells tolled sonorously. Dawa Nine danced as an ancient warrior, with silver armor and a silver sword on his hip. Often in his practice, he rose to impossible heights and swooped like a predatory bird to within a feather's-breadth of the treetops.

But Jasper had eyes only for Anna Tingri Five, an attention the fireborn dancer enjoyed and encouraged, much to Onyx's disgust. Jasper pleased Anna Tingri Five by befriending the apprentice who maintained her gear, helping him with small tasks and asking occasional pertinent questions. On idle days he folded Anna

Tingri Five's silk and poured her dinner wine. What he hoped to accomplish with this foolish fawning was beyond Onyx. Until it became clear to her.

One cloudless night in spring, when the fireborn were gathered under a great pavilion tent for their communal meal, Anna Tingri Five stood and cleared her throat (*like the sound of a silver flute clearing its throat,* Onyx thought) and announced that she had revised her plan for the Festival and that she would teach the commoner Jasper to dance.

The fireborn were startled, and so was Onyx, who nearly dropped the pitcher of wine she was carrying. Last month, she had been given a device the size of a pea and the shape of a snail, which she wore behind her ear, and which translated the confusing languages of the fireborn into words she could mostly understand. In that startled moment, the device conveyed a tumult of dismay, disapproval, disdain.

Anna Tingri Five defended her decision, citing examples of novelty dancers who had been admitted to tournaments in supporting roles, citing the elevation of certain commoners to near-fireborn status for certain sacred functions, citing Jasper's fascination with the dance. A few of the fireborn nodded tolerantly; most did not.

Jasper had been training in secret, said Anna Tingri Five, and tomorrow he would make his first flight.

Jasper wasn't present in the tent that night, or Onyx would have given him her best scornful glare. She was forced to save that for the morning, when she joined a crowd of the fireborn for the occasion of his ascent. She watched (he avoided her eyes) as Jasper was strapped and haltered into a bodymaker by Anna Tingri Five's sullen apprentices. She watched with grim attention as Anna Tingri Five escorted him to the launching meadow. She watched as he rose into a mild blue sky, bobbing like a paper boat on a pond. Then he engaged his bodymaker.

Jasper became a mile-high man. A man dressed like a farmer. A flying peasant. An enormous gawking rube.

The false Jasper flexed its county-wide limbs. It turned an awkward, lunging pirouette.

Now the fireborn understood the nature of the dance: they laughed in approval.

Onyx scowled and stalked away.

"It's a silly custom," Onyx said. "Skydancing."

Perhaps she shouldn't have said this—perhaps especially not to Dawa Nine, the troupe's other keynote dancer. But he had come to her, not vice versa. And she guessed that he deserved to hear her true and honest opinion.

"You only say that because you're jealous."

Dawa Nine was a tall man. His skin was dark as hard coal, even darker than Onyx's skin. His head was well-shaped and hairless. He had lived nine lives and that was enough for him. He aimed to dance his way into immortality, and the most immediate obstacle in his path was Anna Tingri Five. "I am not jealous," Onyx said.

It was noon on a spring day and the sun was shining and he had come to her tent and asked to speak with her. Onyx had agreed. But what could Dawa Nine have to say that would interest Onyx? She cared very little about the fireborn or their ambitions. In five days, the troupe would leave Buttercup County for the windswept granaries of the Great Plains. Onyx planned to leave them there and make her own way to the cities of the Atlantic Coast. She had saved enough copper dollars to make the journey easier.

"Be honest," Dawa Nine said. His voice was not a flute. His voice was the wind hooting through the owl-holes of an old tree, and his smile was soft as moonlight. "With yourself, if not with me. You came here with Jasper, and he was your everyday boyfriend, and now he's flying with a beautiful fireborn dancer. What sane woman wouldn't be jealous?"

"It's not like I ever would have married him," Onyx protested.

"In that case, you should stop paying him such close attention."

"I'm not! I'm *ignoring* him."

"Then let me help you ignore him."

I'm doing fine in that department, thought Onyx. "What do you mean?"

"Work as my apprentice."

"No! I don't want to fly. I don't want to be some dancer's clown."

"I'm not suggesting that you learn to fly, Miss Onyx. But you can husband my machinery and harness my bodymaker. The boy who does it for me now is a mere One, and you're smarter than he is—I can tell."

Onyx took this for fact, not flattery. And—yes—Jasper would be gratifyingly annoyed to find Onyx working for Anna Tingri Five's bitter rival. "But what do *you* get out of this, Old Nine? Not just a better apprentice, I'll bet."

"Of course not. You're a commoner. You can tell me about Jasper. Who he is, what he wants, how he might dance—what Anna Tingri Five might make of him."

"I will not be your spy," Onyx said.

"Well, think about it," said Dawa Nine.

Dawa Nine's offer was on Onyx's mind as the troupe packed its gear and left Buttercup County.

The fireborn all rode robots, and robots carried their gear and supplies, and even Onyx and Jasper were given robots to ride. The troupe found and followed the road that ran through Buttercup Town, and Onyx was able to wave to her parents from the comfortable shoulder of a tall machine. They waved back fearfully; Jasper's father was also present, also waving and weeping; and Onyx burned with the pangs of home-leaving as they passed the hotel, the counting house where she had worked, the general store, the barber shop. Then Buttercup Town was behind them, and her thoughts moved differently.

She thought about commoners and the fireborn and the Eye of the Moon.

Now that she had dined and slept and bathed with them, the fireborn were far less daunting than they had seemed to her in stories. Powerful, yes; masters of strange possibilities, yes; rich beyond calculation, surely. But as striving and envious as anyone else. Cruel and kind. Thoughtless and wise. Why then were there two kinds of people, commoners and fireborn?

Legend had it that commoners and fireborn had parted ways during the Great Hemoclysm centuries ago. But not even the fireborn knew much about that disaster. Some said the Eye of the Moon had watched it. Some said the Eye of the Moon had only just come into existence when the world began to burn. Some said the Eye of the Moon had somehow *caused* the Hemoclysm (but Onyx kept that notion to herself, for it was a heresy; the fireborn considered the Eye a holy thing).

Onyx cared little about the Eye. It was where the fireborn went after they had lived their twelve allotted lives—or sooner, if they tired of life on Earth and could claim some worthy achievement. In the Eye, supposedly, the fireborn wore whatever bodies they chose and lived in cities made entirely of thought. They could travel across the sky—there were Eyes, some claimed, on other planets, not just the moon. One day the Eye would rule the entire universe. Or so it was said.

As a child on a pew in Buttercup County's Church of True Things, Onyx had learned how Jesu Rinpoche had saved wisdom from the Hemoclysm and planted the Four Doors to the Moon at the corners of the Earth. The story of the Fifth Door, in which Jasper so fervently believed, was a minor heresy much favoured by old pipe-smoking men. What was the truth of it all? Onyx didn't know. Probably, she thought, nine-tenths of these tales were nonsense. She had been called cynical or atheistic for saying so. But most of everything people said was nonsense. Why should this be different?

All she really knew was that there were commoners and there were fireborn. The fireborn traveled at will and played for a living and made robots that mined mountains and cultivated harvests. The commoners lived at the feet of the fireborn, untroubled unless they *made* trouble. That was how it had been since the day she was born, and that was how it would be when she left the world behind. Only dreamers like Jasper believed differently. And Jasper was a fool.

Jasper's foolishness grew so obvious that Onyx gave up speaking to him, at least until they argued.

The troupe descended in long robotic marches from the mountains to the hinterland, where the only hills were gentle drumlins and rolling moraines, and where the rivers rippled bright and slow as Easter ribbons. Some days, the sky was blue and empty. Some days, clouds came rolling out of the west like gray monsters with lightning hearts.

The road they followed was paved and busy with traffic. They made their camps by the roadside where wild grass grew and often stayed encamped for days. A month passed in this lazy transit, then another. Where the plains had been farmed, a vast green bounty mounded and grew ripe. The Harvest approached.

Jasper's dancing skills improved with practice, though Onyx was loathe to admit it. Of course, he wasn't as good as the fireborn dancers, but he wasn't supposed to be. He was a foil, as Dawa Nine explained to her: a decorative novelty. The theme of Anna Tingri Five's dance was the misbegotten love of a fireborn woman for a young and gawkish commoner. It was a story the fireborn had been telling for centuries, and the tale was always tragic. It had been set to music many times, though Anna Tingri Five would be the first to dance it. Jasper was required only to clump about the sky in crude yearning poses, and to adopt a willing stillness while Anna Tingri Five beckoned him, teased him, accepted him, loved him, and forsook him in a series of highly symbolic set-dances. The rehearsals were impressive, and with her head turned to the late-summer sky, Onyx even felt a kind of sour pride: *That's our Jasper a mile high and another mile tall*, she thought. *That's the same Jasper who walked behind a mule cart in Buttercup County ten months ago.* But Jasper was as stupid and bemused as the peasant he portrayed in the dance.

And then, one night as she served wine, Onyx discovered Jasper with Anna Tingri Five in a dark corner of the fireborn pavilion, the two of them exchanging bird-peck kisses.

Onyx left the pavilion for the bitter consolation of the prairie night. Jasper guessed what she had seen and followed her out, calling her name. But Onyx didn't stop or look back. She didn't want to see his traitorous face. She went straight to Dawa Nine instead.

Jasper caught her the next day, as she passed along a row of trees where a creek cut the tabletop prairie. The day was warm. Onyx wore a yellow silk skirt one of the fireborn women had given her, and a yellow silk scarf that spoke in gestures to the wind. The troupe's lesser dancers rehearsed among clouds high above, casting undulant shadows across the wild grass.

"Don't you trust me?" Jasper asked, blocking her path.

"Trust you to do what? I trust you to do what I've seen you doing," said Onyx.

"You have no *faith*!"

"You have no *sense*!"

"All I want is to learn about the Eye of the Moon and how to get there," Jasper said.

"I don't care about the Eye of the Moon! I want to live in a city and look at tall buildings! And all I have to do to get there is walk toward the sunrise!"

"I'll walk alongside you," said Jasper. "Honest, Onyx!"

"Really? Then let's walk!"

". . . after the Dance, of course, I mean. . . ."

"Hah!"

"But I owe her that much," he said, not daring to pronounce the name of Anna Tingri Five for fear of further provoking Onyx. His big eyes pleaded wordlessly.

"She cares nothing for you, you mule!"

These words wounded Jasper in the tender part of his pride, and he drew back and let his vanity take command of his mouth. "Bet you're wrong," he said.

"Bet how much?"

"Ten copper dollars!"

"*It's a bet!*" cried Onyx, stalking away.

The Harvest Festival came at summer's decline, the cooling hinge of the season. The troupe joined a hundred others for the celebration. Onyx marvelled at the gathering.

There were many harvests in the world but only a few Festivals. Each of the world's great breadlands held one. Prosaically, it was the occasion on which the fireborn collected the bounty of grain and vegetables that had been amassed by their fleets of agricultural robots, while commoners feasted on the copious leavings, more than enough to feed all the mortal men and women of the world for the coming year. That was the great bargain that had sealed the peace between the commonfolk and the fireborn: food for all, and plenty of it. Only overbreeding could have spoiled the arrangement, and the fireborn attended to that matter with discreet lacings of antifertility substances in the grain the commoners ate. Commoners were born and commoners died, but their numbers never much varied. And the fireborn bore children only rarely, since each lived a dozen long lives before adjourning to the Eye of the Moon. Their numbers, too, were stable.

But the Harvest Festival was more than that. It was an occasion of revelry and pilgrimage, a great gathering of people and robots on the vast stage of the world's steppes and prairies, a profane and holy intermingling. The fireborn held exhibitions and contests, to be judged by the Council of the Twelve-Lived and marvelled at by commonfolk. Jugglers juggled, poets sang, artisans hawked their inscrutable arts. Prayer flags snapped gaily in the wind. And of course: *skydancers danced*.

Several troupes had arrived at the site of the North American festival (where the junction of two rivers stitched a quilt of yellow land), but the troupe Onyx served was one of the best-regarded and was allotted the third day and third night of the Festival for its performances.

By day, the lesser dancers danced. Crowds gawked and marvelled from below. Warm afternoon air called up clouds like tall white sailing ships, and the skydancers danced with them, wooed them, unwound their hidden lightnings. The sky rang with bells and drums. Sunlight rebounding from the ethereal bodies of the avatars cast rainbows over empty fields, and even the agricultural robots, serene at the beginning of their seasonal rest, seemed to gaze upward with a metallic, bovine awe.

Onyx hid away with Dawa Nine, who was fasting and praying in preparation for his night flight. The best dancers danced at night, their immense avatars glowing from within. There was no sight more spectacular. The Council of the Twelve-Lived would be watching and judging. Onyx knew that Dawa Nine was deeply weary of life on Earth and determined to dance his way to the moon. And since the day she had discovered Jasper and Anna Tingri Five exchanging kisses, Onyx had promised to help him achieve that ambition—to do whatever it was in her power to do, even the dark and furtive things she ought to have disdained.

She could have offered Dawa Nine her body (as Jasper had apparently given his to Anna Tingri Five), but she was intimidated by Dawa's great age and somber manner. Instead, she had shared secrets with him. She had told him how Jasper worked Anna Tingri Five's gear, how he had learned only a few skydancing skills but had learned them well enough to serve as Anna's foil, how he had mastered the technical business of flight harnesses and bodymakers. He had even modified Anna Tingri Five's somatic generator, making her avatar's vast face nearly as subtle and expressive as her own—a trick even Dawa Nine's trained apprentices could not quite duplicate.

None of this information much helped Dawa Nine, however; if anything, it had deepened his gloomy conviction that Anna Tingri Five was bound to outdance him and steal his ticket to the Eye. Desperate measures were called for, and time was short. As the lesser dancers danced, Dawa Nine summoned Onyx into the shadow of his tent.

"I want you to make sure my bodymaker is functioning correctly," he said.

"Of course," said Onyx. "No need to say, Old Nine."

"Go into the equipment tent and inspect it. If you find any flaws, fix them."

Onyx nodded.

"And if you happen to find Anna Tingri's gear unattended—"

"Yes?"

"Fix *that*, too."

Onyx didn't need to be told twice. She went to the tent where the gear was stored, as instructed. It was a dreadful thing that Dawa had asked her to do—to tamper with Anna Tingri Five's bodymaker in order to spoil her dance. But what did Onyx care about the tribulations of the fireborn? The fireborn were nothing to her, as she was nothing to them.

Or so she told herself. Still, she was pricked with fleabites of conscience. She hunched over Dawa Nine's bodymaker, pretending to inspect it. Everything was in order, apart from Onyx's thoughts.

What had Anna Tingri Five done to deserve this cruel trick? (*Apart from being fireborn and haughty and stealing kisses from Jasper!*) And why punish Anna Tingri Five for Jasper's thoughtlessness? (*Because there was no way to punish Jasper himself!*) And by encouraging this tampering, hadn't Dawa Nine proven himself spiteful and dishonest? (*She could hardly deny it!*) And if Dawa Nine was untrustworthy, might he not blame Onyx if the deception was discovered? (*He almost certainly would!*)

It was this last thought that troubled Onyx most. She supposed that she could do as Dawa had asked: tamper with the bodymaker and ruin the dance Anna Tingri Five had so carefully rehearsed—and it might be worth the pangs of conscience it would cause her—but what of the consequences? Onyx secretly planned to leave the Festival tonight and make her way east toward the cities of the Atlantic Coast. But her disappearance would only serve to incriminate her, if the tampering were discovered. The fireborn might hunt her down and put her on trial. And if she were accused of the crime, would Dawa Nine step forward to proclaim her innocence and take the responsibility himself?

Of course he would not.

And would Onyx be believed, if she tried to pin the blame on Dawa?

Hardly.

And was *any of that* the fault of Anna Tingri Five?

No.

Onyx waited until an opportunity presented itself. The few apprentices in the tent left to watch a sunset performance by a rival troupe. The few robots in the pavilion were downpowered or inattentive. The moment had come. Onyx strolled to the place where Anna Tingri Five's bodymaker was stored. It wouldn't take much. A whispered instruction to the machine codes. A plucked wire. A grease-smeared lens. So easy.

She waited to see if her hands would undertake the onerous task.

Her hands would not.

She walked away.

Onyx left the troupe's encampment at sunset. She could not say she had left the Festival itself; the Festival was expansive; pilgrims and commoners had camped for miles around the pavilions of the fireborn—crowds to every horizon. But she made slow progress, following the paved road eastward. By dark, she had reached a patch of harvested land where robots like great steel beetles rolled bales of straw, their red caution-lights winking a lonesome code. A few belated pilgrims moved past her in the opposite direction, carrying lanterns. Otherwise she was alone.

She stopped and looked back, though she had promised herself she would not.

The Harvest Festival smoldered on the horizon like a grassfire. A tolling of brass bells came down the cooling wind. Two skydancers rose and hovered in the clear air. Even at this distance Onyx recognized the glowing avatars of Jasper and Anna Tingri Five.

She tried to set aside her hopes and disappointments and watch the dance as any commoner would watch it. But this wasn't the dance as she had seen it rehearsed.

Onyx stared, her eyes so wide they reflected the light of the dance like startled moons.

Because the dance was different. The dance was *wrong!*

The Peasant and the Fireborn Woman circled each other as usual. The Peasant should have danced his few blunt and impoverished gestures (*Supplication, Lamentation, Protestation*) while the Fireborn Woman slowly wove around him a luminous tapestry of *Lust, Disdain, Temptation, Revulsion, Indulgence, Ecstasy, Guilt, Renunciation* and eventually *Redemption*—all signified by posture, motion, expression, repetition, tempo, rhythm, and the esotery of her divine and human body.

And all of this happened. The dance unfolded in the sky with grace and beauty, shedding a ghostly rainbow light across the moonless prairie. . . .

But it was the Fireborn Woman who clumped out abject love, and it was the Clumsy Peasant who danced circles of attraction and repulsion around her!

Onyx imagined she could hear the gasps of the crowd, even at this distance. The Council of the Twelve-Lived must be livid—but what could they do but watch as the drama played out?

And it played out exactly as at rehearsal, except for this strange inversion. The Peasant in his tawdry smock and rope-belt pants danced as finely as Anna Tingri Five had ever danced. And the Fireborn Woman yearned for him as clumsily, abjectly, and convincingly as Jasper had ever yearned. The Peasant grudgingly, longingly, accepted the advances of the Fireborn Woman. They danced arousal and completion. Then the Peasant, sated and ashamed of his weakness, turned his back to the Fireborn Woman: they could not continue together. The Fireborn Woman wept and implored, but the Peasant was loyal to his class. With a last look backward, he descended in a stately glide to the earth. And the Fireborn Woman, tragically but inevitably spurned, tumbled away at the whim of the callous winds.

And kept tumbling. That wasn't right, either.

Tumbling this way, Onyx thought.

It was like the night so many months ago when the January sky had come down close and Anna Tingri Five had fallen out of it. Now as then, the glowing avatar stiffened. Its legs, which could span counties, locked at the knee. The wind began to turn it sidelong, and parts of the skydancer grew transparent or flew off like evanescent colored clouds. Broken and shrinking, it began to fall.

It came all apart in the air, but there was something left behind: something small that fell more gently, swaying like an autumn leaf on its way from branch to winter.

It landed nearby—in a harvested field, where copper-faced robots looked up in astonishment from their bales of straw.

Onyx ran to see if Anna Tingri Five had been hurt. But the person wearing the bodymaker wasn't Anna Tingri Five.

It was Jasper, shrugging out of the harness and grinning at her like a stupid boy.

"I doctored the bodymakers," Jasper said. "I traded the seemings of them. From inside our harnesses everything looked normal. But the Peasant wore the Fireborn Woman's body, and the Fireborn Woman appeared as the Peasant. I knew all about it, but Anna Tingri Five didn't. She danced believing she was still the Fireborn Woman."

"You ruined the performance!" exclaimed Onyx.

Jasper shrugged. "She told me she loved me, but she was going to drop me as soon as the Festival ended. I heard her saying so to one of her courtiers. She called me a 'dramatic device.'"

"You could have told me so!"

"You were in no mood to listen. You're a hopeless skeptic. You might have thought I was lying. I didn't want you debating my loyalty. I wanted to show it to you."

"And you're a silly dreamer! Did you learn anything useful from her—about the Fifth Door to the Moon?"

"A little," said Jasper.

"Think you can find it?"

He shrugged his bony shoulders. "Maybe."

"You still want to walk to the Atlantic Coast with me?"

"That's why I'm here."

Onyx looked back at the Harvest Festival. There must be chaos in the pavilions, she thought, but the competition had to go on. And in fact, Dawa Nine rose into the air, right on schedule. But his warrior dance looked a little wobbly.

"I crossed a few connections in Dawa Nine's bodymaker," she confessed. "He's a liar and a cheat and he doesn't deserve to win."

Jasper cocked his big head and gave her a respectful stare. "You're a saboteur too!"

"Anna Tingri Five won't be going to the moon this year, and neither will Dawa Nine."

"Then we ought to start walking," said Jasper. "They won't let it rest, you know. They'll come after us. They'll send robots."

"Bet you a copper dollar they can't find us," Onyx said, shrugging her pack over her shoulder and turning to the road that wound like a black ribbon to a cloth of stars. She liked the road better now that this big-headed Buttercup County boy was beside her again.

"No bet," said Jasper, following.

Ruminations in an Alien Tongue

VANDANA SINGH

Vandana Singh was born and raised in India, and currently resides in the United States with her family, where she teaches physics and writes. Her stories have appeared in several volumes of Polyphony, *as well as in* Lightspeed, Strange Horizons, InterNova, Foundation 100, *Rabid Transit Press,* Interfictions: An Anthology of Interstitial Writing, Mythic, Trampoline, *and* So Long Been Dreaming: Post-colonial Science Fiction & Fantasy. *She published a children's book in India,* Younguncle Comes to Town, *and a chapbook novella,* Of Love and Other Monsters. *Her other books include another chapbook novella,* Distances, *and her first collection,* The Woman Who Thought She Was a Planet. *Her most recent book is an original anthology, co-edited with Anil Menon,* Breaking the Bow.

Here's an autumnal and contemplative story about a gifted mathematician exploring an enigmatic alien artifact found on another planet, one with the power to move things through space, time, and a tangled skein of alternate-possibility universes. When the things so moved are people, *though, bitter complications can ensue . . .*

BIRHA ON THE DOORSTEP

Sitting on the sun-warmed step at the end of her workday, she laid her hand on the dog's neck and let her mind drift. Like a gyre-moth finding the center of its desire, her mind inevitably spiraled inward to the defining moment of her life. It must be something to do with growing old, she thought irritably, that all she did was to revisit what had happened all those years ago. Yet her irritation subsided before the memory. She could still see it with the shocking clarity of yesterday: the great, closed eyelid set in the enormous alien stronghold, opening in response to her trick. The thick air of the valley, her breath caught in her throat, the orange-and-yellow uniforms of the waiting soldiers. She had gone up the ladder, stepped through the round opening. Darkness, her footsteps echoing in the enormous space, the light she carried casting a small, bobbing pool of illumination. This was the alien stronghold considered invincible by the human conquerors, to which the last denizens of a dying race had crawled in a war she had forgotten when she was young. She had expected to find their broken, decayed bodies, but instead there was a silence like the inside of a temple up in the mountains. Silence, a faint smell of dust, and a picture forever burned into her mind: in light of her lamp, the missing soldier, thunderstruck before the great mass of machinery in the center.

That was the moment when everything changed. For her, and eventually for humankind. She had been young then.

"Hah!" she said, a short, sharp sound, an old woman laughing at her foolishness. It felt good to sit here on the doorstep, although now it was turning a little cold. On this world the sun didn't set for seven years as counted on the planet where she had been born. She knew she would not live to see another sunset; her bones told her that, and the faint smell in her urine, and her mind, which was falling backward into a void of its own making.

But the clouds could not be ignored, nor the yellow dog at her knee, who wanted to go inside. There would be rain, and the trees would open their veined, translucent cups to the sky. There would be gyre-moths emerging from holes in the ground, flying in smooth, ever-smaller circles, at the center of which was a cup of perfumed rain—and there would be furred worms slithering up the branches to find the sweet moth-meat. In the rain under the trees, the air would quiver with blood and desire, and the human companion animals, the dogs and cats and ferrets would run to their homes lest the sleehawks or a feral arboril catch them for their next meal. Yes, rain was a time of beauty and bloodshed, here at the edge of the great cloud forest, among the ruins of the university that had been her home for most of her life.

She got up, noting with a grim satisfaction that, in *this* universe, old knees creaked. She went in with the dog and shut the door and the windows against the siren-like calls of the foghorn-trees, and put some water on to boil. Rain drummed on the stone walls of her retreat, and she saw through the big window the familiar ruined curve of the university ramparts through a wall of falling water. Sometimes the sight still took her breath away. That high walk with the sheer, misty drop below was where she had first walked with Thirru.

A VERY SHORT RUMINATION

When I was born my mother named me Birha, which means "separated" or "parted" in an ancient human language. This was because my mother was about to die.

DIFFICULT LOVES

Thirru was difficult and strange. He seemed eager to make Birha happy but was like a big, foolish child, unable to do so. A large, plump man, with hair that stood up on end, he liked to clap his hands loudly when he solved a difficult problem, startling everyone. His breath smelled of bitter herbs from the tea he drank all day. Even at their pairing ceremony he couldn't stop talking and clapping his hands, which she had then thought only vaguely annoying and perhaps endearing. Later, her irritation at his strangeness, his genius, his imbecility, provoked her into doing some of her best work. It was almost as though, in the discomfort of his presence, she could be more herself.

One time, when she was annoyed with Thirru, she was tempted by another man. This man worked with her; his fingers were long and shapely over the simulator controls, and he leaned toward her when he spoke, always with a warmth that made her feel as though she was a creature of the sunlight, unfurling in the rays of morning. He made her feel younger than she was. She didn't like him very much; she distrusted people with charm as a matter of principle, but he was more than charm. He was lean, and wore his dark hair long and loose, and every posture of his was insouciant, inviting, relaxed as a predatory animal; when he leaned toward her she felt the yearning, the current pulling her toward him. At these moments she was always stiff and polite with him; in privacy she cursed herself for her weakness. She avoided him, sought him out, avoided him, going on like this for days, until, quite suddenly, she broke through the barrier. She was no longer fascinated by him. It wasn't that his charm had faded; it was only (she congratulated herself) the fact that she had practiced the art of resisting temptation until she had achieved some mastery. You practice and it becomes easier, just like the alien mathematics on which she was working at the time. Just like anything else.

This freedom from desiring this man was heady. It was also relaxing not to feel drawn to him all the time, to be able to joke and laugh with him, to converse without that terrible, adolescent self-consciousness. She could even let herself like him after that.

In this manner she carried herself through other temptations successfully. Even after Thirru's own betrayal she wasn't tempted into another relationship. After the reconciliation they stayed together for an entire cycle, some of which was marked by an easy contentment that she had never known before, a deep wellspring of happiness. When they parted, it was as friends.

But what he left behind, what all old loves left behind were the ghostly imprints of their presence. For her, Thirru came back whenever she looked up at the high walk where she had first walked with him. Thirru was the feel of damp stone, the vivid green of the moss between the rocks, the wet, verdant aroma of the mist. She didn't have to go there any more; just looking up at the stone arch against the clouds would bring back the feel of his hands.

After Thirru, she had had her share of companions, long and short term, but nobody had inspired her to love. And when the man came along who came closest, she was unprepared for him. His name was Rudrak, and he was young.

What she loved about him was his earnestness, his delight in beautiful things, like the poeticas she had set up on the long table. He was an engineer, and his passion was experimental craft designed to explore stars. She loved his beautiful, androgynous face, how it was animated by thought and emotion, how quick his eyes were to smile, the way his brow furrowed in concentration. That crisp, black, curling hair, the brown arm flung out as he declaimed, dramatically, a line from a classic play she'd never heard of. When he came, always infrequently, unexpectedly, always on a quest for the woman Ubbiri, it was as though the sun had come out in the sky of her mind. Conversation with him could be a battle of wits, or the slow, easy, unhurried exchange of long-time lovers. She never asked him to stay for good (as though it were possible); never told him she loved him.

Now she was pottering about in her kitchen, listening to the rain, wondering if he would come one more time before she died. The last time he had come was a half-cycle ago (three and a half years on her birth planet, her mind translated out of habit). There was not much more than a half-cycle left to her. Would he come? Pouring her tea, she realized that despite the certainty with which she loved this man, there was something different about this love. She felt no need for him to reciprocate. Sometimes she would look at her arms, their brown, lean strength, the hands showing the signs of age, and remember what it was like to be touched, lovingly, and wonder what it would be like to caress Rudrak's arm, to touch his face, his lips. But it was an abstract sort of wondering. Even if she could make him forget Ubbiri (and there was no reason for her to do that), she did not really want him too close to her. Her life was the way she liked it: the rising into early mornings, the work with the poeticas, which was a meditation in sunlight and sound, then the long trek up the hill to the now-abandoned laboratory. Returning in the early evening before the old bells rang sunset (although the sun wouldn't set for half a cycle yet) into the tranquility of her little stone house, where the village girl entrusted with the task would have left her meal warming on the stove just the way she liked it. The peace of eating and reading by herself, watching the firelings outside her window, in the temporary, watery dark created by the frequent gathering of clouds. In those moments the universe seemed to open to her as much as it seemed shut to her during the long day. She would stare out at the silhouettes of trees and wonder if the answers she was seeking through her theories and equations weren't instead waiting for her out there in the forest, amidst the ululations of the frenet-bird and the complex script of the firelings' dance. In those moments it would seem to her as though all she had to do was to walk out into the verdure and pluck the answer from the air like fruit from trees; that it was in these moments of complete receptivity that the universe would be revealed to her, not in the hours at the simulators in the laboratory. That the equations would be like childish chatter compared to what was out there to know in its fullness.

She took her tea to her favorite chair to drink. On the way she let her fingers brush lightly over the wires of the poeticas that stood on wood frames on the long table. The musical notes sounded above the crash of the rain, speaking aloud her ruminations in the lost alien tongue. Rudrak had left his ghost behind here: the remembrance of his body leaning over the instruments, brushing them as he might, in some other universe, be brushing the hair from her face. Asking how this sequence of notes implied those words. Since she had walked into the alien stronghold so many years ago, since the time that everything had changed, Rudrak had visited her nine times. Each time he remembered nothing of his previous visits, not even who she was. Each time she had to explain to him that Ubbiri was dead, and that he should come in, and wouldn't he like some tea? She went through the repetition as though it was the first time, every time, which in a way it was. A sacred ritual.

Rudrak.

Would he come?

A RAMBLING RUMINATION

Simply by virtue of being, we create ripples in the ever-giving cosmic tree, the kalpa-vriksh. Every branch is an entire universe. Even stars, as they are born and die, leave permanent marks in the shadow universe of their memory. Perhaps we are ghosts of our other selves in other universes.

It was not right for Ubbiri to die. There is a lack of symmetry there, a lack even of a proper symmetry breaking. Somewhere, somehow, Ubbiri's meta-world-line and mine should connect in a shape that is pleasing to the mathematical eye. Sometimes I want to be Ubbiri, to know that a part of me did wander into another universe after all, and that separated, the two parts were joined together at last. There is something inelegant about Ubbiri's return and subsequent death. Ubbiri should have shared consciousness with me. Then, when Rudrak asks: "I am looking for Ubbiri. Is she here?" for the ump-teenth time, I, Birha, will say yes. She's here.

Instead this is what I say:

"I'm sorry, Ubbiri passed away a long time ago. She told me about you when she died. Won't you come in?"

What is the probability that I am Ubbiri? If so, am I dead or alive, or both?

Ubbiri is dead. I am Birha, and Birha is alone.

THE DISCOVERY

When Birha was neither young nor old, when Thirru had already moved off-planet, a young soldier volunteered to test-fly an alien flyer, one of two intact specimens. The flight went well until upon an impulse he decided to swoop by the alien ruins in the valley below the university. During the dive he lost control of the flyer, which seemed to be heading straight for a round indentation like an eye in the side of an ancient dome. The indentation revealed itself to be a door by opening, and then closing behind the flyer.

When Birha was consulted about the problem, she suspected that the door worked on an acoustical switch. Calculating the frequency of sound emitted by the alien flyer at a certain speed in the close, thick air of the valley took some time. But when a sound wave of the requisite frequency was aimed at the door, it opened almost immediately, with a sigh as though of relief.

She volunteered to go alone into the chamber. They argued, but she had always been stubborn, and at the end they let her. She was the expert on the aliens after all.

The interior was vast, shrouded in darkness and her footsteps echoed musically. She saw the flyer, in some kind of docking bay, along with a dozen others. There were no decaying alien bodies, only silence. The young man stood in front of the great mass of machinery at the center of the room. In the light from her lamp (which flickered strangely) she saw a complexity of fine, fluted vanes, crystalline pipes as thin as her finger running in and out of lacy metalwork. The whole mass was covered in a translucent dome that gleamed red and blue, yellow and green, in the light from her lamp. There was a door in the side of the dome, which was ringed by pillars.

"My hand . . ." the soldier was staring at his hand. He looked at Birha at last. "My hand just went through that pillar . . ."

Birha felt a loosening of her body, as though her joints and tendons were coming apart, without pain. If she breathed out too hard, she might fling herself all over the cosmos. Her heart was beating in an unfamiliar rhythm. She put her hand in her pocket and took some coins out. Carefully she tossed each one in the air. Thirteen coins came down on the floor, all heads.

"There's nothing wrong with you," she told the aviator. "It's the machine. It's an alien artifact that changes the probabilities of things. We're standing in the leakage field. Look, just come with me. You'll be all right."

She led him into the light. The round door was propped open by a steel rod and there were crowds of people waiting at the foot of the ladder. The young man was still dazed.

"It tickled," he said. "My hand. When it went through the pillar."

A RUMINATION ON THE ALIENS

The aliens! What do we know about them? We know now they are not dead. They went through the great probability machine, the actualizer, to another place, a place we'll never find. The old pictures show that they had pale brown, segmented bodies, with a skeletal frame that allowed them to stand upright. They were larger than us but not by much, and they had feelers on their heads and light-sensitive regions beneath the feelers, and several limbs. They knew time and space, and as their culture was centered around sound, so was their mathematics centered around probability. Their ancient cities are filled with ruined acoustical devices, enormous poeticas, windchimes, and Aeolian harps as large as a building. Their music is strange but pleasant to humans, although its frequency range goes beyond what we can hear. When I was just an acolyte at the university, I chose to study what scripts were left after the war. They were acoustical scripts, corresponding to the notes in a row of poeticas on the main streets of their cities. I was drunk with discovery, in love with the aliens, overcome with sorrow that they were, as we thought then, all dead. For the first time since I had come to this planet, I felt at home.

To understand the aliens I became a mathematician and a musician. After that those three things are one thing in my mind: the aliens, the mathematics, the music.

RUDRAK'S STORY

A bristleship, Rudrak told Birha, is like no other craft. It burrows into the heart of a star, enduring temperatures beyond imagination, and comes out on the other side whole and full of data. The current model was improved by Rudrak in his universe, a branch of the cosmic tree not unlike this one. He did it for his partner, Ubbiri, who was writing a thesis on white dwarf stars. Ubbiri had loved white dwarf stars since a cousin taught her a nursery rhyme about them when Ubbiri was small:

Why are you a star so dim
In the night beyond the rim
Don't you want someone to love?
In the starry skies above?

Ubbiri had to write a thesis on white dwarf stars. As dictated by academic custom in that culture, her thesis had to connect the six points of the Wheel of Knowing:

Meta-networking, Undulant theory, Fine-Jump Mathematics, Time-Bundles, Poetry and Love. To enable her to achieve deep-knowing and therefore to truly love the star, she took a ride on the new bristleship with Rudrak. They discovered that when the ship went through the starry core, it entered another reality. This was later called the shadow universe of stars, where their existence and life history is recorded in patterns that no human has completely understood. Some poets call this reality the star's memory-space, or its consciousness, but Ubbiri thought that was extending metaphor beyond sense. The data from the bristleship told her that this star, this love, had been a golden star in its youth and middle age, harboring six planets (two of which had hosted life), and much space debris. In the late season of its existence it had soared in largeness, dimming and reddening, swallowing its planetary children. Now it was content to bank its fires until death.

After this discovery, Rudrak said, the two of them lived quiet lives that were rich and full. But one day before he was due to take off for another test flight, Ubbiri noticed there was a crack on the heat shielded viewscreen of the bristleship. Rudrak tested it and repaired it, but Ubbiri was haunted by the possibility of the tiny crack spreading like a web across the viewscreen, and breaking up just as Rudrak was in the star's heart.

Perhaps that was what she thought when Rudrak disappeared. Rudrak only knew that instead of passing through the shadow universe before coming out, the bristleship took him somewhere else, to a universe so close to his own that he did not know the difference until he had crashlanded on a planet (this planet) and been directed to people who knew the truth. They led him to Birha, who sheltered him for fifteen days, allowed him to mourn, and to come slowly to life again. Each time she sent him back to his universe, as protocol demanded, by way of the alien probability machine, the actualizer. Somehow he was caught in a time-loop that took him back to the day before the ill-fated expedition. He had returned to her in exactly the same way nine times. His return visits were not predictable, being apparently randomly spaced, and her current (and last) calculation was an attempt to predict when he would come next.

Each visit was the same and not the same. Surely he had had less gray hair the last time? And that healed cut on his hand—hadn't that been from his last trip, when he was trying to help her cut fruit and the knife had slipped? And hadn't his accent improved just a little bit since last time? They'd had to teach him the language each visit as though it was new, but perhaps it became just a hair's breadth easier each time?

She tried to make each experience subtly different for him. She was afraid that too drastic a change might upset whatever delicate process was at work in the time-loop. He was like a leaf caught in an eddy—push too hard and the time stream might take him over a precipice. But a little tug here, a tug there, and perhaps he'd land safely on a shore, of this universe or that one.

So far nothing had worked. His bewilderment was the same, each time he appeared on her doorstep, and so was his grief. It was only these small, insignificant things that were different. One time he wore an embroidered collar, another time a plain one. Or the color of his shirt was different.

Birha worked on her calculations but the kalpa-vriksh gave senseless, contradictory answers.

A RUMINATION ON TIMMAR'S ROCK

I remember when I first came to the university, I used to pass a flat-topped boulder on the way to class. There was a depression on the flat surface of the rock in the exact shape of the bottom of a water bowl. When I met Thirru he told me that the great Timmar Rayan, who had founded the School of Wind and Water, had sat there in daily meditation for three entire cycles, placing his water bowl in the same spot every time. Over the years the depression had developed. I have always marveled that something as unyielding as rock can give way before sheer habit, or regularity, or persistence, whatever you might call it. Practice, whether in mathematics or in love, changes things. Sometimes.

UBBIRI'S ARRIVAL

It was one thing to realize that the alien device in the center of the chamber was some kind of probability-altering machine. That it was the fabled actualizer hinted at in alien manuscripts, which she had always thought of as myth, was quite another thing. This knowledge she owed to Ubbiri, who was discovered lying on the floor of the chamber not three days after Birha had first opened the round door. Ubbiri was immediately incarcerated for questioning and only after several ten-days, when her language had been deciphered and encrypted into a translation device, had Birha been allowed to speak to her. They said the old woman was mad, babbling about shadow universes and tearing at her silver hair, but Birha found her remarkably sane. Ubbiri told her that she had tired of waiting for her partner, who had disappeared during a flight through a certain white dwarf star, and when he didn't return, she had taken an old-model bristleship and dived into the heart of the star. When the ship passed through the core she defied its protestations and stepped out of it, seeking either him or death in the shadowy depths of the other reality. Instead she found herself lying on the floor of the chamber, aged beyond her years.

Over the course of four ten-days of conversation Birha determined that the constants of nature were a hairs-breadth different where Ubbiri came from, so it was very likely another universe entirely. She realized then that the machine at the center of the room did not merely change probabilities. It was an actualizer: a probability wave intereference machine, and the portal inside it led to whatever branch of the kalpa-vriksh you created by changing the parameters. But the portal only opened if you'd satisfied consistency checks and if (as far as the machine could tell) the universe was stable. Somehow the pathways to other universes intersected within the cores of stars, hence Ubbiri's surprising arrival.

Not long after, Ubbiri died. She left a note stating that there were three things she was grateful for: her white dwarf star, Rudrak, and spending her last days with Birha.

A quarter-cycle after Ubbiri's death, Rudrak came for the first time into Birha's life.

A RUMINATION ON THIRRU, OR RUDRAK

There is a rift valley between us, a boundary that might separate two people or two universes. I've been exploring there, marveling at the tortured geometries of its sheer walls, the pits and chasms on its floor. Through them I've sometimes seen stars. So far I've avoided falling in, but who knows? One day maybe I'll hurtle through the layer between this universe and that, and find myself a meteor, a shooting star falling into the gravity well of a far planet.

What if a meteor changed its mind about falling? Would the universe allow it? Only if the rock fell under the sway of another imperative that lifted it beyond gravity's grasp. But where, in that endless sky, would it find the rift from which it had emerged? It would have to wander, searching, until the journey became an end in itself. And then, one day when the journey had changed it beyond recognition, it would find the rift and it would stand on the lip of it, wondering: should I return?

But I am not a rock. I am a person, slowly ripening in the sun of this world, like a pear on a tree. I am not hard, I am not protected by rocky layers.

Still, I cannot soar through your sky without burning.

THEORIES OF PROBABILITY

What the actualizer did was to change probabilities. So sometimes things that were highly improbable, like walking through a wall, or tossing five thousand coins so that heads came up every time—all those things could become much more likely.

Birha thought that in some sense people had always known about the other branches of the kalpa-vriksh. So many of humankind's fantasies about the magical and the impossible were simply imaginative leaps into different regions of the cosmic tree. But to go to the place of your imagining in the flesh, that wasn't possible before the actualizer's discovery. If you adjusted the parameters the actualizer would tweak the probability amplitudes to make your fairytale universe. Or perhaps it only opened a portal to an already existing one. What's the difference? So much for you, entropy, for heat death, for death. Make it more likely that you live from fatal cancer than an ant bite . . .

But you couldn't always predict how the amplitudes would work for complex systems like universes, and whether programming in coarse features you desired would give too much creative freedom to subsystems, resulting in surprises beyond imagining, and not always pleasant ones. Thus a mythology had already grown around the actualizer, detailing the possible and impossible other universes and their dangers. One made-up story related how they put in the parameters, the universal physical constants and the wave-function behavior in space and time, and there came to be an instability in the matter of that universe that made people explode like supernovas when they touched each other with love. It was a fanciful lie but it made a great opera.

In her idle moments, Birha wondered whether there was a curtain through which she could slip to find the place that always stays still amid the shifting cosmos, like the eye of a storm. But the foghorn trees were calling in the rain, and she was nodding over a bowl of soup, like the old woman she was. She looked at the veins standing out on the backs of her hands, and the thick-jointed fingers and thought of the body, her universe, which was not a closed system at all. Was there any system that was completely closed? Not in this universe, at least, where the most insulated of systems must interact with its environment, if only very slowly. So was our universe completely disconnected from the others, or did they bleed into each other? Exchange something? Not energy in any form we recognized, perhaps, but something more subtle, like dreams. She wanted to know what connected the universes, she wanted to step back from it all and see the kalpa-vriksh in its entirety. But she was caught in it as surely as anyone else. A participant-observer who must deduce the grand structure of the cosmic tree from within it, who must work at it while being caught in it, a worm in a twig, a fly in amber, to feel the knowing, the learning, like a new intimacy, a love.

"All matter is wavelike in some sense," she told the dog. "The actualizer generates waves, and through interference changes the probability amplitudes. The tiny bubble universe so formed then resonates with an existing universe with the same properties, and a doorway opens between them."

The dog sighed, as though this was passé, which in a way it was, and wagged his tail.

A RUMINATION, DOZING IN THE SUN

One day I dreamed I was the light falling off the edge of a leaf, nice and straight, but for the lacy diffraction at the edge. At night I flew into the clouds, to the well of stars, and became a piece of the void, a bit of dark velvet stitched onto the sky. In the afternoon I am just an old woman dozing in the sun with a yellow dog sitting by her, wondering about stars, worried about the universes. If I could be the tap of your shoe, the glance out of the corner of your eye when you see that man or this woman, if I could be the curled lip of the snarling arboril, or a mote in the eye of a dog. What would I be, if I were to be any of this?

I am myself and yet not so. I contain multitudes and am a part of something larger; I am a cell the size of a planet, swimming in the void of the night.

WHEN THEY LEFT

After the actualizer's discovery it became a subject of study, a thing to explore, and ultimately an industry dealing in dreams. Streams of adventurers, dreamers, and would-be suicides, people dissatisfied with their lives, went through the actualizer to find the universe that suited them better. The actualizer became a wish-fulfillment machine, opening a path to a universe just like this one, but with your personal parameters adjusted ever so slightly, the complexity matrices shifted just so (this was actually not possible: manipulating individual meta-world-lines was technically an unsolved problem, but tell that to the dreamers). Among the last to go were the people who had worked with Birha, her colleagues and students. They claimed not to be deceived by the dream-merchants; their excuse was academic, but they went like so many other people into the void. The exodus left certain towns and regions thinly populated, some planets abandoned. Imagine being dissatisfied enough to want to change—not towns, or planets, but entire universes! It was all Birha could do in the early days to stand there and watch the insanity until finally her dear companions were sundered from her by space, time, and whatever boundary kept one universe from another. Some people came back but they were strangers, probably from other planets in her universe. She had discovered the infinite branches of the cosmic tree, but it was not hers to claim in any way. She was the only one who wouldn't travel its endless ways.

Who knew how long her erstwhile companions would be gone, or in what shape they'd come back, if they came back? She was too old to travel, and she liked the pleasures of small things, like tinkering with the tuning on the poeticas, designing and constructing new ones, and sipping the pale tea in the morning. She liked watching the yellow dog chase firelings. But also she was a prickly old woman, conservative as they come about universes and parameters, and she liked this one just fine, thank you. She liked the world on which she lived, with the seven-year daycycle. No, she wouldn't go. She was too obstinate and she disapproved of this meddling with the natural unfolding of things. Besides there was the elegance of death. The neatness of it, the way nothing's wasted after. It seemed as though only in this universe was death real. She liked to sit on the sunny doorstep and talk to the dog about it all. Dogs, she thought, don't need other universes, they are already perfect for the one in which they exist. She wondered if humans were refugees from some lost other branch of the Tree, which is why we were so restless. Always dissatisfied, going from planet to planet, galaxy to galaxy, branch to branch of the Cosmic Tree, and maybe rewriting our own life-histories of what-has-been. But we are not all like that; there have always been people who are like the dog, like Birha, perfectly belonging in the worlds of this universe.

A RUMINATION ON POETICAS

A poetica consists of a series of suspended rods or wires under tension, mounted vertically on a frame. A sounding stick run by an ingenious mechanism of gears and a winding mechanism not unlike an old-fashioned clock brushes over the rods at a varying speed, forward and backward. A series of levers controls which rod or wire is struck. While this instrument can be designed to be played by an adept, it can also be fully automated by the mechanism, which is built to last. The enormous ones on public display recount the histories and great epic poems of the people, and are made of wood and stone and metal. Some kinds are designed to be played by the wind, but in these instruments, the sounds, and therefore the meanings, are always new, and ambiguous.

It took me years to learn the musical language of the aliens, and more years to learn to build miniature poeticas.

To sound these ruminations I have had to interpolate and invent new syllables, new chords and phrases, in order to tell my story. There are no words in their language for some of what I feel and think, and similarly there are sounds in their tongue I'll never understand.

We call them aliens but this is their world. We took it from them. We are the strangers, the interlopers, the aliens.

BIRHA'S LOVES

So Birha waits, watching the clouds gather over the university ramparts, walking every day to the abandoned laboratory, where her calculations give her both frustration and pleasure. Following the probability distribution of a single meta-world-line is tremendously difficult. Through the skeins and threads of possibility that arc across the simulator's three-dimensional result-space, she can discern several answers that fit the constraints. A problem with a multiplicity of answers as scattered as stars. Rudrak will be back in 0.3, or 0.87, or 4.6 cycles. Or in 0.0011, or 5.8, or 0.54 cycles. She is out of temper with herself and the meta-universe at large.

As she goes down the slope in the cloud-darkness that passes for evening, tripping a little bit because she wants to be in the stone house before the rain starts, it occurs to her that her irritation signifies love. For Thirru, for the man who temporarily attracted her, for the lesser loves of all the years after, for Rudrak, for all her long-gone colleagues and students, for the yellow dog who lives with her, for the village girl who brings the evening meal and cleans up in silence. For Timmar's rock, for the aliens and their gift to her, for the cloud forest, for that ever-giving Tree, the cosmic kalpa-vriksh, and especially her branch of it. And for death, who waits for her as she waits for Rudrak.

As she thinks this, her impatience at Rudrak's non-arrival dissipates the way the mist does when the sun comes out. In the stone house she is out of breath, her chest hurts. There is an aroma of warm food and the yellow dog looks up from where he is lying and wags his tail lazily. She sits down to eat, dropping bits for the dog, sipping the pale tea. She thinks how it might be good for her to go out, when the time comes, into the deep forest and let her life be taken by a stinging death-vine, as is the custom among some of the natives. The vine brings a swift, painless death, wrapping the body in a shell of silken threads until all the juices are absorbed. The rest is released to become part of the rich humus of the forest floor. She feels like giving herself back to the world that gave her so much, even though she was not born here. It is comforting to think of dying in this way. The yellow dog will be happy enough with the village girl, and the old stone house will eventually be overcome by the forest. The wind will have to learn to play the poeticas, and then it will interpolate its own story with hers. Only closed systems are lonely. And there is no such thing as a closed system.

Three days later as the bell for morning tolls, there is a knock on the door. There is a man standing there. A stranger. No. It takes her a moment to recognize Rudrak, with his customary attitude of bewilderment and anxiety. The change is just enough to render him not quite familiar: more silver hairs, a shirt of a different fashion, in blue with an embroidered sash. He's taller, stoops a little, and the face is different too, in a way that she can't quite explain. In that long moment of recognition the kalpa-vriksh speaks to her. The mistake she had made in her calculations was to assume that through all the changes between universes, through space and through time, Rudrak would be Rudrak, and Birha, Birha, and Ubbiri would always remain

Ubbiri. But finally she's seen it: identity is neither invariant nor closed. No wonder the answers had so much scatter in them! The truth, as always, is more subtle and more beautiful. Birha takes a deep breath of gratitude, feels her death only a few ten-days away.

"I'm looking for Ubbiri," says this almost-stranger, this new Rudrak. His accent is almost perfect. She ushers him in, and he looks around, at the pale sunlight falling on the long table with the poeticas, which are sounding softly. His look of anxiety fades for a moment, to be replaced by wonder.

"This looks familiar," he says. "Have I been here before?"

Tyche and the Ants

Hannu Rajaniemi

Hannu Rajaniemi was born in Ylivieska, Finland, but currently lives in Edinburgh, Scotland, where he received a PhD in string theory. He is the cofounder of ThinkTank Maths, which provides consultation service and research in applied mathematics and business development. He is also a member of Writers' Bloc, an Edinburgh-based spoken-word performance group. Although Rajaniemi has a relatively small body of work, he has had a big impact on the field. His story from 2005, "Deus Ex Homine," originally from the Scottish regional anthology Nova Scotia, *was reprinted in several Best of the Year anthologies, including this one, and was one of the most talked-about stories of the year, as was his* Interzone *story "His Master's Voice" in 2008. His first novel,* The Quantum Thief, *was published in 2010 to a great deal of critical buzz and response. His most recent novel,* The Fractal Prince, *is receiving similar acclaim.*

Here he tells a tale of political warfare and a cyberattack on the barren surface of the Moon, all seen through the focus of a child's whimsical fantasy world.

The ants arrived on the Moon on the same day Tyche went through the Secret Door to give a ruby to the Magician.

She was glad to be out of the Base: the Brain had given her a Treatment earlier that morning, and that always left her tingly and nervous, with pent-up energy that could only be expended by running down the grey rolling slope down the side of Malapert Mountain, jumping and hooting.

"Come on, keep up!" she shouted that the grag that the Brain had inevitably sent to keep an eye on her. The white-skinned machine followed her on its two thick treads, cylindrical arms swaying for balance as it rumbled laboriously downhill, following the little craters of Tyche's footprints.

Exasperated, she crossed her arms and paused to wait. She looked up. The mouth of the Base was hidden from view, as it should be, to keep them safe from space sharks. The jagged edge of the mountain hid the Great Wrong Place from sight, except for a single wink of blue malice, just above the gleaming white of the upper slopes, a stark contrast against the velvet black of the sky. The white was not snow—that was a Wrong Place thing—but tiny beads of glass made by ancient meteor impacts. That's what the Brain said, anyway: according to Chang'e the Moon Girl, it was all the jewels she had lost over the centuries she had lived here.

Tyche preferred Chang'e's version. That made her think of the ruby, and she touched her belt pouch to make sure the ruby was still there.

"Outings are subject to being escorted at all times," said the sonorous voice of the Brain in her helmet. "There is no reason to be impatient."

Most of the grags were autonomous: the Brain could only control a few of them at the time. But of course it would keep an eye on her, so soon after the Treatment.

"Yes, there is, slowpoke," Tyche muttered, stretched her arms and jumped up and down in frustration.

Her suit flexed and flowed around her with the movement. She had grown it herself as well, the third one so far, although it had taken much longer than the ruby. Its many layers were alive, it felt light, and best of all, it had a powerskin, a slick porous tissue made from cells that had mechanosensitive ion channels that translated her movements into power for the suit. It was so much better than the white clumsy fabric ones the Chinese had left behind; the grags had cut and sown a baby-sized version out of those for her that kind of worked but was impossibly stuffy and stiff.

It was the only second time she had tested the new suit, and she was proud of it: it was practically a wearable ecosystem, and she was pretty sure that with its photosynthesis layer, it would keep her alive for months, if she only had enough sunlight and brought enough of the horrible compressed Chinese nutrients.

She frowned. Her legs were suddenly gray, mottled with browns. She brushed them with her hand, and her fingers—slick silvery hue of the powerskin—came away the same colour. It seemed the regolith dust clung to the suit. Annoying: she absently noted to do something about it for the next iteration when she fed the suit back into the Base's big biofabber.

Now the grag was stuck on the lip of a shallow crater, grinding treads sending up silent parabolas of little rocks and dust. Tyche had had enough of waiting.

"I'll be back for dinner," she told the Brain.

Without waiting for the Base mind's response, she switched off the radio, turned around and started running.

Tyche settled into the easy stride the Jade Rabbit had shown her: gliding just above the surface, using well-timed toe-pushes to cross craters and small rocks that littered the uneven regolith.

She took the long way around, avoiding her old tracks that ran down much of the slope, just to confuse the poor grag more. She skirted around the edge of one of the pitch-black cold fingers—deeper craters that never got sunlight—that were everywhere on this side of the mountain. It would have been a shortcut, but it was too cold for her suit. Besides, the ink-men lived in the deep potholes, in the Other Moon beyond the Door.

Halfway around, the ground suddenly shook. Tyche slid uncontrollably, almost going over the edge before she managed to stop by turning around mid-leap and jamming her toes into the chilly hard regolith when she landed. Her heart pounded.

Had the ink-men brought something up from the deep dark, something big? Or had she just been almost hit by a meteorite? That had happened a couple of times, a sudden crater blooming soundlessly into being, right next to her.

Then she saw beams of light in the blackness and realised that it was only the Base's sandworm, a giant articulated machine with a maw full of toothy wheels that ground Helium-3 and other volatiles from the deep shadowy deposits.

Tyche breathed a sigh of relief and continued on her way. Many of the grag bodies were ugly, but she liked the sandworm. She had helped to program it: constantly toiling, it went into such deep places that the Brain could not control it remotely.

The Secret Door was in a much shallower crater, maybe a hundred metres in diameter. She went down its slope with little choppy leaps and stopped her momentum with a deft pirouette and toe-brake, right in front of the Door.

It was made of two large pyramid-shaped rocks, leaning against each other at a funny angle, with a small triangular gap between them: the Big Old One, and the Troll. The Old One had two eyes made from shadows, and when Tyche squinted from the right angle, a rough outcrop and a groove in the base became a nose and a mouth. The Troll looked grumpy, half-squashed against the bigger rock's bulk.

As she watched, the face of the Old One became alive and gave her a quizzical look. Tyche gave it a stiff bow—out of habit, even though she could have curtsied in her new suit.

How have you been, Tyche? the rock asked, in its silent voice.

"I had a Treatment today," she said dourly.

The rock could not nod, so it raised its eyebrows.

Ah. Always Treatments. Let me tell you, in my day, vacuum was the only treatment we had, and the sun, and a little meteorite every now and then to keep clean. Stick to that and you'll live to be as old as I am.

And as fat, grumbled the Troll. Believe me, once you carry him for a few million years, you start to feel it. What are you doing here, anyway?

Tyche grinned. "I made a ruby for the Magician." She took it out and held it up proudly. She squeezed it a bit, careful not to damage her suit's gloves against the rough edges, and held it in the Old One's jet-black shadow, knocking it against the rock's surface. It sparkled with tiny embers, just like it was supposed to. She had made it herself, using Verneuil flame fusion, and spiced it with a piezoelectric material so that it would convert motion to light.

Oh? said the troll. Well, maybe the old fool will finally stop looking for the Queen Ruby, then, and settle down with poor Chang'e.

It's very beautiful, Tyche, the Old One said. I'm sure he will love it.

In with you, now, the Troll said. You're encouraging this old fool here. He might start crying. Besides, everybody is waiting.

Tyche closed her eyes, counted to ten, and crawled through the opening between the rocks, through the Secret Door to her Other Moon.

The moment Tyche opened her eyes she saw that something was wrong. The house of the Jade Rabbit was broken. The boulders she had carefully balanced on top of each other lay scattered on the ground, and the lines that she had drawn to make the rooms and the furniture were smudged. (Since it never rained, the house had not needed a roof.)

There was a silent sob. Chang'e the Moon Girl sat next to the Rabbit's house, crying. Her flowing silk robes of purple, yellow, and red were a mess on the ground like broken wings, and her makeup had been running down her pale, powdered face.

"Oh, Tyche! It is terrible, terrible!" She wiped a crystal tear from her eye. It evaporated in the vacuum before it could fall on the dust. Chang'e was a drama queen, and pretty, and knew it, too. Once, she had had an affair with the Woodcutter just because she was bored, and borne him children, but they had already grown up and moved to the Dark Side.

Tyche put her hands on her hips, suddenly angry. "Who did this?" she asked. "Was it the Cheese Goat?"

Tearful, Chang'e shook her head.

"General Nutsy Nutsy? Or Mr. Cute?" The Moon People had many enemies, and there had been times when Tyche had led them in great battles, cutting her way through armies of stone with an aluminium rod the Magician had enchanted into a terrible bright blade. But none of them had ever been so mean as to break the Peoples' houses.

"Who was it, then?"

Chang'e hid her face behind one flowing silken sleeve and pointed. And that's when Tyche saw the first ant, moving in the ruins of the Jade Rabbit's house.

It was not like a grag or an otho, and certainly not a Moon Person. It was a jumbled metal frame, all angles and shiny rods, like a vector calculation come to life, too straight and rigid against the rough surfaces of the rocks to be real. It was like two tetrahedrons inside each other, with a bulbous sphere at each vertex, each glittering like the eye of the Great Wrong Place.

It was not big, perhaps reaching up to Tyche's knees. One of the telescoping metal struts had white letters on it. ANT-A3972, they said, even thought the thing did not look like the ants Tyche had seen in videos.

It stretched and moved like the geometrical figures Tyche manipulated with a gesture during the Brain's math lessons. Suddenly, it flipped over the Rabbit's broken wall, making Tyche gasp. Then it shifted into a strange, slug-like motion over the regolith, first stretching, then contracting. It made Tyche's skin crawl. As she watched, the ant thing fell into a crevice between two boulders—but dextrously pulled itself up, supported itself on a couple of vertices and somersaulted over the obstacle like an acrobat.

Tyche stared at it. Anger started to build up in her chest. In the Base, she obeyed the Brain and the othos and the grags because she had Promised. But the Other Moon was her place: it belonged to her and the Moon People, and no one else.

"Everybody else is hiding," whispered Chang'e. "You have to do something, Tyche. Chase it away."

"Where is the Magician?" Tyche asked. *He would know what to do.* She did not like the way the ant thing moved.

As she hesitated, the creature swung around and, with a series of twitches, pulled itself up into a pyramid, as if watching her. *It's not so nasty-looking,* Tyche thought. *Maybe I could bring it back to the Base, introduce it to Hugbear.* It would be a complex operation: she would have to assure the bear that she would always love it no matter what, and then carefully introduce the newcomer to it—

The ant thing darted forward, quickly like a falling meteorite, and a sharp pain stung Tyche's thigh. One of the thing's vertices had a spike that quickly retracted. Tyche's suit grumbled as it sealed all its twenty-one layers, and soothed the tiny wound. Tears came to her eyes, and her mouth was suddenly dry. No Moon Person had ever hurt her, not even the ink-men, except to pretend. She almost switched her radio on and called the grag for help.

Then she felt the eyes of the Moon People, looking at her from their windows. She gritted her teeth and ignored the bite of the wound. She was Tyche. She was brave. Had she not climbed to the Peak of Eternal Light once, all alone, following the solar panel cables, just to look at the Great Wrong Place in the eye? (It had been smaller than she thought, tiny and blue and unblinking, with a bit of white and green, and altogether a disappointment.)

Carefully, Tyche picked up a good-sized rock from the Jade Rabbit's wall—it was broken anyway. She took a slow step towards the creature. It had suddenly contracted into something resembling a cube and seemed to be absorbed in something. Tyche moved right. The ant flinched at her shadow. She moved left—and swung the rock down as hard as she could.

She missed. The momentum took her down. Her knees hit the hard chilly regolith. The rock bounced away. This time the tears came, but Tyche struggled up and threw the rock after the creature. It was scrambling away, up the slope of the crater.

Tyche picked up the rock and followed. In spite of the steep climb, she gained on it with a few determined leaps, cheered on by the Moon People below. She was right at its heels when it climbed over the edge of the crater. But when she caught a glimpse of what lay beyond, she froze and dropped down on her belly.

A bright patch of sunlight shone on the wide highland plain ahead. It was crawling with ants, hundreds of them. A rectangular carpet of them sat right in the middle, all joined together into a thick metal sheet. Every now and then it undulated like something soft, a shiny amoeba. Other ant things moved in orderly rows, sweeping the surroundings.

The one Tyche was following picked up speed on the level ground, rolling and bouncing, like a skeletal football, and as she watched from her hiding place, it joined the central mass. Immediately, the ant-sheet changed. Its sides stretched upwards into a hollow, cup-like shape: other ants at its base telescoped into a high, supporting structure, lifting it up. A sharp spike grew in the middle of the cup, and then the whole structure turned to point at the sky. *A transmitter,* Tyche thought, following it with her gaze.

It was aimed straight at the Great Wrong Place.

Tyche swallowed, turned around and slid back down. She was almost glad to see the grag down there, waiting for her patiently by the Secret Door.

———

The Brain did not sound angry, but then the Brain was never angry.

"Evacuation procedure has been initiated," it said. "This location has been compromised."

Tyche was breathing hard: the Base was in a lava tube halfway up the south slope of the mountain, and the way up was always harder than the way down. This time, the grag had had no trouble keeping up with her. It had been a silent journey: she had tried to tell the Brain about the ants, but the AI had maintained complete radio silence until they were inside the Base.

"What do you mean, *evacuation*?" Tyche demanded.

She opened the helmet of her suit and breathed in the comfortable yeasty smell of her home module. Her little home was converted from one of the old Chinese ones that had been here when the Brain arrived, snug white cylinders that huddled close to the main entrance of the cavernous lava tube. She always thought they looked like the front teeth in the mouth of a big snake.

The main tube itself was partially pressurised, over sixty metres in diameter and burrowed deep into the mountain. It split into many branches expanded and reinforced by othos and grags with regolith concrete pillars. She had tried to play it there many times, but preferred the Other Moon: she did not like the stench from the bacteria that the othos seeded the walls with, the ones that pooped calcium and aluminium.

Now, it was a hotbed of activity. The grags had set up bright lights and moved around, disassembling equipment and filling cryogenic tanks. The walls were alive with the tiny, soft, starfish-like othos, eating bacteria away. The Brain had not wasted any time.

"We are leaving, Tyche," the Brain said. "You need to get ready. The probe you found knows we are here. We are going away, to another place. A safer place. Do not worry. We have alternative locations prepared. It will be fine."

Tyche bit her lip. *It's my fault.* She wished the Brain had a proper face. It had a module for its own, in the coldest, unpressurised part of the tube, where its quantum processors could operate undisturbed, but inside it was just lasers and lenses and trapped ions, and rat brain cells grown to mesh with circuitry. How could it understand about the Jade Rabbit's house? It wasn't fair.

"And before we go, you need a Treatment."

Going away. She tried to wrap her mind around the concept. They had always been here, to be safe from the space sharks from the Great Wrong Place. And the Secret Door was here. If they went somewhere else, how would she find her way to the Other Moon? What would the Moon People do without her?

And she still hadn't given the ruby to the Magician.

The anger and fatigue exploded out of her in one hot wet burst.

"I'm not going to go not going to go not going to go," she said and ran into her sleeping cubicle. "And I don't want a stupid Treatment," she yelled, letting the door membrane congeal shut behind her.

Tyche took off her suit, flung it into a corner and cuddled against the Hugbear in her bed. Its ragged fur felt warm against her cheek, and its fake heartbeat was reas-

suring. She distantly remembered her Mum had made it move from afar, sometimes, stroked her hair with its paws, its round facescreen replaced with her features.
That had been a long time ago and she was sure the bear was bigger then. But it was
still soft.

Suddenly, the bear moved. Her heart jumped with a strange, aching hope. But it
was only the Brain. "Go 'way," she muttered.

"Tyche, this is important," said the Brain. "Do you remember what you promised?"

She shook her head. Her eyes were hot and wet. *I'm not going to cry like Chang'e*,
she thought. *I'm not.*

"Do you remember now?"

The bear's face was replaced with a man and a woman. The man had no hair
and his dark skin glistened. The woman was raven-haired and pale, with a face like
a bird. *Mum is even prettier than Chang'e*, Tyche thought.

"Hello, Tyche," they said in unison, and laughed. "We are Kareem and Sofia,"
the woman said. "We are your mommy and daddy. We hope you are well when you
see this." She touched the screen, quickly and lightly, like a little bunny hop on the
regolith.

"But if the Brain is showing you this," Tyche's Dad said, "then it means that
something bad has happened and you need to do what the Brain tells you."

"You should not be angry at the Brain," Mum said. "It is not like we are, it
just plans and thinks. It just does what it it was told to do. And we told it to keep
you safe."

"You see, in the Great Wrong Place, people like us could not be safe," Dad continued. "People like Mum and me and you were feared. They called us Greys, after the
man who figured out how to make us, and they were jealous, because we lived longer
than they did and had more time to figure things out. And because giving things silly
names makes people feel better about themselves. Do we look grey to you?"

No. Tyche shook her head. The Magician was grey, but that was because he was
always looking for rubies in dark places and never saw the sun.

"So we came here, to build a Right Place, just the two of us." Her Dad squeezed
Mum's shoulders, just like the bear used to do to Tyche. "And you were born here.
You can't imagine how happy we were."

Then Mum looked serious. "But we knew that the Wrong Place people might
come looking for us. So we had to hide you, to make sure you would be safe, so they
would not look inside you and cut you and find out what makes you work. They
would do anything to have you."

Fear crunched Tyche's gut into a little cold ball. *Cut you?*

"It was very, very hard, dear Tyche, because we love you. Very hard, not to touch
you except from afar. But we want you to grow big and strong, and when the time
comes, we will come and find you, and then we will all be in the Right Place together."

"But you have to promise to take your Treatments. Can you promise to do that?
Can you promise to do what the Brain says?"

"I promise," Tyche muttered.

"Goodbye, Tyche," her parents said. "We will see you soon."

And then they were gone, and the Hugbear's face was blank and pale brown
again.

"We need to go soon," the Brain said again, and this time Tyche thought its voice sounded more gentle. "Please get ready. I would like you to have a Treatment before travel."

Tyche sighed and nodded. It wasn't fair. But she had promised.

The Brain sent Tyche a list of things she could take with her, scrolling in one of the windows of her room. It was a short list. She looked around at the fabbed figurines and the moon rock that she thought that looked like a boy and the e-sheets floating everywhere with her favourite stories open. She could not even take the Hugbear. She felt alone, suddenly, like she had when she climbed to look at the Great Wrong Place on top of the mountain.

Then she noticed the ruby lying on her bed. *If I go away and take it with me, the Magician will never find it.* She thought about the Magician and his panther, desperately looking from crater to crater, forever. *It's not fair. Even if I keep my promise, I'll have to take it to him.*

And say goodbye.

Tyche sat down on the bed and thought very hard.

The Brain was everywhere, but it could not watch everything. It was based on a scanned human brain, some poor person who had died a long ago. It had no cameras in her room. And its attention would be in the evacuation: it would have to keep programming and reprogramming the grags. She picked at the sensor bracelet in her wrist that monitored her life signs and location. That was the difficult bit. She would have to do something about that. But there wasn't much time: the Brain would get her for a Treatment soon.

She hugged the bear again in frustration. It felt warm, and as she squeezed it hard, she could feel its pulse—

Tyche sat up. She remembered the Jade Rabbit's stories and tricks, the tar rabbit he had made to trick an enemy.

She reached into the Hugbear's head and pulled out a programming window, coupled it with her sensor. She summoned up old data logs, added some noise to them. Then she fed them to the bear, watched its pulse and breathing and other simulated life signs change to match hers.

Then she took a deep breath, and as quickly as she could, she pulled off the bracelet and put it on the Hugbear.

"Tyche? Is there something wrong?" the Brain asked.

Tyche's heart jumped. Her mind raced. "It's fine," she said. "I think . . . I think I just banged my sensor a bit. I'm just getting ready now." She tried to make her voice sound sweet, like a girl who always keeps her promise.

"Your Treatment will be ready soon," the Brain said and was gone. Heart pounding, Tyche started to put on her suit.

There was a game that Tyche used to play in the lava tube: how far could she get before she was spotted by the grags? She played it now, staying low, avoiding their camera eyes, hiding behind rock protrusions, crates and cryogenic tanks, until she was in a tube branch that only had othos in it. The Brain did not usually control them directly, and besides, they did not have eyes. Still, her heart felt like meteorite impacts in her chest.

She pushed through a semi-pressurising membrane. In this branch, the othos had dug too deep for calcium, and caused a roof collapse. In the dim green light of her suit's fluorescence, she made way her up the tube's slope carefully. *There.* She climbed on a pile of rubble carefully. The othos had once told her there was an opening there, and she hoped it would be big enough for her to squeeze through.

Boulders rolled under her, suddenly, and she banged her knee painfully. The suit hissed at the sudden impact. She ignored the pain and ran her fingers along the rocks, following a very faint air current she could not have sensed without the suit. Then her fingers met regolith instead of rock. It was packed tight, and she had to push hard at it with her aluminium rod before it gave away. A shower of dust and rubble fell on her, and for a moment she thought there was going to be another collapse. And suddenly, there was a patch of velvet sky in front of her. She widened the opening, made herself as small as she could and crawled towards it.

Tyche emerged onto the mountainside. The sudden wide open space of rolling grey and brown around her felt like the time she had eaten too much sugar. Her legs and hands were wobbly, and she had to sit down onto the regolith for a moment. She shook herself: she had an appointment to keep. She checked that the ruby was still in its pouch, got up and started downwards with the Rabbit's lope.

The Secret Door was just the way Tyche had left it. She eyed the crater edge nervously, but there were no ants in sight. She bit her lip when she looked at the Old One and the Troll.

What's wrong? the Old One asked.

"I'm going to have to go away."

Don't worry. We'll still be here when you come back.

"I might never come back," Tyche said, choking a bit.

Never is a very long time, the Old One said. Even I have never seen never. We'll be here. Take care, Tyche.

Tyche crawled through to the Other Moon, and found the Magician waiting for her.

He was very thin and tall, taller than the Old One even, and cast a long cold finger of a shadow in the crater. He had a sad face and a scraggly beard and white gloves and a tall top hat. Next to him lay his flying panther, all black, with eyes like tiny rubies.

"Hello, Tyche," the Magician said, with a voice like the rumble of the sandworm.

Tyche swallowed and took out the ruby from her pouch, holding it out to him.

"I made this for you." *What if he doesn't like it?* But the Magician picked it up, slowly, eyes glowing, held it in both hands and gazed at it in awe.

"That is very, very kind of you," he whispered. Very carefully, he took off his hat and put the ruby in it. It was the first time Tyche had ever seen the Magician smile. Still, there is a sadness to his expression.

"I didn't want to leave before giving it to you," she said.

"That's quite a fuss you caused for the Brain. He is going to be very worried."

"He deserves it. But I promised I would go with him."

The Magician looked at the ruby one more time and put the hat back on his head.

"Normally, I don't interfere with the affairs of other people, but for this, I owe you a wish."

Tyche took a deep breath. "I don't want to live with the grags and the othos and the Brain anymore. I want to be in the Right Place with Mum and Dad."

The Magician looked at her sadly.

"I'm sorry, Tyche, but I can't make that happen. My magic is not powerful enough."

"But they promised—"

"Tyche, I know you don't remember. And that's why we Moon People remember for you. The space sharks came and took your parents, a long time ago. They are dead. I am sorry."

Tyche closed her eyes. *A picture in a window, a domed crater. Two bright things arcing over the horizon, like sharks. Then, brightness—*

"You've lived with the Brain ever since. You don't remember because it makes you forget with the Treatments, so you don't get too sad, so you stay the way your parents told it to keep you. But we remember. And we always tell you the truth."

And suddenly they were all there, all the Moon People, coming from their houses: Chang'e and her children and the Jade Rabbit and the Woodcutter, looking at her gravely and nodding their heads.

Tyche could not bear to look at them. She covered her helmet with her hands, turned around, crawled through the Secret Door and ran away, away from the Other Moon. She ran, not a Rabbit run but a clumsy jerky crying run, until she stumbled on a boulder and went rolling higgedly-piggedly down. She lay curled up in the chilly regolith for a long time. And when she opened her eyes, the ants were all around her.

The ants were arranged around her in a half-circle, stretched into spiky pyramids, waving slightly, as if looking for something. Then they spoke. At first, it was just noise, hissing in her helmet, but after a second it resolved into a voice.

"—hello," it said, warm and female, like Chang'e, but older and deeper. "I am Alissa. Are you hurt?"

Tyche was frozen. She had never spoken to anyone who was not the Brain or one of the Moon People. Her tongue felt stiff.

"Just tell me if you are all right. No one is going to hurt you. Do you feel bad anywhere?"

"No," Tyche breathed.

"There is no need to be afraid. We will take you home." A video feed flashed up inside her helmet, a spaceship that was made up of a cluster of legs and a globe that glinted golden. A circle appeared elsewhere in her field of vision, indicating a tiny pinpoint of light in the sky. "See? We are on our way."

"I don't want to go to the Great Wrong Place," she gasped. "I don't want you to cut me up."

There was a pause.

"Why would we do that? There is nothing to be afraid of."

"Because Wrong Place people don't like people like me."

Another pause.

"Dear child, I don't know what you have been told, but things have changed. Your parents left Earth more than a century ago. We never thought we would find you, but we kept looking. And I'm glad we did. You have been alone on the Moon for a very long time."

Tyche got up, slowly. *I haven't been alone.* Her head spun. *They would do anything to have you?*

She backed off a few steps.

"If I come with you," she asked in a small voice, "will I see Kareem and Sofia again?"

A pause again, longer this time.

"Of course you will," Alissa the ant-woman said finally. "They are right here, waiting for you."

Liar.

Slowly, Tyche started backing off. The ants moved, closing their circle. *I am faster than they are*, she thought. *They can't catch me.*

"Where are you going?"

Tyche switched off her radio, cleared the circle of the ants with a leap and hit the ground running.

Tyche ran, faster than she had ever run before, faster even than when the Jade Rabbit challenged her to a race across the Shackleton Crater. Finally, her lungs and legs burned and she had to stop. She had set out without direction, but had gone up the mountain slope, close to the cold fingers. *I don't want to go back to the Base. The Brain never tells the truth either.* Black dots danced in her eyes. *They'll never catch me.*

She looked back, down towards the crater of the Secret Door. The ants were moving. They gathered into the metal sheet again. Then its sides stretched upwards until they met and formed a tubular structure. It elongated and weaved back and forth and slithered forward, faster than even Tyche could run, a metal snake. The pyramid shapes of the ants glinted at its head like teeth. Faster and faster it came, flowing over boulders and craters like it was weightless, a curtain of billowing dust behind it. She looked around for a hiding place, but she was on open ground now, except for the dark pool of the mining crater to the west.

Then she remembered something the Jade Rabbit had once said. *For anything that wants to eat you, there is something bigger that wants to eat it.*

The ant-snake was barely a hundred meters behind her now, flipping back and forth in sinusoid waves on the regolith like a shiny metal whip. She stuck out her tongue at it, accidentally tasting the sweet inner surface of her helmet. Then she made it for the sunless crater's edge.

With a few bounds, she was over the crater lip. It was like diving into icy water. Her suit groaned, and she could feel its joints stiffening up. But she kept going, towards the bottom, almost blind from the contrast between the pitch-black and the bright sun above. She followed the vibration in her soles. Boulders and pebbles rained on her helmet and she knew the ant-snake was right at her heels.

The lights of the sandworm almost blinded her. *Now.* She leapt up, as high as she could, feeling weightless, reached out for the utility ladder that she knew was on the huge machine's topside. She grabbed it, banged painfully against the worm's side, felt its thunder beneath her.

And then, a grinding, shuddering vibration as the mining machine bit into the ant-snake, rolling right over it.

Metal fragments flew into the air, glowing red-hot. One of them landed on Tyche's arm. The suit bubbled it up and spit it out. The sandworm came to an emergency halt, and Tyche almost fell off. It started disgorging its little repair grags, and Tyche felt a stab of guilt. She sat still until her breathing calmed down and the suit's complaints about the cold got too loud.

Then she dropped to the ground and started the climb back up, towards the Secret Door.

There were still a few ants left around the Secret Door, but Tyche ignored them. They were rolling around aimlessly, and there weren't enough of them to build a transmitter. She looked up. The ship from the Great Wrong Place was still a distant star. She still had time.

Painfully, bruised limbs aching, she crawled through the Secret Door for one last time.

The Moon People were still there, waiting for her. Tyche looked at them in the eye, one by one. Then she put her hands on her hips.

"I have a wish," she said. "I am going to go away. I'm going to make the Brain obey me, this time. I'm going to go and build a Right Place, all on my own. I'm never going to forget again. So I want you all to come with me." She looked up at the Magician. "Can you do that?"

Smiling, the man in the top hat nodded, spread his white-gloved fingers and whirled his cloak that had a bright red inner lining, like a ruby—

Tyche blinked. The Other Moon was gone. She looked around. She was standing on the other side of the Old One and the Troll, except that they looked just like rocks now. And the Moon People were inside her. *I should feel heavier, carrying so many people,* she thought. But instead she felt empty and light.

Uncertainly at first, then with more confidence, she started walking back up Malapert Mountain, towards the Base. Her step was not a rabbit's, nor a panther's, nor a maiden's silky glide, just Tyche's own, for the first time.

the wreck of the
"charles dexter ward"

SARAH MONETTE AND ELIZABETH BEAR

Elizabeth Bear was born in Connecticut, and now lives in Brookfield, Massachusetts, after living for several years in the Mohave Desert near Las Vegas. She won the John W. Campbell Memorial Award for Best New Writer in 2005, and in 2008 she took home a Hugo Award for her short story "Tideline," which also won her the Theodore Sturgeon Memorial Award (shared with David Moles). In 2009, she won another Hugo Award for her novelette "Shoggoths in Bloom." Her short work has appeared in Asimov's Science Fiction, Subterranean, SCI FICTION, Interzone, The 3rd Alternative, Strange Horizons, On Spec, and elsewhere, and has been collected in The Chains That You Refuse and New Amsterdam. She is the author of three highly acclaimed SF novels, Hammered, Scardown, and Worldwired, and of the alternate history fantasy Promethean Age series, which includes the novels Blood and Iron, Whiskey and Water, Ink and Steel, and Hell and Earth. Her other books include the novels Carnival, Undertow, Chill, Dust, All the Windwracked Stars, By the Mountain Bound, Range of Ghosts, a novel in collaboration with Sarah Monette, The Tempering of Men, and two chapbook novellas, Bone and Jewel Creatures and Ad Eternum. Her most recent book is a new collection, Shoggoths in Bloom. Forthcoming are a new novel, Shattered Pillars, and a new novella, The Book of Iron. Visit her Web site at www.elizabethbear.com. Her solo story "In the House of Aryaman, A Lonely Signal Burns" appears elsewhere in this anthology.

Sarah Monette was born and raised in Oak Ridge, Tennessee, one of the secret cities of the Manhattan Project. Having completed her PhD in Renaissance English drama, she now lives and writes in a ninety-nine-year-old house in the upper Midwest. Her Doctrine of Labyrinths series consists of the novels Melusine, The Virtu, and The Mirador. Her short fiction has appeared in many places, including Strange Horizons, Aeon, Alchemy, and Lady Churchill's Rosebud Wristlet, and has been collected in The Bone Key. Upcoming is a new novel in the Doctrine of Labyrinths series, Corambis. Her Web site is located at www.sarahmonette.com.

Bear and Monette have collaborated before, on the story "The Ile of Dogges" and on the novel, A Companion to Wolves, as well as on other stories set in the same universe as this one, such as "The Boojum" and "Mongoose." Here they join forces again to take us on a quest for a lost spaceship—one that it might be a good idea not to find!

PART ONE

Six weeks into her involuntary tenure on Faraday Station, Cynthia Feuerwerker needed a job. She could no longer afford to be choosy about it, either; her oxygen tax was due, and you didn't have to be a medical doctor to understand the difficulties inherent in trying to breathe vacuum.

You didn't have to be, but Cynthia was one. Or had been, until the allegations of malpractice and unlicensed experimentation began to catch up with her. As they had done, here at Faraday, six weeks ago. She supposed she was lucky that the crew of the boojum-ship *Richard Trevithick* had decided to put her off here, rather than just feeding her to their vessel—but she was having a hard time feeling the gratitude. For one thing, her medical skills had saved both the ship and several members of his crew in the wake of a pirate attack. For another, they'd confiscated her medical supplies before dumping her, and made sure the whole of the station knew the charges against her.

Which was a death sentence too, and a slower one that going down the throat of a boojum along with the rest of the trash.

So it was cold desperation that had driven Cynthia here, to the sharp side of this steel desk in a rented station office, staring into the face of a bald old Arkhamer whose jowls quivered with every word he spoke. His skin was so dark she could just about make out the patterns of tattoos against the pigment, black on black-brown.

"Your past doesn't bother me, Doctor Feuerwerker," he said. His sleeves were too short for his arms, so five centimeters of fleshy wrist protruded when he gestured. "I'll be very plain with you. We have need of your skills, and there is no guarantee any of us will be returning from the task we need them for."

Cynthia folded her hands over her knee. She had dropped a few credits on a public shower and a paper suit before the interview, but anybody could look at her haggard face and the bruises on her elbows and tell she'd been sleeping in maintenance corridors.

"You mentioned this was a salvage mission. I understand there may be competition. Pirates. Other dangers."

"No to mention the social danger of taking up with an Arkhamer vessel."

"If I stay here, I face the social danger of an airlock. I am a good doctor, Professor Wandrei. I wasn't stripped of my license for any harm to a patient."

"No-oo," he agreed, drawing it out. She knew he must have her C.V. in his heads-up display. "But rather for seeking after forbidden knowledge."

She shrugged and gestured around the rented office. "Galileo and Derleth and Chen sought forbidden knowledge, too. That got us this far." Onto a creaky, leaky, Saturn-orbit station that stank of ammonia despite exterminators working double shifts to keep the toves down. She watched his eyes and decided to take a risk. "An Arkhamer Professor ought to be sympathetic to that."

Wandrei's lips were probably lush once, but years and exposure to the radiation that pierced inadequately shielded steelships had left them lined and dry. Despite that, and the jowls, and the droop of his eyelids, his homely face could still rearrange itself beautifully around a smile.

Cynthia waited long enough to be sure he wouldn't speak before adding, "You know I don't have any equipment."

"We have some supplies. And the vessel we're going to salvage is an ambulance ship, the *Charles Dexter Ward*. You should be able to procure everything you need aboard it. In my position as a senior officer of the *Jarmulowicz Astronomica*, I am prepared to offer you a full share of the realizations from the salvage expedition, as well as first claim on any medical goods or technology."

Suspicion tickled Cynthia's neck. "What else do you expect to find aboard an ambulance, Professor?"

"Data," he said. "Research. The *Jarmulowicz Astronomica* is an archive ship."

Next dicey question: "What happened to your ship's surgeon?"

"Aneurysm," he said. "She was terribly young, but it took her so fast—there was nothing anyone could do. She'd just risen from apprentice, and hadn't yet taken one of her own. We'll get another from a sister ship eventually—but there's not another Arkhamer vessel at Faraday now, or within three days' travel, and we'll lose the salvage if we don't act immediately."

"How many shares in total?" A full share sounded good—until you found out the salvage rights were divided ten thousand ways.

"A full share is one percent," he said.

No self-discipline in space could have kept Cynthia from rocking back in her chair—and self-discipline had never been her strong point. It was too much. This was a trap.

Even just one percent of the scrap rights of a ship like that would be enough to live on frugally for the rest of her days. With her pick of drugs and equipment—

This was a trap.

And a chance to practice medicine again. A chance to read the medical files of an Arkhamer archive ship.

She had thirteen hours to find a better offer, by the letter of the law. Then it was the Big Nothing, the breathsucker, and her eyes freezing in their tears. And there wasn't a better offer, or she wouldn't have been here in the first place.

"I'll come."

Wandrei gave her another of his beatific smiles. He slid a tablet across the rented desk. Cynthia pressed her thumb against it. A prick and a buzz, and her blood and print sealed the contract. "Get your things. You can meet us at Dock Six in thirty minutes."

"I'll come now," she said.

"Oh," he said. "One more thing—"

That creak as he stood was the spring of the trap's jaw slamming shut. Cynthia had heard the like before. She sat and waited, prim and stiff.

"The *Charles Dexter Ward?*"

She nodded.

"It was a liveship." He might have interpreted her silence as misunderstanding. "A boojum, I mean."

"An ambulance ship *and* a liveship? We're all going to die," Cynthia said.

Wandrei smiled, standing, light on his feet in the partial gravity. "Everybody dies," he said. "Better to die in knowledge than in ignorance."

The sleek busy tug *Veronica Lodge* hauled the cumbersome, centuries-accreted monstrosity that was the *Jarmulowicz Astronomica* out of Saturn's gravity well. Cynthia stood at one of the Arkhamer ship's tiny fish-eye observation ports watching the vast misty curve of the pink-gray world beneath, hazy and serene, turning in the shadows of her moons and rings. Another steelship was putting off from Faraday Station simultaneously. She was much smaller and newer and cleaner than the *Jarmulowicz Astronomica*, which in turn was dwarfed by the boojums who flashed bioluminescent messages at each other around Saturn's moons. The steelship looked like it was headed in-system, and for a moment, Cynthia wished she were on board, even knowing what would be waiting for her. The *Richard Trevithick* had not been not her first disaster.

She could not say, though, that she had been lured on board the *Jarmulowicz Astronomica* under false pretenses. The ship's crew of scholars and their families badly needed a doctor. Uncharitably, Cynthia suspected that they needed specifically a non-Arkhamer doctor, who would keep her mind on her patients.

The lost doctor—Martha Patterson Snead had been her name, for she had come to the *Jarmulowicz Astronomica* from the *Snead Mathematica*—might have been a genius, but as the *Jarmulowicz Astronomica* said goodbye to the *Veronica Lodge* and started on her stately way toward the *Charles Dexter Ward*, Cynthia found herself treating a great number of chronic vitamin deficiencies and other things that a non-genius but conscientious doctor should have been able to keep on top of.

Cynthia's patients were very polite and very grateful, but she couldn't help being aware that they would have preferred a genius who let them die of scurvy.

Other than nutritional deficiencies, the various cancers of space, and prenatal care, the most common reason for Cynthia to see patients were the minor emergencies and industrial accidents inevitably suffered in lives spent aboard a geriatric steelship requiring constant maintenance and repair. She treated smashed fingers, sprained wrists, and quite a few minor decompression injuries. She was splinting the ankle of a steamfitter's apprentice and undergraduate gas-giant meteorologist—many Arkhamers seemed to have two roles, one relating to ship's maintenance and one relating to academic research—when the young man frowned at her and said, "You aren't what I expected."

She'd forgotten his name. She glanced at the chart; he was Jaime MacReady Burlingame, traded from the *Burlingame Astrophysica Terce*. He had about twenty Terran years and a shock of orange hair that would not lie down, nor observe anything resembling a part. "Because I'm not an Arkhamer?" she asked, probing the wrist joint to be sure it really was a sprain and not a cracked bone.

"Everybody knows you're not one of us." He twitched slightly.

She held him steady, and noted the place. But when she glanced at his face, she realized his distress was over having said something more revealing than he intended. She said, "Some people aren't pleased about it?"

He looked away. She reached for the inflatable splint, hands gentle, and did not push. People told doctors things, if the doctors had the sense to keep quiet.

His pale, spotted fingers curled and uncurled. Finally, he answered, "Wandrei got in some trouble with the Faculty Senate, I hear. My advisor says Wandrei was high-handed, and he's lucky he has tenure."

Cynthia kept her head down, eyes on her work. Jaime sighed as she fitted the splint and its numbing, cooling agents began to take effect. "That should help bring the inflammation down," she told him. But as Jaime thanked her and left, she wondered if she ought to be grateful to Wandrei or if she ought to consider him her patron.

But she wasn't grateful—he had taken advantage of her desperation, which was not a matter for gratitude even if it had saved her life. And the Arkhamers didn't seem to think in terms of patronage and clients. They talked about apprentices and advisors, and nobody expected Cynthia to be Wandrei's apprentice.

She also noticed, as the days drew out into weeks, that nobody was approaching her about taking an apprentice of her own. She was just as glad, for she had no illusions about her own abilities as a teacher, and no idea how one person could go about imparting a medical school education from the ground up, but it made her feel acutely isolated—on a ship that was home to several hundred people—and she lay in her hammock during her sleep shift and worried about what would happen to the shy, solemn Arkhamer children when she was no longer on board. At other times, she reminded herself that the *Jarmulowicz Astronomica* was part of a network of Arkhamer ships, and—as Wandrei had said—they would acquire another doctor. They were probably in the middle of negotiating the swap or the lease or the marriage or whatever it was they did. But when she was supposed to be asleep, she worried.

They knew they were nearing the *Charles Dexter Ward* for days before he showed up on even the longest of the long-range scanners. The first sign was the cheshires, the tentacled creatures—so common on Arkhamer vessels—which patrolled the steelship's cabins and corridors, hunting toves and similar trans-dimensional nuisances that might slip through the interstices in reality and cause a potentially deadly infestation. One reason Arkhamer ships were tolerated at stations like Faraday was because the cheshires would hunt station vermin just as heartily. Boojums took care of their own pest control.

Normally, the cheshires—dozens or hundreds of them, Cynthia never did get a good count—slept and hunted seemingly at random. One might spend hours crouched before the angle of two intersecting bulkheads, tendrils all focused intently on one seemingly random point, its soft body slowly cycling through an array of colors that could mean anything or nothing at all . . . only to get up and slink away after a half-day of stalking as if nothing had happened. Cynthia often had to shoo two or three out of her hammock at bunk time, and like station cats they often returned to steal body heat once she was asleep. But as the *Jarmulowicz Astronomica* began encountering the spacetime distortions that inevitably accompanied the violent death of a boojum, the ship's cheshires became correspondingly agitated. They traveled in groups, and any time Cynthia encountered two sleeping, there was also one keeping watch . . . if a creature with sixteen eyes and no eyelids could be said to sleep. Cynthia tried not to speculate about their dreams.

The second sign was the knocking. Random, frantic banging, as if something outside the ship wanted to come in. It came at unpredictable intervals, and would sometimes be one jarring boom and sometimes go on for five minutes. It upset the cheshires even more; they couldn't hear the headache-inducing noise, being deaf, but they could feel the vibrations. Every time Cynthia was woken in her sleep shift by that terrible knocking, she'd find at least one and usually more like three cheshires under her blankets with her, trying to hide their wedge-shaped heads between her arms and her body. She'd learned from her child patients, who lost their shy formality in talking about their playmates, how to pet the cheshires, how to use her voice in ways they could feel, and she would lie there in the dim green glow of the one working safety light and pet the trembling cheshires until she fell asleep again.

The knocking was followed by what the Arkhamers called pseudoghosts—one of them explained the phenomenon in excruciating detail while Cynthia cleaned and stitched a six-inch long gash on her forearm: not the spirits of the dead, but microbursts of previous and future time. "Or, rather, future probabilities, since the future has yet to be determined."

"Of course," Cynthia said. The girl's name was Hester Ayabo Jarmulowicz; she was tall and skinny and iron-black, and she had laid her arm open trying to repair the damage done to an interior bulkhead by the percussive force of the knocking. "So the woman I almost ran into this morning before she vanished in a burst of static—was that Martha Patterson?"

"Probably," Hester said. "Not very tall, wiry, freckled skin?"

"Yes. Keep your arm still, please."

"That was Doctor Patterson. Before Doctor Patterson, we had Doctor Belafonte, so you may see him as well."

"And your future doctors, whoever they may be?"

"Very likely," Hester said.

Cynthia saw Dr. Patterson several times, and once an old man who had to be Dr. Belafonte, but the only future ghost she saw was herself—her hair longer, grayer, her clothes shabbier—standing beside the exam table with a scowl on her face that could have been used for spot-welding.

What frightened Cynthia most—aside from the nauseating, almost electric shock of walking into the medical bay and seeing *herself*—was the way that scowl had looked as if it had been carved into her face.

It made no sense. Why would she still be on the *Jarmulowicz Astronomica*? She didn't want to stay, and the Arkhamers clearly didn't want to keep her. But then she thought, in the middle of autoclaving her instruments, *Wandrei trapped me once.*

That was not a nice thought, and it brought others in its wake, about pitcher plants and the way they started digesting their prey before the unfortunate insects were dead, about the way her future self's face had looked as if it were eroding around that scowl.

She schooled herself for being morbid and tried to focus on her patients and on her reading in the ship's archives (Wandrei had at least kept his word about that), but she was very grateful, as well as surprised, when, a few days after their conversation about pseudoghosts, Hester Ayabo marched into the medical bay and announced, "Isolation is bad for human beings. I am going to eat lunch with you."

Cynthia toggled off the display on the patient file she had been updating. "You are? I mean, thank you, but—"

"You can tell me about your studies," Hester said, midway between an invitation and a command. She gave Cynthia a bright, uncertain, sidelong look—*like a falcon,* Cynthia thought, *trying to make friends with a plow horse*—and Cynthia laughed and got up and said, "Or you can tell me about yours."

Which Hester was glad to do, volubly and at length. She was an astrobiologist—the same specialty as Wandrei, and Wandrei was in fact a member of her committee, which seemed to be a little like being a parent and a little like being a boss. Hester studied creatures like boojums and cheshires and the dreadful bandersnatches, creatures that had evolved in the cold and airless dark between the stars—or the cold and airless interstices of space-time. She was very excited by the chance to study the *Charles Dexter Ward,* and on their third lunch, Cynthia found the nerve to ask her, "Do you know how the *Charles Dexter Ward* died?"

Hester stopped in the middle of bringing a slice of hydroponically cultivated tomato to her mouth. "It is something of a mystery. But I can tell you what we do know."

It was more than Wandrei had offered; Cynthia listened avidly.

As Wandrei had told her, the *Charles Dexter Ward* had been an ambulance ship—or, more accurately, a mobile hospital. He had been in service for more than ten solar, well known throughout the farther and darker reaches of the system. His captain was equally well-known for disregarding evidence of pirate status when taking patients on board; though there was no formal recognition of neutrality once you got past the sovereignty of Mars, the *Charles Dexter Ward* was one boojum that no pirate would attack. "Even the Mi-Go," Hester said, "although no one knows why."

Cynthia tried to hide the reflexive curl of her fingers, even though there had been no hint of special meaning in Hester's tone. "What became of his crew?"

"Probably still aboard," Hester said. "Possibly some are even alive. Although you can't eat boojum. It's not what we'd consider meat."

"How did the *Jarmulowicz Astronomica* find out about him?"

"Another Arkhamer ship picked up a distress buoy. They couldn't stop for her"—and Hester's sly look told Cynthia that, friends or not (were they friends?) Hester would never tell an outsider why—"but they sent us a coded burst as closest relative. We may not beat other salvage attempts, even so. The beacon just said that the ship was moribund—no reason given. Possibly, the captain didn't know, or if something happened to him, it might have been junior crew who sent the probe. And nobody tells us students much anyway."

Cynthia nodded. She put her hand on her desk, about to lever herself to her feet, as Hester sucked down a length of tofu. "Huh," Cynthia said. "Do boojums die of natural causes?"

Lips shining with broth, Hester cocked her head at her. "They have to die of something, I suppose. But our records don't mention any that have."

By the time they were within a hundred kilometers of the dead boojum, the banging and the manifestations were close to constant. Cynthia dodged her own shadow in Sick Bay almost reflexively, as she might a surgical nurse with whom she had established a practiced partnership. It was a waste of mental and physical energy—*I could just walk through myself*—but she couldn't bring herself to stop.

Hester brought her cookies, dropping the plate between Cynthia and the work screen on which she was studying what schematics she could find of the *Charles Dexter Ward*—spotty—and his sister ships—wildly varying in architecture. Or growth patterns. Or whatever you called a boojum's internal design.

"We'll be there next watch," Hester said. "You ought to rest."

"It's my work watch," Cynthia said. The cookies were pale, crisp-soft, and fragrant with lemons and lavender. It was everything she could do to nibble one delicately, with evident pleasure, and save the others for later. Hester did not take one, though Cynthia offered.

She said, "I've another dozen in my locker. I like to bake on my rec watch. And you *should* rest: the President and the Faculty Senate have sent around a memo saying that everybody who is not on watch should be getting as much sleep as possible."

Cynthia glanced guiltily at her wristpiece. She had a bad habit of forgetting she'd turned notifications off. Something like a giant's fist thumped against the hull; she barely noticed. "I should be cramming boojum anatomy, is what I should be doing."

Hester smiled at her, but did not laugh. "You've been studying it since we left Faraday. You have something to prove?"

"You know what I have to prove." But she took a second cookie anyway, stared at it, and said, "Hester. If you only see one ghost . . . does that mean that there's only one future?"

"An interesting question," Hester said. "Temporal metadynamics aren't really my field. It may mean there are futures in which there are no people in that place. It may mean that that one particular future is locked in, I guess."

"Unavoidable?"

"Inescapable!" She grinned, plush lips a contrast to the wiry narrowness of her face and body. "I'm going to go take my mandated nap. If you have any sense you will too. You're on the away team, you know."

Cynthia's startle broke the cookie in half. "Read the memo," Hester advised, not unkindly. "And get some sleep while you can. There's unlikely to be much time to rest once we reach the *Charles Dexter Ward*."

PART TWO

The corpse of the *Charles Dexter Ward* hung ten degrees off the plane of the ecliptic, in a crevice of spacetime where it was very unlikely that anyone would just stumble across it. Cynthia had been called to the bridge for the first time in her tenure as ship's surgeon aboard the *Jarmulowicz Astronomica*. She stood behind the President's chair, wishing Professor Wandrei were somewhere in sight. She'd been too nervous to ask after his current whereabouts, but an overheard comment suggested he was at his instruments below. She, on the other hand, was watching the approach to the ruined liveship with her own eyes, on screens and through the biggest expanse of transparent crystal anywhere on the ship.

She rather wished she wasn't.

The boojum was a streamlined shape tumbling gently in the midst of its own web of tentacles. Inertia twisted them in corkscrews as the boojum rotated grandly around its center of mass, drifting farther and farther from the solar system's common plane. It was dark, no bioluminescence revealing the details of its lines. Only the sun's rays gently cupping the curve of the hull gave it form and mass.

Around it, where Cynthia would expect to see the familiar patterns of stars burning in the icy void of the up-and-out, the Big Empty, the sky was shattered. A great mirrored lens, wrenched loose and broken into a thousand glittering shards, cast back crazy reflections of the *Jarmulowicz Astronomica*, the *Charles Dexter Ward*, and the steelship already moored to the dead boojum, a ship so scarred and dented that all that could be deciphered of its hull markings was the word CALICO. It was a small ship—it couldn't boast more than a two- or three-man crew—and didn't worry Cynthia. What did worry her were all those jagged bits of mirror, all those uncalculated angles of reflection. The very things a mirror like that was meant to blind would be drawn to this jostling chaos, and with the boojum dead, neither the *Jarmulowicz Astronomica* nor her competition had much in the way of defense— unless the stupid stories Cynthia had been hearing all her life were true and the Arkhamers had some sort of occult weaponry that nobody else knew about.

Unfortunately, she was pretty sure they didn't.

"All right," said the President, loudly enough to cut through the two or three muttered discussions taking place at various points on the bridge. "We have three immediate objectives. One, obviously, is the reason we're here"—and she nodded at the derelict before them—"the second is salvaging and neutralizing that reflecting lens, and the third is making contact with the *Calico* over there. We need to see if we can come to a mutually beneficial agreement. Please talk to your departments. By no later than the top of the next shift, I want a roster of volunteers for EVA. I know some departments badly need the practice." She glanced at an elderly Arkhamer Cynthia did not know; there was clearly a story there by the way the man blushed and stammered, but Cynthia doubted she'd ever hear it.

"What about the *Calico*?" a voice said from the doorway. It was Wandrei, and if he was in disgrace, he didn't seem to mind.

"Professor Wandrei," the President said coolly. "Are you volunteering?"

"Of course," Wandrei said, smiling at her affably. "And since I imagine they've docked at the most useful point of—ah—ingress, may I suggest that you send the planned away team with me?"

There was a fraught silence. Cynthia stared fixedly at the nearest of the *Charles Dexter Ward*'s blank, glazed eyes and cursed herself for thirty-nine kinds of fool. Finally, the President said, "Thomas, you're plotting something."

"I pursue knowledge, Madam President," said Wandrei, "as we all do. Or have you forgotten that I sat on your tenure committee?"

One of the junior scholars gasped. Cynthia did not look away from the boojum's dead eye, but she could hear the smile in the President's voice when she said, "Very well. Take Meredith and Hester and Dr. Feuerwerker, and go find out what the *Calico* is doing. And remember to report back!"

The *Jarmulowicz Astronomica* possessed two landing craft, a lumbering scow called the *T.H. White* and an incongruously sporty little skimmer called the *Caitlin R. Kiernan*. The skimmer seated four, if nobody was too fussy about his or her personal space, and Hester knew how to fly it—which meant, Wandrei said, herding his team toward the *Caitlin R. Kiernan*, that they didn't need to wait for one of the two people on board who could fly the *T.H. White*.

The President was right, Cynthia thought, as she strapped herself in next to Meredith. Wandrei was plotting something. He was almost bouncing with eagerness, and there was a gleam in his eye that she did not like. But she couldn't think of anything she could do about it from here.

Hester ran through her pre-flight checks without letting Wandrei hurry her. Meredith—a big blonde Valkyrie whose specialty was what she called boojum mathematics—apologized for crowding Cynthia with her shoulders and said, "Could you see a cause of death, Dr. Feuerwerker?"

"No," Cynthia said. "He just looked dead to me. But I don't know if I'd recognize a fatal wound on a boojum if I saw one."

"It probably didn't leave a visible mark," Wandrei said from where he was riding shotgun. "So far as our research has discovered, there are only two ways to kill a boojum. One is to cut it literally to pieces—a tactic which backfires disastrously far more often than it succeeds—the other, to deliver a systemic shock powerful enough to disrupt all of the creature's cardio and/or synaptic nodes at once."

"That's one mother of a shock," Cynthia said, feeling unease claw its way a little deeper beneath her skin.

"Yes," said Wandrei and did not elaborate.

Hester piloted the *Caitlin R. Kiernan* with more verve than Cynthia's stomach found comfortable; she gripped her safety harness and swallowed hard, and Meredith said kindly, "Hester is one of the best young pilots we have."

"When I was a child, I wanted to jump ship on Leng Station and become a mechanic," Hester said cheerfully. "I tried a couple of times, but they always brought me back." She piloted the *Caitlin R. Kiernan* in a low swooping arc across the *Charles Dexter Ward*'s forward tentacles, and they could see that Wandrei's guess had been correct; the *Calico* had succeeded in prying open one of the *Charles Dexter Ward*'s airlocks, and the ship was moored partly within the boojum.

Cynthia hoped the Arkhamers had a better way in than that.

As it turned out, they didn't. And Cynthia was unsettled to watch Meredith and Hester strap sidearms on over their pressure suits. Were they really expecting that much trouble from the crew of the *Calico*? And didn't salvage law give her first picking? Or would the Arkhamers' earlier intercept and beacon trump that?

Cynthia had never encountered a dead boojum before, and she had braced herself with the knowledge that there would be any number of things she wasn't expecting. But no amount of bracing or foreknowledge could ever have been sufficient for the stench of the *Charles Dexter Ward*—a fetor so intense Cynthia would have sworn she could pick up the scent through her helmet, and before the airlock cycled. What that said about the spaceworthiness of the *Caitlin R. Kiernan*, Cynthia did not care to consider.

What the cycling outer airlock door revealed was more of a shock than it might have been if she hadn't already been dragging her tongue across her teeth in a futile effort to scrape the stench of death away. The membranes between the struts were not glossy with health, appearing dull and tacky instead, but the amazing stink that left her lightheaded and pained even within the oxygenated confines of her helmet had led her to expect—well, what course *did* decay take, on a boojum? Writhing infestations? Deliquescence? Suppurating lesions?

There was none of that.

Just the ridged stretch of intact-seeming corridor disappearing into the curvature of the dead ship, and the reek of putrescence. *Don't throw up in your helmet*, Cynthia told herself. That would be one sure way of making things even less pleasant.

The *Charles Dexter Ward* retained good atmospheric pressure—though Cynthia couldn't have attested to the air quality—and she didn't need to tongue on her suit intercom for Wandrei and the others to hear her when she said, "Isn't anything we salvage from this mess going to be unusable due to contamination?"

Meredith said, "Anything sealed should be fine. And we wouldn't want unsealed medical supplies anyway."

"I can smell it through my suit."

Wandrei looked at her with curious intensity. "Really?" he said, brow wrinkling behind his faceplate. "I don't smell anything."

"Maybe your suit has a bad filter," Meredith said. "We do our best to check them, but, well." She shrugged—a clumsy gesture, but Cynthia understood. When everything the Arkhamers owned, from their clothes to their ship, was second-hand, salvaged, scavenged, there was only so much they could do.

"That's probably it," she said, although she wasn't sure—and from the look he gave her before he turned away, Wandrei wasn't sure, either.

"Let's see if we can't find the crew of the *Calico*," he said.

I am walking in a dead body, Cynthia said periodically to herself, but aside from the eye-blurring stench that no one else could smell, the only sign of death was the darkness. Every boojum Cynthia had ever traveled on had used its bioluminescence to illuminate any space its human crew and passengers were using. But the *Charles Dexter Ward* stayed dark.

They proceeded cautiously. Cynthia remembered Hester saying the crew of the *Charles Dexter Ward* might still be alive somewhere in their dead ship, and there was the nagging question of the *Calico*'s crew—a question that got naggier and naggier the farther they went without finding a single trace of them.

"We know they weren't on their ship," Hester muttered. "Corinne hailed them until she was hoarse."

"And they haven't been salvaging," Meredith said. "None of the doors since the airlock has been forced open."

"My question," Cynthia said, "is how long they've been here. And if they aren't salvaging, what are they doing?"

That was two questions, and actually she had a third: what did Wandrei know that she and Hester and Meredith didn't? He didn't seem worried, and she had noticed after a while that, although he wasn't in a hurry, he did seem to know where he was going. She didn't want to be the one to mention it, though. Not a good idea for the politely tolerated outsider.

"What else *can* you do on a dead boojum?" Hester demanded.

"Maybe," Cynthia said after a moment. "Maybe they weren't here for salvage in the first place. Maybe they needed a hospital. Not all doctors are as laissez-faire as Captain Diemschuller."

"The *Calico's* too small for piracy," Meredith said, "but I agree with your general principle. If they aren't here for salvage—how do we find the operating theaters?"

Her question went unanswered as they came to a corridor junction and caught sight of another human being.

He was in shirtsleeves rather than a pressure suit, wearing the uniform of the Interplanetary Ambulance Corps, dark blue with red piping and *CDW* embroidered on his sleeve. Across his chest were blazoned a row of symbols including a caduceus, a red crescent, and the Chinese ideogram for "heart." Despite being distracted by the medical symbols, Cynthia knew there was something wrong with him several seconds before she was able to identify why she thought so. And the man—youngish and tall, his skin fishbelly pale in their floodlights—stood and stared at them, his face so perfectly blank that Cynthia finally realized that was the problem. No relief, no anger, no fear—not even curiosity.

"Hello!" she said, starting forward and forcing brightness into her voice as if she could compensate for his nullity. "I'm Dr. Feuerwerker with the *Jarmulowicz Astronomica*. Is your captain—" And then she was close enough to see him clearly, close enough to see that the shadow at his midsection was not a shadow but a hole, jagged-edged and gaping, where his stomach used to be, close enough to see the greenish tinge to his pale skin.

Her voice was thin and screechy in her own ears when she said, "He's dead."

"*What?*" said Hester

"He's *dead*. He's been dead for weeks."

"But he's standing up. A dead body couldn't . . ." Hester's voice dried up with a faint click as the dead man turned, giving them a good view of his disemboweled torso, and started walking down the hall away from them. His locomotion wasn't perfect, but it was damn good for someone who'd probably been dead for three months.

Hester started to blaspheme, and Meredith ungently hushed her. This was not the place to be attracting that kind of attention.

"It might be a parasite," Cynthia said, having run frantically through her knowledge of what could animate a corpse. "Something that got through a gap in spacetime when the *Charles Dexter Ward* died. We have to tell the *Jarmulowicz Astronomica*"—surprised, Cynthia realized her concern was not for herself, stuck here in the belly of a dead boojum, but for Jaime and the shy children and the cheshires Cynthia couldn't count—"can we call them from here? How far back—"

"Calm yourself, Dr. Feuerwerker," said Wandrei. "What you see is not the work of a parasite. It is the pursuit of knowledge."

That brought her up short. She looked at him, calm and sweating behind the faceplate of his pressure suit, and swallowed against a curl of bright nausea. "You knew about this?"

The twitch at the corner of his lips was more disturbing than the dead man striding away from them. Hastily, Cynthia turned her attention forward again. There were medical-school stories of the horrors Arkhamer doctors got up to. Cynthia had never credited them, considering them part of the general anti-Arkhamer bigotry that permeated so many institutions of higher learning—and so many spacedock taverns.

Now she wondered if she had been too willing—in her conscientious open-mindedness—to assume there was no truth behind the slander. *Ooh, ethics now, Dr. Feuerwerker? That's a new look on you.*

She stepped forward, following the dead man. Wandrei and the other women jogged to catch up, their pressure suits rustling with the sudden movement. As Wandrei fell back into stride beside Cynthia, she said, "So when did the *Charles Dexter Ward* sign on an Arkhamer doctor?" Wandrei remained silent, though she waited after each sentence before adding the next. "That's what got the ship killed, isn't it? That's the real motive behind coming here."

"Reanimation isn't a topic we commonly pursue," Wandrei said. "But if . . . if someone has made it work—think of the advance to human understanding. To medicine."

"To shipping," Meredith said.

"There are a number of applications," Hester was beginning, when Cynthia almost-shouted, "Are you fucking *nuts?* Every scare story I've ever heard about raising the dead says that either dying or coming back drives people mad. Are you really suggesting—"

"Are you a scientist, Dr. Feuerwerker?" Wandrei asked. "Then I suggest you wait for the data."

The walking cadaver did not move particularly fast. When she caught up to him, he turned to her, jaw moving. If he was trying to say something, the lack of lungs and diaphragm impeded the process. Upon closer inspection, he was a Major and a registered nurse. The name on his shirt pocket read *Ngao.* His eyes, dull and concave where the ship's environment had begun dehydrating them, fastened on Cynthia's face through the helmet.

His jaw worked again.

Was he conscious? she wondered, the chill running up her back so real that her head wrenched to one side. Did he know he was dead? Eviscerated? Did he ever try to touch his stomach and have his fingers brush his spine? She wanted to apologize, even though Major Ngao's fate was none of her doing. But she, too, had sought after forbidden knowledge—not reanimation, at least the irony wasn't that cruel. She'd muttered those same words about *science* and *the pursuit of knowledge* and told herself that Chen and Derleth would be pleased. That Galileo would be pleased.

Had it been a lie? She didn't know. Chen and Derleth and Galileo had been dead for centuries. She couldn't ask them—and even this lunatic on the *Charles Dexter Ward* couldn't bring them back. She remembered her burning certainty that the truth was there, attainable and valuable beyond any price—and she remembered Captain Nwapa's expression, too, that one flicker of horror before the captain got her game-face back. It took a lot to rattle a boojum captain, and Cynthia was not proud of the achievement.

Wandrei said crisply, "Take us to Dr. Fiorenzo," before Cynthia could find any words that weren't trite and false—*and probably pointless, really, Dr. Feuerwerker, the man's missing nine-tenths of his vital organs, do you think he has any attention to spare for you?* And if nothing else, Cynthia thought grimly, now at least she had a name to hang the nightmare on.

The corridors of the *Charles Dexter Ward* were dark and silent as Cynthia followed the Arkhamers following the dead man. From time spent on the *Richard Trevithick* and other boojums, she knew a little about their internal architecture, and she'd done her best to stay oriented, so she was fairly sure that they were heading away from the rending plates and tearing diamond teeth of the *Charles Dexter Ward*'s mouth (and she couldn't help wondering if his crew had called him Charlie, the same way the *Richard Trevithick*'s crew always referred to their boojum as Ricky—it was a stupid thought and wouldn't be banished). The anatomy of boojums adhered to no principle that Terran mammals abided by, including bilateral symmetry, but if you were headed away from the mouth, you were probably headed toward the cloaca. And most ships' systems were stuck as deep in the bulk of the boojum as the bioengineers could get them.

The *Charles Dexter Ward* being a hospital ship, there was not one specific area that Cynthia would have identified as the sickbay. Rather, she and the others had passed corridor after corridor of clinical chambers and wards, rooms that Cynthia was sure would have reeked of disinfectant and that eternal powdery medicinal smell were it not for the eye-watering putrescence overwhelming everything. They found the operating theaters, which looked as if they'd been the scenes of intense guerilla fighting, and Cynthia's pace slowed automatically, trying to reconstruct what had happen, where the defenders had been, how the line of attack had run, whether that was all human blood in horrible sticky pools, or if some of it was other colors.

"Dr. Feuerwerker," Meredith said, pointing, and she saw that farther down the corridor, in the direction that Major Ngao was plodding, uninterested in what might have been the site of his own death, there was, for the first time in hours, a gleam of light that they hadn't brought with them from the *Caitlin R. Kiernan*.

And as they followed the dead man—he dripped, occasionally, an irregular trail of brownish fluid on the corridor floor—around the bend in the dead boojum's corridor, Cynthia saw an open pressure hatch, a slice of light spilled across the floor, and a glimpse of one of the medical labs.

Within it, she could just make out some white-coated movement.

She followed Wandrei, she thought, because she had so little idea what else to do. *This is how war crimes happen. People get overwhelmed and follow orders. If you were as brilliant as one of these Arkhamer doctors, you'd know what to do besides whatever Wandrei tells you.*

And then she bit her lip inside the helmet and thought, *If I were as brilliant as one of these Arkhamer doctors, the* Richard Trevithick *might be as dead as Charlie here.*

That thought chilled whatever part of her the quietly guiding dead man had missed.

Something brushed Cynthia's right glove, then grabbed it. Her throat closed with fright, and she turned as she tried to pull away, looking down to see what horrible thing had caught her. But it was a suit gauntlet, tight against her own, and when she looked up again, she met Hester's gaze dimly, through two helmet bubbles glazed with the reflected light of the lab up ahead. She'd stopped, lost in thought. The idea of being left out here in the dark with the stars knew what made her heart jump like a ship's rat in the claws of a cheshire.

She squeezed back and caught a flash of Hester's teeth, bright against the darkness of her face. They moved forward together, though any comfort from the other woman's presence was abrogated by a series of scraping sounds that Cynthia's medical ear easily identified as metal on bone.

Five more steps brought them into the lab. Cynthia found herself fascinated by the way the light—clip-on work lighting trailing to batteries, and not biolume—caught on the scratches on Meredith's and Wandrei's pressure suits as they stepped out of the shadows of the corridor. She was avoiding looking past them, at whatever the lab contained, and their broad shoulders mercifully blocked most of the view.

Then Wandrei stepped to one side, to make room for her and Hester, and raised both hands to open the catches on his helmet. As he lifted it off, Cynthia had to fight the urge to reach out and slam it back into place—as if a standard, somewhat worn pressure suit was any protection in a situation like this.

Cynthia stayed on suit air anyway. It made her feel a little better, and she noticed Meredith and Hester were in no hurry to uncouple their helmets either.

"Dr. Fiorenzo," Wandrei said pleasantly. "Allow my to introduce my colleagues. I take it you've had some success?"

"Limited," Fiorenzo answered in a light contralto, turning from a dissection table upon which the twitching remains of something that couldn't possibly still be alive were pinned. She did not seem at all surprised to see them—and that Wandrei apparently did not need to introduce himself. "I'm pleased you're here. After the accident . . . Charlie dead and all the crew . . ."

Her face revealed grief, tension, relief. What would it be like, trapped alone parsecs off any shipping lane, inside an enormous dead creature slowly rotting around you?

The introductions were a scene of almost surreal cordiality. Fiorenzo was a narrow-shouldered, olive-skinned woman. Her face was smooth everywhere but at the corners of her eyes as she smiled, and she wasn't old enough to be going salt-and-pepper yet, though what few strands of grey there were stood out like silver embroidery on black velvet against the darkness of her hair. She wore it in a pixyish crop, like a lot of practical-minded spacers.

I thought you'd be older, Cynthia didn't say, in the hellish mundanity of pleasantries carried out while the relic of Major Ngao stood against the far bulkhead, arms folded across his chest, watching cloudy-eyed but seemingly intent, as if he were following the conversation. She was spared from having to shake hands because Fiorenzo was gloved, and she was spared from having to come up with something else to say when Fiorenzo paused at her name, frowned, and said, "Feuerwerker. They threw you off the *Richard Trevithick* just before—Damned shame. That was good research. It's about time somebody found out what's in one of those biosuspension canisters!"

Cynthia managed not to step back, rocked by a peculiar combination of the warmth of a fellow scientist's regard and the horror of who, exactly, was praising her. Her jaw was still working on an answer when Fiorenzo continued, "Well, you're welcome here now. We'll find some things out, you and I! Maybe even a thing or two about the Mi-Go!"

"Thank you," Cynthia said weakly. She let Fiorenzo, Meredith, and Wandrei step away. Hester crowded close and leaned their helmets together in order to whisper: "What did you *do*?"

"I thought everybody knew already."

"Tell me anyway."

Cynthia couldn't quite figure out where to start. She was still fumbling when Hester broke and asked outright, "You were trying to reverse engineer a Mi-Go canister?"

"A vacant one," Cynthia said in weak protest. "Not one with somebody inside."

"Sweet breathsucker," Hester said. "Haven't you heard about what happened to the *Lavinia Whateley?*"

A boojum privateer. Vanished without a trace after pirating a cargo of the Mi-Go's canisters of disembodied brains. Rumor was that all hands and even the ship herself had wound up disassembled and carted off to the outer reaches of the solar system, living brains forever locked in metal tins, going immortally mad.

Cynthia nodded tersely, lips thin. "I didn't say it was a good idea."

Hester looked like she wanted to say something else, but Wandrei called her over. Cynthia stayed where she was, not wanting to intrude on an Arkhamer conversation.

Although . . . *was* Fiorenzo an Arkhamer? Cynthia'd learned enough to recognize the names of the Arkhamer ships—all of them named for one of the nine which originally set out from Earth—and *Fiorenzo* wasn't one of them. But Wandrei called her Doctor Fiorenzo, and she'd introduced herself the same way—Julia Filomela Fiorenzo. No "Jarmulowicz" or "Burlingame" or "Dubois." So either she wasn't a Arkhamer—whom the Arkhamers *treated* like an Arkhamer, and Cynthia wasn't buying that for a second—or she *was* an Arkhamer and her ship had disowned her.

Well, gosh, Dr. Feuerwerker. I wonder why.

Her ship had disowned her, but Wandrei hadn't—and Cynthia remembered the comments about Wandrei getting in trouble, remembered the President's suspicions, and knew that, yes, Wandrei had brought them out here, not on a mission of mercy, but to check in on Fiorenzo's experiments. Experiments which the rest of the *Jarmulowicz Astronomica* did not know about, or at least did not know were still on-going.

Sweet merciful Buddha of the Breathsucker, Cynthia thought and looked down to discover that she'd wandered over much closer than she'd meant to get to the dissection table where Fiorenzo had been working when they came in.

The creature on it had once been human. It should not still be alive.

Or possibly it wasn't. She twisted her head, forcing her gaze away from the wet holes where the thing's face had been, and found Major Ngao watching her. Watching? Staring at? Staring through? She had to squeeze her eyes shut and bite down hard on her lip to keep the bubble of hysteria from escaping, and when she opened her eyes again, she was staring down at the dead, twitching creature's chest.

Where, under the blood, the words *Free Ship Calico Jack* were still, just barely, legible on the scraps of its uniform.

Cynthia stepped back, a big over-dramatic step that caught everyone's attention, Fiorenzo's voice dying in the middle of a sentence: "the bodies just aren't fresh enough. I need—"

"Dr. Feuerwerker?" Wandrei said, with that nasty snide tone that every teacher in the universe used when they'd caught you not paying attention in class.

Cynthia opened her mouth, without the least idea what was going to come out— and more than half convinced it was going to be, *There's nothing to ensure freshness like harvesting them yourself, is there, Dr. Fiorenzo?* But some remnant of self-preservation interfered, and what she said was:

"How did the *Charles Dexter Ward* die?"

"What?" Fiorenzo said; Wandrei was frowning. Cynthia repeated the question.

"Oh. There was . . . the mirror broke," Fiorenzo said with a vague gesture. "And the doppelkinder came. They killed the crew and the ship."

"How did you escape?" Meredith asked, wide-eyed.

"Luck, I think," Fiorenzo said with a shrug that almost looked like a spasm, and a bitter laugh. "I was the pathologist, and I was in the morgue when it happened. I think they just couldn't smell me. And you know they don't last very long."

Yes, like homicidal mayflies. They rarely lasted more than a few hours after they'd killed their primary host. Cynthia nodded and did not—did *not*—look at the dissection table. "And you've been here ever since?"

Fiorenzo offered a sad, slanted little smile. "There's been nowhere I can go."

Fiorenzo wanted, she said, to transfer her most promising experiments to the *Jarmulowicz Astronomica*. As she and Wandrei and Meredith started a discussion of how that might be accomplished, Hester caught Cynthia by the arm and dragged her grimly out into the hallway, still within the light of Fiorenzo's rigged operating theater, but well out of earshot.

There Hester stopped and leaned into Cynthia's helmet again. "She's lying."

"About what?" Cynthia said, her mind still stuck blankly on that poor twitching thing strapped down on Fiorenzo's operating table.

"Doppelkinder can't kill a boojum. They won't even go after one. Boojums don't recognize their own reflections."

"Wait. What?"

"Doppelkinder hunt in mirrors," Hester began with exaggerated patience.

"Not that," Cynthia said. She'd been terrified of doppelkinder since her first Civil Defense class when she was five. "Boojums don't see themselves in mirrors?"

"Two-dimensional representations don't mean anything to them. Cheshires are the same way." Hester managed a smile, although it wasn't a very good one. "That's why there's that folk saying about how you can't fool a cheshire. The most cunning optical illusion ever created won't even make them twitch."

"And doppelkinder are dependent on optical illusions," Cynthia said, finally catching up to what Hester was trying to say.

"They don't eat people's eyes for the nutritional value."

"Right. But if the doppelkinder didn't kill the *Charles Dexter Ward*, what did?"

Hester folded her arms and gave Cynthia a flat obdurate stare. "I think *she* did."

"Fiorenzo?" Cynthia spluttered a little, then caught herself and regrouped. "Not that I don't believe she would do it in a heartbeat, but *why?* Why the boojum, I mean? And for the love of little fishy gods, *how?*"

Hester's gaze dropped. "You were supposed to talk me out of it. It's a crazy idea, and I know it's because I'm jealous."

"Jealous?"

"If Professor Wandrei had even *once* shown this kind of interest in my work . . ." She trailed off, her face twisting.

"I understand," Cynthia said and dared to offer Hester's shoulder a clumsy pat. "But, Hester, I don't think you're wrong. I'm pretty sure she killed the crew of that little scavenger ship." And she told Hester about the uniform.

"We have to tell Professor Wandrei," Hester said, taking a step back toward Fiorenzo's little island of lunatic light.

This time it was Cynthia who caught hold of Hester's arm. "Do you really think he doesn't know?"

She hated herself a little for the sick expression on Hester's face, the knowledge that she, Cynthia Feuerwerker, had just opened her mouth and killed something irreplaceable.

Hester said, barely whispering even though they were still helmet-to-helmet, "What should we do?"

Cynthia opened her mouth to say, *What CAN we do?* and all but physically choked on her own words. Because that was how war crimes happened. That was how you ended up a future-ghost on a Arkhamer ship with the lines of a scowl bitten so deep in your face you never really stopped frowning.

And Hester was watching her hopefully. Hester, knowing what she'd done, was still willing to believe that Cynthia would do the right thing.

Cynthia took a deep breath. "If she killed the *Charles Dexter Ward*, how did she do it? I mean, you and Wandrei said there were only two ways, and she clearly didn't cut him to pieces, so . . . ?"

"She must have rigged some kind of galvanic motor," Hester said. "If she hooked it up to the UPS—and a hospital ship would have to have one, even a liveship—that would take care of the power requirements . . ."

Cynthia got a good look at the wideness of Hester's eyes before she realized that here in the dark corridor, even with their helmets leaned up together, she shouldn't have been able to make out the details of her friend's expression. Hester stepped back slowly, her features revealed more plainly as Cynthia's shadow no longer fell across her face. Cynthia forced her gaze to the right.

All along the passageway, bioluminescent runners were crawling with unexpected brilliance. Fiorenzo had reanimated the *Charles Dexter Ward*.

"Aw, shitballs," Hester said.

PART THREE

Looking away from the light that showed the *Charles Dexter Ward* was no longer entirely dead was as hard as opening a rusted zipper. But Cynthia did it, and didn't let herself look back. She pulled Hester a little further down the corridor and said, "Now we *really* need to know how she killed him. And whether it'll work a second time."

"It should," Hester said. "Whatever force is animating him, a big enough shock should disrupt it. We just have to find her machine."

"I like your use of the word 'just.' Something like that—would it be portable or not?" The *Charles Dexter Ward*'s bioluminescence was continuing to ripple and pulse in an arrhythmic not-quite-pattern that was like nothing Cynthia had ever see a boojum do before. It was already giving her the mother of all headaches, and if it was a reflection of the *Charles Dexter Ward*'s state of mind, then she couldn't believe it was a good auspice.

"One that could kill a boojum? Definitely not."

"So wherever she built it, that's where it is. But how do we *find* it? It's a boojum—how do we even *look*?"

"Um," said Hester and tugged Cynthia another few steps away from Fiorenzo's lab. "The closed stacks have a schematic. Professor Wandrei said not to share it with—"

"Outsiders," Cynthia finished wearily, and Hester ducked her head like a reproved child. And of *course* the Arkhamers had a second, inner archive to which Cynthia had not been given access. It was their secrets that kept them alive and independent. "It's okay. You don't have to—"

"No, at this point it's only stupid and self-destructive," Hester said. "Here."

Cynthia's heads-up was filled with a spidery green constellation: the human-scale paths through the *Charles Dexter Ward*. She had only a moment to appreciate them before her pressure suit ballooned taut and a sudden sharp pressure in her ear canals distracted her. Reflexively, she opened her mouth and closed her eyes—every spacer knew and feared that sensation—but it was just a pressure fluctuation, not a hull breach. She closed her mouth again and blew until her ears popped.

When she opened her eyes, Hester was looking at her, head swaying in relief. "Good idea, staying suited."

Cynthia took a tentative breath and gagged. The reek of putrescence that had poisoned every breath since she stepped through Charlie's airlock was thick enough to taste now, and she wasted thirty seconds re-checking her perfectly functioning suit seals. "By Dodgson's blessed camera," she swore, then belatedly realized she didn't know how Hester felt about taking sacred names in vain. "I think that took a year off my life."

"So long as it's just one," Hester said. She ran a gloved hand up one of Charlie's dead interior bulkheads, tracing the rippling patterns of necroluminescence. Her fingers found an indentation, and Cynthia could see her face screw up with disgust through the bubble of the helmet. When she pushed in, her glove vanished to the knuckles. Charlie's flesh made a squelching sound.

Hester hooked and ripped; mucilaginous strings of meat stretched and rent. She tossed a panel to the deck; it rang like ceramic. Behind, a cavity lined with readouts and conduits lay revealed. Hester, wincing, reached for a small rack of what Cynthia recognized as wireless connectors. She tugged one loose, made a face, and—before Cynthia could decide that she really ought to stop her—slotted it into a jack on her suit.

"Hester—"

"Shush," Hester said. "I spend enough time researching the damned things. A dead one shouldn't bo—oh."

"What?"

"*Run.*"

They ran. Suits rustling and rasping, booted feet thudding dully on the decking. Off to the left, something scurried. Cynthia's head snapped around, but Hester put a hand on her arm and pulled.

"Tove," she said.

Normally, you would never see a tove on a boojum, but Charlie's death had strained the fabric of space-time, making inter-dimensional slippage easier, and a dead boojum could not eat its own parasites as was their usual habit. Cynthia thought about the shattered ward-mirror, intended to defend against nastier creatures than toves: doppelkinder, raths, and other predators. It worked because it reflected nothing but the Big Empty—even at dock, those warped enormous mirrors wouldn't reflect on a human scale and thus could not be exploited by doppelkinder, just as they blinded raths. Mirrors were not standard equipment on all ships, but for a hospital ship like Charlie they were an extra line of safety. *Charlie broke it dying,* she guessed. Fiorenzo had invented the doppelkinder—who didn't hunt boojums and who would never have left Major Ngao's eyes intact—as an alibi.

Then she heard something else, not the scuttling of a tove, but a wetter sound, a bigger sound. She didn't have the strength of will not to glance back, and there, barely illuminated by Charlie's twitchy necroluminescence, she saw human silhouettes, a reaching arm with the remains of an Ambulance Corps uniform, the glare of an eyeball in a half-skinned face.

Hester swung through a hatchway, pulling Cynthia with her, and slammed the emergency plate located behind glass on the other side. A blast door dropped with decapitating force. If the *Charles Dexter Ward* were to be hulled, it was in the interests of crew and ship that pressure doors should guillotine any unfortunate they caught. It was a case of one life for many, and spacers learned not to stand in doorways.

"That won't keep them for long," Hester panted. "But we can stop for a second."

Cynthia tried to slow her breathing, to get more use out of her canned air. "Where in the nine names of Hell did they come from?"

"Charlie opened a door," Hester said.

Cynthia squinted, but that didn't make what Hester was saying make any more sense. "I'm missing some context—"

Hester tapped Charlie's connector, plugged into her opposite forearm jack. "I've got access to his logs, and I think . . . I think he didn't like Fiorenzo killing his crew, because it's pretty clear from the logs that she *was*. I think that's why she electrocuted him. But the reanimated crew was killing the living crew, and she doesn't seem to be able to control what she makes. So she lured them into a vacuum bay and sealed the door—"

But vacuum can't kill things that are already dead.

"Charlie let his crew out," Cynthia said.

Hester nodded, the boojum's crawling green and violet necroluminescence rippling across her corneas and the bubble of her suit. "He can open any door I override. And they're probably not very . . . safe. Anymore."

"No," Cynthia agreed. "Not safe." Her throat hurt. She made herself stop swallowing and worked enough spit into her mouth to say, "We'd better keep moving. We have to find Fiorenzo's device. Before her mistakes find us."

PART FOUR

"She said she was in the morgue," Cynthia muttered.

"What?" Hester said, distracted by shooting the rotting hand off their lead pursuer.

"Dr. Fiorenzo. She said when it happened, she was in the morgue. And she was the pathologist. If she was going to hide something *anywhere*, she'd hide it there."

"I imagine you didn't get too many people dropping in for a friendly chat," Hester said. "So where's the morgue from here?"

By the time Cynthia had enough breath to reply—running in a pressure suit was no picnic, and although Fiorenzo's reanimated corpses weren't very fast, they were undistractable and relentless—Hester had found the answer herself. "One up and two over. Okay then."

Cynthia had spent time on a handful of boojums—as passenger, as crew, that last nasty week on the *Richard Trevithick* as a prisoner—and there was no standard system of orientation. Some boojums had no internal signposts at all; unless the captain gave you the schematic, you were dependent on a crew member to guide you around. The *Charles Dexter Ward* was probably the best and most thoughtfully labeled boojum Cynthia had ever seen, and even so it was essentially markers to help you plot your position on a gigantic imaginary three-dimensional graph, onto which Charlie only problematically mapped.

But it was better than nothing.

And it was better than being torn apart by these mindless, malevolent things that Fiorenzo had created out of what had once been men and women. And surely, Cynthia thought, remembering the row of symbols on Major Ngao's uniform, the men and women who deserved it *least*. She had been appalled by Fiorenzo and afraid of her and a little (*admit it, Cynthia*) envious, but now she began to be truly angry. Not at the pursuit of forbidden knowledge, but at the wanton destructiveness.

"Up is good," Hester panted beside her. "The ladder'll take them longer."

"I just wish it would stop them," Cynthia said. "Or that *anything* would." Thus far, though they'd kept ahead of the reanimated, they hadn't managed to lose them—certainly not to stop them.

"Here," Hester said. The ladder was stainless steel dulled with Charlie's slow decomposition; Hester had to override the hatch at the top with Cynthia crammed against her lower legs to avoid the frustrated grabs of the reanimated beneath them.

Hester helped Cynthia through the hatch and they slammed it closed again. Then they took off running—two shambling scientists pursued by more shambling corpses than they could stop to count.

The morgue, when they found it, was long and low and cold—and all too obviously the right place. It crawled with the same decayed-looking light as the rest of the *Charles Dexter Ward*, but here that light limned empty body bags and open lockers. Cynthia was careful to close and dog the door behind them before they proceeded down the length. Her skin crawled at the idea of locking herself in here, blocking her own route of escape . . . but what waited outside was worse. They'd managed to leave the reanimated behind, but Cynthia had no confidence that that would last.

They came around a corner to find Doctor Fiorenzo crouched behind an autopsy table, huddling with Professor Wandrei over a gaping hole in the decking. The ragged, ichorous edges framed something that looked like an exposed boojum neural cluster. The former Major Ngao was silently handing Fiorenzo tools. Fiorenzo had a veterinary syringe in her hand, a medieval-looking device with a needle easily four inches long. It was filled with some colorless fluid. Cynthia could make out two more empties on the floor.

Meredith . . . Cynthia didn't have to get close to see the lines of black stitchery holding the crushed edges of her neck together. Her head lolled to one side, tongue drooping from her slack mouth, and her eyes were half-lidded and beginning to glaze.

Cynthia wondered how Fiorenzo had arranged to have one of the pressure doors catch Meredith, and how long it would be before she got around to Wandrei. And how he could be so blind as not to see that he would be Fiorenzo's next experiment.

Hester raised and aimed her pistol. Wandrei must have glanced up just then, because he made a warning sound.

Fiorenzo rose to her feet and turned. Light shivered along the needle of the syringe as she lowered it to a non-threatening position beside her thigh.

The thing that had been Meredith took a shuffling step closer and Cynthia hid her cringe. For a moment, Cynthia waited, searching for words. Wondering why Hester hadn't pulled the trigger.

"Doctor Feuerwerker—" Wandrei began.

Somehow, Cynthia silenced him with a glance. It must have been scathing; even her eyes felt scorched by it.

Fiorenzo's eyes met Cynthia's. "You're a doctor. A researcher. You should understand!"

"I understand that you're a mass-murderer, and you're putting everyone in this sector of space at risk. Your monsters—your *victims*—aren't far behind us. What are you going to do when Charlie lets them in here?"

"I'm getting close!"

"No, you're *not*." Cynthia waved a little wildly at Major Ngao. "Maybe you've made him not-dead, but you haven't made him alive. You can't. You can't make Meredith alive and you can't make that poor bastard off the *Calico* alive. You can animate the meat, but that's not the same thing and you know it. This boojum isn't *alive*. What it is, is *wrong*."

The *Charles Dexter Ward* shuddered beneath their feet, as if in agreement. Cynthia lurched into Hester, Wandrei and the two dead people went down, and even Fiorenzo had to grab at a safety-bar to keep her feet. Cynthia was reaching for Hester's arm, to lift her sidearm back on target—

Fiorenzo slammed the syringe with which she had been about to inject the *Charles Dexter Ward* through lab coat and trousers and into her own thigh.

Cynthia stared, disbelieving. Fiorenzo straightened, smiling, and was starting to say something when she seized, crashing to the deck as stiff and solid as a bar of iron. Cynthia said over her to Wandrei, "We have to stop this."

"Science, Dr. Feuerwerker," Wandrei began, and Cynthia shouted, "Science schmience!" which startled him into shutting up.

Cynthia was a little startled herself, but she plunged on while she had the initiative, "Fiorenzo's leavings out there aren't science. They're walking nuclear waste. And what she did to Meredith is murder."

"That was an accident," Wandrei said.

Hester made a bitter noise that wasn't a laugh. "Do you really believe that?"

Wandrei didn't answer her. He said, "Dr. Fiorenzo has achieved a remarkable—" and that was when he made the mistake of letting Meredith get too close.

Cynthia and Hester had not stopped to ponder the intentions of their reanimated pursuers, not with Charlie's stuttering necroluminescence all around them and the carnage everywhere they looked. But if they *had* wondered, any last niggling doubt would have been unequivocally dispelled.

Meredith tore Wandrei to pieces, starting with his mandible.

Hester screamed; so did Wandrei, for a while. *By the Queen of Hearts, is that his endocardium?* Cynthia dragged Hester back, both of them sprayed with Wandrei's blood like stationer graffiti, and said, her voice low and frantic, "We have to find the machine. Now. While the door's still closed and Meredith is . . . distracted."

Hester's gulp might have been a sob or a hysterical laugh, but she nodded.

They looked around, trying to ignore the gory welter in the center of the room. There wasn't much there beyond dissection tables and refrigeration units. A microscope locked down on a stand, a centrifuge . . .

"Why would you have so many refrigeration units when the universe's biggest refrigerator is right outside your door?" Cynthia muttered. "One, sure, for samples and emergencies, but . . ."

They skirted the edges of the room, both keeping an uneasy eye on their roommate, but Meredith seemed to have forgotten about them, which was all to the good. The first refrigerator unit was just that, a nice Tohiro-Nikkonen that now needed very badly to be cleaned out. The second was a jury-rigged *something*—from the look on Hester's face, she had no more idea than Cynthia did. But next to that, back in the corner where it was awkward to reach, lower and bulkier—"That's it," Hester said. "Has to be."

"Can you figure out how to turn it on?" Cynthia said. She stole a glance at Fiorenzo—still seizing—and Meredith. Still . . . busy.

"Watch me," Hester said confidently and wiggled into the cramped space. "Or rather, don't watch me. Watch for company." And she passed Cynthia her pistol.

"You got it," Cynthia said, although it wasn't clear that the pistol would be any more use than a wedding bouquet if the reanimated found them and Charlie decided to open the doors.

Pursuant to that thought, she asked, "Can you communicate with him at all? Charlie, I mean?"

"I've tried," Hester said. "I don't know if it's just that I *can't* or that he doesn't recognize me as crew."

"Rats," Cynthia said. "Because it occurred to me that the best way to get rid of the reanimated would be for Charlie to eat them."

"Oh," said Hester. "Well. That would certainly be tidy. Although I'm not entirely sure that he *could*. It doesn't look to me as if Fiorenzo's reanimated can actually digest anything."

"Well, there goes that idea," Cynthia said. "But he could still chew on them, couldn't he?"

"If they went to his mouth. But he probably can't just . . . reabsorb them."

The *Charles Dexter Ward* shuddered again; Hester was knocked against the wall, and Cynthia ended up in a drunken sprawl against the galvanic motor.

"I think," Hester said dryly, "that something isn't quite right."

"Do you think that's what the second dose of serum was for?"

"Probably."

"Do you think without it, he'll die again?" Horrible, to sound so hopeful. Horrible, to be in a situation where that was the optimum outcome.

"Ngao hasn't," Hester said.

Cynthia was trying to think of an answer that was neither obscene nor dangerously blasphemous when motion caught her eye. She jerked around, but it wasn't Meredith or Ngao; it was a tove.

"There weren't any toves in here, were there?" They'd encountered a tove colony several corridors away from the morgue, thick on the ceiling and walls, and starting to creep across the floor. The smell cut through even the stench in Cynthia's nostrils, and she and Hester both had to fight not to gag at the crunch and lingering squish of toves under their boots.

"No," Hester said. "Why?"

Cynthia aimed carefully and shot the tove. "Just hurry up, okay?" All by themselves, toves weren't much more than a nuisance—at least, not to a healthy adult. But where toves went, raths were sure to follow, and raths were dangerous. And where raths went, would surely come bandersnatches, and while a bandersnatch could probably deal with Fiorenzo's mistakes, it would happily annihilate the rest of them as well.

"Fiorenzo's got it backwards, you know," Hester said in a would-be-casual voice, instead of calling Cynthia on the evasion.

"Oh?" Cynthia said warily. Hester was under tremendous pressure and had just watched one member of her family murder another at extremely close range. Cynthia wouldn't blame her in the slightest for falling apart, but they desperately needed it not to be right now.

"The fresher the body, the worse the results," Hester said. "Meredith being Exhibit A. She must have reanimated Meredith within *minutes*."

Only as long as it takes to sew a head back on, Cynthia thought. Aloud, she said, "I see what you mean."

"So she's wrong," Hester said fiercely. "I had to say it to someone. The odds of having the opportunity to refute her theories in print . . ."

Cynthia wanted to close her eyes, but she had to keep watch on Meredith, Fiorenzo, Ngao . . . and everything else. She said, "I understand."

"Okay," Hester said, scrambling back to Cynthia's side. "The machine is drawing power, and I've started it cycling. Now we just have to attach the leads to Charlie's nervous system." She brandished a thick double-handful of cables, and Cynthia followed her gaze to the hole Fiorenzo had dug in the deck of the morgue, with Wandrei's remains on one side and Fiorenzo's rigor-stiff figure on the other. Ngao was standing patiently where Fiorenzo had left him. Meredith had moved to the door, which she was pawing at with obvious confusion. But she wasn't Charlie's crew; he wasn't opening it for her.

"Can't we just, I don't know, rip him open ourselves?"

"It would take too long," Hester said with a crispness that betrayed her own reluctance. "Besides, I don't have the specialized diagnostic equipment we'd need to find a node, and Fiorenzo must have cannibalized hers—or maybe *left* it somewhere."

Cynthia swallowed her arguments. "Okay. Will the cables reach?"

"I suspect that node is where she attached them the first time," Hester said. "But let's find out."

Hester paid the cables out carefully; Cynthia kept pace, trying to keep her attention on far too many threats at once. A cheshire's sixteen eyes had never sounded so good. Cynthia and Hester's movement attracted Meredith's attention, and she started in their direction, not in the all-out berserker charge of the other reanimated, but in that slow-seeming sidle that had lethally fooled Wandrei.

Cynthia shot her, aiming as best she could for the knee. They had learned, by the good old scientific method of try-it-and-find-out, that the pistol could not damage a reanimated corpse enough to unanimate it. But it could cripple one. The trick was to make sure any bits you knocked off were too small to do any damage when they kept coming after you.

At this range, even Cynthia couldn't miss. Meredith didn't make a sound—she couldn't, with severed vocal cords—but the silent rictus of shock (*pain?* Cynthia wondered bleakly, *betrayal?*) was almost worse. She went down, and continued dragging herself forward—but her hands couldn't get much purchase on the deck plates protecting the *Charles Dexter Ward*'s tissue, especially slick as they were with Wandrei's fluids.

Hester had reached the dark and wetly shining hole. She knelt clumsily, then looked up, a brave if not very convincing effort at a smile on her face. "You'd better," she started; then voice and smile failed together, her face going slack with an emotion Cynthia couldn't identify—until a voice behind her, a grating, hollow snarl said, "*Stop.*"

And then she knew, because she could feel her own face mirroring Hester's: it was horror.

Cynthia turned. Dr. Fiorenzo was struggling to her feet. She stretched. She examined her hands. She took a carotid pulse.

She smiled. "All it took," she said calmly, "was a fresh enough specimen. Really, Dr. Feuerwerker, you of all people should appreciate my success."

Cynthia stepped backward. Once, twice. She worried about stepping into the pit, about tripping over Hester. About edging too close to Meredith and her undead strength. But she couldn't take her eyes away from Fiorenzo. And she couldn't—viscerally couldn't—let Fiorenzo close the gap between them. No matter how sweet and reasonable she sounded.

Something brushed Cynthia's ankle. She almost squeezed off a shot—the last in the pistol—before realizing that it was Hester, mutely offering up the power cables. They were too thick to manage one-handed. Cynthia would have to let go of the gun.

"Not live," she said.

Hester said, "I'll worry about that."

Carefully, watching Fiorenzo the whole time, Cynthia handed Hester the gun and took the cables. They were heavy. How had Hester handled them so easily?

"Dr. Fiorenzo," she said. "Stop."

Fiorenzo took another step, but she was eyeing the cables cautiously. Cynthia was at the limit of their length, and the pit was behind her. She could retreat no farther.

"I assure you, I'm no threat," Fiorenzo said. "This process will *save* lives."

Cynthia heard Hester scrambling. Did she intend to get past Fiorenzo somehow? No, she was edging to the side, still keeping Cynthia as her buffer. *Thanks a lot.* But if their positions were reversed, would Cynthia be doing any differently?

"It will save your life," Fiorenzo said.

And lunged.

Her strength was incredible. Cynthia swung the cables against her head, again and again, until Fiorenzo pinioned her arms. They rolled to the floor. Fiorenzo landed on top. Fiorenzo's teeth worried at the seam of Cynthia's pressure suit; Cynthia got a foot up and kicked, but couldn't knock her off.

"*Incoming!*" Hester yelled. Fiorenzo's head jerked up, and Cynthia thought, *What damned good is—*

The report of the pistol would have been deafening in the confined space of the morgue, if not for Cynthia's suit filters. Fiorenzo thrashed for a second, the left side of her skull blossoming into a cratered exit wound. Cynthia threw herself free and rolled across the decking.

"Cables!" Hester yelled.

Cynthia grabbed them from the middle and yanked. The ends came slithering toward her, sparking against the deck. Heavy yellow sparks. Cynthia grabbed them by the insulation and lifted.

Fiorenzo rolled to a crouch, then stood. She laughed, one eye bobbing gently on the end of its optic nerve against her cheek. She sprang forward like a racer—

Cynthia jabbed the cables into her chest.

Fiorenzo arched back as the current went through her, hands splayed and clawing. She didn't scream; there was no other sound to cover the crack of electricity, the hiss of cooking flesh.

She slumped. Cynthia jumped backward, but Fiorenzo's outflung hand still fell across her boot. She turned wildly; Meredith was still crawling toward her. Hester crouched by the controls, sliding the master switch back to *off*.

"Decomp tie-ins," Hester said. "You use the bolt nearest the panel." She stepped over Fiorenzo's corpse, her boot disturbing the gentle wisps of steam still rising, and dropped into the hole again. "And hand me the fucking cables again, would you please?"

Following orders was the easiest, most pleasant thing that Cynthia had ever done. She clipped and locked her safety line to the bolt. She slid the power control back to *full*.

"Do it!" she shouted to Hester.

And Hester must have done it, because the *Charles Dexter Ward* convulsed. Cynthia was jerked hard against her tether and then slammed back into the machine— and that was with only enough slack to attach the line. Everything unanchored went flying; she heard the crunch as Meredith hit a bulkhead, and then she was jerked forward again and blacked out.

She couldn't have been out for more than a minute, she reckoned later; she could hear things still cascading in thumps and crunches. But the ship himself was not moving, and more importantly, more tellingly, his necroluminescence was gone. The only light was Hester's suit lamp, and Cynthia fumbled her own on.

"Thank the ancient powers and the Buddha," Hester said in a thin fervent voice. "I thought you were dead."

Cynthia swallowed bright copper where she'd bitten the inside of her mouth. "Ow."

"Yes." Hester was undoing her safety line and dragging herself upright. Cynthia undid her own line with shaky fingers, and then her head cleared and she made it to her feet in one adrenaline-sour jerk. She twisted around, scanning, but Meredith was nowhere within the limited range of her light. She saw one of Ngao's legs and part of his spine; he had been torn apart by the force of Charlie's convulsions. As she watched, the foot twitched.

"Do you think we can make it back to the *Caitlin R. Kiernan* alive?" Hester said.

Cynthia squared her shoulders, wincing a little, and answered: "I think we can try."

EPILOGUE

In his (second) death throes, the *Charles Dexter Ward* had taken a chunk out of the *Jarmulowicz Astronomica*, like a kid biting a chunk out of an apple. The casualties were five dead and thirteen injured, and they would have been worse except that everyone possible had been press-ganged into helping with the broken ward-mirror. The medical bay was gone, and now Cynthia knew why she'd only ever seen the one future-ghost, because there had only been one future path in which there was still a medical bay—the future path, she knew with cold uncomfortable certainty, in which she had not stood up to Wandrei and Fiorenzo, in which the *Charles Dexter Ward* had not died twice.

Cynthia patched up the crew as best she could with bandages made of cloth and splints repurposed from any number of functions, and the crew patched up the *Jarmulowicz Astronomica*. The mass funeral was devastating; Cynthia stood with Hester and let Hester's grip leave bruises on her hand.

She bunked in with Hester, which was tight but doable. On her first sleep shift, after she finished brushing what she hoped was the last of the *Charles Dexter Ward*'s death stench out of her mouth, she came into Hester's room and found two smug cheshires in the hammock slung crossways above Hester's bunk. She surprised herself by bursting into tears.

"I'm okay, I'm okay," she said, fending off Hester's concern. "I just didn't expect them to find me."

"They know you," Hester said, as if it were all that simple.

The *Jarmulowicz Astronomica* sent out a distress signal, and before leaving the *Charles Dexter Ward*, they set warning beacons around the boojum's carcass. The Universal Code didn't have an entry for *REANIMATED*; Hester told Cynthia that the Faculty Senate passed a motion to submit a proposal to add it before agreeing that the best they could do for now was *EPIDEMIC* alternating with *BANDER-SNATCH*, and trust that it would be dire enough to warn people away.

And there was always the story, Cynthia thought, and that would do more good than a hundred beacons. Their distress call was answered, less than a week out, by a liveship, the *Judith Merrill*, and her crew lost nearly all their native distrust of Arkhamers in their desire for the details—Cynthia, as a non-Arkhamer, was pestered nearly to death. But she was willing to tell the story as often as necessary to make people believe it, and she knew perfectly well that half the reason she got so many questions was the *Judith Merrill*'s crew double-checking what the Arkhamers told them. Everyone knew Arkhamers lied.

She was amused, though, and also touched that their greatest concern was for what Fiorenzo had done to the *Charles Dexter Ward*. They were fiercely protective of their ship, and while they were horrified by the idea of Fiorenzo reanimating the dead, it was Charlie they wanted to lynch her for. It was the wreck of the *Charles Dexter Ward* that was going to make the story, and Fiorenzo would be merely its villain, not a scientist striving—however wrong-headedly—for knowledge.

With the *Jarmulowicz Astronomica* in a cargo bay, Cynthia and Hester (and a random assortment of cheshires) were sharing a dormitory cubicle somewhere under the *Judith Merrill*'s left front fin. The purser had offered to put her somewhere else, but Cynthia had turned him down. Until they reached Faraday Station, her contract bound her to the *Jarmulowicz Astronomica*. And even after that, friendship would bind her to Hester.

And, the bare truth was, she didn't want to try to sleep alone.

When Cynthia reached their cubicle at the start of her next sleep shift, she said, "What makes forbidden knowledge forbidden, anyway?"

Hester looked up with visible alarm.

"No, I haven't found another Mi-Go canister," Cynthia said, amazed to find that she was able to joke about it. "I was just thinking about Fiorenzo and, well, how do you figure out where to draw the line? Because apparently I don't know."

"You do know," Hester said. "You knew Fiorenzo was wrong before I did."

"I knew Fiorenzo was *suicidal*. That's not quite the same thing."

"No," Hester said. "You looked at Ngao and you knew it was wrong. You saw the person suffering first, not the scientific achievement."

Cynthia winced. She had looked up Major Ngao—Major Kirawat Ngao, R.N. M.Sc.—but had had to draw back from attempting to contact his next of kin. What could she say? *I'm sorry your loved one was murdered and reanimated by an unscrupulous scientist, and is still animate and possibly conscious—though in pieces—in the belly of a dead boojum.* That was rank cruelty.

It was Ngao and the rest of the *Charles Dexter Ward*'s crew that she still felt worst about; Charlie himself was at least peacefully dead—even the pseudoghosts had faded out before the *Jarmulowicz Astronomica* was picked up by the *Judith Merrill*, showing that the spacetime disruptions were healing. But the reanimated were trapped in their dead ship, and the best that could be hoped for was that Fiorenzo's serum might someday wear off.

"Someday," which might just be another word for "never."

"You said yourself," Hester continued, pursuing the argument and jarring Cynthia out of a sad and pointless spiral of thought, "that you wouldn't put anyone in a canister, and I suspect you wouldn't have experimented at all if it had still had a brain in it."

"No," Cynthia said, then muttered rebelliously, "I still think we could find really valuable applications for the knowledge."

"Which is exactly what we told you about Fiorenzo," Hester said.

"Ouch," Cynthia said. She swung into her hammock and rearranged the cheshires to give her space.

"Mostly, I've always thought 'forbidden knowledge' was another way of saying, 'don't do that or the bandersnatches will get you,'" Hester pursued thoughtfully. "Or, I suppose, the Mi-Go."

"Which is frequently true," Cynthia said.

"Yes, but it never stops us." Hester looked up at Cynthia, her eyes dark. "Maybe that's the worst part of human nature. Nothing *ever* stops us. Not for long."

"Not for long," Cynthia agreed and petted the tentacled horror on her lap until it cuddled close and began to purr.

invisible men

CHRISTOPHER BARZAK

Christopher Barzak lives in Youngstown, Ohio, and teaches writing at Youngstown State University. His short fiction has appeared in Asimov's Science Fiction, Strange Horizons, Eclipse Online, Realms of Fantasy, Salon Fantastique, Firebirds Soaring: An Anthology of Original Speculative Fiction, Lady Churchill's Rosebud Wristlet, Flytrap, Apex Magazine, The Beastly Bride: Tales of the Animal People, *and elsewhere. His novels include* One For Sorrow *and* The Love We Share Without Knowing. *His most recent book is a collection,* Birds and Birthdays. *Coming up is a new collection,* Before and Afterlives.

Here he takes another look at a science fiction classic, retold from a somewhat different perspective.

She said he was an "ex-peer-i-ment-al in-vest-i-gat-or, don't you know?" And lucky for me, I don't catch her looking at me much, so I rolled my eyes at myself in the glass I was cleaning, then set it up on its shelf with my eyes rolling in its surface for a long time after.

She always likens herself to our Lord in Heaven, and clutches her hand at her heart like some poor widow, though she just married for a second time not a year ago, and you'd think she'd be happier with Mr. Hall around to help. Especially when *he* came round and took rooms from them. I might be a bit of a dull-headed girl—that's what my mother always told me, Lord keep her—but I ain't so dull I can't see something's wrong with a person when he comes into the Coach and Horses with his head all wrapped up like some bloody mummy, and thick blue goggles for glasses. Really, I should wince and say to her, "Do you think that's normal, miss?"

Oh, shut up, you silly girl. Move it along. You're slower than a cow! Help indeed! Snap, snap! Clap, clap! She's got many ways of dealing with me. But I ain't no girl, and I ain't no cow. I got sixteen years, and four of them I been working like anyone. What she sees ain't me, but some other girl. Cause ain't I the one who cleared the straw he spilled from those crates of his all over the floor of his room? And ain't I the one who scrubbed at a stain on the floor he'd made with all his chemicals and such?

She wanted to take him his tea and his eggs and ham. *She* wanted to stand at his shut door and listen to his moaning and sobbing, hand clutched at her heart like some mother. *She* wanted to try speaking with him like she was on his level—whatever it was, it was surely above hers by the way he spoke—and all I could do was laugh behind my hand in the kitchen when he chased her out of that room with a chair, the chair floating in midair like a ghost, and she came shrieking down the staircase.

Mrs. Hall gave me a hot time of it, she did, taking out her troubles with him on the likes of me while he was staying here. But I didn't let her muck me about too much. And there was always talk to be had when she wasn't round the bar, but upstairs leaning her ear against that door of his. Teddy Henfrey was here one day after all that mess with the Invisible Man started, and I caught him looking up at the pub's ceiling, shaking his head. "Here, Millie," he said, "what's Mrs. Hall on to up there? Still trying to get old goggle-eyes to talk?"

I kept wiping glasses and shook my head. "I don't right know, Teddy," I said. "I keep to my own or she'll give me a hot time of it."

And Teddy said, "Ain't like you're to blame for anything, Millie. And anyway, you're mostly back in the kitchen where nobody can see you."

"True enough," I told Teddy. "But when *she* wants to, she can see me all right. When she wants to."

Teddy Henfrey is the village clock-mender. He had a bad round of it with old goggle-eyes on the very day he showed up at the Coach and Horses. Mrs. Hall asked Teddy to come mend a clock in her new guest's room, but that clock had been dead some three months and she'd never once made a glance in its direction. Then goggle-eyes come through the door of the inn on the last day of February, snow blowing all round him, and him wrapped up in a greatcoat, muffler, and a hat with a brim so wide it cast a shadow over his face. And wouldn't you know, not two hours after she brought him his eggs and ham, Mrs. Hall was going on about that clock in his room needing mending.

It was just so she could get in there while Teddy went to work. Anyone could see that. Wanting a look at things, she was. We didn't know goggle-eyes weren't visible when he showed up, of course—we thought he'd been hurt in a fire or some other kind of accident—but if we'd known the truth of him then, I would've liked to say to her, "He's invisible, miss. He ain't blind, too, is he?"

But I must remind myself I've got a place, and that ain't so bad, considering I got no people. Ma died four years ago, and that's when I come to the Coach and Horses, where she'd done the work before me. Dad's been gone since I was little. Drowned, Ma told me, in the river one black night when he was wandering round like a fish with two legs. So I suppose it could have been me coming through that door on the last day of February, shouting, "In the name of human charity! A room and a fire!"

It was the Invisible Man, though. And what happened after that, none of us would've guessed.

What happened was this. Mrs. Hall wouldn't leave the man well enough alone. She kept trying to get his story out of him. Whenever she got a chance, she'd make a reason to barge in, even though he'd said to leave him be. She took him ham and eggs, like I've said, and then, after he waited for her to leave, she came back to the kitchen and saw she'd forgotten the mustard I'd made. "I declare!" she shouted. "Slow as treacle, you are, Millie! Help indeed!" She took the mustard upstairs then, and I pulled a face at her backside, but when she come down again a few minutes later, her face was all wrinkled with trouble.

"What is it, miss?" I asked, truly worried at that point. It's not often Mrs. Hall looks like someone run her over with a carriage.

She stood there for a while, blank, and then finally she started speaking. Said that his injuries must have something to do with his mouth, cause when she pushed in with the mustard, he put his serviette up to his face and wouldn't move it for nothing till she turned to leave.

"Something terrible must have happened to him," I said, and she nodded, staring off into a distance.

You'd have thought that would have been enough to keep a person from going on and bothering with him any more, but not Mrs. Hall. In fact, it wasn't a half hour passed before she took herself back up there, and this time it was to try and make a friend of him.

I suppose I made my own reasons for being round where she was, too. Cause it was something to watch her get to work on him, it was. She was smooth as a confidence man if ever I saw one. Stood there in his room and started telling him about her sister's boy, Tom, who'd cut his arm on a scythe last summer, and how Tom was three months getting better. "My sister was tied up with her little ones, though," she told him, "and there were all those bandages of Tom's to do and undo every day. So I took to changing the bandages as a way of helping, and by the end of that summer I knew my way round wrapping and unwrapping people." She paused after she finished her story, to make her point, and what she told the Invisible Man at the end of her ramble was, "If I may make so bold as to say it, sir—"

Before she could finish making so bold, though, old goggle-eyes interrupted to say, "Will you get me some matches? My pipe is out."

I had to put my hand over my mouth when I heard that one out in the hall where I'd been putting away the bedding. He pulled her right up, he did. But she got him those matches he asked for, and she never did make so bold as to say anything else.

Later that day was when she brought in Teddy Henfrey, like I mentioned, to make a show of fixing that dead clock. But Teddy stayed over his welcome. Kept trying to fix things about that clock that didn't need fixing, just so he could get a look at our strange houseguest. So it weren't just Mrs. Hall who was curious. I suppose anyone with a mind that notices things wanted a look at him. But when it was clear Teddy was wasting his time on that clock, goggle-eyes told him that's exactly what he was doing, and sent him right off. I hear Teddy went round town in a tizzy about how a man must do a clock at times, surely!

That was probably the first mistake, if you want to start counting the important ones, the ones that started other things happening. Mrs. Hall let Teddy in the man's room for her own reasons, and when the Invisible Man threw Teddy out, Teddy went about town like a cloud spewing thunder and lightning. It was Teddy, you see, who ran across Mr. Hall coming back from his conveyance route to Sidderbridge Junction and told him, "You got a rum-looking customer at the Coach and Horses, Hall!"

And when Mr. Hall said he didn't know what Teddy was on about, Teddy told him how Mrs. Hall let a room to a stranger, and how she didn't even know the bloke's name, and how he was all done up with bandages over his face, and how tufts of black hair curled out of the man's wrappings like the horns of the devil.

He planted a seed in Mr. Hall right then, and when Mr. Hall come round the Coach and Horses a bit later, all totted up with whisky, he started giving Mrs. Hall a time of it. And when Mrs. Hall just kept on as if he weren't even there, he started saying things like, "You women don't know everything!" and that's when Mrs. Hall turns round real slow, to give him a dark eye, and says, "You mind your own business, Hall, and I'll mind mine!"

I dare say I had a laugh about that one. Caught it in my hand, though, and slipped it in my pocket. She was always giving me a hot time of it, she was, but she'd take her tongue out and do Mr. Hall a bad turn whenever the feeling came on her. Couldn't help but feel a bit bad for him, but also a bit like I weren't the only one she didn't see till she wanted to.

It was the next day, though, that things really started to seem strange, if that's possible. His luggage was brought over from the rail station, and it was all in large crates. Mr. Fearenside and Mr. Hall started to unload them from the cart outside the inn, and you could see how heavy the crates were by the strain in their faces, how red their cheeks turned, like roses in winter.

The Invisible Man came through the pub where I was collecting plates for a table, and brushed right past me like a cold wind. He was wearing his greatcoat and was muffled in that hat and gloves and scarf, just like the day before. I went to the window and rubbed away the fog of my breath to watch him go clattering down the steps, shouting that Mr. Fearenside and Mr. Hall were taking too long, and why weren't his things already unloaded. It were a bad idea for him to go down so quick and angry like that, though, cause Mr. Fearenside's dog was under the wagon, see, and out it come, barking and yapping, and took a nip at the Invisible Man's hand. Old goggle-eyes pulled back his leg and gave the dog a good kick, but that just stirred the thing even more, and the next thing it did was lunge at his leg and take away a piece of his trousers.

Then—*snap! snap!*—Mr. Fearenside give his dog two licks of a whip, and the dog went yelping back under the wagon.

Goggle-eyes come through the pub door directly, cursing under his breath. I take a glance at the place where the dog tore his trousers, expecting to see a leg in there, and thinking I might get a chance of seeing what ails his skin as to require all those wrappings. But there ain't any leg I can see as that bit of his trouser opens and shuts like the flap of a carnival tent, giving glimpses of darkness behind it.

Seemed nothing was in there at all. Just darkness. And I thought, *How can that be? Man needs a leg to keep walking.*

He slammed his door when he reached his bedroom, and after a few minutes, Mr. Hall come in to see if the guest got hurt in a bad way. But Mr. Hall made the mistake—the second big mistake—of going in without knocking.

There was a tussle of some sort up there. Anyone with ears in the house could hear it. First Mr. Hall made an awful sound, then the door slammed shut again. A minute later, Mr. Hall's back in the pub, rubbing his head like someone's given him a great clout upside it.

"Are you all right, sir?" I asked, and he looked up, noticing me as if it's the first he's ever seen me. He didn't say anything, though. Just tugged at his mustache and winced, shook his head like a dog wringing itself out, then went back out to help with the unloading.

The crates were brought in then, one after another, once goggle-eyes came out of his room wearing a new pair of trousers. And what a spectacle, the things those crates carried! Towers of books. Glass tubes, glass bottles. And all kinds of powders and fluids of all sorts of colors. A burner and a balance. The Invisible Man put his things wherever he could find a bit of room. On the mantel. On the bookshelf. On the windowsill. On the floor, when he had no more room to speak of. Quite a sight it all was, too. Took the breath right from me when I peeked round the door to see inside. It appeared he was about to open a chemist's shop right there in the Coach and Horses!

He got right to work, too, for the rest of the day, with the door locked so Mr. and Mrs. Hall couldn't come in whenever they wanted. Sometimes I'd take a journey up the stairs to get a dustbin or a set of bedding for another room, and would take my time to listen near his door. Bottles clinked. Fluids dripped. I could hear a pencil scratch across paper, and thought of him then, bent over one of those big books, all taken up by some idea or experiment that possessed him. And while I was lost in thought of him like that was when *she* came round the corner and gasped like I were burgling.

"Millie!" she said, and I jumped back from his door, embarrassed at first, and then angry with her. Ain't it her, after all, who'd been doing the same thing I'd been doing right then, and even more?

The door opened on us then, and goggle-eyes looked back and forth between us. I shivered, being that close to him, seeing him look down at me through those blue spectacles of his. And his nose—what a shiny thing it was to see this close. Like a toy nose he might have purchased at a shop somewhere, it was. Mrs. Hall took the chance to look past him into the room right then, and before goggle-eyes could give us a bad time, she gasps and says, "My word, but it looks like a barn in here! All that straw, sir!"

"Put it on my bill, if you must," goggle-eyes muttered.

Mrs. Hall didn't stop there, though. No, she was in motion. Pushed right past him into the room and found her way to a golden stain he'd made on the floor with some of his chemicals, just like a hound, and said, "Sir, my floor!"

And goggle-eyes just said, "The bill, put it on the bill, I told you!"

I took the chance to slip away while they haggled over the price of his damages. Later, though, Mrs. Hall said to go in and sweep things up, the straw and all, and try to get that golden stain out.

I did as told, but I never did tell anyone what happened later that day when I went up there. Not even that writer, Mr. Wells, when he came round months after, looking to collect the scraps of the story from us.

———

This is what happened that day, the day I've never told a soul about.

I show up at his door and knock gently, as Mrs. Hall said to, and when he doesn't come to the door, I call through it, "Millie, sir. Here to sweep up, if you'll let me."

But still no answer comes. I look over my shoulder, back down the stairwell. I can hear Mrs. Hall down in the kitchen making tea. Then I look back at his door, turn the knob, and odd but it ain't locked as usual. And when I push in, the room's empty. Not the straw or mess, of course. Him. Old goggle-eyes ain't there. But I've not seen him come down and I've been working in the parlour all morning. And I've not seen him go out the pub way either, and I been working in there all afternoon. And as Mrs. Hall made it a thing for me to knock, like she expects him to be in there working on his experiments, I can't imagine she seen him leave the Coach and Horses either.

So I go in and think, Maybe this is better, not having to see him. Just doing my business of picking up after, and getting away without having to work around him. There are lots of things out of order in there, so I start first with the straw, since it's most noticeable, and sweep it all up into a pile in the hall to pick up later. Then I start in on the stain, putting my elbow and shoulder into it. It ain't coming out well, though I do manage to make it fade a little. I rub and rub and finally I sigh, sit up on my knees, and stretch my arms above me, letting my fingers flicker in the air, stretching them too.

And that's when I feel it. Something creeping under my arms, like spiders crawling on my skin. I put my arms down quick and the feeling goes away. I look both right and left, but no one's in there. Just me. I bend over again, thinking I've got to get a day free if Mrs. Hall will allow it. I'll tell her the spiders-on-my-arms story, I'm thinking, and that might help my case. And while I'm rubbing at that golden stain on the floor, thinking about this, I feel the spiders go crawling down my spine.

I sit up again and say, "Who's there?"

That's when the spiders come walking over my right cheek, and I shiver. I open my mouth, ready to scream, and that's when his hand goes over my mouth, catching my scream fore I can get it out of me.

"Shh, shh, girl," he says. "Shh, shh." Like I'm a baby crying. So I stop making a fuss and he says, "I will release you if you promise to be quiet." I nod once, and then his hand comes off my mouth.

"Who?" I say. And then, "What are you?"

He says, "Who I am is not important, Millie. What I am is invisible."

"Are you a ghost?" I say, looking round the room at nothing. I hear footsteps on the floor, creaking in a room where no one's walking. I stand, ready to run.

"Ah," he says, chuckling. "A village girl, through and through. No, my young one, I am no ghost. I am a scientist, you see."

And I say, "I don't see nothing."

He laughs at that. The room laughs at that. I say, "What's so funny about the truth?"

He says, "The truth? The truth is humorous more often than not, if you have the right perspective."

I don't say anything to that. I'm too busy looking round the room, trying to hear where the footsteps come from. He's circling me like wolves circle lambs cut off from the herd.

Then the footsteps stop, and he says, "I have discovered something, Millie. A powerful thing. The secret of invisibility. A way for no one to ever see you."

I say, "Not many people care to see me as it is. What's so powerful about that?"

"Well, exactly," he says, and his voice changes so it sounds like he's latched on to something. "Exactly, Millie. You're already an unseen, of sorts, aren't you? And what good does it do you? If you were truly invisible, though, you could do what you can't now. You could take a greater payment for the work you do. You could damage those who regularly abuse your services."

I wince, thinking I'm not understanding what I'm hearing. "Sir," I say. "Are you talking about thieving?"

"I'm talking about taking what you deserve," he tells me. "Taking what you deserve and much, much more." He says, "Millie, I can offer you a moment in history, if you should like to join me."

"History?" I say, blinking. "What good is a moment in history, sir?"

"You will never die, Millie. Your name will live on forever if you join my ranks of the invisible. You will be remembered."

His fingers—I know that's what they are this time round—caress my cheek again, a soft stroke. I notice that old goggle-eyes has his greatcoat hanging up in the corner now, and his hat on the table, and his gloves beside it. His trousers hang over the back of a chair. His shoes sit beside the legs of his chemistry table. "It's you," I say, "ain't it? You ain't wearing any clothes, are you?"

He don't answer me none, and I hear his steps move away from me. Then, from the table with all his tubes and bottles set up on it, a needle filled with blue fluid lifts into the air like a bottle fly, and starts drifting toward me.

"Would you like to test my new serum, Millie?" he says. "Would you like to be powerful like I am?"

I back up without saying anything. The needle follows. At the door, I take hold of the knob and say, "Sir, nothing's happened here today. I want you to understand that. You can go about your business and I'll go about mine. Not a word they'll have from me, but I promise they'll have it if you don't leave me be."

I close the door without a word back from him. I turn to find the mound of straw in the hall behind me. I lean over then, pick up as much as I can carry, and take it downstairs. Mrs. Hall don't see me take it out the kitchen door. She's busy doing sums of some sort on the account book. Totting up what goggle-eyes owes her, surely.

The rest of that day was taken up by thinking about what happened, and after a while my thoughts just kept spinning out like a spider web, and at some point in the spinning, I started thinking on my mother.

I hadn't thought about her for a while. It'd been four years since she died. I was twelve then, and working at the Coach and Horses kept me busy enough over the following years that I didn't think much about anything but my duties. I can't say when for sure I'd stopped fingering my memories of Ma, but surely it was sometime between washing the dishes and making up beds.

My mother had been a good woman, even if she were sometimes hard on me. Like I said, she sometimes called me dull-headed, and would come home from the

Coach and Horses and shoo me off cause she'd been caring after others all day, and there I was wanting a bit of her when she didn't have a drop left. Usually, though, after she got her feet up and her wind back, she'd sit me on her lap and brush my hair. She'd tell me stories. In all her stories, I was the heroine. Millie who went to London on the back of a flying horse. Millie who found a cave where the fair folk live, and brought them home to help her poor mother cook and clean. Cause of Ma, I had many ideas of myself that I can't say I'd thought of on my own. But they were none of them the *me* I was after she died, after I went to take her place at the Coach and Horses.

I wonder sometimes, what sort of idea of herself did Ma have? She never put herself in her stories as a heroine, just me. And whenever I tried to include her, she'd say, "Aww, Millie, my love, your old mother's not an adventurer like you are."

Quite an adventure it was, too, after she died. Going to live with the Halls, working there like my mother did. And then the funeral service, when some of her friends from the village came to pay their respects, that was shorter than I'd expected. I suppose I'd imagined something grander, rows of flowers, a violin playing somewhere, at least a piano, or a choir—even one melancholy singer, really—might have marked my mother's passing. But, no, that was not to be. At least the vicar Mr. Bunting was nice about her, from what I remember. He mentioned the smile she had for anyone who entered the Coach and Horses. I remember thinking how odd that was, though, cause she weren't ever smiling when she came home from there.

She has a stone marker in the churchyard now, but her name ain't on it. Sometimes, when I have a free day, I sit with her there, and trace my fingertip over the dirt on the stone. I spell her name. Rose. I trace the letters over and over, until it burns the tip of my finger.

That's what I kept coming back to after that incident in the Invisible Man's room. How he said I could have a moment in history. My mother never had a moment in history. Her name ain't even on that stone in the churchyard. All that's left of her is that stone itself, and whatever I can recall of her.

What would Ma have thought of the Invisible Man, I wonder? Would she have had a smile for him, like the vicar Mr. Bunting said she had for anyone? I certainly didn't give goggle-eyes any smiles for the rest of the time he stayed at the Coach and Horses. Which was a long time, indeed. He came in on the last day of February and stayed all through March and April. Everyone in the village had something to say about him, too, they did. Even the people who'd never chanced to see him. Children made up songs and rhymes. They called him the Bogey Man, and sometimes you'd see a whole pack of them running down a lane, and someone would pull them up and ask where they were all going in a hurry, and they'd say, "John seen the Bogey Man walking this way! We're going to see him!" And then they'd be off again, singing their Bogey Man songs.

Teddy Henfrey stopped coming to the Coach and Horses after a while. Said it made him feel too uncomfortable, being there, hearing old goggle-eyes thrashing about in his room, doing his experiments. Mr. Hall complained he was driving business away. But I thought it was really Teddy Henfrey doing the driving, cause he was the one going round the village telling people how he won't go back to the Coach and Horses for a pint until that Bogey Man is gone. Mrs. Hall told Mr. Hall, "Bills settled punctual is bills settled punctual, whatever you'd like to say about it." She said maybe she'd made a mistake, marrying a man who didn't know the ways of an inn like her father had, and that they'd wait till summer to do anything about it. Mr. Hall went off muttering something fierce, and for the rest of that day everyone stayed away from him.

I can't say goggle-eyes went out much in the two months he come to stay here. Mostly he worked in the parlour he'd set up as a chemist's shop, and spent his nights walking his bedroom floor. Even though Mrs. Hall spent time listening at his door, she couldn't make heads or tails of anything she heard in there, but I never stopped to have a listen any longer. When it was time for sleep, I swept past his door fast as a mouse, and ran up the stairs to the attic, hoping he didn't hear me.

But everyone knew he was up in that room of his in the Coach and Horses, even if they didn't see him but now and then, when he took walks round the village for fresh air, usually at twilight or late in the evenings. And so talk began to spread, wondering about what sort of work he did, or if he were a criminal all bandaged up like that to hide himself from the authorities. And when this kind of talk began to make its way back to the Coach and Horses, Mrs. Hall come right out to the center of the pub one night when we had a decent crowd, and called everyone's attention to her.

"I've heard all your nonsense talk," she said in a firm voice, "and I'll say this once and once only. He is an ex-peer-i-ment-al in-vest-i-ga-tor, is what he is! Now stop your tale telling."

"A scientist," Mr. Hall muttered from behind the bar. And when Mrs. Hall shot him a look, he went back to pouring.

"Yes, quite right," said Mrs. Hall, turning back to her audience. "A scientist." She seemed to think the folks at the pub would hear all that as an explanation, and go back to their business. Which I thought odd, since Mrs. Hall's been living in Iping all her life, and surely she must know that everyone talking about anything different going on in the village is their exact business.

"Here, Millie!" Mr. Fearenside said that same night, after most everyone had left and I was cleaning up the tables. "What do you make of old goggle-eyes? You have to live right here with him, after all. What's your story?"

I looked up from the table I'd been wiping down and met Mr. Fearenside's eyes for a moment, then looked toward the staircase that led up to the Invisible Man's room. He could be standing there, on that bottom step, for all I knew. He could be watching me, waiting to see me break my word with him. I'd felt his eyes on me many a time over March and April, and I was worse than a cat all that time, jumping at no cause a time or two every day it might seem to anyone looking. I could feel him watching me, waiting for me to tell his secret. So when I turned back to Mr. Fearenside, I said, "I ain't got no story, Mr. Fearenside. I don't see nothing and nothing don't see me. Simple as that."

"Clever girl, Millie!" said Mr. Fearenside.

And Mrs. Hall appeared in the pub right then to say, "Brought her up right, I can see now."

I didn't say anything to that. Just went back to wiping and taking up glasses. But for the rest of the night I kept thinking, *How?* How could she say that? *She* didn't bring me up. It were my mother's hands that molded me.

And right then, as I thought that, I started to cry a little. Tried getting the tears out of my eyes fore anyone saw them, but it was no use. Mrs. Hall saw straightaway and said, "Now what, Millie? I swear, always crying about something, you are!"

What happened next, everyone knows by now. It's been months gone by since they found and killed him over in Port Burdock, and even now there's always something about the other invisible folks he made that keep going round the countryside, terrifying innocent people and stealing. What happened was, Mr. Cuss, the village doctor, turned up at the Coach and Horses at the end of April. Had a professional interest in our guest, he said, since old goggle-eyes were all wrapped up in bandages. Said others were worried he was sick with something that might go round. But Mrs. Hall told Mr. Cuss he don't have a reason to see her guest if her guest ain't asked to be seen. Mr. Cuss went right on by her, though, into goggle-eyes' room, where they must have had some kind of conversation, because he didn't come out again for at least ten minutes.

Whatever they talked about ended in a short cry of surprise from Mr. Cuss, and then we heard a chair flung to the side, and that sharp bark of a laugh that belonged to goggle-eyes. Then the quick patter of feet to the door where Mrs. Hall and I both stood listening with our ears turned. It opened, and there stood Mr. Cuss. His face was pale as whitewash, and he held his hat against his chest like he were going to give us bad news. He looked back and forth at us, but in the end he said nothing, not a whisper, just went past us and down the stairs as if the devil himself were on his heels, and then the pub door closed behind him.

The Invisible Man laughed softly in the room beyond, and Mrs. Hall, without peering in, asked if she could get him anything. "No," he said. His voice sounded black as the blacking I'd put on the stove that morning. "There is nothing anyone can get me now, Mrs. Hall. It is over."

Mrs. Hall stood there for a minute, twisting her hands in her apron, waiting to see if he might say more. Maybe she hoped he'd ask for something and make her useful, I can't right say. But when she turned and saw me, she jumped back an inch, as if she'd forgotten I'd been at the door with her all that time. "Millie," she said. "Kitchen." Then she went down the hall to her own room, shut the door, and didn't come out until the next day, when we heard that the vicar Mr. Bunting and his wife had been burgled. And on Whit Monday, no less.

The story made it round town like the plague everyone feared old goggle-eyes might carry underneath those bandages of his. Before noon everyone knew the vicar and his wife had woken in the small hours of the morning by the sound of coins rattling downstairs. And when they went to check on the noise, found a candle lit. And the door unbolted. But no one there. They swore they watched the door of their house open and close on its own like it had a spirit in it. And then, when they checked their cash drawer, it was empty.

That same afternoon, while I was making a soup in the kitchen, a great racket happened up in old goggle-eyes' room. I heard Mrs. Hall screaming like her head must have come right off and started flying round the rooms on its own, and then it come down the steps and found me like that, making soup in the kitchen. I looked up, dropped my knife, and went up directly.

I found Mr. Hall holding her up in the hallway. Old goggle-eyes' door was closed up behind them. She slouched in Mr. Hall's arms like she might faint at any time, so I got my arm under her other side and together Mr. Hall and I brought her down to the pub and I poured her a cup of rum to calm her. She and Mr. Hall took turns then, telling me what had happened.

Seems they went up because old goggle-eyes' door was open, but he weren't in there, and his clothes were all laid out, and his bed cold, which meant he'd been gone all morning, but without clothes, and all of his bandages left behind too. Mrs. Hall said he'd put spirits into her furniture, cause didn't her mother's own chair lift up and chase her right out of the room? I didn't stop her to say it weren't any spirits in that chair, but old goggle-eyes himself lifting it and chasing her out the door with it. How could I? If the Halls knew I'd known our guest had been invisible all this time and didn't tell, I'm not sure what would happen. They might take me out the door directly, and leave me to find my own way. So I kept my mouth shut and kept nodding as Mrs. Hall brought the story round to when I'd come up the stairs after hearing her screaming.

"Out," she told Mr. Hall now, after she'd finished the story. "Lock the doors on him! I don't want him here any longer! All of those bottles and powders! I knew there wasn't something right with him. No one should have that many bottles!"

I held her hand while she sipped her drink, and didn't say what came to my mind right then. Ain't it her who defended him some weeks ago? Ain't it her who said he was an *ex-peer-i-men-tal in-vest-i-ga-tor*, like that were something above the rest of us? I figure she'd had a bad enough time already. When she finished her rum, I poured another to help her get along a little further.

She asked me to go across the way to get Mr. Wadgers, the blacksmith, to come and have a look at that furniture. She admired Mr. Wadgers, she said. She said she wanted his opinion on the strange occurrences at the Coach and Horses. So I ran over and brought Mr. Wadgers back, telling him very little, as I didn't want to put an idea into his mind before he had a chance to think for himself.

"Thank you, Millie," said Mrs. Hall when we returned. She sighed and began telling Mr. Wadgers about our morning, and I thought the madness had surely passed, that old goggle-eyes had had a good time of giving her a fright, and now he'd go back to his experiments. But soon as Mrs. Hall's sigh escaped her lips, wouldn't you know, the door upstairs creaks open, and down the stairs he comes, dressed in his bandages and hat and coat and muffler, just like when he first appeared in the late February entrance to the Coach and Horses. "I didn't see him come in," said Mrs. Hall as he walked past, as though none of us were there for the seeing, and went to his chemistry parlour, where he shut the door.

Mr. Hall got up and followed after Mr. Wadgers told him he should do so. He knocked at the door, opened it a sliver, and demanded an explanation for old goggle-eyes' sudden appearance. But the only thing old goggle-eyes had to say was, "Go to the devil! And shut that door behind you!"

And for the rest of that morning all we could hear was him in there clinking his bottles and tubes together, tossing about all those chemicals.

It was later, after we'd all gone back to our regular ways, that Mrs. Hall brought the thing to an end. It was her, I'd say, that had the courage to do so. She gave me instructions not to feed old goggle-eyes a crumb, and to not heed his calls. Instead, we went about our business, and ignored him as he threw bottles into his fireplace and cursed the gods. I cringed whenever I heard him shouting in there, but Mrs. Hall said, "Be a rock, Millie," and so I was still as the stone that marks my mother's grave in the churchyard.

At midday, though, he opened his door and demanded Mrs. Hall attend to him. His shouts filled up the Coach and Horses. Mrs. Hall hitched up her skirts and went right to him, her fright from the morning having passed her by, and said, "Is it your bill you're wanting, sir?"

"Why have I not received my breakfast?" he asked.

And Mrs. Hall said, "Why isn't my bill paid? That's what I'd like to know."

I put my hand over my mouth, knowing that I could shut myself up and hold my voice inside me, even if Mrs. Hall had no way of doing so for her own sake.

He told her he had the money he owed, but Mrs. Hall wasn't backing down. She said, "Yes, but I wonder where you found it. The vicar and his wife been burgled this very morning, and yesterday you had none." Then she began demanding he tell her what he'd done to her chairs—had he put spirits in them? And she demanded to know what he was on to in there with all those bottles and fluids. She demanded to know how his room was empty that morning and how he got in and out with none of us seeing. She demanded to know his name. "Who are you?" she said.

An endless list of demands, it was, and when Mrs. Hall reached the end of it, old goggle-eyes stamped his foot like the hoof of the devil and said, "By Heaven! I will show you!"

Mind you, I was in the kitchen when all this was happening. I could hear Mrs. Hall's voice going up and up, though, and stopped washing the dishes for a moment to listen harder. And just as I took my hands out of the water, Mrs. Hall screamed. And the scream was something louder and more frightening than anything she'd made when the chair flew at her earlier that morning.

I had my hands in my apron, drying them off, when I come out the kitchen into the pub, and there, right in front of me, his back to me, was old goggle-eyes. But he'd taken the bandages off his head, and his goggles and hat. He was a headless man standing there, and even though I'd already been in a room with him when he was invisible, I couldn't help but catch Mrs. Hall's screams and join her in sending one up to our Lord in Heaven.

It was a bad thing to do, though, it was. For it only called his attention. Old goggle-eyes turned round when he heard me, and though I couldn't see his face, I knew he was going to kill me. He'd blame me, I knew, for his discovery. Even if it were Mrs. Hall who'd forced him to reveal himself. To reveal that there weren't a self underneath all those bandages.

I turned and ran back into the kitchen then, and he came after, calling, "Millie, Millie!" But I kept on going. I took the stairs up to the next floor, and then the stairs up to my room in the attic. I locked the door, then opened my window, flung my head out and saw people running not only out of the pub beneath me, squealing and screaming, but also up and down the street people were abandoning the Whit Monday festivities to see what was happening down at the Coach and Horses.

Gypsies and sweets sellers, the swing man, wenches and dandies—they all came running down to the inn, and soon I could hear their voices burbling up from below like the soup I'd left on the stove. It was like how the vicar Mr. Bunting talked to us one Sunday about the tower of Babel, and all the many voices, and how no sense could be made of anything. I didn't move from my seat on the ledge of my dormer window, only looked over my shoulder every now and then to see if my door were still closed. I had the key in the palm of my hand, sweaty and hot. And later, when Mrs. Hall come up to say through the door that all was fine again, that the Invisible Man were gone now, they'd chased him off after a struggle, and won't you come out Millie, I opened that hand and saw how I'd held the key so tight it had cut into my skin and raised my blood.

What did he want from me, I wonder sometimes, when he ran after me into the kitchen, calling my name out? I was afraid then, and didn't stop to ask. But when I look back now, I sometimes think I can see round that fear to hear his voice again. To understand that he weren't angry at me, like I thought. He'd sounded frightened as I was. The same way I sometimes come into a room and see a mouse, and both of us jump at the sight of each other. What did he want from me? Someone told me that, after I ran away, the constable came and found him sitting at the kitchen table eating a crust of bread and some cheese. Was that all he'd wanted? Really? Had he just been hungry?

I can't right know the answer to that question. After that day, he only came back to Iping once more, with a tramp he forced to help him steal his books out of the room where he stayed here at the Coach and Horses. When he had those books again, they say he went on to other places and grew madder and madder, and stole more and more, and even involved himself in murder before a mob in Port Burdock hunted him down and killed him. It took a few weeks before the various stories told by various people in the various nearby ports and villages he terrorized were brought out and put together, so that a bigger story could be seen. And that was mostly cause of the writer, Mr. Wells, who came round after everything seemed to be over, drawing us all out to speak with him. Everyone, that is, except me.

He was a curious man, Mr. Wells, with eyes that pierced through me in a way that made me feel too seen. So much so that, when it was my turn for an interview, I said, "I don't have anything I can tell you, sir. I'm sorry."

"And why is that, Millie?" he asked as I sat at a table in the pub with him, rubbing my fingertips over the palm of my hand where the key had cut into me. "I hear, after all, that you were here almost all the time, and that he chased you into the kitchen on the day he revealed himself."

"I don't see nothing, sir," I told him. "And nothing sees me."

Mr. Wells waited for me to look up from my fidgeting before he spoke again. And when I did, he said, "I don't believe that for an instant, Millie."

But he let me alone, he did, and I was grateful.

It was clear that the Invisible Man had given the same offer he'd made me to others. Mrs. Hall read the news to me every morning in the months that followed his reign of terror. One day she said, "Look here, Millie! Not two months after he's been killed in Port Burdock and there are others like him taking on his filthy business. Thieving and firing houses! What a world we live in! If I had it my way, I'd see them all out of the country!"

"Would you now, miss?" I said. "And how would you see to it, them being invisible and all?"

She gave me a sour face and said, "Millie, you know what I mean."

I met her eyes when she said that, instead of looking down at the floor like I used to when she scolded. I never say what I think aloud, of course, but there are words that eyes can say just as well as any mouth can. And what my eyes said that morning when they met hers was, "You was wrong about him all along, weren't you?" An experimental investigator, indeed.

I think about the description of his death Mrs. Hall read from Mr. Wells' report some months later, usually when I'm alone and can use my time to imagine what happened after he was finished with us here at the Coach and Horses. She said that the people of Port Burdock welcomed him with fists and knees and boots when they finally cornered him. She said that they welcomed him with the flash of their teeth and a spade to the head, swung heavily. She said that, when he no longer moved and they began to back away, he started to appear within the circle they'd made round him.

First, an old woman saw a hand. Just the nerves and veins and arteries and bones could be seen beneath the invisible flesh. But then there were his feet as well. And then, slowly, his skin began to appear, moving inward from his toes and fingers toward the center of his body, like waves returning to the sea. He was all bashed up and bloody. His skin was white, his eyes red like a rabbit's. Nearly an albino, he'd been.

Mrs. Hall says he'd been a working boy who grew up and went to university somehow. Said his teachers ignored him. Said he stole from his own father to pay for his experiments, and that his father killed himself when he found the money gone, for he needed it to pay a debt.

I shake my head and say, "It's a bad business, it is."

And Mrs. Hall says, "I don't know who these scientists think they are. Playing as if they were our Lord in Heaven."

I don't say, "I meant his teachers ignoring him, miss."

Mrs. Hall says, "They'll get these other ones, too. You wait and see."

I say, "Indeed, miss."

Sundays, when I go round to Ma's grave after church, I think on the scene when they killed him, and wonder if the other people he injected with the serum he offered me were there when it happened, watching, invisible, protected if they did not speak and make themselves known. Did his anger at the world that didn't see him get into them as well? Surely it must have, as they've continued his terrible ways after his passing. That is what he leaves behind. Now, no one will forget him.

And then I wonder about his offer. A moment in history. Sometimes, when I'm looking at my mother's stone, tracing the letters of her name into the dirt that covers it, I wonder if I should have taken him up on it. For what good is life without the howls of anger in a world that thinks so highly of itself, even when there is great wrongness in it?

To be seen, to be known. It seems, when I look out at the faces of the people in the village, that's what most want. But we live in a world where not everyone can possibly be seen. We put too much on seeing to know one another, and the eye is a friend who often lies. At least this is something I've noticed in my time pouring drinks and making beds at the Coach and Horses. It might be better, I sometimes think, if we were all blind.

Proof of my time here. That is my desire. But there's little most can do to have this. The choices for our memorials are few, like Ma's unmarked stone here. I trace her name again, and again. We must take what we are given, then, like the vicar Mr. Bunting is always reminding us, and be happy. We must be happy, I think, with our anger, with our outraged mobs, with our eagerness to tear at the world that binds us. We must be content with what we have.

ship's brother

ALiETTE DE BODARD

Aliette de Bodard is a software engineer who was born in the United States, but grew up in France, where she still lives. Only a few years into her career, her short fiction has appeared in Interzone, Asimov's Science Fiction, Clarkseworld, Realms of Fantasy, Orson Scott Card's Intergalactic Medicine Show, Writers of the Future, Coyote Wild, Electric Velocipede, The Immersion Book of SF, Fictitious Force, Shimmer, *and elsewhere, and she won the British SF Association Award for her story "The Shipmaker." Her novels include* Servant of the Underworld, Harbinger of the Storm, *and* Master of the House of Darts, *all recently reissued in a novel omnibus,* Obsidian and Blood. *Her most recent book is a chapbook novella,* On a Red Station, Drifting.

The engrossing story that follows takes us to the far future of an alternate world where a high-tech conflict is going on between spacefaring Mayan and Chinese empires, and women give birth to children who are prenatally altered in the womb to become the control systems of living spaceships. This one deals with the ultimate sibling rivalry, as a brother traumatized by witnessing the birth of his "sister," who then becomes the starship The Fisherman's Song, *develops a lifetime enmity for her, and eventually enters into an adversarial relationship with her and her kind that has dramatic consequences for the rest of the family. . . .*

Y ou never liked your sister.

I know you tried your best; that you would stay awake at night thinking on filial piety and family duty; praying to your ancestors and the bodhisattva Quan Am to find strength; but that it would always come back to that core of dark thoughts within you, that fundamental fright you carried with you like a yin shadow in your heart.

I know, of course, where it started. I took you to the mind-ship—because I had no choice, because Khi Phach was away on some merchant trip to the Twenty-Third Planet—because you were a quiet and well-behaved son, and the birth-master would have attendants to take care of you. You had just turned eight—had stayed up all night for Tet, and shaken your head at the red envelopes, telling me you were no longer a child and didn't need money for toys and sweets.

When we disembarked from the shuttle, I had to pause—it was almost time for your sister to be born, and I felt my entire body had grown still—my lungs afire, my muscles seized up, and your sister in my womb stopping her incessant thrashing for a brief, agonizing moment. And I felt, as I always did during a contraction, my thoughts slipping away, down the birth canal to follow your sister; felt myself die, little by little, my self extinguishing itself like a flame.

Like all Minds, she was hungry for the touch of a human soul; entwined around my thoughts, and in her eagerness to be born, she was pushing outwards, dragging me with her—I remembered pictures and holos of post-birth bearers, their faces slack, their eyes empty, their thought-nets as pale as the waning moon, and for a moment—before my lips curled around the mantras of the birth-masters—I felt a sliver of ice in my heart, a hollow of fear within my belly—the thought that it could be me, that it would be me, that I wasn't strong enough . . .

And then it passed; and I stood, breathing hard, in the center of the mind-ship they had laid out for my daughter.

"Mommy?" you asked.

"I'm fine, child," I said, slowly—breathing in the miracle of air, struggling to string together words that made sense. "I'm fine."

We walked together to the heartroom, where the birth-master would be waiting for us. Within me, your sister was tossing and turning—throbbing incessantly, a beating heart, a pulsing machine, the weight of metal and optics within my womb. I ran my hands on the metal walls of the curving corridors, feeling oily warmth under my fingers—and your sister pulsed and throbbed and spoke within me, as if she were already eager to fly within the deep spaces.

You were by my side, watching everything with growing awe—silenced, for once, by the myriad red lanterns hung on rafters; by the holos in the corridors depicting scenes from *The Tale of Kieu* and *The Two Sisters in Exile*; by the characters gleaming on doors and walls—you ran everywhere, touched everything, laughing; and my heart seemed full of the sound of your voice.

The contractions were closer together, and the pain in my back never seemed to go away; from time to time, it would rack my entire body, and I bit my tongue not to cry out. The mantras were in my mind now; part of the incessant litany I kept whispering, over and over, to keep myself whole, to hold to the center of my being.

I had never prayed so hard in my entire life.

In the heartroom, the birth-master was waiting for us, with a cup of freshly brewed tea. I breathed in the flowery smell, watched the leaves dance within the shivering water—trying to remember what it felt to be light on my feet, to be free of pain and fatigue and nausea. "She's coming," I said, at last. I might have said something else, in other circumstances; made a comment from the Classic of Tea, quoted some poet like Nguyen Trai or Xuan Dieu; but my mind seemed to have deserted me.

"She is," the birth-master said, gravely. "It's almost over now, older aunt. You have to be strong."

I was; I tried; but it all slid like tears on polished jade. I was strong, but so was the Mind in my belly. And I could see other things in the room, too—the charms against death, and the bundle at the back of the room, which would hold the injector—they'd asked me what to do, should the birth go wrong, should I lose my mind, and I had told them I would rather die. It had seemed easy, at the time; but now that I stood facing a very real possibility it seemed very different.

I hadn't heard you for a while. When I looked up, you were still; watching the center of the room, utterly silent, utterly unmoving. "Mommy . . ."

It looked like a throne; if thrones could have protrusions and metal parts; and a geometry that seemed to continually reshape itself—like the spikes of a durian fruit, I'd thought earlier on, when they hadn't yet implanted your sister in my womb, but now it didn't feel quite so funny or innocuous. Now it was real.

"This is where the Mind comes to rest," the birth-master said. He laid a hand in the midst of the thing, into a hollow that seemed no bigger than a child's body. "As you see, all the proper connections are already in place." A mass of cables and fibers and sockets, and other things I couldn't recognize—all tangled together like a nest of snakes. "Your mommy will have to be very brave."

Another contraction racked through me, a wave that went from my womb to my back, stilling the world around us. I no longer felt huge or heavy; but merely detached, watching myself with growing anger and fear. This, now; this was real. Your sister would be born and plugged into the ship, and make it come alive; and I would have done my duty to the Emperor and to my ancestors. Else . . .

I vaguely heard the birth-master speak of courage again, and how I was the strongest woman he knew; and then the pain was back, and I doubled over, crying out.

"Mommy!"

"I'm—fine—" I whispered, trying to hold my belly—trying to keep myself still, to gather my thoughts together—she was strong and determined, your sister, hungry for life, hungry for her mother's touch.

"You're not fine," you said, and your voice suddenly sounded like that of an adult—grave and composed, and tinged with so much fear it brought me back to the world, for a brief moment.

I saw on the floor a puddle of blood that shone with the sheen of machine oil—how odd, I thought, before realizing that I was the one bleeding, the one dying piece by piece; and I was on the floor though I didn't remember kneeling, and the pain was flaring in my womb and in my back—and someone was screaming—I thought it was the birth-master, but it was me, it had always been me . . .

"Mommy," you said, from somewhere far away. "Mommy!" Your hands were wet with blood; and the birth-master's attendants were dragging you away, thank the ancestors. There were strong hands on me, whispering that I should hold, ride the crest of the pain, wait before I pushed, lest I lose myself altogether, scatter my own thoughts as your sister made her way out of my womb. My tongue was heavy with the repeated mantras, my lips bloodied where I had bit them; and I struggled to hold myself together, when all I longed for was to open up like a lotus flower; to scatter my thoughts like seeds upon the wind.

But through the haze of pain I saw you—saw, in the moment before the door closed upon you, the expression on your face; and I knew then that you'd never forget this, no matter how it all ended.

Of course, you never forgot, or forgave. Your sister was born safely; though I remained weak ever after, moving slowly through my own home, with bones that felt made of glass; and my thoughts always seemed to move sluggishly, as if part of me had really followed her out of the birth canal. But it all paled when they finally let me stand in the ship; when I felt it come to life under my feet; when I saw colors shift on the wall, and metal take on the sheen of oil; when the paintings slowly faded away, to be replaced by the lines of poetry I'd read to your sister in the womb—and when I heard a voice deeper than the emptiness of space whisper to me, "Mother."

The mind-ship was called *The Fisherman's Song*; and that became your sister's name; but in my heart she was always Mi Nuong, after the princess in the fairytale, the one who fell in love with her unseen fisherman.

But to you, she was the enemy.

You put away the Classics and the poets, and stole my books and holos about pregnancies and Minds—reading late at night, and asking me a thousand questions that I didn't always have the answer to. I thought you sought to understand your sister; but of course I was wrong.

I remember a day seven years after the birth—Khi Phach was away again to discuss shipments with some large suppliers, and you'd convinced me to have a banquet. You'd come to me in my office and told me that I shouldn't be so preoccupied with my husband and children. I almost laughed; but you looked so much in earnest, so concerned about me, that my whole body suddenly felt light, infused with warmth. "Of course, child," I said; and saw you smile, an expression that illuminated your entire being.

It was a huge banquet: in addition to our relatives, I'd invited my scholar classmates, and some of your friends so you wouldn't get bored. I'd expected you to wander off during the preparations, to find your friends or some assignment you absolutely had to study; but you didn't. You stood in the kitchen, fetching bits and pieces, and helping me make salad rolls and shrimp toasts—and mixed dipping sauces with such concentration, as if they were all that mattered in the world.

Your sister was there too—not physically present, but she'd linked herself to the house's com systems, and her translucent avatar stood in the kitchen: a smaller model of *The Fisherman's Song* that floated around the room, giving us instructions about the various recipes, and laughing when we tore rice papers or dashed across the room for a missing ingredient. For once, you seemed not to mind her presence; and everything in the household seemed . . . harmonious and ideal, the dream put forth by the Classics.

At the banquet, I was surprised to find you sitting at my table—it wasn't so much the breach of etiquette, I had never been over-concerned with such strictures, as something else. "Shouldn't you be with your friends?" I asked.

You glanced, carelessly, to the end of the room, where the younger people sat: candidates to the mandarin exams, like you; and a group of pale-skinned outsiders, who looked a bit dazed, doing their best to follow the conversations by their side. "I can be with them later," you said, making a dismissive gesture with your hands. "There's plenty of time."

"There's also plenty of time to be with me," I pointed out.

You pulled your chair, and sat down with a grimace. "Time passes," you said at last. "Mother . . ."

I laughed. "I'm not that frail." Though I felt weak that particular night, my bones and womb aching, as if in memory of giving birth to your sister; but I didn't tell you that.

"Of course you're not." You looked awkward, staring at your bowl as if you didn't know what to say anymore. Of course, you were fifteen—no adult yet, and ancestors know even Khi Phach had never mastered the art of small conversation.

I glanced at Mi Nuong. Your sister didn't eat; and so she spent the banquet at the back of the room, at a table with the avatars of other ships—knowing her, she'd be steering the conversation at the table to literature, and then disengage and listen to everyone's ideas. It seemed as though everything was going well; and I turned back to the people around my table.

After a while, I found myself deep in talk with Scholar Soi, one of my oldest friends from the Academy; and paying less attention to you, though you intervened from time to time in the discussion, bringing up a reference or a quotation you thought apt—you'd learnt your lessons well.

Soi beamed at you. "Wonderful boy. Ready to sit for your mandarin exams, I'd say."

You looked pale, then, as if you'd swallowed something that had got stuck in your throat. "I'm not sure, elder aunt."

"Modesty becomes you. Of course you're ready. The fear will go away once you're sitting in your exam cell, facing the dissertation subject." She smiled fondly at that. You still looked ill; and I resolved to speak to you afterwards, to tell you that you had nothing to fear.

"In fact," Soi said, "we should have something right here, right now. A poetry competition, to give everyone a chance to shine. What do you think, child?"

I'd expected you to say no; but you actually looked interested. If there was one thing you shared with your sister and with me, it was your love of words. "I'd be honored, elder aunt."

"Younger sister?" Soi asked me, but I shook my head.

I don't know how Soi did it, but she soon got most of the guests gathered around a table laden with wine cups—making florid gestures with her arms as she explained the rules. The outsiders, who didn't speak the language very well, had all declined, except for one; but it was still a sizeable audience. You stood at the forefront of it, eagerly hanging on to Soi's every word.

As Soi handed out turns for composing poetry, I found Mi Nuong hovering by my side. "I thought you'd be with them," I said.

"What about you, Mother?"

I sighed. "He's fifteen, and proud of his learning. He doesn't need to compete with his forty-year-old mother."

"Or with his sister." Mi Nuong's voice was uncannily serene; but of course, navigating the deep spaces, the odd dimensions that folded space back upon itself, she saw things we didn't.

"No," I said at last. I wasn't blind; and had seen the way you avoided her.

"It doesn't matter, Mother," Mi Nuong said, still in the same serene tones. "He'll come around."

"You sound like you can see the future."

"Of course not." She sounded amused. "It would be nice, though." She fell silent, then; and I knew what she was thinking: that she didn't need to see the future to know that she'd outlive us all. Minds lived for centuries.

"Don't—" I started, but she cut me.

"Don't worry about me. It's not that bad. I have so many more things to worry about, it doesn't really loom large." She sighed—I knew she was lying to reassure me, but I didn't press the point. "Look at him. He's still such a child."

And she wasn't, not anymore—Minds didn't age or mature at the same rate as humans. Perhaps it was her physiology, perhaps it was the mere act of crossing deep spaces so often, but she sounded disturbingly adult; even older than I sometimes. "You can't hold him to your standards."

She laughed—girlish, carefree. "Of course not. He's human."

"But still your brother?" I asked.

"Don't be silly, Mother. Of course he's my brother. He's such an idiot sometimes, but then so am I. It's what ties us together." Her voice was brimming with fond amusement; and her avatar nudged slightly closer to me, to get a better view of the contest. Everyone was laughing now, as a very tipsy scholar attempted to compose a poem about autumn and wine, and mangled words. The lone outsider stood by your side, and didn't laugh: his eyes were dark and intent, and he had a hand on your shoulder as he spoke to you—it looked as if he was trying to reassure you, which I couldn't fault him for.

"He worries for nothing," Mi Nuong said. "He'll win with ease."

And, indeed, when your turn came, you got up, gently setting aside the outsider's hand—and made up a poem about crab-flowers, making puns and references to other poems effortlessly, as if it was all part of some inner flow you could dip into. People stood, silent, as if struck with awe; and then Soi bowed to you, as younger to elder, and everyone else started to crowd around you in order to give you congratulations.

"See? I told you. He'll fly through his examinations, get a mandarin posting wherever he wants," Mi Nuong said.

"Of course he will," I said. I'd never doubted it; never questioned that you had my talent for literature, and Khi Phach's cunning and practical intelligence.

I looked at you—at the way you stood with your arms splayed out, basking in the praise of scholars; at your face still flushed with the declaiming of poetry—and you looked back at me, and saw me sitting with your sister by my side; and your face darkened in that moment, became as brittle as thin ice.

I felt a shiver go down my spine—as if some dark spirit had touched me and cast a shadow over all the paths of my future.

But the shadow never seemed to materialize: you passed your mandarin exams with ease—and awaited a posting from the government, though you closeted yourself with your friends and wouldn't confide any of your plans to us.

The summer after your exams, we went to see Mi Nuong—you and me and Khi Phach, who had just returned from his latest expedition. We took a lift to the orbital that held the spaceport—watching the fractured continents of the Eighteenth planet recede to a string of pearls in the middle of the ocean.

You sat away from us, reading a book a friend had given you—the outsiders' *Planet of Danger and Desire*, which was the latest rage that summer—while Khi Phach and I watched the receding continents, and talked about the future and what it held in store for us.

At the docks, the screens blinked above us, showing that your sister had just arrived from the First Planet. We stood outside the gate, waiting for her passengers to disembark—a stream of Viets and Xuyans, wearing silk robes and shirts, their faces still tense from the journey—from the odd sounds and sights, and the queer distortions of metal and flesh and bones one experienced aboard a mind-ship in deep spaces.

There were dignitaries from the Court itself, in five-panel brocade, their topknots adorned with exquisite jade and gold, talking amongst themselves in quiet tones—and a group of saffron-cloaked monks carrying nothing but the clothes on their back, their faces calm and ageless, making me ache for their serenity. Last of all came a vacant-eyed mother who hadn't survived the birth of her Mind, being led by her husband like a small child. My hands must have tensed without my realizing it, because Khi Phach grabbed me so hard I felt bruised, and forced me to look away.

"It's over," he said. "You'll never need to carry another Mind again."

I looked at my hands, tracing the shape of my bones through translucent skin—it had never been the same since Mi Nuong's birth. "Yes. I guess it is."

When we turned back, you weren't with us. I glanced at Khi Phach, fighting rising panic: you were an adult after all, hardly likely to be defenseless or lost. "He must have gone to another dock," Khi Phach said.

We searched the docks; the shops; the entire concourse, even the pagodas set away from the confusion of the spaceport's crowd, before we finally found you.

You were at the back of the spaceport, where the outsider hibernation ships berthed—watching another stream of travelers, their pale skins glistening from the fluid in the hibernation cradles, their eyes still faraway, reeling from the shock of waking up—the knowledge that the thin thread of ansible communications was their only link to a home planet where everyone they had ever held dear had aged and died during the long journey.

Khi Phach called out your name. "Anh!"

You didn't turn; your eyes remained on the outsiders.

"You gave us quite a fright," I said, laying a hand on your shoulder, feeling the tension in every one of your muscles. I thought it was stress; worry at the new life that opened up for you as a mandarin. "Come, let's see your sister."

You were silent and sullen the entire way; watching Khi Phach introduce himself to the crewmember that guarded the access to the ship, telling him we were family—her face lit up, and she congratulated him on such a beautiful child. I'd expected you to grimace in jealousy, as you always did when your sister was mentioned; but you didn't even speak.

"Child?" I asked.

I felt you tense as we walked into the tunnel leading to your sister's body; as the walls became organic, as faint traceries of poetry started appearing, and a persistent hum rose into the background: your sister's heartbeat, reverberating through the entire ship.

"This is stupid," you said, as we entered.

"What is?" Khi Phach asked.

"Mind-ships." You shook your head. "It's not meant to be that way."

Khi Phach glanced at me, inquisitively; for once, I was stuck for words. "Outsiders do it better," you said, your hands shut into fists.

We stopped, in the middle of the entrance hall—rafters adorned with red lanterns, poetry about family reunions, your sister's way of welcoming us home—I knew she was listening, that she might be hurt, but it was too late to take this outside, as you'd no doubt intended all along. "Better?" I said, arching an eyebrow. "Leaving for years in hibernation, leaving everything they own behind?"

"They don't take mind-ships!" You weren't looking at me or Khi Phach; but at the walls, your sister's body wrapped all around you. "They don't go plunging into deep spaces where we were never meant to go, don't go gazing into things that make them insane—they don't—don't birth those monstrosities just to navigate space faster!"

There was silence, in the wake of your words. All I could think of was all that I'd ignored; the priests' books that you'd brought home, your trips to the nearby Sleeper Church, and your pale-skinned outsider friends—like the one who had spoken to you so intently at the banquet.

"Apologize to your sister," Khi Phach said.

"I won't."

His voice was cold. "You just called her an abomination."

"I don't care."

I let go of you, then; moved away with one hand over my heart, as if I could make the words go away. "Child. Apologize. Please," I said, in the tone that I'd used when you were little.

"No." You laid a hand on the walls, feeling their warmth; and pulled back, as if burnt. "Look at you, Mother. All wasted up, for *her* sake. All our women, subjugated just so they can birth those things."

You sounded like Father Paul; like an outsider yourself, full of that same desperate rage and aggressiveness—though, unlike them, you had a home to come back to.

"I don't need you to defend me, child," I said. "And we can resume that discussion elsewhere—" I waved a hand, forestalling Khi Phach's objections—"but not here, not in your sister's hearing."

A wind rose through the ship, picking up sound as it whistled through empty rooms. "Abomination . . ." Mi Nuong whispered. "Come tell me what you think—to my face. In my heartroom."

You stared upwards; as if you could *see* her; guess at the mass of optics and flesh plugged into the ship—and before either of us could stop you, you spun and ran out of the ship, making small, convulsive noises that I knew were tears.

Child . . .

I would have run, too; but Khi Phach laid a hand on my shoulder. "Let him cool off first. You know you can't argue with him in that state."

"I'm sorry," I said to Mi Nuong.

The lights flickered; and the ship seemed to contract a little. "He's frightened," Mi Nuong said.

"Which is no excuse." Khi Phach's face was stern.

But he hadn't been there at the birth; he didn't remember what I remembered; the shadow that had lodged like a shard within your heart, that colored everything. "I should have seen it," I said. Because it was all my fault; because I should have never brought you to the ship that day. What had I been thinking, trusting in strangers to protect my own child?

"You shouldn't torment yourself," Mi Nuong said.

I laid a hand on a wall—watching lines of poetry scroll by, songs about fishermen flying cormorants over the river, about wars dashing beloved sons like strings of pearls—about the beauty of hibiscuses doomed to pass and become nothing, just as we, too, passed away and became nothing—and I thought about how small, how insignificant we were within the world—about letting go of grief and guilt. "I can't stop," I said. "He's my son, just as you are my daughter."

"I told you before. He'll see it."

"I guess," I said. "Tell me about your trip. How was it?"

She laughed; giggled like a teenage girl. "Wonderful. You should see the First Planet, it's so huge—it has all those palaces and gardens, covering it from end to end; and pagodas that go all the way through the atmosphere, joined to orbitals, so that prayers genuinely go out into the void . . ."

I remember it all; remember it vividly, every word, every nuance that happened that day. For, when we came home, you weren't there anymore.

You'd packed your things, and left a message. I guess you were a scholar in spite of everything, because you didn't send a mail through the terminal, but wrote it with pen and paper: crossed words over and over until they hardly made sense.

I can't live here anymore. I apologize for being an unfilial son; but I have to seek my fortune elsewhere.

Khi Phach started moving Heaven and Earth to find you; but I didn't have to look very far. Your name, barely disguised, was on the manifest for an outsider hibernation ship headed out of the Dai Viet Empire, to an isolated planet on the edge of a red sun—a trip sponsored by the Sleeper Church. The hibernation ship had left while we were still searching for you; and there was no calling it back, not without starting a war with the outsiders. And what pretext could we have given? You were an adult; sixteen already, with the mandarin exams behind you; old enough to do what you wanted with your life.

You wouldn't age in your hibernation pod; but by the time you arrived, twenty years would have elapsed for us, making the distance between us all but insurmountable.

Khi Phach fumed against the Church, speaking of retribution and judgment, making plans to bring this before the local magistrate. I merely stood still, watching the screen that showed the hibernation ship going farther and farther away from us—feeling as though someone had ripped my heart out of my chest.

Many years have passed, and you still haven't come back. Khi Phach took his anger and bitterness into his grave; and I stare at his holo every morning when I rise—wondering when I, too, will join him on the ancestral altar.

Your sister, of course, has hardly aged: Minds don't live like humans, and she'll survive us all. She's with me now—back from another trip into space, telling me about all the wonders she's seen. I ask about you; and feel the ship contracting around me—in sadness, in anger?

"I don't know, Mother. The outsider planets are closed to mind-ships."

I know it already, but I still ask.

"Have you—" I bite my lips, pull out the treacherous words one by one—"have you forgiven him?"

"Mother!" Mi Nuong laughs, gentle, carefree. "He was just a child when it happened. Why should I keep grudges that long? Besides . . ." Her voice is sadder, now.

"Yes," I say. "I've seen the holos, too." Gently, carefully, I pull your latest disk—finger it before triggering the ansible record it contains. An image of you hovers in the midst of the ship, transparent and leeched of colors.

"Mother. I hope this finds you well. I have started work for a newscast—this would please you, wouldn't it, my being a scholar after all?" You smile, but it doesn't reach all the way to your eyes; and your face is pale, as if you hadn't seen the sun in a long time. "I am well, though I think of you often."

The messages all come through ansible; so do money transfers—as if money could reduce the emptiness of space between us, as if it could repay me for your absence. "I was sorry to hear about Father. I miss you both terribly." You pause then, turn to look at something beyond the camera—I catch a glimpse of slim arms, wrapped around you—a quick hug, to give you strength, but even that doesn't light up your eyes or your face—before you look at the camera again. "I'm sorry. I—I wish I were home again."

I turn off the disk, let it lie on the floor—it becomes ringed with scrolling words, with poems of sorrow and loss.

"He's happy," Mi Nuong says, in a tone that makes clear she believes none of it. "Among the outsiders."

Walking on a strange land, in a strange world—learning new customs in an unfamiliar language—away from us, away from your family. "Happy," I say.

I finger the disk again. I know that if I turn it on again, I'll hear your final words, the ones that come at the end of the recording, spoken barely loud enough to be heard.

I miss you all terribly.

Us all. Father and Mother—and sister. This is the first time you've ever admitted this aloud. And I've seen the other, earlier holos; seen how your eyes become ringed with shadows as time passes; how unhappiness eats you alive, year after year, even as you tell me how good life is, among the outsiders.

I'll be long gone when your pain becomes heavier than your fear, heavier than your shame; when you turn away from your exile and return to the only place that was ever home to you. By the time you come back, I'll be dust, ashes spread in the void of space; one more portrait on the ancestral altar, to be honored and worshipped—I'll have passed on to another life, with the Buddha's blessing.

But I know, still, what will happen.

You'll walk out of the outsiders' docks, pale with the lack of sun, covered in the slime of your hibernation pod—shaking with the shock of awakening, your eyes filled with the same burning emptiness I remember so well, the same rage and grief that all you've ever held dear has been lost while you traveled.

And, like an answer to your most secret prayer, you'll find your sister waiting for you.

EATER-OF-BONE

ROBERT REED

Robert Reed sold his first story in 1986, and quickly established himself as one of the most prolific of today's writers, particularly at short fiction lengths, and has managed to keep up a very high standard of quality while being prolific, something that is not at all easy to do. Reed stories such as "Sister Alice," "Brother Perfect," "Decency," "Savior," "The Remoras," "Chrysalis," "Whiptail," "The Utility Man," "Marrow," "Birth Day," "Blind," "The Toad of Heaven," "Stride," "The Shape of Everything," "Guest of Honor," "Waging Good," and "Killing the Morrow," among at least a half dozen others equally as strong, count as among some of the best short work produced by anyone in the last few decades; many of his best stories have been assembled in the collections The Dragons of Springplace and The Cuckoo's Boys. He won the Hugo Award in 2007 for his novella "A Billion Eves." He is also a prolific novelist, having turned out eleven novels since the end of the '80s, including The Lee Shore, The Hormone Jungle, Black Milk, The Remarkables, Down the Bright Way, Beyond the Veil of Stars, An Exaltation of Larks, Beneath the Gated Sky, Marrow, Sister Alice, and The Well of Stars, as well as two chapbook novellas, Mere and Flavors of My Genius. His most recent book is a new chapbook novella, Eater-of-Bone. Coming up is a new novel, Slayer's Son. Reed lives with his family in Lincoln, Nebraska.

The tense and exciting novella that follows is related to Reed's longrunning series of stories about the "Great Ship," a Jupiter-sized spaceship created eons ago by enigmatic aliens that endlessly travels the Galaxy with its freight of millions of passengers from dozens of races, including humans. In this story, set at a tangent to the main "Great Ship" sequence, human colonists from the Ship have crashed and been marooned on a planet inhabited by smaller, weaker aliens. Because of their comparatively greater size and strength, and because of the repair nanomechanisms in their blood, which make them effectively immortal, or at least very, very hard to kill, the natives see them as monsters, and over hundreds of years, their relationship with humans has evolved into a state of constant warfare. To the surviving humans, though, the real monsters are other humans. . . .

1

With cured gut and twitch-cord, the Nots had constructed their trap—a marriage of old cleverness and deep rage designed to catch dreaded, unworldly monsters such as her. But the device had lain undisturbed since summer, and the winter rains had washed away some of the leaf litter and clay that served as its camouflage. Knowing what to expect, the young woman easily spotted the taut lines and anchor points, and experience told her where a single soft footfall would trigger the mechanism, causing the ground to fall away. An extraordinarily deep hole had been dug into the hillside. One misstep, and she would plunge into blackness, every kick and helpless flail bringing down the loose dirt that would suffocate and then temporarily kill. She had seen this design before. The Nots were masters when it came to doing the same ancient tricks again and again. Only once in her experience had this type of mechanism worked as designed, but the vivid memory of that exceptionally miserable night was enough to make the woman step backwards—a reflexive, foolish reaction, since traps occasionally came in pairs, and one careless motion could be more dangerous than twenty smart, studied footfalls.

But her bare foot fortunately hit only damp dirt, and she felt nothing worse than a jikk-incisor gouging her exposed Achilles.

She knelt slowly and pulled the thorn free, placing a thumb across the wound to force the first drop of blood to remain inside her body. Her skin grew warm beneath her touch, and then there was no wound. Sucking on her thumb, she tasted iron and salt and a dozen flavors of grime, and after some consideration, she carefully, carefully traced out a wide ellipse that eventually placed the trap upwind from her.

Riding the breeze was the aroma of a mature piss fungus. Saliva instantly filled her mouth. Her present hunger had been building for days. She couldn't resist taking a quick step forward while sucking down the scent, wild eyes searching the forest floor until she saw the trap's bait tucked behind a stand of spent silver yddybddy.

Her bare foot struck nothing but dirt; another youthful impulse went unpunished.

Again she made herself stop. Again she retreated cautiously. Then from a safe vantage point, she studied the Nots' trap. Her empty stomach rolled and shrank ever closer to nothing, but she didn't let her instincts run free. Only when she had a workable plan did she coax herself back the way she had come earlier, climbing the slight slope, tracing two of the exposed twitch-cords and deciphering where the third was hidden. Her best knife was an ancient nanocarbon blade wrapped inside a plastic scabbard. She decided to use a worn sapphire knife instead, digging into the cold gray clay until the last cord was discovered. It took five hundred breaths to fully uncover each of the cords. Working together, dozens of Nots had pulled the cords to their natural limits. Extend them just a little more, and their latent energies would be unleashed. The trapdoor would be wrenched open, and the piss fungus would vanish into the killing hole. That was why she found a stand of mature pegpokes, breaking off the strongest three pokes and sharpening them, and then with the heaviest rock she could lift, pounding each one into the ground. Every stake had to be buried next to one of the twitch-cords, as close to the bait as she dared. Then she spent the rest of her rich morning weaving short heavy ropes that she tied to the pokes and then spliced into the cords, leaving no slack. Finally she eased her green blade under the middle cord and sliced it with a single clean motion, and with the pegpoke absorbing the load, the long portion of the cord slapped and twisted its way uphill, leaving the invisible trapdoor undisturbed.

Once the other cords were cut, the trap was utterly helpless, its bait free for the stealing.

With the knife in her right hand, she crept close to the yddybddy and paused, staring at the dense yellow folds of fungus tucked behind the finger-like branches. Her mind and then her mouth imagined the feast to come. She would eat today and tomorrow too, and the fungus' hard fibrous heart would remain as traveling rations. Close to tears, she took a tiny step forward, feeling the ground and trapdoor sag slightly—just as she had expected. Then she took another step and heard what might have been a soft fart, and she turned in time to watch a single coil of elastic nanofibers spring from the ground beside her. She leaped back in time to save her leg but fell into another trap built along the same fierce lines. A second spring unraveled and flung out blindly, grabbing her by the right arm and yanking her down, and she kicked and flopped and dove back against the burning pressure as a thousand rit-hairs ate into her bicep and the burning joint of her elbow.

Two more traps were sprung, both missing her. She lay still and silent on the muddy ground, watching the coils lash at the air overhead, gradually losing their tension before dropping down and finally giving up. Then she stood, very slowly, looking at her bloodied arm, breathing hard, the air thick with the stink of an injured and terrified human monster.

For a long moment, there was no sound but her panic. Then from the hilltop came a strong wet woosh that continued up and up—a peculiar and important noise ending with another two breaths of silence, followed by an explosion and a brilliant flash of hard white light.

What had been so carefully contrived had done its gruesome work, and the rocket was a message telling the trap builders to come fast and marvel at their great luck.

There was no guessing how much time remained.

A decision that should have taken consideration and endless pain was made in an instant, without hesitation. With her free left hand, she yanked the precious nanocarbon knife out of its scabbard, making a first sloppy gouge to guide the following cuts. No blade could cut the fibers inside the coil, and trying would be an absolute waste of time. As she had been taught, she sliced up into her living shoulder, working too fast to let her natural misery killers take hold. Teeth clenched, body shaking, she choked back a scream as muscles and blood vessels and the main gray nerve were severed, and then she paused for a three-breath moment, allowing those gaping wounds to stop bleeding before using the knife's keen point to dismantle the joint where the arm entered her body—the body that she was saving, leaving her dying limb in the trap's tenacious grip.

Maybe the one arm would be enough, she told herself. Maybe its long bones would satisfy her enemies.

Though there was absolutely no good reason to hope so.

The long nameless hillside was covered with young forest, low and dense and as purple as a sick bruise, and a tiny woman with just a single arm could slip easily through gaps that might confound others. Not that that blessing occurred to her at that moment. What mattered was the desperate need to cover the greatest possible distance as fast as possible. Because it was a difficult direction, she ran sideways to the natural slope, pushing through the densest timber, and then she climbed a ridge and paused for ten breaths, listening as she gathered herself, wishing that nobody would come quite this soon. Then she attacked the steep ground, tearing downhill, leaping whenever she could and trying hard to touch only bare stone, making it a little harder to track her progress.

The country was dark purple to the brink of black, and it was drenched by rain. Even at a full sprint, she recognized dozens of smells—winter blossoms and sacks of fresh rainwater and fungi spores and bug dusts and the rocky soaked dirt itself. Westerwinds held their hiding places until she was in the midst of them, and then they broke for the sky—elegant green faces wrapped around empty gray eyes, fleshy mouths screaming and their voices always sounding like curses. Perhaps a hundred of the creatures lifted around her, and in a moment of pure fantasy, she wondered if she could lob off her legs too and grab one of them by its neck, letting the bird carry her away from this miserable place.

That long slope ended with a river that might or might not have been the same river she had followed for the last dozen days. The skin on the water was growing thin with the wintery gloom, but the dead white bubbleweed was stiff enough to support her weight, at least along the forested shore. Travel in the open was dangerous, but at least she wouldn't leave easy tracks and the river made for quick running. Her sapphire knife had been lost with her arm. Her nanocarbon knife was still clenched in her left hand, lost blood clinging to the long gray blade, already infested with colonies of iron-eating bugs. She plunged the blade into the river's skin and knelt and drank what poured from the wound. The water was warm, laced with winter algae and fish shit. As she drank, she wiped her knife against her trousers and then finished cleaning it with the hem of the little poncho covering her upper reaches, and then she pushed her only weapon back into its scabbard and stood again, discovering that her legs couldn't hold her very slight weight.

She settled again, knees falling to the rubbery, interwoven face of the river. Something large passed below. She felt the river's skin lift and then saw a long fin cutting into the bubbleweed, and a single black eye pushed through the hole that she had made, standing on a short thick stalk, considering the meal that seemed to be in easy reach.

An instinctive revulsion made her afraid, and that fear gave her enough strength to stand and run again. She followed the river past the next sharp turn, down to where the current picked up velocity and anger. Here the skin thinned until it couldn't be trusted. Downstream was open water sprinkled with sharp corundum stones and sudsy foam, little fetchers skimming low while giant moth-planes hovered high above, wings thin as dreams, stiff and wide, baking in the muted orange glow of the midday sky.

She crossed back to solid ground and stopped and looked upstream, watching the walkable stretch of river.

No enemies were visible.

She leaped from one rock to the next, and the next, and when she misjudged the distance, both of her bare feet slipped and she dropped hard, cracking something inside her hip that instantly caught fire, her abused little body struggling to push that fresh misery aside.

Where the river slowed, the skin reappeared, and she ran with a limp across the face of it.

After the next bend, where trailing eyes wouldn't see, she crossed over to the far bank before coaxing her legs to hurry, convincing herself that she had outraced every foe.

But she was nearly spent. Passion and fear gave out in the same instant. Gasping, she dragged her trembling, half-starved body past the ancient trunk of an enormous sky-hugging tree. Had she ever seen leaves such as this? Never, no. The river was heading north, pushing into country unlike that of her birth, and with their delicate but broad purplish leaves, the trees welcomed her with deep shadows and brushy cover and the rich fatty stink of a nearby grief-hive.

The hive was fixed to the water-swollen trunk of a massive tree. It was an old hive covered with living and dead griefs, and the entire colony buzzed, warning her of their presence and their very difficult mood.

Using her surviving arm, she picked up a slab of mudstone and walked up to the tree, closing her eyes for no reason. The insects could never hurt her. With a sweeping motion, she broke into the hive. The griefs went insane. Wings and rubbing legs roared. They picked up their dead and carried the desiccated bodies before them, driving barbed stingers into her poncho and her thin brown flesh. But toxins powerful enough to sicken a hundred Nots did nothing to her alien tissue. The stingers would feel like tiny pricks on her most sensitive day, which wasn't today, and she barely noticed as she flung the rock twice again, battering the woodish walls, crashing into the queen's quarters and exposing the rich golden wax that would give her a lingering bellyache as well as a fortune in calories.

Here was enormous luck, but the cool voices of the Dead reminded her that good fortune always demands the bad.

That first mouthful of wax made her gag and cough, and she had to push her hand between her tiny teeth to hold the bite in place. Chewing was work. Swallowing was misery. But her injured body responded immediately, unleashing enzymes tailored to break stubborn bonds, reshaping the peculiar lipids into other, more digestible fats that were already awakening glands and ducts that for too many days had done nothing but dream of food.

Twenty breaths, and she felt drunk.

Twenty more, and she was kneeling on the moldy floor of the old forest, her jaw working at a second mouthful while her hand kneaded what would become her third bite. That was when she noticed a pleasant heat building inside her wounded shoulder. She swallowed again and took another bite and then looked at the shoulder, studying the hairless pink bulge emerging from the gore—a totipotent structure ripe with everything needed for true muscle and nerves and bone. If she could eat her fill and then sleep, a short workable right arm would emerge, complete with a tiny new hand begging to be used. Her body would be only a little smaller as a consequence, and the rest of her bones only a little more frail. Several days of determined feasting would be needed to recover her lost mass, and richer meals than this had to be found before she found her strength again. But inside this splendid, unexpected moment, it was easy to believe that her life had suddenly changed. In this obscure corner of a country that she didn't know, she had stumbled across a wilderness full of grief-hives and other easy treasures; and for the next thousand years she would rule this forest—a monster of importance inflicting miseries on the local Nots as well as more dangerous and far more persistent enemies.

Motion caught her attention.

Smoothly and slowly, she turned her head, looking down the slope and out onto the river.

The rain was stronger now, gray and steady, splashing against the river's sun-starved skin. She heard the rumble of the rain and smelled it and smelled the river too, and then she saw a solitary figure running with a strong relaxed gait along the river's far bank. The intruder was built not too differently from her, but it was wearing more and better clothing—a wardrobe that changed color to match any background—and the creature had the posture of a hunter following a promising trail, the back tilted forward, head up and watching, and both hands carrying some kind of long, awful weapon.

Her first thought, odd and wrong, was that she must have wonderful eyes if she noticed that monster at such a distance.

But then the second hunter stepped out from behind a nearby tree. This was what had moved first, plucking her out of her daydream: A male human, tall and gloriously strong, his face rounded and hairless, that big spoiled body as well fed as any she had ever seen before.

To someone else, the man said, "Nothing."

Then, after too long of a pause, he added, "Here."

Her half-filled belly ached, and the stub of her new arm flinched. Otherwise she remained on her knees, still as death.

The man paused long enough to look in several directions but never straight at her. Like his partner across the river, he carried a weapon—an ancient gun sporting a long barrel, its magazine probably full of explosive rounds. His armored helmet was topped with some kind of radio transmitter. Riding his broad back was a leather pack large enough to hide somebody's severed limb. She watched the diamond barrel aim at nothing, and then it dipped. But it didn't dip far. Then she watched both the gun and man retreat back down to the river, and he stepped onto the rain-soaked skin, and once more he said a few words, too soft for her to make out but their tone sounding nervously happy.

They knew where she had been.

A moment later, the man slipped out of sight. But the figure next the far bank was running upstream now, the gait youthful and bold. The man's partner wanted to cross where the skin was thick enough. Then both of the humans, and perhaps others, would converge on this damp little place, ready to wage war against the poor little monster lurking here.

Instinct told her to run. Now.

But the endless need for food was too much. She stood slowly and with her surviving hand brushed away the griefs and yanked free another lump of hard wax, and she ate it much too fast, suppressing the urge to vomit. When her mouth was empty, she began to cry, fear and fatigue and honest, precious joy finding room inside her. Dying was better with a full stomach. How often had she heard that said? Many times, her mother had repeated those grim old words, and to prove their wisdom, the woman's death had been a blessing at the end of a miserable long famine. And that was why her daughter stood up now and reached high, risking everything to steal even more food from the furious griefs.

The two hunters reappeared, climbing the riverbank together. They could have been brother and sister, or maybe products of some tiny population where inbreeding ran deep. Definitely they had similar faces and identical mannerisms. They acted bold. With their camouflaged clothes and long guns, they looked exceptionally competent, immune to every fear, ready for any surprise. But their broad bright eyes dispelled those illusions. They were a young couple, she realized. They might be dangerous in a thousand awful ways, but during their little lives, they had done nothing quite like this repugnant, awful work.

Kneeling behind a low ridge of packed clay, she studied them.

Inside the woman's pack was a gaunt brown arm, mangled but still alive. It bent and then straightened. When the lost hand closed on nothing, the injured girl ached. Severed limbs could reattach themselves, she was thinking. Flesh always recognized its own kind. If she could just hide where she was, and if they followed her tracks too closely, and then if she charged with her knife, dodging their shots and cutting their throats . . . well, then it would be easy then to take back what was hers and steal their weapons too, pumping bomb after bomb into their helpless bodies.

"The Creation was built on grand, foolish blunders," her mother used to teach, in days not long ago, yet irretrievably remote.

Leaving her knife resting inside its scabbard, the young woman crept back into the darkest shadows.

Young as they were, these hunters were not idiots. Speaking in whispers, they spread apart, guns lifted and the man walking after a set of footprints that would look old and rain-worn by now. At least for another twenty breaths, they would never guess that she was this close. That gave her enough time to find a ridge of shale that offered a trackless route up the hillside. Then with the rain sounds covering her little noises, she jogged, climbing the slope until the ground softened, and then after sucking down a single deep breath, she forced her tiny body into a desperate sprint.

The forest ended at the top of the hill. Where the high ground flattened, the Nots had attacked the native trees, using explosive summer fires and corundum axes to create a single long field dotted with burnt stumps and winter crops. Purplish earweed and coldharm and the blue-black cindercane grew lush and thick with the chill rain. She paused at the field's edge, listening past the raindrops, resting while she compared what were a series of exceptionally poor choices. And then she moved again, slipping along the edge of the forest and wishing that was best.

By very little, an aluminum-hulled bomb missed the back of her head and fell into the shaggy field, detonating with a hard, awful thud.

Weak despite wounds and her overstuffed belly, she ran into the cindercane, pressing hard even when she left behind a broad trail any fool could follow.

Duplicity was dropped, replaced with a bold taunt.

"Follow if you dare!" she was telling them.

Her first Not was a youngster, half-grown and consumed by its little work. She saw the long exoskin—like a poncho with a tall hood, washed milky gray with the season—and she saw the wooden hoe being lifted high and the warm rain sliding off the creature's greased back, merging with the ground where roots like fingers worked to absorb and protect what came only in the winter. She couldn't see any face, but she heard the creature speaking to itself. Nothing about the voice was sensible: Neither the words or their meanings, nor the emotions, or even if this was true speech at all. But the creature made its soft private sounds, and then down went the hoe, beheading a single green plant growing in the midst of all that happy black cane.

Before the hoe lifted again, she called out.

The Not turned abruptly, its face showing beneath the folds of thin gray flesh. Staring into the shadows, memory supplied the features: Two pairs of eyes and a beak-like mouth and flat nostrils and purple skin laid across stiff protein-woven bones that bore no resemblance to hers.

The young Not saw her and gave a weak holler.

Believing it was doomed, the creature bowed to the monster and wished it well, and then it lifted its head again, perhaps more startled than pleased to discover that she had already run past it, offering not so much as a brutal slap.

A few strides beyond the Not was the main trail.

She paused, just for an instant. But there was no way to decipher which direction was best, and so she made her guess and never looked back, even when the next hard thud rolled across the plateau.

One of the hunters had shot the Not.

The trail was narrow and curling, and then all at once it was straight and wide, leaving the cane field for ground more established and far more open. The burnt stumps were gone. The crops were perennials like elder and pack-a-long. A pair of adult farmers were walking home at the end of a wet good day, hands filled with implements too important to leave in the mud. This time she made no sound. She ran between them, and even exhausted, she pushed one farmer down and looked back at his friend until that creature thought to yell out a warning into the gathering night.

She didn't know the precise translation, but that single sharp word would mean her.

A human monster.

Which she was. A horrible murderous creature, and she was running loose in the village now. Little ellipsoid homes appeared, low-built and solid, made from stacked stone blocks and living earth, skins of water set out in the yards, absorbing the weak sunlight. She found dozens of Nots trapped in moments of very ordinary life, and in ways she had never felt before, she was envious. There was comfort in this place, alien but recognizable. She ran down a street of foot-packed mud, straight into the heart of a tiny community—a rough lonely place perched on the brink of a monster-infested wilderness. Yet here lived souls that enjoyed the luxury of dry shelter and a world of food that they raised for themselves, their brief, endless lives punctuated with countless little feasts.

Her enemies wouldn't follow her into this dangerous realm, she hoped.

But they did. From the street behind her came gunfire and screams, the screams growing louder as her pursuers drew close. Then she heard the booming thuds of a single drum set in the village center—a great bowl of wood covered with the exoskins of ancestors. Someone was beating the drum with authority, warning the populace of monsters running loose. Now the children and elderly would hide. Every able body would race indoors long enough to retrieve a spear, or maybe a bow and lucky arrow, and then they would rush out again to stab at a trio of organisms that were impossible to kill.

Two determined enemies became a mob of a hundred and two. She couldn't run faster, and then her legs slowed even more, turning clumsy. She had never breathed this deeply, but all the oxygen in the world couldn't cure the kind of fatigue eating away at her muscle and reflexes. She was stupid with exhaustion. Straight ahead of her, a tall Not stepped out of his home, and she was slow enough that he had ample time to aim what looked like a very long arrow. She saw the creature's face, the skin nearly black with the purple and the glassy beak exposed when the nervous lips pulled back, and she saw the arrow fly off the bow and heard the thunk and knew full well that she should leap to one side or the other, spoiling the shot. But despite trying to react, she couldn't. The arrow's head was hard, well-sharpened sapphire that cut through her poncho and the skin just beneath her tiny left breast, meeting the ribs and then bouncing. But the blade didn't fall free. She felt the impact and spun around, astonished by how easily her balance was lost. More Nots were emerging from their little houses. She saw anger and terror. Or she saw nothing. Who could say what the Nots felt, in any situation, in any given day? But she imagined them being fearful, and then brave because of their fear. They saw her stumble and nearly drop to the ground, and maybe a dozen of them were holding sharp implements that could be used to hack at a monster such as her, reducing her to shreds before she could find her feet again.

But she didn't lose her balance completely.

Her last hand caught the packed mud and pushed, and her bare toes bit deep and helped shove her into full stride again. Then the hand lifted and blindly broke the arrow shaft and pulled it from her chest, tossing it aside before the muddy hand dug into the gore, pulling out the jagged gemstone.

The little road came to empty ground that led out toward a gray wet sky. She ran, and a thrown rock struck her in the back, between her shoulder blades. More rocks fell on the street with hard squishing sounds. Then all at once the shouting changed complexion. It took her a moment to realize that the faces had turned away, and now every mouth was cursing the monsters chasing after her.

It was astonishingly easy, this irrational and useless belief that the Nots had taken sides in another species' contest.

But that's exactly what she felt.

Unable to help herself, she paused at the edge of the village, and she breathed and turned around while placing her hand against one knee and bending forward, drinking at the dense air while her little Nots made their stand.

A hundred voices shouted insults, or they begged the gods for help, or they tried to coax bravery out of every hiding cousin and lover and brother.

The thunk-thunk-thunk of bows was a sweet noise.

Then the crowd charged at the two monsters, hoes and simple clubs lifting high and then dropping, battering one another as much as their mortal enemies.

She felt distant; she felt safe.

Even when she knew she was wrong, she entertained a bold little confidence that produced the best smile in days and days and days.

Then the hard pop of human guns began, and the nearly instantaneous booms of explosives. Concussions broke against her face. What kept the blasts from being louder were all those packed brave foolish and doomed bodies filling up the street. Nots flew back into Nots, and all their bravery was lost in an instant. The villagers tried to run and couldn't, packed too close, and the young man and the young woman shot another ten or twelve rounds at pointblank range, accepting the burns and bony shrapnel that was sure to come from that tactic.

The one-armed girl took a tentative step backward.

Whole exoskins were ripped free of their bodies, and voices died in the midst of screaming, and then the mob dissolved into panicked figures fleeing and others falling, and the humans emerged from the carnage, shouting at their assailants with a few old Not curses.

She knew to run but couldn't.

Spellbound, she stared at bodies not too unlike hers. These monsters were peppered with arrows and at least one long spear, and knife wounds and gashes from heavy rocks. But the man and woman were far stronger than her, and larger, and what would have dropped her ten times just made them angrier and more sure.

It was the bride who took time to kneel and aim carefully.

As her gun kicked, the one-armed girl—her target—remembered to leap sideways.

What saved her was the range, which was too close. And it was the tiny distance that she had moved sideways, insuring that the single round passed into the guts but missed the spine or hips or ribs. It hit hard and dug into her and through her, and her first impression was that some heavy old piece of her body had been removed. At last, she was light again and full of energy. In that half-moment before the explosion, she could tell herself that she was blessed. And then came the white-hot blast that threw her forward, that casual violence shoving her into the wet face of the road.

She died, but only for a moment.

Then she was aware enough to know that her back was scorched, and her hair, and her clothes were blown away and her guts were battered or missing entirely. She came back into life unaware of how much time had passed, but then sitting up, she realized that only a moment or two was lost. The human man was just beginning to run at her, and his pretty mate stood and smiled, and the severed arm carried in the pack twisted and grabbed at the sky—a blind reflexive gesture that wouldn't last much longer.

She rose to her feet somehow.

So much of her belly was missing that she had to use her one arm to keep herself upright, that meal of chewed wax dripping free even after the bleeding had stopped. She turned and began to do what passed for running. Neither quick nor graceful, she headed into the open country. Her only advantage was that pain and deprivation had stolen away all of her good sense. Any rational mind would have given up now. But she had nothing left except instinct, and both legs remained intact, and maybe the hunters were too confident or too injured to put an end to this chase. Maybe the Nots had counterattacked. She didn't know. Crossing a pasture of hairvetch, at some point she stumbled her way onto a spine of eroded gneiss that quickly narrowed. But she couldn't see beyond her next two steps, what with the rain falling harder suddenly and the invisible sun setting and her own numbing desire to do nothing but keep her eyes half-closed, dancing with sleep until that moment when her left foot stepped into the open air, dragging her body and other leg over the sudden lip of cliff.

Twice on the tumbling journey down, she struck boulders. Then the cliff pulled away, and she fell past beside thick beds of slates and mudstones undermined by an ocean that she had never seen before and didn't see now—a realm of deep cool nearly living water topped with a winter-starved skin that split when her body, led by her unconscious head, finally struck.

2

The limp, burnt body was a prize too rich to ignore. Fish licked the salty flesh and bit hard into the rusty red muscle. But even tiny meals made throats burn and bellies sicken, and the indigestible was often spat out again. Her proteins were unlike anything natural, spun from amino acids peculiar to distant worlds and immortal beings. Her stubborn blood was laced with antioxidants often toxic to the local biology. Buried inside her chemical bonds were the scarcest, most dangerous metals and lanthanides and heavy halogens. And worst of all, between her dead cells slept fleets of machine-like phages. If just one of those ingested phages lost its ancient safeguards, then it would duplicate itself at a staggering pace—billions of machines trying mightily to transform native flesh into the healthy body of a human female. But even with those dangers, her body was steadily bitten and masticated and then vomited up again. Nervous systems failed; metabolisms collapsed. Her drifting corpse created a zone of misery, the dark winter water full of twitching fins and abortions as well as a succession of increasingly grim fish kills. But that slaughter proved endurable for some species, and for a lucky few, there was uncommon wealth. Deep-swimmers tasted the mayhem, and once the rough soup was diluted enough, they rose up to drink their fill. A flight of hack-a-leens descended on the water's skin, claws cutting through and the long necks leading down to where they would nab tiny, precious meals. After two nights and a day, the deep expanse of the bay had absorbed much of her potassium and phosphorus, while her stolen iron and calcium fueled a million quiet wars; and during the second day, a remarkable midwinter bloom made the water glow with a vivid, milky light.

Much as it had in life, the woman's body continued to wander. Bloodless and burnt, gutted and chewed upon—yet she felt nothing. Many days and nights passed without being noticed. Occasionally one of her dark eyes would open, but the mind behind it perceived nothing but a vague cold gray. In tiny, ineffectual steps, intricate mechanisms would strive to make repairs to her body, or at least staunch the steady losses. A sleeping organ might wake for a moment, pushing ions into important places and spinning a few new proteins; but even tiny actions were a waste, and the work quickly ended. Processes rather like rot took hold, causing her flesh to bloat. She floated with her back up and her dead face down, the final arm and her legs spread wide. With the barest metabolism, her temperature matched that of the winter sea. The nameless river supplied the first steady push that carried her out of the bay, and the tides pulled her farther from the land. Then a wild storm broke, shredding the last of the summer skin. Waves rose up in high neat rows, marching toward a horizon she could neither see nor imagine, and what little remained of the woman was carried out into a realm as empty and black as space.

Each season had its wealth, its champions. Winter was dark but deliciously wet, and with the skin peeled off the wind-churned water, oxygen passed freely into the deepest realms. The muddy floor of the ocean was home to a nation: a thousand unimagined beasts, at least not imagined by the dead woman. These were huge creatures, and by any measure, their minds were substantial. Winter was their time to rise to the surface, feeding and breeding. Soon they discovered the mystery drifting above their home, and with sonar and then giant blue-black eyes, they studied the intruder with care. There was perhaps a passing resemblance of form, but this was no Not. That was one point of agreement. Ancient tales spoke of monsters descending from the sky, but that must have been a different species from this creature. The corpse carried no trace of wings. Nothing about the visitor seemed grand or special, and after so much abuse, even her original shape was a subject of considerable debate.

"Eat it," one beast suggested.

"I will not," its companion replied.

"Why not?"

"It is not dead."

Only detritus and their own children were suitable food.

"But it is dead," the first creature argued. "Have you seen it move? In all of the time we have danced here, has the creature taken any action?"

Just then, the dead eyes opened.

Perhaps the sound of whistling voices woke her. Perhaps it was chance. Whatever the reason, the right eye came alive, followed by the left, and the mind behind the eyes fell out of its coma just enough to perceive two vast shapes drifting beneath, carefully keeping their giant selves out of reach.

The two watery beasts stared up at her, perplexed and intrigued.

Weakly, she managed to kick both of her rotted, bloated legs. And the last bits of muscle made her arm flinch, pulling her hand against her belly, gingerly touching the still-gaping hole.

"It lives," the first beast decided.

But its companion was less sure. "Perhaps that was a reflex."

Whatever the carcass was, it was unnatural. And it was evil. No other conclusion was possible.

"We should destroy it," said the first beast.

"But why?"

"To rid the world of an abomination."

There was a compelling logic to that opinion, yes.

"Consider the honor," the first beast argued.

"I give this honor to you," said its companion.

Slowly, the first beast swam upward and opened its broad mouth and then inhaled, neatly pulling the carcass into its wide throat and then its belly. Then with a lying voice, it said, "Delicious."

"Really?"

"You must eat the next one of these," it argued. "You will never taste anything like it, I promise."

Phages designed to defend and repair human flesh suddenly woke, bathed in free oxygen and eager to work. But even worse were the rare elements carried in the dead blood—heavy metals freed by the stomach acids, effortlessly spreading into every cell inside that exceptionally long body. Bright cries of misery carried back into the depths. Every recent meal was thrown out of the anguished mouth and anus. Then before nightfall, thankfully, the poor creature was dead.

Consumed by acids and smaller than ever, the human corpse calmly resumed its facedown floating.

The surviving beast grieved for its lost friend and wrestled with its own guilt, and then in a moment of despairing bravery, it vowed that if this monster couldn't be destroyed, at least it would be removed from the ocean.

The nearest land was an island, black and rough and rain-soaked, and when the tide was high, the water beside its shore was open and very deep. Carrying the monster on its head, the beast swam close and then flung the danger as far as possible, watching with satisfaction as the immortal body landed on a tall stack of rocks. And there it did nothing but lie in a motionless heap, those tiny black alien eyes neither opened nor closed, nothing to see but the rain and darkness and their inevitable doom.

3

The cistern was overflowing, and before it was capped it needed to be laced with copper salts—a useful trick to keep thieves out of the stored rainwater. That's why the man was kneeling in the gully. The fanhearts spotted him and dropped through the tall trees, screaming some nonsense about a mysterious visitor. Then the flock's white-throated elder settled on the slope above, long wings spread wide and her throat twisting to say one alien word. "Human," the bird managed with a crackling squawk. "Human, human, human!"

The man poured in the last of the salt. Then he looked up, and with a rough approximation of the fanheart language, he asked, "Where?"

"Rookery, dawnward, pillars," she reported in her own tongue. And when he did nothing, she said again, "Human."

His companions meant well. But in matters like these, they were almost always wrong. What they'd found could be any sort of creature cast up on the shoreline, or it was nothing at all. But most likely it was a dead Not—some fisherman tossed from his boat, probably. Fanhearts were incurable optimists. They loved to make large promises, hoping for a taste of his praise.

Before anything else, what he needed to do was fit the sapphire plug into the cistern's mouth, and then he covered the plug with plastic and clay and random rocks, hiding its presence. Then he finally climbed to his feet, telling them, "Thanks. Human will go view."

The flock was thrilled that their ancient friend might believe them. They drew furious circles overhead, voices bright and enthusiastic. The rookery was an easy flight but a long walk, and the pillars in question stood beyond the barricade. Preparation was important. On the remote possibility they were right, the human climbed down the hillside and stepped inside his home. There he filled a large pack with supplies, selecting one gun to carry and two more for his belt. Then he donned a fresh poncho and secured his front door before walking out from under the shadow of the old gyreboy, attacking the cold chilled rain.

With eyes closed, he could have walked the next thousand steps. This portion of the island was so much his own that it felt as if his soul extended past his flesh, embracing the corundum hills and the crumbling beds of mudstone and the mature black forest that fed the wild game that lived as it wished, knowing nothing of genuine danger. This was a retreat, a private paradise. One creature ruled here, and the creature's reputation was considerable—a titanic and fearless monster known well by the local Nots. "The Giant", they had dubbed their human, or whistles to that effect: Even among his horrible species, he was huge and strong—the ultimate monster—and the tiny natives knew better than risk slinking into his dark realm.

The man walked smoothly, with grace and economy, his swollen pack creaking as the straps rubbed and the baggage shifted.

His fanhearts kept tabs on his progress, and they sent ahead scouts to check on the body lying above the surf—one after another returning with the breathless news that nothing had changed since the last glimpse.

Now and again, he let himself believe there was a human visitor. But even if that were the case, what was likely? Peaceful conversation was doubtful. And even if the two of them could talk politely, what were the odds that he could actually trust this intruder?

By and large, human beings were monsters.

From the forest edge, he announced his presence—a bright screaming shout familiar to every local Not—and then he donned an appropriate mask and stepped into the open, dropping the pack to throw it over the barricade, and then with a smooth motion, jumping after it.

The pillars and the black tidal flats lay exposed. Standing on high ground, he peered through a telescope, seeing enough to make his slender hopes collapse. The pillars were masses of corundum, pale brown and tough after spending their youth being tortured far beneath some ancient crust. He remembered clearly when those landmarks were still part of this island, and not just at low tide. He studied the terrain between him and them. Then he looked at the sea beyond, dark and exceptionally rough, the wind building waves that tore loose bundles of wiry black baleen weed. The weed had been flung across the top of the pillars, and even at this distance, he could see which tangle had confused his friends. A body-shaped lump lay in the open, one leg extended and another crumpled up in a decidedly unnatural pose. And what looked like a single bony arm rose up into the rain, stumps instead of fingers and no second arm to be seen. The mistake was natural. The fanhearts had too much respect for humans to approach without being invited, which was why they circled high overhead, the entire flock screaming happily as he let the pack drop and strode across the soggy mud, and with hands and bare feet climbed his way up onto the natural table.

The body didn't move for him.

He approached, knelt. And then for a full ten breaths, he saw nothing but a mangled, unfamiliar species of baleen weed. Because human flesh could never be this color or texture, and because a human body, mangled even to this degree, would still actively fight to cure its various ills.

Then the woman's mouth opened, exhaling once.

He fell back on his butt.

And she inhaled, slowly and with little effect, before her mouth pulled shut, her battered face turning back into the rough black weed.

For another ten breaths, the man could do nothing but sit, measuring the wounds but not bothering to imagine their history. He had seen worse, yes. Many times. But there came a point where the victim couldn't be helped. Not by the likes of him, no. True death might be exceptionally rare, but between the Eternal and the maimed lay countless states of near-extinction.

"Do you hear me?" he asked.

The mouth stirred, slowly pulling open. But only to manage another breath, supplying fire to what had to be a very thin metabolism.

The right arm was missing. Her belly was ripped through. Her left leg had been shattered by a hard impact, and the poor woman's flesh had been chewed and sucked dry, and then scorched by stomach acids. But worse than any wounds was her general health. Gingerly, he picked up the shattered leg and looked into the torn rancid meat. Human bone didn't break so easily. Not unless it was malnourished, and severely malnourished at that. And the remaining muscle felt soft and simple, squirming between his thumb and finger—a washed-out, iron-depleted tissue perpetually on its last gasp.

Two choices presented themselves.

Cautious by nature, he looked at both possibilities before making his decision. He retrieved his pack and quickly yanked out what he needed, and with small rocks as anchors, he pitched a shelter over his guest and his supplies, keeping the rain off both of them and allowing him the privacy to remove his mask.

The tide was coming back in now. He scanned the shoreline, wondering how many Nots were hiding in the woods.

"Stand guard," he told his friends.

The fanhearts scattered, granting him a small measure of quiet.

He had many blades and quality foods, but what counted here was simple. Inside an important satchel was a medical kit. Inside the kit were vials, each labeled in codes known only to him. By guesswork more than experience, he added a little powder from each vial, mixing them into a bladder half-filled with pure water. The concoction that he was mixing was worth an incalculable fortune. He put the ingredients together for the first time in ages, and then with a diamond dagger, he sliced deeply into the woman's chest and set the bladder against the new, unnoticed wound, counting the drips as they came, stopping with every fifty-five.

His patient did not move and her breathing didn't quicken, and for that matter, her breathing didn't slow any either.

But after two hundred and twenty measured drops, something changed. It was the stump of her missing arm that moved first. Which he expected. It twirled once and shivered for a few moments, and then the entire body passed into what looked like misery. He slipped the dagger back into her chest and held his hand against the hilt, waiting for the beat of a heart and measuring its sluggish force, counting the times it beat and pulling out the dagger again and added another portion of the metallic soup.

How long had his guest gone hungry?

And what kinds of brutal adventures had she endured?

Because he was very much out of practice, he spoke to her. She would hear few if any of his words, and the odds of her understanding his meanings were minimal. But making noise to a captive audience was easy, and more than he would have guessed, it was fun.

"Did a leviathan gulp you down, daughter? And did you make the poor bastard pay for his foolishness?"

Spasms shook her.

With three bare fingers, he reached into the gaping hole in her belly, measuring the ruined tissue, wondering which course was best.

Food, he decided.

He fed himself, pulling provisions from his stores and paying only minimal attention to what kind of food. Some dried finfair and glow-in-day meat and the sugary lackadaisical fruit, followed by a lump of cold wax from a grief nest.

As he chewed on the wax, one sunken eye opened.

He pulled the wax from his mouth and passed the lump over the double-pits of her chewed-off nose, and a random breath must have found the scent because her mouth opened, revealing starved little teeth, sickly yellow and widely spaced on a pair of pale, almost ghostly gums.

He stuffed the wax back into his mouth, chewed hard and swallowed.

And then he waited, counting the minutes.

Then he found the largest bowl in his pack and sat beside the woman, legs apart and the bowl between his knees. Vomiting was a difficult trick, but he had eaten too much and that helped his stomach agree to this purge. He threw up every morsel as well as the rich juices of his digestive tract, and then with a spoon and his free hand, he guided the feast into her gaping mouth.

The meal lasted all day and most of the night.

Sometimes he spoke to her, explaining the logic of everything. She was short of essential metals, which kept her constantly weak. Her body needed energy, but it had no working stomach. So he let his stomach do the hard labors, breaking bonds and reconfiguring the alien proteins, creating a stew that could be absorbed and transformed into fresh muscle and better bone.

He told her that she had somehow landed on his island. He didn't approve of luck, but he used that old word now, congratulating whatever conspiracy of forces had managed to place her here, and now she was safe and dry under his tent, and for the present moment, she didn't need to worry about anything.

He mentioned that he was very, very old.

Later, speaking in a whisper, he confessed that he was lonely and preferred his life to be that way. Other ways of living always turned out badly, and to prove that sorry fact, he told her a few stories that reached back across the ages. They were his stories, mostly. But he hadn't repeated them in a very long time, which made him wonder if they could be somebody else's tales, stolen by a sloppy old brain. Then he realized that he was feeling both wildly fortunate and exceptionally sad. And with that, the bowl of food and bile was drained and he was hungry enough to feed himself, sharing nothing with his unexpected guest.

That was in darkest part of the night.

The fanhearts were sleeping in their rookery, which was their right. And a new winter storm was building, winds tearing at the tent and the fierce rain drumming and his own voice lost when he told his patient his name.

It had been ages since he said the simple word, "Mercer."

If she heard him, nothing showed. She was shaking as if cold, but her half-dead body was hot as coals, and the stub-arm was as long now as a healthy hand, and the shattered leg had pulled close to her hip, bones meeting and gathering the necessary resources before attempting any new growth. Her skin was a bright red, almost glowing in the dark. And then her heat fell away, and the color left, and she suddenly lay still.

He pulled a fungus from its sack and blew on it, causing the flesh to glow brightly enough to illuminate the entire tent.

Carefully, he set a hand between his patient's breasts, measuring the beat and strength of the rebuilt heart. But she didn't stir, even when he groped her. Even when he cried hard and wiped his eyes with both hands. And then he lay beside her and took her new hand with both of his and closed his eyes and remembered back to the last time when he had slept this way, with another.

4

The first trace of day pushed its way through a gray-gold skin—the cured hide of an exceptionally large tattler, she realized. New eyes gazed straight up, investing their first moments in the careful study of a rope made from cured gut as well as the delicate, beautifully interwoven veins preserved within the taut fabric. Then she closed her eyes and examined her mind, astonished to discover that not only were her thoughts coming quickly and easily, but that every idea was relaxed if not happy. This was someone else's mind at work. Compulsive, enduring fear had been the spine of her life, but that had been stolen away, and she missed it. How she could survive until dusk without the cherished terror? Yet despite the stakes, she coolly and dispassionately wondered what force had done this damage to her, and how could she move through the world if she didn't believe that every step taken and every step avoided carried the possibility of tragedy and death?

Again she opened her eyes. But this time she ignored what she saw, paying strict attention to how the world felt through her new skin. She was naked. With her left hand, she touched the bare flank of her leg, newborn flesh still without hair and free of punctures and the muscle beneath as hard as it had been in a long while, if ever. Then her new right hand flexed, discovering fresh bones cradled inside a strong grip. Here was a third hand. Whose? She momentarily imagined that she must have recovered her stolen limb. Her rested, recharged mind took that single impossibility and wove an elaborate tale of revenge and victory. But then that third hand flinched, and she noticed the heat of a body close beside her, and very carefully, she turned her head to one side, discovering the dim profile of a man lying on the rock floor of the small shelter.

Suddenly her old friend, Fear, returned from its hiding place.

She choked off a gasp and killed the urge to leap up. She didn't know this face, and she had no idea how she had arrived here, in these thoroughly bizarre circumstances. She could imagine any scenario, and none would be right, and she might as well believe that this was her genuine life and this man was her mate and every misery and little success that she recalled was nothing but a dream.

The next wild moments were spent studying the man's nose and closed eyes and the occasional twitch of his wide, relaxed mouth.

His breaths were long and patient and exceptionally shallow.

Beneath the shelter—presumably his tent—the air smelled of exhaled air and body oils and subtle pheromones for which no name existed. A big, half-emptied pack lay just above her head. The slit doorway lay at her feet. Even for a human, the man beside her was large, longer than her by a good middle and thick about the middle in a fashion that she had never seen in their species. Dressed for cold weather, he wore full-length trousers and a loose shirt made from some kind of blackish Not fabric. His long feet and very large hands were bare. The rust-colored hair was shaggy and dense, woven into an elaborate rope that vanished between his back and the stone ground. His beard was thick and closely cropped. Like a corpse, he seemed unnaturally comfortable. Just once, he took a deep breath, and she lifted her head high enough to look down on his face, watching the wet balls of his eyes bounce beneath their brown lids, dreaming who-knew-what kind of dream while he slept unaware.

Silently, she reached across her body with her old left hand, one finger and the tip of the thumb gently touching both sleeping eyes.

He woke instantly, totally.

What charmed her, then and forever, was that he acted as confused as she felt, if only for a moment or two. Who was this woman? How did he come here? Perhaps they were equal in this fashion—two souls thrown beneath the same tent, lost together and joined together out of simple shared ignorance.

Who was thinking these thoughts?

Because the ideas couldn't be hers, she decided. In her busy brief life, the woman had never felt her mind slipping so quickly between subjects and possibilities.

The man spoke to her quietly, and he seemed to smile.

It took a moment to realize that she understood his words, despite the twisting accent and the unfamiliar voice. What he said was, "Hello," followed by, "How do you feel?"

She had never felt this way, so how could she answer him?

Then he said, "Mercer."

She opened her newly rebuilt mouth—the strong tongue pushing against fresh hard teeth—and with a voice that she recognized only to a point, she asked, "What did you say?"

"My name is. Mercer."

She repeated the word softly.

"And yours?"

She said, "Dream."

It was a little joke, reflexive and swift. She was telling him that she didn't believe any of this. But he seemed to accept her answer, lifting his head and turning his entire body. A second tattler skin, folded three times, served as their shared mattress. It squeaked under his bulk. He squeezed her newborn hand and then let it drop, reaching for her bare body and then stopping himself abruptly, pulling back the hand before repeating her new name.

"Dream," he said, with feeling.

Perhaps he didn't believe her, but he seemed gracious. She hadn't known many men, but even her thin experiences gave her reason to believe that this creature would either agree to almost any answer she decided to give, or he would believe nothing she said.

"Where am I?" she asked.

"Do you know the Lake-of-Lakes?"

A dim memory tugged. "Yes," she said.

"This is an island . . . the sunken backbone of an old mountain range stuck far out from the northwestern shore."

"An island?"

"My island."

She absorbed that odd news. "Who do you live with?"

Several responses seemed to have occurred to him. But instead of answering, he asked his own reasonable questions. "Where are you from? What family is yours? And how did you find your way across the water, in the winter, without any boat?"

An enormous story filled her head, but she told only what she remembered from her last conscious days. She ended with the giant eyes floating beneath her and a vast toothy mouth reaching for her helpless body.

"I think that river was the Ticklewater," he offered.

She had never heard that name before.

"What did your Nots look like?"

The farmers were narrower than most of their species, she recalled, and their flesh was a ruddy purple, and they seemed to have a fondness for cindercane and sapphire arrowheads. Then he asked about their tools and the construction of their homes, and she discovered of details waiting to be told, fueling what sounded like an expert opinion.

"They come from the Northern Clad," he reported. "Outcasts and now settlers, probably. Probably from one of the weak sect-families claiming some of those marginal lands."

She had always known that the Nots had relationships and a kind of culture, but the concept of "clad" meant little to her. And even though she had heard the term "sect-family," its subtle implications lay beyond her reach and her interests.

Genuinely baffled, she asked, "How do you know this?"

The man reacted with a shy smile.

Then he sat up, and with quick precise motions, he stuffed tools and vials into a variety of skin satchels that in turn had to be shoved inside the pack. She caught a glimpse of a rifle butt, but she couldn't be sure if a working weapon was attached to it. Two small pistols rode his belt, secured inside their holsters by cord and complicated knots. Between the pistols was a simple mask carved from nightwood, orange flourishes painted around the eye and mouth holes. He secured the mask to his face and then looked back at her, his gray eyes burning inside the orange slashes. "Stay here," he instructed. Then he climbed through the slit opening and pulled the pack out of sight.

She considered following after him, or maybe slipping out the back end of the tent and running away. But her impression was that Mercer was standing nearby, giving her this important opportunity to disobey him.

Twenty breaths later, he returned, dropping folded clothes at her feet, along with a second black and orange mask. A voice both happy and hurried told her to dress herself. He said that the mask was essential, and she shouldn't ask for explanations yet. And when she didn't quite hurry, he announced, "I want to go home now."

The clothes were his extras, far too large for her new body.

He stood back, watching as she dressed. Then with a quiet, almost sweet tone, he added, "I'll take you home with me and feed you, Dream. If you'd allow me that kindness."

She would. Yes. For the moment, why not?

Mercer dismantled and packed both tattler skins. Then they climbed down from a stack of brown corundum boulders, hurrying across a stretch of low ground that just a hundred breaths ago had been underwater. The man had no trouble carrying the enormous pack. With him in the lead, they fled the wet shoreline, crossing onto a wide apron where last summer's scrubtar gave way to winter weeds. Fanhearts were flying nearby, their screams rather different from how the mainland varieties would sound. For two breaths, the man paused to look off to the east, studying what seemed to be nothing but a tiny tangle of woods. Then he continued west, leading her toward an enormous half-built wall—corundum and slate and mudstone bricks stacked high enough to slow them, with upright poles giving the barrier the illusion of height.

On the other side of the wall, the world changed. Suddenly they were pushing hard into a dark wet realm that didn't seem to know either fire or the axe. They paused just long enough to remove and stow their masks. Then they began to walk with quick long strides. At first she assumed somebody had been hiding in those little woods that he had stared at. Unseen enemies were chasing them, their arrival imminent and worth avoiding at all cost. Why else move with such a quick, half-blind gait, hanging to the obvious trails? Why so thoroughly ignore the ground underfoot and the black canopy created by the tallest trees that she had ever seen? An army of Nots could be hiding inside these shadows; yet the man seemed to look at nothing but the ground ten or twenty steps ahead of them, holding what had to be a punishing pace. He acted oblivious to the world. Which made him a fool. She came to that uncharitable conclusion, and it would take days for that wrong impression to vanish, at least to where she wouldn't feel pity every time that she looked into his ageless, almost unreadable face.

On bare feet, they climbed through the ancient woods, reaching the crest of the hill exactly where it was easiest to cross. Judging by the noise, every corner of this wilderness was full of life. Croaking voices and singing voices and voices carried on wings constantly jabbered away, and sometimes the man would make his own little sounds, as if pretending to be a dewlane beast or some kind of buzz. She couldn't make sense of what he was saying, much less why it was worth the effort. Her savior might as well have been trading thoughts with the rain, as much good as it would do. But she didn't offer questions or betray any doubt with her newly reconstituted face. And perhaps Mercer was worried by the silence, because he paused suddenly on a wide, hard-worn portion of the trail. "Can I trust you to be good?" he asked.

"Yes," she lied, almost convincing herself of her honesty.

And perhaps he believed the weak promise. Though the half-grin hinted that no, even this peculiar fool had his limits.

Guarding that old trail were mounds and heaps that looked unlike anything she had ever seen before. She smelled death leaking from them, and between the gray leaves of widow fungi, she saw the glossy white remains of recent bodies. Animal

carcasses had been dropped here to rot. No, she realized, these weren't animal carcasses. She noticed a single dead Not laid on the pile, its narrow three-toed feet near
the ground and its badly decomposed face staring up at nothing, the soft protein-
aceous skull still emerging from the purple flesh, its complicated jaws pulled apart
to reveal the spine of what had been its own sexual member, jutting from the back
of its mouth.

She stopped, staring at that oddity.

"He was one of mine," said Mercer.

Her response was to glance at him and then stare again at the pile, trying to
count the bodies that had built this impressive feature.

"He was a good citizen," the man added.

"One of yours?"

Something in the moment was grimly satisfying. But he didn't offer explanations, preferring instead to ask, "What else do you notice?"

"Where?"

"Anywhere."

She saw everything worth noticing, while this crazed man was oblivious to the
most essential details.

"This trail," he prompted.

She hated to walk on foot-worn ground. No reasonable soul strolled down common avenues.

"Guess," he prompted. "How many feet created this trail?"

And when she didn't respond, he said, "Two feet. One pair. And how long would
you imagine it took that man to cut the ground this way?"

She watched him pull one long foot back across the yellowish corundum.

"I don't have a guess," she confessed quietly.

"Of course you don't. Only one living person knows how to measure that much
time."

"You know?"

He nearly laughed. But even then, he stubbornly refused to give explanations.
Again he walked, even faster than before now, and she followed the path willingly,
but with every step she tried to decide where she would jump if trouble came, and
where to flee, and if he didn't survive this day, how much of that swollen, burdensome pack could she carry on her own.

His home was buried inside a stubborn old hill. The front door was red and massive—a slab of native ruby rock protected by at least one booby trap that he took the
trouble to disable now. Then he slid the door open on a greased rail, revealing a
series of tunnels created by the careful blasting of faults and natural cavities. With
tangible pride, he mentioned that he had built his home by himself and added to it
whenever he had the chance, and in the next breath he asked his guest what she
thought about his humble sanctuary.

"I can see it," she complained.

Her critique was ignored.

"Every trail leads to it," she mentioned. Then she added, "Nots live this way. In
the open, easy to find."

Except she had never seen Nots that lived underground, much less built on such a colossal scale. And the idea that one man would need so much space, just for his body, was difficult to accept.

"Why did you do all this work?"

"You can't offer any guesses?"

She shook her head.

Most of the rooms were empty of furnishings or decorations, connected to one another but never by simple, obvious routes. The windowless places were lit by pampered stands of cool shadow-fighting fungi. Doorways and hallways and hidden dark chambers would probably cause a Not to become lost, and even an invading human might grow disoriented. Perhaps that gave this home's owner advantages inside here, she reasoned. But were those blessings worth all of the trouble?

"Security isn't my first purpose," he confessed.

He wanted her to beg for explanations. But instead she asked, "How long did it take you? To pile up all these rooms?"

His smile was broad and warm.

"On average," he replied, "I add one fresh chamber every ten years."

They had been walking through his maze for a long while, and not once had they crossed their path.

"How many rooms in all?"

"Would one thousand rooms impress you?"

It was an enormous, useless number—the kind of swollen figure that had never come into play during her narrow existence.

"I'm not impressed," she lied.

Then her mind dropped back to an earlier question. "How long have you walked your trail? To wear at the stone that way . . . how many years have you wasted marching the same few directions . . . ?"

They had entered a spacious room nestled deep inside the hill. Blue fires burned inside thick globes of glass, washing away every shadow. Electric currents flowed inside a variety of odd, seemingly magical machines. Unlike the air outside, this volume felt dry and pleasantly warm, little winds finding their way in and then out again. On every surface, she could smell the man. The furnishings looked used and treasured. Rock walls were softened with polished and oiled slabs of wood. Yet even in the middle of this castle-like arrangement of carved rock, she could hear the squawks and trillings coming from the surrounding forest.

"We'll live here and in these next two rooms," Mercer announced.

At last, he let his gigantic pack crash to the floor.

"My kitchen is fully stocked," he promised. "Whatever is to your taste is yours. Rest hard, and then I'll explain whatever you can understand."

"What can I understand?"

"That might take us time to puzzle out," he mentioned. Then he opened the pack and pulled out a short-barreled rifle—an ancient design, but with the carved butt that she had seen before and a grip coated with black plastic, the long magazine probably filled with explosive rounds.

She couldn't help but stare at the treasure.

"You still have wounds to heal," he warned. "It's going to take a lot of patience for your body to forget its old life."

"Are you leaving?"

"For the rest of the day, maybe longer." He gestured with the rifle's barrel, adding, "My bathroom is the final room. When you need to relieve yourself, go in the water-chair in the corner. Don't just shit on my floor."

Even in simple matters, nothing here made sense.

The man stepped into the hallway and then looked back at his guest, delivering two warnings. "If you wander anywhere, even for a short distance, I'll know. And eventually I will learn everything that you have done."

She didn't believe him. But she nodded, promising, "I'll stay here."

"And rest."

"Yes."

Then with a delicate menace, he added, "Humans like you have found their way to my island. And some of them, sometimes for a very long while, were my welcome guests."

Inside those words lay emotion, ageless and raw, and she knew enough to pay close attention.

"Where are those guests now?" she asked.

"Back to the mainland, I assume."

Then he snorted and laughed softly, and turning his back to her, he added, "Unless they've ended up where everybody ends up. Which is a place I don't know much about, and you don't know much about, and neither of us wants to learn the truth about it any time soon."

5

She wasn't an ignorant soul, regardless what her host might believe. She understood that the world swam away from the sun each year, the weakening light helping to trigger the cold and wet that was winter. And better than some, she appreciated how the transformation of life helped bring about each new season. In the blistering brilliance of summer, every lake and quiet river was covered with blackish blankets of knotted algae and bladderweed. Those floating jungles absorbed sunlight and its invisible mate, heat, and like a lid on a pot, the living skin trapped the rising vapors. Clouds soon vanished. Rain all but ceased. Forests sipped at their stockpiles of water, but by summer's end, the trees often burned. Yet the world always swam away from the sun again. The pall of smoke and fading daylight reached a trigger point, and that's when fish ate up the algae faster than it could grow, and that signaled the bladderweed to make its seed and then shrivel away. Now the world's water lay exposed to the desiccated air. Clouds blossomed in a single afternoon. The world suddenly grew cooler and darker. And then the winter storms began, racing across the land, drowning fires and slaking countless thirsts.

Her mother was an orphan and life-long wanderer, and she had taught her only surviving child everything worth knowing about their world. Imagine a round skull sporting two faces, she had explained. The face beneath their feet was covered with old mountains and mud flats, enormous shallow lakes and endless rivers. But the sibling's face carried less land, and every dry surface was rough and young, dotted with sharp peaks that needed no excuse to spit fire at the sky. Both skies shared the same stars and moons. But the other face stared up at a vast and exceptionally strange world. Being naturally proud, the Creator had saved its most startling colors for its largest child—distinct bands of earwish purple and human blood that were always in motion, endlessly swirling around bone-white clouds and bottomless holes that were bluer than even the youngest cindercane. Her mother had never seen that giant world with her own eyes, but she confidently described how their little home danced around it, and when the sun slid behind the giant's bulk, the best human eye could make out the flickering fires of storms—great silent lightning bolts powerful enough to incinerate all the world's Nots and all the humans too.

Their world was a moon, much the same as the two moons visible on clear summer nights. And her mother tried to explain to her daughter how the rock beneath their toes suffered as a consequence. Each swirling journey around the giant world made the sister moons jealous, and they worked together to crush and twist the old stone. They wanted to murder this world, but by tugging at its heart, their hatred made the heart beat. That was why there were quakes and geysers as well as the legendary fire-mountains. Though how moons could hate moons was a mystery, and more than once the young girl had been warned not to waste her head on questions that could not be answered.

One day Mercer asked what she believed about the sky, and then he listened carefully to her explanations for the seasons and the purpose of the gas world and the consequences of their sister moons' greed. He never made comments, not even with those expressive pale eyes of his. Then when she was finished, at last, he said, "All right," and leaned closer. "And what about everything else?"

"What else is there?"

"Beyond the moons," he said. "Please, Dream. Tell me what you think about the sky."

With a clear, certain voice—very much her mother's voice—she repeated the lessons of her childhood. The stars were suns like theirs, but most were childless. And between the stars lay nothing but black sand and the exhalations of the dead. With assurance, she told how any clear night revealed a vast, sterile realm. There wasn't any purpose in naming those distant lights. Except to find marks for navigation, watching the sky was a sorry waste.

Mercer seemed to expect those words. He shook his head and laughed weakly, and then he spoke to the floor, asking, "Where did this sad, useless model of the universe come from?"

"From my mother's mouth," she snapped. "And what do you mean? Why shouldn't I ignore what I don't need to know?"

He accepted her rebuff, smiling at nothing for a breath or two. Then with a soft coaxing voice, he mentioned, "We were discussing the weather. Every human has his or her favorite season. And yours, I'm guessing, is summer."

"Why?"

"Because I like winter, and we are rather different souls, it seems."

Lucky or wise, he was correct: She was born in the middle of a wildfire. Since then she had always loved the fierce, honest glare of each day. Given her choice, she preferred slinking through baked forests and oppressive glades, every piece of vegetation swollen with stored rainwater and fire-resistant saps. It was easier to spot danger when all life suffered equally. Even though the sun was a swollen monster and every tree was ready to explode into fire and ash, the living world always managed to survive, and wasn't that the greatest blessing? And of course the summer nights were bright, and by dawn they were tolerably cool, and a solitary human could enjoy good nights and the occasional great night as she made her way across the endless, enduring world.

But the sun always grew small again, weakening before it vanished behind the endless storms, and those cool gray times brought new threats and many more teeth.

"Fire," Mercer repeated, without reason.

She paused.

Then he spoke again, offering a single word that meant nothing to her.

"What was that?"

Again, he said, "Oxygen."

She waited for an explanation.

"This atmosphere is thick with the element," he mentioned. Then he winked, adding, "Which is only reasonable. There isn't enough iron lying about to cause any meaningful amount of rust. Not to mention all the ways this vegetation tears apart water and carbon dioxide, making odd sugars and churning out the oxidizers as a byproduct."

She studied his hairy chin, his bright gray eyes. The way his hands made a pair of cups, and the erect posture with which he filled a chair constructed from smooth rope and gray driftwood.

"Did your mother ever tell you?" he began.

Then he paused.

"What?" she finally asked. "Did she tell me what?"

"Where we came from," he said with a slow, serious tone. "The human species, I mean."

She knew three stories, each as unreliable as its siblings. Every explanation brought their species down from the sky. The Gold Moon was her favorite, if only because when the night was deep and that moon was full, she found herself wasting time staring up at its beautiful smooth face.

Either moon was their first homeland, she explained. Or they had climbed up from the world of gas and lightning. How her ancestors left any one of those places, and why they should come to this barely livable world, were unanswered, unanswerable mysteries. But she doubted the reasons were as simple as the old fables claimed—a trick played on the naïve humans by some malicious, unnamable god.

Mercer laughed gently, nodding as if he agreed.

"You have a different story to tell me. Don't you?"

"But not today," he remarked. "We're talking about the seasons now."

Except that she had nothing else to offer.

Mercer's smile changed. It was a subtle difference, but she recognized what lay behind those glad eyes and the healthy white teeth. He was smiling as men have always smiled at women, probably since the Creation. Staring hard at her eyes, pretending that his words had little importance, he whispered, "Winter is a good time for humans to conceive."

"Early winter is best," she added. "The baby arrives early in the second summer, when everything grows but nothing burns yet."

That lucky date had been passed, she was telling him.

Mercer nodded, pretending to accept her wisdom. But the smile remained. Leaning forward in his chair, the ropes creaked as his voice rose slightly, remarking, "I don't think you've been healthy nearly long enough. Not to conceive, much less carry the child successfully. Winter or summer, you're far too depleted to be fertile."

She had assumed as much, yes.

"We won't have to worry," he mentioned. "If anything should happen between us, I mean."

Something was going to happen. She had known it from the moment she woke beneath the tattler's skin. She could deflect his interest today, and probably tomorrow, but unless she was prepared to accept a frightful cost for her stubbornness, they would sleep together. So she did what she had done in similar circumstances during her busy, brief life.

She rose to her feet.

To this man, nothing was as real as the woman that he had saved on the rocky shoreline. Food and sleep had healed a body that had never been entirely whole before. She was a strong lovely creature with short black hair and eyes that made the hair seem pale by comparison. With him staring only at her, she pulled off the clothes that had been his but she had retailored to fit herself. Then in that rich, perfect instant when hunger and surprise were in rough balance, she mentioned, "I won't take any pleasure from this."

That was a useful lie.

Mercer suddenly acted shy—this strange ancient man full of stories that he never quite told. Leaning back in his chair, he managed to say, "You won't like this, will you?"

"But if it is a duty, I will comply."

He sighed as if injured. Perhaps he would change his plans. But then he stood and approached her, nervous and perhaps eager to impress, and before long he realized that she was not the passionless vessel that he had been warned about.

Later, as he climbed on top of her again, and then again, she saw in his wide eyes that he was intrigued, and perhaps in useful ways, he was a little bit impressed by what the ocean had brought to him.

6

The island was shaped like a short powerful arm, and the man's private empire stretched from the broad shoulder to the elbow—a rough landscape of high hills and brief winter streams too swift to be absorbed by the forest, each torrent plunging into cisterns or the deep water offshore. And on his ground, the man proved to be neither blind nor foolish. Not one speck of dirt was new to him. Every tiny change was noted and measured for importance. Each day, he took his guest farther and showed her more, mentioning tiny facts and offering anecdotes to help her see with his eyes. Fungi and griefs existed for no purpose but to give him easy meals. Every animal with a memory knew him by sight or by smell. There were only a few species of trees, but even the kinds that she recognized towered above the specimens growing on the mainland. Winter pushed ahead, the sun continued to dim, and the rain fell hard and then harder. Then one day the invisible sun seemed brighter by a little ways. Yet the season refused to weaken, its rains lashing down even as the clouds filled with sunlight and the first teasing hints of heat.

On the final ridge before the island's elbow, a giant magna-wood grew halfway to the clouds, providing a natural watching post.

One morning, Mercer invited her to crawl with him up into the tree, into a blind made of rope and wooden planks and camouflaging bark. A squall line suddenly passed over their hiding place, and they filled their time pleasantly enough. Then the storm was finished, and it was possible to see all the way to the island's far end—a long narrow and plainly fertile landscape that ended with crooked fingers with half a dozen black bays between.

"Look through here," he advised.

A tube hung on a cord. She peered into the tiny end, and suddenly the distant places were thrown against the back of her astonished eye.

Quietly, he explained the nature of light and how the clear plastic shells of young haphazard-bugs could be cut to size and polished, producing superior lenses that would bend light and magnify the universe around them. But oxygen always distorted the hydrocarbons, and these lenses had to be replaced each year. The gas was a frequent villain in Mercer's stories. She let go of the telescope and mentioned as much, adding, "For you, it's worse than the Nots."

That was an amusing observation. He laughed and winked, and then he took his own look at the island's far end.

She had heard about enormous Not villages—landscapes that were covered to the horizon with their willowy, skin-draped bodies. But she had never seen as many of the creatures as she had just then, peering through the shells of dead bugs. Giant houses were built close to dozens of wide, well-traveled roads, and between the roads lay fields where winter crops and young groves of wood were kept for lumber. Beyond the farms were stone buildings, some as tall as trees, and there docks and countless little boats not just floating in the narrow bays but riding the wind out into the open water, using the long nets that could never be deployed in summer. The inhuman, incomprehensible creatures numbered in the thousands, and if they were aware that two human monsters were watching over them, no sign of anxiety or hatred could be seen.

"My enemies," he whispered.

She sat close enough to feel the heat of his body. With unassisted eyes, she could see every piece of the Nots' realm. The telescope might have its value, but narrowing a soul's vision carried risks too.

"You think my neighbors aren't my enemies?"

"I know they help you," she admitted.

"And how do you know this?"

Now she had reason to laugh. "I see where you go when you leave me. Not every day, but sometimes. And you come back from these visits with things you can't find or make for yourself. Like last night's food."

They had feasted on real monster fare—green leaves and long white roots, bitter but rejuvenating, and fresh, and crisp, and precious.

Mercer said nothing.

So she guessed, "The Nots grow those plants for you."

He smiled.

She pointed, singling out the green smudge in a distant field.

"That isn't quite accurate."

"No?"

"Because of me, they cultivate those old weeds. That's all."

"What does that mean?"

"Our meal was an offering," he explained. "A good-natured attempt to earn my gratitude. At set times, a few of my neighbors approach the barricade to leave gifts at the feet of my likeness."

"What likeness?"

"Down there," he said, gesturing at the bottom of the hill. "You can't see it now. But it's a rather impressive statue."

"Of you?"

"As well as they can manage it," he mentioned. "Since none of them have ever seen my face and survived."

"All right," she said. "Name some other enemies."

"Oxygen, always," he whispered.

She gazed off in a new direction.

"By the way," he said. "Life did come from one of the moons."

"I knew that."

"But I mean the life that is not us. What we think of as the natives plants and animals." Mercer pointed his telescope at one patch of clouds, perhaps knowing where the moon was hiding. "For the first two or three billion years, this world was too hot, too volcanic. It remained sterile until a few spores drifted down here from the Gold Moon that you seem to like so much."

She hadn't expected this answer.

"Our original home can't be seen," he continued. "Not by any number of polished bug asses. But I promise you: our cradle didn't have as much free oxygen in its atmosphere as there is in this one. And if we had arrived here wearing our original bodies, we would have died. Since oxygen is always a little bit toxic, and in these doses, inevitably fatal."

That final word was offered with a loud voice and a sly tilt of the head.

She repeated one word as a question. "Fatal?"

"Long ago, we were rather like the Nots. Except for every detail, of course. We had a different home world and a very different history, and our future wasn't at all like theirs, and our outlook wasn't even remotely similar. Plus we enjoyed a huge array of technological wonders that we had invented ourselves or that we were given."

When she looked south across the open water, like now, she thought she could almost see the mainland lurking in the squall line. But that was an illusion. Nothing was out there but the watery horizon, Mercer had promised. The currents and then the leviathans had carried her an enormous distance, which was why this was an isolated and remarkably safe island.

"In our youth, we could and often did die."

"We can die now," she pointed out.

"But not like Nots die. Not like bugs and birds either." With an ageless hand, he dismissed everything that wasn't human. "In ancient times, a fall from this height would have shattered our bodies, and even if we survived, we'd have been crawling through our days as cripples."

"We are different than them," she conceded. "I know that."

He released his telescope to look at her eyes.

"We're aliens," she said, repeating one of his favorite words.

"How long have those Nots and I shared this island?"

"One hundred years."

He grinned. "Why that number?"

"It's about as long as they can live, or so I've heard."

"Clever," he admitted. Then he rephrased the question, asking, "When did Nots carve that statue of me?"

She offered a huge number.

He said, "Triple that number. And in human years too."

Which were twice as long as Not years, he had told her.

"In that long ago time, I came here. I discovered their ancestors inhabiting this ground, and for generations, we fought. I killed them, and they tried their best to defeat me. But our war eventually turned into something else. Something more. Larger and more subtle, and in ways neither side can define precisely, we have created a relationship larger than any hatred. Deeper than simple worship. More enduring than any love."

"Do you understand their language?"

"Don't you?"

She shrugged, admitting, "I haven't met anyone who does."

"Then why ask me that?"

"Because you know so much about the Nots down there. And apparently, you hear news about Nots living beyond the horizon too."

"My neighbors like to talk. Yes."

"Do they understand you?"

He smiled with pride. "By various routes, and only when necessary, they understand exactly what I am saying to them."

"Some humans pick a little village and terrorize it," she said. "But there's usually more than one human working together, and the Nots don't have the numbers or wealth that your little neighbors have."

"What do you see out there?" he asked.

"One of those bays . . ."

"Yes?"

"I don't understand what I'm seeing." She took the telescope, squinting at a line of stone barely holding itself above the high tide.

He seemed pleased that she was puzzled.

"I saw you talking to those friendly fanhearts of yours," she mentioned. "And then the flock flew out over the open water, moving south."

"On patrol," he said.

She considered what that might mean.

The man kept returning to the oxygen. "Once we were rather like the Nots. But then we learned tricks and improved our bodies and minds, and we left our green world for other places. Good, promising worlds."

She had no idea what he might say next.

"There was once a ship of human colonists, a boat built for deep space and bound across the emptiness. And for years and years, everything happened according to a very thorough plan. And then quite suddenly, nothing went right. There was a tragedy. There were regrettable mistakes. Those immortal humans had to watch helplessly as their new home was lost. Inside their injured starship, they could do nothing but push on and on, deeper into a realm without uranium, with little iron, and often without the elements essential to making a good human mind."

She listened carefully to each word. Who knew what would prove valuable tomorrow or in a hundred years? But she learned more by piecing together little clues and asking what he didn't expect.

"What do your fanhearts hunt for?"

The man smiled, but he was unwilling to answer.

"In the winter," she continued, "when the ocean water is open, I think strange Nots sail out this far."

"I can't remember a winter when they don't wander by."

"Why come here?"

"For every imaginable purpose."

"As raiders?"

"Some."

"And what do you do then?"

The gray eyes held steady.

She smiled. "This is what I think. Raiders attack your precious Nots, and they call up their resident monster to wreak vengeance."

He let her enjoy her imagined success.

Then he dropped his mouth to her ear, and with an intense and distinctly proud whisper, he mentioned, "These Nots, my Nots, have enemies. But what truly terrifies them isn't their own kind. And from what little I know of your life story, Dream . . . I think you know full well what murderous horrors make my neighbors beat the warning drums in terror."

7

A body might persist across centuries and millennia, healing from every injury and insult; and it was much the same for the personality trapped inside that tenacious, wondrous skull. Mercer had always been an organized creature, and in ordinary times he had been pragmatic and stubborn. But despite living a life that was strange by any measure, he was still the man that he had always been. Patterns mattered to him. Routine was his most reliable, trustworthy friend. And because he was an organized creature who kept thorough, precise records of the island's weather and the passage of its seasons, he knew at once that this auspicious summer had arrived eighteen days before the mean date for such milestones—an early heat by a considerable ways, though still three days short of the ancient and probably unbreakable record.

He woke in the dark and immediately knew why he was awake. With eyes closed, he smelled the drier air, and he heard the telltale noises coming through the ventilation pipes and distant microphones: scared scrubbers croaking and a male draconia begging for mates and the distant fanhearts warning their babies that the easy days were finished. For one sweet moment, he could remember every first summer night. It was as if those hundreds and thousands of milestones had been pushed together and supercooled, forming a condensate where each swam united with all; and for just that instant, it felt that if he could lie still with eyes shut, then perhaps he could inhabit every one of these promising days, forever.

But his eyes had to open, one illusion surrendering to another.

She was close beside him and hard asleep, and he wanted her to remain that way. But in his life, he had known perhaps only three people more alert than this wild girl. Unfamiliar sounds never seemed to pass unnoticed. An unexpected touch could startle, even scare. Obviously that was how she had survived in the world. But Mercer was possibly the most graceful person that she had ever met, and what he heard from outside didn't sound that different from last night's prattle. He managed to slip out of their bed, never disturbing her breathing, never interrupting the jittering eyes or the fearful dreams that they signified.

For an instant, he allowed himself the pleasure of staring at the woman's strong new body.

Then on bare toes, he moved into the darkened hallway, navigating by memory, climbing stairs and then a creaky rope ladder before entering an important room perched high inside his rambling, oversized house. His first chore was to find a sharp knife and slice off his braided hair. One haircut each year was his habit: It earned him a useful length of free rope and a cooler scalp for the coming season. Then he turned to the masks perched on the various shelves, organized according to a rigorous private code, each mask with its purpose, and its occasion, and a distinct aesthetics. Nots liked to see faces, which was why he kept his hidden—a visceral, instinctive unease always gave him a slight advantage. And they had sensitive, quirky eyes. Mercer selected a bold bright gigantic mask, and he opened a jar and used two fingers, surrounding the eyeholes with a radiant gel made from the guts of a roach-like bug found nowhere but in this island's caves. The gel lent the mask a wild, fiery glow, particularly in the near-infrared. Then he secured it to his face. Except for the giant mask, he wore nothing. He carried nothing. He was a fearless god, or at least he wanted to appear fearless. Then the naked god slipped through a hidden doorway, stepping out into a deep crevice and its secret path.

The strong south wind had pushed away every cloud, revealing a hundred thousand nameless suns. In principle, this summer could be a lie. It was possible that the wind would shift, winter returning tomorrow or the day after. But that had happened only once, which was effectively the same as never. Looking at the brilliant stars and the soft, clouded face of the Gold Moon, he knew the summer was genuine, and with it would come many hot days and drought, explosive fires and the possibility of new wealth.

"Poor in metal, rich in sky."

Who first said those words? One of the colonists had described their new world with that bittersweet phrase, probably during the first summer. But ancient memories, and particularly the trivial ones, were difficult. Was it Lota? Or Tesstop? Though it sounded like Ming. Unless of course Mercer said it, which wouldn't be the first time that he had allowed his ghosts to steal his best lines.

"Poor in metal, rich in sky," he whispered, breaking into a steady run.

The Milky Way was surrounded by thousands of ancient star clusters, and on occasion, one of the clusters would pass through the body of the galaxy—like a breath of dense smoke dropping through a thin wisp of fog. Disaster and lousy luck had pushed the colonists' ship past their target world and then past both of the viable alternates. They were riding a dying machine, streaking through a dense cluster of elderly suns. But there was one world in this difficult wilderness that had life as well as land and bearable water. Its lone sun was smallish and stable, and not even the most paranoid models saw any looming collisions with neighboring suns. Where the majority of the old local planets had lost their tectonics, this tidal-wracked body retained that critical blessing. But what made it their home inevitable was pure chance: They happened to spot the world with just enough time to spare, the last sips of hydrogen fuel placing them in orbit around the brown dwarf primary. One hundred and ninety-one colonists and crew were still alive, in one form or another. Most were grateful to finally escape the battered, inadequate ship. A rough little settlement was established near the equator, hugging a deep bay that would eventually serve as their harbor; and the colony's first fifty years brought nothing but measured successes as well as those good days when the community could tell itself, with honest conviction, that at least some portion of their hopes would come true.

But the scarcity of metal was an endless burden. With a starship's power and a hundred talented engineers, they would have slashed deep into this old stony world, wrenching free enough treasure to make up the shortfalls. But their ship little more than a stripped and starving hulk, and the mission's various disasters had decimated what began as a minimal engineer corps. These were inventive, intelligent people, yes. Ad hoc pumps pulled river's worth of seawater through atomic filters. Plastics and diamond were manufactured in impressive quantities. Their best biologists were little more than gifted hobbiests, but they were still able to manipulate a succession of earth plants, inventing new species that breathed the dense rich atmosphere. But then their main reactor failed for the final time, and a series of technical solutions proved miserably unworkable. After that, emotion ruled over reason. Decent people quarreled and eventually picked sides, and during one awful winter, most of the technological innovations and all of the deep decent thoughts that humans had brought from the stars were pushed aside.

Mercer survived that winter war, and he didn't suffer much during the following year's long rebellion. But an organized, pragmatic soul had to recognize the inevitable. Their tiny colony existed only as a name on a few unread maps. In another year, or perhaps two, the last shreds of organization would collapse. People that he had known for ages—friends and a few lovers—would try to murder him. Or even worse, those trusted faces would coax him into their battles, using smiles and implicit threats.

The colonists considered Mercer to be organized and passionless, and that's why he served as the semi-official shopkeeper. One summer night, a distant volcano sent a dense cloud of ash over the sky, covering the brown dwarf's glowering face. The shopkeeper used that lucky darkness to slip into various locked storerooms, collecting items of value. Then he made two piles of supplies, and he forced himself to leave the larger pile, stuffing the smaller one into a pack that he could carry without too much pain, and if necessary, run with.

Before dawn, Mercer abandoned the human realm. By then, there were only three working plasma guns. Each faction had congealed around its own murderous gun. What he carried was one of the broken guns, and if confronted, his plan was to bluff. And if that bluff didn't fool anybody, he had a diamond-barreled kinetic gun in easy reach. That would drop a few bodies, at least temporarily. People were already slow to heal, what with the shortages of calories and key nutrients. But fortunately there was no need to play games or to fight. No one noticed the shopkeeper as he slipped over the town's rock wall and ran down to the ocean's edge. One last time, Mercer paused and listened to the night breeze, some tiny piece of him believing that a woman had just called his name. But this was only another one of his ghosts speaking. The voice that he had heard, sweet little Deleen's, had been silenced last year, executed for undefined crimes against the irritable, ineffectual state.

The moons were down, the tide out. The summer skin lay against the wet shore, thick and hard as wood, and each stride felt momentous. He walked quickly until the blazing sun rose, and then after a long look at the flat terrain behind him, Mercer continued to walk, ignoring sleep and food for three full days.

Reaching this isolated chunk of land took years.

Alone, he had wandered countless places and watched whatever this world would show him, and on rare occasions, he had interacted with the sentient organisms called Nots by no one but his exceptionally rare species.

In despairing moments, he talked to his ghosts. His memories. Not to the dead colonists, but to people he had known in his previous life. Most of them were probably still alive, scattered across a thousand successful colonial worlds. They were thriving today, he could assume. In their comfortable immortality, those happy souls would eat whatever they wished and sleep without care, and when the mood struck, they could become experts in the narrowest, dreamiest fields. Undoubtedly a few old friends had studied their local sentients, learning curious secrets and sharing their findings with an increasingly human galaxy.

To his ghosts, Mercer often explained the Nots.

The biology of this place wasn't unique, but along many lines, it had pushed what was possible to the rational limit. Life here most certainly evolved on one of the outer moons. Since the White Moon was smallest and cooled first, it was the most likely candidate. But that world was little more than a titanic drop of water with mud and stone trapped at the core. In those depths, peptide nucleic acids were utilized for genetic material—built from the commonest elements, yet tough enough to withstand a wide range of temperatures and pH. Huge, cumbersome proteins were spawned. A patient metabolism must have evolved. Then some forgotten comet splashed into that living water, sending up storms of viable spores. Ten billion years ago, the Nots' world would have been a hot, sterile realm. The spores fell, and a precious few of them survived, and the subsequent ten billion years of natural selection had taught the invaders to use more of the periodic table, but not much more. In tiny amounts, iron was embraced. And phosphorus. And sulfur. But life is a perniciously conservative business, after all. With an abundance of free oxygen and water, living cells and their makeshift chemistries could afford to be inefficient. Even when the sea was covered with a deep, suffocating layer of living skin, plenty of dissolved oxygen remained in the depths, nourishing the minimal gills. And despite a steeply elliptical orbit, the world's seasons remained predictable. Carnage and small successes had led to an astonishing array of creatures, and those species continued playing hard at life, utilizing nothing but the same few, utterly functional ingredients.

Where the Nots thrived, humans struggled.

In their blood and bones, the colonists held the talent to endure huge abuse and repair even the most catastrophic wound. But magic was never free, and their particular magic demanded huge stores of chemical energy as well as most of the periodic table—dozens of elements far, far rarer than the ancient rust running through their arteries.

Tiny, sophisticated organs hid inside Mercer's ageless body, and he had never fully understood what any of them accomplished.

But they were vital, and they were shamelessly greedy. Those intricate machines relied on oddities like selenium and bismuth, terbium and silver, and in this diluted realm, sweat and pee and every lost drop of blood carried away what was essential and often irreplaceable.

Before the Nots' world, Mercer felt no particular interest in the workings of his heart and lungs. But after abandoning the colony, he had no choice: If he didn't replace his losses, atom by atom, and if he didn't build up reserves to carry him across the lean centuries, then his body would literally fall to pieces.

Success was never easy, much less inevitable. But the life that he had fashioned on this island, by himself and for the benefit of no one else, was an accomplishment worthy of celebration. Without hesitation, he would set his life story against the best in human history. There were days when his success felt boundless, and he couldn't help but smile with a smug, defiant pride. And there were summer nights, like this good night, when he was certain that he would never have to abandon this familiar ground or the fanhearts, or the Nots for whom he felt every emotion, including a deep, aching love.

He reached the barricade as the Gold Moon fell from sight.

Every Not had a simple but important calendar woven into its peculiar mind. To survive, Mercer had decided to plant himself inside his neighbors' consciousness, which included dividing their year into a string of memorable dates. Ages ago, the first night of every summer brought death. Masked and alone, the human monster would suddenly march out of the hills to terrorize the farmers and fishermen, slaughtering all those who dared fight him. Nots might be slow learners, but their most vivid memories were often transcribed into their genetics and carried into their offspring. He wrote on their souls, using terror and hatred as well as a god's endless patience. And by defeating his neighbors, he eventually taught those tiny creatures to accept and then embrace what was inevitable.

The Nots tried and tried and tried to kill the alien in their midst.

For centuries, they would send out their champions and their slaves, and they hired mercenaries who came here on the winter boats. The best of those professional killers had experience fighting similar monsters. The colony was lost, but their offspring were spreading across every landmass. Mercer was just the oldest of a dangerous breed. But he was a large strong opponent, and experienced, and he was fighting on ground that he knew better than anyone, and most important, he was far too shrewd to fool.

In the end, Mercer had the power to murder the last of the local Nots—a tiny population huddling inside a stone fort built in desperation, set far out on one of the island's distant fingers. He arrived there on the first night of a long-ago summer, but without warning or explanations, he showed mercy. In ways that even the simplest Not could understand, the human monster betrayed a charity of spirit. He spent half of that night marching circles about the fort. Then he suddenly slid his long diamond sword back into its scabbard and set to work, wrenching free one of the fort's smaller stones. A well-fed human, trained and rested, was stronger than six Nots. He carried that rock to the tip of the finger. The tide was high. He looked at the open water and then glanced back at the cowering faces, and when every eye was fixed on him, he threw the rock into the brackish sea.

Then he returned to the fort and claimed a second stone and threw it on top of the first.

In all, he tossed only a dozen rocks into the bay. At dawn, he strode back into his hills, back to bed in his small underground home again. And the Nots, misunderstanding his message, dismantled the fort and tossed every last block into the bay, creating a tiny second island.

That marked a momentous truce that held for a full year. Then the first summer night came again, and he returned and again threw rocks into the open water.

Gradually, very gradually, his intentions became clear.

Several generations of Nots grew old and died away, but the monster's arrival remained a linchpin to their year. Afterwards, when they began adding rocks to the growing cofferdam, he rewarded them with gifts of wild meat and planks sliced from one of the giant magna-wood trees. As he slowly learned their ancient, inherited language, and they learned about his mind, understandings were reached. Principles became law. A bright young Not paid close attention to this ritual with the rocks, and after making an intellectual leap, she managed to explain her inspiration to others. Ignorant of the science, they nonetheless finished the cofferdam before the water grew warm. With a hill's worth of packed mud, they sealed the bay off from the sea, even at high tides. And as the sun grew huge in the pale green sky, the bay evaporated, leaving behind nothing but thin white grime that their monster demanded for no conceivable reason.

But when two pirate boats came that following winter, Mercer generously slaughtered every last one of those invaders.

By then, no one but him could remember when dropping the ceremonial rock was not a tradition. Just once, Not youngsters got the foolish idea that they could kill the god while he was naked, unarmed and unaware. They took the trouble to ambush Mercer as he slipped through the barricade. But even with a couple arrows buried in his guts, he proved far more dangerous than any of those tiny fools. The rock that would have been thrown on the dam crushed skulls instead. He ripped off heads with his bare hands, and he stomped on squirming bodies, and cursing in their little language, he told everyone in earshot just how pissed he was, promising a hard long miserable summer in exchange for this undeserved treachery.

That was three thousand summers ago, and since then, nothing like it had happened again.

But for the glowing mask, he was naked: A fearless image striding onto the Nots' rich ground. At a random point, Mercer bent low, picking up a worthy stone. Then he began to run again, powerful ageless legs carrying him down a rocky lane that was created more by his feet than any of theirs. It was night still, farmhouses and apartment buildings dark with the hour. But he knew that most of his neighbors were awake and watching, hiding out of respect more than fear, but their inherited fear never quite removed. Before dawn, he would run out on the same fingertip of land and throw the rock on top of the well-repaired dam, and if there was time, he would examine the various flumes and subsidiary dams that helped increase the production of salts and other precipitates: The summer's treasure destined to fill a few dozen jars that he kept inside a locked room hidden in his forbidden home.

Summer had arrived, and at a perfect moment like this, there was no reason to suppose that the next billion summers didn't belong to him as well—a balanced and endless life that would outlast human civilization and perhaps his species too.

Eventually this cluster of old suns would abandon the Milky Way. Hotter, richer stars would blow up and die away. But here he would remain, running down a tame road not too different from this road, while above, in the increasingly darkening sky, the last relics of the universe steered inexorably toward the Cold Death.

8

The world was bathed in sunlight. Not one winter cloud remained, and for the first days of this exceptionally early summer, the surrounding sea was brilliant and clear, cold to the eye and to the touch. But when the surface water warmed just enough, countless spores and seeds were shaken awake. One calm afternoon saw the transparent water fill with blue-black ink, and the following night brought the calming glow often called summer-milk. Furious biochemical reactions created that wistful silver-white light. She already knew this, but Mercer was full of obscure details and a willingness to share everything he knew. Thrilled with the sound of his voice, he happily explained how nothing mattered to that watery vegetation except to be near the surface once the summer bloom was finished. For heatweave and kather, and in particular, the giant ocean bladderweeds, the goal was to be planted on the very top, sooty-black leaves to the sky. For cooperative fickles and tuts and old-henry-balls, success was to supply the foundation for this buoyant, closely packed jungle, their deep roots pulling up the water desperately needed by the sun-broiled canopy.

The origins of this elaborate system mattered. Mercer claimed as much, and she offered agreeable noises whenever he glanced her way. But when he spoke about evolutionary pressures and microchemistries and the wondrous vagaries of chance, her mind wandered. Her life—what little there had been of it—had depended on hard, determined effort. The vagaries that mattered were her next meal and a stolen knife or two, and with luck, some hidden shelter where she could sleep for ten thousand uninterrupted breaths. She never needed to know how this rigid black summer skin spread across the world's water, or where it grew best, or precisely how an array of simple, catalyst-impoverished organisms managed to build such a marvel out of light and air and drink.

Mercer still used her joke name. "Dream," he called her. And she let him, since the past didn't matter except when its lessons allowed her to reach the future. And by future, she meant only her next few days, or in her most expansive moments, the rest of this unexpected summer.

From a dozen vantage points, she gazed out at the fresh skin of the ocean, judging its thickness and its rigidity, and most important, how far from this long rocky patch of land it had managed to reach.

There was open water to the north, she observed.

"A deep cold current runs out there," Mercer reported. "A polar current. By mid-summer, you won't see water. But the skin never gets thick, and the mix of species changes constantly."

South was a more interesting direction.

"How close is the mainland?" she asked.

He offered one of his ludicrous figures, using a measurement system that still made no sense to her.

She glanced at him, frowning.

And he laughed, and winked, and then only with his face, he revealed the first traces of concern. "As I told you, Dream. The continent is a very long distance from us."

"But will this skin reach all that way?"

"Maybe," he allowed. "But there's an undersea canyon between us and the rest of the world. And several big rivers keep the currents pushing. In your average summer, the skin finishes late, and it's never stable or strong."

"But you keep saying: This is a hot early summer."

And when he didn't reply, she asked, "Does the sea-skin ever come early enough and grow hard enough to let everything that wants to walk, walk?"

She was wondering if she could leave the island.

But Mercer didn't understand her thinking, or he chose to ignore it. "Since I've been living here," he quietly reported, "this island has been joined to the continent five times. Five different summers."

So many thousands of years had passed, yet he knew the precise number. She had no doubt that Mercer could tell stories about each of those long summers. But the topic was too speculative to hold her interest, which was why she said nothing else, staring out across the flat black face of the sea.

She wasn't stupid. Mercer said as much a little too often, as if trying to convince himself. He liked to explain how her brain was nearly the same as the one he carried inside his hard old skull. Between their ears sat a bioceramic wonder—the culmination of design and evolution. Even if the flesh was peeled from her bones, and the bones themselves were burnt and crushed, her brain would endure. Impacts and chemical explosions meant nothing. The hottest fires were ignored. Nuclear temperatures were required to consume what held her soul. Mercer mentioned that there used to be murderous weapons called plasma guns, but the last of them were disabled ages ago. Nothing in this solar system could manage that kind of blaze, unless it was the sun itself.

With similar minds, they had similar talents.

Though her head was emptier than his, he might mention . . . speaking of past experiences as well as a multitude of bad old habits.

"Five difficult summers," he allowed.

Winter meant open water, and water brought boats. But they were usually small craft piloted by lost fishermen or raiders navigating through the starless rain, using the taste of the land to guide them here. For the island, summer brought relative peace. Yet this year was the exception, and the water barrier would soon vanish. And just as critical, life on the mainland was going to be hard. The heat would be brutal. Cataclysmic fires would push through the interior. What if all the Nots in the world one night dreamed of escape, and then every last one of them decided to march across the water, hunting for safer land?

And Nots weren't even the most dangerous threat.

Mercer said as much with his southward glance, lips tight and one hand playing with the red stubble of his hair.

The girl woke early that next morning, alone in bed, and after a pissing into the special wooden bowl, she tracked him through his enormous house. Using scent and toe prints in the dust, she found her way to a huge yet cramped room normally hidden behind a bland beige slab of corundum. Here was Mercer's armory—an enormous stockpile of weapons of every age, every design. On the racks and deep shelves and stacked in neat, scrupulously organized heaps were enough implements to make an army of killers. Slaughtering Nots was usually easy work. A long blade of tempered glass proved effective in most circumstances, particularly when wearing the nanoarmor that hung from high hooks—breastplates and helmets, breeches and leggings designed to shrug off all but the worst blows from the natives. But something—an intuition; a nightmare; some private voice—had compelled Mercer to clean the firing mechanisms and test the aim of several fancy, terrible weapons that she understood too well.

With a fingertip, she touched the diamond barrels and plastic triggers and the carved wooden stocks that fit against only a human shoulder. Some instinctive piece of her was scared, warning her that she didn't belong here, begging her to flee before the ghosts of this place woke.

Mercer stared at the rifle in his big hands. "Last night, I had an exceptionally lousy dream," he confessed.

"Dreams have meaning," she told him.

He made a rough, dismissive sound.

"They tell you what you won't hear any other way," she assured.

"And it's always the same message. You're worried about something real, and your mind finds a lazy way to remind you."

"In my dreams," she began.

Then she hesitated.

He closed the rifle's breech and looked up, watching her eyes. More out of politeness than curiosity, he asked, "What about your dreams?"

"That's how the dead speak to us."

He looked almost relieved. "You believe that?"

"My dead speak," she continued. "My mother, and others too."

"Memories," he said with a shrug. "That's all they are."

"No, no," she insisted. "They come from the Afterlife."

He repeated the doubtful grunt.

But not a whisper of skepticism lay in her voice. "The dead come to help me find my way."

Mercer wanted to laugh. She saw that in his careful face, in the hard grip of his hands. But he decided to push the topic back to where it began. "I don't want to worry you. And probably nothing will come of this. But today, before anything else, I want you to find three good guns that fit your body, your tastes. Your talents. This is a haphazard collection, but I can adapt my munitions. Whatever you choose, we will make it work."

Most of the guns belonged to distinct, easily recognized species. They could be grouped by age and shape and the quality of their materials, and by the quirky designs of their barrels and firing mechanisms, plus the occasional flourish left behind by famous, nameless builders, all of whom were long dead. Humans had spread across this world, but they were never common. Few had the skills, much less the tools, to create machinery like this. But there were the occasional lush times, and the gifted crafts-man would outfit an extended family and even its allies. As a rule, these weapons were tough, easy to repair and deeply cherished. In her life, she had held three guns, only one of which was loaded. But inside this room, she counted a hundred guns and then stopped counting. Each one could throw a kinetic round or an explosive charge over long distances. In a marksman's grip, they would disable their target by shredding muscles and organs and temporarily shattering every human bone.

"How many have come here?" she asked.

Mercer pretended not to hear.

"How many of us have you have faced?" she persisted. "Do your dreams re-member?"

Given any choice, he would evade that question. But then he looked at her, just for a moment, and she saw several emotions swirling behind his eyes, including a self-astonished pride.

"Three hundred and thirteen," he allowed.

"They walked here?"

"Some did." He nodded. "Most came in winter, sailing their own boats. But our species has more trouble than Nots do when it comes to navigating without stars or good maps. Besides, my fanhearts always spot those raiders first, and I'm usually waiting for them when they make landfall."

She watched his jaw tighten, eyes narrowing.

"Summers are worse," he allowed. "Fanhearts have to fly north to feed over open water. So I don't have the usual eyes. And with clear skies, the humans can know where they are heading, and if they also have a plan . . ."

His voice trailed away.

This ancient creature was a marvel: By his admission, he had defeated more than three hundred monsters, and he had survived every battle, managing to steal away their weapons and ammunition and who knew what other tools that had been car-ried here from the distant coast.

She wondered what was lurking inside the other locked rooms.

But she didn't ask, turning away from him, pulling a particular gun off its wooden rack.

Behind the rack sat a row of thick glass tanks, filled with something green, each topped with an elaborate valve.

She touched one tank.

"Don't," he cautioned.

She pulled her hand away slowly.

"Chlorine gas," he explained. "Awful, wonderful stuff. It would force our bodies into alternate metabolisms, and we'd have to regrow our lungs before we could take a normal breath again."

She nodded, wondering where the gas came from. "Is it for Nots?"

"If there's a lot of them, and if the wind offers to help me."

She nodded without comment. The gun in her hands had a long thin barrel, designed to send a tiny charge across considerable distances. The diamond barrel had a trace of yellow, and it was slick on the outside, and she knew immediately which species of gun this was.

"That's too big for you," he mentioned.

Too big by a lot, she thought.

"You'd be happier with something stubby. Accurate enough, but small, and with a lot more punch." He stopped working long enough to pull two candidates off another rack.

But she kept staring at the weapon in her hands.

"I saw two guns just like this," she mentioned. "And not that long ago."

"Where was that?"

She smiled at him. "Where did this come from?"

"The same as every other gun. From the mainland."

Mercer might know quite a lot about the Nots, understanding their clads and sect-families. But the politics of human monsters seemed rather more mysterious to him.

"After you destroy their bodies," she began.

He waited, and then asked, "What do I do with them?"

"With those immortal brains, yes."

They watched each other's face.

She was a tiny, tiny fraction of this man's age, and she lacked his experiences and all of his hard-earned wisdom. But her life, such as it was, had taught her what mattered most. With confidence, she said, "If I was in you, I'd take everything that I could use of them. Everything. Then I'd walk out on the sea with their heads, and where I knew it was very deep, I would tie rocks to them and cut a hole through the water's skin, and I'd drop them down where nothing would ever find them."

The man flinched.

Then with a tone edging near embarrassment, Mercer admitted, "I've considered that. A few times. But it seems like too much."

"So what do you do?"

With the wide barrel of what would become her favorite gun, Mercer pointed at the floor. "I have another room, a special room," he admitted. "Where I keep their skulls, labeled and safe."

Flashing a little smile, she asked, "Where are they?"

"No." He spoke quietly, yet the voice could not have been sharper. Some line of trust was being defined. "Dream, no. Never. And please don't ask me that again."

9

She watched the dense black skin cover the sea, and she didn't quit asking herself when would be the best time to run. Because she knew that she couldn't stay in this little place forever. A summer as remarkable as this might never come again. Yes, she was thriving for now. Her body had never been so healthy or felt half this strong. But to stand two moments on the same patch of rock felt unnatural. The life that she knew—the hard, inspired, honest, unburdened life that her mother had taught her—beckoned. Perhaps if this Mercer man were ordinary, or even just comprehensible, she would want to linger. But he was different from any human she had ever known—a strange and unimaginably ancient creature, secretive beyond all reason and far too in love with his ancient ways.

When Mercer wasn't working, he was busily thinking new projects to attack. In his home were rooms filled with vats, and he would build hot fires and breathe the smoky fumes, enduring that misery while he refined some peculiar metal or semi-conductor or odd salt. In the depths of the hill were a series of connected rooms filled with the turbines that gave light and electricity. One distant room, isolated and sealed, was where he made his fresh explosives and special, Not-killing poisons. One great long chamber was his "shop", and it was full of complicated machines that did little more than sleep. But occasionally he would wake one of the machines, using it to repair some broken device or shape a useful piece of sapphire or build an entirely new machine that had no function except to impress his guest. He even boasted that he could weave nanofibers and culture pure diamond, although he didn't presently have the time or need. And of course he was constantly leaving her, for a day and sometimes for longer, attending to one of the nameless but very important tasks that involved his Nots or the surrounding sea.

It was a time-eating burden, being the monster deity.

But when he returned home again, Mercer enjoyed his rest. Sitting on a chair or in their shared bed, he loved to reach inside his cavernous head, offering another tale about vanished ages and invisible worlds. As a rule, his stories had no ends and usually no discernable lesson. Often they were little more than noise. Yes, the old man was unquestionably bright, and his life on this island was an astonishing accomplishment; but sometimes she wondered if the human mind wasn't as durable as he claimed: Some kind of erosion or madness was infecting his soul. He had become such an expert at living one very narrow life that he couldn't see his sorry decay, much less conjure up any fresh answers to questions long set aside.

And the man had his rules: Some were small, others enormous, but they were usually unbreakable. He didn't want her crossing the barricade, ever. Which was fine, since she wanted nothing to do with his precious Nots. But there so many rooms that she couldn't enter either, and so many topics that were strictly forbidden. She didn't need to know anything about the original human colony. The names of his old friends and lovers couldn't matter less to her. But knowing that she was forbidden to ask about his Dead only made her want to know more. And worse still, Mercer began to control what she ate and how much. That was for the sake of her body, he claimed. And maybe he was right. But even when she was a child, no one had so thoroughly defined her life. Even her mother had let her explore and make her own spectacular blunders, preparing her daughter for that day when every last taboo would be lifted.

The girl didn't often guess at the future, but when her mind drifted, she could imagine herself remaining here for years, and perhaps many years. But the next instant always brought an obvious, dangerous question: Why would a man such as Mercer live alone? She wasn't the first woman to find her way to his front door and not make herself into his enemy. But he was evasive when telling her how many others there had been. With words and long glances, he implied that every guest eventually returned to the mainland. But she had to wonder what happened if the love had turned sick. Maybe those past lovers hadn't left him. Maybe their bioceramic brains were labeled and stacked inside the forbidden tomb.

Her working plan was to wait until a few days before winter, and then slip away without warning. That's why she stole nothing but tiny items that wouldn't be missed. Yet she compiled a longer list of treasures—items too important to leave behind—and when the time came, she planned to grab them up too.

There was a favorite rifle that threw big explosive rounds, and a quiet pistol that fired kinetic rounds, and she knew a sack already filled with both flavors of ammunition.

She planned to steal vials from his stocks of minerals, but only a sampling of the full inventory—if she were too greedy, she reasoned, then he would probably have to chase after her.

A tattler skin shelter.

Tools, of course.

Spare clothes.

And enough dried piss-fungus to keep her belly full for thirty days. If she could carry all of that, she resolved, and if she reached land before the storms and darkness descended, that would ensure an easy winter and a better summer than any she had ever known.

As long as she kept her guns and used the ammunition sparingly, she would be a powerful force in the worlds of Nots and of humans.

If if if if if . . .

But which country was best? In her head was a loose conglomeration of facts and offhanded words that came from every voice she had ever heard. But there was a painful lack of precision. What she needed was a map, drawn out and defined in terms that she could understand. She had owned and lost a few simple maps in her days. In Mercer's living quarters was an odd machine that showed images that resembled maps. The lines and incomprehensible writing always made her eyes ache. But when he left one morning on some grand errand, she set to work trying to memorize some kind of maze—an interwoven array of tunnels and rooms far larger than his little house. But the only image resembling a world proved gray and dry and strangely smooth, save for a few odd mountains standing high above one hemisphere.

By some means or another, Mercer discovered what she had been doing in his absence, and he was pleased. That smooth world seemed to be another one of his endless fascinations.

"What is this object?" he asked, bringing the gray world back onto the screen. "Any guesses, Dream?"

It was obviously important. But since Mercer responded best to ignorance, she shrugged and said, "No. No guesses."

"I came from here."

"Is that the earth?" she asked doubtfully.

Her response saddened him. He shook his head for a moment before saying, "It's not a world. It is a starship."

"You came here on that ball?"

"Hardly."

She waited, knowing the rest would soon emerge.

And it did. For a long while, he talked about an ancient, empty vessel found drifting between the galaxies, and he explained how humans had claimed it for themselves and then took their glorious prize on a long circular voyage around the galaxy. He had ridden inside that ship for a long time, and then in a much, much tinier vessel, he had come here.

"This ball moves in a circle?"

"If it's still on course," he said. "Yes."

"So it will eventually find us here," she concluded.

He shook his head. "The starship never came this way to begin with, and I doubt that its captains would be interested in a place as remote and impoverished as this. I'm sorry."

"Why are you sorry? Are your hands steering this fat ship?"

"The Great Ship. That's its name."

Which was not much of a name, she decided, in secret. With a dismissive shrug, she pointed out, "Whatever this ball is . . . if it isn't coming back here, then it might as well not exist . . . and why waste your time thinking about it . . . ?"

It was her mother who warned her that she was going to have a baby. And in that same urgent dream, she told her that the child was destined to die. But then the dead woman laughed, reminding her that every child meets that fate. The trick was to feed both of them well enough to assure a strong birth, and then she should teach her son—and it would be a boy—everything of practical substance. Then if the boy were fortunate as well as strong, that sorry last day could be avoided for the next thousand hard and wondrous years.

Then the young woman woke, discovering that it was the middle of the night, the man lying close beside her.

Now what?

Her first instinct was to run and run now. A life of ceaseless wandering demanded nothing less. But she was trapped, at least for the moment. Caught in the bed of this slumbering giant, she had no choice but keep still, breathing softly, carefully considering her reasons for whatever she did next.

Nutrition was everything for the developing fetus.

Mercer could lecture for days about tiny, nameless organs and essential rare-earths and how exceptionally difficult it was for a body to build a new mind. But she didn't need fancy ideas to appreciate how selfish and rude the unborn were. They absorbed the wealth from every bite of food, every sip of water. And if that thievery weren't adequate, they would happily reach inside their poor mother's bones, stripping away her own reserves of precious elements.

Every pregnancy was a tiny war, and when one side dominated too well, both fighters could perish.

Her mother had carried at least ten fetuses during her life, and she had used all of the reliable tricks, including sucking the sweat from her clothes and drinking her own urine. Of course she ate as much as possible, which meant some disgusting and dangerous foods. Yet only one of the ten fetuses survived into adulthood. Three siblings died as malnourished infants. The other six developed too slowly, and when famine struck, their living home had no choice but to stop the pregnancy and reabsorb what could never be finished.

Remain with Mercer, and there wouldn't be any famines.

But this was his island, his home. In so many ways, she was the stranger in a forest that knew him by sight, and she couldn't imagine that day when she wouldn't feel like the ignorant, dependant guest.

Stay here, and her child would almost certainly become an adult.

But to what end? One child might be the first of five babies, or fifty. There would come a day when the fat land and its surrounding water wouldn't feed their family. In boats and on foot, her offspring would have to return to the mainland—attempting to survive in a busy, dangerous realm for which none of them were halfway prepared.

But if she returned to the mainland now, armed and strong, she had a respectable chance of seeing her first child grow into the life she knew best—a wandering, inventive existence that would survive long after this piece of land collapsed into the tide-swept sea.

Mercer was a fluke.

He was a species of one.

What she felt for him was too fresh to weigh, too weak with all the gaps and wise questions. On the matter of children, she didn't know what his opinion might be, with her, or for that matter, with any other woman.

But she couldn't ask. She didn't dare. Not without alerting him to a host of uncomfortable possibilities.

Hard thought led to one half-viable tactic. Then she lay awake until dawn, and when Mercer woke, she offered her fond hands and mouth, making love to him before lying on his long bare chest and belly, her knees tucked and her new hand drawing circles in the dense rusted-red hair on his chest.

"When will we tell them?" she whispered.

He heard the question, but the words didn't seem to make sense. A long moment of concentration was needed before he asked, "Tell who?"

"Your Nots."

"And what are we telling them?"

"That I'm here." She looked at his face, and when he finally returned her gaze, she smiled. "I'm living here with you. We should announce that two gods are now ruling over this island."

He said, "Soon," with his mouth.

But nothing else about him seemed sure.

"And I want to make my own mask," she persisted.

He said nothing.

"And I want to walk beside you," she continued. "Past the barricade, right down to the bay where the big buildings stand. I want every last Not to see the two of us together, holding hands."

"Not yet."

"When?"

"I'm not sure."

"Why not?"

"Because they aren't ready."

She paused long enough to make him believe that she was considering that weak answer. Then with less of a smile, she asked, "When will they be ready?"

"Nots are more instinct than culture. More ant than man." His own instinct was to lecture, perhaps to explain what an ant was. But then he doubted himself. Being the teacher wouldn't help, and in a rare moment of self-restraint, he stopped talking.

And she surprised herself. Her first reaction was to feel fire surging through her body. Who would have guessed that jealousy would be her response? Jealousy directed at a pack of Nots that seemed to possess this strange old man? Then she surprised herself a second time when she remained silent, choking back the justifiable anger, keeping it hidden behind a wide, meaningless but very believable smile.

"Everything on this island hangs in a balance," Mercer said. "Forces match forces, genes guide every important thought, and I'm not at all sure how they would react if they saw us walking as equals."

She gave him a few moments to believe whatever he wanted to believe.

Then she quietly reminded Mercer, "Nothing is balanced. The world only pretends to be, darling. And most of us are waiting for chance to throw everything out of whack."

Three days later, fanhearts that had been feeding over the open water to the north and west returned home with important news. Nots were walking across the sea's skin—a multitude of strange Nots, if those chattering voices could be believed—and they seemed to be marching for the island.

Mercer appeared ready for the news.

He spoke to his friends, deciphering distance and speed. Then he dressed in armor and selected a few weapons before telling the girl he would be gone for at least one night and probably two. "I'll turn them before they get close," he explained calmly.

She nodded, saying nothing.

"I want them to run home scared," he continued. "I want stories told that will frighten their descendants for generations."

"I'll wait here," she volunteered.

They kissed, and he left.

She counted five hundred breaths and then dragged a big pack out of its hiding place and finished collecting the various treasures that had to carry her and her son for the next year or two. Then with the pack on her shoulders and her rifle in one hand, she passed through the front door. She felt the forest watching her. Every tree was swollen with last winter's rain, but the dark air beneath those high branches was hot and treacherously dry. To be fair to Mercer, she took time to seal the stone door, and then she set each of the three booby traps that would stop the curious and delay the malicious. Then she believed that she was leaving. But stepping onto the footworn path, she remembered a final treasure that was far too tempting, and she changed course.

In the high heat of summer, the magna-wood bladders were inflated with watery saps, each one of them close to bursting. She dropped the pack and rifle, muscling her way up the rope to the watching post. The bladders squirmed under her toes, and ripe fire retardants leaked through the pores, saturating the exceptionally dangerous air. She coughed some. Then she reached the hidden post and wasted a few moments staring across the Nots' half of the island.

Little moved in the blazing, shadowless heat. The green crops had been harvested or they had died. The Nots' summer crops were black and tall, patient hands having killed every weed and unwelcome mouth. With the little telescope, she studied the long bay with its mouth jammed full of rocks and mud and mortar, the trapped water halfway evaporated. That stagnant pond had to be bitter with salts by now. She saw Nots working on the dam, struggling to patch some tiny leak. Then she panned to the right and the left, and in the bright space alongside one building, she noticed perhaps a thousand Nots enjoying the last of the day's brutal light.

With her new diamond knife, she cut the little telescope free.

Then she climbed down fast and shouldered the pack and hurried toward the south. Out from under the trees, the sun was enormous and fierce. But the day was nearly finished, and the blistering heat wouldn't grow any worse. She was soon shuffling across the sea's skin, making even better time than she had hoped. The footing was excellent. Except for the occasional muted wave, the sea remained still. The tides lifted the entire skin and then let it drop again, but all of the world's water was obeying those stately motions, and when the sun was gone, she broke into a slow but determined run.

It had been a lot of days since she felt any fatigue.

The sensation proved pleasant, like a cherished friend returning on cue. The ache of her legs and her shoulders helped keep her awake through the night. The heat faded, but only to a point. And then the sun returned as a broad red glow breaking across a flat horizon.

She paused to drink and rest, sitting on her swollen pack.

The glow brightened, and the sun's face emerged, brilliant orange light licking across the black surface of the world.

In the distance, on the brink of visibility, she saw dots.

One dot, and then two more.

Then she counted again, making out ten distinct objects moving lazily along the horizon.

If she could see them, then she might be visible to their eyes. But a stand of some purplish parasite grew on the skin's surface—a watery little tangle of limbs and seed pods that she didn't know—and moving slowly, she dragged her pack behind the inadequate cover and sat again, guessing the distance and counting her breaths as she waited for this second band of uninvited Nots to pass out of view.

Either they were closer than they looked, or they were moving faster than she expected.

The sun was hanging free in the sky when they passed north of east, and it would have been easy to pick up her pack now and march on, confident that no one would notice her. But she had stolen the telescope, and it seemed important to use what belonged to her, particularly now that she wouldn't have to stare directly into the sun. Setting the device on a knee, she looked into the eyepiece and pulled the inner tube out until the focus was found, and for a long while she didn't breathe—she forgot to breathe—and then her body begged for oxygen and she managed a deep gulp and steadied her arm and the leg and closed her extra eye and bent down again, fighting to get the focus just so, counting the bodies until she was certain of everything, except what she would do next.

10

On the perfectly flat terrain, Mercer had the tallest, farthest seeing eyes.

And his first glance was enough.

The Nots belonged to one of the fishing sect-families—they could well be the entire family, judging by the drag-carts and youngsters and the purplish-black sun-boiled exo-skins. He found them at midday—dozens of motionless lumps scattered across a random stretch of the sea's skin. Each had its poncho-like skin spread out as widely as possible, the adults forming a tidy ring with their faces watching outwards, protecting their possessions and the little ones who slept in the middle. Only in the summer, and at this high latitude, only near noon, was there enough light to thoroughly feed the hungry Not. If mayhem was the goal, his timing was perfect. Lob a few incendiaries into the middle of them, and the rest would panic along predictable lines. After all, Nots were simple, reliable souls. He had lived close to them for thousands of years, and when was the last time one of them had managed to surprise him? Which was why he decided not to waste ammunition on creatures that would never damage his interests, even by accident.

These were fishers, after all.

Come summer, they hid their boats on shore and moved out onto the lakes and sea, and where currents seemed favorable, they would slice through the skin, spearing and hooking what the sun and chum lured to the surface.

As Nots went, they were poor, almost landless souls.

And they were probably a long ways from home, judging by their indifference to the island and the famous monster that ruled its forested hills.

Mercer dropped to his knees and waited.

Let them rest. Let them eat sunshine and feel the heat quickening their watery blood. If he killed any of them, it would be a simple clean warning act—an old body or a weakling child that wouldn't live through the next winter. But he hadn't decided what to do yet. He had always wrung a certain pleasure in being what he was, but even at the worst, the monster held tight to a knot of compassion. Empathy was another old habit. Even in rage, Mercer had the capacity to measure his violence, to hold back the blade and the bomb, understanding exactly what was necessary and then using only a little more than that.

What would he tell the girl when he returned home?

People like her, these solitary wanderers, were often the most wonderful guests. Weak bodies and their hard upbringings meant they could be trusted, at least in measured doses. An old man's charities were readily accepted. Easy food and dry shelter meant a paradise worth cherishing. They would even accept his little wisdoms, or at least pretended to believe whatever truths he tried to share with them. And like this girl, those poor humans understood how even the tiniest mistake could bring violence and disaster.

Which was only reasonable. Consider the girl: For her, compromise and compassion were last resorts. She appreciated the merits of blind determination, small-scale thievery, and how the mangled hand often delivered the winning blow. But she couldn't understand why a creature like him would vanquish his enemies, but then fail to sink the dead into the deepest ocean trench. It made no sense to her, and her response was to stare at him—a fierce baffled stare—some piece of her soul probably wondering if she had ever known anyone more foolish than this soft old fossil.

It was a measure of Mercer's fondness for the girl that as he watched these helpless fishers, he decided to offer her a lie.

If asked, he would describe a nonexistent slaughter. He would tell her that he killed every Not child and most of the adults, sending a few survivors running back to the mainland. And if she didn't inquire, he would act grim but fierce nonetheless, using his eyes and a tight mouth to convey an understandable, respectable viciousness.

"If she's waiting for me," he whispered softly.

Because he knew she was planning to leave. A shopkeeper in his former life, he always kept thorough inventories of his stocks and tools and anything else of value, and he knew exactly what was being stolen and how much she might carry comfortably. None of this surprised him. In some ways, he was almost pleased. It was the dangerous guest who took nothing. In his experience, if you weren't a thief in small ways, you were plotting to remove the owner and acquire everything that was his. But as much as Mercer liked this girl, he didn't allow himself to feel sentimental or unreasonably attached: After all, she was a wild child who had reached maturity despite several decades of hard deprivation, and as miserable as every breath had been, the life she knew was too familiar to surrender. Particularly when it meant sharing the bed and food with a strange, eons-old creature.

He knew what would happen. When he had stabbed her in the chest and dripped those essential and precious minerals into her dead heart, he understood that she would eventually leave.

He had hoped for a normal summer and a longer stay, of course.

In his fantasies, she gave them time to make a child. That birth and the demanding infant would keep the wild girl here for a several more winters, giving Mercer time enough to teach her more about this world and the universe beyond, and in little ways, explain what he could about himself. Nothing of lasting importance would be accomplished, probably. Once Dream left, she would never return to the island. Dozens of women had come to his doorstep, accepting his charity and instruction, and then along very predictable avenues, they had built a small boat or walked across the summer sea, abandoning him forever.

That's why he had always kept a little space between the girl and his heart.

Too well, he understood that the human spirit was enduring, and deep habits were just as immortal as a favorite hand or the language of your youth.

In his best dreams, women long lost and probably long dead returned to him. But they were nothing more, or less, than precious memories. The girl was superstitious to believe in ghosts, but that didn't mean Mercer held those who had passed in any less esteem, or what the brain recalled from ages past was any less sacred than what a few ghosts would mean if they were real, and if they cared enough to visit from the Afterlife.

Memory had a vivid, inexhaustible hold on Mercer's soul.

And perhaps that was why he found this girl more intriguing than most. From the first time he saw her face filled with life, she looked familiar. In the nose and black eyes and the shape of her delicate suspicious mouth, she resembled the woman he had lived with last in the lost colony.

Dead little Deleen.

How long ago was that now?

Forever, it seemed. And it was yesterday, too.

Deleen never had children. But every woman's eggs were harvested by the two-doctor clinic, and there was always the possibility that after Mercer left, some other woman had used those eggs to begin her own family. But even if that was true, the resemblance had to be an accident. How many generations had those genes passed through? How many nameless families had began and died before this girl, Deleen's descendant or not, was flung onto the rock above the high-tide mark?

Coincidences were only that. But they provided a solid measure of his longings too. As he sat on the blackish skin of the sea, on his knees, watching the Nots do nothing, Mercer again warned himself that she was going to leave, and perhaps she had slipped away already, taking only a fraction of the treasures that he would have willingly bestowed on her, if only she'd had the foresight and courage to ask.

And with that, he dropped that difficult subject.

A mind polished by endless centuries of solitude had that talent. In the next breath, he was thinking about small solvable problems and the endless chores waiting in his busy life. What gift would he grant his own Nots next, and what did he need to build next inside his machine shop, and what would be the shape and purpose of the newest room that he eventually carved deep inside that ancient hillside?

His eyes drifted shut, and for an instant, he napped.

Then he was awake, utterly and perfectly alert. One of the Nots had stood, and Mercer's first thought was that the creature had noticed him kneeling behind a patch of graylick weed. But the angle of those double-paired eyes was wrong. Then he heard a voice speaking in a simple, planet-wide language that was defined by the genetics—an instinctive language that had changed only slightly and very grudgingly since the humans' arrival.

"Smoke," the voice said.

The other adult Nots began climbing to their feet, looking where the first Not looked, repeating the "smoke" squawk again and again.

Before he turned, Mercer knew that his island was burning. But he wasn't particularly surprised, since it was such a hot dry summer. The forested uplands had plenty of fuel, but he knew that the healthiest of the giant trees could resist the flames. Probably one of the south drainages was on fire, he decided. That's where they came first and hit hardest . . .

But that guess was completely wrong.

His hilly end of the island stood on the horizon, the eastern region just out of view. The thick column of smoke sprang from a single blaze, and its position meant either that the sea north of his territory was on fire—a strict impossibility—or the Nots' lands beyond were caught up in some unlikely, tremendous blaze.

He leaped to his feet.

That's when the Nots saw him. And that's when they began to scream—a single reflexive chorus splitting the air, everyone using one of the few words that had arisen during these last hundred millennia:

"Eater-of-Bone!" cried the little creatures. "Eater-of-Bone!"

11

Twenty-seven humans.

More than once she counted the running bodies, never believing the tally but the impossible number always waiting at the end of her count.

Twenty-seven, and every last one of them was an adult.

Not in any experience of hers, nor even inside any old, unlikely story, had she heard of so many people sharing one another's air. Except for Mercer's fables about lost colonies and left-behind worlds, that is. How could so many mouths find enough food? How could so many skulls share the same destination? And her best guess was that there were six or maybe seven women, which meant the extra men were laying awake nights, plotting ways to win or steal what was as valuable to them as any nourishment.

She watched how they ran, studying their gaits and weighing their packs by the bounce. Every last one of them carried guns, usually a long rifle, and they kept their distance from one another, as if expecting somebody to fire on them any moment. They were determined people with a goal, a mission. They had to be running toward Mercer's half of the island. But no, that reasonable, wrong assumption was soon thrown aside. They were steering for the Nots, and in particular, for those long fingery bays where the big stone buildings stood just above the high water mark.

The strangers never looked back.

What mattered to them lay straight ahead.

But even when she was certain that they couldn't see her, she remained behind the parasite plant, counting her breaths and watching the runners grow too tiny to see anymore, and that's when she finally eased out into the open again, staring at her bulging pack.

Except for the guns and ammunition, she left everything.

She didn't run as fast as the others, and she followed a different line, retracing her own steps as the sun lifted and the heat lifted and the sea's skin responded by growing fiercely hot and dry beneath bare toes. The day reached noon. The Nots would be outside now, basking in the sun. Every so often, she changed her mind and told her legs to stop, and when they refused, she became confused. Where was her trusted fearfulness hiding? How would returning accomplish anything at all? But she was relieved as well as puzzled. Fanciful, improbable plans swirled inside a head that had never been so rested or well fed, and she kept returning to the simple faith that her intuitions actually knew what they were doing.

The first explosion sounded like the crack of a dried pegpoke.

She stopped running and listened, and just when she decided that the sea was making the snapping noise—a consequence of tides and currents abusing the thick skin—she saw half a dozen flashes of light and the bright yellow lick of flames rising up from the shoreline.

The Nots' buildings were burning.

She knelt on the sea and watched, silently telling herself to turn now, turn and go back. The mainland beckoned, and a life of relative wealth and constant invention.

But then a traitorous thought pushed her back onto the suicidal path.

She imagined Mercer.

This creature that she barely knew was inside her. She could see him, and she heard his smooth old voice talking to no one but her. He was weepy and furious about what was happening to his Nots, to his island. One life had spent eons in a tiny place, and all those habits had gathered on the soul because of it . . . an illusion of eternity that meant more to him than any sensible notion . . . and she had absolutely no doubt how he would react to this brutal assault.

More buildings began to burn.

Even across such a distance, she heard the Nots' wild screams.

She rose again, and her shoulders slumped, and she managed to take half a dozen steps backward. Then a single fanheart dove out of the smoke-pierced sky, spotting her and diving close to shout nothing that made sense and that she understood nonetheless.

Again, she ran toward the island.

She felt trapped inside a strange woman. Reasonable terror and brilliant cowardice had been tossed aside. With the fanheart circling overhead, she finally reached the shore. The tide was high. Open, weed-choked water lay between her and a mudstone bank. She didn't hesitate, feet plunging into the warm deep edge of the sea. One arm pulled and both legs kicked, and she held the stubby rifle high until her left foot kicked the sharp lip of bedded stone, slicing open the skin behind her toes. Then she hurried up the bank and into the great forest that welcomed her with shade and the rich smell of burning flesh. Kneeling for a moment, she pushed at the cut until it was healed. The wind was blowing down the length of the island. Through gaps in the canopy, she saw black smoke and glimpses of an afternoon sun. Obviously her enemies knew much about the island and its inhabitants. An army like this could be everywhere, but she filled only one little place, forever shifting and never unaware. When she reached a familiar trail, she paused long enough to convince herself that only her feet and Mercer's had passed this way. Then she crept down to his front door, discovering that each of the booby-traps remained active, untouched.

She disabled them, and before she entered, she set them again.

But waiting beside the door itself—that great slab of ruby rock—sat a little wooden box that she didn't recognize.

She began to step back, and then thought better of it.

Standing on the only ground she trusted, she called out. Ten times, she risked making the kinds of noise that should have drifted through the house's breathing holes. Mercer would have heard her with her first word, and where was he? Gone already, she decided. But she yelled an eleventh time regardless, and that was when a body kicked the ground behind her, and his careful, very soft voice asked, "What are you doing?"

She turned.

He was dressed for war. A huge man with muscles and tough bone, he nonetheless looked tiny inside unfamiliar armor and beneath the various munitions. Steel boots covered his feet. The ancient mask was as clear as clean water. His face was exactly as she had expected: A tight jaw and the red beard and the squinting, uncompromising eyes, little beads of sweat running through the whiskers and the throat jumping a little as the voice said, "I thought you'd left me."

"No," she lied.

Dark, skeptical eyes stared at nothing but her eyes.

"I did leave," she finally admitted. "But I changed my mind."

He insisted on saying nothing.

"I saw them coming," she explained. Then she reported their numbers and the equipment that she had seen and the arrow-certainty of their motion.

Mercer's only response was a slight silent nod.

Once again, she looked at his gear. Where did all that shiny armor come from? She hadn't seen it hanging in the armory, she realized. And his rifle was different from the others, although she couldn't decide exactly what made it so unlikely. So strange.

Sensing those questions, he said, "Hyperfiber."

What was that word?

"I stole several sheets of it when I abandoned the colony." He rapped hard on the flat breastplate. "This was scavenged off our starship."

"Your gun?"

"I designed it and built it myself." He aimed at the sky, adding, "It has an exceptionally long reach and some very special shells."

"I don't care," she said.

"See?" He pulled one bullet from the breech and tossed it up.

She caught it, astonished by its weight.

"Metal," he said.

The object was long and tapered at one end, its smooth face reflecting the world around it.

He said, "That one is lead and silver, mostly."

"I don't care," she repeated. "You can't beat them."

"You think I should run away?"

But she knew he wouldn't. And that was why she shook her head. "We can go underground," she said. "We'll fight them when they come here." She almost believed those words, and every other crazy utterance that spilled out of her mouth. She and Mercer had their booby traps and the hard old hill, plus a maze of tunnels in which to hide. Their armory and living quarters were stocked and ready for a long, long siege. Sure, an army of monsters was coming, but they'd brought only what they could carry, and most of them were men, and eventually their little peace with one another would break down, and they would fight with each other instead of the two of them.

"Why did you come back?" he interrupted.

He might as well have asked about the far side of the White Moon. She had no ready answer, or even a half-convincing lie.

"You did leave me," he pointed out. "And then you didn't."

It made no sense to her either.

She admitted, "I don't know why."

He dropped his gaze.

Then she said, "Maybe," before her voice fell away.

"Maybe what?"

Every breath tasted of smoke and burning Nots. She managed a deep breath before saying, "I'm pregnant."

If anything, he looked offended. He shook his head, saying, "Then I'll ask again. Why? Why endanger yourself and the baby?"

There was no answer to give.

Looking at her own hands, she had to admit, "I don't know this person."

"Maybe what it was . . . is . . ."

His voice trailed off.

She said, "What?"

"No."

"What?" she pressed.

Then she took a sloppy step forward.

The new trap was triggered, a simple gun inside that wooden box aimed at her back. A copper bullet was driven past her ribs and through her ribs and heart, and she dropped hard on her rump, feeling nothing but warmth and surprise.

Mercer leaped, dropping the rifle and slashing the air with a diamond sword. An insulated wire ran from the box to her chest, and he cut the wire an instant before a staggering jolt of electricity ran up into the wound, cooking her insides. Then he knelt and yanked at the bullet until it dropped free, and gently, he set a hand over the tidy little hole.

"I don't think your siege plan is awful," he finally admitted. "But whoever they are, these people know me. I'm sure of that. My guess? One of their women lived here, long ago. Or some old girlfriend of mine talked to one of the men and told too much. Either way, they're probably prepared for a long fight. So if I am going to beat them, I have to do it now. Today. Before everyone's dead but them and me."

He had to save his Nots, he meant.

She coughed hard, tasting the sweet iron in her blood.

He pulled off his helmet and kissed her twice, and then he opened the ruby door and dragged her limp body inside. Then he kissed her once again, on the belly that betrayed no trace of a baby yet.

"You'll heal quickly enough," he promised.

She already felt her toes wiggling.

"These other monsters have made plans," he allowed. "Careful plans. But then again, there's one element they won't see coming."

"Me?"

"When you have your legs again," he began.

"What do you want?"

He told her.

She nodded, coughing one last time.

Then he put on the helmet again and touched a switch, causing the faceplate to turn black as a winter night. Then quietly, tenderly, he said, "I love you. Whatever your name is, I do love you."

12

Generations of laborers had invested their lives shaping a titanic block of gray-white basalt. Sapphire chisels had dug into the stone, creating the rough approximation of a human form. Then mud laced with diamond grit was used to smooth and polish, finishing arms and legs and the powerful torso, and finally, the frightful, mocking mask laid over a face that none had ever witnessed. Here was stark evidence for the power of honesty over any singular artistic genius: Every detail was rendered with relentless perfection—the hard fibers of each muscle, every vein in the menacing fists, and those gray-white eyes, big as platters, staring forever into the Nots' homes. This was the island's lawful ruler. Not Mercer, but this gigantic testament to fear and adoration. Without any prompting on his part, the sculptors had captured the individual hairs trailing down his long bare back, and they understood the precise angle of every bone as well as the bare human ass, and several of those exceptionally thorough creatures had even managed to replicate what was the most unremarkable male genitalia.

Mercer slipped past the stone god, kneeling behind a long slab of polished magna-wood. Two old Nots and a child had died recently. Relatives had prepared them for the Afterlife, peeling away their exoskin to reveal spidery bodies that were treated with their family blood before being carefully laid out on the altar, waiting for the honor of being carried into the monster's realm. A Not's rotting flesh produced a horrific stink. Mercer held his breath, reading the sun-washed country before him. Twenty-seven invaders? That still seemed like an enormous, unlikely number. Yet he trusted the girl's eyes, and even if she hadn't returned to warn him, Mercer would have recognized the awful stakes. His home had been invaded, obviously. What this army wanted was nothing less than to kill him and then live here forever. And all of this smoke and carnage was nothing more, or less, than a brazen, carefully planned message meant for an audience of one.

They were taunting him.

One way or another, they would draw him into their fight; and somewhere in the ruins, a careful trap was being set.

Yet that could play to Mercer's advantage. People crouching inside secret holes often felt too safe for their own good. Whoever these invaders were, they probably expected him to sneak down through the crops and between the intact buildings. But they couldn't where he would come from, or when. Twenty-seven pairs of eyes looking into the shadows, expecting a slinking, fearful soul . . . and that's why Mercer forced himself to stand and breathe deeply, ignoring his nausea as well as a host of reasonable, useful fears . . .

He ran.

Holstered pistols bounced, but his rifle was tied securely to his left shoulder, and with his armor and light pack cinched tight, he could easily maintain this long efficient stride. Against every instinct, he kept to the perfect middle of the lane. He didn't bother watching for hazards that he likely wouldn't see anyway. Let the bastards hide where they wanted. What mattered were speed and surprise. His only focus was the ground straight ahead. When the lane twisted left and began to drop, he consciously lifted his pace. And where the farmland started to dissolve into the tall stone apartment buildings, Mercer pushed his body and cargo into a blurring sprint.

Pure human genetics couldn't have managed this relentless pace. Mercer forced his fit, well-fed body to unleash all of its talents. Metabolisms lifted while pains were obscured. His heart roared. His lungs massaged every breath. Oxygen made his bright blood sing.

Like two streams merging, his lane joined with a neighbor, and moments later he sprinted out into a wide stretch of open ground—the Nots' version of a public plaza. The space was paved with tightly-fitted corundum stones and lined with tall mirrors that gathered the low northern sunlight. A little Stonehenge stood in the middle plaza, showing with shadow exactly where they sat inside this summer. Here was where Mercer fully expected to suffer. Some sniper would suddenly notice him and aim a little too quickly, opening fire before he was ready, and then this miserable waiting would end . . .

Yet nothing happened.

The next few moments of running lasted for ages, and then Mercer escaped the open ground, slipping back between tall buildings again. He was surprised. Disappointed, in a fashion. And then as he thought about the situation, he became terrified.

Was he going to have to run back and forth like a madman, begging to be noticed? Or worse, could his enemies have anticipated his tactics?

The invaders weren't here. He thought it and then believed it: Somehow they had slipped past all the watching, friendly eyes that guarded Mercer's forest—the fanhearts and dewlanes and such. They had lured him here, and now they would steal his home.

He hoped Dream had healed enough to run away . . . using her legs and paranoia to keep her safe . . .

Thinking of her, Mercer slowed his pace just a touch.

Crack.

The first round missed, skipping off the pavement ahead of him, bouncing and detonating with a hot red flash. His momentum carried him through the explosion. Then he jumped to the left for no reason but to jump, to ruin the next shot. But the marksman guessed right and put an explosive charge into his chest, and the blast slammed against the hyperfiber armor and every rib beneath.

Mercer felt his feet lifting.

Then he found himself on his back, but perfectly conscious.

He rolled and stood and ran blindly toward the nearest door—a dozen tattler skins woven together and painted with yellow lettering that told all who passed the significance of this building. He was barely through that opening when two explosions went off together, flinging him onto the little Not stairs that led up into the nesting house.

Mercer picked himself up and climbed.

At the top of the stairs, a single guardian remained at his post—a sturdy, mature Not armed with authority and habit as well as a sapphire-tipped spear. The creature barked the traditional warning at the intruder, and Mercer replied by declaring his identity and demanding help. But the building was being peppered with grenades and kinetic rounds. The Not heard nothing that convinced him to quit, and he must have believed that this was one of the invaders. He lifted his spear and drove the tip downward, aiming for a gap in the unbreakable armor. Mercer had no choice but shove the Not aside, and when the creature stubbornly tried to find his feet again, Mercer used a short sword to finish the useless fight.

The nursery was built to never burn, which was helpful.

And it was tall, which gave him a sniper's power.

But there were several doors and endless windows intended for ventilation, and that meant that no one fighter could keep the army at bay for long.

The gunfire fell off, vanished.

Mercer slipped into a long narrow room where the windows faced south, admitting the afternoon sun into a realm where unborn Nots lay inside their transparent cocoons—the first exoskins wrapped tight around half-defined bodies that were hung from the stone ceiling, each of those unfinished faces habitually following the sliding of the day's light.

A pair of the cocoons had been shot.

Mercer measured the wounds and guessed the likely angles of fire, and he crawled between two windows and shucked off his pack and his rifle and pulled a dulled piece of mirror out of a pocket, using the dark reflection to study both of the facing buildings without letting the sunlight offer up his position.

Someone launched one kinetic round.

On the lane below, a single Not screamed and died.

Mercer made himself do nothing. Nothing. He would let the monsters sit and wonder if he'd managed to get away from them somehow. Make them crazy, at least for a little while. The next few minutes were spent unfolding and then studying a piece of high-technology—the highly detailed map of the city, including not only what the Nots had built in the last ten generations, but also every chamber and abandoned sewer and paved-over cave that no living creature besides him was aware of.

Nots were gathering in the lane below. Their long feet moved in a rough unison, a desperate muttering building. Dozens of them had crawled out of their hiding places. There could be a hundred of them, even more. Then he heard prayers to vanished gods, and thankfully, prayers intended for him. The Nots had learned about this fight at the nursery, and they were coming to rescue their children. Which wouldn't have happened if the enemy had struck him in the open, in the Stonehenge. That would have been better for everybody, Mercer told himself.

"But you can't live forever," he muttered to himself. "Not wasting your head thinking about what-ifs, you can't . . ."

The snipers opened up on the converging Nots.

Prayers turned to wailing screams. Across the lane, two windows sprouted guns, and Mercer lowered his mirror and lifted his rifle and turned on the laser sight, and then he came around smoothly, kneeling low, waiting for the first human face to fill the eyepiece before punching three fast shots between the eyes.

He pulled back, grabbed his gear and rolled and then ran hard.

Grenades dove through three windows, spinning and then exploding, sticky gobs of napalm splashing across walls and the helpless cocoons.

Mercer dropped beside another window and pulled out a single bomb. One of treasures that he stole from the original colony was the chemical knowledge of his species, and with the resources and ample time, he had managed to concoct some wonderfully potent species of pyrotechnics.

A hundred Nots were dying below him.

Again he wheeled and aimed, punishing the next human face with a single round of lead and gold and silver, and then he set the fuse and flung the bomb at the open window, his aim not quite perfect but the gray aluminum casing slipping across the sill and bouncing inside maybe two seconds before the blast incinerated flesh and bone, half of the apartment building shaken to pieces and collapsing onto the street below.

A fresh handful of humans joined the fight, spraying explosives through the nursery windows.

But Mercer had slipped away. He was charging down the back stairs, pack and rifle held high in one hand and maybe two dozen Nots coming up into the nursery from the flanking side of the building. They could smell burnt flesh, pure death. A peace that had lasted longer than their lives had been lost, and every old instinct forced them to act crazy and stupid, rushing up those same stairs even when they couldn't do anything that would matter.

The human monster shoved his way into them.

His plan was find the latrine at the building's low end and open the floor with a shaped charge and work his way up along the sewer line. In principle, he could reach the farmland without being seen again. But the smarter plan would be to pop up periodically, hitting his enemies with a few shot and blasts, making sure that their focus wouldn't fade.

He wanted to make a very specific retreat.

That was the goal.

But Mercer didn't expect to round one corner in the narrow hallway and find a human monster ready for him.

He threw his pack at the figure.

She had a long rifle meant to fire little bombs, and she managed to avoid firing until the pack had fallen at her feet.

Too late, he threw his rifle to his shoulder.

Her first shot struck the hyperfiber plate over his belly, bouncing off and detonating at his feet.

Mercer was flung back, his boots torn apart, feet burnt to the bone.

But then he had his shot to take, and he even managed to fix the laser on that point on her neck where half a dozen solid rounds would probably break the spine and cut the head clean off.

What made him pause was a mystery.

Maybe it was the woman's age, which seemed very young, or how terrified she looked to him just then. Or maybe he was startled, noticing the swollen belly that made her nanofiber armor next to useless. Or it was her gun, which was the same type that Dream had seen in his armory—the model carried by that young couple who had tried so hard to kill her just last winter.

In an impoverished world, human bone could be a precious resource for any woman expecting to give birth.

Was her pregnancy to blame?

Unless there was no hesitation at all. Maybe the first blast hurt Mercer worse than he had realized, and he wouldn't have gotten off any kind of return fire before she shot again, blindly but with extraordinary luck.

The man was flat on his back, on the hard stone floor, and the bomb passed between his belly plate and chest plate.

His hyperfiber contained the blast, making it worse.

Guts were shredded and his heart quit and those scorched lungs opened up to the air, and he howled and dragged himself backward, and she fired one last time, aiming carefully and missing by quite a lot.

Mercer shot her once in the forehead.

The bullet knocked her off her feet, giving his body time to rouse several anaerobic metabolisms. Then he dragged himself close enough to use the diamond sword, hacking at that long limp neck until it was cut through, and he set two of his big bombs on long timers and left them under his pack, and he took only his rifle and sword and a pair of grenades, crawling to the latrine door, flinging in one grenade and then another, battering a wide hole in the floor before he pulled his near-corpse to the edge.

He clung there, smelling the rancid chemistry of an alien sewer.

Mercer asked himself if life could be worth this kind of misery.

Then he rolled and fell into the gaping hole, his impact cushioned by water and the stinking gelatinous filth. And because the building above him was about to collapse, he forced his battered body to stand, and he convinced his exhausted legs to march upstream, his guts held in place under his hand while his thoughts, such as they were, revolved around the woman that was still waiting for him.

13

She began to work even before her feet quit tingling. Following Mercer's precise instructions, she slipped into the armory and found everything that she needed and filled the same huge pack that the man had used when he came to rescue her, all but dead on the shoreline. Then she stomped her toes a few times, just to make certain that her legs had recovered. Shouldering the pack took three attempts, and the hike proved far harder than she had imagined. But there was still daylight when she reached the hilltop, and she dropped the pack against the magna-wood tree with its camouflaged blind. The next few hundred breaths were spent studying the slope to the south. The big fires down by the sea were beginning to die back. She wasn't certain about the timetable, which meant that she might already be late. But Mercer had been explicit: The trap would work or it wouldn't work; they would never get a second chance.

The incendiaries were not particularly large, but he had promised that they had a hard kick. And the fuses could have been any brown cord, which was why she invested a few moments cutting an extra length of fuse and wrapping it around the magna-wood trunk before setting one end on fire.

In two hurried breaths, the entire fuse turned to sparks and ash.

As she had hoped, the water-gorged bladders protected the old wood. No premature fire had been started. She fixed her first bomb to the trunk's base, on the south side, and tied in the brown cord and laid it back to where she would sit unseen. Then she grabbed several bombs and all of the fuses and worked her way down the slope, selecting only in the largest and the weakest trees.

Mercer had gone past the barricade to put up a good brief fight. He wanted to do just enough to get every human's attention and rage, and then he would lead that army on a long, painful retreat, bringing them here during the night, hopefully leading them through this particular drainage.

Her job was to mine this slope and then hide, waiting for that perfect moment when she would drop the entire forest on their heads.

The little bombs would spray fire, and if enough of the trees' watery bladders were punctured, and if enough deep wood was splintered and exposed to the atmosphere, then what would begin as an avalanche would turn into an enormous, cleansing bonfire.

With each bomb set and each cord laid back up on top of the hill, she found herself more and more believing in Mercer's plan.

About when she expected to hear gunfire, the muted explosions began to drift from below. She paused occasionally, listening carefully, trying to piece together an accurate picture of the war. But then came a final big thud followed by silence, and she returned to her work as the sun set and night rose up from the dried streambed and then fell from a sky full of close bright and astonishingly colorful stars.

Her hands knew what to do in the dark, and she soon discovered that every bomb was set and there was no more fuse to cut and splice and lay out.

Satisfied, she returned to the hilltop and the hidden place where thirty cords lay together, waiting for any excuse to burn.

She listened for another battle, preferably from some place nearer.

None came.

But she didn't let herself worry. Not yet. Having fixed her future to Mercer, she found herself willing to accept his skills and experience, and his confidence, and what she considered to be his bottomless well of luck.

The man was coming, she told herself.

As time passed, the Gold Moon rose over the eastern sea, washing the hillside with its slippery wet light. Maybe in the next breath or two, Mercer's armored body would appear. She pictured him shoving his way up along the drainage, defiant and unbowed, firing back a few times just to make his pursuers hold their pace, and then pausing at a predetermined point and signaling his survival to her with that bright red laser.

She had to believe that he was coming, didn't she?

But then at some point, without warning, her mother interrupted her unheard-of devotion.

"Run," the dead woman advised.

In the softest whisper, the daughter asked, "What?"

"That man is lost," declared the ghost. The phantom. The memory. "You know where you left your pack. So run to it now and push on, and don't bother looking back."

She said, "No."

Then after a long listen to the silence, she admitted, "He should have been here by now."

"Lost," the phantom repeated.

Perhaps so.

"And if those monsters find you, then you're lost as well."

She told herself to remain in her hiding place. To give Mercer time, to give him every chance. But her body was suddenly possessed with energy, nervous but ready, and the best she could do was make herself stand slowly, stepping nowhere, watching the valley below and discovering a numbing despair that had been secretly brewing for a long while.

From the opposite slope came the hard quick voice of an ollo-lol.

To give her mind some job, she began to count her quick breaths.

"Remember what I told you, daughter?" the phantom continued. "Before my death, you were kneeling over me, tending to me. But the dying have few needs, except to be heard."

"I listened," she reported, interrupting her count.

"What a beauty, life is. I told you. And I promised you that small moments in every day would contain some lovely good thing to soothe the eye or sweeten the nose or linger inside the happy ear."

"Quiet," she begged.

But the phantom refused to obey. Quietly but with force, it reminded the grown daughter, "I promised you one treasure for your day."

She realized that she was weeping, and she had been weeping for a long while now.

"What was the treasure, daughter?"

"No."

"I was dying—"

"You weren't dead yet," she muttered, probably too loudly.

"I was lost," the phantom said.

Starvation on top of endless malnutrition had shriveled her mother's badly depleted body. The woman had insisted that her child eat everything available, which was very little, and that final deprivation meant that even cuts that should have healed in moments refused to knit. Organs, named and otherwise, were plunging into hibernation. Old wounds were resurfacing, and each labored breath could have been the last.

"You did what you had to do, daughter."

The strength drained from her legs. Slowly, she dropped to the ground and wrapped her arms across her bare knees, sobbing peacefully.

"I was lost—!"

"I could have buried your body," she interrupted. "Hidden you and come back again, with food. With nutrients."

"That wouldn't have happened," the phantom replied.

"In my pack," she said, looking south toward the sea. "I have enough treasures to make you over again. Bring you to life and back with me—"

"Your child needs those gifts, darling."

"I didn't have to," the young woman muttered, mouth against one knee, the salty taste of her own flesh making her guilt even worse. "Your bones . . . they were just a few little sticks at the end . . ."

"Mine became yours," the phantom assured her.

But that sorry truth just made her sicker, and sadder, and she pulled the palms of her hands across her wet eyes and choked back a deep sob and let little gasps leak out while the phantom said, "Sticks, yes. Spent, yes. But still with little nodules of minerals that you needed worse than any dead lost soul would need them . . . and that was the beautiful heart of your day, daughter . . . regardless what you pretend to think . . ."

Another ollo-lol spoke in the darkness.

She looked up, looked around. What would she do now?

"Run," the dead mother advised one last time.

Then the young woman rose to her feet again, finding the strength to retrieve her rifle from the hiding place. What she would do next wasn't decided. She didn't know her mind yet, and it might have taken another thousand breaths before she finally gave up the wait. But then came the sudden thunder of bombs exploding to the east and south, and she turned in time to see a flash rising from where the barricade divided the island into its two halves, both His.

She ran.

Then halfway down the rocky slope, she stopped. What good could she do in this fight? Her task—his hope—was for her to be where he expected her to be, waiting for the signal. Always, impulses seemed to rule over reason inside her. She chastised herself and managed to turn around, starting to climb again, when a voice she didn't know screamed, "The forearm! The left forearm! And his damned gun too, I got it!"

Mercer was injured.

"Blood," the voice said. A woman's voice. "Look for blood trails."

Badly hurt, she realized.

Some man asked, "Which way?"

Another man said, "Here's a track, here . . . !"

Where the dry stream poured down onto the farmland, human shapes were moving. Brush was snapping; she heard overlapping orders. A single man stood in the moonlight for a long moment, presenting an easy shot. The enemy believed that the war was won. Whatever had happened before made them feel safe and powerful, and obviously they didn't have any hint that she was standing nearby, eager to spray explosives down across their heads.

Instead of firing, she crept silently along the slope, trying to guess where Mercer was.

A kinetic pistol fired.

Half a dozen larger weapons slashed at the trees, starting fires that sputtered and died as the ripped bladders bled over them.

Then somebody yelled, "Quiet," and then, "What do you see?"

In the chill light of the moon and endless stars, she saw the familiar shape struggling to run. He was still some distance ahead of his pursuers. The hyperfiber armor still encased the powerful body, but it was obvious that nothing had worked as planned. Mercer was staggering. Two steps, and he dropped to his knees while the stump of one arm flailed senselessly, and then he rose again and did nothing after that, too spent to manage even one weak step.

Mercer was still too far down the drainage.

Exposed, and caught in his own trap too.

She ran, pushing down the slope while working upstream, running out onto a bed of dried, dusty pebbles. She was above him. Even facing her, he didn't seem to notice anything amiss. Walking was everything that he could manage, and he did it erect, shattered feet dragging on the rocks and the armor catching the moonlight, making him all the more obvious, and what sounded like a spongeworm squishing every time his nearly useless lungs managed to take another breath.

The army closed on their victim.

She heard the monsters talking openly, happily. An infectious mood, a kind of celebration, erased all but the last shreds of caution. She even heard two voices near the front arguing passionately about which one of them should get the final pleasure.

On her toes, she ran toward Mercer.

His helmet was missing. A burnt face managed to see her as a shape approaching, and he lifted his final pistol and tried to fire with the empty chamber, perhaps puzzled by the useless series of clicks.

She kneeled and aimed over his head, flinging half a dozen explosive rounds over his head.

The blasts flung him to the ground.

She had never heard so many humans speaking at once, and every last one of them was cursing.

"A new gun," someone decided. "He must have stashed one."

Nobody wanted to get battered now, at the end. So they hunkered down, waiting for Mercer to make a fresh mistake.

He was fighting to stand one last time. Lying on his chest, he looked helpless. She came close and dropped flat to put her mouth against his ear, and tasting ashes, she said, "I'm here."

He didn't answer. But his body seemed to relax, slightly.

She grabbed his surviving arm and tugged hard, once and then again, and he decided to obey what he felt, pulling one leg up and then his body, allowing her to slip under that arm and helping him to come upright. But every step was miserably slow. He was astonishingly, frighteningly light. Something awful had happened, and that he could heal enough to stagger this far was miraculous. But that lightness meant that a rested and strong woman, no matter how small, could push herself under his bulk and shove up hard enough to let his shattered body lay limp over her shoulders, and with her rifle in one hand and the other arm between his shrunken legs, she could run straight for nearly a hundred rapid breaths.

A dried waterfall stood like a wall before them.

Behind them, voices argued and debated and gradually pushed closer. And then as she wondered what to do, a man's voice declared, "There's fresh prints here. He's got a friend."

She bent low and swallowed an enormous amount of air, and then with a clean shove, she flung him over the brink of the dried falls.

He was unconscious now.

Shaking from fatigue, she dragged him up to where the winter currents had cut into the bank, creating a tiny shelter roofed with ruddy corundum. Into the less-burnt ear, she said, "Stay," and then she retrieved her rifle and ran hard up the hill, terrified that she wouldn't have time enough or that her trap had been diagnosed or that any of a thousand little mistakes could have doomed both of them.

Below her, countless rifles fired at every shadow.

She reached the fuses without drawing anyone's fire. Time mattered, but so did precision. She used the flint lighter to light one short fuse that she had lashed around the others, and then stood back, one long breath spent wondering what to do when this didn't work. Shoot the fuses with her rifle? Or detonate the trees one by one, maybe?

Her doubts evaporated.

Several dozen serpents sprang to life, spark and fire streaking across the dry ground, setting tiny fires before reaching the incendiary bombs. The watching post's tree exploded first, the ancient trunk gouged out and bladders bursting, and then as more trees exploded below, the giant bent and fell, dislodging rocks as well as the explosive underbrush, the shattered mess sliding rapidly downhill.

Fifty breaths, and the hillside quit falling.

No voices were heard. No weapons, no sobs. The drainage below Mercer and the waterfall was jammed with downed timber, and as promised, much of that exposed wood was burning. Bladders had been shattered, soaking the mess with water and fire retardants. But when those desperate measures had done their best, the ancient forest burst into a single consuming blaze, hot enough to create a funeral pyre for every miserable monster trapped beneath.

With the heat, she couldn't reach Mercer's hiding place.

But he would be safe enough where he was, she reasoned. In that damp, near-underground place, he would burn only a little and heal those new wounds before dawn, most likely. This creature that never believed in any long future found herself talking to the almost-dead man, telling him the story of his unlikely survival and imagining what he might tell her about his various adventures facing down nearly thirty of the most deadly monsters in the world.

She baked in the fire, and because she wanted to feel sure, she scanned both her slope and the facing slope, in the unlikely chance that one or two of the humans had escaped the others' fate.

Whole trees detonated, but the opposite, north-facing slope was too wet and far too steep to catch fire.

Every once in a while, she noticed movement. But what she saw was high on the next ridge, and they plainly weren't human shapes, and it was easiest to believe that tattlers and other animals were running through the forest.

By dawn, the giant fire was reduced to red-hot coals and a thick column of black smoke.

Rifle in hand, she began to walk toward Mercer. But even now the heat was intense. Her flesh threatened to blister, and each little breath hurt her throat and her chest.

She thought about retreating.

But then she saw the Nots braving the furnace. Fifty of them, all adults. And then she realized that no, they were just the first of several waves, and she couldn't count how many hundreds were climbing down the opposite slope. Some of the Nots carried bladders stolen from the forest trees, busily soaking themselves and their neighbors with the cooling liquid. Like a flood, they flowed into the dried streambed, smelling the air and ground and finally discovering what they knew was somewhere close by.

Mercer was dragged out into the open.

She stopped, standing on her toes, not certain what to think but incapable of feeling much concern. His Nots must have followed the invaders up into the forbidden forest. Unseen, they had watched the last fight and the horrible fire, and now they were dragging their great protector out of his hiding place. There were so many of the tiny creatures crowding in close now. Despite a lifetime of mistrust and paranoia, she couldn't understand what they wanted from the god they had worshipped for hundreds of generations—not until one Not lifted a stone-tipped hoe over its head, driving the cutting edge into Mercer's burnt and helpless face.

Twenty other Nots took their swings with the same hoe, and then the pole shattered with a sharp crack.

Sapphire knives were pulled from hidden belts.

A thunderous chorus of cries rose up from the opposite slope.

Suddenly what might have been ten thousand shapes flowed out of the shadows, out from under the trees, fighting one another for the honor to help with or at least witness what was plainly a wondrous, long-anticipated event.

The girl saw nothing that happened after that.

Finally obeying her mother's wise advice, she ran off those hills and across the summer sea, retrieving her waiting pack before continuing to the south, chasing after her new, old life.

14

Summer was nearly done when the great ruby door was finally pried open, but even then booby-traps continued killing and maiming, including the sudden release of a wicked green gas that slaughtered dozens of good citizens. After that tragedy, there was fearful talk and fearful thoughts. What if the female monster—that mutilated beast thrown out of the sea—was hiding in the hills, waiting to inflict her terrible revenge? Traps were built and baited with piss fungi, yet nothing touched them. The sharpest eyes and noses examined every piece of the island, but no recent trace of her or any other living Eater-of-bone was found. When the darkest, wettest days of winter descended, the Elders held a council, and it was decided that their enemies indeed had been vanquished. The ancient premonitions were true: With an ocean of patience and a handful of courage, the Nots at long last had won their well-deserved freedom.

Yet even when the monster's lair proved toothless and empty, it was studied only with slowest possible deliberation. An intricate maze of tunnels had to be measured and marked. Room after room after room was carefully examined. Maps were drawn. Scribes made exhaustive inventories. The monster's furniture and his elaborate wardrobe brought endless fascination. But those were normal, knowable objects. His home was littered with mysterious wonders that needed to be examined and memorized. Those rare souls with the necessary skills gazed directly at the human-built machines, and they whispered with learned voices, and then only when they felt ready did they give their honest verdict.

"We have no idea what this device does," was the usual pronouncement.

They were the Hunters-of-unthinkable-thoughts.

At the beginning of time and the world, a lady Not had watched the monster throw rocks into the bay, and from the action, she had somehow discerned an important piece of his greater purpose. She had urged her people to mimic his insanity that next year. And her descendants learned from the monster how to build the dam and drain the bay and then carefully scrape up a white film, vanishingly thin that meant so much to the invincible Eater-of-bone.

It was the Hunters who always studied what refused to be understood. To strengthen their talents, they formed a narrow sect-family, gradually improving their blood line— countless generations of wizard-like savants whose culminating moment was to stand together in the heart of that cave-like home, debating the purpose and merits of this piece of brass and of that broken cylinder of cultured diamond.

At winter's end, a fleet of raiding Nots landed near the burnt remains of the mineral works. But before they could move off the shoreline, they were struck dead by a rain of aluminum bullets and tiny bombs.

That day, a new force sat upon the world.

Then came the holy first night of summer. Much talk had been invested in the proper best way to mark this event. One young Hunter—a lady Not with an astonishing talent for holding the odd and unimaginable behind her fiery eyes—argued successfully for a reversal of the traditional ceremony. As a nation, the Nots streamed past the uprooted statue of their vanquished god, and they passed through new gaps cut in the barricade, and then holding tight to a respectful silence, they marched up into the hill country. The strongest carried the weakest; no one was left behind. At the lead was the courageous young male who had first struck at their sworn enemy, his only weapon being the common, now famous hoe.

What he carried tonight, nestled in careful hands, resembled a round stone, grayish in color and surprisingly light in weight, decorated with a multitude of folds and little fissures mirroring the ancestral mind of human beings.

The Hunters followed closely behind, carrying the twenty-seven souls of the wicked, blessed invaders.

Into the lair went the honored leaders.

The rest of the Nots waited silently in the darkness of the forest, crowded beneath a giant gyreboy tree.

Twenty-eight monsters were carried into a distant room.

Set about that room, in neat rows and labeled in a precise, still unreadable tongue, were more than three hundred Eaters-of-bone—the previous residents of this common grave.

Some Nots had argued for sinking all of these horrors in the sea.

But other voices had won out, at least for the moment. And to make that moment eternal, the young Hunter reminded all in her presence that little was known about the creatures they were at war with. The origins and magic of these demons remained deep mysteries. But time was deeper, and patience could be eternal. Using the relics in the monster's sanctuary, some future generation might finally tease away all of the ignorance, and wiser souls would find themselves holding all of the tools used by their unwelcome visitors.

Who could say where the next billion years would lead?

Perhaps someone of power would find a compelling reason to give these dead monsters their faces again, and their limbs, and their animal voices.

But not their freedom, she hoped.

As did all of the good Nots . . .

15

"My name is," she began.

"Mother," said the boy, grinning.

"Are you sure?"

And he laughed at one of their oldest, most cherished jokes. Of course she was his mother, and that was the only name she would even need from him. It was still just the two of them working as one. Other solitary humans lived in this forest of sky-hugging trees. But since these were relatively wealthy times for monsters, at least in this one northern corner of the world, there was no serious fighting. Nor were there any treaties of alliance, either. Cooperation demanded need, and none of the resident monsters saw good reasons to join forces, even for a day.

"I want a story," the young boy said.

They were sitting in the dark, under the tattler skin, listening to the rain hit and flow off onto the muddy ground.

Mother said, "All right."

"Which story?" he asked eagerly.

"The island," she promised.

"About my father?"

"What about your father?"

"I want to hear how he saved you and cared for you . . . right up until . . ." Then his young voice trailed off into a sad, practiced silence.

"Another night, I think."

"Then what will you tell me?"

She wrapped her arms around her tough little monster, and she squeezed him until both of them ached, and after a while she said, "I am going to tell you about the stars, and about the universe beyond the stars, and our great species, and the wonders you can see only with our mind's eyes . . ."

Michael Alexander, "The Children's Crusade," *F&SF*, May/June.

———— & K.C. Ball, "The Moon Belongs to Everyone," *Analog*, December.

Molshree Ambastha, "Kalyug Amended," *Breaking the Bow*.

Charlie Jane Anders, "Intestate," *Tor.com*, December 17.

Eleanor Arnason, "The Woman Who Fooled Death Five Times," *F&SF*, July/August.

Chet Arthur, "The Sheriff," *F&SF*, September/October.

Kate Bachus, "Things Greater Than Love," *Strange Horizons*, March 19.

Dale Bailey, "Mating Habits of the Late Cretaceous," *Asimov's*, September.

Neelanjana Banerjee, "Exile," *Breaking the Bow*.

John Barnes, "Swift as a Dream and Fleeting as a Sign," *Edge of Infinity*.

Stephen Baxter, "A Journey to Amasia," *Arc 1.1*.

————, "Project Herakles," *Analog*, January/February.

————, "Obelisk," *Edge of Infinity*.

Neal Barrett, Jr., "Trash," *Postscripts* 26/27.

Peter S. Beagle, "The Ape-Man of Mars," *Under the Moons of Mars*.

————, "Great-Grandmother in the Cellar," *Under My Hat*.

————, "Olfort Dapper's Day," *F&SF*, March/April.

Elizabeth Bear, "The Death of Terrestrial Radio," *Shoggoths in Bloom*.

————, "No Decent Patrimony," *Rip-Off!*.

————, "The Depths of the Sky," *Edge of Infinity*.

————, "Faster Gun," *Tor.com*, August 8.

————, "The Salt Sea and the Sky," *Brave New Love*.

Chris Beckett, "The Caramel Forest," *Asimov's*, December.

Gregory Benford, "The Sigma Structure Symphony," *Tor.com*, March 28.

Michael Bishop, "Unfit for Eden," *Postscripts* 26/27.

Holly Black, "Little Gods," *Under My Hat*.

Michael Blumlein, "Bird Walks in New England," *Asimov's*, July.

————, "Twenty Two and You," *F&SF*, March/April.

Gregory Norman Bossart, "The Telling," *Beneath Ceaseless Skies*, Nov 29.

Elizabeth Bourne, "Beasts," *Interzone* 240.

Richard Bowes, "A Member of the Wedding of Heaven and Hell," *Apex Magazine*, March 6.

————, "The Queen and the Cambion," *F&SF*, March/April.

————, "Seven Smiles and Seven Frowns," *Lightspeed*, May.

Keith Brooke, "War 3.01," *Lightspeed*, February.

Eric Brown, "The Scribe of Betelgeuse V," *Postscripts* 26/27.

Ben Bova, "A Country for Old Men," *Going Interstellar*.

Tobias S. Buckell, "A Tinker of Warhoon," *Under the Moons of Mars*.

————, "Press Enter to Execute," *Fireside*, Spring.

Karl Bunker, "The Remembered," *Interzone* 242.

Pat Cadigan, "In Plain Sight," *The Future Is Japanese*.

Jack Campbell, "Highland Reel," *Rip-Off!*.

Tracy Canfield, "The Chastisement of Your Peace," *Strange Horizons*, January 30.

Sarah K. Castle, "The Mutant Stag at Horn Creek," *Analog*, July/August

Adam-Troy Castro, "My Wife Hates Time Travel," *Lightspeed*, September.

Rob Chilson, "The Conquest of the Air," *Analog*, July/August.

Gwendolyn Clare, "All the Painted Stars," *Clarkesworld*, January.

David Ira Cleary, "Living in the Eighties," *Asimov's*, April/May.

Geoffrey W. Cole, "Cradle and Ume," *New Worlds*, September 2.

James S.A. Corey, "Drive," *Edge of Infinity*.

Paul Cornell, "A New Arrival at the House of Love," *Solaris Rising 1.5*.

———, "The Ghosts of Christmas," *Tor.com*, December 19.

Matthew Corradi, "City League," *F&SF*, May/June.

Stephen D. Covey, "The Road to NPS," E, "Ninety Thousand Horses," *Analog*, January/February.

Albert E. Cowdrey, "Asylum," *F&SF*, May/June.

———, "The Goddess," *F&SF*, September/October.

———, "Greed," *F&SF*, March/April.

———, "Hartmut's World," *F&SF*, July/August.

———, "The Ladies in Waiting," *F&SF*, November/December.

———, "Mindbender," *F&SF*, January/February.

Nan Craig, "Scrapmetal," *Arc 1.3*.

Ian Creasey, "Joining the High Flyers," *Asimov's*, August.

———, "Souvenirs," *Asimov's*, April/May.

Tom Crosshill, "Fragmentation, or Ten Thousand Goodbyes," *Clarkesworld*, April.

Benjamin Crowell, "Kill Switch," *Asimov's*, July.

Tony Daniel, "Checksum Checkmate," *Baen.com*, January 16.

Indrapramit Das, "Muo-Ka's Child," *Clarkesworld*, September.

———, "Sita's Descent," *Breaking the Bow*.

Colin P. Davies, "Land of Fire and Ashes," *Abyss & Apex*, 1st Quarter.

Grania Davis, "Father Juniper's Journey to the North," *F&SF*, September/October.

Aliette de Bodard, "A Dance of Life and Death," *Pandemonium*.

———, "Heaven Under Earth," *Electric Velocipede 24*.

———, "Immersion," *Clarkesworld*, June.

———, "On a Red Station, Drifting," *Immersion Press*.

———, "Scattered Along the River of Heaven," *Clarkesworld*, January.

———, "Starsong," *Asimov's*, August.

———, "Two Sisters in Exile," *Solaris Rising 1.5*.

A.M. Dellamonica, "The Sweet Spot," *Lightspeed*, July.

Craig Delancey, "The Ediacarian Machine," *Analog*, March.

Charles De Lint, "Barrio Girls," *Under My Hat*.

Alan DeNiro, "The Flowering Ape," *Asimov's*, June.

Junot Diaz, "Monstro," *The New Yorker*, June 4 & 11.

Peter Dickinson, "Troll Blood," *F&SF*, September/October.

Paul di Filippo, "A Palazzo in the Stars," *Solaris Rising 1.5*.

———, "Karin Coxswain, or, Death As She Is Truly Lived," *Rip-Off!*

Ian Douglas, "The Johnson Maneuver," *Armored*.

Aidan Doyle, "Ghost River Red," *Lightspeed*, July.

Andy Duncan, "On 20268 Petercook," *Tor.com*, April 11.

Thoraiya Dyer, "The Wisdom of the Ants," *Clarkesworld*, December.

T.D. Edge, "Big Dave's in Love," *Arc 1.2*.

Jennifer Egan, "Black Box," *The New Yorker*, June 4 & 11.

K.M. Ferebee, "The Keats Variation," *Strange Horizons*, June 4—11.

Peter M. Ferencz, "The Womb Factory," *Clarkesworld*, April.

C.C. Finlay, "The Cross-Time Accountants Fail to Kill Hitler Because Chuck Berry Does the Twist," *Lightspeed*, May.

Michael F. Flynn, "Buried Hopes," *Captive Dreams*.

——, "Hopeful Monsters," *Captive Dreams*.

——, "The Journeyman: On the Short-Grass Prairie," *Analog*, October.

——, "Places Where the Roads Don't Go," *Captive Dreams*.

Jeffrey Ford, "A Natural History of Autumn," *F&SF*, July/August.

Susan Forest, "7:54," *On Spec*, Summer.

Peter Freund, "Stray Magic," *Under My Hat*.

Emily Gilman, "The Castle That Jack Built," *Beneath Ceaseless Skies*, January.

Molly Gloss, "The Grinnell Method," *Strange Horizons*, September 3—10.

Kathleen Ann Goonan, "A Love Supreme," *Discover*, October.

Theodora Goss, "Beautiful Boys," *Asimov's*, August.

——, "England Under the White Witch," *Clarkesworld*, October.

——, "Woola's Song," *Under the Moons of Mars*.

Steven Gould, "Rust with Wings," *After*.

Simon R. Green, "Find Heaven and Hell in the Smallest Things," *Armored*.

Daryl Gregory, "Begone," *Rip-Off!*.

Eric Gregory, "The Sympathy," *Lightspeed*, April.

Dave Gullen, "All Your Futures," *Arc 1.3*.

Guy Haley, "iRobot," *Interzone 243*.

Nick Harkaway, "Attenuation," *Arc 1.2*.

M. John Harrison, "In Autotelia," *Arc 1.1*.

Maria Dahvana Headley, "Game," *Subterranean*, Fall.

——, "Give Her Honey When You Hear Her Scream," *Lightspeed*, June.

Samantha Henderson, "Beside Calais," *Strange Horizons*, May 14.

Howard V. Hendrix, "Red Rover, Red Rover," *Analog*, July/August.

Nalo Hopkinson, "The Easthound," *After*.

Kat Howard, "The Least of the Deadly Arts," *Subterranean*, Winter.

Sarah A. Hoyt, "The Big Ship and the Wise Old Owl," *Going Interstellar*.

Louise Hughes, "Over the Waves," *Strange Horizons*, August 13.

Matthew Hughes, "The Immersion," *Postscripts 26/27*.

——, "Wearaway and Flambeau," *F&SF*, July/August.

Dave Hutchison, "Sugar Engines,"

Alexander Jablokov, "The Comfort of Strangers," *F&SF*, January/February.

N.K. Jemisin, "Valedictorian," *After*.

Xia Jia, "A Hundred Ghosts Parade Tonight," *Clarkesworld*, February.

C.W. Johnson, "The Burst," *Asimov's*, January.

Kij Johnson, "Mantis Wives," *Clarkesworld*, August.

——, "Wolf Trapping," *Apex Magazine*, July 3.

Matthew Johnson, "The Afflicted," *F&SF*, July/August.

——, "The Last Islander," *Asimov's*, September.

Gwyneth Jones, "Bricks, Sticks, Straw," *Edge of Infinity*.

Michaele Jordan, "Wizard," *F&SF*, July/August.

Vylar Kaftan, "Lion Dance," *Asimov's*, October/November.

——, "Seeking Captain Random," *Interzone 240*.

James Patrick Kelly, "Declaration," *Rip-Off!*.

——, "The Last Judgment," *Asimov's*, April/May.

Caitliln R. Kiernan, "Fake Plastic Trees," *After*.

——, "Random Thoughts Before a Fatal Crash," *Subterranean*, Spring.

Hideyuki Kikuchi, "Mountain People, Ocean People," *The Future Is Japanese*.

Swapna Kishore, "Regressions," *Breaking the Bow*.

Ellen Klages, "The Education of a Witch," *Under My Hat*.

——, "Household Management," *Strange Horizons*, November 2.

David Klecha and Tobias S. Buckell, "Jungle Walkers," *Armored*.

Ted Kosmatka, "The Color Least Used By Nature," *F&SF*, January/February.

Mary Robinette Kowal, "The Lady Astronaut of Mars," *Rip-Off!*.

——, "Weaving Dreams," *Apex Magazine*, October 2.

Nancy Kress, "After the Fall, Before the Fall, During the Fall," *Tachyon*.

——, "Writer's Block," *Rip-Off!*.

——, "We Can Do This," *Arc 1.3*

Naomi Kritzer, "High Stakes," *F&SF*, November/December.

——, "Liberty's Daughter," *F&SF*, May/June.

——, "Scrap Dragon," *F&SF*, January/February.

Ellen Kushner, "The Three-fold World," *Under My Hat*.

Jay Lake, "Lehr, Rex," *Apex Magazine*, March 6.

——, "The Weight of History, the Lightness of the Future," *Subterranean*, Spring.

Marc Laidlaw, "Forget You," *Lightspeed*, April.

Margo Lanagan, "Crow and Caper, Caper and Crow," *Under My Hat*.

Geoffrey A. Landis, "Demiurge," *F&SF*, March/April.

Joe R. Lansdale, "The Metal Men of Mars," *Under the Moons of Mars*.

Ann Leckie, "Night's Slow Poison," *Electric Velocipede 24*.

Karalynn Lee, "Unsilenced," *Beneath Ceaseless Skies*, October.

Rand B. Lee, "Theobroma Valentine," *F&SF*, September/October.

Yoon Ha Lee, "The Battle of Candle Arc," *Clarkesworld*, October.

Ursula K. Le Guin, "Elementals," *Tin House 53*.

David D. Levine, "The Last Days of the Kelly Gang," *Armored*.

Marissa Lingen, "On the Acquisition of Phoenix Eggs (Variant)," *Lightspeed*, January.

——, "Uncle Flower's Homecoming Waltz," *Tor.com*, February 1.

Jennifer Linnaea, "He Reminds Us," *Strange Horizons*, November 12.

Ken Liu, "A Tale of Guan Yu, the Chinese God of War, in America," *Daily SF*, Feb. 1.

—— "Arc," *F&SF*, September/October.

——, "The Bookmaking Habits of Select Species," *Lightspeed*, August.

——, "The Five Elements of the Heart Mind," *Lightspeed*, January.

——, "Good Hunting," *Strange Horizons*, October 9–October 29.

——, "Memories of My Mother," *Daily SF*, March 19.

——, "Mono no Aware," *The Future Is Japanese*.

——, "The People of Pele," *Asimov's*, January.

——, "The Message," *Interzone 242*.

——, "Real Faces," *F&SF*, July/August.

——, "The Silk Merchant," *Apex Magazine*, July 3.
——, "To the Moon," *Fireside*, Spring.
——, "The Waves," *Asimov's*, December.
Sarah Lotz, "Charlotte," *Solaris Rising 1.5*.
——, "Home Affairs," *AfroSF*.
——, "If I Die, Kill My Cat," *Magic*.
——, "Inspector Bucket Investigates," *Pandemonium*.
Karin Lowachee, "Nomad," *Armored*.
Will Ludwigsen, "The Ghost Factory," *Asimov's*, October/November.
Ian R. MacLeod, "Tumbling Nancy," *Subterranean*, Summer.
Bruce McAllister, "Free Range," *Asimov's*, June.
——, "Stamps," *Asimov's*, August.
——and Barry N. Malzberg, "Going Home," *Asimov's*, January.
Paul McAuley, "Antarctica Starts Here," *Asimov's*, October/November.
——, "Bruce Springsteen," *Asimov's*, January.
Simon McCaffery, "The Cristobal Effect," *Lightspeed*, June.
Meghan McCarron, "Swift, Brutal Retaliation," *Tor.com*, January 12.
John G. McDaid, "Umbrella Men," *F&SF*, January/February.
Edward McDermott, "Nothing But Vacuum," *Analog*, October.
Jack McDevitt, "Lucy," *Going Interstellar*.
——, "Maiden Voyage," *Asimov's*, January.
——, "Waiting at the Altar," *Asimov's*, June.
Sandra McDonald, "Mehra and Jiun," *War and Space*.
——, "Searching for Slave Leia," *Lightspeed*, November.
——, "Sexy Robot Mom," *Asimov's*, April/May.
——, "Your Final Apocalypse," *Clarkesworld*, December.
——and Stephen D. Covey, "The Road to NPS," *Edge of Infinity*.
Sophia McDougall, "Mailer Daemon," *Magic*.
Sean McMullen, "Electrica," *F&SF*, March/April.
Nick Mamatas, "Arbeitskraft," *Mammoth Book of Steampunk*.
Arkady Martine, "Laco Downstairs," *Abyss & Apex*, 4th Quarter.
Eugene Mirabelli, "This Hologram World," *Asimov's*, October/November.
Mary Anne Mohanraj, "The Princess in the Forest," *Breaking the Bow*.
Sarah Monette, "Blue Lace Agate," *Lightspeed*, January.
——, "Coyote Gets His Own Back," *Apex Magazine*, July 3.
Pat Murphy, "About Fairies," *Tor.com*, May 9.
Linda Nagata, "A Moment Before It Struck," *Lightspeed*, August.
——, "Nahiku West," *Analog*, October.
Shweta Narayan, "Falling into the Earth," *Breaking the Bow*.
Mari Ness, "And the Hollow Space Inside," *Clarkesworld*, February.
Alec Nevala-Lee, "Ernesto," *Analog*, March.
——, "The Voices," *Analog*, September.
Garth Nix, "A Handful of Ashes," *Under My Hat*.
——, "You Won't Feel a Thing" *After*.
——, "Sidekick of Mars," *Under the Moons of Mars*.
Efe Okogu, "Proposition 23," *AfroSF*.
Nnedi Okorafor, "African Sunrise," *Subterranean*, Fall.
Issui Ogawa, "Golden Bread," *The Future Is Japanese*.

An Owomoyele, "If the Mountain Comes," *Clarkesworld*, June.
——, "Water Rights," *Edge of Infinity*.
K.J. Parker, "One Little Room an Everywhere," *Eclipse Online*, October.
——, "Let Maps to Others," *Subterranean*, Summer.
Richard Parks, "In the Palace of the Jade Lion," *Beneath Ceaseless Skies*, July.
——, "Three Little Foxes," *Beneath Ceaseless Skies*, October.
Benjamin Parzybok, "Bear and Shifty," *Lightspeed*, October.
Joe Pitkin, "A Murmuration of Starlings," *Analog*, June.
Rachel Pollack, "Jack Shade in the Forest of Souls," *F&SF*, July/August.
Steven Popkes, "Breathe," *F&SF*, October/November.
Gareth L. Powell, "Another Apocalypse," *Solaris Rising 1.5*.
——, "Railroad Angel," *Interzone 241*.
William Preston, "Unearthed," *Asimov's*, September.
Tom Purdom, "Bonding with Morry," *Asimov's*, April/May.
——, "Golva's Ascent," *Asimov's*, March.
Chen Qiufan, "The Flower of Sahazui," *Interzone 243*.
Hannu Rajaniemi, "Topsight," *Arc 1.1*.
Cat Rambo, "So Glad We Had This Time Together," *Apex Magazine*, January 3.
Melanie Rawn, "Mother of All Russiya," *Lightspeed*, May.
Kit Reed, "Results Guaranteed," *Asimov's*, October/November.
Robert Reed, "Bright Lights," *Strange Horizons*, May 14.
——, "Emergence," *Postscripts* 26/27.
——, "Exchange," *Arc*.
——, "Flowing Unimpeded to the Enlightenment," *Lightspeed*, October.
——, "The Girl in the Park," *Asimov's*, July.
——, "Katabasis," *F&SF*, November/December.
——, "One Year of Fame," *F&SF*, March/April.
——, "Murder Born," *Asimov's*, January.
——, "Noumenon," *Asimov's*, September.
——, "The Pipes of Pan," *Asimov's*, December.
——, "Prayer," *Clarkesworld*, May.
Jessica Reisman, "The Bottom Garden," *Postscripts* 26/27.
Alter S. Reiss, "If the Stars Reverse Their Courses, If the Rivers Run Back from the Sea,"
    F&SF, November/December.
Mike Resnick, "A Weighty Affair," *Postscripts* 26/27.
——, "The Evening Line," *Rip-Off!*.
——, "The Second Civil War," *Solaris Rising 1.5*.
——, "The Wizard of West 34th Street," *Asimov's*, December.
Alastair Reynolds, "Trauma Pod," *Armored*.
——, "Vainglory," *Edge of Infinity*.
Ted Reynolds, "View Through the Window," *Asimov's*, August.
Joel Richards, "Patagonia," *Asimov's*, March.
Leonard Richardson, "Four Kinds of Cargo," *Strange Horizons*, November 5.
M. Rickert, "Burning Castles," *Under My Hat*.
Gray Rinehart, "Sensitive, Compartmented," *Asimov's*, April/May.
Mecurio D. Rivera, "Missionaries," *Asimov's*, June.
Adam Roberts, "An Account of a Voyage from World to World," *Pornokitch*.
——, "Martin Citywit," *Pandemonium*.

Margaret Ronald, "The Governess and the Lobster," *Beneath Ceaseless Skies*, May.

Benjamin Rosenbaum, "Elsewhere," *Strange Horizons*, June 18.

Christopher Rowe, "The Contrary Gardener," *Eclipse Online*, October.

Rudy Rucker and Bruce Sterling, "Loco," *Tor.com*, June 20.

Kristine Kathryn Rusch, "Safety Tests," *Edge of Infinity*.

——, "The Voodoo Project," *Asimov's*, January.

Pervin Saket, "Test of Fire," *Breaking the Bow*.

Sofia Samatar, "Honey Bear," *Clarkesworld*, August.

Jason Sanford, "Heaven's Touch," *Asimov's*, August.

——, "Mirrorlink," *Interzone 243*.

Felicity Savage, "The Sound of Breaking Up," *The Future Is Japanese*.

John Scalzi, "Muse of Fire," *Rip-Off!*.

Catherine Shaffer, "The North Revena Ladies Literary Society," *Analog*, July/August.

Delia Sherman, "The Witch in the Wood," *Under My Hat*.

David J. Schwartz, "Bear in Contradicting Landscape," *Apex Magazine*, February 7.

Ekaterina Sedia, "A Handsome Fellow," *Asimov's*, October/November.

——, "Whale Meat," *The Future Is Japanese*.

Gord Sellar, "The Bernoulli War," *Asimov's*, August.

Priya Sharma, "Lady Dragon and the Netsuke Carver," *Interzone 243*.

Lewis Shiner, "Application," *F&SF*, November/December.

——, "Canto MCML," *F&SF*, January/February.

Felicity Shoulders, "Long Night on Redrock," *Asimov's*, July.

——, "Small Towns," *F&SF*, January/February.

Cory Skerry, "Sinking Among Lilies," *Beneath Ceaseless Skies*, April.

Alan Smale, "The Mongolian Book of the Dead," *Asimov's*, October/November.

Bud Sparhawk, "Scout," *Asimov's*, June.

Allen M. Steele, "Alive and Well, A Long Way From Anywhere," *Asimov's*, July.

——, "The Big Whale," *Rip-Off!*.

Bruce Sterling, "Goddess of Mercy," *The Future Is Japanese*.

——, "My Pretty Alluvian Bride," *Arc 1.3*

——, "The Peak of Eternal Light," *Edge of Infinity*.

Andy Stewart, "Typhoid Jack," *F&SF*, May/June.

S.M. Stirling, "The Jarsoom Project," *Under the Moons of Mars*.

Charles Stross, "A Tall Tail," *Tor.com*, July 20.

Tim Sullivan, "Repairmen," *F&SF*, March/April.

Ken Sursi, "The Seven Samovars," *Lightspeed*, September.

Michael Swanwick, "Day of the Kraken," *Tor.com*, September 26.

——, "The Fire Gown," *Tor.com*, August 18.

——, "The Mongolian Wizard," *Tor.com*, July 4.

——, "Pushkin the American," *Postscripts 26/27*.

——, "The Woman Who Shook the World-Tree," *Tor.com*, March 21.

Rachel Swirsky, "The Sea of Trees," *The Future Is Japanese*.

John Alfred Taylor, "Chromatophores," *Asimov's*, October/November.

Karin Tidbeck, "Rebecka," *Jagganath*.

Lavie Tidhar, "A Brief History of the Great Pubs of London," *Pandemonium*.

——, "Black God's Kiss," *Postscripts 26/27*.

——, "The Ballad of the Last Human," *The Mammoth Book of Steampunk*.

——, "Chosing Faces," *Arc 1.3*.

——, "Earthrise," *Redstone SF* #28.

——, "The Indignity of Rain," *Interzone* 240.

——, "The Lord of Discarded Things," *Strange Horizons*, October 15.

——, "Love Is a Parasite Meme," *Apex Magazine*, April 13.

——, "The Red Menace," *Rip-Off!*.

——, "Robotnik," *Dark Faith 2*.

——, "The Stoker Memorandum," *Daily Science Fiction*,

——, "Strigoi," *Interzone* 242.

——, "This, Other World," *Breaking the Bow*.

Steven Utley, "Crime and Punishment," *Postscripts* 26/27.

——, "The End in Eden," *Analog*, October.

——, "Shattering," *Asimov's*, October/November.

——, "The Tortoise Grows Elate," *F&SF*, March/April.

——, "Zip," *Asimov's*, July.

Catheryene M. Valente, "Coming of Age in Barsoom," *Under the Moons of Mars*.

——, "Fade to White," *Clarkesworld*, August.

Genevieve Valentine, "A Bead of Jasper, Four Small Stones," *Clarkesworld*, October.

——, "A Game of Mars," *Under the Moons of Mars*.

——, "Aurum," *Abyss & Apex*, 1st Quarter.

——, "The Gravedigger of Kostan Spring," *Lightspeed*, February.

Jeff VanderMeer, "Komodo," *Arc 1.2*.

James Van Pelt, "Mrs. Hatcher's Evaluation," *Asimov's*, March.

Carrie Vaughn, "Don Quixote," *Armored*.

——, "Harry and Marlow and the Talisman of the Cult of Egil," *Lightspeed*, February.

Juliette Wade, "The Liars," *Analog*, October.

Wendy N. Wagner, "Barnstormers," *Ideomancer*, June.

Kali Wallace, "The Widdershins Clock," *Asimov's*, June.

Tracie Welser, "A Body Without Fur," *Interzone* 240.

K.D. Wentworth, "Alien Land," *F&SF*, January/February.

Kate Wilhelm, "The Fullness of Time," *F&SF*, July/August.

Edward Willett, "A Little Space Music," *On Spec*, Spring.

Liz Williams, "Cad Coddeu," *Magic*.

Sean Williams, "The N-Body Solution," *Armored*.

Tad Williams, "Every Fuzzy Beast of the Earth, Every Pink Fowl of the Air," *Rip-Off!*.

——, "Three Lilies and Three Leopards," *Subterranean*, Winter.

Walter Jon Williams, "The Boolean Gate," *Subterranean Press*.

Chris Willrich, "Grand Tour," *F&SF*, May/June.

——, "The Mote Dancer and the Firelife," *Beneath Ceaseless Skies*, March.

——, "Star Soup," *Asimov's*, September.

Robert Charles Wilson, "Fireborn," *Rip-Off!*.

Gene Wolfe, "Dormannna," *Tor.com*, March 7.

Nick Wood, "Azania," *AfroSF*.

Alberto Yanez, "Recognizing Gabe: un cuento de hadas," *Strange Horizons*, January 16.

Dorothy Yarros, "The Fourth Exam," *Strange Horizons*, September 17.

Caroline M. Yoachim, "Mother Ship," *Lightspeed*, April.

——, "The Philosophy of Ships," *Interzone* 243.

Jane Yolen, "Andersen's Witch," *Under My Hat*.